THE
CIRCLE
SERIES

TED DEKkER

THOMAS NELSON
Since 1798

NASHVILLE   DALLAS   MEXICO CITY   RIO DE JANEIRO

teddekker.com

DEKkER FANTASY

BOOKS OF HISTORY CHRONICLES

THE LOST BOOKS (YOUNG ADULT)
Chosen
Infidel
Renegade
Chaos
Lunatic (WITH KACI HILL)
Elyon (WITH KACI HILL)
The Lost Books Visual Edition

THE CIRCLE SERIES
Black
Red
White
Green
The Circle Series Visual Edition

THE PARADISE BOOKS
Showdown
Saint
Sinner

Immanuel's Veins
House (WITH FRANK PERETTI)

DEKkER MYSTERY

Kiss (WITH ERIN HEALY)
Burn (WITH ERIN HEALY)

THE HEAVEN TRILOGY
Heaven's Wager
When Heaven Weeps
Thunder of Heaven

The Martyr's Song

THE CALEB BOOKS
Blessed Child
A Man Called Blessed

DEKkER THRILLER

THR3E
Obsessed
Adam
Skin
Blink of an Eye

CONTENTS

Published in Nashville, Tennessee, by Thomas Nelson. Thomas Nelson is a registered trademark of Thomas Nelson, Inc.

Thomas Nelson, Inc., titles may be purchased in bulk for educational, business, fund-raising, or sales promotional use. For information, please e-mail SpecialMarkets@ThomasNelson.com.

Published in association with Creative Trust, Inc., 5141 Virginia Way, Suite 320, Brentwood, TN 37027.

ISBN: 978-1-59554-922-8 (SE for B&N)
ISBN: 978-1-59554-792-7

Printed in the United States of America

18 QG 10 9 8 7

BLACK

THE BIRTH OF EVIL

Switzerland

CARLOS MISSIRIAN was his name. One of his many names.

Born in Cyprus.

The man who sat at the opposite end of the long dining table, slowly cutting into a thick red steak, was Valborg Svensson. One of his many, many names.

Born in hell.

They ate in near-perfect silence thirty feet from each other in a dark hall hewn from granite deep in the Swiss Alps. Black iron lamps along the walls cast a dim amber light through the room. No servants, no other furniture, no music, no one except Carlos Missirian and Valborg Svensson seated at the exquisite dining table.

Carlos sliced the thick slab of beef with a razor-sharp blade and watched the flesh separate. *Like the parting of the Red Sea.* He cut again, aware that the only sound in this room was of two serrated knives cutting through meat into china, severing fibers. Strange sounds if you knew what to listen for.

Carlos placed a slice in his mouth and bit firmly. He didn't look up at Svensson, although the man was undoubtedly staring at him, at his face— at the long scar on his right cheek—with those dead black eyes of his. Carlos breathed deep, taking time to enjoy the coppery taste of the filet.

Very few men had ever unnerved Carlos. The Israelis had taken care of that early in his life. Hate, not fear, ruled him, a disposition he found useful as a killer. But Svensson could unnerve a rock with a glance. To say that

3

this beast put fear in Carlos would be an overstatement, but he certainly kept Carlos awake. Not because Svensson presented any physical threat to him; no man really did. In fact, Carlos could, at this very moment, send the steak knife in his hands into the man's eye with a quick flip of his wrist. Then what prompted his caution? Carlos wasn't sure.

The man wasn't really a beast from hell, of course. He was a Swiss-born businessman who owned half the banks in Switzerland and half the pharmaceutical companies outside the United States. True, he had spent more than half his life here, below the Swiss Alps, stalking around like a caged animal, but he was as human as any other man who walked on two legs. And, at least to Carlos, as vulnerable.

Carlos washed the meat down with a sip of dry Chardonnay and let his eyes rest on Svensson for the first time since sitting to eat. The man ignored him, as he almost always did. His face was badly pitted, and his nose looked too large for his head—not fat and bulbous, but sharp and narrow. His hair, like his eyes, was black, dyed.

Svensson stopped cutting midslice, but he did not look up. The room fell silent. Like statues, they both sat still. Carlos watched him, unwilling to break off his stare. The one mitigating factor in this uncommon relationship was the fact that Svensson also respected Carlos.

Svensson suddenly set down his knife and fork, dabbed at his mustache and lips with a serviette, stood, and walked toward the door. He moved slowly, like a sloth, favoring his right leg. Dragging it. He'd never offered an explanation for the leg. Svensson left the room without casting a single glance Carlos's way.

Carlos waited a full minute in silence, knowing it would take Svensson all of that to walk down the hall. Finally he stood and followed, exiting into a long hall that led to the library, where he assumed Svensson had retired.

He'd met the Swiss three years ago while working with underground Russian factions determined to equalize the world's military powers through the threat of biological weapons. It was an old doctrine: What did it matter if the United States had two hundred thousand nuclear weapons trained on the rest of the world if their enemies had the right biological weapons? A highly infectious airborne virus on the wind was virtually indefensible in open cities.

One weapon to bring the world to its knees.

Carlos paused at the library door, then pushed it open. Svensson stood by the glass wall overlooking the white laboratory one floor below. He'd lit a cigar and was engulfed in a cloud of hazy smoke.

Carlos walked past a wall filled with leather-bound books, lifted a decanter of Scotch, poured himself a drink, and sat on a tall stool. The threat of biological weapons could easily equal the threat of nuclear weapons. They could be easier to use, could be far more devastating. *Could.* In traditional contempt of any treaty, the U.S.S.R. had employed thousands of scientists to develop biological weapons, even after signing the Biological and Toxin Weapons Convention in 1972. All supposedly for defense purposes, of course. Both Svensson and Carlos were intimately familiar with the successes and failures of former Soviet research. In the final analysis, the so-called "superbugs" they had developed weren't super enough, not even close. They were far too messy, too unpredictable, and too easy to neutralize.

Svensson's objective was simple: to develop a highly virulent and stable airborne virus with a three- to six-week incubation period that responded immediately to an antivirus he alone controlled. The point wasn't to kill off whole populations of people. The point was to infect whole regions of the earth within a few short weeks and then control the only treatment.

This was how Svensson planned to wield unthinkable power without the help of a single soldier. This was how Carlos Missirian would rid the world of Israel without firing a single shot. Assuming, of course, such a virus could be developed and then secured.

But then, all scientists knew it was only a matter of time.

Svensson stared at the lab below. The Swiss wore his hair parted down the middle so that black locks flopped either way. In his black jacket he looked like a bat. He was a man married to a dark religious code that required long trips in the deepest of nights. Carlos was certain his god dressed in a black cloak and fed on misery, and at times he questioned his own allegiance to Svensson. The man was driven by an insatiable thirst for power, and the men he worked for even more so. This was their food. Their drug. Carlos didn't care to understand the depths of their madness; he only knew they were the kind of people who would get what they wanted, and in the process he would get what he wanted: the restoration of Islam.

He took a sip of the Scotch. *You would think that one, just one, of the thousands of scientists working in the defensive biotechnological sector would have stumbled onto something meaningful after all these years.* They had over three hundred paid informants in every major pharmaceutical company. Carlos had interviewed fifty-seven scientists from the former Soviet bioweapons program, quite persuasively. And in the end, nothing. At least nothing they were looking for.

The telephone on a large black sandalwood desk to their right rang shrilly.

Neither made a move for the phone. It stopped ringing.

"We need you in Bangkok," Svensson said. His voice sounded like the rumble of an engine churning against a cylinder full of gravel.

"Bangkok."

"Yes, Bangkok. Raison Pharmaceutical."

"The Raison Vaccine?" Carlos said. They had been following the development of the vaccine for over a year with the help of an informant in the Raison labs. He'd always thought it would be ironic if the French company Raison—pronounced ray-ZONE, meaning "reason"—might one day produce a virus that would bring the world to its knees.

"I wasn't aware their vaccine held any promise for us," he said.

Svensson limped slowly, so slowly, to his desk, picked up a piece of white paper and scanned it. "You do remember a report three months ago about unsustainable mutations of the vaccine."

"Our contact said the mutations were unsustainable and died out in minutes." Carlos wasn't a scientist, but he knew more than the average man about bioweapons, naturally.

"Those were the conclusions of Monique de Raison. Now we have another report. Our man at the CDC received a nervous visitor today who claimed that the mutations of the Raison Vaccine held together under prolonged, specific heat. The result, the visitor claimed, would be a lethal airborne virus with an incubation of three weeks. One that could infect the entire world's population in less than three weeks."

"And how did this visitor happen to come across this information?"

Svensson hesitated.

"A dream," he said. "A very unusual dream. A very, very convincing dream of a future world populated by people who think his dreams of this world are only dreams. And by large white bats who talk."

Now it was Carlos's turn to hesitate.

"Bats."

"Who know more than is humanly possible, it seems. We have our reasons for paying attention. I want you to fly to Bangkok and interview Monique de Raison. If the situation warrants, I will want the Raison Vaccine itself, by whatever means."

"Now we're resorting to mystics?"

Svensson had covered the CDC well, with four on the payroll, if Carlos remembered correctly. Even the most innocuous-sounding reports of infectious diseases quickly made their way to the headquarters in Atlanta. Svensson was understandably interested in any report of any new outbreak and the plans to deal with it.

But a dream? Thoroughly out of character for the stoic, black-hearted Swiss. This alone gave the suggestion its only credence.

Svensson glared at him with dark eyes. "As I said, we have other reasons to believe this man may know things he has no business knowing, regardless of how he attained that information."

"Such as?"

"It's beyond you. Suffice it to say there is no way Thomas Hunter could have known that the Raison Vaccine was subject to unsustainable mutations."

Carlos frowned. "A coincidence."

"I'm not willing to take that chance. The fate of the world rests on one elusive virus and its cure. We may have just found that virus."

"I'm not sure Monique de Raison will offer an . . . interview."

"Then take her by force."

"And what about Hunter?"

"You will learn by whatever means necessary everything Thomas Hunter knows, and then you will kill him."

1

One Day Earlier

THE WATER cascaded over Thomas Hunter's head and ran down his face like a warm glove. It was just that, water, but it washed away all his concern and anxiety and set his mind free for a few minuets. He'd been here a while, lost in a distant world that hung on the edge of his mind without any detail or meaning. Just escape. Pure escape, the closest he ever got to heaven these days.

A fist pounded the door. "Thomas! I'm outta here. You're going to be late."

A mental image of a much older Kara flashed through his mind. She was graying, perhaps in her fifties, and she was asking him to take her with him. Just that: "Take me with you, Thomas."

And then the image was gone. He blinked under streams of water, suddenly disoriented. How long had he been here? For the briefest moment he was at a loss as to how he'd even gotten here.

Then it all came crashing in on him. He was in the shower. It was late morning. His shift at Java Hut started at noon. Right? Yes, of course.

He shook the water from his head. "Okay." Then added, "See you tonight."

But Kara was probably already out the door, headed to her shift at the hospital. The thing about his sister: she might only be in her early twenties like him, but what she lacked in age, she more than made up for in maturity. Not that he was irresponsible, but he hadn't made the transition from life on the streets in Manila to life in the States quite as smoothly as Kara.

He stepped out of the shower and wiped the steamed mirror with his

9

forearm. He ran both hands through his wet hair and examined his face as best he could with streaks of water clinging to the glass.

Not bad. Not bad, chicks dug a little stubble, right? He'd lost some of his edge over the last couple years in New York, but Denver would be different. The troubles with loan sharks and shady import partners were behind him now. Soon as he got back on his feet, he would reenter society and find a way to excel at something.

In the meantime, there was the coffee shop he worked at, and there was the apartment, gratis, thanks to Kara.

He dressed quickly, grabbed a day-old sugar donut on his way out and headed up Ninth, then through the alley to Colfax, where the boutique coffee shop better known as Java Hut waited. The Rockies stood against a blue sky, just visible between high-rise apartments as he made his way up the street. Mother was still in New York, where she'd settled in after the divorce. It had been a tough road, but she was set now.

Indeed, the world was set. He just had to put some time in, regroup, and let life come to him as it always had, with fistfuls of dollars and a woman who could appreciate the finer things in life. Like him.

Okay, only in his dreams at the moment, but things were looking up. Maybe he'd finally get back to one of those novels he'd written when his dream of conquering the publishing world was alive and well.

Thomas entered the coffee shop two minutes past noon and let the door slam shut behind him.

"Hey, Thomas." The new dark-haired hire, Edith, smiled and gave him a wink.

Okay . . . interesting. Pretty enough. But being a magnet for trouble, Thomas didn't make a habit of flirting with women he knew nothing about.

"Hey."

She tossed him a green apron. "Frank would like you to show me the ropes."

"Okay." He stepped around her and behind the counter.

"We close together tonight," she said.

Right. Frank had started up these ten-hour shifts a week earlier. "Okay."
"Yeah."

He refused to look at her, knowing what was on her mind already. It was the farthest thing from his mind.

The day passed quickly and he managed to close with her without either betraying his general disinterest in her or offering any encouragement. But showing her the ropes, as she called it, had taken longer than usual, and he didn't get out till ten thirty that night.

He headed down the street, headed for the apartment. Another day, another dollar. Not fistfuls, but at least it was steady. More than he could say for his, uh . . . more ambitious gigs. All was good. All was . . .

But then suddenly all wasn't so good. He was walking down the same dimly lit alley he always took on his way home when a *smack!* punctuated the hum of distant traffic. Red brick dribbled from a one-inch hole two feet away from his face. He stopped midstride.

Smack!

This time he saw the bullet plow into the wall. This time he felt a sting on his cheek as tiny bits of shattered brick burst from the impact. This time every muscle in his body seized.

Someone had just shot at him?

Was shooting at him?

Thomas recoiled to a crouch, but he couldn't seem to tear his eyes off those two holes in the brick, dead ahead. They had to be a mistake. Figments of his overactive imagination. His aspirations to write novels had finally ruptured the line between fantasy and reality with these two empty eye sockets staring at him from the red brick.

"Thomas Hunter!"

That wasn't his imagination, was it? No, that was his name, and it was echoing down the alley. A third bullet crashed into the brick wall.

He bolted to his left, still crouching. One long step, drop the right shoulder, roll. Again the air split above his head. This bullet clanged into a steel ladder and rang down the alley.

Thomas came to his feet and chased the sound in a full sprint, pushed by instinct as much as by terror. He'd been here before, in the back alleys of Manila. He'd been a teenager then, and the Filipino gangs were armed with knives and machetes rather than guns, but at the moment, tearing down the alley behind Ninth and Colfax, Thomas's mind wasn't drawing any distinction.

"You're a dead man!" the voice yelled.

Now he knew who they were. They were from New York. Right? He had no enemies in Denver that he was aware of. New York, on the other hand . . . Yeah, well he'd done a few stupid things in New York.

This alley led to another thirty yards ahead, on his left. A mere shadow in the dim light, but he knew the cutaway.

Two more bullets whipped by, one so close he could feel its wind on his left ear. Feet pounded the concrete behind him.

Thomas dove into the shadow.

"Cut him off in the back. Radio me."

Thomas rolled to the balls of his feet, then sprinted, mind spinning. Radio?

The problem with adrenaline, Makatsu's thin voice whispered, *is that it makes your head weak.* His karate instructor would point to his head and wink. *You have plenty of muscle to fight, but no muscle to think.*

If they had radios and could cut off the street ahead, he would have a very serious problem.

One access to the roof halfway down the alley. One large garbage bin too far away. Scattered boxes to his left. No real cover. He had to make his move before they entered the alley.

Fingers of panic stabbed into his mind. *Adrenaline dulls reason; panic kills it.* Makatsu again. Thomas had once been beaten to a pulp by a gang of Filipinos who'd taken a pledge to kill any Americano brat who entered their turf. They made the streets around the army base their turf. His instructor had scolded him, insisting that he was good enough to have escaped their attack that afternoon. His panic had cost him dearly. His brain had been turned to rice pudding, and he deserved the bruises that swelled his eyes shut.

This time it was bullets, not feet and clubs, and bullets would leave more than bruises. Time was out.

Short on ideas and long on desperation, Thomas dove for the gutter. Rough concrete tore at his skin. He rolled quickly to his left, bumped into the brick wall, and lay face down in the deep shadow.

Feet pounded around the corner and ran straight toward him. One man. How they had found him in Denver, he had no clue. But if they'd gone to this much trouble, they wouldn't just walk away.

The man ran on light feet, hardly winded. Thomas's nose was buried in the musty corner. Noisy blasts of air from his nostrils buffeted his face. He clamped down on his breathing; immediately his lungs began to burn.

The slapping feet approached, ran past.

Stopped.

A slight tremor lit through his bones. He fought another round of panic. It had been five years since his last fight. He didn't stand a chance against a man with a gun. He desperately willed his pursuer's feet to move on. *Walk. Just walk!*

But the feet didn't walk. They scraped quietly. He had to move now, while he still had the advantage of surprise. He threw himself to his left, rolled once to gain momentum. Then twice, rising first to his knees, then to his feet. His attacker was facing him, gun extended, frozen.

Thomas's momentum carried him laterally, directly toward the opposite wall. The gun's muzzle-flash momentarily lit the dark alley and spit a bullet past him. But now instinct had replaced panic.

What shoes am I wearing?

The question flashed through Thomas's mind as he hurtled for the brick wall, left foot leading. A critical question.

His answer came when his foot planted on the wall. Rubber soles. One more step up the wall with traction to spare. He threw his head back, arched hard, pushed himself off the brick, then twisted to his right halfway through his rotation. The move was simply an inverted bicycle kick, but he hadn't executed it in half a dozen years, and this time his eyes weren't on a soccer ball tossed up by one of his Filipino friends in Manila.

This time it was a gun.

The man managed one shot before Thomas's left foot smashed into his hand, sending the pistol clattering down the alley. The bullet tugged at his collar.

Thomas didn't land lightly on his feet as hoped. He sprawled to his hands, rolled once, and sprang into the seventh fighting position opposite a well-muscled man with short black hair. Not exactly a perfectly executed maneuver. Not terrible for someone who hadn't fought in six years.

The man's eyes were round with shock. His experience in the martial arts obviously didn't extend beyond *The Matrix*. Thomas was briefly tempted to shout for joy, but if anything, he had to shut this man up before *he* could call out.

The man's astonishment changed to a snarl, and Thomas saw the knife in his right hand. Okay, so maybe the man knew more about street fighting than was at first apparent.

He ducked the knife's first swipe. Came up with his palm to the man's chin. Bone cracked.

It wasn't enough. This man was twice his weight, with twice his muscle, and ten times his bad blood.

Thomas launched himself vertically and spun into a full roundhouse kick, screaming despite his better judgment. His foot had to be doing a good eighty miles an hour when it struck the man's jaw.

They both hit the concrete at precisely the same time, Thomas on his feet ready to deliver another blow; his assailant on his back, breathing hard, ready for the grave. Figuratively speaking.

The man's silver pistol lay near the wall. Thomas took a step for it, then rejected the notion. What was he going to do? Shoot back? Kill? Incriminate himself? Not smart. He turned and ran back in the direction they'd come.

The main alley was empty. He ducked into it, edged along the wall, grabbed the rails to a steel fire escape, and quickly ascended. The building's roof was flat and shouldered another taller building to the south. He swung up to the second building, ran in a crouch, and halted by a large vent, nearly a full block from the alley where he'd laid out the New Yorker.

He dropped to his knees, pressed back into the shadows, and listened past the thumping of his heart.

The hum of a million tires rolling over asphalt. The distant roar of a jet overhead. The faint sound of idle talk. The sizzling of food frying in a pan, or of water being poured from a window. The former, considering they were in Denver, not the Philippines. No sounds from New York. He leaned back and closed his eyes, catching his breath.

Fights in Manila as a teenager were one thing, but here in the States at the ripe age of twenty-five? The whole sequence struck him as surreal. It was hard to believe this had just happened to him.

Or, more accurately, *was* happening to him. He still had to figure a way out of this mess. Did they know where he lived? No one had followed him to the roof.

Thomas crept to the ledge. Another alley ran directly below, adjoining busy streets on either side. Denver's brilliant skyline glimmered on the horizon directly ahead. An odd odor met his nose, sweet like cotton candy but mixed with rubber or something burning.

Déjà vu! He'd been here before, hadn't he? No, of course not. Lights shimmered in hot summer air, reds and yellows and blues, like jewels sprinkled from heaven. He could swear he'd been . . .

Thomas's head suddenly snapped to the left. He threw out his arms, but his world spun impossibly and he knew that he was in trouble.

Something had hit him. Something like a sledgehammer. Something like a bullet.

He felt himself topple, but he wasn't sure if he was really falling or if he was losing consciousness. Something was horribly wrong with his head. He landed hard on his back, in a pillow of black that swallowed his mind whole.

And then . . .

And then Thomas Hunter dreamed, and the world would never be the same.

2

THE MAN'S eyes snapped open. A pitch-black sky above. No lights, no stars, no buildings. Only black. And a small moon.

He blinked and tried to remember where he was. Who he was. But all he could remember was that he'd just had a vivid dream.

He closed his eyes and fought to wake. He'd dreamed that he was running from some men who wanted to hurt him, presumably from New York. He'd escaped like a spider up a wall. Then he'd stared out at the lights. Such beautiful, brilliant lights. Now he was awake.

He sat up, disoriented. The shadows of tall, dark trees surrounded a rocky clearing in which he'd been sleeping. His eyes began to adjust to the darkness, and he saw a field of some kind ahead.

He stood to his feet and steadied himself. On his feet, leather moccasins. On his body, dark pants, tan suede shirt with two pockets. He instinctively felt for his left temple, where a sharp ache throbbed. His fingers came away bloody.

He'd been struck in his dream. He turned and saw a dark patch glistening on the rock where he'd fallen. He must have fallen, struck his head against the rock, and been knocked unconscious. But where was he? Maybe the knock to his head had given him amnesia.

What was his name? *Thomas.* The man in his dream had called him Thomas Hunter.

Thomas felt the bleeding bump on his head again. The surface wound above his ear matted his hair with blood. It had knocked him senseless, but thankfully no more.

He lowered his hand and stared at a tree without full comprehension.

Square branches jutted off from the trunk at a harsh angle before squaring and turning skyward, like claws grasping at the heavens. The smooth bark looked as though it might be made of metal or a carbon fiber rather than organic material.

Why did this sight disturb him?

"It looks perfectly good."

Thomas spun to the voice.

A redhead dressed in blue trousers stood on a rock behind him, looking at a small puddle of water nestled in a boulder at the edge of the clearing. There was something strange about the water, but he couldn't put his finger on it. Did . . . did he know this man?

"The water looks clean to me," the man said.

Thomas cleared his throat. "What's . . . what happened?"

"I think we should try it."

"Where are we?" Thomas asked.

"Good question." The man looked at him. A thin grin twisted his lips. "You really don't remember? What, you get knocked in the head or something?"

"I must have. I . . . I can't remember a thing."

"What's your name?"

"Thomas. I think."

"Well, you know that much. Now all we have to do is find a way out of here."

"And, umm . . . I know this sounds crazy, but what's your name?"

"Seriously? You don't remember?" The man walked over to the water and knelt on one heel.

"No."

"Bill," the man said absently. "My name is Bill." He reached down and touched the water. Brought it to his nose and sniffed. His eyes closed as he savored the scent.

Thomas glanced around the clearing, willing his mind to remember. Odd how he could remember some things but not others. He knew that these tall black things were called trees, that the material on his body was called clothing, that the organ pumping in his chest was a heart. He even knew that this kind of selective memory loss was consistent with amnesia. But he couldn't remember any history. Couldn't remember how he got here. Didn't know why Bill was so mesmerized by the water. Didn't even know who Bill was.

"I had a dream about being chased down an alley," Thomas said. "Is that how we got here?"

"If only it were that simple. I dreamed of Lucy Lane last night—if only she really did have an obsession over me." He grinned.

Thomas closed his eyes, rubbed his temples, paced, and then faced Bill again, desperate for some sense of familiarity. "So then . . . where are we?"

"This water smells absolutely delicious. We need to drink. How long has it been since you had water?" Bill was looking at the liquid on his finger. That was another thing Thomas knew: They shouldn't drink the water. But Bill seemed to be considering it very seriously.

"I don't think—"

A breathy snicker cut the night. Thomas scanned the trees.

"You hear that?"

"Are we *hearing* things now?" Bill asked.

The sound came again, a soft rattle more than a snicker. "Something's out there."

"You're hearing things."

Bill dipped three fingers into the water. This time he lifted them above his mouth and let a drop fall on his tongue.

The effects were immediate. He shuddered and stared at his wet finger. Slowly his mouth twisted into a smile. He placed his fingers into his mouth and sucked with such relief, such rapture, that Thomas thought he'd lost his mind on the spot.

Bill suddenly dropped to his knees and plopped his face into the small pool of water. He drank, like a horse from a trough, sucking down the water in long, noisy pulls.

Then he stood, trembling, licking his lips.

"Bill?"

"Huh?"

"What are you doing?"

Bill jerked his head around and scowled. "I'm drinking the water. I suggest you do the same before you die. Drink the water, Thomas. Drink it or he'll rip—" He caught himself midsentence and blinked.

His took several deep breaths, then looked at the water at his feet, lost in thought. After a moment he knelt and reached for the water, as if it drew him beyond mere thirst. He sampled the liquid again, groaning with what could only be pleasure. This man named Bill, whom he presumably knew, was either in desperate need of water or had flipped his lid completely. Odd, because Thomas wasn't that thirsty. Was he?

Bill stood and scanned the forest, now drawn as much by the dark trees as he had been by the water.

"You have to try the water, Thomas. You absolutely have to drink the water."

Then, without another word, Bill walked into the black forest and vanished into the night.

"Bill?" Thomas peered into the night where Bill had disappeared. Should he follow? He ran forward and pulled up by the boulder.

"Bill!"

Nothing.

Thomas took three long steps forward, planted his left hand on one of the boulders surrounding the puddle of water, and vaulted in pursuit. A chill flashed up his arm. He glanced down, midvault, and saw that his index finger rested in the puddle of water.

The world slowed.

Something like an electrical current ran up his arm, over his shoulder, straight to his spine. The base of his skull buzzed with intense pleasure, pulling him to the water, begging him to plunge his head into this pool.

Then his foot landed beyond the rock and another reality jerked him from the water. Pain. The intense searing pain of a blade slicing through his leather moccasins and into his heel.

Thomas gasped and dived headlong into the field past the boulder. The instant his outstretched hands made contact with the ground, pain shot up his arms and he knew he had made a dreadful mistake. Nausea swept through his body. Razor-sharp shale sliced through his flesh as though it were butter. He recoiled, shuddering as the shale pulled free from deep cuts in his forearms.

He groaned and fought to retain consciousness. Pinpricks of light swam in his clenched eyes. High above, a million leaves rustled in the night breeze. The snickers of a thousand—

His eyes snapped open. *Snickers?* His mind wrestled between throbbing pain and the terrible fear that he wasn't alone.

From a branch not five feet above him hung a large, lumpy growth the length of his arm. Next to the growth hung another, like a cluster of black grapes. If he hadn't fallen, he might have hit his head on the clumps.

The growth nearest him suddenly moved.

Two wings unfolded from the growth. A triangular face tilted toward him, exposing pupil-less eyes. Large, red, pupil-less eyes. A thin pink tongue snaked out of black lips and tested the air.

He jerked his eyes to the other growths. A thousand black creatures clung to the branches surrounding him, peering at him with red eyes too large for their angular faces.

The bat closest to him curled its lips to expose dirty yellow fangs.

Thomas screamed. His world washed with blackness.

3

HIS MIND crawled out of darkness slowly, beating back images of large black bats with red eyes. He was breathing in quick, short gasps, sure that at any moment one of the growths would drop off its branch and latch onto his neck.

Something smelled putrid. Rotten meat. He couldn't breathe properly past the stuff in his face, this bat guano or this rotten meat or—

Thomas opened his eyes. Something was sitting on his face. It was clogging his nostrils and had worked its way into his mouth.

He jerked up, spitting. No bats. There were big black bags and there were swollen boxes and some of them had broken open. Lettuce and tomatoes and rotten meat. Garbage.

High above, the building's roof drew a line across the night sky. That's right, he'd been hit on the head and he'd fallen into the alley, into a large garbage bin.

Thomas sat in slimy vegetables swamped with a moment of intense relief. The bats had just been a dream.

And the men from New York?

He hauled himself up by the lip, glanced down a vacant alley. Pain throbbed over his temple and he winced. His hair was matted with blood, but the bullet must have only grazed him.

There were two possibilities here, depending on how much time had elapsed since he'd fallen. Either the shooter was still making his way toward Thomas, or the shooter had already come and gone without digging through the garbage bin.

Either way, Thomas had to move now, while the alley was empty. His apartment was only a few blocks away. He had to reach it.

Then again, if they knew where he lived, wouldn't they just wait for him there?

He crawled out of the bin and hurried down the alley, glancing both ways. If they knew where he lived, they would have waited for him there in the first place, rather than risk confronting him in the open as they had.

He had to get to the apartment and warn Kara. His sister's nursing shift ended at one in the morning. It was now about midnight, unless he'd been out a long time. What if he'd been out for several hours? Or a whole day?

His head ached, and his new white Banana Republic T-shirt was soaked with blood. Ninth Street still roared with traffic. He would have to cross it to get to his apartment, but he didn't fancy the idea of scurrying down the sidewalk to the next intersection for all to see.

Still no sign of his attackers. He crouched in the alley and waited for traffic to clear. He could vault the hedge, cross the park, and get to the complex over the concrete wall in the back.

Thomas closed his eyes, took a deep breath, and let it out slowly. How much trouble could one person possibly get into in the span of twenty-five years? Never mind that he'd been born an army brat in the Philippines, son of Chaplain Hunter, who'd preached love for twenty years and then abandoned his wife for a Filipino woman half his age. Never mind that he'd grown up in a neighborhood that made the Bronx look like a preschool. Never mind that he'd been exposed to more of the world by the age of ten than most Americans were exposed to in a lifetime.

If it wasn't Dad leaving, it was Mom going ballistic and then sinking into bottomless depression. That's why these men were here now. Because Dad had left Mom, and Mom had gone ballistic, and Thomas, good old Thomas, had been forced to bail Mom out.

Admittedly, what he'd done to bail her out was a bit extreme, but he'd done it, hadn't he?

A fifty-yard gap opened in the traffic, and he bolted for the street. One horn blast from some conscientious citizen, whose idea of a desperate situation was probably a dirty Mercedes, and Thomas was across. He vaulted the hedge and sprinted across the park under the shadows of lamp-lit aspens.

Amazing how real the bat dream had felt.

Three minutes later, Thomas rounded the exterior stairs to his third-floor apartment. He took the stairs two at a time, eyes still peeled for any sign of the New Yorkers. None. But it would only be a matter of time.

He slipped into his flat, eased the door closed, twisted the deadbolt home, and dropped his head on the door, breathing hard. This was good. He'd actually made it.

He glanced at the clock on the wall. Eleven p.m. Half an hour since that first bullet had plowed into the brick wall. He'd made it for all of one half hour. How many more half hours would he have to make it?

Thomas turned and walked to the chest under the window. The flat was a simple two-bedroom apartment, but one glance and even the most jaded traveler would know its inhabitants were not your average, simple people.

The north side of the room looked like it could be a set piece of one of Cirque du Soleil's extravagant acts. A large ring of masquerade masks circled a huge globe, six feet in diameter, cut in half and hung to give the appearance it protruded from the wall. A chaise lounge rested below amid at least twenty silk throw pillows of various designs and colors. Spoils of Thomas's travels and episodic seasons of success.

On the south wall, two dozen spears and blowguns from Southeast Asia surrounded four large, ceremonial shields. Below them stood no fewer than twenty large carvings, including a life-sized lion carved out of ironwood. These were the remnants of a failed attempt at importing exotic artifacts from Asia to sell in art houses and at swap meets. If Kara knew that the real purpose of the venture had been to smuggle crocodile skins and bird of paradise feathers in the carvings' carefully hollowed torsos, she would have undoubtedly thrown him out by the ear. The streets of Manila had taught her a few lessons as well, and his older sister could handle herself surprisingly well. Maybe too well. Fortunately, he'd come to his senses without the need for such persuasion.

Thomas dropped to his knees and threw open the lid of an old chest. He twisted around, saw that the door was indeed firmly locked, and began rummaging through the musty wood box.

He grabbed handfuls of papers and dumped them on the floor. The receipt was yellow; he was sure of that. He'd buried it here four years ago when he'd first come to Denver to live with his sister.

A thick ream of paper came out in his hands. He grunted at the manuscript, struck by its weight. Heavy. Like a stone. Dead on arrival. This wasn't the receipt, but it arrested his attention anyway. His latest failed endeavor. An important novel entitled *To Kill with Reason*. Actually it was his second novel. He reached into the box and pulled out the first. *Superheroes in Super Fog.* The title was admittedly confusing, but that was no reason for the self-appointed literary wizards scouring the earth for the next Stephen King to turn it down. Both novels were either brilliant or complete trash, and he wasn't yet sure which. Kara had liked them both.

Kara was a god.

Now he had two novels in his hands. Enough dead weight to pull him to the bottom of any lake. He stared at the top title, *Superheroes in Super Fog,* and considered the matter yet again. He'd given three years of his life to these stacks of paper before entombing them in this grave with a thousand rejection slips to keep them company.

The whole business made his stomach crawl. As it turned out, dishing out coffees at Java Hut actually paid more than writing brilliant novels. Or, for that matter, importing exotic carvings from Southeast Asia.

He dropped the manuscripts with a loud thump and shuffled through the chest. Yellow. He was looking for a yellow slip of paper, a carbon-copy sales receipt. The kind written by hand, not tape from a machine. The receipt had a contact name on it. He couldn't even remember who had loaned him the money. Some loan shark. Without that receipt, Thomas didn't even know where to start.

Then it was there, in his hand.

Thomas stared at the slip of paper. Real, definitely real. The amount, the name, the date. Like a death sentence. His head swam. Very, very, real.

He lowered his hand and swallowed. At the bottom of the chest lay an old blackened machete he'd bought in one of Manila's back alleys. He impulsively grabbed it, jumped to his feet, and ran for the light switch by the door. The place was lit up like a bonfire. It was these kinds of stupid mistakes that got people killed. So says the aspiring fiction writer.

He slapped off the lights, pulled back the curtains, and peered out. Clear. He released the drape and turned around. Faces peered at him. Kara's masquerade masks, laughing and frowning.

His knees felt weak. From loss of blood, from the trauma of a bullet to the head, from a growing certainty that this fiasco was only just beginning and it would take more than a whole lot of luck and a few karate kicks to keep it from ending badly.

Thomas hurried to the kitchen, set the machete on the counter, and called his mother in New York. She answered on the tenth ring.

"Hello?"

"Mom?"

"Tommy."

He released a silent breath of relief. "It's Tommy. Um . . . you're okay, huh?"

"What time is it? It's after one in the morning."

"Sorry. Okay, I just wanted to check on you."

His mother was silent.

"You sure you're okay?"

"Yes, Tommy. I'm fine." Pause. "Thanks for checking though."

"Sure."

"You kids doing okay?"

"Yes. Sure, of course."

"I talked to Kara on Saturday. She seems to be doing well."

"Yeah. You sound good." He could always tell when she was struggling. Depression was difficult to hide. Her last serious bout had been over two years ago. With any luck the beast was gone for good.

More to the point, it didn't sound like there were any gunmen in her apartment, holding her hostage.

"I have to run," he said. "You need anything, you call, okay?"

"Sure, Tommy. Thanks for calling."

He dropped the receiver in its cradle and steadied himself on the counter. He was really in a pickle this time, wasn't he? And no quick solutions were coming to mind.

He had to get off his feet.

Thomas grabbed the machete and hurried to his bathroom, head swimming. He stood in front of the mirror and ran his fingers along his head wound again. No more bleeding, that was good. But his whole head throbbed. For all he knew, he had a concussion.

It took him less than five minutes to clean up, change his clothes, and don a baseball cap. He walked back out to the living room and collapsed on the couch. Kara could dress the cut properly when she got home.

He lay back and thought about calling her at work but decided an explanation over the phone would be too difficult. The room began to spin, so he closed his eyes.

He had an hour to think of something. Anything.

But nothing came.

Except sleep.

4

THOMAS WASN'T sure if it was the heat or the buzzing that woke him, but he woke with a start, snapped his eyes open, and squinted.

Impressions registered in his mind like falling dominoes. The blue sky. The sun. The black trees. A lone bat perched high above him, like a deformed vulture. Thomas held perfectly still and stared up through slits, determined to make sense of what was happening.

He'd just had another incredibly lifelike dream of a place called Denver.

For a fleeting moment he felt relieved that his dream was only that, a dream. That he really hadn't been shot in the head and that his life really wasn't in danger.

But then he remembered that he really *was* in danger. He had banged his head on a rock and cut his foot on the shale and passed out under the red gaze of a hungry bat. He wasn't sure what he should fear more, the horrors in his dream or the horrors here.

Bill.

Thomas opened his eyes wide and ran them in circles to view as much as he could without having to move. He couldn't see where the buzzing came from. Stark, square branches jutted from the leafless trees. Lifeless, charred trees.

He concentrated, grasping for memories. None that preceded his fall came to mind. The amnesia had locked them out. His surroundings looked oddly familiar, as if he'd been here before, but he felt disconnected from the scene.

His head ached.

His right foot throbbed.

The bat didn't look as threatening as it had last night.

Thomas slowly pushed himself up to his elbow and glanced around the black forest. To his left, a large black field of ash lay between him and a small pond. Fruit that he hadn't seen last night hung on the trees in a stunning variety of colors. Red and blue and yellow, all hanging in an im-possible contrast to the stark black trees. Something seemed very wrong here. More than the strange surroundings, more than the fact that Bill had disappeared. Thomas couldn't put his finger on it.

Except for the one high above, the bats were gone. He knew about the bats, didn't he? Somewhere back in his lost memories, he was completely familiar with bats. He knew that they were dangerous and evil and had very sharp teeth, but he couldn't remember other details, like how to avoid them. Or how to wring their necks.

A blanket of black rose from the field. The buzzing swelled.

Thomas scrambled to his feet. What he'd thought was black soot on the field was actually a blanket of flies. They buzzed a few feet off the ground and then settled again. As far as the clearing extended, the squirming, black-winged insects crawled over one another, forming a thick, living carpet.

He backed up, fighting a sudden panic. He had to get out of here. He had to find someone who could tell him what was going on. He didn't even know what he was running from.

But he *was* running, wasn't he?

That's why he was having those crazy dreams of Denver. He was dreaming of running in Denver because he really *was* running. Here, in this black forest.

He glanced back in the direction he assumed he'd come from, then quickly realized he had no idea which direction he'd truly come from. Behind him, the sharp shale that had sliced into his feet and arms. Beyond the shale, more black forest. Ahead, the field of flies and then more black forest. Everywhere, the black, angular trees.

A cackle rasped through the air to his right. Thomas turned slowly. A second bat within spitting distance stared at him from its perch on a branch. It looked like someone had stuffed two cherries into the flier's eye sockets and then pinned its eyelids back.

Movement in the sky. He glanced up. More bats. Streams of them, filling the bare branches high above. The bat nearby did not flinch. Did not blink. The treetops turned black with bats.

Eyes fixed on the lone creature, Thomas backed into a rock and reached out his hand to steady himself. His hand touched water.

A chill surged through his fingers, up his arm. A cool pleasure. Yes, of course, the water. Something was up with the water; that was another thing he remembered. He knew he should jerk his hand out, but he was off balance and his eyes were fixed on the black bat, who stared at him with those bulging red eyes, and he let his hand linger.

He dropped to his elbow and pulled his hand out of the water, turning to it as he did.

The small pool of water pulsed with emerald hues. Immediately he felt himself drawn in. His face was eighteen inches from this shimmering liquid, and he desperately wanted to thrust his head into the puddle, but he knew, he just knew . . .

Actually, he wasn't sure what he knew.

He knew he couldn't break his stare and look off somewhere else, like at the buzzing meadow or at the canopy still filling with black bats.

The bats screeched in delight somewhere in the back of his mind.

He slowly dipped a finger into the puddle. Another shot of pleasure surged through his veins, a tingling sensation that he liked. More than liked. It was like Novocain. And then he felt another sensation joining the first. Pain. But the pleasure was greater. No wonder Bill had—

A shriek pierced the sky.

Thomas's eyes sprang open and he stared numbly at his hand. Red juice dripped from his fingers. Red juice or blood.

Blood?

He stepped back.

Another shriek high above him. He looked at the sky and saw that a

- lone white bat was streaking through the ranks of black beasts, scattering them from their perches.

The black creatures gave chase, obviously opposing the presence of the white flier. With a piercing cry, the white intruder looped over and dived through the squawking throngs again. *If the black bats are my enemies, the white one might be my ally.* But were the black bats his enemies? He looked back at the water. Pulsing, wonderful. It occurred to Thomas that he wasn't thinking clearly.

A shrill call like a trumpet sounded from the white bat's direction. Thomas turned again and saw that the white bat had circled and was streaking over the meadow, trumpeting as it blasted through the horde of black flies. And then Thomas caught a single, brief glimpse of the white bat's green eyes as it swooped by.

He knew those eyes!

If he wanted to live out this day, he had to follow that white flier. He was sure of it. Thomas tore his feet from the ground and lurched toward the meadow. His flesh throbbed from the cuts of yesterday's fall and his bones felt like they were on fire, but everything was suddenly quite clear. He had to follow the white creature or he would die.

He forced his legs forward and ran into the meadow despite the pain. He'd made it this far into the black forest by running, hadn't he? And now it was time to run again.

At first the flies let him pass. An unbroken swarm lifted from the pond and buzzed in chaotic circles, as if confused by the sudden turn of events. Thomas was midfield, racing toward the black trees on the far side, when they began attacking. They came in from his left, swarming, slammed into his body and face like dive bombers on suicide runs.

He cried out in panic, raised his arms to cover his eyes, and nearly beat a hasty retreat. But he had come too far already.

His shoulders suddenly felt like they were on fire, and with a single terrified glance Thomas realized the flies were already through his shirt, eating his flesh. He slapped madly at his skin and sprinted for the trees. The flies blanketed his body, chewing.

Fifty yards.

He swatted at his face to clear his vision, but the little beasts refused to budge. They were getting in his ears and his nose. They furiously attacked his eyes. He screamed, but the flies bit at his tongue and he clamped his mouth shut. He wasn't going to make it.

A chorus of screeches filled the air behind him. The black bats.

Fangs sank into his left calf. Pain shot up his spine, and the last threads of reason fell from his mind. Time and space ceased to exist. Only reaction remained. The only messages that managed to get through the buzz in his brain were to his muscles, and they said run or die, kill or be killed.

He smashed at his calf. The black bat fell away but took a chunk of flesh with it.

Twenty yards.

Another bat attached itself to his thigh. Thomas clamped his mouth to keep from screaming and pumped his arms with every ounce of strength remaining in his strained muscles.

He plunged into the forest, and immediately the flies cleared.

The bats did not.

His shirt was tattered and his skin was red. Covered in blood. He stumbled through the trees, nauseated, legs numb from the loss of blood.

A black bat landed on his shoulder, but each nerve cut by the beast's sharp teeth was already inflamed with pain, and Thomas barely noticed the black lump on his shoulder now. Another attached itself to his buttocks. He ignored the bats and lurched drunkenly through the trees.

Where was the white bat? There. Left. Thomas swerved, hit a tree head-on, and dropped to the ground. He tried to catch his fall with his right arm, but his forearm broke with a tremendous snap. White-hot pain flashed up his neck.

The bats lodged on his body lost their places and screeched in protest, beating their wings furiously. He struggled to his feet and lurched forward, right arm dangling uselessly at his side. The bats landed on Thomas's jerking body, struggled for footing, and began chewing again.

He stumbled on, vaguely aware that his moccasins and most of his clothes were now gone, leaving only a loincloth. He could feel fangs working on his thigh.

A voice, slippery and deep, echoed quietly through the trees. "You will find your destiny with me, Thomas Hunter."

The voice had come from one of the bats behind him, he could swear it. But then he broke from the forest onto the bank of a river and the thought was lost.

A white bridge spanned the flowing water. A towering, multicolored forest lined the far bank, dazzling like a box of crayons topped with a bright green canopy. The sight stopped him.

Green. A mirage or heaven.

Thomas limped toward the bridge, hardly aware of the bats squawking on his back. His breathing came in great gasps. His flesh quivered. The black bats fell from his back. The lone white bat flapped eagerly on a low branch across the river. His ally was large, maybe as high as Thomas's knees with a wingspan three times that. Its kind green eyes fixed on him.

He knew this bat as well, didn't he? At least he knew that his hope rested in this creature now.

In his peripheral vision, Thomas saw that thousands of the black creatures were lining the stark trees behind him. He wobbled onto the bridge and gripped its rail tightly for support. His mind began to drift with the water below. Slowly but steadily he hauled himself across the bridge, over the rushing waters, all the way to the other side. He collapsed into a thick bed of emerald green grass.

He was dying. That was the last thing he thought before the pain shoved him into the world of unconsciousness.

5

SOMETHING WOKE him. A noise or a breeze—something had pulled him from his dreams.

Thomas blinked in the darkness. Breathed hard, tried to clear his mind. The bats weren't simply figments of his imagination. Nothing was. His name was Thomas Hunter. He'd fallen on a rock and lost his memory, and he'd just escaped the black forest. Barely. Now he'd just passed out and he was dreaming.

Dreaming that he was Thomas Hunter, being chased by loan sharks he'd stiffed for $100,000 four years ago in New York. Assuming that really was the party responsible for the wound on his head—he couldn't be sure.

Problem was, this dream of Denver felt as real as the black forest had. There had to be a way to tell if he really was, at this very moment, physically lying on a bed of green grass or staring at the ceiling of an apartment in Denver, Colorado. He could test the reality of this environment by standing up and walking around, but that wouldn't help if his dreams felt like reality. He would be able to see if his skin was stripped off or if his arm was broken, but since when did dreams reflect reality? He'd broken his arm in the black forest, but here in this dream of Denver, he could be totally healthy. In dreams, the condition of one's body didn't necessarily correlate.

Thomas moved his arm. No broken bone. He had to find a way to push past this dream and wake up on the riverbank before he died there, lying on the grass.

The door opened and Thomas reacted without thinking. He grabbed the machete, rolled to the ground, and came up in position one, blade ex-tended toward the door.

"Thomas?"

Kara stood at the door, facing him with wide eyes. She certainly looked real enough. Standing right there, still wearing her white nurse's outfit, long blonde hair pulled up off her neck, blue eyes as bright and feisty as ever. He straightened.

"Expecting someone?" She flipped the switch.

Light flooded the apartment. If this was real and not a dream, light could attract the night crawlers. The New Yorkers.

"Does it look like I'm expecting someone?" Thomas asked.

"What's the machete for?" She nodded at his right hand.

He lowered the blade. This couldn't be a dream, could it? He was here in their apartment, not lying unconscious by some river.

"I had a crazy dream."

"Yeah, how so?"

"It felt real. I mean *really* real."

Kara tossed her purse on the end table. "Nightmare, huh? Don't they all?"

"This wasn't like just any dream that feels real. I keep falling asleep in my dream, and then waking up here."

She stared at him, uncomprehending.

"What I'm saying is that I only wake up here if and when I fall asleep there."

A blank stare. "And?"

"And how do I know I'm not dreaming here, right now?"

"Because I'm standing here, and I can tell you that you're not dreaming right now."

"'Course you would. You'd be in the dream, wouldn't you? That's why you'd think you're real. That's why I think you're—"

"You've written one too many novels, Thomas. It's late, and I need to get some sleep."

She was right. And if she was right, their problems weren't as simple as a case of the delusional novelist being chased by black bats.

Kara turned and started for her room.

"Uh, Kara?"

"Please. I don't have the energy for another crisis right now."

"What makes you think this is a crisis?"

She turned. "You know I love you, brother, but trust me, when you wake up with a machete in your hand, telling me I'm just part of your dream, I think to myself, *Tommy's going off the deep end.*"

She made a good point. Thomas glanced at the window. No signs of anything.

"Have I gone off the deep end before?" he asked. "I don't remember doing that."

"You *live* off the deep end." She paused. "I'm sorry, that's not fair. Apart from buying $20,000 worth of statues you can't sell and trying to smuggle crocodile skins in them and—"

"You knew about that?"

"Please." She smiled. "Good night, Thomas."

"I was shot in the head tonight." His urgency suddenly returned. He ran to the window and peered past the curtain. "If this isn't a dream, then we have a very big problem."

"Now you *are* dreaming," she said.

He yanked off his hat. The cut must have been obvious, because her eyes went wide.

"I kid you not. I was chased by some guys from New York and got shot in the head. I passed out in a garbage can but escaped before they could find me. And you're right, I'm not dead."

Kara hurried over, incredulous. "You got shot in the head?" She touched his scalp gently, as a nurse would.

"It's fine. But we may not be."

"It's a head wound! You need a dressing on this."

"It's just a surface wound."

"I'm so sorry, Tommy. I had no idea."

He closed his eyes and took a deep breath. "If you only knew. I'm the one who should be sorry." Then under his breath, "I can't believe this is happening."

"You can't believe *what's* happening?"

"We have a problem, Kara," he said, pacing. She was going to kill him, but he was beyond that now. "Remember when Mom lost it after the divorce?"

"And?"

"I was there with her in New York. She couldn't work, she got into some serious debt, and they were going to take everything away from her."

"You helped her out," Kara said. "You sold out your end of the tour company and bailed her out."

"Well, I helped her out. And then I came to help you out."

She tilted her head. "But you *didn't* sell your end of the tour company. Is that what you're going to say?"

"No, I didn't sell out. It was already a bust."

"Don't tell me you borrowed money from those crooks you used to talk about."

He didn't answer.

"Thomas? No!" She lifted her hands in exasperation and turned away. "No." She spun back. "How much?"

"Too much to pay back right away. I'm working on it."

"How *much?*"

He dug out the receipt, handed it to her, and walked back to the curtain, as much now to avoid her eyes as to check the perimeter again.

"One hundred dollars?"

"Thousand," he said.

She gasped. "One hundred thousand? That's insane!"

"Well, unless I'm dreaming, it's real. Mom needed sixty to come clean, you needed a new car, and I needed twenty-five for my new business. The carvings."

"And you just took off from New York, hoping they would be fine with that?"

"I didn't just take off. I left a trail to South America and then split with full intention to pay them back in time. I have a buyer in Los Angeles who's interested in the carvings—should bring in fifty, and that's without the contraband. Just took a little longer than I expected."

"A *little* longer? What about Mom? You're endangering her?"

"No. No connection they ever knew about. As far as the records go, she got her money from the divorce settlement. But that's not important. What is important is that they found me, and I doubt they're interested in anything other than cash. Now."

The full meaning of what he was saying settled over Kara. Any sympathy she'd felt for his bullet wound seemed to vanish. "Of course they found you, you idiot! What do you think this is—Manila? You can't just walk away with $100,000 of the mob's money and expect to live happily ever after. They let one person get away with it, and every Thomas, Dick, and Harriet will be robbing them blind!"

"We don't know it's them."

"You just said it was."

"I just got shot, for crying out loud!"

"We'll be lucky if we *both* don't get shot! What were you thinking, moving here?"

Her statement hit him broadside. He took a deep breath and closed his eyes. The whole business suddenly felt impossibly heavy to him. He'd risked more than she could ever know to help out their mother. He'd left a life behind in New York to protect her, to make a clean break, to get back on his feet with the import business. That he would endanger Kara by bringing this debt to Denver had never occurred to him.

What was he thinking moving here, she wanted to know? He was thinking that they'd both been abandoned by their parents. That they didn't have any real friends. Or any real home. That they were suspended between countries and societies and left wondering where they fit in. He wanted to be Kara's brother—to help her and to be helped by her.

"I was twenty-one," he said.

"So?"

"So I wasn't thinking. You were having a tough time."

Her hands dropped to her thighs with a slap. "I know. And you've always been there for me. But this . . . I just can't believe you were so stupid."

"I'm sorry. Really, I'm sorry."

Kara looked at him and began to pace. She was steaming all right, but she couldn't bring herself to take his head off. They'd been through too much together. Being raised as outcasts in a foreign land had woven an inseverable bond between them.

"You can be an idiot, Thomas."

Then again, the bond wasn't beyond being stretched now and then.

"Look," he said, "I know this isn't good, but it's not all bad."

"Of course not. We're still alive, right? We should be eternally grateful. We're walking and breathing. You have a cut on your head, but it could have been much worse. We should be toasting our good fortune."

"They don't know where we live."

"See, that's the problem here," she said. "It's already gone from *I* to *we*. And there's nothing *we* can do about it."

The pain in Thomas's head was making a strong comeback. A wave of dizziness swept over him, and he walked unsteadily for the chaise lounge. He sat hard and groaned.

Kara sighed and disappeared into her room. She came out a few seconds later with some gauze, a bottle of peroxide, and a tube of Neosporin and sat by him.

"Let me see that."

He faced the wall and let her dab the wound with peroxide.

"If they knew where we lived, they would be here already," he said.

"Hold still."

"I don't know how long we have."

"I'm not going anywhere," she said emphatically.

"We can't stay here, and you know that. They found me in Denver, probably through the dinner theater. I should've thought about that—the theater advertises all over the country. My name's in the credits."

She wound the gauze around his head and taped it. "Seems appropriate that a production of *Alice in Wonderland* would end up being your demise, don't you think?"

"Please. This isn't funny anymore."

"Never was funny."

"You've made your point, okay? I was a fool, I'm sorry, but the fact is, we *are* still alive, and some pretty bad people *are* trying to kill me."

"Have you called the police yet?"

"That won't stop these guys." He ran his fingers along the bandage and stood. His world tipped crazily.

"Sit down," Kara ordered.

She was being bossy, but he deserved to be bossed at the moment. Besides, allowing her to boss him would help repair any breach in their relationship.

He sat.

"Take these." She handed him two pills. He threw them into his mouth and swallowed without water.

Kara sighed again. "Okay, from the top. You have some mob thugs after you for stiffing them out of $100,000. After four years your sins have finally caught up with you, presumably through the Magic Circle dinner theater or the Java Hut. They shot at you and you escaped. But you were on foot, so they know you live close by, and it's only a matter of time before they find you again. Right?"

"That's about it."

"To top it all off, the blow to your head is tempting you to think that you live in another world. Still right?"

He nodded. "Maybe. Sort of."

She closed her eyes. "This is insane."

"Maybe. But we still have to get out of here."

"And exactly where are we supposed to go? I have a job. I can't just pick up and take off."

"I'm not saying we can't come back. But we can't just wait here for them." He stood and began to pace, ignoring a sudden whirl of disorientation. "Maybe we should go back to the Philippines for a while. We have passports. We have friends who—"

"Forget it. It's taken me ten years to make the break from Manila. I'm not going back. Not now."

"Please, you have more Filipino in you than American. You can't run forever."

"Who's got the bullet wound in his head? *I'm* not running anymore. I'm here. I'm an American, I live in Denver, Colorado, and I like who I've become."

"So do I. But if they came this far to settle a debt, they'll hound me for the rest of my life!"

"You should have thought about that earlier."

"Like I said, you made your point. Don't beat me into the ground with it." He took a deep breath. "Maybe I can fake my death."

"How on earth did you manage to talk them out of $100,000 to start with?"

He shrugged. "I convinced them I was an arms dealer."

"Oh, that's just great."

The pain pills were starting to make him woozy. Thomas sat again, leaned back, closed his eyes. "We have to do something."

They sat quietly for a long minute. Kara had always insisted she was happy here in Denver, but she was twenty-six and she was beautiful and she hadn't dated in three years despite her talk of getting married. What did that mean? It meant she was a stranger in a strange land, just like him. Try as they may, they couldn't escape their past.

"I'm sure you'll think of something," Kara said. "I don't think I can leave."

"I'm not going to leave you alone here. Not a chance." His head was spinning. "What did you give me?"

"Demerol." She stood and walked to the window. "This is completely insane."

Thomas said something. Something about leaving immediately. Something about needing money. But his voice sounded distant. Maybe it was the Demerol. Maybe it was the knock on the head. Maybe it was because he was really lying on the bank of a river, stripped of his skin, dying.

Kara was saying something.

"What?" he asked.

". . . in the morning. Until then . . ."

That's all he got.

6

AT THE foot of the arching bridge, on thick green grass, the bloodied man lay facedown as though he had been dead for days. The black beasts on the opposite shore had deserted the charred trees. Two white creatures leaned over the prone body, their wings folded around their furry torsos, their short, spindly legs shifting so that their bodies swayed like penguins.

"Hurry, into the forest," Michal said.

"Can we drag him?" asked Gabil.

"Of course we can. Grab his other hand."

They bent, though not so far—they stood only about three feet if they stretched—and hauled the man from the bank. Michal led them over the grass, through the trees, into a small clearing surrounded by fruit trees. The ground was clear of debris and rocks, but they couldn't be doing the man's belly any favors. Soon it wouldn't matter.

"Here." He dropped the man's arm. "I assume he can't hear us."

"Of course he can't understand us. No sir," Gabil said, kneeling beside the man. "How can he understand us when he's unconscious?"

Michal nudged the man in the shoulder with a frail foot resembling a bird's. "You say you *led* him out from the black forest?" Not that he should doubt his friend, but Gabil did have a way of milking a story. It was more of a comment than a question.

Gabil nodded and scrunched his lightly furred forehead. The expression looked out of place on his round, soft face.

"He's lucky to have lived." Gabil stretched one wing in the direction they'd come. "He barely made it through the black trees. You should have seen the Shataiki that had him. Ten at least." Gabil hopped around the

41

fallen body. "You should have seen, Michal. You really should have. He must be from the far side—I don't recognize him."

"How could you possibly recognize him? His skin is missing."

"I saw him before they took his skin. I'm telling you, this one's never been in these parts before." Gabil stood over the prostrate body again, swaying.

"Well, he didn't drink the water; that's what really matters," Michal said.

"But he may have if I hadn't flown in," Gabil said enthusiastically.

"And you flew in because . . . ?" They rarely confronted the black bats anymore. There was a time, long ago, when heroic battles had been fought, but not for a millennium now.

"Because I saw the sky black with Shataiki about a mile in, that's why. I went in high, but when I saw him, I couldn't leave him. There were a thousand of the beasts flying mad circles around me, I'm telling you. It was nothing short of spectacular."

"And how did you manage to escape a thousand Shataiki?"

"Michal, please! It's I! The *conqueror* of Shataiki." He raised his wing in a mock salute. "Flies or beasts, black or red, urge them on. I'll dispatch them to darkness." He waited for a response from Michal and continued when he received none.

"Actually, I took them by surprise. Out of the sun. And did I tell you about the flies? I blasted through a horde of flies like they were the air itself."

"Of course you did." And then after a moment of thought, "Well done."

Michal tilted his head and studied the man's rising back. Fresh blood still oozed from three gaping holes at the man's neck, his buttocks, and his right thigh where the Shataiki had eaten him to the bone. His flesh quivered under the hot sun. There was something strange about the man. It was strange enough that someone from one of the distant villages had entered the black forest at all. It had happened only once before. But the strangeness was more than that. He could smell the stench that came from the man's ragged breathing—like the breath of the Shataiki bats.

"Well, let's get on with it then. You have the water?"

"Hello?"

They both turned as one. A young woman stood at the edge of the clearing, eyes wide. Rachelle.

Rachelle stared at the bloodied body, stunned by the gruesome sight. Had she ever seen anything so terrible? Never! She hurried forward, red tunic swishing below her knees.

"What . . . what is it?" A man, of course. She could see that by the muscles in his back and legs. He lay on his belly, head turned toward her, a bloody mess. "Who is he?"

The Roush, Michal and Gabil, exchanged a glance. "We don't know," Michal said.

"He's no one we know," Gabil blurted. "No sir, this one's from one of the other villages."

Rachelle stopped, mesmerized. One arm lay at an odd angle, cleanly broken below the elbow. Empathy swelled in her chest. "Dear. Oh dear, oh dear." She dropped to her knees by his shoulder. "How could anything like this possibly have happened?"

"The bats. I led him from the black forest," Gabil said.

Alarm flashed. "The bats? He's been *in* the black forest?"

"Yes, but he didn't drink the water," Michal said.

Silence settled over them. This was the work of the Shataiki! She'd never actually seen one, much less encountered their fangs, but here on the grass was evidence enough of the terrible beasts' brutality. So much blood. Why hadn't the Roush healed him immediately? They knew as much as she how blood defiled a man. It defiled man, woman, child, grass, water, anything that it touched. It wasn't meant to be spilled. And on the rare occasions that it was, there were accommodations.

Rage displaced her alarm. What kind of thinking could influence any creature to do this to a man?

"This is why Tanis has talked about an expedition to destroy the bats!" she said. "It's horrible!"

"And any expedition would put Tanis in the same condition!" Michal snapped impatiently. "Don't be ridiculous."

Rachelle returned her gaze to the bloodied body. He was breathing steadily, lost to this world. Such a poor, innocent soul.

Yet an air of mystery and intrigue seemed to rise from the man. He had entered the black forest without succumbing to the water. What kind of man could do such a thing? Only a very strong man.

"The water, Gabil," Michal said.

The smaller Roush withdrew a gourd of water from under his wing.

Rachelle wanted to reach out. To touch the man's skin. The thought surprised her.

Could *he* be the man? This thought surprised her even more. How could she dare think of choosing a man she didn't know for marriage?

Michal had taken the pouch from Gabil. He pulled the cork from its neck.

How absurd that she should think of this brutalized man as anything more than someone who desperately needed the water and Elyon's love. But the thought swelled in her mind. She felt herself irrevocably drawn to it, like blood to the heart. Since when did men and women qualify the ones they chose? All men were good, all women were good, all marriages perfect. So then why not this man if she felt so suddenly drawn by compassion for him? He was the first she'd ever seen in such desperate need of Elyon's water.

Michal waddled forward. He tilted the flask.

Rachelle lifted her hand. "Wait."

"Wait?"

She wasn't sure what had come over her, but emotion tugged at her heart in a way she'd never quite felt before. She looked at Michal. "Is . . . do you think he's marked?"

The two Roush exchanged another glance.

"What do you mean?" Michal asked.

The man's forehead, which would bear the mark of union, was covered in blood. She was suddenly desperate to wipe the blood and see if he bore the telltale one-inch circle that signified his union to another woman. Or the half circle that meant he was promised. But she hesitated; spilled blood was the undoing of Elyon's creation and should be avoided or immediately restored.

Michal lowered the water pouch. "Please, you can't seriously be thinking—"

"It's a wonderful idea!" Gabil said, hopping up and down. "How wonderfully romantic."

"Why not?" Rachelle asked Michal.

"You don't even know him!"

"Since when has that made any difference to any woman? Does Elyon exercise such discrimination? And I *did* find him."

"What you're feeling is empathy, certainly not—"

"Don't be so quick to decide what I'm feeling," Rachelle said. "I'm telling you I have a very strong feeling for this man. The poor soul has been through the most awful ordeal imaginable."

"No, it's not the worst imaginable," Michal said. "Trust me."

"But that's not the point. The point is, I feel very strongly for this man, and I think I may be meant to choose him. Is that so unreasonable?"

"No, I don't think it's unreasonable at all," the smaller Roush said. "It's very, very, very romantic! Don't be so cautious, Michal; it's a delicious thought!"

"I have no idea if he's marked," Michal said, but he seemed to have softened.

Rachelle was twenty-one, and she'd never once felt such a strong desire to choose a man. Most women her age had already chosen and been chosen. She certainly was eligible. And it really didn't matter whom she chose, more that she did choose. That was the custom.

She snatched up a handful of grass and brought it to the man's forehead. Careful not to let it make any contact with her skin, she wiped the blood away.

No mark!

Her heart pounded. The custom was rare but clear. Any eligible woman who brought wholeness to an eligible man showed her invitation. She was choosing him. The man would then accept her invitation and choose her by pursuing her.

Rachelle stood slowly. "There's no mark."

Gabil hopped. "It's perfect, perfect!"

Michal looked at her, then at the man. "It seems highly unusual, not even knowing which village he comes from. But I suppose you're right. It's your choice. Would you like to bring him wholeness?"

Her bones trembled. It seemed so daring. So audacious. But she knew, staring down at the man, that the reason she hadn't made her choice until this day was because she was more adventurous than most. Was he a good man? Of course. *All* men were good. Would he pursue her? What man would not romance a woman who had invited him? And what woman would not romance a man who had chosen her? It was the nature of the Great Romance. They all knew it. Thrived on it.

In this most unusual and daring situation, she was ready to choose this man. She was suddenly more ready to choose and be chosen by this man than she could express to any Roush, even the wisest, like Michal. How could they understand? They weren't human.

"I would," Rachelle said. "Yes, I would." She reached a trembling hand for the pouch. "Give me the water."

A smile tugged at Michal's mouth. His left brow arched. "You are sure?"

"Give me the pouch. I am very sure!"

"So you are." He handed her the water.

Rachelle took the gourd. She impulsively brought the pouch to her lips and sipped the sweet green water. A surge of power washed through her belly and she shuddered.

"Well, come on, Gabil," Michal said. "Roll him over."

Gabil stopped his pacing, clasped the man's arm, and hauled him over onto his back. "Oh dear," he said. "Yes sir. He *is* bad off, isn't he? Yes sir. Oh, may Elyon have mercy on this poor being." His broken arm now lay doubled over on itself.

The emotion that had compelled Rachelle swallowed her. She could hardly wait another second to bring wholeness to this man. She sank to her knees, tilted the pouch over his face, and let the clear green water trickle onto his lips.

The water seemed to glow a little and then spread over the man's face, as though searching for the right kind of healing for this pulp. Immediately red lumps of flesh began to recede and blend in with pink skin. The skin rippled. Shapes of a nose and lips and eyelids rose from the face.

She poured the water over the rest of the man's body now, and as quickly as the liquid spread over his skin, the blood dissipated, the redness faded, the cuts filled in with new flesh. The bruises beneath his skin lost their purple color. The man's broken forearm suddenly jerked from where it lay and began straightening. Gabil yelped and stepped back from the flailing appendage. With a loud pop the arm snapped true.

Rachelle gazed at the transformed man before her, amazed at his beauty. Golden skin, strong face, muscles that rippled, veins running up his arms. Elyon's water had healed him completely.

She'd just chosen this man as her mate, hadn't she? The thought was almost more than she could comprehend. She had actually just chosen a man! There was still his choosing of her, naturally, but—

The man heaved a tremendous breath. Gabil uttered a small cry, which alarmed Rachelle even more than the man's sudden movement. She scrambled back and jumped to her feet.

The man's eyes flickered open.

———⟨∞⟩———

Bright light filtered into Thomas's eyes and slowly brought him to his senses. His mind scrambled for orientation. A blue sky above. Brilliant green canopy shimmering in the breeze.

This wasn't Denver.

He wasn't lying on the couch after consuming Demerol after all. Denver had all been a dream. Thank heavens. Which meant . . .

The black bats.

Thomas jerked himself to a sitting position and faced a forest of trees that shone with amber- and topaz- and ruby-colored trunks. He twisted to his left. Two white creatures gazed at him with curious emerald eyes. Like white cousins to the black bats, with rounded features.

The smaller of the two looked behind him. Thomas followed his stare. A woman with long brown hair, wearing a red satin dress, stood ten feet from him, eyes wide with wonder.

He rose to his feet, immediately aware that his body wasn't brutalized. It wasn't even bloody.

The woman watched him without moving. The small furry creatures looked up quizzically. He heard rushing water nearby. Where was he? Did he know this woman? These creatures?

"Is there a problem?" the larger of the two white furries asked.

Thomas stared. He had just heard speech come from the lips of an animal. But that was nothing unusual, was it? Not at all. He shook his head to clear his thoughts, but they remained muddled.

"You came from the black forest," the creature said. "Don't worry, you didn't drink the water. I am Michal, this is Gabil, and that"—he pointed his wing at the woman—"is Rachelle." He said her name as if it should mean something to him. "How do you feel?"

"Yes, how do you feel?" the other one, Gabil, repeated.

Details of his sprint through the black forest strung through his mind. Everything felt vaguely familiar, but his memory didn't extend beyond last night, when he'd awakened after knocking his head on the rock. He felt for the wound on his skull. Gone.

He looked down at his body and slowly ran a hand over his bare chest. No cuts, no bruises, not even a hint of the carnage he remembered from the chase.

Thomas looked at the woman. "I feel fine."

She arched a brow and smiled. "Fine?" She stepped forward on bare feet and stopped at arm's length. "What is your name?"

He hesitated. "Thomas Hunter?"

"So nice to make your acquaintance, Thomas Hunter."

She reached out her hand and he tried to take it, but instead she slid her fingers over his palm. That was the greeting. He'd forgotten even that much.

"You are a beautiful man, Thomas Hunter," she said. "I have chosen you." She said it softly, her eyes bright as stars. Clearly this information implied something significant, but Thomas didn't have the foggiest notion what it could be. He said nothing.

She dipped her head, stepped back, and drilled him with a positively infectious stare, as if she'd just shared a deep, delightful secret.

Without another word, she turned and ran into the forest.

KARA AWOKE at three o'clock in the morning with a splitting headache. She tried to ignore the pain and slip back into sleep before waking completely, but the moment she remembered the predicament Thomas had brought home, her mind resisted.

She finally climbed from the covers, entered her bathroom, and washed down two Advil with a long drink of cool water. If the apartment had any shortcoming, it was the absence of air conditioning.

She headed out to the living room and stopped by the chaise. Thomas lay under the batik quilt she'd thrown over him, his position virtually unchanged from when she'd left him a couple of hours ago. Dead to the world.

Tangled brown hair curled over his eyebrows. Mouth shut, breathing steadily and deeply. A square, clean-shaven jaw. Lean, strong body. Mind as wide as the oceans.

She'd been unfair to question his decision to bring his troubles to Denver. He'd come for her sake; they both knew that. He was the baby of the family, but he'd always been the one to take care of them all. The only reason he hadn't responded to Harvard's acceptance as initially planned was because Mother needed him after the divorce. And the only reason he hadn't resumed his education after he'd settled Mother in was because his older sister needed him. He'd put his own life on hold for them. She might play tough with him, but she could hardly blame him for his alternative exploits. He'd never been one to sit back and let the world pass him by. If it wasn't going to be Harvard, it would be something else as extravagant.

Something like borrowing $100,000 from a loan shark to pay off

Mother's debt and start a new business. Given enough time, he would pay it back, but time wasn't on their side.

Yes, the problem belonged to both of them now, didn't it? What on earth would they do?

She considered waking him to make sure he was sound. Despite her dismissal earlier, this business of his vivid dream was unlike him. Thomas never did anything without careful consideration. He wasn't given to fancy. His consideration might be quick and creative—even spontaneous—but he didn't walk around speaking of hallucinations. The blow to his head had clearly affected his thinking.

What was he dreaming now?

She recalled their short transfer stateside when she was in tenth grade and he in eighth. He'd wandered around school like a lost puppy for the first two weeks, trying to fit in and failing. He was different and they all knew it. One of the football players—a junior linebacker with biceps larger than Thomas's thighs—had called him a spineless-gook-Chinese-lover one afternoon, and Thomas had finally lost his cool. He'd put the boy in the hospital with a single kick. They left him alone after that, but he never made many friends.

He was so very strong during the days, but she could hear his soft cries late at night in the room next to hers. She'd come to his rescue then. In the years since, she'd thought maybe her dissociation with the all-American male had started then. She'd take her brother over a steroid-stuffed football player any day of the week.

Kara stepped forward, leaned over, and kissed his forehead. "Don't worry, Thomas," she whispered. "We'll get out of this. We always have."

━━━⦿⦿⦿━━━

Thomas stood in the clearing and looked at the two white creatures. They were odd to be sure, with their furry white bodies and thin legs. The wings weren't made of feathers, but of skin, like a bat's wings, white like the rest of their bodies.

All familiar, but only oddly so.

"The black bats," he said. "I dreamed black bats chased me from the forest."

"That was no dream," Gabil replied in an excited tone. "No sir! You were lucky I came along when I did."

"I'm sorry, I don't . . . I can't quite remember what's going on."

The two creatures studied him with blank stares. "You don't remember anything?" Michal asked.

"No. I mean, yes, I remember being chased. But I hit my head on a rock last night and I was knocked out." He paused and tried to think of the best way to explain his disorientation. "I can't remember anything before I hit my head."

"Then you've lost your memory," Michal said. He waddled forward. "You do realize where you are?"

Thomas stepped back instinctively and the creature stopped. "Well . . . actually not entirely. Sort of, but not really." He rubbed his head. "I must have really bumped my head."

"Well then. What *do* you know?" Michal asked.

"I know that my name is Thomas Hunter. I somehow got into the black forest with someone named Bill, but I fell and smashed my head on a rock. Bill drank the water and just wandered—"

"You saw him drink the water?" Michal demanded.

"Yes, he definitely drank the water."

"Hmm."

Thomas waited for him to explain his reaction, but the creature just waved him on. "Go ahead. What then?"

"Then I saw you"—he looked at Gabil—"and I ran."

"That's all? Nothing more?"

"No. Except my dreams. I remember my dreams."

They waited expectantly.

"You want to know my dreams?"

"Yes," Michal said.

"Well, they make no sense. Completely different from this. Crazy stuff."

"Well then. Tell us this crazy stuff."

Denver. His sister, Kara. The mob. A fully formed world with amazing detail. He told the creatures the gist of it all in a long run-on sentence, but he felt self-conscious telling them his dreams, no matter how vivid they had seemed. Why would they want to know his dreams anyway? The creatures looked at him, unblinking, absorbing his brief tale without reacting.

They and the colored forest behind them were perfectly normal. He just couldn't remember them.

"That's all?" Michal asked when he'd finished.

"Mostly."

"I didn't think anyone but the wise ones knew the histories so vividly," Gabil said.

"What histories?"

"You don't know what the histories are?" Michal asked. "You're speaking about them as if you know them well enough."

"You mean my dreams of Denver are real?"

"Of course." Michal waddled in the direction the woman had run, then turned back. "I don't know about your running around with men in hot pursuit, but the histories of ancient Earth are real. Yes, of course they are. Everyone knows about them." He paused and looked at Thomas with skepticism. "You honestly don't know what I'm talking about?"

Thomas blinked and looked at the colored forest. The tree trunks glowed. So very foreign, yet so familiar.

"No," he said, rubbing his temples. "I just can't seem to think straight."

"Well, you seem to be thinking quite straight when it comes to the histories. They're an oral tradition, passed on in each of the villages by the storytellers. Denver, New York—everything you dreamed about is taken from the histories roughly two thousand years ago."

Gabil hopped sideways like a bird. "The histories!"

Michal cast a side glance at the other as if impatient. "My dear friend, I do believe you have a classic case of amnesia, though I can't understand why the water didn't heal that as well. The black forest has sent you into a state of shock—no surprise there. Now you're dreaming that you live in a world that existed thousands of years ago where you're being chased by men with ill intent. Your mind has created a detailed dream using what you know about the histories. Fascinating, really."

"Utterly fascinating!" Gabil said.

Another glance from Michal.

"But if I lost my memory, why would I remember the histories?" Thomas objected. "It's almost as if I know more about these histories than I do about . . . you."

"As I said, amnesia," Michal explained. "The mind is an amazing thing, isn't it? Selective memory loss. It seems you can remember only certain things, like the histories. You're hallucinating. You're dreaming of the histories. Reasonable enough. I'm sure the condition will pass. As I said, you've been through quite a shock, not to mention the knock to your head."

Made sense. "Just a dream. Hallucinations because I've knocked my head senseless."

"In my estimation," Michal said.

"So . . . what's the difference between this Earth and the one I dream about? What's changed?"

"Well, everything. It's practically another reality, through technically simply the past. In the other place, the histories, the forces of good and evil could not be seen. Only their effects. But here, both good and evil are more . . . intimate. As you experienced with the black bats. An incomplete differentiation, but simple enough, wouldn't you say, Gabil?"

"I would say, simple enough."

"Well then, there you have it."

The explanation didn't seem quite so simple to Thomas, but he let it suffice. A single word suddenly popped into his mind. Horde. He spoke it without thinking.

"Horde. What's that mean?"

"Horde?" Michal repeated. "It means nothing. Well, I take that back. In the histories there was once a Mongol Horde. An army that roamed China, I believe. Perhaps that's what you're thinking of."

"Yeah." But Thomas wasn't sure. "What happened to ancient Earth?"

"Oh dear, now you ask too much," Michal said, turning. "That story is not so simple. We would have to start with the great virus at the beginning of the twenty-first century—"

"The French," Gabil cut in. "The Raison Strain."

"Not really the French," Michal said. "A Frenchman, yes, but you can't say it was . . . never mind. They thought it was a good thing, a vaccine, but it mutated under intense heat and became a virus. The whole business ravaged the entire population of Earth in a matter of three short weeks—"

"Less than three," Gabil inserted. "Less than three weeks."

"—and opened the door to the Deception."

"The *Great* Deception," Gabil said.

"Yes, the Great Deception." Michal gave his friend a let-me-tell-the-story look. "From there we would have to move on to the time of the tribulations and wars. It would take a full day to tell you how ancient Earth saw the end and how then man was reborn. Sort of a take two, as they might say in the histories. Clearly you don't know all of your history, do you?"

"Obviously not."

"Perhaps your mind has inserted itself at a particular point and is stuck there. The mind, a wonderfully tricky thing, you know?"

Thomas nodded.

"How do I know *this* isn't the dream?" he asked.

Both creatures blinked.

"I mean, isn't it possible? In the Denver place I have a sister and a history, and things are really happening. Here I can't remember a thing."

"Clearly you have amnesia," Michal said. "You don't think my easily excited friend here and I are real? That isn't grass under your feet, or oxygen passing through your lungs?"

"I'm not saying that . . ."

"You've lost your memory, Thomas Hunter, if that's indeed your real name. I would guess it's the name from your dreams—they used double names in ancient Earth. But it'll do until we can figure out who you really are."

"We can see you," chirped Gabil. "You're no dream, Thomas!"

"So you really can't remember *anything* about this place?" Michal asked. "The lake, the Shataiki? Us?"

"No, I can't. I really can't."

Michal sighed. "Well, then I suppose we'll have to fill you in. But where to start?"

"With us," Gabil, the shorter one, said. "We are mighty warriors with frightening strength." He strutted to Thomas's right on his short, spindly legs, like a furry Easter egg with wings. A huge white baby chick. Tweety on steroids. "You saw how I sent the black bats flying for cover! I have a thousand stories that I could—"

"We are Roush," Michal interrupted.

"Yes, of course," Gabil said. "Roush. Mighty warriors."

"Some of us are evidently mightier warriors than others," Michal said with a wink.

"Mighty, mighty warriors," said Gabil.

"Servants of Elyon. And you, of course, are a man. We are on Earth. You know *none* of this? It seems quite elementary."

"What about the man who drank the water?" Thomas asked. "Bill."

"Bill was no man. If he was a man and he drank the forbidden water, we would probably all be dead by now. He was a figment of your imagination, probably formed by the Shataiki to lure *you* to the water. Surely you remember the forbidden water."

Thomas paced and shook his head. "I'm telling you, I don't know anything! I don't know what water is forbidden, or what water is drinkable, or who these Shataiki bats are, or who the woman was." He stopped. "Or what she meant when she said she's chosen me."

"Forgive me. It's not that I doubt you can't remember anything; it's just very strange to talk to someone who's lost his memory. I am what they call a wise one—the only wise one in this part of the forest. I have perfect memory. Dear, dear. This is going to be interesting, isn't it? Rachelle has chosen a man with no memory."

Gabil smiled wide. "How romantic!"

Romantic?

"Gabil finds nearly everything romantic. He secretly wants to be a man. Or perhaps a woman, I think."

The smaller Roush didn't argue.

"At any rate, I suppose we should start with the very basics then. Follow me." Michal headed toward the sound of the rushing water. "Come, come."

Thomas followed. The thick carpet of grass silenced his footfalls. It didn't thin out under the trees but ran heavy and lush right through. Violet and lavender flowers with petals the size of his hand stood knee-high, scattered about the forest floor. No debris or dead branches littered the ground, making walking surprisingly easy for the two Roush hopping ahead of him.

Thomas lifted his eyes to the tall trees shining their soft colors about him. Most seemed to glow with one predominant color, like cyan or magenta or yellow, accented by the other colors of the rainbow. How could the trees glow? It was as if they were powered by some massive underground genera-tor that powered fluorescent chemicals in large tubes made to look like trees. No, that was technology from ancient Earth.

He ran his hand gently across the surface of a large ruby tree with a purple hue, surprised at how smooth it was, as if it had no bark at all. He took in the tree's full height. Breathtaking.

Michal cleared his throat and Thomas jerked his hand from the tree.

"Just ahead," the Roush said.

"Just a moment more," Gabil piped in.

They exited the forest less than fifty yards from the meadow, on the banks of the river. The white bridge he'd stumbled over spanned flowing water. On the far side, the black forest. Tall trees lined the bank as far as he could see in either direction. Behind the trees, deep, dark shadows. The memory of them sent a wave of nausea through Thomas's gut.

Not a black bat in sight.

Michal stopped and faced him. He might not be the more excitable of the two Roush, but at the moment he was eager enough to take on the role of teacher. He stretched one wing toward the black forest and spoke with authority.

"That is the black forest. Do you remember it?"

"Of course. I was in it, remember?"

"Yes, I do remember that you were in it. I'm not the one with the memory problem. I was just double-checking so as to give us a common point of reference."

"The black forest is the place where the Shataiki live!" Gabil said.

"If you don't mind, I'm telling the story here," Michal said.

"Of course I don't mind."

"Now. This river you see runs around the whole planet. It separates the green forest from the black forest." He absently flipped his wing in the direction of the far bank. "That's the black forest. The only way into the black forest from this side is over one of three Crossings." He pointed to the white bridge. "The river runs too fast to swim, you see? No one would dare attempt to cross except over one of the bridges. Do you follow?"

"Yes."

"Good. And you can remember what I just told you, correct?"

"Yes."

"Good. Your memory was wiped clean, but it seems to be working with any new data. Now." He paced and stroked his chin with delicate fingers on the underside of his right wing. "There are many other men, women, and children in many villages throughout the green forest. Over a million now live on Earth. You likely stumbled into the black forest over one of the other two Crossings on the far side and then were chased here by the Shataiki."

"How do you know I don't come from nearby?"

"Because, as the wise one given charge over this section of the forest, I would know you. I don't."

"And I am the mighty warrior who led you from the black forest," Gabil said.

"Yes, and Gabil is the mighty warrior who cavorts with Tanis in all kinds of imagined battles."

"Tanis? Who's Tanis?" Thomas asked.

Michal sighed. "Tanis is the firstborn of all men. You will meet him. He lives in the village. Now, Elyon, who created everything you see and all creatures, has touched all of the water. You see the green color of the river? That is the color of Elyon. It's why your eyes are green. It's also why your body was healed the moment the water touched it."

"You poured water on me?"

"No, not I—"

"Rachelle!" Gabil blurted out.

"Rachelle poured the water over you. Trust me, it's not the first time you've touched his water." Michal's cheeks bunched into a soft smile. "But we'll get—"

"Rachelle has chosen you—"

"Gabil! Please!"

"Yes, of course." The smaller Roush didn't seem at all put off by Michal's chiding.

Michal went on. "As I was saying, we'll get to the Great Romance later. Now, the black forest is where evil is confined. You see, good"—he pointed to the green forest—"and evil." He pointed to the black forest. "No one is permitted to drink the water in the black forest. If they do, the Shataiki will be released to have their way with the colored forest. It would be a slaughter."

"The water in the black forest is evil?" Thomas asked. "I touched it—"

"Not evil. Not any more evil than the colored trees are good. Evil and good reside in the heart, not in trees and water. But by custom, water is given as an invitation. Elyon invites with water. The black Shataiki invite with their water."

"And Rachelle invited you with water," Gabil said.

"Yes. In a moment, Gabil," Michal said. But the more stately Roush couldn't hide a slight smile. "For many years, the people have agreed not to cross the river as a matter of precaution. Very wise, if you ask me." The Roush paused and looked about. "That is the heart of it. There are a thousand other details, but hopefully they will return to you in short order."

"Except for the Great Romance," Gabil said. "And Rachelle."

"Except for the Great Romance, which I will let Gabil tell you about, since he's so eager."

Gabil didn't miss a beat. "She's chosen you, Thomas! Rachelle has. It is her choice and now it's yours. You will pursue her and woo her and win her as only you can." He grinned delightedly.

Thomas waited for Gabil to continue. The creature just kept grinning.

"I'm sorry," Thomas said. "I don't see the significance. I don't even know her."

"Even more delicious! It's a wonderful twist! The point is, you don't bear the mark on your forehead, so you are eligible for any woman. You will fall madly in love and be united!"

"This is crazy! I hardly know who I am—romance is the farthest thing from my mind. For all I know, I'm in love with another woman in my own village."

"No, that wouldn't be the case. You would bear another mark."

Surely they didn't expect him to pursue this woman out of obligation. "I still have to choose her, right? But I can't. Not in this condition. I don't even know if I'll like her."

The two Roush stared, stupefied.

"I'm afraid you don't understand," Michal said. "It's not a matter of liking. Of course you'll *like* her. It is your choice, otherwise it wouldn't be choosing. But—and you must trust me on this—your kind abound in love. He made you that way. Like himself. You would love any woman who chooses you. And any woman you choose would choose you. It's the way it is."

"What if I don't feel that way?"

"She's perfect!" Gabil said. "They all are. You *will* feel that way, Thomas. You will!"

"We're from different villages. She would just go away with me?"

Michal raised his eyebrow. "Minor details. I can see this memory loss could be a problem. Now we really should be leaving. It will be slow on foot, and we have quite a road before us." He turned to his friend. "Gabil, you may fly, and I will stay with Thomas Hunter."

"We must go," Gabil said. He unfurled his wings and leaped into the air. Thomas watched in amazement as the white furry's body lifted gracefully from the earth. A puff of air from the Roush's thin wings lifted the hair from his forehead.

Thomas stared at the magnificent forest and hesitated. Michal looked back at him patiently from the tree line. "Shall we go?" He turned back to the forest. Thomas took a deep breath and stepped after the Roush without a word.

⁂

They proceeded through the colored forest for ten minutes in silence. The sum of it was that he lived here, somewhere, perhaps far away, but in this wonderful, surreal place. Surely when he saw his friends, his village, his . . . whatever else was his, his memory would be sparked.

"How long will it take to return me to my people?" Thomas asked.

"These are all your people. What village you live in isn't terribly significant."

"Okay, but how long before I find my own family?"

"Depends," Michal said. "News is a bit slow and the distances are great. It could take a few days. Maybe even a week."

"A week! What will I do?"

The Roush pulled up and stopped. "What will you do? Are your ears not working as well? You've been chosen!" He shook his head and continued. "Dear, dear. I can see this memory loss is quite impossible. Let me give you some advice, Thomas Hunter. Until your memory returns, follow the others. This confusion of yours is disconcerting."

"I can't pretend. If I don't know what's happening, I can't—"

"If you follow the others, perhaps everything will come back to you. At the very least, follow Rachelle."

"You want me to pretend to be in love with her?"

"You *will* be in love with her! You just don't remember how it all works. If you were to meet your mother but didn't remember her, would you stop loving her? No! You would assume you loved her and thereby love her."

The Roush had a point.

Gabil suddenly swept down from the treetops and lit next to Thomas, plump face grinning. "Are you hungry, Thomas Hunter?" He held up a blue fruit with his wing. Thomas stopped and stared at the fruit.

"No need to be afraid, no sir. This is very good fruit. A blue peach. Look." Gabil took a small bite out of the fruit and showed it to Thomas. The juice glistening in the bite mark had the same green, oily tinge he recognized from the river.

"Oh, yes," Michal said, turning back, "another small detail, in the event you don't remember. This is the food you eat. It's called fruit and it, too, along with the water, has been touched by Elyon."

Thomas took the fruit gingerly in his hands and looked at Michal.

"Go ahead, eat it. Eat it."

He took a small bite and felt the cool, sweet juice fill his mouth. A flutter descended into his stomach, and warmth spread through his body. He smiled at Gabil.

"This is good," he said, taking another bite. "Very good."

"The food of warriors!" Gabil said. With that the short creature trot-waddled a few feet, leaped off the ground, and flew back into the sky.

Michal chuckled at his companion and walked on. "Come. Come. We must not wait."

Thomas had just finished the blue peach when Gabil brought another, a red one this time. With a swoop and a shrill laugh, he dropped the fruit into Thomas's hands and took off again. The third time the fruit was green and required peeling, but its flesh was perhaps the tastiest yet.

Gabil's fourth appearance consisted of an aerobatics show. The Roush screamed in from high above, looping with an arched back then twisting into a dive, which he managed to pull out of just over Thomas's head. Thomas threw up his arms and ducked, sure the Roush had miscalculated. With a flurry of wings and a screech, Gabil buzzed his head.

"Gabil!" Michal called out after him. "Show some care there!"

Gabil flew on without a backward glance.

"Mighty warrior indeed," Michal said, stepping back along the path.

Less than a mile later, the Roush stopped on a crest. Thomas stepped up beside the furry creature and looked down on a large green valley covered in flowers like daisies, but turquoise and orange, a rich carpet inviting a roll. Thomas was so surprised at the sudden change in landscape that he didn't at first notice the village.

When he did, the sight took his breath away.

The circular village that nestled in the valley below sparkled with color. For a moment, Thomas thought he must have stumbled onto Candyland, or possibly Hansel and Gretel lived here. But he knew that was a lost story from the histories. This village, on the other hand, was very, very real.

Several hundred square huts, each glowing with a different color, rested like children's playing blocks in concentric circles around a large pinnacled structure that towered above the others at the village's center. The sky above the dwellings was filled with Roush, who floated and dived and twisted in the afternoon sun.

As his eyes adjusted to the incredible scene, he saw a door open from a dwelling far below. Thomas watched a tiny form step from the door. And then he saw that dozens of people dotted the village.

"Does it jog any memories?" Michal asked.

"Actually, I think it does."

"What do you remember?"

"Well, nothing in particular. It's just all vaguely familiar."

Michal sighed. "You know, I've been thinking. There may be some good that comes out of your little adventure in the black forest. There's been talk of an expedition—an absurd idea that Tanis has somehow latched onto. He seems to think it's time to fight the Shataiki. He's always been inventive, a storyteller. But this latest talk of his has me in fits. Maybe you could talk him out of it."

"Does Tanis even know how to fight?"

"Like no other man I know. He's developed a method that is quite spectacular. More flips and twirls and kicks than I would know what to do with. It's based on certain stories from the histories. Tanis is fascinated with them—particularly the histories of conquests. He's determined to wipe out the Shataiki."

"And why shouldn't he?"

"The Shataiki may not be great warriors, but they can deceive. Their water is very inviting. You've seen. Maybe you could talk some sense into the man."

Thomas nodded. He was suddenly eager to meet this Tanis.

Michal sighed. "Okay, stay here. You must wait for me to return. Do you understand?"

"Sure, but . . ."

"No. Just wait. If you see them leaving for the Gathering, you may go with them, but otherwise, please stay here."

"What's the Gathering?"

"To the lake. Don't worry; you can't miss it. There'll be an exodus just before dusk. Agreed?"

"Agreed."

Michal unfolded his wings for the first time in two hours and took to the air. Thomas watched him disappear across the valley, feeling abandoned and unsure.

He could see now that the dwellings must have been made out of the forest's colored trees. These were his people—a strange thought. Maybe not his very own people, as in father, mother, brother, sister, but people just like him. He was lost but not so lost after all.

Was the woman Rachelle down there?

He sat cross-legged, leaned against a tree, and sighed. The houses were small and quaint—more like cottages than houses. Paths of grass separated them from one another, giving the town the appearance of a giant wheel with spokes converging on a large, circular building at the hub. The structure was at least three times as high and many times wider than any of the other dwellings. A meeting place, perhaps.

To his right, a wide path led from the village to the forest, where it vanished. The lake.

Thoughts ran circles around his mind. It occurred to him that Michal had been gone a long time. He was looking for an exodus and he was looking for Michal, but neither was coming fast. He leaned his head back on the tree and closed his eyes.

So strange.

So tired.

8

THOMAS OPENED his eyes and knew immediately that it had happened again.

He was lying on the beige chaise in the apartment in Denver, Colorado. Covered by a batik quilt. Light streamed through a gap in the drapes on his left. On his right, the back of the couch, and beyond it, the locked door. Above, the ceiling. Orange-peel texture covered by an off-white paint. Could be clouds in the sky, could be a thousand worlds hiding between those bumps. Thomas lay perfectly still and drew a deep breath.

He was dreaming.

Yes, of course he was dreaming. This couldn't be real because now he knew the truth of the matter. He'd been knocked on the head while in the black forest. The blow had robbed his memories and kicked him into these strange dreams where he actually thought he was alive on ancient Earth, being chased by some men with *ill intent,* as Michal had put it.

He was, at this very moment, dreaming of the histories of ancient Earth.

Thomas sat up. Amazing! It all looked so real. His fingertips could actually feel the texture of the quilt. Kara's mosaic of masquerade masks looked as real as real could be. He was breathing, and he could taste his musty morning mouth. He was engaging this dream with nearly as much realism as if he were actually awake, touching the trees of the colored forest, or biting into the sweet fruit brought to him by Gabil. This wasn't quite as real, but very convincing.

At least he knew what was happening now. And he knew why the dream felt so real. What an incredible trip.

He swung his feet to the floor and pushed the quilt aside. So, what could he do in his dreams that he couldn't do in real life? He stretched his fingers and curled them. Could he float?

He stood. As he expected, no ache in his head. 'Course not, this was only a dream. He bounced on the balls of his feet.

No floating.

Okay, so he couldn't float like in some of his dreams, but he was sure there were plenty of unusual things he could do. He couldn't get hurt, truly hurt, in his dreams, which gave him some interesting possibilities.

Thomas took a few steps and then stopped. Interestingly enough, dream steps actually felt very similar to real steps, although he could tell the difference. His legs didn't feel totally real. In fact, if he closed his eyes—which he did—he couldn't really feel his legs. He could feel his feet, sure, but as far as he knew there could be air rather than flesh and bone connecting his feet to his hips.

Dream standing. Incredible.

He walked around the room in awe of how utterly real everything felt. Not quite as real as walking with Michal and Gabil, of course, but if he didn't know he was in a dream, he might actually think this room was real. Amazing how the mind worked.

He ran his hand over a black cassowary carving he'd imported from Indonesia. He could feel every bump and nick. It probably even—Thomas bent to sniff the wood—yes, it did smell like smoke, exactly as he'd imagined. The wood had been hardened by burning. Had the carver been dreaming when he carved—

"Thomas?"

He wondered if that was Michal calling him. The Roush had returned from wherever he'd flown off to and was trying to wake him. Thomas wasn't sure he wanted to be awakened quite yet. This dream—

"Thomas."

Actually, the voice sounded higher, more like Gabil's voice.

"What are you doing?"

He turned around. Kara stood by the couch, dressed in a blue-flowered camisole and boxers. He should've known. He was still dreaming.

"Hi, sis."

She wasn't really his sister, of course, because she didn't really exist. Well, in this dream reality she did, but not in *real* reality.

"You okay?"

"Sure. Never been better. Don't I look okay?"

"So . . . so you're not freaking out over what happened last night, I take it?"

"Last night?" He paced to his right, wondering if Michal might wake him up at any moment. "Oh, you mean the chase through the alleys and the shot to the head and the way I handily dispatched the bad dudes? Actually, this may come as a shock to you, but none of that really happened."

"What do you mean? You made that all up?" Her face lightened a shade.

"Well, no, not really. I mean, it did happen here. But here isn't really real. The cow can't really jump over the moon, and when you dream that you're falling but you never actually land, it's because you're not really falling. This isn't real." He grinned. "Pretty cool, huh?"

"What on earth are you talking about?" Her eyes shifted to the end table where the bottle of pain pills sat. "Did you take any more medication?"

"Ah, yes. That would be the Demerol. No, I didn't, and no, I'm not hallucinating." He stretched out his arms and announced the truth of the matter. "This, dear sister, is a dream. We're actually *in* a dream!"

"Stop messing around. You're not funny."

"Say whatever you like. But this isn't really happening right now. You'll say I'm crazy because you don't know any better—how can you? You're part of the dream."

"What do you call the bandage on your head? A dream? This is insane!" She headed for the breakfast bar.

Thomas felt the bandage around his head. "I'm dreaming about this cut because I fell on a stone in the black forest. Although not everything correlates exactly, because I don't have a broken arm here like I did there."

Kara faced him, incredulous. For a moment she said nothing, and he thought she might be coming to her senses. Maybe with the right persuasion, dream-people could be convinced that they lived only in your dreams.

"Have you given our situation with the New Yorkers any more thought?" she asked.

Nope. She was still in denial.

"You're not listening, Kara. There *was* no chase last night. This cut came from the black forest. This is a dre—"

"Thomas! Stop it! And stop smiling like that."

Her sincerity certainly sounded real. He flattened his mouth.

"You can't be serious about this nonsense," Kara said.

"Dead serious," he said. "Think about it. What if this really is a dream? At least consider the possibility. I mean what if all of this"—he swept his arms about—"what if it's all just in your mind? Michal told me this was happening, and it is, exactly like he said it was. Trust me, that was no dream. I was attacked by Shataiki. You wouldn't know about those, but they're big black bats with red eyes . . ."

He stopped. Maybe he should go light on the details. To Kara such realities would sound preposterous without having lived them firsthand.

"In reality, I live in the future. I'm waiting for Michal, but he's taking forever, so I sat down and put my head back on a tree. I just fell asleep. Don't you see?" He grinned again.

"No, actually I don't."

"I just fell asleep, Kara. I'm sleeping! Right at this very minute, I'm asleep under a tree. So you tell me, how could I be standing here if I know I'm asleep under a tree waiting for Michal? Tell me that!"

"So you live in a world with big black bats and . . ." She sighed. "Listen to yourself, Thomas! This isn't good. I need you sane now. Are you sure you didn't take any more of those pills?"

Thomas felt his frustration building, but he remained calm. It was, after all, just a dream. He could feel however he wanted to in a dream. If a great big ghost with fangs rushed him right now, he could just face it and laugh and it would vanish. No need to trounce all over Kara—she could hardly be blamed. If he couldn't convince her, he would just play along. Why not? Michal would wake him up at any moment.

"Fine, Kara. Fine. But what if I can prove it to you?"

"You can't. We have to figure out what we're going to do. I need to get dressed and then get you to the hospital. You have a concussion."

"But what if I can prove we're in a dream? I mean really? I mean, just move your hand around like this." He swept his hand through the air. "Can't you tell that it's not real? I can. Can't you feel that something's not quite right? The air feels thinner—"

"Please, Thomas, you're starting to scare me."

He lowered his hand. "Okay, but what if I could prove it logically?"

"That's impossible."

"What if I could tell you how the world is going to end?"

"Now you're a prophet? You live in a world with black bats, and you can read the future? None of that sounds stupid to you? Think, Thomas, think! Wake up."

"It's not stupid. I can tell you how the world is going to end because, in reality, it *has* ended, and it has been recorded in the histories."

"Of course it has."

"Exactly. It will begin with the Raison Strain—some kind of virus that comes from a French company. Everyone thinks it's a vaccine, but it mutates under intense heat and will ravage the world sometime this year. I'm not quite sure on that last detail."

"That's your proof? That the world is going to end sometime this year?" She wasn't buying the argument.

Thomas suddenly had another thought. Quite a fun thought, actually. He walked for the front door, twisted the deadbolt, and flung it open.

"Okay, I'll prove it to you," he said and stepped outside.

"What are you doing? What if they're out there?"

"They're not out here because they don't exist. Am I talking to a wall here?" The light stung his eyes. He stepped across the front walkway and gripped the railing. They were three floors up. The parking lot below was concrete.

Kara ran to the doorway. "Thomas! What are you doing?"

"I'm going to jump. In dreams you can't really get hurt, right? If I jump—"

"Are you crazy? You *will too* get hurt! What do you call the bullet wound on your head?"

"I told you, that was from a rock in the black forest."

"But what if you're wrong?"

"I'm not."

"What if you are? What if there's even a slight possibility that you are? What if it's the other way around?"

"What do you mean?"

"What if this is the real Earth, but you think the other one is because it feels so real?"

"The cut on my head from the fall, it's real. How can you—"

"Unless it really was a bullet that cut your head, and so you dreamed something, like the rock. Step back, Thomas. You're not thinking clearly."

Thomas looked down, suddenly struck with that possibility. Out here in the morning light, his confidence waned. What if she was right? He had hurt his head in both the black forest and in his dream here. What if there was a real connection? Or what if he had the dreams backward?

"Thomas. Please."

He backed away from the railing, heart suddenly hammering. What was he thinking?

"You think that's possible?" he asked.

"Yes! Yes, I think. I know!"

He rubbed his fingers together, then looked at her. Actually, now that he thought about it, she was his sister. If he was only dreaming, did that mean Kara didn't really exist?

The morning newspaper lay by the front door. If she was right, then it meant they really *were* in trouble. He grabbed the paper.

"Okay, get inside."

She did, quickly, and he pulled the door closed.

"You have me worried," Kara said. She took the newspaper from him and led him into the kitchen. "This isn't good timing. That bullet obviously did more harm than we thought."

She dropped the paper on the counter, turned the water on, and scanned the front page as she washed her hands.

"I'm sorry, honestly, I'm just . . ." Actually, Thomas didn't know what he just was. Clearly, it was decision time. He had to assume that he was in Denver after all, and not as part of a dream, but in reality. What that said about the black forest and Michal made his head spin. He didn't have the brain capacity to figure it out at the moment. If he really had been chased down by New Yorkers last night, he and Kara had their hands full.

Panic rolled up his belly. They had to get out of town.

"Thomas?"

He looked up. "We have to get out of here."

She wasn't listening. Her wet hands hung over the sink, unmoving. Her eyes were fixed on the newspaper to her left.

"What did you say that virus was called?"

"What virus? The Raison Strain?"

"A French company?"

He walked up to her and looked at the paper. A bold black headline ran across the top:

CHINA SAYS NO

"China says no?"

She lifted the paper, unconcerned with the dark water blotches her hands made on the page. He saw the smaller headline then, halfway down and on the left, the business-page headline:

FRENCH ASSETS:
RAISON PHARMACEUTICAL TO ANNOUNCE NEW VACCINE, SELLS U.S. INTERESTS

Thomas took the paper, flipped to the business page, and found the article. The company's name suddenly seemed to fill the entire page. Raison Pharmaceutical. His pulse pounded.

"What—" Kara stopped, apparently confused by this new information. She leaned in and quickly read the short story with him.

Raison Pharmaceutical, a well-known French parent of several smaller companies, had been founded by Jacques de Raison in 1973. The company, which specialized in vaccines and genetic research, had plants in several countries but was headquartered in Bangkok, where it had operated without the restrictions often hampering domestic pharmaceutical companies. The company was best known for its handling of deadly viruses in the process of creating vaccines. Its contracts with the former Soviet Union were at one time quite controversial.

In the last few years, the firm had become better known for its release of several oral and nasal vaccines. The drugs, based on recombinant DNA research, weren't dose-restrictive—a fancy way of saying they could be taken in large quantities without side effects. Dibloxin 42, a smallpox vaccine, for example, could be deposited in a country's water supply, effectively administering the vaccine to the whole population without fear of overdosing any one person, regardless of how much water was consumed. A perfect solution for the Third World.

Several of the vaccines, however, would be subjected to a whole new gamut of rigorous testing procedures if Congress passed the new legislation introduced by Merton Gains before he became deputy secretary of state.

Raison advised this morning that in a matter of days it would announce a new multipurpose, airborne vaccine that would effectively eliminate the threat of several problematic diseases worldwide. Dubbed the Raison Vaccine—

Kara uttered a short gasp at the same time Thomas read the sentence.

"Dubbed the Raison Vaccine, the vaccine promises to revolutionize preventive medicine. Stocks are bound to react to the news, but the gains may be tempered by the announcement that the firm's Ohio plant will close in the interests of focusing on the Raison Vaccine, developed by the Bangkok facility."

The article went on, offering details about the stock market's anticipated reaction to the news. Thomas's hand trembled slightly.

"How did you know about this?" Kara asked, looking up.

"I didn't. I swear I've never seen or heard this name until right now. Except . . ."

"Except in your dreams. No, that's impossible."

Thomas laid the paper down and set his jaw. "Tell me how else I could have known about this."

"You must have heard about—"

"Even if I knew about the company, which I didn't before last night, there's no way I could have known about the Raison Vaccine—not without reading this paper. But I did!"

"Then you read the paper or heard it on the news last night."

"I didn't watch the news last night! And you saw the paper outside, exactly where it always is in the morning."

She crossed one arm and nibbled at her fingernail, something she did only when she was beyond herself. Thomas recalled his discussion about the Raison Strain with Michal as if it had occurred only a moment ago, which wasn't that far from the truth. For all he knew, he had been asleep under the tree for only a few minutes.

But this wasn't really a dream, was it?

"You're actually telling me that something's happening in your dreams that gives you this information?" she demanded. "What else did you learn about the future?"

He considered that. "Only that the Raison Vaccine has some problems and ends up as a virus called the Raison Strain, which infects most of the world population in a . . ."

"In a what?"

Thomas scratched his head. "In a very short time."

"How short?" She exhaled sharply. "Listen to me, I can't believe I'm even asking these questions."

"In a few weeks, I think."

Kara paced the kitchen, still biting her fingernail. "This is just crazy. Yesterday the extent of my life's challenges consisted of whether I should cut my hair short, but that was before I came home to my crazy brother. Now the mob is breathing down our necks, and it just so happens that the whole world is about to be infected by a virus no one but my dreaming brother knows about. And how, pray tell, does he know about this virus? Simple: Some black bat with red eyes in the real world told him. Excuse me if I don't don my gas mask posthaste."

She was venting, but she was also troubled or she wouldn't *be* venting.

"Not a black bat," Thomas said. "A white one. A Roush. And the Roush have green eyes."

"Yes, of course; how silly of me. Green eyes. The bat with green eyes told him. And did I mention the tidbit about this world all being a dream? Well, if it's a dream, we really don't have to worry, do we?"

She had a point there.

Thomas walked into the living room and turned around to see she'd followed him. Her face was pale. She really was worried, wasn't she?

"But you don't believe for a second that you and I are in a dream right now," he said. "Which can only mean that the other stuff is a dream. Fine. That's worse. It means this is real. That a virus is about to threaten the world."

Kara walked to the window and eased back the drape. She still wasn't buying it, but her confidence had been shaken.

"Anyone?" he asked.

"No." She released the curtain. "But if I'm to believe you, a few killers from New York are the least of our problems, right?"

"Look, could you please lose the condescending tone here? I didn't ask for this. Okay, maybe I did set us up for the mob, but I've already begged your forgiveness for that. In the rest of this, I'm as innocent as you. Can I help what my dreams are?"

"It just sounds so stupid, Thomas. You at least see that, don't you? It sounds like something a kid would dream up. And frankly, the fact that you're so . . . youthful isn't playing in your favor here."

Thomas said nothing.

Kara sighed and sat on the arm of the couch. "Okay. Okay, just say that there's something to your dreams. Exactly what are these dreams about?"

"For the record, I'm not agreeing that they are dreams," he said. "At the very least, I have to treat each scenario like it is real. I mean, you want me to treat this room like it's really here, right? You don't want me to jump off the balcony. Fine, but believe me, it's just as real there. I'm sleeping under a tree there right now. But the moment I wake up from my little nap under the tree, I'll have a whole set of new problems."

"Fine," she said, exasperated. "Fine, let's pretend both are real. Tell me about this . . . other place."

"All of it?"

"Whatever you think makes sense."

"It *all* makes sense."

Thomas took a deep breath and told her about waking up in the black forest and about the bats that chased him and the woman he'd met and about the Roush leading him to the village. He didn't think there was any evil in the colored forest. It seemed confined to the black forest. He told it all to her, and as he spoke, she listened with an intensity that undermined periodic scoffs until they stopped altogether.

"So every time you fall asleep in either place, you wake up in the other place?"

"Exactly."

"And there's no direct time correlation. I mean, you could spend a whole day there and wake up here to find out only a minute had passed."

"I think so. I've been there for a whole day but not here."

She suddenly stood and walked into the kitchen.

"What are you doing?" Thomas asked.

"We're going to test these dreams of yours. And not by jumping over guardrails."

"You know how to test this?" He hurried after her.

She grabbed the newspaper and flipped through it. "Why not? You claim to have gained some knowledge from this place. We'll see if you can get some more."

"How?"

"Simple. You go back to sleep, get some more information, and then we wake you up to see if you have something we can verify."

He blinked. "You think that's possible?"

She shrugged. "That's the point—to find out. You said they have histories of Earth there. You think they would have the results of sporting events?"

"I . . . I don't know. Seems kind of trivial."

"History loves trivia. If there's history, it will include sporting events." She'd stopped on a sports section and glanced down the page. Her eyes stopped and then looked over the paper at him.

"You know anything about horse racing?" she asked.

"Uh, no."

"Name me a horse that's on the racing circuit."

"Any horse?"

"Any horse. Just one."

"I don't know any horse. Runner's Luck?"

"You're making that up."

"Yes."

"That's not the point. I'm just satisfying myself that you don't know any of the entries in today's race."

"Which race?"

"The Kentucky Derby."

"That's running today?" He reached for the paper and she pulled it back.

"Not a chance. You don't know the horses racing; let's not spoil that." She folded the paper. "The race is in"—she glanced at the clock on the wall—"six hours. No one on Earth knows the winner. You go and talk to your furry friends. If you come back with the name of the horse that wins, I will reconsider this little theory of yours." A slight smile lifted her small mouth.

"I don't know if I can get that kind of detail," Thomas said.

"Why not? Fly over to the golden library in the sky and ask the attending fuzzball for a bit of history. What can be so hard about that?"

"What if it's not a dream? I can't just do whatever I want there any more than I can do whatever I want here. And the histories are oral. They won't know who won a race!"

"You said that some of them knew everything from the histories."

"The wise ones. Michal. You think Michal is going to tell me who won the Kentucky Derby this year?"

"Why not?"

"It doesn't sound like something he'd tell me."

"Oh, stop it."

"I'm sleeping on a hill right now—I can't just go on some crazy search for something this trivial."

"As soon as you fall asleep here, you'll wake up there," she said. "You want to prove this to me—here's your chance."

"This is ridiculous. That's not how it works."

"So you're begging off?"

"The race is in six hours. What if I can't go back to sleep over there?"

"You said there wasn't necessarily any time correlation. I'll let you sleep for half an hour, and then I'll wake you. We can't afford to sit around here for much longer than that anyway."

Thomas ran his fingers through his hair. The suggestion sounded absurd to him, yet his own demands that she believe him were as absurd to her. More so. Actually, he had no reason to believe that he *couldn't* get the information. Maybe Michal would understand and tell him right away. As long as Kara woke him up in time . . .

It just might work.

"Okay."

"Okay?"

"Okay. How do I fall asleep?"

She looked at him as if she hadn't really expected him to agree. "You sure you don't know any of the horses?"

"Positive. And even if I did, I wouldn't know who is going to win, would I?"

"No." Kara gave him one last suspicious glance and headed for her bedroom, taking the paper with her. She returned thirty seconds later shaking a bottle of pills.

"You're going to drug me?" he asked. "How will you wake me up if I'm conked out? I can't walk around drugged all day."

"I've got some pills that will wake you up in a hurry too. It's admittedly a bit extreme, but I think our situation is a bit extreme, don't you?"

She was a nurse, he reminded himself. He could trust her.

Ten minutes later he lay on the couch, having ingested three large white tablets. They were talking about where they would go. They had to get out of town. To his surprise, Kara was warming to the idea. At least until they figured this all out.

What . . . what about . . . what . . . the Raison Strain, he was asking her.

She still wasn't sold on the Raison Strain. That's why she'd fed him the pills. Big, monstrous, white pills that were big enough to be . . .

"Can you tell me which village he comes from?" Michal asked.

"Not as near as you might imagine. Not as far as you might think."

This meant: *No, I choose not to tell you at this time.*

"Rachelle has chosen him. I should just lead him into the village?"

"Why not?"

This meant: *Don't interfere with the ways of humans.*

Michal shifted on his spindly feet. He dipped his head in reverence. "He concerns me," he said. "I fear the worst."

His master's voice answered softly, unconcerned. "Don't waste your time on fear. It's unbecoming."

Two valleys to the east, the man who called himself Thomas Hunter was slumped against a tree, lost in sleep. Dreaming of the histories in vivid detail. Surely this couldn't be good.

Michal had left the man and flown to a nearby tree to consider his options. He had to think the situation through carefully. Nothing of the kind had ever happened, at least not in his section of the forest. He couldn't just usher Thomas into the village and present him to Rachelle with this complete memory loss of his. He didn't even seem to know Elyon, for heaven's sake!

When Hunter fell asleep, Michal decided he must seek higher guidance.

"He thinks that this might be a dream," Michal said, looking up. "He thinks that he lives in the histories in a place called Denver, and that he's dreaming of the colored forest, of all things! He's got it backward! I tried to tell him, but I'm not sure he believes me entirely."

"I'm sure he'll eventually figure it out. He's quite smart."

"But at this very moment he's lying against a tree above the village, dreaming that he lives before the Great Deception!" Michal swept his wings behind his back and paced. "He seems to know the histories in stunning detail—a family, a home, even memories. He's bound to engage Tanis!"

"Then let him engage Tanis."

"But Tanis . . ." Could he say it? Should he say it? "Tanis is teetering!" he blurted out. "I fear a small nudge might push him over the edge. If he and Hunter start talking, there's no telling how creative Tanis might get."

"He was created to create. Let him create."

How could he say it so easily, standing there with hardly an expression? Didn't he know what kind of devastation Tanis could bring them all?

"Of course I know," the boy said. Now his soft green eyes shifted. "I knew it from the beginning."

Michal felt a lump rise in his throat. "Forgive my fear. I just can't imagine it. May I at least discourage them? I beg you—"

"Sure. Discourage them. But let them find their own way."

The boy turned and walked to a large white lion. He ran his hand along the lion's mane, and the beast fell to its belly. He looked out to sea, shielding his eyes from Michal's sight.

The Roush wanted to cry. He couldn't explain the feeling. He had no right to feel such remorse. The boy knew what he was doing. He always had known.

Michal left the upper lake, circled high, and slowly winged his way to where Thomas Hunter slept under the tree above the village.

9

THOMAS HEARD the rush of wings and felt himself falling from his dream. Tumbling, tumbling into real light, breathing real air, smelling something that reminded him of gardenias. He opened his eyes.

Michal was just pulling his wings in, not ten feet away. They were back in the colored forest. He'd been sleeping against a tall amber tree, dreaming as if he lived in the histories of Earth again. This time he'd returned with a challenge from Kara. Something about—

"It's been a full day for you, I can see," Michal said, waddling over. Another rush of wings to Thomas's left announced Gabil, who incorporated a roll into his landing.

Thomas stood up, fully awake. The grass was green; the forest glowed in blues and yellows behind him; the village waited in all its brilliance. He stepped forward, suddenly eager to descend the hill and reconnect with his past.

"Are we going?"

"Absolutely going," Gabil said.

"Yes," Michal said. "Although I'm afraid you've missed the Gathering." He looked over his shoulder, and Thomas saw the last of a huge group disappearing down a path that led into the trees several miles away. As far as he could see, the village had emptied.

"I'm terribly sorry, but it will take us too long to catch up. You'd best just wait in the village until they return."

"What took you so long?"

"Perhaps I should have taken you to the village first, but I wanted to make sure. This is quite unusual, I'm sure you must realize. You didn't drink the water in the black forest, but the Shataiki clearly had *some* effect on you. Your memory at least. I had to be sure I did the right thing."

They headed down the hill in the afternoon's waning light, Michal first, followed by Thomas, and Gabil hopping along to bring up the rear.

The histories. He'd dreamed that Kara had insisted this colored forest was a dream and Denver was real. She'd sent him on a mission.

The winner of the Kentucky Derby.

Would the histories record something so insignificant as the winner of a horse race? If so, only someone with a perfect memory could possibly recall it. Someone like Michal.

But asking Michal to check something he'd dreamed of had a ring of insanity to it. Then again, it was no more absurd than insisting to Kara that *she* was a dream. So then, which was it?

Here in the colored forest, Michal had offered a perfectly reasonable explanation for his dreams of Denver: Thomas had hit his head and was dreaming of ancient Earth. Logical.

There in Denver, however, he had no explanation for how he could be dreaming about the Raison Strain, especially since the related events hadn't happened yet. He was getting the information from Michal, from the histories. But that would only prove that this world in which he'd found the histories was real. If this was real, then the other had to be a dream. Unless they were both real.

"How many people live in this village?" Thomas asked.

"Here? This is the smallest village. There are three tribes on the planet, each with many villages. But this is the first. Tanis is the firstborn."

"Over one thousand in this village," Gabil piped up.

"Fifteen hundred and twenty-two," Michal said. "There are seven villages in this tribe, and they all come to the same Gathering. The other two tribes, one of which is yours, are very far away and much larger. We have over a million living now."

"Huh. How long do we live? I mean how long has—"

Michal had stopped, and Thomas nearly tripped over him.

Gabil bumped into him from behind. "Sorry. Sorry."

Michal was staring at Thomas as if he'd lost his mind.

Thomas stepped back. "What's wrong?"

"There *is* no death here. Only in the black forest. You're confusing reality with ancient Earth. Losing your memory I can understand, but surely you can separate what is real from your dreams."

"Sure," Thomas said, but he wasn't sure. Not at all. He would have to think through his questions more carefully.

Michal sighed. "In the event you're not so sure as you say, let me give you a quick refresher on your history. Tanis, the leader of this village, whom we've discussed, was the firstborn. He was united with Mirium, his wife, and they had eighteen sons and twenty-three daughters over the course of the first two hundred years. His first two sons left, one to the east and one to the west, a month's journey each, to form the three tribes. Each tribe is completely self-contained. There is no commerce or trading, but visitors are quite common and interunions aren't unusual. Three times a year the other two tribes make a journey here for a very, very large celebration, known as the Great Gathering, not to be confused with the Gathering each tribe experiences every night."

Michal looked longingly toward the path the villagers had taken. "You'll find a preoccupation with the Gathering. It's the focus of each day. By midday most of the people are preparing for it in one way or another. It's a very simple yet very extravagant life I would gladly exchange a year of torment for. You are exceedingly fortunate, Thomas Hunter."

The evening stood still.

"That makes me a descendant of Tanis?" Thomas finally asked.

"Many generations removed, but yes."

"And my immediate family will be coming here for a celebration. When?"

"In . . . what, Gabil? Sixty days?"

"Fifty-three!" the smaller Roush said. "Only fifty-three."

"Gabil is the master of games at the celebrations. He knows them intimately. At any rate, there you have it."

Michal continued his duck-walk down the hill.

"I had another dream," Thomas said.

"Yes?" Michal said. "Well, dreams are quite common, or have you forgotten that as well?"

"It picked up where the one before left off. I was wondering if you could help me with something. Did the histories record sporting events?"

"The histories recorded everything."

"Really! Could I get, say . . . the winning horse from the Kentucky Derby for a particular year?"

"The histories are oral, as I mentioned. They were written . . . are written . . . in the Books of Histories, but these Books are"—he paused here—"no longer available. They are very powerful, these Books. At any rate, the oral traditions were given to Tanis and passed on."

"No one would know who won the Kentucky Derby?"

"Who would care about such trivia? Do you know what kind of mind it would require to hold such an insignificant detail?"

"So then no one knows it."

Michal hesitated. "I didn't say that. What Tanis knows of the histories is more than any other human. It's more than enough. Too much knowledge of some things can be worrisome. Tanis has tried many times to pry more information out of me. His thirst for knowledge is insatiable."

"But you have a perfect memory. You don't know who won the Kentucky Derby this year?"

"And if I do?"

"Can you tell me?"

"I could. Should I?"

"Yes! My sister wants to know."

Again Michal stopped. "You remember your sister? You're beginning to remember?"

"No, the sister in my dreams," Thomas said, feeling foolish.

"Now that's something, don't you say, Gabil?" Michal said. "His sister, in his dreams about the histories, wants to know something about the histories. Sounds quite circular."

"Round and round and round, for sure."

Thomas diverted his eyes. "Yes, I guess you could say that."

"I'm not sure I *should* tell you," Michal said.

"Then is there anyone else who could tell me?"

"Teeleh," Gabil hissed. "He was a wise one."

Thomas knew without having to ask who Teeleh must be.

"The leader of the Shataiki," Thomas said.

"Yes," Michal said. Nothing more.

Thomas directed the discussion back to the horse race. "Please, I just need to know if what you're saying ties directly into what I'm dreaming. It might help me put the dreams aside."

"Perhaps. I'm not in the business of digging up the histories. We are making our own here, and it's enough. You already have enough of the histories running through your mind to distract you and confuse even me. I will tell you on one condition."

"I won't ask again. Agreed."

Michal frowned. "Exactly. You will not ask about the histories again."

"And as I said, I agree. Which horse?"

"The winner of the Kentucky Derby was Joy Flyer."

"Joy Flyer!" Gabil cried. "A perfect name!" He ran ahead and took flight. He gained altitude quickly, executed one loop, and winged in the direction of the Gathering.

Joy Flyer.

The village looked familiar to Thomas, but not so much that his heart didn't begin to increase its pace as they approached.

They walked under a great blue-and-gold arch at the entrance and then down a wide brown path between rows of colored huts. Thomas stopped at the first house, taken by the ruby glow of the wood. A lawn wrapped around the dwelling in a thick, uniform carpet of green, highlighted by flowers growing in symmetrical clusters. What appeared to be carvings of brightly colored sapphire and golden wood accented the lawn, giving it a surreal beauty.

"Do you remember?" Michal asked.

"Sort of. But not really."

"It could take a while, I understand. You will stay with Rachelle's family."

"Rachelle! The woman who chose me?"

"Yes."

"I can't stay in her house! I don't have a clue about this Great Romance."

"Follow your instincts, Thomas. And if your instincts don't offer enough guidance, then pretend. Surely you can pretend to be in love."

"What if I don't want to be in love?"

"Stop that nonsense!" Michal ordered. "Of course you want to be in love. You're human." He turned up the path. "You're frightening me, young man."

Thomas walked down the path, lost in thought at first, but then quickly distracted by the beauty around him. Both sides of the road were lined with beautifully landscaped lawns that bordered each colored cottage. The homes shone more like pearl than wood. Flowers like the daisies on the valley floor grew in wide swaths across the bright green lawns. Large cats and parrots meandered and fluttered about the village in harmony as though they, too, owned a part of this marvelous work of art.

The refined nature of the village kept Thomas in awe as they made their way toward the large central structure. Although not necessarily symmetrical, every object, every carving, every flower, and every path was in exactly the right location, like a perfectly executed symphony. Move one path and the vision would crumble. Move one flower and chaos would ensue.

The Thrall, as Michal had called it, was huge compared to the other structures, and if the village was a work of refined art, then this was its crowning glory. Thomas paused at the bottom of wide steps that ascended to the circular building. The jade-colored dome looked as though it had been made out of some flawless crystalline material that allowed light to pass through it.

He gingerly placed his foot on the first step and began the ascent. Ahead, Michal struggled up the steps one by one, ignoring him for the moment. Thomas followed him and then turned at the top to view the village from this elevated vantage.

The village looked as if massive jewels—ruby and topaz and emeralds and opals and mother-of-pearl—had been transported here and then carved into solid structures over hundreds of years. What kind of technology could have possibly created this? So simple and elegant, yet so advanced.

"Who did this?"

Michal looked up at him. "You did this. Come."

Thomas followed him into the Thrall.

The scope of the large auditorium was at once intimidating and spectacular. Four glowing pillars—ruby, emerald, jasper, and a golden yellow— rose from the floor to the iridescent domed ceiling. There was no furniture in the room. All of this Thomas saw at the first glance.

But it was on the great circular floor, centered under the dome, that he rested his gaze.

He stepped past Michal and walked lightly to the floor's edge. The floor seemed to draw him into itself. He slowly knelt and reached out his hand. He couldn't see a single blemish on its hard, clear surface, like a pool of resin poured over a massive unflawed emerald. He stroked the floor, breathing steadily. A sudden, slight vibration shot up his arm and he quickly withdrew his hand.

"It's quite all right, my friend," Michal said behind him. "It's a sight that I never get used to myself. It was made from a thousand green trees. Not a blemish to be found. The creativity you humans display never ceases to amaze me."

Thomas stood. "This is like the water?"

"No. The water is special. But Elyon is the Maker of both. I will leave you here," he said, turning for the door. "Duty calls. Johan and Rachelle will come and collect you here as soon as they return from the Gathering. And remember, if in doubt, please play along." He waddled out of the building, and Thomas thought he heard the Roush say, "Dear, dear. I hope Rachelle hasn't bitten off more than she can chew."

Thomas started to protest. Waiting alone in this magnificent room struck him as a little terrifying. But he couldn't think of a reason why he should be terrified—beyond his memory loss, this was all very familiar to him. As Michal said, he had to play along.

10

THOMAS DIDN'T have to wait long. A boy, maybe twelve, with light blond hair and dressed in a blue tunic, burst into the Thrall. A yellow bandanna wound about his head. He spun on his heel for a quick look around and then turned and ran backward, urging someone else to follow.

"Come on!"

He was followed by the woman Thomas recognized as Rachelle. She wore the same red satin dress but now with a bright yellow sash draped over one shoulder.

The thrill of the sight was so unexpected, so sudden, that Thomas found himself frozen in the corner shadows.

"Do you see him, Johan?" Rachelle asked, glancing around.

"No. But Michal said he would be here. Maybe . . ." Johan saw Thomas and stopped.

Rachelle stood in the middle of the floor, staring into the corner where Thomas stood watching.

Thomas cleared his throat and stepped into the light. "Hi."

She looked at him, unabashed. For a few long seconds, all motion seemed to cease. Her eyes shone a rich jade, like a pool of water. She was fully grown and yet slender. Early twenties. Her skin was bronzed and milky smooth.

A soft, shy smile slowly replaced her thoughtful gaze.

"You are very pleasing to look at, Thomas," she said.

Thomas swallowed. This sort of statement must be completely normal, but because of his amnesia, it felt . . . ambitious. Daring. Wonderful. He had to play along as Michal had demanded.

"Thank you. And so are you. You are very"—he had to stop for a breath—"pleasing to look at. Daring."

"Daring?" she asked.

"Yes, you look daringly beautiful." Thomas felt his face blush.

"Daring!" Rachelle looked over at Johan. "Did you hear that, Johan? Thomas thinks I'm daring."

Johan glanced from one to the other and laughed. "I like you, Thomas."

Rachelle looked at him, amused, like a young, shy girl, but she wasn't bashful, not in the least. Was he supposed to do something here?

She offered him her hand. He reached for it, but, like before, she didn't shake it. Without removing her eyes from his, she gently touched his fingers with hers.

He was so shocked by the touch that he didn't dare speak. If he did, surely idiotic mumbling rather than words would come from his mouth. Her caress lingered on his skin, sensuous yet completely innocent at once.

Thomas's heart was pounding now, and for a brief moment he panicked. She was touching his hand, and he was frozen to the floor. This was the Great Romance?

He didn't even know this woman.

She suddenly took his hand in hers and pulled him toward the door. "Hurry, they are waiting."

"They are? Who are?"

"It's time to eat," Johan cried. He threw the door open, pulled up, and then rushed down the steps toward two men on the path below. "Father! We have Thomas Hunter. He is a very interesting man!"

Two thoughts struck Thomas at the comment. One, Rachelle was still touching his hand. Two, these people seemed to have no shame. Which meant *he* had no shame, because he was one of these people.

Rachelle released his hand and ran down the steps. The man Johan had called Father embraced the boy and then turned to Thomas. He wore a tunic that hung to his thighs, tan with a wide swath of blue running across his body from right shoulder to left hip. The hem was woven in intricate crossing patterns with the same colors. A belt of gold ran around his waist and held a small water pouch.

"So. You are the visitor from the other side." He clasped Thomas's arm, pulled him into an embrace, and slapped his back. "Welcome. My name is Palus. You are most welcome to stay with my family." He drew back, frowning, eyes bright, delighted. "Welcome," he said again.

"Thank you. You are most kind." Thomas dipped his head.

Palus jumped back and swept his arm toward the other man. "This is Miknas, the keeper of the Thrall," he said proudly. "He has overseen all the dances and celebrations on the green floor for well over a hundred years. Miknas!"

Miknas looked about forty. Maybe thirty. Hard to tell. How old was the firstborn, Tanis? Thomas dismissed the question for the moment.

"It's an honor," Thomas said.

Miknas stepped forward and embraced Thomas in the same way Palus had. "The honor is mine. We rarely have such special visitors. You are most welcome. Most, most welcome."

"Come, walk to our house." Palus led them down the path.

They stopped at the arching sapphire entrance of a home close to the Thrall, and each took turns embracing Miknas farewell, bidding him a wonderful meal. Palus led them down several rows of homes to a cottage as brilliant green as its surrounding lawn, then up the walk and past a solid green door into his domed abode.

Thomas entered the dwelling, hoping that here, in such intimate surroundings, the familiarity of his past would return. The wood here in the home had the appearance of being covered in a smooth, clear resin several inches thick. The furniture was carved from the same wood. Some pieces glowed a single color, and others radiated in rainbow moirés. Light emanated from all the wood. The light was not reflective as he had first guessed but came from the wood itself.

Incredible. But not familiar.

"This is Karyl, my wife," Palus said. Then to his wife, "Rachelle has touched his hand."

Thomas smiled at Rachelle's mother awkwardly, eager to avoid any further discussion on the matter. "You have a beautiful home, madam."

"Madam? How quaint. What does it mean?"

"Hmm?"

"I've never heard this expression before. What does 'madam' mean?"

"I think . . . I think it's an expression of respect. Like 'friend.'"

"You use this expression in your village?"

"Maybe. I think we might."

They all watched him in a moment of silence, during which he felt terribly conspicuous.

"Here," Karyl said finally, stepping toward a bowl into which she dipped a wooden cup, "we invite with a drink of water." She brought the cup to him, and he sipped. The water was cool at his lips but felt warm all the way to his belly, where its heat spread. He dipped his head and returned the cup.

"Thank you."

"Then you must eat with us. Come, come."

She took his arm and led him to the table. A large bowl of fruit sat in the center, and he recognized the colors and shapes. They were the same as those Gabil had given him earlier.

His sudden hunger for the fruit surprised him. Everyone had taken a seat at the round table now, and he was aware of their eyes on him. He forced himself to look away from the fruit, and he met Rachelle's eyes.

"You're most kind to have me in your home. I must admit, I'm unsure of what I should do. Did they tell you that I'd lost my memory?"

"Michal mentioned that, yes," Palus said.

"Don't worry, I will teach you anything you need to know." Rachelle picked up a fruit topaz in color, looked him directly in the eye, and bit into it. She chewed and lifted the fruit to his lips. "You should eat the kirim," she said, holding his eyes with hers.

Thomas hesitated. Was this like the touching of hands?

"Go ahead." Now Karyl urged him on.

They all waited, staring at him as though insistent on his tasting the fruit. Even Johan waited, anticipation painted in his bright, smiling eyes.

Thomas leaned forward and bit into the fruit. Juice ran down his chin as his teeth broke the skin and exposed the flesh. The moment the nectar hit his tongue he felt its power ripple down his body like a narcotic, stronger than the fruit Gabil had given him earlier.

"Take it," Rachelle said.

He took the fruit, brushing her fingers as he did. She let her hand linger, then reached for another fruit. The others had reached into the bowl and eagerly ate the fruit. It wasn't a narcotic, of course, but a gift from Elyon, as Michal had explained. Something that brought pleasure, like all of Elyon's gifts. Food, water, love. Flying and diving.

Flying and diving? There was something about flying and diving that struck a chord. What, he didn't know. Not yet.

Thomas took another bite and beamed at his hosts. Johan was the first to begin laughing, a bite of yellow flesh still lodged in his mouth. Then Palus joined in the laughter, and within seconds they were joined by Rachelle and Karyl. Still chewing slowly, Thomas shifted his gaze around the table, surprised at their odd behavior. His mouth formed a dumb grin, and he rested his eyes on Johan. He was one of them; he should be laughing as well. And now that he thought about it, he wanted to laugh.

Johan's shoulders shook uncontrollably. He had thrown his head back so his chin jutted out, his laughing mouth facing the ceiling. A nervous chuckle erupted from Thomas's throat and quickly grew to laughter. And then Thomas began to laugh uncontrollably, as though he had never laughed before, as though a hundred years of pent-up laughter had broken free.

Johan slipped out of his seat and rolled onto the floor, laughing hysterically. The laughter was so great that none of them could finish the fruit, and it was a good ten minutes before they gathered themselves enough to eat again.

Thomas rubbed the tears from his eyes and took another bite of the fruit. He was struck by the obscure idea that he must be floating through a dream. That he was in Denver having an incredible dream. But the hard surface of the table told him this was no dream.

The scene was surreal to be sure: sitting in a room lit by drifting colors that emanated from resined wood, seeing the hues of turquoise and lavender and gold hang softly in the air, eating strange and delicious fruit that made him delirious, and laughing with his new friends for no apparent reason other than his simple delight at the moment.

And now, sitting in silence, except for the sound of slurping fruit, feeling totally content without uttering a word.

Surreal.

But very real. This was supper. This was the common eating of food.

Johan suddenly sprang up from his chair. "Father, may we start the song now?"

"The song. The dance." A grin formed on Palus's face.

Without clearing the table, Karyl rose and glided to the center of the room, where she was quickly joined by Johan, Rachelle, and Palus. Thomas watched, feeling suddenly awkward, unsure whether he was expected to rise or stay seated. The family didn't seem concerned, so he remained seated.

He noticed the small pedestal in the center of the room for the first time. The four joined hands around a bowl perched on the pedestal. They raised their heads, began singing softly, stepped gingerly around the pedestal in a simple dance.

The moment the notes fell on his ears, Thomas knew that he was hearing much more than just a tune. The plaintive melody, sung in low tones, spoke beyond its notes.

It quickened and broke out in long, flowing notes containing a kind of harmony Thomas could not remember. Their dance picked up intensity—they seemed to have forgotten him completely. Thomas sat, captivated by the great emotion of the moment, stunned by the sudden loss of understanding, surprised by the feeling of love and kindness that numbed his chest. Johan beamed at the ceiling, exhibiting sincerity that seemed to transport him well beyond his age. And yet Palus looked like a child.

Rachelle stepped with distinguished grace. Not a movement of her body was out of place. She danced as though she had choreographed the dance. As though it flowed from her first and then to the others. She was lost in innocent abandon to the song.

He wanted to rush out and join them, but he could hardly move, much less twirl.

Then they each sang, but when young Johan finally lifted his head, smiled at the ceiling, and opened his mouth in a solo, Thomas knew immediately that he was the true singer here.

The first tone flowed from his throat clear and pure and sharp and so very, very young. The tones rose through the octave, higher and higher until Thomas thought the room might melt at his song.

But the boy sang higher, and still higher, bringing a chill to Thomas's spine. No wasted breath escaped Johan's lips, no fluctuation in tone, no strain of muscles in his neck. Only effortless song spun at the boy's whim.

A moment's pause, and the tone began again, this time in a rich, low bass deserving of the best virtuoso. And yet sung by this *boy!* The tones filled the room, shaking the table to which Thomas clung. He caught his breath and felt his jaw part. The entrancing melody swept through his body. Thomas swallowed hard, trying to hold back the sentiment rising through his chest. Instead he felt his shoulders shake, and he began to weep.

Johan continued to smile and sing. His tune reached into each chamber of Thomas's heart and reverberated with truth.

The song and dance must have gone on late into the night, but Thomas never knew, because he slipped into an exhausted sleep while they still sang.

11

THAT'S IT, come on. Wake up."

Someone was squeezing his cheeks together and shaking his head. Thomas forced lead-laden eyes open, surprised at how difficult the task was. He squinted in the light. His sister sat beside him, long blonde hair backlit by a halo of light.

He struggled to sit up and finally managed with a pull from Kara. He felt like he was moving in molasses, but that was to be expected—dreams often felt that way. Slogging instead of sprinting, floating instead of falling.

"You should wake up pretty quick," Kara said. "You feel okay?"

She was talking about the drugs. Sedatives followed by enough caffeine to wake a horse, if he remembered right.

"I gethh," he slurred. He swallowed a pool of saliva and said it again, concentrating on his pronunciation. "I guess." His head felt as though a rhino had stomped on it.

"Here, drink this." Kara handed him a glass of water. He took a long slug and cleared his throat. The fog started to clear from his mind. This could be a dream, or that could be a dream, but at the moment he didn't want to think about it.

"So?" Kara asked, setting the glass aside.

"So what?"

"So, did you dream?"

"I don't know." He looked around the room, disoriented. "Am I dreaming now?" He reached out and bumped her forehead with his palm.

"What are you doing?" she demanded.

"Just checking. To see if my hand went through your head, like in a dream. Guess not."

"Please, indulge me. For all I've done for you over the years, do me this one favor: Pretend this isn't a dream. And that whatever went through your noodle while you were sleeping was a dream."

"I'm sleeping now."

"Thomas, stop it!"

"Okay!" He tried to stand, got halfway up, and settled back down. "But it's not easy, you know."

"I'm sure it's not." She stood, picked up the glass, and headed for the kitchen. "The fact is, you didn't learn anything from the white fuzzy creatures in the colored forest, right? I suggest we start giving some serious thought to getting out of this mess you got us into."

"The winner was Joy Flyer. Is. Will be . . . whatever."

Kara blinked once. Twice. Thomas knew he'd hit a home run.

"You see?" he said. "I didn't have a clue who Joy Flyer was because you wouldn't even show me which horses were in the race. I'd never heard of the name before today. There's no way I could have guessed that. But the histories have recorded that a horse named Joy Flyer will win today's Kentucky Derby."

She snatched the newspaper off the counter and stared at the sports page. "How do you spell it?"

"How should I know? I didn't read it; Michal told me. Don't be—"

"Joy Flyer's a long shot." She stared at the paper. "How did you even know that name?"

"I told you, I didn't."

This time Kara didn't argue. "The race isn't for another five hours. We don't know that he will win."

"The race was run a long time ago, on ancient Earth, but I can understand your unease with that kind of thinking." Truth be told, even he felt plenty of unease with that kind of thinking.

"This is absolutely incredible! You're actually getting facts about the future in your dreams as if they're history?"

"Didn't I tell you that an hour ago?"

"How long were you there? What else can you tell me?"

"How long? Maybe, what? Four, five hours?"

"But you only slept for half an hour. What else did you learn?"

"Nothing. Except for what I said about the Raison Strain."

For a moment they faced each other in perfect stillness. Kara grabbed the rest of the paper and noisily crashed through it.

"What else did you find out about the Raison Strain?" she demanded, scanning the story on the French pharmaceutical company.

"Nothing. I didn't ask anything about—"

"Well, maybe you should have. You had the presence of mind to ask about a horse race. If this virus is about to wipe out a few billion people, you'd think you would have the presence of mind to ask about it."

"So now you're starting to listen," Thomas said, standing successfully this time. He looked around and reached for the bandage above his right ear. He pulled it off and felt for the wound. Odd.

"Kara?"

"It says here that Raison Pharmaceutical operates almost exclusively just outside Bangkok where its founder, Jacques de Raison, runs the company's new plant. His daughter, Monique de Raison, who is also in charge of new drug development, is expected to make the announcement in Bangkok on Wednesday."

"Kara!"

She looked up. "What?"

"Can you . . ." He walked toward her, still feeling the scar on his skull. "Is this normal?"

"Is what normal?"

"It feels . . . I don't know. I can't feel it."

Kara pushed his hand aside, spread his hair with her fingers, and stepped back, face white.

Thomas faced her. "What is it?"

She stared, too stunned to answer.

"It's gone," Thomas said. "I was right. This was an open wound eight hours ago, and now it's gone, isn't it?"

"This is impossible," Kara said.

Actually, it did sound a bit crazy.

"I'm telling you, Kara. This thing's real. I mean, real-real."

A tremble had come to Kara's fingers.

"Okay." He ran his fingers through his hair. The mob from New York City was still gunning for him, but the Raison Strain was the real threat here, wasn't it? For whatever reason, and through whatever device, he now possessed knowledge of the most damning proportions. Why him—third-culture vagabond from the Philippines, Java Hut extraordinaire, aspiring Magic Circle actor, unpublished novelist—he had no idea. But the significance of what he knew began to swell in his mind.

"Okay," he said, lowering his arm. "Maybe we can stop it."

"Stop it? I'm having trouble believing it, much less stopping it."

"Bangkok," Thomas said.

"What, pray tell, are we going to do in Bangkok? Storm the Raison facilities?"

"No, but we can't just stay here."

She broke off and walked for the kitchen desk. "We have to tell someone about this."

"Who?"

"CDC. Centers for Disease Control. The headquarters are in Atlanta."

"Tell them what?" Thomas asked. "That a fuzzy creature told me the Raison Strain was going to wipe out half the world?"

"That's what you're saying, isn't it? This Raison Vaccine is going to mutate and kill us all like a bunch of rats? The whole thing's crazy!"

He rubbed the scar on his head. "So is this."

Her eyes lifted to where the bullet had grazed his head not ten hours ago. She stared at his temple for a long moment and then turned for the phone. "We have to tell someone."

He assured himself that her frustration wasn't directed so much at him as at the situation. "Okay, but you can't tell some pencil pusher at the CDC," Thomas said. "You'll come off sounding like a kook."

"Then who? The local sheriff?" She scanned a list she'd placed in the front of the phone book, found the number, and dialed.

Thomas brushed past her and began flipping through the phone book. The Roush had said that the Raison Strain led to the "Great Deception." His mind fully engaged the problem now.

"What if I know this because I'm supposed to stop it?" Thomas asked. "But who really would have the power to stop it? The CDC? More like the FBI or the CIA or the State Department."

"Believe me, it'll sound just as crazy to the State Depar—" Kara turned, phone still plastered to her ear. "Yes, good morning, Melissa. This is Kara Hunter calling from Denver, Colorado. I'm a nurse. Who would I speak to about a . . . um, potential outbreak?" She paused. "No, actually I'm not calling on behalf of the hospital. I just need to report something I find suspicious." Another pause. "Infectious disease. Who would that be? Thanks, I'll hold."

Kara turned back to Thomas. "What do I tell him?"

"I'm telling you, I really think—"

She held up her hand. "Yes, hello, Mark." Kara took a breath and told him her concerns about the Raison Strain, stumbling along as best she could. She met with immediate resistance.

"I can't really tell you precisely why I suspect this. All I want is for you to have the vaccine checked out. You've received a complaint from a credible source. Now you need to follow up . . ."

She blinked and pulled the receiver from her ear.

"What?" Thomas demanded. "He hung up on you?"

"He said, 'Duly noted,' and just hung up."

"I told you. Here."

Thomas took the receiver and punched in a number he'd found in Washington, D.C. Three calls and seven transfers finally landed him in the office of the Bureau for International Narcotics and Law Enforcement Affairs assistant secretary, who evidently reported to the under secretary for global affairs, who in turn reported to the deputy secretary of state. None of this mattered that much; what did matter was that Gloria Stephenson seemed like a reasonable person. She at least listened to his claim that he, one, had information of utmost importance to U.S. interests, and, two, he had to get that information to the right party immediately.

"Okay, can you hold on a minute, Mr. Hunter? I'm going to try to put you through."

"Sure." See, now they were getting somewhere. The phone on the other end rang three times before being answered.

"Bob Macklroy."

"Yes, hi, Bob. Who are you?"

"This is the office of the Bureau for International Narcotics and Law Enforcement Affairs assistant secretary. I am the secretary."

The big gun himself. "Uh, morning, Mr. Macklroy. Thank you for taking my call. My name is Thomas Hunter, and I have information about a serious threat here that I'm trying to get to the right party."

"What's the nature of the threat?"

"A virus."

There was a moment of silence. "Do you have the number for the CDC?" Macklroy asked.

"Yes, but I really think this goes beyond them. Actually, we tried them, but they pretty much blew us off." It occurred to Thomas that he may not have all day with someone as important as Macklroy, so he decided to give it to the man fast.

"I know this may sound strange, and I know you don't have a clue who I am, but you have to hear me out."

"I'm listening."

"Ever hear of the Raison Vaccine?"

"Can't say that I have."

"It's an airborne vaccine about to hit the market. But there's a problem with the drug." He told Macklroy about the mutation and ensuing devastation in one long run-on sentence.

Silence.

"Are you still there?" Thomas asked.

"The earth's entire population is about to be decimated. Is that about it?"

Thomas swallowed. "I know it sounds crazy, but that's . . . right."

"You do realize there are laws that prohibit defaming a company without—"

"I'm not trying to defame Raison Pharmaceutical! This is a serious threat and needs immediate attention."

"I'm sorry, but you have the wrong department. This is something the CDC would typically handle. Now, if you'll excuse me, I have a meeting I'm late for."

"Of course, you're late for a meeting. Everyone who wants to get off the phone is always late for a meeting!" Kara was motioning for him to calm down. "Look, Mr. Macklroy, we don't have a lot of time here. France or Thailand or whoever it is that has jurisdiction over Raison Pharmaceutical has to check this out."

"Exactly what is your source for this information?"

"What do you mean?"

"I mean, how did you come across this information, Mr. Hunter? You're making some very serious allegations—surely you have a credible source."

The words slipped out before he could stop them. "I had a dream."

Kara put both palms to her forehead and rolled her eyes.

"I see. Very good, Thomas. We're wasting tax dollars here."

"I can prove it to you!" Thomas said.

"I'm sorry, but now I really *am* late for a meet—"

"I also know who's going to win the Kentucky Derby this afternoon," he yelled into the receiver. "Joy Flyer."

"Good day, sir."

The phone went dead.

Thomas stared at Kara, who was pacing and shaking her head. He dropped the receiver into its cradle. "Idiots. No wonder the country's falling apart at the seams."

A car door slammed in the parking lot outside.

"Well," Kara said.

"Well what?"

"Well, at least we've reported it. You have to admit, it sounds a bit loopy."

"Reporting it isn't enough," Thomas said, walking for the living room windows. He pulled aside one of the drapes.

"Why don't we make up some signs and stand on the corner; maybe that will get their attention," Kara said. "Armageddon cometh."

Thomas dropped the drape and jumped back.

"What?"

"They're here!" Three of them that he had seen. Working their way, door to door, on their floor.

Thomas sprang for his bedroom. "We have to get out of here. Grab your passport, money, whatever you have."

"I'm not dressed!"

"Then hurry!" He glanced at the door. "We have a minute. Maybe."

"Where are we going?"

He ran for his bedroom.

"Thomas!"

"Just go! Go, go!"

He grabbed his traveling papers and stuffed them in a black satchel he always used when he traveled. Money—two hundred bucks was all he had here. Hopefully Kara had some cash.

His toothbrush, a pair of khakis, three T-shirts, boxers, one pair of socks. What else? Think. That was it; no more time.

Thomas ran into the living room. "Kara!"

"Just hang on. I could *kill* you!"

Their yelling would wake the neighborhood. "Hurry!" he whispered hoarsely.

She mumbled something.

What else, what else? The bills? He grabbed the basket of bills, crammed them into his bag, and snatched up the machete from the coffee table.

Kara ran out, hastily dressed in black capris and a yellow tank top. Her hair was tied in a ponytail, a white bag under her arm. She looked like a canary ready for a cruise to the Bahamas.

"We're coming back, right?" she asked.

"Keep down and stay right behind me," Thomas said, running for the rear sliding-glass door. He pulled back the drape—back lot looked clear. They slipped out, and he closed the door behind them.

"Okay, quick but not obvious. Stay behind me," he repeated. They hurried down metal stairs and angled for Kara's Celica. No sign of the men who were probably pounding on their front door at this very moment.

"Keys?"

She pulled them out and handed them to him. "How do you know it was them?" she asked.

"I know. One of them had a bandage on his head. Same guy I met last night. I put my foot in his mouth."

They climbed in and he fired the car. "Get down."

Kara slouched in the front seat for two blocks before sitting up and straining back for sight of any pursuit.

"Anything?" Thomas asked.

"Not that I can see." She faced him. "Where are we going?"

Good question.

"Your passport is up-to-date, right?"

"Please, Thomas, be serious. We can't just run off to Manila or Bangkok, or wherever!"

"You have a better idea? This is real! Those are *real* men with *real* guns back there! The Raison Vaccine is a *real* vaccine, and Joy Flyer is a *real* horse!"

She looked out her side window. "The Kentucky Derby hasn't been raced yet," she said quietly.

"How long did I say we had before the Raison Strain became a threat?" he asked.

"You weren't even sure what year it happened." She faced him. "If all these things really *are* real, then you need some better information. We can't just traipse all over the globe because Joy Flyer really is a horse."

"What do you suggest, finding out exactly how to fix the problem in the Middle East in one fell swoop?"

She looked at him. "Could you do that?"

"'Course not."

"Why not?"

Yes, why not?

"What was it the black bats said to you?" Kara asked. "Something about them being your destiny? Maybe you should talk to them instead of these white furry creatures. We need specifics here."

"I can't. They live in the black forest! It's forbidden."

"Forbidden? Listen to you. It's a *dream,* Thomas! Granted, a dream with some pretty crazy ramifications, but just a dream."

"Then how do I know all this stuff? Why is my head wound gone?"

"I don't know. What I do know is that *this*"—she jabbed at the console—"isn't a dream. So your dreams are special. You're somehow learning things in there you shouldn't know; I give you that. I'm even *embracing* that. I'm saying, learn more! But I'm not going to go running off to Bangkok to save the world without the slightest idea of what to do once we get there. You need more information."

They entered the interchange between I-25 and I-70, headed for Denver International Airport.

"So at least you *are* admitting that this information's important. And real."

She set her head back. "Yes. So it seems."

"Then we have to respond to it. You're right, I need more information. But I can't very well fall asleep at the wheel, can I? And you can't keep drugging me."

"Okay."

"Macklroy seemed to think the CDC was the right place to go with this information."

"That's what I thought."

"Okay. So let's go to Atlanta. How much money do you have?"

She raised an eyebrow. "Just fly to Atlanta? I can't just leave my job without some notice."

"Then call them. But the phone obviously isn't the best way to get the attention of the CDC. They probably get a hundred kooks a day calling in crazy stories. So we go to the CDC headquarters in person."

"Not Bangkok?"

"No. Atlanta. You know we can't go back to the apartment—who knows how long they'll stake the place out?"

She considered the matter. Closed her eyes.

"Okay," she finally said. "Atlanta."

12

TRY AS he may at Kara's urging, Thomas couldn't sleep on the flight to Atlanta. Not a wink.

Slowly but surely, Kara was laying aside her disbelief that something very significant was actually happening to Thomas, although she still wasn't buying the notion that he'd actually stumbled onto the end of the world, so to speak. As she put it, just because he was admittedly experiencing some kind of precognition when he slept, didn't mean everything his highly active imagination latched onto was real. Who ever heard of fuzzy white bats anyway?

Thomas desperately wanted to convince her that it could easily be the other way around. That there was no real evidence the Boeing 757 they were flying in wasn't actually part of some crazy dream. Who was to say which reality was more compelling?

"Think about what Dad used to say when we were kids," he said. "The whole Christian worldview is based on alternate realities. We fight not against flesh and blood but against principalities or whatever. Remember that? In fact, most of the world believes that most of what actually happens, happens without our being able to see it. That's a religious mainstay."

"So? I don't believe that. And neither do you."

"Well, maybe we *should* believe that. Not necessarily the Christianity part, but the whole principle. Why not?"

"Because I don't believe in ghosts," she said. "If there is a God and he made us with five senses, why wouldn't he show himself to us through those senses? A dream makes no sense."

"Maybe he does show himself to us, but we don't see. Maybe it's not our senses that are the problem, but our minds."

She twisted in her seat and looked at him. "Is this the same Thomas who used to tell Dad how crazy his silly faith was?"

"I'm not saying anything's changed. I'm just saying that it's something to consider. Like *The Matrix*. Remember that movie? Everyone thinks it's one way, when actually it's another way."

"Only the real world is a colored forest with fuzzy white bats, and all this is just a dream. I don't think so."

"The fuzzy white bats healed my head and told me who will win the Kentucky Derby. And if I'm imagining one reality, it would be more likely that I'm imagining *this* one. In the other reality, both realities make sense— this one as a history and that one as the present. In this reality, the other reality makes no sense unless this reality isn't really a reality. Or unless it really is the future."

"Enough. You're giving me a headache. Go to sleep and find out how we solve the Middle East crisis."

"We don't. The Raison Strain hits us before then. Which is now."

"Unless the Raison Strain is stopped," she said. "Is it possible to change the future? Or better yet, change history?"

He didn't bother to respond.

They landed in Atlanta an hour later and spent thirty minutes on a run of errands. Kara owed the hospital in Denver an explanation and had some banking to do; Thomas checked on the availability of flights to several overseas destinations, just in case. It was half past three before they met up in ground transportation.

"So," Thomas said, holding the door open that led to the taxi line. "How much do we have?"

"We? About $5,000, and it's in my account. I don't recall you depositing any money in my account."

He'd found a 10:00 p.m. flight to Bangkok through Los Angeles and Singapore, but the short-notice tickets would cost $2,000 apiece. Not good. He frowned.

"You expected more?" she asked.

"I thought you'd saved up over twenty thousand," he said.

"That was three months ago. I've made some purchases since. Five will hold us. As long as we don't go running off to Manila or Bangkok." She shut her door.

The yellow cab pulled up to the Centers for Disease Control headquarters on Clifton Road at 4:15, forty-five minutes before the government building presumably closed. Kara paid the driver and faced the front doors with Thomas.

"Okay, exactly what is our primary goal here?" she asked.

"To wake the dead," Thomas said.

"Let's be a little more precise."

"Someone in there has to take us seriously. We don't leave until someone with the power to do something agrees to look into the Raison Strain."

Kara glanced at her watch. "Okay."

They entered the building and approached a counter cordoned off with protective Plexiglas and identified by a black sign as "Reception." Thomas explained their objective to a red-headed woman named Kathy and, when informed that they would have to see a caseworker, asked to see one immediately. He was handed a stack of forms containing a host of questions that seemed to have nothing to do with infectious diseases: birth date, Social Security number, grade school achievements, shoe size. They retreated to a row of cushioned waiting chairs, filled the forms out quickly, and returned them to Kathy.

"How long will we have to wait?" Thomas asked.

Her phone buzzed and she answered it without offering a response to Thomas. One of her coworkers was evidently having mice problems in her house. Thomas tapped his fingers on the counter and waited patiently.

Kathy set her phone down, but it rang again.

Thomas held up his finger. "Simple question: How long?"

"As soon as someone's available."

"It's already 4:35. When will someone be available?"

"We'll do our best to get you in today," she said and picked up the phone. Same party. Another critical question on tactics to hold back swarms of attacking mice. Something about wearing rubber gloves when removing the varmints from traps.

Thomas sighed audibly and walked back to the waiting chairs. "Kathy was raised in an idiot factory," he said.

"Patience, Thomas. Maybe I should do the talking." Kara glanced at her watch again.

"I have a bad feeling we're wasting our time here," he said. "Even if we do report this, how long will it take for the bureaucracy to work? It takes months, sometimes years, to get FDA approval for a drug. How long does it take to reverse that? Probably months and years. I'm telling you, we have to go to Bangkok. They're making the announcement in two days. All we have to do is explain the problem to them—to this Monique de Raison. They'll check out our concerns, find the problem, and deal with it."

Kara looked at her watch and stood. "I doubt it would be that simple. I have to check something. Be right back."

Thomas let his steam gather for another ten minutes before approaching Kathy for another round. This time she stopped him before he could ask the obvious question.

"Excuse me, sir, are you hard of hearing, or just stubborn? I thought I said I'd call you when a caseworker was available."

He stopped, shocked by her rudeness. No one else was within earshot—a fact obviously not lost on Kathy, or she wouldn't dare offer this verbal abuse.

"Excuse me?" he stammered.

"You heard me," she snapped. "I'll call you if we have a caseworker available before we close."

Thomas stepped up to the counter and glared through the Plexiglas. "This can't wait until tomorrow."

"You should've thought about that earlier."

"Listen, lady, we flew all the way from Denver to see you! What if something dead serious was wrong with me? How do you know I don't have a disease that could wipe out the world?"

She sat back, clearly smug in a certainty that she had won with this last absurdity of his. "This isn't a clinic. I don't think you have—"

"You don't know that! What if I had polio?" Wrong disease. "What if I had Ebola or something?"

"It says Raison something." She lazily pulled out his form. "Not Ebola. Sit down, Mr. Hunter."

Heat flared up his neck. "And what *is* the Raison Strain?" he demanded. "Do you even know? As a matter of fact, the Raison Strain makes the Ebola virus look like a common cold. Did you know that? The virus may just have broken out in—"

"Sit down!" Kathy rose to her feet, fists clenched by her hips. She pointed dramatically to the waiting chairs. "Sit down immediately."

Thomas could never be sure if it was his martial arts instincts or his generous intelligence that took over in the next moment—either way, at least his courage couldn't be faulted.

He locked stares with the woman behind the Plexiglas for a full five seconds. The sight of her quivering jowls was the last straw. He suddenly grabbed his own neck with both hands and began to choke himself.

"Ahhhh! I think I might have been infected," he gasped. He stumbled forward and smashed his head into the Plexiglas. "Help!" he screamed. "Help, I'm infected with the Raison Strain!"

The woman stood rigid and shaking with fury, still pointing at the chairs. "Sit down!"

Thomas smashed his cheek against the glass, tightened his choke hold, and stuck out his tongue. "I'm dying! Help, help!"

"Thomas!" Kara ran toward him from the hall.

He started to sag and rolled his eyes.

A half-dozen workers ran into the cubicles behind the receptionist.

"Stop it!" Kathy shrieked. "Stop it!"

"Thomas, what are you doing?" Kara demanded frantically.

He winked at her discreetly and then banged his head against the glass, this time hard enough to give himself a headache.

"Excuse me!" A man dressed in a gray suit had materialized behind the receptionist. "What seems to be the problem here?"

"He . . . he wants to see a caseworker," she said.

Thomas lowered his hands and stood up. "Are you in charge here?"

"Can I help you?"

"Forgive me for the antics, but I'm a bit desperate and a junior-high fit was the only thing that came to mind," Thomas said. "It's absolutely criti-cal that we speak to someone from the infectious diseases department immediately."

The man glanced at Kathy's red face. "We have procedures for a reason, Mr. . . ."

"Hunter. Thomas Hunter. Trust me, you'll be very interested in what I have to say."

The man hesitated and then stepped through a door in the Plexiglas. "Why don't you come into my office?" He extended his hand. "My name is Aaron Olsen. Please excuse our delay. It gets a bit hectic around here at times."

Thomas shook the man's hand and followed him, escorting Kara.

"Next time you're going to lose your hearing, warn me, will you?" Kara whispered.

"Sorry."

Kara couldn't hide a grin.

"What?" Thomas asked.

"Nothing," she said. "I'll tell you later."

Aaron Olsen stared at Thomas from behind a large cherry-wood desk, elbows propped on the surface, face stoic and impossible to read in the wake of Thomas's detailed explanation of the fuzzy white bats.

Thomas sat back and let out a long breath. A gold placard on Aaron's desk said he was the assistant director, and he explained that his department was indeed infectious diseases. And, although he'd started by explaining that the World Health Organization's rapid response unit was the right party to contact, he had agreed to listen to their story and had done so without emotion.

They were finally getting somewhere.

"So," Aaron said, and for the first time a slight grin nudged his lips.

"I know it sounds strange," Thomas said. "But you have to consider the facts here."

"I am, Mr. Hunter, and that's what's troubling me. Am I missing something here, or are you actually telling me that this information came from a dream?"

Kara leaned forward. "You say that like it's preposterous." Her defensive tone was striking. "Did you hear a word of what he just told you? He knows about the Raison Vaccine! He knew about it before it was made public."

"The Raison Vaccine has been touted in private circles for a few months now—"

"Not in *his* private circles."

Thomas held up a hand. "It's okay, Kara." What had come over her? She was suddenly his ardent advocate. He faced Olsen. "Okay, let's go over this again. What exactly is confusing you?"

The man smiled, incredulous. "You're saying this came from a dream—"

"Not exactly," Thomas said. "An alternate reality. But let's forget that for a minute. Regardless of how I know, I do have specific knowledge of things that haven't happened yet. I knew that a French company was going to announce a vaccine called the Raison Vaccine before it was public knowledge. I also know that the Raison Vaccine will mutate under extreme heat and become quite deadly. It will infect the world's population in less than three weeks. All we're asking you to do is check it out. What's so complicated about that?"

Olsen looked from Thomas to Kara and back. "So let me summarize here. A man walks into the building, begins to scream for help while choking himself, and then claims some bats have visited him in a dream and told him that the world is about to end—in what, three weeks?—when a vaccine overheats and turns into a deadly virus. Is that about it?"

"Three weeks *after* the virus is released," Thomas clarified. Olsen ignored him.

"Are you aware that intense heat kills things like viruses, Mr. Hunter? Your warning is flawed on the surface, regardless of the source."

Kara came to his defense again. "Maybe that's why Raison Pharmaceutical is ignorant of the problem, assuming they are. Maybe drugs aren't tested under extreme heat."

"You're a nurse," Olsen said. "You're buying all this dream nonsense?"

"Like Thomas said, it's not necessarily dream nonsense. Just check it out, for goodness' sake!"

"How do you propose I do that? Send out a bulletin that announces the fuzzy white bats have issued a warning about the Raison Vaccine? Pretty clear case of defamation, don't you think?"

"Then explain to me how I knew that Joy Flyer was going to run in the Kentucky Derby," Thomas said.

Olsen shrugged. "Public information."

"But it wasn't public that Joy Flyer was going to win," Kara said. "Not two hours ago when I placed my bet."

Thomas faced her. "What bet?"

"Joy Flyer won?" Olsen said. He glanced at his watch. "You're right, the results should be in. You sure Joy Flyer won? He was a long shot."

"You bet on Joy Flyer?" Thomas demanded. "How much?"

"Yes, Thomas, I did. And yes, he did win, long shot or not."

"Bummer." Olsen shook his head and looked out the window. "I had a thousand bucks on Winner's Circle."

"You're missing the point," Kara said. "Thomas learned that Joy Flyer was going to win from the same source that gave him these details about the Raison Vaccine."

"How much?" Thomas asked again.

Olsen sighed. "None of this can be substantiated. For all I know, you didn't even bet on Joy Flyer. And if you did, you could be claiming to have been tipped off by some angel to substantiate this other story. For all I know, you have stock in Raison Pharmaceutical's competitor and are looking to trash Raison. I can't do a thing with this information except put it through the normal channels."

"So you're dismissing it? Just like that?" Kara demanded.

"No, I said I'd report it." Olsen sat up and straightened some papers. "You've made your report—I suggest you go collect your winnings." He smiled condescendingly.

Kara stood abruptly. "You're a fool, Olsen. Don't you dare toss that report. If there's even a small chance that we're right, you could be messing with a very dangerous situation here. I just bet $15,000, most of my life savings, on a long shot named Joy Flyer because of what my brother knows. There's $345,000 sitting in an account with my name on it right now because I listened to him. I suggest you do the same."

She marched to the door.

"Exactly!" Thomas said, standing. Three hundred forty-five thousand?

The cab had waited as instructed.

"That's true? You really won that much?"

"If we paid off your debt to the boys in New York, do you think they'd leave us alone?"

"With a little interest, sure. You're serious?"

"You've bailed me out more than once." She shrugged. "Now it's my turn. Besides, it's as much your money as mine."

"Where to?" the driver asked.

Thomas searched his sister's eyes. "Airport," he said. Then to Kara, "Okay?"

"Where?" she asked.

"Bangkok. A flight leaves at ten. We no longer need visas, I checked."

She stared at the back of the driver's seat. "Why not? Airport."

"Airport it is." The cab pulled out.

Thomas nodded. "Okay, good. We don't have a choice, right?"

"Of course we don't," she said quietly. "We never have a choice with you, Thomas. Staying put isn't in your vocabulary."

"This is different. We can't pretend this isn't happening."
She looked out her window. "We need more information."
"We will. I promise. As soon as I can fall asleep."
"That should be when? Somewhere over the Pacific?"

13

CARLOS MISSIRIAN walked through Bangkok International Airport eight hours after Valborg Svensson had given him the order to come. The company's jet served him well. His mind retraced the conversation with the Swiss.

"Our man at the CDC received a nervous visitor today who claimed that the mutations of the Raison Vaccine held together under prolonged, specific heat," Svensson had said. "The result, the visitor claimed, would be a lethal airborne virus with an incubation of three weeks. One that could infect the entire world's population in less than three weeks."

"And how did this visitor happen to come across this information?"

Svensson had hesitated. "A dream," he said. "A very unusual dream."

Carlos's shoes clacked on the concrete floor. Perhaps they had found the virus, although it was difficult to imagine they'd done so by this sort of means. He took a deep breath. The time would soon come when taking a long pull of air would bring death instead of life. An odorless virus borne on the wind, searching for human hosts. Not a simple disease as innocuous as Ebola that took weeks to spread properly, but a genetically engineered virus that traveled with the world's air currents and infected the entire world's population. An epidemic that could poison this very airport in a matter of minutes, incubate over a number of weeks, and then kill within twenty-four hours of its first symptom.

There was no defense for such a virus. Except an antivirus.

He rented a Mercedes and drove into the city. Monique de Raison was due to deliver an address at the Sheraton in twenty-four hours. He would wait until then. This gave him ample time to prepare. To plan for whatever contingencies might disrupt his primary course of action. To narrow any possible avenues of escape or disruptions to the kidnapping.

They'd chased down hundreds of leads over the last five years. A dozen times they'd been very hopeful of uncovering a virus with precisely the elusive characteristics they required. Once they were quite certain that they actually had it. But never had they acted on such an irregular report. Certainly not a dream. What had convinced Svensson to trust such a report, Carlos didn't know. But the more he thought about it, the more he liked the idea.

Why not? Why couldn't the answer to his prayers be delivered through a dream? Was this beyond Allah? He'd never been a mystic, but this didn't mean that God hadn't spoken to Mohammed through visions in the cave. If this single weapon could deal such a blow to his enemies, wasn't it conceivable that Allah would open man's mind to it through something as mystical as a dream? The fact that this Thomas Hunter not only had such a dream but that he'd proceeded to the CDC with it seemed to suggest providence.

Furthermore, if any pharmaceutical research firm had the resources to develop such a virus, it would be Raison Pharmaceutical. He'd never met Monique de Raison, but her meticulous research in the field took what the Russians had accomplished to a whole new level. Carlos served death with force, not through the veins, but that didn't mean he was ignorant concerning the intricacies of bioweapons.

He could still hear Svensson's low, grinding voice that late night seven years earlier as they overlooked Cairo. "When you were six, in Cyprus, your father was a computer scientist who moonlighted as a strategic adviser to the PLO," Svensson said. "He was kidnapped by Israeli Mossad agents. He never came home."

"Okay, so you know your history," Carlos said, somewhat surprised that this man knew what few could possibly know.

"I would expect most young boys would turn bitter. Maybe one day act out deep-seated resentment. But these are pale words to describe you, yes?"

Carlos watched the tall Swiss draw deep on his cheroot. "Maybe."

"You left home at age twelve and spent the next fifteen years training with a long list of terrorists, including a two-year stint in an Al Qaeda training camp. You finally left this nonsense of petty terrorism. You're interested in bigger fish."

Carlos did not like this man.

"But your years of training have suited you well. Some say that there isn't a man alive who could live through five minutes of hand-to-hand combat with you. Is that true?" Another deep drag of smoke.

"I'll leave the business of judging me to others," Carlos said.

The man smiled. "Do you know what it would take to subdue the earth?"

"The right weapon," Carlos said.

"One virus."

"As I said, the right weapon."

"One virus and one antivirus."

Carlos dismissed the sudden urge to cut the man's throat right there on the roof of the Hilton, not because Svensson presented any immediate threat, but because the man looked evil to him with his black eyes and twisted grin. He did not like this man.

"One virus, one vaccine, and one man with the will to use both," Svensson said, and then slowly turned to Carlos. "I am that man."

"Frankly, I don't care who you are," Carlos said. "I care about my people."

"Your people. Of course. The question is, What are you willing to do for your people?"

"No," Carlos said evenly, "the question is, What *will* I do? And the answer is, I will remove their enemies."

"Unless, of course, the Israelis remove you first."

Three months later they had struck a simple agreement. Svensson and his group would offer a base of operations in the Alps, an unprecedented level of intelligence, and the means to conduct a biological attack. In return, Carlos would provide whatever muscle Svensson required in his personal operations.

The broader plan involved nations and leaders of nations and was masterminded by the man Valborg Svensson answered to: Armand Fortier. Carlos had met Fortier on only two occasions, but after each, any doubts he'd harbored had been swept out to sea. Every conceivable detail had been excruciatingly planned and then planned again. Contingencies for a hundred possible reactions to the release of any virus that met their requirements. The primary nuclear powers were the greatest prize—each had been softened and judged in ways they could not begin to imagine. Not yet. One day the historians would look back and lament the missed signals, so many subtle signs of the coming day. No one would pay such a price as the United States. The final result would forever change history in a matter of a few short weeks. It was almost too much to hope for.

And yet it was a very real possibility. If a hundred million Americans woke up one morning and learned they had been infected with a virus that would kill them in a matter of weeks, and only one man had the cure and was demanding their cooperation in exchange for that cure . . .

This was true power.

All they needed was the right weapon. The one virus with its one cure.

Carlos took a deep breath and blew it out past pursed lips. The American was on his way. Thomas Hunter. According to his sources, Hunter would be arriving in Bangkok in a matter of hours. By this time tomorrow, Carlos would know the truth.

He breathed a prayer to Allah and eased the Mercedes toward the off-ramp.

14

THOMAS AWOKE with duplicitous images running circles in his head. He was in a soft bed, and light was streaming through a small window above him. This was Rachelle's home. Johan's home. In the colored forest where he lived.

He groaned, shook the dreams of the histories from his mind, rubbed his eyes, and struggled out of bed. The room was small and plain, but turquoise and golden hues from the wood gave it a rich beauty.

He slowly opened the door. Memories of the previous evening flooded his mind. He dipped his hands into a small basin of water by the bedroom door and splashed water over his face.

"Thomas!"

Thomas whirled around, startled by the cry. Johan stood in the doorway, grinning. "Do you want to play, Thomas?"

"Play? Um, actually I have some things I have to do. I have to find my village." Not to mention figuring out what to do about the romance business.

"Then maybe Tanis and my father can help you find your village. He's waiting for you."

"Your father? With Rachelle?"

The boy grinned very wide. "You want to see Rachelle?"

"Uh, no, not necessarily. I just wondered if—"

"Well, I think she wants to see you. I think that's what my father wants to talk to you about. Yes, I do. And it's very exciting! Don't you think?"

"I . . ." Was he understanding this right? The whole village knew? "I'm not sure what you mean."

Johan beamed. "They said that you hit your head and lost your memory. Is that fun?"

"Not especially."

"But if you come with me, you will have fun. Come on! They're waiting." He ran off through the door.

Thomas followed. His memory was still lost, even after a good sleep.

He stepped outside and allowed his eyes to adjust to the light. Everywhere, small groups of people busied themselves. He stared at a group of women to his right who sat on the ground working with leaves and flowers—they seemed to be making tunics. Some were quite thin, others fairly plump, their skin tone varied from dark to light. All watched him with knowing glints in their emerald eyes.

He turned to his left, where two men massaged a piece of red wood with their bare hands. Beside them a woman manned a fruit stand, ten or fifteen wood boxes filled with different fruits. Several others bordered the path farther down. A low note rang through Thomas's ears, singing from a source he couldn't place. All of this he took in immediately, searching his memory for any recognition. His memory failed him completely.

Johan took his hand. "These are my friends," he said, pointing to two children who stared wide-eyed at Thomas from the lawn. "This is Ishmael and Latfta. They are singers like me."

They both had blond hair and green eyes; both stood a tad taller than Johan. "Hello, Thomas."

"Hello, Ishmael and Laffta."

The one on the left lifted a hand to his mouth and giggled. "Latfta!" he blurted out. "My name is Latfta!"

"Oh, sorry. Latfta?"

"Yes. Latfta."

Thomas braved another look at the women. One of them, a plump woman with beautiful eyes and long lashes, began to giggle. A glance across the path betrayed her.

There, under the eaves of a house twenty feet away, leaning against the amber wall with arms crossed and head tilted, stood Rachelle. Bare feet. Simple blue dress. Tousled hair. Brilliant green eyes. Tempting smile.

She was stunning, and she was suddenly walking toward him. For an incredible moment the motion around Thomas seemed to cease. Only her dress, flowing mid-thigh, and her hair swirling in her own breeze, and those emerald eyes swallowing him.

Rachelle winked.

His heart nearly ceased. Surely the whole village had seen it. Every eye was undoubtedly fixed on her seductive approach. This incredible display of . . .

Rachelle suddenly diverted her eyes, flattened her mouth, and veered to her right. She walked right past him and then past the other women without a single word. And if he wasn't mistaken, she had squared off her shoulders. A man chuckled. Thomas felt his face flush.

"What did I tell you?" Johan whispered.

He and his little friend pulled Thomas out onto the path. He followed, avoiding eye contact with anyone, looking instead directly ahead as if he were going somewhere important, stealing glances to take in the village. He wasn't sure what had just happened, but he wasn't about to reveal his ignorance of the matter.

There was no evil on this side of the black forest, Michal had told him. So then Rachelle couldn't dislike him, right? Wasn't dislike a form of evil? Yet a deity—such as his father's God in the histories—could dislike without being evil. So surely his creation could dislike without being evil. They would dislike evil. But would they love one person over another? Would they choose one man or woman over another? Evidently.

Johan stopped within twenty paces. "Marla! Good morning, Marla!"

A mature woman stepped into the path and ruffled Johan's hair. "Elyon is smiling, Johan. Like the sun in the sky, he's smiling over you." Her eyes darted over Thomas. "Is this the stranger?"

"Yes."

"Then you must be Thomas Hunter. Most welcome to this side." She touched his cheek and studied him for a moment. "I am the daughter of

Tanis. I would say that your mother came from my brother Theo's line. Yes, the same cheeks, the same eyes, the same mouth." She lowered her hand. "My brother always was a handsome one. Welcome."

"Thank you. So you think my father's name is Theo?"

She laughed. "Not likely. But a descendant, more than likely. You don't remember?"

"I . . . no, I hit my head."

"Did you, now? How interesting. Take care of him, Johan."

"Tanis and Palus are waiting for him," Johan said.

"Tanis, of course. Perhaps the four of you could mount my father's famous expedition." She smiled and winked.

They passed by a woodworker who was shaping a piece of red wood. Thomas paused to watch the man work. The wood moved under the crafter's massaging fingers. He shifted for a better perspective and watched carefully. There could be little doubt about what he saw. The wood was actually moving under the woodworker's bare hands, as if he were successfully coaxing it to reshape itself.

"What's he doing?" Thomas whispered.

"He's making a ladle. Maybe a gift for someone. You don't remember?"

"That's incredible. No, I guess I don't."

Johan talked excitedly to Ishmael and Latfta. "You see? He doesn't remember. He's going to love the storytellers!" Then to Thomas. "Tanis is a storyteller." Johan pulled a small piece of red wood formed to look like a miniature lion from his pocket and handed it to Thomas. "Keep this," he said. "Maybe it will help you remember." Johan and Latfta grabbed his hands once again and pulled him along like a prized trophy.

―⸺∞⸺―

They found Johan's father, Palus, talking to a man beyond the brilliant topaz arch that led into the village. The stranger's moccasins were strapped tight, and a dark brown tunic, made from something like leather that came from one of the trees, Michal had informed him yesterday, hung above his knees. His eyes were green, of course, set into a strong tanned face that looked not a day older than thirty. The man's legs were lean and well muscled. He looked born to run through the forest. A warrior by all appearances.

This must be Tanis. Firstborn. The oldest man on Earth.

"Ah, my dear young man, good morning to you," Tanis said. "So very, very glad that you've come into our village."

"That's very kind of you," Thomas said. He scanned the forest at the crest of the hill beyond. "Have you seen Michal?"

"Michal? No. Have you seen Michal, Palus?"

"No, I haven't. I'm sure he'll be along."

Tanis looked at Thomas, left eyebrow raised. "Well, there you have it then. Michal will be along."

"He was going to find my village for me," Thomas said.

"Oh, yes, I'm sure he will. But I think it will take him some time. In the meantime, we have some wonderful ideas."

"Maybe I should try to help him. Won't my family be worried?"

"No, no, certainly not. You really have lost all of your memory, haven't you? What a thing, to experience everything as if it were the first time. It must be both exhausting and quite stimulating."

"Wouldn't my village worry about me?" Thomas asked.

"Worry? Never! They will assume you are with Elyon, as you most definitely are. Do you think he hasn't allowed this?"

They all stared at Thomas, waiting for an answer. Silence lingered.

"Of course he has," Thomas said.

"There you go, then! Come, let us talk." Tanis led him up the hill. Palus walked abreast, followed by the three children. Overhead, several Roush winged through the air.

"Now, I would like to know a few things before we begin," Tanis said. "I would like to know if you've forgotten the Great Romance."

"Before we begin what?"

"Before we begin to help you."

"With what?"

"With the Great Romance, of course."

There it was. He couldn't escape this romance of theirs.

Tanis exchanged glances first with Palus, and then with the children. "So then you do forget. Wonderful!" He walked in a tight circle, thinking. Raised a hand. "Not wonderful that you've forgotten, mind you. Wonderful that you have so much to discover. As a storyteller, I must say the prospects we have here are incredible! Like an unmarked wood. Like a pond without a single ripple. Like a—"

"Well then, get on with it. Tell him!" Palus said.

Tanis stopped, hand raised. He dipped his head.

"Yes, of course. The Great Romance. Sit, sit, all of you."

The others quickly sat on the sloping grass, and Thomas eased down beside them. Tanis walked back and forth, tan tunic flowing.

"The Great Romance," Tanis announced, one digit in the air. He spun to the children. "Tell him what the Great Romance is, Johan."

Johan leaped to his feet. "It is the game of Elyon!" He dropped to his seat.

"A game. Yes, it is a game, I suppose. As much as any story is a story. Exactly. Well, there you have it then. The *game* of Elyon. I'm going to assume, perhaps correctly, that you know nothing, Thomas. In either case, I want to tell you anyway. The Great Romance is the basis for all of the stories."

"You mean the histories?" Thomas asked.

"Histories? No, I mean stories. The histories are fascinating, and I would love to talk to you about them. But the Great Romance is the root of our stories, stories that confront us with the eternal ideals. Love. Beauty. Hope. The greatest gifts. The very heart of Elyon. Do you understand?"

"Um . . . actually it sounds a bit abstract."

"Ha! The opposite, Thomas! Do you know why we love beautiful flowers? Because we love *beauty!*"

They all nodded. Thomas looked at them blankly.

"The point is, we were created to love beauty. *We* love beauty because *Elyon* loves beauty. We love song because Elyon loves song. We love *love* because Elyon loves love. And we love to be loved because Elyon loves to be loved. In all these ways we are like Elyon. In one way or another, everything we do is tied to this unfolding story of love between us and Elyon."

Thomas nodded, more because the response seemed appropriate than because he understood.

Tanis nodded with him. "Elyon's love for us and ours for him, the Great Romance, you see, is first." One index finger in the air. "And second"—his other index finger in the air—"that same love expressed between us." He paused, raised both fingers above his head like goalposts, and announced emphatically, "Between man and woman!"

Palus searched Thomas's face expectantly. "Do you remember? Surely you remember."

"Love. Yes, of course I remember love."

"Between a man and a woman," Palus pressed.

"Sure. Yes, between a man and a woman. Romance."

Tanis clapped once, loudly enough to pass for a thunderclap. "Exactly! Romance!"

"Romance!" a voice cried behind them. Three Roush led by none other than Gabil drifted in for a landing. The other two quickly introduced themselves as Nublim and Serentus. When Thomas asked if the names were male or female, Gabil laughed. "No, Roush are not like that. No romance, not like that at all."

"Unfortunately, not like that at all," Nublim said.

"Do you want to play?" Johan asked Gabil, jumping to his feet.

"Of course!"

As if on cue, all three children ran after the Roush, sending them hooting in flight down the hill.

The two village elders immediately put their arms around Thomas's shoulders and turned him uphill.

"Now the question, my dear friend, is, of course"—Tanis looked across at Palus—"Rachelle."

It was all starting to make sense to Thomas, but the implications were surprising. So bold. So unabashed. The village leader, this firstborn, and Palus were actually trying to set him up with Rachelle!

All he could manage was, "Rachelle."

Palus clapped again. "Exactly! You have it! My daughter, Rachelle! She's chosen you!"

"And that's why we are here to help you," Tanis said. "You've lost your memory, and we're going to help you remember. Or at least learn again. We think—"

"Perhaps I should say . . . ," Palus began, hand uplifted.

"Yes, of course, you should say it."

"We know there will be a wonderful romance between you and my daughter, Rachelle, but we realize you may not know how to proceed."

"Well . . ."

"It's perfect! I saw it in your eyes the moment we met yesterday."

"You saw what?"

Tanis led him farther up the hill. "You find her beautiful, yes?"

"Yes."

"She must know this if you are to win her."

Thomas wanted to ask the one question begging a voice here. Namely, what if he didn't want to win her? But he couldn't bring himself to betray his promise to Michal to play along or dampen the enthusiasm of Rachelle's father.

"I could write your story," Tanis continued. "A wonderful play of love and beauty, but then it would be mine, not yours. You must tell your own story. Or, in this case, live it. And to understand how love unfolds, you must understand how Elyon loves."

The sheer momentum of their zeal carried Thomas. He asked the question he knew Tanis was demanding he ask. "And how does Elyon love?"

"Excellent question! He chooses."

"He chooses," Palus repeated.

"He pursues."

"He pursues," said Rachelle's father, fist clenched.

"He rescues."

"He rescues."

"He woos."

"He woos."

"He protects."

It was like a Ping-Pong match.

"He protects. Ha!"

"He lavishes," Tanis shouted.

Palus stopped. "Is that one of them?"

"Why not?"

"I mean, is that normally placed with the others?"

"It should be."

They looked at each other for a moment.

"He lavishes," cried Palus.

"This, my dear Thomas, is what you should do to win Rachelle's heart."

"Elyon does all this?"

"Yes, of course. You've forgotten him as well?" This seemed to astound both of them.

"No, not entirely. It's coming back, you know." He quickly diverted the discussion back to Rachelle. "Forgive my"—he tapped his head—"density here, but exactly what does a woman need rescuing from? There is no evil this side of the black forest. Right?"

Again, they stared at each other.

"My, my, it is strange, this memory loss of yours," Tanis said. "It's a game, man! A play! Something to take pleasure in. You give a flower to a maiden, why? Because she *needs* nourishment? No, because she *wants* it."

"What's that got to do with rescuing? What would she need rescuing from?"

"Because she wants to *feel* rescued, Thomas. And she wants to *feel* chosen. As much as you are desperate to be chosen. We all are. Elyon chooses us. He rescues us and protects us and woos us and, yes, lavishes love on us. This is the Great Romance. And this is how you will win Rachelle's heart."

Thomas wasn't sure he wanted to ask again, but honestly he still didn't understand their concept of rescuing.

"Tell him, Palus," Tanis said. "I think maybe a story would be a good idea here. I could write it for you to read before you go into battle for this love."

"Battle?" Thomas said. "Now it's a battle?"

"Figuratively," Palus said. "You know, you win a woman's heart as you would win a battle. Not as if you were fighting the Shataiki in flesh and blood, of course, because we never do that."

"Not yet we don't," Tanis said. "But there may come a time. Very soon, even. We've been thinking of an expedition to teach those terrible bats a lesson or two."

Michal's concern.

"They are confined to the black forest," Thomas said. "Why not just leave them there to rot?"

"Because of what they have done!" Tanis cried. "They are evil, despicable creatures who need a lesson teaching, I'm telling you! We know from the histories what they are capable of. Do you think I'm content to just sit back and let them plot their way across the river? Then you don't know me, Thomas Hunter. I have been working on a way to finish them for good!"

There was no lack of passion in his diatribe. Even Palus seemed slightly taken aback. There was something amiss in his reasoning, but Thomas couldn't put his finger on it.

"Either way, we often pretend to fight with the same kind of passion and vigor we would in a real fight with the Shataiki," Palus said. "Show him, Tanis. Just show him."

Tanis made a stance similar to those of the martial arts from Thomas's dreams of the histories. "Okay then—"

"You know martial arts?" Thomas asked.

Tanis stood up. "That's what they called it in the histories. You know the histories?"

"Well, I'm dreaming of them. In my dreams I know the martial arts."

"You're dreaming of the histories, but you forget everything here because you hit your head," Palus said. "Now, that is something."

"That's what Michal thinks."

"And Michal is very wise." Tanis glanced around, as if checking for the white furry. "How much detail do you dream about? How much do you know?"

"I don't know what happens after the Raison Strain, but before then, I know quite a bit."

"You can tell me how Napoleon won his wars? What strategy he used?"

Thomas tried to think. "No, I don't know that I ever studied Napoleon. But I suppose I could find out. I could read a history book in my dreams."

The notion seemed to stun Tanis. "My, my. You can do that?"

"Actually, I've never tried. But I'm doing it the other way." He shifted on his feet. "What I mean is, it's occurred to me. Do you know anything about the Great Deception? The virus?"

"Not enough. Not nearly enough, but more than most. It happened before the great tribulations, I do know that. The only two around these parts who would know all the histories are the wise ones. Michal and Teeleh, though Teeleh is no longer a wise one. Michal is convinced the histories are a distraction that could lead us down the wrong path. And Teeleh . . . If I ever were so fortunate as to lay my eyes on Teeleh, I would tear him limb from limb and burn the parts!"

"Michal is right," Thomas said. "An expedition would be pointless. I've been in the black forest and I can tell you, the Shataiki are wicked. They very nearly killed me."

This last admission proved to be nearly too much for Tanis. "You've been *in* the black forest? Over the Crossing?"

He was so excited that Thomas wondered if he'd taken the wrong turn by telling him. But Michal had suggested it, hadn't he? How could he dissuade Tanis without this admission?

"Yes. But I barely survived."

"Tell us, man! Tell us everything! I've seen the black forest from a distance and seen the black bats flying overhead, but I've never worked up the nerve to approach the river."

"That's how I lost my memory. I fell in the black forest. Gabil led me out, but not before the bats had nearly chewed me to the bone."

"That's it? I need more detail, man. More!"

"That's about it."

Tanis eyed him in wonder. "I can see that you and I would make an excellent team," he said. "I could teach you how to fight, and you could teach me the histories!"

"Rachelle is waiting," Palus said patiently.

Although Thomas wasn't altogether in sync with the Great Romance, it suddenly sounded far better than delving into details of the black forest or the histories with Tanis. Either way, Tanis knew less than Thomas did about the virus. He would be no help in uncovering more detail.

Unless the answers were in the black forest, and Tanis could help him get those answers from the black forest.

"Yes, the Great Romance," Thomas said.

Tanis nodded. "Okay, but later we must talk. We must!" He spread his arms and looked up the hill. "Okay then, pretend that Palus is Rachelle. Just pretend now, it's only a story. There she is, and here you are." He pointed to the ground by his feet. "First, I will say that you have given her many flowers and wooed her with many words, telling her precisely how she makes your heart melt and why her hair reminds you of waterfalls and . . . well, you get the idea." He was still standing with arms spread, slightly crouched as if to receive an attack.

"You see, this will soften her heart. Whisper in her ear and keep your voice low so that she knows you are a strong man." He stopped and considered Thomas for a moment. "Perhaps later I can give you some of the right things to say. Would you like that? I am very good at romance."

Thomas was too far into their game to suggest anything but wholehearted endorsement now. "Yes," he said.

"Okay, that's wooing. You will become very good at this activity. We woo our women every day. But back to the rescue." He flexed his legs. "Now, as I was saying, Palus is Rachelle and you are here. Down the hill comes a flock of the black bats. The Shataiki. You can dispatch them easily enough, of course, because you're a man of great might. The object here, though, isn't only to dispatch the vermin, but to rescue your beauty while you do so. Are you following me?"

"Yes, I think so. Dispatch the vermin and rescue the beauty."

"Exactly. With your legs flexed as so, you throw one arm out to Rachelle and ready the other to beat back the bats. Then you cry in a loud voice, so that she knows everyone in the valley can hear your statement of valor." And here Tanis thundered to Palus, "Come, my love, throw yourself into my arm of iron, and I will strike the withering beasts from the air with my other, a fist of stone."

Tanis motioned to Palus with his hand.

"What?" Palus asked.

"Show him. Run and jump into my arm. You're Rachelle, remember? I won't drop you."

"Jump? How?"

"I don't know, just run and jump. Make it look real, as a woman might jump. Perhaps feetfirst."

"I don't think Rachelle would run and jump. She's quite a confident woman, you know. What do you think of sweeping me off my feet instead?" Palus asked. "You could strike a few of the bats that are diving in to eat me, then pluck me to safety while whispering wondrous words into my ear, then battle the beasts with your free arm."

Tanis arched an eyebrow. "Very clever. How many beasts would you say I should fell before I sweep you off your feet?"

"If you were to send a hundred back to hell, she would be very impressed."

"A hundred? Before I jump to her rescue? It seems over the top."

"Then fifty. Fifty is plenty."

Tanis seemed totally taken with the notion. "And what if we were to say that the big one, Teeleh himself, were leading the attack from two sides, leaving me no way for escape? I dispatch fifty easily enough, but then they are too many and all hope seems lost. At the last moment, Rachelle could direct my attack, and with a brilliant reversal I send the big one screeching for his life. The rest flee in disarray. Perfect!"

"Do you actually want to do it?" Palus asked.

In answer Tanis suddenly spun uphill. "Don't worry, my love! I will rescue you!" he thundered, looking at Palus.

He took three steps and then leaped into the air, executed a spectacular roundhouse, landed on his hands, rolled forward, and came up with two stunning kicks Thomas wouldn't have thought possible in succession.

Tanis ended his first attack in a back handspring that placed him at Palus's side. He swept the man from his feet and struck out with another kick.

The momentum carried both off balance. They tumbled to the ground, rolled once, and came up laughing.

"Well, I suppose that one needs a bit of practice," Tanis said. "But you do get the idea. I wouldn't suggest anything so extravagant with Rachelle the first time you see her. But she will want to be surprised by your inventiveness. To what lengths would you go to choose her, to save her, to love her?"

Thomas couldn't remotely imagine doing anything bold. Whispering lavish words of woo could prove challenging enough. Had he ever done anything like this before his amnesia? Evidently not, or he would bear the mark of union on his forehead.

"How did you do that kick?" Thomas asked.

Tanis bounded to his feet. "Which one?"

Palus held up his hand. "Forgive me, but I must take my leave. Karyl waits." They bid him well and he headed for the village. The children were playing with several Roush on the other side of the valley, taking turns riding on a pair of the white creatures' backs as they locked wings and swooped down the hill.

"Which kick?" Tanis asked again.

"The first one. The one-two-back?"

"Show me what you mean," Tanis said.

"Me? I can't kick like that."

"Then I'll teach you. A woman loves a strong man. It was once the way

men fought, you know. In the histories, I mean. I have created a whole system of hand-to-hand combat. Try the kick. Show me."

"Now?"

"Of course." Tanis clapped twice. "Show me."

"Well, it was something like . . ." Thomas stepped forward and executed a roundhouse with a second kick, somewhat similar to the one he'd
seen Tanis do. Surprisingly the roundhouse felt . . . simple. He could execute it with far more ease here than in his dreams of the histories. The
atmosphere?

Unfortunately the second kick came up short. He landed on his side
and grunted.

"Excellent! We'll make a warrior of you yet. I think Rachelle will be
very impressed. Would you like to be my apprentice?"

"At fighting?"

"Yes, of course! I could teach what very few have learned, even here.
We could talk of the histories and discuss ways to deliver a crushing blow
to the putrid bats of the black forest."

"Well, I would like to learn from you—"

"Perfect! Come, let me show you the second kick."

Tanis was gifted and spared no passion in explaining precisely how to
move so as to maximize the number of moves in the air. When he took off,
he used his arms as a counterbalance, allowing for surprising maneuvers.
Within an hour, Thomas was able to execute some of the moves without
landing on his head. Short of the movies, no living person could move like
this in the histories, surely. There had to be a difference in the atmospheres.
Or was it the water?

The hour wore Thomas weak.

"Enough! Now we talk," Tanis finally announced, seeing Thomas
struggle for breath. "We will learn more fighting tomorrow. But now I
want to know more about the histories. I would like to know, for example,
what kind of weapons they had. I know some, devices that made large
sounds and delivered terrible blows to hundreds at once. Have you ever
heard of such a thing?"

"A gun?" Alarm rose through Thomas's chest. Tanis really was seriously considering this expedition of his into the black forest. But he couldn't! It was far too dangerous.

"What is a gun?" Tanis asked. "I am considering an expedition, Thomas. Such weapons could be a great help. A very great help, indeed. You could go with me, since you've been there!"

He spoke with such enthusiasm and innocence.

"You don't know the black forest, Tanis. Entering would be the death of anyone who tried."

"But you! You're alive!"

"I was lucky. And trust me, no swift kicks would have helped me any. There's way too many of them. Millions!"

"Exactly. Which is why they must be defeated!"

"You have agreed with the others not to cross the river."

"A precaution. There are times to leave caution in the valley and strike out for the mountain."

"I don't think this is that time," Thomas said. It occurred to him that he needed some water. He was desperately thirsty. Faint, in fact. They were walking up the hill, and he stopped to catch his breath. "Are you driven by anger against them, or curiosity?"

Tanis looked at the forest in thought. "Anger, I think. Perhaps it's not the right time. At the least, I could write a wonderful story about such a thing." He faced Thomas. "Tell me what else you know."

This wasn't going as Michal intended.

Dizziness suddenly swamped him. He shook his head. "Please, Tanis, you don't understand."

"But I want to!"

Thomas's world tipped and suddenly began to fade. He dropped to one knee. Felt himself falling. Reached out his hand.

Black.

15

EXCUSE ME, sir?" A hand touched Thomas's shoulder.

He sat up, half awake. A stewardess leaned over him. "Please bring your seat up." Kara's seat was empty. Bathroom.

Thomas tried to clear his mind. "We're landing?"

"We've begun our descent into Bangkok." She moved on.

They were in the cattle class of a Singapore Airlines 747. The yellow-and-blue upholstery that covered the seat directly in front of him was beginning to tear. On the seat-back monitor, a red line showed the flight's progress over the Pacific. This was the dream.

The plane smelled like home. Southeast Asia home. Soy soup, peanut sauces, noodles, herbal teas. His mind flashed back over the last eight hours. The flight to Singapore had been a long, sleepless affair during which Kara and Thomas had flipped through channels on the small embedded screens and reminisced about their years in Southeast Asia. Years of learning how to be a chameleon, switching skins between cultures.

Like switching mind-sets between his dreams now. He'd been bred for this.

"Scoot over, will you?" Kara bumped his knee, and he slid over to the center seat so she wouldn't have to climb over him.

"Welcome back to the land of the living." She fastened her seat belt. "Talk to me."

"About what?"

"About why ants build nests in the desert. What do you mean, about what?" she whispered. "What did you find out?"

He stared at her, struck by how much he loved his one and only sister. She came off tough, but her walls were paper thin.

"Thomas?"

"Nothing."

Her left brow arched. "Excuse me? You just slept for five hours. We're flying across the ocean to Bangkok *because* of your dreams. Don't tell me they stopped working."

"I didn't say that. In fact, I think I am learning something. I think I may know why this is happening."

"Enlighten me."

"I think maybe these dreams of what happened in the histories are arming me with information that could stop something terrible in the future. I think maybe Elyon is allowing me to have these dreams. Maybe to stop Tanis from his expedition."

She just stared at him.

"Okay, so maybe it's the other way around. Maybe I'm supposed to stop something from happening here."

"I have $345,000 in my bank account that says it's the latter. Which is why you were going to find out what in the world we're supposed to do in Bangkok, remember? And you come back with nothing?"

"It's not like that. Believe me, when I'm there, I'm not exactly concerned about my dreams of this place. Trust me. I have bigger problems. Like who I am. Like how this Great Romance thing works."

"Great romance? Please don't tell me you're actually falling for this girl who healed you." He'd filled Kara in on the details of his dream before falling asleep.

The last meeting with Rachelle flooded Thomas's mind. The way she had looked at him, smiled at him, walked by him without a word. His face must have shown something because Kara turned away.

Kara rolled her eyes. "Oh, please. You can't be serious."

"Actually, she's very interesting."

"Uh-huh. Of course she is. And built like a goddess, no doubt. Did she find you irresistible and smother you with kisses?"

"No. She walked away. But Tanis, the leader of the tribe, and Palus, her father, are showing me how to win the beauty."

"Okay, Thomas. Win the beauty. Everyone is entitled to a fantasy now and then. In the meantime, we have a problem here."

The plane entered a turn and Kara looked across Thomas at Bangkok's metropolitan skyline, not so different from New York's. The fairly modern and very exotic city packed nearly eight million people like sardines. Midday. To the east, Cambodia. To the south lay the Gulf of Thailand, and several hundred miles across it, Malaysia.

"I'm not pretending to know how this works, but you've got me scared, Thomas," she said quietly.

He nodded. "Me too."

She faced him. "No, I mean really. I mean, this isn't a dream here. For all I know, the other isn't a dream either, but I can't have you treating this reality like some dream. You hear me? You know things you shouldn't know—terrifying things. For all I know, you may be the only one alive to stop it."

She had a point. Not that he was treating this 747 like a dream no matter how much it felt like a dream. On the contrary, he was the one who'd convinced her they had to come in the first place. Would he have done that if it were only a dream? No.

"And no offense," Kara said, "but you're starting to look pretty haggard. You have bags under your eyes, and your face is drooping."

"Drooping?"

"Tired. You haven't had a decent sleep since this whole thing started."

True enough. He felt like he hadn't slept at all. "Okay," he said. "I hear you. Any ideas?"

"As a matter of fact, yes. I think I can help you. I can keep you focused."

"I am focused. We wouldn't be here if I hadn't insisted."

"No, I mean really focused. As long as you keep tripping between these dreams and realities, you're bound to keep second-guessing yourself, right?"

"A little. Maybe."

"Trust me, a lot. Right now you probably still think you're in the colored forest, sleeping somewhere, and that Bangkok is some dream based on the histories of Earth. Well, you're both right and wrong, and I'm going to make sure you realize that."

"You lost me."

"I'm going to assume that both realities are real. After all, it is a possibility, isn't it? Alternate universes, divergent realities, time distortions, whatever. The point is, from here on we assume that both realities are absolutely real. The colored forest really does exist, and there really is a woman there named . . . what's her name?"

"Rachelle."

"Rachelle. There really is a beautiful babe over there named Rachelle who has the hots for you."

"I didn't say that."

She held up her hand. "Whatever. You get the idea. It's all real. You have to do whatever you're meant to do there, even if it's nothing more than falling madly in love. I'll help you with that. Give you ideas, advice. Maybe I can help you land this hot chick."

"Assuming I'm interested in landing the first hot chick who winks at me. What do you take me for?"

"Okay, I won't call her a hot chick. Does that help? You're missing the point. It's real. That's the point. The colored forest really exists. Everything that happens there is as real as real can be. And I won't let you forget that. Not one word about it being a dream anymore. We pretend it's another country or something. The furry bats are real."

This last sentence she said a bit loud, and a tall, dark-haired European with a gray mustache looked their way. Kara returned his stare.

"Can I help you?"

The man looked away without responding.

"You see, that's what we're going to get. That's why we have to stick together on this, because you know it, Thomas, this world is real too."

The huge plane bounced on the runway, and the overhead bins creaked with the strain of the landing.

"We really have landed in Bangkok and the Raison Vaccine really is going to be announced tomorrow and you really do know something about that."

"So we go a hundred percent in both realities," Thomas said.

"Not me. You. I just help you do that."

It was the most sensible thing he'd heard in forty-eight hours. He wanted to hug her right there. "Agreed."

"Okay." She took a deep breath. "Now that we're in Bangkok, what do we do?"

"We find out everything we possibly can about Raison Pharmaceutical."

"Okay." Kara nodded. "How?"

"We go to their complex outside the city," Thomas said.

"Okay. Then what?"

"Then we stop them from shipping any samples or product. Better yet, we stop them from making this announcement tomorrow."

"This is where the plan loses focus for me," Kara said. "I'm not exactly a stockbroker, but I've seen my share of new drugs released into the market, and I'll guarantee you, calling off an announcement would send their stock into a dive. It's up 100 percent in anticipation of this announcement already."

Thomas nodded. "And we have to convince them to destroy any existing samples of the vaccine. And the means to make it."

"This whole thing is definitely out of focus. Who says we even get past the main gate? This is a high-security facility, right?"

"I guess we're going to find out."

She sighed and shook her head. "The next time you go back to the other place, you need more information. Period. In the meantime, is there anything you need here that will help you there?"

She looked at him, dead serious.

"I told you, Thomas, we treat both . . . what should we call them? Worlds? We treat both worlds, or whatever they are, as if they are real. And as a matter of fact, they have to be. So if we need information here, maybe you need information there too."

He shook his head. "No, not really. There's nothing happening there. I mean, I'm lost and I can't remember anything, but I don't see how anything here can help that."

"I wouldn't assume there's nothing happening there. How about this winning the beauty thing? Need some advice on how to land the chick?"

"Please—"

"Fine. On how to find true love then?"

"No."

"Just don't pass gas around her."

"You're not taking this seriously."

"That's exactly what I'm doing. You have enough idealism to fill a hundred novels. What you need is practical advice. Brush your teeth, wear deodorant, and change your underwear."

"Thanks, sis. Priceless advice." He twisted his mouth in a half-grin. "I think she's pretty religious."

"Then go to church with her. Just make sure it's not some cult. Stay away from the Kool-Aid."

"Actually, we're all quite religious. I'm pretty sure this Elyon is God."

She raised her eyebrow. "You don't believe in God, remember? Dad believed in God, and it about killed us all. God is where I'd draw the line with this chick. Girl. Keep religion and politics out of it. Better yet, find a different woman."

———— ✐✐✐ ————

It took them an hour to make their way through Bangkok International Airport and negotiate the rental of a small green Toyota Tercel from the Avis desk. Thomas still had his international driver's permit from the Philippines, and he welcomed the thought of weaving his way through Third World traffic again. Kara spread the map on the dash and took the role of navigator, maybe the more difficult task of the two.

She traced a line on the map. "Okay, Raison Pharmaceutical is out by the Rama Royal Park, east of town. We go south on the Vibhavadi Rangsit to the Inthara cutoff, east to the Inthara Expressway, and then south all the way to the Phra Khanong district." She looked up as he pulled into traffic. "Just don't get us killed. This isn't Denver."

"Have faith."

A horn blared and he swerved.

"I'm not into faith, remember?" she said.

"Maybe now would be a good time to start."

He'd have to get used to the horns again—they were as ubiquitous as road markings here. The main roads were properly marked, but they acted as guides more than restrictions. The position of a car and the volume of its horn were nine-tenths of the law: The first and the loudest had the right of way. Period.

He hit his horn now, to warm up to the idea. Another horn went off nearby, like mating calls. No one seemed to mind. Except Kara.

"Yes?" Kara said.

"Yes. Sounds good, doesn't it?"

Thomas drove into the city. A brown haze hung over towering midtown skyscrapers. In the distance, the sky train. Dilapidated taxis, held together with baling wire, and Mercedes crowded the same surface streets with motorcycle taxis and Tuk-Tuks—a three-wheeled cross between a car and a motorcycle.

And bicycles. Lots of bicycles.

Thais went about their daily business, some teetering along on bicycle carts that would unfold into frying stands, others piloting dump trucks, still others strolling in the orange garb of monks.

He cracked the window. It was early afternoon—the smells of the city were nearly overpowering. But to Thomas they were intoxicating. There was exhaust, there was a touch of stale water, there was fried noodles, there was . . .

This could easily be the Philippines. Home. Ten years ago, one of the rascals on the street might have been him, mixing it up with the locals and then stopping by a stand for some satays with peanut sauce.

Thomas felt a knot rise in his throat. It was the most beautiful sight he'd seen in years.

They drove in reflective silence for twenty minutes. Kara stared out the windows, caught up in her own thoughts. A soupy nostalgia overtook them both.

"I miss this," Kara said. "It almost feels like a dream. Maybe we're both dreaming."

"Maybe. Exotic."

"Exotic."

They passed the Phra Khanong district midafternoon and headed out into the delta. The city sounds faded behind them. The concrete gave way to a carpet of trees and rice paddies known as the Mae Nam Chao Phraya delta—*the rice bowl of Asia*—a hot, steamy, fertile sea of vegetation infested with insects and creatures rarely seen.

Like a primordial soup from which would come the most deadly virus the earth had ever known.

"It's hard to believe we're actually here," Thomas said.

"Halfway across the world in twelve hours. Nothing like the jet age. Turn left up here. It should be about a mile up the road."

Thomas turned onto a private road that led into an area hidden by heavy jungle growth. The asphalt was black, freshly poured. There was no other traffic.

"You sure this is right?" Thomas asked.

"No. Just following the clerk's directions. It's kind of . . . spooky."

Good word.

The complex rose out of the delta like a wraith in the night. The jungle had been cleared directly ahead. There was a gate. Two or three guards. Manicured lawns. And a massive white building that stretched across several acres. Behind the building, the jungle reclaimed the land.

Thomas stopped the car a hundred yards from the front gate. "This it?"

"Raison Pharmaceutical." She nodded at a sign he'd missed to their left.

He cracked his door, set one foot out, and stood. The jungle screeched around him—a billion cicadas screaming their warning. The humidity made breathing hard.

He plopped back down, eased the door closed, started the car moving again. They rolled up to the gate without speaking.

"This is it," Thomas said. A guard dressed in a gray uniform complete with shiny pistol approached them. "Why are you so quiet?"

"What am I supposed to say, 'Let's go back. This doesn't feel right to me. Please don't do anything stupid'?"

"Please, this is me," he said, rolling down the window.

"Exactly."

The guard glanced at the license plate and stepped forward. "What is your business?"

"We're here to see Monique de Raison. Or Jacques de Raison. It's very important we see them."

The man scanned his clipboard. "I have no scheduled arrivals. What is your name?"

"Thomas Hunter."

He flipped one page and lowered the board. "You have an appointment?"

Kara leaned over. "Of course we do. We've just arrived from the United States. The Centers for Disease Control. Check again; we have to be there."

"And your name?"

"Kara Hunter."

"I have neither on my list. This is a secured facility. No one in without a name on the list."

Thomas nodded patiently. "No problem. Just give them a call. Tell them that Thomas Hunter is here from the CDC. It's absolutely imperative that I see Monique de Raison. Today. We didn't fly all the way from Atlanta for nothing." He forced a grin. "I'm sure you understand."

The man hesitated, then walked into the booth.

"What if he doesn't let us in?" Thomas asked.

"I knew this would happen."

"Maybe we'd be more convincing in a Mercedes."

"Here comes your answer."

The guard approached. "We have no record of a visit today. Tomorrow there will be an event at the Sheraton Grande Sukhumvit. You may see her then."

"I don't think you understand. I need to see her today, not tomorrow. It's critical, man. Do you hear me? Critical!"

The man hesitated, and for a moment Thomas thought he might have made the right impression. He lifted a radio and spoke quietly. The door to the guardhouse opened and a second guard approached. Shorter than the other one, but his sleeves were rolled up over bulging muscles. Dark glasses. The kind who liked American T-shirts with Sylvester Stallone's Rambo persona stamped across the chest.

"Please leave," the first guard said.

Thomas looked at him. At the other, who'd stopped by the hood. He rolled up the window.

"Any suggestions?"

Kara was biting one of her nails. But she wasn't demanding that they retreat.

The guard by the hood motioned him to turn the car around.

"How important is it that we stop this announcement of theirs?" Kara asked.

"Depends if you think we can really change history."

"We're past that," she said. "The answer is yes. Focus, remember? This is real. That's why we're here."

"Then it depends on whether stopping the announcement will change history." The guard was starting to get a tad animated. Thomas reached over and locked the car. "Depends on whether they actually plan on shipping the vaccine tomorrow."

"Can we assume anything else? This isn't a game we can play over if we lose the first time."

A fist rapped on the window. The guards were both motioning vigorously now. The one with the bunched biceps put his hand on his holster.

"They wouldn't kill an American, would they?" Thomas asked.

"I don't know, but I think this is getting out of hand, Thomas. We should leave."

Thomas grunted and slammed the steering wheel. Maybe they were power-less to change history. Maybe they were the two martyrs who'd tried to change history but got gunned down at the gates to Raison Pharmaceutical. Or maybe changing history required extraordinary measures.

"Thomas . . ."

The guards were slamming his hood now. "Hold on."

He sprang the latch, shoved the door open, and rose from the car.

Both guards went for their guns.

"Whoa." Thomas lifted his hands. "Easy. I just want to talk. Just one thing, I promise. I'm on official business with the United States government. Trust me, you don't want to hurt me."

"Get back in the car, sir!"

"I'm getting back in, but I want to say something first. The Centers for Disease Control has just learned that the vaccine this company is planning to announce tomorrow has a fatal flaw. It mutates under extreme heat and becomes a virus that we believe may have far-reaching implications."

He walked toward the short one with the big muscles. "You have to listen to me!" He spoke loudly and slowly. "We are here to stop a disaster. You two, Fong and Wong, will go down as the two imbeciles who didn't listen up when the Americans came to warn Monique de Raison. You have to tell her this!"

Both guards were stepping back, guns in hand, intent but clearly caught off guard by his audacity. Oddly enough, Thomas wasn't terribly frightened by their guns. Yes, they had his stomach twisted in a knot, but he wasn't scrambling back in terror. The whole scene reminded him of the hillside lesson Tanis and Palus had given him. Taking on a hundred Shataiki with a few well-placed kicks.

He looked from one guard to the second and resisted a strong impulse to try the kick he'd learned from Tanis—the double-back kick that had at first looked impossible. He could do it too. They were perfectly placed. Saliva gathered in his mouth. He knew he could pull it off. Just like that:

one, *whack,* twist; two, *whack.* Just like Tanis had taught him. Before they could react.

'Course, it was crazy. And what if, just what if, that had been only a dream? He would be doing flips in his mind but falling flat on the asphalt here in reality.

"You hear me?" he asked. "I have to talk to someone."

They stood their ground, crouched, ready for anything.

"Do you guys like Jet Li?"

"Back!" screamed the one with biceps. "Back, back!"

"Listen to me!" Thomas yelled in a sudden fit of frustration.

"Back, back, back, or I shoot!" Biceps screeched.

Thomas blinked at the man. And what would Tanis say to that?

"Okay. Relax." He turned to climb back in the car.

Perfect.

Right now, at this very moment, the situation was perfect for that particular kick. If they shot, they would hit each other. If he just . . .

Thomas planted his left hand on the hood, scissored into the air. *Whack,* gun, *whack,* head. Continue the motion with the momentum, pirouette.

That was one. The other one stared with wide eyes.

A gun boomed.

Missed him.

Whack, gun. *Whack,* head.

Land. Perfect.

Thomas stood by the hood, stunned by what he'd just done. Both guards lay on their backs. Biceps had shot harmlessly. He had done this? His heart pumped with adrenaline. He felt like he could take on the flock if he had to.

"Thomas!"

Kara. Yelling.

He ran for the guardhouse, found the button that opened the gate. Pushed it. Motors whirred, and the gate ground slowly open. He bolted for the car.

Kara stared at him with round eyes.

"Hold on!" he yelled and shoved the stick into drive. He pointed the car for the gap in the gate. They roared toward the white building.

Immediately another problem presented itself. A round hole in the windshield. Bullet hole.

Kara slumped down. "They're firing!"

Four more guards had materialized from the main building. They had rifles and they were firing.

Reality crashed in on Thomas. He whipped the wheel to his right and punched the accelerator. The car veered into gravel. Spun through a wide donut. Two more bullets cracked through the back window.

"Hold on!"

The moment the tires regained traction on the asphalt, the Toyota surged forward. Through the gate. By the time they passed the Raison sign, they were doing 120 kph.

Thomas kept the accelerator pegged until they hit the intersection. Traffic on the main road limited his speed. It took another mile for his heart to match pace.

Kara blew out a long breath. "What was that?"

"Don't start. It was crazy, I know."

"No argument."

It appeared that they'd made a clean getaway.

"What exactly did you do back there?" Kara asked.

"I don't know. I really didn't plan on going after them like that. It just happened. We had to get in; they were in the way. You seemed to think we should—"

"No, I'm talking about that kick. I've never seen you do anything like that."

That fact had lingered in his own mind for the last five minutes.

"I haven't done anything like it. Not here."

"Not here, meaning . . . ?"

"Well, actually . . . it's something Tanis taught me."

"In the other reality?"

"It feels almost like instinct. Like my brain has learned a few new tricks and is using them automatically. They say we could walk through walls if we used all of our brainpower, right? Crazy, huh?"

She stared ahead, awed. "No, not crazy. It actually makes sense. In this wacky dream thing of yours. And we're treating them like they're both real, remember?"

"So what I learn there, I can use here. And what I learn here, I can use there."

"Evidently. Not just knowledge but skills." They drove in silence for a few seconds. "Now what?"

"Now we get a room at the Sheraton Grande Sukhumvit and hope we can make an impression on Monique de Raison tomorrow."

"Maybe you can woo her," Kara said.

"Woo her?"

"Never mind."

Thomas sighed. "Don't be ridiculous."

"What we need is for you to sleep. And dream."

He nodded. "Sleep and dream."

16

THOMAS! WAKE up. Open your mouth."

Thomas felt the cool juice run down his throat. He jerked up, sputtered, and spit a lump of something from his mouth.

"Easy, lad."

Tanis grinned beside him, yellow fruit in hand. Michal stood beside him.

"What happened?" Thomas asked.

"You passed out," Tanis said. "But a bite of fruit and you came back quickly enough."

"You are weak; perhaps the effects of your fall in the black forest still linger," Michal said. "How do you feel now?"

"Fine."

He felt a bit disoriented, but otherwise well enough. He'd dreamed of Bangkok. Fighting two guards. Then retreating to a luxurious hotel called the Sheraton Grande Sukhumvit where he and Kara had taken a suite, walked the streets, and finally collapsed into bed, groggy with jet lag.

Thomas shook his head.

"How long was I . . . out?"

"Only a few minutes," Tanis said.

Yet he'd dreamed of a whole day in Bangkok.

Two thoughts rang through his head. One, he had to treat both worlds as if they were real. Two, he had to get more information.

Which meant he might have to retrace his steps to the black forest after all. With Tanis's help. Unless he could persuade Michal to help him out.

What was he thinking? He could never go back to the black forest!

"Please," Tanis said, handing Thomas the fruit, "have some more."

Thomas bit deep into the fruit and immediately felt the nectar flow into his gut. He bit again and again and suddenly realized he'd lost himself in the process. He had already finished the fruit.

"Did . . . did you dream?" Tanis asked.

"Dream?" Thomas stood.

"Just now, did you dream of the histories?"

Thomas glanced at Michal, who arched a fuzzy eyebrow.

"I was only out for a few seconds," Thomas said.

"Dreams do not keep time," Tanis said.

There was no hiding it from the leader.

"Yes, as a matter of fact, I believe I did dream."

"Did you go to the history books and read about Napoleon?"

What was Michal thinking of this exchange? Tanis wasn't hiding anything. No, of course not. He was purely innocent.

"No," Thomas said. "Why would I do that?"

"Have you forgotten, man? I will teach you how to fight, and you will open my mind to the histories. It was our understanding!"

"It was?"

"It was my understanding. What do you think, Michal? Since Thomas Hunter seems to have unusual access to the histories and I am a very gifted fighter, I thought we would make a wonderful team, he and I. If we ever were to mount an expedition to the black forest, Thomas could be very helpful. Yes?"

The Roush frowned thoughtfully. "Hmm . . ."

Thomas assumed that Michal would disapprove outright. But he didn't. He seemed in some way subservient to Tanis.

"It's an interesting idea, the two of you pairing up. But the expedition is a foolish notion on all counts. It would be like seeking a cliff to lean over. Are you so interested in seeing whether you will fall?"

"Then at the very least, Thomas could teach me more of the histories," Tanis said. "I understand why you won't. As you say, interfering with us is not your job, yes? The histories could interfere, you say. Understood. But

Thomas Hunter is not a Roush. And the fact that he's here, having these dreams, must mean Elyon has willed it. Perhaps caused it! It's only natural that we form this bond. Wouldn't you agree?"

Innocence clearly didn't compromise the man's intelligence.

"The histories are oral for a reason," Michal said cautiously. "I would think very carefully before tempting that tradition."

Thomas stepped forward. "Actually . . ." He stopped, remembering his promise to the Roush.

Michal eyed him. "Yes, Thomas? Actually what?"

"Well, to be perfectly honest, there were a few questions that I had about the histories too. I seem to be stuck in a certain time, just before the Great Deception. In my dreams, my sister and I seem to think we might be able to prevent the virus from being released. We think that may be our purpose. Maybe you could help me to do this. Make any sense?"

"No. Not really," Michal said. "How can you stop something that has already happened? You see, these dreams are not helpful. They are keeping you in a state of disorientation. They might actually be the *cause* of your continued amnesia. You should be focusing on other things now, not trivia from the distant past. Does *that* make sense?"

"You're right, you're right. Perfect sense, but in my dreams it doesn't make perfect sense."

"And you want me to encourage these dreams? How about you, Tanis? Does this make sense to you?"

"Perfect. But if the dreams persist, they may have another purpose. How to make weapons, for example."

"Weapons! Why would you need weapons?" Michal demanded.

"To fight the Shataiki, of course!"

"You will fight them with your heart!" the Roush cried. "Forget the weapons! I will tell you something from the histories now, and then I will never speak to either of you of them again. There was a saying I want you to remember. It was used poorly then, but it will serve you both well now. Make love, not war, they said. Think of this, Tanis, when you consider making your weapons. Make love, not war."

Tanis looked stricken. He threw his hands wide, palms up. "You question my motives? Is there a man you know who is more versed in the Great Romance than I? No! I would rescue, as Elyon would rescue. If I would need a weapon to dispatch the black bats, is it even questionable? Is anything I suggest wrong?"

"No. And yes, you are a great lover of Elyon. I would never question your motives or your passions, Tanis. Do you hear me? Never!"

Tanis's eyes flashed desperately. He lifted a fist to the sky and cried out, "Elyon, oh, Elyon, I would never withhold my love from you! I would dive into your bosom and drink deep of your heart! I will never forsake you. Never!"

Tears wet Michal's eyes. It was the first time Thomas had seen such emotion from the stoic Roush, and it surprised him.

Tanis paced back and forth quickly. "I must write a story for Elyon. I must speak of my love and the Great Romance and the rescuing of everything that is his! I have been inspired. Thank you, thank you both for this." He turned to Thomas. "We will talk later, my young apprentice. You are ready to win the beauty?"

His reference to the anticipated romance between him and Rachelle made Thomas feel suddenly lightheaded. "Yes, I think so. I think it's all coming back." Slowly. Too slowly.

"That's my boy!" Tanis slapped him on the back. "Wonderful. Remember, he chooses."

Thomas nodded. "Chooses. Got it."

"He pursues."

A pause. He was expected to repeat. "He pursues."

"He rescues."

"He rescues."

"He woos."

"He woos."

"He protects."

"He protects."

"He lavishes."

"That was the extra one."

Tanis pumped his fist. "He lavishes. It's a good one, and I'm going to include it in the story I will write now."

Thomas mimicked Tanis with his fist. "He lavishes!"

"And so will you."

"And so will you."

"No, I. You say, 'So will *I*.'"

"And so will I," Thomas said.

"And now I am off. A story is in the making!" Tanis dipped his head at both of them. "Until the Gathering." He ran a few yards and whirled around.

"Should I tell her you are waiting?"

"Who?"

"The beauty! Rachelle, lad! Rachelle, the beauty!"

Now? He wasn't even sure how to win a beauty. But especially now, in front of Michal, he had to follow the Roush's advice. Pretend.

"Sure," Thomas said.

"Ha!" Off he ran.

Michal watched Tanis run. "Stunning, wonderful, magnificent."

"You can't seem to make up your mind about him," Thomas said.

"He is human! I can't help but admire any human."

"Right. Yes, of course."

Tanis was already a tiny figure, running up the main street, probably telling the whole world that the dashing visitor from the other side was on the hill now, prepared to woo and win his beauty. Rachelle.

Michal turned from the valley. "The Great Romance. The Gathering. You have no idea what I would give to have what you have." He hopped a few yards and gazed longingly at the horizon. "It's all a bit much at times. I can hardly stand to sit by and watch."

That was it. There was no way Thomas could question Michal's decision on withholding the histories after a spiel like that. It was all a bunch of nonsense any—

From the corner of his eye he saw a figure racing through the village below, and his heart bolted in his chest. It was Rachelle. He couldn't see her face from this distance, but he saw her blue dress. She was racing for the arching village entrance, like a child sprinting to catch the ice-cream truck.

Tanis had told her.

Panic swept through his bones. What had he gotten himself into? Wasn't this all going a bit fast? He'd been in the valley for less than a day. Love seemed to be a currency they were all swamped with. Naturally, without evil to rob their hearts, it would be.

Which meant he, too, was full of love. It would all come back. This was the way it worked.

Rachelle slowed at the entrance and started to meander up the hill. It was hard to imagine that anyone would be so eager to meet him, much less be romanced by him. Was he so appealing? Attractive?

"Michal!" He cleared his throat. "Michal."

The Roush was staring down the hill, swaying with anticipation.

"Michal, you have to help me."

"And take the fun out of it? It's in your heart, Thomas. Win her!"

"I don't know *how* to win her! I forget how!"

"No, you don't; no, you don't forget! Some things you can't forget."

"She's walking up here!" Thomas paced quickly. "I don't know what she expects."

"You're nervous; that's good. That's a good sign."

"It is?"

"It betrays your true feelings!"

Thomas stopped and stared at him. True enough. Why was he so nervous? Because he did want very much to impress the stunning woman sauntering up the hill toward him.

The realization only made it worse. Much worse.

"At least give me a pointer," he said. "Should I just stand here?"

"Didn't Tanis tell you? Okay." Michal lifted his wing and guided Thomas up the hill, toward the forest. "Okay, not speaking from experience but from what I've seen, and I have seen a few to be sure, I would suggest you wait in the trees up there." His wings quivered. "Intrigue and mystery are what you're after, I think. Dear, dear. I should go. She's coming closer. I should go."

Michal waddled off, hopped twice, and took to the air.

"Michal!"

But Michal was gone.

Thomas whirled back, saw that Rachelle was making good time up the hill, hands behind her back, looking nonchalantly away. He ducked down, despite his full knowledge that she'd seen him, and ran for the top.

He was beginning to think he'd gone too far into the trees. That the large amber tree behind which he'd hidden camouflaged him too well. She'd missed him. He wasn't even sure why he was hiding. Did rescuing the beauty look anything like hide-and-seek?

But he couldn't stand out in the open with his arms folded, pretending to be a mighty warrior. On the other hand, Tanis might do that. Maybe he should.

He poked his head around the tree.

No sign of her. The forest glowed in a dazzling display of color. Red and blue and amber in this section. Birds chirped overhead. A light breeze swept the rich scent of roses through his nostrils.

But no sign of Rachelle.

He stepped out, suddenly worried that he'd lost her. Should he call out? No, that would only make it clear that he'd lost her. She wanted to be chosen, which sounded more like seeking and finding than calling out like a frightened boy lost in the forest. And although it was true that part of his anxiousness was motivated by this unabashed approach to romance, in all honesty he was very much attracted to her. Perhaps meant for her.

A flash of blue caught the corner of his eye. He jerked to his right.

Gone! His heart pounded. But it had been her, about fifty yards that way, between two huge trees.

Rachelle suddenly walked into the open, stopped, stared directly at him, and then disappeared without so much as a smile.

Thomas stood rooted for a full five count. *Go after her, you idiot! Run!*

He ran. Around a tree. Crashing through the underbrush like a stampeding rhino.

Stop! You're making too much noise!

He pulled up behind a tree and looked around it. Nothing. He walked forward in the direction she'd gone. But there was nothing. She'd vanished?

"Psst."

Thomas spun around. Rachelle leaned against a tree, arms crossed. A provocative smile crossed her lips. She winked. Then she slipped around the tree and was gone.

He ran after her. But again she'd vanished. This time he sprinted from tree to tree, looking, winded now.

When she did appear, it was like the last time, suddenly and casually, leaning against another tree behind him. She raised her eyebrow and grinned. Then again she was gone.

It struck Thomas then that he hadn't been paying any mind to the rescuing part of this romance. Maybe that's why she was leading him on. He'd chosen her by running after her, but she was waiting for him to show his strength. The time for subtlety had passed.

The show Tanis and Palus had put on raced through his mind.

He yelled the first thing that came to mind. "Hark, what see I? It is a streak of black in the trees!" He ran in the direction Rachelle had vanished. "Come hither, my dear!" He desperately hoped that wasn't too forward. "Come so that I mightest protectest thou!"

Mightest protectest thou? Was that the way Tanis had put it?

"Oh, dear!"

Rachelle!

She jumped out from behind a tree to his left, eyes round, one hand raised to her lips. "Where?"

Where? He shoved a finger in the opposite direction. "There!"

She cried out and ran toward him. The breeze whipped her blue dress around the leggings she wore. She grabbed his shoulder and hid behind him.

Thomas was so stunned by his sudden success that he lost track of the black bats for a moment. He stared at her face, now only inches from his own. The forest fell silent. He could smell her breath. Like lilacs.

Her eyes shifted to meet his. They held for a moment.

"Are you going to stare at me or take on the bats?" she asked.

"Oh, yeah."

Thomas jumped out ambitiously and cocked his arms to take on the phantom enemy with a few spectacular chops and kicks.

"They are coming in hoards. Don't worry, I can take them all. Ha, ya!" He sprang into the air, kicked with his right foot, then twirled through a full three-sixty before striking out again.

He'd gone for it impulsively, pushed by an inordinate desire to show his strength and skill. But the fact that he'd actually twisted through a full revolution in the air stopped him cold. Where had he learned that?

Just now he'd learned that.

In his self-admiration he lost track of his movements and crashed to the forest floor with a mighty thump.

"Ugh!"

Thomas clawed his way to his knees, breath knocked clean out of his lungs. Rachelle ran up and dipped to one knee.

"Are you okay?" Her hand touched his shoulder.

He gasped. "Yeah."

"Yes?"

"Sure."

She quickly pulled him to his feet. A smile slowly twisted her lips. "I can see that you've forgotten some of your . . . mighty moves," she said. She glanced around. "The next time it might look something like this."

She leaped in the direction of the invisible Shataiki. "Ha!" She kicked. Not a simple forward kick, but a perfectly executed roundhouse that dropped her back to earth in the ideal position for a second move.

She looked back, winked. "Tanis taught me."

Then she went after the enemy in a long series of spectacular moves that stopped Thomas's breath for a second time. He counted one, two, three backflips in the mix. At least a dozen combination moves, most of them in the air.

And she did it all with the grace of a dancer, careful to accommodate her dress as she flew.

This chick was good. Very good.

She landed on her toes, facing Thomas at twenty feet, all business.

"Ha!" she said and winked again.

"Ha. Wow."

"Wow."

He swallowed.

She quickly lowered her guard and assumed a more feminine stance. "Don't worry, we'll just pretend you did that. I won't tell a soul."

He cleared his throat. "Okay."

She studied him for a moment. Her eyes twinkled. The game wasn't over. Of course not. It was probably just starting.

Or so he was beginning to hope.

Choose, pursue, protect, woo. The words echoed in his mind.

"You are very . . . strong," he said. "I mean graceful."

She started to walk toward him. "I know what you mean. And I like both strong and graceful."

"Well, you're also very kind."

"Am I?"

"Yes, I think so."

He wanted to tell her that she was beautiful. That she was intriguing and full of life and compelling. But suddenly he found the words too much. It was all too much, too fast. For a man with all of his senses properly engaged, this might be the natural way to romance a woman, but for him, having lost his memory . . .

Rachelle stopped at arm's length. Searched his eyes.

"I think it was a wonderful game. You are a mysterious man. I like that. Maybe we can pick this up later. Good-bye, Thomas Hunter."

She turned and walked away.

Just like that? She couldn't just walk away, not now.

"Wait!" He ran up to her. "Where are you going?"

"To the village."

Her interest seemed to have evaporated. Maybe this choosing and wooing business was more involved than he'd thought.

"Can I walk with you?"

"Sure. Maybe I can help you remember a few things along the way. Your memory certainly needs some prodding."

Before he could respond to her obvious needling, a large white beast stepped out of the trees toward them. A tiger, pure white with green eyes. Thomas stopped abruptly.

Rachelle looked at him, then at the tiger. "That, for example, is a white tiger."

"A tiger. I remember that."

"Good."

She walked to the animal, hugged it around the neck, and ruffled its ears. The tiger licked her cheek with a large tongue and she nuzzled its nose. Apparently all in the course of a day. Then she insisted that he come over and scratch the tiger's neck with her. It would be easier for him to remember if he engaged the world actively.

Thomas wasn't sure how to read her comments. She said them all with a smile and with apparent sincerity, but he couldn't help thinking that she was edging him on or chiding him for his lackluster romancing.

Or she could be playing hard to get. Could that be part of the Great Romance?

On the other hand, she may have already decided he wasn't quite what she'd hoped for. Maybe the game was at its end. Could you un-choose, once having chosen?

They walked a few steps with tiger in tow. Rachelle plucked a yellow fruit from a small leafed tree.

"What is this?" she asked.

"I . . . I don't know."

"A lemon."

"A lemon, yes, of course, I remember that too."

"And if you put the juice of this lemon on a cut, what happens?"

"It heals?"

She curtsied. "Very good." They walked on and Rachelle picked a cherry-sized purple fruit from a low tree with wide branches. "And this one?"

"I don't think I know that one."

She circled him as she held up the fruit. "Try to remember. I'll give you a hint. Its flesh is sour. No one likes them much."

He grinned and shook his head. "No. Doesn't ring any bells."

"If you eat it"—she imitated a small bite with perfectly formed white teeth—"your mind reacts."

"No, no. Still nothing."

"Rhambutan," she said. "It puts you to sleep. You don't even dream." She tossed it back to the tiger, but the beast ignored it.

They'd come to the edge of the forest. The village sat peacefully in the valley, glimmering with the brightly colored homes leading concentrically to the great Thrall.

Rachelle gazed down the hill and spoke without looking at him. "You are even more mysterious and wonderful than I imagined when I chose you."

"I am?"

"You are."

He should respond in kind, but the words weren't coming.

"You might want to work on your memory, of course," she said.

"Actually, my memory works well in some areas."

She faced him. "Is that so? What areas are those?"

"In my dreams. I'm having vivid dreams that I live in the histories. And all of that I remember. It's almost as real as this place."

She searched his eyes. "And do you remember how to romance in these dreams?"

"Romance? Well, I don't have a girlfriend or anything, if that's what you mean, no. But maybe I do know some things." Kara's advice on romance came back to him. Now would be a good time to turn up the wooing quotient. "But nothing like this. Nothing so wonderful and beautiful as you. No one who captures my heart so completely with a single touch or a passing smile."

The corner of her mouth tugged into a faint smile. "My, you are remembering. You may dream all you like, my dear."

"Only if I can dream about you," he said.

She reached up and touched his cheek. "Good-bye, Thomas Hunter. I will see you soon."

He swallowed. "Good-bye."

Then she was walking down the hill.

Thomas walked back from the crest so that he wouldn't be visible from the valley. The last thing he wanted at the moment was for Tanis or Palus to come flying up for a report.

He knew he wouldn't be dreaming of Rachelle, despite his sentiments to do so. He'd be dreaming of Bangkok, where he was expected to deliver some critical information on the Raison Strain.

He stopped by a large green tree and looked east. The black forest was about an hour's walk. The answers to a dozen questions could be there. Questions about what had happened to him in the black forest. Where he'd come from. Questions about the histories. The Raison Strain.

What if he were to go? Just one quick visit, to satisfy himself. The others might not even know he was missing. Michal might. But he couldn't continue on with these impossible dreams or without knowing exactly how he'd come to be in the black forest in the first place. One way or the other, he had to know precisely what had happened, was happening, to him. He might find those answers only in the black forest, just as Tanis might find his satisfaction only in an expedition there.

But not now.

He leaned against the green trunk and crossed his arms. His legs had a rubbery feel to them, like noodles. He hadn't realized that romancing required so much energy.

17

OF COURSE she likes me," Thomas said. He'd slept half the night, but felt as though he was running on fumes here.

Kara looked at him across the wrought-iron table. "I think wishful thinking is rearing its beautiful head, dear brother. For all you know, winking means, 'Take a hike.'"

They were seated in the café adjacent to the atrium where Raison Pharmaceutical would make its grand announcement as soon as the entourage arrived. The main courtyard milled with dozens of reporters and local officials awaiting this momentous occasion. You'd think they were receiving the president. In Southeast Asia—any excuse for a ceremony. Thomas was surprised they didn't have a ribbon to cut. Any excuse to cut a ribbon.

Thomas scanned the crowd for the hundredth time, considering yet again his options. Getting to Monique de Raison shouldn't be a problem. Convincing her to order additional testing of the drug didn't seem unreasonable either. The real challenge would be the timing. Getting to Monique before the announcement if possible; convincing her to do more testing *before* shipping.

"I have a bad feeling about this," he said. He felt like a worn leather sole. His eyes hurt and his temples throbbed.

"You sure you're okay?" Kara asked. "I know you've been insisting you're peachy all morning, but you really do look horrible."

"I'm tired is all. Soon as we deal with this thing, I'll sleep for a week."

"Maybe not."

"Meaning what?"

"Meaning the dreams. They're real, remember? Maybe the reason you're not getting any rest is because you're *not*."

"Because when I'm asleep there, I'm awake here and vice versa."

"Think about it," Kara said. "You're tired in both places. You just fell asleep on the hill overlooking the valley while contemplating the Great Romance."

"No, I was contemplating returning to the black forest at the urging of my sister."

Thomas heard a commotion by the front doors. A guest's baggage had toppled from a cart, and several bellhops were frantically throwing it back on.

"You're right that I'm just as tired there. I keep falling asleep. It's one of the only things that's similar. Everything else is different. I wear different clothes; I talk differently—"

"How do you talk?"

"More like them. You know, eloquent and romantic. Like a hundred years ago."

She grinned. "Charming."

"You'd be surprised."

"Oh, brother."

Thomas felt the first of a blush warm his face. "I know it sounds sappy, but things are just different there."

"Clearly. The point is, you can't keep going like this. You're exhausted, you're nervous, you're sweating, and you're chewing on your fingernail. You have to get some rest."

Thomas pulled his finger from his mouth. "Of course I'm sweating. It's hot."

"Not in here it's not."

For the first time Thomas seriously considered his physical condition. What if she was right and he wasn't getting any real sleep at all? He instinctively ran his fingers through his dark curls in an attempt to put them in order. It helped that his hairstyle was a tad avant-garde, or "messy," as Kara put it. He wore a pair of Lucky jeans, featherweight black boots, and a

black T-shirt, tucked in at Kara's insistence given the occasion. The shirt
had an inscription in white schizoid letters:

I've gone to find myself.
If I get back before I return, please keep me here.

"Maybe I'm sleeping, but my mind's so active that I'm not getting good
rest," he said.

The loitering crowd suddenly surged toward the atrium.

Thomas jumped to his feet, knocking over his chair. "She's here!"

"Did I mention edgy?" Kara asked. "Calm and collected, Thomas.
Calm and collected."

He righted the chair and then strode toward the entrance with Kara
hurrying to keep pace.

"Slow down."

He didn't slow down.

The door opened and two husky men dressed in black stepped into the
reception area. Thai *sak* tattoos marked their forearms. There were basically
two varieties of tattoos in Thailand: *khawm* designs meant to invoke the
power to love, and *sak* designs meant to invoke the power against death.
These were the latter, worn by men in dangerous lines of work. Clearly
security. Not that Thomas cared—he wasn't planning on jumping the
woman. Their eyes made quick work of the room.

Two red cords draped through golden posts formed a temporary path
toward the atrium. The men blocked the space between the last post and
the entrance, pushed the doors open, and swept their arms to guide their
employer.

The strong, confident face of the woman who stepped into the lobby
of the Sheraton Grande Sukhumvit commanded attention. She wore
expensive-looking navy heels without nylons. Sculpted calves. Navy blue
skirt and blazer with a white silk blouse. Gold necklace with a nondescript
gold pendant that looked vaguely like a dolphin. Flashing blue eyes. Dark,
shoulder-length hair.

Monique de Raison.

"My, my," Kara said.

Flashbulbs popped. Most of the guests waited in the atrium, where a podium had been set up amid a virtual jungle of exotic flowering plants. Monique gave the room one glance and then walked briskly toward the atrium.

Thomas angled for the ropes. "Excuse me!" They hadn't heard him. And she was a fast walker.

Thomas hurried to intercept them. "Excuse me, Monique de Raison."

"Thomas! You're yelling!" Kara whispered.

Monique and her security goons were ignoring him. Behind the lead three, an entourage of Raison Pharmaceutical employees were filing into the lobby.

"Excuse me, are you deaf?" he demanded. Yelled.

This time the security men swiveled in his direction. Monique turned her head and drilled him with a stare. The sight of an American strutting for her clad in a black T-shirt and jeans clearly didn't impress. She diverted her stare and walked on as if she'd passed nothing more than a curious-looking dog on the street.

Thomas felt his pulse surge. "I'm here with the Centers for Disease Control. I lost my bags and don't have the right clothes. I have to talk to you before you make your announcement." He didn't yell now, but his voice carried loudly enough.

Monique stopped. The security stepped to either side, glaring like two Dobermans begging to pounce. She faced Thomas at ten feet. Her eyes glanced at the inscription on his chest. Maybe he should have worn the shirt inside out. Kara bumped into his side.

"This is my assistant, Kara Hunter. My name is Thomas." He stepped forward, and the guard to her right immediately moved forward as a precaution.

"I just need a minute," Thomas said.

"I don't have a minute," Monique said. Her voice was soft and low and carried a slight French accent.

"I don't think you understand. There's a problem with the vaccine."

Thomas knew before the last word left his mouth that it was the wrong thing to say. Any such suggestion or any endorsement of any such suggestion would be poison to the value of Raison Pharmaceutical stock.

Monique's brow lifted slightly. "Is that so?"

No turning back now. "Yes. Unless you want me to spill the beans here, in front of them all, I suggest you take a moment, just one teeny-weeny moment, and talk to me." His confidence surged. What could she say to that?

"Afterward," she said and turned on her heels.

He took a long step in her direction. "Hey!"

The security man closest put up a hand. Thomas had half a notion to take him on right here, right now. The man was twice his size, but he'd picked up a few new skills as of late.

Kara grabbed his arm. "Afterward will work."

The entourage came abreast with curious stares. Thomas wondered if anyone would recognize him from the incident at the gates yesterday. Undoubtedly the whole thing had been caught by security cameras.

"Okay, afterward. Try to keep your head low. Someone might recognize us."

"My point exactly. We talked about this, remember? No scene. I didn't come to Bangkok to get thrown in jail."

The announcement was surprisingly short and to the point. Monique delivered it with all the poise of an experienced politician. Raison Pharmaceutical had completed the development of a new airborne super-vaccine engineered to vaccinate against nine primary viruses, including SARS and HIV. This was followed by a laundry list of details for the world health community. Not once did she look in Thomas's direction.

She waited till the end to drop the bomb.

Although the company was waiting for FDA approval in the United States, the governments of seven countries in Africa and three in Asia had placed orders for the vaccine, and the World Health Organization had given its blessing after receiving assurances that the vaccine would not spontaneously spread beyond a specified geographical region, due to engineered limitations that shortened the vaccine's life. The first order would be delivered to South Africa within twenty-four hours.

"Now, I'll be happy to answer a few questions."

The mind works in strange ways. Thomas's had worked in the strangest of ways over the last few days. In and out of realities, crossing the seas, waking and sleeping in starts and fits. But with Monique de Raison's final statement, everything came into simple focus.

There was a Raison Vaccine. It would mutate into a virus that would make SARS look like a case of the hiccups. It was now being shipped to South Africa. He, Thomas Hunter from Denver, Colorado, and Kara Hunter from the same were the only people on the face of the earth who knew this.

It had all seemed somewhat dreamlike until this moment. Now it was tangible. Now he was staring at Monique de Raison and hearing her tell the world that boxes of the drug that would kill millions was boxed and ready for shipment. Maybe shipped already. Maybe it was in the back of some transport plane now, being baked by the hot sun. Mutating.

The sum of his predicament shoved him out of his chair.

"Thomas."

"Did you hear that?"

"Sit."

She pulled at his arm. He sat. The reporters were asking her questions. Bulbs kept flashing.

"We have to stop that shipment."

"She said she'd talk to us *afterward*," Kara insisted between clenched teeth. "A few more minutes."

"What if she won't listen?" Thomas asked.

"Then we try the authorities again. Right?"

He'd considered the possibility that Monique was a brick upstairs and would scoff, but, listening to her, she seemed far too intelligent. He really hadn't considered anything other than her willingness to cooperate. That's the way it went in dreams. Ultimately, it all really does work out. Or you wake up.

Suddenly he wasn't sure of either.

"Right, Thomas?"

"Right."

"What does that mean?" she asked.

"It means *right*."

"I don't like the way you said—"

A smattering of applause rippled through the courtyard. Thomas stood. Monique was finished. Music swelled. This was it.

"Let's go." He headed to the front, eyes fixed on Monique, who was straightening papers at the podium. A rope lined with three security men now separated the platform from the dispersing audience. Several reporters were summarily turned away when they approached the platform.

Monique caught his eye, looked away as if she hadn't noticed, and headed stage right.

"Monique de Raison!" Thomas called. "A moment, if you don't mind."

Heads turned and the hubbub eased.

Here they went again. Thomas walked straight for her. A guard moved to intercept.

"It's okay, Lawrence. I'll speak to them," she said quietly.

Thomas stared the man off. They were wearing guns, this one on his waist. Thomas stepped onto the stage, helped Kara up, and crossed to where Monique had stopped. He had no doubt that if he hadn't made a scene she would be in the limousine already. As his *sensei* was fond of saying, there was no better way to disarm an opponent than with an element of surprise. Not necessarily through timing as most assumed, but as often through method. Shock and awe.

Despite the fact that Monique looked neither shocked nor awed, he knew he'd gotten under her skin at least. More important, he was talking to her.

"Thank you for your time," Thomas said. The time for shock and awe was now passed. Diplomacy. "It is most kind of you to—"

"I'm already late for an interview with the *TIME* magazine bureau chief. Make your point, Mr. . . ."

"Hunter. You don't have to be rude."

She sighed. "You're right. I'm sorry, but it's been a very busy week. When a man walks up to me and lies to my face, my patience is the first to go."

"A simple test will easily demonstrate whether or not I'm lying."

"So then you are with the CDC?"

"Oh. That lie." He lifted a hand to his shoulder as if taking an oath. "You got me. I had to get your attention somehow. This is Kara, my sister."

"Hi, Kara." They shook hands. But she hadn't shaken his hand.

"I really do have to go," Monique said. "Please, to the point."

"Okay, to the point. You can't ship the vaccine. It mutates under intense heat and becomes a deadly virus that kills billions of people."

She stared at him, unmoved. "Oh. Is that all?"

"I can explain exactly how I know this, but you wanted the bottom line, so there it is. Have you submitted the vaccine to intense heat, Miss de Raison?"

"One of the things they teach in freshman biology is that intense heat kills things. The Raison Vaccine is no exception. Our vaccine begins to spoil at 35 degrees centigrade. One of our greatest challenges was keeping it stable for warmer regional climates. This is the most ludicrous thing I've ever heard."

Heat flared up Thomas's back. "Then you haven't tested it at high heat?"

"Show a little respect, Monique," Kara bit off. "We didn't fly over the Pacific to be dismissed like beggars. The fact is, Thomas has a point here, and you'd be a fool not to listen."

Monique forced a smile. "I would love to. I really would. I have to go." She started to turn.

Something went off in Thomas's head like a gong. She was dismissing them. "Wait."

She didn't wait, not a beat.

Thomas eased back toward the guard called Lawrence and spoke quietly, in as menacing a tone as he could muster without raising the alarm.

"If you don't stop at this very moment, we'll go to the papers. My father-in-law owns the *Chicago Tribune*. They'll have to scrape your stock prices off the floor with razor blades."

A ridiculous claim. Monique didn't honor it with a single misstep. She was beyond the pale.

It occurred to Thomas that what his mind was telling him to do now couldn't be justified in any sense of the word. Except in his world. The world in which a virus called the Raison Strain was about to forever alter human history.

The two guards Thomas had first encountered were making their way to assist Monique's exit, but Lawrence still had his back turned. Monique wasn't his primary responsibility.

Thomas was at the guard's back with a single side step. In one quick move, he slipped his hand under the man's jacket, grabbed the gun, and whipped it out. He bounced to his right, away from the man's grabbing hands. The man hesitated, mouth agape, probably appalled that he'd so easily lost his weapon.

Thomas ran forward on the balls of his feet, reached Monique before an alarm could be raised.

Shoved the gun in her back.

"I'm sorry, but you have to listen to me."

She went rigid. Both guards saw the gun at the same time. They crouched, weapons immediately drawn. Shouts now, dozens of them.

"Thomas!"

Including Kara's.

Thomas had his left arm around Monique's waist, pulling her close so that his chin was over her left shoulder, breathing hard in her ear. He kept the gun in her back and stepped sideways, toward an exit sign.

"One move and she dies!" he cried. "You hear me? I'm not having a good day today! I'm very, very upset, and I don't want anyone to do anything stupid."

People were running for the door. Screaming. What were they screaming for? He wasn't pointing the gun at their backs.

"Please," Monique gasped. "Please get ahold of yourself."

"Don't worry," Thomas whispered. "I won't kill you." The fire door was only ten feet away now. He stopped and glared at the two guards who had their pistols trained on him.

"Put the guns down, you idiots!" he yelled.

Monique flinched. He was yelling in her ear.

"Sorry."

The guards slowly lowered their guns to the floor.

"And you," he shouted in Kara's direction. "I want you as a hostage too. Get over here or I kill the girl!"

Kara looked frozen by shock.

"Move it!"

She hurried over.

"Get the door."

She complied and stepped into the hall beyond.

Thomas pulled Monique through the door.

"Anyone follows us, any police or any authorities, and she's dead!"

He slammed the door closed with his foot.

18

THE PARADISE Hotel was a flea-infested joint frequented by street traders. Or the odd sucker who responded to the promise of exotic, all-inclusive Internet vacation specials. Or in this case, the kidnapper trying desperately to get his point across to a very stubborn French woman.

Monique had guided them under duress. Kara had appropriately and repeatedly expressed her horror over what Thomas had done. Thomas had insisted this was the only way. If the rich French snob refused to care about a few billion lives, then they had no choice but to persuade her to care. This was what persuasion looked like in the real world.

The old, rusted elevator doors in the underground parking garage screeched open. Kara walked to the rental car at a fast clip, newly acquired room keys in hand.

"Okay," Thomas said, waving the 9-millimeter at Monique for show. "We go up, and we go quiet. I meant it when I said I would never kill you, but I might put a bullet in your pinkie toe if you get snobby. We clear? The gun will be in my belt, but that doesn't mean you can start hollering."

Monique glared at him, jaw muscles flexed.

"I'll take your silence as a chorus of agreement. Let's go."

He shoved the door open and waved her out.

"Top floor?" he asked Kara.

"Top floor. I don't know if I can do this, Thomas."

"You're not doing this. I am. I'm the one having the dreams. I'm the one who knows what he shouldn't know. I'm the one who has no choice but to talk some sense into this spoiled brat."

"You don't have to yell."

A car nosed into the lot.

"Sorry. Okay, into the elevator." He pressed the button for the fifth floor and breathed some relief when the doors slid shut.

"What is it with you French, anyway? Is it always business before saving the world?"

"This from the man with the gun in my back?" Monique asked. "Besides, as you can see, I don't live in France. Their politics are disagreeable to my father and me."

"They are?" She didn't respond. Thomas wasn't sure why he found the reve-lation surprising. Her perfume filled the small car quickly. A musky, flowery scent.

"If you cooperate, you'll be out of here in half an hour."

She didn't respond to that either.

No surprise, the rooms weren't as palatial as unsuspecting travelers might have been led to believe. Orange carpet turned brown. Flowered bedcovers on two double beds. A wicker dresser, crusted with enough dirt to wear out a power washer. The television worked, but only in green and without sound.

Thomas directed Monique to take the room's only chair, a flimsy wood job, into the far corner and sit still. He put the gun on the dresser beside him and turned to his sister.

"Okay. I need you to sneak out of this dump, find the police, and demand to talk to Jacques de Raison. Tell the police that you escaped. Tell them I'm a wacko or something. I need you clear of this, you understand?"

"Smartest thing I've heard all morning." She looked at Monique. "What do I tell her father?"

"You tell him what we know. And if he doesn't agree to stop or recall the shipment, you tell him that I said I'm going to start shooting."

Thomas faced Monique. "Only pinkies, of course. I don't like making threats, but you understand the situation."

"Yes. I understand perfectly. You've gone completely mad."

He nodded. "You see, that's why we need this backup plan, Kara. If she doesn't come around, maybe her father will. More important, it gets you off the hook. Make sure it's clear that I'm threatening his daughter, not you."

"And where do I tell them you are?"

"Tell them you jumped out of the car. You don't have a clue where we are."

"That's a lie."

"There's a lot at stake. Lies will be forgiven at this point."

"I hope you know what you're doing. How will I know what's going on?"

"Through Jacques. I'm sure he'll take a call from his daughter in the event we need to make contact. If you need to reach me, call, but make sure it's safe."

She walked over to the bedstand, lifted the phone receiver to her ear, and set it down, evidently satisfied that it had a dial tone. She'd lived in Southeast Asia too long to trust any such thing to chance.

Kara stepped forward and gave Thomas a hug. "This is nuts."

"I love you, sis."

"Love you, too, brother." She pulled back, gave Monique a last look, and headed for the door.

"Good luck wooing that one," she said and closed the door softly behind her.

"Yes, good luck wooing this one," Monique said. "The unabashed American male flexing his muscles. Is that what this is?"

Thomas picked up the gun, leaned on the dresser, and looked at his hostage. There was only one way to do this. He had to tell her everything. At least now she had to listen.

"Farthest thing from my mind, trust me. The fact of the matter is, I really did cross the ocean to talk to you, and I really am risking my neck to do so. Why would I risk so much to talk to a rude French woman, you ask? Because unless I'm sadly mistaken, you may be the only person alive who can work with me to stop a terrible thing from happening. Contrary to the overall impression I may have given you, I really am a very decent guy. And under all your fierce determination, I think you're probably a very decent girl. I just want to talk, and I just want you to listen. I'm very tired and I'm at my wit's end, so I hope you don't make this more difficult than it has to be. Is that too much to ask?"

"No. But if you expect me to burn the thousands of stockholders who've stuck out their necks for this company, you'll be disappointed. I won't spread a malicious rumor just because you say you'll shoot my pinkie toes off if I don't. If I were to guess, you've been hired by one of our competitors. This is some ridiculous plot to hurt Raison Pharmaceutical. What on earth would convince you that this makes any sense?"

Thomas stood, walked to the window, peered out. The street bustled with thousands of Thailand's finest, oblivious to the drama unfolding five stories above their heads.

"A dream," he said. He faced her. "A dream that is real."

Carlos Missirian waited patiently in the Mercedes across the street from the Paradise Hotel. In a few hours it would be dark. He would make his move then.

A satay vendor wheeled his cart past the car. Carlos pressed a button on the door and watched the tinted window slide down. Hot air rolled into the cool car. He held out two five-baht coins. The vendor hurried over with a small tray of meat sticks, took the coins, and handed him the satays. Carlos rolled the window up and pulled a small slice of warm, spicy meat from the stick using his teeth. The taste was inspiring.

His father had often told him that good plans are useless without proper execution. And proper execution depended on good timing more than any other factor. How many terrorist plots had failed miserably because of bad timing? Most.

He'd been caught off guard by the appearance of the American at the press conference. Thomas Hunter, a desperate-looking maniac who had watched the proceedings from a seat two rows in front of his own. It had been his own intention to approach the Raison woman after the conference and suggest an interview using false credentials he'd scavenged from an Associated Press contact. Failing that, he would have taken more direct measures, but he'd long ago learned that the best plan is usually the most obvious one.

He'd taken several steps toward the podium when the American had barged up front and pulled off his incredible stunt. What more obvious way to deal with an adversary than to march up, steal a weapon, and kidnap her in broad daylight in front of half the world's press corps? Surprisingly, the plot had worked. Even more surprisingly, they had gotten away. If Carlos hadn't habitually positioned his own car for a quick exit, they might have escaped him as well.

The fact that the American had gone to such lengths carried its own meaning. It meant that the CDC hadn't paid him any attention. This was good. It meant that the American had a very, very high level of confidence in this so-called dream of his. This was also good. It meant that the American intended to force Raison Pharmaceutical into pulling the drug. This wasn't so good.

But that would soon change.

He'd followed the green Toyota here, to the Paradise Hotel. The news was turning the kidnapping into a major story. Word had already reached the American wires. The police scanners in Bangkok were busy coordinating a frenzied search, but no one had a clue where the crazed American had vanished to.

Except Carlos, of course.

He placed the satays between his teeth and slid another piece off the stick. The American was doing his job for him. He had nicely isolated Monique de Raison in a hotel room. Thomas's blonde cohort had left on foot an hour ago. This bothered Carlos some, but the other two were still inside. He was sure of it. From his position he had a full view of every exit except an emergency exit in the alley, which he'd found and subsequently disabled.

The situation had fallen perfectly into his hands. How convenient that he could deal with them both at the same time. It was now simply a matter of timing.

Carlos looked in the rearview mirror, brushed a speck of dirt from the scar on his cheek, and leaned back with a long, satisfied breath.

Timing.

———— ✤ ————

Monique watched Thomas pace and wondered if there was any way, however unlikely, that the tale he'd spun over the past two hours was anything more than absolute nonsense. There always was that possibility, of course. She'd given herself to the pursuit of impossible new drugs precisely because she didn't believe in impossibilities unless they were proved mathe-matically. Technically speaking, his story could be true.

But then, technically speaking, his story was hogwash, as the Americans liked to say.

For the past five minutes he'd been silent, pacing with the gun dangling from his fingers. She wondered if he'd ever used a gun before. At first she had assumed so, judging by the way he handled it. But now, after listening to him, she wondered.

The air-conditioning unit rattled noisily but produced nothing more than hot air. They were both drenched in sweat. She had removed her jacket over an hour ago.

If she weren't so furious with the man for all this nonsense, she might pity him. Honestly, she pitied him anyway. He was completely sincere, which meant he had to be wrong in the head. Maybe insane. Which meant that, although he gave no signal that he was capable of shooting her toes off, he might very well be the kind who suddenly snapped and decapitated his victim or some other such terrible thing.

She had to find a way to break through to whatever reason he might have.

Monique took a deep breath of the stuffy air. "Thomas, can we talk on my level for a moment?"

"What do you think I've been trying to do for the past two hours?"

"You've been talking on your level. It may all make perfect sense to you, but not to me. We're not accomplishing a thing, hidden away in this suffocating room. The vaccine is most likely in flight by now, and within forty-eight hours it will be in the hands of a hundred hospitals around the world. If you're right, we're only wasting time by sitting here."

"You're saying that you'll recall the shipments?"

She had considered lying to him a hundred times, but her indignation prevented her from doing so. He wouldn't believe her anyway.

"Would you believe me if I said yes?" she asked.

"I'd believe you if we made the call together. A call to the *New York Times* from Monique de Raison would go a long way."

She sighed. "You know I can't do that." They were getting nowhere. She had to earn his trust. Negotiate a settlement to this standoff.

"But if I truly did believe you, I would. You do understand my predicament, don't you?"

He didn't answer, which was answer enough. She pressed forward.

"You know, I grew up on a vineyard in the south of France. Much cooler than here, I'm glad to say." She smiled. For his sake. "We came from a poor family, my mother and I. She was a servant in our vineyards. Did you know that my family used to make wine, not drugs?"

He just stared at her.

She continued. "I never knew my biological father; he left when I was only three. Jacques was one of the Raison sons. He fell in love with my mother when I was ten. My mother died when I was twelve. That was fourteen years ago. We've come a long way since then, Father and I. Did you know that I studied at UCLA Medical School?"

"Why are you telling me all of this?"

"I'm making conversation."

"We don't have time for conversation," Thomas said. "Haven't you been listening to me?"

She answered as calmly as possible. "Yes. I have. But you haven't been speaking on my level. Remember? I'm telling you who I am so that you can address me as a real, living person, a woman who is confused and a bit frightened by all your antics."

"I don't know how I can be clearer. Either you believe me, or you don't.

You don't. So we have a problem." He held up his hand. "Don't get me wrong, I would love to sit and chat about how our fathers abandoned us. But not now, please. We have more pressing matters on our hands."

"Your father left you?"

He lowered his hand. "Yes."

"How sad." She was making progress. Not a lot, but some. "How old were you?"

"Sixteen. We lived in the Philippines. I grew up there. He was a chaplain."

The revelation cast Thomas in a completely new light. An army brat. Son of a chaplain, no less. Based in the Philippines. She spoke some Tagalog herself.

"Saan ka nakatira?" *Where did you live?*

"Nakatira ako sa Maynila." *I lived in Manila.*

They stared at each other for a long second. His face softened.

"This isn't going to work," he said.

She sat up. He was folding so quickly? "What do you mean?" she asked.

"I mean this psychobabble approach of yours. It isn't going to work."

"This . . ." He was forcing *her* to fold? "How dare you reduce my childhood to psychobabble! You want to talk to me? Then talk to me like a human, not some bargaining chip!"

"Of course. You're a frightened woman, trembling under the hand of her fearsome captor, right? You're the poor abandoned child in desperate need of a hero. If anything, *I'm* the poor abandoned loser who's worked his way into a pretty hopeless predicament. Look at me!" He shoved both arms out. "I'm a basket case. I have the gun, but it might as well be you. You know I wouldn't touch you, so what threat am I? None. This is crazy!"

"Well, you said it, not me. You talk about black bats and colored forests and ancient histories like you actually believe all that nonsense. I have a PhD in chemistry. You really think some crazy dream would have me trembling on my knees?"

"Yes!" he shouted. "That's exactly what I expect! Those black bats know your name!"

Hearing him say it like that sent a chill through her gut. He glared at her, slapped the gun on the dresser, and yanked his shirt off over his head.

"It's hot in here!" He threw the shirt on the floor, snatched up the gun, and marched for the window.

His back was strong. Stronger than she would have guessed. It glistened with sweat. A long scar ran over his left shoulder blade. He wore plaid blue boxer shorts under his jeans—the tag on the elastic waistband read Old Navy.

Monique had considered rushing him before he'd told her that he was the blurred image in the security footage at the front gates yesterday. Looking at him now, even with his back turned, she was glad she'd rejected the idea.

Thomas suddenly dropped the curtain and turned. "Tell me about the vaccine."

"I have."

He was suddenly very excited. "No, more. Tell me more."

"It wouldn't make any sense to you, unless you understand vaccines."

"Humor me."

She sighed. "Okay. We call it a DNA vaccine, but in reality it's actually an engineered virus. That's why—"

"Your vaccine is a virus?" he demanded.

"Technically, yes. A virus that immunizes the host by altering its DNA against certain other viruses. Think of a virus like a tiny robot that hijacks its host cell and modifies its DNA, usually in a way that ends with the rupturing of that cell. We've learned how to turn these germs into agents that work for us instead of against us. They are very small, very hardy, and can spread very quickly—in this case, through the air."

"But it's an actual virus."

He was reacting as so many reacted to this simple revelation. The idea that a virus could be used to humanity's benefit was a strange concept to most.

"Yes. But also a vaccine, though unlike traditional vaccines, which are usually based on weaker strains of an actual disease organism. At any rate, they are hardy enough, but they do die under adverse conditions. Like heat."

"But they can mutate."

"Any virus can mutate. But none of the mutations in our tests have survived beyond a generation or two. They immediately die. And that's in favorable conditions. Under intense heat—"

"Forget about the heat. Tell me something that no one could possibly know about—" He lifted his hand. "No, wait. Don't tell me." He paced to the bed and back. Faced her. The gun had become an extension of his arm; he waved it around like a conductor's baton.

"Would you mind watching where you point that thing?" she said.

He looked at the gun then tossed it on the bed. Lifted his hands.

"New strategy," he said. "If I can prove to you that everything I've told you is true, that your vaccine really will mutate into something fatal, will you call it off?"

"How would you—"

"Just go with me. Would you call it off and destroy the vaccine?"

"Of course."

"You swear it?"

"There's no way to prove it."

"But *if? If,* Monique."

"Yes!" He was unnerving her. "I said I would. Unlike some people, I don't lie out of habit."

He ignored the jab, and she regretted her insinuation.

A smile twisted his mouth. "Okay. Here's what we're going to do. I'm going to go to sleep and get some information that I couldn't possibly know, and then I'm going to wake up and give it to you."

His eyes were bright, but the brilliance of his plan escaped her. "That's absurd."

"That's the point. You think it's absurd because you don't believe me. Which is why when I wake up and tell you something I can't know, you'll believe me! I can't believe I didn't think of this before."

He really believed that he could enter this dream world of his, discover real information from the histories, and return to tell her about it. He really was mad.

On the other hand, if he was sleeping, she could . . .

"Okay. Fair enough. Go to sleep then."

"See? It makes sense, doesn't it? What kind of information should I look for?"

"What?"

"What could I bring back that would persuade you?"

She thought about it. Preposterous. "The number of nucleotide base pairs that deal specifically with HIV in my vaccine," she said.

"The number of nucleotide base pairs. Okay. Give me something else, in case I can't get that. The histories may not have recorded something that specific."

She couldn't hold back some amusement at his enthusiasm. It was like negotiating with one of the children right out of Narnia. "My father's birth date. They would have the year of his birth, right? Do you know what it is?"

"No, I don't. And I can come back with more than just his birth date if you want." He picked up the gun and walked to the window yet again.

"What do you keep looking at?"

"There's a white car that's been parked down the street for the last few hours. Just checking. It's getting dark."

He spun back. "Okay. How do we do this? I'll sleep on the bed."

"How long will this take?"

"Half an hour. You wake me up half an hour after I fall asleep. That's all I need. There's no correlation between time here and time there."

He walked to the bed and sat down, pulled off the cover, and ripped the sheet off.

"What are you doing?"

He tore the sheet in two. "I can't just let you wander around while I'm sleeping. I'm sorry, but I'm going to have to tie you up."

She stood up. "Don't you dare!"

"What do you mean, don't you dare? I'm the one with the gun here, and you're my prisoner, in case you forgot. I tie you up, and if you yell for help, I wake up and shoot off your pinkie toes."

He was impossible. "You're going to leave me sitting here while you fall asleep? How do I wake you up if I'm tied up?"

He grabbed one of the pillows and tossed it over by the air conditioner. "You throw this pillow at me. Move over to the air conditioner."

"You're going to tie me to the air conditioner?"

"Looks pretty solid to me. The anchor rod will hold you. You have a better idea?"

"And how will I throw the pillow if my hands are tied?"

He thought about that. "Good point. Okay, I'll tie you so that you can reach the bed with your foot. You kick the bed until I wake up. You don't yell."

She stared at him. Then the air conditioner.

"Didn't think so. Hurry up. The sooner I fall asleep, the sooner we can get this over with." He waved the gun. "Move."

It took him five minutes to rip up the sheet halves and form a short tether. He made her lie down on her back to measure the distance to the bed. Satisfied that she could reach it, he bound her hands behind her back. Not just her hands, but her fingers, so that she couldn't move them to untie anything. And her feet, so she couldn't stand.

He worked over her quickly, unconcerned that his sweaty torso was smudging her silk blouse. The whole thing was desperately absurd. But he clearly didn't think so. He was scurrying around like a rat on a mission.

When he'd finished, he stood back, admired his handiwork, carried the gun to the bed, and plopped down on his back, spread-eagle.

He closed his eyes.

"I can't believe this stupidity," she mumbled.

"Quiet. I'm trying to sleep here. Do I need to gag you?" He sat up, pulled off his boots.

Her teeth! She might be able to tear the cloth cords with her teeth.

"Do you really think you'll be able to fall asleep like this? I mean, I will be quiet, I promise, but isn't this just a bit ridiculous?"

"I think you've made yourself clear on that point. And actually I don't know if I can fall asleep or not. But I'm about ready to drop from exhaustion as it is, so I think there's a pretty good chance."

He plopped back down and closed his eyes.

"Maybe I could sing you a lullaby," Monique heard herself say. It was a surprising thing to say at a moment like this.

He turned his head and looked at her, sitting against the wall under the air conditioner. "Do you sing?"

She turned away and stared at the wall.

Five minutes passed before she braved a glance his way. He lay exactly as she'd last seen, bare chest rising and falling steadily, arms to either side. Very well built. Dark hair. A beautiful creature.

Totally mad.

Was he asleep? "Thomas?" she whispered.

He sat up, rolled out of bed, and picked up a fragment of sheet.

"What is it?" she asked.

"I'm sorry, but I have to gag you."

"I wasn't talking!"

"No, but you might try to bite your way out. I'm sorry, I really am. I can't sleep unless I'm totally at ease, you understand, and I think a strong jaw might be able to tear this stuff." He wrapped the strip around her mouth and tied it behind her head. She didn't bother protesting.

"Not that I think you have a strong jaw. I didn't mean it like that. I actually like the sound of your voice."

He stood, crossed to the bed, and dropped onto his back once again.

19

THOMAS AWOKE with a start and jumped to his feet on the hill overlooking the village. He scrambled to the lip of the valley. Dusk. The people were already heading up the valley to the lake. The Gathering.

Two thoughts. One, he should join them. If he ran, he could catch them. Two, he had to get to the black forest. Now.

He'd dreamed how many times since waking in the black forest? Yet something had changed. For the first time, he'd awakened with a compulsion to treat this dream of Bangkok, this lucid fabrication in his mind, as real. It was no longer only a conscious choice that he was making, it was something in his heart. He really *did* have to treat the dreams as real. Both of them, in the event either or both *were* real.

If Bangkok was real, then he needed Monique's cooperation. The only way to get Monique's cooperation was to prove himself by retrieving information. Information he hoped he could find in the black forest.

Thomas spun around and sprinted down the path that led to the Shataiki.

He had to learn the truth. The Great Deception, the Raison Strain, Monique de Raison—he had to know why he was having these dreams. He'd survived the black forest once; he would survive it again.

His feet slapped the earth as he jogged. The path soon faded, but he knew the direction. The river. It lay directly ahead. The slight glow from the trees lit the forest—even in the dead of night he would be able to find his way back.

He slowed to a walk and caught his breath. Then he fell back into a jog. This time he wouldn't actually enter the forest. He would call out. And if the black bats didn't respond? Then he would see. Either way, he couldn't return without some answers.

What had Monique suggested he learn? The number of nucleotide base pairs in the HIV vaccine.

The journey must have lasted an hour, but there was no way for Thomas to know. When he finally broke into the clearing he recognized as the place he'd first been healed, he pulled up, panting hard. Just past the meadow lay a short stretch of forest, which ended at the river's edge. He stepped out into the meadow and jogged forward. A snapshot of the hotel room in Bangkok flashed through his mind and he plodded on, across the meadow and through the forest toward the rushing river.

The trees gave way to riverbank without warning. One second forest, the next only grass. And the river.

The scene took his breath away. He leaped back into the safety of the trees and flattened himself against a massive red tree. He waited for a moment and then carefully peered out onto the bank of the green river. The bridge the Roush had called the Crossing glimmered fifty yards upriver, white in the rising moonlight. The river glowed, translucent and sparkling with the colored light cast by the trees. Beyond the river lay the outline of ragged black trees in the darkness.

Thomas stared into the black forest and began to shiver. There was no way he could enter that blackness again. He imagined red beady eyes lying in wait just beyond the black barrier. Or above. He slowly raised his eyes to the treetops across the river, but there was only darkness. He listened to the sound of the night, trying to filter out the river.

Was that a snicker?

Then he saw a lone dark shadow flee from the upper branches. He quickly pulled back into the colored forest's cover, his heart pounding in his ears. A Shataiki! But it had fled. Maybe it hadn't seen him.

He shut his eyes and took a deep breath. He should leave this place. He should turn and run.

But he didn't. Couldn't.

He stood by the red tree for ten minutes, slowly gathering his courage.

The river bubbled on, undisturbed. The forest stood black, unmoving beyond. Nothing changed. Slowly his fear gave way to resolve again.

Thomas stepped from the forest and stood on the bank, washed in moonlight. No bats. Just the bridge to his left, the river, and the dead trees beyond. He took a few more steps, angling for the bridge. Still nothing changed. The river still rushed on, the trees behind him still glowed in oblivion, and the blackness ahead remained pitch dark.

Thomas took a deep breath and walked quickly toward the bridge. He gripped the rail of the white structure, and for the first time it dawned on him that the wood of the bridge, unlike any wood he had seen outside the black forest, did not glow. It had been constructed by the Shataiki, then? He paused and looked again at the black trees looming taller now. He should call out from here. What he should yell, he didn't know. Hello? Or maybe . . .

A speck of red suddenly flickered in the corner of his right eye. Thomas jerked his head toward the light. He saw them clearly now, the dancing red eyes just beyond the tree line across the river. He tightened his grip on the rail and caught his breath.

Another flicker of red off to his left made him turn his head, and he saw a dozen Shataiki step out of the forest and stop, facing the river. And then, as Thomas watched with terror, a thousand sets of red gleaming eyes materialized, emerging from their hiding places.

Thomas told himself to turn and run, but his feet felt rooted to the earth. He watched with dread as the Shataiki poured silently out of the forest, creating a line as far as he could see in either direction. The creatures squatted like sentinels along the tree line, gazing at him with blank red eyes set like jewels on either side of their long black snouts. And then the treetops began filling as well, as if a hundred thousand Shataiki had been called to witness a great spectacle, and the black trees were their bleachers.

Thomas's legs began to shake. The pungent smell of sulfur filled his nostrils, and he checked his breathing. This whole thing was a terrible mistake. He had to get back to the colored forest.

The wall of Shataiki directly ahead of him suddenly parted. Thomas watched as a single Shataiki walked toward the bridge, dragging brilliant blue wings on the barren earth behind him. This one stood taller than a man, much larger than the rest. Its torso was gold and pulsed with tinges of red. Stunning. Beautiful. The night air filled with the clucks and clicks of a hundred thousand bats as the huge Shataiki slogged toward the crossing. It moved slowly. Very slowly, favoring its right leg.

Thomas watched without moving. The beast's green eyes were set deep into its triangular face, fixed on Thomas. Pupil-less, glowing saucers of green. Frightening and yet oddly comforting. Luring. Thomas could hear the scraping of its talons along aged planks, the whisper of its huge wings, as it slowly ascended the bridge. The Shataiki made its way to the center and stopped.

He raised one wing slightly and the throngs behind him fell silent.

Somewhere in the back of Thomas's paralyzed mind, a voice began to re-assure him that this Shataiki could certainly mean no harm. No creature so beautiful could harm him. He had come to talk. Why else would he have come out to the center of the bridge? According to the Roush, no Shataiki could cross the bridge.

"Come." The Shataiki sang as much as spoke. Hardly more than a whisper.

The leader was telling him to come. And why should he give that suggestion any mind? He could speak from here just as easily as from up there.

"Come," the leader repeated.

This time, the Shataiki opened his mouth. Thomas saw its pink tongue. As long as he stayed on this side of the bridge and out of the creature's reach, he would be safe. Right?

Thomas stepped cautiously onto the bridge. The Shataiki made no move, so Thomas stepped up the Crossing toward the beast. He stopped five meters from the Shataiki and looked directly into his eyes. They glistened like giant emeralds in the moonlight. A chill ran down Thomas's spine. He had to be the one called Teeleh. But he wasn't what Thomas had expected.

The creature let his shoulders droop and turned his head slightly. He retracted his talons and allowed a gentle smile to form on his snout.

"Welcome, my friend. I had hoped you would come." Now he spoke plainly, in a low voice without a hint of music. "I know this may all seem a little overpowering to you. But please, ignore them. They are imbeciles who have no mind."

"Who?" Thomas said. But it came out like a grunt so he said it again. "Who?"

"The sick, demented creatures behind me." The beautiful bat withdrew a red fruit from behind his back and offered it to Thomas. "Here, my friend, have a fruit."

Thomas looked at the fruit, too terrified to move any closer to the beast, much less reach out to take something from it.

"But of course. You are still frightened, aren't you? Pity. It is one of our best." The Shataiki raised the fruit to his lips without removing his eyes from Thomas and bit deeply into its flesh. A stream of juice dribbled through his furry chin and spotted the planks at his feet. "Possibly our very best. Certainly the most powerful." He smacked his lips. He lifted his chin to swallow the fruit and tucked the uneaten portion behind his back again.

He withdrew a small pouch. "Are you thirsty?"

"No, thanks."

"Not thirsty. I understand. We'll have plenty of time for eating and drinking later, won't we?"

Thomas began to relax a little. "I didn't come to eat or drink." Was it possible Teeleh could be a friend to him? The creature certainly disapproved of the other black bats. "How did you know I was coming?"

"I have powers you can't imagine, my friend. To know you were coming was nothing. I have legions at my disposal. Do you think I don't know who comes and who goes? I think you underestimate me."

"If you have such power, then why do you live in the black trees instead of in the colored forest?" Thomas asked, looking past the beast at the throngs milling in the trees across the river.

"The colored forest, you call it? And who in their right mind would want to live in the colored forest? You think their fruit can compare with my fruit? No. Is their water any sweeter than ours? Less. They are nothing but slaves."

Thomas shifted on his feet. There was only one rule here. No matter what happened, he could never drink the water. As long as he followed that simple standard, he would be perfectly safe.

"What is that in your pocket?" the bat suddenly demanded.

Thomas reached into his pocket and withdrew the small glowing carving that Johan had handed him in the village.

Teeleh recoiled. "Throw it over the side. Throw it over!"

Thomas reacted without thought. He tossed the red lion over the edge of the bridge and gripped the rail to steady himself.

Slowly Teeleh lowered his arm and stared at Thomas with his wide, green eyes.

"It is poison to us," the beast said.

"I didn't know."

"Of course not. They have deceived you."

Thomas let the statement go. "What do they call you?" he asked.

"What does who call me?" the beast asked.

"Them." Thomas nodded at the bats.

The Shataiki raised his chin. "I am called Teeleh."

"Teeleh." He'd expected nothing else. "You're the leader of the Shataiki."

"Foolish minds may call what they do not know whatever they wish. But I am the ruler of a thousand legions of subjects in a land full of mystery and power. This they call the black forest." The black bat swung a huge wing toward the forest behind him. "But I call it my kingdom. Which is why I've come to speak to you. To set your mind free. There are some things you should know."

Thomas could hardly ignore the obvious fact that the creature wanted something from him. This show of power couldn't be arbitrary. But he had no intention of giving them anything. He'd come for one purpose only, to gather some information about the histories.

Despite his confusion over the true nature of this creature, Thomas couldn't allow Teeleh to gain the upper hand.

"And there are some things that you should know as well," Thomas said. "It's forbidden for me to drink your water, and I have no intention of doing it. Please don't waste your time."

Teeleh's eyes brightened. "Forbidden, you say? Who can forbid another man to do anything? No, my friend. No one is forbidden unless he chooses to be forbidden." The Shataiki spoke fluidly, as though he'd argued the subject a thousand times. "What better way to keep someone from experiencing my power than to say he will suffer if he drinks the water? Lies. Surely you, more than the rest, should know that such small-minded talk only locks people in cages of stupidity. They follow a god who demands their allegiance and robs them of their freedom. Forbidden? Who has the right to forbid?"

The reasoning was compelling. But it had to be fast talk. Thomas chose his next words carefully. "I also know that if even one of us drinks your water, the whole land will be turned over to those sick, demented creatures, as you call them, and we will become your slaves."

The air suddenly filled with angry snarls of outrage from the army of Shataiki in the trees. Startled by the outcry, Thomas retreated a step.

"Silence!" Teeleh thundered. His voice echoed with such force that Thomas instinctively ducked.

The beast dipped its head. "Forgive them, my friend. I don't think you would blame them if you knew what they have been through. When you have lived through deception and tyranny and you survive, you tend to overreact to the slightest reminder of that tyranny. And believe me, those behind me have faced the greatest form of deception and abuse known to living souls." He paused and twitched his head as though he were trying to loosen a stiff neck.

In many ways the Shataiki's actions *were* consistent with creatures who'd been abused and imprisoned. Thomas felt a sliver of pity run through his heart. For such a beautiful creature as Teeleh to be imprisoned in the black forest seemed unjust.

"Now come," Teeleh said. "You must surely know that the myths you speak of are designed to deceive the people of the colored forest—to control their allegiance. You think you know, but what you've been told is the greatest kind of deception. And I've come to make that clear to you."

Did Teeleh know that he'd lost his memory?

"Why did you try to kill me?" he asked.

"I would never do such a thing."

"I was in your forest and barely got out alive. If I hadn't made the Crossing when I did, I would be dead now."

"But you didn't have my protection," the beast said. "They mistook you for one of them."

"Them?"

"Surely you don't actually believe that you're one of them, do you? How quaint. And clever, I might add. They're actually using your memory loss against you, aren't they? Typical. Always deceiving."

So he did know about the memory loss. What else did he know?

"How did you know about the memory loss?" Thomas asked.

"Bill told me," the creature said. "You do remember Bill, don't you?"

"Bill?"

"Yes, Bill. The redhead who came here with you."

Thomas took a step back. The creature before him shifted out of focus. "Bill is *real?*"

"Of course he's real. You're real. If you're real, then Bill's real. You both came from the same place."

Thomas couldn't mistake the sense that he was standing at the edge of a whole new world of understanding. He'd come with a few questions about the histories, and yet before asking those questions, a hundred others had been deposited in his mind.

He glanced back at the colored forest. What did he really know? Only what the others had told him. Nothing more. Was it possible that he had it all wrong?

His heart thumped in his chest. The air suddenly felt too thick to breathe. Easy. Easy, Thomas. He couldn't reveal his ignorance.

"Okay, so you know about Bill. Tell me about him. Tell me where we came from."

"You still don't remember?"

He eyed the bat circumspectly. "I remember some things. But I'll keep those to myself. You tell me what you know, and we'll see if that matches what I remember. Say the wrong thing, and I'll know you're lying."

The smile faded from Teeleh's lips. "You came from Earth."

"Earth. This is Earth. Be more specific."

Teeleh regarded him with a long stare. "You really don't know, do you? You're a sharp one, I'll give you that, but you just don't know."

"Don't be so sure," Thomas said, careful to keep anxiety out of his voice.

"Don't be so sure that you're sharp? Or that you know?"

"Just tell me."

"You and your copilot, Bill, crashed less than a mile behind me," Teeleh said. "Which is why I'm here. I think I've found a way back."

It was all Thomas could do to hide his incredulity. What a preposterous suggestion! It actually eased his tension. If Teeleh was stupid enough to think he'd fall for such a ridiculous fabrication, he was much less an opponent than Michal had suggested. Hopefully the bat still knew the histories.

For now he would play along, see how far this creature would take the story.

"So. You know about Bill and the spaceship. What else do you know?"

"I know that you think the spaceship is preposterous because you really don't remember a thing."

Thomas blinked. "Is that so?"

"The truth of it is this: You are stranded on a distant planet. Your ship, *Discovery III,* crashed three days ago. You lost your memory in the impact. You're standing on this bridge talking to me because you don't fit in with the simpletons in the colored forest, which is natural. You don't."

Thomas's ears were burning. He wondered if this creature could see that as well.

He cleared his throat. "What else?"

"It's good to hear, isn't it? The truth. Unlike the pitifully deceived people of the colored forest, I will tell you only the truth."

"Fine. Tell me the truth then."

"My, my, we are hungry. The truth is, if you knew what I know about that colored forest and those who live in it, you would despise them."

The throngs of Shataiki had lost their respect for the silence. A sea of voices muttered and squealed under their collective breath. Somewhere in the darkness, Thomas could just hear a dozen arguments raging in high pitch.

"We have been imprisoned in this forsaken forest," Teeleh said. "That is the truth. For a Shataiki to touch the land across this river means instant death. It is tyranny."

The throngs of bats screeched their outrage.

Teeleh lifted a wing.

Quiet fell over the forest like a blanket of fog.

"They make me ill," Teeleh muttered. He looked back to make sure his legions were in order.

"What about the histories?" Thomas asked. The question he'd come to ask sounded out of balance in this new realm of truth.

"The histories. Yes, of course. I suppose you're dreaming of the histories, are you?"

"They're real? How can there be histories of Earth if this isn't Earth?"

The question seemed to set the big bat back. "Clever. Very clever. How can we have histories of Earth if we aren't on Earth?"

"And how do you know I'm dreaming of the histories?"

"I know you're dreaming because I've drunk the water in the black forest. Knowledge. The histories of Earth are really the future of Earth. To you, they're history, because you've tasted some fruit from the forest behind me. You're seeing into the future."

The revelation was stunning. Thomas didn't remember eating any fruit. Perhaps before he hit his head on the rock? In its own way it made perfect sense. And there was a way to test this assertion.

"Fair enough," Thomas said. "Then you should be able to tell me what happens in this future. Tell me about the Raison Strain."

"The Raison Strain. Of course. One of humanity's most telling periods. Before the Great Tribulation. Often called the Great Deception. I'll speak of it as history. It was a vaccine that mutated into a virus under extreme heat."

Teeleh licked his lips delectably. "Nobody would have ever known, you know. The vaccine never would have mutated because no natural cause would ever produce a heat high enough to trigger the mutation. But some unsuspecting fool stumbled upon the information. He told the wrong party. The vaccine fell into the hands of some very . . . disturbed people. These people heated the vaccine to precisely 179.47 degrees Fahrenheit for two hours, and so was born the world's deadliest airborne virus."

There was something very odd about what Teeleh was saying, but Thomas couldn't put his finger on it. Regardless, the creature's information matched his dreams.

"Come closer," Teeleh said.

"Closer?"

"You want to know about the virus, don't you? Just a little closer."

Thomas took a half step. Teeleh's claw flashed without warning. It barely touched his thumb, which was gripping the rail. A small shock rode up his arm, and he jerked the hand back. Blood seeped from a tiny cut in his thumb. It was smeared.

"What are you doing?" he demanded.

"You want to know; I'm helping you know."

"How does cutting me help me know?"

"Please, it's nothing but a scratch. I was merely testing you. Ask me a question."

The whole business was highly unusual. But then so was everything about Teeleh.

"Do you know the number of nucleotide base pairs for HIV?" he asked. "In the Raison Vaccine, that is."

"Base pairs: 375,200. But you know that it wasn't the actual Raison Strain that brought such destruction," Teeleh said. "It was the antivirus. Which conveniently also ended up in the hands of the same man who unleashed the virus. He blackmailed the world. Thus the name, the Great Deception."

Thomas's head buzzed. "The antivirus?"

"Yes. Cutting the DNA at the fifth gene and the ninety-third gene and splicing the two remaining ends together." Teeleh suddenly grew very still. His voice softened. "Tell them that, Thomas. Tell them 179.47 degrees for two hours and tell them the fifth gene and the ninety-third gene, cut and spliced. Say that."

"Say the numbers?"

"Don't you want to know? Say them."

"One hundred and seventy-nine point four seven degrees for two hours."

"Yes, now the fifth gene."

"Fifth gene . . ."

"Yes, and the ninety-third gene."

"Ninety-third gene," Thomas repeated.

"Cut and spliced."

"Cut and spliced."

"And you'll need her back door as well."

"The back door as well?"

"Yes. Now forget that I told you that."

"Forget?"

"Forget." Teeleh withdrew the same fruit he'd offered before. "Here. Have a bite of fruit. It'll help you."

"No, I can't."

"That's just not true. I've just proved that those rules are a prison. How thick can you be?"

Teeleh stood, unmoving, the fruit perched lightly in his fingers. He spoke in a quieter voice now. "The fruit will open whole new worlds to you, Thomas, my friend. And the water will show you worlds of knowledge you have only dreamed of. Worlds your friends in the colored forest know nothing about."

Thomas looked at the fruit. Then up at the green eyes. What if there really was a spaceship behind those trees? It was as likely a scenario as anything else he'd considered.

"Assuming this is all true, where is Bill?"

"Would you like to see Bill? Maybe I can arrange that for you."

"You said you had a way to get us home."

"Yes. Yes, I can do that. We've found a way to fix your ship."

"Can you show it to me?" Thomas's heart pounded as he asked the question. Seeing the ship would end the debate raging in his mind, but Thomas had no guarantee the Shataiki wouldn't tear him to pieces. They'd tried once already.

"Yes. Yes, and I will. But first I need one thing from you. A simple thing that you could do easily, I think." Again the leader paused, as if tentative about actually asking what he had come to ask.

"What?"

"Bring Tanis here, to the bridge."

Silence engulfed them. Not a single Shataiki lining the forest seemed to move. All eyes glared with anticipation at Thomas. His heart pounded. Other than the gurgling of the river below, it was the only sound he now heard.

"And if I do that, then you will guarantee me safe passage to my ship? Repaired?"

"Yes."

Thomas reached a hand to the rail to steady himself.

"You just want me to bring him to the bridge, right? Not across the bridge."

"Yes. Just to the river here."

"And what guarantee do I have that you will lead me safely to the craft?"

"I will bring the craft here to the bridge as well. You may enter it with no Shataiki in sight, before I speak to Tanis."

If the Shataiki could actually show him this ship, the *Discovery III,* it would be proof enough. If not, he wouldn't cross the bridge. No harm.

"Makes sense," he said cautiously.

The living wall of black creatures lining the forest now hissed collectively like a great field of locusts. Teeleh stared at Thomas, raised the fruit to his lips, and bit deeply again. He licked the juice that ran onto his fingers with a long, thin, pink tongue. All the while his unblinking eyes stared at Thomas. Could he trust this creature? If what he said were true, then he had to find the spacecraft! It would be his only way home.

The leader stopped his licking. He stretched the fruit out to Thomas. "Eat this fruit to seal our agreement," Teeleh said. "It's our very best."

He'd done this once already. According to the creature, it was why he was dreaming. Thomas forced his fear back, reached out to the Shataiki, took the fruit from his claw, and stepped back.

He glanced up at the creature smiling before him. Raised the half-eaten fruit to his mouth. He was about to bite down when the scream shattered the night.

"Thomasssss!"

Thomas jerked the fruit from his mouth and swung to his right. Bill? The voice sounded slurred and ragged.

Then he saw the redhead. Bill had emerged from the forest and was struggling weakly against the claws of a dozen Shataiki. His clothes had been stripped entirely, and his naked body looked shockingly white in the tangle of shrieking black Shataiki who now tore at him. Blood matted the redhead's hair and streaked his drawn face. Dozens of cuts and bruises covered the man's pale flesh. He looked like an abused corpse.

The blood drained from Thomas's head. Nausea washed over him.

Teeleh swung around, his eyes blazing with an intensity that Thomas had not yet seen. Thomas's fingers went limp, and the fruit fell to the wooden deck with a deadening thump.

"Take your hands off him!" Teeleh screamed. He unfurled his wings and raised them above his head. "How dare you defy me!"

Thomas watched, stunned. Immediately the Shataiki released Bill.

"Take him to safety. Now!"

Two bats pulled Bill by the hands. He stumbled into the trees.

Teeleh faced Thomas. "As you can see, Bill is indeed real. I must keep him, you understand. It's the one assurance I have from you that you will return with Tanis. But I promise you, no more harm will come to him."

"Thomas!" Bill's voice cried from the trees. "Help me . . ." His voice was muted.

"Very real, my friend," Teeleh said. "He's been through a bit of turmoil lately and isn't thrilled with the way the others have treated him, but I can promise you my full protection."

Thomas couldn't tear his eyes from the gap in the trees where Bill had vanished. It was real? Bill was real. Confusion clouded his mind.

A lone cry suddenly shrieked behind Thomas. He spun his head and saw the white Roush swoop in from the treetops. Michal!

"Thomas! Run! Quickly!"

Thomas whirled around and tore toward the forest. He slammed into a tree and spun around, gasping for air. Teeleh stood stoically on the bridge, drilling him with those large green eyes.

"Hurry," Michal called. "We must hurry!"

Thomas turned from the scene and dived into the forest after Michal.

20

FINDING THE room had been a simple matter of handing the desk clerk a hundred U.S. dollars and asking which room the blonde American girl had taken several hours earlier. She was probably the only American who'd checked in all day.

Room 517, the clerk said.

Carlos stepped into the fifth-floor hall, saw that it was clear, and walked quickly to his left. 515. 517. He stepped to the door, tested the knob. Locked. Naturally.

He stood in the vacant hall for another three minutes, ear pressed to the door. Aside from the rattling air conditioner, the room was completely silent. They could be sleeping, although he doubted it. Or gone. Unlikely.

He reached into his pocket, withdrew a pick, and very carefully turned the tumblers in the lock. There was more than enough white noise to cover his entry. The American had a gun, but he wasn't a killer. One look at his face and Carlos had seen that. And guns weren't terribly familiar to him, by the way he'd gripped the 9-millimeter in the hotel lobby.

No, what they had here was an American who was crazed and bold and perhaps even a worthy adversary, but not a killer.

If your enemy is strong, you must crush.

If your enemy is deaf, you must shout.

If your enemy fears death, you must slaughter.

Basic terror-camp doctrine.

Carlos rolled and cracked his neck. He was dressed in a black blazer, T-shirt, slacks, patent leather shoes. The clothes of a Mediterranean businessman. But the time for facades was at an end. The jacket would only encumber his movements. He eased the silenced gun from his breast pocket and slipped it under his belt. Shrugged off the jacket. Draped it over his left arm and handled the pistol. Twisted the knob with his left hand.

Carlos took a deep breath and leaned hard into the door, enough force to snap any safety device.

A chain popped and Carlos was through, gun extended.

Force and speed. Not only in execution but in understanding and judgment. He saw what he needed to see before his first full stride.

The woman bound to the air conditioner. Gagged. Cords made from sheets.

The American lying shirtless on the bed. Asleep.

Carlos was halfway across the room before the woman could respond, and then only with a muffled squeak. Her eyes flared wide. Powerless.

The American was his only concern then. He jerked the gun to his right, ready to put a bullet in the man's shoulder if he so much as flinched.

He was moving quickly, without wasted movement. But in his mind everything felt impossibly slow. It was the way he'd flawlessly executed a hundred missions. Break a simple movement into a dozen fragments and you can then influence each fragment, make corrections, changes. It was a supreme advantage he had over all but the very best.

Carlos reached the girl in four strides. He dropped to his right knee and slugged her with a quick chop to her temple, all the while keeping the gun trained on the American.

The woman moaned and sagged. Unconscious.

Carlos held his position for a count of three. The American's chest rose and fell. The 9-millimeter gun lay on the bed by his fingers.

Easy. Too easy. Almost disappointingly easy.

He rose, retrieved the American's gun, hurried to the door. Closed it quietly. He returned to the bed and studied the situation, gun hanging at his side. A windfall in any sense of the word. Two for the price of one, as the Americans would say. An unconscious woman and a sleeping man, helpless at his feet.

The man had several scars on his chest. Very well muscled. Lean fingers. The perfect body for a fighter. Perhaps he'd underestimated this one.

What was driving Thomas Hunter? Dreams? They would soon know, because he would take them both. The world would be looking for the crazed American who'd kidnapped Monique de Raison, never suspecting that they were both now in the hands of a third party. Svensson would wet himself over this one.

The air conditioner rattled steadily to his left. Outside, the street crawled with night business. The other woman could return at any moment.

Carlos walked to the Raison woman, removed her gag. Withdrew a marble-sized ball from his pocket. It was a product of his own making. Nine parts high explosive, one part remote detonator. He'd used it successfully on three occasions.

He pulled the woman to a sitting position, squeezed her cheeks to part her lips, and slipped the ball into her mouth. Using his left hand, he squeezed her windpipe with enough sudden force to make her gasp involuntarily. At the same moment, while her mouth gaped, he shoved the ball down her throat with his forefinger.

She gagged. Swallowed. He clamped his hand over her mouth, and she struggled against him, regaining consciousness. When he was sure she'd swallowed the ball completely, he brought his fist across her temple.

She slumped to the floor.

Monique de Raison now carried enough explosive in her belly to disembowel her with the push of a single button. Undetonated, the explosive ball would pass out of her system in roughly twenty-four hours, but until then she was his prisoner to a range of fifty meters. It was the only way to get both her and the American to cooperate. She would comply with his instructions for obvious reasons. And if Carlos judged the American correctly, Hunter would comply to protect the girl.

"Wha—" The American's head jerked in his sleep. He was mumbling. "What?"

Carlos stepped to the base of the bed. He considered waking the man with a bullet through the shoulder. But they still had to descend to the basement and walk to the car. He could risk neither the mess nor the time of a bleeding shoulder.

"Say them?" Hunter mumbled. "Say them . . . 179.47 degrees for two hours . . . the fifth gene and the ninety-third gene, cut and spliced. The back door as well."

What was the idiot mumbling?

". . . Now forget . . ."

An interesting sight, this American jerking about, mumbling in his sleep. His dreams. Fifth gene, ninety-third gene, cut and spliced. You'll need the back door. Meaningless. Carlos stored the information out of habit.

He lifted the gun and trained it on the American's chest. One shot and the man would be dead. Truly tempting. But they needed him alive if possible. It reminded him of the time he'd assassinated another American. The owner of a pharmaceutical company whom Svensson wanted out of the way.

Carlos let the moment linger.

Michal flew below the treetops and glanced back wordlessly from time to time. Thomas plunged ahead, mind numb. Something very significant had just happened. He'd snuck away from the village. He'd met with Teeleh, a thought that sent a chill down his spine every time he saw the creature in his mind's eye. He'd actually agreed to betray—

No, not betray. He could never do that.

But he had!

And he'd seen a redhead named Bill, who was his copilot, barely alive. The horror of it all seeped into his mind, an indelible ink. He felt like a child stumbling through the streets of Manila.

Thomas finally settled into a dumb hopelessness and lost himself in the drumming of his feet.

When they finally broke over the crest of the valley, Michal didn't turn down toward the lighted village as Thomas expected. Instead, he turned up the valley where the wide road disappeared over the hill. Thomas came to a panting halt and leaned over, hands on his knees, gulping the night air. The Roush flew on for a hundred yards before noticing Thomas had stopped. With a flurry of wings he turned and glided back down the hill.

"Would it be better if we walked now?" he asked.

Thomas motioned toward the village. "Are we going?"

"Tonight you will meet Elyon," Michal answered.

"Elyon?" Thomas stood up, alarmed.

The Roush turned and began walking toward the path.

"Michal! Please. Please, I have to know something."

"Oh, you will, Thomas. You will."

"Bill. You saw him? The Shataiki said he was my copilot. We crash-landed . . ."

Michal turned back and studied him. "This is what the deceiver told you?"

"Yes. And I saw him, Michal. *You* saw him!"

"I will tell you what I saw, and you must never forget it. Do you understand me? Never!"

"Of course!" Emotion swelled in Thomas's chest. He placed his palms on his temples, desperate for clarity. "Please, just tell me something that makes sense."

"I saw nothing but lies. Teeleh is a deceiver. He will tell you anything to lure you into his trap. Anything! Knowing full well that you would quickly doubt what he told you, he showed you this redhead you call Bill."

"But if Bill is real—"

"Bill isn't real! What you saw was a figment of your imagination! A creation of that monster! From the beginning he was planted to deceive you."

"But . . . Bill warned me! He ran out of the forest and yelled at me!"

"What better way for Teeleh to convince you that he was real? He knew that you would likely break your agreement with him to betray the others." Michal shuddered with the last word. "But now that he has pulled this stunt and you're tempted to think Bill, whatever he really is, is friendly, you are more likely to return. It will haunt you until you finally return."

The Roush stared at him with eyes that made Thomas want to cry.

"Never!" he said. "I would never return if that's true!"

Michal didn't reply right away. He turned and waddled down the hill. "Even now you doubt," he said.

Thomas let Michal walk on, suddenly sure that the Roush was both right and wrong. Right about the Shataiki's deception, wrong about him going back. How could he? He wasn't from the histories; he wasn't from some distant planet called Earth. He was from here, and here was Earth.

Unless Teeleh was right.

He followed the Roush at a respectable distance. They walked over the hill and into a second valley. Here a new landscape unfolded before his eyes. The gentle roll of the hills gave way to steep grades covered with trees much taller than those behind them.

Thomas gazed at the landscape in wonder. The steep grades became cliffs and the trees grew massive, so the light they shed brightened the canyon to near daylight. Every branch seemed to carry fruit. It must have been from this forest that the huge columns of the Thrall had been harvested. Flawless pillars that shone in hues of ruby and sapphire and emerald and gold, lighting the path with an aura that Thomas could almost feel.

This was his home. He'd lost his memory, but this incredible place was his home. He quickened his pace slightly.

Red and blue flowers with large petals covered a thick carpet of emerald grass. The cliffs looked as though they were cut from a single large, white pearl, which reflected light from the trees so that the entire valley glowed in the hues of the rainbow. Thomas could hear the rushing of a river that occasionally wound its way close enough to the path that he could see the green, luminescent water as it rushed by.

Home. This was home, and Thomas could hardly stand the fact that he'd ever doubted it. Rachelle should be here with him, walking up this very path.

They had walked no more than ten minutes when Thomas first heard the distant thunder. At first he thought it must be the sound of the river. No, more than a river.

A tingle ran over his skin. The thunder grew. He picked up his pace again. Michal also moved faster, hopping along the ground and extending his wings to maintain balance. Whatever was drawing Thomas also drew him.

The foliage to his left suddenly rustled and Thomas stopped. A white beast the size of a small horse but resembling a lion sauntered into the path, eying him curiously. Thomas took a step back. But the lion walked on, purring loudly. Thomas ran to catch Michal, who hadn't stopped.

He saw other creatures now. Many looked like the first, others like horses. Thomas watched a large white eagle land on a lion's back and fix its eyes on him as he stumbled down the path.

The thunder grew, a rumble low and deep and powerful enough to send a faint tremor through the ground. Michal had left his hopping and skipping and had taken back to the air.

Thomas sprinted after the Roush. Vibrations rose through the earth. He ran around a sweeping bend in the road, heart pounding.

And then the path ended. Abruptly.

Thomas slid to a halt.

Before him sprawled a great circular lake, glowing fluorescent with the same emerald water that contained the black forest. The lake was lined with huge, evenly spaced, gleaming trees, set back forty paces from a white sandy shore. Animals circled the lake, sleeping or drinking.

On the far side, a towering pearl cliff shimmered with ruby and topaz hues. Over the cliff poured a huge waterfall, which throbbed with green and golden light and thundered into the water a hundred meters below. The rising mist captured light from the trees, giving the appearance that colors arose out of the lake itself. Here, there could hardly be a difference between day and night. To his right, the river he had seen along the path flowed from the lake. Michal had descended to the lake's shore and lapped thirstily at the water's edge.

All of this Thomas registered before his first blink.

He took a few tentative steps down the shore, then stopped, feet planted in the sand. He wanted to run to the water's edge and drink as Michal drank, but he suddenly wasn't sure he could move.

Below, Michal continued drinking.

A chill descended Thomas's spine, from the nape of his neck to the soles of his feet. An inexplicable fear smothered him. Sweat seeped from his pores despite a cool wind blowing across the lake.

Something was wrong. All wrong. He stepped back, mind grasping for a thread of reason. Instead, the fear gave way to terror. He spun and ran up the bank.

The moment he crested the bank, the fear fell from him like loosed shackles. He turned back. Michal drank. Insatiably.

In that moment, Thomas knew he *had* to drink the water.

There on the beach, his feet spread and planted firmly in the soft white sand, his hands clenched at his sides, Thomas's mind snapped.

He was vaguely aware of the low groan that broke from his lips, barely audible above the falling water. The animals loitered. Michal drank deeply below him. The trees stood stately. The waterfall gushed. The scene was frozen in time, with Thomas mistakenly trapped in its folds.

The waterfall suddenly seemed to crash a little harder, and a large surge of spray rose from the lake. Mist drifted toward him. He could see it coming. It billowed over the shore. It hit him in the face, no more than a faint sprinkling of moisture, but it could have been the shock wave of a small nuclear weapon.

Thomas gasped. His hands fell to the sand. Eyes wide. The terror was gone.

Only the desire remained. Raw, desperate desire, pulling at his aching heart with the power of absolute vacuum.

No one watching could have been prepared for what he did next. In that moment, knowing what he must do—what he wanted most desperately—Thomas tore his feet from the sand and sprinted for the water's edge. He didn't stop at the shore and stoop to drink as the others did.

Instead, he dived headlong over the bent posture of Michal and into the glowing waters. Screaming all the way.

The instant Thomas hit the water, his body shook violently. A blue strobe exploded in his eyes, and he knew that he was going to die. That he had entered a forbidden pool, pulled by the wrong desire, and now he would pay with his life.

The warm water engulfed him. Flutters rippled through his body and erupted into a boiling heat that knocked the wind from his lungs. The shock alone might kill him.

But he didn't die. In fact, it was pleasure that racked his body, not death. Pleasure! The sensations coursed through his bones in great, unrelenting waves.

Elyon.

How he was certain he did not know. But he knew. Elyon was in this lake with him.

Thomas opened his eyes and found they did not sting. Gold light drifted by. No part of the water seemed darker than another. He lost all sense of direction. Which way was up?

The water pressed in on every inch of his body, as intense as any acid, but one that burned with pleasure instead of pain. His violent shaking gave way to a gentle trembling as he sank into the water. He opened his mouth and laughed. He wanted more, much more. He wanted to suck the water in and drink it.

Without thinking, he did that. He took a great gulp and then inhaled unintentionally. The liquid hit his lungs.

Thomas pulled up, panicked. Tried to clear his lungs, hacking. Instead, he inhaled more of the water. He flailed and clawed in a direction he thought might be the surface. Was he drowning?

No. He didn't feel short of breath.

He carefully sucked more water and breathed it out slowly. Then again, deep and hard. Out with a soft whoosh.

He was breathing the water! In great heaves he was breathing the lake's intoxicating water.

Thomas shrieked with laughter. He tumbled through the water, pulling his legs in close so he would roll, and then stretching them out so he thrust forward, farther into the colors surrounding him. He swam into the lake, deeper and deeper, twisting and rolling as he plummeted toward the bottom. The power contained in this lake was far greater than anything he'd ever imagined. He could hardly contain himself.

In fact, he could not contain himself; he cried out with pleasure and swam deeper.

Then he heard them. Three words.

I made this.

Thomas pulled himself up, frozen. No, not words. Music that spoke. Pure notes piercing his heart and mind with as much meaning as an entire book. He whipped his body around, searching for its source.

A giggle rippled through the water. Like a child now.

Thomas grinned stupidly and spun around. "Elyon?" His voice was muffled, hardly a voice at all.

I made this.

The words reached into Thomas's bones, and he began to tremble again. He wasn't sure if it was an actual voice, or whether he was somehow imagining it.

"What are you? Where are you?" Light floated by. Waves of pleasure continued to sweep through him. "Who are you?"

I am Elyon.
And I made you.

The words started in his mind and burned through his body like a spreading fire.

Do you like it?

Yes! Thomas said. He might have spoken, he might have shouted, he didn't know. He only knew that his whole body screamed it.

Thomas looked around. "Elyon?"

The voice was different now. Spoken. The music was gone. A simple, innocent question.

Do you doubt me?

In that single moment, the full weight of his terrible foolishness crashed in on him like a sledgehammer. How could he have doubted this?

Thomas curled into a fetal position within the bowels of the lake and began to moan.

I see you, Thomas.
I made you.
I love you.

The words washed over him, reaching into the deepest marrow of his bones, caressing each hidden synapse, flowing through every vein, as though he had been given a transfusion.

So then, why do you doubt?

It was the Thomas from his dreams—from his subconscious—that filled his mind now. He had more than just doubted. That was him, wasn't it?

"I'm sorry. I'm so sorry." He thought he might die after all. "I'm sorry. I am so sorry," he moaned. "Please . . ."

Sorry? Why are you sorry?

"For everything. For . . . doubting. For ignoring . . ." Thomas stopped, not sure exactly how else he had offended, only knowing that he had.

For not loving?
I love you, Thomas.

The words filled the entire lake, as though the water itself had become these words. Thomas sobbed uncontrollably.

The water around his feet suddenly began to boil, and he felt the lake suck him deeper into itself. He gasped, pulled by a powerful current. And then he was flipped over and pushed headfirst by the same current. He opened his eyes, resigned to whatever awaited him.

A dark tunnel opened directly ahead of him, like the eye of a whirlpool. He rushed into it and the light fell away.

Pain hit him like a battering ram, and he gasped for breath. He instinctively arched his back in blind panic and reached back toward the entrance of the tunnel, straining to see it, but it had closed.

He began to scream, flailing in the water, rushing deeper into the dark tunnel. Pain raged through his entire body. He felt as if his flesh had been neatly filleted and packed with salt; each organ stuffed with burning coals; his bones drilled open and filled with molten lead.

For the first time in his life, Thomas wanted desperately to die.

Then he saw the images streaming by, and he recognized where he must be. Images from the Crossing, from his dreams, strung out here for him to see.

Images of him spitting in his father's face. His father the chaplain.

"Let me die!" he heard himself shrieking. *"Let me diiiieeee!"*

The water forced his eyes open and new images filled his mind. His mother, crying. The images came faster now. Pictures of his life. A dark, terrible nature. A red-faced man was spitting obscenities with a long tongue that kept flashing from his gaping mouth like a snake's. Each time the tongue touched another person, they crumpled to the floor in a pile of bones. It was his face he saw. Memories of lives dead and gone, but here now and dying still.

And he knew then that he had entered his own soul.

Thomas's back arched so that his head neared his heels. His spine stressed to the snapping point. He couldn't stop screaming.

The tunnel suddenly gaped below and spewed him out into soupy red water. Blood red. He sucked at the red water, filling his spent lungs.

From deep in the pit of the lake a moan began to fill his ears, replacing his own screams. Thomas spun about, searching for the sound, but he found only thick red blood. The moan gained volume and grew to a wail and then a scream.

Elyon was screaming! In pain.

Thomas pressed his hands to his ears and began to scream with the other, thinking now that this was worse than the dark tunnel. His body crawled with fire, as though every last cell revolted at the sound. *And so they should*, a voice whispered in his skull. *Their Maker is screaming in pain!*

Then he was through. Out of the red, into the green of the lake, hands still pressed firmly against his ears. Thomas heard the words as if they came from within his own mind.

I love you, Thomas.

Immediately the pain was gone. Thomas pulled his hands from his head and straightened out slightly in the water. He floated, too stunned to respond. Then the lake was filled with a song. A song more wonderful than any song could possibly sound, a hundred thousand melodies woven into one.

I love you.
I choose you.
I rescue you.
I cherish you.

"I love you too!" Thomas cried desperately. "I choose you; I cherish you." He was sobbing, but with love. The feeling was more intense than the pain that had racked him.

The current suddenly pulled at him again, tugging him up through the colors. His body again trembled with pleasure, and he hung limp as he sped through the water. He wanted to speak, to scream and to yell and to tell the whole world that he was the luckiest man in the universe. That he was loved by Elyon, Elyon himself, with his own voice, in a lake made by him.

But the words would not come.

How long he swam through the currents of the lake, he could never know. He dived into blue hues and found a deep pool of peace that numbed his body like Novocain. With the twist of his wrist, he altered his course into a gold stream and trembled with waves of absolute confidence that come only with great power and wealth. Then a turn of his head and he rushed into red water bubbling with pleasure so great he felt himself go limp once again. Elyon laughed. And Thomas laughed and dived deeper, twisting and turning.

When Elyon spoke again, his voice was gentle and deep, like a purring lion.

Never leave me, Thomas.
Tell me that you'll never leave me.

"Never! Never, never, never! I will always stay with you."

Another current caught him from behind and pushed him through the water. He laughed as he rushed through the water for what seemed a very long time before breaking the surface not ten meters from the shore.

He stood on the sandy bottom and retched a quart of water from his lungs in front of a startled Michal. He coughed twice and waded from the water. "Boy, oh boy." He couldn't think of words that would describe the experience. "Wow!"

"Elyon," Michal said, his short snout split with a gaping grin. "Well, well. It *was* a bit unorthodox, diving in like that."

"How long was I under?"

Michal shrugged. "A minute. No more."

Thomas slopped onto the shore and dropped to his knees. "Incredible."

"Do you remember?"

He looked back at the waterfall. Did he remember?

"Remember what?"

"What village you come from. Who you are," Michal said.

Did he?

"No," Thomas said. "I remember everything since falling in the black forest. And I remember my dreams."

Where he was sleeping, he thought. Waiting to awake. But he knew that he wouldn't wake there until he fell asleep here. It could be two days here and one second there. That's the way it worked.

Assuming he ever dreamed again. He certainly didn't want to. The lake had revived him completely. He felt like he'd slept a week.

He dropped to his back and lay on the sandy beach, gazing up at the moon.

21

MONIQUE BLINKED. Her head throbbed. She was lying on her side. Her vision was blurred. Her cheek was pressed into the carpet. She could see under the bed ten feet away. She'd fallen asleep?

Then she remembered. Her pulse spiked. Someone had broken in while Thomas was sleeping! He'd come in like a whirlwind and smashed her head before she could do anything. Something else had happened, but she couldn't remember what. Her throat was sore; her head felt like a balloon.

But she was alive, and she was still in the room.

She had to wake Thomas!

Monique was about to lift her head when she saw the shoes under the end of the bed. They were connected to pants. Someone was standing at the end of the bed.

She caught her breath and froze. He was still here! Thomas's breathing sounded ragged. He was hurt? Or sleeping.

Monique closed her eyes and tried to think. The strips of bedsheet still bound her arms and feet. But her mouth. He'd taken the gag off. Why? Was this her rescuer? Had the police come to take her away? If so, then why had the man knocked her unconscious?

No, it couldn't be anyone who had her safety in mind. For all she knew, he was crossing the room at this very minute, knife in hand, intending to finish the job.

She opened her eyes wide. The shoes hadn't moved. She rolled her eyes upward as far as she could, desperate for a glimpse of her attacker.

Black shirt. There was a long scar on his cheek. His arm was extended. He had a gun in his hand. The gun was pointed at Thomas.

Monique panicked. She jerked up as hard as she could and screamed. "Thomas!"

The man spun to her, pistol leveled, eyes wide. Thomas bolted upright on the bed, like a puppet on strings. The man dropped to one knee and whipped the gun back toward Thomas.

"Don't move!"

But it was too late. Thomas was already moving.

He threw himself to his left. The gun spit. A pillow spewed feathers. Monique saw the American fall from the bed, hit the floor on the other side. He moved with lightning speed, as if he'd bounced off the carpet.

Then he was in the air, flying for the black-clad intruder.

Phewt! The gun spit again, ripping a hole in the headboard. Thomas entered a scissors kick, like a soccer player lining up for a goal. His foot connected with the man's hand.

Crack!

The gun flew across the room and slammed into the wall above Monique's head. It fell to the floor at her side.

She was powerless to get it. But she swung her legs to cover it.

Thomas had rolled up onto the bed after his kick and now stood by the ruptured pillow, facing the attacker in a familiar ready stance.

The man glanced at her, then at Thomas. A smile twisted his lips. "Very good. I did underestimate you after all," he said. Mediterranean accent. Schooled. Not a thug. Monique pushed herself up, ignoring a splitting pain in her head.

"Who are you?" Thomas demanded. His eyes were wide, but otherwise he was surprisingly calm. "I don't want to hurt anyone."

"No? Then perhaps I did underestimate you."

"You're the one who wants the vaccine," Thomas said.

The man's left eye narrowed barely. Enough for Monique to know that Thomas had struck a chord.

"How did you know?" Thomas asked.

"I have no interest in a vaccine." The man's eyes darted to a jacket lying by the door. Thomas saw it as well.

"I tipped you off, didn't I?" Thomas demanded. "If I hadn't said anything to anybody, you wouldn't be here. Isn't that right?"

The man shrugged. "I only do what I'm hired to do. I have no idea what you're talking about." He eased toward the front door. Brushed his hands against each other and raised them in a show of surrender. "In this case, I was hired to return the girl to her father, and I must tell you that I fully intend to do that. I have no interest in you."

Thomas shook his head. "No, I don't believe you. Monique, 375,200 base pairs. HIV vaccine. Am I right?"

She stared at him. They hadn't published that information yet. How could—

"Am I right?" he demanded.

"Yes."

"Then listen to me." Thomas looked at her, then at the attacker. Tears filled his eyes. He looked desperate. "I don't know what's happening to me. I don't want to hurt anyone. I really don't, you hear me? But we have to stop this man. I mean, no matter what happens, we have to stop him. They're real, Monique. My dreams are real. You have to believe me!"

The man had taken another step toward the door. She answered to calm Thomas more than to agree with him. "Yes, okay. I do. Watch him, Thomas! He's going for the jacket."

"Leave the jacket," Thomas said.

The man arched an eyebrow. He seemed to be enjoying himself.

"This is absurd," he said. "You think you can actually stop me from doing what I want? You're unarmed." He casually reached into his pocket and pulled out a switchblade. The blade snapped open. "I am not. And even if I were, you would have no chance against me."

"You promise?"

"You want me to—"

"Not you! Her. You believe me, Monique? I need you to believe me."

His conviction made her hesitate.

"This could end badly, Monique. I really, really need you to understand what's happening here."

"I believe you," she said.

The man suddenly lunged for his jacket.

Monique had never seen anyone move as fast as Thomas did then. He didn't jump; he didn't step. He shot, like a bullet. Straight at the floor between the bed and the front door where the jacket lay folded.

He rolled once, sprang to his feet, and hit the black-clad man broadside with the heels of both hands.

———⊗———

Carlos had killed many men with his bare hands. He'd never, in a dozen years of the finest training, seen a man move as fast as the American. If he could get to the transmitter in the jacket, there would be no fight. He was now certain Thomas Hunter would capitulate when faced with the prospect of the French woman's terrible death.

He saw Hunter hit the floor and roll, and he knew precisely what the man intended to do. He even knew that what the man had gained by putting gravity to work in his favor might mean Hunter would reach him before he could reach the jacket. But he had to make a decision, and, all things considered, he decided to finish his attempt for the jacket. It was the only way to avoid a fight that would undoubtedly end in Thomas Hunter's death.

The fact was, he wanted Hunter alive. They needed to learn what else he knew.

The man reached him too quickly. Carlos shifted to accept Hunter's blow. The American hit him on his left arm, hard. But not hard enough to knock him from his feet.

Carlos whipped the knife in his right hand across his body. The blade sliced into flesh. The American dropped to his belly. Rolled over the jacket and came up ready. Blood seeped from cuts in both his forearms.

He flung the jacket across the room. Unfazed. He bounced on the balls of his feet twice and threw himself at the wall adjacent Carlos, feetfirst.

This time he knew the man's trajectory before he could line up his kick. He was going for the knife.

Carlos sidestepped, blocked the man's heel as it came around, and stabbed up with the knife. The blade sank into flesh.

Hunter grunted and twisted his legs against the blade, forcing it out of Carlos's hand. He landed on both feet, blade firmly planted in his right calf. He snatched it out and faced Carlos, blade ready.

The reversal was completely unexpected. Enraging. Enough—he was running out of time.

Carlos feigned to his left, ducked low, and jerked back. As expected, the move drew a quick stab with the knife. Still on his heels, he dropped back to one hand and swung his right foot up with his full strength. His shoe caught Hunter in the wrist. Broke it with a sharp crack. The knife flew across the room.

He followed his right foot with his left to the American's solar plexus.

Hunter staggered back, winded.

The phone rang.

Carlos had taken far too long. His first concern had to be the girl. She was the key to the vaccine. Another ring. The blonde? Or the front desk. Taking the American was no longer an option.

He had to finish this now.

<hr />

Nausea swept through Thomas's gut. The phone was ringing, and it occurred to him that it might be Kara. The ringing seemed to unnerve his attacker slightly, but he wasn't sure it mattered any longer. The man with the face scar was going to take Monique.

Both of Thomas's arms were bleeding. His wrist was broken, and his right leg was going numb. The man had disarmed him without breaking a sweat. Panic began to set in.

The man suddenly broke to his left, bounded for Monique. She swung both feet at him in a valiant effort to ward him off.

"Get away from me, you—"

He swatted her feet to one side and scooped up the gun. He turned casually and pointed the weapon at Thomas.

Thomas's options were gone. It was now simply a matter of survival. He straightened. "You win."

The gun dipped and bucked in the man's hand. A bullet plowed through Thomas's thigh. He staggered back, numbed.

"I always win," the man said.

"Thomas!" Monique stared in horror. "Thomas!"

"Lie on the bed," the man ordered.

"Don't hurt her."

"Shut up and lie on the bed."

Thomas limped forward. His mind was fading already. He wanted to say something, but nothing was coming. Surprisingly, he didn't care what the man did to him now. But there was Kara, and there was Monique, and there was his mother, and they were all going to die.

And there was his father. He wanted to talk to his father.

He heard himself whimper as he fell onto the bed.

Phewt! A bullet tugged at his gut.

Phewt! A second punched into his chest.

The room faded.

Black.

⎯⎯⎯❧⎯⎯⎯

Deputy Secretary of State Merton Gains ducked out from under the umbrella and slid into the Lincoln. He'd grown used to the showers since moving to Washington from Arizona. Found them refreshing, actually.

"Boy, it's really coming down," he said.

George Maloney nodded behind the wheel. "Yes it is, sir." The Irishman didn't show a hint of emotion. Never did. Gains had given up trying. He was paid to drive and paid to protect.

"Take me to the airport, George. Take me to drier parts of Earth."

"Yes sir."

Miranda had insisted on living in their Tucson home for at least the winters, but after two years, the Washington life wore thin, and she found excuses to return home even in the warmer months. Truth be told, Merton would do the same, given a choice. They were both bred in the desert, for the desert. End of story.

Rain splashed unrelentingly on the windows. Traffic was nearly stalled.

"You'll be back on Thursday, sir?"

Gains sighed. "Tucson today, California tomorrow, back on Thursday; that's right."

His cell phone vibrated in his breast pocket.

"Very well, sir. Maybe this rain will be gone by then."

Gains withdrew the phone. "I like the rain, George. Keeps things clean. Something we can always use around here, right?"

No smile. "Yes sir."

He answered the phone. "Gains here."

"Yes, Mr. Gains, I have a Bob Macklroy on the phone for you. He says it could be important."

"Put him on, Venice."

"Here you go."

At times Washington seemed like a college reunion to Gains. Amazing how many jobs had ended up in the hands of Princeton graduates since Blair had been elected president. All qualified people, of course; he couldn't complain. He'd done his own share of upping the Princeton quotient, mostly through recommendations. Bob here, for example, was not exactly a Washington insider, but he was working as the assistant secretary in the Bureau for International Narcotics and Law Enforcement Affairs office in part because he had played basketball with now Deputy Secretary of State Merton Gains.

"Hello, Bob."

"Hi, Merton. Thanks for taking the call."

"Anytime, man. Tim treating you good down there?"

Bob didn't bother answering the question directly. "He's in Saõ Paulo for a few days. We're not sure if you're exactly the right person. This is a bit unusual, and we're not quite sure where to take this. Tim thought the FBI might be—"

"Try me, Bob. What do you have?"

"Well . . ." Bob hesitated.

"Just tell me. And speak up a bit, it's raining hard. Sounds like a train in here."

"Okay, but it's all very strange. I'm just telling you what I know. It seemed appropriate with your involvement in the Gains Act."

Gains sat up a bit. This evasiveness wasn't like Bob. Something was up, not only in his voice but in this mention of the narrowly defeated bill Merton had introduced two years earlier when he was a senator. It was up again, with some alterations and his name still attached. The bill would impose strict restrictions on the flood of new vaccines hitting the market by demanding they pass a comprehensive battery of tests. Two years had passed since his youngest daughter, Corina, had died of autoimmune disease after mistakenly being administered a new AIDS vaccine. The FDA had approved the vaccine. Gains had successfully had it barred, but other vaccines were entering the market every month, and the casualties were mounting.

"If you don't spit it out, I'm going to send some muscle over there to force it out of you," he said. It was something he could say only to a man like Bob, the locker room cutup who'd once owned the best three-point shot in college ball. They all knew Merton Gains would go out of his way to step over an ant if it wandered onto the sidewalk.

"I'll remember to keep my door locked," Bob said. He sighed. "I got a strange call a couple of days ago from a man who called himself Thomas Hunter. He—"

"The same Thomas Hunter from the situation in Bangkok?" Gains asked. The incident had fallen in his lap earlier today. An American citizen identified as Thomas Hunter from flight records had kidnapped Monique de Raison and another unidentified woman in the lobby of the Sheraton. The French were up in arms, the Thais were demanding intervention, even the stock market had reacted. Raison Pharmaceutical wasn't exactly unknown. The timing couldn't have been worse—they'd just announced their new vaccine.

In Gains's mind, the timing was about right.

"Yes, I think it could be," Bob said.

"He called you? When?"

"A few days ago. From Denver. He said that the Raison Vaccine would mutate into a deadly virus and wipe out half the world's population. Nutcase stuff."

Not necessarily. "Okay, so we have a nut case who's managed to wing his way over to Thailand and kidnap the daughter of Jacques de Raison. That much the world already knows. He say anything else?"

"Actually, yes. I didn't think about it until I saw his name today on the wires. Like you said: a nut case, right?"

"Right."

"Well, he told me that the winner of the Kentucky Derby was Joy Flyer."

"So? Wasn't the Derby three days ago?"

"Yes. But he called me before the race. He got the information from his dreams, the same place he learned that the Raison Vaccine—"

"He actually told you the name of the winner before the race?"

"That's what I'm saying. Crazy, I know."

Gains looked out the side window. Couldn't see a thing past the streams of water sliding down the glass. He'd heard of some crazy things in his time, but this was shaping up for prime bar talk.

"Did you place a bet?"

"Unfortunately, I put the call out of my mind until today, when I saw his name again. But I did some checking. His sister, Kara Hunter, won over $300,000 on the race. They were in Atlanta where they made a bit of a scene at the CDC."

Something definitely wasn't right here. "So we have two nut cases. I haven't seen her profile."

"She's a nurse. Graduated with honors. Sharp gal, from what I can see. Not your typical nut case."

"Don't tell me you're actually thinking this kid knows something."

"I'm just saying he said he knew about Joy Flyer, and he did. And he says he knows something about this Raison Vaccine. That's all I'm saying."

"Okay, Bob. Suffice it to say that Thomas Hunter is thoroughly deluded—the street corners of America are filled with similar types, usually of the variety who carry signs and rant loudly about the end of the world. This is good. At least we have motivation. You're right, though, this needs to get to the CIA and the FBI. Have you written it up?"

"In my hand."

"Then get it out. The profilers will have a heyday with this. Fax me a copy, will you?"

"Will do."

"And do me a favor. If he calls again, ask him who's winning the NBA championship."

That got a chuckle.

Gains folded his phone and crossed his legs. And what if Thomas Hunter did know something other than who would win the Kentucky Derby? Impossible, of course, but then so was knowing who would win the Kentucky Derby.

Hunter had flown out of Atlanta. The headquarters for the CDC were in Atlanta. That would make sense. Hunter thinks a virus is about to ravage the world, he goes to the CDC, and when they grin at his preposterous claims, he goes straight to the source of the so-called virus.

Bangkok.

Interesting. A true-blue nut case. Certifiable.

Then again, how often did lunacy win you $300,000 at the horse track?

22

"THOMAS."

A sweet voice. Calling his name. Like honey. Thomas.

"Thomas, wake up."

A woman's voice. Her hand was on his cheek. He was waking, but he wasn't sure if he was really awake yet. The hand on his cheek could be part of a dream. For a moment, he let it be a dream.

He relished that dream. This was Monique's hand on his cheek. The strong-headed French woman who'd been horrified that he might actually die. *Thomas!* she'd cried. *Thomas!*

No, no. This wasn't Monique. This was Rachelle. Yes, that was better. Rachelle was kneeling beside him, caressing his cheek with her hand. Leaning over him, whispering his name. *Thomas.* Her lips were reaching out to touch his lips. Time to wake the handsome prince.

"Thomas?"

He jerked his eyes open. Blue sky. Waterfall. Rachelle.

He gasped and sat up. He was still on the beach where he'd fallen asleep during the night. He glanced around. No animals were in sight. No Roush. Only Rachelle.

"Do you remember?" she asked.

He did remember. The lake. Diving deep. Ecstasy. It still lingered here on the sound of the waterfall.

"Yes. I'm beginning to remember," he said. "What time is it?"

"Midday. The others are preparing."

He also remembered the Crossing and Teeleh's claim that he'd crash-landed. "They're preparing for what?"

"For the Gathering tonight." She said it as though he should know this.

"Of course." He looked at the lucent waters that stretched across the lake, tempted to swim again. Could he just dive in anytime he wanted to? He pushed himself to his knees. "Actually, I don't remember everything just yet."

"What don't you remember?"

"Well . . . I don't know. If I knew, I would remember. But I think I understand the Great Romance. It's about Elyon."

Her eyes lit up. "Yes."

"It's about choosing and rescuing and winning love because that's what Elyon does."

"Yes!" she cried.

"And it's something we do because we are like Elyon in that way."

"You're saying that you want to choose me?"

"I am?"

She arched a brow. "And now you're trying to be tricky about it by pretending that you're not. But really you're desperate for my love, and you want me to be desperate for your love."

He knew that she was exactly right. It was the first time he could admit it to himself, but hearing her say it, Thomas knew that he was falling in love with this woman who knelt by him on the banks of the lake. He was meant to woo her, but she was wooing him.

She was waiting for him to say something.

"Yes," he said.

Rachelle jumped to her feet. "Come!"

He pushed himself up and brushed the sand from his seat. "What should we do?"

"We should walk through the forest," she said with a mischievous glint in her eyes. "I will help you remember."

"Remember the forest?"

They started up the slope. "I was thinking other thoughts. But that would be nice too."

She turned back and stopped. "What is that?"

He followed her eyes and saw it clearly. A large blotch of red discolored the white sand where he'd slept.

Blood.

He blinked. His dream? The fight in the hotel flashed through his mind.

No, it couldn't be. It was only a dream. He *had* no wounds.

"I don't know," he said. "I swam through some red waters in the lake, maybe from that?"

"You never know what will happen with Elyon," she said. "Only that it will be wonderful. Come."

They left the lake. But the red stain on the sand lingered in Thomas's mind. There was the possibility, however remote, that he was different from Rachelle. That he really wasn't from here. That Rachelle was falling in love with someone who wasn't what he seemed.

That Teeleh was right.

An hour later the thought was gone.

They walked and laughed, and Rachelle toyed with his mind in lovely ways that only strengthened his resolve to win her. Very slowly they began to set aside the charade and embrace something deeper.

She showed him three new combat moves Tanis had shown her, two aerial and one from a prone position, in the event one fell while fighting, she said. He managed them all, but never with the same precision she demonstrated. Once she had to catch him when he toppled off balance toward her.

She had rescued him. He found it immensely appealing.

He immediately returned the favor by fighting off a hundred phantom Shataiki, sweeping her from her feet in the process. Unlike Tanis and Palus, he did not fall. It was quite a feat, and he began to feel very good about himself.

Rachelle sauntered beside him, hands clasped behind her back, lost in thought.

"Tell me more about your dreams," she said without looking at him.

"They're nothing. Nonsense."

"Oh? That's not what Tanis thinks. I want to know more. How real are they?"

Tanis was talking about his dreams? The last thing on Earth Thomas wanted to do right now was discuss his dreams. Particularly with Rachelle. But he couldn't very well lie to her. "They seem real enough. But they're the histories. A totally different reality."

"Yes, so you've said. So it's like you're really living in the histories?"

"When I'm dreaming? Yes."

"And what do you think of this place"—she motioned to the trees—"in your dreams?"

It was the worst question she could have asked. "Actually, when I'm dreaming it's like I'm there, not here."

"But when you're there, do you remember this place?"

"Sure. It's . . . it's like a dream."

She nodded. "So I'm like a dream?"

"You're not a dream." Thomas could feel himself sinking. "You're walking right beside me, and I have chosen you."

"I'm not sure I like these dreams of yours."

"And neither do I."

"You have a mother and a father in these dreams?"

"Yes."

"You have a full life, with memories and passions and all that makes us human?"

This was positively not good.

She stopped on the path when he didn't respond. "What are you doing in your dreams?"

He had to tell her at some point. She'd forced the issue now. "You really want to know?"

"Yes. I want to know everything."

Thomas paced, thinking of the best way to put it so that she could understand. "I'm living in the histories, before the Great Deception, trying to stop the Raison Strain. Trust me, it's a horrible thing, Rachelle. It's so real! Like I'm really there, and all of this here is a dream! I know it's not, of course, but when I'm there, I also know *that* is real." Was this a good way to put it? Somehow he doubted there was a good way to put it.

He continued before she could ask another question. Better that he control the direction of his confession.

"And yes, I have a full history in my dreams. Memories, a family, the full textures of real life."

"That's absurd," she said. "You've created a fantasy world with as much detail as the real one. Even more because in your dreams you haven't lost your memories. You have your own history there, but here you don't. Is that it?"

"Exactly!"

"It's preposterous!"

"I can hardly stand it. It's maddening. Just before you woke me up by the lake, I was fighting a man who was intent on killing me. I think he did kill me! Three shots with a gun to the body." He tapped his chest.

"Really? A gun? Some kind of fanciful weapon, I assume. And why were you fighting this man?"

Thomas spoke without thinking. "He was trying to capture Monique."

"Monique. A woman?"

"A woman who means nothing to me!" No, that wasn't completely honest. "Not in a romantic way."

"You're in love with another woman in your dreams?"

"Of course not. Not at all. Her name is Monique de Raison, and she may be the key to stopping the Raison Strain. I'm helping her because she may help me save the world, not because she's beautiful. I can't just ignore her because you don't want me dreaming about her."

Too much information.

He was sure he saw a flash in Rachelle's eyes. Jealousy obviously was a sentiment that flowed from Elyon's veins. "You talk as if your dreams are more important than reality. Do you doubt that any of this is real?" She swept her hand to indicate the forest again. "That I am real? That our romance is real?"

"Never. Only when I'm dreaming."

He had to stop before he lost her completely.

Rachelle stared at him for a long time. He decided to keep his mouth shut. It was doing him no favors. She crossed her arms and looked away.

"I don't like these dreams of yours, Thomas Hunter. I really wish that you would stop them."

"I'm sure they will stop. I don't like them either."

"You are here. With me. I watched you sleep on the shores of the lake just an hour ago. Believe me when I say you weren't fighting a man, and you weren't killed. Your body was here! If I'd pinched you, you would have woken."

"That's right. And there was no Monique. It's just a dream, I know. I'm here. With you."

Her features softened. "Maybe your dreams are nothing more than a fascinating discovery. But I'm not sure how I feel about your dreaming of another woman when I'm in your arms. Do you understand?"

"Perfectly."

Rachelle didn't seem completely satisfied. "Other than trying to save the world, what do you do in the histories?"

"Well . . . I think I'm a writer. Though not a very good one, I'm afraid."

"A storyteller! You're a storyteller. Maybe that's why you're dreaming. You've hit your head, lost your memory, and forgotten how to tell stories like you did in your own village. But your subconscious hasn't forgotten. You're making up a grand story in your dreams!"

She just could be right. In fact, more likely than not.

"Maybe. What is Tanis saying?"

"That he and you might be successful in mounting an expedition to the black forest using information from your dreams of the histories. I think it's just a storyteller's fantasy, but he's quite excited."

Alarm spread through Thomas's mind. Clearly Michal's warning hadn't affected Tanis.

"He said that?"

"Yes. If I hadn't insisted on coming to the lake alone to find you when

Michal told us you were here, he would have come too. He says that he has some new ideas to share with you."

Thomas made a mental note to avoid the man until he sorted this out.

"I'm glad you came alone," he said.

"So am I."

"And I'll try not to dream."

"Or better, dream of me."

⚬⚬⚬

The gathering that night washed away any fears and doubts lingering in Thomas's mind. They swept up the path to the lake, silent during the last half of the fifteen-minute trek. Thomas ran onto a patch of white sand on the right side of the lake. He absently realized that the red blotch was gone.

As far as memory permitted, this was his first Gathering.

A warm mist from the waterfall already floated across the group. Many of the people were already prone on the sand, their hands outstretched toward the thundering water.

Thomas fell to his knees, heart pounding with anticipation. It had been too long, far too long. A warm mist suddenly hit his face. His vision exploded with a red fireball and he gasped, sucking more of the mist into his lungs.

Elyon.

He was aware of the wetness tickling his tongue. The sweetest taste of sugar laced with a hint of cherry flooded his mouth. He swallowed. The aroma of gardenia blossoms mushroomed in his nostrils.

Ever so gently, Elyon's water engulfed him, careful not to overpower his mind. But deliberately.

The red fireball suddenly melted into a river of deep blue that flowed into the base of Thomas's skull and wound its way down his spine, caressing each nerve. Intense pleasure shot down every nerve path to Thomas's extremi-ties. He dropped to his belly, body shaking in earnest.

Elyon.

The waterfall's pounding increased in intensity, and the mist fell steadily on his back as he lay prostrate. His mind reeled under the power of this Creator, who spoke with sights and colors and smells and emotions.

Then the first note fell on his ears. Flew past his ears and bit into his mind. A low note, lower than the throaty roar of a million tons of fuel thundering from a rocket's base. The rumbling tone shot up an octave, rose to a forte, and began etching a melody in Thomas's skull. He could hear no words, only music. A single melody at first, but then joined by another melody, entirely unique yet in harmony with the first. The first caressed his ears; the second laughed. And a third melody joined the first two, screaming in pleasure. And then a fourth and a fifth, until Thomas heard a hundred melodies streaming through his mind, each one unique, each one distinct.

All together not more than a single note from Elyon.

A note that cried, *I love you.*

Thomas breathed in great gasps now. He stretched his arms out before him. His chest heaved on the warm sand. His skin tingled with each minute droplet of mist that touched him.

Elyon.

Me too! Me too! he wanted to say. *I love you too.*

He wanted to yell it. To scream it with as much passion as he felt from Elyon's water now. He opened his mouth and groaned. A dumb, stupid groan that said nothing at all, and yet it was him, talking to Elyon.

And then he formed the words screaming in his mind. "I love you, Elyon," he breathed softly.

Immediately, a new burst of colors exploded in his mind. Gold and blue and green cascaded over his head, filling each fold of his brain with delight.

He rolled to one side. A hundred melodies swelled into a thousand— like a heavy, woven chord blasting down his spine. His nostrils flared with the pungent smell of lilac and rose and jasmine, and his eyes watered with their intensity. The mist soaked his body, and each inch of his skin buzzed with pleasure.

Thomas shouted, "I love you!"

He felt as though he stood in an open doorway on the edge of a vast expanse, bursting with raw emotion that was fabricated in colors and sights and sounds and smells, blasting into his face like a gale. It was as though Elyon flowed like a bottomless ocean, but Thomas could taste only a stray drop. As though he were a symphony orchestrated by a million instruments, and a single note threw him from his feet with its power.

"I love youuuu!" he cried.

He opened his eyes. Long ribbons of color streamed through the mist above the lake. Light spilled from the waterfall, lighting the entire valley so it looked as though it might be midday. The entire company lay prone as the mist washed over their bodies. Most shook visibly but made no sound that could be heard above the waterfall. Thomas let his head drop back to the sand.

And then Elyon's words echoed through his mind.

I love you.
You are precious to me.
You are my very own.
Look at me again, and smile.

Thomas wanted to scream. Unable to contain himself, Thomas let the words flow from his mouth like a flood.

"I will look at you *always*, Elyon. I worship you. I worship the air you breathe. I worship the ground you walk on. Without you, there is nothing. Without you, I'll die a thousand deaths. Don't ever let me leave you."

The sound of a child giggling. Then the voice again.

I love you, Thomas.
Do you want to climb up the cliff?

Cliff? He saw the pearl cliffs over which the water poured.

A voice called over the lake. "Who has made us?" Tanis was on his feet, crying out this challenge.

Thomas struggled to his feet. The rest were scrambling to their feet. They yelled together above the thundering falls, "Elyon! Elyon is our Creator!"

Like a display of fireworks, the colors continued to expand in his mind. He gazed about, momentarily stunned. None of the others looked his way. Their display was simple abandonment to affection, foolish in any other context, but completely genuine here.

The voice of the child suddenly echoed through his mind again.

Do you want to climb the cliff?

Thomas spun toward the forest that ended at the cliff. Climb the cliff? Behind him the others started running into the lake.

Giggling again.

Do you want to play with me?

Now inexplicably drawn, Thomas ran up the shore toward the cliff. If the others noticed, they showed no sign. Soon only his own panting accompanied the thundering falls.

He cut into the forest and approached the cliffs with a sense of awe. How could he possibly climb this? He considered turning back and joining the others. But he had been called here. To climb the cliffs. To play. He ran on.

He reached its base, looked up. There was no way he could climb the smooth stone wall. But if he could find a tree that grew close to the cliff, and if the tree was tall enough, he might be able to reach the top along its branches. The tree right beside him, for example. Its glowing red trunk reached to the cliff's lip a hundred meters up.

Thomas swung himself up onto the first branch and began his ascent. It took him no more than a couple of minutes to reach the treetop and climb out to the cliff. He dropped from the branch to the stone surface below. To his left he could hear the thundering waterfall as it poured over the edge. He stood up and raised his eyes.

Before him, water lapped gently on a shore not more than twenty paces from the cliff's edge. Another lake. A sea, much larger than the lake. Shimmering green waters stretched to the horizon, neatly bordered by a wide swath of white sand, which edged into a towering blue-and-gold forest topped by a green canopy.

Thomas stepped back and drew a deep breath. The white sandy swath bordering the emerald waters was lined with strange beasts who stood or crouched at the water's edge. The animals were like the white lions below, but these seemed to glow with pastel colors. And they lined the beach in evenly spaced increments that continued as far as he could see.

He spun to the waterfall and saw at least a hundred creatures hovering above the water cascading down the cliff, like giant dragonflies. Thomas eased back toward a rock behind him. Had they seen him? He studied the creatures hovering with translucent wings in a reverent formation. What could they possibly be doing?

So this was Elyon's water. A sea that extended as far as the eye could see. Maybe farther.

"Hello."

Thomas turned around. A little boy stood not five feet from him on the shore. Thomas stumbled back two steps.

"Don't be afraid," the boy said, smiling. "So, you're the one who's lost?"

The small boy stood to Thomas's waist. His brilliant green eyes stared wide and round beneath a crop of very blond hair. His bony shoulders held thin arms that hung loosely at his sides. He wore only a small white loincloth.

Thomas swallowed. "Yes, I suppose so," he said.

"Well, I see you're quite adventurous. I believe you're the first of your kind to walk these cliffs." The boy giggled.

Incredible. For so small and frail a boy, he held himself with the confidence of someone much older. Thomas guessed he must be about ten. Although he certainly didn't talk like a ten-year-old.

"Your name is Thomas?" the boy asked.

He knows my name. Is he from another village? Maybe my own? "Is this okay? I can be up here?"

"Yes. You're perfectly all right. But I don't think any of the others could get past the lake to bother climbing the cliff."

"Are you from another village?" he asked.

The boy stared at him, amused. "Do I look like I'm from another village?"

"I don't know. No, not really. Am I from another village?"

"I suppose that's the question, isn't it?"

"Then do you know who called me?"

"Yes. Elyon called you. To meet me."

There was something about the boy. Something about the way he stood with his feet barely pressing into the white sand. Something about the way his thin fingers curled gently at the end of his arms; about the way his chest rose and fell steadily and the way his wide eyes shone like two flawless emeralds. The boy blinked.

"Are you like a . . . Roush?"

"Am I like a Roush? Well, yes, in a way. But not really." The boy raised an arm to the hovering dragonfly creatures without looking their way. "They are like Roush, but you may think of me however you want now." He turned his head to the line of lionlike creatures lining the sea. "They are known as Roshuim."

Thomas eyed the boy. "You . . . you're greater, aren't you? You have greater knowledge?"

"I know as much as I've seen in my time."

The boy definitely wasn't talking like a small boy. "And how long is that?" Thomas asked.

The child looked at him quizzically for a moment. "How long is what?"

"How long have you lived?"

"A very long time. But far too short to even begin to experience what I will experience in my time."

The boy scratched the top of his head with one hand. He spoke again, staring out to the sea. "What is it like to come to Elyon after ignoring him for so long?"

"You know that? How do you know that?"

The boy's eyes twinkled. "Do you want to walk?"

The boy turned to the white sandy shore and walked casually without looking back. Thomas glanced around and then followed him.

It was as light as day, although Thomas knew it was actually night.

"I saw you looking out over the water. Do you know how great this sea is?" the boy asked.

"It looks pretty big."

"It extends forever," the boy said. "Isn't that something?"

"Forever?"

"That's pretty clever, isn't it?"

"Elyon can do that?"

"Yes."

"Well, that's . . . that's pretty clever."

The boy stopped and walked to the water's edge. Thomas followed him tentatively. "Scoop up some of the water," the child said.

Thomas stooped, gingerly placed his hand into the warm green water and felt its power run up his arm the moment his fingers touched its surface—like a low-voltage electric shock that hummed through his bones. He scooped the water out and watched it drain between his fingers.

"Pretty neat, huh? And there's no end to it. You could travel at many times the speed of light toward the center, and never reach it."

It seemed incredible that anything could extend forever. Space, maybe. But a body of water? "That doesn't seem possible," Thomas said.

"It does when you understand who made it. It came from a single word. Elyon could open his mouth, and a hundred billion worlds like this would roll off his tongue. Maybe you underestimate him."

Thomas looked away, suddenly embarrassed by his own stupidity. Did he underestimate him? How could anyone ever *not* underestimate someone so great?

The child reached up his frail hand and placed it in Thomas's. "Don't feel bad," he said softly.

Thomas wrapped his fingers around the small hand. The boy looked up at him with wide green eyes, and more than anything Thomas had ever wanted to do, he desperately wanted to reach down and hold this child. They began walking again, hand in hand now. "Tell me," Thomas asked. "There's one thing that I've been wondering about."

"Yes?"

"I've been having some dreams. I fell in the black forest and lost my memory, and ever since then I've been dreaming of the histories."

"I know."

"You do?"

"Word gets around."

"But can you tell me why I'm having these dreams? Honestly, I know this sounds ridiculous, but sometimes I wonder if my dreams are really real. Or if *this* is a dream. It would help if I knew for certain which reality was real."

"Maybe I could help with a question. Is the Creator a lamb or a lion?"

"I don't understand."

"Some would say that the Creator is a lamb. Some would say he's a lion. Some would say both. The fact is, he is neither a lamb nor a lion. These are fiction. Metaphors. Yet the Creator is both a lamb and a lion. These are both truths."

"Yes, I can see that. Metaphors."

"Neither changes the Creator," the boy said. "Only the way we think of him. Like me. Am I a boy?"

Thomas felt the boy's small hand, and his heart began to melt because he knew what the boy was saying. He couldn't speak.

"A boy, a lion, a lamb. You should see me fight. You wouldn't see a boy, a lion, *or* a lamb."

Five minutes of silence passed without another word. They only walked, a man and a boy, hand in hand. But it wasn't that. Not at all.

And then Thomas remembered his question about the dreams.

"What about my dreams?"

"Maybe it's the same with your dreams."

"That both are real?"

"You'll have to figure that out."

They walked on. It might have been a cloud, not sand, that they walked on, and Thomas wasn't sure he'd know the difference. His mind was reeling. His hand was by his side, moving as he walked. In it was this boy's hand. A tremble had set into his fingers, but the boy didn't show he noticed.

Clearly he did.

"What about the black forest?" Thomas asked. "I've been in it. I may have taken a drink of the water. Is that why I'm dreaming about the histories?"

"If you'd chosen Teeleh's water, everyone would know."

Yes, that made sense.

"Then maybe you can tell me something else. How is it that Elyon can allow evil to exist in the black forest? Why doesn't he just destroy the Shataiki?"

"Because evil provides his creation with a choice," the child said as though the concept was very simple indeed. "And because without it, there could be no love."

"Love?" Thomas stopped.

The boy's hand slipped out of his. He turned, brow raised.

"Love is dependent on evil?" Thomas asked.

"Did I say that?" A mischievous glint filled the boy's eyes. "How can there be love without a true choice? Would you suggest that man be stripped of the capacity to love?"

This was the Great Romance. To love at any cost.

The child turned back to the sea and gazed out.

"Do you know what would happen if anyone did choose Teeleh's water instead of Elyon's water?" the boy asked.

"Michal said the Shataiki would be freed. That they would bring death."

"Death. More than death. A living death. Teeleh would own them; this is the agreement. Their minds and their hearts. The smell of their death would be intolerable to Elyon. And his jealousy will exact a terrible price."

The boy's green eyes flashed as though strobes had been ignited behind them. "The injustice will be against Elyon, and only blood will satisfy him. More blood than you can possibly imagine."

He said it so plainly that Thomas wondered if he'd misspoken. But the boy wasn't the kind who misspoke.

Again, a word popped into his mind. Horde. He didn't know what to do with the thought so he said the word aloud.

"Horde. Does it mean anything to you?"

The boy hesitated. "This is before the time of the Horde. Or after, depending on how you see it. It means nothing to you now."

Thomas felt his curiosity connected to the word vanish. His concern for the people in the colored forest returned.

"If the people become Teeleh's, is there a way to win them back?" he asked.

No response.

"Anyway, I can't imagine anyone ever changing or leaving this place," Thomas said.

"You don't have to leave, you know."

"Except when I dream."

"Then don't dream," the boy said.

The idea suddenly sounded like such a simple solution. If he stopped dreaming, Bangkok would be no more?

"I can do that?"

"You could. There is a fruit you could eat that would stop your dreams."

"Just like that, no more histories?"

"Yes. But the question is, do you really want to? You'll have to decide. The choice is yours. You will always have that choice. I promise."

It was early in the morning when the boy finally led Thomas back to the cliff, and after a great big bear hug, Thomas descended the red tree, made his way back to the village, and quietly sneaked into bed in the house of Palus.

He might have been mistaken, but he was sure that he could hear the sound of a boy's voice singing as he drifted off to sleep.

23

"THOMAS."

A sweet voice. Calling his name. Like honey. *Thomas.*

"Thomas, wake up."

A woman's voice. Her hand was on his cheek. He was waking, but he wasn't sure if he was really awake yet. The hand on his cheek could be part of a dream. For a moment he let it be a dream.

He relished that dream. This was Rachelle's hand on his cheek. The strong-headed woman who kept showing him up with her fighting moves.

"Thomas?"

His eyes snapped open. Kara. He gasped and jerked up.

"Thomas, are you okay?" Kara, face white, stood back staring at the bed. "What is this?" But Thomas's eyes were on the air conditioner where rolled white sheets had been cut and Monique had been freed. She was gone.

"Thomas! Talk to me!"

"What?" He looked at her. "What's—" The sheets were wet. Soaked in red. Blood?

Thomas scrambled out of the bed. He'd been lying on sheets soaked in his blood. He grabbed his chest and belly as visions of the attacker shooting into his body flashed through his mind. Two silenced shots. *Phewt! Phewt!*

Yes, there was that, but, more important, there was the lake and the boy. He looked up at Kara.

"God is real," he said.

"What?"

"God. He's . . . wow." His head spun with the memory of the lake. He could feel a wild grin tempt his face, but his mind wasn't working in full cooperation with all of his muscles yet.

"Well, at least I dreamed that he's real," he said. "Not just real, like wow he exists, but . . . real, like you can talk to him. I mean, maybe touch him."

"Very nice," she said. "In the meantime, here, where I live, we're standing next to a bed covered in your blood!"

"I was shot," he said.

She stared at him, unbelieving. "Are you sure? Where?"

"Right here. And here." He showed her. Chest and gut. "I swear I was shot. Someone broke in; we fought; he shot me. And then he must have taken Monique."

"I called you. Was that before or after?"

"You called before. He was here when you called." Suddenly Bangkok was making more sense than the lake. "Actually, I think your call unnerved him. The point is . . ." Yes, what was the point?

"The point is what?"

"I'm not dead."

Kara looked at his stomach. Then his eyes. "I don't get it. You're saying that you were healed in your dreams?"

"It's not the first time."

"But you were shot, right? You were shot and killed. How's that possible?"

"I don't know that I was killed. I lost consciousness. But there, in my dreams, I was lying on the shores of the lake. The air was full of mist from the waterfall. Water. The water is what heals. I was probably healed before I could die."

He pulled the sheets from the bed, grabbed the mattress. Flipped it over. Kara hadn't removed her stare.

"You're dead serious."

"No, not dead."

She looked away, paced to the end of the bed. Turned back. "Do you understand the implications?"

"I don't know, do I?" He quickly untied the homemade ropes from the air conditioner. "There's a lot I'm not clear on. But one thing I am sure of is that Monique is gone. The guy who took her wasn't your everyday thug."

She was still preoccupied with his healing. Thomas stopped.

"Look, I'm not indestructible, if that's what you're thinking. There's no way."

"And how would you know?"

"Because I think you're right—both realities are real, at least in some ways. Evidently, if I get shot here and then fall asleep and get water poured on me there before I die, I get healed. But if I get killed here and there's no water around to heal me, I just might die."

"You're like Wolverine or somebody now? You get hit in the head or shot in the chest, and there's not a mark on you! That's incredible!"

It *was* incredible. But there was more, wasn't there? A simple bit of information that had nagged at him since he'd talked to Teeleh, that bat in the other place. The details began to buzz in his brain, and he felt the first hints of panic.

"Well, that's not all," he said. "For starters, I'm pretty sure that the guy who shot me and took Monique is the guy who's going to blackmail the world with the Raison Strain."

Thomas began to pace. He'd bundled up the bloody sheets and now held them in his right hand.

"Or at least the guy works for whoever is planning this. That's not all. I'm pretty sure that the only way they even *know* the Raison Vaccine has the potential to mutate into a deadly virus is because *I* spilled the beans to someone who told them."

"That can't be. That would mean without you the mutation wouldn't happen? You're saying you're the *cause* of this thing?"

"That's exactly what I'm saying. I learn about the Raison Strain as a matter of history in my dreams, I tell someone, 'Hey, such and such is going to happen,' and they decide to make such and such actually happen. Like a self-fulfilling prophecy. If I'd kept my mouth shut and not told the State Department or the CDC, no one would even know the Raison Strain was possible."

She chewed on that for a moment. "So you've caused the very virus you're trying to stop? That's a trip."

"Where can we stash these sheets?"

"Under the bed." They stuffed the bedding under the frame.

"But if that's true," Kara said, "can't you change something now that would ruin the rest of what happens? You go back to the histories, find out that X-Y-Z happened, then return and make sure that doesn't happen."

"Maybe. Maybe not. I can't get information about the histories that easily anymore."

"What about the black forest?"

"I went to the black forest! I'm not going back again, no way!"

"What if it's a dream? And it saves us here?"

"There's more." Thomas turned slowly, remembering his conversation with Teeleh. But there was something he was missing from it, he was sure. He'd gone to prove himself to Monique, and he'd done that. But he'd also learned about the antivirus.

He'd repeated the antivirus.

"What if . . ." A chill snaked down his spine. He turned back to Kara, stunned by the thought. "What if I inadvertently told them how to do it?"

"To make the virus?"

"No, they know that. Intense heat. They can figure it out. But that doesn't do anyone any good. You put the virus in the air and three weeks later, everyone's dead. Including the person who releases it. But if you have an antivirus, a cure or a vaccine to the virus, you can—"

"Control it," Kara finished. "The threat of force. Like having the only nuclear arsenal in the world."

"And I think I might have given it to them."

"How?"

"Teeleh. He tricked me. Just before he gave me the information, he cut me." He was speaking through a daze, as if to himself. "I could swear I heard myself saying it out loud."

"So then you also have it. What good is the virus to them, if you have the antivirus?"

"Do I?" He cocked his head. He couldn't remember it. "I . . . can't think of it right now."

"I'm not going to pretend to understand all of this, but we have to get out of here. The police bought my story, and I talked to Monique's father. I called because he agreed to hold the shipments. I nearly killed myself getting here unseen when you didn't pick up. I think I can get us in to see Raison, but he's pretty bent out of shape. When he finds out that Monique's gone again . . ."

She sighed.

They left the room looking lived in but not massacred.

———∞———

"You what?"

The sharp nose on Jacques de Raison's angular face was red, and for good reason. He'd just lost, then found, then lost his daughter, all within eight hours.

"I didn't lose her," Thomas objected. "She was taken from me. You think I would take her just to lose her?" He glanced from the dark-haired Raison to Kara and then back. He had to get the situation back in hand. Or at the very least back in mind.

"Please, if you'll have a seat, I'll try to explain."

Jacques glared at him, tall and commanding, the kind of man who had grown accustomed to getting what he wanted. He sat in a wing chair by his desk, eyes fixed on Thomas.

"I'll give you five minutes. Then I call the authorities. Three governments are looking for you, Mr. Hunter. I'm quite sure they'll make quick work of you."

Thomas had driven from the hotel to Raison Pharmaceutical. Kara wanted to know what had happened in the colored forest, so, with only a little encouraging, he told her. He told her about meeting Teeleh at the Crossing. About the lake. About the boy. They finally agreed that none of it proved God really did exist, but Thomas was having trouble reconciling the reasoning with his experience. He changed the subject and told her about Rachelle.

The world was facing a crisis inadvertently caused by Thomas, and he was off learning the fine points of romancing Rachelle. It didn't seem right, Kara had said.

Getting past the gates and in to see Jacques de Raison required no fancy footwork on Thomas's part this time. Three ambitious guards nearly took off both their heads in the courtyard before Raison Pharmaceutical's prestigious founder marched in and suggested they lower their rifles. They dipped their heads and backed off.

Jacques de Raison had ushered them into this library, with its tall bookcases and a dozen high-backed black leather chairs positioned around a long mahogany table. Now he and Kara had the prodigious task of convincing this man that his true enemy was the Raison Strain, not Thomas Hunter.

Jacques' eyes dropped to a large bloodstain on the pocket of Thomas's Lucky jeans. His shirt, which had been off at the time of his shooting, had been spared the carnage.

Thomas took a deep breath. "The fact of the matter is, Mr. Raison, your daughter and I were attacked. I was shot and left for dead. Monique was taken by force."

"You were left for dead," the man said. "I can see that."

Thomas waved off his cynicism. "I clean up good. The man who shot me was the same person I was trying to protect your daughter from in the first place. I knew there was a potential problem. I tried to convince her of it, and when she refused, I forced her hand."

"That's utter nonsense."

"My five minutes aren't up. Just listen to me for a minute here. You may not like it, but I may be the only one who can save your daughter. Please listen."

"Please, Mr. Raison," Kara said evenly. "I told you before, this goes way beyond Thomas or Monique."

"Yes, of course; the Raison Vaccine will mutate and infect untold millions."

"No," Thomas said. "Billions."

"Monique submitted the vaccine to the most ardent series of tests, I assure you."

"But not to heat," Thomas said. "She told me that herself."

"The fact is, you can't substantiate any of this," Raison said. "You kidnap my daughter at gunpoint, and then you expect me to believe you did it for her own good. Forgive my suspicions, but I think it's more likely that you have her hidden away right now. At any moment I'll get a call from an accomplice demanding money."

"You're wrong. What you will get is a call demanding either information or samples of the vaccine. Test it yourself. The virus mutates under extreme heat. How long would it take to confirm that?"

It was the first thing Thomas had said that seemed to sink in.

"She is my only daughter," he said. "There is nothing I love more. Do you understand this? I will do whatever it takes to bring her home safely."

"So will I," Thomas said. "How long to test the vaccine?"

"You really do believe this? It's preposterous."

"Then the tests will show that I'm wrong. If I'm right, then we know we have a very big problem. How long?"

"Two weeks under normal circumstances," Raison said.

"Forget normal."

"A week. There are a number of variables. Exact temperature, length of exposure, other external elements."

"A week is too long, way too long!" Thomas crossed to the long mahogany table and spun around. "If I'm right, just for the sake of argument, and they knew exactly how to initiate this mutation, how long would it take them to have a usable virus?"

"I can't answer—"

"Just pretend, Jacques. Best-case scenario, how long?"

He studied Thomas. "Could be a couple of hours."

"A couple of hours. I suggest either you start taking me at my word or you start your tests, because if you're right, God help us all."

"Could take weeks. This is all impossible to believe."

The phone on Raison's desk rang.

"Then you'd better do some soul-searching, because Monique's life rests in your ability to believe."

The man stood and snatched up the phone. "Yes." He was silent for five seconds. "Who is this? Who . . ." Silence. Fear spread through the man's eyes. "How will I know . . . hello?"

The phone went limp in his hand. "They've . . . they've given me seventy-two hours to turn over all our research and all existing samples of the vaccine, or they will kill her."

Thomas nodded. A lump gathered in his throat. "You'd better turn this facility into one giant testing lab. Twenty-four–seven. And you're going to need a lot more than the virus. You're going to need a new antivirus."

24

THE IMMINENT threat posed to his daughter, Monique, seemed to wilt Jacques de Raison. Only at his urging did the Bangkok authorities agree to delay taking Thomas into custody. He would go, they promised. The French and the Americans were both breathing down their necks. But considering the fact that another party had evidently swooped in to take Monique, and considering Thomas's insistence that he might be able to help, they would keep him under house arrest in the mansion at Raison Pharmaceutical.

Thomas spent an hour with Kara, working through their options. The most obvious solution to the entire mess was to recall the antivirus Teeleh had given Thomas in his dreams. But half an hour of Kara's prying and another ten minutes of Thomas beating his head against a metaphorical wall yielded nothing. His mind was simply blank on the details. In the end, only one plan made any sense to either of them.

"I need to talk to him," Thomas announced outside Raison's office.

"He is busy," the guard said.

"Did you see the tape of the man who fought your two gate guards the other day?"

The guard paused. "You're threatening me?"

"No. I was wondering if you saw it. But yes, I am that man. Please, I really need to speak to him."

The man looked Thomas over. "One moment." He poked his head in the door, asked a question, then pushed the door open.

Thomas walked in. Jacques de Raison looked up from his desk, haggard and distracted.

"Any progress?" Thomas asked.

"I told you a week! Seventy-two hours? There's a much simpler solution to this. If I give them what they want, they will give me Monique. We will deal with them later, through the world courts."

"Unless I'm right," Thomas said. "Unless by giving them everything you have, you severely hamper any attempt to produce an antidote to the Raison Strain."

Raison slammed his fist on the desk. "There *is* no Raison Virus!"

"Monique will tell you differently when we find her. By then it will be too late."

"Then I'll give them what they want and keep what I need to reproduce the vaccine."

"If you give them what they want, it'll slow you down. The Raison Virus will do its work in three weeks."

They faced off. Thomas felt oddly resigned. There were only two things he could do now: Find Monique, who alone might be able to find a way out of the mess her vaccine would make, and prepare the world for the Raison Strain. Somehow he had to do both.

"Mr. Raison, I want you to consider something. I don't think they have any intention of releasing Monique anytime soon, even if you do meet their demands. She's too valuable to them. Alive. If I'm right—"

"If I'm right, if I'm right—how many times are you asking me to assume that you're right?"

"As many as it takes. If I'm right, the only way to get Monique back to safety is to go after her." Thomas sat in one of the leather chairs facing the man. "For that we need help. And there's one way to get help."

"I have money, Mr. Hunter. If it's muscle we need—"

"No, we need more than a little muscle here. We need eyes and ears everywhere. And we need to be able to move quickly. For that we need governments. If I'm right—yes, I know, there I go again—the lid is going to blow off this whole thing in the next few days. I suggest we ease the pressure now and bring in some partners."

He said it almost exactly the way he and Kara had rehearsed it.

Actually, given a little space and the right training, he might make a pretty decent diplomat. Something he should take up with Tanis.

"What do you want me to do, inform the world that my vaccine is actually a deadly virus? It will kill the company. I would be better off to meet their demands."

"I'm not suggesting you tell the world any such thing. Not yet." Thomas made the decision then, looking at the haggard man in front of him. "I'm suggesting you let me speak to a few key players confidentially."

"You want me to put my company's future in your hands?"

"Your company's future is already in my hands. If I'm right, there won't be a company in the future. If I'm wrong, my claims will be written off as the ravings of a maniac, and your company will be just fine. Which is why I, not you, need to make selective contact with a few leaders. A call from you, admitting that your vaccine might be quite deadly, would require them to take certain actions. Raison Pharmaceutical would be dead and buried by morning. I, on the other hand, have more latitude. I don't officially represent Raison Pharmaceutical."

The man was mulling over Thomas's idea. "I'm not sure what you're asking."

"I'm asking that you let me—assist me to—make contact with the outside world. My hands are tied without you. I'm in captivity here. Let me spill the beans about the danger the Raison Strain presents to the world. It will give them reason to throw some resources behind finding Monique. Nothing like a virus to motivate the right people."

Thomas knew by the look in Jacques de Raison's eyes that he was already warming to the idea. "I would have plausible deniability," Raison said.

"Yes. I'll make the calls without your official endorsement. That will insulate you even while making an appeal for help."

It was a flawless idea. He should've gone into politics.

"You're simply asking for the use of a phone? You can't just place calls to world governments and expect them to be answered."

"I want to use your personal contacts. Only those approved by you, of course. The U.S. State Department, the French government, the British. Maybe Indonesia—they have a large population nearby. The point is, we need to convince a few people with resources to take the kidnapping of your daughter as more than an industrial espionage case. We need them to consider the possibility of risk to their own national security and help us find Monique."

"And you really think I would let you do that?"

"I don't think you have a choice. This whole thing is about to hit the fan anyway. This gives us a chance. To warn the right people. To find Monique."

***

Jacques de Raison went one step further than lending Thomas use of his contacts and a phone. He lent his secretary, Nancy.

"Tell him that if he doesn't clear a line to the secretary in the next hour, I'm going to . . ." Thomas paused, considering. "Whatever. Tell him I'm going to set off a nuke or something. Don't any of these people have the foresight to even *consider* that we could be in a bit of trouble here?"

Kara watched her brother pace. They'd been at it for five hours, and the results could hardly be worse. The French were not only hopeless but, in her thinking, downright rude. She'd expected much more cooperation from Raison's home country. Evidently their current administration wasn't excited about the fact that Raison Pharmaceutical had left France in the first place. They seemed interested enough in putting on a good face in this kidnapping mess, but when it came right down to getting a politician to break his schedule for a ten-minute phone call with Thomas, all interest evapo-rated. It was a legal matter, they said.

The British had been a little more congenial. But the bottom line was still roughly the same. The Germans, the Italians, even the Indonesian government—no one was in the mood to listen to the rantings of a crazed prophet who'd kidnapped the woman in Bangkok.

Kara walked toward her brother. The fact that it was three in the morning didn't help matters much. He was practically sleepwalking. Then again, if he was right and this was the dream, he *was* sleepwalking.

"Thomas." She rubbed his back. "You okay?"

He tried to smile. "Not really. I've gone from being terrified that there's a comet coming to being horrified that no one believes there's a comet coming."

"What do you expect? There's been a comet coming every year for two thousand years. It never lands. So now a twenty-five-year-old in jeans claims to live in his dreams, where he learns the world is about to end. He threatens to blow up the castle unless the king believes him. Why should the secretary of state break his meeting with the prince of Persia to take your call?"

"Thanks for the encouragement, sis."

"Look, I know none of this matters if no one will listen, but there is another way, you know."

He studied her face. They walked away from the desk. "You mean go back . . ."

"Well?" Kara said. "I know sleeping seems like the wrong thing here, but why not? For starters, if you don't sleep soon, you're going to fall into a coma anyway. And it's worked before, right? What if you could find out where she is?"

He shook his head. "This is different. The other stuff was a matter of histories. This is too specific. And like I said, I don't want to go back to the black forest, which is the only place I think I can get information."

He said it with so much conviction. He really did live with the constant awareness of his dreams. And he was changing.

The Thomas she knew as her brother had always been articulate, but he carried himself with a greater purpose now. He talked with more authority. Not enough to convince the French and the British, but enough to exchange a few rounds with some pretty powerful people before being sent packing, for his brazen approach to diplomacy as much as anything.

Her brother had somehow been chosen. She didn't understand how or why, and, truthfully, she wasn't ready to think it all through just yet.

But she couldn't escape the growing certainty that this man who worked in the Java Hut in Denver just a few days ago was becoming someone very, very important.

"Then don't go back to the black forest. But there's a connection between your dreams and what's happening here, Thomas. Your dreams caused this, after all. There has to be a way to get more information. Go to sleep; nothing's happening here anyway."

He sighed. "You're right, I've got to sleep."

"You still can't remember the antivirus."

He shook his head. "No."

"I wish there was a way you could take me."

"Take you there? I'm not actually going anywhere, am I?"

"No. Your mind is though. Maybe there's a way to take my mind with you." She smiled. "Crazy, huh?"

"Yeah, crazy. I don't think that's possible."

"Neither is breathing in a lake," she said.

"Sir!"

Thomas spun. It was Raison's secretary, holding up a phone.

"I have the deputy secretary of the United States. Merton Gains. He's agreed to talk to you."

———— ∞ ————

Deputy Secretary Merton Gains sat at the end of the conference table, listening to the others express opinions on a dozen different ways to look at yet another looming budget crisis. Paul Stanley was still out of town, but the secretary of state had never shown a reluctance to throw Gains in the mix when he was unavailable.

Half the cabinet was present, most of the notable ones excluding defense, Myers. A dozen aides. President Robert Blair sat across and down the table from Gains, leaning back as his advisers begged to differ. The subject was tax cuts again. To cut or not to cut. How hard to push. The economic fallout or gain, the political fallout or gain. Some things never changed, and the argument over taxes was one of them.

Which was only part of the reason Gains found his mind wandering. The rest of the reason was Thomas Hunter.

Fact: If his daughter hadn't died from a vaccine two years ago, he never would have spearheaded legislation to heighten scrutiny of new vaccines.

Fact: If he hadn't written the bill, his friend Bob Macklroy never would have thought to call him about Thomas Hunter.

Fact: If Hunter hadn't called Bob and told him about the winner to the Kentucky Derby, Joy Flyer, Gains wouldn't have taken Hunter's call.

Fact: Hunter's prediction had been accurate.

Fact: Hunter had gone to the CDC and reported the potential outbreak. And he'd been pretty much stuffed.

Fact: Hunter had kidnapped Monique de Raison, the one person, he claimed, who could stop the virus by not shipping it in the first place.

Fact: Monique had been kidnapped again by someone else who now wanted the Raison Vaccine.

This was where the facts started fusing with Hunter's claims.

Claim: The party that took Monique did so because they, like Thomas, knew the vaccine could be turned into a deadly weapon and hoped to get what they needed through coercion.

Claim: This party also could have access to an antidote within reach.

Claim: If the world didn't get off its collective high horse, find Monique de Raison, and develop an antidote, very bad times that would make the budget crisis look like a game of dominoes were only days around the corner.

Hearing Thomas Hunter lay down the entire story, Gains couldn't help but entertain the few chills that had swept through his bones. This wasn't unlike the kinds of scenarios he'd pitched to the Senate more than once. And here it was, staring him in the face as a claim by a brazen man who was either totally deluded or who knew more than any man had any business knowing. There was something about Hunter's sincerity that tempted him to listen to more. And so he had.

Much more.

He'd even promised any help he could in the matter of Monique de Raison. What if? Just what if? Obviously old man Raison hadn't thrown Hunter out on his ear.

". . . Merton?"

Gains cleared his throat. "No, I don't think so." He glanced up. The president was looking at him with that lazy I-can-read-your-mind look. It meant nothing, but it had won him the presidency.

"Just one thing," Gains said. "I assume you all heard about the kidnapping in Bangkok yesterday. Monique de Raison, daughter of Jacques de Raison, founder of Raison Pharmaceutical."

"Don't tell me," President Blair said. "It was one of our military boys."

"No."

"My understanding is that the man originally involved was blindsided by a third party who now holds the woman," CIA Director Phil Grant said. "We're shifting some assets to lend a hand. I wasn't aware there was any new movement in the case."

"There isn't. But I've run across some information that I'll get over to your office, Phil. It seems there's a question about the stability of the Raison Vaccine, the real subject of this kidnapping. It's an airborne multipurpose vaccine that was supposed to enter the market today. Let's just say the incident in Bangkok has exposed the possibility, however slight, that the vaccine may not be stable."

"I haven't heard about this," the health secretary said. "I had the understanding the FDA was ready to approve this vaccine next week."

"No, this is new and, I might add, hearsay. Just a heads-up."

The table remained quiet.

"I'm not sure I understand, Merton," the president said. "I know you have a unique interest in vaccines, but how does this affect us?"

"This has nothing to do with the Gains Bill. It probably doesn't affect us. But if there is any truth to Hunter's claims and an unstable airborne vaccine does become a deadly virus, we could have a very significant health challenge on our hands. Just wanted to get the thought on the table." Wrong time, wrong place. You don't just stand up in a cabinet meeting, inform the leaders of the country that the sky might soon fall, and expect straight faces. Time for a bit of spin.

"Anyway, I'll get the report to each of you. It could affect health and finance at the least. Possibly homeland security. If word of this leaks, the country could react badly. People get very nervous about viruses."

There was a moment's pause.

"Seems straightforward enough," the president said. "Anyone else?"

25

THOMAS AWOKE to excited shouts outside the cottage. His confusion from the transition lasted only a moment. It was becoming customary. Every time he woke up, he had to make the switch, this time from a discussion with Deputy Secretary of State Merton Gains. They were making progress, real progress. He threw on his tunic and rushed from the house.

What greeted his eyes vanquished all thoughts of Bangkok and his success with Merton Gains.

There was a gigantic bright light suspended against the colored forest halfway up the sky. That the bright light hung in the sky wasn't so surprising—suns were known to do that. That the forest was up there as well was a different matter.

He jerked his head up and stared at the sky. Only there was no sky. The green forest was above him!

The people streamed toward the center of the village, chattering excitedly, dancing in delight as though their world suddenly going topsy-turvy was a great thing.

Thomas turned, his mouth gaping, and gazed at the changed landscape. The forests rose from where they should have been and curved upward to where the sky had been. Far above him he could see meadows. And there, just to his right, at an elevation that must be over ten thousand feet, he was sure he saw a herd of horses galloping through a vertical meadow.

"It's upside down!"

"Yes, it is."

Thomas whirled to find Michal squatting next to him, smiling at their new world.

"What's going on? What happened?"

"Do you like it?" the Roush asked with a childish smirk.

"I . . . I don't know what it is."

"Elyon is playing," Michal said. "He does this often, actually." Then he turned and leaped into the air after the others running for the Thrall. "Come. You will see."

Thomas ran after Michal, almost tripping over a carving that someone had left in the yard. "You mean this is supposed to happen? Everything is safe?"

"Of course. Come. You will see."

It was as if the entire landscape had been painted on the inside of a gigantic sphere. The effects of gravity had been somehow reversed. Directly ahead of them, the road leading to the lake curved upward to meet it, only now the lake was slanted upward and the waterfall thundered horizontally. The only thing missing was the black forest.

The scale of things also had changed dramatically, so that the sky, which should have been many hundreds of miles above them, seemed much closer. Conversely, the other villages, which should have been visible, were not. Thomas could see creatures running through the fields at impossible angles. Tens of thousands of birds dived about crazily. Half as many Roush swooped through the air as far as Thomas could see, twisting and turning and flying in giant loops that reminded Thomas of Gabil. It was nothing less than a circus.

They reached the Thrall and joined the others who, like Thomas, stared with wide eyes at the sight before them.

It was Johan who first discovered that the atmosphere had changed as well. Changed so much, in fact, that he could stay in the air longer than usual when he jumped. Thomas saw the young boy jumping, as if in slow motion.

"See, Thomas. See this?" Johan jumped again, harder this time.

He floated ten feet up and hung there.

"Thomas!" he cried. "I'm flying!"

Sure enough, Johan floated higher, about a hundred feet above the ground now, faltering slightly, screaming with laughter. Three other boys joined Johan in the air. Then the air began to fill with others who took to the air like children in their dreams.

"Thomas," Michal said. Thomas stood frozen by the sight. "Thomas, try it."

Thomas looked at the Roush with apprehension. "I can fly?"

"Of course. Elyon has changed the world for us. You'd better do it while you can because it won't last forever, you know. He is just playing. Try it."

Thomas reached out instinctively and grasped the fur on Michal's head for stability. He jumped tentatively and found a lightness that surprised him. He smiled and jumped again, with more force. This time he floated several feet off the ground. The third time he leaped with all his strength, and he soared off balance into the air.

Johan buzzed by, squealing with delight. He had obviously learned how to maneuver. Thomas found that he could gain momentum by shifting his body weight. There was just enough gravity to allow forward motion.

Within minutes, Thomas flew with the rest of them. It wasn't long before Rachelle, Johan, and Michal joined him, and they set off to explore their new world. Chattering like children between peals of laughter, they flew to the inverted globe's highest crest and looked down on the village far below. They landed on a meadow, its flowers hanging upside down and pointing to the village now barely visible below. They walked upside down, hearts fluttering like butterflies, stepping carefully at the odd angle. Then they leaped off the grass, skimmed the trees down one side to the lake, and plunged into its jade waters.

In the warm green waters flush with light, they heard delighted laughter through the full range of the scale, from a deep, rumbling chuckle to a high, piercing giggle. And with wide-eyed glances to see if the others had also heard, they knew at the first chuckle that it was Elyon. If they were beside themselves with the staggering scope of the adventure, Elyon was beside himself at bringing it to them. And they laughed with him.

The hours fled. They played like children in an amusement park. There were no lines, and all rides were open. They flew and explored and

twisted and turned, and it wasn't until after midday that the world began
to reshape itself.

———— ✺ ————

Within an hour it was back to normal.

And Thomas remembered Bangkok.

Rachelle approached him, laughing throatily. "Now that, my dear
Thomas, is what I call a fabulously good time!" She spontaneously threw
her arms around his neck and squeezed him tight.

Thomas was so surprised that he neglected to return the hug. Rachelle
pulled back, but she didn't release him. She cocked her left leg behind her
and stared into his eyes.

"Would you like to kiss me?"

"Kiss?" He could smell her sweet breath.

"I am helping you restore your memory, or have you forgotten that
as well?"

"No." He swallowed.

"So then I would like to help you remember what it is like to kiss. I
will have to show you, of course."

"Have you kissed anyone before? I mean, another man?"

"No. But I've seen it done. It's very clear in my mind. I'm sure I could
show you exactly how it's done." Her eyes flashed. She ran a tongue over
her lips. "Perhaps you should wet your lips first; they look quite dry."

He did it.

She leaned forward and touched her lips gently to his.

Thomas closed his eyes. For a moment everything seemed to shut
down. But in that same moment, a new world blossomed into existence.

No, not a new world. An old world.

He had done this before.

Rachelle's lips separated from his. "Trust me, dear, you're not in a
dream. We'll see if that sparks your memory."

Heat spread down Thomas's neck. He'd done this before. He'd kissed
a woman before! He was sure of it.

He must have looked stunned, because Rachelle offered a satisfied smile. It was true, her kiss had taken his breath away, but there was more. It had brought something back.

"Tanis is coming to speak to you," she said. "He still insists that you're his apprentice in the fighting arts, but I think he's more interested in the histories." She put a finger on his lips. "Just remember, they're dreams. Don't get carried away."

Rachelle turned and stepped down the path, looking pleased and supremely confident despite her best efforts to appear nonchalant.

Thomas's mind immediately chased a new thought that had presented itself while she warned him about the histories. Suppose both realities were not only real, but woven together? Like the boy had said at the upper lake, the lion and the lamb, both real. Both images of the same truth.

The same reality.

What if . . .

"Rachelle?"

She turned back. "Yes?"

If the two realities were interwoven, maybe he was meant to rescue in both. Rachelle here, Monique there. Could Rachelle lead him to Monique?

"You're staring at me," Rachelle said. "Is something wrong?"

"That was very wonderful," he said. *Very wonderful?*

She winked. "It was meant to be."

"Could I ask you a question?"

"Of course."

"If there was one place from which you would like to be rescued, where would it be?"

"That is your job. To rescue me."

He hurried forward, taken with the possibility that worked his mind. "Yes, but if there was one place. Say you were trapped and I was to rescue you. Where would that be? Please, I have to know so that I can rescue you."

"Well, I'm not exactly a storyteller. But . . ." She faced the forest and considered the question. "I would say that I would be held in a . . ." She spun toward him. "A great white cave full of bottles. Where a river and the forest meet."

"Really? Have you ever seen such a cave?"

"No. Why should I have? I am fabricating this for you, like a storyteller would."

"Is it here, in this forest, or somewhere far away?"

"Close by," she said after a moment's thought.

"And how would I find this cave?"

"By following the river, of course."

"And which direction is it from here?"

She looked at him curiously, as if objecting to his pressing for details. "That way," she said, pointing to her right. "East."

"East."

"Yes, east. I'm sure of it. The cave is a day's walk to the east."

He nodded. "Then I will rescue you."

"And when you rescue me, I should want another kiss," she said in complete seriousness.

"A kiss."

"Yes. A real kiss, not one from your silly dreams. A real kiss for a real woman who has fallen hopelessly in love with you, my dear prince."

She turned and walked down the path.

Thomas walked quickly, if for no reason other than that he was thinking quickly.

Rachelle's kiss had spawned a whole new thread of possibility. It found its origin in this one thought: What if the two realities were more than just interwoven; what if they *depended* on each other?

What if what happened in Bangkok depended on what he did here? And what if what happened here depended on what happened in Bangkok? He already knew that if he was healed here, he was healed in Bangkok. And what skills he learned here, he could also use in Bangkok. But to think that the realities might *depend* on each other . . .

It was a staggering thought. Yet in so many ways it made sense. In fact, he was quite sure he'd come to the same conclusion in Bangkok. If it were another way, the boy would have said so. Elyon would have discouraged his dreams. But he hadn't. He'd left the choice up to him.

God wasn't a lamb or a lion or a boy. He was all of them if he chose to be. Or none of them. They were metaphors for the truth.

The truth. One truth. Two sides of one truth. Lion and lamb. The colored forest and Bangkok. Possible?

He still wasn't sure which reality was real, but he was that much more convinced now that *the truth* in both realities was real. And he had to be very careful to treat both as real.

Kara had said that.

Of course, this didn't mean that just because he loved Rachelle he was meant to love Monique. But it was quite possible he was meant to rescue Monique. That was why he was learning how to rescue Rachelle in this Great Romance.

It had to be. And if so, he may have just discovered *how* to rescue her. Or at least where to rescue her. He should sleep immediately, dream of Bangkok, and test this theory.

Thomas stopped on the path. If he was meant to rescue Monique in the histories, then what was he supposed to do here, if this reality also depended on his dreams?

Thomas stopped on the path. If Monique was real, wasn't it possible that Bill was also real? That they really had crash-landed in a spacecraft as Teeleh had insisted?

What if that was the only reality?

Maybe everything else was only a dream. He was really from Earth, being terribly affected by this strange planet. His stomach turned. The thought suddenly felt terribly compelling. It would explain everything.

He had to at least eliminate that as a possibility. The only way to know was to return to the black forest. He should at least consider—

"Thomas! Thomas Hunter, there you are!"

Tanis ran out of the forest, waving a crooked red stick in his right hand. "I have looked everywhere for you. Did you enjoy the change this morning?"

"Incredible," Thomas said. "Spectacular!"

"The last time, he split the whole planet in two," Tanis said. "You may have forgotten, because it was before you lost your memory, but we could see the stars above and below. Then the fissure filled halfway with water and we dived. The dive itself lasted a full hour." Tanis chuckled and shook his head.

"That's amazing," Thomas said.

"This?" Tanis waved the stick. "You like it?"

"I meant your story's amazing—falling for an hour. What is that?"

"Well, it's something I've come up with based on something I remember from the histories. Maybe you know what it's called." He held it up proudly.

It was a stick, shaped and bent like waves with a hook on the end.

Thomas shook his head. "No, I can't say that I recognize it. What does it do?"

"It's a weapon!" Tanis cried. He jabbed the air like a clumsy swordsman. "A weapon to scare off the vermin!"

"Why would that work?"

"You don't know? The Shataiki are terrified of the colored forest. This is a weapon from the colored forest. It follows that they would be terrified of it as well. We could use these weapons on our expedition."

Thomas took the device. It was a sword of sorts from the histories. A very poor one. But the fact that it was made from the colored wood made for some interesting applications. Thomas could hardly forget Teeleh's reaction to the small piece of colored wood from Johan.

Thomas swung the sword. It had an awkward feel. He looked at Tanis, saw the man was watching him with interest.

"This is called a sword. But you've forgotten to give it a sharp edge."

Tanis jumped forward. "Show me."

"Well, it needs to be flat here and sharp along this edge so that it can cut."

Tanis reached for the sword. "May I?"

Thomas gave it to him. The man went to work with his hands. He was a storyteller, not a craftsman, but he had enough basic skill to quickly reshape the sword by coaxing the wood into what looked more like a sword. Thomas watched, confounded by the sight. Rachelle had explained the process to him, but he'd failed miserably at all of his own attempts. Reshaping molecules with his fingers was something he would evidently have to relearn.

"There!" Tanis shoved out the sword.

Thomas took it and ran his fingers along the now flat, sharp blade. Amazing. This in a matter of moments. What else could Tanis build with the proper guidance?

Thomas felt a stab of caution.

"It would never work." He tossed the sword back to Tanis. "Remember, I've been in the black forest. One small sword against a million Shataiki— not a chance. Even if they are afraid of the wood."

"Agreed!" Tanis said. "It would never work." He hurled the sword into the forest. It clattered against a tree and fell to the ground.

"Now, about the histories—"

"I don't want to talk about the histories right now," Thomas said.

"Your dreams are wearing you out? I understand completely. Then more training. As my apprentice, you have to apply yourself, Thomas Hunter. You're a quick study, I saw that the first time you attempted my double-back, but with the right practice you could be a master! Rachelle has taught you some new moves. Show me." He clapped twice.

"Right here?"

"Unless you'd rather do it in the village square."

Thomas glanced around. They were in a small meadow. Birds chirped. A white lion watched them lazily from where it lay by a tall topaz blue tree.

"Okay." Thomas took two long steps, launched himself into the air, twisted, and rolled into a forward flip. He landed squarely on his feet, back to imaginary opponent. Amazing how easy it felt.

"Bravo! Wonderful. I call that the reverse, because your opponent will never see your heel coming around on the flip. It would knock a black bat dizzy. Here, tear your tunic up the thigh to give you more freedom of movement."

Thomas did so. The leather pants they often wore wouldn't present this challenge, but the tunics could be restrictive during wild kicks.

"Good. Show me another."

Thomas showed him five more moves.

"Now," Tanis said, stepping forward. "Hit me!"

"I can't hit you! Why would I want to hit you?"

"Training, my apprentice. Defense. I will pretend you are a bat. You're bigger than a bat, of course, so I'll pretend you're three bats, standing on each other's shoulders. Now, you come for me and try to hit me, and I'll show you how to protect yourself."

"Sparring," Thomas said.

"What?"

"It was called sparring in the histories."

"Sparring! I love it! Let's do some sparring."

They sparred for a long time, a couple of hours at least. It was the first time Thomas had been exposed to the full breadth of the fight method developed by Tanis, and it made the martial arts of his dreams feel simple by comparison.

True, all aerial maneuvers were easier here, in part, presumably, because of the atmosphere. But he suspected the moves were easier also because of the method itself. Hand-to-hand combat was far more about the mind than muscle, and Tanis had both in abundance. Not once was Thomas able to land a blow on the leader, though he got closer with each attempt.

Amazingly, Thomas's stamina seemed nearly inexhaustible. He was growing stronger by the day. Recovering from his fall in the black forest.

"Enough," Thomas finally said.

Tanis lifted a finger. "Enough for the day. But you are improving with astonishing speed. I am proud to call you my apprentice. Now"—he put his hand on Thomas's shoulder and turned him toward the forest—"we must talk."

The histories. The man was incorrigible.

"Tell me, what kind of weapon do you think would work against the Shataiki?"

"Tanis, have you ever confronted the Shataiki? Have you ever even stood on the banks of the river and watched them?"

"I've watched them from a distance, yes. Black bats with talons that look like they could pop a head off in short order."

"But why haven't you gone closer, if you know they can't cross the river to harm you?"

"Where's the wisdom in that? They are tricky beasts; surely you've seen that. I would think that even to talk to them could prove fatal. They would employ all sorts of connivances to trick you into their water. Honestly, I am astounded you survived yourself."

"If you know all of this, why are you so adamant about an expedition? It would be suicide!"

"Well, I wouldn't talk to them! And you survived! Also, you know many things that might shift the balance of power. Before you came to us, I might never have seriously considered an attack, even though I wrote many stories about it. With your knowledge, we can defeat the vermin, Thomas! I know it!"

"No! We can't! They fight against the heart, not measly swords!"

"You think I don't know this? But tell me, wasn't it true that in the histories there was a device that could level the entire black forest in one moment?"

A nuclear bomb. Of course, any use of a nuclear weapon would be a landmark recorded in the histories.

"Yes. It was called a nuclear bomb. Do you know when such a device was used in the histories?"

"Not specifically," Tanis said. "Several times, if I remember. But mostly after the Great Deception. In the time of the tribulations. Are you saying that even with such a device we couldn't destroy the Shataiki?"

Thomas considered this. He looked to the east where the black forest waited in darkness. What was it Michal had said? The primary difference between this reality and the histories was that here everything found an immediate expression in physical reality. You could virtually touch Elyon by entering his water. You could see evil in the Shataiki. So maybe Tanis was on to something. Maybe evil could be wiped out with the right weapons.

Thomas shook his head. It sounded wrong. All wrong.

"I'm not suggesting this nuclear bomb," Tanis said. "But I'm making a point. What about a gun, as you call it? With enough guns, couldn't we hold them off at the river?"

A gun. Thomas shrugged. "A gun is only a small device. They come in bigger sizes but . . . this is ridiculous. Even if I could figure out how to make a gun, I wouldn't."

"But you could, couldn't you?"

Possible. He couldn't bring a gun here, of course. Nothing physical had ever followed him in his dreams. But knowledge . . .

"Maybe."

"Then think about it. It might be a useless idea, I must agree. But sending the lot of those beasts scrambling is a thought worth savoring. I have something else that you must see, Thomas. Come."

He steered Thomas to the forest, not the least bit put off or discouraged by Thomas's dismissal of his ideas.

"Now? Where?"

"Just here by the river that leads from the lake. I have an invention you must help us try."

He headed into the forest, and Thomas hurried to catch him. "Who is 'us'?" Thomas asked.

"Johan. He is my first recruit. We have made something that an adventuresome soul like you will appreciate. Hurry. He is to meet us there." Tanis began to run.

—⁂—

They broke out onto the banks of a river slightly smaller than the one at the black forest. Johan sat on a large yellow log they'd felled. He jumped to his feet and ran for Thomas.

"Thomas! First we fly, and now we float." He hugged Thomas's waist. "Did you see the stick Tanis made? Where is the stick, Tanis?"

"I threw it into the forest," the elder said. "Thomas said it was a terrible idea, and I agreed. It would never work."

"Then how will we—"

"Exactly!" Tanis boomed. He stuck a finger in the air. "We won't!"

"We *won't* float our log down the river to attack the Shataiki?"

"That's what you were planning?" Thomas asked. He looked at the tree and saw that they'd hollowed out half of it. He'd dreamed about one of these. It was a canoe.

"It was an idea," Tanis said. "We talked it up yesterday and we shaped this log so that it might float, but the sword was a bad idea, you said so yourself. Don't tell me you want me to fashion another, because I really am having my doubts about it now. Unless we could send a bomb down the river in this log."

They both stared at Thomas with round green eyes. Innocent to the bone. But still filled with desire. The desire to create, the desire to romance, to eat, to drink, to swim in Elyon's lake.

The tension between satisfaction and desire was odd, to be sure. Dissatisfaction led to mischief as well as good.

He faced Johan. "Do you want to take this canoe onto the water?"

His eyes lit up. "Yes."

"And would you be unhappy if we didn't try?"

Johan cast a blank stare. "Unhappy?"

"What on earth are you talking about, man?" Tanis boomed. "You're speaking in riddles here. Is this a game of wits?" He seemed quite taken with the idea.

"No, not a game. Just my memory. A way to help my recollection of the way things are. There is happy, so there must be unhappy. There is good, so there must be evil. I was simply asking if Johan here would be unhappy if we didn't push the boat onto the water."

"Yes, there is evil, and we dispatch it regularly. And since there is happy, there must be *un*happy too. I can see what you're saying. I feel anger at the bats, of course, but unhappy? You have me tied in a knot, Thomas Hunter. Help me out."

They felt desire without dissatisfaction, Thomas thought. The best of both worlds.

He, on the other hand, did feel dissatisfaction. Or at least *un*satisfaction. Perhaps because he'd been in the black forest. He hadn't taken a drink of the water, but he'd been in there, and his mind had been affected somehow.

Either that, or he wasn't from this place at all. He'd come in a spaceship.

"Just a story, Tanis," Thomas said. "Just an idea."

Tanis exchanged a glance with the boy. Then back. An idea.

"Well then, should we give it a try?"

Johan started jumping in anticipation. The invention was quite an event. Thomas ran his hand along the canoe.

"How will you steer it?"

"With the sword," Tanis said. "But I think any good stick would do."

"And how did you bring the tree down?"

"As we always do. With our hands."

"Okay, let's give it a try."

They tied a vine around its bow and then to a tree on the bank. Thomas braced himself. "Are you ready?"

"Ready!" they both cried.

Together they heaved and watched the glowing yellow canoe slip out into the running water. "It works!" Tanis beamed. But almost as soon as he said it, the boat began to sink. Within a few seconds, it had disappeared under the gurgling green waters.

"It's too heavy," Thomas said with a frown.

Tanis and Johan stared at the bubbles that still broke the surface. "Another story sinks," Tanis said.

Johan found this so funny that he dropped first to his knees and then to his back in uncontrolled fits of laughter. Tanis was soon joining in, and they quickly turned the laughing fits into a game of sorts: who could laugh the longest without taking a breath.

Thomas tried, at their urging, and lost handsomely.

"Well, now," Tanis finally said, "what do you say we try another tomorrow?"

"I would find something else," Thomas said. "I really don't think floating down to the black forest is such a great idea anyway."

"Perhaps you are right."

"Tanis?"

"Yes, what is it?"

"Rachelle told me of a fruit that makes you sleep so deeply that you don't remember your dreams."

"So deep that you don't even dream," he said. "Would you like me to find you some?"

"No. No, I need to dream. But is there also fruit that just makes you sleep?"

"And still dream?"

"Yes."

"Of course!"

"The nanka!" Johan cried. "Do you want some?"

An amazing thought. To be able to enter his dreams at will. Or to turn them off by not dreaming.

"Yes. Yes, I would like that. Maybe one of each."

26

"WHAT?" THOMAS sat up on the couch.

"Sorry, you said five hours, but I fell asleep," Kara said. "It's been eight."

"What time is it?"

"Close to noon. What is it? You look like you've seen a ghost."

His head swam. "Am *I* a ghost?"

Kara ignored the question. "You found something out, didn't you? What is it?"

Thomas rolled off the couch and stood. "I think I can turn off my dreams," he said.

"Completely?"

"Yes, completely. Not here. There. I can stop dreaming of this."

"And what good would that do you? This is pretty important."

"This is also a major distraction to me. I'm trying to remember my life, and instead I keep running up against this."

"So you would just fall asleep and wake up and never dream of any of this again? It would just . . . disappear?"

"Yes, I think it would."

"Well, don't you dare turn off your dreams, Thomas. You don't know what would happen. What else did you learn?"

The rest of his dream came to him in a barrage of images that ended with Rachelle telling him where she would like to be rescued.

He turned to her, wide-eyed. "That's it!"

"What's it?"

"It's a map. Is Raison awake?" He ran toward the doors. "A map, Kara!" he said, turning. "We have to find a map."

"What's going on?" she demanded.

"I think she told me where to find Monique. Is Jacques awake?"

"Yes." Kara ran after him through the door. She followed him straight to the office. "Who told you?"

"Rachelle!"

"How would Rachelle know?"

"I don't know. She just made it up. Maybe she doesn't know." Thomas ran past a stunned guard and threw the door open. The old man sat at his desk, dark circles prominent under his eyes. He spoke urgently into his phone.

"I think I may have it!" Thomas shouted.

Raison dropped the phone into its cradle. "You know where Monique is?"

"Maybe. Yes, I think maybe I do. I need a map and someone who knows this area."

"How could you know?"

"Rachelle told me. In my dreams."

The man's face sagged noticeably. "That's very encouraging."

Thomas felt his patience slip. "Well, it should be. For all I know, *you're* the dream!" He jabbed his finger at Jacques. "You ever consider that? Don't be so . . . so stuck up." He'd been better with the diplomacy last night.

"Now I'm a dream," Raison said. "Very, very encouraging. Mr. Hunter, if you think I will—"

"I don't think you will do anything. Except help me find your daughter. What if I'm right?"

"The what-ifs again."

"I know where Monique is!" he shouted.

Kara stepped forward. "I would listen to him, Mr. Raison. I don't think he's been wrong yet."

"Of course, the big sister speaks. My daughter's kidnappers-turned-saviors have spoken. The little people in their dreams have told them where my daughter is. Then let's warm up the helicopter and scoop her up, shall we?"

Thomas stared, dumbfounded at Raison's arrogance. Jacques was stressed out. He needed a shock to his system.

He spun around and strode for the door. "Fine. We'll let her rot in the cell she's in."

Kara delivered one last salvo. "How dare you mock me, you walking ox! You have no idea what a terrible mistake you're making."

They got to the door before he spoke.

"I'm sorry. Wait."

"Wait?" Thomas said, turning. "Now you want to sit around and wait?"

"You made your point. Tell me where you think she is."

Thomas hesitated. He had the upper hand; he intended to keep it. Tell-ing the man that Monique was in a—what was it, a great white cave full of bottles where a river and the forest meet, a day's walk to the east? Wouldn't do.

"Get me a map and someone who knows southern Thailand. And then I want Deputy Secretary Merton Gains on the line. Then I'll tell you where Monique is."

"You're making demands again? Just tell—"

"The map, Jacques! Now."

<hr />

They had a large map of Thailand and the gulf countries on the conference table. Jacques insisted that he knew the region well enough, but Thomas wanted a local. The bulky Thai guard who limped into the room was none other than one of Thomas's security guard casualties.

Muta Wonashti was his name. Thomas stretched out his hand. "Taga saan ka?" *Where are you from?*

The man paused at Thomas's use of his language. "Penang."

"Welcome to the team. Sorry about the other day."

The man seemed to straighten. He walked up to the map, limp now gone.

Jacques glared. "Satisfied?"

"Is Gains on the line?"

Nancy stepped forward with a phone. "He's waiting."

"You have no idea how embarrassing this will be if you are wrong," Jacques said. "I've expended considerable equity on you."

"Not on me, Jacques. On your daughter." Thomas took the phone. "Secretary Gains?"

"Speaking," Gains's familiar voice said. "I understand that you have some new information."

"That's correct," Thomas said. "I really can't keep trying to prove myself at every turn, Mr. Gains. It's slowing us down."

There was a pause.

"You see? You still don't know whether or not to believe me. I'm not saying I blame you; it's not every day someone tells you a virus is about to wipe out the world, and they know so because they've dreamed it."

"I will remind you that I did hear you out," Gains said. "And I did mention the situation to the president. In this world, that's sticking my neck out for you, son. I'm sticking my neck out for a kidnapper who's having crazy dreams."

"Which is why I'm calling. To the point: I've had a dream and in this dream, I've learned where they're keeping Monique de Raison. In front of me I have a map. I want you to begin to accept me on my terms if it turns out that I'm right about where Monique is. Fair enough?"

Gains thought about it.

"If I'm right, Mr. Secretary, and there is a virus, we'll need a few believers. I need someone on the inside."

"And that would be me."

"No one else is volunteering at the moment."

"You say you found out where they have Monique from your dreams. No other information?"

"Bona fide, 100 percent dream. Not a hint of any other intelligence."

"So if you actually find her, you think it proves that your dreams are valid and should be taken seriously," Gains said.

"It won't be the first time I'm right. I need an ally."

"Okay, son, you have a deal. Put Mr. Raison on the line."

"I don't suppose you could get me a team of Rangers or Navy SEALs?" Thomas asked.

"Not a chance. But the Thai have good people. I'm sure they'll cooperate."

"They still think I'm the kidnapper," Thomas said. "Cooperation isn't exactly flowing over here."

"I'll see if I can't get them to ease up."

"Thank you, sir, you won't regret this." He handed the phone to an impatient Raison, who listened and ended the call with a polite salutation.

"Now, please tell me. I've done everything you've asked."

Thomas leaned over the map. "A great white cave full of bottles a day's walk to the east where a river and the forest meet," he said. "Where is that?"

"What's that?"

Thomas looked up. "That's where she is. We just have to figure out what that means."

The man's face lightened a shade. "That's your . . . that's what this is all about? A white cave full of bottles?"

"Yes, but Rachelle wouldn't know what a laboratory looked like. A white cave full of bottles has to be a laboratory, right? They took her to an underground laboratory a day's walk to the east where a river meets the forest. That's about twenty miles."

"How many kilometers?" the tracker asked.

"Roughly thirty."

"The Phan Tu River cross plain here." The squatty fighter drew his finger along a blue river line on the map. "It end here at the jungle. Thirty kilometer east. No lab. Concrete. No longer in use."

Thomas stared at the man. "A concrete plant? Right there?"

"Yes."

Jacques de Raison ran both hands through his hair. "How do you know this is accurate? And how—"

"You have a helicopter, Mr. Raison," Thomas said. "Is your pilot here?"

"Yes, but surely this is a matter for the authorities. You can expect—"

"I can expect that whoever attacked us in that hotel room is smarter than any team the Thai military can throw together on a moment's notice. I can expect that *they* will expect a possible rescue mission by the Thai government and are thoroughly prepared. And I can expect you would do anything, Mr. Raison, anything at all to see your daughter alive again. Am I missing something here?"

He responded momentarily. "You're right."

"Send me in with a radio and a guide, say Muta here, drop us off a few miles out, and we can at least locate her, maybe do more. At this point, we're operating on one of my dreams, not enough to bring out the U.S. Marines. But if we can get something on the ground, we have a whole new story."

The man paced, squinting and scratching at his head. "And you think you're the one to go in?"

"I know a few new tricks."

Kara raised her brow. "He does indeed."

"And I practically grew up in the jungle."

"You're under house arrest. This is just not feasible—"

Thomas slapped the map. "Nothing is feasible, Mr. Raison. Nothing! Not my dreams, not the virus, not your daughter's kidnapping. We're running out of time here. If anyone can rescue your daughter, I can. Trust me. I'm *supposed* to rescue your daughter."

27

CARLOS PATIENTLY led Svensson down the concrete steps. His bad leg made stairs nearly impossible. The Swiss had flown into Bangkok during the night and arrived at the old lab an hour earlier. Carlos had never seen the kind of rabid intensity that had emerged in him.

"Open it," he said at the steel door.

Carlos slid the latch and shoved the door open. The white lab gleamed under two rows of bare fluorescent bulbs. Svensson had built or converted two dozen similar labs throughout the world for an eventuality like this one. The discovery of a possible virus. If a virus presented itself in South Africa, they needed to be in South Africa. Ultimately they would return to the much larger labs and production facilities of the Alps, of course, but only when they had what they needed firmly secured and the environment it came from thoroughly analyzed.

Here, in Southeast Asia, they had six labs. Raison Pharmaceutical's move from France to Thailand precipitated the building of this particular one. And now it was paying its dividends.

The lab was equipped with all the equipment expected of any medium-sized industrial lab, including refrigeration and heating capabilities. Monique sat in the corner, gagged with duct tape and bound to a gray chair. Carlos hadn't hurt her. Yet. But he'd talked to her at length. The fact that she refused to engage him with more than a grunt convinced him he would have to hurt her soon.

"So, this is the woman the world is screaming about," Svensson said, moving slowly over the white tile floor. He stopped three feet from Monique. "The one who's chosen not to see the light yet?"

Carlos stood with his hands clasped in front of him. He didn't answer. Wasn't expected to answer. Wouldn't have anyway. He'd done his part; now it was time for Svensson to do his part.

The Swiss's big bony hand flashed out and slapped loudly against Monique's cheek. The woman's head jerked to the side and her face flushed red, but she didn't breathe a sound.

Svensson smiled. "You've seen me. And you obviously recognize me. I believe we even met once, at the Hong Kong drug symposium two years ago. Your father and I are practically bosom buddies, if you stretch things a bit. Do you see the problem in this?"

She didn't respond. She couldn't.

"Remove it, Carlos."

Carlos stepped forward, ripped the gray duct tape from her mouth.

"The problem is that I've committed myself to you," Svensson said. "You can now finger me. Until the time comes when I no longer care if I'm identified by you, I have to keep you under lock and key. Then, depending on how you treat me now, I will either let you live or have you killed. Does this make any sense to you?"

She drilled his face with a stare and said nothing.

"A strong woman. I may be able to use you when this is over. Soon, very soon." Svensson stroked his mustache and paced in front of her. "Do you know what happens to your Raison Vaccine when it's heated to 179.47 degrees and held at that temperature for two hours?"

Her eyes narrowed for a brief moment. Carlos didn't think she knew. In fact, *they* didn't know for sure.

"No, of course you don't," Svensson said. "You've never tested the vaccine under such adverse conditions; there'd be no need to. So let me make a suggestion: When you apply this specific heat to your miraculous drug, it mutates. You do know it's capable of mutating, because according to our internal sources, it also mutates at a lower heat, but the mutations never could sustain themselves for more than a generation or two."

Monique's eyes widened briefly. She'd just learned there was a spy in her own lab. Perhaps now she would take them seriously. Carlos was surprised that Svensson told her so much. Clearly he didn't expect her to live to tell.

"Yes, that's right, we are quite resourceful. We know about the mutations and we also know that other, much more dangerous mutations hold under more intense heat. Your Raison Vaccine becomes my Raison Strain, a highly infectious, airborne virus with a three-week incubation period." He smiled. "The whole world could have the disease before the first person showed any symptoms. Imagine the possibilities for the man who controlled the antivirus."

A tremble took Monique's face. It was the kind of response that undoubtedly had Svensson's heart pounding like a fist. He'd called her bluff, suggested an incredible possibility they'd only just pieced together themselves. And she was responding with terror.

Monique de Raison's face was screaming her answer. And no other answer could have been better. She, too, knew all of this. Or at least suspected it with enough conviction to drain the blood from her face. She'd spent a few hours alone with Thomas Hunter, the dreamer, and she'd come away somehow convinced that her vaccine did indeed pose a real risk.

"Yes, the vaccine to the AIDS virus has 375,200 base pairs . . . isn't that what this Hunter told you? And he was right. So much information for a simpleton from America. It's too bad we don't have him as well. Unfortunately, he's dead."

Svensson turned and started to walk toward the door.

"I hope Daddy loves his daughter, Monique. I really do. We're going to do some wonderful things in the days to come, and we would like you to help us."

He limped slowly, right foot clacking on the concrete. Svensson was in his game.

Carlos pulled out the transmitter. "Don't forget the explosive in your belly," he said. "I can detonate it by pressing this button, as I've told you. But it will detonate on its own if it loses a signal past fifty meters. Think of it as your ball and chain. Don't think anyone will come for you. If they do, they will only kill you."

She closed her eyes.

Perhaps he wouldn't have to hurt her after all. Better that way.

The helicopter was a standby, an old bubble job that held four and ran on pistons. Thomas and the guide dropped into a rice paddy three miles south of the concrete plant and angled for the jungle to their right. The banger lifted and banked for home. They were now dependent on the radios, Muta's nose, and Thomas's tricks.

They slogged through the water to high ground, then followed the tree line at an easy jog. Both carried machetes, and Muta carried a 9-millimeter on his hip. The foliage slowed them down, forcing them to hack their way through vines and underbrush. Three miles took them a full hour.

"There!" Muta thrust his machete out at the clearing ahead. Half a dozen concrete buildings in various degrees of deterioration. An overgrown parking lot with large tufts of grass growing between the concrete slabs. A rusted conveyor nosing into thin air.

Only one building was large enough to conceal any underground work. If they had Monique there, underground, the first building on their left looked like the best bet. Although, at the moment, all bets looked pretty weak.

He'd made bold statements and fired off thundering salvos, but standing here on the edge of the jungle, with cicadas screeching all around and the hot afternoon sun beating on his shoulders, the notion that the genesis of a worldwide virus attack lay hidden in this abandoned concrete plant struck him as ludicrous.

What if he was wrong? The question had dogged him since the helicopter had abandoned them an hour earlier. But now it went from question to haunting certainty in one giant leap. He was wrong. This was nothing more than an abandoned concrete plant.

"It is abandoned?" Muta said.

He knows it too.

"You get behind the shed," Thomas said, pointing to a small structure thirty feet from the entrance to the main building. "Cover me with your gun. You can shoot that thing straight, right?"

Muta tsked in offense. "You kick so good; I shoot better. In military I shoot many gun. Nobody shoot so good as me!"

"Keep it down!" Thomas whispered. "I believe you. Can you hit a man at the door from this distance?"

The man eyed the door a hundred yards off. "Too far."

Good. He was honest, then.

"Okay, you cover me. As soon as I clear the entry, you run up and follow me in." He looked at the machete in his hand. Most of his fighting skills consisted of fist- and footwork, but what good would hand-to-hand combat do him in a place like this? True, he did have some tricks, but his main trick was falling asleep and coming back healthy. A very cool trick, to be sure, but not exactly a knockout blow in a fight.

"Ready?"

Muta released the clip from his pistol, checked it once, and slammed it home in a show of weapon-handling prowess. "You go; I follow."

Not exactly a raid by U.S. Rangers.

"Go!"

He jumped over the berm and ran low to the ground, machete extended. Muta ran behind, feet thudding on the earth.

Thomas was halfway to the door when the doubts began to pile up in earnest. If the man he'd fought in the hotel room was inside this building, he'd be firing bullets. A machete might be less useful than a wet noodle. But hand-to-hand was out of the question; the man was much too skilled and powerful.

He slid to a halt, his back against the wall, the door to his left. Muta pulled up at the shed, gun extended.

Thomas tried the doorknob. Unlocked. He pulled it. Braved a quick look and withdrew. The interior was dark. Vacant.

Vacant, very, very vacant. He swallowed and waved Muta forward. The man ran across the open ground, gun waving.

Thomas stepped into the building.

"They're in," Carlos said, eying the monitor.

"Let them come," Svensson said. "Send a message to her father as soon as you leave. In view of his disregard for the terms we set forward, we have reduced the time for his compliance to one hour. Give him new drop-off instructions. Use the airport."

Svensson strode for the door. "Bring her to the mountain," he said. "I trust this will be the last complication."

They'd seen the pair as soon as the sensors picked them up at the perimeter. They'd even released the security bolts on the doors to let the men in. Like mice to a trap.

How Raison had found this place, Carlos couldn't begin to guess. Why he'd sent only two men, even more mysterious. Either way, Carlos was prepared. What happened to these two was inconsequential. But the lab's cover had been compromised. Svensson would be gone through the tunnels in a matter of minutes, even with his bad leg. Carlos would follow as soon as he had the vaccine.

Carlos stood. "I'll bring her within twenty-four hours. Yes, this will be the last complication."

Svensson was gone.

Carlos took a deep breath and faced the monitor. Perhaps this was better. The mountain complex in Switzerland had a far more extensive lab. The entire operation would be launched from yet another secured facility. The six leaders who'd already agreed to participate, should Svensson succeed, had established links with the base. The complication would change—

Carlos blinked at the monitor. The lead man's face had come into full view for the first time. This was either Thomas Hunter or Thomas Hunter's twin.

But he'd killed Hunter. Impossible! Even if the man had survived a bullet to the chest, he would be in no condition to run through the jungle.

Still, there he was.

Carlos stared at the image and considered his options. He would let the mouse into his trap, yes. But should he kill him this time?

It was a decision he wouldn't rush. Time was now on his side. At least for the moment.

Vacant. Very vacant and very dark.

A flight of stairs to his right descended into blackness.

"There." He pointed the machete at the stairwell.

He ran for the stairs and descended on the fly, using the light from the gaping door above to guide his steps. A steel door at the bottom. He tried the handle. Open. The door swung in. A dark hall. Doors on either side. At the end, another door.

A thin strip of light ran like a seam beneath the far door. Thomas's heart pounded. He kept his machete leveled in both hands. Two careful steps forward before remembering his backup. Muta.

He eased back, glanced up the stairs. No Muta.

"Muta?" he whispered.

No Muta. Maybe Muta had gone back to cover the front door. Maybe he'd been taken out. Maybe . . .

Thomas began to panic. He breathed deliberately, shrouded in the darkness. It was a nightmare and he was the lone fugitive, panting down deserted dark hallways with the phantoms at his heels. Only his phantom had a gun, and Thomas had already felt a couple of its slugs.

No way he could go back up those stairs now. Not if there was someone up there waiting.

He ran toward the door at the hall's end. Rubber soles muted his footfalls. He was passing other doors on either side. *Whoosh, whoosh,* like windows into gray oblivion. Doors into terror. He ran faster. Suddenly it was a race to get into the door with the light.

He crashed into it, desperate for it to be open. It was. He burst through, blinded by light. He slammed the door shut. Shoved a bolt home and gasped for breath.

"Thomas?"

Thomas spun. Monique was strapped to a chair in the corner beyond a row of white tables with bottles on them. This was the room Rachelle had wanted to be rescued from, almost exactly as he'd imagined it. But this wasn't Rachelle; this was Monique.

Her eyes were wide and her face white. "You . . . you're dead," she said. "I saw him shoot you."

Thomas walked to the middle of the floor, mind reeling. She was actually here. He wasn't sure if it was an intense sense of relief or a general kind of madness that made him want to cry.

He was suddenly running again, straight for her. "You're here!" He slid behind her and ripped at the duct tape that bound her hands to the chair legs. "Rachelle told me you'd be here, in the white cave with bottles, and you're here." An uncontrolled sob was in the mix, but he recovered quickly. "This is incredible; this is absolutely incredible."

He pulled a trembling Monique to her feet, threw his arms around her, and hugged her dearly. "Thank God you're safe."

She felt stiff, but that was to be expected. The poor soul had been taken at gunpoint and—

"Thomas?" She gently pushed him away. Glanced at the door.

Thomas fell back a step and followed her glance. The door was locked from this side. Monique wasn't doing backflips at his rescue, and he wondered why.

"I came to rescue you," he said. The reality of what he was doing, where he was, suddenly crashed in around him. He blinked.

"Thomas, we have a problem."

"We have to get out of here!" He grabbed her hand and pulled. Then doubled back for the machete he'd set on the ground. "Come on!"

"I can't!" She jerked her hand free.

"Of course you can! It's true, Monique, all of it. I knew about the

AIDS pairs, I knew about the Raison Strain, and I knew how to find you. And I know that if we don't get out of here, we're going to have more problems than either of us can imagine."

She spoke quickly in a half whisper, hands on her belly. "He forced me to swallow an explosive device. If I go more than fifty meters from him, it will kill me. I can't leave!"

Thomas looked at her stricken face, her hands trembling over her stomach. His mind went blank.

"You have to get out, Thomas. I'm sorry, I'm so sorry for not listening. You were right."

"No, it's not your fault. I kidnapped you." He stepped up to her and for a moment she was Rachelle, begging to be rescued. He almost reached out and swept her hair from her forehead.

"You have to get out now, and tell them it's all true," she said, glancing at the corner.

Thomas saw the small camera and froze. Of course, they were being watched. Muta had been taken out because Monique's kidnapper had seen them coming all the way. They had let Thomas walk into this trap. There would be no way out!

Monique stepped up to him and pulled him tight. Her mouth pressed by his ear. "They are listening; they are watching. Kiss my face, my ears, my hair, like we've known each other for a long time."

She didn't wait for him but immediately pressed her lips against his cheek. She was giving whoever was watching something to think about.

"They have the wrong numbers," she said, louder, but not too loudly. "Only you."

"Only . . ."

"Shh, shh," she hushed him. And then very softly. "His name is Valborg Svensson. Tell my father. They intend to use the Raison Vaccine. Tell him it mutates at 179.47 degrees after two hours. Don't forget. Take the ring carefully off my finger and get out while you can."

Thomas had stopped kissing her hair. He felt the ring, pulling it off.

"Keep kissing me."

He kept kissing.

"I can't leave you here," he said.

"They will need me alive. And if they think you have more information that they need, they won't kill you."

"I'm right about the virus, then."

"You're right. I'm sorry for doubting."

He felt a strange panic grip his throat. He couldn't just leave her here! He was meant to rescue her. Somehow, in some way beyond his understanding, she was the key to this madness. She was at the heart of the Great Romance; he was sure of it.

"I'm staying. I can fight this guy. I've learned—"

"No, Thomas! You have to get out. You have to tell my father before it's too late! Go."

She gave him one last kiss, on the lips this time. "The world needs you, Thomas! They are powerless without you. Run!"

Thomas stared at her, knowing that she was right, but he couldn't leave her like this.

"Run!" she yelled.

"Monique, I can't leave—"

"Run! Run, run, run!"

Thomas ran.

It happened so fast, so unexpectedly, that Carlos found himself off guard. One second he had them both trapped in the laboratory at the end of the long hall. The next Monique was suggesting that Hunter still knew something they did not. That perhaps she and Hunter had planned this together, an interesting thought.

And then Hunter was running.

The American made the hall before Carlos reacted.

He leaped over the body of the guard who'd come with Hunter, threw open the door, and sprang into the hall. Hunter hit him broadside before he had time to bring his weapon around. Then the man was past and sprinting for the stairs.

Carlos let the force of the impact spin his body toward the fleeing figure. He extended his gun, aimed at the man's back. Two choices.

Kill him now with an easy shot through the spine.

Wound him and take him alive.

The latter.

Carlos pulled the trigger. But Hunter had anticipated the shot and dodged to his left. Fast, very fast.

Carlos shifted left and fired again.

But the slug sparked against the steel door. The man was through the door and on the stairs. Carlos felt momentarily stunned. He recovered. Took after the man in a full sprint.

"Run!" the woman screamed from behind.

She stood in the doorframe of her prison.

Carlos ignored her and raced up the stairs, three at a time. Hunter was gone already? Carlos reached the door and flew through it.

The American was at the shed. Cutting behind. Carlos squeezed off a quick shot that took a chunk of concrete from the corner just above Hunter's head. He veered into the open and sprinted for the tree line.

Carlos started his pursuit, knowing the shed would offer a perfect brace for a fully exposed shot at the man. He'd taken only one step before pulling up.

If he and the woman were separated by more than fifty meters, the explosive in her belly would end her life. They needed her alive. She knew and wasn't following.

The man was stretching the distance.

Carlos could leave the transmitter, but the woman might decide to follow, find the transmitter, and escape with it. She was his ball and chain.

Carlos swore under his breath, leaned against the doorframe, and steadied his outstretched gun. The man was only twenty yards from the jungle, a bobbing blotch in the gun sight.

He squeezed off a shot. Another. Then two more in rapid succession.

Smack!

The last bullet hit the man squarely in the back of his head. Carlos saw the man thrown forward with the signature impact of the slug, saw the spray of blood. Hunter disappeared into the tall grass.

Carlos lowered the gun. Was he dead? No one could have survived such a hit. He couldn't leave to check as long as the woman was free and the transmitter was in his pocket. But Hunter was going nowhere soon.

Movement.

The grass. He was crawling?

No, he was up, there, along the trees. Running!

Carlos jerked the gun up and emptied the last clip with three more shots. Hunter vanished into the trees.

Carlos closed his eyes and settled a rage pounding in his skull. Impossible! He was sure he'd hit the man in the head.

Twice the man had eluded him after direct hits. Never again. Never!

The woman's ingenuity was quite unexpected. Admirable in fact.

He walked down the stairs and stared at Monique, who stood in the doorway, arms crossed. He very nearly put a bullet through her leg. Instead, he walked down the hall and slugged her in the gut.

Perhaps he would have to hurt her after all.

28

IT HAPPENED in three segments, branded in Thomas's memory, still hot from the burning. He'd been dodging a spray of bullets, sprinting for the forest, only a few steps from the first tree and sure he'd escaped. Segment one.

Then a bullet had struck his skull. It felt as though a sledgehammer had hit the back of his head. He was flying forward, headlong, parallel to the ground. Everything screamed with pain and then everything went black. Segment two.

He didn't remember landing. He was either dead or unconscious before he hit the ground. But he did remember rolling over after hitting the ground. He was panting and lying on the ground, staring at the blue sky.

He wasn't dead. He wasn't unconscious. And a quick check of his head confirmed that he wasn't even wounded. He was only winded. Segment three.

He'd scrambled for the jungle and run into the trees, chased more by thoughts of what had just happened to him than by the last few bullets.

He'd been shot in the head. He'd lost consciousness before dying. But in the moment before dying he'd awakened in the colored forest, and although he couldn't remember it, he knew he'd been healed by a fruit or the water. For all he knew, the whole journey had lasted only one second.

When he returned to the jungle, it took him two hours to reestablish contact with the base, get to the landing zone, and make the return trip in the helicopter. Time to think. Time to consider a quick trip back to the compound to get Monique out. Or retrieve Muta.

But he knew neither would be there.

A police helicopter checked the place out before his own pickup and confirmed his suspicions. Not a soul.

Even if she had still been there, he couldn't take her. He might be able to withstand the odd lethal blow, but she couldn't. He felt both indestructible and powerless, an odd mix.

Maybe he hadn't been hit. Was there blood on the grass back there? He'd been in too much of a hurry to look. It was all a bit fuzzy. Just the three segments.

Alive, dead, alive.

———

"You what?"

"I paid it," Jacques de Raison said.

Thomas stepped into the office, dumbstruck. His dungarees were caked with mud, his shirt torn from the three-mile run back to meet the pickup, and his boots were leaving marks on Raison's floor.

"You actually gave them the vaccine?"

"They gave me one hour, Mr. Hunter. My daughter's life is on the line—"

"The whole world's on the line!"

"For me it's one daughter."

"Of course, but what about the information I radioed in?"

"The hour was up. I had to make a choice. They wanted only a sample of the vaccine and a file with a copy of our master research data left in a car two miles from the airport. Monique will be in our custody within two days. I had to do it."

Thomas dug into his pocket, pulled out the ring. A gold band with a ruby perched in a four-point setting. He tossed it to Raison.

"What's this?"

"That's the ring your daughter gave me to persuade you that I was telling the truth. If you heat the vaccine to 179.47 degrees and hold that temperature for two hours, it will mutate. The man who has this information is named Valborg Svensson. He also may have the only antivirus."

Jacques de Raison's face lightened a shade. He toyed with the ring absently. "Why didn't you bring her out?"

"Are you listening to me? I understand you're distressed, but you have to pull yourself together. I found her, exactly as I said I would. If you don't buy the ring, then the fact that Svensson changed the deal on you because I found them is enough."

The man dropped heavily to his chair.

"Now they have the vaccine?" Thomas ran a hand through his hair. This was the worst of all worlds. Nothing he was doing was having any real impact on the unfolding drama. Maybe there was no way to stop this matter of the histories.

Kara hurried in. "Thomas! Are you okay?"

"I'm fine. They have the vaccine. They have Monique; they have the vaccine; they know exactly how to force the mutation; they may have the antivirus."

"But the dream. It was real."

"Yes."

"Yes, Peter, I want you to change the testing parameters. Try the vaccine at 179.47 degrees and maintain the heat for two hours."

Jacques de Raison seemed to have come out of his stupor. He was on the phone with the lab. "Watch for mutations and get back to me immediately."

He dropped the phone into its cradle.

"Forgive me, Mr. Hunter. It's been a very hard two days." All business now. "I believe you. At any rate, the tests will speak for themselves in two hours. In the meantime, I suggest we contact the authorities. I know Valborg Svensson."

"And?"

"And if it is true, if it is him . . ." Dots were being connected behind those soft blue eyes of his. "God help us," he said.

"It is him," Thomas said. "Monique insisted. I want to speak to Deputy Gains immediately."

Jacques de Raison nodded. "Nancy, get the secretary on the phone."

∞∞∞

Merton Gains sat alone at his desk and listened to Jacques de Raison for several minutes in a mild state of shock. Six hours ago, hearing Thomas Hunter lay out his test to prove himself, the idea had seemed fanciful. Now that he'd actually done it, Gains felt distinctly unnerved.

He had heard Bob Macklroy explain that Hunter had predicted the Kentucky Derby's outcome. He'd talked to Thomas and reported the possible problems with the Raison Vaccine in the cabinet meeting. He even agreed to test Hunter's dreams. But his indulgences had all seemed quite harmless until now.

Thomas Hunter had gone to sleep, learned Monique de Raison's location, gone to that location, and brought back virtual proof that the virus was in fact in the works.

"He would like to speak to you."

"Put him on," Gains said. "Thomas? How are you?"

"I'm not doing exceptionally well, sir. I hope you're going to be reasonable now, as we agreed."

"Now hold on, son. You have to slow down on me."

"Why? Svensson's obviously not slowing down."

He had a point. "Because, for starters, we don't know there actually is a virus yet. Right? Not until they run the tests."

"Then the Raison Strain will come into existence in exactly two hours. I'm giving you a head start. You have to stop Svensson!"

"We don't even know where this Valborg Svensson is!"

"Don't tell me no one could find this guy. He's not exactly unknown."

"We will find him. But we have no probable cause to—"

"I gave you probable cause! Monique told me he was planning on using the virus; what more do you need?"

Two words pounded in Merton Gains's mind. *What if?* What if, what if, what if? What if Hunter really was right and they were only days away from an unstoppable pandemic? Everyone knew that technology would eventually be used for something other than improving the human condition. The cool air spilling from the vent above his desk suddenly felt very cold. His door was closed, but he could hear the soft footfalls of someone passing by in the hall.

America was purring down the proverbial highway like a well-oiled truck. Banks were trading billions in dollars; Wall Street was noisily swapping nearly as many stocks. The president was due to make a speech on his new tax plan in two hours. And Merton Gains, deputy secretary of state, had a phone to his ear, hearing someone five thousand miles away tell him that in three weeks four billion people would be dead.

Surreal. Impossible.

But what if?

"First of all, I need you to slow down. I'm with you, okay? I said I would be with you, and I am. But you understand how the world runs. I need absolute proof if we expect anyone to listen. These are incredible claims we're dealing with. Can you at least give me that?"

"By the time I get you proof, it will be too late."

"I need you to work with me, at my pace. The first thing we need is the results of those tests."

"But you can at least find Svensson," Thomas said. "Please tell me you can find this guy. The CIA or the FBI?"

"Not in two hours, we can't. I'll get the ball rolling, but nothing happens that fast. If we have a B2 in the air circling Baghdad, we can drop a bomb in an hour, but we don't have B2s in the air or even out of the hangar. We don't even know where Baghdad is on this one; you got me?"

Hunter sighed. "Then I'll tell you what, Mr. Gains. We're toast. You hear me? And Monique . . ." His voice trailed off.

What if? What if?

Gains stood and paced, phone held tightly to his ear. "I'm not saying we can't do anything—"

"Then do *something!*"

"As soon as we hang up, I'll be on the phone with the director of the CIA, Phil Grant. I'm sure they're already all over this thing. For all we know, the Thai police already have whoever picked up the package in custody. At least the car. The kidnapping case is in full swing now, but the virus is a different matter altogether. So far, this looks like corporate espionage to everyone but you and maybe Raison."

"You don't know how slow the wheels of justice turn in Southeast Asia. And it's the virus that will bite us in the backside, not corporate espionage."

"I'll make some calls. But I need proof!"

"And in the meantime I twiddle my thumbs?"

Gains thought about that. "Do what you've been doing. You've done some pretty amazing things in the last few days. Why stop now?"

"You want me to go after Monique? Isn't this just a bit over my head now?"

"I think this is over everyone's head. You're the one with the dreams. So dream."

"Dream. Just like that? Dream."

"Dream."

⁂

The three segments—alive, dead, alive—still buzzed madly in Thomas's brain. He couldn't talk about them. They terrified him.

"What did he say?" Kara asked.

"He told me to wait."

"Just wait? Doesn't he realize we don't have time to wait?"

"And he told me to dream."

Kara walked around the couch. "So he believes you."

"I don't know."

"He's at least beginning to believe that your dreams have some significance. And he's right—you have to dream. Now."

"Just"—he snapped his fingers—"like that, huh?"

"You want me to knock you out? The secretary is only half right. You don't just have to dream, you have to do the right things in your dreams.

Which means doing whatever it takes to get more information on the Raison Strain."

"The black forest," he said.

"If that's what it takes."

Thomas now had two very compelling reasons to return to the black forest, one reason for each reality. The situation here had become critical—he had to accept more risk in uncovering the truth about the histories. And in the colored forest, if he recalled correctly, he was beginning to wonder if he really had crash-landed on a spacecraft.

"Maybe I can talk to Rachelle again. Find out where she wants to be rescued from again. It worked once, right?"

"It did. And what exactly does that mean? Is she somehow Monique? You're talking to Monique in your dreams?"

He sighed. "I don't have a clue. Okay. Knock me out."

Kara dug in her pocket and handed him three tablets.

29

THOMAS SAT up. It was morning. He was in Rachelle's house.

For several long moments he sat there, frozen by a barrage of thoughts from his dream in Bangkok. The situation had gone critical—he had to uncover the truth about the Raison Strain.

True enough, unless that was all a dream.

But there was another reason, wasn't there? He had to learn the truth about Teeleh's claim that Bill and the spacecraft were real. He had to eliminate the confusing possibilities, or he would never settle into the truth.

And yesterday Tanis had shown him how he might be able to mount his own little expedition into the black forest. The colored sword. It was poison to Teeleh.

He jumped out of bed, splashed water on his face, and pulled on his clothes. After leaving Tanis and Johan yesterday, Thomas had intended to eat the nanka that Johan had brought him and fall asleep. But as it turned out, he didn't need any help sleeping just yet. By the time he reached the village, it was almost time for the Gathering. He couldn't miss the Gathering.

Something strange had happened to him that evening while he was in the lake's waters. A momentary shift in his perspective. He'd imagined being shot in the head, but the vision was fleeting.

When he got back from the Gathering, they ate a feast of fruits as they had the first night. Johan sang and Rachelle danced along with Karyl and Palus told a magnificent tale.

But what was Thomas's gift?

Dreaming stories, he told them. He didn't dance like Rachelle or sing like young Johan or tell stories like Palus and Tanis, but he sure could dream stories.

And so he did. He dreamed about Bangkok.

"Good morning, sleepy dreamer." Rachelle leaned against the door, backlit by the sun's rays. "What did we do in your dreams? Hmm? Did we kiss?"

Thomas stared at her, caught by her beauty. The sound of women giggling drifted in from outside.

"Yes, my tulip, I believe I did dream about you."

She crossed her arms and tilted her head. "Maybe this dreaming of yours has more possibilities than I first imagined."

In fact he *had* dreamed about Rachelle. Or at least he had dreamed of talking about his dream of Rachelle. Could he talk to her as if she were Monique?

He crossed to her and leaned against the wall. "If you were held captive and would like me to rescue you, where would—"

"We did this just yesterday," she said. "Are you forgetting again? You still haven't rescued me from the cave with the bottles."

"Well, no . . . you couldn't be rescued."

"You never tried," she said.

He stared at her for a moment, lost. Clearly it wasn't so simple.

"I think I'll go to the forest and think about how to do it," he said.

She stepped aside. "Be my guest."

The women he'd heard laughing were up the path when he stepped past her into the sunlight. They glanced back, whispering secrets.

"Okay, I'll be back."

"Don't be long," Rachelle said. "I want to hear what you've concocted. All of the delicious details."

"Okay."

"Okay."

He made it out of the village after being stopped only twice. Thankfully not by Johan or Tanis. Even more thankfully not by Michal or Gabil. He didn't need the distraction at the moment. Or any dissuasion. He had to keep his mind on this task of his, and if Rachelle wasn't going to shed light on his dreams of Monique, he had to try the black forest before he lost his resolve.

It took him an hour to find the exact clearing where he'd met Tanis yesterday. There, twenty feet to his left, lay the sword. He wouldn't have been surprised if Tanis had returned for it himself. But he hadn't.

He picked up the sword and swung it through the air like a swashbuckler, thrusting and parrying into thin air filled with imaginary Shataiki. It felt uncommonly good. There wasn't much of a handle, but the stick fit his grip perfectly. The blade was thin enough to see through and sharp enough to cut.

He would at least test the Shataiki's reaction to this new weapon of his. What did he have to lose? Surely the beasts would have sentries posted. Within minutes of his appearance at the Crossing, the place would be covered with the bats, and he would pull out the sword and see how they reacted. If the test went especially well, he would see where it might lead.

Thomas glanced at the sun. It was midmorning. Plenty of time.

He reached the white bridge in well under an hour at a steady run. A few days ago it would have taken him longer. He was as fit as he could ever recall.

He stopped at the last line of trees and studied the Crossing. The arching bridge looked unchanged. The river still bubbled green beneath the plain white wood. The black trees on the opposite bank looked as stark as he remembered—like a papier-mâché forest created by a child, branches jutting off at ungainly angles.

The unmistakable flutter of wings drifted across the river. Sentries. Thomas pulled back and dropped to one knee. For a moment the whole notion struck him as both ridiculous and absurdly dangerous. Who was he to think that he could fight off a thousand black Shataiki with a single sword?

He lifted the weapon and ran his finger along its edge. But it wasn't just any sword. If he was right, the wood alone would scatter the vermin. A surge of confidence rippled down his back.

A small stick lay at his knee, red like the sword in his hand. Not too different from what he imagined a small dagger might look like. Thomas snatched it up and slipped it under his tunic at his back. Grasping the sword with both hands, he stood and stepped into the open.

He walked slowly, sword before him. Within twenty paces he reached the bridge. No sign of the bats. He paused at the foot of the bridge, then walked up the planks.

Still no sign of the Shataiki.

He reached the crest of the bridge before he saw them. A dozen, two dozen, a thousand, he couldn't tell, because they were hidden just beyond the tree line with only a few red, beady eyes to show for their presence. But they were most definitely there.

He made a slight waving motion with the sword. The bats made no move. Were they afraid? Or were they just waiting for their leader? Wafts of acidic sulfur drifted past his nostrils. They were definitely there.

"Come out, you filthy beasts," he muttered, straining to see them. Louder now, "Come out, you filthy beasts!"

The eyes didn't move. Only an occasional shift among them even told him they were alive. He took a step forward and called again. "Bring me your leader."

For a long minute there was no movement. Then motion. To his left.

Teeleh's magnificent blue wings wrapped around his golden body and dragged on the ground as he stepped into the open. Thomas had forgotten just how beautiful the larger bat looked. Now, with the sun shining off his skin, the creature looked as though he had just flown down from the upper lake. At thirty paces, only his green, unblinking eyes disconcerted Thomas. He would never grow accustomed to pupil-less eyes.

Teeleh refused to look directly at Thomas, but aimed a stately gaze across the river. No other bats followed.

Thomas swallowed, shifted the sword in his sweating palms, and brought it to his left to bear on the Shataiki leader. The creature gave

Thomas a fleeting glance and returned his eyes to the opposite bank. With a loud flap, he unfolded his wings to their full breadth, shrugged his shoulders, and then wrapped them around his body once again.

"So. You think with your new sword you have power over me. Is that it, human?" The beast still refused to look at him.

Thomas could think of nothing smart in response.

The Shataiki finally shifted his piercing gaze to Thomas. "Well? Are you going to just stand there all day? What is it you want?"

Thomas cleared his throat. "I need to know more about the histories. About the Raison Strain. And then I want you to show me the ship," he said quietly.

"We have an agreement," Teeleh said. "You bring me Tanis, and I show you the ship. Is your memory still slipping? Until you can keep your agreements, you can forget about the histories as well. What does it matter anyway? They are only dreams. Your reality lies behind me, in the black forest, where we have already repaired it."

"I didn't break any agreement. You said you would trade a repaired ship for Tanis. I want to see the ship first. He is waiting to come when I call him."

The Shataiki's eyes widened. Thomas knew then that the Shataiki didn't know what happened outside their miserable black forest. Teeleh was having difficulty finding a response, and Thomas knew in that moment that he could beat this beast.

"You're lying," Teeleh said. "You are as deceiving as the others who've filled you full of lies."

Thomas slowly stepped over the bridge toward the Shataiki. "I lie, you say. And what would this lie gain me? Surely you, the father of lies, should know that lies are spun for gain. Isn't that your chief weapon? And what do I gain by this lie?"

The Shataiki remained silent, face taut, eyes unblinking. Thomas stepped off the bridge and the bat took a step backward. The stench of sulfur from the forest was almost unbearable. "Now, I think that you will show me my ship. What harm is there in that? You didn't lie to me, did you?"

The black leader considered the words. He suddenly relaxed and grinned. "Very well. I will show you. But no tricks. No more lies between us, my friend. Just cooperation. I'll help you, and you can help me."

Thomas had no intention of helping this creature, and the fact that Teeleh didn't seem to understand that gave him even more courage. In the end he was just a big bat with pretty skin and green cherries for eyes.

Thomas walked forward, sword extended.

On the other hand, Thomas had just crossed the bridge and now stood in the black forest. Was he crazy? No, he had to continue. He had to know. If there was a ship as Teeleh claimed, the histories meant nothing. If there was no ship, he would trade information on the histories for another promise to deliver Tanis. He would never fulfill his promise, of course. This was the battle of the minds, and Thomas could beat this overgrown fruit fly.

Teeleh stepped to the side and kept a respectable distance from the sword. A flock of wings took noisy flight when he reached the tree line. Thomas glanced back at the colored trees one last time before stepping into the dark forest.

30

THE MOMENT Thomas stepped into the black forest, Teeleh took to the trees with a mighty *swoosh*. Thomas gripped the red sword with renewed intensity. No fruit, no green, nothing but black. Like walking through a burned-out forest at night.

He stopped. "Which way?"

Teeleh looked down from a tree just ahead. The bat looked too large for the spindly branch he clung to. His beady eyes stared at Thomas, a cross between wonder and disbelief. Or was Thomas simply projecting his own disbelief that he was actually heading in willfully?

Teeleh swept into the air and flew on without responding. He wanted Thomas to follow.

Thomas followed. His heart hammered steadily. He knew he didn't belong here, but still he kept pushing one foot in front of the other.

Clicking and fluttering all around him. No voices. Only the sound of endless wings beating the air and countless claws grabbing at branches as the bats moved from tree to tree.

The air was cool. It was dark down here on the forest floor. Without leaves to block the sun, he would've thought . . .

Thomas looked up. The trees did have a canopy—a hundred thousand black bats directly above, peering down with red eyes. Wordless. Flapping, clicking. They formed a giant black umbrella that followed him deeper and deeper into the forest.

Light from a clearing dawned ahead, and Thomas picked up his pace, drawn by the prospect of getting out from under the living canopy.

Coming into the forest was a mistake. He knew that now. He didn't care if there was a spaceship ahead; the shroud of evil hovering above him would never allow him to escape alive. He would catch his breath in this clearing and return to the Crossing. Maybe he could negotiate with—

Thomas stopped. Sunlight reflected off a shiny metal surface across the bare meadow. A ship?

His heart bolted.

A spaceship.

Thomas stumbled forward three steps.

He knew it! He was a pilot from Earth. He had gone through a wormhole or something and crash-landed on this distant planet trapped in time. Here there was good and there was evil, and the two hadn't mixed. But he was different because he was from Earth.

Thomas sprinted toward the spaceship. A dark flock of Shataiki flew in circles above the meadow, whooping and sneering in shrill pitches. The craft sat on its belly, majestic. He remembered this. It was a space shuttle with broad wings. The white shell looked shiny and new. There was a flag on its tail, Stars and Stripes. United States. Big blue letters on the side read *Discovery III.*

Thomas reached the ship just as the drove of Shataiki settled on trees above the craft. He glanced their way and, seeing no change in their behavior, ran his hand along the smooth metal of the fuselage. No tears, no patches. Restored.

Thomas rounded the craft and pulled the release latch. With a hiss that startled him, the door swung slowly up. The hydraulics still worked. He shoved the sword through the opening and clambered in after it.

The sword glowed in the darkness, giving off just enough light for Thomas to see his old cockpit. He couldn't remember any of it, but apparently it, too, had been completely repaired. He stood and walked to the main control panel, using the sword to light his way. The master power switch rested in the *off* position. Surely there could be no power after such a long time. Then again, whoever repaired this craft surely knew mechanics as well as they knew upholstery.

Thomas held his breath, reached down, and flipped the red toggle.

Immediately the air filled with a hum. Lights blinked on all around him. He wiped at the sweat gathered above his eyes and gazed at the lighted instruments before him. He stroked the leather captain's chair and smiled in the cabin's artificial light. But the smile immediately faded. He had no clue what to do with this magnificent craft.

Bill. He needed Bill. *Please let Bill be alive.*

Thomas flipped the switch back off, returned to the door, and lowered himself through the hatch.

If the Shataiki had killed Bill . . .

He shoved the sword into the ground and turned to close the hatch. He grabbed the door with both hands and pulled down against the hydraulic pressure.

Wings fluttered behind him. He released the door and whirled around just in time to see Teeleh descending on the sword still stuck in the earth. His heart leaped into his throat. How could the bat touch the sword? It was like poison, Tanis had said!

But even as he thought it, he realized that the sword had changed. It no longer glowed with the red luster it had just seconds ago. The Shataiki ripped the useless stick out of the ground with a snarl.

"Now you are mine, you fool! Seize him."

Every last nerve in Thomas's body froze at the words. A dozen shrieking Shataiki streaked out of the trees and descended on him before he could convince his muscles to move.

The ship! He could get into the ship!

Thomas spun around. There was no ship.

THERE WAS NO SHIP!

Michal's words strung through his mind. *He is the deceiver.*

A scream wrenched itself from his chest, the kind of full-throated scream that shreds vocal cords. Talons bit into his flesh. He gasped, swallowing the scream.

The small stick at his back! He had to reach it.

Thomas grasped at his back, but the world tipped and he landed on the ground, hard. He tried to strike out. Furry bodies suffocated him. He had to get the colored wood from his waist, but the bats were in his face, digging at his flesh. He instinctively brought his knees up in a fetal position and buried his face in his arms.

"Bring him to the forest!"

A single talon swiped at his back and cut to his spine. Thomas arched his back and groaned. They lashed twine around his neck and feet, and he was powerless to fight against it. Then they began to pull, dragging him a few inches at a time along the ground, wheezing and groaning against his weight.

"Use this, you imbeciles," he heard a Shataiki screech. Bitter, high-pitched arguing. "This way . . ."

"No, you fool . . ."

"Hurry . . ."

"Let go, or I'll cut your hand off!"

"Out of my way . . ."

He was being dragged slowly along the forest floor. They'd tied a tow-rope to his bindings, and no fewer than a hundred black bats were successfully pulling him along the ground.

Sharp objects cut into his back. He moaned and felt the world spin around him. The last thing he saw was the clearing beyond his feet.

The one without a spaceship.

———— ∞∞∞ ————

Thomas awoke to the violent, stinging drag of a taloned claw across his face.

"Wake up!" a distant voice screamed at him. "Wake up! You think you can just sleep through this? Wake up!"

He pried his eyes open and saw a fire dancing at his feet. Where was he? He struggled to raise his head. A clawed fist beat down on his cheek, snapping his head to one side. He began to slip away.

Another loud slap on his right cheek brought him back. "Wake, you useless slab of meat!" Teeleh's voice.

Thomas opened his eyes and saw that he'd been strapped to an upright device by his wrists and his ankles. Scores of the hairy creatures danced about a huge fire roughly thirty feet away. Thousands of beady eyes dotted the dark forest.

He lifted his eyes slowly. Maybe hundreds of thousands. Teeleh stood on a platform to his right.

A Shataiki swooped in from his perch, screeching with delight. "He's awake! He's awake! Can I—"

With a throaty snarl, a huge black beast whirled and swatted the smaller Shataiki from the air. The bat fell to the ground with a thud. Others quickly pounced on him and dragged his twitching body into the shadows.

A hush fell over the gathering. Fire crackled. Shataiki wheezed. A sea of red eyes hovered over him. But it was the image of the large bat, drilling him with glowing red eyes, that struck terror in Thomas's heart.

This was Teeleh.

He'd changed. His skin was pitch-black and cracked, oozing a clear fluid. His wings were flaking, shedding long swaths of fur. Lips peeled back to reveal crusted, yellow fangs. A fly slowly crawled over one of his eyes—red now—but the beast didn't appear to notice.

Thomas rolled his head from left to right. The device on which they had hung him creaked with his movement. He was bound to a crude wooden beam planted upright with a similar beam fixed perpendicular. A cross. They had bound him to the cross with twine. Streaks of blood ran from a dozen gashes on his chest.

He slowly turned farther to his right. The beast's red eyes bulged larger than he remembered. If his hands had been free, he could have reached out and clawed the morbid balls from the fiend's face. As it was, he could only stare into Teeleh's torrid eyes and fight his own terror.

"Welcome to the land of the living," Teeleh said. His once musical voice sounded low and guttural, as if he was speaking past a throat full of phlegm. "Or should I say, the land of the dead. We make no real distinction here, you know." The assembled Shataiki hissed with a laughter that sent chills down Thomas's spine.

"Silence!" the leader thundered.

The laughter ceased. The large beast's vocal range was incredible.

He could switch from a high-pitched squeal to a deep-throated growl effortlessly.

The huge Shataiki turned back to Thomas, leaned forward, and opened his mouth. His breath was moist and smelled like a septic tank. Thomas tried to recoil. He managed a flinch.

Teeleh extended a claw to his face. "You have no idea how delighted I am that you came back to us, Thomas." He began to delicately stroke Thomas's face with the tip of his talon.

"It would have been such a disappointment if you had stayed away." He spoke in a soft, purring voice now. A sick smile pulled his lips back to reveal yellow fangs. Bits of fruit flesh were lodged between his teeth.

"I have always loved you hairless animals, you know. Such beautiful creatures." He ran the back of his furred claw down Thomas's cheek. "Such soft skin, such tender lips. Such . . ."

"Master, we have him," another Shataiki suddenly blurted, staggering from the trees.

The leader's eyes flashed at being interrupted. But then his expression changed to one of amusement and he spoke without turning to face the new Shataiki.

"Bring him in," he commanded. And then to Thomas, "I have prepared a special treat for you, Thomas. I think you will like it."

The throng looked on as a dozen Shataiki dragged another cross into the clearing. A creature had been fixed to the beams. They managed to erect the cross and drop it into a fresh hole not ten feet from Thomas.

A man.

The man's naked body sagged, battered almost beyond recognition. Wide swaths of flesh had been stripped from his torso.

Thomas groaned at the sight.

"Lovely, isn't it?" the beast sneered. He giggled in delight. "You do remember this one, don't you?"

Bill.

"I know what you're thinking," Teeleh said. "You're thinking that the spaceship isn't real and so Bill isn't real. But you're wrong on both counts."

Bill's bloodstained body moved ever so slowly on the cross. The poor soul's hands had been nailed to the horizontal member of the wooden cross, not tied as Thomas's had been. A large spike also jutted from a deep wound in his feet. His eyes had swollen shut, leaving only thin lines. His upper lip had been split open. A tangled mat of red hair fell to the man's shoulder. Thomas closed his eyes and trembled with horror.

The man managed to part one eye to a slit. Tears leaked from his eyes when he saw Thomas. He spoke in a soft, gravelly voice.

"I'm his lover. I . . . I have to die for my lover. I have failed him!" This last he blurted, and then he wept quietly, eyes shut, face twisted in agony.

Teeleh laughed. "You like it? He's alive, waiting for you to rescue him." At that the throng roared with laughter. Thomas kept his eyes closed. A fresh wave of nausea washed through his stomach.

Teeleh let the laughter continue for a few short moments. "Enough!"

Once again to Thomas, with a mocking tone: "Now, here is your means of escape, Thomas. You really do have to escape, because unless you do, you'll never be able to bring me Tanisssss."

Tanis?

Without removing his eyes from Thomas, Teeleh motioned to the darkness. A lone Shataiki hopped toward the platform, dragging Thomas's sword. He lifted it up to the leader and promptly disappeared into the trees. Teeleh took the dark sword and twirled it in the air.

"And to think that you thought you could defeat me with one measly sword. You see, it's useless. Nothing can withstand my power."

A snicker ran through the audience of Shataiki. Teeleh took a step closer to Thomas, eyes glaring. "I told you, this is my kingdom, not his. Here, if you don't take up the sword, you lose its power. You're a fool to think you can defeat me on my own land."

The Shataiki suddenly swung the sword broadside at Thomas's midsection. With a thump, the hard wood struck his bare flesh. He heaved in pain. The night grew fuzzy for a moment and he thought he might pass out.

"Now we will see how bright you are." Teeleh shoved the sword out toward Bill. "Take this sword and kill this slab of flesh. Kill him, and I will release you. Otherwise, I will let you both hang here for a very long time."

The night turned deathly silent.

Kill Bill?

Bill wasn't real, Michal said.

But Bill was real.

Or was he just a figment?

Or was it a test? If he killed Bill, he would be obeying Teeleh by killing another man who in fact could be real. He would be following the wish of Teeleh, regardless of whether Bill was real.

On the other hand, if he *refused* to kill Bill because he believed Bill to be alive, then he was also following the word of Teeleh, who, contrary to Michal, claimed that Bill was real.

No matter what he did, Teeleh would claim a victory.

On the other hand, who cared what Teeleh claimed? Thomas had to survive.

He lowered his head and struggled for a decent breath. He could seem to get enough air into his lungs only when he pushed up and gave his chest muscles room to function.

"What are you waiting for, you fool? You think this miserable soul deserves to live? Look at him!"

Thomas wasn't sure he had the strength to raise his head again. Another blow to his midsection changed his mind.

"Look at him!" the Shataiki snarled.

Thomas raised his head. Even if Bill were real, he wouldn't feel the sword in his current condition. Death would put him out of his misery. How had they managed to keep the poor soul alive this long? He shuddered.

"I told him I would crucify him if he failed to help you drink, " Teeleh said. "Now you can be the one to thrust the sword into his side. Be merciful and kill this pig."

There was no way out. If Thomas didn't kill this poor soul, they would both die. He closed his eyes, took another pull of air, and groaned.

"What was that, a yes?"

"Yes."

The hushed mob of Shataiki erupted in a frenzy of excited whispers and hisses.

"A wise choice," Teeleh said softly. "Pull him down! Let the human show us what he's made of."

A dozen black bats immediately flew to the cross and began to pick at the twine that held Thomas. His right hand came free first and he slumped forward at an odd angle that almost pulled his left shoulder out of joint. His feet fell free next, and for an unbearable moment he hung only by his left arm. The rope tore loose and he crashed to the ground.

The Shataiki began singing in odd, twisted voices that pierced eerily into the night—grossly absent of melody, yet heavy with meaning.

"Kill . . . kill . . . kill . . ."

The leader leaped off the platform and stood to one side. The fire seemed to burn brighter as the throng pressed in closer.

Thomas pushed himself up to a kneeling position. He faced the cross on which Bill hung.

Teeleh spread his wings to their full breadth. The volume of the Shataiki's song slowly grew, drumming deep into Thomas's mind.

"Now, my son. Show me your submission by taking the sword with which you came to kill me, and kill this man instead." With that, the Shataiki shoved the sword deep into the earth at Thomas's knees.

The freakish pounding of voices behind the leader continued, and in that moment Thomas doubted very much they would set him free without horrific consequences. Coming into the forest had been a terrible—

Thomas suddenly flinched.

"What?" Teeleh demanded.

The stick at his back. The dagger! Had they taken it? No, they hadn't even seen it. It was under his tunic. It had been in contact with his flesh the whole time.

"Take the sword!" Teeleh thundered.

Thomas felt a surge of energy spread through his bones. He gripped the blackened sword with his hands and used it as a crutch to drag himself to his feet.

The chanting grew louder. Its pitch rose higher.

Thomas's head swam, and without the sword to steady himself he might have collapsed. He leaned on the black stick and waited for his legs to steady. Teeleh stood still, no more than three paces to his right, wings now wrapped around his shoulders in stately fashion. Thomas gripped the sword with both hands and pulled it free from the ground.

He looked up at the body that hung on the cross, close enough to touch. He slowly raised the sword in his right fist.

The chanting rose to a roar, and the leader grinned wickedly.

Still shaking on his feet, Thomas slipped his left hand behind his back and under his tunic.

There. It was still there! He gripped the dagger with his fingers and jerked it into the open.

The effect was immediate. A hundred thousand Shataiki fell mute, as if somewhere in the back, behind the stage, some little idiot bat had tripped over a cord and pulled the plug.

Thomas stared at the glowing red dagger in disbelief. He swung to Teeleh, holding the knife out before him.

The large black Shataiki's face was frozen in the firelight. Teeleh took a step back from the blade. Thomas waved the knife a few inches and watched in amazement as the beast leaped back in fear. He felt the corners of his mouth edge up. Adrenaline poured new strength into his muscles.

He staggered to the edge of the clearing. Bats scattered, screeching.

Bill. He couldn't leave Bill.

Thomas spun around. But there was no Bill. Of course there was no Bill. Just as there was no spaceship.

Thomas looked at Teeleh. "You see what Elyon can do with only one *human?*" he asked quietly. "One human and one small blade of wood, and you're nothing but a sack of leather."

The leader's face twisted in rage. He thrust a wing forward. "Attack him!" he screamed. A single Shataiki with inordinate courage streaked from a low branch toward Thomas. A dozen others followed.

Maybe he had spoken too early. He shifted the dagger toward the first onrushing bat and stiffened for the impact.

But the shrieking bat's extended talons, followed by the rest of its body, fell limp the instant the glow from the extended dagger touched its skin. Its momentum carried the bat hurtling into the ground, where it crumpled in a heap of dead fur.

Two other bats made the same journey before the rest broke off the attack, shrieking in defeat. Thomas shifted his shaking limbs. He looked back toward Teeleh, who stood trembling.

"Never!" he shouted. "Not now, not ever. You will never win."

With that, Thomas turned from the throng and staggered into the forest, dagger held high.

⚬⚭⚬

The bats kept their distance, but it sounded like every last one of them was following. Flapping, clicking, and now shrieking.

He still had to find the Crossing. How far had they carried him after attacking him at the clearing? It had been roughly midday, and then night when he came to on the cross. Now it was moving toward morning.

He hadn't dreamed while unconscious. Or if he had, he couldn't remember what he'd dreamed. Strange. What was happening in Bangkok? Maybe nothing. Maybe there was no Bangkok, just as there was no spaceship and no Bill. Maybe that's why he wasn't dreaming anymore.

It was the rising sun that saved him. A very soft glow in the east. Thomas pulled up in a clearing. If that was east, then the river was directly ahead, north.

A black canopy moved against the dim sky.

"Get away!" Thomas shouted, waving the dagger.

Shrieks echoed and the canopy lifted from the trees. Then settled again. Somewhere out there Teeleh watched.

Watched and waited.

He hit the river an hour later. No Crossing. The question was: Right or left? His back and chest burned with deep cuts. If he couldn't find the Crossing soon, he would just jump into the river and swim across. Could he do that?

Thomas turned east and jogged along the river. The bats followed in the trees. On the other side of the river, the colored forest glowed like a rainbow.

He was seriously considering a dive into the river when he caught the glint of white directly ahead.

He pulled up, panting. There, arching lazily over the bubbling green waters, a white bridge stretched from the dark, harsh ground on which he stood to a lush landscape, bursting with color and life.

The Crossing.

He swallowed at the sight and surged forward on wobbly legs. He had made it.

He had actually made it! Twice now he'd talked to Teeleh and survived. The big, ugly bat wasn't all that powerful after all. It was simply a matter of knowing how to defeat him. Knowledge was the key. You know what to do, and you—

Thomas stopped midstride.

There, near the bridge on the opposite shore, silhouetted by the lucent forest, stood the unmistakable figure of a human.

Tanis!

The man stared at Thomas, frozen like a statue. In his hands he held a red sword like Thomas's. A sword?

A rush filled the air. Teeleh settled to the ground, directly opposite Tanis. He was no longer the black creature, but the beautiful bat, glowing blue and gold. A chill swept down Thomas's spine.

The Shataiki folded his wings and opened his mouth wide. At first nothing happened. And then he began to make a noise.

The sound that issued past Teeleh's trembling pink tongue was unlike any Thomas had ever heard. It was not speech. It was song. A song with long, low, terrifying notes that seemed to crackle in heavy vibration, slamming into Thomas's chest.

It was as though the beast had harbored the song for a thousand years, perfecting each tone, each word. Saving it for this day.

Words came with the song now.

"Firstborn," the leader sang out, spreading his wings. In his right wing he carried a fruit. "My friend, come in peace."

The song reverberated through the air. A lovely song. A song of peace and love and joy and fruit so delicious that no person could possibly resist.

And Thomas knew that he must, at all costs.

Tanis watched Teeleh with bulging eyes.

Thomas found his voice. He began to yell, to scream at Tanis. But Teeleh only sang louder, drowning him out.

There were two melodies, spun as one, twisted and entwined into a single song. On one strand, beauty. Breathtaking life. On the other, terror. Endless death.

He looked at Tanis. The expression of delight plastered on the man's face told Thomas that Tanis could not hear the other notes. The twisted ones. He heard only the lovely song. The pure tones of song that rivaled those spun by Johan, or those sung by—

And then he recognized one of the melodies. It was from the lake! A song from Elyon!

Thomas struggled to his feet as the song's meaning became clear. He forced air through his lungs. "Run, Tanis!" Thomas screamed across the river. "Run!"

Tanis stood transfixed by the large Shataiki.

"Tanis, run!" Thomas bellowed.

He reached the Crossing and staggered up its arch. His vision swam from exhaustion and pain, but he forced his feet on. Behind him, Teeleh's song continued to fill the air.

"Get out of here!" Thomas gasped. He crashed into Tanis. Knocked him from his feet. The sword spun into the river.

"Have you lost your mind?"

The man stammered something and scrambled to his feet.

"Run! Just run!" Thomas propelled Tanis into the forest.

Behind them Teeleh's voice rang out a new chorus. "I have powers beyond your imagination, Tanisssss!"

And then the sounds from the Crossing fell away.

They reached the clearing in which Thomas had first been healed, fifty paces from the river, and Thomas knew that he could not manage another step. His world tipped crazily, and he collapsed on the grass. For a moment he was vaguely aware of Tanis kneeling over him with a fruit in his hands.

Then he was aware of nothing but the distant beating of his heart.

31

THOMAS SAGGED on the couch, looking peaceful and sad at the same time, Kara thought. But behind his closed eyes, only God knew what was really happening. He'd been sleeping two hours, but if she was right, two hours could be two days in the colored forest, assuming he didn't sleep there.

Amazing. If only there was a way for him to bring Rachelle back with him. Or for her to go with Thomas.

The bustle of security and secretaries and white-coated lab technicians had eased for the moment, leaving them alone in the large room they were coming to think of as their situation room.

Six hours had passed since Raison had ordered the tests. And still no answer. No definitive answer, anyway. There'd been a ruckus just after Thomas had fallen asleep, when Peter had barged into the situation room, mumbling incoherently. Peter turned on his heels and hurried into Raison's office, white smock flying behind.

But when Kara ran in, Raison insisted the results weren't conclusive. Even mixed. They had to be sure. Absolutely positive. Another test.

She glanced at her watch. If she didn't wake him soon, he wouldn't sleep well tonight, when he might very well need to. She shook him gently.

"Thomas?"

He bolted up. "Tanis!"

Thomas's eyes jerked about the room. He yelled the name of the first-born from the colored forest. "Tanis!"

"You're in Bangkok, Thomas," Kara said.

He looked at her, closed his eyes, and dropped his head. "Man. Man, oh man, that was bad."

"What happened?"

He shook his head. "I'm not sure. I went into the black forest."

"And? Did you learn anything?"

"There's no ship. He's black! Teeleh is—" He swallowed.

Kara rubbed his back. "Easy. It's okay. You're here now."

He quickly reoriented himself.

"Did you learn anything about the Raison Strain?"

"No . . . he wouldn't tell me. I . . ." Thomas gripped his head, and she saw that his hands were trembling. "Crazy. It was crazy, Kara."

She put her arm around him and pulled him close. "You're okay, Thomas. Easy."

He looked up. "Did anything happen?"

"Nothing positive. They're still testing."

Thomas sighed and sat back into the couch. Kara stood and paced the carpet, thinking. "You sure you're okay? I've never seen you wake this upset."

"I'm fine," he said, but he wasn't fine.

"Maybe we should bring in a psychologist," Kara said. "Maybe there's more of a connection to your dreams than we're understanding. Or maybe there's a way to control them more. Give you suggestions while you're sleeping or something."

"No. The last thing I want is a shrink crawling around in this crazy mind of mine. The fact is, they have the Raison Strain by now, and I know Teeleh will never tell me what we need to know. It's hopeless."

"And is it hopeless there as well?"

"Where?"

"In the colored forest?"

He stood abruptly, gaze lost. He walked to the window and peered out. *He's fried to the bone.*

"I don't know," Thomas said. He faced her. "If I don't get back, it might be! Something's happening to Tanis. If he crosses . . ." Thomas hurried over to her. "I have to get back, Kara. You have to help me get back!"

"You just woke up! We need you here. And you're asleep there right now, right?"

"I'm unconscious there," he said.

"You'll wake when you wake. It doesn't matter how long you're awake here. The times don't correlate, remember? For all you know, someone could be kneeling over you right now, waking you. You can't control that. What you can control is how long you stay awake here. We need you to be awake now. We need your mind here. The results from the tests will be coming down any minute."

He thought about it and then nodded. They sat on the couch, side by side.

"You're sure that you can't get any more information from the black forest?"

"I'm sure."

"And Rachelle wasn't helpful?"

"No."

"Then what do we have left?"

He frowned in thought. "Monique. I think there's something about Monique. We need to find her. Maybe there's something else I can do in the colored forest to find her."

"I think you're right; she's the key."

"I had her, Kara. She was right there in my arms. I could have thrown her over my shoulders and made it. At the very least, I should have stayed."

"You had Monique in your arms?"

"She kissed me; that was her distraction while she told me about Svensson and the virus. But that's not the point."

"Maybe it is the point," Kara said. "You obviously have a thing for her, and you hardly know her."

"That's ridiculous."

"Maybe not. Any other time, maybe. But right now it makes sense." She stood from the couch. "All this talk of rescuing Rachelle, while at the same time Monique is in desperate need of exactly that. And maybe the connection is even stronger. Maybe you're right. Maybe you *have* to rescue Monique. Maybe it's not a matter of stopping Svensson, but rescuing

Monique. Maybe your dreams are telling you that. Why else are you falling in love with her?"

He started to object but thought better of it.

"I mean, from everything I've heard, stopping someone from spreading a virus is almost impossible anyway. Fine, let the authorities do that."

"Great, and Thomas goes after Monique. No need for professionals, CIA, Rangers, SWAT teams. No fear, Thomas is here."

"You managed pretty well this morning," Kara said.

He turned back to the window, hands on hips. "I can't do this anymore."

"Yes, you can," Kara said. "And for all we know, it's just starting. Maybe you need a few new skills."

He didn't answer.

"I'm serious, Thomas. Look at you. You don't die; you don't fight like any man I've seen. You—"

"Trust me, that guy could break my neck with one kick. Fact is, he *did* kill me. Twice."

"You don't sound very dead to me. Listening to you on the phone, you're sounding anything *but* dead these days. You're even turning into a bit of a romantic. Stop being so stubborn about this. I'm just supporting you."

He took a deep breath. "I'm just Thomas, Kara. I didn't ask for this. I don't want to do this. I'm tired, and I feel like a wet rag." He suddenly looked like he was on the verge of tears.

Kara walked up to him and put an arm around his waist. He lowered his head on her shoulder.

"I'm sorry, Thomas. I don't know what else to say. Other than I love you. You're right, you're just Thomas. But I have a feeling Thomas is a much bigger person than anyone, including myself, can possibly guess. I think we've all just seen the beginning."

The door flew open to their right. Jacques de Raison stepped in, face blank.

"So?" Thomas said. "You have it?"

"Monique's right. You're right. The vaccine mutates at 179.47 degrees. As far as we can tell, the resulting virus is extremely contagious and very probably quite lethal."

"What a surprise," Thomas said.

—⊷—

Valborg Svensson wore a soft smirk that refused to budge from his face. In his right hand he held a sealed vial of yellow fluid that diffused the glare of an overhead spotlight. His left hand rested on his lap, quivering slightly. He squeezed his fingers together.

"Who would ever have guessed?" he said. "History changed because of a few drops of such an innocuous-looking yellow liquid and one man who had the stomach to use it."

Eight technicians milled in the lab below, talking, stealing furtive glances up at the window behind which he sat. Mathews, Sestanovich, Burton, Myles . . . the list went on. Some of the world's most accomplished and, as of late, highest-paid virologists. They had sold their souls for his cause. All in the name of science, of course. With a little misdirection from him. They were simply developing lethal viruses for the sake of antiviruses. How many of them truly believed what they were doing was so innocuous, Svensson didn't care. The fact was, they all took his money. More important, they all understood the price of compromising confidentiality.

"Bring her up," he said.

Carlos left without a word.

How many billions had he invested in this venture? Too many to count offhand. They meticulously explored the most advanced science, and yet, in the end, it came down to a vaccine and a bit of luck.

Svensson knew the history of biowarfare well enough to recite in his sleep.

1346: Tartars send soldiers infected with the plague over the wall in the siege of Caffa on the Black Sea.

1422: Attacking forces launch decaying cadavers over castle walls in Bohemia.

American Revolution: British forces expose civilians to smallpox in Quebec and Boston. The Boston attempt fails; the one in Quebec ravages the Continental Army.

World War I: Germans target livestock being shipped into Allied countries. Overall impact on war: negligible.

World War II: Unit 731 of the Imperial Japanese Army directs biowarfare on a massive scale against China. As many as ten thousand die in Manchuria in 1936. In 1940, bags of plague-infected fleas are dropped over the cities of Ningbo and Quzhou. By the end of the war, the Americans and the Soviets have developed significant bioweapons programs.

Cold War: Both the United States and the Soviet Union bioweapons programs reach new heights, exploring the use of hundreds of bacteria, viruses, and biological toxins. In 1972, more than one hundred nations sign the Biological and Toxin Weapons Convention, banning production of biological weapons. There is no enforcement. In 1989, Vladimir Pasechnik defects to Britain and tells of the Soviets' genetically altered superplague, an antibiotic-resistant inhalation anthrax. The Soviet program employs thousands of specialists, many who scatter when the Soviet Union crumbles. Some of these specialists take up residence in Iraq. Others take up residence in the Swiss Alps, under the thumb of Valborg Svensson.

Dawn of the twenty-first century: The first truly successful use of any biological weapon is unleashed. The Raison Strain redefines modern power structures.

The last wasn't yet a matter of history, of course. But the vial in Svensson's hand said it would be soon. In reality, biological weapons were still in their infancy, unlike nuclear weapons. Anyone who understood this also understood that whoever won the unspoken race to perfect the right bioweapon would wield more power than any man who had ever preceded him. Period.

The door opened and Carlos marched a disheveled Monique de Raison forward.

"Sit," Svensson said.

She sat with a little encouragement from Carlos.

"Do you know what would happen if I dropped this vial?" Svensson asked. He didn't expect an answer. "Nothing for three weeks, if your friend is right. And I will say that our people think he very well may be. He was right about the virus, why not about the incubation period?"

Still no reaction. She believed this much already.

"If you only knew the trouble we've accepted over numerous years to be in this position today. Monoclonal antibody research, gene probes, combinatorial chemistry, genetic engineering—we've scoured every corner of Earth for the right breakthrough."

Her eyes remained on the vial.

"And today I have that breakthrough. The Raison Strain—it has a nice ring to it, don't you think? What I need now is the antivirus, or an antidote. There are two ways I can proceed with this task. One: I can have my people work on the numbers we already have. They will eventually develop precisely what I need. Or, two: I can persuade you to develop what I need. You know more about these genes than anyone alive. Either way, I will have an antivirus. But I rather prefer a quick solution to one that drags out for days or weeks or months, don't you?"

"You honestly think I would lift a finger to help you with any part of this . . . this insanity?" She had the look of someone who was seriously considering an assault. If her hands weren't bound, she might have tried. Her spirit was entirely noble.

"You already have," he said. "You've created the vaccine, and you've provided more research than I could have hoped for. Now it's time to help us with the cure. A cure doesn't interest you, Monique?"

"Without the antivirus, you have nothing."

"Not true," Svensson said. "I have the virus. And I will use it. Either way."

"Then throw it on the floor now," she said evenly. "We'll die together."

He smiled. "Don't tempt me. But I won't, because I know that you will help us. If nothing else, the fact that this virus now exists will force your hand. Every day that passes without a way to protect the world's population against this disease is a day closer to your torment."

"You think my father isn't already working on an antivirus?"

"But how long will it take him? Months, best case. I, on the other hand, have some idea where to begin. I'm confident we can do it in a week. With your help, of course."

"No."

"No?"

"No."

She would change her mind within twenty-four hours.

"I'll give you twelve hours to change your mind on your own. Then I will change it for you."

She didn't react.

"No more word, Carlos?"

"None."

The first call from the authorities had come two hours ago. A courtesy call from his own government, requesting an interview of the highest priority. It meant that they suspected him already. Fascinating. It was Thomas Hunter, of course. The dreamer. Carlos had said he'd killed the man in the hotel room, but the media said differently. Carlos either had lied deliberately or, more likely, had been bested by this man. It was something he would keep in mind.

The authorities didn't have enough for a search warrant. He'd granted them their interview, but not for two more days. By then it wouldn't matter.

"Everything is ready?"

"Yes."

"Then I will handle the next move. I want you to eliminate the American."

He watched Carlos. Not a flinch, just a steady gaze. "I shot the American twice. You're saying that he's not dead?"

The woman glanced up at Carlos. She, too, knew something.

"He's alive enough to be in the news. He's also the source of the antivirus. I want him dead at all costs."

Monique turned to him. "Are you aware that your right-hand man is lying to you? One of the men who came for me outside Bangkok was Thomas Hunter. Carlos knows that. Why is he hiding this from you?"

"Thomas Hunter?" Carlos looked at the woman with some surprise. "I don't think that's possible. He may not be dead, but he has two bullets in his chest. And he's a civilian, not a soldier."

Her accusation was meant to sow distrust. Smart. But he had far more reason to distrust her than Carlos.

The man from Cyprus faced him. "I will leave immediately. Thomas Hunter will be dead within forty-eight hours. On this you have my word."

Svensson looked back into the lab. The technicians were huddled over three different work stations now, assessing the information Carlos had reported from Thomas Hunter, this string of numbers.

Svensson now faced two very significant risks. One, that his operation would be found out. Unlikely, considering all their meticulous planning, but a risk nonetheless. Timing was now critical.

The second significant risk was that neither his people nor Monique could develop an antivirus in time. He was willing to accept that risk. His name was now out there; sooner or later they would know the truth. If he didn't succeed now, he would either spend the rest of his life in a prison or die. The latter was more appealing.

"I will be contacting the others in a few hours. Meet us at the control facility as soon as you've eliminated Hunter. Take her."

———

Thomas stared at the monitor that displayed what the electron microscope had uncovered. The Raison Strain. He tried to imagine how a sea of these tiny viruses could possibly hurt a flea, much less slaughter a few billion people. They looked like an Apollo lunar-lander, a miniature pod on legs that had landed its host cell.

"That's the Raison Strain?"

"That's the Raison Strain," Peter said. "Looks harmless, doesn't it?"

"Looks like a tiny machine. So the mutation is sustained even when the temperatures come down?"

"Unfortunately, yes. It's terribly unusual, you know. No regulation or protocol even suggests testing vaccines at such a high temperature. No one could have possibly guessed that mutation was even possible at such a temperature."

Thomas straightened. Jacques de Raison stood by Kara and a half dozen other technicians in white coats.

"And how can you tell what the virus will do?"

Peter looked at Raison, who nodded. "Show him."

Peter led them to another computer monitor. "We're basing the conclusions on a simulation. Two years ago this would have taken a month, but thanks to new models that we've developed in conjunction with DARPA, we're down to a few hours." He tapped several keys and brought the screen to life.

"We feed the genetic signature of the virus into the model—in this case human—and then let the computer simulate the effect of infection. We can squeeze two months into two hours."

"Put it on the big screen, Peter," Raison said.

The image popped up on an overhead screen.

"Hold on . . . there."

A single cell appeared.

"That's a normal cell taken from a human liver. Lodged on its outer membrane you can see the Raison Strain, introduced through the blood supply—"

"I don't see it."

"It's very small, one of the reasons it fares so well as an airborne agent." Peter stepped up and pointed to the left side of the cell with a wand. "This small growth here. That's the Raison Strain."

"That's the deadly beast?" Thomas said. "Hard to believe."

"That's it on day one, before lysogeny—"

"Could you explain it in layman's terms? Pretend I'm a fifth grader." Peter smiled awkwardly.

"Okay. Viruses aren't cells. They don't grow or multiply like cells do. They consist basically of a shell that harbors a little bit of DNA. You know what DNA is, right?"

"Blueprint for life and all that."

"Good enough. Well, that shell we call a virus is able to attach to a cell wall and squirt its viral DNA inside. Think of it as a nasty little bug. The squirted DNA makes its way into the DNA of the host cell, in this case a liver cell, so that the host cell will be forced to make more viral shells as well as pieces of identical viral DNA. Follow?"

"This little bug can do all that? You'd think it has a mind of its own."

"That and more. Viruses are assembled; they do not grow. They take over the host and turn it into a factory for more viral shells, which repeat the process."

"Like the collective Borg in *Star Trek*," Thomas said.

"In many ways, yes. Like the Borg. The way they kill the cell is by making so many shells that the cell literally explodes. This is called lysogeny."

"Somehow I missed all this in biology."

Peter continued. "Some viruses linger and wait until the host is under stress before constructing themselves. That's called latency. In this case our virus is a very slow starter, but after two weeks it becomes very aggressive, and its exponential growth overtakes the body in a matter of days. Watch."

Peter returned to the keyboard and punched in a command. Slowly the image on the screen began to change. The virus injected the host cell like a scorpion. The liver cell started to change and then hemorrhaged.

"Lysogeny," Thomas said.

"Exactly."

The view expanded, and thousands of similar cells went through the same process.

"A human body infected by this virus will literally eat itself up from the inside out."

He hit another key. They watched in silence as the same simulation was shown on a human heart. The organ began to break apart as its countless cells hemorrhaged.

"Quite deadly," Peter said.

"How long?" Thomas asked.

"Based on this simulation, the virus will require under three weeks to build enough momentum to affect organ functionality." He shrugged. "It is then a matter of days, depending on the subject."

Thomas faced Raison. "I take it we are now in agreement?"

"Yes. Clearly."

"And you've informed the CDC?"

"We're in the process now. But you must understand, Mr. Hunter: This is a scenario, not a crisis. Outside this laboratory, the Raison Strain doesn't even exist. It would never occur in nature."

"I realize that. But I have it on pretty good authority that someone is going to go around nature. It may be too late, but on the off chance it's not, we have to mobilize as if it is a crisis. We need to stop Svensson, and we need an antivirus within a couple of weeks."

"That's impossible," Raison said.

"So I keep hearing," Thomas muttered. He turned to Peter. "You can't create an antivirus with all this computing power?"

"I'm afraid it's an entirely different matter. Two months, best case, but not three weeks."

Thomas caught Kara's stare. She had that look. This would be up to him. But he didn't want it to be up to him.

"If we had Monique," Peter said, "we might have a chance. She engineers certain particulars into all of her vaccines to protect them against theft or foul play. It's essentially a backdoor switch that's triggered by the introduction of another uniquely engineered virus, which renders the vaccine impotent. If her engineering survived the mutation, her unique virus could also kill Svensson's lethal strain."

"So she may have the key?"

"Maybe. Assuming the mutation didn't destroy her back door."

The room went silent.

"You don't have this switch of hers? She keeps this where, in her head? That seems stupid."

"Until a vaccine is approved by the international community, she keeps the key to herself. It's her way of making sure no one, including employees, steals or tampers with the technology."

"And she keeps no records."

"It's not a complicated matter if you know which genes to manipulate," Peter said. "If there are records, no one here knows where they would be. Either way, it's a long shot. The switch may have mutated along with the vaccine."

"Naturally, we will search," Jacques de Raison said. "But as you can see, we must find my daughter."

"Agreed," Thomas said. "We should also wake up the world."

Thomas left the meeting exhausted and, worse, powerless. He was still under house arrest for kidnapping. He made a dozen phone calls but was quickly reminded of why he came to Bangkok in the first place. News of this sort wasn't received well from a source as unlikely as him. Especially now that he was quite famous for kidnapping Monique.

Fortunately Raison Pharmaceutical commanded far more respect.

Reports of the potential mutation of the Raison Vaccine hit all the appropriate teletypes and computer screens throughout the massive bureaucracy of health services.

It did not send the world scrambling for answers.

It was not a crisis.

It was hardly even a problem.

It was only a possible scenario in one of the models held by Raison Pharmaceutical.

Thomas collapsed into bed at nine that night, weary to the bone but frazzled by the knowledge that the probability of this particular scenario was 100 percent.

It took him a full hour to fall asleep.

32

TANIS SAT alone on the hill overlooking the village. The events of the morning still buzzed about in his mind. For the first time in his life, he'd actually seen the creature from the black forest, and the experience had been astounding. Exhilarating. Most surprising had been the song. This stunning creature was not the terrible black beast of his vivid imagination and stories.

He had saved Thomas. That was justification enough for his visit to the black forest. So then, it was a good thing he'd gone.

Tanis had stayed with Thomas for a short time before leaving. Oddly, he had no desire to be with the man when he awoke.

He'd returned and spent some time in the village. Rachelle had asked him if he'd run into Thomas, and he'd told her that he had, and that Thomas was sleeping.

He'd wandered around the village feeling very much in place and at peace. By midday, however, he felt as though he must go somewhere by himself to consider the events continuing to nag his mind. And so he had come here, to this hill overlooking the entire valley.

Tanis had gone to fetch the sword he'd thrown in the woods yesterday and found it missing. And not only that, but Thomas was also missing. He wasn't sure why he'd concluded that Thomas had taken the sword to the Crossing—perhaps because this very thought was on his own mind—but after searching high and low for the man, he decided to make another sword and go in search at the Crossing.

What interested him most was the fact that Thomas had come from the black forest and lived to tell of it. Not just once, but twice.

The creature . . . now the creature had been something else altogether. He'd never imagined Teeleh as he appeared. Indeed, he hadn't imagined that such a beautiful being could have existed in the black forest at all. Admittedly, he looked rather unique with those green eyes and golden fur. But the song . . .

Oh, what a song!

The fact of the matter was that Tanis wanted very much to meet this creature again. He had no desire to cross into the black forest and drink the water, of course. That would mean death. Worse yet, it was forbidden. But to meet the black creature at the river—that had not been forbidden.

And Thomas had done it.

Tanis glanced at the sun. He had been sitting on the hill, turning the events over in his mind, for over an hour now. If he were to leave now, he could reach the black forest and return without being missed again.

He stood shakily to his feet. The eagerness he felt was odd enough to cause a slight confusion. He couldn't remember ever feeling such strange turmoil. For a moment he thought he should just return to the village and forget the creature at the black forest completely. But he quickly decided against it. After all, he wanted very much to understand this terrible enemy of his. Not to mention the song. To understand one's enemy is to have power over him.

Yes, Tanis wanted this very much, and there was no reason not to do what he so greatly desired. Unless, of course, it went against the will of Elyon. But Elyon had not prohibited meeting new creatures, regardless of where they lived. Even across the river.

With one last look to the valley floor, Tanis turned his back and struck out for the black forest.

⸺∞⸺

Thomas woke with a start. The sweet smell of grass filled his nostrils. He'd dreamed again. Bangkok. They were running ragged in Bangkok because they'd finally accepted the virus at face value. The Raison Strain now existed, if only in laboratories. He had to find Monique, but he had no idea how. And here—

He jerked up. *Tanis?*

He scrambled to his feet and looked around. "Tanis!"

The rush of the river drifted from the east. It was midafternoon. Tanis must have left him near the Crossing and returned to the village.

It took him an hour to reach the valley, fifteen minutes of that retracing his way north after missing the path that led to the village. He had to reach Tanis and explain himself. If ever the man was capable of confusion, it would be now. And the fact that Tanis had made himself another sword after their discussion only yesterday didn't bode well for the man.

He was bitten with the bug. His curiosity was turning. His desire was outpacing his satisfaction. He'd gone to the Crossing because he was tired of not knowing.

Well, now he knew, all right. The only question was, How much knowledge would suffice? And for how long?

Of course, Thomas had gone across as well. But he was different; there could no longer be any question about that. He hadn't taken any water, but according to Teeleh, he'd eaten the fruit before losing his memory, and he'd managed to survive. It was like a vaccine, perhaps.

No, that couldn't be right. Still, Thomas was quite sure that he was different from Tanis. Maybe the people from his village far away had more liberties. But that made even less sense. Maybe he *was* from Bangkok. He might be from Bangkok when he was dreaming, but in reality he was from here. This was his home, and his dreams of Bangkok were wreaking havoc here.

He should eat the rhambutan fruit and rid himself of these silly dreams. They were meddling with a tenuous balance. If not for him, Tanis wouldn't have gone to the black forest today.

"Thomas!"

A Roush swept in from his right.

"Michal!"

The Roush hit the ground hard, bounced once, and flapped furiously to keep from crashing.

"Michal?"

"Oh, dear, dear! Oh, my goodness!"

"What's wrong?"

"It's Tanis. I think he is headed for the black forest."

"Tanis? The black forest?" Impossible! He'd just been to the black forest a few hours ago!

"He was headed straight for it when I left to find you. And he was running. How is that for being sure?" Michal hopped about nervously as though he had stepped on a hot coal.

"For the sake of Elyon, why didn't you stop him?"

"Why didn't I stop *you*? It's not my place; that's why! He's mad! You're both mad, I tell you. Just plain mad. Sometimes I wonder what the point was. You humans are just too unpredictable."

Thomas tried to think clearly. "Just because he's running in that direction doesn't mean he's going to enter the black forest."

Michal's eyes flashed. "We don't have time to discuss this! Even if we go now, you could be too late. Please. Do you know what this could mean?"

"He can't be that stupid," Thomas said. He meant to reassure Michal, but he didn't even believe himself.

Neither did Michal. "Please, we must go now."

The Roush ran along the grass, flapping madly. Then he was in the air. Thomas sprinted to catch him.

An image of the boy at the upper lake filled his mind. That had been two days ago. What had come over them? He suddenly felt suffocated with panic.

"Elyon!" he breathed.

But Elyon had grown completely silent.

"Michal!" he yelled.

The Roush was preoccupied with his own thoughts. Thomas quickened his pace. There was no way he could let Tanis do anything even remotely so unreasonable as talk to Teeleh.

Not while he was alive.

⸎

The scene that greeted Tanis when he broke onto the banks of the river stopped him cold.

As far as he could see in either direction, black creatures with red eyes crowded the trees along the edge of the black forest like a dense, shifting black cloud. There had to be a million of them. Maybe many more.

His first thought was that Thomas had been right—there were far too many to easily dispatch with a few well-placed kicks.

His second was to run.

Tanis jumped back under the cover of the trees. He had never heard that so many other creatures shared their world. He held his breath and peered around a tree at the wondrous sight.

And then he saw the beautiful creature standing on the white bridge. The one he had seen at sunrise! The beast wore a bright yellow cloak and a wreath fashioned with white flowers around his head. He gnawed on a large fruit, the likes of which Tanis had never seen, and stared directly at him with glowing, green eyes.

Silence. All but the river was deathly silent. It was as if they had expected him. What a lovely creature Teeleh was.

He caught himself. These were the Shataiki. Vermin. They were meant to be beaten, not coddled. But, as the histories had so eloquently recorded, to defeat your enemy you must know him. He would speak to the big beautiful one only. And he would pretend to be a friend. In this way he would outwit the creature by learning his weaknesses, then return one day and be rid of him.

And he would do it holding the colored wood.

He grabbed a small green stick about the length of his arm and stepped out onto the bank.

"Greetings," he called. "I am Tanis. By what name are you called?"

He knew, of course, but Tanis didn't want to tip his hand. The beast tossed the half-eaten fruit behind him and rubbed the juice from his mouth with a hairy blue wing. He smiled with crooked yellow teeth. "I am Teeleh," he said. "We have waited for you, my friend."

Tanis glanced back at the colored forest. Well, then. Here was the creature he had come to meet. Tanis felt an uncommon flutter in his heart and stepped out to meet Teeleh, the leader of the Shataiki.

He stopped at the foot of the bridge and studied the creature. Of course! This was trickery! How could the leader of the Shataiki be different from his legions?

"You're not what I expected," he said.

"No? And what did you expect?"

"I had heard that you were quite clever. How clever is it to pretend you're different than you really are when you know you'll be found out?"

Teeleh chuckled. "You like that, don't you?"

"I like what? Exposing you for what you are? Are you afraid to show me who you really are?"

"You like being clever," Teeleh said. "It's why you've come here. To be clever. To learn more. More knowledge. The truth."

"Then show me the truth."

"I intend to."

Teeleh's eyes turned first, from green to red. Then his wings and body, slowly to gray, then black. All the while his smile held true. Talons extended from his feet and dug into the wood. It was a shocking transformation, and Tanis gripped the colored stick tighter.

"Is that better?" The bat's voice had changed to a low, guttural growl.

"No. It's much worse. You're the most hideous creature I could ever have imagined."

"Ah, but I possess more knowledge and truth than you could ever have imagined as well. Would you like to hear?"

The invitation sounded suspect, but Tanis couldn't think of an appropriate way to decline. How could he reject the truth?

Teeleh's snout suddenly gaped wide, so that Tanis could see the back of his mouth, where his pink tongue disappeared into a dark throat. A low, rumbling note rolled out, followed immediately by a high, piercing one that seemed to reach into him and touch his spine. Teeleh's song ravaged him with its strange chorus of terrible beauty. Powerful and conquering and intoxicating at once. Tanis felt an overwhelming compulsion to rush up the bridge, but he held firm.

Teeleh closed his mouth. The notes echoed, then fell silent. The bats in the forest peered at him without a stir. Tanis felt a little disorientated by all these new sensations.

"This is new to you?" Teeleh asked.

Tanis shifted the makeshift sword to his left hand. "Yes."

"And do you know why it's new?"

It was a good question. A trick? No, just a question.

"Are you afraid of me?" Teeleh asked. "You know that I can't cross the bridge, yet you stand at the bottom in fear."

"Why would I be afraid of what can't harm me?"

No, that's not entirely true. He can hurt me. I must be very careful.

"Then walk closer. You want to know more about me so that you can destroy me. So walk closer and see me clearly."

How did the beast know this?

"Because I know far more than you do, my friend. And I can tell you how to know what I know. Come closer. You're safe. You have the wood in your hand."

Teeleh could have guessed his thoughts; they weren't so unique. At any rate, he should show this beast that he was not afraid. What kind of warrior quivered at the bottom of the bridge? He walked up the white planks and stopped ten feet from Teeleh.

"You are braver than most," the bat said, eying his colored sword.

"And I am not as dense as you think I am," Tanis said. "I know that even now you're trying your trickery."

"If I use this . . . trickery and persuade you by it, wouldn't that mean I am smarter than you?"

Tanis considered the logic. "Perhaps."

"Then trickery is a form of knowledge. And knowledge is a form of truth. And you want more of it; otherwise, as I said, you wouldn't be here. So if by using trickery I persuade you to accept my knowledge, it can only be because I am smarter than you. I have more truth."

It was confounding, this logic of his.

"The reason my song is new to you, Tanis, is because Elyon doesn't want you to hear it. And why? Because it will give you the same knowledge that I have. It will give you too much power. Power comes with the truth; you already know that."

"Yes. But I won't have you talking about Elyon like this." Tanis jabbed his stick forward. "I should stick you through now and be done with this."

"Go ahead. Try it."

"I might, but I'm not here for battle. I'm here to learn the truth."

"Well, then. I can show it to you." Teeleh pulled a yellow fruit from behind his back. "There is in this fruit some knowledge. Power. Enough power to make all the creatures behind me cringe. Wouldn't you like that? One word from you, and they will squeal in pain. Because they will know you have the truth, and with that truth comes great power. Here, try it."

"No, I can't eat your fruit."

"Then you don't want the truth?"

"Yes, but—"

"Is it forbidden to eat this fruit?"

"No."

"Of course not. If there was harm in eating this fruit, Elyon would have forbidden it! But there is no harm, so it is not forbidden. There is only knowledge and power. Take it."

Tanis glanced back at the colored forest. What the bat said was true. There was no harm in eating the fruit. There was no evil in it. It wasn't forbidden.

"Just one bite," Teeleh said. "If you find that what I've said isn't true, then leave. But you owe it to yourself to at least try it. Hmm? Don't you think?" The large beast made no effort to hide his talons, which tapped impatiently on the wood bridge.

Tanis looked past the large black bat and hesitated. "Well, you know I won't drink any of your water."

"Heavens no! Just the fruit. A gift of truth from me to you."

Tanis held the colored stick firmly and stepped forward to take the fruit.

"Keep the wood to your side, if you don't mind," Teeleh said. "It is the color of deception, and it doesn't sit well with my truth."

Tanis stopped. "See, I already have the power. Why do I need yours?"

"Go ahead, wave it at my subjects and see how much power you have."

Tanis glanced at the throngs behind Teeleh. He motioned at them with the sword, but none so much as flinched.

"You see? How can you compare your power to mine, unless you first know? Know your enemy. Know his fruit. Taste what Elyon himself has invited you to taste by *not* forbidding it. Just keep your stick at your side so that it doesn't touch me."

Tanis now wanted very much to try this mysterious yellow fruit in Teeleh's claw. He lowered the sword to his side, ready to use it at a moment's notice, stepped forward, and took the fruit. It felt daring, but he was a warrior, and to defeat this enemy he had to employ his own trickery.

He stepped back, just out of Teeleh's reach, and bit into the fruit. Immediately his world swam in stunning color. Power surged through his blood, and his mind felt numb.

"Do you feel the power?"

"It's . . . it's quite strong," Tanis said. He took another bite.

"Now, raise your hand and command my legions."

Tanis looked at the black bats that lined the trees. "Now?"

"Yes. Use your new power."

Tanis lifted an unsteady hand. Without a single word, the Shataiki began to shriek and turn away. The sound made him cringe. Terror swept through their ranks. This with a single outstretched arm.

"You see? Lower your arm before you destroy my army."

Tanis lowered his arm.

"Can I take this fruit with me?"

"No. Please hand it back."

Tanis did so, though somewhat reluctantly. The Shataiki continued their ruckus.

"Not to worry, my friend. I have another fruit. More truth. More power. This one will open your mind to the forbidden truth. That is the truth only the wise ones possess. You can't command armies with power alone. You must have the mind to lead. This fruit will show it to you."

Tanis knew he should leave, but there was no law forbidding even this.

"It's the same fruit your friend Thomas ate," Teeleh said.

Tanis looked up, shocked. "Thomas ate your fruit?"

"Of course. It's why he's so wise. And he knows the histories because he drank my water. Thomas has the knowledge."

The revelation made Tanis dizzy. That was how Thomas knew the histories. He reached out his hand.

"No, for this fruit you must put your sword on the railing here, on my side of the bridge. I can't touch it, of course. But you must hold this fruit with both hands."

The bat's reasoning sounded very strange, but then Tanis's mind wasn't entirely clear. As long as the sword was right there where he could grab it if needed, what harm would there be in setting it down? If anything, it put a greater barrier between him and the bat.

Tanis stepped forward and set the stick on the railing. Then he reached both hands for the fruit in Teeleh's outstretched claw.

When they broke from the forest, Tanis already stood before the horrid beast, like a dumb sheep bleating to its butcher. Thomas skidded to a halt. Michal landed on a branch to his right.

"Michal!" Thomas rasped.

"We're too late!" the Roush said. "Too late!"

"He's still talking!"

"Tanis will decide."

"What?"

Thomas turned back to the scene before him. Thomas stood frozen by the moment. He could barely hear his friend's voice above the shrieking bats.

"This is the fruit that Thomas ate?" Tanis took the fruit from the grinning black beast with both hands.

Thomas released the tree he had gripped with white knuckles and leaped forward. *No, Tanis! Don't be such an utter fool. Throw it back at him!*

He wanted to yell it, but his throat was frozen.

"It is indeed, my friend," Teeleh said. "Thomas is a very wise man indeed."

Half the Shataiki lining the trees now noticed him. They flew into a fit, pointing in panic, shrieks now earsplitting.

Thomas raced across the bank toward the arching bridge. "Tanis!"

But Tanis didn't turn. Had he already eaten?

Tanis took one step backward, and Thomas was sure that he was about to fling the fruit back at the beast and leave him standing on the bridge's crest. The man paused and said something too softly for Thomas to hear above the bats. He stared at the fruit in his hands.

"Tanis!" Thomas cried, rushing onto the bridge.

Tanis calmly brought the fruit to his mouth and bit deeply.

The throng of bats in the trees behind Teeleh suddenly fell silent. The wind whistled quietly and the river below murmured, but otherwise a terrible stillness swallowed the bridge.

"Tanis!"

Tanis whirled around. A stream of juice glistened on his chin. The fruit's yellow flesh was lodged in his gaping mouth.

"Thomas. You've come!"

He closed his lips over the piece between his teeth and held the bitten fruit out toward Thomas. "Is this the same fruit you ate, Thomas? I must say, it is very good indeed."

Thomas slid to a halt halfway up the arch. "Don't be a fool, Tanis! It's not too late. Drop it and come back." He shook as he spoke. "Now! Drop it now!"

"Oh, it is you," the beast behind Tanis sneered. "I thought I heard a voice. Don't worry, Tanis, my friend. He would like to be the only one to eat my fruit, but you know too much now, don't you? Has he told you about his spaceship?"

Tanis swiveled his head from Thomas to the beast and back again, as though unsure of what he was expected to do.

"Tanis, don't listen to him. Get ahold of yourself!"

Tanis's eyes seemed to float in their sockets. The fruit was taking its toll on the man.

"Thomas? What spaceship?" Tanis asked.

"He's afraid to tell you the truth," Teeleh snarled. "He drank the water!"

"It's a lie!" Thomas said. "Do *not* cross the bridge. Drop the fruit."

Tanis wasn't listening. Yellow juice from the fruit trickled down his cheek, staining his tunic. He turned back to the beast and took another bite.

"Very powerful," he said. "With this kind of power, I could defeat even you."

"Yesssss." The hideous bat grinned. "And we have something you cannot possibly imagine."

He withdrew a leather pouch.

"Here, drink this. It will open your eyes to new worlds."

Tanis looked at the bat, then at the pouch. Then he reached one hand for the pouch.

Teeleh turned, and in doing so he bumped into something Thomas hadn't seen before. A stick resting on the railing. A dark stick that had lost its color. The wood slid off the railing and fell into the river.

Thomas whirled around. Michal was watching in silence. "Elyon!" Thomas screamed. Surely he would do something. He loved Tanis desperately. "Elyon!"

Nothing.

He spun back to the bridge. What was happening was happening because of him. In spite of him. He felt as powerless and as terrified as he could ever remember feeling.

Teeleh walked slowly, ever so slowly, favoring his right leg. Down the bridge to the opposite bank. "More knowledge than you can handle," he said. "Isn't that so, my friends?" he bellowed to the throngs lining the forest.

"Yesss . . . yessss," rasped a sea of voices.

"Then bid our friend drink," he cried out, stepping onto the opposite bank. "Bid him drink!"

"Drink, drink, drink, drink," the Shataiki chanted slowly, in one throbbing, seductive tone. A song.

Thomas felt the hair on his neck stand on end. Tanis looked back at him, eyes glazed over, a grin twisting his face. He released a nervous chuckle.

Thomas's mind began to swim in panic. Tanis was falling for it!

In final desperation, he lunged up the arch toward the intoxicated man. "Tanis, don't. Don't do it!" he cried over the bewitched song. "You have no idea what you're doing!"

Tanis turned back to the chanting throng and took a step toward the opposite shore.

Images of Rachelle and little Johan flashed before Thomas's eyes. This was not going to happen, not if he could help it.

He leaped forward, gripped the railing with his left arm, and flung his other arm around the man's waist. Planting his feet hard, he jerked Tanis back, nearly pulling him from his feet.

With a snarl Tanis swung around and planted a kick on his chest. Thomas flew back and sat hard on the deck.

"No, Thomas! You are not the only one who can have this knowledge! Who are you to tell me what I must do?"

"It's a lie, Tanis! I didn't drink!"

"You're lying! You're dreaming of the histories. No one has ever dreamed of the histories."

"Because I fell!"

A brief look of confusion crossed the firstborn's face. He turned away with a tear in his eye, lifted the pouch to his lips, and poured the water into his mouth.

Then he walked over the bridge and stepped onto the parched earth beyond.

What happened next was a sight Thomas would never forget as long as he lived. The moment Tanis set foot on the ground next to the large black bat, a dozen smaller Shataiki stalked out to greet him. Thomas scrambled to his feet just as Tanis extended a hand in greeting to the nearest Shataiki. But instead of taking his hand, the Shataiki suddenly leaped from the ground and slashed angrily at the extended hand with his talons.

For a moment, time seemed to cease.

The pouch dropped from Tanis's hand. His half-eaten fruit tumbled lazily to the ground. Tanis lowered his eyes to his hand just as the white walls of a deep gash began to fill with blood.

And then the first effects of his new world fell on the elder like a vicious, bloodthirsty beast.

Tanis screamed with pain.

Teeleh faced the black forest, standing tall and stately.

"Take him!" he said.

The groups of Shataiki who had greeted Tanis dived for him. Tanis threw his hands up in defense, but in his state of shock it was hopeless. Fangs punctured his neck and his spine; a wicked claw sliced at his face, severing most of it in one terrible swipe. Then Tanis disappeared in a mess of flailing black fur.

Teeleh raised his wings in victory and beckoned the waiting throngs that still clung to the trees. "Now!" he thundered above the sounds of the attack on Tanis. "Now! Did I not tell you?" He lifted his chin and howled in a voice so loud and so terrifying that it seemed to rip the sky itself open.

"Our time has come!"

A ground-shaking roar erupted from the horde of beasts. Above the cheer Thomas heard the leader's throaty, guttural roar. "Destroy the land. Take what is ours!"

Teeleh swept his wings toward the colored forest.

—◦◦◦—

Thomas watched, frozen by horror, as a massive black wall of bats took flight. The wall ran as far as he could see in either direction and seemed to move in slow motion for its sheer size. A dark shadow crept across the ground. It moved over the black forest, then up the bridge toward Thomas. The white wood cracked and turned gray along the forward edge of the shadow. The pungent odor of sulfur swarmed him.

Thomas whirled and ran just ahead of the shadow. He leaped off the bridge and hit the grass in a full sprint. Michal was gone!

"Michal!" he screamed.

He dared a quick glance back at the trees that marked the edge of the colored forest. The grass behind him was turning to black ash along the leading edge of the shadow, as if a long line of fire had been set ablaze beneath the earth and was incinerating the green life above it.

But he knew the death didn't come from below. It came from the black bats above. And what would happen to his flesh when the shadow overtook him?

He screamed and pumped his legs in a blind panic, knowing full well that panic would only slow him down. "Elyon!"

Elyon wasn't responding.

The shadow from the wall of black bats above reached him when he tore into the clearing just beyond the riverbank. He tensed in anticipation of the searing pain of burning flesh.

The burned grass under his feet crackled. The colored light from the trees on either side winked out, and the green canopy began crumbling in heaps of black ash. The air turned thick and difficult to breathe.

But his flesh didn't burn.

The shadow moved on, just ahead of him. His strength began to fade.

The wall of bats was moving toward the village. No! It would reach them long before Thomas could sound any warning.

The animals and birds howled and shrieked in aimless circles of confusion.

Here in the shadow was death. Ahead, before the shadow, there was still life. The life of the colored forest. The life that allowed Tanis to execute incredible maneuvers in the air with superhuman strength. The life that had fed Thomas's own strength over the previous days.

One last wedge of hope lodged stubbornly in Thomas's mind. If only he could catch the shadow. Pass back into the life ahead of it. If only he could summon the last reserves of his strength from any fruit on the trees, from any life in the land.

If he could just stay ahead of the bats.

The fruit was falling from the charred trees and thudding to the ground like a slow hail. Thomas veered to his left, dipped down and grabbed a piece of fruit, and bit off a chunk of flesh. He swallowed without chewing.

Immediately, strength returned.

Clenching his hands around the fruit, he tore forward. Juice seeped around his knuckles. He shoved another bite in his mouth and swallowed and ran.

Slowly, very slowly, he gained ground on the shadow. Why the bats didn't swoop down and chew him to pieces, he didn't know. Perhaps in their eagerness to reach the village they ignored this one human below.

He sucked down two more chunks of fruit and chased the shadow for ten minutes in a full sprint before catching it. But now his panic had left him. The moment he passed in front of the canopy of bats, his strength surged.

He snatched a piece of unspoiled fruit and ripped off a huge bite.

Sweet, sweet release. Thomas shivered and sobbed. And he ran.

With a strength beyond himself, he ran, gaining on the shadow, on the approaching throng shrieking high above him. First fifty yards, then a hundred, then two hundred. Soon they were a massive black cloud well behind him.

From a hill he could see their approach with stunning clarity. From this vantage point he saw what was happening in a new light. The black forest was encroaching on the green in a long, endless line that blocked the sun and burned the land to a crisp.

He raced on, vision blurred with tears, screaming in rage.

The sky above the valley was empty when Thomas broke from the forest. It was, in fact, the only sign that there was anything at all askew. At any other time at least a dozen Roush would be floating in lazy circles above the village, or tumbling along the grass with the children. Now there wasn't a single one to be seen. No Michal, no Gabil.

Below, the villagers went about peacefully, ignorantly. Children scampered between the huts, laughing in delight; mothers cuddled their young as they sang softly and stepped lightly in dance; fathers retold their tales of great exploits—all unaware of the approaching throng that would soon tear into them.

Thomas tore down the hill. "Oh, Elyon," he pleaded. "Please, I beg you, give me a way."

He ran into the village screaming at the top of his lungs. "Shataiki! They're coming! Everyone grab something to defend yourselves!"

Johan and Rachelle skipped toward him with smiles on their faces, waving eagerly. "Thomas," Rachelle called. "There you are."

"Rachelle!" Thomas rushed up to her. "Quick, you have to protect yourself." He glanced up the hill and saw the wall of bats above the crest. Thousands of the black creatures suddenly broke rank and poured into the valley.

It was too late. There was no way they could defend themselves. These weren't the ghosts with phantom claws that they had learned how to combat with fancy aerial kicks. Like Tanis, they would be pummeled by the bloodthirsty beasts.

Thomas whirled around and grabbed both of their hands. "Come with me!" he demanded, sprinting down the path. "Hurry!"

"Look!" Johan yelled. He'd seen the coming Shataiki. Thomas glanced over and saw the boy's wide eyes looking back at the beasts now descending on the village.

"The Thrall!" he cried. "The Thrall. Run!"

Rachelle sprinted by his side, face white. "Elyon!" she cried. "Elyon, save us!"

"Run!" Thomas yelled.

Johan kept wanting to turn around, forcing Thomas to repeatedly jerk him back down the path. "Faster! We have to get into the Thrall!"

Thomas urged them up the stairs, two at a time. Behind them, screams filled the village. "Don't look back! Go, go, go!" He shoved them roughly through the doors and spun back.

No fewer than ten thousand of the beasts dived into the village, claws extended. The screams from the villagers were overwhelmed by a high-pitched shrieking from thousands of open Shataiki throats. Talons swiped like sickles; fangs gnashed ravenously in anticipation of meat.

To his right, a Shataiki descended on a young boy fleeing down the street. He fell to the ground, smothered by a dozen bats, who sank their talons into his soft flesh. The boy's screams became one with the Shataiki's shrieks.

Not ten paces from the boy, a woman flailed her arms wildly at two beasts who had attached themselves to her head and gnawed madly at her skull. The woman whirled about, screaming, and despite the blood covering her face, Thomas recognized her. Karyl.

Thomas groaned in shock. All around the village, the helpless fell easy prey to the bloodthirsty Shataiki.

And still they came. The sky was now black with a hundred thousand of the creatures, streaming over the hills into the valley. He knew it was this way in every village.

Thomas slammed the large doors shut, gasping. He threw the large bolt and turned to Rachelle and Johan, who stood on the green floor, holding each other's hands innocently.

"What's happening?" Rachelle asked in a trembling voice, her wide green eyes fixed on Thomas. "We have to fight back!"

Thomas ran across the floor and shut the rear doors that led to an outer entrance.

"Are these the only two entrances?" he demanded.

"What is—"

"Tell me!"

"Yes!"

No Shataiki could get into the Thrall without breaking down the doors. He turned back.

"Listen to me." He paused to catch his wind. "I know this is going to sound strange, and you may not know what I'm talking about, but we've been attacked."

"Attacked?" quipped Johan. "Really attacked?"

"Yes, really attacked," he said. "The Shataiki have left the black forest."

"That's . . . that's not possible!" Rachelle said.

"Yes, it is. Possible and real."

Thomas walked over to the front doors and tested them. He could barely hear the sounds of the attack beyond the walls of the Thrall. Rachelle and Johan remained still, hand in hand, at the center of the jade floor where they had danced a thousand dances. They had no way to understand what was really happening outside. They had no idea how dramatically the colorful world they had known so well just a few moments ago had forever changed.

Thomas walked up to them and put his arms on their shoulders. And then the adrenaline that had rushed him through the forest and into this great hall evaporated. The full realization of the devastation racking the land beyond the Thrall's heavy wooden doors descended upon him like ten tons of mortar. He hung his head and tried to remain strong.

Rachelle placed a hand on his hair and stroked it slowly. "It is all right, Thomas," she said. "Don't cry like this. Everything will be just fine. The Gathering is in a short time."

Like a flood, despair swept through Thomas's chest. They were doomed. He strained to maintain a semblance of control. How could Tanis have been deceived so easily? What a fool he'd been to even *listen* to the black beast! To even go near the black forest.

"Please, don't cry," Johan said. "Please, don't cry, Thomas. Rachelle is right. Everything will be fine."

An agonizing half hour crept by. Rachelle and Johan tried to ask him questions about their plight. "Where are the others? What will we do now? How long will we stay here? Where do these black creatures live?"

Each time, Thomas shrugged them off as he paced about the great room. The jade hall would become their coffin. If he did answer Rachelle or Johan, it was with a nondescript putoff. How could he explain this betrayal to them? He couldn't. They would have to discover it themselves. For now, their only objective was to survive.

At first the Shataiki attacks on the outer Thrall came in waves, and at one point it sounded as though every last one of the dirty beasts had descended on the dome, beating and scratching furiously to gain entrance. But they could not.

An hour must have passed before Thomas noticed the change. They had sat in silence for a good ten minutes without an attack.

He stood shakily to his feet and crossed the floor to the front doors. Silence. The bats either had left or waited quietly on the roof outside, waiting to attack the moment the doors opened.

Thomas faced Rachelle and Johan, who still, after all this time, stood in the center of the green floor. It was time to tell them.

"Tanis drank the water," he said simply.

They stiffened, mouths gaping. Together they dropped their heads, obviously unfamiliar with the new emotions of sorrow washing through them. They knew what this meant, of course. Not specifically, but in general they knew something very bad had happened. It was the first time anything bad had happened to either one of them.

Silently their shoulders began to shake, gently at first, but then with greater force until they could stand it no longer, and they threw their arms around each other and sobbed.

The sting of tears returned to Thomas's eyes. How could such a tragedy have happened at all? For a long time they clung to each other and cried.

"What will we do? What will we do?" Rachelle asked a dozen times. "Can't we go to the lake?"

"I don't know," Thomas responded quietly. "I think everything's changed, Rachelle."

Johan looked at Thomas with a tear-streaked face. "But why did Tanis do that when Elyon told us not to?"

"I don't know, Johan," Thomas said, taking the boy's hand. "Don't worry. Earth may have changed, but Elyon will never change. We just have to find him."

Rachelle tilted her head back and raised her hands, palms up. "Elyon!" she cried. "Elyon, can you hear us?" Thomas looked on hopelessly. "Elyon, where are you?" Rachelle cried again.

She dropped her hands and looked despondently at Thomas and Johan. "It's different," she said.

He nodded. "Everything is different now." He glanced up at the green-domed roof. *Except for the Thrall.* "We will wait until morning and then, if it seems safe, we will try to find Elyon."

33

THE NIGHT had been pure agony for Thomas. He'd awakened screaming, soaked in a cold sweat, at two in the morning. He couldn't go back
to sleep, and he couldn't bring himself to tell Kara about the nightmare.
He could scarcely comprehend what it all meant himself. The images of
the black wall of bats spreading over the land and then tearing into the
village hung on him like a sopping, heavy cloak.

The early morning hours had been torture, relieved only in part by the
onset of a new distraction.

"Do we have Internet access?" he asked Kara at six.

"Yes. Why?"

"I need a distraction. Who knows, maybe a little crash course in survival may help me out in the land of bats."

She looked at him, taken aback.

"What?" he asked.

"I thought we were more interested in how that reality can save
this world than how to build weapons to blow away a few black bats
for Tanis."

If only she knew. He couldn't bring himself to tell her, not yet. She
would never understand how utterly real it all felt.

"I need a distraction," he said.

"So do I," she said.

They spent the next three hours browsing subjects on Yahoo! that
Thomas thought might come in handy. Maybe Tanis had been onto something with this idea of his to build weapons. If they were right, the only
things that were transferable between the realities were skills and knowl-

edge. He couldn't take a gun back with him, but he could take back the knowledge of *how* to build a gun, couldn't he?

"What good is a plan to build a gun if you don't have metal to build it with?" Kara asked. "Will the wood there sustain an explosion?"

"I don't know."

He doubted there was any more wood that could be reshaped. Or anyone who could reshape it. He clicked off the weapons page and searched for the basics. Finding ore and building a forge. Swords. Poisons. Survival skills. Combat strategy. Battle tactics.

But in the end he came to the horrible conclusion that no matter what he did, the situation in the colored—or was it all black now?—forest was ultimately hopeless.

Things were hardly better here. They had proof that the Raison Vaccine could mutate into one very bad virus, and no one seemed to want to make sure it didn't. True, in less than a day he'd been dropped in by helicopter with Muta, found Monique, barely escaped with his scalp in one piece, and finally confirmed the reality of the Raison Strain, but Thomas still felt like nothing was happening. If Merton Gains was working his promised magic, he was doing it way too slowly.

Jacques de Raison entered the room midmorning, and Thomas spoke before the Frenchman could explain his presence.

"I feel like an animal trapped in a cage," Thomas said. "I walk around like an idiot under this house arrest while they sit around and talk about what to do."

"They've lifted the house arrest," Raison said. "At my request."

Thomas faced the haggard-looking pharmaceutical giant. "They have? When?"

"An hour ago."

"Now you tell me?"

The man said nothing.

"I need a cell phone," Thomas said. "And I need a few phone numbers. Can you do that?"

"I think that can be arranged."

"Our car is still here?"

"Yes. In the parking lot."

"Can you have it brought around? Kara, you ready to leave?"

"Nothing to get ready. Where to?"

"Anywhere but here. No offense, Jacques, but I can't just sit around here. I'm free to go, right?"

"Yes, but we're still looking for my daughter. What if we need you? Secretary Gains could call at any minute."

"That's why I need a cell phone."

———

Their feet clacked along the Sheraton lobby's tile floor. Thomas pressed the cell phone to his ear patiently, scanning the room. Hundreds of people loitered in the grand atrium, completely clueless that the young American named Thomas Hunter and the pretty blonde at his elbow were bargaining for the fate of the world.

Patricia Smiley came back on the line for the fourth time in the last half hour. He was driving her rabid, but he didn't care.

"It's Thomas Hunter again," he said. "Please, please tell me he's not in a meeting or on the phone."

"I'm sorry, Mr. Hunter, I told you before, he's on the phone."

"Can I be frank? You don't sound sorry, Patricia. Did you tell him I was on the phone? He's waiting for my call. Did I tell you I was in Bangkok? Put him on; I'm dying over here!"

"Raising your voice won't—" Her voice went mute. She was talking to someone in the office. "I'll put you through now, Mr. Hunter."

Click.

"Hello?" Had she hung up on him? "Don't you dare hang up on me, you—"

"Thomas?"

Merton Gains.

"Oh. I'm sorry, sir. I was just on the phone with . . ." He stalled.

"Never mind that. I'm sorry I haven't been able to get through sooner, but I've been clearing my schedule. How you looking for ten o'clock tonight?"

Thomas stopped.

"What?" Kara asked at his elbow.

"Ten o'clock for what?"

"For me. My flight leaves in an hour. I'll have the director of the CIA with me. We still have some calls to make, but we think we can get Australian Intelligence, Scotland Yard, and the Spanish there as well. Ten, fifteen people. It's not exactly a summit, but it's a start."

"For what? Why?"

The phone hissed.

"For you, boy. I want you to have everything ready, you understand? Everything. You tell them the whole thing, from start to finish. I'll have Jacques de Raison there to present their findings on the virus. I'll have a CDC representative on the plane to hear those findings. The president has given me discretion on this, so I'm running with it. From this point forward, we treat this as a real threat. With any luck, we'll have the ears of a few other countries by day's end. Trust me, we'll need them. I don't have a lot of believers here at home."

"You want me to present this at the meeting?"

"I want you to tell them what you told me. Explaining dreams isn't something that comes naturally to me."

"I can do that." Thomas wasn't sure if he really could, but they were way beyond such insignificant considerations. "And someone is locating Svensson, right? He has to be stopped."

"We're working on that. But we're dealing with international laws here. And Svensson is a powerful man. You don't just drop the hammer on him without evidence."

"I have evidence!"

"Not in their minds, you don't. He's agreed to an interview tomorrow. Don't worry; we have a ground team paying him a visit in a few hours. They'll set up surveillance. He's not going anywhere."

"That could be too late."

"For crying out loud, Thomas! You want fast; this *is* fast! I have to catch a flight. I'll instruct my secretary to patch your calls through. You're at the Sheraton, right?"

"Right."

"Ten o'clock at the Sheraton. I'll have a conference room reserved." Merton Gains paused. "Have you . . . learned anything else?"

The nightmare swept through Thomas's mind. The Fall. A sense of impending dread settled in his gut like a lead brick. "No."

"Fine."

"Okay."

He hung up.

"What was that?" Kara asked. "He's coming?"

"He's coming. With an entourage. Ten o'clock."

"That's twelve hours. What happens in the next twelve hours? You're briefing them, right? So we need more information."

Thomas suddenly felt faint. Sick. He settled into a chair in the open dining room and stared out at the lobby.

"Thomas?" Kara slid into a chair opposite him. "What is it?"

He massaged his temples. "We have a problem, Kara."

"Why do you say that? They're finally starting to listen."

"No, not with them. With me. With whatever's happening to me."

"Your dreams?"

"The colored forest has come apart at the seams," he said.

"What . . . what do you mean?"

"The colored forest. It's not colored anymore. The bats have broken past the river and attacked—" Thomas broke off.

She stared at him as if he'd lost his mind. "That's . . . is that possible?"

"It happened."

"What does that mean?"

"I don't know." He hit his hand on the table. The plates clattered. A couple seated two tables away looked over.

Again, not as loud. "I don't know; that's the problem. As far as I know,

I won't even go back. And if I do go back, I have no idea what the land will be like."

"It's that bad?"

"You can't imagine."

"This explains your sudden interest in weapons."

"I guess."

"Then you have to sleep! You can't meet with all those people without knowing what's going on over there. Our whole case hinges on this . . . these dreams of yours. You're saying it's over? We have to get you to sleep!"

"I'm not going to *tell* them what's going on over there!" he said. "That's for us, Kara. It's bad enough talking about what I learned in my dreams, but there's no way I can give them any specifics. They'll lock me up!"

"But you still have to know. For yourself."

They sat quietly for a moment. She was right—he had to find out if he could go back. They had twelve hours.

"Tell me what happened," Kara said quietly. "I want to know every-thing."

Thomas nodded. It had been a while since he'd told her everything. "It'll take a while."

"We have time."

⸻

Twelve hours had come and gone, and Svensson hadn't forced Monique to change her mind as promised. But one look at his face when he opened the door to her white-walled cell, and Monique suspected that was about to change.

They'd moved her during the night. Why or where she had no idea. What she did know was that the plan unfolding about her had been the subject of immense planning and foresight. She'd picked up enough between the lines to conclude that much.

Virologists had speculated for years that one day a bioweapon would change history. In anticipation of that day, Valborg Svensson had laid exhaustive plans. His stumbling upon the Raison Virus might have been a fluke, but what he would now do with it was anything but. Actually, he hadn't stumbled upon it at all. He'd invested in a vast network of informants so that at the first sign of the right virus, he could pounce on it. In effect, he had many thousands of scientists working for him.

This man standing tall in the doorway to her white room was a brilliant man, Monique thought. And perhaps completely insane.

"Hello, Monique. I trust we've treated you well. My apologies for any discomfort, but that will change now. The worst is behind you, I promise. Unless, of course, you refuse to cooperate, but that is beyond my control."

"I have no intention of cooperating," she said.

"Yes, well, that's because you don't know yet."

She didn't indulge him with the obvious question.

"Would you like to know?"

She still didn't. He chuckled. "You have a strong backbone; I like that. What you don't know is that in exactly fourteen hours, we—yes, we; I'm certainly not alone in this, not even close, although I would like to think I play a significant role—are going to release the Raison Strain in twelve primary countries."

Monique's vision swam. What was he saying? Surely he wasn't planning to . . .

"Yes, exactly. With or without an antivirus, the clock starts ticking in fourteen hours." He grinned wide. "Astonishing, isn't it?"

"You can't do that . . ."

"That's what some of the others argued. But we prevailed. It's the only way. The fate of the world is now in my hands, dear Monique. And yours, of course."

"The virus could wipe out the earth's population!"

"That's the point. The threat has to be real. Only an antivirus can save humanity. I trust you would like to help us create that antivirus. We have a very good start already, I must say. We may not even need you. But your name is on the virus. It seems appropriate that it also be on the cure, don't you think?"

34

THE FIRST thing Thomas realized was that he was back. He was waking up in the Thrall with Rachelle and Johan curled by his feet. He'd dreamed of Bangkok and was getting ready to enter a meeting with some people who were finally willing to consider the Raison Strain.

They'd spent the evening huddled together on the Thrall's floor. The night seemed colder than usual. Depression hung in the room like a thick fog. Rachelle had even tried to dance once, but she just couldn't find the right rhythm. She gave up and sat back down, head in her hands. They soon grew silent and finally drifted off to sleep.

Sometime in the middle of the night, they were awakened by a scratching on the roof, but the sound passed within a few minutes and they managed to return to sleep.

Thomas was the first to wake. Morning rays lit the translucent dome. He quietly stood, walked to the large doors, and pressed his ear against the glowing wood. If anything alive was waiting beyond the doors, it made no sound. Satisfied, he hurried across the room to a side door that Rachelle said led to storage. He opened it and descended a short flight of steps to a small storage room.

A clear jar containing about a dozen pieces of fruit sat against the far wall. Some bread. Good. He closed the door and returned upstairs.

Rachelle and Johan still slept, and Thomas decided to leave them to their sleep as long as he could. He walked over to the main doors and put an ear to the wood again.

He listened for a full minute this time. Nothing.

He eased the bolt open and cracked the door, half expecting to hear a sudden flurry of black wings. Instead, he heard only the slight creak of the hinges. The morning air remained absolutely still. He pushed the door farther open and cautiously peered around. He squinted in the bright light and quickly scanned the village for Shataiki.

But there were none. He held his breath and stepped out into putrid morning air.

The village was deserted. Not a soul, living or dead, occupied the once lively streets. There were no dead bodies as he had expected. Only patches of blood that had soaked the ground. Nor were there Shataiki perched on the rooftops, waiting for him to leave the safety of the Thrall. He twisted to look at the Thrall's roof, thinking of the scratching during the night. Still no bats.

But where were the people?

Apparently even the animals had been chased from the valley. The buildings no longer glowed. The entire village looked as though it had been covered by a great settling of gray ash.

"What happened?" Rachelle and Johan stood dumbstruck.

"It went dark inside," Johan said, staring past Thomas with wide eyes.

He was right; the wood inside had lost its glow as well. It must have been somehow affected by the air he had let in when he opened the door. He turned back to the scene before him.

Thomas felt nauseated. Scared. His pulse beat steady and hard. Had evil entered him somehow, or was it just out here in this physical form? And what about the others?

"It's all changed!" Rachelle cried. She grabbed Thomas's arm with a firm, trembling grip. Frightened? She'd known caution before. But fear? So she, too, felt the effects of the transformation even without being torn to shreds.

"What . . . what happened to the land?" Johan asked.

The meadows surrounding the village were now black. But the starkest change in the land was the forest at the meadow's edge. The trees were all charred, as though an immense fire had ravaged the land.

Black.

For a long time they stood still, frozen by the scene before them. Thomas looked to his left where the path snaked over scorched earth toward the lake. He placed his arms around Johan and Rachelle.

"We should go to the lake."

Rachelle looked at him. "Can't we eat first? I'm starving."

Her eyes. They weren't green.

He lowered his arm and swallowed. The emerald windows to her soul were now grayish white. As though she'd contracted an advanced case of cataracts.

It took every ounce of his composure not to jump. He stepped back cautiously. Her face had lost its shine and her skin had dried. Tiny lines were etched over her arms.

And Johan—it was the same with him!

Thomas turned around and looked at his own arm. Dry. No pain, just bone dry. The nausea in his gut swelled.

"Eat? Don't you want to go to the lake first?"

He waited for a response, afraid to face them. Afraid to look into their eyes. Afraid to ask whether his eyes were also gray saucers.

They weren't responding. See, they were afraid too. They'd seen his eyes and were stunned to dumbness. They stood on the steps of the Thrall, ashamed and silent. Thomas certainly felt—

He heard a loud smacking sound and spun around, fearing bats. But it wasn't bats. It was Rachelle and Johan. They'd descended the steps and were stuffing some fruit he hadn't seen into their mouths.

Whose fruit? Everything else here appeared to be dead.

Teeleh's.

"Wait!" He took the steps in long leaps, rushed over to Rachelle, and ripped the fruit from her mouth.

She whirled around and struck him, her hand flexed firm and her fingers curved to form a claw. "Leave me!" she snarled, spewing juice.

Thomas staggered in shock. He touched his cheek and brought his hand away bloody. Rachelle snatched up another fruit and shoved it into her mouth.

He shifted his gaze to Johan, who ignored them totally. Like a ravenous dog intent on a meal, he greedily chewed the flesh of a fruit.

Thomas backed to the steps. This couldn't be happening. Not to Johan, of all people. Johan was the innocent child who just yesterday had walked around the village in a daze, lost in thoughts about diving into Elyon's bosom. And now this?

And Rachelle. His dearest Rachelle. Beautiful Rachelle, who could spend countless hours dancing in the arms of her beloved Creator. How could she have so easily turned into this snarling, desperate animal with dead eyes and flaking skin?

A flurry of wings startled Thomas. He spun his head to the blackened entrance of the Thrall. Michal sat perched on the railing.

"Michal!"

Thomas bounded up the steps. "Thank goodness! Thank goodness, Michal! I . . ." Tears blurred his vision. "It's terrible! It's . . ." He turned to Rachelle and Johan, who were making quick work of the fruit scattered below.

"Look at them!" he blurted out, flinging an arm in their direction. "What's happening?" Even as he said it, he felt a sudden desire to cool his own throat with the fruit.

Michal stared ahead, regarding the scene serenely. "They are embracing evil," he said quietly.

Thomas felt himself begin to calm. The fruit looked exactly like any fruit they'd eaten at a table set by Karyl. Intoxicating, sweet. He shivered with growing desperation. "They've gone mad," he said in a low voice.

"Perceptive. They're in shock. It won't always be this bad."

"Shock?" Thomas heard himself say it, but his eyes were on the last piece of fruit, which both Rachelle and Johan were heading for.

"Shock of the most severe nature," Michal said. "You've tasted the fruit before. Its effect isn't so shocking to you, but don't think you're any different from them."

Johan reached the fruit first, but his taller sister quickly towered over him. She put one hand on her hip and shoved the other at the fruit. "It's mine!" she screamed. "You have no right to take what is mine. Give it to me!"

"No!" Johan screamed, his eyes bulging from a beet-red face. "I found it. I'll eat it!" Rachelle leaped on her younger brother with nails extended.

"They're going to kill each other," Thomas said. It occurred to him that he was actually less horrified than amused. The realization frightened him.

"With their bare hands? I doubt it. Just keep them away from anything that can be used as a weapon." The Roush looked at them with a blank stare. "And get them to the lake as soon as you can."

Rachelle and Johan separated and circled each other warily. From the corner of his eyes, Thomas saw a small black cloud approaching. But he kept his eyes on the fruit in Johan's fist. He really should run down there and take the fruit away himself. They'd eaten more than enough. Right?

Thomas cast a side glance at Michal. The Roush had his eyes on the sky. "Remember, Thomas. The lake." He leaped into the air and swept away.

"Michal?" Thomas glanced at the sky that had interested the Roush. The black cloud swept in over blackened trees. Shataiki!

"Rachelle!" he screamed. These black beasts terrified him more now than they had in the black forest.

"Rachelle!" He bounded down the stairs and seized first Rachelle and then Johan by their arms, nearly jerking them from their feet. He glanced at the skyline, surprised at how close the Shataiki had come. Their shrieks of delight echoed through the valley.

Rachelle and Johan had seen, too, and they ran willingly. But their strength was gone, and Thomas had to practically drag them up the stairs into the Thrall. Even with Rachelle finally pulling free and stumbling up the steps on her own, they just managed to flop into the dark Thrall and shove the doors closed when the first Shataiki slammed into the heavy wood. Then they came, shrieking and beating, one after another.

Thomas scrambled back, saw the door was secure, and dropped to his seat, panting. Rachelle and Johan lay unmoving to his right. He had no idea how to follow Michal's last request. It would be hard enough to sneak undetected to the lake by himself. With Rachelle and Johan in their present catatonic state, it would be impossible.

Neither of them stirred in the Thrall's dim light. The once brilliant green floor was now a dark slab of cold wood. The tall pillars now towered like black ghosts in the shadows. Only the weak light filtering in through the still-translucent dome allowed Thomas to see at all.

He rolled over and pushed himself to his feet. The Shataiki still slammed unnervingly against the door, but the period between hits began to lengthen. He doubted they could find a way to break into the building. But it wasn't the Shataiki he feared most at the moment. No, it was the two humans at his feet who sent shivers up his spine. And himself. What was happening to them?

The fruit in the storage room. Thomas scrambled to his feet and pounded down the steps. Had the air destroyed that fruit as well? Actually, now that he thought about it, the fruit in the forest had dropped to the ground as he ran by, but it hadn't turned black. Not right away.

He slammed into the door and pulled up. This door had been closed before they'd opened the main Thrall doors. If he opened it, would the air that now filled the Thrall destroy the fruit?

He would have to take that chance. He threw the door open, stepped in, and slammed it behind him. The jar stood against the far wall. He bounded over, grabbed one fruit out, and immediately stuffed rags in the top. He had no clue if this would work, but nothing else came to mind.

Thomas lifted the one red fruit up and blew out a lungful of air.

Bad air, he thought. *Too late.*

The fruit didn't wilt in his hand. How long would it last?

He shoved the fruit into his mouth and bit deep. The juice ran over his tongue, his chin. It slipped down his throat.

The relief was instantaneous. Gentle spasms ran through his stomach. Thomas dropped to his knees and tore into the sweet flesh.

He'd eaten half the fruit before remembering Rachelle and Johan. He grabbed an orange fruit from the jar, stuffed the rag back into its neck, and tore up the stairs.

Rachelle and Johan still lay like limp rags.

He slid to his knees and rolled Rachelle onto her back. He placed the fruit directly over her lips and squeezed. The skin of the orange fruit split. A trickle of juice ran down his finger and spilled onto her parched lips. Her mouth filled with the liquid and she moaned. Her neck arched as the nectar worked into her throat. In a long, slow exhale, she pushed air from her lungs and opened her eyes.

Eyeing the fruit in Thomas's hand with a glint of desperation, she reached up, snatched the fruit, and began devouring. Thomas chuckled and pressed his half-eaten fruit into Johan's mouth. The moment the young boy's eyes flickered open, he grabbed the fruit and bit deeply. Without speaking they ravenously consumed flesh, seeds, and juice.

If Thomas wasn't mistaken, some color had returned to their skin, and the cuts they had sustained during their argument were not as red. The fruit still had its power.

"How do you guys feel?" he asked, glancing from one to the other. They both stared at him with dull eyes. Neither spoke.

"Please, I need you with me here. How do you feel?"

"Fine," Johan said. Rachelle still did not respond.

"We have more, maybe a dozen or so."

Still no response. He had to get them to the lake. And to do that he had to keep himself sane.

"I'll be right back," he said. He left them cross-legged on the floor and returned to the basement, where he ate another whole fruit, a delicious white nectar he thought was called a sursak.

Eleven left. At least they weren't spoiling as quickly as he'd feared. If Rachelle and Johan showed any further signs of deterioration, he would give them more, but there was no guarantee they would find any more. They couldn't waste a single one.

The next few hours crept by with scarcely a word among them. The attacks at the door had stopped completely. Thomas tried his patience with futile attempts to lure them into discussing possible courses of action now that they had found a temporary haven from the Shataiki.

But only Johan engaged him, and then in a way that made Thomas wish he hadn't.

"Tanis was right," Johan bit off. "We should have launched a preemptive expedition to destroy them."

"Has it occurred to you that that's what he was doing? But it obviously didn't work, did it?"

"What do you know? He would have called *me* to go with him if he was going to battle. He promised me I could lead an attack! And I would have too!"

"You don't know what you're saying, Johan."

"I wish we would have followed Tanis. Look where you got us!"

Thomas didn't want to think where this line of reasoning would lead the boy. He turned away and broke off the conversation.

Two hours into the unbearable silence, Thomas noticed the change in Rachelle and Johan. The gray pallor was returning to their skin. They grew more restless with each passing hour, scratching at their skin until it bled. In another hour, tiny flaking scales covered their bodies, and Johan had rubbed his left arm raw. Thomas gave them each another fruit. Another one for him. They were now down to eight. At this rate, they wouldn't last the day.

"Okay, we're going to try to make it to the lake."

He grabbed both by their tunics and helped them to their feet. They hung their heads and shuffled to the back entrance without protesting. But there didn't seem to be a drop of eagerness in them. Why so reluctant to return to the Elyon they once were so desperate for?

"Now, when we get outside, I don't want any fighting or anything stupid. You hear? It doesn't sound like there are any black bats out there, but we don't want to attract any, so keep quiet."

"You don't have to be so demanding," Rachelle said. "It's not like we're dying or anything."

It was the first full sentence she had spoken for hours, and it surprised Thomas. "That's what you think? The fact is, you're already dead." She frowned but didn't argue.

Thomas pressed his ear against the door. No signs of Shataiki. He eased the door open, still heard nothing, and stepped out.

They stood on the threshold and looked over the empty village for the second time that day. The bats had left.

"Okay, let's go."

They walked through the village and over the hill in silence. An eerie sense of death hung in the air as they walked past the tall trees looming black and bare against the sky. The bubbling sound of running water was gone. A muddy trench now ran close to the path where the river from the lake had flowed. Had they waited too long? It had been only a few hours since Michal urged him to go to the lake.

Lions and horses no longer lined the road. Blackened flowers drooped to the ground, giving the appearance that a slight wind might shatter their stems and send them crumbling to join the burned grass on the ground. No fruit. None at all that Thomas could see. Had the Shataiki taken it?

Thomas stayed to the rear of Rachelle and Johan, carrying the jar of fruit under one arm and a black stick he had picked up in the other hand. His sword, he thought wryly. He expected a patrol of beasts to swoop down from the sky and attack them at any moment, but the overcast sky hung quietly over the charred canopy. With one eye on the heavens and the other on the incredible changes about him, Thomas herded Rachelle and Johan up the path.

It wasn't until they approached the corner just before the lake that Johan finally broke the silence. "I don't want to go, Thomas. I'm afraid of the lake. What if we drown in it?"

"Drown in it? Since when have you drowned in any lake? That's the most ridiculous thing I've heard."

They continued hesitantly around the next bend. The view that greeted them stopped all three in their tracks.

Only a thread of water dribbled over the cliff into a small grayish pond below. The lake had been reduced to a small pool of water. Large white sandy beaches dropped a hundred feet before meeting the pool. No animals of any kind were in sight. Not a single green leaf remained on the dark circle of trees now edging the dwindling pool.

"Dear God. Oh, dear God. Elyon." Thomas took a step forward and stopped.

"Has he left?" Rachelle asked, looking around.

"Who?" Thomas asked absently.

She motioned to the lake.

"Look." Johan had fixed his eyes on the lip of the cliff.

There, on the high rock ledge, stood a single lion, gazing out over the land.

Thomas's heart bolted. A Roshuim? One of the lionlike creatures from the upper lake? And what of the upper lake? What of the boy?

The magnificent beast was suddenly joined by another. And then a third, then ten, and then a hundred white lions, filing into a long line along the crest of the dried falls.

Thomas turned to the others and saw their eyes peeled wide.

The beasts at the head of the falls were shifting uneasily now. The line split in two.

The boy stepped into the gap, and Thomas thought his heart stopped beating at first sight of the boy's head. The lions crumpled to their knees and pressed their muzzles flat on the stone surface. And then the boy's small body filled the position reserved for him at the cliff's crest. The boy stood barefooted on the rock, dressed only in a loincloth.

For a few moments, Thomas forgot to breathe.

The entire line of beasts bowed their heads in homage to the boy. The child slowly turned and gazed over the land below him. His tiny slumped shoulders rose and fell slowly. A lump rose in Thomas's throat.

And then the boy's face twisted with sorrow. He raised his head, opened his mouth, and cried to the sky.

The long line of beasts dropped flat to their bellies, like a string of dominoes, sending an echo of thumps over the cliff. A chorus of bays ran down the line.

The air filled with the boy's wail. His song. A long, sustained note that poured grief into the canyon like molten lead.

Thomas dropped to his knees and began gasping for air. He'd heard a simi-lar sound before, in the lake's bowels, when Elyon's heart was break-ing in red waters.

The boy sank to his knees.

Tears sprang into Thomas's eyes, blurring the image of the gathered beasts. He closed his eyes and let the sobs come. He couldn't take this. The boy had to stop.

But the boy didn't stop. The cry ran on and on with unrelenting sorrow.

The wail fell to a whimper—a hopeless little sound that squeaked from a paralyzed throat. And then it dwindled into silence.

Thomas lifted his head. The beasts on the cliff fell silent but remained prone. The boy's chest heaved now, in long, slow gasps through his nos-trils. And then, just as Thomas began to wonder whether the show of sor-row was over, the small boy's eyes flashed open. He stood to his feet and took a step forward.

The boy threw his fists into the air and let loose a high-pitched shriek that shattered the still morning air. Like the wail of a man forced to watch his children's execution, with a red face and bulging eyes, screaming in rage. But all from the mouth of the small boy standing high on the cliff.

Thomas trembled in agony and threw himself forward on the sand. The shriek took the form of a song and howled through the valley in long, dreadful tones. Thomas clutched his ears, afraid his head might burst. Still the boy pushed his song into the air with a voice that Thomas thought filled the entire planet.

And then, suddenly, the boy fell silent, leaving only the echoes of his voice to drift through the air.

For a moment, Thomas could not move. He slowly pushed himself up to his elbows and lifted his head. He ran a forearm across his eyes to clear his vision. The child stood still for a few moments, staring ahead as though dazed, and then turned and disappeared. The beasts clamored to their feet and backed away from the cliff until only a deserted gray ledge ran along the horizon. Silence filled the valley once again.

The boy was gone.

Thomas scrambled to his feet, panicked. No. No, it couldn't be! Without looking at the others, he sprinted down the white bank and into the dwindling water.

The intoxication was immediate. Thomas plunged his head under the water and gulped deeply. He stood up, threw his head back, and raised two fists in the air. "Elyon!" he yelled to the overcast sky.

Johan ran only a step ahead of Rachelle, down the bank and facefirst into the water. Now numb with pleasure, Thomas watched the two dunk their heads under the surface like desperately thirsty animals. The contrast between the terror that consumed the land and this remnant of Elyon's potent power, left as a gift for them, was staggering. He flopped facedown into the pool.

But there was a difference, wasn't there?

Elyon?

Silence.

He stood up. The water seemed to be lower.

Rachelle and then Johan stood from the water. A healthy glow had returned to their skin, but they looked down, confused.

"What's happening?" Rachelle asked.

The pond was sinking into the sand. Draining. Thomas splashed water on his face. He drank more of it. "Drink it! Drink it!"

They lowered their heads and drank.

But the level fell fast. It was soon at their knees. Then their ankles.

"So, now you know," a voice said behind Thomas.

Michal stood on the bank. "I'm afraid I have to go, my friends. I may not see you for a while." His eyes were bloodshot, and he looked very sad.

Thomas splashed out of the pond. "Is this it? Is this the last of the water? You can't go!"

Michal shifted away and stared at the cliff. "You're not in a position to be demanding."

"We'll die out here!"

"You're already dead," Michal said.

The last of the water seeped into the sand.

Michal took a deep breath. "Go back to the Crossing. Walk through the black forest due east from the bridge. You'll come to a desert. Enter the desert and keep walking. If you survive that long, you may eventually find refuge."

"Through the black forest again? How can there be refuge in the black forest? The whole place is swarming with the bats!"

"Was swarming. The other villages are much larger than this one. The bats have gone for them. But you'll have your hands full enough. You have the fruit. Use it."

"The whole planet is like this?" Rachelle asked.

"What did you expect?"

Michal hopped twice, as if to take off. "And don't drink the water. It's been poisoned."

"Don't drink any of it? We have to drink."

"If it's the color of Elyon, you may drink it." He hopped again, readying for flight. "But you won't be seeing any of that soon."

He took off.

"Wait!" Thomas yelled. "What about the rest? Where are the rest?"

But the Roush either didn't hear or didn't want to answer.

They left the charred valley and ran for the Crossing.

Thomas stopped them within the first mile and insisted they all spread ash over their bodies—the bats might mistake them for something other than humans. They picked their way through the landscape like gray ghosts. The ground was littered with fallen trees, and their unprotected feet were easily cut by the sharp wood, slowing them to a walk at times. But they pressed forward, keeping a careful eye to the skies as they went.

There were still a few pieces of fruit here and there that hadn't dried up, and what juice remained still held its healing power. They used the juice on their feet when the cuts became unbearable. And when the shriveled fruit became scarce, they began using the fruit from the jar. They were soon down to six pieces.

"We'll each take two," Thomas decided. "But use them sparingly. I have the feeling this is the last we'll see."

Slowly and silently they made their way toward the Crossing. It was midmorning before they saw the first Shataiki formation, flying high overhead, at least a thousand strong. The Shataiki were headed toward the black forest and flapped on. They either did not see the party of three or were fooled by the ash.

An hour later they reached the Crossing. The old grayed bridge arched over a small stream of brown water. The rest of the riverbed was cracked dry.

Johan ran to the bank. "It looks okay."

"Don't drink it!"

"We're going to die of thirst out here!" he said. "Who says we have to listen to the bat?"

The bat? Michal.

"Then eat some fruit. Michal said not to drink the water, and I for one will follow his advice. Let's go!"

Johan frowned at the water then reluctantly joined them on the bridge.

The far bank showed a dark stain where the Shataiki had torn Tanis to shreds, but otherwise there was nothing peculiar about the black forest. It looked just like the ground they had already traversed.

"Come on," Thomas urged after a moment. He swallowed a lump in his throat and led them over the bridge and into the black forest.

They slowly made their way through the forest, stopping every hundred meters or so to wipe more juice on the soles of their feet.

"Use it sparingly," Thomas insisted. "Leave enough to eat." He hated to think what would happen when they ran out.

Shataiki sat perched in the limbs above, squealing and fighting over petty matters. Only the more curious looked down at the trio passing beneath them. *It must be the ash, Thomas* thought. Deceptive enough to confuse the mindless, deceptive creatures.

They had picked their way through the forest for what seemed a very long time when they came to a clearing.

"The desert!" Rachelle said.

Thomas glanced around. "Where?"

"There!" She pointed directly ahead.

Black trees bordered the far side of the clearing. And beyond a fifty-foot swath of trees, glimpses of white sand. The prospect of getting out of the forest was enough to make Thomas's pulse scream in anticipation.

"That's my girl. Come on!" He stepped forward.

"So I'm still your girl?"

Thomas turned back. She wore a sly smirk. "Of course. Aren't you?"

"I don't know, Thomas. Am I?"

She lifted her chin and walked past him. She was. At least he hoped she was. Although it occurred to him that the Great Romance had been blackened like everything else in this cursed land.

He shoved the thoughts from his mind and trudged after her. Their need for survival was greater than any romance. He quickly passed her and led the way. He might not be the man he was, but he could at least put on a front of protection. Famed warrior, Thomas Hunter. He grunted in disgust.

They had reached the field's midpoint when the first black Shataiki dived from the sky and settled to the ground ahead of them. Thomas looked at the bat. *Keep moving. Just keep moving.*

He adjusted his course, but the bat hopped over to block his passage.

"You think you can pass me so easily?" the Shataiki sneered. "Not so easy now, eh?"

Johan jumped forward and put up his fists as if to take the bat on. Thomas lifted a hand to the boy without removing his eyes from the Shataiki. "Back off, Johan."

"Back off, Johan," the bat mimicked. Its pupil-less red eyes glared. "Are you too weak for me, Johan?" The bat raised one of its talons. "I could cut you open right here! How does that feel? Welcome to our new world." The Shataiki cackled with delight and bit deeply into a fruit it had withdrawn from behind.

"Want some?" he taunted and then laughed again as though this had been a hilarious assault.

Thomas took a step in the direction of the bat. The Shataiki immediately flared his wings and snarled. "Stay!" A flock of Shataiki had now gathered in the sky and circled above them, taunting. "You tell him," one with a raspy voice taunted.

"You tell him," another mimicked.

And the first Shataiki did. "You stay put!" it yelled now, even though Thomas hadn't moved.

Thomas reached into his pocket and squeezed his last fruit so that the juice from the flesh seeped out between his fingers.

He turned calmly around and faced Rachelle and Johan. "Use your fruit," he whispered. "When I say, run."

"Face me when I talk to you, you—"

It was as far as the Shataiki got. Thomas flung the dripping fruit at the Shataiki. "Run!" he yelled.

The fruit landed squarely in the Shataiki's face. Burning flesh hissed loudly. The beast screamed and swatted at his face. A strong stench of sulfur filled the air as Thomas rushed by, followed by Johan then Rachelle.

"It's a green fruit!" a bat cried from among those that circled the scene. "They have the green fruit! They're not dead. Kill them!"

Thomas tore through the field. No less than twenty Shataiki dived toward them from behind.

"Use your fruit! Rachelle!"

She spun and hurled her fruit at the swarm. They scattered like flies. Rachelle flew by him. Then Johan. But the bats had reorganized and were coming again. Johan clutched their last fruit between his fingers. They shouldn't have thrown the fruits.

"Wait, Johan! Don't throw it." They ran into the trees. "Give me your fruit."

Johan ran on, desperate to reach the white sand.

"Drop it!"

The fruit fell from his fingers. Thomas scooped it up and whirled around. A hundred or more of the bats had materialized from nowhere. They saw the fruit in his hand and passed him. Straight for Johan.

"Back!" Thomas screamed. He raced for the boy, reached him, and shoved the fruit into the face of the first bat to reach them.

The Shataiki shrieked and fell to the ground.

And then they were through the trees and running on white sand.

"Stay together!" Thomas panted. "Stay close."

They ran a hundred yards before Thomas glanced back and then stopped. "Hold up."

Rachelle and Johan stopped. Doubled over, heaving for breath.

The bats flew in circles over the black forest, screeching their protests. But they weren't following.

They weren't flying into the desert.

Johan jumped into the air and let out a whoop. Thomas swung his fist at the circling bats. "Ha!"

"Ha!" Rachelle yelled, flinging sand at the forest. She laughed and stumbled over to Thomas. "I knew it!" Her laughter was throaty and full of confidence, and Thomas laughed with her.

She straightened and walked up to him wearing a tempting smile. "So," she said, drawing a finger over his cheek. "You're still my fearless fighter after all."

"Did you ever doubt?"

She hesitated. He saw that her skin was drying out again.

"For a moment," she said. She leaned forward and kissed him on the forehead. "Only for a moment."

Rachelle turned and left him standing with two thoughts. The first was that she was a beautifully mischievous woman.

The second was that her breath smelled a bit like sulfur.

"Rachelle?"

"Yes, dear warrior?"

He took a big bite out of their last fruit and tossed her the rest. "Have some fruit. Give the rest to Johan."

She caught it with one hand, winked at him, and bit down hard. "So, which way?"

He pointed into the desert.

———

The last of their exuberance vacated them at midday, when the sun stood directly overhead.

They navigated by the ball of fire in the sky. Deeper into the desert. East, as Michal had said. But with each step the sand seemed to grow hotter and the sun's descent into the western sky slower. The flats quickly gave way to gentle dunes, which would have been manageable with the right shoes and at least a little water. But these small hills of sand soon led to huge mountains that ran east to west so that they were forced to crawl up one side and stagger down the other. And there was not a drop of water. Not even poisoned water.

By midafternoon, Thomas's strength began to fail him. In his cautiousness, he'd had much less fruit since leaving the lake than either of them, and he guessed that it was beginning to show.

"We're walking in circles!" Rachelle said, stopping at the top of a dune. "We're not getting anywhere."

Thomas kept walking. "Don't stop."

"I will stop! This is madness! We'll never make it!"

"I want to go back," Johan said.

"To what? To the bats? Keep going."

"You're marching us to our deaths!" he yelled.

Thomas whirled around. "Walk!"

They stared at him, stunned by his outburst.

"We can't stop," Thomas said. "Michal said to walk east." He pointed at the sun. "Not north, not south, not west. East!"

"Then we should take a break," Rachelle said.

"We don't have *time* for a break!"

He marched down the hill, knowing they had no choice but to follow. They did follow. But slowly. So as not to be too obvious, he slowed and let them catch up.

The first hallucinations began toying with his mind ten minutes later. He saw trees that he knew weren't trees. He saw pools of water that weren't the least bit wet. He saw rocks where there were no rocks.

He saw Bangkok. And in Bangkok he saw Monique, trapped in a dark dungeon.

Still he plodded on. Their throats were raw, their skin was parched, and their feet were blistering, but they had no choice. Michal had said to walk east, and so they would walk east.

He began to mumble incoherently in another half hour. He wasn't sure what he was saying and tried not to say anything at all, but he could hear himself over a hot wind that blew in their faces.

Finally, when he knew that he would collapse with even one more step, he stopped.

"Now we will rest," he said and collapsed to his seat.

Johan plopped down on his right, and Rachelle eased to her seat on his left.

"Yes, of course, now we have time for a rest," Rachelle said. "Half an hour ago it would have killed us because Michal said to walk east. But now that you're babbling like a fool, now that our mighty warrior has deemed it perfectly logical, we will take a rest."

He didn't bother to respond. He was too exhausted to argue. It was a wonder she still had the energy to pick a fight.

They sat in silence on the tall dune for several minutes. Thomas finally braved a glance over at Rachelle. She sat hugging her knees, staring at the horizon, jaw firm. The wind whipped her long hair behind her. She refused to look at him.

If he had it in him, he might tell her to stop acting like a child.

Ahead the dunes rose and fell without the slightest hint of change.

Michal had told them to come to the desert because he knew the Shataiki wouldn't leave their trees. But why had he insisted they go deeper into the desert? Was it possible that the Roush was sending them to their deaths?

"You're already dead," he'd said. Maybe not in the way Thomas had first assumed. Maybe "dead" as in, *I know you'll follow my direction because you have no other choice. You'll walk into the desert and die as you deserve to die. So really, you're already dead.*

Dead man walking.

"You're still dreaming about Monique."

The hallucinations were back. Monique was calling to him. Kara was telling him—

"I heard you speak her name. At a time like this, she's on your mind?"

No, not Monique. Rachelle. He faced her. "What?"

Her eyes flashed. "I want to know why you're mumbling her name."

So. He'd mumbled about the woman from his dreams—her name, maybe more—and Rachelle had heard him. She was jealous. This was insane! They were facing their deaths, and Rachelle was drawing strength from a ridiculous jealousy of a woman who didn't even exist!

Thomas turned away. "Monique de Raison, my dear Rachelle, doesn't exist. She's a figment of my imagination. My dreams." Not the best way to put it, actually. He emphasized his first point. "She doesn't exist, and you know it. And arguing about her definitely won't help us survive this blasted desert."

He stood to his feet and marched down the hill. "Let's move!" he ordered, but he felt sick. He had no right to dismiss her jealousy so flippantly. Just this morning he'd stared at her and Johan fighting over the fruit, horrified by their disregard for each other, yet he was no different, as Michal had pointed out.

Johan was the last to stand. Thomas had already reached the next crest when he looked back and saw the boy facing the way they'd come.

"Johan!"

The boy turned slowly, looked back one last time, and headed down the dune after them.

"He wants to go back," Rachelle said, walking past him. "I'm not sure I blame him."

They walked another two hours in forlorn silence, taking breaks every ten or fifteen minutes for Rachelle's and Johan's benefit now as much as his own. The wind died down and the heat became oppressive.

Every time Thomas felt the onset of hallucinations, he stopped them. He might not be much of a leader any longer, but he was leading the way by default. He had to keep his mind as clear as possible under the circumstances.

They walked with the dread knowledge that they were walking to their deaths. Slowly, painfully now, the mountainous dunes fell behind them, one by one. The only change was the gradual appearance of boulders. But no one even mentioned them. If boulders didn't hold water, they didn't care about boulders.

The valley they were in when the sun dipped below the horizon was maybe a hundred yards wide. A cropping of boulders rose from the valley floor.

"We'll stop here for the night," Thomas said. He nodded at the boulders. "The rocks will block any wind."

No one argued. Thomas collapsed by the rocks and set his head back in the sand as the setting sun cast a rich red glow across the desert floor. He closed his eyes.

The sky was black when he opened them again. Whether it was complete exhaustion or the unbearable silence that kept him from sleep, he wasn't sure. Johan had rolled into a ball and lay under the rocks. Rachelle lay twenty feet away, staring at the sky. He could see the moonlight's reflection in her glassy eyes.

Awake.

It was an absurd situation. They were as likely going to die out here as live, and the only woman he could ever remember loving was lying twenty feet away either fuming or biting her tongue, or hating him, he didn't know which.

But he did know that he missed her terribly.

He pushed himself to his feet, walked over to her, and lay down beside her.

"Are you awake?" he whispered.

"Yes."

It was the first word she'd spoken since telling him that Johan wanted to go back, and it was amazing how glad he was to hear it.

"Are you mad at me?"

"No."

"I'm sorry," he said. "I shouldn't have yelled at you."

"I guess it's been a day to yell," she said.

"I guess."

They lay quietly. Her hand lay in the sand, and he reached over and touched it. She took his thumb.

"I want you to make me a promise," she said.

"Okay, anything you want."

"I want you to promise not to dream about Monique ever again."

"Please—"

"I don't care what she is or isn't," Rachelle said. "Just promise me."

"Okay."

"Promise?"

"I promise."

"Forget the histories; they don't mean a thing anymore anyway. Everything's changed."

"You're right. Forget dreams about Bangkok. They seem silly now."

"They are silly," she said, then she rolled over and pushed herself to one elbow. The moonlight played on her eyes. A beautiful gray.

She leaned over and gently kissed him on the lips. "Dream of me," she said. She settled on her side and curled up to sleep.

I will, Thomas thought. *I will dream only about Rachelle.* Thomas closed his eyes feeling more content than he'd felt since trudging into this terrible desert. He fell asleep and he dreamed.

He dreamed about Bangkok.

35

THE CONFERENCE room boasted a finely finished cherrywood table large enough to seat the fourteen people in attendance with room to spare. A lavish display of tropical fruits, European cheeses, cold roast beef, and several kinds of bread had been set as a centerpiece. They sat in wine-colored leather chairs, looking important and undoubtedly feeling the same.

Thomas, on the other hand, neither looked nor felt much more than what he actually was: a twenty-five-year-old wannabe novelist who'd been swallowed by his dreams.

Still, he had their attention. And in contrast to the events in his dreams, he felt quite good. Fourteen sets of eyes were fixed on him seated at the head of the table. For these next few minutes, he was as good as omniscient to them. And then they might decide to lock him up. The Thai authorities had gone out of their way to make it clear that regardless of the circumstances, he, Thomas Hunter, had committed a federal offense by kidnapping Monique de Raison. What they should do about it was unclear, but they couldn't just ignore it.

He looked at Kara on his immediate right and returned her quick smile.

He winked but didn't feel nearly as confident as he tried to look. If there were any skills he needed now, they were diplomatic ones. Kara had suggested he try to find a way to cultivate those in the green forest, as he had his fighting skills. Clearly, that was no longer an option.

Lately, the reality of the desert seemed more real to him than this world here. What would happen if he died of heat exhaustion in the desert night? Would he slump over here, dead?

Deputy Secretary Merton Gains sat to Thomas's left. Very few back in Washington knew that he'd left earlier in the day for this most unusual meeting. Then again, very few were aware the news that had punctuated the wires over the last forty-eight hours had anything to do with more than a crazed American who'd kidnapped Raison Pharmaceutical's chief virologist on the eve of the Raison Vaccine's long-awaited debut. Most assumed Thomas Hunter was either cause-driven or money-driven. The question being asked on most news channels was, Who put him up to it?

Gains's square jaw was in need of a shave. A young face betrayed by gray hair. Opposite him sat Phil Grant, the taller of the two dignitaries from the States. Long chin, long nose with glasses riding the end. The other American was Theresa Sumner from the CDC, a straightforward woman who'd already apologized for his treatment in Atlanta. Beside her, a Brit from Interpol, Tony Gibbons.

On the right, a delegate from the Australian intelligence service, two high-ranking Thai officials, and their assistants. On the left, Louis Dutêtre, a pompous, thin-faced man with sagging black eyebrows from French intelligence whom Phil Grant seemed to know quite well. Beside him, a delegate from Spain, and then Jacques de Raison and two of his scientists.

All here, all for him. He'd gone from being thrown out of the CDC in Atlanta to hosting a summit of world leaders in Bangkok within the span of just over a week.

Gains had explained his reason for calling the meeting and expressed his confidence in Thomas's information. Thomas had laid out his case as succinctly and clearly as he could without blowing them away with details from his dreams. Jacques de Raison had shown the simulation and presented his evidence on the Raison Strain. A string of questions and comments had eaten away nearly an hour.

"You're saying that Valborg Svensson, whom some of us know quite well by the way, is not a world-renowned pharmaceutical magnate after all, but a villain?" the Frenchman asked. "Some man hidden deep in the mountains of Switzerland, wringing his hands in anticipation of destroying the world with the invincible virus?"

A gentle chuckle supported several smiles on either side of the table.

"Thank you for the color, Louis," the CIA director said. "But I don't think the deputy secretary and I would have made the trip if we thought it was quite that simple. True, we can't verify any of Mr. Hunter's assertions about Svensson, but we do have a rather unusual string of events to consider here. Not the least of which is the fact that the Raison Strain appears to be real, as we've all seen with our own eyes tonight."

"Not exactly," the CDC representative said. Theresa. "We have some tests that reportedly show mutations, granted. But we don't have true behavioral data on the virus. Only simulations. We don't know exactly how it affects humans in human environments. For all we know, the virus can't survive in a complex, live, human host. No offense, but simulations like this are only, what, 70 percent?"

"Theoretically, 75," Peter said. "But I'd put it higher."

"Of course you would. It's your simulation. In reality you've injected mice?"

"Mice and chimps."

"Mice and chimps. The virus seems comfortable in these hosts, but we don't have any symptoms yet. Am I right? They've survived a couple of days and have grown, but we have a long way to go to know their true effect."

"True," the Raison employee said. "But—"

"Excuse me, could you restate your name?" Gains said.

"Striet, Peter Striet. Everything we see about this virus gives us the chills. True, the testing is only a day old, but we've seen enough viruses to make some pretty educated guesses, with or without the simulations."

"We need to know how long it will live in a human host," Theresa said.

"Are you volunteering?"

More chuckles.

She didn't think it was funny. "No, I'm recommending caution. The initial outbreak of MILTS infected only five thousand and killed roughly one thousand. Not exactly an epidemic of staggering proportions. But the fear it spread dealt a massive economic blow to Asia. An estimated five

million people in the tourism industry alone lost their jobs. Do you have
any idea what kind of panic would ensue if word about a planet-killing
virus hit the Drudge Report? Life as we know it would stop. Wall Street
would close. No one would risk going to work. Don't tell me: You've
bought a boatload of duct tape stock?"

"I'm sorry?"

"Six billion people would tape themselves into their homes with duct
tape. You'd get rich. Meanwhile, millions of elderly and disadvantaged
would die from neglect at home."

"Overstated, perhaps, but I think she makes an excellent point," the
Frenchman said. Several others threw in their agreement. "I agreed to come
precisely because I understand the explosive nature of what is being so
loosely suggested."

That would be him doing the loose suggesting, Thomas realized.
Kara's jaw flexed. For a moment he thought she was going to tell the
Frenchman something. Not this time. This was different, wasn't it? The
real deal. Not exactly a college debate.

The Frenchman pressed his point. "This could easily be nothing more
than Chicken Little crying that the sky is falling. There is the issue of ir-
responsibility to be considered."

"I resent that remark," Gains said. "On more than one occasion,
Thomas has proved me wrong. His predictions have been nothing short
of astounding. To take his statements lightly could prove to be a terrible
mistake."

"And so could taking his statements seriously," Theresa said. "Let's say
there is a virus. Fine. When that virus presents itself, we deal with it. Not
when it becomes a widespread problem, mind you, but when it first rears
its ugly little head. When we have even a single case. But let's not suggest
it's a problem until we have absolute certainty that it is. Like I said, fear and
panic could be much larger problems than any virus."

"Agreed," the Spanish delegate said. "It is only prudent." The man's
collar was too tight, and half his neck folded over his shirt. "Until we have
a solution, there is no benefit in terrifying the world with the problem.

Especially if there is even the slightest chance that there may not be a problem."

"Precisely," the Frenchman said. "We have a virus. We're working on a way to deal with that virus. We have no real indication that the virus will be used maliciously. I don't see the need for panic."

"He has my daughter," Raison said. "Or does that no longer concern you?"

"I can assure you that we'll do everything we can to find your daughter," Gains said. He glared at Louis Dutêtre. "We've had a team on the ground at Svensson's laboratories for several hours."

"We should get a report at any time," Phil Grant said. "Our deepest sympathies, Mr. Raison. We'll find her."

"Yes, of course," Dutêtre said. "But as of yet, we don't know that Svensson had anything to do with this understandably tragic kidnapping. We have hearsay from Mr. Hunter. Furthermore, even if Svensson is somehow connected to her disappearance, we have no reason to believe the kidnapping in any way predicts a malicious use of a virus—a virus we haven't proved to be lethal, I might add. You're making a leap of faith, gentlemen. Something I'm not prepared to do."

"The fact of the matter is, we have a virus, deadly or not," Gains said. "The fact of the matter is, Thomas told me there would be a virus before any physical evidence surfaced. That was enough to get me on a plane. Granted, this isn't something we want to leak, but neither can we ignore it. I'm not suggesting we start barring the doors, but I am suggesting we give contingencies some thought."

"Of course!" Dutêtre continued. "But I might suggest that your boy is the real problem here. Not some virus. It occurs to me that Raison Pharmaceutical is now in the toilet, regardless of how this plays out. I wonder what Thomas Hunter is being paid to kidnap and fabricate all of these tales."

Heavy silence descended on the room as if someone had dropped a thousand pounds of smothering flour on everyone. Gains looked stunned. Phil Grant just stared at the smiling Frenchman.

"Thomas Hunter is here at my request," Gains said. "We did not invite—"

"No," Thomas said. He held his hand out to Gains. "It's okay, Mr. Secretary. Let me address his concern."

Thomas pushed his chair back and stood. He put a finger on his chin and paced to the right, then back to the left. The air seemed to have been sucked out of the room. He had something to say, of course. Something pointed and intelligent.

But suddenly it occurred to him that what he thought was intelligent might very well sound like nonsense to the Frenchman. And yet, in his silence, stalking in front of them at this very moment, he had complete if momentary power. The realization extended his silence at least another five seconds.

He could trade power too.

"How long have you been working in the intelligence community, Mr. Dutêtre?" Thomas asked. He shoved a hand into his pocket. His khaki cargo pants weren't exactly the going dress in this room, but he shoved the thought from his mind.

"Fifteen years," Dutêtre said.

"Good. Fifteen years, and you get invited to a gig like this. Do you know how long I've been at this game, Mr. Dutêtre?"

"Never, from what I can gather."

"Close. Your intelligence is off. Just over one week, Mr. Dutêtre. And yet I was also invited to this gig. You have to ask yourself how I managed to get the deputy secretary of state and the director of the CIA to cross the ocean to meet with me. What is it that I said? What do I really know? Why are these men and women gathered here in Bangkok at my request?"

Now the room was more than silent. It felt vacant.

"In a word, Mr. Dutêtre, it is extraordinary," Thomas said. He put the tips of his fingers on the table and leaned forward. "Something very extraordinary has occurred to compel this meeting. And now you're sounding very plain and boring to me. So I've decided to do something that I've done a number of times already. Something extraordinary. Would you like that, Mr. Dutêtre?"

The Frenchman glanced at Phil Grant. "What is this, a pony show?"

"Would you like to see me float into the air? Maybe if I did that you'd be convinced?"

Someone made a sound that sounded like a half chuckle.

"Okay, I will float for you. Not like you might expect, hovering in mid-air, but what I'm going to do will be no less extraordinary. Just because you don't understand it doesn't change that fact. Are you ready?"

No comment.

"Let me set this up. The fact is, I knew who would win the Kentucky Derby, I knew that the Raison Vaccine would mutate, and I knew exactly under what circumstances it would mutate. Mr. Raison, what's the probability that you, much less I, could do that?"

"Impossible," the man said.

"Theresa, you must have a good working knowledge of these matters. What would you say the probability would be?"

She just stared at him.

"Exactly. There *are* no probabilities, because it's impossible. So for all practical purposes, I already have floated for you. Now I'm saying I can float again, and you have the audacity to call me a fraud."

The Frenchman was smiling, but it wasn't a pleasant smile. "So you remember exactly how the virus mutates, and you think you may have given some information about the antivirus to this Carlos character, but you forget how to formulate it yourself?"

"Yes. Unfortunately."

"How convenient."

"Listen to me carefully," Thomas said. "Here comes my floating trick. The Raison Strain is a highly contagious and extremely lethal airborne virus that will infect most of the world's population within the next three weeks unless we find a way to stop it. Delaying one day could make the difference between life and death for millions. We will learn of its release within seven days, when the community of nations, perhaps through the

United Nations, receives notice to hand over sovereignty and all nuclear weapons in exchange for an antivirus. This is the course history is now on."

Louis Dutêtre leaned back in his chair and tapped a pencil on his knuckles. "And what you would like to do is bring on World War III before it's here. Monsters aren't conquered by heroes on white horses in this world, Mr. Hunter. Your virus may kill us all, but believing in your virus *will* kill us all."

"Then either way, we're all dead," Thomas said. "You can accept that?"

Gains lifted a hand to stall the exchange. "I think you see his point, Thomas. There are complications. It may not be black and white. We can't run around yelling virus. Frankly, we don't have a virus yet, at least not one that we know will be used or even could be used. What do you propose?"

Thomas pulled his chair out and sat. "I propose we take Svensson out before he can release the virus."

"That's impossible," the CIA director said. "He has rights. We're moving, but we can't just drop a bomb on his head. Doesn't work that way."

"Assuming you're right about Svensson," Gains said, "he would need a vaccine or an antivirus to trade, right? So that gives us some time."

"Nothing says he has to wait until he has the antivirus before releasing the virus. As long as he's confident he can produce an antivirus within a couple of weeks, he could release the virus and call our bluff, claiming to have the antivirus. Right now the race is to stop Svensson before he can do any damage. Once he does his damage, our only hope will ride with an antivirus and a vaccine."

"And how long would that take?" Gains asked, turning to Raison.

"Without Monique? Months. With her?" He shrugged. "Maybe sooner. Weeks." He didn't mention the possible reversal of her genetic signature, as Peter had explained to Thomas yesterday.

"Which is another reason why we have to go after Svensson and determine if he has Monique," Thomas said. "The world just may depend on Monique in the coming weeks."

"And what suggestion do you have short of taking out Svensson?" Gains asked Thomas.

"At this point? None. We should have taken out Svensson twenty-four hours ago. If we had, this would all be over now. But then what do I know? I'm just a wannabe novelist in cargo pants."

"That's right, Mr. Hunter, you are," the Frenchman said. "Keep that in mind. You're firing live bullets. I won't have you galloping around the world shooting your six-guns. I for one would like to pour a little water down your barrels."

Grant's phone chirped, and he turned to answer it quietly.

"I would like to consider some contingency planning in the event we do end up with a problem," Gains said. "What are your thoughts on containment, Mr. Raison?"

"It depends on how a virus would break out. But if Svensson is behind any of this, he will know how to eliminate any containment possibilities. That's the primary difference between natural occurrences of a virus and forced occurrences as in bioweapons. He could get the virus into a hundred major cities within a week."

"Yes, but if—"

"Excuse me, Merton." Grant snapped his cell shut. "This may all be moot. Our people have just finished a sweep of Svensson's facilities in the Swiss Alps. They found nothing."

Thomas sat up. "What do you mean, nothing? That's not—"

"I mean, no sign of anything unusual."

"Was Svensson there?"

"No. But we spoke to his employees at some length. He's due back in two days for an interview with the Swiss Intelligence, which we will also attend. He's been at a meeting with suppliers in South America. We confirmed the meeting. There's no evidence that he's had anything to do with a kidnapping or any massive conspiracy to release a virus."

Silence engulfed them.

"Well, that's good news, I would say," Gains said.

"That's not news at all," Thomas said. "So he's not at his main lab. He could be anywhere. Wherever he is, he has both Monique and the Raison Strain. I'm telling you, you have to find him now!"

Gains put his hand out. "We will, Thomas. One step at a time. This is encouraging; let's not pour water over it just yet."

With those words Thomas knew that he had lost them all. Except Kara. Merton Gains was as much of an advocate as he could expect. If Gains was expressing caution, the game was over.

Thomas stood. "I really don't think you need me to discuss contingencies. I've told you what I know. I'll repeat it one more time for those of you who are slow tonight. History is about to take a plunge down a nasty course. You'll all know that soon, when unthinkable demands come from a man named Valborg Svensson, although I doubt he's working alone. For all I know, one of you works for him."

That kept them in a state of mild shock.

"Good night. If for some inexplicable reason you need me, I'll be in my room, 913, hopefully sleeping. Heaven knows someone has to do something."

Kara stood and lifted her chin evenly. They walked out side by side, brother and sister.

❦

Exhaustion swamped Thomas the moment the conference room door thumped shut behind him. He stopped and gazed down the empty hall, dazed. He'd been running through this madness for over a week without a break, and his body was starting to feel like it was filled with lead.

"Well, I guess you told them," Kara said quietly.

"I have to get some rest. I feel like I'm going to drop."

She slipped her arm through his and guided him down the hall. "I'm putting you to bed, and I'm not letting anyone wake you until you've caught up on your sleep. That's final."

He didn't argue. There was nothing he could do at the moment anyway. There might not be anything more he could do. Ever.

"Don't worry, Thomas. I think you said what needed saying. They'll have a change of attitude soon enough. Right?"

"Maybe. I hope not."

She understood. The only thing that would change their attitudes would be an actual outbreak of the Raison Strain, and nobody could hope for that.

"I'm proud of you," she said.

"I'm proud of you," he said.

"For what? I'm not doing anything! You're the hero here."

"Hero?" He scoffed. "Without you I would probably be in some fighting ring downtown trying to prove myself."

"You have a point," she said.

They entered the elevator and rode up alone.

"Since you seem agreeable to my suggestions, do you mind if I make another one?" Kara asked.

"Sure. I'm not sure if my tired mind is up to understanding anything more at the moment."

"It's something I've been thinking about." She paused. "If the virus is released, I don't see how anyone can physically stop it. At least not in twenty-one days."

He nodded. "And?"

"Especially if it's already a matter of history, as you've learned in the green forest, which is where all this is coming from, right?"

"Right."

"But why you? Why did this information just happen to be dumped in your lap? Why are you flipping between these realities?"

"Because I'm connected somehow."

"Because you're the only one who can ultimately make a difference. You started it. The virus exists because of you. Maybe only you can stop it."

The elevator stopped on the ninth floor and they headed for their suite.

"If that's true," he said, "then God help us all because, believe me, I don't have a clue what to do. Except sleep. Even then, we've been abandoned. Three days ago my entire understanding of God was flipped on its end, at least in my dreams. Now it's been flipped again."

"Then sleep."

"Sleep. Dream."

"Dream," she said. "But not just dream. I mean *really* dream."

He led her into the room. "You're forgetting something."

"What?"

"The green forest is gone. The world's changed." He sighed and plopped into a chair by the table. "I'm in a desert, half-dead. No water, no fruit, no Roush. I get shot now, and I really do die. If anything, the information will have to flow the other way to keep me alive there." He cocked his head. "Now there's an idea."

"You don't know that. I'm not saying you should go out and get shot and see what happens, mind you. But there's a reason why you're there. In that world. And there's a reason you're here."

"So what exactly are you suggesting?"

She dropped her purse on the bed and faced him. "That you go on an all-out search for something in that reality that will help us here. Take your time. There's no correlation between time there and time here, right?"

"As soon as I fall asleep there, I'm here."

"Then find a way not to be here every time you sleep. Spend a few days in that reality, a week, a month, however much time you need. Find something. Learn new skills. Whoever you become there, you will be here, right? So become somebody."

"I am somebody."

"You are, and I love you the way you are. But for the sake of this world, become someone more. Someone who can save this world. Go to sleep, dream, and come back a new man."

He looked at his sister. So full of optimism. But she didn't understand the extent of the devastation in the other reality.

"I have to get some sleep," he said, walking toward his room.

"Dream, Thomas. Dream long. Dream big."

"I will."

36

THOMAS'S MIND flooded with images of a young boy standing innocently at the center of a brightly colored room, chin raised to the ceiling,
eyes wide, mouth gaping.

Johan. And his skin was as smooth as a pool of chocolate milk. His
deep-throated song suddenly thundered in the room, startling Thomas.

He rolled over in his sleep.

For a moment the night lay quiet. Then the boy began to sing again.
Quietly this time, with closed eyes and raised hands. The sweet refrains
drifted to the heavens like birdsong. They ascended the scale and began to
distort.

Distort? No. Johan always spun a flawless song to the last note. But
the sound climbed the scale and grew to more of a wail than a song. Johan
was wailing.

Thomas's eyes sprang open. The morning's soft light flooded his vision.
His ears filled with the sound of a child singing in broken tones.

He pushed himself to an elbow, gazed about, and rested his eyes on the
boulder twenty paces from where he and Rachelle lay. There, facing the forest they had left behind, sitting cross-legged on the boulder with his back
turned to them, Johan lifted his chin in song. A weak, halting song to be
sure. Strained and off key. But a song nonetheless.

Rachelle raised to a sitting position next to him and stared at her
brother. Her skin was dry and flaking. As was his own. Thomas swallowed
and turned back to Johan, who wailed with his arms spread wide.

"Elyon, help us," he sang. "Elyon, help us."

Thomas stood up. Johan's whole body trembled as he struggled for notes. The boy sounded as though he might be crying. Crying under the waning power of his own notes, or perhaps because he could not sing as he once did.

Beside Thomas, Rachelle rose slowly to her feet without removing her eyes from the scene. Tears wet her parched cheeks. Thomas felt his chest constrict. Johan raised his small fists in the air and wailed with greater intensity—a heartbreaking rendering of sorrow and yearning and anger and pleading for love.

For long minutes they stood facing Johan, who lamented for all who would hear. Grieving for all who would take the time to listen to the cries of an abandoned, tortured child slowly dying far from home. But who could possibly hear such a song in this desert?

If only Michal or Gabil would come and tell them what to do. If only he could speak one more time, just one last time, to the boy from the upper lake.

If only he could close his eyes and open them again to the sight of a boy standing on the rise of sand to their left. Like the boy standing there now. Like—

Thomas froze.

The boy stood there, on the rise beside the boulders, staring directly at Johan. The boy from the upper lake!

As though conducted by an unseen hand, both Johan and Rachelle ceased their sobbing. The boy took three small steps toward the boulder and stopped. His arms hung limply by his sides. His eyes were wide and green. Brilliant, breathtaking green.

The boy's delicate lips parted slightly, as if he were about to speak, but he just stood, staring. A loose curl of hair hung between the boy's eyes, lifting gently in the morning breeze.

The two boys gazed directly at each other, as if held by an invisible bond. Johan's eyes were as round as saucers, and his face was wet from tears. To Thomas's right, Rachelle took a single step toward Johan and stopped.

And then the little boy opened his mouth.

A pure, sweet tone, crystal-clear in the morning stillness, pierced

Thomas's ears and stabbed at his heart like a razor-tipped arrow. He caught his breath at the very first note. Images of a world far removed flooded his mind. Memories of an emerald resin floor, of a thundering waterfall, of a lake. The notes tumbled into a melody.

Thomas dropped to his knees and began to cry again.

The child took a step toward Johan, closed his eyes, and lifted his chin. His song drifted through the air, dancing on their heads like a teasing angel. Rachelle sat hard.

The boy opened his arms, expanded his chest, and let loose a deep, rumbling tone that shook the ground. Then the boy formed his first lyrics, encased in notes rumbling gently over the dunes.

> *I love you.*
> *I love you, I love you, I love you.*

Thomas closed his eyes and let his body shake under the power of the words. The tune rose through the octave, piercing the still air with full-bodied chords.

> *I made you,*
> *and I love the way I made you.*

The song reached into Thomas's heart and amplified the resonance of each chord a thousandfold so that he thought his heart might explode.

And then, with an earsplitting tone, like a concert of a hundred thousand pipe organs blowing the same chord, the air shattered with one final note and fell silent.

Thomas lifted his head slowly. The boy still gazed at Johan, who had slipped down from the boulder and stood with both arms stretched out toward the boy.

Their first steps seemed tentative, taken almost simultaneously toward each other. The two boys suddenly broke free from the ground and raced toward each other with wide arms.

They collided there on the desert floor, two small boys about the same height, like two long-lost twins reunited. They all heard the slap of bare chest against bare flesh followed by grunts as the boys tumbled to the sand, giggling hysterically.

Rachelle began to laugh out loud. She clapped excitedly, and although Thomas assumed she'd never met the young boy, she knew his name. "Elyon!" She said the name like an ecstatic child. "Elyon!" She wept and laughed as she clapped.

The boys sprang to their feet and chased each other around the boulder, tagging each other in play, still giggling like schoolchildren passing a secret.

And then the boy turned toward Thomas.

Still kneeling, Thomas saw the boy run directly for him. His eyes flashed like emeralds, a twisted grin lifted his cheeks. The boy sprinted right up to Thomas, slid to a stop, put an arm around his neck, and placed his soft, warm cheek against Thomas's. His hot breath brushed Thomas's ear. "I love you," the boy whispered.

A roaring tornado rushed through his mind. Forceful winds blasted against his heart with pure, raw, unrefined love. He heard a feeble grunt fall from his mouth.

Then the boy was on to Rachelle. He repeated the embrace and Rachelle shook with sobs. The boy turned and sprinted from the camp. He stopped a dozen paces to the east and twirled around, eyes sparkling mischievously.

"Follow me," he said, then turned back to the dune and ran up its slope.

Johan raced past Thomas and Rachelle, panting.

Thomas struggled to his feet, eyes fixed on the boy now cresting the dune. He tugged Rachelle to her feet. They followed the boy like that— Johan leading, Thomas and Rachelle running behind.

No one spoke as they ran through the barren desert. Thomas's mind was still numb from the boy's touch. Sweat soon drenched Thomas's clothes. His breathing came in gasps as he clambered up the sandy dunes, following this little boy who ran as though he owned this sandbox. *But I'd follow him anywhere. I'd follow him over a cliff, believing that after leaping I'd be able to fly. I'd follow him into the sea, knowing I could breathe underwater.* It was the boy's song. It was his song, his eyes, his tender feet, the way his breath had rushed through Thomas's ears.

They ran on in silence, keeping their eyes fixed on the boy's naked back, glistening with sweat. He loped steadily into the desert—slowing up the face of sandy slopes and then bounding down the other side. Not fast enough to lose them, not slow enough to allow them any rest.

The sun stood high when Thomas staggered over a crest marked by the boy's footprints. He pulled himself up not ten feet from where Johan had stopped. The boy stood just ahead of Johan. Thomas followed their gaze.

What he saw took his breath away.

Below them, in the middle of this desolate white desert, lay a huge valley. And in this valley grew a vast green forest.

Thomas stared, mouth hanging open dumbly. It had to be several miles across, maybe more. Maybe twenty miles. But in the far distance where the trees ended, the valley floor rose in a mountain of sand. The desert continued. The forest wasn't colored. Green. Only green. Like the forests in his dreams of Bangkok.

"Look!" Rachelle extended her arm. Her pointing finger quivered. Then Thomas saw it.

A lake.

To the east, several miles inside the forest, the sun glinted off a small lake.

The boy whooped, thrust his fists into the air, and tore down the sandy slope. He tumbled once and came to his feet, flying fast.

Johan ran after him, whooping in kind. Then Thomas and Rachelle, together. Whooping.

It took them twenty minutes to reach the edge of the forest, where they slid to a stop. The trees stood tall, like sentinels intent on keeping the sand from encroaching. Brown bark. Large, leafy branches. A flock of red-and-blue parrots took flight and squawked overhead.

"Birds!" Johan cried.

The boy looked back at them from the forest's edge. Then, without a word, he stepped between two trees and ran in.

Thomas ran after him. "Come on!"

They came, running behind.

The canopy rose overhead, shading the sun. They passed between the same two trees the boy had slipped through.

"Come on, hurry!"

The sound of their feet brushing through sand changed to a soft crunch when they hit the first undergrowth.

Thomas strained for glimpses of the boy's back between the trees. There, and there. He raced on, hardly aware of the forest now. Behind him, Rachelle and Johan had the easier task of following him.

Thomas glanced up at the canopy. It all looked vaguely familiar. For a moment it seemed as if he were rushing into the jungles of Thailand. To rescue Monique.

The boy never ran out of sight for more than a few seconds. Deeper into the jungle they ran. Straight for the lake. There were birds on almost every tree it seemed. Monkeys and possums. They passed through a meadow with a grove of smaller trees heavy with a red fruit. Not the same kind of fruit they'd eaten in the colored forest, but very similar.

Thomas snatched up a fallen apple and tasted it on the run. Sweet. Delicious. But no power. He grabbed another and tossed it back to Rachelle. "It's good!"

A pack of dogs barked from the other end of the meadow. Wolves? Thomas picked up his pace. "Hurry!"

They hurried. Through tall trees squawking with birds, past large bushes bursting with berries, over a small creek sparkling with water, through another brightly flowered meadow and past a startled stampede of horses.

Rachelle and Johan were as frightened as the horses. Thomas was not.

And then, as suddenly as they had entered the forest, they were out. On the lip of a small valley.

A gentle slope descended to the shores of a glistening green lake. A thin blanket of haze drifted lazily above sections of the glassy surface. Trees, heavy with fruit, lined its shore. Colors of every imaginable hue splattered the trees.

Wild horses grazed on the high green grass of the valley floor. A bubbling creek meandered into the lake from the base of the cliff to their right, and then back out, down the valley.

The boy walked back to them, grinning. He wasn't breathing hard like they were. Only a light sweat broke his brow.

"Do you like it?" he asked.

They were too stunned to respond.

"I thought you would," he said. "I want you to take care of this forest for me."

"What do you mean?" Thomas asked. "Are you going?"

The boy tilted his head slightly. "Don't worry, Thomas. I'll come back. Just don't forget about me."

"I could never forget!"

"Most of them already have. The world could get very bad very quickly. It will be easier to spill blood than water. But"—he pointed to the lake—"if you bathe in the water once a day, you'll keep the disease away. Never allow blood to defile the water."

Then the boy gave them a list of six simple rules to follow.

"The others lived?" Rachelle asked. "Where . . . where are they?"

The boy eyed her softly. "Most are lost, but there are others like you who will find one of seven forests like this one." He smiled mischievously. "Don't worry, I have an idea. My ideas are usually pretty good, don't you think?"

"Yes. Yes, definitely good."

"When you think it can't get any worse, there will be a way. In one incredible blow we will destroy the heart of evil." He walked up to Rachelle, took her hand, and kissed it. "Just remember me."

He walked to Johan and looked into his eyes. For a moment Thomas thought he saw a dark look cross Elyon's eyes. He leaned forward and kissed Johan on the forehead.

Then he came to Thomas and kissed his hand.

"Could you tell me one thing?" Thomas asked quietly. "I dreamed of Bangkok again last night. Is it real? Am I supposed to rescue Monique?"

"Am I a lion or a lamb? Or am I a boy? You decide, Thomas. You are very special to me. Please . . . please don't forget me. Don't ever, ever forget me. I have a lot riding on you." He winked.

Then he turned around, ran down the bank, planted his foot on a rock, and launched himself into a swan dive. His body hung in the air above the lake for a moment, and then broke the surface with barely a ripple before disappearing.

He has a lot riding on me. The idea terrified him.

Johan was the first to move. He plummeted down the shore and into the lake with Thomas and Rachelle hard on his heels. They dived in together, one, two, three splashes that almost sounded as one.

The water wasn't cold. It wasn't warm. It was clean and pure and crystalline clear, so that Thomas could immediately see the rocks on the bottom.

This lake had a bottom.

And apart from the wonderfully clean feeling it gave him, the water didn't shake his body or tingle against his skin as in the other lake. He knew immediately that he couldn't breathe it.

But he did drink it. And he did laugh and cry and splash around like a child in a backyard pool. And the water did change them.

Almost immediately their skin returned to normal, and their eyes . . .

A soft green replaced the gray in their eyes.

For a while.

"We will build our home here," Thomas said, looking around at the clearing. "It's only a stone's throw from the lake, and there's plenty of sunshine. Our first order of business will be to build a shelter."

"No, I don't think so," Rachelle said.

He looked at her, taken aback by her tone.

"Our first order of business will be to deal with Monique," she said.

"Come on, Rachelle."

"I want you to tell me everything. All of your dreams."

He spread his arms. "But they're nothing. They're just dreams!"

"Is that why you asked the boy about them just an hour ago? Is that why you mumble her name in your sleep? Even last night after you promised me you wouldn't, you whispered her name as if she is the sweetest fruit in the land! I want to know it all."

"Maybe we should bathe again."

"After you tell me. If you hadn't noticed, there is you and there is me in the land now. One man and one woman. Or is it one man and two women? Have you chosen me, or not?"

"I did choose you. That's why you're here. Did I pull another woman into the Thrall to protect? No, I pulled you because I chose you, and we will marry immediately. And I want to tell you about Monique anyway." He walked over to the boulders and sat. These dreams would be his ruin. "Where's Johan?"

"He's gone exploring. Tell me about your dreams."

Thomas looked back into the forest. "You let him go? What if he gets lost? I'm worried about him. We have to keep our eyes on him."

"Don't change the subject. I want to hear everything."

So Thomas told her. She sat beside him on the rock at the center of the clearing, and he told her almost everything he could remember dreaming, leaving only a few parts sketchy.

He told her about being shot at in Denver and about flying to Bangkok and about kidnapping Monique and about the Raison Strain. Then he told her about the entire world constructed in his dreams, or at least as much of it as he could remember, because when he wasn't dreaming it seemed distant and vague.

"Do you know what this sounds like to me?" Rachelle said when he'd finished.

"No, what?"

"It sounds like you're imagining something similar to what happened to us, here. I told you where I would like to be rescued, and so you dreamed of exactly such a place to rescue another woman. And here the black forest has threatened to destroy us and now does, and so you dream of a blackness that will destroy another world. A plague. Bangkok is a figment of your dreams that reflects what's happening in your real life."

"Maybe I can stop the virus where I failed to stop Tanis."

"No, you're not going to stop it."

"Why not?"

"First of all, it's a dream! Listen to you. Even now you're talking of making a difference in a world that doesn't even exist! It's no wonder Michal refused to fuel your dreams with more information from the histories."

Rachelle stood and crossed her arms. "Second, if you're right, the only way to stop it is to find this Monique woman you seem to have grown somewhat attached to. I won't have it."

"Please, I hardly know her. It's not romantic. She's a figment of my imagination; you said so yourself."

"I won't have you dreaming of a beautiful woman named Monique while I'm suckling your child," Rachelle said.

That stopped him cold.

"So you really do want to bear children?"

"Do you have a better idea?" She paused. "I don't see another man around. And I do love you, Thomas, even if you do dream of another woman."

"And I love you, Rachelle." He reached for her hand and kissed it. "I would never dream of another woman. Ever."

"Unfortunately it seems as though it's beyond your control. If we only had the rhambutan fruit, I would feed it to you every night so that you would never dream again."

Thomas stood.

"What?"

"The boy . . ."

"Yes? What about the boy?"

"He told me at the upper lake that I would always have the choice not to dream."

She searched his face. "And yet you dreamed last night. Was that your choice?"

"No, but what if there *is* rhambutan fruit?"

"The fruits aren't the same anymore."

"But maybe he left this one. How else would I not dream? He made me a promise."

Her eyes lit up. She scanned the edge of the forest.

"Okay, let's bathe."

⎯⎯⎯⎯⎯⎯⎯⎯

They spent several hours searching for rhambutan fruit and, while they were at it, material they could use to build a shelter in the clearing.

By midday their hope of finding any rhambutan in this forest had faded, but then so had Thomas's urgency to find it, although he didn't share this with Rachelle. The dreams seemed distant and abstract in the face of their new surroundings. The whole notion that he was dreaming of another woman of whom Rachelle should be jealous seemed absurd.

He watched her walk ahead of him through the forest, and he knew without the smallest shred of doubt that he could never love any woman as he loved her. She had the spirit of an eagle and the heart of a mother. He even liked the way she argued with him, full of mettle.

He loved the way she walked. The way her hair fell over her shoulders. The way her lips moved when she talked. She was beautiful, even with dry skin and gray eyes, though when she first stepped from the pool with smooth skin and green eyes, laughing in the sunlight, she was breathtaking.

The idea that she had anything to fear from a dream was absurd. He suggested that she keep looking while he turned his attention to the shelter they had to build. He had some ideas on how to build one. He might even know how to make metal.

And what ideas are those, she wanted to know.

Something from my dreams, he'd made the mistake of saying.

Maybe the rhambutan was a good idea after all.

Johan had finally returned from his scouting trip and helped Thomas with the first lean-to, constructed out of saplings and leaves. Thomas knew how it should look, and he knew how to make it.

"How did you know to tie those vines like that?" Johan asked when they'd finished the roof. "I've never seen anything like it."

"This," Thomas said, rubbing the knots lovingly, "is how they do it in the jungles of the Philippines. We'll strap palm leaves to these—"

"Where's the Philippines?" Johan asked.

"The Philippines? Nowhere, really. Just something I made up."

And it was true, he thought. But with less conviction now.

Rachelle strode into camp about the time Thomas was thinking they should go looking for her.

"How are my men? My, that is a handy-looking thing you have there." She studied the lean-to. "What on earth is it?"

"This is our first home." Thomas beamed.

"Is it? It looks more like one wall." She walked around it. "Or a falling roof."

"No, no, this is more than a wall," Thomas said. "It's the entire structure. It's perfect! You don't like it?"

"Functional enough, I suppose. For a night or two, until you can build me bedrooms and a kitchen with running water."

Thomas wasn't sure how to respond. He rather liked the open feel of the place. She was right, of course. They would eventually have to build a house, and he had some ideas of how to do that as well. But he thought the lean-to was quite smart.

She looked at him and winked. "I think it's very clever," she said. "Something a great warrior would build." Then she brought her hand from behind her back and tossed him something. "Catch."

He caught it with one hand.

It was a rhambutan.

"You found it?"

She smiled. "Eat it."

"Now?"

"Yes, of course now."

He bit into the flesh. The nectar tasted like a cross between a banana and an orange but tart. Like a banana-orange-lemon.

"All of it," she said.

"I need all of it for it to work?" he asked with the one bite stuffed in his cheek.

"No. But I want you to eat all of it."

He ate all of it.

<hr />

Rachelle watched Thomas sleep. His chest rose and fell steadily to the sound of deep breathing. A slight gray pallor covered his body, and she knew that if she could see his eyes they would be dull, like her own. But none of this concerned her. The lake would wash them both clean as soon as they bathed.

What did concern her were these dreams of his. Dreams of the histories and dreams of this woman named Monique. She told herself it was more about the histories. After all, an argument could be made that a preoccupation with the histories had gotten Tanis into trouble. But her concern was as much about the woman.

Jealousy had been an element of the Great Romance, and she made no attempt to temper it now. Thomas was her man, and she had no intention of sharing him with anyone, dream woman or not.

If Thomas was right, eating Teeleh's fruit in the black forest before he'd lost his memory had started his dreams in the first place. Now she desperately prayed that what remained of Elyon's fruit would wash his mind clean of them.

"Thomas." She leaned over and kissed his lips. "Wake up, my dear."

He moaned and rolled over. A pleasant smile crossed his face. Deep sleep? Or Monique? But he'd slept like a baby and not once mumbled her name.

Rachelle couldn't extend her patience. She'd been awake for an hour already, waiting for him to wake.

She slapped his side and stood. "Wake up! Time to bathe."

He sat up with a start. "What?"

"Time to bathe."

"It's late. I've been sleeping this whole time?"

"Like a rock," she said.

He rubbed his eyes, stood up, and marched out to the fire. "Today I will begin building your house," he announced.

"Wonderful." She watched his face. "Did you dream?"

"Dream?" He seemed to be searching his memory.

"Yes, did you dream?"

"I don't know. Did I?"

"Only you would know."

"No. The fruit must have worked. That's why I slept so well."

"You can't remember anything? No phantom trips to Bangkok? No rescuing the beautiful Monique?"

"The last thing I dreamed about was falling asleep in Bangkok after the meeting. That was two nights ago." He spread his hands and grinned purposefully. "No dreams."

She knew he was telling the truth. The fruit did as the boy had promised. "Good," she said. "Then it works. You will eat this fruit every day."

"Forever?"

"It's also very healthy and makes a man fertile," she said. "Yes, forever."

So Thomas ate the rhambutan fruit every day and not once did he dream of Bangkok. Or of anything.

Weeks passed, then months, then years, then fifteen years, and not once did Thomas dream of Bangkok. Or of anything.

He became a mighty warrior who defended the seven forests against the desert Hoards who marched against them. But not once did he dream. Not of Bangkok, not of anything.

Perhaps Rachelle was right. Maybe he would never dream again. Maybe he would eat the rhambutan fruit every day forever and never again dream of Bangkok.

Or of anything.

37

VALBORG SVENSSON stood at the head of the table and eyed the gathered dignitaries. All from governments that had been coaxed for three years with promises of power. Until now, none of them knew enough to damage him significantly. And if they did know more than they should, they hadn't damaged him, so the point was moot. There were seven, but they needed only one country from which to build their power base. All seven would be useful, but they needed the keys to one of their kingdoms as a backup. If they only knew.

Carlos was in Bangkok now, only hours away from eliminating Hunter once and for all. Armand Fortier was making the necessary arrangements with the Russians and the Chinese. And he, Valborg Svensson, was dropping the bomb that would make everything possible. So to speak.

He extracted his pointer and tapped off the cities on the wall map to his left. "The Raison Strain has already entered the air space of London, Paris, Moscow, Beijing, New Delhi, Cape Town, Bangkok, Sydney, New York, Washington, D.C., Atlanta, and Los Angeles. These are the first twelve. Within eight hours, we will have twenty-four entry points."

"Enter the air space—as in . . ."

"As in the virus is airborne. Delivered by couriers over twenty-four commercial aircraft, spreading as we speak. It's highly contagious, more so than any virus we've seen. Fascinating little beast. Most require some kind of assistance to get around. A cough, fluid, touch, high humidity at least. But this pathogen seems to do quite well in adverse environmental conditions. A single virus shell is enough to infect any adult."

"You've already done it?"

"Naturally. By our most conservative models, three million people will be carriers by day's end. Ninety million within two days. Four billion within one week."

They sat dumbfounded. Not a single one truly comprehended what he'd just said. Not that he blamed them. The reality was staggering. Too significant to digest in one sitting.

"The virus is gone? There's no way to stop it?"

"Gone? Yes, I suppose it is gone," Svensson said. "And no, there's no way to stop it."

They were all jumping into the mix now. "And who will be infected?"

"Everyone. Myself, for example. And you. All of us are infected." He pointed to a small vial on the counter. "We were infected within minutes of stepping into this room."

Silence. The yellow liquid sat undisturbed.

Their objections came in a barrage of angry protests. "You have a vaccine; we should be inoculated at once! What kind of sick joke is this?"

"A very sick joke," Svensson said. "There is no vaccine."

"Then what, an antivirus?" the man demanded. "I demand to know what you're doing here!"

"You know what we're doing. Unfortunately, we don't have the antivirus quite yet either. But not to worry, we will very soon. We have less than three weeks to perfect one, but I'm confident we'll have it by the end of the week. Maybe sooner."

They looked at him like a ring of rats frozen by a wedge of cheese. "And if not?"

"If not, then we will all share the same fate with the rest of the world."

"Which is what?"

"We aren't precisely sure. An ugly death, we're quite sure of that. But no one has yet died from the Raison Strain, so we can't be sure about the exact nature of that death."

"Why?" To a man they were incredulous. "This was *not* what we discussed."

"Yes, it was. You just weren't listening very well. We have a list of instructions for each of your countries. We trust you will comply in the most expeditious fashion. For obvious reasons. And I really wouldn't think about trying to undermine our plans in any way. The only hope for an antivirus rests with me. If I am inhibited, the world will simply die."

The gentleman from Switzerland, Bruce Swanson, shoved his seat back and stood, face red. "This is not what I understood! How dare you proceed without consulting—"

Svensson slipped a pistol out from under his jacket and shot the man in the forehead at ten paces. The man stared at him, his new third eye leaking red, and then he toppled backward, hit his head on the wall, and crumpled to the floor.

Svensson lowered the pistol. "There is no way to stop the virus," he said. "We can only control it now. That was the point from the beginning. Dissension will only hinder that objective. Any argument?"

They did not argue.

"Good." He set the gun on the table. "As we speak, the governments of these affected countries are being notified of our demands. These governments won't react immediately, of course. This is preferred. Panic is not our friend. Not yet. We don't need people staying home for fear of catching the disease. By the time they realize the true nature of our threat, containment will be out of the question. It virtually is already."

He took a deep breath. The power of this moment, standing over seven men—six living—was alone worth the price he'd paid. And it was only the very beginning. He'd resisted a smile, but now he smiled for them all.

"It's a wonderful day, my friends. You find yourselves on the right side of history. You will see. The die has been cast."

Markous had been guaranteed two things for this assignment: his life and a million dollars cash. Both he valued enough to cut off his own leg if needed. The cash he had already received. His life was still in their hands. He doubted neither their will nor their ability to take his life or give it.

He stood in the bathroom stall and flicked the small vial with his fingernail. Hard to believe that the yellow liquid could do what they insisted it would do. Unnerved by a few drops of amber fluid.

He held his breath and pulled the rubber cork out of the vial's neck. Now only air separated him—his nose and his eyes and his skin—from the virus. Had he been infected already? No, how could he be?

He exhaled the air from his lungs, held his breath at the bottom, and then slowly inhaled, imagining invisible spores streaming into his nostrils. If it were scented, like a perfume, he would notice. But the objective was not to notice.

So then, he was now infected.

Markous impulsively splashed some of the fluid on his jacket, his hands, rubbed his face. Like a cologne. He tested it with his tongue. Tasteless. He drank a little and swished it around his mouth. Swallowed.

Markous stepped from the men's room. Travelers crowded Bangkok International Airport despite the early hour. He looked both ways, straightening his tie. Rarely did he mix with women at nightclubs or other common social institutions, despite his handsome Mediterranean features. But at the moment, spreading a little love seemed appropriate.

He saw what he was looking for and walked toward a gathering of four blue-suited flight attendants talking by a phone bank.

"Excuse me." All four women looked at him. Their luggage tags read "Air France." He smiled gently and zeroed in on a tall brunette. "I was just walking by, and I couldn't help but notice you. Do you mind?"

They exchanged glances. The brunette lifted an eyebrow self-consciously.

"Could you please tell me your name?" Markous asked. She wasn't wearing a nametag.

"Linda."

He stepped closer. His hands were still moist with the liquid. He imagined the millions of cells swimming in his mouth.

"Come here, Linda. I would like to tell you a secret." He leaned forward. At first she hesitated, but when two of the others chuckled, she spread her hands. "What?"

"Closer," he said. "I won't bite, I promise."

Her face was red, but she complied by leaning a few inches.

Markous stepped into her and kissed her full on the mouth. He immediately pulled back and raised both hands. "Forgive me. You are so beautiful, I simply had to kiss you."

The shock registered on her face. "You . . . what do you think you're doing?"

Markous grabbed the hand of the woman next to the brunette. He coughed. "Please, I'm terribly sorry." He backed out quickly, dipping with apology. Then he was gone, leaving four stunned women in his wake.

He walked by the airport's first-aid station, where a mother was asking a nurse for something while her two blond-headed children played tag about the waiting bench. An older man with bushy gray brows watched him take his still-moist jacket off and hang it on the coatrack. With any luck, the man would report the jacket and security would confiscate it. Before he took five paces, the mother, her two children, the nurse, and the old man were infected.

How many more he infected before leaving the airport, he would never know. Perhaps a hundred, though none with such tenderness as his first. He stopped in a morning market on his way through the city and worked his way down the crowded aisles. How many here, he couldn't guess. At least several hundred. For good measure, he tossed the shirt he'd soaked into the Mae Nam Chao Phraya River, which wound its way lazily through the city center.

Enough. By end of day, Bangkok would be crawling with the virus. Job done.

Carlos parked his car in the Sheraton's underground parking structure at eight o'clock and rode the elevator to the lobby. The morning crowd was already bustling. He crossed to the main elevators, waited for an empty car, and stepped in. Ninth floor.

The meeting with Deputy Secretary Gains and the gathered intelligence officers had gone late last night, and his latest intelligence had it that Hunter was still in his room. Asleep. The source was impeccable.

In fact, the source had actually been *at* the meeting.

If they only knew to what extent Svensson had gone to execute this plan. The only caveat was Hunter. A man who learned from his dreams. A man none of them could possibly control. A man Carlos had killed twice already.

This time he would stay dead.

The elevator bell rang and Carlos slipped down the hall, tried and found the room next to Hunter's, which was open as arranged.

There were two critical elements in any operation. One, power; and two, intelligence. He'd engaged Hunter once, and despite the man's surprising skill, he'd handled him easily enough. But he'd underestimated the man's endurance. Hunter had somehow managed to survive.

This time there would be no opportunity for a fight. Superior intelligence would prove the victor.

Carlos approached the door that adjoined the suite next door to this one. He withdrew a Luger and screwed a silencer into its barrel.

Superior intelligence. For example, he knew that at this very moment this door was unlocked. The inside man had made sure of that. Past this door, one door on the left, was the door to Thomas Hunter's room. Hunter had been sleeping in the room for seven hours now. He would never even know he'd been shot.

All of this Carlos knew without the slightest doubt. If anything changed—if his sister, who slept in the suite's other bedroom, woke, or if Hunter himself woke—the video operator would simply page him, and the receiver on Carlos's belt would vibrate.

Intelligence.

Carlos opened both doors separating the suites and walked to the room on his left. Cartridge chambered. All was silent. He reached for the doorknob.

A phone rang. Not the main house phone—the one in the sister's room on his right. Immediately his pager vibrated. He ignored the pager and paused to listen.

—∞∞—

The phone beside Kara's bed rang once. She opened her eyes and stared at the ceiling. Where was she?

Bangkok. She and Thomas had attended a meeting the night before with deputy secretary of state Merton Gains because the Swiss, Valborg Svensson, had kidnapped Monique de Raison for one reason only: to develop the antivirus to the virus he would unleash on the world. At least that was what Thomas had tried to persuade them of. They hadn't exactly run to him and kissed his feet.

The phone rang again.

She sat up. Thomas was hopefully still asleep in the suite's other bedroom. Had he dreamed? Was he still dreaming? She'd suggested he dream a very long time and become someone new, an absurd suggestion on the face of it, but then so was this whole alternate-world thing he was living through. The spread of evil in one world, the threat of a virus in the other one.

The phone was ringing. She'd taken the phone in Thomas's room off the hook last night. He wouldn't hear it.

She grabbed the receiver. "Hello?"

"This is Merton Gains. Kara?"

She switched the phone to her right ear. "Yes. Good morning, Mr. Secretary."

"I'm sorry to wake you, but it seems that we have a situation on our hands."

"No, no, it's okay. What time is it?" *What time is it?* She was speaking to the deputy secretary of state, and she was demanding he tell her what time it was?

"Just past eight in the morning local," Gains said. His voice sounded strained. "The State Department received a fax from a party claiming to be Valborg Svensson."

A chill washed down Kara's spine. This was what Thomas had predicted! Not so soon, but—

"He's claiming that the Raison Strain has been released in twelve cities including Washington, D.C., New York, Los Angeles, and Atlanta," Gains said, voice now very thin.

"What?" Kara swung her legs off the bed. "When?"

"Six hours ago. He claims that the number will be twenty-four by the end of the day."

"Twenty-four! That's impossible! They did it without the antivirus! Thomas was right. Has any of this been verified?"

"No. No, but we're working on it, believe me. Where is Thomas?"

She glanced at the door. "As far as I know, he's sleeping next door."

"How long has he been sleeping?"

"About eight hours, I think."

"Well, I don't have to say it, but it looks like he may have been right."

She stood. "I realize that. You realize that this could have been prevented—"

"You may be right." He wasn't the one who'd doubted Thomas. She had no right to accuse him. What was she thinking? He was the deputy secretary of state for the United States of America, for heaven's sake!

"If this new information turns out to be right, your brother may be a very important person to us."

"He may be or he may not be. It could be too late now."

"Can I talk to him?"

She hesitated. Of course they could talk to Thomas. They were powerful men who could talk to anyone they wanted to. But they'd taken too long to talk to him already.

"I'll wake him," she said.

"Thank you. I have some calls to make. Bring him down in half an hour. Will that be enough time?"

"Yes."

The line clicked off.

Kara got halfway to the bedroom door and stopped. Half an hour, the secretary had said. *Bring him down in half an hour.* If she woke Thomas now, he'd demand to go down immediately. Besides, he'd hardly slept a decent stretch in over a week. And if he was dreaming, which she had no reason to doubt, then every minute of sleep—for that matter, every second—could be the equivalent of hours or days or even weeks in his dream world. A lot could happen. Answers could come.

Six hours ago, Svensson had released the virus. It was a mind-bending thought. She should wake her brother now, not later.

Right after she used the toilet.

Carlos had heard enough. He hadn't anticipated hearing their reaction like this, but he found it quite satisfying.

He twisted the knob. Cracked the door. The sound of breathing.

He readied his gun and slipped in.

Thomas Hunter lay on his back, sleeping in a tangle of sheets, naked except for boxer shorts. Sweat soaked the sheets. Sweat and blood. Blood? So much blood, smeared over the sheets, some dried and some still wet.

The man had bled in his sleep? *Was* bleeding in his sleep. Dead?

Carlos stepped closer. No. Hunter's chest rose and fell steadily. There were scars on his chest and abdomen that Carlos couldn't remember, but nothing to suggest the slugs Carlos was sure he'd put into this man in the last week.

He brought the gun to Hunter's temple and tightened his finger on the trigger.

He couldn't resist a final whisper. "Good-bye, Mr. Hunter."

38

RACHELLE WAS wrong.

Thomas did not eat the fruit forever.

He only ate it for fifteen years. Not once in those fifteen years did he dream, but then, in the worst of times, when they didn't think it could possibly get any worse, just as the boy had foretold, Thomas dreamed again.

And when he did, he dreamed that a gun was hovering by his left temple. Three words whispered menacingly in his ear: "Good-bye, Mr. Hunter."

THE JOURNEY CONTINUES WITH RED . . .

RED

THE HEROIC RESCUE

Bangkok

KARA GOT halfway to her door and stopped. She and Thomas were in a large hotel suite with two bedrooms. Beyond her bedroom door was a short hall that ran to the living room and, in the other direction, to the adjoining suite. Across that hall—her brother's room, where he lay dead to this world, dreaming, oblivious to the news she'd just heard from Deputy Secretary Merton Gains.

The virus had been released exactly as Thomas had predicted just last evening.

Half an hour, Secretary Gains had said. *Bring him down in half an hour.* If she woke Thomas now, he'd demand to go down immediately. Every minute of sleep—for that matter every second—could be the equivalent of hours or days or even weeks in his dream world. A lot could happen. Answers could come. She should let him sleep.

Then again, Svensson had released the virus. She should wake her brother now.

Right after she used the bathroom.

Kara hurried to the side room, flipped the light switch, turned on the water. Closed the door.

"We've stepped off the cliff and are falling into madness," she said. Then again, perhaps the fall to madness had started when Thomas had tried to jump off the balcony in Denver. He'd dragged her to Bangkok, kidnapped Monique de Raison, and survived two separate encounters with a killer named Carlos, who was undoubtedly still after them. All this because of his dreams of another reality.

421

Would Thomas wake with any new information? *The power was gone from the colored forest,* he'd said. The colored forest itself was gone, which meant that his power might be gone as well. If that was the case, Tom's dreams might be useless except as fantasies in which he was falling in love and learning to do backflips off a pinhead.

The water felt cool and refreshing on her face.

She flung the water from her hands and stepped to the toilet.

1

THOMAS URGED the sweating black steed into a full gallop through the sandy valley and up the gentle slope. He shoved his bloody sword into his scabbard, gripped the reins with both hands, and leaned over the horse's neck. Twenty fighters rode in a long line to his right and left, slightly behind. They were unquestionably the greatest warriors in all the earth, and they pounded for the crest directly ahead, one question drumming through each one's mind.

How many?

The Horde's attack had come from the canyon lands, through the Natalga Gap. This was not so unusual. The Desert Dwellers' armies had attacked from the east a dozen times over the last fifteen years. What was unusual, however, was the size of the party his men had just cut to ribbons less than a mile to the south. No more than a hundred.

Too few. Far too few.

The Horde never attacked in small numbers. Where Thomas and his army depended on superior speed and skill, the Horde had always depended on sheer numbers. They'd developed a kind of natural balance. One of his men could take out five of the Horde on any bad day, an advantage mitigated only by the fact that the Horde's army approached five hundred thousand strong. His own army numbered fewer than thirty thousand including the apprentices. None of this was lost on the enemy. And yet they'd sent only this small band of hooded warriors up the Gap to their deaths.

Why?

They rode without a word. Hoofs thundered like war drums, an oddly comforting sound. Their horses were all stallions. Each fighter was dressed in the same hardened-leather breastplate with forearm and thigh guards. These left their joints free for the movement required in hand-to-hand combat. They strapped their knives to calves and whips to hips, and carried their swords on their horses. These three weapons, a good horse, and a leather bottle full of water were all any of the Forest Guard required to survive a week and to kill a hundred. And the regular fighting force wasn't far behind.

Thomas flew over the hill's crest, leaned back, and pulled the stallion to a stamping halt. The others fell in along the ridge. Still not a word.

What they saw could not easily be put into words.

The sky was turning red, blood red, as it always did over the desert in the afternoons. To their right stretched the canyon lands, ten square miles of cliffs and boulders that acted as a natural barrier between the red deserts and the first of seven forests. Thomas's forest. Beyond the canyon's cliffs, red-tinged sand flowed into an endless sea of desert. This landscape was as familiar to Thomas as his own forest.

What he saw now was not.

At first glance, even to a trained eye, the subtle movement on the desert floor might have been mistaken for shimmering heat waves. It was hardly more than a beige discoloration rippling across the vast section of flat sand that fed into the canyons. But this was nothing so innocuous as desert heat.

This was the Horde army.

They wore beige hooded tunics to cover their gray scabbed flesh and rode light tan horses bred to disappear against the sand. Thomas had once ridden past fifty without distinguishing them from the sandstone.

"How many, Mikil?"

His second in command searched the horizon to the south. He followed her eyes. A dozen smaller contingents were heading up the Gap, armies of a few hundred each, not so much larger than the one they'd torn apart thirty minutes ago.

"Hundred thousand," she said. A strip of leather held her dark hair back from a tanned forehead. A small white scar on her right cheek marred an otherwise smooth, milky complexion. The cut had been inflicted not by the Horde, but by her own brother, who'd fought her to assert his strength just a year ago. She'd left him unscathed, underfoot, soundly defeated.

He'd died in a skirmish six months after.

Mikil's green eyes skirted the desert. "This will be a challenge."

Thomas grunted at the understatement. They'd all been hardened by dozens of battles, but never had they faced an army so large.

"The main body is moving south, along the southern cliffs."

She was right. This was a new tactic for the Horde.

"They're trying to engage us in the Natalga Gap while the main force flanks us," Thomas said.

"And they look to succeed," his lieutenant William said.

No one disagreed. No one spoke. No one moved.

Thomas scanned the horizon again and reviewed their bearings. To the west the desert ended in the same forested valley he'd protected from the Horde threat for the past fifteen years, ever since the boy had led them to the small paradise in the middle of the desert.

To the north and the south lay six other similar forests, inhabited by roughly a hundred thousand Forest People.

Thomas and Rachelle had not met their first forest dweller until nearly a full year after finding the lake. His name was Ciphus of Southern, for he came from the great Southern Forest. That was the year they gave birth to their first child, a daughter they named Marie. Marie of Thomas. Those who'd originally come from the colored forest took designation according to which forests they lived in, thus Ciphus of Southern. The children who were born after the Great Deception took the names of their fathers. Marie of Thomas.

Three years later, Rachelle and Thomas had a son, Samuel, a strong lad, nearly twelve now. He was wielding a sword already, and Thomas had to speak loudly to keep him from joining the battles.

Each forest had its own lake, and Elyon's faithful bathed each day to keep the painful skin disease from overtaking their bodies. This ritual cleansing was what separated them from the Scabs.

Each night, after bathing, the Forest People danced and sang in celebration of the Great Romance, as they called it. And each year the people of all seven forests, roughly a hundred thousand now, made the pilgrimage to the largest forest, called the Middle Forest—Thomas's forest. The annual Gathering was to be held seven days from today. How many Forest People were now making the exposed trek across the desert, Thomas hated to imagine.

Scabs could become Forest People, of course—a simple bathing in the lake would cleanse their skin and wash away their disgusting stench. A small number of Scabs had become Forest People over the years, but it was the unspoken practice of the Forest Guard to discourage Horde defections.

There simply weren't enough lakes to accommodate all of them.

In fact, Ciphus of Southern, the Council elder, had calculated that the lakes could function adequately for only three hundred thousand. There simply wasn't enough water for the Horde, who already numbered well over a million. The lakes were clearly a gift from Elyon to the Forest People alone.

Discouraging the Horde from bathing was not difficult. The intense pain of moisture on their diseased flesh was enough to fill the Scabs with a deep revulsion for the lakes, and Qurong, their leader, had sworn to destroy the waters when he conquered the much-coveted resources of the forest lands.

The Desert Dwellers had first attacked thirteen years ago, descending on a small forest two hundred miles to the southwest. Although the clumsy attackers had been beaten back with rocks and clubs, over a hundred of Elyon's followers, mostly women and children, had been slaughtered.

Despite his preference for peace, Thomas had determined then that the only way to secure peace for the Forest People was to establish an army. With the help of Johan, Rachelle's brother, Thomas went in hunt of metal, drawing upon his recollection of the histories. He needed copper and tin, which when mixed would form bronze, a metal strong enough for swords. They'd built a furnace and then heated rocks of all varieties until they found the kind that leaked the telltale ore. As it turned out, the canyon lands were full of ore. He still wasn't sure if the material from which he'd fashioned the first sword was actually bronze, but it was soft enough to sharpen and hard enough to cut off a man's head with a single blow.

The Horde came again, this time with a larger force. Armed with swords and knives, Thomas and a hundred fighters, his first Forest Guard, cut the attacking Desert Dwellers to shreds.

Word of a mighty warrior named Thomas of Hunter spread throughout the desert and forests alike. For three years after, the Horde braved only the occasional skirmish, always to their own terrible demise.

But the need to conquer the fertile forest land proved too strong for the swelling Horde. They brought their first major campaign up the Natalga Gap armed with new weapons, bronze weapons: long swords and sharp sickles and large balls swinging from chains. Though defeated then, their strength had continued to grow since.

It was during the Winter Campaign three years ago that Johan went missing. The Forest People had mourned his loss at the Gathering that year. Some had begged Elyon to remember his promise to deliver them from the heart of evil, from the Horde's curse, in one stunning blow. That day would surely come, Thomas believed, because the boy had spoken it before disappearing into the lake.

It would be best for Thomas and his Guard if today was that day.

"They'll be at our catapults along the southern cliffs in three marks on the dial," Mikil said, referring to the sundials Thomas had introduced to keep time. Then she added, "Three hours."

Thomas faced the desert. The diseased Horde army was pouring into the canyons like whipped honey. By nightfall the sands would be black with blood. And this time it would be as much their blood as the Horde's.

An image of Rachelle and young Marie and his son, Samuel, filled his mind. A knot swelled in his throat. The rest had children too, many children, in part to even odds with the Horde. How many children in the forests now? Nearly half the population. Fifty thousand.

They had to find a way to beat back this army, if only for the children.

Thomas glanced down the line of his lieutenants, masters in combat, each one. He secretly believed any of them could capably lead this war, but he never doubted their loyalty to him, the Guard, and the forests. Even William, who was more than willing to point out Thomas's faults and challenge his judgment, would give his life. In matters of ultimate loyalty,

Thomas had set the standard. He would rather lose a leg than a single one of them, and they all knew it.

They also knew that, of them all, Thomas was the least likely to lose a leg or any other body part in any fight. This even though he was forty and many of them in their twenties. What they knew, they'd learned mostly from him.

Although he'd not once dreamed of the histories for the past fifteen years, he did remember some things—his last recollection of Bangkok, for example. He remembered falling asleep in a hotel room after failing to convince key government officials that the Raison Strain was on their doorstep.

He could also recall bits and pieces of the histories, and he drew on his lingering if fading knowledge of its wars and technology, an ability that gave him considerable advantage over the others. For in large part, memory of the histories had been all but wiped out when the black-winged Shataiki had overtaken the colored forest. Thomas suspected that now only the Roush, who had disappeared after the Great Deception, truly remembered any of the histories.

Thomas transferred the reins to his left hand and stretched his fingers. "William, you have the fastest horse. Take the canyon back to the forest and bring the reinforcements at the perimeter forward."

It would leave the forest exposed, but they had little choice.

"Forgive me for pointing out the obvious," William objected, "but taking them here will end badly."

"The high ground at the Gap favors us," Thomas said. "We hit them there."

"Then you'll engage them before the reinforcements arrive."

"We can hold them. We have no choice."

"We always have a choice," William said. This was how it was with him, always challenging. Thomas had anticipated his argument and, in this case, agreed.

"Tell Ciphus to prepare the tribe for evacuation to one of the northern villages. He will object because he isn't used to the prospect of losing a battle. And with the Gathering only a week away, he will scream sacrilege, so I want you to tell him with Rachelle present. She'll make sure that he listens."

William faced him. "Me, to the village? Send another runner. I can't miss this battle!"

"You'll be back in time for plenty of battle. I depend on you, William. Both missions are critical. You have the fastest horse and you're best suited to travel alone."

Although William needed no praise, it shut him up in front of the others.

Thomas faced Suzan, his most trusted scout, a young woman of twenty who could hold her own against ten untrained men. Her skin was dark, as was the skin of nearly half of the Forest People. Their varying shades of skin tone also distinguished them from the Horde, who were all white from the disease.

"Take two of our best scouts and run the southern cliffs. We will join you with the main force in two hours. I want positions and pace when I arrive. I want to know who leads that army if you have to go down and rip his hood off yourself. In particular I want to know if it's the druid Martyn. I want to know when they last fed and when they expect to feed again. Everything, Suzan. I depend on you."

"Yes sir." She whipped her horse around. "Hiyaaa!" The stallion bolted down the hill with William in fast pursuit.

Thomas stared out at the Horde. "Well, my friends, we've always known this was coming. You signed on to fight. It looks like Elyon has brought us our fight."

Someone humphed. All here would die for the forests. Not all would die for Elyon.

"How many men in this theater?" Thomas asked Mikil.

"With the escorts out to bring the other tribes in for the Gathering, only ten thousand, but five thousand of those are at the forest perimeter," Mikil said. "We have fewer than five thousand to join a battle at the southern cliffs."

"And how many to intercept these smaller bands of Horde that intend to distract us?"

Mikil shrugged. "Three thousand. A thousand at each pass."

"We'll send a thousand, three hundred for each pass. The rest go with us to the cliffs."

For a moment all sat quietly. What strategy could possibly overturn such impossible odds? What words of wisdom could even Elyon himself offer in a moment of such gravity?

"We have six hours before the sun sets," Thomas said, pulling his horse around. "Let's ride."

"I'm not sure we *will* see the sun set," one of them said.

No voice argued.

2

CARLOS MISSIRIAN stared at Thomas Hunter.

The man lay on his back, sleeping in a tangle of sheets, naked except for boxer shorts. Sweat soaked the sheets. Sweat and blood. Blood? So much blood, smeared over the sheets, some dried and some still wet.

The man had bled in his sleep? *Was* bleeding in his sleep. Dead?

Carlos stepped closer. No. Hunter's chest rose and fell steadily. There were scars on his chest and abdomen that Carlos couldn't remember, but no evidence of the slugs Carlos was sure he'd put into this same man in the last week.

He brought his gun to Hunter's temple and tightened his finger on the trigger.

3

A FLASH from the cliff. Two flashes.

Thomas, crouched behind a wide rock, raised the crude scope to his eye and scanned the hooded Scabs along the floor of the canyon. He'd fashioned the spyglass from his memory of the histories, using a resin from the pine trees, and although it hardly functioned as he suspected it should, it did give him a slight advantage over the naked eye. Mikil kneeled beside him.

The signal had come from the top of the cliffs, where he'd positioned two hundred archers each with five hundred arrows. They'd learned long ago that their odds were determined by the supply of munitions almost as much as by the number of men.

Their strategy was a simple, proven one. Thomas would lead a thousand warriors in a frontal assault that would choke the enemy along its front line. When the battlefield was sufficiently cluttered with dead Scabs, he would beat a hasty retreat while the archers rained thousands of arrows down on the crowded field. If all went well, they could at least slow the enemy down by clogging the wide canyon with the dead.

Two hundred cavalry waited with Thomas behind a long row of boulders. They kept their horses seated on the ground with gentle persuasion.

They'd done this once before. It was a wonder that the Horde was subjecting itself to—

"Sir!" A runner slid in from behind him, panting. "We have a report from the Southern Forest." Mikil shifted next to him.

"Go on. Quietly please."

"The Horde is attacking."

Thomas pulled the scope from his eye, then peered through it again.

He lifted his left hand, ready to signal his men's charge. The runner's report meant what?

That the Horde now had a new strategy.

That the situation had just gone from terrible to impossible.

That the end was near.

"Give me the rest. Quickly."

"It's said to be the work of Martyn."

Again he pulled the glass from his eye. Returned it. Then this army wasn't being led by their new general, as he'd suspected. They'd been tracking the one called Martyn for a year now. He was a younger man; they'd forced that much out of a prisoner once. He was also a good tactician; they knew that much from the shifting engagements. And they suspected that he was a druid as well as a general. The Desert Dwellers had no declared religion, but they paid homage to the Shataiki in ways that were slowly but surely formalizing their worship of the serpentine bat on their crest. Teeleh. Some said that Martyn practiced the black arts; others said he was guided by Teeleh himself. Either way, his army seemed to be advancing in skill quickly.

If the Scab called Martyn led his army against the Southern Forest, could this army be a diversion? Or was the attack on the Southern Forest the diversion?

"On my signal, Mikil."

"Ready," she replied. She slipped into the saddle of her seated horse.

"How many?" Thomas asked the runner.

"I don't know. We have fewer than a thousand, but they are in retreat."

"Who's in charge?"

"Jamous."

He jerked the lens from his face and looked at the man. "Jamous? Jamous is in retreat?"

"According to the report, yes."

If such a headstrong fighter as Jamous had fallen back, then the engaging force was stronger than any he'd fought before.

"There is also the warrior named Justin there."

"Sir?" It was Mikil.

He turned back, saw movement cresting the swell a hundred yards ahead, and took a deep breath. He lifted his hand and held it steady, waiting. Closer. The stench from their flaking skin reached his nostrils. Then their crest, the bronzed serpentine bat.

The Horde army rose into view, five hundred abreast at least, mounted on horses as pale as the desert sands. The warriors rode hooded and cloaked, grasping tall sickles that rose nearly as high as their serpent.

Thomas slowed his breathing. His only task was to turn this army back. Diversion or not, if he failed here, it made no difference what happened at the Southern Forest.

Thomas could hear Mikil breathing steadily through her nose. *I will beg Elyon for your safety today, Mikil. I will beg Elyon for the safety of us all. If any should die, let it be that traitor, Justin.*

"Now!" He dropped his hand.

His warriors were moving already. From the left, a long row of foot soldiers, silent and low, crept like spiders over the sand.

Two hundred horses bearing riders rolled to their feet. Thomas whirled to the runner. "Word to William and Ciphus! Send a thousand warriors to the Southern Forest. If we are overtaken here, we will meet in the third forest to the north. Go!"

His main force was already ten yards ahead of him, flying for the Horde, and Thomas wouldn't allow them to reach the battle first. Never. He swung into his saddle and kicked the stallion into a gallop. The black leaped over the boulders and raced for the long line of surprised Desert Dwellers, who'd stopped cold.

For a long moment the pounding of hooves was the only sound in the air. The sea of Scab warriors flowed down into the canyon and disappeared behind the cliffs. A hundred thousand sets of eyes peered out from the shadows of their hoods. These were the very ones who despised Elyon and hated his water. Theirs was a nomadic world of shallow, muddy wells and filthy, stinking flesh. They were hardly fit for life, much less the forests. And yet they would likely defile the lakes, ravage the forests, and plant their desert wheat.

These were the people of the colored forest gone amuck. The walking dead. Better buried at the base of a cliff than allowed to roam like an unchecked plague.

These were also warriors. Men only, strong, and not as ignorant as they had once been. But they were slower than the Forest Guard. Their debilitating skin condition reached down into their joints and made dexterity a difficult prospect.

Thomas pounded past his warriors. Now he was in the lead, where he belonged. He rested his hand on the hilt of his sword.

Forty yards.

His sword came free of its scabbard with the loud scraping of metal against metal.

Immediately a roar ascended from the Horde, as if the drawn sword confirmed Thomas's otherwise dubious intentions. A thousand horses snorted and reared in objection to the heavy hands that jerked them back in fear. Those in the front line would surely know that although victory was ultimately ensured today, they would be among the first to die.

The Forest Guard rode hard, jaws clenched, swords still lowered by their legs, easy in their hands.

Thomas veered to the right, transferred his sword to his left hand, and raked it along the breasts of three Scabs before blocking the first sickle that compensated for his sudden change in direction.

The lines of horses collided. His fighters screamed, thrusting and parrying and beheading with a practiced frenzy. A pale horse fell directly in front of Thomas, and he glanced over to see that Mikil had lost her sword in its rider's side.

"Mikil!" With her forearm, she blocked a nasty swipe from a monstrous Scab sword and twisted in her saddle. Thomas ripped at the cords that held his second scabbard and hurled it to her, sword and all. She caught it, whipped the blade out, twirled it once through the air and swung downward at a charging foot soldier.

Thomas deflected a swinging sickle as it sliced for his head, jumped his stallion over the dying horse, and whirled to meet the attacker.

The battle found its rhythm. On every side blades broad and narrow, short and long, swung, parried, blocked, swiped, sliced. Blood and sweat soaked man and beast. The terrible din of battle filled the canyon. Wails and cries and snorts and moans of death rose to the sky.

So did the battle cries of one thousand highly trained warriors facing an endless reservoir of skillful Scabs.

Not three years ago, under the guidance of Qurong, the Horde's cavalry never failed to suffer huge losses. Now, under the direct command of their young general, Martyn, they weren't dying without a fight.

A tall Scab whose hood had slipped off his head snarled and lunged his mount directly into Thomas's path. The horses collided and reared, kicking at the air. With a flip of his wrist, Thomas unleashed his whip and cracked it against the Scab's head. The man screamed and threw an arm up. Thomas thrust his sword at the man's exposed side, felt it sink deep, then wrenched it free just as a foot soldier swung a club at him from behind. He leaned far to his right and slashed backward with his sword. The warrior crumpled, headless.

The battle raged for ten minutes in the Forest Guard's unquestioned favor. But with so many blades swinging through the air, some were bound to find the exposed flesh of Thomas's men or the flanks of their horses.

The Forest Guard began to fall.

Thomas sensed it as much as saw it. Two. Four. Then ten, twenty, forty. More.

Thomas broke form and galloped down the line. The obstruction from fallen horses and men was enough. To his alarm he saw that more of his men had fallen than he'd first thought. He had to get them back!

He snatched up the horn at his belt and blasted the signal for retreat. Immediately his men fled, on horse, on foot, sprinting past him as if they'd been firmly defeated.

Thomas held his horse steady for a moment. The Scabs, hardly used to such wholesale retreat, paused, apparently confused by the sudden turn of events.

As planned.

The number of his men among the dead, however, was not planned. Maybe two hundred!

For the first time that day, Thomas felt the razored finger of panic slice across his chest. He whirled his horse and tore after his fighters.

He cleared the line of boulders in one long bound, slipped from his horse, and dropped to one knee in time to see the first barrage of arrows from the cliff arc silently into the Horde.

Now a new kind of chaos ensued. Horses reared and Scabs screamed and the dead piled high where they fell. The Horde army was temporarily trapped by a dam made of its own warriors.

"Our losses are high," Mikil said beside him, breathing hard. "Three hundred."

"Three hundred!" He looked at his second. Her face was red with blood and her eyes shone with an unusual glare of defiance. Fatalism. "We'll need more than bodies and boulders to hold them back," she said. She spit to the side.

Thomas scanned the cliffs. The archers were still sending arrows down onto the trapped army. As soon as the enemy cleared the bodies and marched fresh horses up, twenty catapults along each cliff would begin to shower the Horde with boulders.

Then it would begin again. Another head-on attack by Thomas, followed by more arrows, followed by more boulders. He quickly did the math. At this rate they might be able to hold off the army for five rounds.

Mikil voiced his thoughts. "Even if we hold them off until nightfall, they'll march over us tomorrow."

The sky cleared of arrows. Boulders began to fall. Thomas had been working on the counterweight catapults for years without perfecting them. They were still useless on flat ground, but they did heave big rocks far enough over a cliff to make good use of gravity. Two-foot boulders made terrible projectiles.

A dull thump preceded the ground's tremor.

"It won't be enough," Mikil said. "We'd have to bring the whole cliff down on them."

"We need to slow the pace!" Thomas said. "Next time on foot only, and draw the battle out by withdrawing quickly. Pass the word. Fight defensively!"

The boulders stopped falling and the Horde cleared more bodies. Thomas led his fighters in another frontal assault twenty minutes later.

This time they played with the enemy, using the Marduk fighting method that Rachelle and Thomas had developed and perfected over the years. It was a refinement of the aerial combat that Tanis had practiced in the colored forest. The Forest Guard knew it well and could play with a dozen Scabs under the right circumstances.

But here in crowded quarters with so many bodies and blades, their mobility was limited. They fought hard for thirty minutes and killed nearly a thousand.

This time they lost half of their force.

At this rate the Horde would be through their lines in an hour. The Desert Dwellers would stop for the night as was their custom, but Mikil was right. Even if the Guard could hold them off that long, Thomas's warriors would be finished in the morning. The Horde would reach his undefended Middle Forest in under one day. Rachelle. The children. Thirty thousand defenseless civilians would be slaughtered.

Thomas searched the cliffs. *Elyon, give me strength.* The chill he'd felt earlier was spreading to his shoulders.

"Bring up the reinforcements!" he snapped. "Gerard, your command. Keep them on that line, by whatever means. Watch the cliff for signals. Coordinate the attacks." He tossed the lieutenant the ram's horn. "Elyon's strength," he said, holding up his fist.

Gerard caught the horn. "Elyon's strength. Count on me, sir."

"I am. You have no idea how much I am." Thomas turned to Mikil. "With me." They swung into their horses and pounded down the canyon.

His second followed him without question. He led her up a small hill and then doubled back along the path toward an overlook near the top.

The battlefield stretched out to their right. His archers were raining arrows down on the Scabs again. The dead were piled high. To see the Horde's front lines, an observer might think that the Forest Guard was routing the enemy. But a quick look down the canyon told a different story.

Thousands upon thousands upon thousands of hooded warriors waited in an eerie silence. This was a battle of attrition.

This was a battle that could not be won.

"Any word from the three parties to the north?" Thomas asked.

"No. Let's pray they haven't broken through."

"They won't."

Thomas dismounted and studied the cliffs.

Mikil nudged her horse forward, then brought it snorting around.

"Yes, I know you're impatient, Mikil." There was something about the cliffs that bothered Thomas. "You're wondering if I've gone mad; is that it? My men are dying in a final battle and I've dismounted to watch it all."

"I'm worried about Jamous. What's your plan?"

"Jamous can take care of himself."

"Jamous is in retreat! He would never retreat. What's your plan?"

"I don't have a plan."

"If you don't come up with one soon, you may never plan again," she said.

"I know, Mikil." He paced.

Mikil spit again. "We can't just sit here—"

"I'm *not* just sitting here!" Thomas faced her, suddenly furious and knowing he had no right to be. Not at her.

"I am thinking! You should start thinking!" He thrust an arm out toward the Horde now being pounded by boulders again. "Look out there and tell me what could possibly stop such a monstrous army! Who do you think I am? Elyon? Can I clap my hands and make these cliffs crush—"

Thomas stopped.

"What?" Mikil demanded. She glanced around for an enemy, sword in hand.

Thomas spun toward the valley. "What was it you said earlier?"

"What? That you should be with your men?"

"No! The cliffs. You said we'd have to bring the whole cliff down on them."

"Yes, but we might as well try to bring the sun down on them."

It was an insane thought.

"What is it?" she demanded again.

"What if there *was* a way to bring the cliff—"

"There isn't."

He ran to the edge. "But *if*! If we could bring down the canyon walls near their rear, we could box them in, bring them down here, and we would trap them for an easy slaughter from above."

"What do you want to do, heat the whole cliff with a giant fire and empty the contents of the lake on it so that it cracks?"

He ignored her. It was reckless, but then so was doing nothing.

"There's a fault along the cliff there. Do you see it?"

He pointed and she looked.

"So there's a fault. I still don't see how—"

"Of course you don't! But if we *could*, would it work?"

"If you could clap your hands and bring down the cliff on them, then I'd say we have a chance of sending every last one of the Scabs to the black forest where they belong."

A battle cry filled the canyon. Gerard was leading his newly reinforced ranks into the battle again.

"How long do you think we can hold them?" Thomas demanded.

"Another hour. Maybe two."

Thomas paced and muttered under his breath. "That may not be enough!"

"Sir, please. You have to tell me what's going on. There's a reason I'm your second in command. If you can't, I am needed back on the battlefield."

"There was once a way to bring a cliff like this down. It was a long time ago, written about in the Books of Histories. Very few remember, but I do."

"And?"

Exactly. And what?

"I think it was called an explosion. A large ball of fire with tremendous strength. What if we could figure out how to cause an explosion?"

She looked at him with a wrinkled brow.

"There was a time when I could get specific information about the histories. What if I could retrieve specific information on how to cause an explosion?"

"That's the most ridiculous thing I've ever heard! We're in the middle of a battle here. You expect to go on some kind of expedition to find information on the histories? You have battle fatigue!"

"No, not an expedition. I'm not sure it would even work. I've taken the fruit so long." The idea swelled in his mind and with it an excitement. "It would be the first time in fifteen years I haven't eaten the fruit. What if I can still dream?"

She stared at him as if he'd gone mad. Below them the battle still raged.

"I would need to sleep; that's the only problem." He paced, eager for this idea now. "What if I can't sleep?"

"Sleep? You want to sleep? Now?"

"Dream!" he said, fist clenched. "I need to dream. I could dream as I used to and learn how to blow this cliff down!"

Mikil had been struck dumb.

"Do you have a better idea?" he asked forcefully.

"Not yet," she managed.

What if he couldn't dream? What if the rhambutan required several days to wear off?

Thomas faced the canyon. He glanced at the far cliff, its fault line clear where the milky white rock turned red. In two hours all of his men would be dead.

But if he did have an explosive . . .

Thomas bounded for his horse and swung into the saddle.

"Thomas!"

"Follow me!"

She followed at a gallop up the path to the cliff's lip. He swept past the first post and yelled at a full run.

"Delay them! Do whatever you must, but hold them until dark. I have a way."

"Thomas! What way?" came the cry.

"Just hold them!" And then he was past.

Do you have a way, Thomas?

He ran all the way down the line of archers and catapult teams, passing encouragement to each battery. "Hold them! Hold them till dark! Slow the pace. We have a way. If you hold them until dark, we have a way!"

Mikil said nothing.

When they passed the last catapult, Thomas pulled up.

"I'm with you only because you've saved my life a dozen times and I've sworn my own to you," Mikil said. "I hope you know that."

"Follow me."

He led her behind an outcropping of boulders and looked around. Good enough. He dismounted.

"What are we doing here?" she asked.

"We're dismounting." He found a rock the size of his fist and weighed it in one hand. As much as he disliked the thought of being hit in the head, he saw no alternative. There was no way he could fall asleep on his own. Not with so much adrenaline coursing through his veins.

"Here you go. I want you to knock me on the head. I need to sleep, but that's not going to happen, so you have to knock me unconscious."

She looked around uncomfortably. "Sir—"

"Knock me out! That's an order. And hit me hard enough to do the job on the first try. Once I'm out, wake me up in ten minutes. Do you understand?"

"Ten minutes is enough to retrieve what you need?"

He stared at her, struck by the sound of the questions.

"Listen to me," she said. "You've turned me into a lunatic. The Horde's druids might practice their magic, but when have we ever? Never! This is like their magic."

True enough. The Horde druids were rumored to practice a magic that healed and deceived at once. Thomas had never seen either. Some said that Justin practiced the way of the druids.

"Ten minutes. Say it."

"Yes, of course. Ten minutes."

"Then hit me."

She stepped forward. "You really—"

"Hit me!"

Mikil swung the rock.

Thomas blocked the blow.

"What are you doing?" she demanded.

"Sorry. It was reflex. I'll close my eyes this time."

He closed his eyes.

His head exploded with light.

His world faded to black.

4

THOMAS HUNTER awoke in perfect stillness, and he knew three things before his heart had completed its first heavy beat.

One, he knew that he wasn't the same man who'd fallen asleep just nine hours ago. He'd lived fifteen years in another reality and had been transformed by new knowledge and skills.

Two, none of those skills, unfortunately, included surviving a bullet to the head, as was once the case.

Three, there was a bullet in the barrel of the gun that at this very moment pressed lightly against his head.

He kept his eyes shut and his body limp. His head throbbed from Mikil's blow. His mind raced. Panic.

No, not panic. How many times had he faced death over the last fifteen years? Even here, in this dream world, he'd been shot twice in the last week, and each time he'd been healed by Elyon's water.

But this time there was no healing water. It had disappeared with the colored forest fifteen years ago.

A soft, low whisper filled his ear. "Good-bye, Mr. Hunter."

———◦◦◦———

Carlos Missirian let the last satisfying moment linger. A line from a movie he'd once seen drummed through his mind.

Dodge this.

Yes, Mr. Hunter, just try to dodge this. He tightened his finger on the trigger.

Hunter's body jerked.

For a split second, Carlos thought he'd shot the gun and sent a bullet through the man's brain, which explained Hunter's sudden jerk.

But there had been no detonation.

And his gun was flying across the room.

And his wrist stung.

In one horrifying moment of enlightenment, Carlos saw that Thomas Hunter had slapped the gun from his hand and was now rolling away from him, far too quickly for any ordinary man.

Nothing of this kind had ever happened to Carlos. It confused him. There was something very wrong about this man who seemed to retrieve information and skills from his dreams at will. If Carlos were a mystic, as his mother was, he might be tempted to think Hunter was a demon.

The man came to his feet and faced Carlos on the opposite side of the bed. He had no weapon and wore only boxer shorts. He was bleeding from a fresh cut on his forearm that Carlos hadn't put there. Curious. Perhaps that explained the blood on the sheets.

Carlos withdrew his knife. Ordinarily his next course of action would be straightforward. He would either bear down on the unarmed man and slash his abdomen or neck, whichever presented itself, or he'd send the knife flying from where he stood. Despite the ease with which actors knocked aside hurling blades in the movies, deflecting a well-thrown stiletto in real combat wasn't an easy task.

But Hunter wasn't an ordinary man.

They faced off, both cautious.

It occurred to Carlos that Thomas had changed. Physically he was the same man with the same loose brown hair and green eyes, the same strong jaw and steady hands, the same muscled chest and abdomen. But he carried himself differently now, with a simple, unshakable confidence. He stood tall, hands loose at his sides. Hunter watched Carlos with unwavering eyes, the way a man might look at a challenging mathematics equation rather than a threatening foe.

Carlos knew that he should be diving for the gun on the floor to his left or throwing the knife he'd drawn. But his fascination with this man delayed his reactions. If Svensson knew the full extent of Hunter's capabilities, he might insist he be taken alive. Perhaps Carlos would take the matter up with Armand Fortier.

"What's your name?" Thomas asked. His eyes glanced sideways, to the gun and back.

Carlos eased to his left. "Carlos."

"Well, Carlos, it seems that we meet again."

They both went for the gun at the same time. Hunter reached it first. Kicked it under the bed. Sprang back.

"I never did like guns," Thomas said. "You wouldn't by any chance be interested in a fair fight, would you? Swords?"

"Swords would be fine," Carlos said. There was no way to get the gun now. "Unfortunately, we don't have time for games today."

The woman would be coming. At any moment she'd knock on the door and wake her brother as promised. If either of them raised an alarm . . .

Carlos lunged for Thomas.

The man sidestepped his thrusting blade, but not quickly enough to avoid it. The edge sliced into his shoulder.

Thomas ignored the cut and leaped toward the door.

You're fast, but not that fast. With two long steps to his right Carlos cut the man off.

"You've slipped through my fingers twice," he said. "Not today." He backed Thomas into the corner. Blood ran down his arm. How he'd once managed to survive a high-velocity slug to the head, Carlos had no clue, but the cut on his arm wasn't healing now. One well-directed slash, and Thomas Hunter's blood would turn the beige carpet red.

Hunter suddenly spread his mouth and yelled at the top of his lungs. "Karaaa!"

Kara had just flushed the toilet when her brother's voice sounded through the walls. "Karaaa!"

He was in trouble?

"Karaaa!"

She flew through the bathroom door. The bedroom door. Across the suite's hall. Slammed into Thomas's door and wrenched the knob. Threw the door open.

Thomas stood in the corner, all boxers and muscles and blood. A man of Mediterranean origin by all appearances had put him there with his knife. Carlos?

They both turned to her at the same time. She saw the long scar on his cheek then. Yes, Carlos. The man about to shove his blade through Thomas was the same who'd shot him a few days earlier.

She looked at Thomas again. He wasn't the same man she'd kissed on the forehead last night before retiring.

She'd told him to dream for a long time and become the kind of man who could save the world. She didn't know who he'd become in his dreams, but his eyes had changed. The sheets on the bed were stained with blood, some of it fresh, some dried black. He was bleeding from his shoulder and his forearm.

"Meet Carlos," Thomas said. "He hasn't heard about the antivirus that we have, so he thinks it's safe to kill me. I thought it would sound more convincing coming from you."

Had Thomas learned something about the antivirus from his dreams? Carlos's eyes jerked between them.

"What neither of you know," Thomas continued, "is that I have to take explosives of some kind back with me. The Horde is slicing my army to ribbons as we speak. I have fewer than five thousand men against a hundred thousand Scabs. I absolutely have to succeed. You understand? Both of you? I have to get this information and get back!"

He was babbling.

"The water doesn't work anymore, Kara. There's a gun under the bed. You don't have much time."

Carlos lunged at Thomas. Her brother slapped away the first blow with his right hand. The man followed with his left fist, which Thomas also deflected. But blocking the successive blows had left him exposed, and Kara had seen enough street fights in Manila to know that this was precisely what his attacker intended.

Carlos drove on, straight into Thomas, using his head as a battering ram. It connected solidly with Thomas's chin. Her brother dropped like a rock.

Kara dove for the bed and hit the carpet with a grunt. She rolled under the bed, saw the gun, and clawed for it.

5

A HORRENDOUS din filled the air.

The din of battle. Of death.

Thomas's eyes snapped open. He sat up and winced at the pounding pain in his head.

"Did you get it?" Mikil asked, dropping to one knee beside him.

"Get what?"

"I knew it!" She stood and walked away.

Of course, he'd gone for the explosives! His mind scrambled. "How long have I been unconscious?"

She shrugged. "Five minutes."

"Five minutes! I told you ten!"

"I didn't wake you. You woke on your own. Maybe it was Elyon waking you to go and lead your men."

"No, I have to go back!"

She looked at him. "Go back where?"

"I didn't have enough time. I have to get back to learn how to make explosives."

"This is nonsense. What would you have me do? Hit you on the head with another rock?"

"Yes!" He clamored to his feet. "It works. I'm dreaming again. I was there, Mikil!"

"And what did you do there?"

"I fought a man who was trying to shoot me with a gun. It's another kind of explosive device. He fights—he's very good. I think he knocked me out."

Thomas turned from her, remembering. "And Kara—" An ache in his shoulder stopped him.

There was a gash about three inches long just above his right bicep. He ran a finger along it, trying to recall if it had come from the battle below or from his dreams.

"Did I have this cut?" he asked her.

"You must have. I don't remember when—"

"No! It wasn't here when I came up. No one cut me while I was sleeping?"

"Of course not."

"Then it's from my dreams!" He grabbed Mikil's arm. "Knock me out! Now! Hurry! I have to get back to save my sister!"

"You don't have a sister."

"Hit me!" he cried. "Just hit me."

"It's not within me to strike my commander twice in the space of ten minutes, even if—"

"I order it." A tremor ran through his hands. "Pretend I'm not your commander. I'm a Scab and smell of rotten meat and I will knock your head off your shoulders if you don't defend—"

She was airborne and he made no attempt to deflect her blow. The leather sole of her boot struck him above his right ear, and he collapsed.

6

KARA'S HAND found the cold steel. She'd never felt such an intense sense of relief. She wrapped her fingers around the gun.

But her relief was premature. She was on her stomach, face planted in the carpet, useless. She twisted and rolled to her back. The gun clanged against the metal bedframe. A thunderous roar ripped through the cramped space.

She'd discharged the gun! Had she hit anyone? Put a hole in the wall or window? Maybe she'd hit Carlos. Or Thomas.

She twisted and saw that Thomas still lay on his back by the far wall. No bullet holes that she could see.

Something bounced on the bed. Carlos.

She fired into the mattress, wincing with the explosion. Again. *Boom, boom.*

She watched Carlos's feet land on the floor. Two long strides and he was into the hall.

Kara jerked the trigger and sent another shot in his general direction.

Carlos vanished toward the adjoining suite at the end of the hall. The door banged.

What if he hadn't really left? What if he was hiding around the wall, waiting for her to stand up and put the gun down before he rushed in and cut her throat?

She scooted into daylight, keeping the gun trained on the doorway as best she could considering all her nervous energy. She carefully stood, edged to the door, and circled to her left in a wide arc until she could see through the door into the hall.

No Carlos.

The door at the end of the hall was open. This man hadn't acted alone. Someone in the hotel had helped him access their suite through the one next to it.

"Thomas?"

Kara ran around the bed and knelt beside him. "Thomas!" She slapped his cheek lightly.

Someone was banging on the front door. They'd heard the shots. Carlos had fled because he knew they would hear the shots. Her accidental discharge may very well have saved both of their lives.

"Thomas, wake up, honey."

He groaned and slowly opened his eyes.

<hr />

Thomas and Kara sat on the sofa in Merton Gains's suite, waiting for the deputy secretary of state to end a string of calls. He'd greeted them briefly, noted the details of the attack on Thomas, ordered more security for his own suite, and then excused himself for a few minutes. The world was unraveling behind closed doors, he said.

They could hear the secretary's muffled voice down the hall behind them. Kara spoke quietly, nearly a whisper.

"Fifteen? Fifteen years? You're sure?"

"Yes. I'm quite sure."

"How's that possible? You're not fifteen years older, are you?"

"My body isn't, nay—"

"Nay?"

"Sorry."

"Nay," she said. "Sounds . . . old."

"As I was saying, I'm about forty there. Honestly I feel forty here as well."

Amazing.

"So these wounds of yours are a definite change in the rules between these two realities," she said, indicating Thomas's arm. "Knowledge and skills have always been transferable both ways, but before the colored forest turned black, your injuries in that world didn't cross over here;

only injuries from this world crossed over there. Now it goes both ways?"

"Evidently. But it's blood that transfers, not merely injuries. Blood has to do with life. Actually, blood defiles the lakes, the boy said. It's one of our cardinal rules. In any case, it's going both ways now."

"But when you first hit your head—when this whole thing first started—it bled in both worlds."

"Maybe I really did wound it in both worlds at the same time. Maybe that's what opened this gateway." He sighed. "I don't know, sounds crazy. We'll assume that knowledge, skills, and blood are transferable. Nothing else."

"And that you're the only gateway. We're talking about *your* knowledge, your skills, your blood."

"Correct."

"It would explain why you haven't aged here," Kara said. "You get cut there and you get cut here, but you don't age the same, or gain weight the same, or sweat the same. Only specific events tied to the spilling of blood show up in both realities." She paused. "And you're a general over there?"

"Commander of the Forest Guard, General Thomas of Hunter," he said without batting an eye.

"How did that happen?" she asked. "Not that I don't think you couldn't be Alexander the Great himself, you understand. It's just a lot to digest. A little detail would help."

"Must sound pretty crazy, huh?" A grin played on his lips. This was the Thomas she knew.

He squeezed the leather cushion by his side. "This is all so . . . so strange. So real."

"That's because it *is* real. Please tell me you're not going to attempt another leap off the balcony."

He released the pillow. "Okay. Obviously both places are real. At least we're still assuming so, right? But you have to understand that after fifteen years in another world, this one here feels more like the dream. Forgive me if I behave rather oddly now and then."

She smiled and shook her head. He was half "rather oddly" and half the old Thomas.

"It's funny?" he asked.

"No. But just listen to you. 'Forgive me if I behave rather oddly now and then.' No offense, brother, but you sound a bit conflicted. Tell me more."

"After the Shataiki spread their poison through the colored forest, a terrible disease overtook the population. It makes the skin flake on the surface and crack underneath. It's very painful. The eyes turn gray and the body smells, like sulfur or rotten eggs. But Elyon made a way for us to live without the effects of this disease. Seven forests—regular forests, not colored ones—still stand, and in each forest is a lake. If we bathe in the lake each day, the disease remains in remission. The only condition we have for living in the forest is that we bathe regularly and keep the lakes from being defiled with blood."

She just looked at him.

"Unfortunately, I'm in a battle with the Horde at this very moment that may end it all."

"What about the prophecy?"

"That Elyon will bring down the Horde with one blow? Maybe dynamite is Elyon's answer." He stood, eager to move forward with this plan. "I have to figure out how to make dynamite before I go back."

"So I take it you're still dreaming," Gains said behind them.

Kara stood with her brother. Hearing the conviction in his voice and seeing the light in his eyes when he talked, she was tempted to think that the real drama was unfolding in a different reality, that the Raison Strain was only a story and the war in Thomas's desert was the real deal.

Gains brought her back to earth.

"Good," he said, rounding the sofa. "I have a feeling we're going to need these dreams of yours. Never imagined I would ever say something like that, but then again, I never imagined we would ever face such a monster either. Can I get either of you a drink?"

Neither responded.

"Again, the lack of security for your suite was my oversight. I hate to admit it, but we've underestimated you from the beginning, Thomas. I can guarantee you that has just changed."

Thomas said nothing.

Gains eyed him. "You sure you're okay?"

"I'm fine."

"Okay." He glanced at Kara, then back. "We need you on this, son."

"I'm not sure I can help anymore. Things have changed."

Gains stepped forward, took Thomas's arm, and guided him toward the window. "I'm not sure you realize the full extent of what's going on, but it's not looking good, Thomas. Raison Pharmaceutical has just concluded the examination of a jacket that was left on a coatrack in the Bangkok International Airport. A man reportedly harassed several flight attendants before walking to the first-aid station, hanging his coat on the rack, and leaving. Any guesses as to what's on the coat?"

"The virus," Kara said.

"Correct. The Raison Strain. As promised by Valborg Svensson. As predicted by none other than Thomas Hunter, which makes you a very, very important man, Thomas. And yes, the virus is airborne. Which means that if the three of us aren't already infected, we will be before we leave for D.C. Half of Thailand will be infected by week's end."

"Leaving for D.C.?" Thomas asked. "Why?"

"The president has suggested that you tell a committee he's pulling together what you know."

"I'm not sure I have anything to add to what you know."

Gains smiled nervously. "I know this hasn't been the easiest week for you, Thomas, but I'm not sure you're seeing the picture clearly here. We have a serious situation on our hands, and we don't have the first idea how to effectively deal with it. But you predicted the situation, and you seem to know more about it than anyone else at the moment. That makes you a guest of the president of the United States. Now. By force if necessary."

Thomas blinked. He glanced at Kara.

"Makes sense to me," she said.

"Any word on Monique?" Thomas asked.

"No."

"But you do understand what's happening now," Thomas said. "Svensson may not have the antivirus yet, but with her help, he will. When that happens, we're finished."

This was more like her old brother.

"I don't know what we are. At this point it's been taken out of my hands—"

"You see? I tell you something and you start in with the doubt. Why should I think that Washington will be any different?"

"I'm not doubting you! I'm just saying that the president has taken this over. I'm not the one who needs persuading; he is."

"Okay. I'll go. But I need your help too. I have to figure out how to create an explosion large enough to knock down a cliff before I fall sleep again."

Gains sighed.

Thomas stepped up, took Gains by the arm in almost the same fashion that Gains had taken his, and walked him slowly toward the same window.

"I'm not sure you realize the full extent of what's going on, but it's not looking good, Merton," he mimicked. "Let me help you. As we speak I am leading what remains of my army, the Forest Guard, in a terrible battle against the Horde. We number fewer than five thousand now. They number a hundred thousand. If I don't find a way to bring the cliff down on top of them, they'll overrun us and slaughter our women and children. That may be so much hogwash to you, fine. But there's another problem. If I die there, I die here. And if I'm dead here, I won't be of much help to you."

"Isn't that a bit of a stretch?"

Thomas thrust out his arm and pulled up his sleeve. "This bandage on my forearm covers a wound I received in battle today. My sheets upstairs are covered with blood. Carlos didn't cut me while I was sleeping. Who did? My temples are throbbing from a rock I took in the head. Believe me, the other reality is as real as this one. If I die there, I can guarantee you I die here."

And the opposite was true as well, Kara thought. *If he died here, then he would die in the forest.*

He pulled down his sleeve. "Now I'll do everything in my power to help you, if you'll help me stay alive. I would say that's an even exchange. Wouldn't you?"

An unsure grin crawled across the secretary's face. "Agreed. I'll see what I can do, on the condition that you won't talk about these kinds of details in front of the media or the establishment in Washington. I'm not sure they will understand."

Thomas nodded. "I see your point. Maybe, Kara, you could do some research for me while the secretary fills me in."

"You want me to figure out how to make explosives?" Her brow arched.

"I'm sure Gains can put a call in to the right people. We're in canyon lands. Lots of rock, rich in copper and tin ores. We make bronze weapons now. Even if we withdraw, we'll only have a few hours to find whatever ingredients you come up with and make explosives. It has to be strong enough to knock down canyon walls along a natural fault."

"Black powder," Gains said.

Thomas faced him. "Not dynamite?"

"I doubt it. Black powder was first made by combining several common elements. That's your best bet." He shook his head. "God help us. We're casually discussing which explosive will best blow up this 'Horde' while breathing in the world's deadliest virus."

"Who can help me?" Kara asked Gains.

He flipped open his cell phone, walked into the kitchen, punched up a number, spoke briefly in soft tones, and ended the call.

"You met Phil Grant last night. Director of the CIA. He's next door, and he'll put as many people as you need on it."

"Now?"

"Yes, now. If black powder can be found and made in a matter of hours, the CIA will find the people who can tell you how."

"Perfect." Thomas said.

Kara liked the new Thomas. She winked at him and left.

———✖———

Thomas turned to Gains. "Okay now, where were you?"

It was all coming back to Thomas. Not that he'd forgotten any of the details, but he'd felt a bit disoriented thus far. He could only be spread so thin. With each passing minute in this world, his sense of its immediate crisis swelled, matching the crisis that depended on him in the other world.

"Washington."

Thomas ran a hand through his hair. "I can't imagine a group of politicians listening to anyone as forthright as me. They'll think I'm insane."

"The world's about to go ballistic, Thomas. The French, the British, the Chinese, Russia . . . every country in which Svensson has released this monster is reeling already. They want answers, and you may be the only person other than those complicit in this plot to give them answers. We don't have time to debate your sanity."

"Well said."

"You made a believer out of me. I've gone out on a limb for you. Don't back out on me, not now."

"Where has Svensson released the virus?"

"Come with me."

———✖———

There was a sense of déjà vu to the meeting. Same conference room, same faces. But there were also some significant differences. Three new attendees had joined through video conference links. Health Secretary Barbara Kingsley, a high-ranking officer of the World Health Organization, and the secretary of defense, although he excused himself after only ten minutes. *Something was odd about his early departure,* Thomas thought.

Eyes flittered about the room on high-strung nerves. The confident glares of last night were gone. Most of them had trouble meeting his stare.

They spent thirty minutes rehashing the reports they'd received. Gains had been right. Russia, England, China, India, South Africa, Australia,

France—all of the countries that had been directly threatened this far were demanding answers from the State Department. But there were none, at least none that offered the slightest sliver of hope. And by end of day, the number of infected cities was promised to double.

Raison Pharmaceutical's report on the jacket left in the Bangkok airport took up fifteen minutes of speculation and conjecture, most of it led by Theresa Sumner from CDC. If, and it was a big *if*, she insisted, every city Svensson claimed to have infected actually had been infected, and if—again it was a big *if*—the virus did indeed act as the computer models showed it would, then the virus was already too widespread to stop.

None of them could quite grasp such a cataclysmic scenario.

"How in the name of heaven could anything like this have possibly happened?" Kingsley demanded. She was a heavy-boned woman with dark hair, and her question was greeted with silence.

This same simple question would be asked a hundred thousand times in as many clever ways as possible in the next week alone, Thomas thought.

"Mr. Raison, maybe you can give me an explanation that I would feel comfortable passing on to the president."

"It's a virus, madam. What explanation would you like?"

"I know it's a virus. The question is how is this possible? Millions of years of evolution or however we got here, and just like that a bug comes out of nowhere to kill us all off? These aren't the Dark Ages, for crying out loud!"

"No, in the Dark Ages the human race didn't have the technology to create anything this nasty."

"I can't believe you didn't see this coming."

It was as close to an accusation as one could make, and it silenced the room.

"Anyone who understands the true potential of superbugs could have seen something like this coming," Jacques de Raison said. "The balance of nature is a delicate matter. There is no way to predict mutations of this kind. Please explain that to your president."

They looked at each other as if at any moment one of them would surely say something that would set this terrible mistake straight.

April fools!

But it wasn't April and no one was fooling.

They rallied around Sumner's repeated announcement that the virus had only been verified in Bangkok. No one else knew quite what to look for, although the CDC was working feverishly to get the right information into the right hands.

"Don't we have a plane to catch?" Thomas finally asked.

They looked at him as if his statement should require some examination. Everything Thomas Hunter said was now worthy of examination.

"The car will take us in thirty minutes," Gains's assistant offered.

"Good. I'm not sure we're doing any good here."

Silence.

"How so?" someone finally asked.

"For starters, I've already told you all of this. And all the talk in the world won't change the fact that we're facing an airborne virus that will infect the world's entire population within two weeks. There's only one way to deal with the virus, and that is to find an antivirus. For that I believe we'll need Monique de Raison. The fate of the world rests on finding her."

He pushed back his chair and stood.

"But we can't speak of finding Monique de Raison here, because in doing so we'll probably tip our hand to Svensson. I believe he has someone on the inside."

Gains cleared his throat. "You're suggesting there's a mole? Here?"

"How else did Carlos know exactly where to find me? How else did he gain access to my suite through the adjoining room? How else did he know I was sleeping when he entered?"

"I have to agree," Phil Grant said. Thomas wondered if the man's trust of his colleagues had kept his own suspicions at bay until now. "There are other ways he could have gained access, but Thomas makes a good point."

"Then I must say that the French government would like custody of Thomas Hunter," Louis Dutêtre said.

All eyes turned to the French intelligence officer.

"Paris has come under attack. Mr. Hunter knew of that attack before it occurred. This places him under suspicion."

"Don't be ridiculous," Gains said. "They tried to kill him this morning."

"Who did? Who saw this mysterious intruder? As far as we know, Thomas is the mole. Isn't that a possibility? My country insists on the opportunity to interrogate—"

"Enough!" Gains stood. "This meeting is adjourned. Mr. Dutêtre, you may inform your people that Thomas Hunter is in the protective custody of the United States of America. If your president has a problem with that, please advise him to call the White House. Let's go."

"I object!" Dutêtre jumped to his feet. "We are all affected; we should all participate."

"Then find Svensson," Gains said.

"For all you know, this man *is* Svensson!"

Now there was an interesting idea.

Gains walked from the room without a backward glance. Thomas followed.

⸙

The small jet winged westward over Thailand, bound for Washington, D.C., six hours after the first fax to the White House informed the world that everything had just changed for Homo sapiens. The CDC had now verified the virus in two new cities: New York and Atlanta. They started with the airports, following indications in Bangkok, and they hadn't needed to go any farther.

Svensson was using the airports.

Had used the airports.

The first critical decision was now upon the world leaders. Should they shut down the airports and by so doing slow the spread of the virus? Or should they avert public panic by withholding information until they had something more concrete?

According to Raison Pharmaceutical, closing the airports wouldn't slow the virus enough to make a difference—it was too widespread already. And panic wasn't a prospect any of the affected governments were willing to deal with yet. For now, the airports would remain open.

Thomas had been awake for only four hours, but now he was eager to fall asleep. He held the thin manila folder in his hands and read the contents for the fifth time.

Kara frowned. "It might not have the kind of power you need—it's pretty slow burning—but Gains was right. Black powder is the only explosive you have any chance of pulling together in the middle of nowhere."

"How am I going to find this stuff?"

"They tell me the kind of firepower you need isn't impossible. The Chinese figured it out nearly two thousand years ago by accident. You can be nearly 50 percent off on the combination of ingredients and still get a decent bang. And the three ingredients you'll need are very common. You just have to know what you're looking for, which you now do. Do you have sugar there?"

"Some, yes. From sugarcane, just like here."

"If you can't get to the charcoal quickly enough, sugar will work as a fuel as well. Here's a list of more substitutes. The ratios are all there. Stall the Horde, and stall them hard. Deploy a thousand soldiers to find what you need."

"A little research and you're ready to start commanding armies?" He grinned. "You'd be good there, Kara. You really would be."

"You like it better there than here?"

He hadn't considered the comparison. "I'm not sure there is a 'there' that's not also 'here.' Hard to explain and it's just a hunch, but both realities are actually very similar."

"Hmm. Well if you ever figure out how to take others with you, promise to take me first."

"I will."

She sighed. "I know this isn't exactly the best time to bring this up, but do you remember the last thing I told you before you disappeared for fifteen years last night?"

"Remind me."

"It was only twelve hours ago. I suggested that you become someone who could deal with the situation here. Now you've come back a general. It just makes me wonder."

"Interesting thought."

"You really have changed, Thomas. And I hate to break it to you, but I really think you've changed for the sake of this world, not that one."

"Maybe."

"We're running out of time. You've got to start figuring things out. Get past all this noncommittal 'maybe' and 'interesting thought' stuff. If you don't, we just may be toast."

"Maybe." He grinned and closed the folder. "But unless I can figure out how to survive as General Hunter there, I won't be around here to figure anything out. Like I said, if I die there, I think I die here."

"And if you die here?" she asked. "What happens if the virus kills us all?"

He hadn't connected the dots in that way, and her suggestion alarmed him. But it only made sense that if he died here along with the rest, he would die in the forest.

"Let's just hope this black powder of yours works, sis."

"Sis?"

"I've always called you that."

She shrugged. "Sounds odd now."

"I *am* odd, sis. I am very, very odd." He sighed, leaned his head back, and closed his eyes. "Time to get back into the ring. I'm almost tempted to ask you to rub my shoulders down. Fourteenth round and I'm dead on my feet."

"Not funny. You have everything you need?"

He tapped his head. "I've read the material a dozen times. Let's hope I can remember it. Let's hope I can find what I need."

"Elyon's strength," she said.

He cracked one eye and looked at her. "Elyon's strength."

"WAKE UP."

His cheek stung. A hand slapped it again several times.

Thomas pushed himself up. "I am awake! Give me a moment!"

Mikil stepped back.

Thomas's mind spun. After so long, transitions of his dreams felt surreal.

He looked at his second in command. Mikil. She could probably walk into any bar in New York and clear the place. She wore battle moccasins, a kind of boot with hardened-leather soles but cured squirrel hide around the ankles and halfway up the calf. A bone-handled knife was strapped to her lean, well-muscled leg. She wore thigh guards for battle and a short hardened-leather skirt that would stop most blows. Her torso was covered in the traditional leather armor, but her arms were free to swing and block. Her hair ordinarily fell to her shoulders, but she'd tied it back today for battle. She'd strapped a red feather to her left elbow, a gift from Jamous, who was courting her. A long scar ran from the dangling feather up to her shoulder, the work of a Scab moments before she'd sent him screaming into hell during the Winter Campaign.

Mikil's eyes had begun to turn gray. The report of skirmishes at the Natalga Gap had come during the night—she'd left the village without her customary swim in the lake. The Forest Guard Oath required all soldiers to bathe at least once every three days. Any longer and they would risk becoming like the Desert Dwellers themselves. The sickness affected not only the eyes and the skin, but the mind as well. The Guard had to either carry large amounts of water with them on campaigns or draw the battle lines close to home. It was the single greatest limiting factor a tactician could be handed.

464

Thomas had once been stranded for four days in the desert without a horse. He had two canteens, and he'd used one for a spit bath on the second day. But by the end of the third day, the onset of the disease was so painful that he could hardly walk. His skin had turned gray and flaked, and a foul odor seeped from his pores. He was still a day's walk from the nearest forest.

In a fit of panic he'd stripped naked, flung himself on the sand, and begged the blistering sun to burn the flesh from his bones. For the first time he knew what it meant to be a Desert Dweller. It was indeed hell on earth.

On the morning of the fourth day, he began to see the world differently. His craving for fresh water diminished. The sand felt better underfoot. He began to think that living life in this new gray skin might not be impossible after all. He wrote the thoughts off to hallucination and expected to die of thirst by day's end.

A group of straying Horde found him and mistook him for one of their own. He drank their stale water and donned a hooded cloak and demanded a horse. He could still remember the woman who'd given him hers as if he'd met her yesterday.

"Are you married?" she asked him.

Thomas stood there, scalp burning under the hood, and stared at the Desert Dweller, taken aback by her question. If he said yes, she might ask who was his wife, which might cause problems.

"No."

She stepped up to him and searched his face. Her eyes were a dull gray, nearly white. Her cheeks were ashen.

She drew back her hood and exposed her bleached hair. In that moment Thomas knew that this woman was propositioning him. But more, he knew that she was beautiful. He wasn't sure if the sun had gotten to him or if the disease was eating his mind, but he found her attractive. Fascinating, at the very least. No, more than that. Attractive. And no odor. In fact, he was sure that if he were somehow miraculously changed back into the Thomas with clear skin and green eyes, she would think that *his* skin stank.

The sudden attraction caught him wholly off guard. The Forest People followed the way of the Great Romance, vowing not to forget the love Elyon had lavished upon them in the colored forest. The Scabs did not.

Until this moment he'd never considered what a man's attraction to a female Scab felt like.

The woman reached a hand to his cheek and touched it. "I am Chelise."

He was immobilized with indecision.

"Would you like to come with me, Roland?" He'd given her the fictitious name knowing that his own was well known.

"I would, yes. But I first must complete my mission, and for that I need a horse."

"Is that so? What is your mission?" She smiled seductively. "Are you a fierce warrior off to assassinate the murderer of men?"

"As a matter of fact, I am an assassin." He thought it might earn him respect, but she acted as if meeting assassins in the desert was a common thing. "Who is this murderer of men?"

Her eyes darkened and he knew that he'd asked the wrong question.

"If you're an assassin, you would know, wouldn't you? There's only one man any assassin has taken an oath to kill."

"Yes, of course, but do *you* really know the business of an assassin?" he said, mentally scrambling for a way out. "If you are so eager to bear my children, perhaps you should know with whom you would make your home. So tell me, whom have we assassins sworn to kill?"

He could tell immediately that she liked his answer.

"Thomas of Hunter," she said. "He is the murderer of men and women and children, and he is the one that my father, the great Qurong, has commanded his assassins to kill."

The daughter of Qurong! He was speaking to Desert royalty. He dipped his head in a show of submission.

She laughed. "Don't be silly. As you can see, I don't wear my position on my sleeve."

The way her eyes had darkened when she spoke his name alarmed Thomas. He knew he was as despicable in the eyes of the Desert Dwellers as they were to him. But to discuss such a thing around the campfire after routing the enemy was one thing; to hear it coming from the lips of such a stunning enemy was quite another.

"Come with me, Roland," Chelise said. "I'll give you more to do than run around making hopeless assassination attempts. Everyone knows that Hunter is far too swift with his sword to yield to this senseless strategy of my father's. Martyn, our bright new general, will have a place for you."

It was the first time he'd heard the new general's name.

"I beg to differ, but I am the one assassin who can find the murderer of men and kill him at will."

"Is that so? You're that intelligent, are you? And are you bright enough to read what no man can read?"

She was mocking him by suggesting that he couldn't read?

"Of course I can read."

She arched an eyebrow. "The Books of Histories?"

Thomas blinked at the reference. She was speaking about the ancient books? How was that possible?

"You have them?" he asked.

Chelise turned away. "No. But I've seen a few in my time. It would take a wise man to read that gibberish."

"Give me a horse. Let me finish my mission, then I will return," he said.

"I'll give you a horse," she said, replacing her hood. "But don't bother returning to me. If killing another man is more important to you than serving a princess, I've misjudged you." She ordered a man nearby to give him a horse and then walked away.

His own Guard had nearly killed him at the edge of the forest. He bathed in the lake on the eve of the fourth day. Normally the cleansing of the disease felt soothing, but at this advanced stage of the disease, the pain was nearly unbearable. Entering the water had been not unlike pulling his skin off. It was no wonder the Scabs feared the lakes.

But the pain was only momentary, and when he emerged from the water, his skin was restored. Rachelle had finally and passionately kissed him on the mouth, now rid of its awful odor. The village had celebrated the return of its hero with more than its usual nightly celebration.

But the memory of that terrible condition with which the Horde lived every day never left him. And neither did the image of the woman from the desert. The only thing that separated her from Mikil was a bucket of Elyon's water.

Regardless of what he might want to think about the Desert Dwellers, one thing was indisputable: They had rejected the ways of Elyon. They were the enemy, and it wasn't their rotting flesh that Thomas hated as much as their treacherous, deceitful hearts. For the sake of Elyon, he and the Forest Guard had taken an oath to wipe the Horde from the earth or die in their attempt to do so.

"Did it work?" Mikil asked.

"Did what work?" His head throbbed. "The dreaming? Yes, yes it worked."

"But no way to bring down the cliff, I take it."

Hoofs pounded around the corner. William and Suzan rode on sweating mounts. The cliff?

The cliff! Black powder.

William pulled up and dropped to the ground. "Thomas! Our lines are breaking! I've brought two thousand from the rear and another two thousand will arrive in the night, but they're too many! It's a slaughter out there!"

"I have it!" Thomas cried.

"You have what?"

"Black powder. I know how to make black powder. In fact, I know a dozen ways to make it."

Suzan dismounted. All three looked at him, at a loss.

"Thomas ordered me to hit him on the head so that he could dream," Mikil said. "Evidently he has the ability to learn things from his dreams."

William blinked. "You do? What could you possibly learn that—"

"I've learned how to make black powder," Thomas said, marching past them. He turned back. "If we can make black powder, we have a chance, but we have to hurry."

"You plan to defeat the whores by sprinkling powder on them?" William demanded. "Have you gone mad?" His designation of the Hordes as whores had become commonplace among the Forest Guard.

"He plans to use the powder to break the cliff off," Mikil said. "Isn't that right, Thomas?"

"Essentially, yes. Black powder is an explosive, a fire that burns very fast and expands." He demonstrated with his hands. "If we could pack black powder into the crack at the top of the cliff and ignite it, the entire cliff might break off."

William was stupefied.

"You actually know how to make this black powder now?" Mikil asked.

"Yes."

"How?"

He recited the information from his memory. "Black powder is composed of three basic ingredients in roughly the following proportions: 15 percent charcoal, 10 percent sulfur, and 75 percent saltpeter. That's it. All we have to do is find these three ingredients, prepare them in tightly packed pouches, lower them—"

"What is sulfur?" Suzan asked.

"What is saltpeter?" Mikil asked.

"This is the most absurd thing I've ever heard anyone without scales for flesh utter!" William said.

Thomas began to lose his patience. "Did I say it would be easy? We're being slaughtered down there! You can't build such a devastating device without a bit of work. Charcoal we have, right? We burn it. A few fast riders can retrieve an ample supply and have it here by midnight. Sulfur is the sixteenth most common element occurring in the Earth's crust. And I do believe this is the same Earth's crust. Never mind that; just know that sulfur is found in caves with pyrite. Never mind that as well. The caves at the north end of the Gap. We'll need to break off the cones, heat them in a large fire, and pray that sulfur flows from the pores. Much like the metal ore."

An excitement was starting to show in Mikil's eyes, but William was frowning. "Even with the reinforcements we're badly outnumbered."

"What about the salt?" Mikil asked.

Thomas ignored William. "Saltpeter." He ran his fingers through his hair. "It's a white, translucent mineral composed of potassium nitrate."

They looked at each other.

"You see?" William asked. "He wants to make our fighters look for postass . . . a name he can hardly say, and in the dark? Because he dreamed—"

"Silence!" Thomas's voice rang over the sounds of battle. "If I fail this time, William, I will give you command of the Guard!"

"Where do we find this saltpeter?" Mikil pushed.

"I don't know."

"Then . . . what do you mean, you don't know?"

"We're looking for a translucent, milky rock that's salty."

William crossed his arms in disapproval.

"And if we do find these ingredients, what then?" Mikil asked.

"Then we have to grind them, mix them, compress the powder, and hope they ignite with enough force to do some damage."

Three sets of eyes locked on his. In the end they would agree because they all knew they had no viable alternative. But never had the stakes been so high.

"You do realize that if we must hold them off while we try this trick of yours, we lose the opportunity to evacuate the forest," William said. "If we leave now, we will have a half day start on the Horde because they won't march during the night. We could gather up the village and head north as planned."

"I realize that. But to what end? The Horde is overtaking the Southern Forest as we speak. Jamous is retreating. The Horde—"

"The Southern Forest?" William said. He hadn't heard.

"Yes. The Horde will take this forest and then move to the next."

Mikil looked to the west where the sounds of battle continued. "Maybe it would be wiser to retreat now, make this black powder of yours, and then, when we know it works, we blast the Horde to hell."

"If they take the Middle Forest—" He stopped. They all knew the loss of this forest was unacceptable. "When will we ever have them in a canyon like this? If this works, we could take out a third of their army in one blow. We can still order the evacuation, even if we aren't there to help." He followed Mikil's gaze westward. His men were dying and he was toying with wild dreams. "What if this is what the prophecy spoke of?"

"'In one incredible blow you will defeat the heart of evil,'" Suzan said, quoting from the boy's promise. "Qurong is leading this army while Martyn is attacking Jamous." A glimmer of eagerness lit her eye. "You think it will work?"

"We will know soon enough."

The moon shone high in the desert sky, surrounded by a million stars. Thomas sat on his stallion and studied the canyon floor. The Horde had settled in for the night, thousands upon thousands of Scab warriors, half sleeping in their cloaks, half milling in small groups. No fires. They'd won the battle and they'd celebrated their victory with a cry that had roared through the canyon like a mighty torrent.

Thomas had ordered his army back in a show of retreat. They'd hauled their catapults from the cliff and shown every sign of fleeing to the forest. Seven thousand of his men had joined the battle here in the canyon. Three thousand had given their lives.

It was the worst defeat they'd ever suffered.

Now their hope rested in a black powder that did not exist.

The Guard waited a mile to the west, ready to make for the forest at a moment's notice. If they could not find the saltpeter within the hour, Thomas would give the order.

They had enough charcoal already. William had led a contingent of soldiers to the caves for sulfur. They hauled nearly a ton of pyrite rock to a pit two canyons removed, where they'd built a fire and coaxed liquid sulfur from the stone. The stench had risen to the sky and Thomas couldn't remember ever being so ecstatic about such a horrible smell.

It was the odor of Scab flesh.

But the saltpeter eluded them. A thousand warriors searched in the moonlight for the white rock, licking when necessary.

"We could bring the archers back and at least give the Horde a parting surprise," Mikil said beside him.

"If we had any arrows left, I would shoot a few myself," Thomas said. He looked up at the moon again. "If we can't find the saltpeter in an hour, we leave."

"That's cutting it close. Even if we do find it, we have to mine it. Then grind it into powder, mix it, and test it. Then—"

"I know what we need to do, Mikil. It's my knowledge, remember?"

"Yes. Your dream."

He let the comment go. She'd always been a strong one, the kind of person whom he could trust to take his place at the head of this army if he were ever killed.

"If we are forced to flee, what will become of the Gathering?" she asked.

"Ciphus will insist on the Gathering. He'll hold it at one of the other lakes if he has to, but he won't neglect it."

She sighed. "And with all this nonsense of Justin coming to a head, I'm sure it will be a Gathering to remember. There's been talk of a challenge." Thomas had heard the rumors that Ciphus might press Justin into a debate and, if necessary, a physical contest for his defiance of the Council's prevailing doctrine. Thomas had witnessed three challenges since Ciphus had initiated them; they reminded him of the gladiator-style matches of the histories. All three usurpers had lost and been exiled to the desert.

"If there isn't, I may challenge him myself," Mikil continued.

"Justin's treachery is the least of our concerns at the moment. He will fall in battle like all of Elyon's enemies."

She dropped the subject and looked westward, toward the Middle Forest. "What will happen if the Horde overtakes our lakes?"

"We may lose our army, we may even lose our trees, but we'll never lose our lakes. Not before the prophecy delivers us. If we lose the lakes, then we will become Desert Dwellers against our will. Elyon would never allow it."

"Then he'd better come through soon," she said.

"You may not remember, but I do. He could clap his hands and end this tonight."

"Then why doesn't he?"

"He just might."

"Sir!"

A runner.

"William calls you. He says to tell you he may have found it."

———◆———

"Here! We'll do it all right here." Thomas gripped the large mallet in both hands and slammed it into the glowing rock. A slab of the cliff crashed down.

It was translucent and it was salty, and of all people to find it, William had. If it wasn't saltpeter, they would know soon enough.

Thomas grabbed a handful of the fragments. "Bring it down. All of it." He turned to William. Bring the charcoal and the sulfur. We will set up a line here for crushing the rock into powder and we'll mix it under that ledge. Put a thousand men on this if you have to. I want powder within the hour!"

He ran to his horse and swung into the saddle.

"Where are you going, sir?"

"To test this concoction of ours. Bring it down!"

They descended on the cliffs with a vengeance, swinging with bronze mallets and swords and granite boulders. Others began to crush the suspected saltpeter into a fine powder. They hauled the charcoal in and ground it further down the line. The sulfur caked the bronze bowls into which they had poured it. The cakes ground easily.

Very few knew what they were doing. Who'd ever heard of such a way to conduct a battle? But it hardly mattered—he'd ordered them to crush the rock, and the powder that was this rock would crush the enemy. He was the same man who'd shown them how to coax metals out of rocks by heating them, wasn't he? He was the man who had survived several days as a Scab and returned to wash in the lake. He was the man who had led them into battle a hundred times and emerged the victor.

If Thomas of Hunter told them to crush rocks, they would crush rocks. The fact that three thousand of their comrades had been killed by the Horde today only made their task more urgent.

Thomas knelt on the large stone slab and looked at a small pile of ground powder he had collected above the quarry.

"How do we measure it?" Mikil asked.

Despite his active participation, William's frown persisted.

"Like this." Thomas spilled the white powder in a line the length of his arm and tidied it so that it was roughly the same width for the entire length. "Seventy-five percent," he said. "And the charcoal . . ." He made another line of charcoal next to the white powder.

"Fifteen percent charcoal. One-fifth the length of saltpeter." He marked the line in five equal segments and swept four of them to one side.

"Now 10 percent sulfur." He poured the yellowed powder in a line two-thirds the length of the black powder.

"Look right to you?"

"Roughly. How exact does it have to be?"

"We're going to find out."

He mixed all three piles until he had a gray mess of powder.

"Not exactly black, is it? Let's light it up."

Mikil stood and backed away. "You're going to light it? Isn't it dangerous?"

"Watch." He made a trail of it and stood. "Maybe it's too much." He thinned the line so that it doubled in length to the height of a man.

William backed up a few steps, but he was clearly less concerned than Mikil.

"Ready?"

Thomas withdrew his flint wheel, a device that made sparks by striking flint against a rough bronze wheel. He started to roll the wheel on his palm but then opted for his thigh guard because his palm was moist with sweat. He lit a small roll of shredded bark.

Fire.

Mikil had backed up another few paces.

Thomas knelt at one end of the gray snake, lowered the fire, and touched it to the powder.

Nothing happened.

William grunted. "Huh."

And then the powder caught and hissed with sparks. A thick smoke boiled into the night air as the thin trail of black powder raced with fire.

"Ha!"

Mikil ran over. "It works?"

William had lowered his arms. He stared at the black mark on the rocks, then knelt and touched it. "It's hot." He stood. "I really don't see how this is going to bring down a cliff."

"It will when it's packed into bound leather bags. It burns too fast for the bags to contain the fire, and *boom*!"

"Boom," Mikil said.

"You've frowned enough for one evening, William. This is no small feat. Let your face relax."

"Fire from dirt. I will admit, it's pretty impressive. You got this from your dreams?"

"From my dreams."

Three hours later they had filled forty leather canteen bags, each the size of a man's head, with black powder, then wound these tightly in rolls of canvas. The rolls were hard, like rocks, and each had a small opening at its mouth, from which a strip of cloth that had been rolled in powder protruded.

Thomas called them bombs.

"Twenty along each cliff," Thomas instructed. "Five at each end and ten along the stretch through the middle. We have to at least box them in. Hurry. The sun will be up in two hours."

They crammed the bombs deep into the fault lines of each cliff for a mile on either side of the sleeping Horde. The strips of canvas rolled in powder ran up and then back, ten feet. The idea was to light them and run.

The rest was in Elyon's hands.

Placing the bombs took a full hour. Light already grayed the eastern sky above. The Horde began to stir. A hundred of the Forest Guard had been sent for more arrows. In the event that only half of the army below was crushed by rock, Thomas determined to fill the remainder with arrows. It would be like shooting fish in a barrel, he explained.

Thomas stood on the lookout, balancing the last bomb in his right hand.

"Are we ready?"

"You're keeping one out?" William asked.

Thomas studied the tightly rolled powder ball. "This, my friend, is our backup plan."

The canyon was gray. The Horde lay in their filth. Forty of Thomas's men knelt over fuses with their flint wheels ready.

Thomas took a deep breath. He closed his eyes. Opened them.

"Fire the north cliff."

A soft whoosh sounded behind him. The archer released the signal arrow. Fire shot into the sky, trailing smoke.

Twenty stood with Thomas on the ledge. They all stared at the cliff and waited.

And waited.

Nausea swept through Thomas's stomach.

"How long does it take?" someone asked.

As if in answer, a spectacular display of fire shot into the sky far down the cliff.

But it wasn't an explosion. The trapped bomb hadn't been strong enough to break its wrappings or the stone that squeezed it tight.

Another display went off closer. Then another and another. One by one the bombs ignited and spewed fire into the sky.

But they did not break the cliff.

Scabs began to scream in the canyon. None had seen such a show of power before. But it wasn't the kind of power Thomas needed.

He dropped the last bomb into his saddlebag and swung onto his horse. "Mikil, do not fire the southern cliff! Hold for my signal. One horn blast."

"Where are you going?"

"Down."

"Down to the Horde? Alone?"

"Alone."

He spun the stallion and kicked it into a full gallop.

Below, the Horde's cries swelled. But by the time Thomas reached the sandy wash, their fear had abated. Fire had erupted from the rocks above them, but not one Scab had been hurt.

Thomas entered the canyon and rode straight for their front lines at a full run. The sky was now a pale gray. Before him stretched a hundred thousand Scabs. Eighty thousand—his men had killed twenty thousand yesterday. None of this mattered. Only the ten thousand directly ahead, packed from side to side and watching him ride, mattered right now.

He leaped over the boulders the Forest Guard had used as a fighting base yesterday. If Desert Dwellers had trees and could make bows and arrows, they could have brought him down then, while he was still fifty yards out.

Thomas slid to a stop just out of spear range. *Elyon, give me strength.*

"Desert Dwellers! My name is Thomas of Hunter! If you wish to live even another hour, you will bring me your leader. I will speak to him and he will not be harmed. If your leader is a coward, then you will all die when we rain fire down from the skies and burn you to cinders!"

He calmed his stamping stallion and reached for the bomb in his saddlebag. He was playing this by ear, and it was a dangerous tune.

A loud rumble suddenly cracked the morning air and rolled over the canyon. A small section of cliff crashed down so far to the back of the army that Thomas could hardly see it. Dust rose to the sky.

A bomb had actually exploded! One bomb in twenty. Maybe a spark that had smoldered and fumed before detonating in a weak spot.

How many had been crushed? Too few. Still, the Horde shifted away from the cliff in a ripple of terror.

Bolstered by this good fortune, Thomas thundered another challenge. "Bring me your leader or we will crush you all like flies!"

The front line parted, and a Scab warrior wearing the black sash of a general rode out ten paces and stopped. But he wasn't Qurong.

"We aren't fooled by your tricks!" the general roared. "You heat rocks with fire and split them with water. We can do this as well. You think we fear fire?"

"Then you don't know the kind of fire that Elyon has given us! If you lay down your weapons and retreat, we will spare your army. If you stay, we will show you the fires of hell itself."

"You lie!"

"Then send out a hundred of your men, and I'll show you Elyon's power!"

The general considered this. He snapped his fingers.

None moved.

He turned and barked an order.

A large group marched out ten paces and stopped. It was a very dangerous tune indeed. If the bomb in his lap didn't detonate, there would be no bluffing.

"I suggest you move to the side," Thomas said.

The general hesitated, then walked his horse slowly away from his men.

Thomas withdrew his flint wheel, lit a two-foot fuse, and let it burn halfway before urging his horse forward. He ran the steed directly at the warriors, hurled his smoking bomb among them, and veered sharply to his right.

The smoldering bag landed in the middle of the Scabs, who instinctively ran for cover.

But there was no cover.

With a mighty *whump,* the bomb exploded, flinging bodies into the air. The concussion hit Thomas full in the face, a hot wind that momentarily took his breath away.

The general had been knocked off his horse. He stood calmly and stared at the carnage. At least fifty of his men lay dead. Many others were wounded. Only a few escaped unscathed.

"Now you will listen," Thomas cried. "You doubt that we can bring these cliffs down on you with such a weapon?"

The general held his ground. Fear wasn't common among the Horde, but this man's steel was impressive. He refused to answer.

Thomas pulled out the ram's horn and blasted once.

"Then you will see another demonstration. But this is your last. If you do not withdraw, every last one of you will die today."

The fireworks started at the far end, only this time on the southern cliff. Thomas desperately hoped for at least one more explosion. One weak spot along the cliff, and one bag stuffed with black powder to send tons of rock—

Whump!

A section of cliff began to fall.

Whump! Whump!

Two more! Suddenly a full third of the cliff slipped off the face and thundered down onto the screaming Horde. A huge slab of rock, enough to cover a thousand men, crashed to the ground, and then slowly toppled over and slammed into the army. The earth quaked, and more rock fell. Dust roiled skyward. Horses panicked and reared.

The Horde weren't given to fear, but they weren't suicidal either. The general gave the order to retreat only moments after the stampede had begun.

Thomas watched in stunned silence as the army fled, like a receding tide. Thousands had been killed by the rock. Perhaps ten thousand. But the greater victory here was the fear he'd planted in their hearts.

His own army cautiously edged to the lip of the northern cliff. What remained of it. Like him, they watched in a kind of stupefied wonder. They could have killed even more Scabs with the arrows that had just arrived, but the Forest Guard seemed to have forgotten those.

It took only minutes for the last of the Horde to disappear into the desert. As was their custom, they killed their wounded as they retreated. There was enough meat in this canyon to feed the jackals and vultures for a year.

Thomas sat alone on his horse staring down the deserted canyon, still unnerved by the devastation they had wrought upon the enemy. This enemy of Elyon.

His whole army had gathered above, seven thousand including those who'd arrived in the night. They began to chase the fleeing enemy with a chant of victory.

"Elyon! Elyon! Elyon!"

After a few minutes the chant changed. From the west toward the east, a single name swept along the long line of warriors. The chant grew until it filled the canyon with a thunderous roar.

"Hunter! Hunter! Hunter!"

Thomas slowly turned his horse and walked up the valley. It was time to go home.

8

CRISIS WAS a strange beast. At times it united. At times it divided.

For the moment, this particular crisis had at least forced a few of Washington's elite to lay aside political differences and submit to the president's demands for an immediate meeting.

Clearly, a virus was neither Democrat nor Republican.

Even so, Thomas sat at the back of the auditorium feeling out of place in this company of leaders—not because he was unaccustomed to leadership, but because his own experience in leadership was vastly different from theirs. His leadership had more to do with strength and physical power than with the manipulative politics that he knew would assert itself here.

He gazed out over the twenty-three men and women whom the president had gathered in the conference hall off the West Wing. Thomas had flown westward, over the Atlantic, and with the time change arrived midday in Washington. Merton Gains had left him with the assurance that he would be called upon to address their questions soon. Bob Stanton, an assistant, would answer any questions in the meantime. Bob sat on one side, Kara on the other.

Funny thing about Kara. Was he older than her now, or still younger? His body was still twenty-five, no denying that. But what about his mind? She seemed to look to him more as an older brother now. He'd given her the details of his victory using the black powder, and she'd mostly listened with a hint of awe in her eyes.

"They're late," Bob said. "Should've started by now."

Thomas's mind drifted back to the victory in the Natalga Gap. There, he was a world-renowned leader, a battle-hardened general, feared by the Horde, loved by his people. He was a husband, and a father to two children.

His fifteen years as commander had been gracious to him, despite the misjudgments that William was kind enough to remind him of.

The chant still echoed through his mind. *Hunter, Hunter, Hunter.*

And here he was what? The twenty-five-year-old kid in the back who was going to talk about some psychic dreams he was having. *Grew up in the Philippines. Parents divorced. Mother suffers from manic depression. Never finished college. Mixed up with the mob. No wonder he's having these crazy dreams. But if President Robert Blair says he goes on, he goes on. Privileges of the office.*

A tall gray-haired man with a beak fit for a year bird walked on the stage and sat at a long table set up with microphones. He was followed by three others who took seats. Then the president, Robert Blair, entered and walked to the center seat. The meeting had the aura of a press conference.

"That's Ron Kreet, chief of staff, on the left," Bob said. "Then Graham Meyers, secretary of defense. I think you know Phil Grant, CIA. And that would be Barbara Kingsley, health secretary."

Thomas nodded. The big guns. The front row was crowded with vaguely familiar faces. Other cabinet members. Senators. Congressmen. Director of the FBI.

"Not often you get such a broad spectrum of power in one room," Bob said.

Ron Kreet cleared his throat. "Thank you for coming. As all of you know, the State Department received a letter by fax roughly fourteen hours ago that threatened our nation with a virus now known as the Raison Strain. You'll find a copy of this fax and all other pertinent documents in the folder you were given."

It was clear that not all of them had read the fax. A number flipped open their folders and shuffled through papers.

"The president has asked to speak to you personally on this matter." Kreet faced Robert Blair. "Sir."

Robert Blair had always reminded Thomas of Robert Redford. He didn't have as many freckles, but otherwise he was a spitting image of the actor. The president leaned forward and adjusted his mike, face relaxed, stern but not tense.

"Thank you for coming on such short notice." His voice sounded shallow. Blair shifted his head to one side and cleared his throat.

"I've thought of a dozen different ways to proceed, and I've decided to be completely candid. I've invited a panel to answer your questions in a moment, but let me summarize a situation that we're now opening up to you."

He took a deep breath. "A group of unconventional terrorists, whom we believe to be associated with a Swiss, Valborg Svensson, has released a virus in numerous cities throughout the world. These cities now include six of our own, and we believe that number will increase with each passing hour. We have verified the Raison Strain in Chicago, New York, Atlanta, Los Angeles, Miami, and Washington."

The room was still enough to pick out heavy breathers.

"The Raison Strain is an airborne virus that spreads at an unprecedented rate. It is lethal and we have no cure. According to our best estimates, three hundred million Americans will be infected by the virus within two weeks."

The room itself seemed to gasp, so universal was the reaction.

"That's . . . what are you saying?"

"I'm saying, Peggy, that if all the people in this room weren't infected ten minutes ago, you probably are now. I'm also saying that unless we find a way to deal with this virus, everyone living between New York and Los Angeles will be dead in four weeks."

Silence.

"You *knowingly* exposed us to this virus?" someone demanded.

"No, you were probably exposed before you set foot in this building, Bob."

Then noise. Lots of it. A cacophony of bewilderment and outrage. An older gentleman stood to Thomas's left.

"Surely you can't be sure of this. The claim will cause a panic."

A dozen others offered slightly less restrained agreement.

The president lifted his hand. "Please. Shut up and sit down, Charles! All of you!"

The man hesitated and sat. The room quieted.

"The only way we're going to make it through this is to focus on the problem. My blood has been drawn. I've tested positive for the Raison Strain. I have three weeks to live."

Smart man, Thomas thought. He'd effectively if only temporarily shut down the room.

The president reached to one side, lifted a ream of paper, and stood it on end using both hands. "The news doesn't get any better. The State Department received a second fax less than two hours ago. In it we have a very detailed and extensive demand. The New Allegiance, as they call themselves, will deliver an antivirus that would neutralize the threat of the Raison Strain. In exchange they have demanded, among other things, our key weapons systems. Their list is very specific, so specific that I'm surprised. It demands that the items be delivered to a destination of their choosing in fourteen days."

He lowered the paper with a gentle thump. "All of the nuclear powers have been given the same ultimatum. This, ladies and gentlemen, is not a group of schoolboys or some half-witted terrorists we're dealing with. This is a highly organized group that has every intention of radically shifting the balance of world power in the next twenty-one days."

He stopped and scanned the room. They were in a freeze frame.

A man in the front voiced the thought screaming through each of their minds. "That's . . . that's impossible."

The president didn't respond.

"Is that possible?" the man asked.

Bob leaned over to Thomas. "Jack Spake, ranking Democrat," he whispered.

"Is what possible?"

"Shipping our weapons in two weeks."

"We're analyzing that now. But they've been . . . selective. They seem to have considered everything."

"And you're telling us that with the brightest scientists and the best health-care professionals in the world, we have *no* way to deal with this virus?"

The president deferred to his secretary of health. "Barbara?"

"Naturally, we're working on that." Feedback squealed and she backed off before regaining the mike. "There are roughly three thousand virologists in our country qualified to work on a challenge of this magnitude, and we're securing their, um, assistance as we speak. But you have to understand that we're dealing with a mutation of a genetically engineered vaccine here—literally billions of DNA and RNA pairs. Unraveling an antivirus may take more time than we have. Raison Pharmaceutical, the creator of the vaccine from which the virus was adapted, is providing us with everything they have. Their information alone will take a week to sort through, even with the help of their own geneticists. Unfortunately, their top geneticist in charge of the project has gone missing. We believe she has been kidnapped by these same terrorists."

The magnitude of the problem was beginning to settle in.

A dozen questions erupted at once, and the president insisted on a semblance of order. Questions on the virus were fired in salvos and answered in fashion.

What about other forms of treatment? How does the virus work? How fast does it spread? How long before people start dying?

Barbara handled them all with a professionalism that Thomas found admirable. She showed them the same computer simulation that he'd seen in Bangkok, and when the screen went blue at the end, the questions came to a halt.

"So basically, this . . . this thing isn't going away, and we have no way to deal with it. In three weeks we'll all be dead. There's nothing . . . nothing at all that we can do. Is that what I'm hearing?"

"No, Pete, we're not saying that," the president said. "We're saying that we don't know of any way to deal with it. Not yet."

To their right a man with black hair and a perfectly round face stood. "And what happens if we give in to their demands?"

Bob leaned over. "Dwight Olsen. Senate majority leader. Hates the president."

The president deferred to the secretary of defense, Graham Meyers.

"As we see it, giving in to their demands is out of the question," Meyers said. "We don't deal with terrorists. If we were to hand over the weapons systems they've demanded, the United States would be left defenseless. We assume that these people are working with at least one sovereign nation. In the space of three weeks, that nation would hold enough power to manipulate whomever it wishes through threat of force. They would essentially enslave the world."

"Having a military doesn't give a nation control of the world," Olsen said. "The USSR had a military and didn't use it."

"The USSR had an opponent with as many nuclear weapons as they did. These people intend to disarm anyone with the will to deter them. You have to understand, they're demanding the delivery systems, the nukes, even our aircraft carriers, for crying out loud! They may not immediately have the personnel to man a battle group, but if they have our delivery systems, they won't need to. They're also demanding evidence, very detailed I might add, that we have disabled all of our early warning systems and long-range radar. Like the president said, we're not dealing with Boy Scouts here. They seem to know what they're talking about."

"What if one of the other countries hands over their weapons?" someone asked.

"We're doing our best to make sure that doesn't happen."

"But the alternative to handing over our weapons is death, right?" Dwight Olsen again.

The president reasserted himself. "Both are death. The only alternative that has any merit in my mind is to beat them up-front before the virus does its damage."

"The virus is already doing its damage."

"Not if we can find them and the antivirus in the next three weeks. It's the only course of action that makes any sense."

"Which I can assure you we're working on as we speak," CIA Director Phil Grant said. "We've temporarily suspended all other cases, over nine thousand, and directed all of our assets at locating these people."

"And what are your chances of doing that?" Olsen asked.

"We'll find them. The trick will be to find the antivirus with them."

The president leaned forward into his mike. "In the meantime, I think it's important that we confront this in the strictest of confidence. We need some ideas. Anything you can think of—I'm all ears. I don't care how crazy it sounds."

A kind of mad chaos overtook the room for the next hour. *They all seemed to function in it, but to say they controlled it would be wrong,* Thomas thought. *The chaos controlled them.*

He watched the verbal sparring, taken by it. It was not so different from his own Council. Here was an advanced civilization doing precisely what his own people did, exploring and vigorously defending ideas, not with swords, but with tongues as sharp as swords.

He stopped keeping track of who asked questions and who answered, but he mulled each one carefully. Americans really did have a kind of uncommon resourcefulness when pressed.

"It would seem that slowing the spread of the virus could at least buy us time," a handsome woman in a navy business suit observed. "Time is both our greatest enemy and our greatest ally. We should shut down travel."

"And cause widespread panic? A threat of this magnitude would bring out the worst in people."

"Then offer them another reason," the woman responded. "Issue a heightened terror alert based on information we can't disclose. They'll assume we're dealing with a bomb or something. Ground air travel and shut the airports. Stop all interstate travel. Anything we can to slow the spread of the virus. Even a day or two could make the difference, right?"

Barbara, the secretary of health, responded. "Technically, yes."

No one objected.

"Frankly, we might be better off concentrating on the antivirus and the means to distribute it on short notice. Getting a vaccine out to six billion people isn't an easy chore."

"But you're saying that everyone here is supposedly infected?" someone asked. "Shouldn't we isolate whatever command and control hasn't been infected? Keep them in isolation as long as is necessary."

"Can you insulate people from this thing?" someone else asked.

"There has to be a way. Clean rooms. Put them on the space shuttle and send them to the space station for all I care."

"To what end? What good are a couple hundred generals in the space station if the rest of the world is dying?"

"Then isolate the scientists who are working on the antivirus. Or give the space station the codes to launch a few well-aimed nukes down the throats of whoever's caused this thing if it ever gets to that."

To what end? Thomas wondered. Retaliation felt hollow in the face of death. The debate stalled.

"We lead this country, we die with this country if it comes down to that," the president finally said. "But I don't see the harm of insulating a thread of command and control and as many scientists as possible."

The chaos gradually gave way to a sober tension. Crisis sometimes divided and sometimes united. Now it united.

At least for the moment.

The meeting was two hours old when the question that brought Thomas forward was finally asked.

The blue-suited woman. The smart one. "How do we know that they actually have an antivirus?"

No answer.

"Isn't it possible that they're bluffing? If it takes us months to create a vaccine or an antivirus, how is it they have one? You said the Raison Strain is a brand-new virus, less than a week old, a mutation of the Raison Vaccine. How did they get an antivirus in under a week?"

The president glanced toward Thomas near the back, then nodded at Deputy Secretary Gains, who stood and walked to an open mike. He'd spoken only a few times during the entire discussion, deferring to his superior, Secretary of State Paul Stanley, as a political courtesy, Thomas assumed.

"There's more to this. Nothing that changes what you've heard, but something that may assist us in a more . . . unconventional way. I hesitate because I'm about to open Pandora's box, but considering the situation, I think it best to go ahead."

Any trace of desire Thomas had to speak to this group suddenly vacated him. He was no more a politician than he was a rat.

"Roughly two weeks ago a man called one of our offices and claimed that he was having some strange dreams."

Thomas closed his eyes. Here they went.

"He came to the conclusion that the dreams were real, because in his dreams there were history books that recorded the histories of Earth. He could go to these history books and learn who won the Kentucky Derby this year, for example. Which he did, *before* the Derby was run, mind you. And he was right. Actually made over three hundred thousand on the long shot. The information in the history books from his dream world was real. Exact."

Thomas was a little surprised there weren't at least a few snickers.

"The reason he called our offices was because he learned something rather disturbing, namely, that a malicious virus named the Raison Strain would be released around the world this week. Again, this was nearly two weeks ago, before the Raison Strain even existed."

They were at least listening.

"No one listened to him, of course. Who would? He went to Bangkok and took matters into his own hands. For the past week he has been feeding us a steady diet of facts, all in advance of their happening."

He paused. No one was moving.

"I flew to Bangkok yesterday on the request of the president," Gains said. "What I have seen with my own eyes would leave you in shock. Like me, you've probably come to the conclusion that our nation is in a very, very bad place. The situation seems hopeless. If there's any one person who can save this country, ladies and gentlemen, it might very well be Thomas Hunter. Thomas?"

Thomas stood and stepped into the aisle. He walked toward the front, feeling self-conscious in the black slacks and white shirt he'd purchased at the mall on their way here from the airport. He must look very, very strange. *Here is the man who has seen the end of the world.* He was as disconnected from their reality as the Hulk or Spiderman.

He covered the mike. "I'm not sure this is going to do any good," he said quietly. The president held him with a steady gaze.

"Make them believe, Thomas," Gains said. "Let them ask their questions." He offered an anemic smile and stepped aside.

Thomas faced the audience. Twenty-three sets of eyes, as unsure and awkward as he was, stared at him.

He felt sweat bead on his forehead. If they knew how uncertain he felt, his information would fall on deaf ears. He had to play his part with as much conviction as he could muster. It didn't matter if they accepted him or liked him. Only that they heard him.

"I know this all sounds pretty crazy to some of you, maybe all of you. And that's okay." His voice sounded loud in the still room. "My name is Thomas Hunter, and the fact is, no matter how I know what I know—no matter how incredible it sounds to you—I do know a few things. If you follow what I'm about to tell you, you may have a chance. If you don't, you'll probably be dead in less than twenty-one days."

He sounded far too confident. Even cocky. But it was the only way he knew in this reality.

"Should I continue?"

"Continue, Thomas," the president said behind him.

His reservations fell like loosed chains. The plain truth was that he probably had more to offer the country than any other person in this room. And not because he wanted to carry such a responsibility. He had nothing to lose. None of them did.

"Thank you."

Thomas strolled to his right, then remembered the mike and walked back, studying them. He may get only one shot at this, so he would give it to them in a language that would at least cause a stir.

"I've lived a lifetime in the past two weeks. I've also learned some things in that lifetime. In particular, that most men and women will yield to the strong currents sucking them into the seas of ruin. Only the strongest in mind and spirit will swim against that current. A bit philosophical maybe, but it's what some people say where I come from, and I agree."

He paused and made eye contact with the navy-suited woman whose question had led to Gains's introduction.

"You'll all be sucked out to sea if you're not very, very careful. I know I must sound like a spiritual adviser to you. Not so. I'm only speaking what I know, and here's what I know."

The woman was smiling gently. Support or incredulity, he didn't know. Didn't care.

"I know that the Swiss will have the antivirus if he doesn't already. I know this because that's what the history books say. Some people survive. Without an antivirus any survival would be impossible."

Thomas took a breath and tried to read them, but the difference between being shocked by a speaker's knowledge and being shocked by his audacity was a difficult thing to gauge.

"Furthermore, I know that the U.S. will eventually yield to his demands and hand over its weapons. I know that the whole world will give in to this man, and even then, half of the world's population will die, though I can only guess which half. This will lead into a time of terrible tribulation."

He sounded like a prophet, or like a schoolteacher lecturing children. It was the last thing he wanted, although he supposed in some unconventional way he was a prophet. Was it possible that he was meant to be here today?

"If you give in to the Swiss, you'll follow the course of history as it's written. You'll be sucked out to sea. Your only hope is to resist those who demand you yield. You'll either find a way to change history, or you'll follow its course and die, as it is written."

"Excuse me."

It was Olsen, the black-haired man who Bob claimed was an enemy of the president. He was grinning wickedly.

"Yes, Mr. Olsen?"

The man's eyes twitched. He hadn't expected to be called by name.

"You're saying that you're a psychic? The president is now counseling psychics?"

"I don't even believe in psychics," Thomas said. "I am simply someone who knows more than you do about a few things. The fact, for example, that you will die in less than twenty-one days due to massive hemorrhaging in your heart and lungs and liver. You will have less than twenty-four hours from the onset of symptoms to your death. I know it all sounds a bit harsh, but then I'm assuming none of you has the time for games."

Olsen's smug grin vanished.

"I also suspect that within one week you will lead a motion to give in to Svensson's demands. That's not from the Books of Histories, you understand. It's my judgment based on what I've observed of you today. If I'm right, you are the kind of man the rest in this room must resist."

Gains chuckled nervously. "I'm sure Thomas isn't entirely sincere. He has unique . . . wit, as I'm sure you can see. Are there other questions?"

"Are you serious?" Olsen demanded, looking at Gains. "You actually have the audacity to parade a circus act in front of us at a time like this?"

"Dead serious!" Gains said. "We're here today because we didn't listen to this man two weeks ago. He told us what, he told us where, he told us when, and he told us why, and we ignored him. I suggest you take every word he speaks as though it were from God himself."

Thomas cringed. He hardly faulted the group for their doubt. They had no reference against which to judge him.

"So you learned about all of this because it's all recorded in some history books in another reality?" the navy-suited woman asked.

"Your name?" Thomas asked.

"Clarice Morton," she said, glancing at the president. "Congresswoman Morton."

"The answer is yes, Ms. Morton. I really did. Any number of events can confirm that. I knew about the Raison Strain over a week ago. I reported it to the State Department and then to the Centers for Disease Control. When neither was helpful, I flew to Bangkok myself. In an admittedly desperate act, I kidnapped Monique de Raison—perhaps you heard about that. I was attempting to help her understand how dangerous her vaccine really was. Needless to say, she now understands."

"So you convinced her before this all happened?"

"She demanded specific information from me. I went into the histories and retrieved the information. She knew then. That was before Carlos shot me and took her. They're undoubtedly using her now to create the antivirus."

"You were shot?"

"A very long story, Ms. Morton. Moot at this point."

Gains was having difficulty suppressing a small grin.

"So if this really is all true, if you can get information about the future as a matter of history—and for the moment I'm going to believe you can—then can you find out what happens next?"

"If I could find the Books of Histories, technically, yes. I could."

She glanced at the president. "And if you can find out what is going to happen, then we might be able to find out how to stop it, right?"

"We might be able to, yes. Assuming history can be changed."

"But we have to assume it can be, or all of this is all moot, as you say."

"Agreed."

"So then can you find out what happens next?"

Thomas had understood where she was going, but not until now did her simple suggestion strike a chord in his mind. The problem, of course, was that the Books of Histories were no longer available. He'd lived with that realization for fifteen years. But rumor was they still existed. He'd never had reason to search them out. Defending the forests from the Horde and celebrating the Great Romance had been his primary passion in the forest. Now he had a very good reason to search them out. They might provide a way out of this mess, precisely as Clarice was suggesting.

"Actually, the Books of Histories . . . are not presently available."

A murmur rippled through the room. It was as if this little bit of information actually interested them. They were incensed. *How convenient. The Books of Histories have gone missing! Yes, of course, what did you expect? It always works that way.*

Or maybe they were disappointed. Some of them at least wanted to believe everything he had said.

And so they should. Decent men and women could see sincerity when it stared them in the face.

"This is absurd!" Olsen said.

"Then I'm afraid that I'm leaning toward the absurd, Dwight," the president said. "Thomas has earned himself a voice. And I think Clarice is on to something. Can you find anything more for us, Thomas?"

Could he? His answer was as calculating as it was truthful. "Maybe."

Olsen muttered something, but Thomas couldn't make it out.

The president closed his folder. "Good. Ladies and gentlemen, please send any additional thoughts and comments through my staff. Good evening. And may God preserve our nation." He stood and left the room.

Now the crisis would divide.

———— ∞∞∞ ————

"Six more cities," Phil Grant said, slapping the folder down on the coffee table. His maroon silk tie hung loose around his neck. He ran a finger under his collar and loosened it even more. "Including St. Petersburg. They're climbing the walls. If the Russians keep this under their hats, it'll be a miracle."

"This . . . this is a nightmare," his assistant said. Thomas watched Dempsey walk to the window and stare out with a lost gaze. "The Russians have decades of experience keeping things under the lid. I'd worry about the United States. If I were a betting man, I'd say Olsen's already leaking this. How many did you say?"

"Twenty. All airports. Like clockwork."

"We *aren't* closing the airports?"

"CDC ran another simulation using the latest data. They say closing the airports won't help at this point. There've been over ten thousand flights in the continental U.S. since the virus first hit New York. Conservative estimates have a quarter of the country exposed already."

Grant put his elbows on his knees and formed a tent with his fingers. A slight tremor shook his hands. Dempsey paced back from the window, frowning. Sweat darkened his pale blue shirt at the armpits. The full reality of what had been delivered to the United States of America was finally and terribly settling into the CIA.

Grant had brought Thomas to the CIA headquarters in Langley forty-five minutes ago.

"You're convinced this psychologist is worth our time?" Thomas asked. "It just seems like a lot of downtime."

"On the contrary, trying to unlock that mind of yours is the only thing that makes sense where you're concerned," Grant said.

"Memories, maybe. But I wouldn't assume that whatever is happening is happening in my head," Thomas replied.

"I'll settle for memories. If you gave the antivirus characteristics to Carlos like you think you may have, that information would be a memory. With any luck Dr. Myles Bancroft can stimulate that memory. You have no information, none whatsoever, on where Svensson might be holing up?"

"None."

"Or where he could have Monique?"

"I assume she's wherever he is. The only communication has been through the faxes, sent from an apartment in Bangkok. We took it down six hours ago. It was empty except for a laptop. He's using relays. Smart to stay off the Web by using facsimile. The last fax came from an address in Istanbul. As far as we know, he has a hundred relays. Took us how long to track down Bin Laden? This guy could be worse. But in a few days I doubt it will matter. As you pointed out earlier, he's undoubtedly working with others. Likely a country. You'll know where to look then."

"But only because he wants us to know. We can't very well bomb Argentina or whatever country he's using. Not as long as he has the antivirus." The director stood and grunted. "The world's coming apart at the seams and we're sitting here, blind as bats," Grant replied.

"Whatever happens, don't let anyone talk the president into compromising," Thomas said.

"I think you'll have the opportunity to do that yourself," Grant said. "He wants to meet with you personally tomorrow."

The phone rang. Grant snatched it up and listened for a moment. "On our way." He dropped the phone in its cradle. "He's ready. Let's go."

—⚬∞⚬—

Dr. Myles Bancroft was a frumpy, short man with wrinkled slacks and facial hair poking out of his orifices, overall not the kind of man most people would associate with the Pulitzer Prize. He wore a small knowing grin that was immediately disarming—a good thing, considering what he played with.

People's minds.

His lab occupied a small basement on the south side of Johns Hopkins's campus. They'd flown Thomas in by helicopter and hurried him down the steps as if he were a man committed to the witness protection program and they'd received warnings of snipers on the adjoining roofs.

Thomas faced the cognitive psychologist in the white concrete room. Two of Grant's men waited with crossed legs in the lobby. Grant had remained in Langley with a thousand concerns clogging his mind.

"So basically you're going to try to hypnotize me, and then you're going to hook me up to these machines of yours and make me fall asleep while you toy with my mind using electrical stimuli."

Bancroft grinned. "Basically, yes. I describe it using more glamorous, fun words, but in essence you have the picture, lad. Hypnosis can be rather unreliable. I won't josh you. It requires a particularly cooperative subject, and I would like you to be that subject. But even if you're not, I may be able to accomplish some interesting results by Frankensteining you." Another grin.

Thomas liked this man immensely. "And can you explain this Frankensteining of yours? In terms I can understand?"

"Let me give it a whirl. The brain does record everything; I'm sure you know that. We don't know precisely how to access the information externally or to record memories, et cetera, et cetera. But we are getting close. We hook you up to these wires here and we can record the wave signatures emitted by the brain. Unfortunately, we're a bit fuzzy on the brain's language, so when we see a zip and a zap, we know it means something, but we don't yet know what zip or zap means. Follow?"

"So basically you're clueless."

"That about summarizes it. Shall we get started?"

"Seriously."

"Well, it's rather . . . speculative, I must admit, but here you go: I have been developing a way to stimulate memories. Different brain activities have different wave signatures. For example, in the simplest of terms, conceptual activity, or waking thought, looks different from perceptual, dream thought. I've been mapping and identifying those signatures for some time. Among countless other discoveries, we've learned that there's a connection between dreams and memories—similar signatures, you see. Similar brain language, as it were. Essentially what I'm going to do is record the signatures from your dreams and then force-feed them into the section of your brain that typically holds memory. This seems to excite the memory. The effect isn't permanent, but it does stimulate the memories of most subjects."

"Hmm. But you can't isolate any particular memories. You just have a general hope that I wake up remembering more than when I fell asleep."

"In some cases, yes. In others, subjects have dreams that turn out to be actual memories. It's like pouring liquid into a cup already brimming with water or, in this case, memories. When you pour the liquid in, the water is displaced over the lip. Quite fun actually. The memory stimulation even seems to help some subjects remember the dreams themselves. As you know, the average person experiences five dreams per night and remembers one at the most. Not so when I hook you up. Shall we begin?"

"Why not?"

"First, some basics. Vitals and whatnot. I need to draw some blood and have it analyzed by the lab for several common diseases that affect the mind. Just covering our bases."

Half an hour later, after a brief battery of simple tests followed by five failed attempts to lure Thomas into a hypnotic state, Bancroft changed tracks and hooked him up to the EEG machine. He connected twelve small electrodes to various parts of his head before feeding him a pill that would calm him without interfering with brain activity.

Then he turned down the lights and left the room. Moments later, soft music began to play through ceiling speakers. The chair Thomas lay in was similar to a dentist's chair. He wondered if there was a pill that could block his dreams. It was the last thought he had before slipping into deep sleep.

—— ∞∞∞ ——

Mike Orear left his office at CNN at six and struggled through traffic for the typical hour it took to reach Theresa Sumner's new home on the south side. He hadn't planned on seeing her tonight, though he wasn't complaining.

She had been called off to some assignment in Bangkok for the CDC and returned earlier today to another private meeting in Washington. A bit unusual, but only a bit. They both lived lives full of curve balls and sudden changes in plan.

Theresa had called him from the tarmac at Reagan International, telling him to get his sorry self to her house tonight by eight. She was in one of her irresistibly bossy moods, and after giving her a piece of his mind, mostly nonsense that made for good drama, he agreed as they both knew he would before she'd even asked. He'd only been to her new house three or four times in the ten months they'd dated, and he never left disappointed.

A white box-looking car—a Volvo—rode to his right and a black Lincoln to his left. Neither of the drivers looked at him when he drilled them with a good stare. This was the rush hour in Atlanta, and everyone was lost in his own world, oblivious to anyone else's. These zombies floated through life as if nothing would ever matter in the end.

Three years ago, his reassignment to the Atlanta office from North Dakota to anchor the late-afternoon hours was a good thing. Now he wasn't so sure. The city had its distractions, but he was growing tired of pursuing them. One of these days he would have to quit playing the tough guy and settle down with someone more like Betty than Theresa.

On the other hand, he liked playing most of this game he was playing.

He could turn the tough act on or off with the flip of a hidden switch, a real advantage in this business. To the audience and some of his peers, he was the genuine North Dakota face with a GQ shadow and dark wavy hair that they could always trust. To others, like Theresa, he was the enigmatic college quarterback who could have made pro if not for the drugs.

Now he threw words instead of balls and could deliver them at any pace required by the game.

He finally pulled his BMW in front of the white house on the corner of Langshershim and Bentley.

He sighed, opened the door, and unfolded himself from the front seat. Her car was in the garage. He could just see the SUV's roof rack through the window.

He sauntered up to the door and rang the bell.

Theresa opened the door and walked back into the kitchen without a word. See, now Betty, the girl he'd dated for two years during college, never would have done that—not knowing he'd driven for an hour to see her. Well, maybe she would as a come-on now and then, but never while wearing this distant, nearly angry look.

Her short blond hair was disheveled and her face was drawn—not exactly the tempting, sexy look he had expected. She pulled a wineglass from her rack and poured Sauvignon Blanc.

"Am I wrong, or did you actually invite me out here?" he asked.

"I did. And thank you. I'm sorry, I just . . . it's been a long day." She forced a smile.

This wasn't a game. She was obviously bothered by something that had happened on her trip. Theresa put both hands on the counter and closed her eyes. He registered alarm for the first time.

"Okay, what's wrong?"

"Nothing. Nothing I can tell you. Just a bad day." She took a long drink and set the glass down. "A very bad day."

"What do you mean you can't tell me? Your job's okay?"

"For the time being." She took another drink. He saw that her hand was trembling.

Mike stepped forward. Took the glass from her hand. "Tell me."

"I can't tell—"

"For crying out loud, Theresa, just tell me!"

She stepped away from the counter and ran her hands through her hair, blowing out a long sigh. He couldn't remember ever seeing her in this condition. Someone had died, or was dying, or something terrible had happened to her mother or the brother who lived in San Diego.

"If you're trying to scare me, you've already done it. So if you don't mind, let's cut the games. Just tell me."

"They'd kill me if I told you. *You* of all people."

"'You' meaning me in the news?" She'd said too much already, and her quick side glance confirmed it. Something had gone down that would make her sweat bullets and send a newsman like him into orbit. And she was sworn to secrecy.

"Don't you kid yourself," he said, grabbing a glass from the rack. "You called me down here to tell me something, and I can guarantee you I won't leave until you do. Now we can sit down and get sloshed before you tell me, or you can tell me straight up while we still have our full wits about us. Your choice."

"What kind of assurance that you don't go public with this?"

"Depends."

"Then forget it." Her eyes flashed. "This isn't the kind of thing that 'depends' on anything you think or don't think." She wasn't in complete control of herself. Whatever had happened was bigger than a death or an accident.

"This has something to do with the CDC, right? What, the West Nile virus is loose in the White House?"

"I swear, if you even breathe—"

"Okay." He lifted both hands, balancing the glass in his right. "Not a word about anything."

"That's not—"

"I swear, Theresa! You have my complete assurance that I won't breathe a word to anyone outside this house. Just tell me!"

She took a deep breath. "It's a virus."

"A virus. I was right?"

"This virus makes the West Nile virus look like a case of hiccups."

"What then? Ebola?" He was half-kidding, but she glared at him, and for a horrible moment he thought he might have hit it.

"You're kidding, right?"

Of course she wasn't kidding. If she was kidding, her upper lip wouldn't be misty with sweat.

"The Ebola?"

"Worse."

He felt the blood drain from his face.

"Where?"

"Everywhere. We're calling it the Raison Strain." The tremor had spread from her hands to her voice. "It was released by terrorists in twenty-four cities today. By the end of the week every person in the United States will be infected, and there is no treatment. Unless we find a vaccine or something, we are in a load of hurt. Atlanta was one of the cities."

He couldn't quite sort all of this into the boxes he used to understand his world. What kind of virus was worse than Ebola?

"Terrorists?"

She nodded. "They're demanding our nuclear weapons. The *world's* nuclear weapons."

Mike stared at her for a long time.

"Who's infected? I mean, when you say Atlanta, you aren't necessarily saying—"

"You're not listening, Mike. There's no way to stop this thing. For all we know, everyone at CNN is already infected."

He was infected? Mike blinked. "That's . . . how can that be? I don't feel like I have anything."

"That's because the virus has a three-week latency period. Trust me, if we don't figure this out, you'll feel something in a couple weeks."

"And you don't think the people deserve to know this?"

"Why? So they can panic and run for the hills? I swear, Mike, if you even look funny at anyone down at the network, I'll personally kill you! You hear me?" She was red.

He set his glass on the counter and then leaned on the cabinet for balance. "Okay, okay, just calm down." There was still something wrong with what she'd told him. He couldn't put his finger on it, but something didn't compute.

"There has to be a mistake. This . . . this kind of thing just doesn't happen. No one knows about this?"

"The president, his cabinet, a few members of Congress. Half the governments in the world. And there is no mistake. I ran some of the tests myself. I've studied the model for the past twelve hours. This is it, Mike. This is the one we all hoped would never come."

Theresa dropped into an armchair, rested her head, closed her eyes, and swallowed.

Mike straddled a table chair, and for a long time neither spoke. The air conditioner came on and blew cold air through his hair from a ceiling vent. The refrigerator hummed behind him. Theresa had opened her eyes and was staring at the ceiling, lost.

"Start at the beginning," he said. "Tell me everything."

—— ∞ ——

There was a problem with the EEG.

Bancroft knew this wasn't true. He knew that something strange was happening in that mind that slept in his chair, but the scientist in him demanded he eliminate every possible alternative.

He switched out the EEG, plugged the twelve electrodes back in, and reset it. Wave patterns consistent with conceptual brain activity ran across the screen. Same thing. He knew it. Same thing as the other unit. There were no perceptual waves.

He checked the other monitors. Facial color, eye movement, skin temperature. Nothing. Not a single cottonpickin' thing. Thomas Hunter had been asleep for two hours. His breathing was deep and his body sagged in the chair. No doubt about it, this man was lost to the world. Asleep.

But that's where the typical indications ended. His skin temperature had not changed. His eyes had not entered REM. The signatures on the EEG did not show a hint of a perceptual signature.

Bancroft walked around the patient twice, running down a mental checklist of alternative explanations.

None.

He walked into his office and called the direct line Phil Grant had given him.

"Grant."

"Hello, Mr. Grant. Myles Bancroft with your boy here."

"And?"

"And I think we have a problem."

"Meaning what?"

"Meaning your boy's not dreaming."

"How's that possible? Does that happen?"

"Not very often. Not this long. He's sleeping, no doubt. Plenty of brain activity. But whatever's going on in that head of his isn't characterized by anything I've seen. Judging by the monitors, I'd say he's awake."

"I thought you said he was sleeping."

"He is. Ergo, the problem."

"I'll be over. Keep him dreaming."

The man hung up before Bancroft could correct him.

Thomas Hunter wasn't dreaming.

9

RACHELLE HEARD the ululating cries on the edge of her consciousness, beyond the sounds of Samuel's singing and Marie's hopeless efforts to correct his tone deafness. But her subconscious had been trained to hear this distant cry, day or night.

She gasped and jumped to her feet, straining for the sound. "Samuel, hush!"

"What is it?" Marie asked. Then she heard the warbling cries too. "Father!"

"Father, father!" Samuel cried.

They lived in a wooden hut, large and circular with two floors, both of which had doors leading to the outside. The doors were one of Thomas's pride and joys. Nearly ten thousand houses circled the lake now, most of them among the trees set back from the wide swath cleared around the waters, but none had a door quite like Thomas's. It was the first and best hinged double door in all the land, as far as Thomas was concerned, because it could swing both ways for fast entry or exit.

The top floor where they slept had a normal locking door that opened onto a walkway, which was part of a labyrinth of suspended walkways linking many homes. The bottom floor, where Rachelle was ladling hot stew into tin bowls, boasted the hinged double door. The hinges were made of leather, which also acted as a kind of spring to keep the doors closed.

Marie, being the oldest and fastest at fourteen, reached the door first and slammed through it.

Samuel was right behind. Too far behind. Too close behind. He met the doors as they released Marie. They smacked him in the forehead and dropped him like a sack of potatoes.

"Samuel!" Rachelle dropped to her knees. "Those cursed doors! Are you okay, my child?"

Samuel struggled to a sitting position, then shook his head to clear it.

"Come on!" Marie cried. "Hurry!"

"Get back here and help your brother," Rachelle yelled. "You've knocked him silly with the doors!"

By the time Marie returned, Samuel was on his feet and running through the doors. This time the doors struck Rachelle on the right arm, nearly knocking her down. She grunted and ran down the stone path after the children.

The doors had hurt her arm, she saw. They had opened a very small cut that could hardly concern her now. She ignored the thin trail of blood and ran on.

Streams of women and children ran the paths that led toward the gate where the high-pitched cries continued with growing intensity. They were definitely home. The only question was how many.

On every side grew winding puroon vines with lavender flowers similar to what Thomas described as bougainvillea and large tawii bushes with white silken petals, each spreading their sweet scent through the air. Like gardenia, Thomas said. Every home was draped in similar flowering vines according to a grand master plan that rendered the entire village a garden of beauty. It was the Forest People's best imitation of the colored forest.

Rachelle ran with a knot in her throat. Thomas may be the best fighter among them, but he was also their leader and the first to rush into the worst battles. Too many times he'd returned carrying the body of the soldier who'd fallen beside him. His good fortune couldn't last forever.

And William's order to prepare for evacuation had set the entire village on edge.

They converged on a seventy-foot-wide stone road that cut a straight line from the main gate to the lake. Night was falling, and the people were ready for celebration in anticipation of the Forest Guard's return. They mobbed the front gate, bouncing and dancing. Torches and branches were raised up high. The army was mounted, but with children on their mother's shoulders, the view was blocked.

A loud voice screamed above the din. This was the assistant to Ciphus—Rachelle could pick out his voice from a hundred yards. He was trying to move the people to the side as was customary.

The crowd suddenly settled and parted like a sea. Rachelle pulled up with Marie on one side and Samuel on the other. Then she saw Thomas where she always saw him, seated on his black stallion, leading his men, who stretched behind him into the forest. A bucket of relief washed over her.

"Father!"

"Wait, Samuel! First we honor the fallen."

The people parted farther, leaving a wide path for the warriors. The *clip-clop* of the horses' hoofs was now clearly audible.

Ciphus approached the front line and Thomas stopped his horse. They talked quietly for a moment. To Rachelle's right, thousands continued to line the road that led to the distant lake, now shimmering in rising moonlight. About thirty thousand lived here, and in the days to follow, their number would swell to a hundred thousand as the rest arrived for the annual Gathering.

Ciphus seemed to be taking longer than usual. Something was wrong. William had been emphatic about the seriousness of the situation when he'd ridden in yesterday to demand they prepare to evacuate, but they had won, hadn't they? Surely they hadn't come to announce that the Horde was only a day's march behind.

Ciphus turned slowly to face the throng. He waited a long time, and for every second he stood, the silence deepened until Rachelle thought that she could hear his breathing. He lifted both hands, tilted his face to the sky, and began to moan. This was the traditional mourning.

Yes, yes, Ciphus, but how many? Tell us how many!

Soft wails joined him. Then in a loud voice he cried, "They have taken three thousand of our sons and daughters!"

Three thousand! So many! They had never even lost a thousand.

The wails rose to fever-pitch cries of agony that reached out to the surrounding desert. First Thomas and then the rest of his men dismounted and sank to their knees, lowered their heads to the ground, and wept.

Rachelle fell to her knees with the rest, until the whole village knelt on the side of the road, weeping for the wives and mothers and fathers and daughters and sons who'd suffered such a terrible loss to the Horde. Only Ciphus stood, and he stood with arms raised in a cry to Elyon.

"Comfort your children, Maker of men! Take your daughters into your bosom and wipe away their tears. Deliver your sons from the evil that ravages what is sacred. Come and save us, O Elyon. Come and save us, lover of our souls!"

The custom of immediately marrying the widows to eligible men would be stretched very thin. There weren't enough men to go around. They were all dying. Rachelle's heart ached for those who would soon learn that their husbands were among the three thousand.

The mourning continued for about fifteen minutes, until Ciphus finished his long prayer. Then he lowered his arms and a hush fell over the crowd now standing.

"Our loss is great. But their loss is greater. Fifty thousand of the Horde have been sent to an appropriate fate on this day!"

A roar erupted down the line. The ground trembled with their throaty yells, motivated as much by the fresh horror of their own loss and their hatred of the Horde as by their thirst for victory.

Thomas swung back into his saddle and walked his horse up the road. At times like this he would sometimes acknowledge the crowd with nods and an uplifted hand, but tonight he rode with sobriety.

His eyes found Rachelle. She ran to him with Samuel and Marie. He leaned over and kissed her on the lips.

"You are my sunshine," he said.

"And you are my rainbow," she replied, tempted to haul him off the horse right now. He felt her teasing tug and grinned. Their sappy exchange was refreshing because it was so genuine. She loved him for it.

"Walk with me."

He kissed Marie and smiled. "As beautiful as your mother." He ruffled Samuel's hair.

They walked down the cheering line like that, Thomas in the saddle, Rachelle, Samuel, and Marie walking proudly on his right side. But there was a tension in Thomas's face. It wasn't only the price they had paid in battle that occupied his mind.

The moment they reached the wide sandy shores to the lake, Thomas dismounted, handed the horse off to his stable boy, and turned to his lieutenants.

"Mikil, William, we meet as soon as we've bathed. Suzan, bring Ciphus and whatever members of the Council you can find. Quickly." He kissed Rachelle on her forehead. "We need your wisdom, my love. Join us."

He hugged Samuel and Marie, whispered something in their ears. They ran off, undoubtedly up to some mischief.

Thomas took Rachelle's hand and led her to one of the twenty gazebos that overlooked a large amphitheater cut from the forest floor. The lake lay two hundred yards distant, just past a swath of clean white sand. They'd cleared the forest over the years, and as the village grew, they expanded the beach by relocating houses that had once been near the lake, such as their own. In their place they planted thick, rich grass and more than two thousand flowering trees, carefully positioned in concentric arcs leading to the sand. Hundreds of rosebushes and honeysuckles spotted the grass in tidy enclaves with benches for sitting. This end of the lake had been landscaped as a garden park fit for a king.

The lake's waters were not for drinking or washing—such water came from the springs—but only for bathing and only then without soap. The lake's shores were reserved for the nightly celebrations, which were getting underway around a large firepit.

Thomas and Rachelle would normally be among the first at the celebration, dancing and singing and retelling stories of Elyon's love that would stretch into the night. It had always been the highlight of their day. But at the moment Thomas's mind was a hundred miles away.

"Thomas. What is it?"

"It's the Southern Forest," he said. "We may lose the Southern Forest."

Thomas paced along the gazebo's half wall deep in thought. Torches blazed from each post. Down the shore, delighted laughter rose from the celebration. A long line of dancers, dressed in fabrics made from dark green leaves and white flowers, had linked arms and were moving in graceful circles around the bonfire. They were undoubtedly light with wine and stuffed with meat. Out on the lake, moonlight shone in a long white shaft.

For so long Thomas's people had waited for Elyon's deliverance. They'd spun a thousand stories about the way he might ultimately deliver them from the Horde. Would he rise from the lake and flood the desert with water to drown them? Or would he ride in on a mighty white horse and lead them in one final battle that rid the earth of the scourge once and for all?

Thomas turned to the gathered elders and lieutenants. "If there are two armies, there may be three. Otherwise, yes, Ciphus, I wouldn't hesitate to lead five thousand men to Jamous's aid tonight. But it's a full day's journey—nearly three days there and back. The Horde has never attacked us on two fronts until now. If our Guard vacate this forest while so many are coming for the annual Gathering—"

"Well, we won't change the Gathering. I promise you that."

"Half of our forces are out escorting the tribes. We're already stretched way too thin. To send more men to the Southern Forest puts us at great risk."

Mikil stood. "Then let me go with just a few of the Forest Guard. Jamous is still fighting, Thomas. You heard the runner!"

The runner had met them at the gates with fresh word from the south. Jamous was holding strong against the Horde. His first retreat had been a strategy to draw the Horde near the forest where his archers had the distinct advantage of cover. They had been fighting for three days now.

"How many men?"

"Give me five hundred," Mikil said.

"That would leave us weak here," William objected. "Here where the whole world will be gathered in less than a week. What if the Horde is weakening us for an assault on the forest, here, next week, when they can take us all in one blow?"

"He's right, Mikil," Thomas said. "I can't let you take five hundred."

"You're forgetting the bombs," Mikil said.

The news of their stunning victory was spreading like fire. He looked at Rachelle. They hadn't been alone yet, when he knew he'd get her true reaction to the fact that he'd started dreaming again. Still, with such a victory, what could she say?

What none of them knew was that he'd dreamed not once, but twice, the second time when they'd stopped for sleep returning from the battle. He'd dreamed that he'd gone before a special meeting called by the president of the United States and then been put to sleep by a psychologist. In his dream world, he was at this very moment lying in a chair in Dr. Bancroft's laboratory.

And he intended to dream again, tonight. He had to. If he could only make Rachelle understand that.

"Using the black powder, we could destroy the Horde!" Mikil said.

"Not on the open desert we won't," William said. "You'll kill a handful with each blast; that's it. And you're forgetting that we don't have any bombs at the moment."

"Then three hundred warriors."

"Three hundred," Thomas said. "But not you. Send another division and tell them to ride along the runners' route." They continually sent messengers on fast horses between the forests in a kind of mail system that Thomas had developed. "If they hear that Jamous has won before they arrive, have them turn back."

She stared at him for a moment, then turned to leave.

"I'm sorry, Mikil. I know what Jamous means to you, but I need you here."

She paused, and then left without another word.

Thomas motioned after her with his head. "Go with her, William. Suzan, organize a sweep of the forest perimeter. Let's be sure there isn't another Horde army lurking."

They both left.

"You really think the Horde would try something like that?" Rachelle asked.

"I wouldn't have thought so a month ago, but they're getting smart about the way they attack. Martyn is changing them."

"So then, we're agreed," Ciphus said. The elder stroked his long gray beard. He was one of the older Council members, seventy. Bathing in Elyon's waters didn't stop the aging process. "The Gathering will proceed as planned in five days."

"Yes."

"Regardless of the Southern Forest's fate."

"You think they may fall?" Thomas asked.

"No. Have any of our forests fallen? But if one does, then all the more reason for the Gathering."

"I suppose so."

Thomas looked at his wife. She was only a few years younger than he was, but she looked half his battle-worn age. There was no doubt in his mind but that she would make an incredible commander. But she was also a mother. And she was his wife. The thought of exposing her to death on the battlefield made him sick.

He walked to her and touched his hand to her cheek. "Have I told you lately how beautiful you are?" he asked. He leaned over and kissed her full on the lips while the others watched silently. Romance had become their religion, and they practiced it daily. When a person wandered into the desert and neglected swimming in Elyon's water, their memory of the colored forest and the love that Elyon had shown them in the old lake also dimmed. But here in the forest, lingering memories had prompted Ciphus and the Council to develop rituals determined to cherish those memories. The Great Romance consisted of rules and celebrations and traditions meant to keep the people from straying. The way that a husband or wife expressed love for his or her spouse was a part of that romance.

Rachelle winked. "Your love for me makes my face shine," she said. He kissed her again.

"Ciphus, what can you tell me of the Books of Histories?" he asked, turning from Rachelle. "They say that the Books still exist. Have you heard of them?"

"We don't need the Books of Histories. We have the lakes."

"Of course. But do you believe they exist?"

Ciphus stared at him past bushy brows. "They aren't books anyone wants," he said. "They were hidden from us a long time ago for good reason."

"I didn't know you were so averse to the Books," Thomas said. "I'm simply asking if you know anything about them."

"This sudden interest in the histories again. You were consumed with them before," Rachelle said. "It's the dreams, isn't it?"

"It's not like you might think, Rachelle, but yes. Nothing's changed there. When I awoke in Bangkok, only a night had passed!" He walked to the rail and gazed at the celebration, now in full swing. "I know it sounds ludicrous, but we may have a very serious problem." He turned to her. "They need me."

"What is Bangkok?" Ciphus asked.

"The world in his dreams," Rachelle said. "When he dreams, he believes that he goes to another place, that he's living in the ancient histories, before the Great Deception. He thinks that he can stop the virus that led to the times of tribulation. You see why the rhambutan is so important, Thomas? Once—only *once*—you sleep without the fruit and your mind is whisked away. Ludicrous!"

"This is why you're interested in the Books of Histories?" Ciphus asked. "To save a dream world?"

Thomas clutched the wound on his shoulder. Suzan had bandaged it with herbs and a broad leaf. A swim in the lake would do it some good, but the deep cut would take some time to heal.

"You see this wound? It didn't come from the Horde. It came from the world in my dreams."

"But surely that world isn't real," the elder said. "Is it?"

"Weren't you listening earlier when I told you about the black powder? I don't know how real it is, but this cut is real enough."

"Then Elyon is using your mind to help us," Ciphus said. "But if you're suggesting that the dreams he's using are real, that's an entirely different matter."

"Call it what you will, Ciphus. My shoulder hurts just the same."

"Please, Thomas." Rachelle drew her hand over his hair. "For all you know the Horde cut you and you just don't remember. Yes? Fascination with the histories pushed Tanis into the black forest to begin with."

"No. I won't have that on my head. His preoccupation was there before I began to dream. Tanis made his own choice."

She removed her hand. "And now you'll make yours," she said. "I will *not* have you dreaming again."

"And what if not dreaming threatens my own life? We are dying there! The virus will kill me. They depend on me, but just as much, my very existence here may depend on my ability to stop the virus there!"

"No, I can't listen to this. Of course they depend on you. Without you they don't exist to begin with!"

"You're willing to risk my life?"

"The last time you dreamed, we all died."

They faced off, romance quickly forgotten. He understood her aversion. What was it she had said? *I will not have you loving another woman in your dreams while I am suckling your child.* Something similar. She was still jealous of Monique.

"These dreams sound like so much nonsense to me," Ciphus said. "I would agree with Rachelle. There is no benefit in dreaming if you lose your mind in them. But if you want to know about the Books of Histories, then you'll have to speak to the old man, Jeremiah of Southern. He is here, I believe."

Jeremiah of Southern? The old man who'd once been a Scab? He was one of very few who had come in and bathed in the lake of his own will. Much of what Thomas knew of the Desert Dwellers he'd learned from the old man. But he'd never mentioned the Books of Histories.

"He's here now?"

The Elder nodded. "For the Gathering."

"Thomas."

He faced Rachelle. She was giving him one of those looks that he adored her for, a fiery glare that threatened without casting any suspicion on her love.

"Please tell me that because you love me you will eat ten rhambutan fruits right now and forget this nonsense forever," she said.

"Ten?" He chuckled. "You want me sick? I would groan all night. That's how you welcome your mighty warrior home?"

Slowly a smile curved her lips.

"Then one fruit. And I promise to chase it down with a kiss that will make your mind spin."

"Now that's tempting," he said. He reached for her hand. "Would you like to dance?"

She took it and spun into him.

"I don't mean to interrupt lovers, but there is another matter," Ciphus said.

"There's always another matter," Thomas said. "What is it?"

"The challenge."

He knew already where the elder was going. "Justin?"

"Yes. We cannot allow his heresy to spread further. As is required, three elders have called for an inquiry before the people as is allowed by law. Do you concur?"

"He insulted my authority once. It would seem natural that I would agree."

"But do you?"

Thomas caught Rachelle's glance. She'd once told him that Justin was harmless and that going on about him only strengthened his popularity. He'd agreed at the time. Although he might not say so in front of Mikil and the others, Thomas still carried respect for the man. He was undoubtedly the best soldier Thomas had ever commanded, which might be one reason Mikil disliked him so much.

On the other hand, there could be no denying the man's flagrant heresy. Peace with the Horde. What utter nonsense.

"Is he really that dangerous?" he asked, more for Rachelle's sake than his. "His popularity is so great. A challenge carries serious consequences."

"But his offense is growing. We believe the best way to deal with him is now, to make an example of any such treasonous talk."

"If he wins your challenge?"

"Then he is permitted to remain, of course. If he refuses to change his doctrine and loses, he will be banished as the law requires."

"Fine." Thomas turned to leave. This was hardly his concern.

"You know that if the people can't decide, then it comes down to a fight in the arena," Ciphus said.

Thomas faced the elder. "And?"

"We would like you to defend the Council if Justin must be fought."

"Me?"

"It only seems natural, as you say. Justin has turned his back on the Great Romance, and he's turned his back on you, his commander. Anyone other than you and the people might think you have no stomach for it. Our challenge will be weak on that face alone. We would like you to agree to the fight if the people are undecided."

"It's pointless, this fight business," Rachelle said. "How can you fight Justin? He served at your side for five years. He saved your life more than once. Does he pose a danger to you?"

"In hand-to-hand? Please, my love, he learned what he knows from me."

"And he learned it well, from what I've heard."

"He hasn't fought in a battle for several years. And he may have saved my life, but he also turned his back on me, not to mention, as Ciphus so rightly says, the Great Romance. Elyon himself. What will the people think if I abandoned even one of our pillars of faith? Besides, there will be no fight."

He faced Ciphus. "I accept."

10

THE HORDE set fire to the Southern Forest at night, after three days of pitched battle. Never before had they done this, partially because the Forest Guard rarely let them close enough to have such an opportunity. But that was before Martyn. They'd ignited the trees with flaming arrows from the desert two hundred yards away from the perimeter. Not only were they using fire, they had made bows.

It had taken Jamous and his remaining men four hours to subdue the flames. By Elyon's grace the Horde hadn't started another fire, and the Forest Guard had managed an hour of sleep.

Jamous stood on a hill overlooking the charred forest. Beyond lay a flat white desert, and just now in the growing light he could see the gathered Horde army. Ten thousand, far fewer than what they'd started with. But he'd lost six hundred men, four hundred in a major offensive just before dusk last evening. Another two hundred were wounded. That left him only two hundred able-bodied warriors.

He'd never seen the Desert Dwellers engage in battle so effectively. They seemed to swing their swords more skillfully and their march seemed more purposeful. They used flanking maneuvers and they withdrew when overpowered. He hadn't actually seen the general they called Martyn, but he could only assume that was who led this army.

Word had come of the great victory at the Natalga Gap, and his men had cheered. But the reality of the situation here was working on Jamous's mind like a burrowing tick. One more major push from the Horde and his men would be overrun.

Behind them not three miles lay a village. It was the second largest village of the seven, twenty thousand souls in all. Jamous had been sent to escort these devout followers of Elyon to the annual Gathering when a patrol had run into the Horde army.

The villagers had voted to stay and wait for the Desert Dwellers' sound defeat, which they were sure would be imminent, rather than cross the desert without protection.

Until yesterday it had seemed like a good plan. Now they were in a terrible situation. If they fled now, the Horde would likely burn the entire forest or, worse, catch them from behind and destroy them. If they stayed and fought, they might be able to hold the army off until the three hundred warriors whom Thomas had sent arrived, but his men were tired and worn.

He crouched on a stump and mulled his options. A thin fog coiled through the trees. Behind him, seven of his personal guard talked quietly around a smoldering fire, heating water for an herbal tea. Two of them were wounded, one where the fire had burned the skin from his calf, and another whose left hand had been crushed by the blunt end of a sickle. They would ignore their pain, because they knew that Thomas of Hunter would do the same.

He looked down at the red feather tied to his elbow and thought of Mikil. He'd plucked two feathers from a macaw and given her one to wear. When he returned home this time, he would ask for her hand. There was no one he loved or respected more than Mikil. And what would she do?

Jamous frowned. They would fight, he decided. They would fight because they were the Forest Guard.

The men had grown silent behind him. He spoke without turning, indicating the desert as he did so.

"Markus, we will hit them on their northern flank with twenty archers. The rest will follow me from the meadow on the south, where they least expect it."

Markus didn't respond.

"Markus." He turned.

His men were staring at three men who'd ridden into camp. The one who led them rode a white horse that snorted and pawed at the soft earth. He wore a beige tunic with a studded brass belt and a hood that covered his head in a manner not unlike the Scabs. Not true battle dress. A scabbard hung on his saddle.

Jamous stood and faced the camp. His men seemed oddly captivated by the sight. Why? All three looked like lost woodsmen, strong, healthy, the kind who might make good warriors with enough training, but they certainly had nothing that would set them apart.

And then the leader lifted his emerald eyes to Jamous.

Justin of Southern.

The mighty warrior who'd defied Thomas by turning down the general's greatest honor now spent his days wandering the forests with his apprentices, a self-appointed prophet spreading illogical ideas that turned the Great Romance on its head. He'd once been very popular, but his demanding ways were proving too much for many, even for some of the pliable fools who followed him diligently.

Still, this man before him threatened the very fabric of the Great Romance with his heresy, and his rhetoric was growing stronger, they said. Mikil had once told Jamous that if she ever met Justin again, she wouldn't hesitate to withdraw her sword and slay him where he stood. She suspected that he had been manipulated by the druids from the deep desert. If the Horde were the enemy from without, men like Justin, who decried the Great Romance and spoke of turning the forest over to the Desert Dwellers, were the enemy from within.

The fact that Justin had turned down his promotion to general and resigned from the Forest Guard two years ago when Thomas needed him most didn't help.

Jamous spit to one side, a habit he'd picked up from Mikil. "Markus, tell this man to leave our camp if he wishes to live." He walked for his bedroll. "We have war to wage."

"You are the one they call Jamous."

The man's voice was soft and low. Confident. The voice of a leader. It was no wonder he'd bewitched so many. It was well known that the Horde's druids bewitched their own with slippery tongues and black magic.

"And you are the one they call Justin," Jamous said. "What of it? You're in the way here."

"How can I be in the way of my own forest?"

Jamous refused to look at the man. "I am here to save your forest. Markus, mount your horse and muster the men. Make sure everyone has bathed. We may have a long day ahead. Stephen, pull out twenty archers and meet me in the lower camp."

His men hesitated.

He whirled. "Markus!"

Justin had dismounted. He possessed the audacity to defy Jamous and approach the fire, where he stood now, hood withdrawn to reveal shoulder-length brown hair. He had the face of a warrior gone soft. All had known of his skill as a soldier before his defection from the Guard. But the lines of experience were softened by his brilliant green eyes.

"The Desert Dwellers will destroy you today," Justin said, reaching a hand out to the fire. He looked over. "If you attack them, they will run over what remains of your army, burn the forest, and slaughter all of my people."

"*Your* people? The people of this forest are alive *because* of my army," Jamous said.

"Yes. They have been indebted to you for many years. But today the Horde is too strong and will crush what's left of your army like they crushed this man's hand yesterday."

He pointed to Stephen, who had taken the sickle.

"You abandoned the army. What would you know of war?" Jamous asked.

"I wage a new kind of war."

"On whose behalf? The Scabs?"

Justin faced the desert. "How much blood will you spill?"

"As much as Elyon decides."

Justin looked surprised. "Elyon? And who made the Scabs? I believe Elyon did."

"Are you saying that Elyon did *not* lead us against the Horde?"

"No. He did. But aren't you really the same as the Horde without the lake? So then if I was to take the water from you and shove you out into the desert, we'd be cutting you to pieces instead of them. Isn't that right?"

"You're saying that I am one of them? Or maybe you're suggesting that *you* are."

Justin smiled. "What I'm really saying is that the Horde lurks in all of us. The disease that cripples. The rot, if you like. Why not go after the disease?"

"They don't want a cure." Jamous grabbed the horn on his saddle and swung up without using the stirrup. "The only cure fit for the Horde is the one Elyon has given us. Our swords."

"If you insist on attacking, maybe you should let me lead your men. We'd have a much better chance of victory." He winked. "Not that you're bad, not at all. I've been watching you since you came, and you're really very, very good. One of the best. There's always Thomas, of course, but I think you're the best I've seen in some time."

"And yet you insult me?"

"Not at all. It's just that I am very good myself. I think I could win this war, and I think I could do it without losing a single man."

Justin had a strange quality about him. He said things that would ordinarily bring out the fight in Jamous, but he said them with such perfect sincerity and in such a noncombative way that Jamous was momentarily tempted to smack him on the back as he would a good friend and say, "You're on, mate."

"That's the most arrogant thing I've ever heard."

"So then I take it you're going to battle without me," Justin said.

Jamous turned his horse. "Markus, now!"

"Then at least agree to this," Justin said. "If I can rid you of this Horde army on my own, ride with me in a victory march through the Elyon Valley to the east of the village."

Jamous's men had started to mount, but they stopped. Justin's companions hadn't moved from their horses. Nothing about this wild proposal seemed to surprise them.

Any hint of play had vanished from Justin's eyes. He stared directly at Jamous again, commanding. Demanding.

"Agreed," Jamous said, interested more in dismissing the man than taking any challenge from him seriously.

Justin held his eyes for a long while. Then, as if time was short, he walked to his horse, threw himself into the saddle, reined it around, and left without so much as a glance.

Jamous turned away. "Stephen, archers. Hurry, before the light is full."

———— ∞∞∞ ————

Justin led Ronin and Arvyl through the trees at a gallop. They could hardly keep up, and he didn't push his mount as he often would when riding alone. There were others beside Ronin and Arvyl—thousands who would cry out his name in the right circumstances, but his popularity had waned as of late. They were a fickle people, given to the sentiments of the day.

He only hoped that he still had enough. His agreement with Martyn depended at least partially on his ability to deliver a crowd as planned.

Living as an outcast had extracted its price. At times he could hardly weather the pain. It was one thing to enter society as an orphan, as he had; it was another to be openly rejected as he was so often now.

At times he wasn't sure why Elyon didn't take his sword to the lot of them. Their Great Romance was no romance of Elyon at all.

Now their fate was in his hands. If they only knew the truth, they might kill him now, before he had the chance to do what was needed.

"Justin! Wait," Ronin called from behind.

They'd come to a grove of fruit trees. Justin pulled up. "Breakfast, my friends?"

"Sir, what do you have in mind? You can't take on the whole Horde army single-handedly!"

Still at a trot, Justin slid a pearl-handled sword from its scabbard, leaned far forward, flipped the blade over his head in a movement that approximated a figure eight, and then reined his horse in.

One, two, three large red fruits dropped from the tree. He caught each in turn and hurled one each to Ronin and Arvyl. "Ha!"

He bit deeply into the sweet nectar. Juice ran down his chin and he shoved his sword home into its scabbard. The fruit he would miss.

Ronin grinned and took a bite of his fruit. "Seriously."

Justin's horse stamped. Slowly the smile faded from his face. He looked off at the forest. "I am serious, Ronin. When I've said that leveling the desert with a single word is a matter of the heart, not the sword, you weren't listening?"

"Of course I was listening. But this isn't a campfire session with a dozen hopeless souls looking for a hero. This is the Horde army."

"You doubt me?"

"Please, Justin. Sir. After what we have seen?"

"And what have you seen?"

"I have seen you lead a thousand warriors through the Samyrian desert plain with twenty thousand Horde before us and twenty thousand behind. I have seen you take on a hundred of the enemy single-handedly and walk away unscathed. I have heard you speak to the desert and to the trees and I have seen them listen. Why do you question my confidence in you?"

Justin looked into his eyes.

"You are the greatest warrior in all the land," Ronin continued. "Greater I believe than even Thomas of Hunter. But no man can possibly go against ten thousand warriors alone. I'm not doubting; I'm asking what you really mean by this."

Justin held him in his gaze, then slowly smiled. "If I ever had a brother, Ronin, I would pray he would be exactly like you."

It was the highest honor one man could give another. In truth Ronin did doubt Justin, even by asking, but now he was wordless.

Ronin dipped his head. "I am your servant."

"No, Ronin. You are my apprentice."

Billy and Lucy watched the three warriors from behind their berry bush, barely breathing. In their hands they gripped wooden swords they had carved only yesterday. Lucy's sword wasn't as sharp or as sword-looking as Billy's because she had a hard time carving with her bad hand. It was good enough to wedge the wood against her leg, but otherwise the shriveled lump of flesh was good only for pointing or clubbing Billy over the head when he got too annoying.

It had been Billy's idea to sneak out of the village while it was still dark and join the battle—or at least take a peek.

His friend had tried to convince Billy that it was too dangerous, that nine-year-old children had no business even looking at the evil Horde, much less thinking they could fight them. Lucy hadn't thought they would actually come, but then Billy had awakened her and she'd followed, whispering her objections most of the way.

Now she was staring at the three warriors on their horses, and her heart was hammering loud enough to scare the birds.

"That's . . . that's him!" Billy whispered.

Lucy withdrew into the bush. They would be heard!

Billy looked at her, eyes wide. "That's Justin of Southern!"

Lucy was too terrified to tell him to shut up. Of course it wasn't Justin of Southern. He wasn't dressed like a warrior. She wasn't even sure that Justin even existed. They'd heard all the stories, but that didn't mean anyone lived who could really do all those things.

"I swear it's him!" Billy whispered. "He killed a hundred thousand Scabs with one hand."

Lucy leaned forward and took another peek. They were like the magical Roshuim of Elyon that her father said would one day strike down the Horde.

———

"And what about you, Arvyl?" Justin asked. "What do you make of—"

He stopped midsentence. Ronin followed his gaze and saw that two children, a boy and a girl, crouched at the edge of the clearing, peering past a berry bush at the three warriors.

They were looking at Justin, of course. They always looked at Justin. Children were always captivated by him. These two looked like twins, blond hair and big eyes, about ten, far too young to have wandered so far from home at a time like this.

Then again, he hardly blamed their curiosity. When had such a battle come so close to them?

Justin had already slipped into another world, Ronin thought with a single glance. Children did this to him. He was no longer the warrior. He was their father, no matter who the children were. His eyes sparkled and his face lit up. At times Ronin wondered if Justin wouldn't trade his life to become a child again, to swing in the trees and roll in the meadows.

This love for children confused Ronin more than any other trait of Justin's. Some said that Justin was a druid. And it was commonly known that druids could deceive the innocent with a few soft words. Ronin had a difficult time separating Justin's effect on children from the speculation that he wasn't who he seemed.

"Hello there," Justin said.

Both children ducked behind the bush.

Justin slid from his horse and hurried toward the bush. "No, no, please come out. Come out, I need your advice." He stopped and knelt on one knee.

"My advice?" the boy asked, poking his head up.

A hand gripped his shirt and pulled him back. The girl wasn't so brave.

"Your advice. It's about today's battle."

They whispered urgently, then finally came out, the boy boldly, the girl cautiously. Ronin saw that they each carried a wooden sword. The girl was shorter and her left hand was bent backward at an odd angle. Deformed.

Justin's eyes lowered to the girl's hand, then up to her face. For a moment he seemed trapped by the sight. A bird sang in the tree above them.

"My name is Justin, and I . . ." He sat down and crossed his legs in one movement. "What are your names?"

"Billy and Lucy," the boy said.

"Well, Billy and Lucy, you are two of the bravest children I have ever known."

The boy's eyes brightened.

"And the most beautiful," he said.

The girl shifted on her feet.

"My friends here, Ronin and Arvyl, aren't convinced that I can single-handedly bring the Horde to its knees. I have to decide, and I think that you might be able to give me some direction. Look in my eyes and tell me. What do you think? Should I take on the Horde?"

Billy looked at Ronin, at a loss. The girl answered first.

"Yes," she said.

"Yes," the boy said. "Of course."

"Yes! You hear that, Ronin? Give me ten warriors who believe like these two and I would bring the entire Horde to its knees. Come here, Billy. I would like to shake the hand of the man who told me what grown men could not."

Justin stretched out his hand and Billy took it, beaming. Justin ruffled the boy's hair and whispered something that Ronin couldn't hear. But both of the children laughed.

"Lucy, come and let me kiss the hand of the most beautiful maiden in all the land."

She stepped forward and offered her good hand.

"Not that one. The other."

Her smile softened. Slowly she lowered her sword. Now both hands hung limp at her sides. Justin held her eyes.

"Don't be afraid," he said very quietly.

She lifted her crippled hand and Justin took it in both of his. He leaned over and kissed it lightly. Then he leaned forward and whispered into her ear.

⟋⟍⟋⟍

To be perfectly honest, Lucy was terrified by Justin. But it wasn't a fearful terrified as much as a nervous terrified. She wasn't sure whether she should trust him or not. His eyes said yes and his smile said yes, but there was something about him that made her knees knock.

When he took her hand and kissed it, she knew he could feel her shaking. Then he leaned forward and whispered into her ear.

"You are very brave, Lucy." His voice was soft and it ran through her body like a glass of warm milk. "If I were a king, I would wish that you were my daughter. A princess."

He kissed her forehead.

She wasn't sure why, but tears came to her eyes. It wasn't because of what he had said, or because he'd kissed her cheek. It was the power in his voice. Like magic. She felt like a princess swept off her feet by the greatest prince in all the land, just like in the stories.

Only it wasn't the beautiful princess the prince had chosen. It was her, the one with the stub for a hand.

She tried her best to keep from crying, but it was very hard, and she suddenly felt awkward standing in front of Billy like this.

Justin winked at her and stood, still holding her own hand. He put his other hand on Billy's shoulder. "I want you both to go home as fast as you can. Tell the people that the Horde will be defeated today. We will march through the Elyon Valley at noon, victors. Can I count on you?"

They both nodded.

He released them both and turned back to where his horse waited. "If only we could all be children again," he said.

Then he swung into his saddle and galloped across the small clearing. Justin pulled up at the trees and spun his horse back.

If Lucy wasn't mistaken, she could see tears on his face. "If only you could all be children again."

Then he rode into the trees.

"Watch our flank!" Jamous thundered. "Keep them to the front!"

Markus drove his horse directly into a pocket of Horde warriors and pulled up just as one took a wide swipe with his sickle. Markus threw his torso backward, flat on the horse's rump. The sickle whistled through the air above. He brought his sword up with his body, severing the Scab's arm at the shoulder.

Jamous used his bow, sending an arrow through the back of the warrior bearing down on Markus from behind. The attacker roared in pain and dropped his sword.

"Back! Back!" Jamous cried.

It was their fourth attack that morning, and the strategy was working exactly as Jamous had designed it to. If they kept beating away at the flanks, their superior speed would keep the slower army from outmaneuvering them for position to the rear. They were like wolves tearing at the legs of a bear, always just out of reach of its slashing claws, just close enough to take small bites at will.

The forest lay a hundred yards to their rear. Jamous glanced back.

No, two hundred. That far?

Farther.

He spun around and stood in his stirrups, surveying the battlefield. A chill defied the hot sun and washed down his back. They were too far out!

"Back to the forest!" he screamed.

Even as he did, he saw the wide swath of Horde slicing in from the east, cutting them off.

He glanced to the west. The enemy ran too far to cut through their lines there. He spun to the west. An endless sea of Horde.

Panic swelled, then receded. There was a way out. There was always a way out.

"Center line!" he cried. "Center line!"

His men fell in behind him for running retreat. When the Horde moved to intercept, they would break off in a dozen directions to scatter them. But always they would move in the direction he first took them.

His horse reared high and Jamous looked desperately for that direction.

"They're cutting us off!" Markus yelled. "Jamous—"

He knew then what the enemy had done. The bear had suffered the wolves' attacks with patience, snarling and swiping as it always did. But today it had slowly, methodically drawn the wolves farther and farther into the desert, far enough so they wouldn't see the flanking maneuver. Too far to outrun it.

The Horde army closed in a hundred yards behind them. At the center a warrior held high their crest, the serpentine Shataiki bat. They were trapped.

The Scabs nearest him suddenly fell back a hundred yards and joined the main army. His men had clustered to his right. Their horses snorted and stamped, worn from battle. No one demanded that he do something. There was little they could do.

Except charge.

The Horde line between them and the forest was their only real option.

But it was already fifty yards wide, too many Scabs to cut through with fewer than two hundred men.

Still, it was their only option. An image of Mikil flashed through his mind. They would say that he had fought like no man had ever fought, and she would carry his body to the funeral pyre.

The Scab army had stopped now. The desert had fallen silent. They seemed content to let Jamous make the first move. They would simply adjust their noose in whichever direction he took them. The Horde army was learning.

Martyn.

Jamous faced his men, who'd formed a line facing the forest. "There's only one way," he said.

"Straight at them," Markus said.

"Elyon's strength."

"Elyon's strength."

Maybe a few of them could cut through the wall to warn the village.

"Spread the word. On my mark, straight ahead. If you make it, evacuate the village. They will be burning."

Had it really come down to this? One last suicide run?

"You're a good man, Jamous," Markus said.

"And you, Markus. And you." They looked at each other. Jamous lifted his sword.

"Rider! Behind!" The call came from down the line.

Jamous twisted in his saddle. A lone rider raced across the desert from the east, half a mile distant. Dust rose in his wake.

Jamous spun his horse. "Steady."

The rider was headed neither for them nor for the Desert Dwellers. He approached halfway between their position and the Horde army. A white horse.

The sound of the pounding hoofs reached Jamous. He fixed his eyes on this one horse, thundering in from the desert like a blinded runner who'd gotten lost and was determined to deliver his message to the supreme commander at any cost.

It was Justin of Southern.

The man still wasn't in proper battle dress. His hood flew behind him with loose locks. He rode on the balls of his feet as if he'd been born in that saddle. And in his right hand hung a sword, low and easy so that it looked like it might touch the sand at any moment.

Jamous swallowed. This warrior had fought and won more battles than any living man except for Thomas himself. Although Jamous had never fought with him, they'd all heard of his exploits before he'd left the Guard.

Justin suddenly veered toward the Horde army, leaned low on the far side of his horse, and lowered his sword into the sand. Still running full speed, he carved a line on the desert for a hundred yards before righting himself and pulling his mount to a stop.

The white stallion reared and dropped back around.

Justin galloped back, not once glancing at either army. The front ranks of the Horde shifted but held steady. He reined tight at the center of the line that he'd drawn and faced the Horde.

The armies grew perfectly still.

For several long seconds Justin stared ahead, his back to Jamous.

"What's he—"

Jamous lifted a hand to quiet Markus.

Justin swung his leg off his saddle and dropped to the ground. He walked up to the line and stopped. Then he deliberately stepped over the line and walked forward, sword dragging in the sand by his side. They could hear the soft crunch of sand under his feet. A horse down the line snorted.

He was only a hundred feet from the main Horde army when he stopped again. This time he thrust his sword into the sand and took three steps back.

His voice rang out across the desert. "I request to speak with the general named Martyn!"

"What does he think he's doing? He's surrendering?"

"I don't know, Markus. We're still alive."

"We can't surrender! The Horde takes no prisoners."

"I think he aims to make peace."

"Peace with them is treason against Elyon!" Markus spit.

Jamous glanced at the army to their rear. "Send one runner wide, to their eastern flank."

"Now?"

"Yes. Let's see if they let him pass."

Markus issued the order.

Justin still faced the army, waiting. A rider broke from Jamous's line and sprinted east, in much the same manner as Justin had. The Scabs made no move to stop him.

"They're letting him go."

"Good. Let's see if—"

"Now they're stopping him."

The Scabs were closing the eastern flank. The rider pulled up and headed back.

Jamous swore. "Well then, let's see how far treason gets us."

As if on cue, the Horde army parted directly ahead. A lone general on a horse, wearing the black sash of his rank, rode slowly out to Justin. Martyn. Jamous could make out his bland Scab face beneath the hood, but not his features. He stopped ten feet from Justin's sword.

The soft rumbling of their voices carried across the desert, but Jamous couldn't make out their words. Still they talked. Five minutes. Ten.

The general Martyn suddenly slid from his horse, met Justin at the sword in the sand, and clasped Justin's hands in the traditional forest greeting.

"What?"

"Hold your tongue, Markus. If we live to fight another day, we will drag him through his treason."

The general mounted, rode back to his men, and disappeared. A long horn blasted from the front line.

"Now what?"

Justin leaped into his saddle, spun his horse, and sprinted straight toward them. He'd come within twenty feet without slowing before it occurred to Jamous that he wasn't going to.

He cursed and jerked his horse to the left.

He could see the mischievous glint in Justin's emerald eyes as he blasted through the line and galloped toward the waiting Horde. Long before he met them, the Scab army parted and withdrew, first east and west, and then south like a receding tide on either side.

Justin pulled up at the tree line.

Jamous glanced back once, then kicked his horse. "Ride!"

It wasn't until he was halfway to Justin that Jamous remembered his agreement. The man had indeed rid him of the Horde, hadn't he? Yes. Not by any means he'd imagined—not by any means he even understood—but he had. And for that at least, Justin was victor.

Today the people would honor him.

11

HE'S STILL sleeping?" Phil Grant asked.

The frumpy doctor pushed the door to his lab open. "Like a baby. I insist that you let me study him further. This is highly unusual, you understand? I've never seen it."

"Can you unlock his dreams with more work?"

"I don't know what I can unlock, but I'm happy to try. Whatever's happening in that mind of his must be scrutinized. Must."

"I'm not sure how much time we have for your musts," Grant said. "We'll see."

Kara walked in ahead of the two men. It struck her as odd that only two weeks ago she'd lived a quiet life as a nurse in Denver. Yet here she was, being traipsed about by the director of the CIA and a world-renowned cognitive psychologist, who were both looking to her brother for answers to perhaps the single greatest crisis that the United States had ever faced. That the world had ever faced.

Thomas lay in a maroon recliner, lights low, while an orchestral version of "Killing Me Softly" whispered through ceiling speakers. She'd spent the afternoon putting their affairs in order: rent on their Denver apartment, insurance bills, a long call to Mother, who'd been climbing the walls with all the news about Thomas's kidnapping of Monique. Depending on what happened in the next day or so, Kara thought she might fly to New York for a visit. The prospect of never seeing her mother again wasn't sitting well. The scientists were all talking as though the virus wouldn't wreak havoc for another eighteen days, but really it could be less. Seventeen. Sixteen. The models were only so accurate. There was every possibility that they all had less than three weeks to live.

"So he's been sleeping for three hours without dreaming?"

Dr. Myles Bancroft walked to the monitor and tapped it lightly. "Let me put it this way. If he is dreaming, it's not like any dream I've ever seen. No rapid eye movement. No perceptual brain activity, no fluctuation in facial temperature. He's in deep sleep, but his dreams are quiet."

"So the whole notion of recording his dream patterns and feeding them back . . ."

"Is a nonstarter," the psychologist finished.

Grant shook his head. "He looks so . . . ordinary."

"He's far from ordinary," Kara said.

"Evidently. It's just hard to imagine that the fate of the world is hung up somewhere in this mind. We know that he discovered the Raison Strain—the idea that he has the antivirus hidden in that mind somewhere is a bit unnerving, considering that he's never had a day of medical training in his life."

"Which is why you *must* let me spend more time with him," Bancroft repeated.

They stared at him in silence.

"Wake him," Kara said.

Bancroft shook Thomas gently. "Wake up, lad."

Thomas's eyes blinked open. Funny how she rarely thought of him as Tom anymore. He was Thomas now. It suited him better.

"Welcome to the land of the living," the doctor said. "How do you feel?"

He sat up. Wiped at his eyes. "How long have I been asleep?"

"Three hours."

———— ∞ ————

Thomas looked around the lab. Three hours. It felt like more.

"What happened?" Kara asked.

They were staring at him expectantly. "Did it work?" he asked.

"That's what we were wondering," Bancroft said.

"I don't know. Did you record my dreams?"

"Did you dream?"

"I don't know, did I? Or am I dreaming now?"

Kara sighed. "Please, Thomas."

"Okay, then yes, of course I dreamed. I returned to the forest with my army after destroying the Horde—the black powder worked wonders—met with the Council, then fell asleep after joining the celebration with Rachelle."

He slid his feet to the floor and stood. "And I'm dreaming now, which means I didn't eat the fruit. She'll have my hide."

"Who'll have your hide?" Grant asked.

"His wife. Rachelle," Kara said.

The director looked at her with a raised brow.

"And I asked about the Books of Histories," Thomas said. "I know the man who may be able to tell me where to find them."

"But you don't remember anything more about the antivirus," Grant pressed.

"No. Your little experiment failed, remember? You can't stimulate my memory banks because you can't record the brain signatures associated with my dreams because I'm not dreaming. That pretty much summarizes it, doesn't it, Doctor?"

"Perhaps, yes. Fascinating. We could be on the verge of a whole new world of understanding here."

Phil Grant shook his head. "Okay, Gains is right. From this point forward we've got to keep this dream-talk to a minimum. We keep the story straight and simple. You have a gift. You're seeing things that haven't happened yet. That's hard enough to buy, but at least there's precedent for it. In the light of our situation, enough people will at least give a prophet a chance. But the rest of this—your wife, Rochel or whatever her name is, your war council, the Horde, the fruit you didn't eat—all of it, strictly off-limits to anyone except me and Gains."

"You want to pitch me as some kind of mystical prophet?" Thomas said. "I'm not as optimistic as you. It'll do nothing for my leverage in the international community. Outside of this room I'm simply a person who may know more about the situation at hand than anyone else in this government because of my association with Monique. I was the last one to speak to her before she was taken. I'm the only one who has engaged the terrorists, and I'm the only one who has accurately anticipated their next move. Considering all of that, I am a man who should be taken very seriously. Judging the rather . . . lukewarm reception I got from the others in the meeting today, I think that might make more sense."

"I won't disagree," Grant said. "Are you anticipating the need for leverage in the international community?"

Thomas walked past him, his sense of urgency swelling. "Who knows? One way or another we've got to beat this thing. I can't believe the Books of Histories still exist! If I can get to them . . ."

He stopped. "I have to know something." Thomas faced them, eyes wide. "I have to know if this cut on my shoulder came from Carlos or from the Horde. In my dreams, that is."

They stared at him without offering any bold statements of support.

"From Carlos," Kara finally said.

"But you didn't see him cut me, right? I was already bleeding when you came into the room. No, I really need to know. They're insisting that the Horde cut me."

"How . . . can you prove it either way?"

"Yes. Cut me." He stuck out his arm. "Make a small incision and I'll see if I have it when I wake up."

All three blinked.

"Just give me the knife then."

Bancroft stepped to a drawer, opened it, and withdrew scissors. "Well, I have these—"

"You're not serious, are you?" Grant demanded.

Thomas took the scissors and drew their sharp tip along his forearm. He had to understand the rules of engagement. "Just a small scratch. For me. I have to know." He winced and handed the scissors back.

"You're suggesting that more than what's in your mind is transferred between realities?" the doctor asked.

"Of course," he said. "I'm there and I'm here. Physically. That's more than knowledge or skills. My wounds show up in both realities. My blood.

Life. Nothing else. My mind and my life. On the other hand, my aging doesn't show here. I'm younger here."

"This . . . this is absolutely incredible," the doctor said.

Thomas faced Grant. "So what's our status?"

The director took awhile to answer. "Well . . . the president's directed FEMA to direct all of its resources to work with the Centers for Disease Control, and he's brought in the World Health Organization. They've now confirmed the virus in thirty-two airports."

"What about the search for Monique? The rest may be pointless unless we find her."

"We're working on it. The governments of Britain, Germany, France, Thailand, Indonesia, Brazil . . . a dozen others are pulling out the stops."

"Switzerland?"

"Naturally. I may not be able to predict a virus, or battle the Horde, but I do know how to look for fugitives in the real world."

"Svensson's gone deep, into a hole somewhere that he prepared a long time ago. One that no one will think to look in. Like the one outside of Bangkok."

"Which you found how?"

Thomas glanced at Kara.

"Could you do that again?" she asked. "The world's changed, but that doesn't mean Rachelle isn't somehow connected to Monique, right?"

Thomas didn't respond. What if he was wrong? He was still Thomas Hunter, the failed writer from Denver. What right did he have advising the CIA? The stakes were astronomical.

On the other hand, he had been right more than once. And he had battled the Horde successfully for fifteen years. That earned him something, as the president had said.

"Will someone please explain?" Grant asked.

Kara faced him. "Rachelle, Thomas's dream-wife, inadvertently led him to Monique the first time. She seemed to know where Monique was being kept. But she became jealous of Monique, because she realized that Thomas was falling in love with her here. So she refused to help him again. It's why he agreed not to dream for fifteen years."

"I must be given more time," Bancroft murmured. "You're in love with two different women, one from each reality?"

"That's a stretch," Thomas said.

It was a thing that Thomas had been trying to squash ever since he'd awakened from the fifteen-year dream, but it lingered there in the back of his mind. It seemed absurd that he would have any feelings for Monique at all. Yes, they'd faced death together, and she'd kissed him as a matter of her own survival. He did find her fiery spirit attractive, and her face refused to budge from his mind's eye. But maybe Rachelle's jealousy was what triggered his romantic feelings for Monique in the first place. Maybe he wouldn't have started to fall for her if Rachelle hadn't suggested that he *was* falling for her.

Now, after fifteen years with Rachelle, any romantic notions he might once have felt for Monique had vanished.

"The whole thing is more than a stretch," Grant said, "starting with your prediction of the Raison Strain. But these are now facts, aren't they? So you get to your Books of Histories and you get to Rachelle and you convince her to help us here. Meaning you sleep and you dream."

He shook his head and started for the door. "With any luck you'll have something more sensible to tell the president when you meet with him tomorrow."

———— ≈≈≈ ————

They'd moved her again. Where, she had no clue.

Monique de Raison stared at the monitor, mind taxed, eyes burning.

It had been less than twenty-four hours since they'd put a sack over her head for the second time in as many days and led her into a car, then onto an airplane. The flight had lasted several hours—she could be anywhere. Hawaii, China, Argentina, Germany. She might have been able to figure out the region by any stray conversation she overheard, but they'd stuffed wax in her ears and taped them. She couldn't even determine the temperature or humidity, because they'd landed during a rainstorm that had wet her hood before she'd been shoved into another car and brought here.

A man of German or Swiss descent whom she'd never met before had pulled the bag off her head and unplugged her ears. He'd left her in this room without speaking.

Another laboratory. Blinding white. A small lab, maybe twenty by twenty, but crammed with the latest equipment. A Field Emission Electron Microscope, a Siemens, stood along one wall. The microscope could effectively examine wet samples as well as specimens treated with liquid nitrogen. State of the art. Next to it, a long table arrayed with test tubes and a Beckman Coulter Counter.

In the corner, a mattress, and in an adjoining room without a door, a toilet and a sink.

The room was constructed of cinder blocks, like the others. On second look, she was sure that whoever had built the other two labs she'd been in had also built this one. How many did they have? And each had been carefully supplied with everything a geneticist or a virologist would need.

She'd curled up on the mattress, dressed in the pale blue slacks and matching blouse they'd given her before the trip, and cried. She knew that she should be strong. That Svensson surely wouldn't actually release the virus as he'd threatened to. That if he did, she might be the only one who could stop it. But the chance of the back door she'd engineered surviving the mutation was terribly small. They had to be bluffing.

Still, she'd cried.

A man in a white smock with red hair and bifocals had entered the room twenty minutes later carrying a brown snakeskin briefcase. "Are you okay?" He actually looked surprised at her condition. "Goodness, what have they done to you? You're Monique de Raison, right? *The* Monique de Raison."

She stood and pushed her bangs from her eyes. A scientist. Her hope surged. Was he a friend?

"Yes," she said.

Only a few days earlier she might have slapped this man for his gawking. Now she felt small. Too small.

A glint sparkled in the man's eyes. "We have a wager. We have a wager."

He motioned to the door. "Who will find it first, you or us." He leaned forward as if what he was about to say was to be kept secret. "I am the only one betting on you."

He was slightly mad, she thought.

"None of us will find it," she said. "Do you realize what's happening?"

"Of course I do. The first to isolate the antivirus will be paid fifty *million* dollars, and the whole team will be paid ten million each. But there are eleven teams, so Petrov—"

She slapped him then. His glasses spun across the room. "He's going to release the virus, you idiot!"

He stared at her. "He already has."

Then he set the case on the floor, walked to his glasses, returned them to his face. "Everything you need is in the case," he said. "You will see all of our work in real-time calculations, and we will see yours."

He headed for the door.

"Please, I'm sorry!" She hurried after him. "You have to help me!"

But he closed the door and was gone.

That was over an hour ago. Now Monique stared at a dizzying string of numbers and tried desperately to focus.

He hasn't released the virus, Monique. The chances of finding an antivirus in time are too low. It would be suicide!

But he'd kidnapped her, hadn't he? He knew he would eventually be caught and would spend the balance of his life in prison. What did he have to lose?

And Thomas . . .

Her mind was swallowed by her two encounters with the American. His harebrained kidnapping of her. He had tied her to the air conditioner in the Paradise Hotel while he slept, while he took his dream-trip to retrieve information that he could not possibly know. The attack by Carlos. She'd seen Thomas shot, and yet he'd survived and come for her again. She'd kissed him. She'd done it to distract whoever was watching, but she'd also done it because he had risked his life for her, and she felt desperate for him to save her. He was her savior.

She didn't know if her irresponsible feelings for him were motivated by his character or by her own despair. Her emotions were hardly trustworthy in a time like this.

Was he still alive?

You have to focus, Monique. They will come for you again. Father will have the whole world looking for you.

She took a deep breath and reapplied her concentration. A model of her own Raison Vaccine filled one corner of the screen. Below it, a model of the Raison Strain, a mutation that had survived after the vaccine had been subjected to intense heat for two hours, exactly as Thomas had predicted. She'd analyzed a simulation of the actual mutation a hundred times over the past hour and saw how it had worked. This was a freak of nature far more complex than anything a geneticist could have come up with on his own.

Ironically, her own genetic engineering, designed to keep the vaccine viable for long periods without contacting any host or moisture, had allowed the inert vaccine to mutate in such adverse conditions.

As far as she could see, there were only two ways in which an antivirus could be developed with any kind of speed—meaning weeks instead of months or years.

The first would be for her to identify the signature she had engineered into her vaccine to turn it off, as it were. She'd developed a simple way to introduce an airborne agent into the vicinity of the vaccine—a virus that would essentially neutralize the vaccine by inserting its own DNA into the mix and rendering the vaccine impotent. It was her personal signature as much as a deterrent to foul play or theft.

If she could find the specific gene she'd engineered, and *if* it had survived the mutation, then introducing the virus she'd already developed to neutralize the vaccine *might* also render the Raison Strain impotent. *If, if,* and *might* being the key words.

She knew the signature like she knew her best friend. The problem now was how to find it in this mangled mess called the Raison Strain.

The only other way to unravel an antivirus in such short order was to chance upon the right gene manipulations. But ten thousand lab technicians could coordinate their efforts for sixty days and not strike the right combination.

Svensson knew something, or he wouldn't risk so much on a long shot. Surely he understood that her signature might not have survived, or that it might not work on the mutated vaccine.

Monique moved the cursor over the key below the diagram of the Strain and brought up a window of its DNA. She would search for her key first.

She slammed her fist on the black Formica desktop. Glass tubes rattled in a tray. She swore through gritted teeth. "This can't be happening!"

"I'm afraid it is."

Svensson! She spun in her chair. The old goat stood in the doorway, smiling patiently, leaning on a white cane.

He moved into the room, dragging his leg, eyes glimmering with self-satisfaction.

"Sorry to leave you alone so long, but I've been a bit preoccupied. The last couple days have been quite eventful."

Monique stood and held the desk to hide a tremble in her hand. The man wore a black jacket, white shirt, no tie. His dark hair was parted in the middle and slicked back with cream. Blue veins stood out on his knuckles.

"What's going on?" she asked, as evenly as possible.

"What isn't?" He closed the door. "But that's unfair. You have no idea how exciting the world has become in the last forty-eight hours, because you've been hard at work trying to save it."

"How can I work if you move me every twelve hours?"

"We're on an Indonesian island, in a mountain called Cyclops. Quite safe here. Don't worry, it will be home for at least three days. Have you made any progress?"

"With what? You've given us an impossible task."

The old man's smile didn't soften, but his eyes glazed. He studied her for an inordinate amount of time.

"You're not as motivated as I'd hoped." He walked toward her. "Please insert this disk," he said, withdrawing a CD-ROM from his breast pocket. "And please don't think of assaulting me. If you think I can't slit your belly open with the flip of my wrist, you're a fool."

She took the disk and slid it into the computer's DVD tray. It retracted.

"The rest of the world has had the benefit of what you're going to see for three days now. I want to make sure you understand everything."

A single virus shell popped onto the screen and she recognized it immediately. The Raison Strain. A clock showed real time at the bottom of the picture.

"Yes, a most efficient mercenary. But you haven't seen what it can actually do."

"This is a simulation," she said. "Anyone can create a cartoon."

"I assure you, not a single piece of hypothetical data has been used for this 'cartoon,' as you call it. I'll leave it for you to analyze later."

She watched as the virus entered a human lung and immediately went to work on the cells of the alveoli. She knew how it would work, penetrating the cells with its own DNA and ultimately rupturing the cells. Soon thousands of virus-infected cells were streaming through the body's network of veins and arteries, searching out new organs. Even so, with this microscopic damage, no symptoms would be evident.

The clock at the bottom sped up and began ticking off hours, then days. It slowed at sixteen. The infected cells had reached a critical mass and were producing symptoms. Their assault on the body's organs resulted in massive internal hemorrhaging and quick failure within two more days.

Like an acid, the virus had eaten the host from the inside out.

"Nasty little beast," Svensson said. "There's more."

Monique had seen a thousand superbug simulations. She'd participated in autopsies of Ebola victims. She had seen and studied as many viruses as any other living person. But she'd never seen such a ravaging animal, not one that was so contagious, so systemic, and so innocuous before reaching maturity and consuming its host like so many piranha.

Monique cleared her throat.

The next frame showed a map of the world. Twelve red dots lit up. New York, Washington, Bangkok, and on, tiny fires popping to life.

"Forgive the melodrama, but there really is no other way to show what the naked eye cannot see."

By the end of day one, the number of cities had reached twenty-four. "Our initial deposit. Everything else is the virus's own doing."

Lines spread over the map, showing air-traffic routes. The lights spread. By the beginning of day three, half the map was solid red.

Now the simulation changed to show the spread of the virus from one host to another. Monique knew the facts well enough: One sneeze contained as many as ten million germs traveling at up to one hundred miles per hour. With this virus, the time between a person acquiring the germ and becoming contagious was a mere four hours. Even assuming each contagious agent infected only a hundred per day, the numbers grew exponentially. By day nine the number had reached six billion.

Svensson reached forward and pressed the space bar. The simulation froze.

"That brings us up to date."

At first she didn't understand. Up to date, meaning what?

"Give or take a few hours," he said.

"You're saying you've actually done it?"

"As promised. And I will admit that not all of the infected cities represent saturation. The red light means the virus is currently airborne, sweeping through that city. We calculate that it will take two weeks for global saturation."

He pulled out a small vial of amber liquid. Uncorked the lid. Sniffed the opening. "Odorless."

She knew the whole truth then. It was hard to grasp, even with his simulations. Computer models and theories and pictures were one thing, but to imagine that what she was seeing had actually happened . . .

He could be lying about all of it, forcing her to slave on an antivirus so that with it he could blackmail the world.

"You need more convincing, I can see." He pressed the intercom button on the phone. "Bring him down." He picked up a clean slide.

Maybe he really had done it.

"This is crazy. The United States would come unglued if—"

"The United States *is* coming unglued!" he shouted. "Every nation with anything resembling a military is coming unglued. The people don't know yet, but the governments have been scrambling for two days already. The CDC has already verified the virus in over fifty of its cities."

The door opened, and a bound man wearing a green shirt and a black bag over his head stumbled in. Carlos entered and shut the door.

Svensson withdrew a scalpel from his pocket and walked to the man. "We picked him up in a Paris nightclub. We have no idea who he is, although he looks like he might be a visitor from the Mediterranean. Perhaps Greek. His mouth is taped, so don't bother asking him any questions. The chances of him being infected are pretty good, considering where he was spending his time, wouldn't you agree?"

Without waiting for an answer, Svensson slashed the man across his chest. The man jerked back and moaned behind his gag. Svensson whipped the slide along the seeping line of blood that darkened the green shirt.

He walked toward the electron microscope, snapped it on, and slipped the slide into place.

"Look for yourself," he said, stepping back.

The man had fallen to his knees, shirt now soaked red.

Monique's head swam.

Svensson walked to the man, pulled out a pistol, and shot him in the head. His victim dropped to the floor.

The Swiss shoved the gun at the microscope. "Look!"

Ears ringing, pulse pounding, Monique walked to the monitor. She worked the familiar instrument without thinking what she was doing. It took too long to focus because she couldn't control her hands. They were shaking and seemed to have forgotten just what to do.

But when she finally found a patch on the slide that cooperated with the intense magnification, she could hardly miss the foreign bodies swimming through the man's blood.

She blinked and increased the magnification. Behind her the room was silent. Just her, breathing through her nostrils. This was it. This was the Raison Strain.

She straightened.

"No more games, Monique. There's no way to stop the spread of the virus. Without an antivirus we will all die. It really is that simple. We know that you engineer a back door into your vaccines. We need you to identify this back door, verify that it hasn't mutated with the vaccine, and then create the virus that will turn the Raison Strain off. I won't lie to you; I'm not telling you everything—you're clever enough to figure that out. But I am telling you what you need to know to play your part in helping humanity survive."

She faced him, suddenly cold. "I don't think you know what you've done."

"Oh, we do. And I, like you, am only playing my part. Everyone must play his part or the game will indeed end badly. But don't think any of this has escaped our calculation. We've anticipated everything."

He glanced at Carlos. "There is the matter of the pesky American, of course. But we're dealing with him. He may not die so easily, but we have other means. I doubt a soul alive understands the breadth of our power."

Thomas was still alive.

She glanced at the crumpled body on the floor. He was dead, but Thomas was alive. A sliver of hope.

"We need the key," Svensson said.

"I'll do my best."

"How long?"

"If it survived the mutation, three days. Maybe two."

Svensson smiled. "Perfect. Now I have a plane to catch. They will take good care of you. You are very important to us, Monique. We'll need brilliant minds when this is over. Please try to think positively."

⁂

"This is an outrage!"

Three of the four men in the room looked at Armand Fortier with shock in their eyes.

"Is it, Jean?" Fortier stood and faced France's leading men: the premier, Boisverte, who had just objected; President Gaetan, who was a weasel and would ultimately capitulate; Du Braeck, the minister of defense, who was the most valuable to Fortier; and the head of the secret police, the *Sûreté*,

Chombarde, who was the only one without round eyes at the moment. Each had been intentionally selected; each was now faced with the decision to live for tomorrow or die tonight, though they didn't understand it in those terms. Not yet.

"Be careful what you say," Fortier said.

"You can't do this!"

"I already have."

As minister of foreign affairs, Fortier had convinced Henri Gaetan to call this emergency session to address Valborg Svensson's recent ultimatum. Fortier had critical information relevant to the virus, he told Gaetan, and suggested that the leaders meet at the Château Triomphe in the Right Bank.

The private conference room beneath the ancient two-story retreat was the perfect setting for new beginnings. Lamps mounted on the stone walls cast an amber light across the plush furnishings. It was more like a private living room than a conference room: tall leather wing chairs budding with brass buttons, a large fireplace licked by greedy flames, a crystal chandelier over the brass coffee table, a fully stocked bar.

And most importantly, heavy walls. Very heavy walls.

Armand Fortier was a thick man. Thick eyebrows, thick wrists, thick lips. His mind, he would say, was sharp enough to cut any woman down to size in a matter of seconds. They never knew what to do with such an assertive statement, but it generally put them in a defensive mind-set so that when he did dominate them, they were not quite so submissive.

It was his only vice.

That and power.

He knew that he could have muscled his way into the presidency long ago, but he wasn't interested in France—the scrutiny leveled at such an office would have worked against him. His appointment as the minister of foreign affairs, however, put him in the perfect position to achieve his true aspirations.

Henri Gaetan was a tall, thin man with deep-set eyes and a jaw line as sharp as Fortier's mind. "What are you saying, Armand? That you work for Valborg Svensson?"

"No."

Fortier had first recruited Svensson fifteen years ago to conduct a much simpler operation: untraceable arms deals with several interested nations, which involved biological weapons research in exchange for lucrative contracts. The deals had earned him billions. The money had fueled Svensson's pharmaceutical empire, with strings attached, naturally.

Fortier hadn't grasped the true potential of the right biological weapon until he watched one of those nations discreetly use an agent of Svensson's against the Americans. The incident had forever altered the course of Fortier's life.

"Then how is this possible?" the president demanded. "You're suggesting that we give in to his demands—"

"No. I'm suggesting that you give in to my demands."

"So he works for you," said Chombarde.

"Gentlemen, perhaps you don't truly understand what has happened. Let me clarify. Half of our citizens are going to work and feeding their children and attending school and doing whatever else they do in this wonderful republic of ours today without the slightest notion that they have been infected with a virus that will overtake every last soul on this planet within two weeks. It is called the Raison Strain, and it will sit quietly for the next eighteen days before it begins its killing. Then it will kill very quickly. There is no cure. There is no way to *find* a cure. There is no way to stop the virus. There is only one antivirus, and I control it. Is there any part of this explanation that escapes any of you?"

"But what you're suggesting is morally reprehensible!" the premier said.

Only the minister of defense, Georges Du Braeck, hadn't spoken. He seemed ambivalent. This was good. Fortier would need Du Braeck's cooperation more than any of the others.

"No sir. Embracing death is morally reprehensible. I'm offering your only escape from that most certain death. Very few men in this world will be given the kind of opportunity I'm giving you tonight."

For a few moments no one spoke.

The president pushed himself to standing and faced Fortier at ten feet. "You're underestimating the world's nuclear powers. You expect them to just load up their aircraft carriers and their merchant fleets and float their entire nuclear arsenals to France because we demand it? They will *launch* them first!"

It was the same objection other heads of much smaller states had voiced when he'd first suggested the plan a decade ago. Fortier smiled at the pompous pole of a man.

"Do you take me for a fool, Henri? You think I have spent less time making calculations in the last ten years than you have after only a few minutes? Please sit down."

There was a tremble in Henri Gaetan's hands. He reached back for a grip on the chair and sat slowly.

"Good. They will object, naturally, but you underestimate the human drive for self-preservation. In the end, when faced with a choice between the bloody death of twenty million innocent children and their military, they will choose their children. We will make sure that the choice is understood in those terms. The British, the Russians, the Germans . . . All will choose to live and fight another day. As I hope you will."

The nature of his threat against each of them personally was starting to sink in, he thought.

"Let me phrase it this way: In fewer than eighteen days, the balance of power on this planet will have shifted dramatically. The course is set; the outcome is inevitable. We have chosen France to host the world's new superpower. As the leaders of France, you have two choices. You can facilitate this shift in global power and live as a part of the leadership you've all secretly wanted for so many years, or you can deny me and die with the rest."

Now they surely understood.

The minister of defense sat with legs crossed, glowing like any good Stalinist faced with such an ultimatum. He finally spoke. "May I ask a few questions?"

"Please."

"There is no physical way for the United States, let alone the rest of the world, to ship all of its nuclear weapons in fourteen days. They have to be evacuated from launching points and armament caches, shipped to the East Coast, loaded on ships, and sailed across the Atlantic."

"Naturally. The list we have given them includes all of their ICBMs, all long-range missiles, most of their navy, including their submarines, and most of their air force, much of which can be flown. The United States will have to take extraordinary measures, but we're demanding nothing of them or anyone else that can't be done. As for the British, India, Pakistan, and Israel, we are demanding their entire nuclear arsenals."

"China and Russia?"

"China. Let's just say that China will not be a problem. They have no love for the United States. China has agreed already and will begin shipments tomorrow in exchange for certain favors. They will be an example for others to follow. Russia is a different story, but we have several critical elements in alignment. Although they will sound off their objections, they will comply."

"Then we have allies."

"In a manner of speaking."

The revelation delivered a long moment of silence. "The Americans are still the greatest threat," said Gaetan. "Assuming the Americans do agree, how can France accommodate all of this"—the president drew his hand through the air—"this massive amount of hardware? We don't have the people or the space."

"Destroy it," the defense minister said.

"Very good, Du Braeck. Superiority is measured in ratios, not sums, yes? Ten to one is better than a thousand to five hundred. We will sink more than half of the military hardware we receive. Think of this as forced disarmament. History may even smile on us."

"Which is why you've chosen the deep water near the Brest naval base."

"Among other reasons."

"And how can we protect ourselves against an assault during this transition of power?" the defense minister asked.

Fortier had expected these questions and possessed answers so detailed that he could never begin to explain everything at this meeting. Inventories of hardware, possible troop movement, preemptive strikes, political will— every possibility had been considered at great length. Tonight his only task was to win the trust of these four men.

"Fourteen days is enough time to ship arms, not deploy troops. Any immediate long-range attack would come by air. Thanks to the Russians, we will have the threat of retaliation to deter any such attack. The only other immediate threat would come from our neighbors, primarily England. We will be at our weakest for the next three days, until we can reposition our forces to repel a ground attack and take on reinforcements from the Chinese. But the world will be in a political tailspin—confusion will buy us the time we need."

"Unless they learn who is responsible now."

"They will have to assume that the French government is being forced. Besides that, they have no guarantee that an attack would secure the antivirus. The antivirus won't be held up in a vial in our parliament for all the world to see. Only I will know where it is."

"Why France?"

"Please, Georges. Wasn't it Hitler who said that he who controls France controls Europe, and he who controls Europe controls the world? He was right. If there were a more strategic country, I would take my leave and go now. France is and always will be the center of the world."

The president had crossed his legs; the head of the *Sûreté* had stopped blinking; the minister of defense was virtually glowing. They were softening.

Only Prime Minister Boisverte still glared.

"Let me give you an example of how this is going to play out, gentlemen. Jean, would you come here?"

The defiant prime minister just stared at him.

He motioned him. "Please. Stand over here. I insist."

The man still hesitated. He was hard to the bones.

"Then where you are will do." Fortier reached into his jacket and pulled out a silenced 9 mm pistol. He pointed the gun at the prime minister and pulled the trigger. The slug punched through the chair just above his shoulder.

The prime minister's eyes bulged.

"You see, this is what we have done. We've fired a warning shot across their bow. Right now they aren't certain of our will to carry through. But soon enough"—he shifted the pistol and shot the man through his fore-head—"they will be."

The prime minister slumped in his chair.

"Don't think of this as a threat, Henri. Jean would have died in eighteen days anyway. We all will unless we do exactly what I have said. Does anyone doubt that?"

The remaining three men looked at him with a calm that pleasantly surprised Fortier.

Fortier slipped the gun back into his pocket and straightened his jacket. "If I die, the antivirus would be lost. The world would die. But I have no intention of dying. I invite you to join me with similar intentions."

"Naturally," Georges said.

Fortier glanced at the president. "Henri?"

"Yes."

"Chombarde?"

The head of the *Sûreté* dipped his head. "Of course."

"And how do we proceed?" the president asked.

Fortier walked around his chair and sat.

"As for the members of the military, the National Assembly, and the Senate, who must know, our explanation is simple: A new demand has come from Svensson. He has chosen our naval base in Brest to accommodate his demands. France will agree with the understanding that we are luring Svensson into our own web. A bluff. Voices of opposition will begin to disappear within the week. I anticipate we will have to call for martial law to protect against any insurgence or riots at week's end. By then we will have most of the world in a vise, and the French people will know that their only hope for survival lies in our hands."

"My dear, my dear," the president muttered. "We are really doing this."

"Yes. We are."

Fortier reached for a stack of folders on the table at his elbow. "We don't have the time to work through all of our individual challenges, so I've taken the liberty of doing it for you. We will need to adjust as we go, of course." He handed each a folder. "Think of this as a game of high-stakes poker. I expect you will each hold your cards close to the chest."

They took the folders and flipped them open. A sense of purpose had settled on the room. Henri Gaetan glanced at the slumped body of the prime minister.

"He's taken an emergency trip to the south, Henri."

The president nodded.

"Thomas Hunter," Chombarde said, lifting the top page from his folder. "The man who kidnapped Monique de Raison."

"Yes. He is . . . a unique man who's stumbled into our way. He may know more than we need him to know. Use whatever force is necessary to bring him, alive if possible. You will coordinate your efforts with Carlos Missirian. Consider Hunter your highest priority."

"Securing a man in the United States could be a challenge at a time like this."

"You won't have to. I am certain that he will come to us, if not to France, then to where we have the woman."

A beat.

"There are 577 members in the Assembly," the president said. "You have listed 97 who could be a problem. I think there may be more."

They reviewed and on occasion adjusted the plans deep into the night. Objections were overcome, new arguments cast and dismissed, strategies fortified. A sense of purpose and perhaps a little destiny slowly overtook all of them with growing certainty.

After all, they had little choice.

The die had been cast.

France had always been destined to save the world, and in the end that's exactly what they were doing. They were saving the world from its own demise.

They left the room six hours later.

Prime Minister Jean Boisverte left in a body bag.

12

THOMAS JERKED awake. He tumbled out of bed and searched the room. It was still dark outside. Rachelle slept on their bed. Two thoughts drummed through his mind, drowning out the simple reality of this room, this bed, these sheets, this bark floor under his bare feet.

First, the realities he was experiencing were unquestionably linked, perhaps in more ways than he ever could have guessed, and both of those realities were at risk.

Second, he knew what he must do now, immediately and at all costs. He must convince Rachelle to help him find Monique, and then he must find the Books of Histories.

But the image of his wife sleeping unexpectedly dampened his enthusiasm to solicit her help. So sweet and lost in sleep. Her hair fell across her face, and he was tempted to brush it free.

Her arm was smeared with blood. The sheet was red where her arm had rested.

His pulse surged. She was bleeding? Yes, a small cut on her upper arm—he hadn't noticed it last evening in all the excitement of his return. She hadn't mentioned it either. But was all this blood from such a small cut?

He glanced at his own forearm and remembered: He'd cut himself in the laboratory of Dr. Myles Bancroft. Yes, of course, he'd been sleeping here when that had happened, and he'd bled here, exactly as he feared he might.

His forearm had rubbed Rachelle's arm. The blood was half his. Half hers.

The realization only fueled his urgency. If he couldn't stop the virus, he would undoubtedly die. They might all die!

Then what? He hurried to the window and peered out. The air was quiet—an hour before sunrise. The thought of waking Rachelle to persuade her to forget everything she'd said about his dreams struck him as a futile task. She would be furious with him for dreaming again. And why would she think his cut was anything but an accident?

The wise man, on the other hand, might understand. Jeremiah.

Thomas pulled his tunic on quietly, strapped his boots to his feet, and slipped into the cool morning air.

Ciphus lived in the large house nearest the lake, a privilege he insisted on as keeper of the faith. He wasn't pleased to be awakened so early, but as soon as he saw that it was Thomas, his mood improved.

"For a religious man, you drink far too much ale," Thomas said.

The man grunted. "For a warrior, you don't sleep enough."

"And now you're making no sense. Warriors aren't meant to sleep their lives away. Where can I find Jeremiah of Southern?"

"The old man? In the guesthouse. It's still night though."

"Which guesthouse?"

"The one Anastasia oversees, I think."

Thomas nodded. "Thank you, man. Get back to sleep."

"Thomas—"

But he departed before the elder could voice any further objections.

It took him ten minutes to locate Jeremiah's bedroom and wake him. The old man swung his legs to the floor and sat up in the waning moonlight.

"What is it? Who are you?"

"Shh, it's me, old man. Thomas."

"Thomas? Thomas of Hunter?"

"Yes. Keep your voice down; I don't want to wake the others. These houses have thin walls."

But the old man couldn't hold back his enthusiasm. He stood and clasped Thomas's arms. "Here, sit on my bed. I'll get us a drink."

"No, no. Sit back down, please. I have an urgent question."

Thomas eased the old man down and sat next to him.

"How can I host such an honored guest without offering him a drink?"

"You have offered me a drink. But I didn't come for your hospitality. And I am the one who should honor you."

"Nonsense—"

"I came about the Books of Histories," Thomas said.

Silence came over Jeremiah.

"I have heard that you may know some things about the Books of Histories. Where they might be and if they can be read. Do you?"

The old man hesitated. "The Books of Histories?" His voice sounded thin and strained.

"You must tell me what you know."

"Why do you want to know about the Books?"

"Why shouldn't I want to know?" Thomas asked.

"I didn't say you shouldn't. I only asked why."

"Because I want to know what happened in the histories."

"This is a sudden desire? Why not ten years ago?"

"It's never occurred to me that they could be useful."

"And did it ever occur to you that they are missing for a reason?"

"Please, Jeremiah."

The old man hesitated again. "Yes. Well, I've never seen them. And I fear they have a power that isn't meant for any man."

Thomas clasped Jeremiah's arm. "Where are they?"

"It is possible they are with the Horde."

Thomas stood. Of course! Jeremiah had been with the Horde before bathing in the lake.

"You know this with certainty?"

"No. As I said, I've never seen them. But I have heard it said that the Books of Histories follow Qurong into battle."

"Qurong has them? Can . . . can he read them?"

"I don't think so, no. I'm not sure *you* could read them."

"But surely someone can read them. You."

"Me?" Jeremiah chuckled. "I don't know. They may not even exist, for all we know. It was all hearsay, you know."

"But you believe they do," Thomas said.

The first rays of dawn glinted in Jeremiah's eyes. "Yes."

So the old man had known all along that they existed with the Horde, and yet he had never offered this information. Thomas understood: The Books of Histories had long ago been taken from Elyon's people and committed to an oral history for some reason. If it made good sense so long ago, then surely it made good sense now. Hadn't Tanis, as Rachelle so aptly pointed out, been led down the wrong path by his fascination with their knowledge? Perhaps Jeremiah was right. The Books of Histories were not meant for man.

Still, Thomas needed them.

"I'm going after them, Jeremiah. Believe me when I say that our very survival may depend on the Books."

Jeremiah stood shakily. "That would mean going after Qurong!"

"Yes, and Qurong is with the army that we defeated in the Natalga Gap. They're in the desert west of here, licking their wounds." Thomas stepped quickly to the window. Daylight had begun to dim the moon.

"You've told me where the commander's tent lies—in the center, always. Isn't that right?" he asked, turning.

"Yes, where he is surrounded by his army. You'd have to be one of them to get anywhere near—"

The old man's eyes went wide. He walked forward, face stricken. "Don't do this! Why? Why would you risk the life of our greatest warrior for a few old books that may not exist?"

"Because if I don't find them, I may die." He looked away. "We may all die."

⸻

Rachelle sat at the table as if in a dream.

Knowing that it was in fact a dream.

Knowing just as well that it was no more a dream than the love she had for Thomas. Or didn't have for Thomas. The thoughts confused her.

The dream was vivid as dreams went. She was working desperately over the table, seeking a solution to a terrible problem, hoping that the solution would present itself at any moment, sure that if it didn't come, life as she knew it would end. Not just in this small room, mind you, but all over the world.

This was where the generalities ended and the specifics began.

The white table, for example. Smooth. White. *Formica.*

The box on the table. *A computer.* Powerful enough to crunch a million bits of information every thousandth of a second.

The mouse at her fingertips, gliding on a black foam pad. The equation on the monitor, the Raison Strain, a mutation of her own creation. The laboratory with its electron microscope and the other instruments to her right. This was all as familiar as her own name.

Monique de Raison.

No. Her real name was Rachelle, and she wasn't really familiar with anything in this room, least of all the woman who bore the name Monique de Raison.

Or was she?

The monitor went black for a moment. In it she saw Monique's reflection. *Her* reflection. Dark hair, dark eyes, high cheekbones, small lips.

It was almost as if she *was* Monique.

Monique de Raison, world-renowned geneticist, hidden away in a mountain named Cyclops on an Indonesian island by Valborg Svensson, who had released the Raison Strain in twenty-four cities around the world.

Whoever searched for her would probably never find her. Not even Thomas Hunter, the man who'd risked his life twice for her.

Monique had some feelings for Thomas, but not the same as Rachelle had for him.

She stared at the screen and dragged her pointer over the bottom corner of the model. One last time she lifted the sheet of paper covered with a hundred penciled calculations. Yes, this was it. It had to be. She set the page down and withdrew her hand.

Something bit her finger and she jerked her hand back. *Paper cut.* She ignored it and stared at the screen.

"Please, please," she whispered. "Please be here."

She clicked the mouse button. A formula popped into a small box on the monitor.

She let out a sob, a huge sigh of relief, and leaned back into her chair.

Her code was intact. The key was here and, by all appearances, un-affected by the mutation. So then, the virus she engineered to disable these genes might also work!

Another thought tempered her elation. When Svensson had what he wanted, he would kill her. For a brief moment she considered not telling Svensson how close she was. But she couldn't hold back information that might save countless lives, regardless of who used that information.

Then again, she might not be close at all. He hadn't told her every-thing. There was something—

"Mother. Mother, wake up."

Rachelle bolted up in bed.

"Thomas?"

Her son stood in the doorway. "He's not here. Did he go out on the patrols?"

Rachelle threw the covering off and stood. "No. No, he should be here."

"Well, his armor's gone. And his sword."

She looked at the rack where his leathers and scabbard usually hung. It stood in the corner, empty like a skeleton. Maybe with all of the people arriving for the Gathering, he'd gone out to check on his patrols.

"I asked in the village," Samuel said. "No one knows where he is."

She pulled back and closed the canvas drape that acted as their door. She quickly traded her bed clothes for a soft fitted leather blouse laced with crossing ties in the back. In her closet hung over a dozen colorful dresses and skirts, primarily for the celebrations. She grabbed a tan leather skirt and cinched it tight with rolled rope ties. Six pairs of moccasins, some decorative, some very utilitarian, lay side by side under her dresses. She scooped up the first pair.

All of this she did without thought. Her mind was still in her dream. With each passing moment it seemed to dim, like a distant memory. Even so, parts of this memory screamed through her mind like a flight of startled macaws.

She'd entered Thomas's dream world.

She'd been there, in a laboratory hidden in a mountain named Cyclops with—or was it as?—Monique, doing and understanding things that she had no knowledge of. And if Monique had found this key of hers, she might be killed before Thomas ever found her.

Her heart pounded. She had to tell Thomas!

Rachelle crossed to the table, snatched up the braided bronze bracelet Thomas had made for her, and slid it up her arm, above the elbow where—

She saw the blood on her arm, a dark red smear that had dried. Her cut? It must have been aggravated and broken open during the night.

The sheets were stained as well.

In her eagerness to find Thomas, she considered ignoring it for the moment. No, she couldn't walk around with blood on her arm. She ran to the kitchen basin, lowered it under the reed, and released the gravity-drawn water by lifting a small lever that stopped the flow.

"Marie? Samuel?"

No response. They were out of the house.

The water stung her right index finger. She examined it. Another tiny cut.

Paper cut. This was from her dreams! Her mouth suddenly felt desert dry.

A thought crashed into her mind. Exactly how she was connected to Monique she didn't know, but she was, and this cut proved it. Thomas had been emphatic: If he died in that world, he would also die in this one. Perhaps whatever happened to Monique could very well happen to her! If this Svensson killed her, for example, they both might die.

She had to reach Thomas before he dreamed again so that he could rescue her!

Rachelle ran into the road, looked both ways through several hundred pedestrians who loitered along the wide causeway, and then ran toward the lake. Ciphus would know. If not, then Mikil or William.

"Good morning, Rachelle!"

It was Cassandra, one of the elder's wives. She wore a wreath of white flowers in her braided hair, and she'd applied the purple juice from mulberries above her eyes. The mood of the annual Gathering was spreading in spite of the unexpected Horde threats.

"Cassandra, have you seen Mikil?"

"She's on patrol, I think. You don't know? I thought Thomas went with them?"

Rachelle ran without further salutation. It was unlike Thomas to leave without telling her. Was there trouble?

She raced around the corner of Ciphus's house and pulled up, panting. The elder was in a huddle with Alexander, two other elders, and an old man she immediately recognized as the one who'd come in from the desert. Jeremiah of Southern. The one who knew about the Books of Histories.

Their conversation stalled.

"He's gone?" she demanded.

No one responded.

Rachelle leaped to the porch. "Where? He's on patrol?"

"A patrol," Ciphus said, shifting. "Yes, it's a patrol. Yes, he's gone—"

"Stop being so secretive," she snapped. "It's not a patrol or he would have told me." She looked at Jeremiah. "He's gone after them. Hasn't he? You told him where he might find the Books and he's gone after them. Tell me it isn't so!"

Jeremiah dipped his head. "Yes. Forgive me. I tried to stop him, but he insisted."

"Of course he insisted. Thomas always insists. Does that mean you had to tell him?" At the moment she was of a mind to knock these old men's heads together.

"Where has he gone? I have to tell him something."

Ciphus shoved his stool back and stood. "Please, Rachelle. Even if we knew where he was, you couldn't go after him. They left early on fast horses. They're halfway to the desert by now."

"Which desert?"

"Well . . . the big desert outside the forest. You cannot follow. I forbid it."

"You're in no position to forbid me from finding my husband."

"You're a mother with—"

"I have more skill than half of the warriors in our Guard, and you know it. I trained half of them in Marduk! Now you will either tell me where he's gone or I will track him myself."

"What is it, child?" Jeremiah asked gently. "What do you have for him?"

She hesitated, wondering how much Thomas had told the man.

"I have information that might save both of our lives," she said.

Jeremiah glanced at Ciphus, who offered no direction. "He's gone to the Natalga Gap with two of his lieutenants and seven warriors."

"And what will he find there?"

"The leader of the Horde, in the desert beyond the Gap. But you mustn't go, Rachelle. His decision to go after these books may lead to tragedy as it is."

"Besides," Alexander said, "we can't afford to send more of our force on yet another crazed mission."

"This has to do with these dreams of his?" Ciphus asked.

"They may not be dreams after all," Rachelle said, and she was surprised to hear the words come from her mouth.

"You as well?"

She ignored the question. "I have information that I believe may save my husband's life. If any of you would even consider holding me back, then his death will be on your hands."

Her overstatement held them in silence.

"If you have any other information that would help me, please, now is not the time to be coy."

"How dare you manipulate us!" Ciphus cried. "If there is any man who can survive this fool's errand, it is Thomas. But we can't have his woman chasing him into the desert four days before the Gathering!"

Rachelle stepped off the porch and turned her back on them. Now her determination to track Thomas down was motivated as much by these men's insults as by her own realization that her husband had been right about his dreams.

"Rachelle."

She turned and faced Jeremiah, who'd walked to the end of the porch.

"They will be due west of the Gap," he said. "I beg you, child, don't go." He paused, then continued with resignation. "Take extra water. As much as your horse can carry. I know it will slow you down, but the disease will slow you down even more."

The tremble in the old man's voice put her on edge.

"He means to become one of them," Jeremiah said. "He means to enter their camp."

Rachelle could not dare believe what she had just heard.

And then she knew it was true. It was exactly what Thomas would do if he knew, if he absolutely *knew*, that both realities were real.

Rachelle sprinted for the stables.

Dear Elyon, give me strength.

———

They were nine of his best, including William and Mikil. With himself, ten.

The three extra canteens of water they each carried weighed them down more than Thomas would have liked. It was a dangerous game that he was playing, and he couldn't risk being caught without the cleansing water.

They had ridden hard all day and now entered the same canyon their black powder had blasted thirty-six hours earlier. The stench rose from thousands of dead buried beneath the rubble and strewn on the desert floor.

They rode the Forest Guard's palest horses. Thomas's steed snorted and pawed at the sand. He urged the horse on and it moved forward reluctantly.

"Hard to believe that we did all this," William said.

"Don't think it's the end of them," Mikil said. "There's no end to them."

Thomas pulled a scarf over his nose and led the warriors into the rocks. The horses carried them through the canyon, past the burlap-cloaked bodies of their fallen enemy. He'd seen his share of dead, but the magnitude of this slaughter made him nauseated.

It was said that the Horde cared less for the lives of their men than the lives of their horses. Any Scab who defied his leader was summarily punished without trial. They favored the breaking of bones to flogging or other forms of punishment. It wasn't unusual to find a Scab soldier with numerous bones broken left to die on the hot desert sand without having shed a drop of blood. Public executions involved drowning the offender in pools of gray water, a prospect that instilled more fear in the Scabs than any other threat of death.

The Horde's terror of water had to be motivated by more than the pain that accompanied cleansing in the lakes, Thomas thought, *though he wasn't sure what.*

He waited until they had passed the front lines of the dead before stopping by a group of several prone bodies. He dismounted, stripped the hooded robe off a Scab buzzing with flies, and shook it in the air. He coughed and threw the cloak over the rump of his horse.

"Let's go, all of you," he said. "Dress."

William grunted and dismounted. "I never would have guessed I'd ever stoop so low as to dress in a whore's clothes." He dutifully began to strip one of the bodies. The rest found cloaks and donned them, muttering curses, not of objection, but of offense. The stench couldn't be washed from the burlap.

Thomas retrieved a warrior's sword and knife. Studded boots. Shin guards. These were new additions, he noted. The hardened, cured leather was uncharacteristic of the Desert Dwellers. The painful condition of their skin tempered their use of armor, but these shin guards had been layered with a soft cloth to minimize the friction.

"They're learning," he said. "Their technology isn't that far behind our own."

"They don't have black powder," Mikil said. "Ask me and I'll say they're finished. Give me three months and I'll have new defenses built around every forest. They don't stand a chance."

Thomas pulled the robe he'd liberated over his head and strapped on the foreign dagger.

"Until they do have black powder," he said, stuffing his own gear behind a boulder. "Have you considered what they could do to the forest if they had explosives? Besides, I'm not sure we have three months. They're growing brave and they're fighting with more intelligence. We're running out of warriors."

"Then what would you suggest?" Mikil asked. "Treason?"

She was speaking of the incident in the Southern Forest. A runner had arrived just before their departure and reported on the Southern Forest's victory over the Horde.

Only it wasn't Jamous who'd driven the Scabs away. He'd lost over half of his men in a hopeless battle in which he was outflanked and surrounded—a rare and deadly position to be caught in.

No, it was Justin, the runner said with a glint in his eye. He'd singlehandedly struck terror into the Horde without one swipe of his blade. He'd negotiated a withdrawal with none other than the great general, Martyn himself.

The entire Southern Forest had sung Justin's praises in the Elyon Valley for three hours. Justin had spoken to them of a new way, and they had listened as if he were a prophet, the runner said. Then Justin had disappeared into the forest with his small band.

"Have I once suggested yielding to the Horde in any way?" Thomas asked. "I'll die waiting for the prophecy's fulfillment if I have to. Don't question my loyalty. One stray warrior is the least of our concerns at the moment. We'll have time enough for that at the Gathering."

He'd told her about the challenge and the Council's request that he defend it, should it come down to a fight.

"You're right," she said. "I meant no disrespect."

Thomas mounted and brought his horse around. "We ride in silence. Pull your hoods over your heads."

They headed out of the canyon, dressed as a band of Desert Dwellers, following the Horde's deep tracks.

The sun set slowly behind the cliffs, leaving the group in deep shadows. They soon emerged from the rock formations and headed due west toward a dimming horizon.

Thomas's explanation of the mission had been simple. He'd learned the Horde had a terrible weakness: They rode into battle with the superstitious belief that their religious relics would give them victory. If a small band of Forest Guard could penetrate the Horde camp and steal the relics, they might deal a terrible blow. He had also learned that at this very moment, Qurong, who'd certainly commanded the army they'd just defeated, carried those relics with him. The relics were the Books of Histories. Who would go with him to deal such a blow to the Horde?

All nine had immediately agreed.

At this very moment, he was lying in a hotel room not ten blocks from the capitol building in Washington, D.C., sleeping. A hundred government agencies were burning the midnight oil, trying to make sense of the threat that had stood the world on its end. Sleep was undoubtedly the furthest thing from their minds. They were busy trying to decide who should know and who should not, which family members they could warn without leaking the word that might send a panic through the nation. They were thinking of ways to isolate and quarantine and survive.

But not Thomas Hunter. He understood one thing very few others could. If there was a solution to Svensson's threat, it might very well lie in his sleep.

In his dreams.

They first saw the sea of fires four hours later, pinpricks of smoking light from oil torches several miles beyond the dune they had crested. Wood was scarce, but the black liquid that seeped from the sand in distant reserves met their needs as well or better than wood. Thomas had never seen the oil reserves, but the Forest Guard frequently confiscated barrels of the stuff from fallen armies and hauled it off as spoil.

They drew up side by side, ten wide, looking west. For several seconds they sat atop the dune in total silence. Even what was left of the army was daunting.

"You are certain about this, Thomas?" William said.

"No. But I am certain that our options are growing thin." He sounded far more confident than he felt.

"I should come with you," Mikil said.

"We stick to the plan," he said. "William and I go alone."

They knew the reasons. First there was the matter of their skin. All but Thomas and William had bathed in the lake before leaving. Then there was Mikil: Horde women didn't normally travel with the armies. Even if her skin turned, entering could be dangerous for her, despite her claim that she could look as much a man in burlap as any of them.

"How is your skin, William?"

His lieutenant pulled up his sleeve. "Itching."

Thomas dismounted, pulled out a bag of ash, and tossed it to him. "Face, arms, and legs. Don't be stingy."

"You're sure this will fool them?" Mikil asked.

"I mixed the ash with some of the sulfur we used for the black powder. It's the scent as much as the—"

"Ugh! This is horrid!" William gasped, nose turned from the bag. He coughed. "They'll smell us coming a mile away!"

"Not if we smell like them. It's their dogs that worry me the most. And our eyes."

Mikil stared into his eyes. "They're paling already. In this light you should be fine. And honestly, in this light with enough of that rotten ash on my skin, I could pass as easily as you."

Thomas ignored her persistence.

Ten minutes later he and William had powdered their skin gray, checked their gear to be sure none of it would be associated with the Guard, and remounted. The others remained on foot.

"Okay." Thomas took a deep breath and blew it out slowly. "Here we go. Look for the fire, Mikil, just as we planned. If you see one of their tents suddenly go up in flames, send the rest in for us on horse, fast and low. Bring our horses. Whatever you do, don't forget to keep your hoods on. And you might want to throw some ash on your face for good measure."

"Send the rest? Lead them, you mean."

"Send them. I need someone to lead the Guard in the event it all goes badly."

She glared at him and set her jaw. "I think you should reconsider going in."

"We go with the plan. As always."

"And as always you refuse any voice of caution. I'm looking at the camp and I'm watching my general about to throw himself into this pack of wolves and I'm starting to wonder why."

"For the same reason we've had all day," he said. "Jamous nearly lost his life yesterday, and we the day before. The Horde is gaining strength, and unless we do something to cripple them, not only Jamous, but all of us along with our children, will die."

Mikil crossed her arms and squatted.

"Let's go," William said. "I want to get out of there before daylight."

"The people need you," Thomas told Mikil softly.

"No, the people need you, Thomas."

She frowned. It was hopeless.

"Elyon's strength," Thomas said.

"Elyon's strength," the others muttered. Mikil said nothing. She would snap out of her brooding mood soon enough, but at the moment he let her make her statement.

Thomas clucked his tongue and eased his horse down the slope.

———— ⌘ ————

"Perhaps we should stop here for the night," Suzan said, staring out at the black desert.

"How can we? I didn't come all this way to wait for him. I could have waited for him at the village."

Rachelle kicked her horse into a trot. They'd ridden hard most of the day and picked their way through the body-strewn canyon in the last hour. She'd seen her share of battlefields, but this one had been terrifying.

Suzan drew abreast. "We can't be sure they even went out—there are too many tracks for me to know."

"I know my husband; he went out. If he left the village without so much as a whisper to me, trust me, he's on a mission. He won't stop for darkness. And you're the best tracker in the Guard, aren't you? Then track."

"Even if we do catch them, what advantage is tonight over tomorrow?"

"I told you, I have information that may save his life. He's going for the Books of Histories because of his dreams, Suzan. He may say it's to give the Guard an advantage, and I'm not saying it wouldn't, but there's more to the story. I have to reach him before he dreams so that he can find me."

"Find you?"

She shouldn't have said so much.

"Before he dreams."

"We're risking our necks over another dream?"

"His dream of black powder saved us all. You were there."

Any further explanation would be futile. Thomas himself hadn't been able to satisfy her, neither fifteen years ago nor last night. She pressed her thumb against the forefinger that had been cut in her own dream. There were two worlds, and each affected the other. With each passing mile, her conviction had grown. With each recollection of Thomas's dreams fifteen years earlier, her understanding had broadened, though she had no clue how it was happening, much less why.

But she could not ignore the pain in her finger.

Forgive me, Thomas. Forgive me, my love.

"It still makes no sense to me," Suzan said, searching the ground for tracks.

"And it may never make sense to you. But I'm willing to stake my life on it. I don't want my husband to die, and unless we reach him, he might."

"Thomas doesn't die easily."

"The virus doesn't care who dies easily."

———

They approached the Horde camp from the northeast, over a small rise that fell into a broad flat valley, with a light breeze in their faces.

Thomas lay on his belly next to William and studied the camp. Tens of thousands of torches on stakes lit the desert night with a surreal orange glow. A giant circular blob of lights spread across the sand. Their tents were square, roughly ten by ten, woven from a coarse thread made from the stalks of desert wheat. The stalks were pounded flat and rolled into long strands that the Horde used for everything from their clothing to bindings.

"There!" William pointed to their right. A huge tent rose above the others south of center. "That's it."

"And it's a good half mile past the perimeter," Thomas said quietly.

They'd left their horses staked behind them where they would be hidden by the dune. The Guard had never attempted to infiltrate a camp before. Thomas was banking on a minimal perimeter guard as a result. He and William would go on foot and hopefully slip in unnoticed.

"That's a lot of Horde," William said.

"A whole lot."

William eased his sword a few inches out of its scabbard. "You ever swung a Scab sword before?"

"Once or twice. The blades aren't as sharp as ours."

"The thought of killing a few with their own weapons is appealing."

"Put it away. The last thing I want is a fight. Tonight we are thieves."

His lieutenant shoved the sword home.

"Remember, don't speak unless directly questioned. No eye contact. Keep your hood as far over your face as possible. Walk with pain."

"I *do* have pain," William said. "The cursed disease is killing me already. You said it won't affect the mind for a while. How long?"

"If we get out before morning, we'll be fine."

"We should have brought the water. Their dogs would never know the difference."

"We don't know that. And if we are taken, the water would incriminate us. They can smell it, trust me."

"You have any idea what the Books look like?" William asked.

"Books. Books are books. Maybe scrolls similar to the ones we use, or the flat kind from long ago. If we find them, we'll know. Ready?"

"Always."

They stood.

Deep breath.

"Let's go."

Thomas and William walked as naturally as they could, careful to use the slightly slower step that the rot forced upon the Desert Dwellers. A ring of torches planted every fifty paces ran the camp's circumference.

There was no perimeter guard.

"Stay in the shadows until we enter the main path that leads to the center," Thomas whispered.

"Right up the middle?"

"We're Scabs. We would walk right up the middle."

The stench was nearly unbearable, if anything, stronger than the powder they'd applied. No dogs were barking yet. So far, so good.

Thomas wiped the sweat from his palms, momentarily touched the hilt of the sword hanging from his waist, and walked past the first torch, through a gap between two tents, and into the main camp.

The retarded pace was nearly unbearable. Everything in Thomas urged him to run. He had twice the speed of any of these diseased thugs, and he could probably race straight up the middle, snatch the Books, and fly to the desert before they knew what had happened.

He squashed the impulse. *Slow. Slow, Thomas.*

"Torvil, you ungracious piece of meat," a gruff voice said from the tent to his right. He glanced. A Scab stepped past the flap and glared at him. "Your brother is dying in here and you're looking for women where there are none?"

For a moment Thomas was frozen by indecision. He'd spoken to Scabs before; he'd even spoken at length to their supreme leader's daughter, Chelise.

"Answer me!" the Scab snorted.

He decided. He walked straight on and turned only partially so as not to expose his entire face.

"You're as blind as the bats who cursed you. Am I Torvil? And I would be so lucky to find a woman in this stinking place."

He turned and moved on. The man cursed and stepped back into the tent.

"Easy," William whispered. "That was too much."

"It's how they would speak."

The Scabs had retired for the night, but hundreds still loitered. Most of the tents had their flaps tied open, baring all to any prying eye. The camp where he'd met Chelise had been strewn with woven rugs dyed in purple and red hues. Not so here. No children, no women that he could see.

They passed a group of four men seated cross-legged around a small, smoky fire burning in a basin of oil-soaked sand. The flames warmed a tin pot full of the white, pasty starch they called sago. Made from the roots of desert wheat. Thomas had tasted the bland starch once and announced to his men that it was like eating dirt without all the flavor.

All four Scabs had their hoods withdrawn. By the light of fire and moon, these did not look like fearless suicidal warriors sworn to slaughter the women and children of the forests. In fact, they looked very much like his own people.

One of them raised light gray eyes to Thomas, who averted his stare.

It took Thomas and William fifteen minutes to reach the camp's center. Twice they had been noticed; twice they had passed without incident. But Thomas knew that getting into the camp in the dead of night wouldn't be their challenge. Finding the Books and getting them out would be.

The large central tent was actually a complex of about five tents, each guarded. From what he could determine, they'd come at the complex from the rear.

The canvas glowed a dull orange from the torches ablaze inside. The sheer size of the tents, the soldiers who guarded them, and the use of color collectively boasted of Qurong's importance. Horde dyes came from brightly colored desert rocks ground into a powder. The dye had been applied to the tent's canvas in large barbed patterns.

"This way."

Thomas veered into an open passage behind the complex. He pulled William into the shadows and spoke in a whisper. "What do you think?"

"Swords," William said.

"No fight!"

"Then make yourself invisible. There are too many guards. Even if we get inside, we'll meet others there."

"You're too quick with the sword. We'll go in as guards. They wear the light sash around their chests, you saw?"

"You think we can kill two without being seen? Impossible."

"Not if we take them from the inside."

William glanced at the tent's floor seam. "We have no idea what or who's inside."

"Then, and only then, we will use our swords." Thomas whipped out his dagger. "Check the front."

William stepped to the edge of the tent and peered around. He returned, sword now drawn. "Clear."

"We do this quickly."

They understood that surprise and speed would be their only allies if the room was occupied. They dropped to their knees, and Thomas ran the blade quickly along the base of the tent with a long ripping slash that he prayed would go unheard.

He jerked the canvas up and William rolled inside. Thomas dove after him.

They came up in a room lit by a flickering torch flame. Three forms lay to their left, and William leaped for one that was rising. These were clearly the servants' quarters. But the cry of a servant could kill them as easily as any sword.

William reached the servant before he could turn to see what the disturbance was. He clamped his hand around the Scab's face and brought the sword up to his neck.

"No!" Thomas whispered. "Alive!"

Keeping hold of the startled servant, William stepped toward the others, smashed the butt of his knife down on the back of the sleeping man's head, and then repeated the same blow on the third.

The Scab in William's arms began to struggle.

"She'll wake the whole tent," William objected. "I should kill her!"

A woman? Thomas grabbed her hair and brought his own dagger up to her throat. "A sound and you die," he whispered. "We're not here to kill, you understand? But we will if we have to."

Her eyes were like moons, wide and gray with terror.

"Do you understand?"

She nodded vigorously.

"Then tell me what I want to know. No one knows that you saw us. I'll knock you out so that no one can accuse you of betrayal."

Her face wrinkled with fear.

"You would rather have me kill you? Be sensible and you'll be fine. A bump on the head is all."

She didn't look persuaded, but neither did she make any sound.

"The Books of Histories," Thomas said. "You know them?"

Thomas felt a moment's pity for the woman. She was too horrified to think, much less speak. He released her hair.

"Let her go."

"Sir, I advise against it."

"You see? He advises against it," Thomas said to the woman. "That's because he thinks you'll scream. But I think better of you. I believe that you're nothing more than a frightened girl who wants to live. If you scream, we'll have to kill half the people in this tent, including Qurong himself. Cooperate and we may kill no one." He pressed the blade against her skin.

"Will you cooperate?"

She nodded.

"Release her."

"Sir—"

"Do it."

William slowly let his hand off her mouth. Her lips trembled but she made no sound.

"Good. You'll find that I'm a man of my word. You may ask Chelise, the daughter of Qurong, about me. She knows me as Roland. Now tell me. Do you know of the Books?"

She nodded.

"And are they in these tents?"

Nothing.

"I swear, woman, if you insist on—"

"Yes," she whispered.

Yes? Yes, of course he'd come for precisely this, but to hear her say that the Books of Histories, those ancient writings of such mythic power, were here at this very moment . . . It was more than he'd dared truly believe.

"Where?"

"They are sacred! I can't . . . I would be killed for telling you. The Great One allows no one to see them! Please, please I beg you—"

"Keep your voice down!" he hissed. They were running out of time. At any moment someone would come bursting in.

Thomas lowered his blade. "Fine then. Kill her, William."

"No, please!" She fell to her knees and gripped his robe. "I'll tell you. They are in the second tent, in the room behind the Great One's bedchamber."

Thomas raised his hand to William. He dropped to one knee and scratched an image of the complex into the sand. "Show me."

She showed him with a trembling finger.

"Is there any way into this room besides through the bedchamber?"

"No. The walls are strung with a . . . a . . . metal . . ."

"A metal mesh?"

"Yes, yes, a metal mesh."

"Are there guards in these rooms here?" He pointed to the adjoining rooms.

"I don't know. I swear, I don't—"

"Okay. Then lie down and I will spare your life."

She didn't move.

"It will be one knock on the head and you'll have your excuse along with the others. Don't be irrational!"

She lay in her bed and William hit her.

"Now what?" William asked, standing from the unconscious form.

"The Books are here."

"I heard. They are also in a virtual vault."

"I heard."

Thomas faced the flap leading from the room. Apparently no alarm had been raised.

"As you said, we don't have all night," William said.

"Let me think."

He had to find more information. They now knew that the Books not only existed, but lay less than thirty yards from where he stood. The find gripped him in a way he hadn't expected. There was no telling how valuable the Books might be. In the other world, certainly, but even here! The Roush had certainly gone out of their way to conceal them. How had Qurong managed to lay his hands on them in the first place?

"Sir—"

Thomas walked to the wall, where several robes hung. He stripped off his own.

"What are you doing?"

"I'm becoming a servant. Their robes aren't as light as the warriors'."

William followed suit. They pulled on the new robes and stuffed the old under the servant's blanket. They would need those again.

"Wait here. I'm going find out more."

"What? I can't—"

"Wait here! Do nothing. Stay alive. If I'm not back in half an hour, then find me. If you can't find me, get back to the camp."

"Sir—"

"No questions, William."

He straightened his robe, pulled the hood over his head, and walked from the room.

———— ∞ ————

The tents were really one large tent after all. Nothing less than a portable castle. Purple and red drapes hung on most walls, and dyed carpets ran across the ground. Bronze statues of winged serpents with ruby eyes seemed to occupy every corner. Otherwise, the halls were deserted.

Thomas walked like a Scab in the direction the servant had shown him. The only sign of life came from a steady murmur of discussion that grew as he approached Qurong's quarters.

Thomas entered the hall leading to the royal chambers and stopped. A single carpet bearing a black image of the serpentine Shataiki bat whom they worshiped filled the wall. To his left, a heavy turquoise curtain separated him from the voices. To his right, another curtain cloaked silence.

Thomas ignored the thumping of his heart and moved to the right. He eased the cloth aside, found the room empty, and slipped in.

A long mat set with bronze goblets and a tall chalice sat in the center of what could only be Qurong's dining room. What Thomas called furniture was sparse among the Desert Dwellers—they lacked the wood—but their ingenuity was evident. Large stuffed cushions, each emblazoned with the serpentine crest, sat around the mat. At the room's four corners, flames licked the still air, casting light on no less than twenty swords and sickles and clubs and every conceivable Horde weapon, all of which hung from the far wall.

A large reed barrel stood in the corner to his right. He hurried over and peered in. Stagnant desert water. The water ran near the surface in pockets where the Desert Dwellers grew their wheat and dug their shallow wells. It was no wonder they preferred to drink it mixed with wheat and fermented as wine or beer.

He wasn't here to drink their putrid water.

Thomas checked the hall and found it clear. He was halfway through the entryway when the drape into the opposite room moved.

He retreated and eased the flap down.

"A drink, general?"

"Why not?"

Thomas ran for the only cover the room offered. The barrel. He slid behind, dropped to his knees, and held his breath.

The flap opened. *Whooshed* closed.

"A good day, sir. A good day indeed."

"And it's only beginning."

Beer splashed from the chalice into a goblet. Then another. Thomas eased as far into the shadow as he dared without touching the tent wall.

"To my most honored general," a smooth voice said. No one but Qurong would refer to any general as *my general.*

"Martyn, general of generals."

Qurong and Martyn! Bronze struck bronze. They drank.

"To our supreme ruler, who will soon rule over all the forests," the general said.

The goblets clinked again.

Thomas let the air escape his lungs and breathed carefully. He slipped his hand under his cloak and touched the dagger. Now! He should take them both now; it wouldn't be an impossible task. In three steps he could reach them and send them both to Hades.

"I tell you, the brilliance of the plan is in its boldness," Qurong said. "They may suspect, but with our forces at their doorstep, they will be forced to believe. We'll speak about peace and they will listen because they must. By the time we work the betrayal with him, it will be too late."

What was this? A thread of sweat leaked down Thomas's neck. He moved his head for a glimpse of the men. Qurong wore a white robe without a hood. A large bronze pendant of the Shataiki hung from his neck. But it was the man's head that held Thomas's attention. Unlike most of the Horde, he wore his hair long, matted and rolled in dreadlocks. And his face looked oddly familiar.

Thomas shook off the feeling.

The general wore a hooded robe with a black sash. His back was turned.

"Here's to peace then," Martyn said.

Qurong chuckled. "Yes, of course. Peace."

They drank again.

Qurong dropped his goblet and let out a satisfied sigh. "It is late and I think the pleasure of my wife beckons me. Round the inner council at daybreak. Not a word to the rest, my friend. Not a word."

The general dipped his head. "Good evening."

Qurong turned to go.

Thomas forced his hand to still. A betrayal? He could kill them both now, but doing so might raise the alarm. He would never get to the Books. And Qurong might assume that their plan had been overheard. He and William could just as easily slit the leader's throat as he slept later.

Qurong drew aside the drape and was gone.

But the general remained. Imagine, taking out Martyn! It was almost worth the risk of discovery.

The general coughed, set his goblet down with care, and turned to leave. It was in his turning that he must have seen something, because he suddenly stopped and looked toward Thomas's corner.

Silence gripped the room. Thomas closed his hand around the dagger. If killing Martyn ruined their plans, then doing so took priority over the Books. They could always—

"Hello?"

Thomas held still.

The general took two steps toward the barrel and stopped.

Now, Thomas! Now!

No, not now. There was still a chance the general would turn away. Taking the man from the side or back would reduce his chances of crying out.

For a long moment, neither moved. The general sighed and turned around.

Thomas rose and hurled the dagger in one smooth motion. If the mighty general even heard the *whoosh* of the knife, he showed no sign of it. The blade flashed in rotation, once, twice, then buried itself in the base of the man's neck, severing his spinal cord before the man had time to react.

Like a sack of rocks cut loose from the rafters, the man collapsed.

Thomas reached him in three long strides and covered the general's mouth with his hand. But the man wouldn't be raising any alarm.

Thomas jerked his knife out and wiped the blood on his robe. A trickle of blood ran down the man's neck. One, two spots on the floor.

Thomas hauled the man to the barrel, hoisted him up, and eased him into the water. Their mighty general would be discovered drowned in a barrel of water like a common criminal.

Thomas found William where he'd left him, standing in the corner, barely visible from the doorway.

"Well?"

"We have to wait. Their fearless leader is with his wife," Thomas said.

"You found the bedchamber?"

"I think so. But like I said, he's busy. We'll give him some time."

"We don't *have* time! The sun will be rising."

"We have time. Their mighty general, Martyn, on the other hand, does not have time. If I'm not mistaken, I just killed him."

Their wait lasted less than thirty minutes. Either Qurong's allusion to his wife was for the benefit of his general, or he'd forgone pleasure for the sake of sleep; no sound other than a soft steady snore reached Thomas's ears when he and William listened at what they assumed to be Qurong's bedchamber.

Thomas pulled back the drape and peered into the room. A single torch lit what looked like a reception room. One guard sat in the corner, head hung between his legs.

Thomas lifted a finger to his lips and pointed at the guard. William nodded.

Thomas tiptoed to a curtain on the opposite end of the room, eyes on the guard. William hurried to the guard. A dull thump and the Scab sagged, unconscious. With any luck, the guard would never confess to being overpowered by intruders. He was a guard after all, not a servant, and guards who let thieves sneak up on their Great One surely deserved to be drowned in a barrel.

Thomas peeled back the curtain. The bedchamber. Complete with one fearless leader spread out, facedown, snoring on a thick bed of pillows. His wife lay curled next to him.

They entered the bedchamber, closed the flap, and let their eyes adjust. A dull glow from both the adjacent hall and the reception room behind them reached past the thin walls.

If the servant girl hadn't misled them, Qurong kept the Books of Histories in the chamber behind his bed. Thomas saw the drape. Even in the dim light Thomas could see the cords of metal woven into the walls all around the bedroom. Qurong clearly had gone to great lengths to keep anyone from slicing their way in.

Thomas eased across the room, dagger drawn. He resisted a terrible impulse to slit the leader's throat where he lay next to his wife. First the Books. If there were no Books, he might need Qurong to lead him to them. If they found the Books, he would kill the leader on the way out.

He reached an unsteady hand out and pulled the drape aside.

Open.

Thomas slipped in, followed by William.

The room was small, dim. Musty. Tall bronze candlesticks stood on the floor in a semicircle, unlit. Above them on the wall, a large, forged serpentine bat. And beneath the bat, surrounded by the candlesticks, two trunks.

Thomas's heart could hardly beat any harder, but somehow it managed exactly that. The trunks were the kind the Horde commonly used to carry valuables—tightly thatched reed, hardened with mortar. But these trunks were banded by bronze straps. And the lids were each stamped with the Shataiki crest.

If the Books were in these two trunks, the Desert Dwellers had embraced them as part of their own evolving religion. The Books had come from Elyon long before the Shataiki had been released to destroy the land. And yet Qurong was blending these two icons, which stood in unequivocal contrast with each other. It was like putting Teeleh next to a gift from Elyon and saying that they were the same.

It was the deception of Teeleh himself, Thomas thought. Teeleh had always wanted to be Elyon, and now he would make sure that in the minds of these Scabs, he was. He would claim history. History was his. He was the Creator.

Blasphemy.

Thomas knelt on one knee, put his fingers under the lid's lip, and pulled up. It refused to budge.

William was already running his thumb along the lip. "Here," he whispered. Leather ties bound rings on both the lid and the trunk.

He quickly sawed at the leather. It parted with a soft snap. They glanced at each other, held stares for a moment. Still nothing but soft snoring from the leader's chamber.

They pulled up on the lid together. It parted from the trunk with a soft scrape.

The problem with being caught in this room was that there was only one way out. There would be no quick escape through a cut in the wall. In essence they were in their own small prison.

They tilted the lid toward the rear together, and as soon as the leading edge cleared the trunk, Thomas knew they had struck gold.

Books.

He lifted quickly. Too quickly. The lid slipped from Thomas's fingers and thumped to the floor. It struck one of the candlesticks, which teetered and started to fall.

Thomas dove for the bronze pole. Caught it. They froze. The snores continued. They set the lid down, sweating profusely now.

The Books of Histories were leather bound. Very, very old. They were smaller than he'd imagined, roughly an inch thick and maybe nine inches long. He estimated there were fifty in this trunk alone.

He lowered his hand and smudged the thin layer of dust that covered one of the Books. Clearly they hadn't been read in a long time. No surprise there; he wondered if any of the Horde could even read. Even among the Forest People, only a few still read. The oral traditions sufficed for the most part.

The book came up heavy for its size. Its title was embossed in corroded foil of some kind: *The Stories of History.* He opened the cover. An intricate cursive script crossed the page. And the next. The same writing from his dreams. English.

Plain English. Yet the daughter of Qurong had said the Books were indecipherable. So the Horde couldn't read then. Unless there was something unique about these books.

He set the book down and lifted another. Same title. Down in the trunk all the other Books he could see bore the same inscription, although some had subtitles as well. He lay the book he held on the floor.

"It's them." William barely whispered.

Thomas nodded. It was most definitely them, and there were many. Too many for Thomas and William to take.

He motioned to the other trunk. They cut the leather thong and pried its lid clear. It too was full of books. They eased the lid back down.

"We'll have to come back," Thomas whispered.

"They'll know we were here! You killed Martyn."

Not necessarily. That could be the work of a disgruntled soldier, Thomas thought. On the other hand, they had cut the leather fasteners on the trunks. They would need to be retied.

They could take a few with them, perhaps one that made reference to—

Qurong coughed in the adjoining room.

He froze. There was simply no time to rummage through the trunks now. They would have to come back with more help and haul them off whole.

Sounds of stirring from the bedroom sent Thomas into action. He motioned with his hands and William quickly understood. It took them longer than Thomas hoped working in silence, but finally both lids were secure. He snatched up the single book he'd withdrawn and stood to examine the trunks. Good enough.

They waited for a long stretch of silence, then slipped past Qurong, ignoring the impulse to finish him. Only after he had the Books. He couldn't risk a full-scale lockdown on the camp due to Qurong's death. With any luck at all, no one would know the bedchamber had been violated. They stole back to the servant's quarters, switched back into the cloaks they'd worn, and squeezed through the cut in the canvas wall.

"Remember, walk slowly," Thomas said.

"I'm not sure I *could* walk fast. My skin is killing me."

The Horde slumbered. If anyone even saw the two on their midnight walk through the middle of camp, they didn't show themselves. Twenty minutes later Thomas and William left the tents behind them and hurried out into the dark desert.

———

"Then we go now!" Mikil said. "We have an hour before the sun will rise. And if they're sleeping, what does it matter if our skin has or hasn't changed? I say we go in and kill the lot of them!"

"Let me wash first," William said, standing. "I'd rather take a sword across my belly than put up with this cursed disease."

Thomas looked at his lieutenant. Neither of them had washed yet—the possibility of returning before the sun rose had delayed their decision.

"Wash," he said.

"Thank you."

William marched to his horse, stripped off his garments, hurled them to one side with a muttered curse, and began to splash water on his chest. He winced as the water touched his skin—after only two days the disease wasn't advanced enough for water to cause undue pain, but he clearly felt it.

"We're losing time, Thomas," Mikil said. "If we're going to go, we have to go now."

She was still furious at having been left out. Thomas could see it in her eyes. She still couldn't understand why they hadn't just slit Qurong's throat while he lay sleeping.

He lifted the book they'd retrieved and opened the cover once again. The first page was blank. The second page was blank.

The entire book, *blank!*

Not a single mark on any of its pages. How could this be? The first book he'd picked up had writing, but this one, the one he hadn't looked in, was empty.

They had to get the other books. Mikil wanted to kill Qurong, but they couldn't do that until they knew more. And until they had both trunks.

He slapped the book closed. "It's too risky. We'll wait and go in tomorrow night."

"You can't last until tomorrow night!" Mikil said. "Another day and you'll lose your mind to the disease. I don't like this, not at all."

"Then I'll bathe and go in tomorrow with the ash, like you. We can't rush into this. The opportunity may never come again. How often does Qurong come so close to our forests? And this plan of his troubles me. We have to think! By the accounts from the Southern Forest, Martyn was courting peace. It may be in our best interests to play along with this plan of theirs without letting on that we know." He stood and walked toward his horse. "There are too many questions. We wait until tomorrow night."

"What if they move tomorrow? And the Gathering is in three days— we can't stay out here forever."

"Then we follow them. The Gathering will wait. Enough!"

A horse snorted in the night. Not one of their horses.

Thomas instinctively dropped and rolled.

"Thomas?"

He pushed himself to one knee. *Rachelle?*

"Thomas!"

She rode into camp, slipped from her horse, and ran to him. "Thomas, thank Elyon!"

Rachelle knew it was Thomas, but his condition stopped her halfway across the sand. Even in the dark she could see he was covered by what looked like gray ash, and his eyes were pale, nearly white. She'd seen the rot, of course. It wasn't uncommon for members of the tribe to gray when they delayed bathing for one reason or another. She'd even felt the onset of the disease a few times herself.

But here in the desert, with the odor of sulfur so strong and his face nearly white, the disease took her by surprise.

"Are . . . are you okay?"

He stared at her, dumbfounded. "We had to go in dressed like one of them," he said. "I haven't bathed. Why are you here?"

His men and Mikil stood around a small circle of bedrolls on the sand. No fire—a clean camp. Their horses stood in a clump beside Thomas. William was only half dressed and was wiping his body down with water. His skin was a mix of clear pink and pasty white.

"How could you do this without telling me?" she demanded. "You haven't bathed since leaving? You've lost your mind!"

He said nothing.

No matter, he was safe; that's what she cared about. She ran back to her horse, pulled out a leather bag full of lake water, and threw it to him.

"Wash. Hurry. We have to talk. Alone."

"What's happened?"

"I'll tell you, but you'll have to wash first. I'm not kissing any man who smells like the dead."

He washed the disease clear, and Suzan told the Guard about their journey. But when Thomas demanded to know why they had taken such a risk, she only glanced at Rachelle.

Thomas jerked a tunic from his saddlebag, snapped it once to clear the dust, pulled it on, and faced the others.

"Excuse us for a moment."

He took her elbow and led her away. "I'm sorry, my love," he said in a hushed tone. "Please forgive me, but I had to come and I couldn't worry you."

He still smelled. A spit bath would never compare to a swim in the lake. "Running off wouldn't worry me?" she asked.

"I'm sorry, but—"

"Don't ever do that again. Ever!" She took a deep breath. "I know why you came. I talked to the old man, Jeremiah. Did you find them?"

"You know I came for the Books?"

"And I'm guessing that you didn't take the fruit last night as I thought we had agreed you would."

"You don't understand; I had to dream."

Rachelle stopped and glanced back at their small camp. Then she looked into his eyes and swept a strand of hair from his face. "I dreamed last night, Thomas."

"You always dream."

"I dreamed of the histories."

He searched her face urgently. "You're sure?"

"Sure enough to chase you halfway across the desert."

"But . . . how is that possible? You've never dreamed of the histories! You're absolutely sure? Because you may have dreamed of something that felt like the histories, or you may have dreamed that you were like me, dreaming about the histories."

"No. I know it was the histories because I was doing things that I have no business knowing how to do. I was in a place called a laboratory, working on a virus called the Raison Strain."

She'd rehearsed this a hundred times in the last twelve hours, but telling him now brought a lump to her throat and a tremble to her voice.

"You were a scientist? You were actually there, *working* on the virus?"

"Not only was I there, but I had a name. I shared the mind of a woman named Monique de Raison. For all I know, I was her."

His body tensed. "You . . . how's that possible?"

"Stop asking that. I don't know how it's possible! Nothing makes sense to me, any more than it ever made sense to you. But I know without question that I was there. In the histories, I shared the mind of Monique de Raison. Look, I have a cut on my finger that proves it. She . . . I . . . I was handling a piece of white parchment . . . no, it was called paper. The edge of the paper cut my finger."

She lifted her finger for him, but there wasn't enough light to see the tiny cut.

"You could have cut yourself here and imagined that you were cutting yourself in a place called a laboratory working on the virus that I've spoken of many times."

"You have to believe me, Thomas! Just like you wanted me to believe you. I was there. I saw the . . . computer. Did you ever talk to me about a device called a computer that computes in a way we can't even imagine here? No, you didn't. Or a micro . . ." She couldn't remember all the names or details; they'd grown fuzzy with each passing hour. "A device that looks into very small things. How could I know that?"

His eyes were wide. He ran his hand through his hair and paced. "This is incredible! You think that you're actually her? But you look different there than here."

"I don't know how it works. I felt like I was her, but also separate. I shared her experiences, her knowledge."

"I'm Thomas in both realities, but I look the same in both. You don't look like Monique."

"You're exactly the same person?"

"Yes. No, I'm younger there. Only twenty-five I think."

"The details get fuzzy the longer you're here," she said.

He suddenly stopped his pacing, looked directly at her, and kissed her on the mouth. "Thank you! Thank you, thank you."

She couldn't help her shallow grin. Here they stood, in the middle of the desert with the Horde not a few miles away, kissing because they had this connection with their dreams.

"Have you dreamed again?" he asked.

Her smile faded. "On my horse, I slept, yes."

"And?"

"And I dreamed of the Gathering."

"But not of Monique. Something must have happened for you to dream that one time." He rubbed his temples. "Something . . . does she know?"

"Monique?"

"When I dream, I'm conscious of myself in the other reality. I know that at this very moment, while I'm awake here, I'm also asleep in a hotel in a place near Washington, D.C. Do you know, is Monique sleeping now?"

Rachelle had no idea. She shrugged. "I don't think she knows about me, or at least she doesn't think of me. Or I should say that she didn't think of me when I was . . . looking through her eyes."

"Perhaps because she hasn't dreamed of you. You know she exists, but she doesn't know *you* exist!"

He was far more excited about his conclusion than she was. "I don't find that comforting," Rachelle said.

"Why not? The point is, you *know*! You have no idea what this means to me, Rachelle. We're somehow bound together in both realities. I'm not the only one anymore. Do you know how many times I've been tempted to think I've lost my mind?"

"So now your lunacy has spread to me. What a delightful prospect. And I don't think we *are* bound together in both realities, as you call them. Not the way I understand bonding." She lowered her voice. "Do you love Monique?"

He blinked. "No. Why?"

"You should!"

Thomas stared at her.

"I mean, if I *am* Monique, then you have to love me."

"But we don't know if you are Monique."

"No. But at the least, she and I are connected."

"Yes."

Rachelle lifted her cut finger. "And what happens to her happens to me."

"It would seem that way."

"A man—Swenson?—this man . . . he will kill Monique."

Thomas didn't say anything for a moment, as though a real under-standing of what she was saying had begun to reach him. Then he gently wrapped his hand around Rachelle's and lifted her finger to his lips. He kissed her cut. "Dreams can't kill you, my love." Thomas's hand was shaking.

"You don't need to pretend. You know it better than I do. You told me the same thing yourself fifteen years ago. You said it again last night. If we die in the histories, we may very well die here. I don't understand it. I'm not sure I want to understand it, but it's true."

"I won't let you die!"

She took a step closer to Thomas so that her body touched his. "Then you must dream, husband. You must stop the virus, because we know from the histories that the virus kills most of them, and I doubt very much that this Swenson has any intention of letting Monique live."

"Then you think I can change the histories?"

She looked into his eyes. "If you can't . . . if we can't, then we both may die. There and here. And if we die here, what will become of the forests? What will become of our children? You must rescue Monique. Because you love me, you must rescue Monique."

Thomas looked stricken.

"I have to get the rest of the Books of Histories! Now, before the Horde moves."

"No. You must dream. I know where Monique is being held."

13

THE OVAL Office. More power flowed from this room than any other room in the world, but watching the hubbub of activity while waiting for his audience with President Blair, Thomas wondered if that power might have short-circuited.

He didn't know precisely who knew about the Raison Strain, but the urgency on their faces betrayed the panicked disposition of half a dozen other visitors who'd evidently demanded and received appointments with the world's highest office.

Some were undoubtedly secretaries or aides in the cabinet itself; others had to represent fires the president felt obligated to put out—opposition leaders threatening to go public, concerned lawmakers with good intentions that would ruin the country, et cetera, et cetera.

If this was the kind of panic that disturbed these stately halls, what was the scene in other governments? From what Thomas could overhear, the governments of the western nations were all but caving in already, only two days into the crisis.

Thomas was seated on the gold sofa with his feet on the presidential seal, facing the president, who sat on an identical couch directly across from him. Phil Grant sat on the couch next to the president. To his right Ron Kreet, chief of staff, and Clarice Morton, who'd come to Thomas's rescue in the meeting yesterday, sat in the green-and-gold armchairs by the fireplace. A painting of George Washington eyed them from its frame between them. Robert Blair, Phil Grant, and Ron Kreet all wore ties. Clarice wore a plum business suit. Thomas had opted for the same black slacks and white shirt he'd worn yesterday—at the moment, they were the only clothes he owned that had any real dress to them, although he doubted it mattered much to this president.

"You're sure about this, Thomas?" the president said.

"I'm as sure as I can be about anything, Mr. President. I know it still sounds like a stretch to you, but this is how I learned about the virus in the first place."

"You're saying that you found the Books of Histories—these history books that may tell us what happens next—but more importantly, you know where they're keeping Monique de Raison."

"Yes."

The president looked at Kreet, who lifted an eyebrow as if to say, *Your call, not mine.*

Thomas had awakened early and spent the first hour trying to track down Gains or Grant—actually anyone who could respond to this new information he'd retrieved from his dreams. Both had stayed up late and were finally asleep, he learned. By the time he convinced Grant's assistant to patch him through, it was almost nine in the morning.

Three minutes later he had both Grant and Gains on a conference call. He had new information, and when he told them what it was, they'd pulled whatever strings needed pulling to move the meeting with the president up.

He'd convinced Kara to take an early flight to New York. Their mother needed her children in a time like this, but Thomas couldn't leave Washington. Not now.

It was eleven, and he'd just made his case to the most powerful man alive. Monique was being held in a mountain called Cyclops, he said.

"So you're saying that your wife, this wife in your dreams, is somehow connected to Monique de Raison. Is that right?" Clarice said.

He sensed that she wanted to believe him. Maybe a part of her did believe him. But the twinkle in her eyes betrayed more than a little doubt.

He looked at the president. "Mr. President, permission to be blunt, Sir."

"Of course."

A woman dressed in a black suit slipped in and whispered something in the president's ear.

"When?"

"In the last two minutes."

He turned to the CIA director. "Phil, I think you're needed. We just received word from the French. Find out what's going on and get back in here as soon as you have the picture."

"I knew it," Grant muttered. "Those sons of . . ." He left the office with the lady in black.

"The French?" Kreet said. "We were right?"

"Don't know." President Blair looked at Thomas. "Five of their leaders including the president and the prime minister were seen walking into an unscheduled meeting yesterday. Only four came out. Some are saying that President Henri Gaetan is no longer who he was yesterday."

"A coup?"

"That's a bit premature," Kreet said. "But it wouldn't surprise us if elements of the French government weren't somehow connected to Svensson."

The president stood and walked to his desk, one hand in his pocket. He rapped the top of his desk, sat against it, and folded his arms.

"Okay, Thomas. Fire away. Tell me why I should listen to you."

"Honestly, I'm not saying that you should. Two weeks ago I was trying to pay rent by holding down a job at the Java Hut in Denver."

"That's not what I need. Why should I listen to you?"

Thomas hesitated. He stood and walked around the couch.

"I'm the only one here who's seeing both sides of history. As the only person seeing both sides of history, there's a good chance that I'm also the only one who can *change* that history. I don't know that as a fact, but I'm fairly confident it's true. If I can't change history, then billions of people, including you, will soon be dead."

The chief of staff raised an eyebrow.

"These are the facts," Thomas said. "And the more time I spend justifying myself, the less time I have to change history."

His delivery seemed to have taken the president off guard. He stared at Thomas silently.

It did sound awfully arrogant, Thomas thought. With his own people, as the supreme commander of the Forest Guard, this kind of presentation would be expected. But here he was still the kid from Denver who had flipped out. At least to some. He only hoped the president wasn't among them.

A slight grin nudged Robert Blair's mouth. "Now that's what I call spunk. I pray to God you're wrong about all of this, but I have to agree that in a strange way you actually make sense."

"Then I'll tell you more, if you like."

"I'm all ears."

Thomas walked to a painting of Abraham Lincoln and faced them again. "I'm sure your people have considered this already, but I've had more time than most of them to think this through. Clearly, it's just a matter of time before the rest of the world discovers what's happening. You can't hide the kind of arms movement Svensson is demanding from the press for long. When they do learn of it, the world will begin to fracture. There's no telling what kind of chaos will ensue. Pressure to comply with Svensson's demands will become astronomical. So will pressure to launch a preemptive strike. Both will end badly."

"And exactly what scenario won't end badly?" the president asked. "You may have given this a lot of thought, son, but I'm not sure you can appreciate the full complexity of the situation."

"Then tell me."

Kreet cleared his throat. "Excuse me, but I really don't think this is the best use of—"

The president held up his hand. "It's okay, Ron. I want him to hear this."

He turned to Thomas. "For starters, short of invoking emergency powers, I don't run this country alone. It's a republic, remember? I can't just do what I want to."

"You can and you have to. Invoke emergency powers."

"I may. In the meantime, the virus has cropped up in over a hundred of our cities. The CDC and the World Health Organization are up to their eyeballs in data they can't begin to unravel in any amount of reasonable time. Apart from this premonition of yours called Cyclops, we have no clue where Svensson's hiding out, assuming he's the person we should be looking for. Dwight Olsen's opposition is already circling the wagons. Knowing him, he'll find a way to blame this whole mess on me and bog down my emergency powers. There are already rumblings of a preemptive nuclear strike, and I think Dwight might reverse himself on this one. If we go down, we go down fighting. You know the drill, and I'm not sure I disagree. Even if we give in to these ridiculous demands of this New Allegiance of theirs, we have no guarantee that they'll give us the antivirus."

"They won't. Which is why you can't give in."

"You know this from these books?"

"If I were their strategist and you were the Horde—if you were my enemy—I wouldn't give you the antivirus. The instruments of battle have changed, but not the minds behind them. It also explains why over half the world's population is wiped out by the virus according to the histories. They plan to give out the antivirus selectively, regardless of any promise to the contrary. I'm quite sure you're not at the top of their list of favorite people."

Clarice stood and crossed the floor. There were now three on the gold carpet—only Kreet remained in his chair. "So you insist we don't give in to their demands, and you insist we don't wage war, assuming we ever pin down a target. What, then?"

The president acknowledged her question with a nod and looked at Thomas evenly.

"I doubt very much any conventional solution will change anything. They would have been tried in the histories and failed. My solution requires you to believe me. I understand that's the challenge here, but in the end you'll find it's the only way."

"Be more specific, Thomas," the president said. "What exactly are you suggesting?"

"First, believe me when I say I know where Monique is. She is your key to securing the antivirus. Second, do whatever is necessary to prevent both nuclear war and the international community's capitulation to Svensson's demands. Bluff if you have to. Start the nuclear weapons on their way. Withhold enough weapons for a credible threat, and if we have no solution when the weapons actually reach their destination—"

"You sound like you know that destination," the president said.

"If I were them, I would choose a European country, for a list of reasons I could give you if you want. France would be ideal."

The president frowned. "Continue."

"If we still have no solution by the time the weapons reach their destination, then pull back. You'll have to persuade other nuclear powers that are closer to France, if I'm right, like England and Israel, to actually send their weapons. If they don't at least appear to cooperate, then we'll have a nuclear war on our hands, and more than the virus will kill people by the millions."

Robert Blair glanced at Ron Kreet. The chief of staff turned his head skeptically. "Israel won't go for it."

"Which is why you begin building the coalition immediately, starting with Israel," Thomas said. "I mean today. You have to commit to this now."

"I still don't hear a plan, Thomas," Clarice said.

Thomas looked at all three. They were lost, he realized. Not that he wasn't, but he did have a slight advantage.

"My plan is for you to delay them by all possible means of trickery and diplomacy and hope that *I* can find a way to stop them."

For a long time they were either too embarrassed or too impressed to respond. Surely the former.

"Let me take a team to Cyclops," he said. "If I'm right, we'll find her. If I'm wrong, I can still relay information from the Books of Histories back to you when I get my hands on them. My remaining here is pointless."

"Even if we do send a team," Kreet said, "I don't see how you're qualified to lead our Rangers. How far do you expect us to go with this . . . dreaming of yours?"

"I think he may be on to something," the president said. "Finish."

"Maybe I could show you something," Thomas said, walking to the center of the room. He glanced at the ceiling. "If you check, you'll find that I have no acrobatics training. I did learn martial arts in the Philippines, but trust me, I could never move like I've learned to move in my dreams while leading the Guard. Stand back."

They glanced at each other, then cautiously stepped back.

Thomas took a single step and launched himself into the air, flipped through one and a half rotations with a full twist, landed on his hands, and held the stand for a count of three before reversing the entire move.

They stared at him, gawking like schoolchildren who had just seen a magic show.

"Maybe one more," Thomas said, "just so you're sure. Pick up that letter opener"—he nodded at a brass blade on the desk—"and throw it at me. As hard as you can."

"No, it's quite all right." The president looked a little embarrassed. "I'd hate to miss and stick the wall."

"I won't let you."

"You've made your point."

"Go ahead, Bob," Clarice said. She eyed Thomas with a new kind of interest. "Why not?"

"Just hurl it at you?"

"As hard as you possibly can. Trust me, there's no way you can hurt me with it. This isn't a ten-foot sickle or a bronze sword. It's hardly a toy."

The president picked up the letter opener, glanced at a grinning Clarice, and hurled the blade. Blair had been an athlete and this blade wasn't traveling slowly.

Thomas caught it by its hilt, an inch from his chest. He held it steady.

"You see, the skills I learn in my dreams are real." He tossed the letter opener back. "The information I learn is as real. I need to lead the team because there's a possibility I may be the only one alive who can get to Monique. I should be on my way already."

The door opened. Phil Grant entered, face drawn.

"We have twenty-four hours to show movement of our arms. The destination is now the Brest naval base in northern France. The government claims they are cooperating with Svensson only because they have no choice. All communications to the matter must be held in strictest confidence. The media must not be alerted. They are working on a solution, but until they come up with one, they insist we must cooperate. In a nutshell that's it."

"They're lying," Thomas said. The others looked at him.

The president faced his chief of staff. "Ron?"

"They probably are lying. But it really doesn't matter either way. Even if Svensson is holding hands with Gaetan himself, we can't very well drop nukes on France, can we?"

The president walked around his desk and dropped into his chair. "Okay, Thomas. I'm authorizing the removal and transportation of the weapons they've demanded. I have a meeting with the joint chiefs in an hour. Until someone offers a reasonable argument to the contrary, we do it your way."

He set his elbows on the desk and nervously tapped his fingers together. "Not a word about any of this dream stuff to anyone. Clear? That includes you, Thomas. No more tricks. You go on assignment from this office and you go with my clearance; that's all anyone needs to know."

"Agreed," Thomas said.

"Phil, get him a clearance. I want him in Fort Bragg by chopper as soon as possible. I'll make sure they give you whatever you need. It's a long haul to Indonesia—make the plans you need in the air if you have to. And if you're right about Svensson being in Cyclops, I just may turn the White House over to you." He winked.

Thomas extended his hand. "I wouldn't know what to do with the White House. Thank you for your confidence, Mr. President."

Robert Blair took his hand. "I'm not sure I'm offering any confidence. As you pointed out, we're just a little short on alternatives at the moment. I just got off the phone with the Israeli prime minister. Their cabinet has already met with the opposition. The hard-liners are insisting the only way they'll deliver any of their weapons is on the end of a missile. He's not inclined to disagree."

"Then you have to convince them that any nuclear exchange would be suicide," Thomas said.

"In their minds, disarming would be suicide. Submitting has landed them in a world of hurt before—they're not going to be easy, and frankly I'm not sure they should be. I doubt Svensson has any plans of giving the Israelis the antivirus, regardless of what they do."

"If the virus doesn't finish us off, a war just might," Thomas said. "A leak to the press might do the same. But then you already know that."

"Unfortunately. We're spinning a story about an outbreak of the Raison Strain on an island near Java. It'll make enough noise to distract anything for a few days. The other governments involved understand the critical nature of keeping this under wraps. But there's no way to hide this for long. Not with so many people involved. Keeping Olsen in line will be a full-time job in itself."

The president drew a deep breath and let it out, eyes closed.

"Let's pray you're right about Monique."

—◦◦◦◦—

Thomas changed back into clothing he felt more comfortable wearing—cargo pants, Vans, and a black button-down shirt. Phil Grant sent three assistants along who had marching orders to coordinate whatever intelligence Thomas needed. He asked for and received a ream of data on the target area, which he'd already gone over once with the CIA. He browsed through the thick folder again.

He knew of the Indonesian island called Papua through a friend of his in Manila, David Lunlow, who attended Faith Academy. David had grown up on the remote island, the son of missionaries. At the time it was called Irian Jaya, but had recently changed its name to Papua because of some misguided political notion that doing so might further its quest for independence from Indonesia.

Papua was unique among the hundreds of Indonesian Islands. The largest, by far. The least populated, and mostly by tribes, scattered across mountains and swamps and coastal regions that had swallowed countless explorers over the centuries. More than seven hundred languages were spoken on the island. Largest city, Jayapura. Fifty miles down the coast, a small airport was attached to a sprawling community of misfits and adventurers. It wasn't unlike the Old West. There was a strong expatriate community whose primary purpose was to give the downtrodden and lost seekers new direction. Missionaries.

It was there, a fifteen-minute Jeep haul from Sentani, that Cyclops waited.

Thomas studied the maps and satellite images of the jungle-covered mountain. How Svensson had ever managed to build a lab in such a remote, inaccessible place, Thomas could hardly guess, but the strategy of it made perfect sense. There was no true military or police threat within a thousand miles. There were no villages or known inhabitants above the base of the mountain. A helicopter approach from the far side would go virtually unnoticed except by the odd bushman, who had no reason to report such a thing and no one to report it to.

Thomas set the map down and stared through a portal at a long stretch of clouds below them. Serene, oblivious. From thirty thousand feet up, the idea that a virus was ravaging the earth below seemed preposterous.

"Sir? Do you need anything else?" She was CIA and her name was Becky Masters.

"No. Thank you."

He returned his attention to the data on his lap, and slowly he began to draw up plans.

They landed and led him into a briefing room two hours later. The Ranger team that he would accompany was commanded by a Captain Keith Johnson, a dark-skinned man dressed in black dungarees who looked like he could take the head off any man with a word or two. He snapped off a salute and called Thomas "sir," but his skittering eyes betrayed him.

Thomas stuck out his hand. "Good to meet you, Captain."

The man took his hand with some hesitation. There were about twenty others in the room, all clean-cut, a far cry from his Forest Guard. But he'd seen enough of the Discovery Channel to know that these men could do serious damage in most situations.

"Men, I'd like you to meet Mr. Hunter. He's been given carte blanche on this mission. Please remember who signs your paychecks." Meaning, *You work for the government, so even if this bozo looks like someone off a movie set, follow orders,* Thomas thought.

"Thank you," Thomas said.

The captain sat without acknowledging him. A map of Papua and Cyclops was already on the overhead projector as he'd requested. He scanned the room.

"I know you've been given the general parameters of the mission, but let me add a few details." He walked to the map and ran through his plan to approach six primary points on the mountain that he and two CIA map readers thought Svensson might have used.

The mission was to rescue Monique de Raison, not to take out the lab or to kill Svensson or any other lab technician who might be at the location. On the contrary, keeping these targets alive was crucial. No explosives could be used. Nothing that might endanger the integrity of the data held in the lab or by those who worked there.

"I have to catch some sleep on the flight," he said, "but we'll have plenty of time to rehearse the rest over the Pacific. Captain, you may want to suggest some modifications. You know your men best, and you'll be leading your men, not me."

None of them, not even the captain, moved a muscle. *They don't know how to respond to me,* Thomas thought. No blame. He wasn't the kind of person people know how to take. These fighters would do what they'd been trained to do, starting with following orders, but in this situation he needed more.

He couldn't keep doing these stupid tricks for doubters. *Look, fellers, look at what I can do.* Soon enough, word would get out and his reputation would speak for itself, but at the moment these fighters had no benefit of the knowledge they should have, given the situation. They didn't know the fate of billions could rest on their shoulders. They didn't know about the virus. They didn't know that the man who stood before them was from a different world. In a manner of speaking.

Thomas walked across the room, studying them. The president had said no tricks. Well, this wasn't really a trick. He stopped near Johnson.

"You look like you might have some reservations, Captain."

Johnson didn't commit either way.

"Okay. So then let's get this out of the way so we can do what we have to do." He walked down the aisle and started to unbutton his shirt.

"I'm smaller than most of you. I'm not Special Forces. I have no rank. I'm not even part of the military. So then who am I?"

He slipped the last button free.

"I'm someone who's willing to take on the captain and any five of you right here, right now, with an absolute promise that I will do each one of you some very serious bodily damage."

He turned at the end of the aisle and headed back up, eying them.

"I don't want to sound arrogant; I just don't have the time it typically takes to win the kind of respect needed for a mission like this one. Do I have any takers?"

Nothing. A few awkward smirks.

He peeled his shirt down to his waist and faced them at the front again. Although normal aging and other physical events didn't transfer between his two realities, blood did. And wounds. And the direct effects of those wounds. Kara had examined them, awed by the graphic change to his body, literally overnight. Twenty-three scars.

He saw them take in the numerous Horde scars that marked his chest. A few of the smirks changed to admiration. Some wanted to try him; he could see it in their eyes, an encouraging sign. If things got hairy, he would depend on these more than the others. He continued before they could speak.

"Good. We wouldn't want to bloody the walls of this room anyway. The reason I've been selected by the president of the United States to lead this mission is because no one else alive qualifies in the same way I do for reasons you'll never know. But believe this: The success or failure of this mission will send shock waves around the world. We *must* succeed, and for that you *must* trust me. Understood? Captain?"

———

Seven hours later, Thomas was on a night flight across the Pacific with Captain Johnson and his team and enough high-tech hardware to sink a small yacht. The transport was a Globemaster C-17, flying at mach point seven, loaded with electronic surveillance equipment. Their flight would last ten hours with three in-flight refuelings.

They still weren't sure what to make of him—big words and a few scars didn't amount to a hill of beans when you got right down to it. And honestly, he wasn't sure about them. What he wouldn't give for Mikil or William at his side.

They would soon find out just who was who.

Thomas reclined in the seat farthest to the back and let the soft roar of the engines lull him into sleep. Into dreams.

14

QURONG STORMED into the dining room, ignoring the pain that flared through his flesh. "Show me his body!"

They'd already pulled the general from the keg of water and laid him on the floor. For a moment Qurong panicked. He'd been with the general just last night, before he'd been killed. The only comfort in this terrible murder was the discovery that a knife, not the water, had ended his life.

"Who did this?" he screamed. "Who!"

The flap snapped open and Woref, head of military intelligence, walked in. "It was the Forest Guard," he said.

Under any other circumstance, Qurong would have dismissed the claim. The very idea that the Forest Guard had been in his own camp was outrageous. But Woref made the claim as if reporting on a well-known fact.

Still, he couldn't digest it. "How?"

"We've taken a confession from one of the servants. Two of them entered through the wall in their quarters. She said that they came for the Books of Histories."

The revelation drained blood from his face. Not because he cared so much for the symbolic relics, although he did, but because of where the Books were kept. His religion was one thing; his life was another altogether.

Qurong strode for his bedchamber.

"There's more, sir." Woref followed him. "We have just received word from a scout that there is a small camp of Forest Guard just three miles to the east."

So then it was true. He walked through the atrium. "Drown the guard on duty last night," he snapped.

The two chests sat where they always did, encircled by the six candlesticks. "Open it," he told Woref.

Few had ever entered the small room, and he doubted that Woref had ever been here. But he knew the trunks well enough; he'd been responsible for their construction nearly ten years ago. The rest of the Books—thousands of them—were in hiding, but he kept these two trunks with him at all times for the aura of mystery they lent him, if not for any tangible power.

None of them could read the Books—they seemed to be written in a language that none of his people could read. Rumor had it that the Forest People could read the words easily enough, but this was the wagging of stupid tongues. How could the Forest People read what none of them had set eyes on?

"The leather has been cut," Woref said, inspecting the straps on either side. "They were in here."

The moment they opened the lid, Qurong knew that someone had been in his bedchamber. The dust on the Books was smeared.

Qurong swept the curtain aside and walked out. Air. He needed more air.

"But they didn't kill me."

"Then they were only after the Books," Woref said.

"And plan to return now that they know we have them?"

"But why would they come after these relics when they could have . . ." Woref didn't finish the thought.

"It's Thomas," Qurong said. Yes, of course it was! Only Thomas would place such value on the Books.

"We have the tenth division south of the—"

"How many of the Guard are in this camp?"

"A dozen. No more."

"Send word immediately. To the tenth division south of the canyons. Tell them to cut off any escape. How long before they could be in place?"

"They have to move a thousand men. Two hours."

"Then in two hours we move in. With any luck we may actually have that dog in a noose."

"And if it is Thomas, would killing him now jeopardize the capture of the forests?" Woref asked.

He ignored Woref's question. There was no secret about the general's interest in securing the forests. Woref was to be given Qurong's daughter, Chelise, in marriage upon the completion of that task. All had their prizes waiting, and Woref's would be the object of his unrequited obsession. But Qurong was no longer quite sure about the wisdom of his agreement to turn Chelise over to this beast.

Qurong walked to a basin of morst, a powdery white mixture of starch and ground limestone, dipped his fingers in, and patted his face. The stuff provided some comfort by drying any sweat on the skin's surface. Any kind of moisture, including sweat, increased the pain.

"How long before the main army from the Southern Forest reaches us?" Qurong asked.

"Today. Perhaps hours. Maybe we should wait until he gets here."

"Is he issuing the orders now? He may have come up with this plan, but as I was last aware, I am still in charge."

"Yes, of course, your excellence. Forgive me."

"If we can kill Thomas, the Forest People will be even less likely to learn of our plans. They still don't know about the fourth army on the far side of their forest. Their firebombs will only go so far against four hundred thousand men."

"They do have other capable leaders. Mikil. William. And they may know more than we think they know."

"None of them compares to Thomas! You will see, without him they are lost. Send the word: Cut them off! Have the rest of our men begin to break camp as if we are leaving for the deep desert. I swear, if Thomas of Hunter is among them, he will not live out this day."

—⊗◈⊗—

A gentle word on the wind woke him. Thomas was falling asleep on the transport plane, but he was also waking, here in the desert, with these words in his ear.

"They're moving."

Thomas sat up. Mikil squatted on one leg.

"It's not a war assembly—they're packing the horses. My guess is back into the desert."

Thomas scrambled up, hurried to the top of the dune, took the eyeglass from William, and peered down. They couldn't see the whole camp; the back end was hidden by a slight rise in the desert. But as far as he could see, the Scabs were slowly loading down their carts and horses.

Rachelle ran up the slope. "Thomas!"

He rolled on his back and sat up. "Did you dream?"

She glanced at William as if to say, *Not here.*

"William, tell the others to prepare to follow the army into the desert," Thomas ordered.

"Sir—"

"How can you possibly go after them now?" Rachelle demanded. "The Gathering is in two days!"

"We have to get the Books!"

She glanced at William again.

"William, tell the others."

"She's right. If we follow them out for a day, it will add another day to our journey home. We'll miss the Gathering."

"Not at the rate these slugs travel. And I think Elyon will understand us missing the Gathering if we are busy destroying his enemies."

"We're stealing books, not destroying the enemy," William said.

"We will destroy the enemy with the Books, you muscle-head!"

"How?"

"Just tell them."

William ran down the dune.

"What happened?" Rachelle asked.

"Did you dream?" he demanded.

"No. Not about the histories. But you did. What happened?"

He stood. "You were right; there is a mountain called Cyclops in Indonesia. Something happened that allowed you to dream."

"Then you're going after Monique?"

"We're on our way now."

"Then let the Books of Histories go. It's too dangerous! You can stop the virus with Monique's help."

"And what if we can't rescue Monique? What if she can't stop the virus? The Books may be able to tell us what we need to know to stop Svensson! The rest can't understand that, but you have to."

She started back down the dune, and he hurried to catch her.

"Rachelle, please, listen to me. You have to go back. I'll send two of my men with Suzan to take you safely—"

"And why should I go if you're out here risking your neck in the desert?"

"Because if anything happens to you out here, Monique might die! Don't you see? We can't risk any harm coming to you. And what about our children?"

"And what about you, Thomas? What happens to Monique or me or the forest or the earth if something happens to you? Our children are in good hands; don't patronize me."

He caught her arm and pulled her around. "Listen to me!"

She swallowed and gazed over his shoulder at the horizon.

"I love you more than life itself," he said. "For fifteen years I've been fighting off these beasts. Nothing will happen to me now, I swear it. Not here. It's there that worries me. We have to stop the virus, and for that we need the Books of Histories."

Her eyes were paling. She'd bathed last night, but only with a rag and some water from the canteens.

"Please, my love. I beg you."

She sighed and closed her eyes.

"You know that I'm right," he said.

"Okay. But promise me you won't let the disease take you."

"Leave your extra water."

"I will."

They stood in silence. The others were casting curious glances up the dune.

Rachelle leaned forward and kissed him lightly on the cheek. "Please come back in time for the Gathering."

"I will."

She turned and walked toward her horse.

———— ✖ ————

Thomas lay on the crest of the dune, watching with the other seven who'd remained behind. Their horses waited behind them, impatient in the rising heat. They'd scavenged as much water as they dared from the four who'd left two hours earlier, enough to keep them for two more days if they were careful. William and Suzan had gone back with Rachelle.

"Is it just my imagination, or are they moving slowly?" Mikil asked.

"They're Scabs. What do you expect?" someone said.

"If they cut out half of all that baggage, they could move twice as fast," she said. "It's no wonder they march so slow."

Thomas scanned the horizon. A tall hill rose to their right. Far beyond this hill lay the Southern Forest, where Jamous had been delivered by Justin, who brokered a peace with the Scabs.

The words he'd heard the night before ran through his mind. *We'll speak about peace and they will listen because they must,* Qurong had said. *By the time we work the betrayal with him, it will be too late.*

Who was *him*? Martyn? No, Qurong had been speaking to the general, who was now dead. Perhaps Justin, but Thomas couldn't accept that. His former lieutenant may have gone off the deep end, but he would never conspire against his own people.

Or would he?

"Sir, there's some movement."

He refocused down the hill. A line of horses had emerged over the distant rise and were headed toward them.

Then another.

Not just two lines of horses. A division, at least, riding at a gallop toward them. Thomas felt his muscles tighten.

"Sir . . ."

"They know," he said. "They know we're here!"

"Then we leave," Mikil said. "We can outrun them without a sweat."

"And the Books?"

"I think that the Books are, for the moment, history," she said. "No pun intended."

"Sir, behind!"

The voice had come from the Guard at the end of the line. Thomas whipped around. Another line of horses was just now edging over the dunes to the east, between them and the forest. A thousand, at least.

It was a trap.

Thomas plunged down the hill. "To the north, hurry!"

He reached his horse first, grabbed the pommel, and kicked the steed before his seat touched the saddle. "Hiyaa!"

The animal bolted. Behind him the other horses snorted and pounded sand.

The army on their left marched into clear view now, a long line that stretched farther than he'd first thought. While he and his men had been watching the breaking camp, the Horde had circled behind. Or worse, this army had been camped to the east or south and had been summoned.

They were now flanked on the east and the west. Surely the Horde knew that they would simply ride north out of the trap. Unless—

He saw the warriors directly ahead. How many? Too many to count, cutting off their escape.

Thomas pulled back on his reins, pitching his horse into a steep rear. Three of his men thundered past him.

"Back!"

They saw the Horde and pulled up.

Thomas jerked his horse around. "South!"

But he'd just laid into the wind when he saw what he feared he would see. The dunes to the south swelled with yet another division.

He veered to his left and plowed up the same dune they'd first hidden behind. There was no sense running blind. He had to see what was happening, and for that he needed elevation.

They brought their horses to stomping fits atop the dune. From here their predicament became abundantly clear. Scabs pounded toward them from every direction. Thomas turned his horse, looking for a break in their ranks, but each time he saw one, it closed.

They had been outwitted by Qurong.

Thomas took quick stock. He'd been in too many close scrapes to panic, too many close battles to consider defeat. But he'd never been eight against so many.

There was no way to fight their way out. Mikil had drawn her sword, but this wasn't a matter of swords. They'd been beaten by a mind, and now they could only win with their own.

These thoughts came over Thomas like a single pounding wave.

But the thoughts that mattered—the ones suggesting a sane course of action—didn't follow in its wake. The sea had gone silent.

Not even his dreams could help now. They could knock him out and he could dream, and they could wake him up in a matter of seconds, but to what end?

Rachelle's words of warning spoke tenderly in his ear. She hadn't used a sweet voice, but now any thought of Rachelle could only be tender.

I am so sorry, my love.

He touched the book that he'd strapped tightly to his waist under his tunic. Maybe he could use it as leverage. Buy time. To what end, he had no clue, but he had to do something. Thomas yanked the book out and thrust it over his head. He stood in his stirrups and screamed at the sky.

"The Books of Histories! I have a Book of History!"

The Horde did not seem impressed. Of course, they hadn't heard him yet.

He released the reins, stood tall with knees tight against the horse, and galloped in a small circle around his men, right hand lifted high with the book between his fingers.

"I have the Books! I have a Book of History!" he cried.

When the circle of warriors reached the dunes surrounding his, they pulled up. Five thousand at least, seated on sweating horses in a huge circle many deep. The sand had turned into men. Scabs.

Perhaps their hesitation was simply a matter of who was willing to die and who wanted to live. They knew that the first few to reach the Forest

Guard would die. Maybe hundreds before they overpowered Thomas of Hunter and his warriors.

They would overpower him, of course. Not one soul who had the scene in their eye could doubt the final outcome.

He yelled at them at the top of his voice. "My name is Thomas of Hunter, and I have the Books of Histories, which your leader Qurong reveres! I dare any man to test my powers!"

Over a hundred horses stepped from the ranks and slowly approached. They bore the red sash of the assassins, the ones who'd sworn to give their lives for Thomas's at a moment's notice. It was said among the Guard that most of them were surviving relatives of men slain in battle.

"It's not working," Mikil said.

"Steady," Thomas muttered. "We can take these."

"These, but there are too many!"

"Steady!"

But his own heart ignored the command and raced ahead of its usually calm rhythm.

The sound of a lone horn cut through the air. The ring of horses pulled up. The horn came again, long and high. Thomas looked for the source. South.

There, atop the tallest hill, stood two riders on pale horses. The one on the left was a Scab. Thomas could see that much from this distance, but nothing more.

The other rider, telling from his tunic, was a Forest Dweller.

"It's him!" Mikil said.

"It's who?"

"Justin." She spit.

Another long horn blast. There was a third man, Thomas saw, seated on a horse just behind the Scab. It was he who blew the horn.

The Forest Dweller suddenly plunged down the hill toward the encroaching Horde. They began to part for his passage. The Horde frequently communicated with various horns, and this blast must have indicated sanctuary of some kind.

The rider rode hard through the Scabs without looking at them. He was still a hundred yards away, in the thick of the Horde army, when Thomas confirmed Mikil's guess. He could never mistake the man's fluid, forward-leaning riding style.

This was indeed Justin of Southern.

Justin rode up the dune and reined to a stop fifteen yards away. For a long moment, he just looked at them. Mikil scowled on Thomas's right. The rest of his men held their places behind him.

"Hello, Thomas," Justin said. "It's been awhile."

"Two years."

"Yes, two years. You look good."

"Actually, I could use a swim in the lake," Thomas said.

Justin chuckled. "Couldn't we all?"

"Including these friends of yours?" Thomas asked.

Justin looked around at the Scab army. "Especially them. Never can get used to the smell."

"I think the smell might be coming from your skin as well as theirs," Mikil said.

Justin stared at her with those piecing green eyes of his. He looked freshly bathed.

"I see you've gotten yourself in a bit of trouble here," he finally said.

Thomas frowned. "Perceptive."

"We don't need your help," Mikil said.

"Mikil!"

Justin smiled. "Maybe you should consider changing your approach. I mean, I love the spirit of it. I'm tempted to join you and fight it out."

There was a twinkle in his eyes that inspired confidence. This was one of the reasons Thomas had selected him to be his second two years ago.

"Have you, by any chance, noticed how large the Horde's armies are these days?" Justin asked.

"We've always been outnumbered."

"Yes, we have. But this isn't a war you're going to win, Thomas. Not this way. Not with the sword."

"With what. A smile?"

"With love."

"We do love, Justin. We love our wives and children by sending these monsters to Hades where they came from."

"I wasn't aware they came from hell," Justin said. "I was always under the assumption that they were created by Elyon. Like you."

"And so were the Shataiki. Are you suggesting we take them to bed as well?"

"Most of you already have," Justin said. "I fear the bats have left the trees and taken up residence in your hearts."

Mikil wasn't one to tolerate such sacrilege, but Thomas had made his will clear, and so she spoke to him, not Justin. "Sir, we can't sit here and listen to this poison. He's riding with them."

"Yes, Mikil, I know how much these words sting such a religious person as yourself." They all knew that she was religious only when it served her. She bathed and followed the rituals, of course, but she would rather plot a battle than swim in the lake any day.

She harumphed.

"There's a saying," Justin said. "For every one head the Horde cuts off, cut off ten of theirs, isn't that it? The scales of justice as it were. The time will come when you'll break bread with a Scab, Thomas."

Someone coughed behind Thomas. Clearly Justin was delusional. Even Thomas couldn't resist a small smile.

"Mikil has a point. Did you come down here to give us a hand, or are you more interested in converting us to your new religion?"

"Religion? The problem with the Great Romance is that it's become a religion. You see what happens when you listen to the bats? They ruin everything. First the colored forest and now the lakes."

Heat spread down Thomas's neck. Speaking against the Great Romance was blasphemy! "You've said enough. Help us or leave."

Justin lowered his eyes to the book in Thomas's hand. "The Books of Histories. The worst and the best of man. The power to create and the power to destroy. Whatever you do, don't lose it. In the wrong hands it could cause a bit of trouble."

"It's empty."

Justin nodded once, slowly. "Take care, Thomas. I'll see you at the Gathering."

Then he turned his horse and galloped past the Scabs, back up the tall dune where he pulled up next to the Desert Dweller.

A long horn blasted once, twice. The call to retreat. At first none of the Horde moved. The assassins seemed confused, and a murmur rumbled over the sand.

The horn blasted twice again, with more force.

The price for disobeying an order such as this was immediate execution for any Scab. They withdrew en masse, in the same directions they'd come from.

Thomas watched, dumbstruck as the desert emptied.

Then they were gone. All of them.

Their salvation had come so fast, with so little fanfare, that it hardly felt real.

He twisted in his saddle to look at Justin.

The hill was bare.

Mikil spit. "I could kill that—"

"Silence! Not another word, Mikil. Your life has just been spared."

"At what cost?"

He didn't have an answer.

15

CYCLOPS.

Stealth was out of the question. They didn't have a week to sweep the jungle in search of a tunnel that might lead into the mountain. What they did have was infrared technology that would electronically strip Cyclops of enough foliage to reveal any suspicious anomalies, such as heat.

They'd landed the tactical C-17 at the Sentani airport, refueled, and immediately climbed back into the skies to take on the mountain looming over the coast. The forecast was fair, the winds were down, and the team had slept well on the flight over the Pacific.

Even so, Thomas couldn't shake his anxiety. What if he was wrong? What if Rachelle had been mistaken?

And another piece of information now complicated things: He'd failed to retrieve the Books of Histories in his dream. Qurong still possessed them all except for the one book with blank pages. The only useful information he had from his dreams was Rachelle's claim that Monique was here, in this mountain.

The transporter flew low, scanning the trees, covering the backside of the mountain in long sweeps. Captain Keith Johnson approached him from the cockpit looking like something out of a comic book with all of his camouflaged equipment: a helmet with a communications rig that allowed him to view the proximity of each of four team leaders through a visor that hovered over his right eye. Parachute. Jungle pack. Two grenades. A green-handled knife with a shiny blade that Mikil might trade her best horse for.

The rest looked the same. Only Thomas was dressed down. Camouflaged jumpsuit, knife, radio, an assault rifle he had no intention of using, and a parachute he had no choice but to use. Buddy jump.

"Just completed the first full sweep," the captain said, dropping to one knee. "Nothing yet. You sure we shouldn't cover the other side?"

"No, this side."

"Then the operator wants to go lower. But you know anyone down there's going to hear us. This thing sounds like a stampede flying over."

Thomas removed his helmet and ran his fingers through damp hair. "You have an alternative?"

They'd been through a dozen scenarios on the flight over. Thomas had offered his thoughts, but when it came to electronic surveillance, he was clearly out of their league. He'd deferred to them.

"No. Not with your time constraints. But I gotta tell you, if they're down there, they're all eyes."

"I'm not sure we don't want them to find us. If we're lucky, we'll force their hand. They can't leave without exposing themselves."

The captain eyed him, then nodded. "I don't mind saying that we're hanging our rear ends out pretty far. This wouldn't be my first choice."

"I realize the danger, Captain, but if it makes you feel any better, the president might put the entire 101st Airborne in these same shoes if he thought it would speed Monique de Raison's recovery. Let's take her down."

⸻

The decision to use the French secret police to deal with Hunter had been Armand Fortier's call. The head of the *Sûreté* had called Carlos directly. They were putting over three hundred agents on the case, each with the order to return Hunter to France immediately or, thus failing, to kill him. They'd already activated a wide network of informants in the United States and learned that the man had flown to Fort Bragg and then disappeared.

Three possibilities, Carlos thought. *One, he was still at Fort Bragg, keeping a very low profile. Two, he was on his way to France to deal directly with Fortier. Or three, he was on his way here, to Indonesia.*

Carlos peered through the binoculars at the approaching transporter and knew that he'd made the right call. No doubt Hunter was in that plane.

The man now unnerved him in a way not even Svensson could. Three times Hunter had miraculously slipped out of his grasp. No, not entirely correct: Twice he had been mortally wounded and then apparently healed, and once he'd slipped from his grasp—the last time.

It wasn't just his nine lives. Hunter seemed to know things that he had no business knowing.

True, it was from the man's dreams that they had supposedly first isolated the Raison Strain. But if Carlos was right, the man was still learning things from his dreams. The plane that now approached, undoubtedly with infrared scanners, was proof enough. He'd elected to let the French track Hunter in the United States while he returned here, where he was sure the man would eventually come. He would come for Monique.

"How many times?" Svensson's voice crackled on the radio.

Carlos keyed his mike. "Seven. They're coming in lower this time."

Static.

"How did they find us?"

"As I said. He knew about the virus, he knew about the antivirus, now he knows where we are. He's a ghost."

"Then it's time to bring your ghost in for a talk. You don't think a crash will kill him?"

"I don't. The rest maybe, but not Hunter."

"Then bring them down. No other survivors."

"We'll evacuate?"

"Tonight, by dark. Fortier wants this man in France."

"Understood."

Carlos stepped from the shielded netting that had kept his heat signature to a minimum, shouldered the modified Stinger launcher, and armed the missile. A direct hit would cut the transporter in half. He wasn't certain that Hunter would survive, of course, but it was a gamble he was gladly willing, even eager, to take. More than a small part of him wanted to be wrong about Hunter's impossible gift. Better for him to die.

He waited for the plane to turn at the far end of the valley and head back toward him. Svensson had dug into the mountain at its center, and the plane was now approaching him at eye level. They would see him this time. He would have one good shot.

It was all that he needed.

———⊗⊗⊗———

"Contact bearing, two-nine-zero."

Thomas heard the electronics operator above the aircraft's din. He twisted and looked out of his window.

"Contact, one—"

"Incoming! Incoming!"

The warning came from the cockpit, and Thomas immediately saw the streaking missile through the window.

He was right then. Monique was here.

He was also staring death head-on.

He grabbed the rail by his seat. The C-17 rolled sharply away from the incoming missile.

"Countermeasures, deployed." The pilot's voice was drowned out by the sudden roar of the four Pratt and Whitney engines as the jet pitched up and groaned for altitude.

"It's gonna hit!" someone yelled.

For a brief moment panic fired the eyes of twenty men who'd faced death before but not in these circumstances. This fight could be over before it started.

Whomp!

The fuselage imploded with a huge flash of fire just behind the cockpit. A ball of heat rolled back through the cabin, hot enough to burn bared skin.

Thomas got his head down before the heat hit him. A roar swallowed him. Hot air. Then cool air. Someone was screaming.

It all happened so quickly that he didn't have to react. He knew they'd been hit by a missile, but he had no understanding of what that meant.

His eyes sprang open. The C-17 floated lazily to his right, cut into three pieces just in front of the wings and at the tail. The middle section was still under full power and now roared past the nose and tail sections.

Thomas was suspended in the air, still strapped to his seat. He didn't seem to be falling, not yet. He'd been thrown from the aircraft, maybe through the exposed tail, and now floated free.

But the trees were less than three thousand feet below him, and this buoyancy wouldn't last more than—

It occurred to him that he was already falling. Like a rock.

Panic immobilized him for a full three count. Thunder to his right jerked him out of it. An oily tower of fire rose from where the main fuselage slammed into the valley under full power. No one could have possibly survived an impact like that.

Thomas twisted in his seat, but the chair just turned with him. He grabbed the harness release, flipped it open, and rolled to his right, fighting his instinct to stay in the relative safety of the metal frame.

Two thousand feet.

The chair caught wind and flipped past him. Now he was free-falling without a seat. He'd jumped from a bungee tower once, but he'd never even worn a parachute before today, much less made a jump.

The nose and tail sections plowed through trees on the opposite mountain slope. No explosions.

One thousand feet.

He grabbed the rip cord and jerked. With a pop the chute deployed, streamed skyward, and snapped open. The harness tugged at him. He gasped, sucked in a lungful of blasting air. His helmet had flown off at some point.

The green canopy rushed up to his feet. Something cracked loudly, and at first he thought it might be his leg, but a branch was crashing down beside him. He'd broken a branch off.

Leaves obscured his view of the ground. The moment his boots struck a solid surface below him, he rolled hard. Too hard. He slammed into a thick tree and collapsed by its long exposed roots, winded and barely aware.

Birds screeched. A macaw. No, a year bird; he'd know the distinctive call anywhere. The long-beaked black bird was sitting atop one of the trees nearby, protesting this sudden intrusion.

I'm alive.

He groaned and forced a breath. Moved his legs. They seemed to be in one piece. What if he was actually unconscious and back in the desert?

He pushed himself up. Slowly his head cleared. The foliage was a mix of reed grass and bushes, thanks to a creek that gurgled thirty yards off. A huge fallen log rested on the bank to his right.

Thomas stood, released the parachute harness, and quickly checked his bones. Bruised, but otherwise intact. His only weapon was the bowie knife strapped to his waist.

Smoke boiled to the sky several miles up the valley. He grabbed the radio at his hip, twisted the volume switch.

"Come in, come in. Anybody, come in."

The speaker hissed. He tried again, got nothing. The transmitter could be dead. But from what he'd seen, he thought it was more likely that the people on the other end were dead. His gut turned. Maybe a few had survived by getting clear like he had, although he couldn't remember seeing any other falling bodies.

Thomas turned, ran up the riverbank, vaulted the log, and landed ankle-deep in sucking mud.

Slow down, slow down. Think!

He scanned the jungle again. If he remembered right, the missile had been fired from a point halfway up the eastern slope. He had to get to the C-17 wreckage. Survivors. A weapon. Radio. Anything that might help him. And before nightfall if he could. He didn't have the same body as Thomas of Hunter in the desert, but he had the same mind, right? He'd been in worse situations. He'd been in one far worse, a hundred Horde assassins within striking distance of his throat, just last night.

Thomas cut back into the jungle, where the canopy shielded the sun and slowed the undergrowth, and headed for the boiling smoke several miles up-valley. His mission took precedence over any survivors, regardless of how inhumane that felt. His purpose here was to find Monique at any cost, even if that cost included the death of twenty soldiers.

He gritted his teeth and grunted.

Several times he resisted the temptation to cut to his right and angle for the source of the missile. But he ran on. They'd surely seen his parachute deploy. They would be ready for him this time.

And this time he wouldn't bounce back from a bullet to his head. He needed more than a knife.

Carlos lifted the radio. "How far?"

"A hundred meters. Running up the river," the voice said softly. "Take the shot?"

"Only if you know you can hit him below the neck. Are you sure it's him?"

A pause.

"It's him."

"Remember, I need him alive." A tranquilizer dart could kill if it hit a man in the head.

Carlos waited. They'd tracked Hunter since his landing, three miles down the valley. Four others had survived the crash: two in similar manner as Hunter, two others broken and bleeding but alive near the crash site. Their survival had been temporary.

If his man didn't take the shot now, they would take him at the wreckage. Better now. The last thing Carlos needed was another of Hunter's escapes.

"Status?"

It was Svensson on the other radio.

Carlos keyed the transmitter. "We have him in our sights."

"So he did survive."

"Yes."

"He's healthy?"

"Yes."

"Keep him that way."

Come out here and keep him healthy yourself, you impossible sloth. Of course he would keep him healthy. As long as the man didn't try anything.

"Target down," his other radio crackled.

He waited, sure that a reversal would immediately follow the report. *Target back up and running.*

But no such report came.

"He's still down?"

"Down."

"Handcuffs tight. And I suggest you hurry. He may not be down for long."

Monique lay on the mattress only half-aware. She'd dreamed of thunder. A loud peal from the crashing skies announcing the end of the world. The people cried out to a huge face in the clouds, which presumably belonged to God. They begged for a hero to save them all from this terrible and unfair turn of events. They wanted a fix. So God had pity. He pointed to a woman with long dark hair named Monique. This was the one who'd first made the Raison Vaccine. This was the one who could now tame it.

Monique opened her eyes and took a deep breath. But there was a problem. Svensson now owned her fix.

The deadbolt slid open and the door creaked.

She closed her eyes. The only thing worse than being trapped in this white room was having to face Svensson or the man from the Mediterranean who smelled like a bar of scented soap. Carlos.

Several sets of feet walked in. Something thudded softly on the concrete floor. What was that? She dared not look now.

The boots left and the door was once again bolted shut from the outside.

Monique waited as long as she could before opening her eyes. She moved her head. There in the middle of the floor lay a body with its face down and turned away from her. Camouflaged jumper and muddy black boots. Hands cuffed behind. Dark hair.

She sat up. Thomas?

It looked like it could be him, but he was dressed wrong.

She hurried across the room and walked around the man. Yes, it was a man—his forearms were too well muscled for a woman. Then she saw his face.

Thomas.

A hundred thoughts raced through her mind. *He'd come for her. He knew where to find her. He had come as a soldier. Were there others?*

To see a man unconscious and handcuffed at her feet would normally turn her stomach, but today was not normal, and today the sight of a friend filled her desperate world with so much joy that she suddenly thought she was going to cry.

She knelt and nudged his shoulder. "Thomas?" she whispered.

He was breathing steadily.

She shook him hard. "Thomas!"

His cheek was pressed against the clean floor, bunching his lips. A day's growth of stubble darkened his face. His wavy hair was tangled and knotted.

"Thomas!"

This time he moved, but only barely before settling back into oblivion.

She stood and stared at his prone body. What kind of man was he really? Her thoughts had been drawn to Thomas Hunter a hundred times in the ten days since he'd first burst into her world and kidnapped her for her own safety. To save the world, he'd said. An absurd suggestion to any person not thoroughly intoxicated.

Now she knew differently. He was special. He knew things he couldn't possibly know, and he made a habit of risking his life to defend that knowledge.

And on a more personal level, to defend her. Save her.

Monique glanced up at the security camera. They were watching, of course. And listening.

She walked to the sink, dipped a beaker into the basin of water (the mountain provided no running water, at least not in her quarters), slipped the hand towel from its rack, and returned to him. She wet the towel and gently wiped his face and neck.

"Wake up," she whispered. "Come on, Thomas, please, we need you awake."

She squeezed more water on his head, his face, his shoulders, and she shook him again. He closed his mouth, swallowed. Finally his eyes fluttered open.

"It's me, Monique."

His eyes turned up to her face, widened, and then squeezed shut with furrowed brow. He groaned and struggled to rise.

She grabbed his handcuffed arm and pulled him, but it didn't seem to help much. He struggled to get his knees under him and his seat in the air. She wasn't sure how to help him—he was awkward yet determined on his own. Finally he managed to bring his head up and sit back on his haunches, eyes closed.

"Are you okay?" she asked. It was a dumb question.

"They shot me," he said.

"You're wounded?" Where? She hadn't seen any blood!

"No. They drugged me."

He just rolled his neck and swallowed.

"You should lie down. Here, let me help you."

"I just got up."

"I have a mattress."

"We don't have time. As soon as they think the drugs have worn off, they'll come for me. We have to talk now. Can you get these handcuffs off?"

She looked at them. "How?"

"Never mind. Man, my head feels like . . ."

His eyes suddenly widened.

"What?" she demanded.

"I didn't dream!"

The dreams again. She wasn't sure what to make of them anymore, but they were certainly more than mere dreams.

"You were drugged," she said. "Maybe that affected you."

He spoke as if he actually was in a dream. "It's the first time I haven't dreamed in two weeks. I mean from this side anyway. There I stopped dreaming for fifteen years by taking the rhambutan fruit."

He was handcuffed and on his knees in a white dungeon, and the world was dying of a virus bearing her name, and he was talking about a fruit.

"Rhambutan," she echoed.

"And we think that you might be connected to Rachelle," he said.

"Rachelle."

He stared at her for a long moment. Then he turned away and whispered under his breath. "Man, oh man. This is crazy."

She didn't know why he thought she would be connected to Rachelle, and for the moment it really didn't matter—he was clearly given to fantasy. What did matter, on the other hand, was the fact that Thomas was the only one who seemed to be able to find her. She glanced at the camera again. They had to be careful.

"They're listening. Sit by my bed with your back to the opposite wall."

He seemed to understand. She helped him across the room and he sat heavily, cross-legged, facing her mattress.

"If we talk quietly, they may not hear us," she said, easing herself onto the mattress.

"Closer," he said.

She scooted closer, so that their knees were nearly touching.

"How did you find me?" she asked.

He stared at her, then past her. "First the virus. It's been released."

"I . . . I know," she said. "How bad is it?"

"Bad. Twenty-four gateway airports. It's spreading unchecked."

"They haven't closed the airports?"

"Won't slow the virus enough to justify the panic." His voice was clearer now—the drug was wearing off quickly. "When I left Washington, only the affected governments were even aware that the virus existed. But they can't keep it quiet for long. The whole world's going to wake up to it one of these days."

She swore softly in French. "I can't believe this happened! We took every precaution. It wasn't just heating the vaccine to a precise heat; it was holding it there for two hours. One hour and fifty minutes or two hours and ten minutes, and the mutation doesn't hold."

"It's not your fault."

"Maybe not, but you do know that my vaccine was actually a virus that—"

"Yes, I know all about your vaccine actually being a virus; you told me that in Bangkok. And it was a brilliant solution to some very big problems. If anyone is to blame here, it's me. I was the one who told the world how your vaccine could be changed into the virus it's become."

"Through your dreams."

"Yes. Where you're connected to Rachelle."

She didn't want to talk to him about these dreams right now. He'd looked at her strangely each time he'd claimed that she was connected to Rachelle.

She refocused the discussion, keeping her voice to a whisper. "Do they know who's behind this? Do they know where we are?"

"The French are involved. Or at least some rogue elements in the French government. That's the prevailing theory. Svensson's not on his own—he's the man behind the virus, but there's a lot more to this than the virus. They call themselves the New Allegiance, and they're demanding huge caches of nuclear arms from all the nuclear countries in exchange for the antivirus."

"They'll never agree!"

"They are already," he said. "China and Russia. The United States is preparing to comply." He blinked and she wondered how true that was. "Others. Israel may be a problem, but with enough pressure they'll probably go along. The prospect of whole populations dying off in a matter of weeks trumps any other logic. This all comes down to the antivirus."

"What about my father? Is the company looking for a way?"

"Your father is screaming bloody murder in Bangkok, but apart from trying to find an antivirus, there's not a lot he can do. Everyone's looking for a way—another reason to delay telling the public. If they do find a way to stop the virus, panic will never have a chance to gain momentum."

"They have leads, then."

"No. Not that I've heard. Not besides you."

"You mean the back door."

"I'm guessing that's why Svensson took you in the first place. Did your key survive the mutation?"

Someone had obviously filled him in. "Yes. And I think I may be able to create a virus that will render the Raison Strain impotent. Hopefully."

He exhaled and closed his eyes. "Thank God."

"Unfortunately, I'm here. And now so are you."

"Did you give it to Svensson? And what do you mean *hopefully?*"

"Hopefully, as in I haven't actually tried it yet. I gave it to them twenty-four hours ago."

"Can you tell me what this virus-killer looks like?"

She knew what he was asking. If they were separated, or if he escaped but not she, he could carry the information to the outside world. But the antivirus in her mind was far too complex for anyone without an education in genetics to remember, much less understand.

"I don't think so."

"You don't think so because you don't know how to or because it's too complicated?"

"I would need to write it down."

"Then write it down."

"It is."

"Where?"

"By the computer." She glanced over his shoulder at the work station. "I would much rather you just take me out of here."

"Trust me, I'm not going anywhere without you. I'd never hear the end of it."

"From whom?"

"From Rachelle," he said.

⬥

Thomas's head slowly cleared. The handcuffs bit deep—there was nothing he could do about them. They had to get out with the antivirus, but there was nothing he could do about that at the moment either. The only thing he *could* do anything about right now was Monique.

He looked into her brown eyes and wondered if Rachelle really was in there somewhere, now, at this very moment. Honestly, looking at Monique now, he wasn't sure that she was Rachelle.

He glanced at Monique's right forefinger. The cut was there, exactly like Rachelle's. He looked into her eyes again. The last time he'd seen Monique was in Thailand last week. But that was fifteen years ago, before he'd married Rachelle. Odd.

Monique's full understanding of the situation might have critical and practical value, however. If they became separated and Monique knew that she could connect with Rachelle, she might find a way to do what Rachelle had done. She might be able to dream as Rachelle if need be.

Thomas considered this as he stared into her eyes.

Monique broke off the stare. "Who's Rachelle?"

Both women shared the same fiery spirit. The same sharp nose. But as far as he could see, that was where the similarities ended.

"Thomas?"

"Rachelle?"

"Yes, Rachelle," Monique said.

"Sorry. Well, you know how I've told you about my dreams. How I learned about the Raison Strain from the Books of Histories in my dreams."

"How could I forget?"

"Exactly. Every time I fall asleep, I wake up in another reality with people and . . . and everything. I'm married there."

"Rachelle is your wife," she said.

She knew! "You remember?"

She stared at him, and for a moment he thought she did remember. "Remember what?"

Why had he said that? "I don't know exactly how it works, but Rachelle dreamed she was you. She told me where to find you."

He paused. "You might be Rachelle. I . . . we don't know."

Monique stood. Thomas couldn't tell if she was offended or just startled. "And what on earth brought you to that conclusion?"

"You have a paper cut on your right forefinger. I know that because Rachelle woke up with a paper cut on her right forefinger. If you and Rachelle are not the same, at least Rachelle is sharing your experiences."

Monique lifted her finger and glanced at a tiny red mark. Then she lowered her hand and slowly looked to Thomas.

"Your wife's in danger."

The door bolt slammed open. Monique's eyes widened and shifted over his shoulder.

⎯⎯⎯∞⎯⎯⎯

Mike Orear had been sure that Theresa was overreacting. She had taken the full brunt of the virus's threat head-on and come away reeling. He didn't doubt any of her facts. It was true, a man named Valborg Svensson had released a virus that had mutated from the Raison Vaccine. The virus was undoubtedly very dangerous and would kill millions, maybe billions, unless it was stopped.

But it would be stopped.

The world didn't just end because some group of deviants got their hands on a vial of germs. His life wouldn't end just because Svensson or whoever was pushing his buttons wanted some nukes. Things just didn't work like that.

That was three days ago, T minus eighteen, give or take a few days if they believed the models at the CDC. Now it was T minus fifteen, and Mike Orear was converting to Theresa's religion of fear.

He sat in his office and studied the spread of legal-pad notes in front of him. They all screamed the same thing, and he knew what they were screaming, but he knew there was a mistake here somewhere. Had to be. Just had to be.

He'd talked to Theresa a dozen times in the last three days, and each time he'd asked if anyone had made any progress on an antivirus, expecting that eventually she would respond in the affirmative. She would say one of the labs in Hong Kong or Switzerland or at UCLA had made a breakthrough.

But she didn't. On the contrary, the labs working on the problem were learning just how unlikely finding any antivirus in less than two months would be.

News about a highly virulent outbreak of a mutated viral vaccine, dubbed the Raison Strain, on a small island south of Java had hit the wires yesterday morning, and the wires were burning hot. The population of the island was roughly two hundred thousand, but there was no airport, and the ferries to and from had been suspended. The island was isolated, and the virus contained. No other shipments of the vaccine had been released.

Given the nature of the virus, the World Health Organization, together with the Centers for Disease Control, had put up unrestricted funds and massive rewards for an antivirus that would save the two hundred thousand people who would otherwise die in less than three weeks. Contracts were being bought out by the government to free up all of the major labs across the country. The healthcare community had gone nearly ballistic.

A red herring, Mike thought, *a red herring for sure.* And even then the networks were reporting a watered-down version of the story. They understood the threat of panic and they were playing ball.

But they didn't know the half of it, Mike thought. Not even a hundredth of it. How could a threat of this magnitude not leak to the press? How many other newsagents were sitting in their offices right now, thinking the same thought? Maybe they were all afraid to run outside and declare to the world that the sky was about to fall. The story was too big. Too unbelievable.

He stood and walked to the mirror on his wall. Opened his mouth and looked at his gums. Stretched his cheeks and peered around his eyeballs. There was no indication at all that he was infected with a killer virus. But he was. He'd given Theresa a blood sample just to be sure, and it had come back positive. He didn't know if he'd caught it from her or from someone else that day, but according to her report, he was a dead man walking.

Mike returned to his desk and stared at his notes. He'd spent most of the last two days scouring the electronic highways and making discreet phone calls in his attempt to piece this puzzle together, and now that it was together, he wasn't sure his effort had been a good idea.

Fact: The president had gone underground for the last four days. The official word was that, due to health concerns, he'd canceled three fund-raising dinners and an alternative-energy lobbying trip to Alaska. He was having some polyps on his colon checked out—routine stuff, they said. He had even gone to the hospital on two occasions. Maybe there was some truth to the polyps story.

Fact: The Russian premier had canceled a trip to the Ukraine due to pressing matters connected with Russia's energy crisis. Another good cover. But Russia's entire naval fleet had also been recalled and was now converging on several major ports. For what purpose?

Fact: No fewer than eighty-four military transport columns had been spotted headed east in the last two days alone. The rails were no exception. There was a lot of military hardware headed to the East Coast. Nothing that would spark a wave of concern to anyone who didn't see the whole picture, but surely some of the officers in charge suspected something, especially if they married this movement of arms with the steady repositioning of navy vessels headed to various eastern seaports.

Fact: The French government had gone virtually AWOL. Two sessions of the National Assembly had been canceled, and a number of papers were asking some troubling questions about the sudden departure of their prime minister, supposedly on an unscheduled vacation. To make matters even more interesting, the bulk of the French army had been called to its northern border for what they called emergency exercises.

Fact: The highest offices in England, Thailand, Australia, Brazil, Germany, Japan, and India, plus another six nations, had gone oddly silent over the past three days.

These were five of twenty-seven facts that Mike had painstakingly compiled over the past forty-eight hours. And they all said that the most powerful people in the world were as concerned with something as Theresa was with this Raison Strain. Maybe more so.

And why had he compiled all of this information? Because Mike knew he couldn't keep his mouth shut for long. When he did open his mouth and let the world know what was really happening while they went about daily life as if all was just peachy, he would have to substantiate his claims with his own data, not data that pointed to Theresa. He felt bound to certain rules, even if the world was in a countdown.

"This is nuts," he mumbled.

Yesterday he'd dropped the finance anchor, Peter Martinson, at the airport for a flight to New York. "Hypothetical question," Mike had said.

"Shoot."

"Let's say you had some information that you knew would affect the markets tomorrow. Say you knew the markets were going to crash, for example. You have an obligation to report it?"

Peter chuckled. "Depends on the source. Insider trading? Off-limits."

"Okay then, let's say you knew that a comet was going to wipe out Earth, but you were sworn to secrecy by the president of the United States because he didn't want to start a panic."

"Then you go out in a flame of glory, spilling your guts to the world just before dying with the rest."

He'd forced a small laugh and changed the subject. Peter had prodded him once but then let it go. He left promising to return with the definitive word on whether the market was going to crash in the next week or so.

A knock sounded on Mike's door. He shuffled the papers together. "Come in."

Nancy Rodriguez, his coanchor on their late-afternoon show, *What Matters*, poked her head in. "You going down to the meeting?"

He'd forgotten that the news director had called the meeting to review a new evening lineup. "Go ahead. I'll be right down."

She pulled the door closed.

He stuffed the papers in his right-hand drawer. *Why was he going to a meeting about a new lineup anyway? Why wasn't he back in North Dakota visiting his parents and friends? Why wasn't he bungee jumping at Six Flags or buying a Jaguar or stuffing lobster down his mouth? Or better still, why wasn't he down at the church confessing to the priest?* The thought stopped him.

A slow wave of heat spread over his head and down his back. This was really happening, wasn't it? It wasn't just a story. It was his life. Everyone's life.

How could he not tell them?

⎯⎯⎯◦⎯⎯⎯

The door opened. "I'll try to get you the paper," Monique whispered. She was speaking about the antivirus.

Thomas twisted. Carlos walked into the room, followed by a man Thomas hadn't yet met. He was tall and walked slowly with a white cane, favoring his right leg. His black hair was greased back. Svensson. He'd seen pictures in Bangkok.

The Swiss looked like he was smothering a temptation to gloat. Carlos, on the other hand, looked more grim.

The man from Cypress pulled the chair from the desk to the middle of the room, walked up to Thomas, grabbed his handcuffs, and hauled him up. Thomas stood and staggered backward before his shoulder joints were unreasonably strained.

"Sit," Carlos ordered, pointing four fingers at the chair. His fingernails were long but neatly manicured. He smelled like European soap.

Thomas walked to the chair and sat. Carlos herded Monique to the sink, where he handcuffed her to the towel rack. Why?

Svensson moved around Thomas slowly. "So this is the man who has given us both the world and a world of trouble. I must say, young man, you look younger than your pictures."

Thomas stared at Monique. He could take care of the old man—even with handcuffs it would hardly be a challenge. But Carlos was another matter. Carlos walked behind him and made the thought pointless by quickly securing his ankles to the chair legs with duct tape.

"I understand you have a few skills that make you quite valuable," Svensson said. "You found us; Armand regards that with some fascination. He wants you in France. But I have some questions of my own to ask first, and I'm afraid I'm going to have to insist that you answer them."

"You need both of us alive until the end," Thomas said.

The scientist chuckled. "Is that so?"

"Only a fool would eliminate the two people who first made this all possible with information they alone had."

Svensson stopped circling. "Perhaps. But I now have that information. At some point your usefulness becomes a matter of history."

"Maybe. But when?" Thomas asked. "When does the virus mutate again? What kind of antivirus will be needed then? Only we know the answers, and even then, we don't know all of them yet. Armand is right."

He didn't know who Armand was, but he assumed it was a person Svensson worked for.

"There will be no more mutations," Svensson said easily. "But I'm happy to announce the formulation of the first antivirus." He pulled a small syringe filled with a clear fluid from his blazer. Now his gloating did spread to his mouth. "And I thought it would be appropriate for both of you to see the fruit of your labor."

He slapped the crux of his left arm with two fingers, removed the plastic shield from the needle with his teeth, and clenched his fist. He found a blue vein in his arm and pushed the needle into it. Two seconds and the liquid was in his bloodstream. He jerked the syringe out and put it into his jacket pocket.

"You see. I am now the only person alive who won't die. That will change shortly, of course, but not before I extract my price. Thank you, both of you, for your service."

He waited as if expecting an answer.

"Carlos."

———— ∞∞∞ ————

Monique saw the long stainless-steel needle before Thomas did, and the bottom of her stomach seemed to fall out. Carlos stepped up to Thomas and let the point hover over his shoulder.

"Penetrating the flesh isn't so painful," Svensson said. "But when he tries to push the needle through your bones, it will be."

"What are you thinking?" Monique cried.

All three looked back to where she stood by the sink.

Svensson was the one who answered. "Loftier thoughts than you, I'm sure. Please try to control yourself."

They hadn't even started on him yet and already her eyes were blurry from tears. She clenched her teeth and tried to still the trembling in her hands.

"It's okay, Monique," Thomas said. "Don't be afraid. I've seen how this ends."

She doubted that he had. He was only trying to confuse them and ease her mind.

"Then let's start with this knowledge of yours," Svensson said. "How did you find us?"

"I talked to a large white bat in my dreams. He told me that you were in a mountain named Cyclops."

Svensson regarded him with a frown. Glanced at Carlos.

The man from Cypress pushed the needle into Thomas's shoulder about a centimeter.

Thomas closed his eyes. "There are books in my dreams called the Books of Histories. They've recorded everything that has happened here. That's how I first learned about the virus."

"History books? I'm sure there are. Then tell me what happens next."

Thomas hesitated. He opened his eyes and looked directly at Monique. She could hardly stand to watch him with that needle sticking out of his arm.

"Over half the world dies from the Raison Strain," Thomas said. "You get your weapons. The times of the Great Tribulation begin."

He kept his eyes on hers. *They were speaking to each other in this strange way,* she thought. She wouldn't look at his arm. She would look only into his eyes, to give him strength.

"Yes, of course, but I was referring to the next few days, not weeks. It doesn't require any precognition to guess how this will end. I want to know how we will get there. Or more to the point, what the Americans will do in the next few days."

He thought about the demand. "I don't know."

"I think you do. We know you've met with the president. Tell me what his plans are."

Monique felt her chest tighten. This wasn't about his dreams. They wouldn't stop until they knew what had passed between Thomas and Robert Blair.

"They didn't tell me what their plans were."

Svensson glanced at Carlos again.

"You want me to make something up?" Thomas said. "I told you, I don't know what the United States will do."

"And I don't believe you."

Carlos pushed and the needle slid in easily before abruptly stopping at the bone. Thomas closed his eyes, but he couldn't hide the tremble that overtook his cheeks.

Carlos leaned on the needle.

Thomas groaned. His body suddenly relaxed and slumped. He'd passed out! Thank God, he'd passed out.

Carlos grunted and withdrew the needle.

"Just a little aggressive, are we?" Svensson said, eying the man.

"I would have expected more from him," Carlos said.

"He still has drugs in his system."

Svensson walked over to the computer, ripped the cord from the wall. He picked up Monique's notes and the pencils she'd used earlier. Satisfied that he'd confiscated her basic tools, he moved toward the door.

"We'll have plenty of time later. I want them ready to move by nightfall."

16

A LOUD bang jerked Thomas from sleep. He cried out and was rolling from the bed before he rightly knew where he was.

The floor greeted him hard, pounding the scream from his lungs.

"Thomas!"

He was in his own house. Rachelle had slammed through the swinging door.

"What is it?" She dropped by his side and helped him to his feet. "Are you okay?"

"Sorry, I just . . ."

"What's this?" She touched his shoulder, where a small trickle of blood ran down his arm. "What's happening?"

"Nothing. It's just a scratch. Nothing." He wiped the blood away, images of this nothing bright in his mind. Carlos had shoved a needle into his arm. The pain had been unbearable. But he had to think it through before telling Rachelle.

He shook the dream from his head and reacquired his sense of this reality.

They'd returned from the desert last night, and one of his men had blurted out the details of how Justin had saved their hides in the desert. The news spread throughout the village like fire.

They were only a day away from the Gathering, and the population had swelled to nearly a hundred thousand, including the large group from the Southern Forest. The air was full of celebration.

He'd slept late.

"What time is it?"

"I'm not sure I believe you. What happened?"

"I'll tell you. But you came in here in an awful hurry. What's going on?"

She seemed to remember why she'd flown in. "They're calling for you. In the Valley of Tuhan. We have to hurry."

"Who's calling for me?"

"The Council. The people. Justin's coming. There's been word all morning; he's coming through the Valley of Tuhan. Half the village is gathered there to receive him already."

"To *receive* him? Whose idea is this? The valley isn't for magicians and politicians!"

She rested her finger on his lips. "Yes, I know, the valley is for mighty warriors. And any man who saves the life of my husband must be a mighty warrior."

"Then it was *your* idea?"

"No. It was rather spontaneous, I think. Dress, dress. We have to go."

"Why do the people want me there?"

"Someone suggested you might want to thank him."

Thomas was bent, strapping his boot, and he nearly fell over at the suggestion.

"Thank him? Who is he, our new king?"

"To hear the people from the Southern Forest, you might think so. Are you jealous? He's harmless."

"Harmless? He's the man I may fight at the challenge tomorrow!"

"Even if there is a fight, you have the option of banishment."

"The Council will want his death. This is the price for disregard of Elyon's love. If he's found guilty, they'll want his death."

"And banishment is death! A living death."

"The Council—"

"The Council is mad with jealousy!" Rachelle said. "Stop this talk. There will be no fight anyway. The people love him!"

"I can't go to the Valley of Tuhan and pay him homage. It would look ridiculous."

"To whom? Your Guard? They're as jealous as the Council. It would look petty if you don't pay a man who saved your life the appropriate respect."

"But the Valley of Tuhan? That's not for every soldier who saves their commander's life. We've only used the valley several times."

"Well, it's being used today, and you *will* come."

He finished dressing and strapped the Book of History to his waist with a broad band of canvas. Rachelle had examined the book upon their return and declared it useless. Yes, he knew, but he wouldn't be separated from it. It might play a role in his mission yet.

They left the house. Evidence of the Gathering was everywhere. White tuhan flowers he liked to call lilies covered the streets; lavender puroon garlands hung from every door. People were dressed for the celebration—light-colored tunics accessorized with hair flowers and bronze bracelets and tin headbands. Not a person they passed didn't acknowledge Thomas with a kind word or a head dipped in respect. Each of their villages had been saved by his Forest Guard numerous times.

He returned each kind word with another. Although the village was brimming with people, it wasn't as crowded as he would have expected the day before the annual Gathering. The people had gone to the valley. The Council would be furious.

They left through the main gate and walked a well-worn path that led directly to the Valley of Tuhan, roughly a mile from the outskirts.

Rachelle glanced back to make sure they were alone.

"So, now tell me. What happened?"

The dream.

"We found Monique."

Her eyes grew round. "I knew it!" She skipped once like a child in her enthusiasm. "It's all true. I told you to believe me, Thomas. That I was there in that white room." She threw her arms around his neck and kissed him on the lips, nearly knocking him off the trail.

"I did believe you," he said. "As I recall, it was you who didn't believe me once upon a time."

"But that was before. So you rescued me?"

"No."

"No?"

"I'm working on it."

"Tell me everything."

He told her. Everything except for the torture.

"So you not only failed to rescue Monique, but now we're both in the dungeon," Rachelle said when he'd finished. She stopped, eyes wide. "This is terrible news. We're in mortal danger!"

"We've always been in danger."

"Not like this."

"The virus presents more of a danger than this. At least we know that the antivirus now exists, and I'm in the vicinity of the people who have it. Maybe I can find a way out."

"We're both in the dungeon, for goodness' sake! We'll be killed, both of us."

He took her hand and they walked on. "That's not going to happen." He looked at the forest. The sound of a distant celebration whispered on the wind.

Thomas sighed. "All around us people are preparing for a celebration and we're talking about being tortured in a dungeon—"

"Tortured? What do you mean tortured?"

"The whole thing. It's torture. Svensson's torturing us with this imprisonment of his."

She seemed satisfied by his quick recovery.

"If you and I live in both worlds, isn't it possible that we all live in both worlds?" she asked.

"I've thought about it. But we may only be sharing the dreams and realities of people in the other world."

"Either way, who is Qurong there? And who is Svensson here? If we could find Svensson here and kill him, wouldn't he die there?"

"We need Svensson alive. He has the antivirus. These are delicate matters, Rachelle. We can't just start killing people."

He challenged her theory on another front.

"Besides, if everyone there also lived here, we would have a much larger population."

"Then maybe we're only part of them. There could be other realities."

"Even then, why aren't people just falling over dead here when they die there from an accident or something?"

"Maybe they aren't truly connected unless they know. We know because of the dreams, but others don't. Perhaps the realities can't be breached without understanding."

"Then how did I first breach these realities?"

She shrugged. "It's only a theory."

Interesting thoughts. And she'd had them on the fly.

She was grinning. "You see the power of a woman's thoughts."

"I think I'm the only gateway between these realities. Blood, knowledge, and skills are the only things that are transferable, and I'm the only gateway."

"Yet I went."

The reason why came to Thomas suddenly and clearly. "You were cut with me. And you were bleeding. Both of us were."

"And maybe this is all nonsense," she said.

"It may be."

The valley of Tuhan had never seen so many people at once, not even after the Winter Campaign, when the nearest forests had come together to honor Thomas.

They first heard the crowd a hundred yards from the valley, a soft murmur of voices that grew with each step. When Thomas and Rachelle finally rounded the last bend in the forest and faced the broad green valley of grass, the murmur became a steady roar.

Thomas stopped, speechless. The valley looked like a large oblong bowl that gently sloped to a flat base. White lilylike flowers called tuhans grew along the banks of a small creek that ran the length of the valley, thus its name, the Valley of Tuhan. A wide path had been worn beside the creek.

But it was the crowd that stopped Thomas. They weren't cheering. They were waiting on the slopes on either side, talking excitedly, thirty thousand at least, dressed in white tunics with flowers in their hair. So many! He knew Justin's popularity had never been as great as it was now. His victory at the Southern Forest and the incident yesterday in the desert had catapulted him to the status of hero overnight. The beat had always been there, of course, but now the fickle crowds had taken up their drums and joined the parade, ready to march en masse.

"Thomas! It's Thomas of Hunter!" someone cried.

Thomas dipped his head at the man who spoke, Peter of Southern, one of the elders from the Southern Forest. Peter hurried over. The news that Thomas had arrived spread down the valley; thousands of heads turned; a cry swelled.

Thomas of Hunter.

He smiled and lifted a hand to the people while looking for any sign of Ciphus or the Council.

"You should be at the front, Thomas," Peter said. "Hurry, he'll be here soon."

"I can see well enough—"

"No, no, we have a place reserved." He took Thomas's arm and pulled him. "Come. Rachelle, come."

A chant had started and they called his name as was the custom. "Hunter, Hunter, Hunter, Hunter." Thirty thousand voices strong.

With their eyes on him and their voices crying his name, he had little choice but to follow Peter of Southern down the slope, where the crowd had parted for him, to the valley floor, where the children had been jumping and dancing only a moment ago. Now they stilled and stared in awe at the great warrior whose name was being chanted.

Peter led him to the front row.

"Thank you, Peter."

The elder left.

His son and daughter, Samuel and Marie, worked their way toward him from the left, glowing with pride but trying not to be too obvious about it. He winked at them and smiled.

The chant hadn't eased. *Hunter, Hunter, Hunter, Hunter.* He lifted his hand and acknowledged the crowd again. They waited on the slopes, natural bleachers. The seventy-yard swath down the middle of the valley was the parade route, and not a soul ventured out to disturb the grass. This was the custom. The path Justin would ride down split the valley in two, only thirty yards from where they stood.

A small girl, maybe nine or ten years of age, with a small white lily in her hair, stared at him with huge brown eyes, ten feet away. *In her shock at being so close to this legend, she'd forgotten how to chant,* Thomas thought. He smiled at her and dipped his head.

Her round mouth split into a wide smile. One of her teeth was missing, he saw. Maybe she was younger than nine.

"She's adorable," Rachelle said, next to him. She'd seen her staring.

Still the crowd chanted his name.

No one gave the signal. No bright light appeared in the sky to signal any change. And yet everything changed in the space of two chants. It was *Hunter, Hunt*— and then silence.

The profound, ringing silence seemed louder to Thomas than the roar that preceded it.

He glanced across the valley and saw that every head had turned to his left. There, where the trees ended and the grass began, stood a white horse. And on the horse sat a man dressed in a white sleeveless tunic.

Justin of Southern had arrived.

Two warriors in traditional battle dress were mounted side by side behind him. *Justin and his merry men,* Thomas thought.

For a long moment that seemed to stretch beyond itself, Justin sat perfectly still. He wore a wreath of white flowers on his head. Bands made of brass were wrapped around his biceps and forearms, and his boots were bound high, battle style. A knife was strapped to his calf and a black-handled sword hung in a red scabbard behind him. He sat in the saddle with the confidence of a battle-hardened warrior, but he looked more like a prince than a soldier.

His eyes searched the crowd, lingered on Thomas for a moment, and then moved on. Still not a sound.

His horse pawed the ground once and stepped into the valley.

A roar shook the ground, an eruption of raw energy bottled in the throats of thirty thousand people. Fists were thrown to the air and mouths

were stretched in passion. Their thunder seemed to fuel itself, and when
Thomas was sure it had reached its peak, the roar swelled.

They were three miles from the village, but there wasn't a doubt in
Thomas's mind that the shutters of every house there were at this very
moment rattling. How many of these people were shouting because the
others were shouting? How many were willing to celebrate, regardless of
the object of that celebration? Apparently, most.

He glanced at Rachelle, who beamed and shouted, caught up in the
moment. He smiled. Why not? Every warrior deserved honor, and Justin
of Southern, though perhaps deserving of other considerations as well, had
certainly earned some honor. Let the Council sweat in their robes. Today
was Justin's day.

Thomas lifted his fist in a salute.

Slowly, with deliberate pronounced steps, Justin rode his horse into
the valley. He stared straight ahead without acknowledging the crowd. His
men marched abreast thirty paces behind.

Now the chant began. The thunder formed a word that roared from the
throats of every man, woman, and child in the valley, perhaps beyond . . .

. . . *Justin, Justin, Justin, Justin* . . .

. . . until it sounded like pounding detonations that exploded with
each roar of his name.

Justin! Justin! Justin! Justin!

Thomas had never seen such a display of worship for one man before.
The fact that Justin accepted the praise without so much as a modest grin
only seemed to justify their adoration. It was as if he knew that he deserved
no less and was willing to accept it.

The air reverberated with their cries. The leaves of the trees along the
creek trembled. Thomas felt the sound reach into his belly and shake his
heart.

Justin! Justin! Justin! Justin!

Justin rode halfway into the valley and stopped his horse. Then he
stood tall in his stirrups, threw his fists to the sky, lifted his head, and began
to scream something.

At first they couldn't hear his words for the roar, but as soon as the people figured out that he was saying something, they began to quiet. Now Justin's cry rose above the din. He was screaming a name. He was bellowing a name at the sky.

Elyon's name.

A chill washed over Thomas. Justin was claiming the authority of the Creator. And this, knowing full well that a challenge had been cast against him. The Council would rage. If Justin wasn't innocent, then he was as devious and manipulating as they came.

Justin cried the name of his Maker, eyes clenched, face twisted, as one who was torn between gratitude and terrible fear. The valley stilled with uncertainty.

With one last unrelenting cry that exhausted every ounce of his breath, Justin screamed the name. *Ellllyyyyonnnnnn!*

Then he settled back in his saddle and slowly faced Thomas.

"I salute you, Thomas of Hunter," he called.

Thomas dipped his head. But he couldn't go so far as to salute the man in return, not with the challenge at hand.

Justin dipped his head in return. He looked at the people, first the far side, turning his horse for a full view, then Thomas's side. His stallion stepped nervously under him. He seemed to be looking for someone.

The children, Thomas thought. *He was looking at the children.*

He spun his horse back around and gazed at the far side again. Then to Thomas's side again, green eyes searching, searching.

Forty feet from where Thomas stood, a young girl stepped out of the crowd, walked a few paces into the meadow, and stopped. Her hair was blond, past her shoulders. Her arms were limp by her sides. One of her hands was shriveled to a stump. She trembled from head to foot and tears ran down her cheeks.

Thomas's first thought was that her mother should call this poor child back immediately. The traditions of the valley were clear enough: No one ever approached any warrior honored on their march. It was a time of order and respect, not chaos.

But then he saw that Justin was staring directly at this child. Surely he hadn't been searching for her.

A small bushy-haired boy stepped out and stopped just behind the girl.

To Thomas's amazement, he saw that tears were on Justin's cheeks. He ignored the gathered throng and exchanged a long stare with this young girl.

"He knows her," Rachelle whispered.

Justin suddenly slid off his horse and faced the girl. Then he dropped to one knee and spread his arms wide.

She ran for him, weeping audibly now. Her white tunic swished around her small legs, and the flowers in her hair fell to the ground as she ran.

The girl collided with Justin in the middle of the field. His arms wrapped around her and he held her tight. A lump rose in Thomas's throat.

The girl showed Justin her hands, which he kissed. He stood and led her ten paces from the horses, where the entire valley could see clearly. He whispered something in her ear and then walked on while she stood still. What was he doing?

Justin swept the crowds with a steady gaze.

"I tell you on this day, that the greatest warriors among you are the children," he cried out for all to hear. "It is with ones like these that you will wage a new kind of war."

He faced the girl, who was beaming from ear to ear now. A twinkle brightened Justin's eyes. He stretched his hand out to her.

"I present to you my princess. Lucy!"

It was impossible to tell if this show was a deception or completely sincere. As either, it was a brilliant performance.

Justin took the white wreath from his head, placed it gently on her head, and stepped back. He settled to one knee, put one hand over his breast, and raised the other to the crowd.

A cry erupted spontaneously.

Thomas thought the girl's face might split in two if she beamed any brighter. Beside him, Rachelle was dabbing her eyes.

Justin motioned excitedly for the boy, who now ran for them.

"And my prince, Billy!"

He swept the boy from his feet and spun him around. Then he led both of the children back to his horse, swung into the saddle, and hoisted them up, Lucy behind and Billy in front. He gave the reins to the boy and nudged the horse.

The thunder began again, now with chants of Lucy and Billy mingled in. Justin took time to acknowledge the crowd now. To look at him riding with such confidence and being so worshiped, one would think he had been a king from the ancient stories instead of a forest vagabond who'd abandoned the Guard and now spoke of treason.

When Justin finally reached the far side of the valley, he set the children down and disappeared into the trees.

"Now do you think there will be a fight at tomorrow's challenge?" Rachelle asked. The din had died and the valley was emptying.

"Justin is either a man who deserves this praise or a man who deserves to die," Thomas said, "in which case he's much more dangerous than I ever could have guessed."

"And who do you think he is?"

Thomas stared at the trees that had swallowed Justin. Was his the face of deception or the face of grace? It hardly mattered in the end, because either way it was definitely the face of treason. Any man who brokered peace with the sons of Shataiki could not be a man who followed Elyon.

"Thomas, you're drifting on me again."

"I think he's a very dangerous man. But we'll let the people decide tomorrow."

"It sounds to me like they've already decided."

"That's because you haven't heard the others yet. Not everyone was here."

17

PRESIDENT ROBERT Blair hadn't slept in twenty-four hours. The air was charged with panic. No one was happy. They were all out of their league, every last one of them. They bore titles like president of the United States and secretary of defense and director of the Central Intelligence Agency, but inside they were all just men and women on the shore, facing a massive tidal wave that blocked their view of the horizon. There was no running; there was no fighting; there was only bracing.

Not true. There was God. It was out of their hands in the hands of God—a scary thought considering his complete lack of understanding in such matters.

And there was Thomas Hunter.

Senate majority leader Dwight Olsen slammed his palm on the table, round face red. "Send them!" He glared at the president. "For Pete's sake, we're running out of time. Give them what they ask for. We have the technology, we can rebuild, we can start over, but we need some breathing space. If you think the American people would condone this game of poker . . ."

He stopped short. *Not thinking too clearly,* the president thought. But then none of them were.

"I *am* thinking of sending the missiles, Dwight. Fully armed and on a collision course with Paris. Israel may beat us to it." He'd already authorized the shipments, but considering Olsen's arrogance, he withheld the revelation for the moment.

"Then you and Benjamin would defy what the Russians, the Chinese, even England is doing. Maybe they have more sense—"

"Shut up!"

Easy, Robert.

"Just shut up and listen to me. You're not thinking this through very clearly. The Russians are complying with Paris because they are in *bed* with Paris. So are the Chinese—we have to assume that based on the intelligence I just laid out to you. Arthur, on the other hand, has convinced our British counterparts to comply with Paris on *my* word that we would not ultimately do so. We will ship our missiles as a sign of good faith, but I'll die before I hand over one pistol to those maniacs so that they can turn around and fire it back at us."

"We have their word—"

"They have no intention of keeping their word!"

"You can't know that," Olsen said.

"They're terrorists, for crying out loud!"

"If either you or Israel does anything stupid, like try a preemptive strike, you'll send us all to our graves based on an assumption that is more likely wrong than right."

The president looked at Graham Meyers. His secretary of defense was listening patiently as were the others. Now Meyers came to his defense.

"Israel won't try that. Our intelligence—"

"Cut the intelligence nonsense," Olsen said. "Who? What intelligence?"

Meyers glanced at the president and Blair dipped his head. *Go ahead, Grant, spill the beans. We're past cat and mouse with this idiot.*

"The same intelligence that located Valborg Svensson," he said.

Olsen blinked. "Svensson. You found him," he said in a doubtful tone.

"Yes, Dwight. We found him," the president said. "They shot down a C-17 that was making a low pass over his compound roughly eight hours ago."

"Where?"

"Indonesia. Furthermore, we received a communiqué two hours ago from the French. They claim they have incontrovertible evidence that Svensson has an antivirus in his possession. Evidently they wondered if we were sure on that point."

Olsen's collar was stained dark with sweat. "And what's being done?"

"The pilot reported their situation before the plane went down. We don't know who survived. Three beacons were activated when their parachutes deployed, but there's been no word since, so we're assuming the worst. A squadron of stealth fighters and three C-17s took off from the Hickam base in Hawaii seven hours ago. An hour ago we dropped forty Navy Seals on the spot where our people believe the Stinger that took down our plane was fired from. This is the kind of intelligence we're talking about."

"So there's a chance we may find Svensson with the antivirus."

"A chance, yes."

"And how did your people find Svensson so easily?"

Blair hesitated, and then decided to finish what he'd started.

"Thomas Hunter," he said. "I'm sure you remember Thomas. The psychic, I think you called him. The communiqué from France also claimed that the New Allegiance had Thomas Hunter in custody and that any further attempts at military action would cost both him and Monique their lives."

The Senate majority leader was taken completely off guard by the revelation.

"Okay, so you have a psychic in your intelligence circles. And I take it this psychic has told you that the United Sates won't receive the antivirus in time. And now you're going to base your entire strategy on this revelation of his. Have you considered the basic logic that if they administer the antivirus to France, the United States is only a seven-hour flight away? It doesn't matter who they give the antivirus to; our scientists can copy it from any carrier."

They'd discussed the scenario already, and there were ways that Svensson could still keep the United States from acquiring and duplicating any antivirus in time. But Thomas had insisted that the United States would not receive the antivirus. In light of his recent success, Blair was prone to believe him.

"Maybe. I'll take it under advisement. Our hope is to avoid getting to that point."

"God knows I hope we can. But if you play hardball with the French on this, I'm going to bring this whole nation down around your ears."

"I'll take that under advisement as well. If our current mission fails, the arms will ship on schedule. I won't do anything rash; you have my word. Only as a very last resort. But don't expect me to roll over yet. Give me at least that much, for heaven's sake. If you really think these guys are going to let us live to fight another day, you're not seeing what I see."

"Well, we always did live in different worlds, didn't we? I hope you can keep the Israelis calm."

"Calm, no. They're climbing the walls behind closed doors over there. But I do have Benjamin's word that they will make a show of compliance, at least for the time being. You do understand that they will not go down without a fight, don't you, Dwight?"

"Fools." Olsen stood to leave. "Meanwhile our country's totally in the dark out there. We have to tell them soon. I can promise you they will be enraged for not being told sooner."

"I would have thought you would count that politically expedient, Dwight."

The man gave him a parting glare, and Blair was sure the man had already considered his political future in all of this. It was perhaps the only reason he hadn't already run to the press.

"Keep this quiet," the president said.

Dwight Olsen turned. "I'll give you two days. If I like what I see, I may play ball. If not, no promises."

"You leak this and I'll have you arrested."

"On what grounds?"

"Treason. Leaking sensitive military operations is an actionable offense. *We* have a virus, but we also have a military action under way."

It was more bluff than actionable, but Blair didn't care.

"Sir." Intercom.

"Yes?"

"Report in from Hawaii."

He caught Olsen's eyes. It was the mission.

The secretary of defense glanced up, eyes wide. "Send it in, Bill."

Ten seconds later Graham Meyers had a red folder in his hands. His eyes scanned the report. Olsen had quietly stepped back into the room.

The president loosened his already sloppy tie. "Well, spit it out, for crying out loud."

"The mission successfully located and entered a large complex on the backside of Cyclops. No casualties. The complex was abandoned."

"What?"

"Abandoned within the last several hours. They're gathering some computers now, but the hard drives have been removed. The place is clean." Grant looked up. "There's evidence to suggest at least one soldier was in one of the rooms. Buttons from one of our uniforms."

"Hunter."

The room was silent.

"They can't be far," someone said.

The president pushed back his chair and stood. "Find him!"

18

THE CELEBRATION had gone late into the night, as was always the case during the three days the Forest People held their annual Gathering. Music and dancing and plays and food, too much food. And drink, of course. Fruit wines and berry ales mostly. Anything and everything that even hinted at their memories of the Great Romance in the colored forest.

The opening ceremonies were held with each tribe marching down the avenue that led to the lake, led by the elders from that tribe. Ciphus led the largest entourage from the Middle Forest, followed by the other forests by their location, from north to south.

Twenty thousand torches burned around the lake as Ciphus recited their creeds and reminded them all why they must adhere to the very fabric of the Great Romance without the slightest deviation, as Elyon would surely have it. Their religion was a simple one, with only six laws at the heart, but the other laws, the ones the Council had refined over the years to assist in following the six, had to be given the same weight, he said. The way to love Elyon was to give yourself completely to his ways, without the slightest compromise.

Thomas had collapsed in bed late, slept with heavy dreams of torture, and awakened with two parallel preoccupations.

The first was this business of finding out who Carlos might be in this reality, if indeed such a thing was even possible, as Rachelle had suggested in passing. A thin thread, to be sure, but following it was the only way he could think of to escape the dungeon with Monique.

The second was the challenge, which was to be held that afternoon. Other than posting notice of it, the Council had been wisely silent about Justin. Still, it had been the talk of the village all morning.

Some wondered why an inquiry was even necessary—the doctrines of Justin weren't so different from any they had followed all these years. He talked about love. Wasn't the Great Romance all about love? Yes, his teachings of peace with the Horde were very difficult to follow, but now he was talking love. Perhaps he'd changed.

Others wondered why Justin wasn't simply banished out of hand—his teachings were clearly an affront to all that was sacred about the Great Romance, *beginning* with his talk of peace. How could anyone make peace with the enemies of Elyon? And his teachings were difficult only because they worked against the Great Romance, they said.

The amphitheater where the challenge would be held was large enough to hold twenty-five thousand adults, which was nearly adequate as only adults could attend. The rest would have to find places in the forest above the large bowl-like structure on the west side of the lake.

The stone slabs that acted as benches on terraced earth were nearly full shortly after noon. By the time the sun hung halfway down the western sky, there was no longer empty space to stand, much less sit.

Thomas sat with Rachelle and his lieutenants in one of the gazebos overlooking the spectacle.

"I should be tracking the Horde into the desert," Thomas muttered.

"Don't think that you won't be called on to do your part here," Mikil said. "When it's finished, we'll go after the Horde and I'll be the first by your side."

She stood next to Jamous. They'd announced their plans for marriage at the celebration last evening. To their right, William scanned the crowd.

Rachelle put her hand on Thomas's arm. She alone understood his dilemma here.

"Even if there is a fight, I won't kill him, Mikil," he said. "Banishment, but not death."

"Fine. Banishment is better than giving him the freedom to poison the minds of our children," she said.

He took a calming breath. "I have to go after the Books of Histories again."

"And this time I will enter the tent," Mikil said. "The rest of this Gathering I can do without. We deal with Justin and then we leave to find your books. And Jamous will come with us."

Jamous kissed her on the lips. "As long as I am with you, I could cross the desert."

"Always," she said.

"Always," he repeated, and they kissed again.

The crowd suddenly hushed.

"They're coming."

Thomas walked to the railing and looked down on the amphitheater. Ciphus was walking down the long slope in his long white ceremonial robe. Behind him, the other six members of the Council. They approached a large platform in the middle of the field. Seven large torches burned in a semicircle around eight tall wooden stools. A stand held a bowl of water between them.

They walked in silence to seven of the stools. The eighth remained empty. If Justin won the inquiry, he would be allowed to sit with the Council in a show of their acceptance of him. Since the Council had cast the inquiry, they were not obligated to accept his doctrine, but in time, even it might be incorporated in the Great Romance.

The members climbed onto their stools and faced a similar, smaller platform with a single stool twenty yards from their own.

"Where is Justin?" Mikil whispered.

Ciphus lifted a hand for silence, though no gesture was needed—no one was moving, much less speaking. If Thomas were to cough, the whole arena would likely hear him.

"The Council will issue its challenge of the philosophies of Justin of Southern in this the tenth annual Gathering of all Forest People," Ciphus cried. His voice rang loud and clear.

"Justin of Southern, we call you forth."

The Council turned back toward the slope down which they had walked. At the crest of the slope, seven large trees marked the only entrance to the amphitheater.

No one appeared.

"He's going to default," Mikil said. "He knows that he's wrong and he's—"

"Who is that?" William asked.

A villager was walking from one of the lower seats. Instead of wearing the more popular short tunic, he was dressed in a longer, hooded beige one. And he wore the boots of a soldier.

"That's him," Jamous said.

The Council still hadn't seen him. The man walked to the lone stool, seated himself, and pulled back his hood.

"Justin of Southern accepts your challenge," he said loudly.

The Council spun as one. Murmurs ran through the amphitheater. A few chuckles.

"He's daring; I'll give him that," Mikil said.

Thomas could practically see the steam coming from Ciphus's ears.

The elder held up his hand for silence, and this time it was required. He walked to the bowl, dipped his hands into the water, and dabbed them dry on a small towel. Behind him the other members took their seats.

Ciphus paced the leading edge of the platform and pulled at his beard. "It is precisely this kind of trickery that I fear has deceived you, my friend," he said, just loudly enough to be heard.

"I have no desire to confuse the important questions you will ask," Justin said. "It is what we say today, not how we look, that will win or lose the hearts of the people."

Ciphus hesitated, then addressed the people. "Then hear what I have to say. The man we see seated before us today is a mighty warrior who has favored the forests with many victories in his time. He is the kind of man who loves children and who marches like a true hero and accepts praise with graciousness. Each of these we all know. For each of these I owe a debt of gratitude to Justin of Southern." He dipped his head at Justin. "Thank you."

Justin returned the bow.

Ciphus was no fool, Thomas thought.

"Nevertheless, it is said that this man has also spread the poison of blasphemy against Elyon throughout the Southern Forest in these past two years. Our task today is only to determine if this is true. We judge not the man, but his doctrine. And as with any challenge, you, the people, will be the judge of the matter when we have concluded our arguments. So then, judge well."

On Thomas's left, murmuring broke out, voices of dissent already. These must be those of the Southern Forest, Justin's strongest supporters. Where were the two men who had entered the Valley of Tuhan with Justin? Ronin and Arvyl, if Jamous had told him correctly. Their voices were in the crowd, surely, but not on the floor as Thomas might have expected. On the other hand, it was like Justin to fight his own battles and defend his own philosophies. He'd probably forbidden them from interfering.

"Silence!"

They hushed again.

"It won't take long. A very simple matter in fact. I think that for this inquiry we could have the children vote and end up with a clear, just verdict. The matter is this."

Ciphus turned to Justin.

"Is it or is it not true that the Horde is truly the enemy of Elyon?"

"It is true," Justin said.

"Correct, we all know this. So then, is it or is it not true that to conspire with the enemy of Elyon is to conspire against Elyon himself?"

"It is true."

"Yes, of course. We all know this as well. So then, is it or is it not true that you advocate creating a bond with the Horde by negotiating peace?"

"It is true."

A gasp flushed through the arena. Shocked mutterings rose from the left and admonishments to let them finish from the right. Ciphus again silenced the crowd with his hand. He measured Justin carefully, undoubtedly thinking that he was plotting some of his trickery.

"You do realize that to conspire with the Horde has always been treasonous to us? We don't compromise with the enemy of Elyon, according to the word of Elyon himself. We subscribe to the boy's prophecy, that Elyon will provide a way to rid the world of this scourge that's upon us. Yet you seem to want to make peace with it. Isn't this blasphemous?"

"Blasphemous, yes," Justin said.

The man had no sense, Thomas thought. With those words he'd conscripted himself to banishment.

"The question is," Justin continued, "blasphemous against what? Against your Great Romance, or against Elyon himself?"

Ciphus was shocked by this assertion. "And you think there is a difference?"

"There is a great difference. Not in spirit, but in form. To make peace with the Horde may defile your Great Romance, but it does not blaspheme Elyon. Elyon would make peace with every man, woman, and child on this world, even though his enemies are found everywhere, even here in this very place."

Silence. The people seemed too stunned to speak. *He'd cut his own throat,* Thomas thought. What he said had a freshness to it, perhaps an idea that he might entertain if he were a theologian. But Justin had decried all that was sacred except Elyon himself. By questioning the Great Romance, he might as well have included Elyon as well.

"You say that we are Elyon's enemy?" There was a tremble in Ciphus's voice.

"Do you love your lake and your trees and your flowers, or do you love Elyon? Would you die for these, or would you die for Elyon? You are no different than the Horde. If you would die for Elyon, perhaps you should die for the Horde. They are his, after all."

"You would have us die for the Horde?" Ciphus cried, red faced. "Die for the enemy of Elyon, whom we have sworn to destroy!"

"If need be, yes."

"You speak treason against Elyon!" Ciphus pointed a trembling finger at Justin. "You are a son of the Shataiki!"

Order abandoned the amphitheater with that one word: *Shataiki.* Cries of outrage ripped through the air, met head-on with cries of objection that Ciphus could say such a thing against this prophet. This Justin of Southern. If they would only let the man explain himself, they would understand, they cried.

Any ambivalence Thomas had felt toward this hearing left him. How could any man who'd served under him dare suggest they die for the Horde? Die in battle defending Elyon's lakes, yes. Die protecting the forest and their children *from* the Horde, yes. Die upholding the Great Romance in the face of an enemy who'd sworn to wipe Elyon's name from the face of the earth, yes.

But die *for* the Horde? Broker peace so that they might be free to work their deceit?

Never!

"How can he say that?" Rachelle asked beside him. "Did he just suggest we lie down and die for the Horde?"

"What did I tell you?" Mikil said. "We should have killed him yesterday when we had the chance."

"If we'd killed him yesterday, we'd be dead today," Thomas said.

"Better dead than indebted to this traitor."

The arena was a mess of riotous noise. Ciphus made no attempt to stop them. He walked to the bowl of water and dipped his hands in once again. He was done, Thomas realized.

The elder conferred with the other Council members one by one.

Justin sat calmly. He made no attempt to explain himself. He seemed satisfied despite having put up no real defense at all. Maybe he wanted a fight.

Ciphus finally raised both hands and, after a few moments, quieted the crowd enough for him to be heard.

"I have made my challenge to this heresy, and now you will decide this man's fate. Should we embrace his teaching or send him away from us, never to return? Or should we put his fate in Elyon's hands through a fight to the death? Search your hearts and let your decision be heard."

Thomas prayed the vote would be clear. Despite his aversion to what Justin had said, he wanted no part in a fight. Not that he feared Justin's sword, but the thought of being dragged down in support of the Council didn't sit well with him either.

On the other hand, there would be a kind of justice in asserting himself over his former lieutenant in one final match before sending him to live with the Horde. Either way, Ciphus would not get his death.

"It's over," he said quietly.

"Then you weren't in the valley yesterday," Rachelle said.

Ciphus lowered his right hand. "If you say this man speaks blasphemy, let your voice be heard!"

A thunderous roar shook the gazebo. Enough. Surely enough.

Ciphus let the cry run on until he was satisfied, then silenced them.

"And if you say we should accept this man's teaching and make peace with the Horde, then let your voice be heard."

The Southern Forest dwellers had strong lungs, because the cry was loud. And it swelled with as much thunder as the first cry. Or was it less? The distinction was not enough for Ciphus to call it.

Thomas's heart rose into his throat. No one outside this gazebo knew that he would defend the Council in a fight. And there would be a fight. No matter how deaf Ciphus wanted to be at this moment, he could not call this a clear decision. The rules were plain—there could be no doubt.

Ciphus lowered both hands and the people quieted. They all knew what was coming. For a long time the elder just stood still, perhaps taken aback that the crowd was so divided.

"Then we will place the fate of this man in Elyon's hands," he said loudly. "I call to the floor our defender, Thomas of Hunter."

The crowd gasped. Or at least half of it gasped. The southern half, which had decided to claim Justin as their own since he'd delivered their forest a week earlier. They clearly couldn't see him fighting their Justin.

The other half began to chant his name.

Rachelle's eyes were dark with fear.

He kissed her cheek. "I taught him; remember that."

He climbed over the railing, and the people made a way for him down through the bleachers. He gripped his sword at his side and vaulted over the short wall that separated the field from the seats. The walk to the main platform seemed long with all the cheering and with Justin drilling him with a stare.

He stood before Ciphus, who shut down the crowd.

"I request you, Thomas of Hunter, supreme commander of the Forest

Guard, to defend our truth against this blasphemy in a fight to the death. Do you accept?"

"I will. But I will seek banishment, not death, for Justin."

"That is my choice to make, not yours," Ciphus said.

Thomas had never heard of such a thing.

"I understood that it was my choice," he said.

"Then you misunderstand the rules. The Council made this rule and now you must abide by it. It will be a fight to the death. The price for this sin is death. I am not willing to consider the living death."

Thomas thought a moment. It was true that the law required death of anyone who defied Elyon. Banishment was a kind of death, a living death, as Ciphus called it. But now, forced to consider it, he realized there could be a problem with banishing Justin. What if he entered the Horde and gained power under Qurong? What if he then led their armies against the forest? Perhaps death was the wiser choice, though not what he desired.

"Then I accept." He dipped his head.

"Swords!" Ciphus cried.

A Council member lifted two heavy bronze swords from the floor by his stool and set them on the stage.

"Choose your sword," Ciphus said.

Thomas glanced at Justin. The warrior watched him with mild interest now. Did the man have a death wish?

Thomas picked up the swords, one in each hand, and walked toward Justin. "Do you have a preference?"

"No."

Thomas flipped both swords into the air. They turned lazily in unison and stuck into the boards on either side of Justin.

"I insist," Thomas said. "I don't want it said that I beat Justin of Southern by picking the better sword."

The crowd reacted with a rumble of approval.

Justin kept his eyes on Thomas without looking at the swords. He stepped forward, yanked out the one to his right. "Neither would I," he said, tossing the weapon so that its blade pierced the earth at Thomas's feet.

Another rumble of approval.

"Fight!" Ciphus yelled. "Fight to the death!"

Thomas plucked the sword out and swung it twice for feel. It was a standard Guard weapon, well balanced and heavy enough to sever a head with one swipe.

Justin put his hand on the sword and waited. Enough of this posturing. The sooner they ended the fight, the better. To know a man in a match of this kind meant watching his eyes. And Thomas didn't like what he saw in Justin's eyes. They were too full of life to cut so easily from his shoulders. The man was full of beguiling influence that unnerved him.

He skipped to his left and leaped to the platform, ten feet from Justin. He briefly wondered if the man was simply going to die without a fight, because he hardly shifted.

Thomas lunged and brought the sword around with enough force to cut the man in half.

At the last moment, Justin pulled his sword up and deflected the blow. A horrendous clash filled the arena. It was exactly what Thomas had expected. In the moment when Justin was blocking his blow, he reached out with his left hand and tapped the man on the cheek.

It was a move he'd taught them all as a bit of a joke once. Mikil dubbed it "The Cheek." What Thomas didn't expect was the hand that shot out from Justin at precisely the same moment. It tapped his cheek.

The crowd roared and Thomas thought he could hear Mikil's cry of approval above the din.

He couldn't help but smile. Good. Very good. Justin smirked. Winked.

Then they went a full round, gripping their swords with both hands. Clash and counterclash, jabbing, sparring, thrusting, moving around the platform—fundamental swordplay to loosen the joints and feel out the opponent. Nothing about the way Justin fought surprised Thomas. He reacted precisely the way Mikil or William or any of his other lieutenants would to each of his attacks.

And he was sure that nothing he did surprised Justin either. That would come later.

They began to add a few of the Marduk moves, feigning, bobbing,

weaving, rolling—off the stage to the field, then along one side of the platform and around the perimeter. Back on top of the stage.

"You're a good man, Thomas," Justin said too softly for the crowd to
hear. "I always liked you. And I still do, very much."

Their swords clanged again.

"You've kept up your skills, I see," Thomas said. "Killing a few of your
Horde friends on the side, are we?"

Justin blocked a blow, and they faced each other in a momentary
stall.

"You have no idea what you've gotten yourself into. Be careful."

Thomas sprinted four steps. It was a classical approach to a vault, but
Thomas didn't vault. He planted his sword as if to flip over it, but instead
of going high he swung low.

Justin had already lifted his sword to ward off the expected jab that
would come when Thomas catapulted himself over his head. But now
Thomas was closer to Justin's ankles. It would end here, when he took
Justin from his feet and followed with his blade.

Thomas swung around his sword, feet first, bracing for the impact of
his shin against Justin's calves.

But suddenly Justin's calves weren't there. At the last moment he'd seen
the reversal, and although he was completely off balance, he'd managed to
launch himself into a backflip. A high somersault off the edge of the platform. Then around in almost perfect form.

He landed on the field, feet spread and hands on his sword, ready for
anything.

Thomas saw it all while he swung through his empty kick, and he used
his momentum to pivot all the way around into a back handspring, off the
platform, into what was called a back-whip.

The full aerial roundhouse move forced an opponent to guard against
a lethal heel to his face, but then morphed into a pirouette, one full rotation to bring the sword, not the feet, around with blazing speed.

Thomas executed the move perfectly. Justin misjudged it. But he threw
himself backward in time to catch the blade as a glancing blow skipped off
his chest.

Instead of continuing into a back handspring, he dropped to his back and rolled in the direction opposite the one in which Thomas's momentum carried him.

Smart. Very smart. If he'd gone for the back handspring, as most warriors certainly would, Thomas could have carried his own momentum into another direct attack before the man had fully recovered.

The crowd knew it too. Their cries had fallen to silence.

Justin came to his feet in a ready stance, eyes blazing with amusement.

"You should have accepted my promotion two years ago instead of losing your head to the desert," Thomas said. "You're a better warrior than the others."

"Am I?" Justin straightened, as if this revelation took him off guard. He tossed his sword on the dirt. "Then let me fight you without a sword. The coming battle won't be won with the sword."

Thomas stepped forward, sword extended. "Pick up your sword, you fool."

"And what, kill you?"

Thomas brought his blade to Justin's neck. The man made no attempt to stop him.

"Kill him!" Ciphus screamed. "To the death!"

"He wants me to kill you."

"If you can," Justin said.

"I can. But I won't."

They were speaking low. "You deceive the people into thinking there can be peace when at this very moment the Horde is planning a betrayal," Thomas said.

Justin blinked.

"Pick up your sword!" Thomas yelled for all to hear.

Justin slowly stepped back and to his left. But he ignored his sword and dropped his hands to his sides, stared at Thomas.

Thomas had given the man from Southern enough latitude; now his antics were infuriating. Thomas attacked. He covered the ground between them in three long strides and swung his sword full strength. The blade would cut the man in two without knowing it had hit anything.

But Justin wasn't there for the sword to hit. Thomas saw the man rolling back to his right, snatching up his sword, and too late he knew that he had been lulled into overcommitting himself to this blow he was already halfway through.

His own words in training screamed through his mind. Never overcommit in close combat!

Yet in anger, he had. He could have killed the man. Now the man might kill him.

With a slower opponent, his error wouldn't have mattered. But Justin moved as fast as he did. His blow came from behind, the broadside of his sword hitting Thomas squarely on the back.

He landed hard. There was grass in his hands. Both hands. He'd lost his sword.

He threw himself to the right, rolling to his back. A blade pressed against his neck and a knee dropped into his solar plexus. Justin kneeled over him, green eyes blazing, and Thomas knew that he was finished.

The breath seemed to have been sucked from the arena along with his own. He stared into his old lieutenant's eyes and saw a fierce fire.

Then the man sprang up, backed away, and tossed his sword high into the air. It twirled in the afternoon sun and fell on its side with a dull thump, twenty yards away.

He strode toward the Council and stopped in front of their platform. "Your challenger has been defeated. Elyon has spoken."

"The match is to the death," Ciphus said.

"I will not kill him for your sin."

"Then Elyon has not spoken," the elder said quietly. "The only reason you are alive now is because Thomas failed to finish. You were defeated first."

"Was I?"

"This isn't over," Ciphus ground out.

"Live!" someone from the crowd shouted. "Let Thomas live!"

A chant began. "Live, live, live, live!"

Thomas pushed himself to his feet, mind spinning. He'd been defeated by Justin in fair combat.

Ciphus clearly wasn't up to defying the people under such ambiguous circumstances. He let them chant.

Justin turned to the crowd. "I will let him live!" he shouted.

The chant settled and died.

He paced slowly, studying the people. "I will show you now, since I have earned the right, the true way to peace." Now he was walking toward the slope that rose to the trees at the entrance. "At this very moment the Horde is conspiring to crush you with an army that will make the battles to the south and west seem like childish skirmishes."

How could Justin know this? And yet Thomas knew that he did. They had to get word to the scouts—search the farthest perimeter.

He spun toward the gazebo, saw Mikil, and motioned for her to make it so. She and William disappeared.

Justin spread his hands out to calm the confused crowd. "Silence! There is only one way to meet this enemy. It is the way of peace, and today I will deliver this peace to you."

He stopped and motioned to the trees. For a moment, nothing. And then a hooded man stepped out.

A Scab!

Wearing the sash of a general.

Justin had smuggled a general from the Horde into the forest. Ten thousand voices cried out. The rest of the crowd gaped in stunned silence.

The tall, hooded man walked quickly, and Justin met him halfway up the slope. They clasped hands and dipped their heads in greeting. Justin faced the arena and spread his arm in a manner of introduction.

"I bring to you the man with whom I will negotiate peace between the Desert Dwellers and the Forest People." He paused.

"The mighty general of the Horde, Martyn!"

Martyn! Was it possible? Then who had he killed in Qurong's tent?

Thomas glanced back at the gazebo. It was already empty. His Guard would not allow this man to leave the village alive. Not now, with this revelation that the Horde was gathering on their exposed flank.

Thomas snatched his sword and ran for the slope. The day had seen enough showmanship. He couldn't kill Justin now, but this general was another matter.

"I have given him my word that you would not kill him," Justin said. "His armies are close now and could swarm the forest and wage a battle that would turn the valleys red with blood. But if Elyon's children all die, then who would be victor?"

The revelation that the Horde was on their doorstep seemed to have tempered the crowd's nerve. The people were actually listening. Thomas saw William and several of the Guard emerge from the trees at the top of the slope behind Justin. Rachelle was with them.

What was she doing? She had no business with them.

He shoved the thought aside and walked toward Justin and the Scab. The Guard moved down the hill to cut off any possible escape.

Justin stepped up to meet him. "Thomas, I beg you to hear me. I have proven my loyalty to you. Now you must allow me this!"

"You are wrong. He has betrayal in his blood!"

They were both weaponless as far as he could see. Thomas's men edged down the slope, swords drawn.

Thomas rushed at the general. Justin seized his arm. "Thomas! You don't know who he is!"

Martyn backed up.

Thomas could see the Scab's white eyes peering from the shadows of his hood. The rare circle tattooed over the man's right eye marked him as a druid, confirming the rumors.

"You think my sword can't draw the blood of the man who has slaughtered ten thousand of my men?" He directed his challenge to Martyn. "Will your magic protect you from a cold blade?"

His men were now only a few paces behind the Scab. Martyn sensed them, glanced back, and stopped. Thomas tore his arm free from Justin's grip and covered the last few steps. He thrust his sword into the bottom of the general's hood and held him at point.

He flicked the blade. Martyn didn't respond to the small cut on his neck. Red blood seeped from the surface wound.

"You think he won't bleed the way my men have bled? I say we send him back to his Horde in pieces."

Justin ran past Thomas, grabbed the general's hood, and yanked it back.

Martyn's face was ashen. A curving scar ran down his right cheek. He blinked pale eyes in the sudden light. He was hardly human, and yet he was fully human. But there was more.

Thomas knew this man.

His heart crashed in his chest.

Johan.

He yanked his sword back.

Johan? And the scar . . . Why did this scar surprise him?

"Johan," Justin said.

Thomas saw Rachelle over the man's shoulder. She was at the crest and she'd heard the words.

"Johan?" she said.

Then she was running. Down the slope. She raced around the general and stared at his exposed face.

"Johan? It's . . . it's you?"

The general showed no emotion at the sight of his sister. His mind had been taken by the disease, Thomas knew. He hadn't been killed in battle as they'd all assumed. He'd been lost to the desert and become a Scab three years ago. It was why the Horde's strategies had become so effective. They were being led by one of the old Forest Guard who had lost his mind to their disease.

Rachelle reached out to him, but he withdrew. She stared at him, grieved. Horrified.

"You must let us go," Justin said. "It's the only way."

William edged closer. "Sir, he's diseased. We can't let him—"

"Then wash him!" Rachelle cried.

"You can't force a man to bathe," Thomas said. "He is what he chooses to be."

"He will bathe! Tell them, Johan. You will wash this curse from your skin. You'll swim in the lake."

His eyes widened with a momentary flash of fear. "If it is peace you want, I can give you peace." Thomas recognized the voice, but barely. It was now deeper. Pained. "Otherwise we bring a curse you have never known to this forest."

William grabbed the man's cloak and drew back his sword. "Enough of this!"

"Let him go!" Thomas ordered.

"Sir—"

"Release him!"

William let the robe go and stepped back.

"I will not kill my own brother!"

His Guard would never agree to the terms of any peace Justin and Martyn drew up, but a truce might stall the Horde long enough for the Guard to prepare if truly there was an army in the plains.

Behind them, Ciphus was silent. Why?

Thomas faced Justin. "Take him. Broker your peace, but don't expect me and my men to go along with it. If we see a single Scab within sight of the forest, we will hunt you both down and drain your blood."

Rachelle gripped his arm. She was trembling.

Martyn replaced his hood and turned. William wouldn't move.

"Let them go, William." Then louder. "These two have my personal word of safe passage from our forest. The man who touches them will face me."

His men parted.

Justin and Martyn, the mighty general of the Horde whose name was also Johan, walked up the slope into the trees and vanished.

19

THOMAS STARED at the man he now knew had masterminded the virus. A thick Frenchman with fat fingers and greasy black hair who looked like he could stand in the face of a hurricane without batting an eye.

This was Armand Fortier.

They had been sedated, Monique told him. Within an hour of him passing out, they'd both been given shots. Men were dismantling the laboratory. They were going to be moved; she got that much from one of them. But to where she didn't know.

Then *she'd* passed out. Neither of them knew how much time had passed since then.

They'd awakened here, in this windowless stone room with a pool table and a fireplace. They were both handcuffed with impossibly tight cuffs, seated in wooden chairs, facing the Frenchman and, behind him, Carlos. Monique was still dressed in her pale blue slacks and blouse, and Thomas still wore the camouflaged jumpsuit.

Thomas had tried to deduce their possible location, but he had no memory of being moved, and there was nothing in this room that couldn't be found anywhere in the world. For all he knew they'd been out for two days. If he was right, the reason he'd dreamed at all was because he hadn't been drugged for that first hour after Carlos had tortured him.

That first hour, he'd dreamed of the inquiry where he'd fought Justin and discovered that Martyn was Johan . . .

"Just so you know, the Americans did try to rescue you," Fortier said. He seemed to find the fact interesting. "And I know from a very reliable source that they were after more than the antivirus. They want you. Everybody seems to want Thomas Hunter and Monique de Raison."

His eyes moved to Monique. "You have this solution in your head. You'd think I would just kill you and eliminate the risk of them finding you. Fortunately for you, I have reasons to keep you alive."

His eyes shifted back to Thomas. "You, on the other hand, are an enigma. You know things you should not. You gave us the Raison Strain, and then you inadvertently gave us the antivirus, both sides of this most useful weapon. But it doesn't stop there. You continue to know things. Where we are. What we will do next, perhaps. What should I do with you?"

Thomas's mind returned to the dream of Justin's challenge.

Johan. The man who'd led the Horde against them so effectively had been Johan. And Johan had a scar on his cheek. Thomas had watched the duo walk into the woods to broker peace with Qurong, a peace that was somehow entwined with betrayal.

The crowd had erupted in fierce debate. Thomas had returned to his Guard, and the Council had joined them to berate his decision to give Johan safe passage from the forest. But how could he kill Johan? And hadn't Justin won the inquiry? They had no right to undermine him now.

The festivities that night had been more dissension than celebration—a strange mix of exuberance by those who believed that Justin was indeed destined to deliver them from the Horde with this peace of his, and animosity by those who argued vehemently against any such treasonous betrayal of Elyon.

Thomas had finally collapsed into a fitful sleep.

"What are you thinking?" Fortier asked.

Thomas focused on the thick Frenchman. He had no doubt that this man would succeed with his virus. The Books of Histories said he would. And, as it was turning out, changing history wasn't as easy as he'd once hoped. Impossible, maybe. All of this—his discovery of the virus in the first place, his attempts to derail Svensson, and now this encounter with Fortier—might very well be written in the Books of Histories. Imagine that: *Thomas Hunter's attempt to rescue Monique de Raison at Cyclops failed when the transport he was flying in was shot down . . .* If he'd been successful in retrieving the Books from Qurong's tent, he could have read the details of his own life! But it seemed that the path of history was continuing exactly as it had been recorded, and he knew its final destination if not the precise course it would take.

The question now was *when*. When would they finally kill him? When would Monique die? When would the antivirus actually be released to the chosen few? When would the rest die their hideous diseased death?

"They searched for you with nearly a hundred aircraft loaded with enough electronic equipment to power Paris for a week," Fortier was saying. "It was quite a spectacle, not all at once or to one region, of course. In circles and to airports throughout the South Pacific. They blocked the air-traffic routes between Indonesia and France. To be quite honest, we barely made it out."

His lips twisted in a small grin. "We wouldn't have if I hadn't foreseen exactly this possibility. You see, you're not the only one who can see the future. Oh, your sight might be different from mine based on this . . . this gift rather than solid deductive reasoning, but I can promise you that I have seen the future, and I like what I see. Do you?"

"No," Thomas said. "I don't."

"Very good. You still have your voice. And you're honest, which is more than I can say for myself."

He turned away.

"I need to know something, Thomas. I know that you know the answer, because I have ears inside your government. I know the president has no intention of actually delivering the weapons that are just now entering the Atlantic. What I don't know is how far the president will carry his bluff. I need to know when to take the appropriate action. We are now fully prepared for a nuclear exchange, you must know. Knowing if and when they might attack would be helpful."

"He won't fire nuclear weapons," Thomas said.

"No? Maybe you don't know your president as well as I do. We anticipate it. Any knowledge you give me won't change the outcome of this chess match; it will only determine how many people must die to facilitate that outcome."

Fortier glanced at his watch. "We are going public in France in three days. Over a hundred less-progressive members of the government will meet untimely ends between now and then. A Chinese delegation is waiting for a meeting with President Gaetan in his office, and I've been asked to join them. Evidently news of the altercations with you in Indonesia have leaked and are causing a stir. The Australians are threatening to go public and must be calmed. One of our own commanders is asking the wrong questions. I am a busy man, Thomas. I have to leave. We'll talk again tomorrow. I hope your memory serves you better then."

He regarded Monique, dipped his head barely, and left the room.

Thomas's mind spun with the details that the Frenchman had just given him. The world was indeed rushing to its well-known end. While he was off dreaming about the Gathering and how it could possibly be that the great general Martyn was really Johan, complete with scarred—

Thomas stopped. He stared at Carlos, who had crossed the room and opened a door that led into darkness.

He turned in profile to Thomas. The scar. Right cheek. Curved like a half moon, exactly as he remembered Johan's.

"Let's go," the man said. "Don't make me drag you."

No, Carlos wouldn't want to drag them. It would mean getting too close—an opportunity for Thomas to do something. The man knew to play things safe.

But none of this interested Thomas at the moment.

The scar.

What if Rachelle was right about how the realities worked? Thomas might be the only true gateway between the realities, but if someone was aware of both realities, then both realities had potential to affect that person. For instance, now that Rachelle believed in both realities, if Monique was cut, Rachelle would also wake up with a cut. And if Monique was killed, Rachelle would also die. Would Monique die if Rachelle did? Thomas hadn't convinced Monique to believe yet. Nor had Monique ever come into contact with Thomas's blood.

The link between the realities was belief? Or Thomas's blood?

Perhaps both. It did make a strange kind of sense. Life and blood and skills and knowledge were all transferable between realities—he'd already experienced that much. Proven it. But why?

Belief.

If someone with even the slightest belief came into contact with Thomas's blood, then their belief would be enough to connect them to his reality with him. It would explain everything! And it wouldn't require that Rachelle and Monique be one and the same.

It was as good a working theory as he'd come up with yet.

"Now. Please," Carlos said, indicating the room.

There was still a hole in his theory. Primarily, why he was Thomas in both realities, why he didn't share this experience with someone else.

Thomas stood. "I have something to say," he said. "Can you get the Frenchman?"

Carlos studied him. "You'll have to wait."

"What I have to say he will want to hear before he meets with the Chinese."

"Then tell me."

"It has to do with how I knew where you were keeping Monique. You knew I'd come, didn't you?" Thomas walked forward a few paces and stopped ten feet from the man. Behind him, Monique kept her seat.

"You could have tracked me down in Washington, but you chose to go to Indonesia and wait for me there, because you knew that I would know," Thomas continued. "Am I right?"

"What does this have to do with the Chinese?"

"Actually, it's not tied directly to the Chinese per se. I just said he should know this before he meets with them."

"And this is?"

"That I am going to escape before he meets with them."

Thomas didn't have any such knowledge, but he needed the man's full attention, and this was the first step.

"Then it would have been a wasted call," Carlos said. "I have no intention of letting you escape. This isn't a useful discussion."

"I didn't say you were going to let us escape. But our escape will involve you. I know this because you're not like them. You're a deeply religious man who follows the will of Allah, and I know you well. Much better than you think I might. We've met before."

Carlos shifted. "If you know me so well, then you know that I'm not easily swayed by a fool who speaks in riddles."

"No, you aren't. But you have been swayed. Deceived. I know that without a doubt. Do you think that Svensson and Fortier have any intention of allowing Islam to thrive after they gain power? Religion is their enemy. They may set up their own, they may even call it Islam, but it won't be the Islam you know. One of the first to die will be you. You know too much. You're much too powerful. You are the worst kind of enemy—they know that. You must as well."

He didn't respond.

"You're not curious as to *how* we met before?" Thomas asked.

"We haven't."

"You don't have the memory of it yet. We've met in the other reality. The one with the Books of Histories. There your name is Johan, and you are the brother of my wife. You're also a great general who has caused me and my Forest Guard more than our share of grief."

Carlos apparently found neither humor nor persuasion in the claim. "The only reason you're alive is because of your witchcraft," he said. "If you cross me again, I will kill you. I see that you're not healing so well these days." He glanced at the bruises and cuts the handcuffs had worn into Thomas's wrists. "I think you will die easily enough. Give me a reason and I will test the theory now."

"My gift is from witchcraft? Or because I'm a servant of El—of God? I'll admit, I haven't followed him in this reality, but I really haven't had a chance, and that's changing. Listen to yourself. You're marked for death *because* of your belief in the one you call God! You serve two demons who kill for their own gain. You think they will let you live?"

He blinked.

"What if I could prove it to you? Brother."

"Don't be absurd."

"But you do believe that I know things I shouldn't," Thomas said. "That's why you waited for me in Indonesia. You knew I would show up. I say that you too believe in a reality where there's more than meets the eye."

Thomas could see the light in his eyes. As a Muslim, such a belief would be natural to him.

———∞———

Carlos was tempted to shoot the man then. If Svensson and Fortier weren't so taken by Hunter's strange gift, he would defy them and kill the man here.

"Your name is Johan and we are destined to be brothers," Thomas said.

His mind ached with this nonsensical revelation. Who'd ever heard of such nonsense?

His mother had. She was a practicing Sufi mystic.

The Prophet, Mohammed, had.

Hunter might be misinterpreting his visions, but he might very well have seen others in his dreams. Maybe even him. Carlos. The man's claims enraged him.

On the other hand, Thomas was smart enough to try something exactly like this to distract him. Handcuffed, the man hardly had a prayer of reaching him, much less escaping from him. But Carlos wouldn't underestimate him.

"I'll consider what you've said. Now if you will please—"

"Then I'll prove it," Thomas said. "I'll cut Johan on the neck without touching you."

The words triggered an alarm in Carlos. Heat spread down his neck.

"Do you believe I can do that? Do you believe that if I'm healed in the other reality, I will be healed in this one? Or that if I die there, I will die here? Do you remember shooting me, Carlos? Still, I'm alive. You live in the other reality with me too, and I've just had a confrontation with you at the Gathering. I cut your neck with my sword."

"Don't be ridiculous! Stop this at once!" But Carlos's mind reared with fear. He had heard the mystics speak like this. The Christians. He'd heard some claim belief that if a man would only open his eyes he could see another world. And a small part of him did believe. Always had.

"Do you believe, Carlos? Of course you do. You always have."

At first, Carlos mistook the sensation in his neck for the rage that filled his veins. But his neck was burning. His flesh was stinging as if it had been cut. It couldn't possibly be true, yet he knew that it was.

He lifted his left hand to his neck.

⁂

Thomas watched with surprise as the skin on Carlos's neck suddenly began to bleed, precisely as it would if he'd just taken a blade to it.

He hadn't just cut Carlos. But enough of Carlos believed his story about Johan to cause the rift in the realities. One of these two worlds might be a dream, but at the moment it didn't matter. At the moment Carlos was bleeding because Johan was still bleeding!

The man lifted his hand to his neck, felt the small wound, pulled his fingers away bloody. His eyes stared in confounded fascination.

Thomas moved then. Two steps and he left the ground. His foot struck Carlos before the man could tear his eyes free from his hand.

The man hadn't even braced for the impact. He crumbled like a chain that had been cut from the ceiling.

Thomas landed on both feet and spun around. Monique was staring, stunned by the developments. Then she was running for him.

"Quick! He has the keys in his right pocket!" Her words piled on top of each other. "I saw them; he has them in his pocket!"

Thomas squatted by the man and felt behind him for the pocket, dug the keys out, and stood. "Back up to me. Hurry!"

They freed themselves in a matter of seconds. Monique's wrists were bleeding because of the cuffs as well. She ignored the cuts. "Now what?"

"You're okay?"

"I'm free; that's better than I've been for two weeks."

"Okay, stay close," Thomas said.

She was staring at Carlos, who lay unconscious, bleeding from a slight wound on his neck. "What just happened?"

"Later. Hurry."

The hallway was empty. They ran to the staircase at the end and were about to climb when Thomas changed his mind. Sunlight poured through a three-foot window directly ahead and above. The latch was unlocked.

He redirected her toward it, pulled himself up, opened the window, and swung into the window well outside. He glanced over the top, saw no guard, and turned back for Monique.

"Jump. I'll pull you up," he whispered.

She caught his hand and he plucked her easily from the floor, wincing with the thought of the pain she must feel in her torn wrists. She struggled a bit to get her knees up on the ledge, but soon they crouched in the window well, window firmly closed behind them. Less than three minutes had passed since Carlos hit the floor.

Monique poked her head up for a look. "We're in the country," she whispered. "A farm."

Thomas saw several large barns and a driveway that disappeared into the forest. This building was covered by old stonework. The sun was already dipping toward the western horizon.

Carlos would wake up soon. They had to put some distance between them and this farm.

"Okay. We go straight for the forest." Thomas studied the closest trees. "Once we run, we don't stop. Can you do that?"

"I can run."

He glanced around one last time. Clear.

Thomas leaped from the window well, pulled Monique up, and ran for the forest, making sure she stayed close. The crunch of twigs and dried leaves welcomed them into the protective trees.

Thomas glanced back. No alarm. Not yet.

Mike Orear guided Theresa Sumner by the arm toward the CDC parking lot. She'd ignored his phone calls for the last twenty-four hours, presumably because she was out of town. But by the looks of the bags under her eyes, he wouldn't be surprised to learn that she'd been holed up here, working on the virus.

He'd driven out to her house last night. No luck. It was eight the next morning before he'd finally driven here.

"Mike, you've made your point. And the answer is no. You can't go public. Not yet." She pulled her arm away.

"Twenty-four hours, Theresa. This isn't about you and me anymore. I made a promise, but I wasn't thinking clearly. You tell whoever needs to know that they have twenty-four hours to come clean, or I'm putting the story on the air."

She reached her white SUV and pulled up, face brave but dog tired. "Then you might as well join the terrorists, because you'll hurt as many people as they will."

"Don't be naive. Are you telling me that if I don't run the story, more people will live?"

She didn't answer. Of course not, the answer was no, because if the virus was real, they were all dead anyway. And this virus *was* as real as she'd said. Real as milk or bread or gasoline. He'd gone from incredulity to a state of constant horror over this impending sickness that was growing in his body at this very moment.

"Which means that you're not making any progress," he said. He turned away. "Great. All the more reason to break this open."

"Are you glad that you know?" she asked. "Has the quality of your life improved because I dragged you into this?"

The last five days had been a living hell. He looked away.

"Exactly," she said. "You want to draw the rest of the world into the same kind of miserable knowledge? You think it'll help us deal with the problem? You think it'll bring us one minute closer to an antivirus or a vaccine? Not a chance. If anything, it slows us down. We'll be dealing with a whole new set of problems."

"You can't just *not* tell people that they're going to die. I don't care how much you want to protect them; it's their lives we're talking about. The president is still holding firm on all this?"

She crossed her arms and sighed. "His advisers are split. But I promise you, the moment the people know, this country shuts down. What am I supposed to do if I can't get a line out to the labs in Europe? Thought about that? Why would the employees at AT&T go to work if they knew they only had thirteen days to live?"

"Because there's a chance we'll all live if they keep the lines open, that's why."

"That would be a lie. You'd just be replacing one lie for another," she said.

"What? Now there's *no* chance we can survive this?"

"Not that I see. We have thirteen *days*, Mike. The closer we look at this thing, the more we realize what a monster it really is."

"I can't accept that. Someone has to be making progress somewhere. This is the twenty-first century, not the Middle Ages."

"Well, it just so happens that DNA is no respecter of centuries. We're all just groping around in the dark."

"You know the word will get out soon anyway. I'm surprised the rest of the press hasn't pieced this together already."

She took a deep breath. "It's only been a week. Patterns take time to recognize unless you know what you're looking for. The military knows what to look for, but they've been told what to expect under various cover stories."

"But for how long? This is insane!"

"Of course it's insane! The whole thing is insane!"

He put his hand on the hood of her Durango. Cold. She'd been here for a while. Maybe all night. Or longer.

"Our story about the quarantined island south of Java is starting to fall apart," she said. "A number of people made it off the island before they shut it down. The press over there is wondering how far it's spread. So are half the labs working with us."

"My point exactly. There's no way they can hold this in. We should have every lab in the world working around the clock on this—"

"We do have practically every lab in the world working around the clock on this!"

"We should have the whole military out, looking for these terrorists—"

"They've got every intelligence agency with anything to offer on it already. But please, these guys have the antivirus—we can't just send a toma-hawk cruise missile after them."

"We know where they are?"

She didn't answer, which meant she either did know or had a very good idea.

"It's France, isn't it?"

No answer.

"Finally, an excuse to nuke France."

"I think there may be some takers."

"Surely not the government proper."

"No. I don't know anything else, Mike." She held up a hand. "No more. I'm wasting time out here." She started back.

"People need to make things right," he said. "With their children. With God. Twenty-four hours, Theresa. I won't implicate you."

She looked back at him. "Do whatever you have to do, Mike. Just think long and hard before you do it."

———

"Where are we going?" Monique panted.

Thomas scanned the meadow that lay ahead of them. Beyond it, a hazy horizon. "Away from Carlos. Do you have any idea where we are?"

"I would say up north. Maybe outside of Paris."

"The *Sûreté* will be scouring the country for us as soon as Carlos sends word," he said. "We have to get to a phone that has service to the United States. The airports will be too dangerous. What about the English Channel?"

"If we could find a way to the Channel without being tracked down. Why not Paris?"

She was French and would pass easily. He might stand out.

"You know Paris well?"

"Well enough to get lost in the crowd."

"We have three days before they go public. When that happens, they'll have to declare martial law. Public transportation may be shut down. We have to get you out of the country before then."

"Then Paris is our best bet. I would say it lies to the west."

"Why?"

"The horizon isn't as clear to the west. Smog."

He considered her reasoning. "Okay, west."

They ran west for nearly two hours before the sun began to dip past the western horizon. They'd encountered several farm buildings, which they skirted after a quick look, but still no paved roads. The problem with using a farm phone was that the *Sûreté* would undoubtedly track any overseas calls originating from this part of the country, a simple task when there couldn't be more than a few hundred in a hundred square miles out here. A pay phone in a place frequented by tourists would be much safer.

The problem with finding such a place was simply that Thomas and Monique were running blind. Not only were they losing light, but they still weren't sure where they were.

They ran on, torn between taking the time to find the right direction and keeping distance between them and any pursuit Carlos gave. Twice Thomas cut back on their own path, struck out due south for several hundred yards, and then continued west again.

Thomas's mind grappled with other issues as they ran. The wound he'd inflicted on Carlos's neck. He had been right: Knowledge and belief of the realities opened a link between them. Not a gateway, mind you—neither Carlos nor Johan had awakened as the other. Not that he knew of, anyway. But some kind of cause-and-effect relationship had been triggered between them. Those who believed in both realities saw the transferable effects in both realities. Blood, knowledge, skills.

You bleed in one; you bleed in the other.

Surely Monique would believe after seeing what had happened to Carlos. With Thomas's prompting, she would likely believe that she was connected to Rachelle. But was this a good thing?

And if he killed Johan, would Carlos die here? Perhaps.

Allowing Johan to live had been the right decision; he was sure of it. Now that he knew the link with Carlos, he would have to reconsider. But how could he kill Rachelle's brother?

And there was another matter that bothered him, something he was having difficulty placing. His memory had been clouded with these dreams, and he couldn't quite say why, but there was a problem with Justin of Southern.

The warrior had defeated him soundly and revealed his intentions of brokering a peace, while the Horde was plotting their final defeat. Mikil had sent out two groups of scouts, but none had yet reported any grave threat. Thomas had reinforced the Guard on each side of the forest, but otherwise he could do nothing except wait while Justin—

He pulled up.

Monique stopped. "What?"

"Nothing." He ran on.

But there was something. There were Qurong's words—the ones he'd overheard in the Horde camp. He could hear them now.

"I tell you, the brilliance of the plan is in its boldness," Qurong had said. "They may suspect, but with our forces at their doorstep, they will be forced to believe. We'll speak about peace and they will listen because they must. By the time we work the betrayal with him, it will be too late."

By the time we work the betrayal with *him*, it will be too late.

Who was "him"? When Thomas learned he hadn't killed Martyn— that the man Qurong had been speaking to *wasn't* Martyn—he'd assumed that "him" had to be Martyn. The thought had passed through his mind as Justin led Martyn from the amphitheater. It was partly why he had no intention of believing in any peace those two brokered. His Guard would be ready.

But what if "him" was Justin of Southern?

Of course! Who better to betray than a hero among the people, a mighty warrior who'd ridden like a king through the Valley of Tuhan and defeated the commander of the Guard in hand-to-hand combat?

It was a trap! Justin must have an alliance with Martyn already. He'd negotiated the Scabs' withdrawal from the Southern Forest. Then he'd ridden back to the main Horde camp with Martyn and arrived in time to save Thomas and his band in a show of good faith. The man atop the hill overlooking Thomas and his men had been *Martyn*.

It all made perfect sense! The battle at the Southern Forest, Qurong's words in the tent, Justin's saving Thomas in the desert, Justin's victory in the challenge, and now this unveiling of Martyn as Johan. Even the march through the Valley of Tuhan.

And it was all to this end. A trap. A betrayal.

What if the betrayal ended in the slaughter of their village? The death of the children? The death of Rachelle? Would Monique die? What if he was killed by the Horde? He was needed here.

Thomas would not be fooled by their betrayal. He would hold the line and refuse any peace offered by Johan and Justin. It would end in a terrible battle, perhaps, but—

Another thought struck him. What if he used this knowledge against the Horde? What if he created a reversal of his own, one that might avoid war altogether? His own peace on his own terms.

Thomas stopped again, heart pounding with an eagerness to dream again. He had to return and deal with Justin's betrayal!

Ahead, at the edge of a clearing, lay a small stone quarry. The lights of a farm cottage glowed several hundred miles down in the valley.

"What now?" Monique demanded, panting.

"It's almost dark. We don't know how far we have to go or where we're really going, for that matter. We have to stop for the night."

"What if he catches up to us?"

"I don't think Carlos will expect us to stop for the night—he'll go on to the city or he'll search the barns and the towns." He nodded at the farm lights ahead.

She looked around. "You want us to stop here?"

He jogged over to the quarry. The ground fell twenty feet, like a bowl. Several huge boulders lay at the bottom.

"We can lay down some branches or straw."

He thought she might protest. But after a moment she agreed. "Okay."

Ten minutes later they had covered the ground with grass and propped several large leafy branches against the largest rock to form a rough lean-to.

Thomas sat on a boulder near the lean-to, strung too tight to even think about sleep. But that was just it—he had to sleep now. He was desperate to sleep. To dream. To stop Justin before the betrayal could destroy both worlds.

"Thomas?"

He looked at Monique, who leaned on the boulder next to him.

"We'll be okay," he said.

"I think you're too optimistic."

"How can I not be optimistic? Three days ago I persuaded the president of the United States that my dreams were real, and he sent me on a fool's mission to find you. It cost some men their lives, but I *did* find you. Now we're free, on our way back to the world with information that will change history."

She looked away, clearly unconvinced. "We're in France. Unless I missed something back there, the people who're doing this have control over France. And you do understand that I have no evidence that the information I have will actually create the antivirus, don't you?"

"Svensson has the antivirus. We watched him inoculate himself."

"But I don't know if what he used is based on the information I gave him."

"Fortier all but said it was yours."

"Why did they keep me separate from the others?"

They sat in silence. Under other circumstances it might have been an uncomfortable silence, but now, on the eve of the world's destruction, with pretension long gone, it was only silence.

"So you really do believe all of this," Monique said.

She meant his dreams. "Yes."

"How is it possible?"

"You didn't have too much trouble believing that I got information from my dreams. That's information out of thin air. Why not more?"

"There's a far cry between dreaming up information and cutting someone's neck without touching him," she said.

"I was also shot dead in the hotel right in front of you."

She paused. "It goes against everything I've ever believed."

He shrugged. "Then you've believed in the wrong things. And if it's any consolation, so have I. When you live it like I have, it begins to feel quite real. Even natural. I'm not saying I understand. I'm not saying that I'm even meant to understand it."

She looked at the sky. "You think about God in all of this?"

"I don't have a good history with religion, despite my father being a chaplain. Maybe that's *because* my father was a chaplain. For the first couple weeks of these dreams, even though I had some incredible dreams of encountering God in the emerald lake, I kept it all in its own little box, reserved for the unexplained. There was the colored forest with its version of God, and there was this Earth, each in its own set of dreams. On this Earth God doesn't exist, I believed. I wasn't ready to think differently."

"And now?"

"Now the reality of Elyon is feeling very compelling again. In my dreams, I mean. For a long time after the Shataiki invaded the colored forest, battle was more real to me than Elyon. I've been commander of the Guard, fighting wars and spilling blood for fifteen years, and not once has anyone reported seeing a black bat or hearing a single word from Elyon. We call our religion the Great Romance, but really it feels more like a list of rules than anything similar to the Great Romance we once had. But now I think the knowledge of Elyon is starting to work its way into me again— in both realities. Make any sense? If Elyon's real there, surely God must be real here."

"It might explain your dreams," she said.

Another long silence.

"I'm still not ready to believe that I'm connected to a woman named Rachelle who is conveniently married to you," she said.

He sighed. "It may be best that you don't believe it. Because if you are connected to her, then anything that happens to Rachelle may also happen to you."

"You mean if Rachelle gets cut, I get cut? Like Carlos?"

"Rachelle has already experienced that very thing. We can't allow anything to happen to you."

"Because it will affect Rachelle as well."

Thomas sighed and leaned back against the boulder.

"Is Rachelle in danger of being killed?"

"As a matter of fact, yes. We all are."

"Then I suppose you'd better dream and save the world."

By her tone he knew that she was frustrated with these ideas of dreams, but he didn't have the energy to win her over now. He decided to give her one parting thought.

"I just may. But I think I'll have to go after Justin to do that."

She didn't ask who Justin was.

The moon was bright and the night cold when they finally agreed that they should sleep. The lean-to was meant to hide them from any prying eyes in the sky, and Thomas insisted they both sleep under the leafy branches.

Despite their initial attempts at modesty, they both accepted the fact that comfort and warmth were more important at the moment than forcing themselves into positions that would keep them up half the night. They lay shoulder to shoulder, arm to arm in the dark and began to drift off.

Thomas was almost asleep when he felt her hand rest on his. His eyes opened. At first he wondered if she was touching his hand in her sleep. He should ease his arm away.

But he couldn't. Not after what he'd put her through.

It took him another fifteen minutes to begin drifting again. They fell asleep like that, wrist to wrist.

⎯⎯∞⎯⎯

Carlos covered the ground in a steady, fast walk. The moon was high enough to light his way, which made the going easier than during the first hour of darkness, before the moon rose.

He traveled alone because this issue of Thomas Hunter had become a very personal matter, and also because he knew he could deal with the problem without ever revealing the full truth of what had happened in the house.

In his hand he held a receiver that accepted a signal from the woman. They'd sewn the transmitter into her waistband a week earlier—no reason not to keep very close tabs on such a valuable asset. If and when she discarded the slacks, he would have a problem, but until she reached a town, she wouldn't have the opportunity. And based on their course, that wouldn't happen before morning.

They had stopped. Even at this pace he would reach them in a matter of hours.

He lifted his hand and touched his neck again. The blood had dried; the cut was hardly more than a scratch. But the manner in which he'd received it played heavily on his mind.

As did what Thomas had said about his own demise after his usefulness had expired. He'd considered the possibility that Fortier would simply dispose of him once the man had what he wanted—there were never guarantees with men like Fortier.

But Carlos wasn't a man without his own plans. This development with Hunter could actually play into his hands. For one, it gave him a perfect reason to kill Hunter once and for all. But it could also ensure his own value until he had the opportunity to take out both Svensson and Fortier. He would tell them that before dying Hunter had confessed something new from these histories of his, a major coup attempt immediately following the transition of power to Fortier. They would keep him alive at least long enough to head off the coup.

Hunter would make no such claim, of course, but there was some truth in the statement. There would be a coup attempt.

Muslims, not a godless Frenchman, would end up the winners in this war of Allah's.

Fortier wasn't the only man who knew how to think.

20

THOMAS GASPED in his sleep and was instantly awake. He jerked up. Black. Silent.

He blinked and strained for sight. The walls slowly came into focus. Monique was in the bed beside him, breathing steadily.

No, not Monique. Rachelle, who'd cried herself to sleep last night after learning the truth about her brother, Johan.

An ache ran up his forearm and he felt his wrist. Bruised and cut. Yes, of course—the handcuffs they'd placed on him were too tight and had bit into his skin. There had been blood on his wrists. He had bled here as well.

The events of both worlds crashed in on him. He'd escaped with Monique and was sleeping under a boulder in the quarry, desperate to dream so that he could come back here and deal with the betrayal.

He swung his feet out of bed, grabbed his boots and clothes, and sneaked into the main room without waking Rachelle. Leaving her alone without a word for the second time in a week struck him as possibly cruel. Yet he didn't dare wake her and run the risk of her interfering with such a perfect plan. What he had in mind had a ring of lunacy to it, and Rachelle would undoubtedly hear that ring and call it out.

Mikil, on the other hand, would jump at the chance.

He dressed quickly, slung his sword over his shoulder, and slipped into the cool morning air. The overcrowded village was still lost in deep dreams of the day's unusual events and the evening's high-pitched celebrations. They'd roasted a hundred goats along the shores of the lake as was the custom on the second night. The dances had gone late, and the talk of Justin and Martyn had gone later.

The warrior from Southern was defended as vigorously by some as he was chastised by others. The idea of peace with the Horde, regardless of the circumstances, was offensive to most. Even Justin's supporters agreed on one thing: If the Horde did march on the forest, it would probably mean that Justin had betrayed them. But not to worry—their hero of the Southern Forest would never betray them. When he said he would broker peace, he had only true peace in mind.

Why Thomas hadn't realized earlier the truth of Qurong's words, he didn't know. Perhaps because his dreaming had confused his mind one too many times. Maybe because he was so taken aback by Martyn's true identity that he couldn't keep his thoughts objective. Either way, he was sure that if he told the counsel what the Horde leader had said in that tent, they would rally an army to head off Justin and Martyn's plan for "peace."

He found Mikil in deep sleep and woke her with a gentle shake. She bounded out of bed, sword in hand.

"It's me!" he whispered.

"Thomas?"

"Yes. Hurry, we have business."

"The scouts have reported in?" She rushed to the window and peered past the shutters.

"No. No word. Hurry."

"Then what?"

"I'll tell you on the way. Meet me at the stables."

He ran for the Guard stables at the edge of the village and was there when she caught up to him.

"Where are we going?"

"Shh, keep quiet. What would you say if I told you that Justin might have betrayal in mind?"

"I would say this is old news. You've learned something new?"

He opened the stable gate. "Saddle up. I'll explain when we're clear."

They walked their horses past the main village entrance, then mounted and rode into the forest.

"Tell me," she demanded, glancing back. "What is it?"

"I dreamed."

"That again. Fine. What did you dream?"

"I dreamed of what I overheard in Qurong's tent." He told her again, word for word, and explained his logic.

She kicked her horse, surged ahead, and then turned it back. "I knew it! He'll be the end of the forest! How many times did I warn you?"

She was right. His silence was confession enough.

"We have to stop this!" she said.

"Why do you think we're on horses before dawn? We ride to the eastern desert, where Qurong last camped. If I'm right, he will still be there, maybe even closer."

"What, you plan on the two of us taking on the whole army?"

"I think our scouts will find that Justin was right: The Horde has gathered in larger numbers than we've guessed. For all we know they have an army to the west, waiting until our preoccupation with the east bares our flank. That would be Martyn's kind of strategy."

"Then you're thinking of negotiation? That's the same plan Justin has! No, Thomas. No peace!"

"I'm thinking that Martyn will listen to another proposal. One that will turn the tables completely."

The sun was hot.

Monique opened her eyes. Sun?

Light streamed through shutters, exposing a thousand particles of lazily floating dust.

Where am I?

I am home.

Who am I?

You are Monique.

She pushed herself to her elbow and blinked. She wasn't entirely herself. Or she was *completely* herself. *Rachelle.*

She lifted her hand and moved her fingers. She was Monique, and she knew that she had to be dreaming while sleeping under the boulder next to Thomas, but she also knew that she was experiencing much more than just a dream. Amazing. This was how Thomas felt when he woke.

She'd dreamed of Thomas's other world because she was holding his hand while she slept? And she was dreaming as Rachelle because she believed that she was connected to Rachelle? It was about belief, Thomas had said. She was sharing Rachelle's life.

Does this mean it's all true? Everything Thomas said is true?

She knew the answer immediately, because as Rachelle she knew this reality was as real as France or Bangkok. What else did Rachelle know?

My husband's name is Thomas. And I have children.

She twisted to his side of the bed. "Thomas!"

But Thomas was gone. Of course, he always woke early. She knew that too. She knew that he was only home one out of every two days because he was the commander of the Guard, a mighty warrior and hero whose name was practically revered in all of the forests.

Her husband, a mighty warrior.

She knew that he had fought Justin yesterday and lost. And she knew that the Horde general, Martyn, was her own brother, Johan.

Rachelle swallowed and set her feet on the floor. This was how Thomas had first felt, waking up in the black forest fifteen years earlier. He'd tried to make her understand, but only now could she. Only he'd awakened without any memory because of his fall.

He'd fallen in the black forest and as a result began dreaming of the histories. This was the reality; that was the dream. She was sure of it. At least at this moment she was sure of it.

Her wrists hurt. The handcuffs. They'd drawn blood, and Thomas said that blood was special. They'd fallen asleep, hand in hand, her wrist touching his. It was why Monique was dreaming of Rachelle at this very moment. It was how she had dreamed of Monique before. She'd cut her shoulder on the door and it had bled in her sleep next to Thomas. A connection had been made in their blood.

Her children . . .

She threw off the blanket, donned a long-sleeved blouse to hide her wrists, and hurried from the room. She found Marie exactly where she expected to find her, digging through the fruit basket for a choice nectar.

"Hi, Mother." Her daughter yawned. "Papa's gone."

"Yes. Your brother's still sleeping?"

"That's all he does anymore."

"He's a growing boy."

She hurried to his room. Yes, indeed, there lay Samuel, arm hanging over the edge of his bed, lost to dreams of fighting the Horde with a sword as tall as he. She walked over and kissed the back of his head.

She was living a second life! In an instant she'd become a whole new person. She could smell Tuhan blossoms. Someone was cooking meat. Laughter drifted in from outside. Everything felt new. This was the time of the annual Gathering when the streets would be full of dancing and stories and the drinking of ale. And she was a magnificent dancer, wasn't she? Yes, of course she was. One of the best.

Her heart was having a hard time keeping up. She understood why Thomas was so persuaded. She had to find Thomas and tell him about this immediately!

Marie had found a large yellow nanka, and its juice ran down her chin.

"Don't be a pig, Marie. Wipe your chin." She looked at the living room. *Her* living room. Thomas's second sword, which normally leaned in the corner, was gone. Odd.

"Do you know where Papa went?" she asked Marie.

"No. He left early. Before the sun was up. I heard him."

Rachelle froze. His words to her in France echoed through her mind. *I'll have to go after Justin to do that,* he'd said.

After Justin?

He'd gone after Justin! Justin was with Martyn. They would be with the Horde. For the second time this week, he'd left her sleeping while he sneaked off on some harebrained mission that only a man as stubborn as Thomas could take beyond mere fantasy.

Justin and Martyn had gone east, according to the scouts. East toward Qurong's army.

She hurried to the bedroom and completed dressing. If Justin was with

Martyn, then he was also with Johan. Did Thomas mean that he was going after her brother?

What if he meant to kill Johan, thinking that in doing so he would kill Carlos? But he couldn't do that. Johan was her brother! They'd all lost family to the Horde fifteen years ago, when Tanis was deceived, but they dealt with it as part of a great tragedy. The thought of losing her own brother to her husband's sword now brought a small panic to her chest.

She had to stop him! And even if he hadn't gone to kill Johan, she had to tell him that she now knew. She was Rachelle. She was Monique! Without a doubt, they were connected.

She wrapped her wrists and managed to make the bandage look like bands with brass accents. The first major task was to get out of the village alone without casting suspicion on her intent. She couldn't walk too fast to Anna's, and when she asked the older mother if she would watch over Marie and Samuel for the day while she went out to gather a special treat for Thomas, she had to sound natural.

Andrew, who oversaw the common stables, would ask questions about why she was taking one of the stallions, but she'd simply tell him that she was in the mood for a wild ride. The Gathering inspired the women as well as the men.

Samuel had dragged himself from sleep by the time she returned with Anna's blessing. She hugged both children, told them to mind their Aunt Anna, and promised to be back by nightfall. If she wasn't back, not to worry, she and Papa had some preparations they had to attend to.

A full hour after waking, Rachelle left behind the last of the curious well-wishers who'd inquired where she was headed on such a magnificent animal. She led the horse through the gates, threw her leg over the saddle, and rode east.

The first hour seemed to last only minutes. With Monique everything felt new and fresh, as if experienced for the first time, which was the case in Monique's mind. The French woman had surely never imagined feeling so powerful, such an accomplished rider, so full of passion as Rachelle was now.

So invigorated was she in fact that she half hoped that one of the Horde would jump out from behind a tree so she could kick him back to where he belonged. Twice she very nearly dismounted to try a few flips. But her thoughts of finding Thomas kept her on the run.

One hour became two and then three and then five. The forest flew by and her mind flew with it. With each passing mile, her eagerness to find Thomas increased. She now knew that he had indeed come this way—his stallion's tracks, which she could read like her own palm, marked the mud at nearly every turn. He'd passed with Mikil. At least he had the sense to bring his best warrior.

She considered the potential danger ahead, but whatever danger her husband had submitted himself to wasn't too much for her. The fate of worlds was at hand, and she had her role to play.

She reached the edge of the forest late in the afternoon and pulled up. The sky and the desert were both blood red this time of day. She'd left the village about two hours after Thomas and had followed his tracks up to this point. If she rode hard, she might reach the place where—

Her heart suddenly rose into her throat. The Horde camp was there, on the horizon, just visible against the red sand. They'd moved closer.

Much closer.

Did they plan to attack? She felt immobilized by panic. The camp seemed larger than she remembered. Nearly double in size. This could only be a gathering for war! Thomas had gone down to them?

She studied his tracks. They went straight on and turned down the canyon. There were two well-traveled paths down to the desert, and Thomas had taken this one. He'd seen the Horde camp and continued. Then she would as well.

Rachelle prodded her horse.

The black stallion had taken only two steps when something struck her broadside.

She gasped and looked down. A stick protruded from her side. The shaft of an arrow. Pain screamed through her body.

Another arrow smacked into her shoulder, and a third into her thigh. She saw the Scabs near the tree line now, a party of five or six. They had bows! She didn't know—

The next arrow hit Rachelle in the back. She kicked the horse into a startled gallop. To her left! She had to get away from them!

There were arrows sticking from her body. Arrows! Panic crowded her mind.

The stallion plunged down a narrow path, over the canyon's lip.

Three more arrows whipped by her head and she ducked. The pain from the others rode up and down her back and leg in waves now.

"Hiyaa!" The path was steep and the horse slipped on the stones but caught itself and leaped over a boulder that suddenly blocked their way. Then around a bend.

Would the Scabs follow?

They were yelling above her now. Laughing.

She reached the sandy bottom and pointed the horse up the first narrow canyon to her right. Hoofs clacked along the stone high above. They were giving chase along the top of the canyon. She pulled the horse close to the left wall and leaned low, wincing with the pain. Terrible pain through her gut.

She was shot. Four arrows—two in her body, one in her leg, one in her arm. She had to hide and then find help.

Should she try to remove the arrows?

We're going to die.

No, no, she couldn't die! Rachelle couldn't die! Not now!

The horse slowed to a trot. Voices echoed, but they seemed to have fallen back. The rocky canyons were like a maze—it was no wonder they had opted to ride along the plateau. But if she worked her way further in, away from the walls near the forest, they would have a difficult time finding her.

Rachelle cut into a side wash, then through a small gap that fed into a long basin. The voices sounded distant now, but her mind wasn't as clear as it had been. Maybe she wasn't hearing as well. She gave the horse its head and examined the arrow in her leg. If she left it in, the movement of the horse might cause the tip to work its way farther in. If she pulled it out, it would bleed badly.

She moaned. The arrow in her side was worse. It had sunk in deep.

Through her internal organs. Even if she could extract it without passing out, she would risk terrible internal bleeding. She could feel the stalk of the one in her back.

It was horrible! She had ridden after her husband like a fool and now would die out here in the canyons, alone!

She didn't know how long she rode, or where the horse took her. Only that her strength steadily faded. The Scabs had lost her, but she didn't know if they were waiting along the edge for her to return, so she kept the horse walking.

You have to find help. You have to go back into the forest and hope for help. She stopped and looked around, but her vision was blurred, and she knew that she would never find the forest in this waning light.

In fact, if she was right, she was at the edge of the desert now, where the canyons gave way to miles of sand. How far had she traveled? If she just kept riding, she might find herself even farther from where she needed to go. And she couldn't keep riding with the arrows in her. The slightest movement shot spikes of pain along her leg and up her spine.

She had to rest. She had to get off the horse and lie down. But she was afraid that if she tried to dismount, she might faint.

"Elyon, help me," Rachelle whispered. "Dear God, don't let me die."

But she knew she would.

21

THOMAS AND Mikil sat across a reed table from Martyn in an open tent that some of the general's aides had erected for their leader after he'd agreed to talk to Thomas. The stench of Scab was almost too much to bear.

The fact that the Horde had nearly doubled in size and moved closer to the forest was an ominous sign, all the more reason for Thomas to approach Martyn.

They'd ridden in waving a white flag—Thomas's idea. No one had ever used a white flag, to his recollection, but the sign was understood quickly enough, and the camp's perimeter guard had held them off at a hundred paces while they checked with their leaders. Another general had finally come out, heard that Thomas of Hunter requested an audience with Martyn, and relayed the question.

"Tell Martyn that Thomas of Hunter requests a meeting with Johan," Thomas said to the general.

"You mean Justin of Southern?"

"No, not with Justin. With Johan. That is the name I know him by. Johan."

Half an hour later they had their meeting.

Johan was clearly there under his stinking, flaking skin. Older now, late twenties. Paint his eyes green and his skin flesh-colored, and no one who'd known the boy could possibly mistake him. The round circle of the druids was shaded on his forehead.

But he moved and spoke like a completely different man. His eyes shifted warily and he kept his movements short to minimize the pain from his disease. Like all of the Horde, he didn't think of the rot as a disease. His mind was sharp, but he'd been swallowed by lies that had long ago persuaded him that this was the way all good men should look and move and feel. Pain was natural. The smell of rotting flesh was more a scent of wholesome humanity than a stench.

Johan looked down at Thomas and wrinkled his nose. "The lakes do that to you?"

"Do what?"

"Give you that terrible smell."

"I suppose so. And your skin is no less offensive to us. You hated the smell yourself, three years ago. Where's Justin?"

Johan hesitated. "He left an hour ago."

"Will he be back?"

"Yes."

"Will you agree to peace with him?"

"That is clearly his intent."

"Is it yours?"

"You tell me; is it?"

The man was talking in riddles. He needed to speak with Johan candidly.

"What I have to say is for your ears only," he said. "Send your men away and I will send my lieutenant away."

"Sir—"

He held up his hand to Mikil. She wouldn't question him further in public.

"Surely you don't fear me," Thomas said. "You're my wife's brother."

"Leave," Johan said to the four warriors behind him.

They hesitated, then backed out. Thomas looked at Mikil who glared disapprovingly, then left. Both parties walked off about fifty paces in opposite directions, then stopped to watch from the open desert.

"Johan," Thomas said. "You don't remember your real name, do you?"

"You mean the name I had as a child. Every boy grows up. Or are all Forest People still children?"

"Is there any of Johan left in you?"

"Only the man."

"And why is it that one of my soldiers can kill five of yours?"

Johan's eye twitched. "Because my men are only just now learning to fight you. I know your ways. Our skills will soon surpass yours."

"You are teaching them new tricks, aren't you? But think back, Johan. Before you lost your way in the desert. You were much stronger than you are now. The skin condition, it's a disease."

The man just held his gaze.

"How did you get lost?"

"Is this why you called me out? To talk about a time when we played with toy swords?"

Johan's mind was as scaled as his flesh, Thomas thought. He wondered if Rachelle could break through his deception.

"No. I've come because I know more than I should." He had to be careful. "I overheard a discussion in your leader's tent several nights ago when I killed the general. I hope you won't hold his death against me."

"The general you killed was a good friend of mine."

"Then please accept my condolences. Either way, I now know that you're conspiring with Justin and Qurong against the Forest People. You will offer them peace, and in the face of overwhelming odds, you think Justin will persuade our people to accept your offer. But you intend to betray us once you have won our trust."

Thomas let the statement stand. Johan made no comment. It was impossible to read his face, shrouded by the dark hood and scaled as it was.

"I'm curious, what will Justin receive for his betrayal?"

"That's none of your concern."

"How long have you been planning this?"

"Long enough."

"I should have known. You're both originally from our forest. First you go missing three years ago, and then you conveniently show up as a general who knows our ways. A year later Justin refuses my appointment and begins to preach his peace. All the while you two are plotting the overthrow of the forest. For all I know you hatched the plan with Justin in the Southern Forest and then chose the life of a Scab. He's been seeding doubt while you've been building your army to take advantage of that doubt. Was it his idea or yours? Will you make Justin supreme leader of the Horde?"

Johan—Martyn, the druid general—stared at him for a long time. But he refused to answer.

"Still, you must be worried about the toll a battle in the forest would have on your army or you'd just march on us now, without any attempt at betrayal," Thomas said. "Betrayal is your equalizer. You hope to catch us with our guard down."

"Is that right? Well, if you know this, our plan is foiled."

Such a quick admission? But Johan didn't have the tone of a defeated man.

"Not necessarily. We each have a problem. Mine is Justin; yours is Qurong. I think that Justin may have enough power to compromise our will for battle."

Johan hesitated. "A surprisingly candid admission."

"I'm not here to play games. Even with your betrayal, the battle would be fierce. Many of your men would die. Most."

"A possibility. And what is my problem?"

"Your problem is Qurong. He will fight this battle even knowing his betrayal has been compromised. In the end, the forest will be red with blood and you will have few people left to govern."

"Isn't that the way it is? War?"

"No." Thomas lowered his voice. It had taken Mikil most of the ride through the forest to embrace the wisdom of what he was about to propose.

"There can never be a true peace between our people; neither of us can accept it. But there can be a truce." He tapped his finger on the table. "Now."

"As Justin has proposed. A truce."

"He's proposed a peace that will end in more bloodshed than anyone can imagine, most of it Horde blood. The only way I see out of this quagmire is for the brother of my wife, Johan, to lead the Horde instead of Qurong. You may have become a man, but will you kill your own sister?"

"I could have you killed for such words," Johan said. He glanced at his men. Clearly he wasn't excited about the mention of treason against his leader.

"You're suggesting a revolt against Qurong, the man who is my father."

"He's not your father."

"His name was Tanis, and I've always seen him as my father."

Tanis. *Tanis?* The firstborn of all men. A father figure to the people of the colored forest. Qurong was Tanis! Thomas felt his chest constrict. He took this in with alarm, though he hoped none showed.

"If you think your armies can survive the explosives we have for them, you're sadly mistaken. Surely you heard about the fate of your Scabs in the canyons. If it's more death you want, tell Qurong to march now, tonight! But I can promise you, for every one of my Guard you kill, our gunpowder will rip the head off a hundred of yours."

It was all a bluff; they had no explosives. But by Johan's slight reaction, Thomas thought it had at least created some confusion.

He continued quickly. "I will ensure your safe passage into the forest with Qurong and Justin. Bring a thousand of your best warriors if you like. Before the people, you will expose the betrayal of Justin and Qurong, and I will swear that what you say is the truth. We will condemn Qurong to death. You will step into the vacancy."

Slowly a smile nudged Johan's mouth. "You are the son of the Shataiki, aren't you?"

"That would be Qurong, the firstborn who brought this sickness upon us in the first place."

"And Justin?"

Thomas shrugged. "He will be discredited. Banished."

"I may kill him?"

The question struck Thomas as strange. "Why?"

"His loyalty to Qurong would be a problem for me."

Thomas hesitated. "Do what you must."

"You think I'm foolish enough to walk into a trap with only a thousand of my men at my side? Qurong will never agree to this."

"He will if I agree to stay here as a guarantee of his safety." It was the most troublesome element of the plan for Mikil. But Thomas had convinced her that the world was at stake. Without some kind of compromise, there would be a bloodbath. Qurong would attack. The forest would be burned. They might kill most of the Horde army, but in the end they wouldn't have their wives or children to justify such a terrible victory.

"Your plan is treasonous," Johan finally said. "I'm not a man who will entertain treason."

"My plan will save your people. And mine. I am the husband of your sister. I beg you, consider your heritage and help me build a truce. With Qurong there is only war. Teeleh has bound him hand and heart. I believe that in your heart there is still room for Rachelle and your own people."

Johan looked at him and finally stood. "Wait here." He walked out into the desert and faced the distant dunes. For a long time he stood with his back to Thomas. Then he walked slowly back into camp.

Mikil ran into the tent. "Well?"

"I don't know."

"Is he considering it?"

"I think."

"I still don't like it. What's to keep a stray soldier with a sickle from taking off your head?"

"I will insist on protection. The last time I checked, I could handle a stray maniac with a single sickle. Besides, you'll have Qurong at the tip of your sword."

She nodded thoughtfully. "Then they don't take you into custody until Qurong is in the forest, under our Guard's watch."

"Of course. Here he comes."

She retreated, eying the approaching general with skepticism.

Johan swept his robe aside and sat down. "I don't care what you say; you are a son of the Shataiki," he said. "But I like your plan. My conditions are as follows: As a sign of good faith, you will not only stay, as you have offered, but you will pull the army on your perimeter back to the center of the forest. I don't want you waging war while I am inside."

Thomas considered the request. Qurong would be their guarantee. As long as Mikil had their leader, they would never attack.

"Agreed."

"My other condition is that you allow me to conduct Qurong's execution as a show of my new authority over my people. It is a language they will understand."

"Understood."

Martyn, general of the Horde whose name was once Johan, dipped his head. "Then we have an agreement."

⁂

They spent another half hour refining details before Thomas and his lone aide mounted and rode away from the camp. His second—Mikil, she was called—would leave for the forest tonight after dark. Qurong, Martyn, Justin, and a thousand warriors would follow the next morning. They would enter the forest in exchange for Thomas, who would then be taken into custody by the Horde army.

Qurong and Thomas would entrust their lives to each other.

The entourage would arrive at the lake in the evening with full assurance that Mikil had set the stage. If she hadn't done so satisfactorily, Qurong and Martyn would retreat. If they were ambushed by the Guard, Thomas would also die. And of course, vice versa.

So it was planned. So it was agreed.

Martyn stared toward the west, where he could just see the distant forest in the twilight. Qurong stood beside him, frowning.

"So they suspect nothing?"

"Nothing. He honestly thinks I would betray you. They are children, as I once was."

"And Justin will agree?"

"Justin will agree. He knows what he's doing."

Qurong grunted and turned back to the camp. "As will they all, soon enough."

22

DARKNESS SWALLOWED the desert. The moon rose and cast an eerie glow over the rising dunes. How many hours had passed? The sun would surely rise soon—she had to hang on until then. That's what Rachelle kept telling herself. If she could just make it to morning, the light would bring new hope.

But now a new problem presented itself: She hadn't bathed for a full day and a half, since the night of the celebration, and her skin was beginning to burn. The pain beneath her skin was now nearly as bad as the dull ache of her wounds.

She lay on one side, feeling the disease slowly eat at her skin, afraid to close her eyes, afraid sleep would take her life, afraid someone might find her and kill her, afraid that she might never see Thomas or Samuel or Marie again. How would they cope without a loving wife and a knowing mother?

They would be lost without her. She didn't think of herself in any inflated way; it was simply a fact. Thomas needed her like he needed water. Samuel and Marie had friends who'd lost their fathers to war, but not their mothers.

She'd managed to crawl off her horse without losing consciousness. The stallion waited patiently, twenty paces away. She wasn't sure whether she wished it would go and find help, or stay in case she needed it to ride out, although she couldn't imagine either actually happening.

She faded in and out of a semblance of sleep. Oddly enough, she was quite sure that she was still asleep under the lean-to with Thomas in France. Perhaps this was all a dream. Was she bleeding from her leg and side there?

So much that she didn't understand.

The hours dragged on. No crickets here. No forest sounds. The silence of the desert was its own sound. It was cold, but that was good because it kept her from slipping into unconsciousness. She had to concentrate to keep from shivering, because shivering sent waves of pain through her back. Maybe she had a fever, because she couldn't remember it ever being—

Was that light? Rachelle stared at the barely graying horizon.

Already! The dawn was coming. She'd made it! Filled with an irrational hope, she moved her arm to sit up. Sharp pain sliced through her belly.

She closed her eyes and winced. Her whole body was going stiff. She couldn't get to her feet, much less to the horse. And when the sun was finished welcoming her to the land of the living, it would only burn her to a crisp. Hope fell to the pit of her stomach like a lead weight.

Her heart plodded on, but it felt slower now. Hardly like a heart at all. Like a horse walking through sand. A *shooshing* sound more than a thudding heart sound. For a moment she imagined herself on a horse, plodding out to the desert. She was hallucinating.

Rachelle cracked her eyes. Saw the horse. Plod, plod, *shoosh, shoosh.* Right toward her as if it were real and the means for her delivery.

That is a real horse, Rachelle.

Now she did hear her heart, and it was bolting in her chest. There, not twenty paces away, stood a pale horse. Its rider was throwing his leg over the saddle to dismount.

This was a Forest Dweller!

She jerked up. Pain filled her eyes with black specks, but she held on. "Hel . . . hello?"

"It's okay," the voice said. "Hold on!"

He—yes, it was a he—was hurrying to her. Thomas?

Her vision cleared and she saw him plainly for the first time. This was Justin of Southern!

Her strength gave way and she sank back down. Tears flooded her eyes, but they weren't from the pain.

Justin ran the last few steps and knelt by her side. His hand gently touched her forehead. "Just relax. Breathe. I'm so sorry, my dear. I came to find you as soon as I heard what the patrol had done, but it took me all night to follow your tracks through the canyons. You're a fighter, no doubt about that."

She didn't know what to say. She wasn't sure she even had the strength to speak intelligently. This was Justin. She wasn't even sure what to *think* about that. Tears were leaking down her cheeks, blurring her vision.

"Shh, shh. It's okay, Rachelle. I promise you it will be okay."

He knew her from when he was under Thomas's command. His hand touched the arrows, each one, as if he was checking to see whether they were too deep to pull.

"I'm dying," she stammered.

"No, I won't let you. But you're turning." He glanced over his shoulder. "Are you carrying water on your horse?"

She glanced at the skin on her arm. Gray. He must not be carrying any, or he'd have retrieved his own.

"Some," she said.

"Where is your horse?"

She looked past him. The horse had gone off?

It was suddenly all too much. There was no way. Even now, having been found, she knew that she could never survive the injuries she'd sustained. And the lake was too far. Her life was seeping from her by the moment.

She closed her eyes and let herself go. Sobs wracked her body. Not sorrow for herself, but for her children and for Thomas.

"Why are you crying?" he asked.

She sniffed and swallowed deep. She would die with her head high, not blubbering like a baby.

"Hear me, my child. I will not let you die today."

He was trying to console her, but she was lying here with arrows protruding from infected wounds, barely clinging to life; his words rang empty. Did he think she was a child to build her hopes on such empty words of promise?

"Don't lie to me," she said.

"No, I would never—"

"Don't lie to me!" she shouted. "I'm dying! And I'm dying because of *you.* He came out here because of your obsession with this impossible peace!" The words came out in a rush that left her breathless. Justin deserved no such tirade, and her anger was really directed at her circumstance more than him, but she didn't care. This was the man who'd defeated her husband in the inquiry. And, at least in part, she was dying now because of it!

Justin stood. Then stepped back. He stared at her, eyes round. She'd hurt him, surprised him. But she was too far gone with pain and dread over her own predicament to care. She rolled her head away from him and cried.

For a long time she stayed like that, and for a long time she didn't know what he was doing. A minute passed. Two. It occurred to her that he might have left. The thought terrified her.

She jerked her head around and looked for him.

He was gone!

But what was this? Someone else was there. A small boy was pacing in front of a large boulder twenty feet away. The boy was crying. His arms hung limp by his side and he was naked except for a loincloth.

Samuel? No, it wasn't Samuel. The sickness was taking her mind. The boy was weeping, beside himself. Sympathy spiked through her heart. But she knew this had to be a figment of her imagination. Yet the boy looked so real. His cries sounded terribly real.

The boy!

This was the boy!

She closed her eyes, opened them. The graying sky was blurry, and she blinked rapidly to clear her vision. The boy was gone.

Justin stood not ten feet away, with his back to her, hands on hips, head hung. Was this also a hallucination? She blinked again. No, this was Justin. But what she'd seen had unnerved her to the core. An image of Justin sweeping the little girl off her feet in the Valley of Tuhan ran through her mind.

The warrior lifted his head and stared at the cliffs. This was the man who had defeated Thomas in battle. Who seemed to be able to have his will with any opponent. It was no wonder that the women and children and fighters from the Southern Forest were so taken with Justin. He was an enigma.

And she'd yelled at him.

But why wasn't he helping her? "I'm sorry," she said. "But I'm going to die here. Please allow a dying woman her liberties."

"You're not going to die," he said softly. "I have too much riding on you to let you die."

She'd heard that before. Where had she heard that?

He faced her. "You think a few arrows and some torn flesh have much to do with death? I will take your pain away, Rachelle, but it is your heart that worries me."

"How can you take away my pain? My skin is gray and there are still arrows in my body. I'm dying and you're just standing there!"

"You're as stubborn as Thomas. Maybe more. And your memory is no better than his either."

He was talking nonsense. A shot of pain traveled through her bones, and she grimaced.

"I want you to listen to me very carefully, Rachelle." He knelt on one knee and clasped her hand in his. He was making no attempt to help her or tend to her wounds. He knew as well as she that there was nothing either of them could do.

"We have brokered a peace between the Desert Dwellers and the Forest People. Qurong will go with Johan and me to the village, where we will offer our terms for peace."

The Council would never accept any terms for peace; didn't Justin know that?

"Thomas will stay in the Desert Dweller's camp as a guarantee for safe passage. Mikil is with Qurong to ensure Thomas's safety. When the Council understands that a second army, twice the size of the one to the east, is camped on the other side of the forest, they will agree to peace. What happens then must happen for the boy. Do you understand? Because of the boy's promise."

"Thomas is in the Horde camp? They'll *kill* him!"

"Mikil will have Qurong and Johan in trade. It must happen this way. No matter what happens, remember that. No matter how terrible or at what cost." He paused. Then he put his other hand on her head, leaned over, and kissed her forehead. "When the time comes, remember these words and follow me. It will be a better way. Die with me. It will bring you life."

Rachelle closed her eyes. She wanted to scream. Her heart felt like it might break free from her chest, and she understood none of it. Not what he said nor her own emotions. "I don't want to die."

"Find Thomas. Your death will save him."

"I can't die!" she cried.

"They're waiting for me." Justin stood. "I must go." He strode to his horse and swung into the saddle. The steed snorted and stamped.

He was leaving her?

"I don't understand," she cried. "Don't leave me!"

"I have never left you. Never!" His eyes flashed with anger, then filled with tears. "We will be together soon and you will understand." He spurred his horse and the stallion galloped into the canyon.

She was too stunned to speak. He was leaving her?

"Remember me, Rachelle! Remember my water."

"Justin!" she screamed.

"Remember me!"

This time his voice echoed long as he pounded down the canyon. The echo of his last word, *me*, seemed to dip into laughter. A child's laughter.

A giggle. A boy's giggle that bubbled like a brook.

She caught her breath. She'd heard that sound before!

The laughter suddenly grew, as if it had taken a turn at the end of the canyon and decided to rush back toward her. Louder and louder, until it seemed to swallow her whole.

Something unseen hit her hard. She gasped. Her whole body jumped off the ground and then arched. She shook in the air for several seconds, then dropped hard back to the sand.

The sound of giggling was sucked back into the canyon, leaving only silence in its wake.

Rachelle sucked in a lungful of air and trembled. But it wasn't from fear. It wasn't from pain. It was from a strange power that lingered in her bones.

Her world momentarily faded.

Then with a flash it returned. What had . . . what had happened?

Monique was gone, for one thing. She'd probably woken.

Rachelle jerked up. No pain. She stared at her side, shocked. Where an arrow had protruded just moments ago, there was only a bloody hole in her tunic. She pulled the garment up and examined her flesh. Blood, but only blood. No wound.

And her skin had lost its gray pallor.

She scrambled to her feet and frantically grasped at the bloody spots. Not a single wound. In fact, she felt as refreshed and whole as if she'd slept the night in perfect peace. She lifted her head up and stared at the canyon.

Remember me.

A chill washed over her skull. They were the words that the boy had spoken to her so long ago before he'd run down the bank and disappeared into the lake. *Just remember me, Rachelle,* he'd said.

I have a lot riding on you.

She couldn't breathe. It was him! Justin was the boy! Only he wasn't a lamb or a lion or a boy now. He was a warrior and his name was Justin! How could she have missed it?

"Justin!" Her call came out like a squeak. She ran. She tore over the sand, desperate to catch him.

"Justin!" This time her cry echoed up the canyon. But he was gone.

Justin was the boy, and the boy was Elyon. Elyon had just touched her. Kissed her forehead! If she had known—

She groaned past a terrible ache that had filled her throat.

"Elyonnnn!"

She fell to her knees. Sobs wracked her body. Panic. Waves of heat that flushed her face. But there was nothing she could do. He'd been within a foot of her and she hadn't fallen to her knees to kiss his feet. She hadn't clung to his hand in desperation.

She'd yelled at him!

She gripped her head and cried long, silent wails that washed away her sense of time. Then slowly she began to come back to herself.

The boy had come back to them. She sniffed and struggled to her feet. Dawn had lightened the sky.

Their Creator had come back to them, and he was going to make peace with the Horde. It was the day of deliverance!

Find Thomas, Justin had said.

She spun and faced the sand dunes. She'd seen the camp to the east. Thomas was being held in the camp. It couldn't be more than a few hours away, even by foot.

She grabbed her tunic and ran into the desert, only briefly thinking about his other words. Your death will save him, Justin had said. But it meant nothing.

She was alive. Elyon had healed her.

23

THOMAS GAZED at the eastern horizon, where the sun was just now rising over the dunes. The lieutenant of the perimeter guard, Stephen, stood beside Thomas, holding the reins of his horse. Behind them, three hundred Forest Guard waited along the tree line. Ahead of them, the contingent from the Horde waited on their horses to make the exchange as agreed. Johan, Qurong, Justin. And behind them, a thousand Scab warriors.

They were about to make history in the desert. Odd to think that at this very moment he was doing nothing more spectacular in the other reality than sleeping next to Monique under a boulder in France, dreaming.

"I don't like it, sir," the lieutenant said. "You're just going to let them take you in shackles?"

"Not 'just,' Stephen. As long as you have Qurong and Martyn, I'm safe."

Thomas and Mikil had spent three hours covering every possible contingency before Mikil headed off to prepare the Guard and the Council for Qurong and Martyn's arrival as agreed. Only Mikil, Thomas, the Council, and Johan knew the truth of what was to happen.

Thomas had spent a fitful night waiting for daybreak. Not a wink of sleep. Despite his tone of confidence with Stephen, he was nervous.

"They have a thousand warriors; you have no one," the man said.

"Are you telling me you and your men can't deal with a thousand warriors in the forest, where they will be lost?"

"No, I'm not saying that. It just strikes me as disproportionate."

"I'm willing to take that chance. Remember, this is a mission of peace. Unless you hear differently from myself or Mikil, no harm to them."

"So Justin has done what he promised," the man said. "He's brokering peace and you're in agreement."

"Justin is brokering peace. For the moment I am in agreement."

"The Council will never accept."

"They will. You will see; they will."

Thomas left his lieutenant's side and walked toward the waiting contingent. The truth, of course, was that instead of brokering their peace in front of the Council, Johan would accuse Qurong of plotting betrayal with Justin. He would tell the congregation that Qurong and Justin were planning to ransack the forest as soon as the Guard had accepted peace. Mikil would step forward and tell the people that on her word, Thomas of Hunter concurred. Qurong would then be convicted and executed, and Justin's fate would be left up to the new leader of the Horde, Johan.

That was the plan. Thomas and Mikil had considered it a dozen times and agreed it would work. It would spare the forest a terrible battle. Just as importantly, they weren't conspiring with the Horde, which would be treason. No, they were conspiring against the Horde leader, Qurong, by using Johan—a Scab, yes, but also Johan. Enough of a technicality to assure the Council's approval, surely.

Gravel crunched under Thomas's feet as he walked. He was the only one not on a horse and armed. For all practical purposes, he was naked.

He reached the midpoint between the two small armies when Justin suddenly dismounted and walked out to meet him. There had been no mention of this, but Johan and Qurong didn't object, and so neither did Thomas.

Justin met him halfway. "Good morning, my brother." The warrior dipped his head.

"Good morning." Thomas returned his gesture.

For a moment they just looked at each other.

"So," Justin said, "it's come down to this after all."

"I guess it has. It's what you wanted, isn't it? Peace?"

"I told them that you would come."

The revelation caught Thomas off guard. "I'm not sure I understand."

"I knew it when I looked in your eyes at the challenge. You don't understand what's happening, but you want peace. You've always wanted peace. And this is the only way for peace, Thomas."

"How did you know that I would come?"

"You taught me to judge my enemy well. Call it a lucky guess." His eyes twinkled. "Johan refused to believe that you would offer yourself as a guarantee for Qurong's safety, but when I saw you ride in yesterday with Mikil, I knew we had won."

Justin had told Johan that he was going to offer an exchange? Johan had known? The general had smiled at the suggestion—perhaps because of Justin's accuracy in predicting it.

But Justin couldn't know the whole truth.

Thomas felt a pang of remorse for his offering up the man in exchange for Qurong's death. But it was the only way.

"Then you're a better tactician than I am," Thomas said, glancing at the Scabs. "If you know so much, tell me this: Will I be safe in their shackles?"

Justin hesitated. "Let's just say that I think you'll be safer in their shackles than I will be in the hands of my own Council."

He stretched out his hand. Thomas took it, and Justin bent to kiss his fingers. "Take courage, Thomas. We are almost home. I'll see you in the lake."

Then Justin turned and walked back to his line.

Thomas hesitated, wondering at this latest exchange. But the die had been cast. He walked to the boulder they'd agreed on and stood tall. Justin remounted and led the Horde contingent forward. As soon as Qurong was within slaying reach of the Forest Guard, a dozen Scabs rushed Thomas and fixed shackles on his wrists.

The Horde army vanished into the trees and Thomas was led away on a horse, hopelessly shackled.

24

MONIQUE BOLTED up, wide awake. Twigs hung in her face. She was in the forest? She'd been wounded by the Desert Dwellers and then Justin had healed her!

No. She was in France. Sleeping beside Thomas. It had been a dream.

A dream! She closed her mouth and swallowed, but her throat was parched and tacky. Beside her, Thomas slept soundly, chest rising and falling. Her hand was in his. She pulled it free and wiped the sweat from her face.

She'd dreamed that she was Rachelle, and yet she knew that it was more than a dream, because she knew that as Rachelle she'd dreamed of being Monique.

Monique stared past the leaves that made up the lean-to, stunned by this change in her perception of reality. She had shared Rachelle's life.

Her bladder was burning. Was it this that had awakened her or the trauma of her dream? Either way, she had to relieve herself. And when she returned, she would wake Thomas and tell him what had happened.

Monique slipped out of the lean-to as quietly as possible and stood. It was only then that she felt the damp spots on her leg. She looked down and saw that her clothes were wet.

Blood! She gasped involuntarily.

The arrows! She touched then pushed on the spots. No pain, no wounds. The dark splotches spread out from where the arrows had struck her. The bleeding hadn't been terrible because the arrows had stopped up the wounds.

Monique felt tremors overtake her body. It had really happened. This

was beyond her. She swallowed and headed, weak-kneed, for the trees just
beyond the quarry.

The moon had fallen into the horizon when Carlos stopped near the edge
of the clearing and took stock of his situation. Through the trees, maybe
three hundred meters down the valley, a farmhouse stood in darkness. He
was approximately halfway between Melun and Paris, headed west toward
the capital. It was midnight.

Thomas and Monique were somewhere within a hundred meters of
him, to the southeast, according to the small screen in his palm. He studied the clearing ahead, careful not to expose himself beyond the tree line.

The quarry. Yes, of course, it would be a natural place to stop. Seventy
paces ahead and to his left. They were in the quarry. Unless the woman had
discovered the tracking device and discarded the transmitter.

Carlos slipped the receiver into his pocket and worked around the
perimeter of the clearing, toward the quarry.

He heard a rustle and froze by a large pine. A rabbit?

The quarry lay just ahead, a depression in the ground that was partially overgrown with stubborn tufts of grass.

Carlos withdrew his pistol and chambered a round. He now wished
he'd thought to bring the silencer—a gunshot might disturb whoever lived
in the farmhouse, although the lay of the quarry would absorb much of the
sound.

He stepped around the tree, crouched down, and walked toward the
edge of the depression. Gravel scattered, knocked by his boot, and he
stopped. He let the sound clear and then eased slowly forward.

The moment he saw the branches set against the boulder, he knew that
he had found them. It would be different this time. He would either kill or
be killed, and he was certain it would be the former.

Monique was standing by a log, ten meters into the forest, but her mind
was still in another forest, in another world altogether.

Monique closed her eyes and clenched her jaw to clear her thoughts. *Reality, Monique. Back to reality.*

But that was the problem—the other *was* reality. The smells, the memories, the sights, the feelings in her heart. All of it!

She pulled the pale blue slacks completely off and hung them from a dead branch that jutted up from the fallen trunk. She could barely see by the starlight, and she didn't want her only clothes to end up with leaves or, worse, bugs in them.

She stood by the log dressed only in her muddied tennis shoes and a cotton blouse, which hung loosely past her underwear. She wouldn't remove her shoes, not with critters under the leaves.

The sound of skittering gravel reached her ears. She froze.

But it was nothing.

He could hear their breathing. Carlos crouched by the edge of the quarry and peered at the dark shadow beneath the branches they'd leaned against the boulder. On the left end, Hunter's boots. He would slip around to the right and put the first two bullets into Hunter's head before turning the gun on the woman. It would have to be quick. Best for both to die in their sleep.

They had what they needed from Monique. Fortier and Svensson might question the events, but they wouldn't second-guess his decision to kill them, despite their desire to keep her alive. They had chosen him for his ability to make such determinations, and they knew enough to leave security in his hands. If Carlos decided that Hunter had to die, then Hunter would die. End of issue. There was too much at stake to quibble over his judgment now. Killing them would ensure that what they knew would never leave France.

Carlos moved slowly, crouching to minimize his profile against the forest behind. Tumbling rocks were his primary concern. Stones clicked softly under his feet, but not enough to wake the average man.

Then again, Hunter wasn't the average man. But he was unarmed, and he was with a woman he would undoubtedly want to protect.

The moment the ground leveled, Carlos rushed in on the balls of his feet. Four long steps, quick pivot. The wedge of darkness beneath the branches opened up to him. He dropped to one knee, extended the nine millimeter's barrel to the head of the man he recognized as Thomas Hunter, and pulled the trigger.

Thunder crashed in his ears.

The body jerked.

There was no second body.

The revelation that the woman wasn't here stopped him short of pulling the trigger a second time. If not here, then where?

He quickly felt Hunter's neck for a pulse, found none, and ran around the boulder, gun still extended. Nothing. He rounded another boulder, but with each step his hope of finding her faded. She wasn't here.

He ran back to where Hunter lay and noted the ground beside his body. Small indentations in the earth confirmed that another body had rested here. No sign of the slacks with the tracking device. He felt for Hunter's pulse one last time, and satisfied that the man was very much dead, he stood and scanned the forest.

She had been here less than five minutes ago. He pulled out the receiver and turned it on. It took only a few seconds to acquire the signal. Directly ahead in the forest. Close. Very close.

Carlos began to run.

<hr />

The odor of sulfur hung low and thick over the Scab camp. It had taken them an hour to reach the huge army, and the sun was already hot on their backs. Twenty warriors rode on either side of Thomas as they approached the same spot where he'd negotiated his treachery with Johan less than twenty-four hours ago.

He'd bathed from a canteen last night, and he was now allowed one additional canteen, which now hung from his belt. He wouldn't drink it, but he would bathe if the meeting at the Council kept him more than a day. Justin would arrive in the evening. The Council would hear the matter, and the reversal would end in Qurong's death. By morning, Johan would be exchanged for Thomas at the forest perimeter. But if there was any delay, he might need the water.

In the meantime, he was consigned to spend the rest of the day and the night in this cursed—

Something hit his head.

He jerked upright and twisted in his saddle. Nothing. But his head was ringing as if a mallet had struck it. Pain spread down his spine. He began to lose focus.

He knew then that something had happened in the other reality. Carlos had found them. He'd been shot. In the head!

Thomas's world suddenly began to spin and darken. He felt himself falling from the horse. Heard his body thud into the ground.

His last thought was that his assumption had been right. If he died in one reality, he also died in the other.

Then everything went black.

Monique had her thumbs hooked in her underwear when the still night exploded with a terrible *boom*.

She instinctively jerked. Behind her! A gunshot in the quarry! She spun, thumbs still hooked, heart pounding.

The trees blocked most of her view, but she peered under a branch by her head and saw in one horrifying moment what had happened. A dark figure stood up by the lean-to, then ran around the boulder, gun in hand.

Carlos! It had to be Carlos! He'd followed them. And he'd just shot . . .

Monique lifted her hand to her mouth and stifled a cry. Thomas!

She nearly ran for him, but she immediately knew that she couldn't—not with Carlos so close. He'd fired point-blank! No one could have survived that.

Monique stood frozen by horror. How could his life end like this? Would he come back? No, he'd told her that his dreams could no longer heal him! Or was that something she'd learned from her own dream? They were terrified that Thomas might be killed here, because they were sure it would mean that he would also die there.

Carlos ran back around the boulder, dropped to his knees, and was checking Thomas's pulse. This confirmed it. Thomas was dead.

Monique fought a nauseating wave of panic. She had to get away! Carlos had already searched the quarry for her . . . he'd assume she'd gone into the trees . . .

She ran then, on her toes, through the forest toward the distant farmhouse. The leaves crinkled under her feet. Too loud! She slid to a stop, turned to the quarry, saw that Carlos was still leaning into the shelter. He hadn't heard her.

She moved quickly, but as quietly as possible now.

Her slacks! No, no time to go back.

Monique was halfway around the quarry when she glimpsed Carlos through the limbs, running toward the section of forest she had occupied only a minute earlier. Had he seen her?

Run! Run, Monique, straight across the quarry, across the meadow to the farmhouse!

No, she shouldn't. In fact, she should do the opposite. She should stop. Monique slid behind a tree and breathed deep and slow to catch her breath. The night was quiet. No rustling of leaves or snapping of twigs from where she'd run. What was Carlos doing? Waiting?

She stood still for what seemed like an hour, though it couldn't have been more than a few minutes. Tears blurred her vision. The thought of Thomas lying there, bleeding on the ground, was enough to make her scream, and it took all of her strength to bury the emotion. She had to survive. Thomas had risked his life to bring her out. She had information the outside world desperately needed.

Monique tiptoed forward, picking her way over the leaves as carefully as possible. She remembered seeing that this strip of woods ended in a meadow to her left. The meadow ran directly to the farmhouse.

It took her only a minute of high-stepping to reach the grass. She stopped for a few seconds, heard no sound of pursuit, and entered the field. Maybe Carlos was waiting by the quarry, watching for her return. Ten steps out she felt the horror of her exposure. If Carlos was anywhere near this side of the forest, he would surely see her! But she'd committed herself.

She began to run. If the man behind had noticed her, there was nothing she could do now except run.

With every step she was terribly aware of the fact that she was leaving Thomas dead behind her. She tried to think of a way to get to him, bring him with her. Wasn't it possible that he was alive?

No, she had to reach safety. She had to survive, and then she had to reach England.

She hadn't noticed the Peugeot in the driveway until now; it was parked near the front of the farmhouse, out of sight of the quarry.

Could she?

Yes, she could. Assuming the keys were in it, she could take the car and explain to the owner later.

She approached it in a crouch. Tried the door. Open! She slid in and searched madly for keys. Visor. Passenger seat. Cup holder. Dash.

They were in the ignition. She twisted and looked out the rear window. Still no sign of pursuit. But if she started the car . . .

Monique gently pulled the door closed, heard the latch click. No lights—she couldn't dare use lights. The driveway was gray enough to see despite the lack of moonlight. She prayed the car had a decent muffler, fired the engine, pulled the stick into drive, and rolled over the dirt, holding her breath to help the silence.

She made two short turns before driving behind a hill. Still too close for lights. Still too close to rev the engine. He might hear or see, even at this distance. For all she knew, Carlos was sprinting across the meadow now. Over the hill to cut her off.

The moment she entered the trees she picked up her speed, but she dared not turn the lights on. Without them, she could hardly see. She drove at ten kilometers per hour for a kilometer. Then two. Still no one behind.

But that wasn't true. Thomas was behind. An image of his body filled her mind. Bleeding from the head. Dead.

She wiped her eyes to see the road.

After five kilometers, Monique turned on the lights and shoved the gas pedal to the floor.

25

DEPUTY SECRETARY Merton Gains adjusted the receiver to give his neck a break. He'd been on hold for ten minutes despite the assurances that the president would take his call immediately. Immediately had always meant a short wait, but ten minutes? This was the new meaning of immediately—the one that came after a week of beating their heads against this brick wall called the Raison Strain.

Gains always vaguely feared it would come down to something like this. It was why he'd introduced his bill to change the way vaccines were used in the United States. Of course, he'd never anticipated a crisis as widespread and terminal as this one, but the danger had always lurked out there. Now it had bitten them in the rear end without so much as a warning.

He'd seen Raison Strain simulations a dozen times. It grew quietly and then struck with a vengeance, rupturing cells in indiscriminate, systemic fashion. *It was precisely how the political fallout from the crisis would develop,* he thought.

At this very moment, a hundred governments were on the verge of ending the silence they'd managed so far. A thousand reporters were sniffing and starting to come up with questions no one could answer. The world's genetics labs were working overtime, and the thousands of scientists on the Raison Strain were murmuring already.

This didn't include the military personnel who had been involved in the massive movement of hardware to the eastern seaports. They'd been trained to keep their questions to themselves and their mouths firmly shut. But all told, over ten thousand people now directly engaged the Raison Strain, and most of those suspected that the new virus that had been restricted to a small island south of Java wasn't nearly so isolated as everyone was saying.

He'd taken a call yesterday from Mike Orear with CNN. The man was on to them. He didn't say how he'd uncovered his information, but he knew that terrorists had released a virus of some kind, and he threatened to break the story in twenty-four hours if the president didn't come clean. It was all Gains could do to hold the man back. He couldn't very well refuse to comment, and a flat denial might push Orear over the edge. Gains had threatened the man with a long list of national security violations, but in the end, it was apparent the man knew too much. Orear had finally agreed to hold off until Gains had spoken with the president.

That was twenty-four hours ago, and the president had seemed surprisingly ambivalent about the prospect of CNN breaking the story. When the news broke, it would boil over and swamp the world. God only knew to what end.

There was only one way to temper the news.

"Merton?" The president's voice took him off guard.

"Yes, hello, Mr. President. I, um . . . I just got off the phone with England, sir."

"I don't mean to push, but I'm late for a meeting with the World Health Organization."

"Yes, sir. I just got off the phone with Monique de Raison. She called me from Dover about twenty—"

"She's alive?"

"She evidently escaped from an undisclosed location in France. She managed to get across the English Channel."

"And Thomas?"

"He was killed during the escape."

The receiver hissed quietly.

"You're sure about this?"

"About which—"

"About Hunter! You're sure he's dead?"

"Monique seems quite sure."

Gains hadn't realized how much stock the president had put in Thomas, and hearing the admission in his tone brought surprising comfort. Amazing that certain things didn't change even in the face of crisis.

"Does she have it?" the president demanded.

"She thinks so. At least a very strong lead."

"Okay. I want her here now. Put her on the fastest plane we have out of our air base in Lakenheath. Use an F-16—use whatever we have that can make the flight. The British are aware of this?"

"I'm waiting for a callback."

"Callback? This isn't a time for callbacks! I want her here in four hours, you understand? And make sure that she's under a heavy guard the whole way. Send an air escort with her. Treat her like she's me. Clear?"

"Yes sir."

26

RACHELLE CRESTED the dune that overlooked the Horde camp when the sun was halfway up the eastern sky.

Find Thomas, Justin had said. The words had haunted Rachelle as she stumbled over the sand. *No matter how terrible,* he had said. What could possibly be so terrible?

She ran down the dune toward the Horde camp. In all truth her spirit soared. Yes, Thomas was in the Horde camp, their virtual prisoner, and yes, there was danger on every side—she could feel it like the sun on her back.

But she'd found Elyon! Justin was the boy; she was sure of it. He'd changed her skin from gray to flesh tone, and he'd healed her wounds with a single word. Elyon had come to save his people! She couldn't wait to tell Thomas.

She understood that Monique had made a connection with her. What Monique was doing now, she had no clue. Unlike Thomas, who seemed to have an awareness of both worlds at all times, her and Monique's connection was apparently sporadic and depended on Thomas.

Rachelle began to yell when she was still two hundred yards out, before anyone had seen her. Whatever happened, she couldn't risk them misunderstanding her intentions as hostile.

"Thomas! I need to see Thomas of Hunter!"

She must have screamed it a dozen times before the first soldiers appeared at the perimeter. And then there were a hundred of them, staring out at the strange sight. This unarmed woman screaming in from the desert, demanding to see Thomas of Hunter.

She pulled up panting, twenty paces from the line of ugly beasts.

"I've been sent to speak to Thomas of Hunter. It's urgent I see him."

They stared at her as if she'd lost her mind. And why would they ever agree to let her see him? Thomas was their insurance.

"What business do you have?" one of them demanded.

"I am here because my lord needs me," she said, remembering what Thomas had told her about the way the Horde women spoke of the men. Several seemed stunned by her request. Was something wrong with Thomas?

"I am here to ensure that nothing is wrong with him. I am sent by our Council to know that he's in good health."

The Scab who'd assumed charge scowled. "Be gone, you wench! Tell your commander that we don't accept spies."

Rachelle panicked. "Then Mikil will cut Qurong's throat!" she screamed.

That set them back.

"If you turn me back, I will go straight to them and tell them that you've betrayed them, and Qurong will die. If I don't return in good health myself, then the same will happen. So don't think of hurting me."

The leader, a general by his sash, studied her for a moment. "Wait here."

He backed away, conferred with several other warriors, sent one of them off with a message, then returned.

"Follow me."

She entered the camp surrounded by a small army. The smell was hardly tolerable, and so many shrouded eyes peering at her made her skin crawl. She tried to breathe in shallow pulls, but it only made her dizzy. So she breathed deeply and forced her mind from the stench.

No women that she could see. Naturally, the Horde didn't allow their women to fight. She couldn't bear to look the men in the eyes, but she refused to look any less than a warrior herself, so she walked tall and straight, praying that she would be directed at the next possible moment into a tent to see Thomas.

They led her to a large tent in the middle of the camp. If she was right, this was the royal tent where Thomas had found the Books of Histories.

A guard parted the front flaps and she stepped in. The general who met her was named Woref, if she understood the guards correctly. His eyes had the look of a snake, and his face looked as though it might crack if he tried to smile.

"Where's Thomas?"

"We did nothing to him. You should know this. His wounds are self-inflicted."

"What wounds? Take me to him!"

He dipped his head and led her down a hallway. The serpentine bat they worshiped was everywhere—decorative paintings on the walls, molded statues in the corners. Teeleh. *Elyon, protect me.* They entered a large room where a half-dozen guards stood at the ready. A long table was spread with an array of fruits and wines and cheeses.

But where—

A body lay on a cushion along one of the walls. The head was bloody.

Thomas? Yes, it was him; she recognized his tunic immediately. He was wounded!

Rachelle ran over to him, dropped to her knees, and stared in horror at a round hole the size of her finger in his head. Blood had run into his hair. Dried.

"Thomas?"

But he was dead. Dead! And by the looks of him, he had been dead for some time.

She couldn't breathe. It wasn't possible! No, this couldn't be happening! Justin had found her, and she had just been saved, and Samuel and Marie were still children, and . . .

What could have made this kind of wound? No weapon of this world.

Something had happened to Thomas in the other reality. She recalled that Monique had been sleeping next to him under the boulder. Carlos must have found them! Now Thomas was dead. But she was still alive!

The thoughts drummed through her head painfully. Her heart didn't feel like it was moving. And behind her the Scabs were staring.

She spun around. "Out! Get out!" she screamed. Her vision was clouded with the pain. "Leave!"

The general scowled but left her alone with the body.

Rachelle sank slowly to her knees, knowing precisely what she had to do. Elyon had told her to find Thomas, not this dead body. Justin had healed her from near death. He carried the power of the fruit in his hands, they said, because he *was* the power of the fruit.

And now she would use that same power.

She rested both hands on his cheeks. Her tears fell on his face. "Wake up, Thomas," she whispered. "Thomas, please."

But he didn't wake up.

Now her voice rose to a soft wail. "Please, please. Save him, Elyon. Wake him from the dead."

Waking from the dead isn't like healing.

"Yes, it is!" she shouted. "Wake up, Thomas! Wake up!"

But he still didn't wake up. There was still a hole in his forehead. He was still dead.

She kissed his cold lips and began to sob. What if Justin didn't know he was dead? No, that was impossible. "Wake up," she cried again, slapping his face. "Wake up!"

Justin had to know. He knew everything. They didn't know; they didn't even remember—

Remember me. Remember my water.

His water. She frantically grasped the canteen still hooked to Thomas's belt. Pulled it free from the clip. Spun off the cap.

She splashed some on his face before she'd really thought it through. The clear liquid ran over his lips and his eyes and filled the small wound on his forehead.

She dumped more on. "Please, please, please . . ."

Thomas's mouth suddenly jerked open.

Rachelle cried out and jumped back. The canteen flew from her hands.

Thomas gasped. The wound closed, as if his skin was formed of wax that had melted to fill itself in. She had seen nothing like it for fifteen years, when she chose Thomas by healing him of the deadly wounds he'd suffered in the black forest.

Thomas's eyes opened.

Rachelle lifted both hands to her lips to stifle a cry of joy. Then she threw her arms around him and buried her face in his throat.

"Get off me, get off me, you . . ."

He didn't know who she was! She lifted her head so that he could see her face. "It's me, Thomas!"

She kissed him on the lips. "Me. You remember my mouth if not my face."

"What . . . where are we?" He struggled up.

"Be quiet; they're outside," she whispered. "We're in the Horde camp."

He jumped to his feet. The blood was still on his face, but his wound was gone. She could hardly take her eyes off his forehead.

"You were dead," she said. "But Elyon's water healed you."

"His water heals again? I . . . how is that—"

"No, I don't think his water's changed. I think he just used it to heal you. Justin is the boy, Thomas."

He lifted a hand to his hair, felt the blood, looked at his fingers. "I was shot. But I didn't dream. I don't have any memory of a dream."

He closed his eyes and rubbed the back of his head. What was it like coming back to life? Hopefully he was putting the pieces of his memory back in place.

"What do you mean, Justin is the boy?"

"I mean he's him. Don't you see? The signs were all there. He's come—"

"He can't be Elyon. He grew up in the Southern Forest. He was a warrior under my command!"

They were whispering, but loudly.

"And who's to say that he's not Elyon? I saw him—"

"No! It's not possible! I know when I see—"

"Stop it, Thomas!"

He stared at her, mouth still open, ready to finish his statement of disbelief. He clamped his jaw shut.

She told him what had happened in the desert. She hurried through the events in a whisper, and when she was finished, he just looked at her, face white.

"And I just saved you with his power. How dare you question me?"

"But Elyon? I fought Elyon?"

"He's come to save us from ourselves, just like he said he would, when we didn't think it could get any worse."

"I . . ." He turned from her. "Oh my God. My dear, dear God, Elyon! I've betrayed him!"

"We all did. And he beat you handily."

"No, with Johan!"

She pulled him around by the arm. "What do you mean?"

"I mean I struck an agreement with Johan that would make Johan the king of the Horde."

"So—"

"So he insisted that he betray both Qurong and Justin. I . . . I agreed."

These words weren't making sense to her. How could anyone betray Justin now? "But once they know that Justin is Elyon, there won't be any such thing."

"It's already started! They are due to reach the forest late this afternoon and work the betrayal. Mikil has informed the Council. Johan intends to kill Justin."

It was suddenly clear to her. Qurong and Johan were influenced by the Shataiki. By Teeleh. They were being used as the creature's instrument against Justin. This wasn't only about the Forest People; it was about Justin!

"We have to stop them!"

Thomas looked around frantically. "How many are outside?"

As if in answer, the flap parted and the general Woref stepped inside. His eyes flashed at the sight of Thomas standing.

Her husband walked toward the man. "Which one of your men tried to kill me?" he demanded.

"None."

Thomas moved quickly. He leaped for the Scab's sword, yanked it free from its scabbard, and ran for the far wall. "Hurry!"

He swung the blade over his head and down, parting the wall from top to bottom, opening it to daylight. He ripped the cut wide and held the sword out to stop the general.

"You follow and you die," he said, and then stepped through the tear into the passageway between the tents. They had already started through the camp before the stunned general gave the alarm.

"The horses!" Thomas yelled, pointing to several that were tied to the side of the tent. They both swung onto a horse. Then they were galloping out of the camp, dodging Scab warriors taken completely off guard by the two horses.

No one tried to stop them—naturally, they'd probably been strictly instructed not to touch Thomas of Hunter. Only the general, and probably now his men, knew what was really happening. It might not have made a difference anyway. The horses outran any words of warning.

They galloped from the Horde's camp straight toward the distant forest.

"Can we make it?" she demanded.

He rode hard just ahead, leaning forward, face drawn.

"Thomas!"

"I don't know!" Thomas snapped. He slapped his horse, coaxing every last ounce of strength from its fresh legs. "Hiyaa!"

The general from whom Thomas and Rachelle had escaped stared out at the dunes that led to the forest. Woref, head of military intelligence, despised the Forest Guard perhaps more than he hated Qurong.

He played the loyal general, but under his pain, not a day went by that he didn't curse the father of the woman who would one day be his. Qurong had forbidden any man from marrying his daughter, Chelise, until the forests had fallen. It was the leader's way of motivating a dozen senior-ranking generals who vied for her hand. If the decision had been left to Woref, they would have burned the forests long ago, then killed every last woman and child who bathed in the lakes and feasted on their flesh for the victory. But Qurong seemed more interested in conquering and enslaving than killing.

"Do we give chase?" his aide asked.

"No," Woref said. They had planned for this contingency. As long as Thomas was delayed by four or more hours, he would be too late. The western army would march.

He glanced at the sun. "Prepare the men to march at nightfall. We are going into the forest."

By week's end, the daughter of Qurong, Chelise, would be his. And then he would look to become Qurong himself.

MONIQUE PEERED at the Washington skyline through the Suburban's tinted windows. The American people didn't know yet; that was her first shock. Most of them probably didn't even know that the Raison Strain even existed, much less that it had infected most of the world's population already.

America's Deputy Secretary of State Merton Gains was on his cell phone, talking in rapid-fire sentences with someone named Theresa Sumner from the CDC in Atlanta. Their plan was to debrief Monique here in Washington before getting her to a yet-undisclosed lab that was already working on the Raison Strain. She'd managed only an hour of dreamless sleep over the Atlantic, and her weariness was beginning to play with her mind—not a good thing, considering the task ahead of her.

The deputy secretary snapped his phone closed. "You sure you're okay?" he asked yet again.

"I'm tired. But otherwise I'm fine. Unless of course you're referring to the Raison Strain, in which case I'm sure that I'm dying like the rest of you."

"That's not what I meant."

She looked over his shoulder at a boy riding a blue bicycle with a fake engine down the sidewalk. His hands were free, and he was holding a soft drink.

"I still can't believe that no one knows."

"It'll break soon enough. Hopefully we'll have some good news to go along with the bad."

"My good news," she said.

"Your good news."

"Then let's hope probability is on our side."

"Where would you put the probability?"

She shrugged. "Sixty percent?"

He frowned, then flipped open his phone and placed another call, this one to someone who was evidently working on a report that Russia's leadership was fracturing.

Monique closed her eyes and let her mind slip back to Thomas. She'd asked about him the moment her feet hit the tarmac, but Gains only knew what she'd told him. No new word. They assumed he was dead.

As did she. The water no longer healed as it had in the hotel room in Bangkok. And even if there was a way to heal Thomas in the forest, he might not be healed here as he had been three times before.

Astounding that she was even thinking like this. She'd lived in Rachelle's skin for less than a day, and only in her dreams, but the experience had been so real that she couldn't deny the existence of Thomas's reality. She'd spent the last ten hours contemplating this strange phenomenon, and with each passing hour her conviction that Rachelle and Justin really did exist strengthened.

Which meant that Thomas had indeed been healed by Elyon's water after being shot on the hotel bed in Bangkok. That time he'd been in the vicinity of water, which healed him immediately, perhaps before he'd actually died. When Carlos had shot him in the head after his first rescue attempt, he'd actually been in the lake, and his healing had been instantaneous. He probably hadn't died either time.

But this time, he had really died. She'd watched Carlos check his pulse. There was no way the killer would have left him without being completely satisfied that he was dead. That meant Thomas would have died in the desert as well. Maybe the Horde had double-crossed him and killed him. Or maybe he'd just died. Even if Justin brought him back to life, there was no guarantee that he would come back to life here.

He was dead. He was really dead this time.

Monique swallowed a lump in her throat. If so, then she would make it well known that he had saved them all. Assuming her antivirus worked. Either way, he had saved her. Carlos would have killed her sooner or later. If not him, then the virus would have.

For that matter, it still might.

"There's something you should know," she said. "The man behind Svensson is the director of foreign affairs, Armand Fortier."

"You know that for a fact?" he asked, surprised. "We'd speculated, but I'm not sure we've confirmed anything."

"Thomas and I met with him. I'm also quite sure that he has someone on the inside over here. Someone who has access to your president."

She might as well have dropped a bomb. He just stared at her. It occurred to her that Fortier's mule could be this very man. She could be telling the wrong man the wrong things and never know the better of it.

"I could be mistaken," she said. "But he seemed to make that claim."

Merton Gains broke off his stare. "Dear God, what next?"

Mike Orear slipped into his chair behind the set of the show he co-anchored with Nancy Rodriguez and fixed his earpiece. Behind him large black letters spelled out the show's name, *What Matters*.

"Ready in five. You right?" Nancy asked.

"As rain."

He'd been in front of the camera too many times to count in his relatively short career, but never had he been so anxious to spill the beans. He'd delayed because of the State Department's adamant demand that he keep his mouth shut. It was non-news, they'd said. But none of that mattered any longer.

What did matter was that he'd awakened this morning with a rash under his arms and on his thighs, and although he succeeded in persuading himself that it had nothing to do with the Raison Strain, the rash reminded him just how real this non-news of his was.

This non-news that the world was dying of the Raison Strain without knowing it.

Windows peered into the studio from a second story above and behind the cameras. The show was directed by Marcy Rawlins, who was reviewing last-minute details with Joe Spencer behind the glass. Any breaking news or changes would come over their earpieces from that room.

"You okay?" Nancy asked.

"I'm fine. Let's roll."

"You look pale."

"I want to change things up a little. Lead with something off the schedule."

"Marcy clear this?"

"No. Trust me, she won't have to."

Nancy arched her brow. "Your skin, not mine."

"No, Nancy, you're wrong. It's your skin too. You'll see."

"What the heck is that—"

"Ten seconds." The program director's voice in their earpieces.

"What's that supposed to mean?" she repeated.

"You'll see."

"Three . . . two . . . one . . ." She gave the on-air signal.

Nancy was already smiling and opening the show. She ran down today's show highlights, none of which Mike heard. His mind was elsewhere.

There was a good reason he hadn't put the story through the normal news channels. Even breaking-news channels, for that matter. Fact was, Marcy probably would have jumped all over it, assuming she believed his sources at all.

But news of this kind would have to be cleared with the brass. Some of them would say that if true, any story of this magnitude should be broken by the president himself or, at the very least, someone with more seniority than Orear. They would hold it while they got up to speed. Might even spike it.

Mike wasn't going to take that chance. A week had passed, and signs that something very significant was in the air were everywhere, and none of his peers seemed to notice. If they did, they sure weren't connecting the dots.

Maybe he intended to do a bit of grandstanding, but not much. How could anyone accuse a condemned man of grandstanding, for heaven's sake? He was dying. They were all dying. That was news and that was that. Time to let the cat out of—

" . . . Mike."

Nancy was giving him that look of nonchalance that some of the best anchors had mastered. *I am a very significant force in the world of news, and the fact that I don't look like I'm swimming in it makes me even more important.*

He looked up into the camera. Wrong one. The one to their left, with the red light on.

"Ladies and gentlemen, I hope you're sitting down. The news I'm about to deliver is of the gravest kind."

He'd thought through his little speech a hundred times, but now it sounded trite and stupid. Delivering his bomb as if it were news lessened its importance. And yet it was that: news.

"Mike, what are you doing?" Marcy's voice in his ear.

He reached up and pulled out his earpiece.

"I . . . I'm not sure how to deliver this. It's not the kind of news any reporter knows how to report." From the corner of his eye he saw that Marcy had a phone to her ear. She slammed it down. The State Department had called? Or the attorney general. That was fast. One of their agents was undoubtedly watching his show.

He had to do this before the program director could pull the plug.

"CNN has learned that a new virus for which there is no known cure, which was previously thought to be isolated on a small island south of Java in the Indonesian islands, has spread far more widely than initially believed, perhaps to most of the world in fact. We have confirmed that the Raison Strain is widespread in the United States and has infected . . ."

So trite. So understated. So impossible to put into words.

" . . . most of us. If this report is correct, and we have it on very good sources that it is, the world is facing a very, very grave crisis."

Impossible or not, all of it had gone out live.

"This has come to us from the highest possible sources. It seems that our government has known for over a week and is making every possible effort to find a vaccine or an antivirus that would counter—"

The red light went off. He'd been pulled off the air.

Mike jerked his head to view the monitor that showed what viewers at home saw, which was at this moment a Lexus ad. The dozen or so technicians in the studio had frozen.

The door to the studio flew open and Marcy stood in the frame, white-faced.

"What was that?"

Mike stood.

"Was that . . ." Nancy pushed back her chair. "Where did you get that?"

"That was the truth, Marcy," he said. "And thank you for cutting to the Lexus ad. It drove the story home for our viewers. Kinda has the feel of the Gestapo jerking the plug, doesn't it?"

"I just got a call from the attorney general," Marcy snapped. "They're watching this. You're going to incite—"

"Of course they're watching this!" Mike yelled. "They're watching because they know that it's true and they know I've got the whole story. Get us backup, Marcy. Call whoever you have to; just get me backup."

"I can't do that! You can't just go on the air and tell the world that they're all about to die! Have you lost your mind?"

He walked straight toward her. "Fine. But if I walk out of this building, I go straight to Fox. Tell them that. You have about thirty seconds to make up your minds. Either way, the full story breaks today."

"Don't you dare threaten me! You're going back on the air, and you're going to tell them that you had no business saying what you did."

Her voice echoed through the room. She still didn't believe him, did she? She was either suffering a terminal case of denial or had lost her compass in the shock of hearing about the virus.

"You tell them, Marcy," he said quietly. A dozen sets of eyes stared at him. The Lexus advertisement had yielded to a Mountain Dew commercial.

The door behind Marcy burst open. "Who's manning the hotline?" This was Wally, the news director. His eyes took in Marcy, then moved to Mike standing on the main floor by the cameras instead of seated in his seat beside Nancy. "What in the blazes is going on down here?"

"You get back in that seat," Marcy said icily.

"I need a news break. Now! NBC is reporting that the French government has just declared martial law," Wally said. "We've confirmed it."

"Martial law?" Mike said. "Why?"

"To control the threat of a virus they claim has affected France."

"The Raison Strain?"

Wally obviously hadn't been watching Mike's little speech.

"How did you know that?"

28

MARTYN, COMMANDER of the Horde army under Qurong, stood beside his leader, facing Ciphus and the rest of the forest Council. Qurong was working his betrayal exactly as he'd planned so many months ago.

Thousands of the villagers had gathered in the amphitheater on short notice. The news that a thousand Scab warriors had entered the village from the backside with Justin had spread quickly. Now they filled the bleachers and peered down in silence to the proceedings on the ground beneath them.

Ciphus stood on the stage near the center, facing Qurong. Mikil and Justin were there on the left with a thousand of the Forest Guard to match his own warriors on the right. The fate of the world was riding on this play of Qurong's. So far everything had progressed precisely as he had anticipated. By morning, the forests would be theirs.

"Hear me, great Ciphus," Qurong said. "I have put my life in your hands to meet with you. Surely you will consider my proposal for a truce until we can work out a lasting peace between us."

This wasn't going as Ciphus had anticipated; that much was clear. Mikil had told the Council that Martyn would give up Qurong, but she'd been wrong.

The Council leader shifted his eyes to Martyn, perhaps expecting, wanting, the commander to step in as Thomas had proposed.

Ciphus cleared his throat. "Of course, we are always willing to listen. But you must realize that we have no basis for peace. You live in violation of Elyon's laws. The penalty for disobeying Elyon is death. Now you want us to deny Elyon his own law by making peace with the Horde? You deserve death, not peace."

This was the classic doctrine of the Forest People. Ciphus was opening the door for Martyn to spring his trap, to offer Qurong's life in exchange for peace. *Not so fast, you old goat.*

"How many of us will you kill to satisfy your God?" Qurong demanded.

"You live in death already!" Ciphus cried. "You would have us make an alliance with death? You have the whole desert; we have but seven small forests. I should ask you, why do you wage war against a small peaceful people?"

Qurong glanced at Martyn. They made no overt signal, but the message was clear. The supreme leader was going to proceed as planned.

"It is because we have no basis for trust between our people that we can't extend true peace," Qurong said. "You won't elevate us above dogs, and we see you for the snakes you really are."

A rumble hurried through the crowd. Ciphus held up a hand.

"You are right; we don't trust you. A dog will see a golden rod and think it has seen a snake. Your eyes are blinded by your rebellion against Elyon."

Qurong smiled, but he didn't take the bait to defend himself.

"Then I will offer you more than the words of a dog today," Qurong said. "I will show you and your people on this day that I am an honorable leader in my own way. If I do so, will you consider a truce between our people?"

Martyn studied the elder. *Come on, you wheezing old bat. You can only accept. I know you.*

Ciphus frowned and finally spoke quietly. "We would consider it."

"Then hear me, all of you," Qurong said. "I have two armies camped outside of your forest at this moment. The two hundred thousand warriors to the east you know of well enough. What you don't know is that we have a second army, twice as large, camped in the western desert."

This news was received by total silence. Perhaps they thought their Guard could deal with both armies. They were wrong for reasons beyond their understanding. In twenty-four hours, their Guard would be defeated.

"I am willing to commit my armies to a campaign that will destroy much of your forest and most of your warriors," Qurong said. "But my victory would not be certain unless I had an element of complete surprise. We both know this."

Here it was, then. Sweat stung Martyn's cracked skin, but he hardly noticed it.

"As a sign of goodwill, I will now show my hand in the hopes of winning your faith. We came here today with betrayal on our minds. We planned to offer you peace, and when you accepted that peace—when your Guard was compromised—we planned to bring the full force of our armies against you in one massive campaign."

The silence deepened, and Martyn was quite sure it was from shock now.

"But I will hold back for the sake of a peace accord!" shouted Qurong. "I have already told you about my army to the west. I have just now revealed my intentions and robbed myself of any victory. I see that peace is more valuable than victory."

Ciphus glanced at Martyn. He hadn't expected quite this. Mikil wasn't prepared for this either. She had the look of a dumb goat.

"Then what do you propose?" Ciphus demanded. "That we offer you peace because you have confessed your intent to ruin us? We are to believe that you've experienced some kind of wholesale conversion since entering our village? A man does not change so quickly. There can be no peace without the appropriate payment. You can't make peace with Elyon while living in your disease!"

"No. I realize that your laws have to be satisfied in order for there to be peace. As do our laws. I propose to meet the requirements of those laws."

"By confessing? It's not enough."

"By the death of the man who would lead us to war. I am not the one who concocted this scheme."

"Then who?"

"It was him." Qurong pointed his finger toward the Forest Guard. Toward Justin.

"Justin."

Confusion swept through the crowd.

"It was Justin who claimed our victory would be complete by offering peace!"

Justin looked at Martyn, expressionless. The people were yelling in such chaos that it was impossible to tell their reaction to this news. Ciphus shouted his silence at the crowd, and slowly they quieted enough for his voice to be heard.

"How dare you accuse one of our own in order to save yourself?" Ciphus said, voice shaking. Martyn wondered if he'd misjudged the man. Surely this emotion was for show.

The elder took a breath and continued, voice lower. "If what you say is true, then yes, we would consider your argument. But what corroboration is there that Justin planned any of this? You take us for fools?"

"I can corroborate!" Thomas's second yelled, stepping forward from the ranks of the Guard. Mikil. "And I can do so with Thomas of Hunter's authority. He is in the Horde camp now, guaranteeing the commander's safety with his own life so that Qurong can expose the truth of this betrayal. Justin is complicit in the plot against the Forest People!"

"What more could show my true intent?" Qurong said. "I give you your traitor and I consign myself to peace."

Ciphus crossed his arms into the sleeves of his robe and paced. "Intent? And what do intentions have to do with peace?"

"Then I will satisfy your own law. I will give you a death at my own expense."

Ciphus stopped his pacing.

"Death to the traitor!" a lone voice cried from the bleachers.

Dissension and argument exploded. But were they for or against Justin? Martyn couldn't tell.

"Your laws require death for defilement of Elyon's love," Qurong shouted. "If treason is not defilement, then what is? Furthermore, he has also waged war against the Desert Dwellers. Our law also requires his death. His death will satisfy both of our laws."

Ciphus seemed to be deep in thought, as if he hadn't considered this thought. He faced Justin.

"Step out."

Justin walked three paces and stopped.

"What do you say to this charge?"

A woman cried over the crowd. "Justin! No, Justin!"

A dozen voices joined. If Martyn wasn't mistaken, children's voices were mixed in. The sound was oddly unnerving.

"Silence!" Ciphus shouted.

They quieted.

"What do you say to these charges?" the elder demanded again.

"I say that I have fulfilled your laws, and I have bathed in the lakes, and I have loved all that Elyon loves."

"Have you conspired to betray the people of Elyon?"

Justin remained silent.

Justin hadn't conspired, but it wouldn't have mattered either way. Hearing the silence, Martyn knew they would win this war. In a day's time, he would defeat these Forest People without lifting a sword.

If they only knew.

It had been Justin's idea for Johan to enter the desert as Thomas had guessed. But now the culmination of their planning would end very differently than even Justin knew.

"Answer me!"

Justin spoke in a low voice—too quiet to be heard past the floor. "Have you become so blind, Ciphus, that you can't remember me?"

"What?"

"Has it been so long since we swam together?"

Ciphus had frozen like a tree. He was actually shaking. "Don't try your deceitful words on me. You're forgetting that I am the elder of Elyon's Council."

"Then you should know the answer to your question."

"Answer me or I'll condemn you myself! You lost the challenge yesterday, except for Thomas's failure to finish you. Perhaps this is the justice of Elyon now. What say you?"

The amphitheater had grown so quiet that Martyn thought he could hear Ciphus breathing. Justin looked up at the people. Martyn thought he was going to say something, but he remained silent. His eyes met Martyn's. The deep green eyes struck terror into his heart.

Justin lowered his head. If Martyn wasn't mistaken, the man was struggling to keep his desperation in check. What kind of warrior could cry before his accusers? When Justin lifted his head, his eyes swam in tears. But he held his head steady.

"Then condemn me," Justin said softly.

"And you realize that condemnation will mean death." The elder's voice was unsteady.

Justin didn't answer. He wouldn't walk the path that Ciphus set before him, but it was close enough. Ciphus lifted both fists and glared at the man below him.

"Answer me when I speak to you in this holy gathering!" the elder shouted. "Why do you insult the man whom Elyon has made your superior?"

Justin looked at the man but refused to speak.

Ciphus lifted both fists above his head. "Then for treason against the laws of Elyon and his people, I condemn you to death at the hands of your enemies!"

Wails cut the air. Shouts of approval. Cries of outrage. It all blended into a cacophony of confusion that Martyn knew would amount to nothing. There was no prevailing voice. No one would defy the sentence of the Council.

"Take him!" Ciphus shouted at Qurong.

"I will accept him on one condition," Qurong said. "He will die according to our laws. By the drowning. We will give him back to your God. Back to Elyon, in your lake."

Ciphus hadn't expected this. If he refused, Martyn had the appropriate contingency plans. The elder conferred with his Council, then turned to give his verdict.

"Agreed. Our Gathering ends tonight. You may deal with him then."

"No, it should be now, with your cooperation. Let his death be a seal for a truce between our armies. His blood will be on both of our hands."

Another short conference.

"Then let our peace be sealed with his blood," Ciphus said.

Thomas and Rachelle came into sight of the village at sunset, winded and worn due to lack of sleep. The ride had been filled with long stretches of silence as the two retreated into their own thoughts. There was little to say after they'd exhausted the telling and retelling of Justin's healing touch and his words. *I have too much riding on you. Remember me.* They were the same as the boy's words.

They heard the first sign of trouble when they passed the gates, the unmistakable wail of mourning for the dead.

"Thomas? What is that?"

He urged his horse into a trot, past the main gate. The women were mourning a death. There had been a skirmish, and some of his Guard had been killed. Or there was news of a battle on the western perimeter. Or this was about Justin.

The sky was already dark gray, but the glow of torches cast an orange hue over the lake at the end of the main road. Lawns and doorways were vacant of the loitering so typical on crowded Gathering evenings. There was a man here and a woman there, but they avoided Thomas's eyes and shuffled with distraction.

A sudden cry of horrible agony echoed distant. Thomas's heart rose into his throat.

"Thomas!" Rachelle sounded frantic. She slapped her horse and galloped past him, straight for the lake.

"Rachelle!" He wasn't sure why he called her name. He kicked his horse, and together they thundered down the wide stone causeway that split the village in two.

They saw the crowd before they reached the end of the street. A sea of people stood on the shore with their backs to the village, staring toward the lake.

"You have to stop them!" Rachelle cried. "It's him!"

"Can you see him?"

They both brought their horses to a rearing halt where the road gave way to the beach. She stared over heads, her eyes wide and her face wrinkled with anguish.

Then Thomas saw what she was looking at. A square wooden tower had been erected to their left, by the shore. Beside the tower, a ring of Horde encircled two Scabs. The Council stood on one side; Qurong and Martyn stood on the other. In the center was a post, and on that post hung a man.

Justin.

One of the Scab's arms went back, then swung forward and struck Justin's ribs. *Crack!* One of his ribs broke with the blow. Justin jerked and sagged against the post.

"Stop!" Rachelle's scream ripped through the air. "Stop!" She grunted with a sob, clenched her jaw, and drove her horse into the crowd.

Villagers unprepared for a stamping, barging steed cried out and scrambled back to make way for the large Scab stallion.

"Back! Out of the way," Thomas yelled. He followed her in.

The Scab hit Justin again, unfazed by the commotion.

"Stop!" Rachelle cried.

The people separated in front of them like falling dominoes. Then they were through. Mikil and Jamous stood with several dozen of the Guard. Another thousand milled on the north side of the lake. The Horde army waited down the shore on the south side. Women and children cried softly, an eerie tone. On the post, Justin's near naked body had stilled.

They hadn't drawn blood. He'd heard of this method of torture employed by the Horde—methodically breaking the bones of a victim without draining any of his life—his blood. They wanted the drowning and the drowning alone to take the man. One look at Justin's swollen body made it clear they'd perfected their torture.

Thomas dropped to the sand and rushed forward. "What's this? Who authorized this?"

"You did," Mikil said.

Rachelle sobbed and ran for Justin. She fell on her knees, gripped his ankles, and bowed so that her hair touched his lumpy, broken feet.

"Get her off of him!" Ciphus ordered.

Rachelle spun back and pleaded. "Thomas!"

Two of the Guard leaped forward and dragged her back.

She struggled against them furiously. "It's him! It's him, can't you see? It's Elyon!"

"Don't be a fool!" Ciphus snapped. "Keep her back."

Thomas couldn't pull his eyes from Justin's brutalized body. They'd pulled his arms above his head and strapped them to the top of the post. His face was swollen. Cheekbones broken beneath the skin. His eyes were closed and his head hung limp. How long had they been beating him? It was hard to imagine that he was the boy, grown now into a man, but with a little imagination, Thomas thought he could see the resemblance.

He faced Mikil. "Release him."

She made no move.

"That's an order. This man isn't who you think. I want him released immediately!"

Mikil blinked. "I thought—"

"She can't release him," Ciphus said softly. "To do so would defy the order of the Council and Elyon himself."

"You're *killing* Elyon!" Rachelle cried.

"That's absurd. Can Elyon die?"

"Justin, please, I beg you! Please, wake up. Tell them!"

"Shut her up!" Ciphus said. "Gag her!"

Jamous pulled out a strap of leather to gag her, but he glanced up at Thomas and stopped. What had gotten into them all? Jamous would actually consider binding his commander's wife?

"Gag her!"

The lieutenant slipped the leather thong around her mouth and muffled a scream. "Thoma . . . mm! Hmmmm!"

On the post, Justin moaned.

Thomas broke from the shock that had frozen him, jerked out his sword, and leaped for his wife.

Mikil stepped forward, hand raised. "No, Thomas. You can't defy the Council."

But Thomas hardly heard her. "Let her go! Have you all gone mad?"

She moved into his path to block him. "Please—"

He swung his elbow and struck her jaw. She landed on her seat with a *thump*. Thomas thrust his sword at Jamous's neck. "Untie my wife!"

"Don't be a fool, Thomas." Mikil spoke in a hurried, hushed tone, ignoring her reddening cheek. "The verdict has been cast. The fate of our people depends on this exchange."

With those words, Thomas knew what had happened. Johan had double-crossed not only Justin, but him as well. Qurong had exchanged a promise of peace for the life of Justin, and the Council had accepted. Justin's death would satisfy the law requiring death for treason against Elyon and allow a peace to be brokered even without requiring the Horde to bathe.

"It will never work," Thomas said. "The peace won't last! You think you can trust these Scabs to keep peace? Qurong is Tanis! He's blinded by Teeleh, and he's found a way to kill Elyon!"

"*You* trusted us," Martyn said.

Thomas held the point of his sword against Jamous's neck. He knew by Martyn's tone that the people didn't know about Thomas and Martyn's agreement to betray Qurong.

"Did you hear me?" Thomas cried to the people. "Qurong is Tanis! This is Teeleh's work, this murder. Open your eyes!"

No one responded. They were deaf and dumb, all of them!

"Please, Thomas," Mikil pleaded quietly. "There's no way to undo this."

Rachelle's eyes were wide and screaming at him. *Free me! Don't let them do this! He's Elyon!*

But Thomas knew that if he killed Jamous and freed his wife, he would be forced to defend both of them against the Guard, whose allegiance to Elyon, and by association to the Council, superseded their allegiance to him. If the Council had cast their verdict, there was no way to undo the verdict without killing the lot of them.

Thomas spun around and strode for Justin's sagging body. He couldn't risk Rachelle's life, but neither could he stand by and let them work their treachery.

Is this really Elyon, Thomas? This swollen man who once served under you and dishonored you by refusing the position Mikil now holds? Elyon?

Rachelle had said so. He would die by her words.

"Stop him," Ciphus said.

This time a dozen of his Guard stepped forward. His first impulse was to fight, and he instinctively braced for them.

"If you kill one of them in the service of defending the Council's orders, then you and your wife will die with Justin," Ciphus said.

They had lost their minds over this killing! His eyes ran along the line of villagers who stood behind the Council and Guard. There was a small girl there, staring around her mother, tears running down her cheeks. He recognized her from the Valley of Tuhan. It was Lucy, the one whom Justin had singled out and danced with. The girl's mother was doing her best to keep her own sobs quiet.

"What has happened here?" he shouted.

"Finish your business," Ciphus told Qurong.

There was a light of defiance in the Horde leader's eyes. He nodded and his men leaned in to continue the beating.

Thomas tossed down his sword. "At least give me the courtesy of speaking to the general," he said. "As one warrior to another. My business is still to defend my people, and I demand a council with Martyn."

Martyn looked at Qurong, who dipped his head.

Thomas turned back to Mikil and indicated Rachelle. "One scratch on her and it will be your neck." He faced the crowd. "What's wrong with you? This is the kind of celebration you choose to end your Gathering?" Only a few seemed to hear.

Thomas gave Ciphus a parting glare, walked past Martyn, and headed toward the water's edge, away from the execution.

Martyn walked to him. Behind them another bone cracked. Thomas held his jaw firm and looked over the lake water, clear and dark in the early night. The orange flames from a hundred torches shone on the glassy surface.

"This wasn't what we agreed to." His voice was shaky, far too emotional for a warrior of his stature, but he was having difficulty even breathing past the lump in his throat, much less speaking with authority.

"It was beyond my control," Martyn said. "I didn't know that the supreme leader would offer Justin's life in exchange for peace. It wasn't our plan."

"You betray everyone except Tanis?"

Martyn didn't bother responding. *Justin had passed out,* Thomas thought. Hoped. The only sound behind them was the thudding of fists and the snapping of bones. He felt nauseated and frantic, and he spoke quickly.

"I beg you, Johan, listen to me. Your men shot a woman last night. Did you hear about it?"

"I heard something, yes."

"The woman was Rachelle. Your sister. You may not remember why you should have any allegiance to your own blood, but surely you remember simple facts. She was your *sister.*"

"And?"

"And Justin found her, barely alive, with four arrows in her. He healed her. There's not a scratch on her. He told Rachelle that he has a lot riding on us. These were the same words he spoke to us fifteen years ago. Do you remember? Or has Teeleh completely consumed your mind? How could Justin have known what the boy told us? Unless he *is* the boy. You're about to kill the same boy who led us to this lake fifteen years ago, when you yourself were still a boy!"

"Even if you are right, why should I care?"

"Because he *made* you, you . . . That is your *Maker* back there!"

Martyn stared out at the lake. Thomas prayed he would come to his senses, and for a moment he began to hope that the deep sentiments of Johan's youth were rising to the surface.

Something had changed behind them. The beating had stopped.

"If that's my Maker back there," Martyn said, "then he would have made me to live with less pain."

"Your pain is your choice, not his! If you would bathe, your pain would be gone."

Martyn spit on the water. "I would rather die than bathe in this cursed lake."

He turned and walked up the shore to the execution.

Thomas could no longer contain the emotion pent up in his chest. He stared out over the lake and let tears spill down his cheeks. If he turned around, the people would see, and he wasn't sure he wanted that. But it was his Creator they were executing.

There was a pause behind him. He swallowed hard. How could it have come to this? Maybe Justin wasn't Elyon. Had Elyon persuaded Johan to enter the desert? How could Elyon's body break? Or worse, die? Elyon would never allow this!

Thomas turned around. The Scabs had strapped a rope around Justin's ankles and were preparing to hang him upside down from the platform. He averted his eyes and walked up the bank, ignoring the Scabs and Council members who watched him. He had to find Marie and Samuel! But as soon as he thought it, he saw them, kneeling beside their mother.

Rachelle lay on her face behind a row of the Guard, weeping. Thomas slipped his arms under her body and lifted her up. "Come with me," he said to his children.

They walked away from the crowd without another word.

⌘

It was their custom to honor the dead by facing rather than turning from their bodies at the funeral pyres. To hide one's eyes because looking at the death was painful insulted the one actually facing that death.

Thomas helped a sagging, despondent Rachelle to the closest gazebo.

Marie and Samuel had both been crying, and now Marie spoke for the first time. "Why aren't we honoring him, Papa?"

He couldn't answer her.

"Put me down," Rachelle said.

She took her children by their shoulders. "We are, Marie. We will honor him."

They hurried up the steps and gazed out over the crowd to the scene below. Thomas stepped up beside them and Rachelle gripped his arm.

They watched the proceedings in stunned silence. The pummeling of Justin's body continued. How they managed to break so many bones was beyond him.

Rachelle's fingers dug into Thomas's elbow each time they struck Justin. But she knew as well as he did that there was nothing they could do for him now.

Surely Ciphus hadn't expected this kind of brutality. The Scabs were defiling the forest with their presence. Their smell drifted over the village like a fog. Those not directly involved let their attention wander and on occasion laughed.

Many of the Forest People watched in stunned silence. Many wept quietly. Many sobbed openly.

They stopped beating him and hauled him up by his feet, so that his head hung five or six feet above the ground. Thomas watched as a Scab walked up, squeezed Justin's broken face, and then pushed him. His body swung like a deer carcass in a smoking shack. His arms hung limp, as if he were surrendering upside down.

Rachelle grunted. "Can't you make them stop? If they have to kill him . . ." She couldn't finish.

It didn't matter. He knew what she was going to say. *If they have to kill him, can't they be forced to do it quickly?* But neither of them could even say such a thing.

"It's their way," Thomas said. "They don't understand suffering like we do. They live with it every day."

"It's not *their* way," she said. "It's the way of Teeleh."

Ciphus held up his hand and walked out to the body. He walked around it, then faced the crowd.

"I know there are those among you who still think that here hangs a prophet." His voice rang over the lake. "Let me ask you, would Elyon allow his prophet to suffer like this? You see, he is flesh and blood like the rest of us. Anyone who dares say that this mess of flesh is actually Elyon has lost his sense. Our Creator could never become so uncreated! He would never let a Scab abuse him, any more than he would let Teeleh abuse him. You see?"

He faced the Horde soldiers. "Hit him."

One of the Scabs stepped forward and hammered Justin's back. No one present could mistake the loud crack.

Ciphus cleared his throat. "You see, just a man."

His words invited a fresh round of abuse from the other Horde guards. Three of them stepped forward and began slugging the body, laughing. Ciphus stepped back, surprised. In his eagerness to deflate Justin, he'd unexpectedly opened this door.

"Thomas," Rachelle pleaded.

It was all he could stand. "Wait here."

He jumped from the gazebo and ran straight for Ciphus. A murmur spread through the section of the crowd that saw him. The elder turned his head before Thomas reached the inner circle.

"Enough! To execute a man is one thing. If you insist on satisfying your blood lust, then do it quickly! But don't humiliate the man who saved the Southern Forest and the Forest Guard just a week ago. Kill him if you must, but don't mock his life."

A thousand voices rose in agreement.

Ciphus seemed relieved. He frowned at Qurong. "It makes sense. Finish this."

"The agreement was to kill him our way. Our way is to take a man's spirit be—"

"You have taken his spirit!" Thomas yelled. "Now you're taking the spirit of the people he served. Finish this!"

Qurong regarded him, then nodded at his men.

One of them grabbed a bucket of water they'd drawn from the lake earlier and splashed it in Justin's face. Justin gasped.

Thomas couldn't tell if Justin had opened his eyes, because the battered man faced the other way. But he did see something else that struck him as odd. Justin's skin was starting to gray. How long had it been since his last bathing? As with all who'd trained with the Guard, he probably bathed every morning as was required. Justin had been in the desert, restricted to canteen water, but there hadn't been a trace of the disease on him this morning.

"Drown him," Qurong said.

Two of the Scabs hastily strapped a large stone on Justin's body so that it would sink. A dozen others who had bound their legs with treated leather to protect them from the water stepped cautiously forward, staring at the lake.

"Drown him!" Martyn shouted in a sudden fit of rage.

They grabbed the tower's hastily constructed supports and began to drag the platform down the shore, to the lake.

Justin's body turned, and now Thomas saw his eyes. The left was swollen shut; the right was barely cracked. Justin's sight met his own and stopped. For a long time Justin looked at him. Even past the swollen flesh there was no fear in his face, no regret, no accusation. Only sorrow.

Was he staring into Elyon's eyes? The thought struck a chord of terror deep in Thomas's mind. This was the boy he'd met on top of the cliffs so long ago, the boy who could sing new worlds into existence. Who could turn the planet inside out, or split the globe in two for a day of play. Who could fill a lake that never ended with water so powerful that a single drop could undo any man or woman.

A tremor ran through Thomas's bones. He'd dived into Elyon's water, breathed it deep, screamed with its pleasure and with its pain. This man who hung by his feet as they hauled the device into the lake was Elyon?

Thomas's chest swelled with grief. Tears were filling his eyes, and he didn't know how to stop them. A lone child began to sob quietly behind him, and he turned. Lucy. She stood alone on the sand, crying.

Thomas impulsively stepped back, dropped to one knee, and drew her in. Neither spoke. He faced the water.

The Horde had pushed the tower ten feet off the shore, cursing bitterly as the water soaked past their leg coverings and ate at their cracked skin. The water was about four feet deep here, and Justin's hands were submerged just past his wrists. He'd closed his eyes again, but his breathing was steady. He was awake.

All except for two of the Scabs hurried out of the water. Their hands were pink where they'd touched the water, and they wiped at them madly, trying to rub them free of the poison that had discolored them. They tore the leather from their legs and beat their flesh to alleviate the pain. Above the waist, their skin was still gray.

The two who'd stayed in the lake climbed up the tower, gripped the rope with both hands, and looked at Qurong.

A small voice, barely more than a whisper, came from Justin. His mouth had opened and he was speaking!

"Remember . . ."

Thomas stopped breathing to hear. What had he said?

"Remember me," Justin said, louder this time, voice choking with emotion now. "Remember me!"

They all heard it and stood frozen.

Justin cried it out again in a terrible groan that echoed over the lake and cut straight to Thomas's heart.

"Remember me, Johan!"

Johan?

Thomas looked to his left. Martyn stood stock still, face hidden by his hood, arms folded. Qurong glanced at his general, then quickly motioned his men to commence the drowning.

Justin was sobbing now. His tears fell into the water below his head. He began to groan loudly. Then he began to scream.

What was it? Why now?

Lucy wailed in his arms, and Thomas drew her in tight, as much for his own comfort as hers. He was sure that his heart had stopped. He couldn't bear to watch this! He couldn't stand by and see any man in such a horrible state of torment.

But he couldn't dishonor the man by turning his head away.

Still Justin screamed, long terrible shrieks that cut the night like a razor. Thomas gritted his teeth and begged the sound to stop.

He noticed the change in Justin's skin just before his head touched the water. The flesh on his chest and legs was now nearly white. It was flaking.

The disease was overtaking Justin before Thomas's very eyes!

This was the source of his groans. The pain . . .

The skin on his chest suddenly began to crack like a dried lake bed.

Someone began to yell behind him. "He has the disease!" But the cry was lost in a long scream of agony from Justin.

Thomas settled to his haunches and began to weep uncontrollably.

Justin's head went under. Bubbles boiled from his mouth. His body jerked and heaved. *He's not holding his breath,* Thomas thought. He was trying to pull the water up into his lungs, but it was difficult, hanging upside down.

Just as the water seemed to take its final, terrible toll on him, the two Scabs jerked him out of the lake. Water poured from his lungs. He gasped and sputtered.

Thomas stood to his feet, horrified by their extended torture.

They lowered him again. Again, Justin's body jerked uncontrollably. Again, the water about his head boiled. Again, his diseased chest pumped deep, drawing, convulsing, spasming in rejection.

Again they pulled him from the water before he could drown.

Thomas tore for the water. "Kill him!" he screamed.

You are demanding the death of Elyon.

"Kill—"

A fist from one of the Scabs landed on his temple before he even knew the man was there. He dropped to the sand and struggled to push himself up.

"Finish it!" Ciphus said. "For the sake of Elyon, just finish this!"

"Our custom is to—"

"I don't care what your custom is! Just kill him!"

A Scab on Thomas's left suddenly rushed at the water. The general Martyn. Johan. He had a sword in his hand.

Thomas caught his breath. Something was wrong with this.

Not until Johan's feet splashed water did Thomas note the leathers on his legs. Johan's hood fell off his head, baring a face twisted in rage for all to see. He bore down on Justin, roaring with fury now.

"Die! Die!"

Before any of them knew his full intent, Johan thrust his sword into Justin's belly, jerked it to one side, and pulled it back out. Blood gushed from the gaping wound and splashed into the water.

"Drown him!" Johan screamed.

The two Scabs on top of the platform dropped the body. Justin hung suspended in the water, body jerking.

Martyn swung around, marched out of the lake, tossed his sword to one side, and pulled his hood back over his head. He walked past Qurong toward the Horde army.

Justin's body stopped jerking.

His skin was cracked and white, unrecognizable as human flesh. But it was the blood that Thomas stared at. Blood spilled for cleansing was permitted. When he'd returned from the desert nearly a Scab himself, he'd been permitted to bathe, even though he was bleeding from several of the cracks in his skin.

But this . . .

Did Ciphus realize that this might be different?

The soldiers reached down and cut the cord. Justin's body slipped into the water with a small splash and sank with the weight of the two large stones strapped to his wrists.

Bubbles rose to the surface. They watched in silence as the water slowly became glassy once again. It was finished. The lake had swallowed the brutality whole, leaving no sign except for a slick of spilled blood.

Thomas looked back at Ciphus. The elder's face was white, fixated on the water.

29

MIKE OREAR adjusted his collar mike and glanced into the camera. He'd never imagined becoming the voice of the Raison Strain, but his gall in breaking the story had somehow caught a wave of appreciation with the viewers. CNN's ratings had shot past Fox News's for the first time in years. The brass extended his airtime to six hours a day, three in the morning, three in the evening. It was the assignment of a lifetime, he knew.

A very short lifetime.

Now, with the news widely known, and after an endless parade of guests—geneticists and virologists and psychologists and the like—the threat he'd made known had come to haunt him in a very, very real way. Before, he had been as consumed with breaking the story as with what the virus meant to him personally. Now, along with the rest of America, he couldn't shake the dread knowledge that he was about to die.

That knowledge changed everything. He wanted to be home with his mother and father. He wanted to go to church. He wanted to be married and have children. He wanted to cry.

Instead, he decided to serve humanity in what way he could, which meant bringing knowledge and comfort and perhaps, just perhaps, aiding the incredible effort underway to beat this virus.

The news of the arms shipments hadn't hit the fan yet. A plea from the Pentagon and the president himself had delayed the announcement for the time being. Their argument was simple and cogent: Let the public adjust to the news of the virus for a few days, then let the president tell them the rest of the story. It had been three days. The president was scheduled to give two major addresses today: the first to the United Nations in New York and the second to the nation at six Eastern tonight. The latter address would tell America the whole story.

A clip of Nancy's interview with a social psychologist from UCLA was on its last leg. Mike scanned his notes. The source who'd given him this information on Thomas Hunter was impeccable. The story itself was beyond belief. He'd decided to hold off on the dreams, but the story hardly needed that much detail. America deserved to know about Thomas Hunter.

He looked into the camera, its red light on him. "Wise words of caution," he said in reference to Dr. Beyer's commentary on panic. "Ladies and gentlemen, I've recently come across some information that I think you'll find fascinating. I realize that under the circumstances, 'fascination' seems like a pretentious word, but we're still people and we still cling to hope, wherever we can find it, however it comes. And frankly, we may owe our hope to the man I'm about to show you. His name is Thomas Hunter."

A head shot of Hunter's stern if somewhat boyish face filled the screen for a moment—a driver's license photo from Colorado. Dark hair, strong jaw. The image slipped to the upper corner of Mike's monitor.

"'Classified' is another word that sounds a bit pretentious now, but there are details about Thomas Hunter that we can't divulge without first confirming. What we can say is that it has come to our attention that this man was single-handedly responsible for calling out the threat this nation faces while facing a sea of doubters. Indeed, if the world had listened to Mr. Hunter a week earlier than they did, we might have avoided the virus altogether. I'm sure some of you remember a story we ran two weeks ago about Hunter's kidnapping of Monique de Raison in Bangkok. It now appears that he did so in an attempt to stop the vaccine from being released."

This was where the story got a bit fuzzy. The whys and hows—and the bit about the dreams—were enough to cast suspicion on the entire story.

"We have reason to believe that many in our government consider this man critical to our ability to defeat this threat. We also have reason to believe that his life may be in danger. I promise you, we'll stay on top of this story and bring you details as soon as we have them."

He turned to Nancy, whom he'd insisted remain as his coanchor. "Nancy."

⁂

Kara Hunter left the taxi at a run and hurried up the concrete stairs to the white building in the middle of a pastoral setting outside of Baltimore, Maryland. The huge blue letters mounted overhead read "Genetrix Laboratories," but she knew that only a year ago the sign had read "Raison Pharmaceutical." The French company had sold it off when they'd centralized their operations in Bangkok.

Monique de Raison was in this building, working feverishly on a solution to her own mutated virus.

Thomas was dead.

Kara had spent the first day in complete denial. Mother had slipped into one of her terrible brooding moods. Then the news of the Raison Strain hit the airwaves and everything changed. Kara went from complete unwillingness to accept Thomas's death to the sinking realization that they were all dead anyway.

The city of New York, like all cities, had first swallowed the story in jaded silence. It took twenty-four hours for the news to sink in. The streets hadn't emptied right away, but by the end of the second day, finding a taxi would have been a chore. Wall Street was still up and running—they were saying that some semblance of life had to go on. The talking heads—the mayor, the governor, the president— all said the same thing. America had to keep functioning. Electricity, water, stocks and bonds. Food, gasoline, cars, and planes. Hospitals. If they shut down, the country would shut down. Panic would kill America as surely as any virus. Every lab in the world was frantically searching for a cure—one would be found.

But Kara knew better.

Today, Kara had developed a fresh case of denial. The news that Thomas might be some kind of hero had been picked up by every channel she surfed. They had dug up his driver's license photo, of all things. There was his young face, trying so hard to be sincere. The picture brought tears to her eyes. She missed him enough that the threat of the Raison Strain felt strangely feeble.

What if he was alive? They hadn't actually found his body, had they? Gains had been tight-lipped. He'd told her that Monique had seen him dead. But how long after his death had she seen him? Yes, the lake's power was gone over there. Yes, he'd been persuaded that this time his death would be final. Yes, it had been two days and not a word from him. Yes, yes, yes!

But this was her only brother here. She wasn't going to let him be dead, not yet.

She'd left Mother this morning, tracked down Monique through one of the deputy secretary's aides, received permission to visit her, and flown straight to Baltimore.

Kara pushed through the door. A haggard receptionist lifted her head. "Can I help you?"

"Yes, my name is Kara Hunter. Monique de Raison is expecting me."

"Yes, Ms. Hunter. This way, please."

The woman led her down a long hall and into a large laboratory. At least twenty work stations were each manned by technicians. To Kara's left, a long glass wall looked into a clean room where blue-capped, white-jacketed, masked technicians worked. Voices buzzed quietly. Intently. These were the people bent on cracking a code that couldn't be cracked in the time given. These were America's heroes, she thought. They paid her no mind as she walked through the lab into another hall and then entered a large office where Monique bent over a thick ream of photos with a scientist who vaguely resembled Einstein, bushy hair, spectacles, and all.

Monique looked up.

"Kara." Her face seemed to sag and her eyes were red. She looked at her comrade. *"Excusez-moi un moment, Charles."*

The man nodded and left.

Monique stepped to Kara and pulled her into a fierce hug. "I'm so sorry, Kara." She sniffed. "I'm so very sorry."

Kara hadn't expected such a touching reception. What had happened between Monique and Thomas? She swallowed a lump rising in her throat. "Are you okay?"

Monique pulled back and turned her face. "Not really, no. I'm not sure that I can deliver."

"They say that your encoding survived the mutation."

"It's not that simple. But yes, the genes I had isolated for modification with the introduction of my own virus did survive. We will know in a couple hours what that means."

"You don't sound hopeful."

"I don't know how to sound." She looked at Kara with sad eyes.

"I came because I'm having difficulty accepting his death," she said.

Monique's eyes watered. She bit her lower lip and eased into her chair behind the desk.

"What happened out there, Monique?"

"I dreamed," she said.

She'd dreamed. This was supposed to mean something? And then it suddenly did.

"You . . . like Thomas, you mean? You dreamed of the forest?"

"Yes. Only not as myself, but as his wife, Rachelle. And honestly, it felt to me like that was the real world and this one was only the dream."

Kara couldn't contain her surprise. "You went there? You saw him there? How?"

"We were sleeping, and I think it might have been something to do with the fact that we were in contact. Our wrists had been injured, both of ours. Maybe our blood . . . I don't know. But I do know that I shared Rachelle's life. I shared all her memories, her experiences."

"You have no doubt about this?" Kara asked, gaping.

"None. And we were both afraid that if he was killed in either reality, he would also die in the other. And also that even if he was by some miracle cured in that reality, he might not be cured in this reality."

"I won't accept that!" Kara said. Even though the same thoughts had occurred to her, she had been hoping Monique would contradict her ideas.

Monique blinked at her outburst.

"Sorry. But if you'd been through what I've been through these past weeks . . ." Kara dropped into a facing chair. "But then you have, haven't you? Then let me be straight with you. I'm not willing to accept this nonsense that he's dead."

"I saw him!"

"You saw him? Did you feel his pulse?"

"I watched Carlos feel his pulse. He was dead." Her voice was strained.

Kara considered something Thomas had told her before leaving on his rescue. He'd concluded that he was the only gateway between the two realities. If he was dead . . .

"You do realize that if your antivirus fails, then the only hope this world has is Thomas."

"Yes."

"And if he's dead, we may be in a world of hurt."

"He got me out; I have the antivirus."

"I thought you weren't so sure."

"We're working on it."

"And I'm working on Thomas."

"They've already dropped a team into the region where I was held," Monique said. She sounded as if she might snap.

"Okay, fine. Let's think this through. We both know that Carlos isn't sloppy enough to let them find him. This isn't about the tactics of special forces. This is about the mind and the heart, and I think you and I might be the ones to find Thomas's mind and heart. If he's alive."

"And if he's not?"

"As I said, I'm not willing to accept that."

Monique stared at Kara. A glimmer of hope lit her eyes. "Do you realize that if Rachelle is killed, I may die?" she asked.

"Tell me everything that happened," Kara said. "Everything."

30

THE HORDE guarded the lake that night. The custom of the Desert Dwellers required that the executed remain a night in the water to complete his humiliation. No one was allowed to enter or bathe until the body was removed.

Ciphus objected but finally capitulated, as much to control the lingering of those loyal to Justin as to yield to the Horde's demands. The beach was cleared, and those who celebrated Justin's death did so in the streets rather than by the lake. Those few who could not wait until morning to bathe did so with the small reserves held in some of the houses.

Thomas found Rachelle in their home, lying on the floor, exhausted and unmoving. Neither had slept for nearly two days. He made her wash and then did so himself. They fell into bed without talking about the execution and fell into a dead sleep.

Oddly, Thomas did not dream of the Raison Strain that night. He hadn't eaten the rhambutan fruit, so he did dream, just not of the virus and France. He should have, though. Unless, of course, he wasn't alive in the other reality any longer, in which case there would be nothing for him to dream about.

But that would mean he was powerless to stop the Raison Strain. Hopefully Monique could stop it. If not, she would die along with the rest of the world in about ten days or so. And Rachelle might very well die with her.

These were the dreamy thoughts running through Thomas's mind when he heard the screams that pulled him from deep sleep early the next morning.

He jerked upright and immediately gasped at a sharp pain that shot through his skin. A quick glance confirmed the worst. The disease was upon him. Not just a light graying, but a nearly fully advanced condition!

He bent his arm, but the pain stopped him. The gray flaking on the epidermis didn't begin to characterize the horrible agony. How had this happened? He had to get to the lake!

Again he bent his arm, this time ignoring the pain, as he knew the Desert Dwellers did. It felt as though the layer of skin just under the epidermis had turned brittle and was cracking when he moved.

Rachelle sat up. "What's that?"

The screams were coming from the west. The lake.

"What . . ." Rachelle cried out with pain and stared at her skin. "Didn't we bathe last night?"

Thomas peeled off his covers and forced himself to stand through the pain. His mind swam with confusion. Maybe they'd accidentally used rainwater instead of water from the lake. It had happened before.

Rachelle had risen and rushed to the window, wincing with each step. "It's the lake. Something's wrong with the lake!"

"Papa!" Marie ran into the room. She too! The disease covered her skin like white ash.

"Get your brother! Hurry!"

"It hurts—"

"Hurry!"

They didn't bother with slippers or boots, only tunics. Thomas and Rachelle led their two children from the house, urging them to move as quickly as possible, which resulted in tears and a pace barely faster than a walk. The screaming had spread; hundreds, thousands of villagers had awakened to the same condition. The disease had swept in over night and infected them all, Thomas thought. They streamed down the main street, desperate for the lake.

Thomas grabbed Samuel's hand and pulled him along. "Ignore it. The faster you get to the water, the sooner the pain will be gone."

"Why is this happening?" Rachelle panted.

"I don't know."

"It's everyone! Maybe it's punishment for the death of Justin."

"I hope only that."

"What do you mean?"

"I don't know, Rachelle!" he snapped.

She hurried beside him in silence. Marie and Samuel were both crying through their pain, but they too knew enough to push ahead. Elyon's lake was their salvation; they knew that like they knew they needed air to breathe. Every cell in their bodies screamed for the relief that the lake alone could give them.

The sight that greeted them on the lakeshore stopped Thomas short. Five thousand, maybe ten thousand diseased men, women, and children stood back from the water's edge, staring aghast or swaying back and forth, moaning.

The water was red!

Not just tinged with red, but red like blood.

Hundreds of brave souls had stepped into the lake and were frantically splashing the red water on their legs and thighs, but most were too terrified to even walk up to the water.

The screams weren't from the pain that would normally be associated with cleansing in such a diseased state, Thomas realized. There was terror in their voices and there were many words, but the ones that seized his mind were those that rose above the others in this sea of chaos.

"The power is gone!"

A man Thomas barely recognized as William, his own lieutenant, staggered from the water. His skin was wet but the disease clung to him like cracked, mildewed leather.

William gripped his head with both hands and looked around in desperation. He saw Thomas and lurched up the shore. "It doesn't work!" He had the look of a crazed man. "The power is gone! The Horde is coming, Thomas!"

Thomas glanced down the shore to his left. Martyn and Qurong stood with arms folded two hundred yards distant. Behind them, the thousand Scab warriors who'd accompanied them watched in silence.

"You mean these?"

William paced frantically, lost to Thomas's question.

"William! What do you mean they're coming?"

"The scouts have come in. Both armies are in the forest."

Both?

"How many? How far?"

"He was innocent! Now we will die for allowing it."

More people were running onto the shores. Even more were fleeing the lake in panic. William was hardly lucid. Thomas grabbed him by the shoulders and shook him.

"Listen to me! How many did the scouts report?"

"Too many, Thomas. It doesn't matter. My men are all diseased!"

Thomas could feel the onset of the same confusion he'd once felt when the disease had nearly taken him before in the desert. But he was still thinking clearly enough to realize what had happened.

Rachelle said it for him. "Johan knew." She gazed at the confusion before them. "He knew that Justin was pure, and he knew that innocent blood would poison the lake." She looked at him with wide eyes. "We're becoming like them. We're becoming like the Horde!"

It was true. This was Martyn's true betrayal. This was how he was waging his battle. They would take the forests without swinging a single blade. The only difference between the Forest People and the Desert Dwellers now was a lake that no longer functioned. In a matter of hours, maybe less, the Forest Guard would look, act, and think like their own enemies.

There wasn't much time. "Give me your sword!"

William stared dumbly.

Thomas reached forward and yanked the blade from William's scabbard. "Call the men! We fight now. To the death!"

His wife was staring at the red lake, eyes wide, but not with horror now. There was another look in them—a dawning of realization.

A shriek split the morning air behind them. Thomas spun and saw a woman pointing to the front gates. He twisted and looked down the main street. The front gates were five hundred yards away—he couldn't make out any detail, but enough to see that an army had arrived.

A Horde army.

"The men, William! Follow me!"

He gripped the sword in his fist and ran across the beach, toward Martyn, shoving from his mind the terrible pain he felt. Feet were padding the sand behind him, but he didn't stop to see who it was.

The plan that had emerged from the fog in his mind was a simple one, with only one end: Qurong's death. In his current condition, he wouldn't have the same advantage that he ordinarily would, but they wouldn't take him down before he killed the Horde leader, the firstborn, Tanis.

"Thomas!"

He recognized the voice. Mikil was running up the bank in a blind panic. He ignored her and raced on. The distant sound of swords clashing carried over the village. Some of his Guard were putting up a defense. But the more ominous sound of boots and hoofs—thousands upon thousands marching in cadence up the main street—made the meager defense sound like a children's sideshow.

One of the Scabs had left Qurong's army and was running to meet him. No, not a Scab warrior, but a Scab general, with a black sash.

Martyn!

"Remember, Thomas, he's my brother," Rachelle said behind him. It was his wife, not William, behind him. And she wanted him to leave Johan unharmed?

He glanced back. "He betrayed Elyon." The Council members, led by Ciphus, had finally arrived at the lake and were testing its waters. The uproar had settled in the hopes that perhaps the elder could fix this terrible problem. No one seemed to worry about the army in the streets—they wanted to bathe. Only to bathe.

Rachelle pulled up next to him. Johan was now only fifty yards from them.

"Thomas, there is another way. Do you remember what Justin told me?"

Thomas slowed and held out his sword with both hands. "The only way I know now is to take Qurong with me. If you want your brother to live, tell him to let me pass."

"You're not listening!" she whispered harshly. "'When the time comes,' that's what he said. Thomas, *this* is that time."

Martyn had withdrawn his sword and slowed to a walk. Thomas stopped and prepared to meet the general in whatever way he had in mind. His skin was crawling with fire, and his joints felt like they'd fractured, but he knew that the Horde fought through the pain all the time. He could do that and more, if not die trying.

"He said he had a better way," Rachelle said. "Justin told me to die with him."

"That's what I'm preparing to do. And with me Qurong will die."

She grabbed his arm and spoke hurriedly. "Listen to me, Thomas! I think I understand what he meant. He said it would bring me life! He knew that we would need life. He knew that he would die. He knew that the lake would no longer give us life because it would be defiled by the shedding of innocent blood. *His* blood!"

The lone figure walking toward them faded from his vision.

Die with me.

"We've died with him already," he said. "Look at us!"

"He said it would bring us *life*!"

Martyn's face was shrouded by his hood. He carried his sword loose, by his side—overconfident, taunting.

Thomas looked at the lake, at the sea of red that sent chills down his spine. Justin's message suddenly seemed quite obvious to him. He couldn't imagine actually doing it, but if Rachelle was right, Justin had asked them to die as he had died.

He'd asked them to drown in this sea of red.

Thomas had swam through a sea of red once, deep in the emerald lake that could be breathed.

A fresh cry erupted from the shore. Evidently Ciphus had failed in his task to prove that all was still fine with his lake. But there was more. Ciphus was screaming above the chaos.

"He's gone!"

Thomas cast a quick glance over his shoulder. The elder stood on the shore, dripping with water. He looked surprisingly like a Scab—with dreadlocks he would look like Qurong himself.

"There is no body!" the elder cried. "They have taken him!"

Thomas spun back to face Martyn. "He's lying," Martyn said. "The body could be anywhere under the water by now. He's setting you up."

"Thomas, you have to listen to me!" Rachelle pleaded.

The disease was making his head swim. He blinked and tried to think clearly. "You're suggesting that we run into the lake and drown ourselves?"

"You would rather live like this?"

Martyn stopped ten feet from them, head low so that shadows hid his face.

Thomas adjusted his grip on the sword. An image of Justin's swollen face filled his mind.

Follow me. Die with me.

It was an incredible demand that Justin had suggested to whoever would listen.

He spoke to Martyn. "What have you done to us?" His voice came out low and unearthly, bitter and full of pain at once.

Martyn lifted his head and Thomas saw his face.

It wasn't the scowl he expected. Tears filled the general's eyes. His face was drawn tight, stricken with fear. Fear!

Martyn was suddenly walking again, closer, sword still by his side.

"Stop there," Thomas ordered.

Martyn took two more steps and then stopped.

This wasn't what Thomas had expected. He could easily take two long steps and thrust his blade into the general's unprotected chest. A part of him insisted that he *should*. He should kill Martyn and then run for Qurong.

But he couldn't. Not now. Not with Rachelle's words ringing in his ears. Not seeing tears in Martyn's eyes. Could this be more trickery?

"I remember," the general said. The remorse in his tone was so uncharacteristic that Thomas blinked. "I remember, Rachelle. He spoke to me, and all night I've remembered."

Rachelle let out a sob and started toward her brother.

He lifted a hand, just barely. "Please, no. They can't see us."

Johan looked past Thomas toward the bank behind them. The first of the Horde army had arrived on the shores. Sporadic cries arose as villagers scattered for safety, but there were no sounds of swordplay or resistance, Thomas noted. The disease had taken most of their minds already. The mighty Forest Guard had been stripped of its will to fight by a disease none of them had defeated before.

Johan looked at Thomas, eyes begging. "I knew he was innocent. I knew his blood would defile the lake. I even knew who he was, but I couldn't remember why I should care. Now I've murdered him. I can't live with this."

"No, there is a better way!" Rachelle said.

"Please, I've decided. I will return to my army with a proposition of surrender from you, and then I will kill Qurong and publicly take the blame for poisoning the water. Ciphus will blame you. I told him that if anything went wrong with our plan, he was to blame you. He'll say that you took the body of Justin and poisoned the water. In the people's state of shock from the disease, they'll believe him. The least I can do is protect you."

"Protect us from what?" Rachelle demanded. "Not the disease."

Thomas lowered his sword. Johan glanced at it, then over his shoulder. Qurong motioned to a line of his warriors, who started to march up the beach toward them.

"Qurong suspects something. We don't have much time," Thomas said. He looked at the water. "Do you remember the boy saying that he had a lot riding on us?"

"I suggest we bow our heads in a sign of mutual agreement," Johan said. "Qurong must see that we've struck some kind of—"

"Forget your plan," Thomas interrupted. "Do you remember the boy saying he depended on us?"

"Yes."

"Justin said the same thing to Rachelle yesterday morning. Then he told her to follow him in his death. It would bring life in a better way, he said. Rachelle's convinced he meant for us to die by drowning in the sea of red, like he did."

Johan glanced at the water.

"Do you believe he was Elyon?" Thomas asked.

"I . . . I don't know. He was . . . he was innocent."

"But do you believe he was Elyon?" Thomas demanded again. "Was he the boy?"

Johan paused and stared out at the glassy red water. "Yes. Yes, I think he was."

Thomas spoke quickly now. "And is it possible to breathe Elyon's red water?"

"Perhaps." A fresh tear leaked from Johan's right eye and ran down his scabbed cheek.

"Then I think she's right," Thomas said. "And I think if we wait any longer, our minds will be confused by the disease with the rest."

Ciphus was delivering a diatribe down the shore. Thomas heard his name repeatedly, but at the moment, the elder's web of lies felt like nonsense next to the things his wife was now suggesting.

"You're suggesting we drown like he did?" Johan asked.

They were all looking at the lake now. A row of warriors had broken from the new arrivals and were approaching from their right. The ones Qurong had dispatched were drawing closer on the left. They were running out of time.

Rachelle spoke with a tremor in her voice. "I'm afraid."

"But that's what he told you?" Johan asked. "To drown like he did?"

"Yes."

Silence.

"And Samuel? Marie?" she said.

"If you're wrong, they're dead with us."

Thomas had been here fifteen years earlier, torn between fleeing Elyon's lake and diving in. Then, it had been a pool of life. This lake looked like a cold pool of death.

Johan uttered a small gasp. He was staring across the lake.

"What is it?"

But Johan didn't have to answer. Thomas and Rachelle saw them together, and instinctively Rachelle grasped his arm. Thomas's first thought was that the trees on the opposite side of the lake had sprouted a thick harvest of cherries.

But these cherries were set in black eye sockets that were attached to furry black bodies.

Shataiki!

A hundred thousand at least, clinging to the trees just beyond the nearest branches, watching them with unblinking stares.

It had been fifteen years since Thomas had seen the bats, black or white. What had changed now? Justin had been killed. The forest was now inhabited by Shataiki. Or had Justin's cry for them to remember opened their eyes as it had opened Johan's mind? Either way, it was both terrifying and revealing at once.

Johan suddenly threw back his hood. Tears slipped down his face in long ribbons now. He gave the bats one last glare and stripped off his cloak, revealing shockingly white and flaky flesh. The sight of their general standing in only a loincloth brought the Scab warriors to a complete halt less than fifty yards on either side.

In that moment Thomas knew what he must do. What he wanted most desperately to do. Whom he must follow. Why Elyon had a lot riding on him. On them.

He didn't bother discarding his tunic. He glanced to his right, caught Rachelle's wide eyes; his left, Johan's frantic stare.

"For Justin," he said.

He ran.

Despite his earlier statement, Thomas almost turned to find his children. The thought of leaving them among the Horde sickened him. But he pushed on—this wasn't the time to stop and make provision for them, no matter what the outcome. His children were now in Elyon's hands. If he survived the next few moments, he would sweep them off their feet and kiss them with joy.

They tore down the bank, Thomas first, with Johan and Rachelle hard on his heels. The Horde grunted in shock to his left and right; he could hear that much. The Shataiki screeched. He wondered if anyone else could hear them.

Then he was airborne.

He hit the water and was immediately swallowed by a cold sea.
Red.

⟨∞⟩

His first impulse was that their decision had been a terrible mistake. That
the disease had softened their reasoning and caused them to do something
so insane as to follow Justin in his death.

He kicked deep so that his feet wouldn't flail on the surface for the
Horde to see.

The water changed on his second stroke, less than five feet under, from
cold to warm. He opened his eyes in surprise. He'd expected a dark abyss
below him—black demons waiting to satisfy their lust for death.

What he saw was a pool of red light, dim and hazy, but definitely light!
He looked left, then right, but there was no sign of Johan or Rachelle.

Thomas stopped kicking. He floated. The water was serene. Silent.
Unearthly and eerie. He could hear the soft thump of his own pulse. Above
him, countless Scabs were watching the water for signs of his emergence,
but here in this fluid he was momentarily safe.

And then the moment passed, and the reality of his predicament filled
his mind.

His eyes began to sting, and he blinked in the warm water, but to
no relief. He was already running out of oxygen; his chest felt tight and
for a moment he considered kicking to the surface to take one more
gulp of air.

He opened his mouth, felt the warm water on his tongue. Closed it.

*It's his water, Thomas. You've been in this lake a thousand times, and you
know that the bottom has always been muddy and black. But now it's light.
You've been here before.*

But this plan suddenly struck him as irrational. What man would willingly suck in a lungful of water? He'd entered intending to throw his own
life away? The disease had ruined him! He'd actually believed for one desperate moment that dying would bring him a new kind of life, but at the
moment, nothing felt quite so foolish.

What of Johan and Rachelle? Would they claw for the surface in panic?

But what choice did he have? Was returning to the living death above any less absurd? He hung limp, trying to ignore the terrible knowledge that his lungs were starting to burn. But that was just it—he didn't have the luxury of contemplating his decision much longer. He was down to a few seconds already.

A jolt of panic, a despair he'd never felt before, ran through his body, shaking him in its horrible fist.

Thomas opened his mouth, closed his eyes. He began to sob. A final scream filled his mind, forbidding him to take in this water. Justin had sucked at the water, but that was Justin.

No, that was Elyon, Thomas.

Then his air was gone. Thomas stretched his jaw wide and sucked hard like a fish gulping for oxygen.

Pain hit his lungs like a battering ram.

He tried to breathe out. In, out, like he once had in the emerald lake. But this wasn't that kind of water. His lungs felt as if they were full of stone. He was going to die. His waterlogged body began to sink slowly.

He didn't fight the drowning. If Justin was Elyon, then this was the right thing for him to do. It was that simple. Justin had told them to follow him in his death, and that is what they were doing. And if Rachelle was wrong about all of this, then he would die as Justin died to show his respect for his innocence. There was no life above the surface anyway.

The lack of oxygen ravaged his body for long seconds, and he didn't try to stop death.

Then he did try. With everything in him, he tried to reverse this terrible course.

Elyon, I beg you. Take me. You made me; now take me.

Darkness encroached on his mind. Thomas began to scream.

Then it was black.

Nothing.

He was dead; he knew that. But there was something here, beyond life. From the blackness a moan began to fill his ears, replacing his own screams. The moan gained volume and grew to a wail and then a scream.

He knew the voice! It was Justin. Elyon was screaming! And he was screaming in pain.

Thomas pressed his hands to his ears and began to scream with the other, thinking now that this was worse than death. His body crawled with fire as though every last cell revolted at the sound. And so they should, a voice whispered in his skull. Their Maker was screaming in pain!

He'd been here before! Exactly here, in the belly of the emerald lake. He'd heard this scream.

A soft, inviting voice replaced the cry. "Remember me, Thomas," it said. Justin said. Elyon said.

Light lit the edges of his mind. A red light. Thomas opened his eyes, stunned by this sudden turn. The burning in his chest was gone. The water was warm and the light below seemed brighter.

He was alive?

He sucked at the red water and pushed it out. Breathing! He was alive!

Thomas cried out in astonishment. He glanced down at his legs and arms. Yes, this was real. He was here, floating in the lake, not in some other disconnected reality.

And his skin . . . he rubbed it with his thumb. The disease was gone. He turned slowly in the water, looking for Rachelle or Johan, but neither was here.

Thomas twisted once in the water and thrust his fist above (or was it below?) his head. He dove deep then looped back and struck for the surface. He had to find Rachelle! Justin had changed the water.

The moment his hand hit the cold water above the warm, his lungs began to burn. He tried to breathe but found he couldn't. Then he was through, out of the water.

Three thoughts mushroomed in his mind while the water was still falling from his face. The first was that he was breaking through the surface at precisely the same time as Rachelle on his right and Johan on his left. Like three dolphins breaking the surface in a coordinated leap, heads arched back, water streaming off their hair, grinning as wide as the sky.

The second thought was that he could feel the bottom of the lake under his feet. He was standing.

The third was that he still couldn't breathe.

He came out of the water to his waist, doubled over, and wretched a quart of water from his lungs. The pain left with the water. He gasped once, found he could breathe easily, and turned slowly.

To his right. Water and strings of saliva fell from Rachelle's grinning mouth. She had just died as well.

To his left. For a brief moment he didn't recognize the man five feet to his left. This was Martyn the Scab, but his skin had changed. Flesh tone. Smooth. Pink like a baby's skin. His eyes shone like emeralds. This was Johan as he once had been, without a trace of the disease. He too had breathed the water.

They stood in the water, three drenched strangers facing a hundred thousand Horde, some dressed in the tunics of Forest People, some dressed in the hooded cloaks of the Desert Dwellers, all dressed in the white skin of disease.

For a while no one spoke. Qurong stood with his army a hundred yards to their right, face shrouded by his hood. Ciphus stood fifty yards to their left, lips drawn. There, directly ahead, were Mikil and Jamous and Marie and Samuel, gaping with the rest.

Thomas walked out of the lake, plowing water noisily with his thighs. In some ways he felt like he was looking at a whole new world. Not only was he a new person, drowned in magic, but the thousands he faced were different. The disease hung on them like dried dung. But when they understood what Elyon had done for them in this lake, they would flock en masse into the red waters. *He would be run over,* he thought wryly.

The Horde warriors who'd been sent to investigate stood fifty paces off. They had their answer, and Thomas doubted they understood it.

He glanced back to where he'd seen the Shataiki. Gone. No, not gone. They were still there, undoubtedly, but he could no longer see them.

He was about to speak, to tell them what had happened, when a shrill voice shattered the silence. "It was them!" Ciphus cried. "They have deceived us and poisoned Elyon's water."

Johan stepped up beside Thomas. "We will tolerate your lies no longer, old man! Are you blind? Do we look poisoned to you?"

"Look at yourselves! The water has stripped you of your flesh!"

"Stripped us?" Thomas asked, dumbfounded. He looked at the people. "It has stripped us of our disease. Can't you see that?"

"Impossible!" Ciphus said. "This is no longer Elyon's lake. This is red water, poisoned by death."

It was what one of the Horde would say, Thomas thought. Ciphus had turned completely. He searched the bank for Marie and Samuel, found them, and saw that Rachelle was already running for them. She knew as well as he, if the disease had taken them all so quickly, they might not be so receptive.

He faced the elder, who'd turned to the people. "The law states with no uncertainty that the body must remain in the water until morning, but you all saw with your own eyes. There is no body!"

Again it was Johan who took up their defense. "No one crossed my line of guards to steal the body. You hardly searched. And this is Horde law that you're quoting, not your own. Since when do you bow to Horde law?"

"It is law!" the elder shouted. "And you were complicit in their plan to steal the body. Who would have suspected the two generals were working together to enslave the entire world in one twisted plot?" He pointed at the lake. "Look at what you've done!"

Johan stepped forward and spoke directly to the people. "The lake isn't poisoned; it has only been changed. Am I dead? Does the disease still cling to my flesh? Am I a Scab? No, I'm free of the disease, and it's because I did what Justin told us to do. To follow him in his death by drowning in the lake and finding new life! This is the fulfillment of the boy's prophecy. This is the blow against evil the boy told us about, and it has come when all other hope is lost." He thrust his hand back toward the lake. "Enter the lake and find his life. Drown, all of you! Drown!"

No one ran for the lake. They stared at him as if he'd lost his senses. The great Martyn who was now Johan no longer commanded the respect he had only minutes earlier.

There was movement beside Qurong on their right. And on their left, Ciphus walked slowly toward them. "Do you hear him?"

Rachelle had shepherded Marie and Samuel to the edge of the water and was whispering in their ears. They were shivering.

"Martyn the general would complete his deception with Thomas by having us all drown!" Ciphus said. "Never!"

"Qurong is coming," Johan whispered urgently. "We don't have much time."

The Horde leader was marching up the shore with several hundred warriors.

Two men broke from the crowd of Forest People and ran down the shore—the two who had traveled with Justin through the Valley of Tuhan. Ronin and Arvyl.

Their faces were stained with tears and their eyes round with fear. "We will follow him to our deaths if we must," Ronin said quietly, looking deep into Thomas's eyes. "What must we do?"

"Swim deep and breathe the water. Let it take you. You'll find life."

They glanced at each other.

"Quickly! They're coming."

The two men stepped in, hesitated, then rushed and dove. They disappeared.

"Now his men, Justin's men!" Ciphus said. "They have all conspired to bring our ruin!"

Qurong was still marching. So then, it had come down to this. The Horde against a family. Surely his second would follow them!

Thomas ran up the shore and grabbed the hands of Mikil and Jamous. "Follow me!"

"Thomas . . ."

"Shut up and follow me, Mikil!" He kept his voice low and hushed. "Do you believe me?"

She didn't answer.

"You killed Elyon. We all did. Now give your life back to him and ride with me!"

Mikil and Jamous stared at each other.

"I think he's right," Jamous said.

"You think Justin was Elyon?" she demanded.

"He spoke to me."

She stared at him with wide white eyes.

"Dive deep and breathe the water; for Elyon's sake, move! Have I ever lied to you? Never. Run!"

It was enough for Mikil. They sprinted down the sandy bank with Thomas right behind. They dove in tandem and splashed just as Ronin and Arvyl broke the surface, flesh pink, mouths wide, retching water.

Thomas grabbed Johan's arm. "Horses, we'll need horses from the auxiliary Guard stable," he whispered. "They'll be saddled and—"

But Johan knew all of this and was already running up the bank. The diseased Forest People scrambled out of his way. He disappeared into a row of houses.

"All of you who will follow Justin in his death and find new life, drown!" Thomas cried. "Drown now!"

The Horde leader was marching faster.

Ciphus remained silent. He too saw Qurong. He too saw the Horde army that had them surrounded, many thousands, mounted on horses, sickles ready. They were under a new order, all of them.

"I beg you! Remember him! This is the day of your deliverance!" Thomas shouted. Behind him the water splashed. Mikil and Jamous had risen.

His frustration boiled to the surface. "What's wrong with you? Are you blind? It's life, you fools! Drown!"

Mikil laughed.

Two children ran down the shore. Lucy and Billy, the two from the Valley of Tuhan. They went in with Marie and Samuel. On their heels several grown men and women, maybe half a dozen, one from here, one from there. They splashed into the water and sank below the surface. One sputtered to the surface and clamored out of the lake. His skin hadn't changed. Two more broke for the lake.

"Enough!" Qurong stood with his fists on his hips, legs spread. "Enter the lake and consider yourself an enemy that we will hunt down and destroy."

"You are Tanis!" Thomas said. "You drank Teeleh's water and brought us the disease. Now you'll wage war on Elyon's children? Justin has brought us peace."

"I have brought you peace!" His voice seemed too loud for a man. It hit Thomas then—this was Teeleh speaking through his firstborn. He was playing the spoiled child who wanted to be as great as Elyon. It had always been Teeleh's way; now, having killed Justin, he would wage war on this unexpected remnant. He would kill the life that Justin had made possible in his death.

"We are one!" Qurong cried with arms spread. "I *am* peace!"

"You are at peace with Teeleh, not Elyon. Not Justin."

"Blasphemy!" Ciphus cried. "You are banished. Any man or woman or child who bathes in this lake will be banished!"

Qurong threw back his hood to expose long knotted dreadlocks over white flaking skin. "Not banished," he roared. "Killed!"

Behind Thomas, the water splashed as others came out of the lake. Oblivious to the exchange, several of the children giggled. Rachelle hurried them from the water with hushed tones.

Thomas scanned the beach. There was only one way clear of the Horde warriors, and that was past Ciphus. Even then, Qurong would give chase.

Where are you, Johan?

A lone man broke from the crowd, ran straight down the shore, and dove in defiance of Qurong's command. William? If Thomas wasn't mistaken, his lieutenant, William, had just joined them.

Where was Johan? How long did it take to open a gate for a few horses? He had to stall Qurong. "If you are with Elyon, then would you condemn women and children to death because they don't have your disease?"

"It is you who have the disease," Qurong said. "You are albinos with poisoned flesh and sickened minds." Spittle flew from his mouth. His eyes were white-hot with anger. Why so furious as this for a few naked prey? "Your disease will divide us and threaten my kingdom, and for that you will drown!"

"We just *have* drowned!" Mikil said. She burst into laughter. "You want to drown us again?"

Thomas held out his hand to quiet her. "Get them ready," he said quietly. "We ride through the forest, north."

"Horses?"

"Johan."

She understood.

"We'll see if you survive my drowning," Qurong said. "Take them!"

His guard broke around him and marched forward.

"Wait!" Thomas shouted. "I have something to exchange!" He reached into his tunic, slipped the leather book from where he'd carried it, and lifted it high.

"A Book of History."

Qurong lifted his hand, and his soldiers stopped. He took a step forward. In his own twisted mind this was a sacred book, but what would he do to own it again? It was, after all, just an artifact.

"You have said that no one is permitted to enter the lake," Thomas said. "If I throw this book in these poisoned waters, will you break your own law and enter to find it?"

"Lay it down."

Johan emerged from the village behind the people, leading a dozen horses. He took one look at the situation and kicked his mount.

Thomas spoke loudly to cover his approach.

"I will lay this book down if you will give me one minute to plead my case in front of the entire Council, as is the custom of our people in a case of this . . ."

The sound of Johan and his horses galloping down the bank was enough to turn every head. The Scabs had just made sense of his sudden appearance and were moving to intercept when their old commander thundered past Qurong.

Thomas shoved the blank Book of History into his tunic, then spun and grabbed the closest child. "Get them on the horses, hurry!"

Rachelle lifted Marie into a saddle behind William. She grabbed Samuel by the arm, jerked him from his feet, and swung him up with William's help. Then she turned for another child.

"Stop them!" Qurong shouted.

"Go, Rachelle! I'll get the others. Ride!"

But she ran for a fourth child.

They were no longer inhibited by the painful disease that slowed the Scabs. Before the first warrior reached them, they'd swung into saddles and were galloping toward the Council, which stood frozen.

All but Thomas and Rachelle, who'd helped the children.

"Mount! Hurry!" Rachelle wasn't going to make it! Thomas ran his horse at the closest warrior, who pulled up and took a meager swipe at him. He ducked the sickle easily enough. Now his wife had mounted.

"Ride! Ride!"

Out of nowhere a single arrow cut through the air and plowed into his mount's neck. The animal reared in pain and Thomas clung to the saddle.

"Thomas!" Rachelle screamed. She knew as well as he that this wound would finish the horse. And the Scabs were now rushing in. A blade struck the rear quarter of his horse.

Rachelle spun her own mount around. "Jump!" She raced up to him, released the reins, and shifted back off the saddle, holding on to the pommel with one hand.

It was a move the Guard knew well; horses often fell in battle. They learned early that at any speed, jumping from one horse to another was nearly impossible unless the rider could hold himself fast in the stirrups and catch the jumper between him and the horse's neck.

Thomas leaped, slammed into her horse's neck, and crashed into the saddle. He bent low and grabbed the reins. His wife hugged him around the waist and held tight.

But now they were going the wrong way. He reined the horse around and galloped to catch the others. It had all happened in a few seconds. Johan had just cleared the Council, but Justin's followers were far from safety.

The hundred Scabs above the beach were spurring their horses to intercept.

"Jamous, William, on your right!" Thomas cried. He veered straight for the Horde. "Hold on!" Rachelle tightened her grip around his belly.

Jamous and William broke from the others and headed for the army. Johan glanced back, took quick stock, and led the others away from the danger at a full sprint.

Thomas leaned forward and screamed as he would in pitched battle. Every Scab soldier there had undoubtedly seen this mighty warrior felling their comrades, and the sight of him and two of his lieutenants racing directly for them caused them to pull on their reins.

The delay was just enough to give Johan the time he needed to lead the others into the trees.

"Break!" Thomas, Jamous, and William veered to the left on the command and raced for the trees after Johan.

It was then, not two horse lengths from the trees, that a soft *thump* punctuated the pounding hoofs.

Rachelle groaned behind him.

Another *thump*.

An arrow smacked into a tree on his right.

Rachelle's grip on his midsection loosened.

"Rachelle?"

She grunted, and there was the unmistakable sound of pain in that grunt.

"Rachelle? Talk to me!"

In answer, a dozen arrows clipped through the branches. And then they were into the forest. His wife had been shot! He had to stop.

"Rachelle!"

The Horde was in heavy pursuit—he couldn't stop.

"Answer me!" he screamed. "Rachelle!"

Nothing. Her hands were slipping, and he grabbed them with his left hand. "William!"

His lieutenant glanced back. "Ride, Thomas! Ride!"

"Rachelle's been shot!" he cried.

William immediately pulled to the side and eased up. Thomas galloped up to him, still at full speed. They dodged several trees and broke into a meadow. William studied the limp body behind Thomas. Rachelle's limp body.

What Thomas saw in his lieutenant's green eyes drove a stake of raw dread through his heart.

Thomas veered off the path just long enough to check Rachelle's pulse. She was alive. But unconscious. Three arrows protruded from her back. He started to sob, still seated on the saddle with the sound of the Horde less than a hundred meters behind. William strapped her wrists together around Thomas's belly, and they rode hard to catch the others.

Elyon, I beg you heal her, he prayed. *I beg you save my wife.*

The others didn't know. Samuel and Marie rode ahead with Mikil and Jamous, who'd taken Marie to lighten Mikil's load. Every minute, Thomas checked Rachelle's wrist for a pulse. Alive, still alive.

William rode behind, silent. Even if they could stop, there was nothing that could be done for Rachelle. She needed rest. She needed to stop riding altogether, but with this pursuit none of that was an option.

You saved me, Justin. You will save my wife.

They had died and come back to life in the lake. Why? So that Rachelle could be killed by the Horde? It made no sense, which could only mean she wasn't going to die. He needed her! The children needed her. The tribe needed her. She was the sweetest person, the wisest, the loveliest, the most loving of them all!

She would not be dying.

William pulled up beside him after twenty minutes. "There are about two hundred in pursuit," he said. "Johan and I will lead them south and join you at the apple grove to the north."

Thomas nodded.

His lieutenant raced ahead and spoke briefly to Johan, who looked back in alarm. He veered to the right and vanished into the trees with William. They would circle back, engage the Horde, and then draw them south according to classic Guard methods.

Thomas rode hard for as long as he dared. Surely William and Johan had engaged the Horde by now. He felt his wife's pulse for the hundredth time. With the horse bouncing under them, the task was now nearly impossible. Maybe her pulse had grown too weak for him to feel without stopping.

"Mikil!"

Thomas pulled his horse up before his second could respond. She saw him stop and called to the others, who had just entered a small clearing.

Thomas untied his wife's wrists, slipped off the horse, and eased her down to the grass. She lay on her side, still. He felt her neck with a trembling hand, desperate to feel the familiar pulse he'd pressed his face against so many times.

It wasn't there.

The others had come behind him, and he heard their startled cries, but his mind didn't care about them right now. He only wanted one thing. He wanted his wife back. But she was lying on the ground and he couldn't find her pulse.

She's dead, Thomas.

No, she couldn't be dead. She was Rachelle, the one who'd been healed by Justin. The one who had led them into the lake. The one who had shown him how to love and fight and lead and live.

"Mama?"

Marie. Tears spilled from his eyes at the sound of his daughter's voice.

"Mama!"

Both of his children fell to their knees over their mother. He tried one more time to feel her pulse, and this time he knew she was dead.

He sank to his haunches and let a terrible anguish wash over him. He drew a deep breath, lifted his chin, and began to sob at the sky.

Mikil was working over the body; a woman was hugging the children, who were also crying; Thomas could do nothing but cry. He'd seen so many die in battle, but today, in the wake of breathing Elyon's water, this death felt somehow different. Raw and terrible and more painful than he ever could have imagined.

Thomas slumped down beside his wife, curled into a ball, and wept.

Mikil took charge. "Mount. Lead them to the apple grove. Wait for us there."

They left him alone. He knew he had to continue. Not all of the Horde would have followed Johan. They would be coming.

He invited them now. Come and kill me as well.

I have a lot riding on you, Thomas of Hunter.

The voice spoke crystal clear in his mind. He opened his eyes. Rachelle's back was a foot from his face. Still.

He closed his eyes, mind numb.

My daughter is with me now. I need her.

"Give her back," Thomas whispered.

"What?" Mikil's voice said.

"Give her back!" he moaned.

For a long time there was only silence. They should have left long ago, but Mikil kept watch and let him lie in grief.

Then the voice spoke again.

Ride, Thomas. Ride with me.

Something was happening in his chest. He opened his eyes and focused on a strange warmth that spread through his lungs and up his neck.

He sat up.

Meet me at the desert, Thomas. Ride.

"Thomas?" Mikil knelt beside him. "I'm sorry, it's . . . it's a terrible tragedy. We should leave."

Thomas stood. The ache in his heart throbbed, but there was this other voice, and he knew that voice. It had spoken to him in the emerald lake long ago. It had spoken in the red lake today. Justin had died. They'd all died. Now Rachelle had died again. But she was alive, because the voice said she was alive. If not here, then somewhere else.

"Help me with her, Mikil."

They put Rachelle's body on the horse in front of Thomas, facing him with her face buried in his shoulder and her arms by his side. He held his wife and he rode and he cried tears that soaked her hair.

But his mourning was for his children and for himself, not for Rachelle. Not for Elyon's daughter. She was with Justin.

When they arrived at the apple orchard, Johan and William were waiting with the others. Johan wept for his sister. He kissed her and smoothed her hair and told them all that he had betrayed her.

"Where are we going?" Mikil asked.

"To the desert," Thomas said, nudging his horse. "We ride to the desert."

31

TO SAY that the world was descending into mad chaos would not be an overstatement, not in anyone's book. Four days had passed since Mike Orear had spilled his guts on CNN, since France had declared martial law, since Monique had returned with the magic elixir firmly in mind, since Thomas Hunter had been killed by a bullet to the forehead. Whether the headlines were in English or German or Spanish or Russian or any other language, they all boiled down to one of a dozen bold statements.

RAISON STRAIN THREAT CONFIRMED

WORLD ON BRINK OF WAR

OVER 5 BILLION ESTIMATED INFECTED

GLOBAL ECONOMIC SHUTDOWN

T MINUS 10 DAYS

GOD HELP US ALL

HOPE FOR ANTIVIRUS

Seeing any such headline was a surreal experience. Neither the writer nor the readers had any clue as to what any of it really meant. Nothing like this had ever happened before. Nothing like this could possibly be happening now. The Raison Strain had been thrust upon the world, and all but a few natives hidden deep in tropical jungles had surely heard the news. But how many believed? Really believed?

Denial.

Naturally, the world was either in full-fledged denial or too stunned to react. This was why there were no riots. This was why there were no protests. This was why the typical ranting and raving on the airwaves hadn't started yet.

Instead, there was an almost disconnected analysis of the situation. The world was collectively glued to the news, praying to God for the word they all knew would soon come—the announcement that Monique de Raison's antivirus had been tested and effectively killed the virus like they all knew it would.

The president spoke to the people twice each day from the White House, calming, reassuring. Tests for the infection were assigned randomly by lottery based on Social Security number. One person in every thousand was permitted to check into the local hospital for a test. The hope that first day that certain sections of the United States had been spared the virus quickly changed to astonishment as one by one each test, each family, each neighborhood, each town and city and state came back positive. CNN used a modified electoral map to show the virus's saturation. When infection was confirmed, the town was painted red. By the beginning of the second day, half the map was red. Twelve hours later, there was nothing to see but red.

Schools canceled classes. Despite the president's pleading for life as usual, half of the country's businesses closed their doors on the second day, and more were sure to follow. Transportation had all but come to a standstill. Thankfully, the public utilities continued their service with minimal staffs under direct orders from the president of the United States.

The first sign that chaos would soon threaten daily life was a run on grocery stores at 8:00 a.m. on the second day. Naturally. Panic would soon set in. It would be impossible to get to a store, much less find one open for business.

The second sign was the tone of the United Nations meeting that the president waited to address at this very minute. Those in attendance were a motley crew if the bags under their eyes and their wrinkled shirts were any indicator. The room was stuffed, every chair filled, every aisle crawling with aides. If there was ever a time for the global community to pull together, it was now. But the responses to the impassioned speeches thus far, from Russia, England, and now France, revealed just how far apart leaders could be when the chips were down.

Organized mayhem.

The French ambassador was spitting out his plea with remarkable conviction. "We are truly the victims of these barbarous terrorists—we, the innocent people of France! Our government has acted only in the best interest of our own citizens and the world community. No matter how impossible it might seem—no matter how suicidal, even—to not yield to their demands would be our true death. Better to live to fight another day than die over a cache of arms!"

A dozen voices shouted in defiance as soon as the translation in their earpieces was complete. Some in agreement, it seemed to Robert; some in vehement opposition. The word "traitor" was in there somewhere—clear enough.

He removed his earpiece. Majority leader Dwight Olsen had been on hold for the past minute. He picked up the black phone in front of him. "Okay, patch me through."

"The president will take your call now."

"Thank you," Olsen's voice crackled. "Good morning, Mr. President."

"I'm up in five minutes. What do you have, Dwight?"

"I understand you're considering declaring martial law."

"I'll do what I think is necessary to keep Americans alive."

"I urge you to remember that people still have their rights. Martial law is pushing too far."

"Call it what you want. I'm calling out the National Guard today. Defense has drawn up a simple plan to deal with various contingencies. Curfew goes into effect tonight. I'm not going to get caught putting down a revolt at home while France is breathing down our necks."

"Sir, I strongly recommend—"

"Not today. I took this call as a courtesy, but my course is set. We'll all be dead in ten days if we can't secure the antivirus. Our best hope for finding it died three days ago with Thomas Hunter—a man you dismissed out of hand, if you remember. Let's hope his death bought us what we need. If not, I don't know what we're going to do. Our ships are halfway across the Atlantic. I've got five days to make the call, you understand. Five days! In that time we keep our citizens alive and we keep them from tearing up the country. Everything else takes a backseat."

"Still—"

"In a few minutes I'm addressing the United Nations," Blair continued. "A copy of my speech will be faxed to you then, but let me give you the gist of it. I'm going to tell them that the United States will do whatever we deem necessary to protect the lives of our citizens and the lives of all who stand with us in the respect of human life. Then I'm going to call upon France to make known to the world the exact methods and means by which it will administer an antivirus in exchange for the weapons that are now streaming to its northern shores. A guarantee. Without any such guarantee, the United States will be forced to assume that the New Allegiance intends to let us die a terrible death after we have been stripped of our weapons."

Dwight wasn't reacting. They both knew where this was heading.

"Under no circumstances will I lead my people to a needless death. If we are to be killed like sheep at the slaughter, then I will deal in kind to those who would threaten my people. With this in mind I'm authorizing the targeting of Paris and twenty-seven other undisclosed locations with nuclear weapons. In five days, short of receiving a guarantee that the United States will indeed be given an antivirus for the Raison Strain, much of France will cease to exist. The innocent citizens will have been fairly warned—make for the south. In a nutshell, you now have my speech. In light of our situation, martial is the least of your concerns."

An aide whispered softly in his ear. "Sir, I have Theresa Sumner from the CDC."

He nodded. The senate majority leader was still silent, reeling.

"If you have a problem with this, take it up with me in the morning briefing. Thank you, Dwight. I have to go."

He set the phone down and took a cell phone from the aide. The deputy secretary of state, Merton Gains, was walking toward him carrying a red folder. Judging by the man's face, the folder undoubtedly contained more bad news. The secretary of state was on his way to the Middle East for a summit with several Arab nations, but it was too soon for news from his meetings. What else could have prompted Gains's entry? Too many possibilities to consider.

The president lifted the cell phone to his ear. "Hello, Theresa."

"Good afternoon, Mr. President." Her voice sounded thin.

"Any word on the tests?"

"Yes." She paused.

Blair took a deep breath. "This isn't sounding good."

"It's not. Monique's encoding survived the vaccine's mutation, but I'm afraid it's no longer effective in neutralizing the virus."

"Meaning it doesn't work."

"Basically, yes."

"Well, does it or doesn't it? Don't give me 'basically.'"

"It doesn't work. And to make matters worse, she's gone missing."

"How could she go missing?"

"We're working on it. She didn't show up this morning. Kara Hunter is frantic. Something about Monique being able to find Thomas."

It was the worst possible news he could have received two minutes before his address. Blair lowered his head and closed his eyes.

"Um, sir?"

"I'm here."

"I just wanted to apologize. I let some details about the Strain slip to—"

"Yes, we know, Theresa. It's okay; it had to come out sooner or later anyway. It worked out. Find Monique. As soon as you do, I want to see her in Washington."

He paused. This was a bad day for news. "And if you don't mind, tell Kara that our forces found the farm Monique described to us outside of Paris. It's deserted. There's no sign of her brother. They also found the lean-to in the quarry, but no body. We had to pull our people. My condolences."

"Okay, I will. There's still hope, sir. We have over ten thousand scientists working on a—"

"Please. You've already done a good job persuading me that finding a solution in time is highly unlikely. We're going to have to find the antivirus that already exists. Assuming they have it."

"Monique thinks they do," Theresa said. "She seems quite confident it's a combination of her code and the information Thomas Hunter gave them."

Merton Gains eased into a chair next to him and shot him a glance.

"Yes, of course. Hunter. It all goes back to Hunter." He sighed. "Okay, thank you. If anything new comes up, tell them to interrupt me."

He closed the phone, mind swimming.

"It looks like it's started," Gains said. "We have reports of widespread rioting in Jakarta and Bangkok." He opened the folder. "There are a number of cities on this report, sir." He stopped and looked up at Blair. "Including Tel Aviv."

The skin at the back of Blair's neck tingled. Israel? He'd spent a full hour on the phone with Isaac Benjamin early this morning, and it was all he could do to keep the man from hanging up on him. Israel was fracturing on every fault line inherent in their delicate political system. They were the only nation with nuclear weapons not to meet France's schedule for compliance, and they'd received a new demand overnight, threatening a first strike if Israel didn't ship their weapons from where they'd been gathered in the ports of Tel Aviv and Haifa.

"Get Benjamin on the phone," he said. "If he's unavailable, I want you to speak to the deputy. We can't stop the rioting, but we'd better keep the Israelis in line."

The UN's secretary general was introducing him at the podium.

"My address is only two minutes; you tell them to sit tight until I can talk to Benjamin."

"The president of the United States."

There was no applause.

Blair approached the podium, shook the secretary general's hand, and faced the circle of countries gathered in New York for answers to this, the world's greatest crisis since man first formed nations.

"Thank you. We're gathered . . ."

It was as far as he got. One of the doors to his right slammed open. The room was deadly silent and every head instinctively turned. There in the doorway stood his chief of staff, Ron Kreet, with an expression that made Blair think he'd swallowed a bitter pill. His face was pale.

Kreet didn't offer a hint of apology. He simply tapped his lips. Meaning he needed to speak to the president. Now.

Blair glanced at the delegates. It was highly unusual, clearly, but Kreet knew this better than most—he'd spent two years as their ambassador to the United Nations.

Something had happened. Something very bad.

"Excuse me for a moment," Blair said and walked off the platform.

32

TWELVE ADULTS and five children. Seventeen. That was how many had entered the lake and escaped as outcasts.

They rode for five hours in a strange silence. Slowly the others began to talk about their experience in the lake. Slowly the others' sorrow over having lost Rachelle was replaced by the wonder of their own resurrection in the red waters. Slowly Thomas and Marie and Samuel were left to their own lingering sorrow.

In the sixth hour, Thomas began to speak to Marie and Samuel about their mother. About how she had saved their lives and the lives of the others by leading them all to the lake. About her courage in placing them on the horses first and then saving his life by coming back for him. About Rachelle's place now, with Elyon, though he really didn't understand this last thing.

They reached the forest's northern edge after seven hours, and all signs of the pursuit were gone.

There they rolled Rachelle in a blanket and buried her in a deep grave as was customary when the circumstances did not favor cremation. They set fruits and flowers by her body and then filled in the grave.

"Mount!" he cried and swung into his saddle.

A fresh determination had filled him over the hours. His destiny was now with Elyon. With every waking moment he would now honor the memory of his wife, and he would cherish the two children she'd given him, but his path was now beyond him.

He sat on his horse and stared at the blistering, red-hued dunes. They'd stopped at a creek and filled the canteens sewn into all saddles. It was spring water, clear and fresh. They wouldn't use it for bathing. Even then, they had only enough to keep them for two or three days at most.

Johan eased his horse next to Thomas. "Now where?"

He cleared his throat. "They won't expect us to leave the forest."

"No, because there's no sense in leaving the forest," Mikil said from behind. "We've never lived in the desert. Where will we find water? Food?"

"I've lived in the desert," Johan said.

"The desert," Thomas said. "All I know is that we ride into the desert."

Johan looked at him. "You say that as if you know something more."

"Only that we are meant to be there."

"The sand will show our tracks," Mikil said.

"Not in the northern canyon lands," Johan countered. "We could lose them for good there."

"We could lose ourselves for good there."

The others had mounted and now sat on their horses in a long line, staring out at the desert.

"Do you think the lakes in the other forests are . . ." Jamous stopped.

"Red?" Thomas said. "I don't know. But they won't work the way they used to. The only way to defeat the disease now is to follow Justin in his death."

"And the disease is gone forever," Lucy said.

Thomas turned to the little girl with bright green eyes. "You know this?"

"That's what I heard."

"From whom?"

"From Justin. In the lake."

He exchanged a knowing grin with the girl's mother, Alisha.

"She's right," Marie said.

"Well. Then maybe Lucy should lead us. Where do you say we should go?" he asked.

Lucy laughed. His own daughter managed a smile, which brought him hope, considering her loss. Thomas returned her smile. Her eyes watered and she turned away.

He faced the red dunes again, resisting his own sorrow.

"Will the Horde find us here, Johan?"

"Not tonight. Tomorrow they will."

"Is . . ." Samuel asked the question no one had asked yet. "Is Justin dead?"

"It depends on what you mean by Justin," Thomas said.

"I mean the Justin who drowned. Not Elyon, but Justin."

Justin. They all pondered the question.

"We saw him drown," Johan said. "And I watched the lake for several hours. He didn't come up. If his body is gone, Ciphus may have stolen it to cast blame on Thomas. But does it matter if Justin is dead or not? It's just a body he was using. Right? We all know that Elyon isn't dead."

Johan had been the one who'd shoved his sword into that body— perhaps he was easing his guilt.

They let the matter rest.

Thomas looked down the line of horses. Five experienced warriors including William and Suzan, five children, and six civilians including Jeremiah, the converted old man who'd once been a Scab. Ronin and Arvyl, of course. And the last three were from the Southern Forest as well.

An unlikely crew, but one he suddenly felt supremely proud of. From so many, these were the few who'd responded to Justin's cry. The fate of the world now rested on the shoulders of people like Marie and Lucy and Johan. Thomas glanced at his arm. The disease would never gray it again. They were truly new people. No longer Forest People, certainly not the Horde. They were outcasts.

They were the chosen. Those who had died. Those who lived.

I love you, Rachelle. I love you dearly. I will always love you.

He wanted to cry again.

"Then we make camp here tonight," he said, looking out at the red hills. "No fires."

"You're saying we waste the rest of the day?" Mikil asked. "What if I'm wrong? What if they do come after us?"

"Then we will post guards. But we wait here."

"What's that?" Samuel asked.

Thomas followed his gaze. A dot on the sand. A rider.

His heart rose into his throat. The horse was riding hard, straight toward them from the desert. A scout?

"Back!" Mikil said, pulling her horse around. "Take cover. If they see us, they'll report it."

The horses responded to the tugs on their reins and retreated behind a row of trees.

They peered from their hiding. The rider was moving as fast as Thomas had ever seen, down the slope of the last dune, leaving a trail of disturbed sand in his wake. A black horse. The rider was dressed in white. His cloak flapped behind him and he rode on the balls of his feet, bent over.

"It's him!" Lucy cried. She dropped off her mother's horse and was running before Thomas could stop her.

"Lucy!"

"It's Justin!" she said.

Thomas blinked, strained for a better view. His heart hammered. And then he knew that the man on the black horse riding pell-mell toward them *was* Justin.

His shoulder-length hair flew with his cape, and even at this distance, Thomas was sure he could see the brilliant green of his eyes. His passion was immediately infectious.

Thomas was frozen by the sudden realization that Justin was actually alive.

Had he come to give Rachelle back to him?

Justin's horse stamped to a halt twenty feet from the trees. His eyes were on Lucy, who was running out to him.

This was Elyon, and Elyon leaned over the side of his horse, grabbed Lucy under her arms, swept her up into his saddle, and spurred his horse into a full sprint. Lucy squealed. He swung the horse back less than fifty paces out and rode in a wide circle, now laughing aloud with the girl.

Thomas urged his horse forward, but he wasn't the only one; they were all rushing from the trees and dismounting.

Justin rode in, lowered Lucy to the ground, and measured them all with a bright, mischievous glint in his eyes.

"Good afternoon," he said.

None of them replied.

"How did you like the lake?"

Thomas slid off his saddle, dropped to one knee, and lowered his head. "Forgive me."

Justin dismounted and walked up to him. "I have. And you followed me, didn't you?" He touched Thomas's cheek. "Look at me."

Thomas lifted his head. There wasn't a blemish on Justin's face to show for the pounding he'd taken. Except for his eyes, he looked every bit human. Yet in those deep emerald eyes Thomas could see only Elyon.

"I knew I could depend on you. Thank you," Justin said.

Thomas wasn't sure he'd heard just right. Thank you? He lowered his head, swamped with emotion. What about Rachelle?

"Look at me, Thomas."

When he looked up, he saw that tears were running down Justin's face. Thomas began to cry. He didn't know there was anything left in him to cry, but there, kneeling, staring into Elyon's crying eyes, he began to shake with long, desperate sobs.

"You understand what you've done, and it's tearing at your mind. You want your wife back, I know. But that's not what I have in mind."

"I'm sorry!" He sounded foolish, but at the moment he only wished he could say whatever was needed to earn Justin's complete forgiveness for his doubt.

"You're a prince to me," Justin said. "I've shown you my mind and my way, but soon I will show you my heart."

"But Rachelle . . ." Thomas's heart felt as though it might explode.

"Is in good hands," Justin finished. "Laughing like she used to in the lake."

His eyes made contact with the others, pausing at each face. "The Great Romance is for you. If only one of you would have followed me, the heavens would not have been able to contain my cries of joy."

Justin's eyes grew impassioned. He hurried over to Johan, lifted his hand, and kissed it. "Johan . . ."

Johan fell to his knees and sobbed before Justin could say more.

"I forgive you." He kissed the man's head. "Now you will ride with me."

Justin stepped to the old man Jeremiah, lifted his hand, and kissed it. "You, Jeremiah, I called you out of the Horde like so many. But you came."

The old man dropped to his knees and began to weep.

Justin ran to Lucy's mother and kissed her hand. "And you, Alisha, I once told you that love would conquer death, but that it wouldn't look like love; do you remember?"

She dropped to her knees, lowered her head, and cried.

"No, no, you followed me, Alisha! You all followed me!"

He went down the line, kissing each of their hands. Their Creator had taken the form of a man and was kissing their hands. They could hardly bear it, much less understand it.

Justin stepped back from the seventeen followers, all still on their knees. He walked to his left, then to his right, like a man overcome by his first viewing of a magnificent painting he himself had painted. "Wonderful," he whispered to himself. "Incredible." His face twisted with emotion. "Wonderful, wonderful, wonderful." He paced, face stricken with emotion.

He suddenly spun from them, fell to his knees, threw his head back, and thrust both hands at the sky.

"Father!" he cried. "My father, she is beautiful!" He burst into a joyful laugh, and his brilliant eyes, full of love, traveled around the small group. "My bride is beautiful! How I have waited for this day."

Thomas immediately understood the significance of what they were watching. He could hardly see it for his own tears, and he couldn't hear too well over the crashing of his own heart, but he knew that this was about the Great Romance between Elyon and his creation. His people.

Elyon was restoring the Great Romance. Teeleh had stolen his first love, but now Justin had reclaimed her. The price had been his own life. He'd taken her disease on himself and he'd drowned with it, inviting them to embrace his invitation to the Romance by following him into the lake to drown with him. To live as his bride!

And Justin had called to his father. Until this moment, Thomas had never thought of such clear distinctions in Elyon's character. But it could hardly be clearer—somehow Elyon the father had given Elyon, his son, a bride. They were the bride. Thomas couldn't help but think that this very moment had been chosen long ago.

Justin stood, rushed to his horse, and grabbed his sword. He thrust its tip into the sand and began to run, dragging the sword. He ran around them as they watched, drawing a large circle.

This was the symbol they had once used to signify the union between a man and a woman. Half a circle on the man's forehead for a betrothal, a full circle for their marriage. He was symbolically making them his bride.

Justin finished the circle and threw his sword on the sand. "You are mine," he said. "Never break the circle that unites us. Do you understand what I'm asking you to do?"

They couldn't speak.

"Your lives have always been about the Great Romance, and in the days to come you will understand that like never before. Your love will be tested. Others will join you. Some will leave the circle. Some will die. All of you will suffer. The Horde will hate you because their hearts have been stolen and their eyes have been blinded by the Shataiki. But if you keep your eyes on me until the end"—he swallowed—"the lake will seem tame compared to what awaits us."

"None of us will ever leave you," Lucy cried.

Justin looked at her as if he himself was going to cry again. "Then guard your heart, my princess. Remember how I love you, and love me the same. Always."

He was looking at Lucy, but he was talking to all of them.

"You won't see me again for some time, but you will have my water. Go to the Southern Forest, then beyond to the farthest southern edge, where you will find a small lake. Johan knows it." He looked over their heads at the forest beyond. "I charge you to bring them to me. One by one, if you must. Show them my heart. Lead them into the red water."

A hundred questions flooded Thomas's mind. He found the courage to speak, though not to stand. "All the lakes are red?"

"All of my lakes are red. To whoever seeks, this water will represent life, just as you found life by following me. To the rest, the lakes will be a threat."

"Are the wars over?" Mikil asked.

"My peace is their war. The war will come against you. For a time, you will find safety in the Southern Forest." He ran to his horse, pulled something out of his saddlebag, and faced them.

"Do you recognize this, Thomas?"

An old leather-bound book. A Book of History!

Justin grinned. "A Book of History." He tossed it to Thomas, who caught it with both hands. "There are thousands, not just the few that Qurong carries in his trunks. This is only one, but it will guide you."

Thomas felt its worn cover and drew his thumb along the title.

The Histories Recorded by His Beloved

He cracked the book open. Cursive text ran across the page.

"Read it well," Justin said. "Learn from it. Ronin will help you discover my teachings from the Southern Forest. He'll show you the way."

Thomas closed the book. "What about the blank book?" He touched the small lump at his waist where the empty book still rested. "Does it have a purpose?"

"The blank books. There are many of those as well. They are very powerful, my friend. They create history, but only *in* the histories. Here they are powerless. One day you may understand, but in the meantime, guard the one you have—in the wrong hands it could wreak havoc."

Justin took a deep breath. "Now I must go." He put his hand on his chest. "Keep your hearts strong and true. Follow the way of the book I have left with you. Never leave the circle."

He eyed them each tenderly, and when his eyes rested on him, Thomas felt both weakened and strengthened by a stare that ran straight through him.

Justin turned toward his horse.

"Wait." Thomas stood. "If this book works only in the histories, that means the histories are real? The virus?"

"Am I a boy, Thomas?" Justin turned back, smiling. "Am I a lamb or a lion, or am I Justin?"

"You are a father and a son?"

"I am. And the water as well."

Thomas's mind swam.

"Will I dream again?"

"Did you dream last night?"

"Yes. But not about the histories."

"Did you eat the fruit?"

"No."

"Well then."

He swung into his saddle and winked. "Remember, never leave the circle." With a slight nudge of his heel, his stallion walked away, and then trotted.

Then he galloped up the same dune from which he'd first come, reared the horse once at the crest, and disappeared into the horizon.

33

THIS HAD better be important," President Blair said.

Kreet's eyes darted around furtively. This wasn't like the battle-hardened general.

"Don't tell me the Israelis have launched," Blair asked.

"They launched a missile into the Bay of Biscay. Cheyenne Mountain recorded a fifty-megaton blast fifteen minutes ago. It was a warning shot. The next one goes into the naval base at Brest. They've given France twenty-four hours to guarantee Israel's survival."

Blair didn't know what to say. They'd discussed this possibility, but hearing that it had actually happened immobilized him. Finally he cleared his throat and turned back for the door.

"Any response from Paris?"

"Too early."

"Okay, keep this quiet. As soon as I'm finished, I want our people out of here. The ambassador stays. Leave him uninformed."

"Excuse me, sir." An aide interrupted by handing Kreet a note. "A priority message."

He took the note, glanced at it. Stared at it.

"What now?" Blair asked.

"It's the French. They've answered Israel's demands."

"And?"

"They've reciprocated."

Someone had cracked the door, preparing to open it for him. One of the European delegates in the main hall was yelling about innocent citizens, but the voice sounded distant, muted by a ring that echoed through Blair's head.

"Cheyenne has picked up a missile headed over the Mediterranean. ETA, thirty minutes . . . that was four minutes ago."

Blair couldn't think straight. Nothing, not even a week of anticipation, could prepare anyone for a moment like this. France had just launched nuclear weapons at Israel.

"We don't know their target. It may be a warning shot in return," Kreet said.

President Blair stepped to the door. "Or it may not be. God help us, Ron. God help us all."

This changed everything.

The basement room used to be a root cellar—cold enough to keep vegetables from rotting. They'd plastered the walls and sealed the ducts, but it was still cold enough to serve its purpose.

Carlos stepped in, flipped on the lights, and walked to the gurney. A white sheet covered the body. He hesitated only a moment, then lifted the corner.

Thomas Hunter's blank eyes faced the ceiling. Dead. As dead as any man Carlos had ever killed. This time there would be no mistake; he'd gone out of his way to make sure of that. On both occasions that the man had seemingly come back to life, the circumstances were suspect. Carlos had never actually confirmed his death, for one thing. And the man's recovery had been almost instantaneous.

This time his body had rested in this sealed room for nearly three days, and he hadn't so much as twitched.

Dead. Very, very dead.

Satisfied, Carlos dropped the sheet over Thomas's face, left the room, and headed down the hall. It was time to finish what they'd all started.

THE JOURNEY CONTINUES
WITH **WHITE** . . .

WHITE

THE GREAT PURSUIT

North Dakota

FINLEY, POPULATION 543. That's what the sign read.

Finley, population 0. That's what the sign could very well read in two weeks, Mike Orear thought.

He stood on the edge of town, hot wind blowing through his hair, fighting a gnawing fear that the gray buildings erected along these vacated streets were tombstones waiting for the dead. The town had bustled with nearly three thousand residents before he'd gone off to school in North Forks and become a football star.

The last time he'd visited, two years earlier, the population had dwindled to under a thousand. Now, just over five hundred. One of countless dying towns scattered across America. But this one was special.

This was the town where his mother, Nancy Orear, lived. His father, Carl, and his only sister, Betsy, too. None of them knew he'd come. They'd talked every day since he'd broken the news of the Raison Strain, but yesterday Mike had come to the terrible conclusion that talking was no longer enough.

He had to see them again. Before they died. And before the march on Washington ramped up.

Mike left his car, slung his jacket over his shoulder, and walked up Central Avenue's sidewalk. He wanted to see without being seen, which, in Finley, was easier done on foot than in a flashy car. But there wasn't a soul in sight. Not one.

He wondered how much they knew about the virus. As much as he did, of course. They were glued to their sets at this moment, waiting for word of a breakthrough, like every other American.

His feet felt numb. Working 24/7 around the studio in Atlanta, he had thought of himself as a crusader on the front lines of this mess, slashing the way to the truth. Stirring the hearts of a million viewers, giving them hope. Breathing life into America. But his drive north along deserted highways awakened him to a new reality.

America was already dying. And the truth was killing them.

The truth that they were about to die, regardless of what the frantic talking heads said. Middle America was too smart to believe that grasping at straws was anything more than just that.

His feet crunched on the dust-blown pavement. Citizens State Bank loomed on his right.

Closed, the sign said. Not a soul.

He'd once held an account at this bank. Saved up his first forty dollars to buy the old blue Schwinn off Toby. And where was Toby today? Last he'd heard, his friend had taken a job in Los Angeles, defying his fear of earthquakes. Today earthquakes were the least of Toby's worries.

The sign in the window of Finley Lounge said it was open—the one establishment probably booming as a result of the crisis. For some the news would go down better with beer.

Mike walked by, unnerved by the thought of going in and meeting someone he might know. He wanted to talk to his mother and his father and Betsy, no one else. In a small inexplicable way, he somehow felt responsible for the virus, though simply letting America in on the dirty little secret that they were all doomed hardly qualified him.

He swallowed and walked on by Roger's Heating. Closed.

Still not a soul on Central or any of the side streets that he could see.

Mike stopped and turned around. So quiet. The wind seemed oblivious to the virus it had breathed into this town. An American flag flapped slowly over the post office, but he doubted any mail was being delivered today.

Somewhere a thousand scientists were searching for a way to break the

Raison Strain's back. Somewhere politicians and heads of states were screaming for answers and scrambling to explain away the inconceivable notion that death was at their doorstep. Somewhere nuclear warheads were flying through the air.

But here in Nowhere, America, better known as Finley, incorporated July 12, 1926, all Mike could hear was the sound of wind. All he could see were vacant streets and a blue sky dotted with puffy white clouds.

He suddenly thought that leaving his car had been a mistake. He should hurry back, jump in, and head to the protest march in Washington, where he was expected by morning.

Instead, Mike turned on his heels and began to run. Past Dave's Auto. On to Lincoln Street. To the end where the old white house his father had bought nearly forty years ago still stood.

He walked up to the door, calming his heavy breathing. No sound, no sign of life. He should at least hear the tube, shouldn't he?

Mike bounded up the steps, yanked the screen door open, and barged into the house.

There on the sofa, facing a muted television, sat his mother, his father, and Betsy, surrounded by scattered dishes, half-empty glasses, and bags of Safeway-brand potato chips. They were dressed in pajamas, hair tangled. Their arms were crossed and their faces hung like sacks from their cheekbones, but the moment they saw him, their eyes widened. If not for this sign of life, Mike might have guessed they were already dead.

"Mikey?" His mother jerked forward and paused, as if trying to decide whether or not she should trust her eyes. "Mike!" She pushed off the sofa and ran toward him, sobbing. Engulfed him in a hug.

He knew then that the march on Washington was the right thing to do. There was no other hope. They were all going to die.

He dropped his head on her shoulder and began to cry.

1

KARA HUNTER angled her car through the Johns Hopkins University campus, cell phone plastered against her ear. The world was starting to fall apart, and she knew, deep down where people aren't supposed to know things, that something very important depended on her. Thomas depended on her, and the world depended on Thomas.

The situation was about as clear as an overcast midnight, but there was one star shining on the horizon, and so she kept her eyes on that bright guiding light.

She snugged the cell phone between her ear and shoulder and made a turn using both hands. "Forgive me for sounding desperate, Mr. Gains, but if you won't give me the clearance I need, I'm taking a gun in there."

"I didn't say I wouldn't get it for you," the deputy secretary of state said. She should be talking to the president himself, Kara thought, but he wasn't exactly the most accessible man on the planet these days. Unless, of course, your name was Thomas. "I said I would try. But this is a bit unconventional. Dr. Bancroft may . . . Excuse me." The phone went quiet. She could hear a muffled voice.

Gains came back on, speaking fast. "I'm gonna have to go."

"What is it?"

"It's need to know—"

"I am need to know! I may be the only link you have to Thomas, assuming he's alive! And Monique for that matter, assuming she's alive. Talk to me, for heaven's sake!"

He didn't answer.

"You owe me this, Mr. Secretary. You owe this to the country for not responding to Thomas the first time."

"You keep this to yourself." His tone left her with no doubt about his frustration at having to tell her anything. But of all people he must know that she might be on to something with this experiment of hers.

"Of course."

"We've just had a nuclear exchange," Gains said.

Nuclear?

"More accurately, Israel fired a missile into the ocean off the coast of France, and France has responded in kind. They have an ICBM in the air as we speak. I really have to go."

"Please, sir, call Dr. Bancroft."

"My aide already has."

"Thank you." She snapped the phone closed.

Surely it couldn't end this way! But Thomas had warned that the virus might be only part of the total destruction recorded in the Books of Histories. In fact, they'd discussed the possibility that the apocalypse predicted by the apostle John might be precipitated by the virus. Wasn't Israel featured prominently in John's apocalypse?

She swerved to avoid a lone bicycler, muttered a curse, and pushed the accelerator. Dr. Bancroft was her last hope. Thomas had been missing for nearly three days, and Monique had disappeared yesterday. She had to find out if either was alive—if not here, then in the other reality.

Bancroft was in his lab; she knew that much from a phone call earlier. She also knew that her brother's records were under the control of the government. Classified. Any inquiry about his earlier session with Dr. Bancroft would require authorization beyond the good doctor. With any luck, Gains had given her at least that much.

Kara parked her car and ran down the same steps she'd descended over a week earlier with CIA Director Phil Grant. The blinds on the basement door were drawn. She rapped on the glass.

"Dr. Bancroft!"

The door flew inward almost instantly. A frumpy man with bags under fiery eyes stood before her. "Yes, I will," he said.

"You will? You'll what?"

"Help you. Hurry!" The psychologist pulled her in, leaned out for a quick glance up the concrete stairwell, and closed the door. He hurried toward his desk.

"I've been poring over this data on Thomas for a week now. I've called a dozen colleagues—not idiots, mind you—and not one of them has heard of a silent sleep brain."

"Did the deputy secretary of state—"

"Just talked to them, yes. What's your idea?"

"What do you mean by a 'silent sleep brain'?" she asked.

"My coined term. A brain that doesn't dream while sleeping, like your brother's."

"There has to be some other explanation, right? We know he's dreaming. Or at least aware of another reality while he's sleeping."

"Unless this"—Bancroft indicated the room—"is the dream." He winked.

The doctor was sounding like Thomas now. They'd both gone off the deep end. Then again, what she was about to suggest would make this dream business sound perfectly logical by comparison.

"What's your idea?" he asked again.

She walked to the leather bed Thomas had slept on and faced the professor. The room's lights were low. A computer screen cast a dull glow over his desk. The brain-wave monitor sat dormant to her left.

"Do you still have the blood you drew from Thomas?" she asked.

"Blood?"

"The blood work—do you still have it?"

"That would have gone to our lab for analysis."

"And then where?"

"I doubt it's back."

"If it is—"

"Then it would be in the lab upstairs. Why are you interested in his blood?"

Kara took a deep breath. "Because of something that happened to Monique. She crossed over into Thomas's dreams. The only thing that links the realities other than dreams is blood, a person's life force, as it were. There's something unique about blood in religion, right? Christians believe that without the shedding of blood there is no forgiveness of sins. In this metaphysical reality Thomas has breached, blood also plays a critical role. At least as far as I can tell."

"Go on. What does this have to do with Monique's dreams?"

"Monique fell asleep with an open wound. She was with Thomas, who also had an open wound on his wrist. I know this sounds strange, but Monique told me she thought she crossed into this other reality because her blood was in contact with his when she dreamed. Thomas's blood is the bridge to his dream world."

Bancroft lifted a hand and adjusted his round glasses. "And you think that . . ." He stopped. The conclusion was obvious.

"I want to try."

"But they say that Thomas is dead," Bancroft said.

"For all we know, so is Monique. At least in this reality. The problem is, the world might still depend on those two. We can't afford for them to be dead. I'm not saying I understand exactly how or why this could work, I'm just saying we have to try something. This is the only thing I can think of."

"You want to re-create the environment that allowed Monique to cross over," he stated flatly.

"Under your supervision. Please . . ."

"No need to plead." A glimmer of anticipation lit his eyes. "Believe me, if I hadn't seen Thomas's monitors with my own eyes, I wouldn't be so eager. Besides, I've been tested positive for the virus he predicted from these dreams of his."

The psychologist's willingness didn't really surprise her. He was wacky enough to try it on his own, without her.

"Then we need his blood," she said.

Dr. Myles Bancroft headed toward the door. "We need his blood."

⸻

It took less than ten minutes to hook her up to the electrodes Bancroft would use to measure her brain activity. She didn't care about the whole testing rigmarole—she only wanted to dream with Thomas's blood. True, the notion was about as scientific as snake handling. But lying there with wires attached to her head in a dozen spots made the whole experiment feel surprisingly reasonable.

Bancroft tore off the blood-pressure cuff. "Pretty high. You're going to have to sleep, remember? You haven't told this to your heart yet."

"Then give me a stronger sedative."

"I don't want to go too strong. The pills you took should kick in any moment. Just try to relax."

Kara closed her eyes and tried to empty her mind. The missile that France had fired at Israel had either already landed or was about to. She couldn't imagine how a nuclear detonation in the Middle East would affect the current scenario. Scattered riots had started just this morning, according to the news. They were mostly in Third World countries, but unless a solution surfaced quickly, the West wouldn't be far behind.

They had ten days until the Raison Strain reached full maturity. Symptoms could begin to show among the virus's first contractors, which included her and Thomas, in five days. According to Monique, they had those five days to acquire an antivirus. Maybe six, seven at most. They were all guessing, of course, but Monique had seemed pretty confident that the virus could be reversed if administered within a day or two, maybe three, of first symptoms.

Too many maybes.

Five days. Could she feel any of the symptoms now? She focused on her skin. Nothing. Her joints, fingers, ankles. She moved them all and still felt nothing. Unless the slight tingle she felt on her right calf was a rash.

Now she was imagining.

Her mind suddenly swam. Symptom? No, the drug was beginning to kick in.

"I think it's time," she said.

"One second."

The doctor fiddled with his machine and finally came over. "You're feeling tired. Woozy?"

"Close enough."

"Do you want any local anesthetic?"

She hadn't considered that. "Just make the cut small." She wanted a mark so that if she did wake up in another reality, she would have the proof on her arm.

"Large enough to bleed," Bancroft said.

"Just do it."

Bancroft wet her right forearm with a cotton ball and then carefully pressed a scalpel against her skin. Sharp pain stabbed up her arm and she winced.

"Easy," he said. "Finished."

He picked up a syringe with some of Thomas's blood. The sample was small—they would use nearly half with this experiment of theirs.

"It would have been easier to inject this," he said.

"We don't know if it would work that way. Just do it the way it happened with Monique. We don't have time to mess around."

He lowered the syringe and pushed five or six drops of Thomas's blood onto her arm. It merged with a tiny bubble of her own blood. The doctor smeared the two together with his gloved finger. For a long moment they both stared at the mixed red stain.

Their eyes met. Soft pop music played lightly over the speakers—an instrumental version of "Dancing Queen" by Abba. He'd turned the lights even lower than when she'd first entered.

"I hope this works," she said.

"Go to sleep."

Kara closed her eyes again.

"Should I wake you?"

Thomas had always claimed that an hour sleeping could be a year in a dream. Her crossing to his world would be precipitated by falling asleep here. Her crossing back would be precipitated by dreaming there.

"Wake me up in a hour," she said.

2

TWO CEREMONIES characterized the Circle more than any other: the union and the passing. The union was a wedding ceremony. The passing was a funeral. Both were celebrations.

Tonight, a hundred yards from the camp beside the red pool that had drawn them to this site, Thomas led his tribe in the passing. The tribe consisted of sixty-seven members, including men, women, and children, and they were all here to both mourn and celebrate Elijah's death.

They would mourn because, although Elijah had left no blood relatives, the old man had been a delight. His stories at the night campfires had been faithfully attended by half the tribe. Elijah had a way of making the young children howl with laughter while mesmerizing his older listeners with mystery and intrigue. Only Tanis had told such brilliant tales, they all agreed, and that was before the Crossing, long ago.

There was more about Elijah to like than his stories, of course: his love of children, his fascination with Elyon, his words of comfort in times when the Horde's pursuit became more stressful than any of them could bear.

But they also celebrated Elijah's passing as they would celebrate anyone's passing. Elijah was now in better company. He was with Justin. None of them knew precisely how nor what those such as Rachelle and Elijah were actually doing with Justin, but Thomas's tribe had no doubts whatsoever that their loved ones were with their Creator. And they had enough of a memory of swimming in the intoxicating water of the emerald lake to anticipate rejoining Elyon in such bliss.

They stood in a circle around the woodpile, looking at Elijah's still body in silence. Some of their cheeks were wet with tears; some smiled gently; all were lost in their own memories of the man.

Thomas glanced at the tribe. His family now. Each man, woman, and child carried a blazing torch, ready to light the pyre at the appropriate moment. Most of the people were dressed in the same beige tunics they'd worn earlier in the day, though many had placed desert flowers in their hair and painted their faces with bright colors mixed from powdered chalk and water.

Samuel and Marie stood to his left beside Mikil and Jamous. They'd grown quickly in this past year, practically a man and a woman now. They both wore the same coin-shaped pendants that all members of the Circle wore, usually on a thin thong of leather around their necks, but also as anklets or bracelets as Samuel and Marie did now.

Johan and William had joined the tribe for tomorrow's council meeting and now stood to Thomas's right.

Beyond the Circle, the red pool's dark water glistened with the light of the torches. A hundred fruit trees and palms rose around the oasis. Before the night was done, they would feast on the fruit and dance under its power, but for now they allowed themselves a moment of sorrow.

Thomas and his small band had found their first of twenty-seven red pools amid a small patch of trees, exactly where Justin said they would. In thirteen months, the Circle had led nearly a thousand Scabs into the red waters, where they drowned of their own will and found new life. A thousand. A minuscule number when compared to the two million Scabs who now lived in the dominant forest. Even so, the moment Qurong became aware of the growing movement, he'd organized a campaign to wipe the Circle from the Earth. They had become nomads, making camp in canvas tents near the red pools when possible, and running when not. Mostly running.

Johan had taught them the skills of desert survival: how to plant and harvest desert wheat, how to make thread from the stalks and weave tunics. Bedding, furniture, even their tents were all eerily reminiscent of the Horde way, though notably colored and spiced with Forest Dweller tastes. They ate fruit with their bread and adorned their tents with wild-flowers.

Thomas returned his thoughts to the body of Elijah on the wood. In the end they would all be dead—it was the one certainty for all living creatures. But after their deaths, they each would find a life just barely imagined this side of the colored forest. In many ways he envied the old man.

Thomas lifted his torch high. The others followed his lead.

"We are born of water and of spirit," he cried out.

"Of water and spirit," the tribe repeated. A new energy seemed to rise in the cool night air.

"We burn this body in defiance of death. It holds no power over us. The spirit lives, though the flesh dies. We are born of water and of the spirit!"

A hushed echo of his words swept through the circle.

"Whether we be taken by the sword or by age or by any cause, we are alive still, passing from this world to the next. For this reason we celebrate Elijah's passing tonight. He is where we all long to be!"

The excitement was now palpable. They'd said their good-byes and paid their respects. Now it was time to relish their victory over death.

Thomas glanced at Samuel and Marie, who were both staring at him. Their own mother, his wife, Rachelle, had been killed thirteen months ago. They'd mourned her passing more than most, only because they'd understood less then than now.

He winked at his children, then shook the torch once overhead. "To life with Justin!"

He rushed the pyre and thrust his torch into the wood. As one, the Circle converged on the woodpile. Those close enough shoved their torches in; the rest threw them.

With a sudden *swoosh,* the fire engulfed Elijah's body.

Immediately a drumbeat rolled through the night. Voices yelled in jubilation and arms were thrust skyward in victory, perhaps exaggerated in hope but true to the spirit of the Circle. Without the belief in what awaited each of them, all other hope was moot.

Elijah had been taken home to the Great Romance. Tonight he was the bride, and his bridegroom, Justin, who was also Elyon, had taken him back into the lake of infinite waters. And more.

To say there wasn't at least some envy among the tribe at a time like this would be a lie.

They danced in a large circle around the roaring fire. Thomas laughed as the celebration took on a life of its own. He watched the Circle, his heart swelling with pride. Then he stepped back from the fire's dancing light and crossed his arms. He faced the dark night where cliffs were silhouetted by a starry sky.

"You see, Justin? We celebrate our passing with the same fervor that you showed us after your own."

An image filled his mind: Justin riding to them on a white horse the day after his drowning, then pulling up, eyes blazing with excitement. He'd run to each of them and grasped their hands. He'd pronounced them the Circle on that day.

The day Rachelle had been killed by the Horde.

"I hope you were right about settling here," a voice said softly at his shoulder.

He faced Johan, who followed his gaze to the cliffs.

"If the Horde is anywhere near, they've seen the fire already," Johan said.

Thomas clasped his shoulder. "You worry too much, my friend. When have we let the threat of a few Scabs distract us from celebrating our sacred love? Besides, there's been no warning from our guard."

"But we have heard that Woref has stepped up his search. I know that man; he's relentless."

"And so is our love for Justin. I'm sick of running."

Johan did not react. "We meet at daybreak?"

"Assuming the Horde hasn't swept us all out to the desert." Thomas winked. "At daybreak."

"You make light now. Soon enough it will be a reality," Johan said. He dipped his head and returned to the revelry.

⌘

They sat on flat rocks early the next morning, pondering. At least Thomas, Suzan, and Jeremiah were pondering, silent for the most part. The other members of the council—Johan, William, and Ronin—might also be pondering, but their cranial activity didn't interfere with their mouths.

"Never!" Ronin said. "I can tell you without the slightest reservation that if Justin were standing here today, in this very canyon, he would set you straight. He always insisted that we would be hated! Now you're suggesting that we go out of our way to appease the Horde? Why?"

"How can we influence the Horde if they hate us?" Johan demanded. "Yes, let them hate our beliefs. You have no argument from me there. But does this mean we should go out of our way to antagonize them so that they despise every albino they see?"

The Horde referred to them as albinos because their flesh wasn't scaly and gray like a Scab's skin. Ironic, because they were all darker than the Horde. In fact, nearly half of the Circle, including Suzan, had various shades of chocolate skin. They were the envy of most lighter-skinned albinos because the rich tones differentiated them so dramatically from the white Horde. Some members of the Circle even took to painting their skin brown for the ceremonies. All of them bore the albino name with pride. It meant they were different, and there was nothing they wanted more than to be different from the Horde.

Ronin paced on the sand, red-faced despite the cool air. "You're putting words in my mouth. I've never suggested we antagonize the Horde. But Justin was never for embracing the status quo. If the Horde is the culture, then Justin was counterculture. We lose that understanding and we lose who we are."

"You're not listening, Ronin." Johan sighed with frustration. "For the first six months, Qurong left us alone. He was too busy tearing down trees to make room for his new city. But now the winds have changed. This new campaign led by Woref isn't just a temporary distraction for them. I know Qurong! Worse, I know Woref. That old python once oversaw the Horde's intelligence under my command. At this very moment he's undoubtedly stalking us. He won't stop until every one of us is dead. You think Justin intended to lead us to our deaths?"

"Isn't that why we enter the red pools?" Ronin asked. "To die?" He grabbed the pendant that hung from his neck and held it out. "Doesn't our very history mark us as dead to this world?"

The medallion cradled in his hand had been carved from green jade found in the canyons north of the Southern Forest. Craftsmen inlaid the medallion with polished black slate to represent evil's encroachment on the colored forest. Within the black circle were tied two crossing straps of red-dyed leather, representing Justin's sacrifice in the red pools. Finally, they fixed a white circle hewn from marble where the red leather straps crossed.

"We find life, not death, in the pools," Johan said. "But even there, we might consider a change in our strategies."

Thomas looked at his late wife's brother. This wasn't the boy who'd once innocently bounded about the hills; this was the man who'd embraced a persona named Martyn and become a mighty Scab leader accustomed to having his way. Granted, Johan was no Martyn now, but he was still headstrong, and he was flexing his muscle.

"Think what you will about what Justin would or wouldn't have wanted," Johan said, "but remember that I was with him too."

Light flashed through Ronin's eyes, and for a moment Thomas thought he might remind Johan that he hadn't only been with Justin; he'd betrayed him. Oversaw his drowning. Murdered him.

But Ronin set his jaw and held his tongue.

"I did make my share of mistakes," Johan said, noting the look. "But I think he's forgiven me for that. And I don't think what I'm suggesting now is a mistake. Please, at least consider what I'm saying."

"What are you saying?" Thomas asked. "In the simplest of terms."

Johan stared into his eyes. "I'm saying that we have to make it easier for the enemies of Elyon to find him."

"Yes, but what does that mean?" Ronin demanded. "You're suggesting that the drowning is too difficult? It was Justin's way!"

"Did I say the drowning was too difficult?" Johan glared at Ronin, then closed his eyes and held up a hand. "Forgive me." Eyes open. "I'm saying that I know the Horde better than anyone here. I know their aversions and their passions." He looked to Jeremiah as if for support. The old man averted his eyes. "If we want to embrace them—to love them as Justin does—we have to allow them to identify with us. We must be more tolerant of their ways. We must consider using methods that are more acceptable to them."

"Such as?" Thomas asked.

"Such as opening the Circle to Scabs who haven't drowned."

"They would never be like us without drowning. They can't even eat our fruit without spitting it out."

Thomas spoke of the fruit that grew around the red pools. Although the red water was sweet to drink, it held no known medicinal value. The fruit that grew on the trees around the pools, on the other hand, was medicinal, and some of it was not unlike the fruit from the colored forest. Some fruits could heal; others gave nourishment far beyond a single bite. Some filled a person with an overpowering sense of love and joy—they called this kind woromo, which had quickly become the most valuable among all the fruits. To any Scab who hadn't entered the red pools, this particular fruit tasted bitter.

"That's right; they don't like our fruit," Johan said. "And they can't be like us—that's my point. If they can't be like us, then we might consider being more like them."

Thomas wasn't sure he'd heard right. Johan wouldn't suggest the Circle reverse what Justin had commanded. There had to be sensible nuances to what he was suggesting.

"I know it sounds odd," Johan continued, "but consider the possibilities. If we were to look more like them, smell like them, dress like them, refrain from flaunting our differences, they might be more willing to tolerate us. Maybe even to live among us. We could introduce them to Justin's teachings slowly and win them over."

"And what about the drowning?" Ronin asked.

Johan hesitated, then answered without looking at the man. "Perhaps if they follow Justin in principle, he wouldn't require that they actually drown." He looked at Ronin. "After all, love is a matter of the heart, not the flesh. Why can't someone follow Justin without changing who they are?"

Thomas felt his veins grow cold. Not because the suggestion was so preposterous, but because it made such terrible sense. It would seem that Johan, of all people, having been drawn out of deception as a member of the Horde, would stand firm on the doctrine of drowning. But Johan had made his case to Thomas once already—his suggestion was motivated by compassion for the Horde.

The survival of the thousand who followed Justin depended on being able to flee the Horde at a moment's notice. But the small nomadic communities were growing tired of running for their lives. This teaching from Johan would be embraced by some of them, Thomas had no doubt.

Ronin spit to one side, picked up his leather satchel, and started to walk away. "I will have no part of this. The Justin I knew would never have condoned such blasphemy. He said they would hate us! Are you deaf? Hate us."

"Then go to Justin and ask him what we should do," Johan said. "Please, I mean no offense, Ronin. I'm just trying to make sense of things myself."

William stepped forward and spoke for the first time. "I have another way."

They all faced him, including Ronin, who had stopped.

"Johan is right. We do have a serious problem. But instead of embracing the Horde's ways, it is my contention that we follow Justin by separating ourselves from the Horde as he himself instructed. I would like to take my tribe deep."

This wasn't the first time William had suggested fleeing into the desert, but he'd never made a formal request of it.

"And how can you follow Justin's instruction to lead them to the drowning if you're deep in the desert?" Ronin challenged.

"Others can lead them to the drowning. But think of the women and children. We must protect them!"

"Justin will protect them if he wishes," Ronin said.

Thomas glanced at Johan, then back at William. The Circle's first deep fractures were already starting to show. For more than a year they'd followed Ronin's lead on doctrine, as instructed by Justin, but these new challenges would test his leadership.

What else had Justin told them that day after drawing a circle around them in the sand?

Never break the Circle.

Ronin glared at each of them. "What's happening here? We're already forgetting why we came together? Why our skin is different? We're forgetting the Great Romance between Elyon and his people? That we are his bride?"

"His bride? That's merely a metaphor," William said. "And even so, we are his bride; the Horde is not. So I say we take the bride deep into the desert and hide her from the enemy."

"We are his bride, and whoever follows us out of the Horde will be his bride as well," Ronin said. "How will the Horde ever hear Elyon's call to love unless it's from our own throats?"

"Elyon doesn't need our throats!" William countered. "You think the Creator is so dependent on you?"

"Keep it down. You'll wake the camp," Thomas said, standing. He glanced at Jeremiah and Suzan, who hadn't spoken yet. "We're on a dangerous course here."

No one disagreed.

"Ronin, read this passage for us again. The one about them hating us."

Ronin reached into his satchel and withdrew the Book of History that Justin had given them before his departure. They all knew it quite well, but the teachings it held were at times difficult to understand.

Ronin carefully peeled the cloth off and opened the cover. *The Histories Recorded by His Beloved.* He flipped through dog-eared pages and found the passage. "Here it is. Listen." His voice lowered and he read with an accustomed somber respect. "When the world hates you, remember that it hated me first. If you belonged to the world, it would love you. But you do not belong to the world. I have brought you out of the world, and that is why it hates you."

"Things change with time," Johan said.

"Nothing has changed!" Ronin said, closing the Book. "Following Justin may be easy, but making the decision never is. Are you second-guessing his way?"

"Slow down," Thomas said. "Please! This kind of division will destroy us. We must remember what we know as certain."

He looked at Jeremiah again. "Remind us."

"As certain?"

"Absolute certainty."

The older man reminded Thomas of Elijah. He stroked his long white beard and cleared his throat.

"That Justin is Elyon. That according to the Book of History, Elyon is father, son, and spirit. That Justin left us with a way back to the colored forest through the red pools. That Elyon is wooing his bride. That Justin will soon come back for his bride."

Now Suzan spoke. "And that most of what we know about who Justin really is, we know from the Book through metaphor. He's the light, the vine, the water that gives life." She gestured to the Book of History in Ronin's hand. "His spirit is the wind; he is the bread of life, the shepherd who would leave all for the sake of one."

"True enough," Thomas said. "And when the Book tells us to drink his blood, it means that we should embrace his death. So how can we hide by running deep into the desert, or by putting ash and sulfur on our skin?"

"He also told us to flee to the Southern Forest," William said. "If what you're saying is true, then why didn't he tell us to run back to the Horde? Perhaps because the bride has a responsibility to stay alive."

William did have a point. The dichotomy was reminiscent of the religion Thomas vaguely remembered from his dreams.

"I intend to leave today and lead a hundred into the deep desert," William said. "Johan's right. It'll only be a matter of time before Woref flushes us out. If you expect any mercy from him, you're mistaken. He'd kill us all to save himself the trouble of dragging us back to the city. This is a matter of prudence for me."

Thomas looked down the canyon, toward the entrance to a small enclave where the tribe was slowly waking. A small boy squatted in the sand by the entrance, drawing with his finger. Smoke drifted from a fire around the cliff wall—they were getting ready to cook the morning wheat pancakes. As the smoke rose, it was swept down-canyon by a perpetual breeze, and most of it dissipated before it rose high enough to be seen from any distance. A thin trail of smoke lingered over the funeral pyre beyond towering boulders a hundred meters from the camp.

Thomas took a deep breath, glanced at the pile of large rocks to his right, and was about to tell William to take his expedition when a man stepped around the largest boulder.

Thomas's first thought was that he was hallucinating. Dreaming, as he used to dream before the dreams had vanished. This was no ordinary man standing before him, drilling him with green eyes.

This was . . .

Justin?

Thomas blinked to clear his vision.

What he saw made his whole body seize. Justin was still there, standing in three complete dimensions, as real as any man Thomas had ever faced.

"Hello, Thomas."

Justin's kind eyes flashed, not with reflected light, but with their own brilliance. Thomas thought he should fall to his knees. He was surprised the others hadn't dropped already. They, like him, had been immobilized by Justin's sudden appearance.

"I've been watching you, my friend. What I see makes me proud."

Thomas opened his mouth, but nothing came out.

"I've shared my mind with you," Justin said. "I've given my body for you." His mouth twisted into a grin and he spoke each word clearly. "Now I will show you my heart," he said. "I will show you my love."

Thomas felt each word hit his chest, as if they were soft objects flung through the air, impacting one at a time. Now I will show you my heart. My love.

Thomas turned his head toward the others. They stared at him, not comprehending. Surely they saw! Surely they heard.

"This is for you, Thomas," Justin said. "Only you."

Thomas looked back at—

Justin was gone!

The morning air felt heavy.

"Thomas!"

Thomas turned back toward the camp in time to see Mikil rushing around the cliff. She pulled up and stared at him, face white.

"What is it?" he asked absently, mind still split.

"I'm . . . I think I know something about Kara," she said.

"Kara? Who's Kara?"

But as soon as he asked, he remembered. His sister. From the histories.

3

WOREF SWUNG his leg over the stallion and dropped to the sand. Behind him, a hundred of his best soldiers waited on horses that stamped and occasionally snorted in the cool morning air. They'd approached the firelit sky last night, camped at the edge of the Southern Forest, and risen while it was still dark. This could be the day that marked the beginning of the end for the albinos.

The lieutenant who'd first located this camp had never been wrong— once again he hadn't disappointed. Still, they'd been in similar situations a dozen times, the albinos within reach, only to return home empty-handed. The Circle didn't fight, but they had perfected the art of evasion.

Woref stared at the canyons ahead. The blue smoke of burning horse manure was unmistakable. Soren had reported a small oasis south of the camp—roughly a hundred trees around one of the poisonous red pools— but the albinos were too smart to use any wood unless it was already fallen. Instead they used recycled fuel, as a Scab would. They'd adapted to the desert well with Martyn's help. Johan's help.

Woref's dreadlocks hung heavy on his head, and he rolled his neck to clear one from his face. Truth be told, he'd never liked Martyn. His defection was appropriate. Better, it had opened the way for Woref's own promotion. Now he was the hunter and Martyn the prey, along with Thomas. The reward for their heads was a heady prospect.

"Show me their retreat paths," he said.

Soren dropped to one knee and drew in the sand. "The canyon looks like a box, but there are two exits, here and here. One leads to the pool, here; the other to the open desert."

"How many women and children?"

"Twenty or thirty. Roughly half."

"And you're sure that Thomas is among the men?"

"Yes sir. I will stake my life on it."

Woref grunted. "You may regret it. Qurong's losing his patience."

A thousand or so dissidents sworn to nonviolence didn't present a threat to the Horde, but the number of defections from the Horde to the Circle was water on Qurong's flaky skin. He was adamant about pre-empting any deterioration in his power base. Thomas of Hunter had defeated him one too many times in battle to take any chances.

"As are we." Soren dipped his head then added, "Sir."

Woref spit to one side. The whole army knew that Thomas of Hunter's head wasn't the only head at stake here. What they didn't know was that Qurong's own daughter, Chelise, was also at stake.

The supreme leader had long ago promised to allow his daughter to marry once the Horde captured the forests, but he had changed his mind when Thomas escaped. As long as Thomas of Hunter was free to lead a rebellion, Chelise would remain single. At the outset of this campaign, he'd secretly sworn his daughter's hand to Woref, pending the capture of Thomas.

At times Woref wondered if Qurong was only protecting his daughter, who'd made it clear that she wasn't interested in marrying any general, including Woref. Her dismissal only fueled Woref's desire. If Qurong refused him this time, he would kill the leader and take Chelise by force.

"They have no intelligence of our approach?" he asked.

"No sign of it. I can't recall an opportunity as promising as this."

"Send twenty to cover each escape route. Death to the man who alerts them before we are ready. We attack in twenty minutes. Go."

Soren ran back and quietly leveled his orders.

Woref squeezed his fingers into fists and relaxed them. He missed the days when the Forest Guard fought like men. Their fearless leader had turned into a mouse. One loud word and he would scamper for the rocks, where the Horde had little chance of ferreting him out. The albinos were still much quicker than Scabs.

Woref had watched the battle at the Natalga Gap, when Thomas had rained fire down on them with the thunder he called bombs. None had been used since, but that would change once they had Thomas in chains. The battle leading up to that crushing defeat had been the best kind. Thousands had died on both sides. Granted, many more thousands of the Horde than the Forest Guard, but they had Thomas on his heels before the cliffs had crushed the Horde.

Woref had killed eight of the Guard that day. He could still remember each blow, severing flesh and bone. The smell of blood. The cries of pain. The white eyes of terror. Killing. There was no experience that even closely compared.

His orders were to bring Thomas in alive, in part because of information the rogue leader could offer, in part because Qurong meant to make an example of him. But if given the excuse, Woref would kill the man. Thomas was responsible for his loneliness these last thirteen months—these past three years, in fact, ever since Chelise had grown into the woman she was, tempting any whole-blooded man with her leveled chin and long flowing hair and flashing gray eyes. He'd known that she would be his. But he hadn't expected such a delay.

He'd objected bitterly to Qurong's decision to delay her marriage after the drowning of Justin. If Martyn had still been with them, Woref's indiscretion that night might have cost him his life. But in the confusion of such wholesale change, Qurong needed a strong hand to keep the peace. Woref had assumed Martyn's place and performed without fault. There wasn't a Scab alive who didn't fear his name.

"Sir?"

Soren stepped up to him, but Woref didn't acknowledge him. He suppressed a flash of anger. *Did I say come? No, but you came anyway. One day no one will dare approach me without permission.*

"They've gone, as you ordered."

Woref walked back to his horse, lifted his boot into the stirrup, paused to let the pain in his joints pass, then mounted. The albinos claimed not to have any pain. It was a lie.

"Tell the men that we will execute one of them for every albino who escapes," he said.

"And how many of the albinos do we kill?"

"Only as many as it takes to capture Thomas. They're more useful alive."

4

"YOUR SISTER," Mikil said. "Kara."

Mikil felt her knees weaken. They stood deadlocked, stares unbroken. The others were looking at both of them as if they'd gone crazy.

"I . . ." Thomas finally stammered. "Is that possible? I . . . I haven't dreamed for thirteen months."

She'd awakened in her tent with the certain knowledge that she wasn't entirely herself. Her mind was full of thoughts beyond those she would ordinarily entertain. In fact, she was considering the strange possibility that she was Thomas of Hunter's sister. Kara.

The moment she considered the possibility, her mind seemed to embrace it. The more she embraced it, the more she remembered Thomas's dreams, and more, Rachelle's dreams. As a woman named Monique.

Then she knew the truth. Kara of Hunter had made a connection with her. Details seeped into her mind. Thomas's sister, who'd just fallen asleep in Dr. Bancroft's laboratory, was dreaming as if she were Mikil at this very moment. Mikil's own husband, Jamous, lay asleep beside her. She had no children. She was well liked if a bit stiff-necked on occasion. She was Thomas's "right-hand man."

But she was also privy to Kara's situation in the histories. She had Mikil's memories and Kara's memories at once. She was technically Mikil—that much was obvious—but she was suddenly feeling nearly as much like Kara.

So Kara had joined her brother in his dreams—at least that was how she thought of it. Now Kara stood gaping at a spitting image of her own brother plus about fifteen years. He wore a sleeveless tunic that accentuated bulging biceps. Below, a short leather skirt that hung midthigh over a well-worn beige tunic. His boots were strapped up high over well-defined calves. The man before her had to be twice as strong as her brother.

"Wow," she said. "You're quite the stud."

Stud? Where had that word come from? Kara.

"A horse?" William said. "You insult him?"

"No, she means something else," Thomas said. "My friends, I would like to introduce you to my sister from my dream world. There, her name is Kara."

William's left eyebrow arched high. "She looks like Mikil to me."

"Yes, but evidently Mikil's brought Kara for a visit."

"Surely you can't be serious," William scoffed.

Mikil grinned. "More serious than you imagine. How else would I know to call him a stud? In the histories it means 'strong,' among other things. Kara's never seen him in this state, and she's surprised by just how strong our Thomas is compared to her brother, who looks the same, less about fifteen years and forty pounds of muscle."

Mikil nearly laughed out loud at the twists in her mind. She felt like both women at once—an exhilarating experience, to say the least.

To Thomas: "Can I speak with you in private? Just a moment."

They stepped to the side and she spoke in a whisper. "You haven't dreamed for thirteen months, you said. Do you know why?"

By his frown, he seemed to be second-guessing his initial conclusion that Kara was dreaming through Mikil. "Where did we grow up?"

"Manila," she said.

"Where does our mother live?"

"New York. Satisfied?"

Slowly a smile crossed his face. "So you're alive, then. The virus didn't kill you?"

"Not yet. We still have ten days to go. You were killed in France by Carlos two, maybe three, days ago. And now Monique's missing as well."

He stared at her, mind grappling with her information.

"Rachelle was killed thirteen months ago by the Horde," he said.

"I know. I'm Mikil. And Kara's sorry . . . terribly sorry."

"So you're saying that thirteen months have passed here but only a couple of days there?" he asked.

"Evidently. And you're saying that you haven't dreamed of Thomas in France in all this time?"

"The last dream I had of Thomas was falling asleep next to Monique."

"Where you were shot by Carlos," Mikil said.

His eyes widened. "Then I was right! I fell from my horse here. I was killed, but Justin healed me through Rachelle."

"But you're not alive in France?" she asked. "When you were brought back before, you came back to life in both realities."

"No. I never died before. I was healed instantly, before I actually died. Both times at the lake. This time I was dead for hours before Rachelle found me."

The exchange stalled.

"By the Hordes who pursue us, what is all this nonsense?" Ronin demanded. They were obviously being overheard.

William grinned. "It's our fearless leader's dream world. Apparently Mikil has joined the game."

Mikil ignored them. "Then you are dead in France, aren't you?"

"I must be."

"But you've only been dead for a couple days. Maybe three."

"So it would seem. And Monique's missing because she died when Rachelle died. She was connected with Rachelle the way you are with Mikil. I haven't dreamed because there's nothing for me to dream."

"And I'm here to bring you back," Mikil said.

Thomas set his jaw. "I can't go back. I don't want to go back. I'm dead there! I'm better off thinking that the histories were a dream."

"I'm no dream. My knowledge of our childhood in the Philippines is nothing like a dream." She shoved out her arm and showed him the cut. "Is this cut a dream? The Raison Strain is only days from showing its first real teeth, France has just fired a nuke at Israel, the world is about to die, and the best I can figure it, you're the only man alive who can stop any of it. Don't tell me it's a dream."

He looked at her skeptically.

"It's been thirteen months—you've lost your edge," she said. "But as you said yourself, you died here when Thomas was killed in France. So now that I'm linked with Mikil, will she also die when the virus kills me in ten days?"

The lights were starting to fire in his mind. She pushed.

"I—Mikil, that is—was wrong to doubt you. The world depends on—"

"Then the world is depending on a dead man," he said.

"This is utter nonsense!" William said. "There are more important matters to deal with than this game. You've lost your mind along with him, Mikil. Now, I would like the blessing of this council to take my tribe deep into the desert to our own faction of the Circle. That is why I've come, not to reminisce about your dreams."

Mikil and Thomas closed ranks with the group.

"You forget so quickly, William?" Thomas said. "How do you think I made the bombs that blew the Horde back to hell? Was that my magic? No, that was information I learned from the histories."

"Yes, your memories of the Books of Histories, recalled in some trance or dream; I can accept that, however unlikely it sounds. But this nonsense of saving people in history . . . please! It's laughable!"

"You've always doubted me, William. Always. I can see now that you always will. Even Justin talked about the blank Book . . ."

Thomas stopped.

Mikil recalled Justin's words to them in the desert thirteen months earlier. She said what Thomas was thinking. "Justin said the blank Book of History created history. But only in the histories. What could that have meant?"

"We've never known," Thomas said. "Never had a reason to care much about the histories since . . ." He looked at Mikil with wide eyes. "Only a couple of days, you say?"

"Believe me, the histories are real. And if you don't care about them because you've gone and died in France, you should care about them because Kara is still alive."

Thomas studied her. He turned to Ronin. "You have the Book?"

"Which Book?"

"The blank Book. This Book that supposedly only works in the histories."

Ronin hesitated, then pulled out a second Book wrapped in canvas. He extracted it from the packaging. He ran a hand over the cover. The title was embossed in a corroded gold foil. *The Story of History.*

"How would a history book make history?" Mikil asked, walking up next to Thomas.

"You're saying that this Book has power in another dimension that is called 'the histories'?" Jeremiah asked. "How is that possible?"

Thomas hurried toward Ronin, suddenly eager. "May I?"

Ronin handed him the Book.

"Could it be?"

"Nonsense," Jeremiah said.

"You said it yourself," Thomas said. "The analogies and metaphors. The stories," he said, his fingers tracing the title. "They're real. Words become flesh and dwell among us. Isn't that how the Beloved's Book begins?"

Thomas opened the Book. Plain parchment. No words. Thomas's eyes met Mikil's, wide with wonder.

She looked at the Book again. "Do you think . . ." But she couldn't say what she was thinking. How was it possible?

"This is the most outlandish thing I've heard," William said. "You expect us to believe that if you write in that Book, something will actually happen, based on the words alone?"

"Why not?" Thomas said.

"Because the whole notion of the word becoming flesh is a metaphor, as you said. Justin was not some scribbling in a book. You're crossing a line here."

"You're wrong," Thomas told him. Then to Mikil, "Where Kara and I come from, no one is required to dive into a pool of red water and drown to follow Justin. They are simply required to die metaphorically." He looked at Kara. "They take up their crosses, so to speak. Tell them, Kara."

She was making the connections as quickly as he was. Neither of them had been practicing Christians, but they'd grown up with a chaplain for a father. They knew the basics of Christianity well enough.

"'Take up your cross and follow me,' Jesus said. He was executed on a cross, as were many of his followers later. But his followers aren't required to die in that fashion."

"Exactly," Thomas said. "Yet here our following isn't metaphorical at all. The same could be said about evil. There the people don't wear a disease on their skin—it's said to be in their hearts. But look at the Scabs. Their refusal to follow Justin in drowning shows up as a physical disease."

William seemed somewhat stunned by this revelation. He glanced at the others, then back at Thomas. "So now you think this Book, which is from here where metaphors express themselves literally, might do the same in this dream world of yours?"

"Who has a quill?" Thomas demanded. "A marker, anything to write with. Charcoal—"

"Here." Ronin held out a charcoal writing stick with a black point.

Thomas took the crude instrument and stared at it.

"Justin was clear that we should hide this Book," William said. "That it is dangerous. We have to come to some kind of agreement on this."

Thomas paced, Book in one hand, pencil in the other. "And Justin said that the Book only works in the histories—the dream world Kara and I come from. For starters, that confirms the histories are real and can be affected. It also means that the Book should be powerless here."

If what Thomas was saying was true, the Book's power might be quite incredible. "What would you write?" Mikil asked. "I mean, what limits would there be? Surely we can't just wipe out the virus with a few strokes of the pen."

Thomas set the Book on the rock. "You're right. I . . . that seems too simple." The others gathered around, silenced by impossible thoughts.

He looked at the cover again. "*The Story of History.* That means it should be a story, right?"

"As in 'once upon a time'?" Ronin asked. "You're saying that if you wrote, 'Once upon a time there was a rabbit,' then a rabbit would appear in your dreams?"

"Too simple," Mikil said. "And what script should we use?" There was a slight difference between the alphabet used in each reality—the one used here was simpler.

"The script of the histories," Thomas said.

"What do you want to accomplish in this other reality?" Ronin asked. "Your main goal—what is it?"

"There's a virus that will destroy most of humanity . . . you know, the Raison Strain," Thomas said. "The one that ushered in the Great Tribulation as recorded in the Books of Histories. Knowledge of the history has become somewhat vague in the fifteen years since Tanis's Crossing, but we all knew it orally once."

"Yes, of course. The Raison Strain. These were the histories that Tanis was fascinated with." Ronin looked at Mikil. "You're saying that these histories are . . . now? Real now?"

"Haven't you been listening to me?" William said. "That's what I've been saying. I've said that he's only recalling memories, but he seems to think that these dreams of his are real."

"Actually, I'm not sure we know how it works," Mikil said. How could she possibly explain her dual reality at this very moment? "Thomas is the expert here, but I can say whether past or present, the histories are not only real, but we must also be able to affect them."

"But surely you don't think you can change what has been written about as a matter of history," William said.

"We don't know that either," Thomas said. "Without the actual Books of Histories, we don't know what was recorded. As far as we know, the histories record our finding this Book and writing in it today."

That kept them all quiet for a moment.

"Then write a story," Ronin finally said.

William grunted in disgust. "Why should I care about any of this? I care about what is real, here. Like the Horde that pursues us every day. I am going to gather my people and take them deep." He stalked off.

Thomas handed Mikil the pencil. "Your recollection of the writing is fresher than mine. You write."

It was an excuse, she thought, but she reached for the instrument anyway. A slight tremble shook her fingers.

"What should I write?"

"Something simple that we can test," Thomas said. "What is our immediate concern?"

"You," Mikil said. "You're dead in France. And Monique."

"You're suggesting we write them back to life?"

"Why not?" Mikil asked.

"Isn't that a bit complicated? It seems a bit much. Absurd maybe."

"Absurd?" Ronin said. "As opposed to the rest of this, which is supposed to make perfect sense?"

"Write it," Thomas said.

Mikil's hand hovered above the blank page. "Once upon a time, Thomas came back to life?"

"More detail."

"I don't think I can do this. What detail? I don't even know what you were wearing."

"Write this," Thomas said. He glanced at her hand, which hadn't moved. "Ready?"

"Okay." She lowered her hand.

"Thomas Hunter, the man who first learned of the Raison Strain's threat, the same man who was shot in the head—"

"Hold on." Mikil touched the charcoal stick to the page. If she wasn't mistaken, a slight heat rode up her fingers. Then again, her nerves were firing hot. She wrote his words verbatim.

"Okay."

Thomas continued. "The same man who was shot in the head, was killed in France by a bullet to the head. Period. But on the third day he came back to life . . . No, forget that. This instead: But at a time when his body was unattended by any of his enemies, he came back to life. The end."

She lifted the stick. "The end? What about Monique?"

"New paragraph. At about the same time that Thomas Hunter came back to life, Monique de Raison found herself in good health and fully able to continue her search for an antivirus in the United States of America. The end."

Johan sighed. "Honestly, these don't sound like stories to me." He looked in the direction William had gone. "This whole thing seems a bit ridiculous in the face of our predicament. Can I suggest we reach . . ."

Johan stopped. His face lightened a shade. Mikil looked at the others who had honed in on Johan's reaction. He was listening.

Then she heard it. The faint thunder of hooves. On the cliffs.

The Horde!

"Move!" Thomas snapped. "Into the tunnel!"

5

THOMAS SNATCHED up the Book and shoved it into his belt as he ran for the tents. Justin had shown his face to him. Then Kara through Mikil. And now the Horde was attacking.

Now I will show you my heart.

In moments they had caught up to William. "Mikil, Johan, get Samuel and Marie into the tunnel with the others! William, the east canyon with me. Five men."

They'd selected this particular wash five days earlier not only for its proximity to the red pool, but because of a hidden passage under two huge boulders in the eastern canyon. The route was almost impossible to see without standing directly in front of it. With any luck the Horde would expect them to take one of the two more obvious escape routes.

How had the Scabs managed to pass their sentries on the cliffs undetected?

The first arrow clipped the rock face on Thomas's left before he reached the tents. He glanced over his shoulder. Mounted archers. Fifty at least.

"Ahead," Mikil shouted. "They've cut off the eastern canyon!"

Cries of alarm sounded throughout the camp. Women ran for their children. The men were already running toward the corral. There was no time to collect dishes or food or clothing. They would do well enough to escape with their lives.

"William?"

"You want only five?" his lieutenant demanded. "The Scabs might not follow us."

They would be the diversion. Under other circumstances he would take at least ten, enough to raise enough dust to draw a pursuit while the others slipped away through the hidden escape route. But Thomas knew that, today, whoever was part of the diversion might not escape.

"Only five," he said. "I have the fire."

He ran to the center of the camp where he was certain to be seen clearly. With any luck they would key in on him. The price on his head was a hundred times that on anyone else's. And Thomas had heard the rumor that Qurong's own daughter, Chelise, whom he had once met deep in the desert, was promised to Woref upon his capture.

The cries quieted quickly. The Circle had been through its share of escapes before. They all knew that screaming was no way to avoid attention. There were enough horses to carry the entire tribe, one adult and one child per horse, with a dozen left over to carry their supplies.

Thomas grabbed the smoldering torch next to the main campfire. Gruff shouting directed the attack overhead. An arrow sliced through the air and thudded into flesh on Thomas's right. He spun.

Alisha, Lucy's mother, was grabbing at a shaft that protruded from her side. Thomas started toward her but pulled up when he saw that Lucy was already running for her mother, gripping one of the fleshy, orange fruits that healed. She reached her mother, dropped the fruit, gripped the shaft with both hands, and pulled hard. Alisha groaned. The arrow slid free.

Then Lucy was squeezing the fruit over the open wound.

Thomas ran to intercept William, who led Suzan and two mounted tribe members. He leaped into the saddle on the run and kicked the horse into a full gallop, leading the others now.

A throaty grunt behind him made him turn his head. It was the old man, Jeremiah. Most of the tribe had already taken their positions under a protective ledge by the stables, but the council had been farthest from the horses when the attack had started. The old man had lagged. A Scab spear had found his back.

In the confusion, no one was running to his aid. If he died, the fruit wouldn't bring him back.

"William, torch!"

He tossed the smoking fire to William, who caught it with one hand and looked back to see the problem.

"Hurry, Thomas. We're cutting this close."

"Light the fires. Go!"

Thomas spun his horse and sprinted for the old man, who lay face-down now. He dropped by Jeremiah, fruit in hand. But he knew before his knee hit the sand that he was too late.

"Jeremiah!" He grabbed the spear, put one foot on the man's back, and yanked it out. The spinal column had been severed in two.

Thomas crushed the fruit in both hands, grunting with anger. Juice poured into the gaping hole.

Nothing. If the man was still alive, the juice would have begun its regeneration immediately.

An arrow slammed into his shoulder.

He stood and faced the direction it had come from. The archers on the nearest cliff stared down at him, momentarily off guard.

"He was once one of you!" he screamed. Without removing his eyes from them, Thomas grabbed the arrow in his shoulder, pulled it out, and threw it on the ground. He shoved the fruit against the wound.

"Now he is dead, as you yourselves are. You hear me? Dead! All of you. You live in death!"

One of them let an arrow fly. Thomas saw that the projectile was wide and let it hiss past without moving. It struck the sand.

Then he moved. Faster than they had expected. Onto his horse and straight toward the eastern canyon.

The first fire was already spewing thick black smoke skyward. William had lit the second on the opposite side of the canyon and was galloping toward the third pile of brush they'd prepared for precisely this eventuality.

Thomas ignored the arrows flying by, leaned over his horse's neck, and plunged into the thick smoke.

———— ◦◦◦◦ ————

Soren raised his hand to give the signal.

"Wait," Woref said.

"The rest will break for the canyon," his lieutenant said. "We should give chase now."

"I said wait."

Soren lowered his hand.

The plan had been to box them in, wound as many as possible from a high angle of attack, and then sweep down to finish them off. Their cursed fruit was powerless against a sickle to the neck. It was a strategy that Martyn himself once would have approved.

Now Martyn was down there among the albinos, trapped with the rest. But suddenly Woref wasn't so sure of the strategy; he hadn't expected the fires.

"They think the smoke will cover them?" Soren said. "The poor fools don't know that we have their escape already covered at the other end."

But this was Thomas they were up against. And Martyn. Neither would think that a bit of smoke would help them escape an enemy that had clearly known their position before the attack.

So why the fires?

"You're certain there are no other routes from this canyon?"

"Not that any of our scouts could find."

Yet there had to be. If he was leading this band of dissidents, which direction would he lead them? Into the desert, naturally. Away from the Horde. Out to the plains where they could simply outrun any pursuit.

"Tell half of the sweep team to cut off the desert to the south," Woref said.

"The south?"

"Do not make me repeat another order."

Soren stood in his stirrups and relayed the order through hand signals. Two mounted scouts, each confirming the message, wheeled their horses around and disappeared.

"The whole tribe will break for the smoke momentarily," Woref said. "I want every archer pouring arrows into the albinos."

"I've already passed the word."

"But why?" Woref muttered to himself. "The smoke will suffocate them if they don't get out quickly."

A whistle echoed through the canyon and, precisely as he'd predicted, nearly fifty head of horses broke from under the ledge of a western canyon wall. Arrows rained down on them. Women clutched their children and rode for the smoke, kicking their mounts for as much speed as the animals could muster.

Multiple hits. They were sitting ducks down there. But they had only fifty yards to run before the smoke swallowed them.

Still, two fell. A horse stumbled and its rider ran on foot. A third clutched an arrow that had struck him in the chest. The one on foot tripped, and three arrows plowed into his back.

Then the albinos were through the gauntlet and into their smoke. Woref's men killed only five. Six, counting the one that the spear had taken earlier. Many more had been shot, but they would survive with the help of their sorcery. This bitter fruit of theirs.

The archers shot a dozen arrows into each of the fallen albinos, then the canyon fell eerily silent.

Woref reined his mount around and trotted along the cliff, eastward, eyes searching for the slightest sign of life beneath the thick smoke. The silence angered him. Surely they wouldn't double back into another onslaught of arrows. There had to be another exit!

Behind him, the sweep team entered the valley, effectively cutting off any attempted retreat.

Thomas had been with the ones who'd lit the fires. Woref's agreement with Qurong was for Thomas. If the parties had split . . .

A cry came from the east. Thomas's group had been sighted.

Woref kicked his horse and galloped up the canyon. He saw them then, five horses raising dust beyond the smoke, speeding directly for his trap.

—◦◦◦—

Thomas led his contingent from the smoke, praying that every Scab eye was on him. He had surveyed every last inch of this canyon and knew where he would set a trap if he were the Horde commander. Their chances of breaking through that trap were small now. If they'd received warning, they would've had a better chance of sprinting past the mouth of the canyon before the trap had been set.

Two brothers, Cain and Stephen, raced beside Suzan to his right. William brought up the rear.

"Do we fight?" William demanded.

"No."

"We're too late! They'll be waiting."

Yes, they would be.

"We could go back," William said.

"No! We can't endanger the others. Have your fruit ready!"

As soon as he said it, he heard the cry ahead. Thirty mounted men rode into the open, cutting off the mouth of the canyon.

Still they galloped, straight for the waiting Horde.

"Justin, give us strength," Thomas breathed.

The Scabs weren't attacking. No arrows, no cries, just these thirty men on horses, waiting to collect them. There was no way past them.

Thomas reined his mount and held up a hand. "Hold up."

They stopped a hundred yards from the Scabs.

"You're going to let them take us?" William asked. "You know they'll kill us."

"And our alternative is what?"

"Mikil and Johan have had the time they need to get the rest through the gap. We can still make it!"

"They'll have men in the canyon by now," Suzan said. She'd been a latecomer to the Circle, and there wasn't a person Thomas had been so glad to have join them. As the leader of the Forest Guard's scouts, she'd studied the Horde more than most and knew their strategies nearly as well as Johan himself.

"And if we're lucky, they won't find the tunnel," Thomas said.

"Then we have to fight! We can beat them—"

"No killing!" Thomas faced Cain and Stephen. "Are you ready for what this may mean?"

"If you mean death, then I'm ready," Cain said.

"I'd rather die than be taken to their dungeons," Stephen said. "I won't be taken alive."

"And how do you propose to force their hands? If they take us alive, then we will go with them peacefully. No fight, are we clear?"

"I helped them build the dungeons. I—"

"Then you can help us escape from their dungeons."

"There is no escape!"

The brothers had been latecomers as well, and their discovery of life on the other side of the drowning was still fresh in their minds. Both were dark-skinned and had shaved their heads as part of a vow they'd taken. They were adamant about showing as much of their disease-free flesh as was decently possible.

"No fighting," Thomas repeated.

They held stares for a moment. Stephen nodded. "No fighting."

They sat five abreast, facing the Horde. Hooves sounded behind them and Thomas turned to see that the team Suzan had predicted was emerging from the thinning smoke.

"We're buying a whole lot of trouble here," William said.

"No, we're buying Mikil's freedom. The freedom of the Circle."

"Mikil? Don't tell me this has to do with these dreams of yours."

The thought had occurred to him. He wasn't sure what they'd done by writing in the blank Book now in his belt, but either he or Kara had to get back. The lives of six billion people were at stake. Not to mention his own sister's life. If Mikil died, Kara would die.

"If I were concerned only with the histories, I would save myself, wouldn't I? We're doing here nothing less than what Justin himself would undoubtedly do."

There was nothing more to be said. Thomas withdrew the Book from his belt and shoved it into his tunic.

——◦◦◦——

Woref rode past his men and studied the standoff in the canyon.

Five.

The other fifty had disappeared.

But among the five was Thomas. If he'd estimated correctly, the others would emerge from these canyons in the south, where his men would deal with them appropriately. His concern was now with these five.

This one.

"Send word: when they find the others, kill them all. I have Thomas of Hunter."

He nudged his horse and rode with his guard to meet the man who was responsible for the grief he'd suffered these past thirteen months. Thomas of Hunter's name was still whispered with awe late at night around a thousand campfires. He was a legend who defied reason. Failing to defeat the Horde with his sword, he'd now taken up the weapon of peace. Qurong would prefer to face a sword any day over this heroic deceit they called the Circle. True, only a thousand had followed Thomas into his madness, but what was a thousand could easily become ten thousand. And then a hundred thousand.

Today he would reduce their number to one.

And today Woref would have his bride.

He stopped ten yards from the albinos. They looked like salamanders with their sickly bare flesh. The breeze brought their scent to him, and he tried his best not to draw it too deep. They smelled of fruit. The same bitter fruit that they used for their sorcery—the variety that grew around the red pools. It was said that they drank the blood of Justin and that they forced their children to do the same. What kind of disease of the mind would push a man to such absurdities?

Two of the prisoners were bald. They looked vaguely familiar. A third was a woman. The mere thought of any man breeding with such a sickly salamander was enough to make him nauseated.

He nudged his horse abreast their leader, Thomas of Hunter. Similarly fashioned medallions hung from each of their necks. He reached down, grasped Thomas's pendant, jerked it free, and held it in his palm. Then he spit on it.

"You are now prisoners of Qurong, supreme leader of the Horde," he said. Then he turned his horse away, overcome by their scent.

"So it would appear," Thomas said.

"Douse them!"

Two of his men rode around the captives and tossed ash on them. The ash contained sulfur and made their stench manageable.

"Where are the others?" Woref asked.

Thomas stared at him, eyes blank.

"Kill the woman," Woref said.

One of the soldiers pulled a sword and approached the black female.

"Killing any of us would be a mistake," Thomas said. "We can't tell you where the others are. We can only tell how they outwitted you, which we will gladly do. But by now they've fled in a direction only they know."

Woref felt a new dislike for this man run deep into his bones. He wondered how smart the rebel would look without lips. But then Qurong wouldn't get the information he needed.

"I know how they escaped," he said. "My scouts missed a break in the cliffs that leads south, into the desert. Your band of rebels is headed into our hands at this very moment."

"Then why do you ask?"

He'd expected a flinch, a pause, anything to indicate the man's surprise at being discovered so easily. Instead, Thomas had delivered this unflinching reprimand.

"You'll pay for your disrespect. I give you my vow. Chain them."

Woref turned his horse around and headed out of the canyon.

⊶⊷

Mikil swept the scope across the desert that surrounded the canyon lands.

"Others?" Johan asked.

"No. Just the one group."

Behind them, fifty sets of round white eyes peered from the dark cavern that hid them. They wound their way through the gap and into an adjacent canyon that led them here, to the edge of the southern desert. But they wouldn't break into the open until they were sure that the Horde was gone.

"They'll be in the cave by now," Johan said. "We have to move soon."

"Unless they followed Thomas out of the canyon."

Johan frowned. "Assuming Thomas made it out of the canyon."

She lowered the glass. "Why wouldn't he?"

He glanced back and spoke in a low voice. "I could have sworn I saw Woref on the cliff. They came on us without warning, which means they had already scouted us out. They would have both escape routes covered. I don't see how anyone, even Thomas, could possibly escape without a fight. And we both know that he won't fight."

The revelation stunned her. Not only as Mikil, who feared for the Circle's future without Thomas to lead them, but as Kara, who suddenly feared for her brother's life.

"Then we have to go back!"

"We have the tribe to think about." He took a deep breath. "First the tribe, then Thomas. Assuming he's alive."

She was about to reprimand him for even suggesting such a thing, but then it occurred to her that, as Mikil, she agreed.

She faced the desert. "Then we stay here," she said.

"They'll follow our tracks."

"Not if we block the tunnel. Think about it. They'll never expect us to stay in these canyons. Anywhere but here, right? And they'll never find this cavern. There's a red pool nearby, water, food. I don't want to go deep if they have my brother."

The emotions mixing in Mikil's chest were enough to make her want to scream. She was Mikil, but she was Kara, and as Kara she'd awakened into a firestorm. Surprisingly she'd felt only a little fear, even with the Horde's arrows narrowly missing her head. Mikil had been up against the Scabs a thousand times, most often in hand-to-hand combat.

On the other hand, it wasn't the status quo for the civilians in her charge. They'd lost six in the attack, including Jeremiah. Her heart felt sick.

But there was another emotion pulling at her. The desire to wake up in Dr. Myles Bancroft's laboratory. Thomas had taken the Book—now she wished she'd taken it. There was no telling how many more opportunities they would have to write in it. The thought of those few words she'd written actually having power on Earth made her spine tingle. She had to get back to see if they had worked. Imagine . . .

Johan scratched his chin and looked around. "If we block the tunnel, they'll see that we blocked it."

"Let them. When they can't find us, they'll assume we went deep."

"They'll still look for our trail."

"Then we'll give them one that takes them away from here, further west and into the desert. With the night winds blowing our tracks, they will be lost by morning."

He was silent, thinking.

"I refuse to go deep as long as Thomas's fate is uncertain."

He nodded. "It could work. But we don't block the tunnel at its entrance. It's too late for that anyway." He ran to his horse and swung into the saddle. "We have to hurry."

6

"KARA. WAKE up."

She felt her shoulder being shaken.

"That's it, dear. Wake up. You've been sleeping for two good hours."

Kara stared at the frumpy figure at her side. Dr. Myles Bancroft wore a knowing grin. Dabbed a handkerchief on his brow.

"Two hours and not one dream," he said.

The lights were still low. Machines hummed quietly—a computer fan, air conditioning. The faint smell of human sweat mixed with a deodorant.

"Did you dream?" he asked.

"Yes." She pushed herself up. He'd wiped the blood from her arm and applied a small white bandage. "Yes, I did."

"Not according to my instruments, you didn't. And that, my dear, makes this not only a fascinating case, but one that is duplicable. First Thomas and now you. Something is happening with you two."

"It's his blood. Don't ask me how this all got started, but my brother is the gateway between these two realities."

"I doubt very much that there are two realities," he said. "Something is happening in your minds that is certainly beyond ordinary dreams, but I can promise you that your body was here the whole time. You didn't walk through any wardrobe to Narnia or take a trip to another galaxy."

"Semantics, Professor." She slid off the bed. "We don't have time for semantics. We have to find Monique."

Bancroft looked at her with a sheepish grin tempting his face, as if he were working up the courage to ask the delicious question: "So what happened?"

"I woke as Mikil, lieutenant to Thomas of Hunter. She and I wrote in a book that has power to bring life from words, narrowly survived an attack by the Horde, and found safe haven in a cavern after blocking our escape route. I finally fell into an exhausted sleep and woke up here."

Hearing herself summarize, a buzz rode down her neck. She'd played both doubter and believer over the last two weeks with Thomas, and she wasn't sure which was easier.

"No wounds."

"What?"

"You don't have any wounds or anything to prove your experiences like Thomas did."

True.

"Have you heard news?" she asked.

"Not particularly, no." He blinked and looked away. "The world is going to hell, quite literally. The great equalizer that most of us knew would eventually get loose finally has. I just can't believe how fast it's all happening."

"The virus? Equalizing as in it's no respecter of persons. The president is as vulnerable as the homeless bum in the alley. And why are you still so interested in dreams, Doctor? You said you were infected, right? You have ten days to live like the rest of us. Shouldn't you be with your family?"

"My work is my family, dear. I did manage to ingest dangerous levels of alcohol when the whole thing first sank in about a week ago. But I've since decided to spend my last days fussing over my first love."

"Psychology."

"I intend to die in her arms."

"Then let me give you a suggestion from one who's seen beyond her own mind, Doctor. Talk to your priest. There's more to all of this than your eyes can see or your instruments record."

"You're a religious person?" he asked.

"No. But Mikil is."

"Then maybe I should talk to this Mikil of yours."

Kara glanced at the bench where she remembered last seeing Thomas's blood sample. It was gone.

"Don't worry; it's safely stored."

"I . . . I need it."

"Not without a court order. It stays with me. You're welcome here anytime. Which reminds me, Secretary Merton Gains called about an hour ago."

"Gains?" The nuclear crisis! "What did he say?"

"He wanted to know if we had reached any conclusion here."

"What did you tell him? Why didn't you wake me?"

"I had to be sure. Some subjects require an unusual amount of time to enter REM. I woke you as soon as I was confident."

Kara started toward the door, suddenly frantic. She had to find Thomas or Monique, dead or alive. But how? And the blood . . .

She turned back. "Doctor, please, you have to give me his blood. He's my brother! The world is in a crisis here, and I—"

"Gains was quite clear," he said. "We can't afford to lose control. He seemed to suggest that this was a possibility, a threat from the inside."

A mole?

"In the White House?"

"He didn't say. I'm a psychologist, not an intelligence officer."

"Fine. What did you tell him about me?"

"That you weren't dreaming. Which probably means you were experiencing the same thing your brother did. He wants you to call him immediately."

She stared at him, then strode for the desk phone. "Now you tell me."

Bancroft shrugged. "Yes, well, I have a lot on my mind. I'm going to die in ten days, did I tell you?"

⸻

Bright light stabbed her eyes. Sunlight. Or was it something else? Maybe that light from beyond. Maybe she'd died from the Raison Strain and was now floating above her body, drifting toward the great white light in the sky.

She blinked. There was pressure on her chest, something biting into her collarbone. Her breathing came hard. No pain though.

All of this she realized with her first blink.

Then she realized that she was in an automobile at a precarious angle, hanging from her seat belt. She grabbed the steering wheel to support herself and sucked in a huge gulp of air.

What had happened? Where was she? Panic edged into her mind. If she shifted her weight, the car might fall!

Green foliage was plastered against the windows. A shaft of sunlight shot through a small triangular break in the leaves. She was in a tree?

Monique blinked again and forced her mind to slow down. She remembered some things. She'd been working on the antivirus to the Raison Strain. Her solution had failed. The chances of finding any antivirus other than the one Svensson possessed were nil. She'd been on her way to Washington—an unscheduled trip of desperation. Kara had convinced her that Thomas might still be their only hope, and in the wake of her monumental failure, Monique intended to make the case to the president himself. Then she would go to Johns Hopkins, where Kara was going to attempt to connect with the other reality by using Thomas's blood.

She'd been driving down a side road at night, following the sign that said Gas—2 miles, when her vision suddenly clouded. That was all she could remember.

Monique leaned to her right. The car didn't budge. She leaned farther and peered out the side window. The car was on the ground, not in a tree. Shrubs crowded every side. The hood was wedged under a web of small branches. She must have fallen asleep and driven off the road. There was no sign of blood.

She moved her legs and neck. Still no pain. Not even a headache.

The car was resting at a thirty-degree angle—nothing short of a crane was going to budge it. She tried the door, found it unobstructed, and shoved it open. Released the shoulder harness.

Her purse. It had Merton Gains's card and her identification. She would need money. The black leather purse was on the floor, passenger side. Holding the steering wheel with her left hand, she lowered herself, grabbed the purse, and pulled herself back up.

Monique eased out of the car and started crawling up the slope with the help of the surrounding shrubs. The road was just above her, maybe twenty-five yards, but several large trees blocked a clear view from the air.

How much time had passed?

The trip up the rocky slope did more damage to her than the car wreck. She tore her black slacks and smudged the front of her beige silk blouse with several falls. Her shoes were black flats, but they had slick soles. She kicked them off halfway up the slope, reached back for them, and muttered a curse when one slid ten feet down before stopping. She decided she was better off without them. Her soles had once favored bare earth over shoes anyway.

When she finally clambered over the crest, she found a two-lane road with a solid yellow line down the middle. The sun was directly above—she'd been unconscious all night and half the day?

To her right she could just see the highway. She stared about, still disoriented. Then she turned to her left and walked toward the small red Conoco sign a mile down the road. Or was it two miles? No, the sign had said 2 miles, but as near as she could see, she was halfway between the highway and the station. One mile. She would take her chances with a phone over thumbing a ride.

Almost immediately she regretted having left her shoes. Fifty yards later she decided that she would thumb a ride to the station if at all possible. Assuming there was a ride to be thumbed. The road was deserted. For that matter, the Conoco station could be deserted as well. Last night she'd seen the lights from the highway—a hopeful sign that the station was open. Most she'd encountered along the road were closed.

The hum of a big rig sounded behind her. She glanced over her shoulder. A large fuel truck with a yellow Shell sign on a chrome tank sped down the highway. The sight stopped her. What was a trucker doing driving fuel down the road, knowing that in ten days he would be dead unless the government managed to find a way to stop the Raison Strain? Did the driver really understand what was happening? The reports she'd heard suggested that most Americans were staying at home, glued to the news. The government was paying huge dividends to certain critical companies if they remained open. Mostly utilities, communications, transportation—the essentials.

She assumed that traffic would be limited to people going home to be with their families. But a trucker? Maybe he was going home too.

She headed back off the road, sticking to the grass shoulder. Not a single car drove by during the twenty minutes it took her to reach the Conoco sign.

The station was closed.

"Hello?"

Her voice echoed under the canopy that covered the deserted fuel islands. She walked for the window. "Hello?"

Nothing. She didn't blame them—the last thing she would do with ten days to live is work at a gas station.

The door was locked. No sign of looting. No need to loot when the looters themselves were also infected. Riots would be instigated by thrill seekers determined to take their fear out on others rather than to seize any goods. It would start soon enough.

In fact, now was as good a time as any.

She picked up the small steel drum that read Garbage, drew it back, and swung it with all her strength at the window. The horrendous crash of breaking glass was loud enough to wake the dead. Good. She needed to wake the dead.

Monique waited for a full minute, giving anyone who might have heard plenty of time to note that she wasn't busy looting. Then she picked her way through the broken glass to the black phone on the counter.

Dial tone.

She dug out the card Gains had given her and stared at the number. What if he was the very mole she had warned him of? Maybe she should call the president himself. No, he was in New York today, speaking at the United Nations.

She dialed the number, let the phone ring, and prayed that Gains, mole or not, would answer.

THOMAS AWOKE on his back. The sheet was over his face. Odd. Although the desert night was cool at times, he wasn't one to smother his breathing by burying his head under the covers like some. Covers also impaired hearing. At this moment he couldn't hear his fellow prisoners breathing, though he knew they were sleeping to his right, chained at the ankles with him. He couldn't even hear the sound of the horses near the camp. Nor the Scabs, talking over morning campfires. Nor the campfires themselves.

He yanked the sheet from his face. It was still night. Dark. He still couldn't hear anything other than his own heart, thumping lightly. No stars in the sky, no campfire, no sand dunes. Only this thin rubber mattress under him, and this cold sheet in his fingers.

Thomas's heart skipped a beat. He wasn't in the desert! He was on a mattress in a dark room, and he'd awakened with a sheet over his face.

He moved his feet. No chains. He'd fallen asleep as a prisoner in the desert and woken in the histories. Alive.

He felt the edge of his bed. Cold steel tubes filled his hand. A gurney. Carlos had shot him, when? Three days ago, Kara had said. He hadn't dreamed for thirteen months in the desert because there was no Thomas here to live the dream. They'd brought his body here, why? For examination? To keep the Americans guessing? And where was here?

France.

Thomas eased his legs from under the sheets and swung them to the cold concrete floor. A loud slap echoed in the room and he jumped. Nothing happened. Something had fallen on the floor.

His eyes adjusted to the darkness. A wedge of light shone through the gap at the bottom of the door. He saw the square shape by his foot. Picked it up. A book. He felt its cover and froze.

The blank Book of History, entitled *The Story of History.* His hands trembled. The Book had crossed over with him!

A chill swept over his body. This Book—its story, its words—had brought him back to life. Here he stood, dressed in a torn jumpsuit, barefooted on a concrete floor in France, holding a Book that could make history with a few strokes of the pen.

Justin had called it dangerous and powerful. Now he knew why.

His sole objective was immediately clear. He had to find a pen, a pencil, anything that could mark the Book, and write a new story. One that changed the outcome of the Raison Strain. And while he was at it, one that included his survival.

Thomas paused at the unexpected thought that the Book wasn't unlike the artifacts from Judeo-Christian history. The ark of the covenant with the power to conquer armies. The serpent in the desert with the power to heal. *Say to this mountain, be thou removed and it shall be removed.* Jesus Christ, AD 30. Words becoming flesh, Ronin had said.

There were now officially four things that crossed between the realities. Knowledge, skills, blood, and this Book, these words becoming flesh.

He could just barely see the outline of a door ten feet away. Thomas walked for the door, tested the knob, found it unlocked, and cracked it ever so slightly. The room beyond was also dark, but not black like this one. He could see a table, a couch. Another door edged by light. A fireplace . . .

He knew this room! It was where he and Monique had met Armand Fortier! They'd brought him back to the farmhouse.

Thomas slipped out, still gripping the Book in his right hand. He covered the room quickly, found nothing of benefit, and moved to the opposite door. Unlocked as well. He'd twisted the knob and cracked the door when the sound of echoing footsteps in the hall reached him.

Thomas stood immobilized. Under no circumstances could he allow the Book to fall into their hands. His escape was no longer as important as the Book's safety.

He eased the door shut and ran on his toes for the cell. He slipped into the dark, shut the door, stepped toward the gurney, and shoved the Book under the thin mattress. Then he lay back down and pulled the sheet over his head.

Relax. Breathe. Slow your heart.

The door opened thirty seconds later. Light flooded the room. The footsteps walked across the floor, paused for a few seconds, then retreated. A man coughed, and Thomas knew it was Carlos. He'd come for something. Surely not to check on a dead body.

The room went black.

Thomas waited a full minute before rising again. He walked to the door, flipped the light on, and surveyed the room. Concrete all around. Except for the gurney and one bookshelf, the room was empty. A root cellar at one time, perhaps. They'd probably put his body here because it was cold and they wanted to preserve it for tests.

He decided that the risk of being caught with the Book was too great. He would find something to write with and return.

Thomas checked the adjoining room, found it clear, and stepped out. This time the hall was clear. He hurried past the same window he and Monique had climbed through just a few nights earlier. Sunlight filled the window well. He was about to mount the stairs that climbed to the next floor when a door across the hall caught his attention. A reinforced steel door, out of place in this ancient house.

He stepped across the hall and opened it.

No sound.

He peered inside. Another long hall. Steel walls. They'd built a veritable fortress down here. This hall stretched far beyond the exterior wall and ended at yet another door.

Now he was torn. He could either climb the stairs, which could lead to a guard station for all he knew, or he could examine the door at the end of this hall. Just as likely to find a guard there.

Thomas eased into the hall and walked fast. Voices came to him while he was halfway down, and he paused. But they weren't voices of alarm. He ran the last twenty paces and pulled up at the door. The voices were from the room beyond.

"They've killed half the fish off our coast with these two detonations, but they won't target our cities!"

They were talking about nuclear detonations? Someone had launched nuclear weapons!

"Then you don't know the Israelis. They know we have no intention of delivering the antivirus, and they have nothing to lose."

"They're still principled. They won't take innocents down with them. Please, I beg you, the Negev desert was bad enough. We can't target Tel Aviv. A power play to realign powers is one thing. Detonating nuclear weapons over densely populated targets is another. They're bluffing. They know the world would turn against them if they targeted civilians. As it would turn against us if we did the same."

"You think that world opinion is still an element in this equation? Then you're more naive than I imagined, Henri." So the man protesting was Paul Henri Gaetan, the French president. "The only language that the Israelis understand is brute force."

A third voice spoke. "Give them the antivirus."

Armand Fortier.

"Pardon me, sir, but I thought—"

"The plan must be flexible," Fortier said. "We've shown the world our resolve to use whatever force is required to enforce our terms. We've blown two massive holes in their desert, and they've blown two holes in our ocean. So what? The Israelis are snakes. Utterly unpredictable except in the defense of their land. If we fire again, they will retaliate. Two-thirds of the world's combined nuclear arsenal is presently loaded on ships, steaming to our shores. Now isn't the time to accelerate the conflict."

"You will leave Israel intact?"

"We will give them the antivirus," Fortier repeated. "In exchange for their weapons."

"What proof will you offer them?" President Gaetan again.

"A mutual exchange on the seas, five days from today."

The room went silent for a few moments. The next voice that spoke was one that Thomas recognized at the first word.

"But you will destroy Israel," Carlos Missirian said softly.

"Yes."

"And the Americans?"

"The Americans don't have the Israelis' backbone. They have no choice but to deliver their weapons, regardless of all their noise. We're listening to everything they say. They're acting out of total confusion now, but our contact assures us they won't have a choice but to comply in the end."

"They might demand an open exchange as well," the French president said.

"Then we will call their bluff. I can afford to make Israel wait until the time of our choosing. The United States will no longer play a role in world politics."

Thomas felt his heart pound. He pulled his ear from the door. He'd heard enough.

"And if Israel does launch in ten minutes as they've promised?"

Thomas stopped. A long pause.

"Then we take out Tel Aviv," Fortier said.

Thomas sprinted back down the hall toward the root cellar. The plan had changed. He had to get word to the United States before Israel had a chance to launch again. He needed a phone. But in searching for a phone, he might find a pen.

Dangerous, Justin had said. Everything was dangerous now.

Thomas ran for the cell door and twisted the knob. Locked.

Locked? He'd opened it just a few minutes ago from this side. He cranked down on the handle. Heat spread down his neck. He stepped back, panicked. Carlos must have engaged the lock when he left.

Thomas ran his hand through his hair and paced. This wasn't good. He needed a phone!

The meeting was still underway. Thomas sprinted up the stairs, took the steps two at a time, and burst through the door at the top. A single startled guard stared at him. He'd clearly never seen a dead man walking before.

Thomas took him with a foot to his temple, one swift roundhouse kick that landed with a sickening thud. Then a clatter as the man collapsed on the metal folding chair he'd been using.

Thomas didn't bother covering his tracks. No time. He did, however, pluck the nine-millimeter from the man's hand. Short of finding a key to the cell, he would blow the door off its hinges. Noisy but effective.

First the phone.

He passed a window and saw a least a dozen guards milling around the driveway, smoking. They were mostly ranking French military, he noted. Not thugs you'd find in the underground. That would be a concern in a few minutes. Phone—where was the phone?

On the wall, naturally. Black and outdated like most things in the French countryside. He dug in his pocket, relieved to find the card Grant had given him in Washington. On the back, scrawled in pencil, a direct line to the White House.

Thomas snatched up the phone and dialed the long number.

Silence.

For a moment he feared the lines were out. Naturally, the French would monitor all calls. Getting through would be impossible.

The line suddenly clicked. Then hissed for a while. He prayed the call would connect.

"You have reached the White House. Please listen closely, as our menu options have changed. You may press zero at any time to speak to an operator . . ."

Hand trembling. Zero.

A switchboard operator answered after four rings. "White House."

"This is Thomas Hunter. I'm in France and I need to speak to the president immediately."

8

THEN YOU were clearly mistaken," Woref said. "Whatever you think you saw was never there."

Soren shook his head. "I could swear that I saw the albino shift an object under his tunic just before falling asleep. He managed to hide something from us during our initial search."

"But there is no object; you said so yourself. Get some sleep while you can. We raise the army in four hours. Leave me."

Soren bowed. "Yes sir." He left his commander alone in the tent.

They'd made good time and stopped for a few hours' sleep in the dead of night. Tomorrow they would enter the city and receive their reward for Thomas of Hunter's capture.

They had forced the albinos to walk most of the way, carrying their chains, and they had fallen asleep almost immediately, according to Soren. Even if Hunter had managed to conceal a weapon in the folds of his tunic, they had little to fear from him now. The once-mighty warrior was a shell of his former self. He'd not only stripped himself of healthy flesh by dipping in the red pools, but he'd lost his manhood in the process. Hunter was nothing more than a diseased rodent, and his only threat to the Horde was the spread of his disease.

Woref removed the hard leather breastplate and set it on the floor beside his cot. A single lamp spewed black smoke. He ran his hand over his hairy chest, brushed away the flecks of dried skin that had fallen on his apron, and pulled on a nightshirt. The day that he would finally take Chelise into his house as wife had come. The thought made his belly feel light.

He drew back the tent flap and stepped into the cool night. They'd camped in a meadow that sloped away from the forest. From his vantage he could see the entire army, settled for the night, some in hastily erected tents, most around smoldering fire pits. They'd celebrated with ale and meat, both delicacies over the standard rations of fermented water and starch.

The prisoners lay uncovered twenty yards to his right, under the standing guard of six warriors. Woref grunted and headed for the tree line to relieve himself.

A deeper darkness settled over him when he stepped past the first trees. The Horde preferred day over night, mostly due to unfounded tales in which Shataiki lured men into the trees to consume them alive. Until this moment, Woref had never given any such myth a second thought.

But now, with blackness pressing his skin, all those stories crashed through his mind. He stopped and gazed at the trunks ahead. Turned and saw that the camp slept as peacefully as a moment ago.

Woref spit into the leaves and walked deeper, leaving the relative safety of the meadow behind. But not far enough to lose complete sight of the camp.

"Wwrrrreffffffffsssssssss."

He stopped, startled by the sound of his name, whispering through the night. The trees rose like charcoal marks against the dark forest. He had imagined . . .

"Woreffff."

He grabbed the hilt of his short sword and spun back.

Nothing. Trees, yes. A thick forest of trees. But he couldn't see the camp any longer. He'd wandered too deep.

"You're looking the wrong direction, my beast of a man."

The sound came from behind. Woref couldn't remember the last time terror had gripped him in its fist. It wasn't just the darkness, nor the whispering of his name, nor the disappearing of the camp. His horror was primarily motivated by the voice.

He knew this voice!

Gravel sloshing at the bottom of a water pail.

He'd never actually heard the voice of Shataiki before, but he knew now, without looking, that the voice behind him belonged to a creature from the myths.

"No need to be afraid. Turn around and face me. You'll like what you see. I promise you."

Woref kept his hand on his blade, but any thought of drawing it had fled with his common sense. He found himself turning.

The tall batlike creature that stood facing him between two trees not ten feet away looked remarkably similar to the bronze-winged serpent on the Horde's crest. This one, though, was larger than any of the stories claimed.

This was Teeleh.

The bat drilled him with round, pupil-less red eyes. Bulging cherries. His fur was black and his snout ran long to loose lips that hung over yellow-crusted fangs.

The leader of the Shataiki grinned and held a red fruit in his wiry and nimble fingers. "That's right. In the flesh."

Teeleh sank his fangs into the fruit's meat. Juice mixed with saliva dripped to the forest floor. He said the name, speaking through smacking lips.

"Teeleh."

Woref closed his eyes for a moment, sure that if he kept them shut long enough, the vision would vanish.

"Open your eyes!" Teeleh roared.

Hot, sweet breath buffeted Woref's face, and he jerked his eyes open. He reached for the tree on his right to steady himself.

"Are all humans so weak?" the bat demanded.

Had Soren or the others heard Teeleh's cry? They would come . . .

"No. No, I don't think anyone will come running to your aid. And if you think you need their help, then you'll prove me wrong. I've been grooming the wrong man."

Woref's terror began to fade. The bat hadn't attacked him. Hadn't bitten him. Hadn't harmed him in any way.

"Do you know what love is, Woref?"

He hardly heard the question.

"You're real," Woref said.

"Love." The bat took another bite. This time he lifted his snout, opened his mouth wide, let the fruit drop into his throat, and swallowed it with a pool of fluid. When his head lowered, his eyes were closed. They opened slowly. "Will you have some?"

Woref didn't respond.

"You don't mind me saying that you humans make me sick, do you? Even you, the one I've chosen."

The leaves in the trees behind Teeleh rustled, and Woref lifted his face to a sea of red eyes glowing in the darkness. The rustling spread to his left, his right, and behind and seemed to swallow him.

A bat the size of a dog dropped to the ground behind Teeleh. Eyes gleaming, furry skin quivering. Then another, beside him. And another. They fell like rotten fruit.

"My servants," Teeleh said. "It's been awhile since I've allowed them to show themselves. They're quite excited. Ignore them."

The bats kept their distance but stared at him, unblinking.

"Do you love her?" Teeleh asked.

"Chelise?"

"He speaks. Yes, the daughter of Qurong, firstborn among the humans who drank my water. Do you love her?"

"She will be my wife." Woref's throat felt parched, his tongue dry like morst in his mouth.

"That's the idea, I know. But do you love her? Not like I love her— I don't expect you to love her so exquisitely—but as the love of a man goes. Do you feel overpowering emotion for her?"

"Yes." The Shataiki were here to bless his union? That might be a good sign.

"And this love you think you have for her, how can you be sure she will return it?"

"She will. Why wouldn't she?"

"Because she's human. Humans make their own choices about their loyalties. That's what makes them who they are."

"She will love me," Woref said confidently.

"Or?"

He hadn't really considered the matter. "I am a powerful man who will one day rule the Horde. It's a woman's place to serve men like me. I'm not sure you understand who you're talking to."

"I am talking to the man who owes me his life."

Teeleh tossed what was left of his fruit to the ground and wrapped his wide, paper-thin wings around his torso. The Shataiki was taking credit for Woref's rise to power?

"Yes, she will be lured by your power and your strength, but don't assume that she will give you her love. She's deceived like the rest of you, but she seems to be more stubborn than most."

They still hadn't made any move against him. Clearly, the Shataiki, regardless of their fierce reputation, meant him no harm. Teeleh seemed more concerned with his marriage to Chelise than with destroying him.

"I'm not sure what this had to do with you," he said, gaining more confidence.

"It has to do with me because I love her far more than you could ever imagine. I broke Tanis's mind, and now I will have his daughter's heart."

Fear smothered Woref again.

"Do you hear what I'm saying? I will possess her. I will crush her and then I will consume her, and she will be *mine.*"

"I . . . How—"

"Through you."

"You're asking me to kill her? Never! I have waited years to make her mine."

The night grew perfectly quiet. For a long time the bat's red eyes drilled Woref. The Shataiki were growing restless, hopping from branch to branch, hissing and snickering.

"Clearly, you don't understand what love is. I want her heart, not her life. If I wanted to kill her, I would use her father." Teeleh rolled his head and momentarily closed his eyes. "You're as wretched as she is. You're all as blind as bats." He unfolded his wings and stepped forward. "But you will win her love. I don't care if you have to beat it out of her."

Teeleh approached slowly, dragging his wings through dead leaves. Woref's limbs began to tremble. He couldn't move.

"I don't care if you have to club it out of her; you will earn her loyalty and her love. I will not lose her to the albinos. And then you will give her to me."

Where he found the sudden strength to resist, Woref wasn't sure, but a blind rage swept over him. "I could never give her to you. She would never love you!"

"When she loves you, she will love me," Teeleh said. Louder now. "He will try to win her love, but she will come to me. Me!"

And then Teeleh leaned forward so that his snout was only inches from Woref's face. The bat's jaw spread wide so that the only thing Woref could see was a long pink tongue snaking back into the black hole that was the bat's throat. A hot, foul stench smothered him.

Teeleh withdrew, snapped his jaw closed with a loud snap.

"I have shown you my power; now I will show you my heart," he said. "I will show you my love."

Teeleh swept his wing around himself and grinned wickedly. With a parting razor-sharp glare, he leaped into the air, flew into the trees, and was gone. The branches shook as his minions scattered into darkness.

Woref felt hot tears running down his cheeks. He still couldn't move, much less understand.

I will show you my heart. My love.

Then Woref was throwing up.

9

"FOLLOW ME," Merton Gains said.

Monique followed him through a short hall to a conference room off the West Wing.

"Kara's in with him. The president's got his hands full with the crisis in the Middle East, and he's got a room full of advisors, but he insisted you come in after hearing Kara. Just tread lightly. They're pretty high-strung in there."

The conference room that Monique walked into was large enough to seat at least twenty people around an oval table. A dozen advisors and military types were seated or standing. A few talked in hushed tones at one side. The rest were staring at three large screens, which tracked the unfolding situation in the Middle East and France.

"Sir, I have Benjamin on the line."

"Put him through," the president said.

The receiver buzzed and he picked it up.

"Hello, Mr. Prime Minister. I hope you have good news for me."

Monique scanned the room for Kara. Their eyes met, and Thomas's sister walked toward her.

"I agree, Isaac, and I don't necessarily blame you for pushing this," the president was saying. "But even in the remotest mountain range, you're bound to have casualties. We don't see how any further escalation will benefit you."

Another pause.

"Naturally. I understand principle." The president sighed. "It's an impossible situation, I agree. But we still have time. Let's not wipe out our cities before we have to."

Kara stopped three feet from Monique, eyes wide. "You disappeared," she said quietly.

"My car ran off the road."

"You were hurt?"

"No. I just blacked out."

"You did?"

Why was this so striking to Kara?

The president had finished his call.

"You were dead," Kara said.

"You mean figuratively. My car slammed into a tree and knocked me out."

"You remember that? Or did you just pass out before the car rolled off the road?"

Kara was right. Monique had no memory of actually flying over the edge. "I passed out first."

"I was there, Monique. With Mikil. I dreamed as Mikil. Rachelle was killed by the Horde thirteen months ago. Because of your unique connection to her, I think you died when she died. You believed that you were Rachelle, right?"

"Rachelle's *dead*?"

"Thirteen months ago."

"But I'm alive. I'm not sure I follow."

"I'll explain later, but I'm pretty sure you were dead."

"And Thomas?"

"Thomas is alive. At least, in the desert he's alive. Rachelle found him dead in the Horde camp and healed him with Justin's power. You know about Justin's power, don't you?"

"Yes. And is Thomas alive here?"

Kara looked deep into her eyes. "You're alive, aren't you?"

"Excuse me," the president said. "You're saying that Monique *died* last night?"

"Sir?"

He held up his hand to silence his chief of staff.

"Monique?"

"Yes, I think she's right. I know it sounds crazy, but if Rachelle was killed in the other reality, I would have died here. We were . . . connected."

"Connected how?"

"Belief. Knowledge." Monique looked at Kara. A small part of her still remembered Thomas's first lieutenant, Mikil, from the short time she'd lived as Rachelle.

"Sir, I think you should take this call," Ron Kreet pressed.

"Who is it?" the president demanded without removing his eyes from Monique.

"He says he's Thomas Hunter."

The president turned around. "Thomas Hunter?"

"I knew it!" Kara whispered. "The Horde didn't kill him!"

"He says he has information critical to the standoff with Israel."

"Put him on speaker."

The chief of staff punched a button and set the receiver in its cradle. "Mr. Hunter, I have the president on the line. You're on a speakerphone. Your sister and Monique de Raison are here as well."

The line remained silent.

"Thomas?" the president said.

"Hello, Mr. President. Monique is alive, then?"

"She's standing right here with Kara."

"The Book works."

"What book?" the president asked.

"I'm sorry, Mr. President. Kara can explain later. Did the others escape?"

"They're safe," Kara said.

"What's this about?" President Blair asked.

"I'm sorry, sir," Thomas said. "I know it isn't making a lot of sense, but you have to listen carefully. The French intend to offer the antivirus to Israel in an open-sea exchange five days from now. The offer is genuine. If Israel calls their bluff and launches another strike, Fortier will retaliate by taking out Tel Aviv."

The president slowly sat. "You're sure about this?"

"Yes sir, I am. I can also tell you that they won't tolerate the existence of a United States postvirus. Can you get me out of here?"

Blair glanced up at a general, who nodded.

"I'll let General Peters give you some coordinates. Are you sure you can make it?"

"No."

Blair paused, then said, "I'm giving the phone to Peters. Godspeed, Thomas. Get back to us."

"Thank you, sir."

The general picked up the phone and talked quickly, feeding Thomas with basic instructions and coordinates for a pickup point fifty miles south of Paris.

"Get the Israeli prime minister on the phone now," the president instructed Kreet. Then to Monique and Kara: "I think I deserve an explanation."

Kara was staring at the floor. She lifted a hand and pulled absently at her hair. "I have to get back and tell Mikil that he's with the Horde."

"You know how to get back?" Monique asked.

"Yes."

———◦⚬◦———

Thomas hung up the phone and took two steps toward the stairs before stopping short. Voices drifted up from the basement.

They were on the stairs!

They would find the guard. Then they would check his cell and find him missing.

He sprinted for the back of the house, through an old kitchen, over a couch in the living room, up to a large window. No guard on the back lawn that he could see. He flipped the latch open.

The window slid up freely. He tumbled to the ground and had the window halfway down when the first alarm came. A loud klaxon that made him jerk.

"Man down!"

Thomas ran for the forest.

Carlos heard the alarm and froze on the bottom step. An intruder? Impossible. They'd evacuated the house only yesterday when the Americans had inserted their special forces in an attempt to locate Thomas. They'd learned of the mission in advance, naturally, and they'd stayed clear long enough for the team to satisfy itself that Monique de Raison's information was simply wrong.

Any intrusion at this point couldn't be part of the American effort. There had been no word. There was always the possibility that their contact had been compromised, but Monique wouldn't have been able to tell them who the contact was, only that they had one. And that was Fortier's mistake, not his.

His radio squawked. "Sir?"

He unclipped the radio from his waist. "Close the perimeter. Cover the exits. Shoot on sight."

He took two steps and stopped. A thought filled his mind. The cut on his neck. The impossible wound from the reality that Thomas claimed to have come from. A bandage now covered the small cut.

Carlos dropped back to the basement and ran toward the back room where the body was kept. The body of Thomas Hunter. He crashed through the first door and inserted his key into the cellar door. He shoved it open and hit the light.

He roared in anger and threw his keys at the wall. They'd taken the body. But how could a team have penetrated his defenses, broken into this room, and taken the body in the space of ten minutes? Less!

Unless this man truly had escaped death before. Unless . . .

But he refused to consider that possibility. Some things pushed a man too far, and the thought of a dead man walking after three days under the sheet was one of them.

Carlos ran from the room, snatching up his radio while he sprinted down the hall.

"Check the windows for footprints. Search the house. Hunter's body is missing. I want him found!"

—∞∞∞—

Now he had a serious dilemma. More serious in some ways than any he'd yet faced. Thomas crouched in the forest watching the frenzied search of the house and its perimeter. They'd found the unlatched window and had concentrated their search on that side of the house. All well and good from his perspective on the opposite side of the property. He had escaped cleanly. They had no idea which direction he'd headed. All he had to do now was reach the coordinates in southern France.

But there was still the Book. There was no way he could leave France without the Book. Not because it might prove useful in his hands, but because it could be devastating in the wrong hands. Assuming the Book still worked. They hadn't tested the Book here yet, but surely . . .

The guards had been searching the house under Carlos's direction for half an hour. What were the chances that they wouldn't find the Book? Very slim.

If he waited until the activity in the house settled down, attempted to recover the Book, and headed south within a few hours, he could still make the pickup.

"Anything?" one of the guards yelled.

"Nothing," a man dressed in the uniform of a high-ranking French military officer answered. He stepped into an old Bentley and slammed the door. "Unless you consider an old empty diary with an entry or two something. It must have been lost by an old patient. Found it under the mattress." He stuck the Book out the window. "Beautiful cover though."

The Book? It was right there in the man's hands. The blank Book of History.

The car roared to life. Thomas rose and almost yelled out without thought. He caught himself and dropped back down. Never mind getting caught—anything he did to draw attention to the Book would be a mistake.

The car sped off with Thomas peering hopelessly after it.

The Book was gone.

He stood still, dumbstruck. The officer had no clue what he'd stumbled upon—Thomas's only small consolation.

Thomas spent the next ten minutes considering his predicament before finally concluding that there was no reasonable way to pursue the Book at this time. For the time being it was simply lost.

Unless Carlos . . . Carlos would know the officer.

Carlos. And who could get to Carlos?

Johan. Carlos had connected with Johan once, when Thomas had cut his neck in the amphitheater. Maybe he could get Johan to dream as Carlos . . .

Thomas turned and ran south. He had to sleep and dream. And he would, but he had only twenty-four hours to reach a helicopter that would transfer him to an aircraft carrier in the Atlantic. They were waiting for him in Washington.

10

CHELISE OF Qurong stood on the balcony of her father's palace and stared at the procession winding its way up the muddy street. They'd captured more of the albino dissidents. Why the people found this a reason for such celebration, she couldn't understand, but they lined the street ten deep, peering and taunting and laughing as if it were a circus rather than a prelude to an execution. She understood their natural fascination with the albinos—they looked more like animals than humans with their shiny hair and smooth skin. Like jackals that had been shaved of their fur. There was a rumor that they might not even be human any longer.

The beast Woref had caught these jackals. He was parading the fruits of his hunt for all the women to see. She wasn't sure how to feel about that. He was uncouth, but not necessarily in a way that was intolerable. So she'd told herself a hundred times since learning his eyes were for her.

She'd never marry him, of course. Father would never allow his only daughter to fall into such hands.

Then again, marriage to such a powerful man who exemplified all that was truly honorable about being human might not be such a bad thing. Every man had his tender side. Surely she could find his. Surely she could tame even this monster. The task might even be a pleasurable one.

Chelise lifted her eyes to the city. Nearly a million people now lived in this crowded forest, though "forest" no longer accurately described the great prize the Horde had overtaken thirteen months ago. At least not here by the lake. Twenty thousand square huts made of stone and mud stretched several miles back from the edge of the lake. The castle stood five stories and was required to be the highest structure in Qurong's domain.

The morning wail still drifted from the temple, where the priests were spouting their nonsense about the Great Romance while the faithful bathed in pain.

She would never speak those thoughts aloud, of course. But she knew that Ciphus and Qurong had fashioned their religion from agreements motivated by political concerns more than by faith. They kept the name and many of the practices of the Forest Dwellers' Great Romance, but they incorporated many Horde practices as well. There was something for everyone in this religion of theirs.

Not that it mattered. She doubted there ever had been such a being called Elyon in the first place.

The lake's muddy waters were considered holy. The faithful were required to bathe in the lake at least once every week, a prospect that had initially terrified most of the Horde. Bathing was a painful experience traditionally associated with punishment, not cleansing.

The fact that Ciphus had drained the red water within a week of Justin's drowning and redirected the spring waters into its basin hardly helped—pain was pain, and no Scab relished the ritual. But as Ciphus said, religion must have its share of pain to prompt faith. And bathing in these muddy waters had none of the red waters' adverse effects. In fact, the bathing ritual was currently in vogue among the upper class. Cleanliness was to be embraced, not shunned, Ciphus said, and this was one teaching that Chelise was beginning to embrace.

She bathed once a day now.

"Excuse me, mistress, but Qurong calls for you."

Chelise faced her maidservant, Elison, a petite woman with long black hair knotted around yellow flowers. Daffodils. Adorning oneself with flowers was the one Forest Dweller practice that Chelise enjoyed adopting more than perhaps any other. They'd never had such a luxury in the desert. As of late, flowers were becoming more difficult to find near the city.

"Did he say why he wants to see me?" Chelise asked.

"Only that he has a gift for you."

"Did he say what kind of gift?"

"No, mistress." Elison grinned. "But I don't think it's fruit or flowers."

Chelise felt her pulse surge. "The villa?"

They all knew that Qurong was building a villa for her in the large walled compound referred to as the royal garden, three miles outside the city. She hadn't seen the villa yet, as Qurong kept the section where it was being built cordoned off. But she'd been to the compound many times, usually to the library to write or to read the Books collected over the past fifteen years. The sprawling gardens and orchards were kept by a staff of twenty servants. Not a blade of grass was out of place. Elyon himself would live here, they said, such was its beauty.

And Chelise would live there too, beside the library where she would sequester herself and write into the night. Maybe even one day discover the key to reading the Books of Histories.

"Perhaps." Her maidservant winked.

Chelise ran into her room. "Quickly, help me dress. What should I wear?"

"I would say that a white gown—"

"With red flowers! Is he waiting?"

"He will meet you in the courtyard in a few minutes."

"A few minutes? Then we have to hurry!"

The palace had been built from wood with flattened reeds for walls and pounded bark for floors—a luxury reserved only for the upper class. The Forest People had built their homes in the same manner, and Qurong had promised that they would all live in such magnificent homes soon enough. Their simple mud dwellings were only temporary, a necessity mandated by the need to build so many houses in a short period of time.

She discarded her simple bedclothes and took the long bleached tunic that Elison had retrieved from her closet. The gown was woven from thread that the Forest People had perfected—smooth and silky, unlike the rough burlap the Horde had made from the woven stalks of desert wheat. The costs of the campaigns against the forests had been staggering, but Qurong had been right about the benefits of conquering them.

"The flowers . . ."

Elison laughed. "The villa won't be going anywhere. Take your time. Sometimes it's best to make a man wait, even if he is the supreme leader."

"You know men so well?"

Elison didn't respond, and Chelise knew that her comment had stung. Maidservants were forbidden to marry.

She sat in front of the resin mirror and picked up a brush. "I will let you marry, Elison. I've told you, the day that I marry, you'll be free to find your own man."

Elison dipped her head and left the room to fetch the flowers.

The mirror's resin had been poured over a flat black stone that reflected her features as a pool of dark water would. She dipped the bristles of her brush into a small bowl of oil and began working out the flakes that speckled her dark hair—an unending task that most women avoided by wearing a hood.

And when will Qurong allow you to marry, Chelise?

When he finds a suitable man for you. This is the burden of royalty. You can't just marry the first handsome man who walks by this castle.

Chelise decided to forget the brushing and settle for the hood after all. She dabbed her fingers into a large bowl of white morst powder and patted her face and neck where she'd already applied paste. The regular variety of the powdery paste soothed skin by drying any lingering moisture such as sweat, but it tended to flake with the skin. This new variety, developed by her father's alchemist, consisted of two separate applications: a clear thin salve, then a white morst powder that contained ground herbs, effectively minimizing the flaking. It might be fine for the common woman to walk around with loose flakes of skin hanging from her tunic, but it wasn't fitting for royalty.

Elison returned with red roses.

"Roses?"

"I also have tuhan flowers," Elison said.

Chelise took the roses and smiled.

They descended the stairs ten minutes later and hurried toward the courtyard. They crossed an atrium that rose all five stories and featured a large fruit tree at its center. Sweet fruit—not the bitter rot that the desert tribes preferred—was the one spoil of the forest that all of the people gorged themselves on. Chelise stopped before the arching entrance to the courtyard, faced Elison, and opened her hands, palms up. "Okay?"

"You're stunning."

"Thank you."

She turned and kissed the base of a tall bronze statue of Elyon—a winged serpent on a pole. "I feel religious today," she said softly, and walked into the courtyard.

Qurong stood in a black tunic beside Woref, who was dressed in full battle gear. Behind them were the albinos under guard.

The sight snatched away any thought of the villa. Chelise stopped, confused. Qurong meant to give her some albinos as a gift? No, that couldn't possibly be it. His gift was to show off his little victory.

Qurong saw her, spread his arms, and smiled wide. "My daughter arrives. A vision of beauty to grace her father's pride."

What was he saying? He rarely spoke in such lofty terms.

"Good morning, Father. I'm told you have a gift."

He laughed. "And I do. But first I want to show you something." Qurong glanced at Woref, who was staring at her directly. "Show her, Woref."

The general dipped his head, stepped to one side, and stood tall like a peacock. For all his fearful reputation, he demeaned himself with this display of pride. Did he think she would tremble with respect at his capturing a few albinos? He should have wiped out the whole band of jackals by now.

She looked at the poor victims. These few were a mockery of his . . .

Something about the albino on the left stopped her. He looked vaguely familiar. Impossible, of course—the only albinos she'd ever seen were the ones dragged in as prisoners these past few months. A couple dozen at most. This man wasn't one of them. Then what was it? His green eyes seemed to look through her. Unnerving. She averted her stare.

The prisoners' hands were bound behind them, and their ankles were shackled. Other than simple loin skirts, they were all naked except for one—a woman. They'd been covered in ash, but their sweat had washed most of it away, revealing broad vertical swaths of fleshy skin.

"You don't know who you're looking at, do you, my dear?"

"What is this?" a voice demanded behind her. Mother had come in. "How dare you bring these filthy creatures into my house?"

"Watch your tongue, wife," Qurong snapped. It was no secret that Patricia ruled the castle, but Qurong wouldn't tolerate brazenness in front of his men.

Patricia stopped beside Chelise and eyed her husband. "Please remove these albinos from my house."

"Thank you for coming, my dear. Your house will be disease-free soon enough. First, please, both of you, look closely and tell me what you see."

Chelise glanced at her mother, who held Qurong with a glare. Her eyes were as white as the moon, but today the moon was on fire.

"For the sake of Elyon, woman! It won't kill you! Look at them!"

Her mother finally obeyed.

Something strange was happening with this ceremonious display, but Chelise was at a loss. They were simply five albinos in chains, headed for the dungeons and then for a drowning. Why would her father take such pride?

She guessed it the moment Qurong spoke.

"You see, even the great Thomas of Hunter is nothing but one more albino in chains."

Thomas of Hunter!

"Which one?" Patricia asked.

But Chelise already knew which one. The once-great commander of the feared Forest Guard was the man who was staring at her. She blinked and looked away again. He looked at her as if he recognized her.

"Take them away," Chelise said.

"So you've captured their leader," her mother said. "This is good news, but their presence in our house is offensive. I'm sure you'll find plenty of commoners to cheer your victory."

Qurong's jaw muscles flexed. Mother was pushing him too far. "It isn't the commoner's victory," he snapped. "It's yours. And it's your daughter's."

Hers? A smile returned to Qurong's face.

"Our daughter's?" Patricia asked.

Now Qurong's eyes were on Chelise. "Yes, our daughter's. Today I am announcing the marriage of my only daughter."

Her mother gasped.

It took a moment for the words to sink in. She felt Elison's hand take her elbow. But what did her marriage have to do with these albinos?

"I am to be married?"

"Yes, my love."

"Well, that is good news indeed," her mother said.

Chelise felt a momentary surge of panic. "Married to whom?"

"To the man who captured him, of course." Qurong stepped to his left and put a hand on his general's shoulder. "To Woref, commander of my armies."

Woref!

Chelise felt the breath leave her lungs. The general's hands hung loosely by his sides—big, thick hands with gnarled fingers. He was twice her size. He lifted a hand and pulled back his hood to reveal his head. Long dreadlocks fell over his shoulders. There could be no mistake about it: this man was part beast.

But he was also Woref, mightiest man in the Horde, next to her father. And even now his gray eyes looked at her hungrily. Desire. This mighty man wanted her as his wife.

Whatever reservation she struggled with was more than compensated for by her mother, who rushed over to the general and bent to one knee. She took his hand and kissed it.

"My daughter is yours, my lord."

She stood as quickly and kissed her husband on the cheek. "You have made me a very happy woman."

Qurong chuckled.

"Well," her mother said, facing Chelise. "Aren't you going to say something?"

Chelise was still too stunned to speak.

Her maidservant squeezed her elbow. "It is a most excellent choice," Elison whispered.

Her compassionate voice filled Chelise with courage. She lowered her head and knelt to one knee. "I am honored to accept this gift, great Qurong of the Horde. You have made me a very happy woman."

With those words her apprehension fled. An excitement she'd never known before flooded her veins. She was going to marry the mightiest man on the earth. She would be the envy of every woman who still possessed the fire to love. She was about to find new life.

She heard him coming toward her. She opened her eyes but dared not lift her head. His muddy battle boots stopped three feet from her. Then one knee. He was kneeling!

Woref's hand touched her chin and lifted her face gently. She stared into his gray eyes. A tremble swept through her bones. Was this terror or desire?

Woref leaned forward and kissed her forehead. He spoke softly, but she couldn't mistake the great emotion in his voice. "You are mine. Forever, you are mine," he said. Then he stood.

The courtyard had fallen completely silent. Now her mother sniffed. She'd never heard the sound from Patricia before.

"When will they marry?" Mother asked.

"In three days," Qurong said. "On the same day that we drown Thomas of Hunter."

11

THOMAS HAD recognized her the moment she stepped into the courtyard. This was Chelise, the daughter of Qurong, whom he'd once met in the desert after the disease had taken him. He'd persuaded her that he was an assassin, and she'd treated him kindly before sending him on his way with a horse. He'd barely made it back to the lake to bathe. He would never forget the pain of that bathing.

He would never forget the kindness of this woman who stared at him with flat gray eyes. She didn't recognize him.

Now he'd just learned that she was being given in marriage to the vilest Scab he'd yet met. Woref. He wasn't sure if she wanted Woref or loathed him, but she'd reacted with enough passion to bring a lump to his throat.

Both Chelise and her mother had used liberal amounts of the morst to cover their faces and smooth out the cracks in their skin. This wasn't done for comfort alone, he thought. Not nearly so much would have sufficed. The powder they used actually covered their skin. In its own way, the Horde's upper class seemed to be distancing itself from the disease. At least the royal women did.

If not for Woref's armor and Qurong's cloak, both which incorporated heavy use of polished bronze buttons, trims, and a winged serpent plate on their chests, both men would have been indistinguishable from any other Scab. They wore their hair long, in knotted dreadlocks, and cracked skin hung in small flakes off their cheeks and noses. They too used morst, but the lightly powdered variety that served the practical purpose of keeping the skin dry, if not smooth.

Seeing the best of the Horde in such close proximity, Thomas was reminded why his people had such an aversion to Scabs. The disease that Justin had drowned to heal was disturbing in the least. Even looking at the disease for too long was frowned upon among some tribes.

Yet Thomas couldn't tear his eyes from Chelise, and at first he didn't know why. Then he understood—he pitied her. This woman who had once treated him with such kindness wanted to be free from the disease, he was sure of it. Or was he simply imposing his will on hers?

When Qurong had announced her marriage, Thomas found himself silently begging her to scream her objections. For a moment he thought she might. Then she'd fallen to her knee and expressed her pleasure, and Thomas's heart had fallen like a rock.

Was she so blind? He felt smothered by empathy.

Qurong had just said something, but Thomas had missed it. The room was quiet. Chelise was looking at him again. Their eyes locked.

Do you recognize me? He willed her to see. *Elyon once sent you to save my life. I am the man who called himself an assassin in front of your tent.*

What had Qurong said that brought this silence?

"Well, then, we have three days to prepare," Qurong's wife said. "Not exactly ample time to prepare a wedding, but considering the occasion, I would say that sooner is better than later." She took her daughter's arm and bowed to her husband and Woref. "My lords." Then she led Chelise from the courtyard.

Three days.

Qurong spoke to Woref: "Take them to the dungeon. Apart from you, no one but Ciphus or myself is to speak to them."

Woref dipped his head. "Sir."

Qurong stepped up to Thomas and eyed him carefully. He lifted his hand and squeezed Thomas's cheeks. "Three days. I'm tempted to finish you now, but I intend to make you speak first." He released his cheeks and absently wiped his fingers on his tunic.

"I will speak now," Thomas said.

Qurong glanced at Woref, then back, grinning. "So easily? I expected the mighty warrior to be more reticent."

"What do you want to know?"

His candor seemed to put the leader off.

"Tell me the locations of your tribes."

"They've moved. I don't know where they are."

Qurong looked at Woref.

"I'm afraid it's true, sir. The tribes move when contact is made."

"You run like a pack of dogs," Qurong said. "The great warriors have turned into frightened pups."

"The bravery of my people is greater than any man who wields a sword," Thomas said. "We could kill your warriors easily enough, but this isn't the way of Justin."

"Justin is dead, you fool!"

"Is he? The Horde is dead."

"Do I look dead?" Qurong slapped him on the cheek. "Did a dead man just strike you?"

Thomas didn't respond. This man was going to drown him in three days—not enough time for Mikil to mount a rescue, not with her duty to protect the tribe first. He had his dreams. If there was any way to turn the tables here, it would come from his dreams.

"Ciphus says you've lost your minds. I see now that he's right. Take them to the dungeons."

He turned away. A guard grabbed Thomas's arm and pulled him around.

"And, Woref," Qurong said, turning back. "Feed him the rhambutan."

He knew?

"We don't want these dreams Martyn spoke about interfering with our plans. If he refuses to eat, kill one of the other prisoners."

Woref led them from the castle back into the street. Thomas stared, still taken aback by the changes.

He'd grown accustomed to the scent of sulfur during the long trip through the desert, but the stink had nearly overpowered him while they were still two miles from the Horde city. Thousands of trees had been cleared to make room for a city that looked more like a garbage pile than a place humans were expected to live. It reminded Thomas of images from the histories, slums in India, only made of mud rather than rusted tin shanties. Flies had infested the place, drawn by the stink.

Thousands of Scabs had lined the road, giving the war party a wide berth. Some mocked in high-pitched tones; some stood with folded arms; all stared with bland eyes. There was no way to tell which ones had once been Forest People. Thomas didn't recognize a single face.

If Thomas wasn't mistaken, Qurong had built his castle on the very spot that his own house had once been built. The wooden structures that had been homes for the Forest People still stood, but they had fallen into disrepair, and the yards had gone to waste.

"Move!"

They marched toward the lake. The homes once occupied by Ciphus and his council were now bordered by twin statues of the winged serpent. Teeleh.

"The lake . . ."

A guard struck William on the head, silencing him.

They'd crested the shore. The red water was gone, replaced by murky liquid. Hundreds of Scabs were sponge bathing along the shore. So this was Ciphus's Great Romance.

Thomas walked against the rattling of his shackles, dumb with disbelief. They'd heard rumors, of course, but to actually see the devastation to their once-sacred home came as a shock. The gazebos that surrounded the lake had been converted into guard towers. And on the opposite shore, a new temple.

A Thrall!

It looked nearly identical to the one that had once stood in the colored forest. The domed ceiling didn't glow, and the steps were muddy from a steady flow of traffic, but it was a clear reconstruction of the Thrall that had stood at the center of the village before Tanis had crossed.

"Take them to the deepest chamber," Woref said. He spit to one side.

"They speak to no one other than myself and the high priest. If they escape, I will personally see to the drowning of the entire temple guard."

He turned and left them without another glance.

They were marched toward the amphitheater where they'd judged and sentenced Justin. But there was no amphitheater now. It had been filled in. No, not filled in, Thomas realized. Covered. They were being marched to an entrance that led into the dungeons where the amphitheater once stood.

Thomas glanced at Cain and Stephen, who had helped with this construction before drowning in the red waters. They both stared ahead, eyes glazed.

"Elyon's strength," Thomas said softly.

The guards either didn't hear him or didn't mind him invoking the common greeting. They themselves now referred to Teeleh as Elyon, though they didn't seem to notice the incongruity of the practice.

The dungeons were dark and smelled of mildew. The albinos were herded down a long flight of stone steps, along a wet corridor, and pushed into a twenty-by-twenty cell with bronze bars. A single shaft of light, roughly a foot square, filtered through an air vent in the ceiling.

The gate crashed shut. The guards ran a thick bolt into the wall, locked it down with a key, and left them.

Something dripped nearby—a single drop every four or five seconds. Water, muddy or pure, would be a welcome taste now. A distant clang of the outer gate echoed down the stairs.

Thomas sank to his haunches along one wall, and the others followed suit. They'd been on their feet since being wakened in the desert for the last leg of their march.

For a long minute no one spoke. William broke the silence.

"Well, we've done it now. This is our tomb." There was no levity in his voice. No one bothered to challenge him.

The outer door clanged again. Boots clomped down the stairs. They could hear any such approach, not that knowing when the executioner entered the dungeon would be any consolation.

A new guard came into view and shoved a container through the bars. "Water," he said. He pointed at Thomas. "Drink it."

Thomas glanced at the others then walked over and picked up the pitcher. He knew by the smell that they'd mixed rhambutan juice with the water, but he had no choice. It went down cool and sweet.

Satisfied, the guard retreated without waiting for the others to drink. They drained the entire pitcher before the outer gate closed.

Once again they sat in silence.

"Any ideas?" Thomas asked.

"We won't dream now," William said.

"Right."

"Which means you can't go to this other world of yours and retrieve any information that might help us out. Like you did when we made the black powder."

"That's right. I'm stuck here. I could spend a month in this dungeon while only minutes or hours pass there."

"And what's happening there?" he asked. William was starting to believe, Thomas saw.

"I'm sleeping on an airplane after barely making a helicopter pickup south of Paris."

The explanation earned him a blank stare.

"You know the daughter of Qurong," Suzan said. "She was the one who gave you a horse once."

His mind was drawn back to Chelise. She was facing her own kind of execution without even knowing it. Why was this a concern of Suzan's?

"You're thinking something?"

"No. Only that she seemed to be taken with you."

William scoffed. "With his death, you mean. She's a Scab!"

"She's also a woman," Suzan said.

"So is her mother. The old witch is worse than Qurong."

"Let her speak," Thomas said. To Suzan: "She's a woman; what of it?"

"She might think differently than her father. Not about us, mind you. But she may be more reasoned than Qurong."

"Reasoned about what?" William asked. "She would just as soon see us dead as her father would."

"Reasoned about the Books of Histories."

Thomas blinked in the dim light. "The Books of Histories?"

"The Horde still has them, right?"

"As far as we know."

"And you have special knowledge concerning the histories."

"I don't see—"

"Didn't you say that she was fascinated by the histories when you met her in the desert?"

Thomas suddenly saw where she was going. He stood slowly.

"If you could win an audience with her," Suzan continued, "and persuade her that you can show her how to read the histories, she might have the influence to delay our execution. Or at least yours."

"But how would I win an audience with her?"

"This is lunacy," William said. "The Horde can't even read the Books of History!"

"We don't know that they can't be taught." Thomas said. "Suzan may be on to something."

"And what would delaying our execution accomplish?" William objected.

"Are you going to argue with everything?" Thomas demanded. "We aren't exactly brimming with alternatives here. Give her a chance."

He turned back to Suzan. "On the other hand, he does have a point. I doubt a Scab can be taught to read the Books of Histories. They can't decipher the truth in them."

"Did the blank Book work?" she asked.

The Book had crossed over into the other reality. When it disappeared, Thomas had offered no explanation to his comrades. "Yes. Yes, as a matter of fact it did."

"Are there more blank Books?"

He hadn't considered the possibility. "I don't know."

"You may not be able to get an audience with Chelise, but Ciphus will see you," Suzan said. "Make him promises concerning the power of the blank Books."

"They don't work in this reality."

"Promises, Thomas. Only promises."

Then Thomas saw the entire plan clearly. He spun to Cain. "How do I get the attention of a guard?"

12

FIVE FULLY armed Scabs led Thomas into the Thrall through a back entrance. The entire structure was built with the original Thrall in mind. Without the option of colored wood, Ciphus had used mud and then covered the mud with dyed thatch work—Horde handiwork. The large circular floor in the domed auditorium was green, again dyed thatch work instead of the glowing resin once shaped by the hands of innocent men. Hundreds of worshipers lay prostrate around the circumference, with only their heads and hands in the green circle.

It was as if they were paying homage to this green lake.

The primary departure from the original Thrall was the large statue of the winged serpent, which stood on top of the dome. A smaller replica hung from its crest inside.

This was Teeleh's Thrall.

Thomas was pushed past the auditorium into a hall and then into a side office, where a single hooded man stood with his back to the door, staring out of a small window. The door closed behind Thomas.

He stood in chains before a large wooden slab, a desk of sorts, bordered on each side with bronze statues of the winged serpent. Candles blazed from two large candlesticks, spewing their oily smoke to the ceiling.

The man turned slowly. Thomas's first thought was that Ciphus had become a ghost. The powder on his face was as white as the robe he wore, and his eyes only a shade darker.

The high priest stared at him like a cat, emotionless, arms folded into draping sleeves that hid his hands.

"Hello, Thomas."

Thomas dipped his head slightly. "Ciphus. It's good to see you, old friend."

For a long time the high priest just looked at him, and Thomas refused to speak again. He would play and win this purposeful game.

Ciphus stepped to a tall flask on his desk and gripped its narrow neck with his long white fingers. He was wearing the same powder as Chelise and her mother had worn, Thomas guessed. The cracked skin was still visible beneath, but not in the same scaly fashion that characterized the scabies.

The priest poured a green liquid into a chalice. "Drink?"

"No, thank you."

"You sure? It's fruit juice."

"We have fruit, Ciphus. Have you tasted it?"

"Your bitter seeds? Your preference for that should be the first indicator that you've lost your senses. The birds and the animals eat bitter seeds eagerly. So do you." He took a sip of the fruit juice.

"Do the seeds eaten by animals also heal them?" Thomas asked.

"No. But animals don't practice sorcery. Which is the one clear indication that you're not truly animals either. So then, what are you, Thomas? You're clearly no longer human; one look at your flesh is proof enough. And you're not really an animal like they all say. Then what are you? Hmm? Other than enemies of Elyon?"

"We are the followers of Justin, who is Elyon."

"Please, not in here," Ciphus said with lips drawn. "We are in his temple; I will not have you utter such blasphemy here." He set the glass down carefully. "You requested an audience. I assume that you intend to beg for your life. You defy me and my council when you have your sword, and now you beg at my feet when I have you in chains, is that it?"

"You don't have me in chains. Qurong does."

"And where is Justin now? I would have thought he would come riding in on a white horse to draw a protective line in the sand for you."

"You can't go on pretending that nothing happened when you killed him, Ciphus."

"Martyn killed him!" Ciphus snapped. "Your precious Johan killed him!"

"And you allowed him to. Johan has found new life. You still live in your death."

"You're wrong. Justin's death *proves* that you're wrong. Only a simpleton could ever be convinced that Elyon would die. Or *could* die, for that matter. You live in this silly condition of yours because of your own foolishness in following Justin's charade. It is Teeleh's judgment against you."

"Teeleh's judgment?"

"Don't try your trickery on me," Ciphus snapped. "Elyon has judged you."

"You said Teeleh's judgment."

"I would never even speak that name in the holy place. Don't put words in my mouth."

He hadn't heard himself. He wasn't only blind to the truth; he was deaf. A man to be pitied, not hated.

"Justin's alive, Ciphus. One day, sooner or later, you'll see that. He will not rest until his bride returns to him."

"What nonsense are you talking about now? What bride?"

"That is what he calls us. You. Any who would embrace his invitation to the Great Romance."

"By drowning? How absurd!"

"By dying to this disease that hangs off your skin and blinds your eyes. By finding a new life with him."

Ciphus frowned and paced along his desk, hands behind his back.

"How did you turn the lake brown?" Thomas asked.

"We drained the defiled water and filled the lake from the spring. We had to get back to the Great Romance; I'm sure you understand. The people went two weeks without bathing, and it was only by the grace of Elyon that he didn't punish us for our indiscretion. An indiscretion that was yours, may I remind you."

"So you're all back to normal here. Bathing away a disease that remains."

"The disease is in the mind, not the skin, you fool. It manifests itself in the cult of yours. What do you call it? The Circle?"

"It represents the circle of marriage."

"So you are married to Elyon?"

"In a manner of speaking, yes."

"And what manner is that?"

"In the same way that he is a lion or a lamb or a boy or Justin."

Ciphus closed his eyes and took a deep breath. "Elyon, give me strength. I can see that you will insist on dying. I had hoped I could help you see sense, Thomas. I really had. The supreme leader listens to me, you know. I may have been able to turn him."

"And you still may."

"Not now. Not with your stubborn heart."

"I'm not suggesting you turn him for my sake," Thomas said. "For yours."

"Hmm? Is that right? I, arguably the most powerful man alive, need your help? How benevolent of you."

"Yes. In all of this building with mud and dabbling in your new lake, you may have missed a point."

Ciphus stared at him. "Go ahead."

"You are not the most powerful man in the world, though arguably you should be. Unfortunately, you are simply a pawn of Qurong's."

"Nonsense!"

"He tolerates you as matter of expedience. His motives are purely political."

"This talk will win you an execution!"

"I've already won an execution. Surely you see what I'm saying, Ciphus. I just came from Qurong's castle. He has no shred of interest in the Great Romance. He knows that making his people subject to a higher power will only strengthen his power over them. He is using you to put a hold on his people."

"There always has been a tension between politics and religion, hasn't there?" Ciphus said. "When you were in your right mind, did the people follow you, or did they follow me?"

"We followed Elyon. The Great Romance was always first! And now you've let that monster in the castle make a fool of you by putting you underneath him."

Ciphus froze halfway through Thomas's point, perhaps as much in fear of being overheard as because of any chord it struck in him. Thomas had to walk a thin line.

"No?" he pushed. "Then consider this: when you decided to allow Justin's execution, I was powerless to stop you. Your word was above mine. But if you now tell Qurong that the council has decided his castle must be torn down, would he do it? I think he might tear down your Thrall instead."

"This is the talk of fools. It is a great privilege for me to serve the people—"

"You mean Qurong. You are the slave of Qurong, Ciphus. Even your blind eyes can see that."

The priest slammed his fist on the table. "And you think that can be changed?" he shouted.

"Good," Thomas breathed. "Then you do see it. Elyon won't be the toy of any man, not even Qurong. How dare you allow him to make the Great Romance his tool? He's reduced your great religion to nothing more than shackles to harness the will of his people. It makes a mockery of Elyon. And of you."

"Enough!" Ciphus had regained control of himself. He set his jaw and folded his arms. "This is pointless. I think our time is over."

"Yes," Thomas said.

Ciphus looked momentarily off guard by Thomas's quick agreement. He dipped his head. "Then you will—"

"Yes, I may have a way to change the imbalance of power between you and Qurong."

The priest's eyes skittered to the door. He blinked rapidly. "You should leave before you earn my drowning as well."

"Exactly. Qurong would drown the high priest for simple words against him. He has it backward. You should have the power to drown him for words against the Great Romance."

Ciphus wasn't ready to capitulate. He knew how dangerous this talk was, because he knew that Thomas spoke the truth. Ciphus *did* serve Qurong. He needed to see the way out before hinting at any agreement.

"The Books of History have a power that is beyond Qurong," Thomas said in a soft voice. "These holy Books may restore the power of the Great Romance to its rightful place. Politically speaking. And with it, you."

A wry smile twisted Ciphus's lips. "Then you don't know, do you? The Books of History, which you were so desperate to find, aren't even legible. Your ploy here has failed."

"You're wrong. They are legible, and I can read them."

"Is that right? Have you ever seen even one of the Books?"

"Yes. And I can read it as if I myself had written it."

The smile faded.

"I also know there are blank Books. They contain a power that would change everything. And I know how to use them."

"How did you know about the blank Books?"

Thomas had guessed that there were more; now he knew. "I know more than you can possibly guess. My interest in the Books of Histories isn't as frivolous as you think. Now they may save both of our lives."

Ciphus picked up his chalice and drank. "You don't realize how bold these statements are."

"I have nothing to lose. And with what I will propose, neither do you."

He emptied the glass and set it down, refusing to make eye contact. "Which is?"

"That you take me to the Books of Histories and let me prove their power."

"Qurong would never allow it. And even if he did, how do I know you wouldn't use this power against me?"

"The Books are truth. I can't use the truth against the truth. You represent truth, don't you? Have I harmed even one man since Justin's death? I am a trustworthy man, Ciphus, mad or not."

The priest eyed him cautiously. "Qurong won't allow it."

"I think he would if the request was properly phrased. It's a matter of the Great Romance. But do you need his permission?"

A light crossed the priest's eyes. He paced, stroking his chin.

"You're sure you can read the Books."

"I'm sure. And I'm sure that you have nothing to lose by testing me. If I'm wrong, you will simply return me to the dungeon. If I can't demonstrate the power, you will do the same. But if I'm right, we will change history together."

"And why would you want to change history with me?"

"I don't necessarily. I want to live. That is my price. If I'm right, you will ensure the survival of me and my friends."

Thomas knew that Ciphus probably couldn't or wouldn't ensure any such thing. He also knew that there was probably no power to show Ciphus. Using one of the blank Books might change things in the other reality—good reason for this plan in and of itself—but the Books would prove powerless here.

No matter. These weren't his primary objectives. He was following another thread. A very thin thread, granted, but a thread.

"Even if I'm wrong about the power, the ability to read the Books of History will give a new power by itself."

"So you can show me how to read them?"

Thomas smiled. "You haven't been listening. You have no idea what you have in your hands, do you? I am your path to the power that's justly yours."

Ciphus picked up his glass, drained the last of the fruit juice, set it down firmly, and walked toward the door. "Then we go."

"Now?"

"What better time? You're right; I don't need Qurong's permission. I have access to the library. I will say that I'm taking you there to extract a full confession from you in writing and to interrogate you on several writings we've found from your Circle."

"I will only show you what I know on one condition."

"Yes, I know. Your life. First the Books."

"No, one other condition. I insist that a third party be present."

"What on earth for?"

"My protection. I want a party to witness our agreement. Someone who's disconnected from your own authority yet has enough authority to corroborate."

"Impossible! It would be tantamount to telling Qurong that I'm working against him!"

"Then choose someone who wants to see the Books of Histories unveiled as much as you do. Surely there's someone Qurong respects enough to listen to in the event you turn against me, yet who doesn't pose a threat to you."

"I don't see it. If you show another person this power, what value is it to me?"

"I won't show them the power. I'll only demonstrate that I can read the Books. This will be enough for them. How about his wife?"

"Patricia. She would just as soon shove a knife into my belly as bathe in the lake."

"Then who is taken with the histories?"

"The librarian, Christoph. But he's hardly better. I don't see the value of this absurd demand. If I'm to trust you, then you'll have to trust me."

"You have reason to trust me. My actions have never undermined you. I, on the other hand, have enough reason to question you."

Ciphus strode deliberately back to his desk. "Then we have no agreement."

"Surely there's someone in the royal court who has enough interest in the histories to bend the rules a bit."

"The royal court is a very small community. There's his wife and his daughter and . . ." Ciphus faced him. "His daughter's quite taken with the histories."

"The one who's to marry Woref? Chelise. Fine, I don't care who it is as long as she is impartial and has a love for the Books. There's no risk to you. We won't tell her that you intend to overthrow her father, only that you've agreed to make my case to Qurong if I can indeed reveal the knowledge contained in the Books. Out of respect to Qurong, you refuse to bother him with the matter until you've verified that I have something to offer."

"No more talk of overthrowing!" Ciphus whispered harshly. "I said no such thing! It's strictly as you said—I'm following up this matter with full intentions of bringing it to Qurong's attention if it has any merits."

"Of course. And you may send Chelise out of the room when it comes time for me to show you the power of the Books."

Ciphus frowned. "Guards!" he called.

"Agreed?" Thomas asked.

"I'll speak with her."

The door opened a few moments later and two guards walked in.

"Return the prisoner to the dungeons."

13

THE ARRANGEMENT was simple, though a bit suspicious to Thomas. Chelise had agreed to wait for them in the inner library at dusk after the librarian had left for the day. Why so late? Thomas wanted to know. Because Chelise often outlasted Christoph in the library, Ciphus said.

Ciphus used his own mounted guard to transport Thomas in chains through several miles of forest to an expansive walled retreat that was surprisingly beautiful. Stunning, in fact. The moment they passed the main gate, he wondered if he hadn't awakened in his dreams, surrounded by a botanical garden in southern France.

But no, he was sleeping in a plane above the Atlantic. This royal garden was very real.

The entire complex was nestled in a large meadow that Thomas remembered well. The botanical garden hedged in by manicured shrubs was new, but the orchard had been here before. Stone paths wound perfect circles around six large lawns, a different fruit tree centered in each one. The orchard was also circular, as was the botanical garden.

This was Qurong's circle, Thomas thought. At the center stood a two-story structure made of fine wood. Three other buildings—homes, by the looks of them—had been built in each corner of the retreat. A fourth was cordoned off behind the garden.

"The villa that Qurong will give Woref and his daughter as a wedding present," Ciphus said. "She doesn't know yet."

"And that's the library?" Thomas asked, nodding at the large building they were approaching.

"Yes."

It looked far too large for any library, much less one built to hold the Horde's Books. Clearly, whatever it housed was more precious to Qurong than the Great Romance. Ciphus could surely see that much now. Maybe for the first time.

They entered through large double doors into an atrium, empty except for an ornately carved black desk and yet one more of the bronze statues of Teeleh.

"Wait here," Ciphus told his guard.

"What about these?" Thomas held out his shackled arms.

Ciphus hesitated. "Free his arms. Leave the leg chains."

Thomas rubbed his wrists. "Thank you."

"Don't thank me yet. After you."

He followed Thomas into a two-story room that looked old despite its relatively new construction. Ten large desks covered the floor, each with its own lamp stand. The walls were lined with shelves, each filled with scrolls and bound books. Two staircases rose to the second floor, where Thomas could see similar bookcases behind a wooden railing.

He looked around, awed by the woodwork. This was the doing of Forest People. Even the books . . .

"May I?" he asked, stepping toward a bookcase.

Ciphus didn't answer.

He withdrew a bound book from one of the shelves. It was the kind he'd taught the Circle's scribes to use from his memories of the histories. Pounded bark bound around reams of crudely formed paper. He opened the book. The script was an elementary cursive form.

"These are our own histories, created by the scribes," Ciphus said. "Qurong is quite taken with history. Everything is carefully recorded, even the most mundane details. During the day every desk is occupied by historians. We have our own temple scribes to record the history of Elyon since the Second Age."

"The Second Age?"

"The Great Romance since our time as one."

"Then you acknowledge that it's changed."

"Everything changes," Ciphus said.

Thomas looked around the room. "The building is larger than this one room. What's in the rest?"

Ciphus indicated a door on the far side. "Chelise is waiting."

Thomas walked around the desks, put his hand on a large brass handle, and pushed the door open. Several torches lit a large room lined with bookcases, floor to ceiling. Thousands of books.

Thomas released the door and stepped in. The cases rose twenty feet and were serviced by a ladder. No ornate desks or candlesticks here, just books, many more than Thomas had imagined.

Leather-bound books.

The Books of Histories?

"These . . . what are these?"

"The Books of Histories, of course."

"This many? I . . . I had no idea there were so many! These are all Books of Histories?"

"Not exactly an encouraging admission from the man who claims to know all there is about the books," a voice said quietly on his right.

Thomas turned. Chelise stood behind a large desk, on which she'd opened one of the Books. She stepped around the desk and walked toward them, black robe flowing around her ankles. She'd left her hood back, revealing long, dark, shiny hair. The contrast between her white face and so much black was quite startling.

"Did you think my father carried all of the Books with him wherever he went?"

Her eyes searched his, and for a moment he thought she might have recognized him from the desert.

She faced Ciphus. "I don't have all night. Either this albino knows something or he doesn't. We can establish that much in a few minutes."

"Matters of the histories are never established flippantly," Ciphus said. "I told you an hour."

"Spare me the eloquence, Priest. Can he read them or not?" She turned to Thomas. "Show us."

Thomas was still too stunned to think straight. He knew that this might be his only opportunity to spend any time with the Books. What were the chances of finding the particular Books that dealt with the Great Deception and the Raison Strain?

"How many are there?"

"Many," Chelise said. "Many thousands."

Thomas walked farther into the room. Torchlight cast a wavering yellow glow over the leather spines. "Are they categorized?"

"How can we categorize what we can't read?" Ciphus asked.

"You can't even read the titles?"

"How can we? They aren't in our tongue."

But they *were* in the common tongue. He looked at a Book on the nearest shelf. *The Histories According to the Second of Five*. What that meant he had no clue, but he could read the words easily enough. They'd all heard that the Horde couldn't read the Books of Histories, but this seemed a bit ridiculous. Were their minds so deceived? And now Ciphus was among them.

"Did you think that the record of everything that has ever happened would be found in two or three Books?" Chelise asked.

"No. I just didn't expect this many." He had to find what he could about the Raison Strain. "Do you know if they are in any order? I would like to look at the one that deals with the Great Deception."

"No, there is no order," Ciphus said. "They were put in place by men who don't read. I thought we'd established that."

"Where did Qurong find them?"

Neither answered.

He looked at Chelise. "You don't know? How could he come into possession of so many Books without a record of where he found them?"

"He says that Elyon showed them to him."

"Elyon? Or was it Teeleh?"

"When I was younger he said Teeleh. Now he says Elyon. I don't know which, and frankly, I don't care. I'm interested in what they say, not where they came from."

"What they say can only be understood by first understanding where they came from. Who wrote them."

"This is your great secret?" Ciphus asked. "You're going to tell us that the only way to read these Books is through your understanding of Elyon? Then don't waste our time."

"Did I say that Elyon wrote them?"

"Do you know who wrote them?" Chelise asked.

He'd sparked some interest in her. *Speak carefully, Thomas. You can't afford to turn Ciphus against you.*

"Where are the blank Books?"

"The blank Books?" Chelise glanced at Ciphus. "I don't care about the blank Books. I can read empty pages as well as you."

Ciphus averted his eyes.

"Then show me the Book you have open," Thomas said.

She let her eyes linger on him, then walked gracefully toward the desk. He followed with Ciphus at his side.

Only he knew that this woman held his fate in her hands. He had to find a way to win her trust. But watching her step lightly across the wood floor, he felt a sliver of hope. Suzan had seen something in her eyes, and he was quite sure he'd seen it too. A longing for the truth, maybe.

Chelise rounded the desk and lowered her hand to the open page. Her eyes studied the page briefly, then rose to meet his. How many times had she looked longingly at these Books, wondering what mysteries they held?

"I leave this one open," she said.

"Why this one?"

"It's the first Book I looked at when I was a child."

Thomas glanced down at the open page. English script. He could read the writing perfectly well. They couldn't know that, except for *The Histories Recorded by His Beloved* and the one Book he'd opened in Qurong's tent, this was the first Book of History he'd read as well.

"And if I can read this Book—if I can tell you what it says—what will you give me?"

"Nothing."

"My death is Woref's wedding gift to you. Wouldn't you think that the life of the man who can read these Books to you would be more of a gift than his death?"

She blinked.

"I'll have no part in this!" Ciphus said. "You said nothing—"

"It's okay, Ciphus," Chelise said. "I think I can speak for myself. Your life is meaningless to me. Even if you can read this Book, which you haven't shown me, you would be useless to me. I couldn't stand to stay in the same room with you long enough to hear you read or learn to read. Years of curiosity have brought me here tonight, but this will be the only time."

The air seemed to have been sucked out of the room. Thomas wasn't sure why her words crushed him, only that they did. He'd faced death before. Although her words were the death sentence to this foolish plan of his, the pain he felt wasn't about his own death. It was about her rejection of him.

"Ciphus has promised me life," he said.

"I said that I would present your case. It will be Qurong who determines your fate, not Chelise. You're a fool for thinking otherwise."

It was at least a lingering hope, but the words fell flat.

He nodded and walked around the desk.

———⟨∞⟩———

Chelise knew that her words had cut him, and she found it rather surprising. What could he possibly have expected? He knew that he was an albino. He knew that his defiance of her father would earn him a death sentence, and yet he persisted in the defiance.

If Ciphus had not been present, she might have said the same thing

with less of a bite. Although it was true, the thought of being alone with
any albino for long made her nervous. Even nauseated.

She watched him walk around the desk, crestfallen. To think that
this man had once defied the great Martyn and even Woref. He looked
anything but the warrior now. His arms were strong and his chest well
muscled, but his eyes were green and his skin . . .

What would it be like to touch skin so smooth?

She dismissed the thought and stepped aside to give him room. He
could have taken the Book from the other side of the desk just as easily.
Instead he walked closer to her.

She was being too sensitive. He undoubtedly hated her more than
she hated him. And if he didn't, he was a fool for misunderstanding her
revulsion of his disease.

Thomas reached his hand to the page and followed the words at the
top. The writing was foreign to her, but he read aloud as if he'd been reading this language all of his life.

"Kevin walked down the road slowly, drawn to the large oak at the end
of the street," he read. "He was quite sure that his heart was breaking, and
the knowledge that his mother would never have to work again did nothing to help heal the wound."

He lifted his hand, but his eyes scanned on, reading.

"What does it mean?" Chelise asked.

"It's a story about a boy named Kevin."

"Not the histories?"

"Yes. Yes, it's the history of Kevin's life, written in story form."

"In story form?" Ciphus said. "We don't write histories in story form.
This is childish."

"Then maybe you should think like a child to understand," Thomas
said. "The boy's just lost his father, and the life insurance is meaningless
to him."

Chelise wasn't sure what he meant by life insurance, but the story
spoke to her. Something about the simplicity perhaps, the emotion, even
the way that the albino had read it had electrified her.

"What's the rest?"

"The rest?" Thomas was turning pages. "It would take me hours to read you the rest."

"How do we know that you're not just fabricating this story?" Ciphus demanded.

"You'll have to learn to read them yourself. Or you, Chelise. What if I could teach you?"

"How?"

"By becoming your servant. I might be able to teach you to read them. All of them. What greater humiliation could Qurong heap upon me, his greatest enemy, than to chain me to a desk and force me to translate the Books? Killing me is too easy."

"Enough!" Ciphus snapped. "You've made your point and it's useless. Please, if you don't mind, I insist that you leave us. I won't have him spouting his lies anymore. Qurong would never approve."

Chelise stilled a tremble in her hands and bowed her head. "I will leave, then."

Ciphus calmed his voice. "But before you do, could you kindly show me where the blank Books have gone to. They aren't on the shelf where I last saw them."

"Of course." She walked to the bookcase where the volumes were kept. She'd seen them just three days earlier.

"This way. I don't know what you could possibly want with Books that have . . ."

She stopped halfway across the room. The bookcase was empty. From floor to ceiling, where hundreds of Books had once rested collecting dust, only empty shelves stood.

"They . . ." She looked around quickly. "They're gone."

"What do you mean, gone? They can't just disappear."

"Then they've been moved. But I just saw them a few days ago. I didn't think anyone had been in here since."

Thomas looked stricken. "How many were there?"

"Hundreds. Maybe a thousand."

"And they're just . . . gone?"

"Where could anyone hide so many Books?" Ciphus asked.

They were both reacting oddly. What was it about these blank Books?

"What does this mean?" Ciphus asked Thomas.

"Without the Books, it means nothing," the albino said.

Ciphus glared at him. "Then you will die in three days."

14

I REALLY don't care if we only have four *hours*, Ms. Sumner. We don't slow down at this point." He was addressing her on the speakerphone.

"I understand, Mr. President."

The president had allowed Kara to stay in the White House, where she'd observed the chaos from as close as she dared, which was mostly in the halls and on the perimeter. Until Thomas's plane arrived in a few hours, she was out of her league.

The president had asked her to come in with Monique an hour earlier while they hammered through the antivirus issue for the hundredth time. They'd been on the phone with Theresa Sumner for the last ten minutes. None of her news was good. Par for the course—*none* of the news Kara had heard over the past twenty-four hours, since the phone call from Thomas, had been good. Defense, intelligence, health, interior, homeland security, you name it—they all were crawling the walls.

To make matters worse, Senate Majority Leader Dwight Olsen was reportedly behind a protest outside the White House. At last report over fifty thousand campers had vowed to wait the White House out in a silent vigil. It had turned into a spiritual gathering of the strangest kind. A sea of somber faces and shaved heads and robes and those who wanted shaved heads and robes.

They'd burned candles and sung soft songs last night. The swelling crowd was flanked by several hundred reporters who'd managed to put aside the normal clamor for this silent waiting of theirs. *Give us some news, Mr. President. Tell us the truth.*

Front and center was the grand master of ceremonies, the CNN anchor who'd first broken the story. Mike Orear. With less than ten days to go, he'd become a prophet in the eyes of half the country. His gentle voice and stern face had become the face of hope to all whose religion was the news, and to many more who would never admit such a thing.

Reporters called it a vigil for all men and women of all races and religions to pray to their God and appeal to the president of the United States, but anyone watching for more than an hour knew it was simply a protest. The crowd was predicted to swell to over two hundred thousand by tonight. By tomorrow, a million. It was turning into nothing less than a final, desperate pilgrimage. To the headwaters of the peoples' troubles and hopes.

To the White House, where at this very moment the president and his government were running on fumes, trying to put out a thousand fires and turn over a thousand stones, desperate to head off disaster and find that elusive solution.

At least that was how Kara saw it.

She looked around at the ragged men in whose hands the world had been forced to put their trust. Secretary of Defense Grant Myers was still bleary-eyed over the nuclear exchange between Israel and France. They'd persuaded Israel not to launch and to play along with France's offer for an open-sea exchange, but the Israeli prime minister was taking a whipping in his own cabinet for that decision. None of them knew Thomas, Kara thought. The recommendation to play ball with France was precipitated by information from Thomas Hunter.

Phil Grant, director of the CIA, listened intently, slowly massaging the loose skin on his forehead. Another headache, perhaps. Within ten minutes he would get up and take more aspirin. She wasn't sure what to make of Phil Grant.

The chief of staff handled most of the communication coming to and going from the president, a steady flow of interruptions that Blair handled with a split mind, it seemed. The rest gathered there were key aides.

Kara couldn't imagine a man better suited to deal with a crisis of this magnitude than Robert Blair. How many people could juggle so many issues, maintain their overall composure, and also remain completely human? Not many. She didn't think any president could truly shed the political skin that earned him the office, but Blair seemed to have. He was genuine to the bone.

President Blair stood and spoke to Kara. "I need Monique with Thomas, at least long enough for us to flesh this thing out. She'll be at your full disposal the minute she's free. Jacques de Raison is on a flight from Bangkok now with several hundred promising samples, as you know. I need those samples in the right hands. As it turns out, I can't think of anyone more qualified to coordinate this than you. Do you disagree?"

"No, Mr. President. But I'm exhausted." Her voice sounded as if it were in a drum. "And to be perfectly honest, I don't share your optimism. I've spoken to Mr. de Raison about the samples, and they would require a month to analyze—"

"I don't care if you need a year to analyze them! I need it done in five days!"

The president's outburst was uncharacteristic but not surprising. Not even startling.

He closed his eyes and took a calming breath. "I'm sorry. If you think someone else is better qualified to handle this, tell me now."

"No sir. Forgive me. It might help to have Monique here."

President Blair glanced at Monique. "I understand."

Monique had been shuttled to the Genetrix Laboratories in Baltimore yesterday and flown back this morning to continue working with Theresa through a dedicated communications link. Nearly every laboratory with a genetics or drug-related research facility had been connected to Genetrix Laboratories after the Centers for Disease Control and the World Health Organization's facilities had proven inadequate. A staff of twenty-five screeners with PhDs in related fields scoured thousands of incoming threads and passed on any that fit the primary model that Raison Pharmaceutical had established to ferret out an antivirus.

Although her backdoor antivirus proved to be insufficient, Monique had brought one critical piece of information back with her: the gene manipulations she'd designed when creating the Raison Vaccine were at least one part of the antivirus. She'd explained the entire scenario to the president minutes ago. Valborg Svensson never would have kept her alive as long as he did unless he needed the information she gave him—namely, the genetic manipulations that completed his antivirus.

Blair rolled his neck and paced. "So am I to understand by your earlier statements that even if we do find an antivirus in the next five days, manufacturing enough and distributing it may be a problem?"

"Monique?" Theresa said, deferring.

"That depends on the nature of the antivirus, but you do understand that people will die. Even if we found the answer today, some will die. Isolated individuals, for example, who have wandered into the wilderness to find peace."

"I understand. But let's take a broader scenario. Our best estimates are that the first catastrophic symptoms of the Raison Strain could manifest in as few as five days, correct?"

"Yes sir."

"But we may have as many as ten days. And the rollout of the disease will take a few days—not everyone was infected in the first days."

"A week for complete rollout—that's correct."

"So we may have over two weeks before some people show symptoms."

"We may. But the incubation period is likely shorter. We may begin to see symptoms in as few as three days in Bangkok and the other gateway cities."

"And we have how long until people begin to die?"

"Best estimate, forty-eight hours from the onset of symptoms. But it's only an educated—"

He held up his hand. "Of course. All of this is." He faced Monique directly. "If we were to receive the antivirus from Armand Fortier in five days, assuming that's the onset of first symptoms, could we manufacture and distribute it quickly enough to save most of our people?"

"It depends—"

"No, Monique, I don't want 'It depends.' I want your best estimate."

She set her elbows on the table and laced her fingers together. "Six billion syringes—"

"We have twenty-eight plants in seven countries manufacturing syringes around the clock. The World Health Organization will supply the syringes it requests in the event you come through."

"Millions who live in Third World countries won't have immediate access to those syringes."

"They were also the last to be infected. We'll have every plane that can fly loaded with the antivirus within an hour of it rolling off the line. We have worked out a detailed distribution plan that will deliver an antivirus in a syringe to most of the world within one week. It'll be a race—I know that—but I want to know who will win that race."

She took a deep breath. "It's possible that a fast-acting antivirus could reverse the virus if administered within forty-eight hours of the first symptoms."

"So if we start with the gateway cities, like New York and Bangkok, and flood the market with an antivirus five days from now, we would have a chance of saving most."

"Assuming the virus waits five days, yes. Most."

"Ninety percent?"

"That would be most, yes."

"Ms. Sumner?"

"I would concur," she said over the speakerphone.

The president walked to the end of the room, hands grasped behind his back. He looked up at a television that showed a riot in progress in Jakarta, triggered by the news that the supposedly contained outbreak in Java hadn't really been contained at all.

"We are holding the world together by a string," President Blair said. "Our ships are scheduled to hand over most of our nuclear arsenal in three days' time. Our only hope of getting the antivirus from the New Allegiance is to disarm ourselves and open ourselves to nuclear holocaust. Even then,

I don't believe that France intends to deal with us, or the Israelis for that matter, straight. They will give what they have to the Russians, the Chinese, but not to us."

He faced them. "We cannot afford to deal with Fortier. Our only real hope rests in you."

His position seemed extreme to Kara, but she no longer trusted her own judgment of extremity. For all she knew, their only hope didn't rest in Monique or Theresa or anyone from the scientific community, but in Thomas. There had to be a reason that all of this was happening.

"Join me when Thomas arrives," the president said. "You may leave."

They left without a word. Ron Kreet was telling the president that he had a call with the Russian premier in two minutes.

"Doesn't sound promising," Kara said to Monique as they walked the hall.

"It never was. I can't imagine this being solved from this end."

This end? "Thomas?"

Monique nodded. "I'm not saying it makes sense to me, but yes. You were there, Kara. It's real, isn't it? I mean, it felt so real when I dreamed of it."

"As real as this. It's like Thomas is a window into another dimension. He lives in both, and our eyes are opened through his blood."

"But I felt more like Rachelle when I was there. Monique to me was only a dream."

"This can't be a dream," Kara said, looking around. "Can it?"

She didn't answer. She didn't need to—they both knew that they weren't going to figure it out now.

"Do you think of him?" Kara asked.

"All the time," Monique said.

Kara glanced at her watch. "He's probably still sleeping. That means he's with the Horde right now. If he's not dreaming with the Horde, there's no telling how many days will pass before he wakes up."

"In that reality."

"Yes."

"How would he not dream?"

"The Horde may know about the rhambutan fruit."

Monique blinked. "Then we should wake him now! What if the Horde executes him?"

"It doesn't matter if we wake him. The time that passes there is dependent on his dreaming there, not his waking here. Trust me, it took me two weeks to wrap my mind around that one. A week could pass with the Horde in the next few minutes of his dreaming on the plane."

They turned into a small cafeteria.

"He'll be here soon enough," Kara said. "Let's hope he has some answers."

15

WOREF STOOD before Qurong in the council chamber, listening to the old man fume about the missing Books of Histories. The librarian, Christoph, had reported them missing this morning. The scribes had turned the library inside out looking for them, but not a sign.

"How could a thousand volumes just vanish into thin air?" Qurong raged. "I want them found. I don't care if you have to search every house in the city."

"I will, your highness. But I have other matters now."

"What other matters? Your matters are more pressing than mine?"

The old fool couldn't hold a thought for more than a few minutes. His obsession with these Books was interfering with far more important matters; surely he knew that.

An image of Teeleh flashed through Woref's mind and he clenched his jaw. He'd decided to deny the beast. He would possess Chelise, yes. And he would love her as he knew how to love. She would be his, and if she resisted his advance, he would use whatever form of persuasion seemed fitting at the time. But Teeleh spoke of love as if it were a crushing force. The thought made him ill.

"I have a wedding tomorrow."

"And your wedding takes precedence over my books? You expect me to attend the wedding of my own daughter in this state?"

"No sir. Never." The realization that Qurong might put off the wedding over such a trivial matter sent a shaft of anger through Woref's heart.

Qurong paced and grunted. "This takes priority. Nothing happens until we find the Books."

"Sir, may I suggest that your wife might not look kindly on the post-ponement—"

"My wife will do as I say. It's you, Woref. Your inflamed passion compromises your own loyalty to your king. You've been hounding my daughter for years now, and when I finally give her to you, you immediately question my authority! I should call the whole thing off."

Woref suppressed his fury. *I will take your daughter. And then I will take your kingdom.*

Teeleh's words whispered in his memory. *I will make her mine.*

"You have my undying loyalty, my king. I will suspend our search for the remaining albinos and personally see to your Books."

Instead of expressing the appropriate apprehension at Woref's suggestion that they pause their campaign, Qurong agreed.

"Good. Turn every stone. Dismissed." He picked up his goblet and walked away, leaving Woref in a mild state of shock.

Qurong stopped by the door as if something had suddenly occurred to him. "You wish to marry my daughter? Then start with her. No one knows the library like she does." He turned around and eyed Woref carefully. "We'll see if you have the skills required to tame a wench. She's in her bedroom."

Woref trembled with rage. How could a father speak in such a way about the woman who would be his? Such a precious, unspoiled bride, at this very moment resting in her bedroom while her own father slandered her.

Teeleh, yes. But her father!

Woref put his hand on the table to calm himself. The day he ran a dagger through Qurong's belly would come sooner than anyone could possibly guess.

You are angry because Qurong is Teeleh's servant, and now you know that you are as well.

He ground his molars and grunted. Yes, it was true, and he despised himself for it.

Woref stepped across the room, entered the atrium, and gazed at the stairs that rose from floor to floor, up to the fifth where Chelise's room waited in silence. He glanced around, saw that he was alone, and hurried toward the stairs.

Desire swelled in his belly. He wouldn't touch Chelise, naturally. In that way he wasn't like Qurong at all. And he would never harm her. Not even Qurong beat his wife. It wasn't becoming of royalty, he had once said. Either way, Woref could never hurt his tender bride.

Then again . . .

No. He only wanted to see her. To gaze upon her face, knowing that tomorrow she would be his. He'd never been on the fifth floor, much less her bedroom. But now Qurong had given him permission. The Books. He couldn't forget to ask about the Books.

He climbed quickly, afraid that at any moment the wife would come out and demand that he leave. It would be like Patricia. She too would have to be silenced one day. Perhaps he'd take her as his second wife. There was a woman he'd enjoy beating.

But not the daughter. Never Chelise.

He stood before her door and knocked gently.

"Come."

He pushed the door open. She sat on her bed with her maidservant. Their eyes flared with surprise.

"Excuse me." He bowed his head. "I'm afraid that Qurong insisted I speak to you immediately."

"Then you would send a servant up to fetch me," Chelise said.

"He insisted I come. It's a matter of grave importance." He looked at the servant. "Leave us."

The woman looked at Chelise and then left when she didn't object.

Woref closed the door and stared at his bride, who now stood by her bed. Her skin was white and beautiful. Not as white as when she had the morst on, but he preferred it this way. The scent of untreated skin stirred him in a way that only a true warrior would understand. Her eyes were white, like twin moons. Her mouth was round and her body slender in the long flowing robe.

He'd never seen such a beautiful creature as she.

"What is it?" she demanded.

He approached her, careful not to look too eager. "Qurong is concerned about some Books that have gone missing from the library," he said. "He thought that you might be able to help us find them."

"Which books?"

"The blank Books of Histories."

"They're gone?"

"All of them."

"How's that possible? There are so many!"

Woref stepped closer. He could smell her breath now, the musky scent of love.

"Please don't come any closer," she said.

He stopped, surprised by her demand. "I meant no disrespect."

"I took none. But we aren't yet married."

"You're mine by betrothal. We will be married."

"Tomorrow." The tone of her voice irritated him. It was as if she was insisting on tomorrow instead of today. As if she might be looking forward to enjoying one last day separated from him. She didn't crave him as he craved her?

He shifted on his feet. "Yes, of course."

"What do I have to do with this?" she demanded.

His irritation grew. He spoke quickly to cover his embarrassment. "Your father seems to think that you may know something about the Books. You've spent more time in the library than even he."

"I have no clue what could have happened to the Books. I don't see why he sent you to interrogate me about his business. Men are not permitted on this floor. Mother wouldn't approve."

"I don't think you understand the significance of this to the supreme leader. And I don't see what your mother's opinion of my coming here has to do with your taking exception. You have been given to me, not to her."

"Tell my father that I know nothing about the Books, and I'll tell my mother that you disapprove of her rules."

"Her rules will mean nothing tomorrow. We'll live by my rules. Our rules."

She smiled. "You may have won my hand, Woref. I have no argument. But you'll have to win my heart as well. You could start by learning that I am my mother's daughter. You may leave now."

Woref wasn't sure he'd heard her correctly. Was she taunting him? Tempting him? Begging to be subdued?

"The situation is more serious than you may realize." He would test her by stepping closer to her. "Qurong will postpone our wedding until the Books are found."

She smiled again. This time it was a tempting smile, he was sure of it. His mind felt dizzy with desire. He took another step, close enough to touch her.

"Postponing our wedding might be wise. It would give you time to learn respect for a woman's desires."

Black flooded Woref's vision. How dare she conspire with Qurong to withhold what was his! She stood mocking him with this smile, perfectly at ease with denying him.

He swung his hand without thinking. It slammed into her cheek with a loud smack. She gasped and flew backward onto the bed.

"Never!" he roared.

The shock of being hit was greater than the pain. Chelise knew that she'd been toying with his emotions, but no more so than she'd done a hundred times before with other men. She'd actually found Woref's presence in her room exhilarating. Naturally it would never do to play into his hands— what kind of signal would that send? He would think of her as nothing more than a doll that he could throw around at his whim until he tired of her completely. Mother had told her the same thing just last night.

Chelise spun to him, aghast. Woref was trembling from head to foot.

"Never!" he roared.

She was too stunned to think straight. He had hit her!

Realization of what he had just done suddenly dawned on Woref's face. He glanced back at the door, and when he faced her again, his eyes were lit by fear.

"What have I done?" He reached out for her. "My precious—"

"Get away from me!" she screamed, slapping his hand aside. She scrambled across the bed and stood on the opposite side. "Don't come near me!"

He walked quickly around the bed, panicked. "No, no, I didn't mean to hurt you."

"Back!"

He dropped to one knee. "I beg you, forgive me!"

"Stop begging! Get on your feet!"

He rose.

"How dare you strike me! You expect me to marry a bull? I was toying with you!"

His awful mistake was finally and terribly setting in. He gripped his head in both hands and paced at the bottom of the bed. Her sudden power over him wasn't lost on her. Her jaw ached. She could never marry this man until they set some things straight between them, but on balance he had just given her his greatest gift. He'd bared his weakness.

"How can I marry a man like you?" she demanded.

"Anything," he said, spinning back. "I swear I will give you anything."

"You'll give me anything today, and then take my life in a fit of rage tomorrow? Do I look like a fool?"

"No, my dear. I swear, never again. My honor as this land's greatest general is in your hands."

"One word to my mother and you would lose it all."

"And spend eternity suffering for one moment's fear of losing you. I can't bear the thought of delaying our wedding, even a single day."

She turned her back on him and stared out the window, surprised by the satisfaction she felt at seeing him grovel. Stripped of his rank, he was a mere man, driven by passion and fear. Perhaps wickeder than most. But still unraveled by his desire for one woman.

She would use this to her advantage. The fact was, she had more on her mind today than her wedding tomorrow. Thoughts of the Books of Histories had filled her dreams and awakened her early. Her desire to understand the mysteries hidden in their pages was greater than any desire she'd known.

Chelise faced Woref, who had recovered from his begging and was regarding her with something that looked more like contempt than remorse.

"Hmm. You will give me whatever I want?"

"Whatever is in my power. I must have your love. Anything."

"Then you'll tell my father that the wedding must be delayed until the blank Books are found—we both insist."

His face darkened.

"It's the price for your lack of control. If you want to earn my love, you can start by showing me that you're a man who can receive as well as give punishment."

He dipped his head. "As you wish."

"And I will also require a gift from you as well."

"Yes, of course. Anything."

"I want a new servant."

"I'll give you ten."

"Not just any servant. I want the albino. Thomas of Hunter."

She might have thrown water in his face. "That's impossible."

"Is it? Unusual, yes. Disagreeable, certainly. But I've heard that this man is able to read the Books of Histories. You intend to execute the one man who can fulfill a dream of mine by revealing the Books to me? His death would not only be an affront to me, but it would be far too honorable for him. Better to keep him chained to a desk as a slave. The people would celebrate you for it."

She'd made the decision impulsively, just now, motivated by spite as much as by what Thomas might offer her. For all she knew, he was only pretending to read from the Books to extend his life.

"Qurong would never allow an albino to live in his castle," he said, with less conviction than he should have.

"He won't live in this castle. He'll live at the royal garden. In the basement of the library, under my supervision. If he can read the Books, my father will agree."

Woref didn't like the idea, but she'd effectively cut his feet off at the ankles. There was a certain logic to the whole idea.

"Ciphus won't agree."

"Ciphus is no fool. He will see my reasoning." *And what about you, Woref? Are you a fool?*

She continued before he could dwell on her insinuation. "Consider it an early wedding present. I am requesting Thomas of Hunter in chains, a much more fitting present for me than his head on a platter."

He only stared at her.

"You said 'anything.' Thomas of Hunter frightens you?"

A look of utter contempt crossed his face. She'd gone too far. He turned and walked from the room.

16

THE DUNGEON might very well have been the cleanest part of the entire city. They'd discussed it at length and decided that, because of the smell that seeped from every living Scab, this hole deep in the ground was one of the best places for them to be. The musty earthen scent of dirt and rocks was preferable. In fact, downright heavenly, Cain said.

"I knew it," Suzan said, pacing by one wall.

"The question is whether they will execute us," William said.

Thomas looked at his companions, sickened that their fate wasn't decided yet. "I'll do everything in my power to get us out."

"And what power is that?" William asked.

They had been told not five minutes ago by a temple guard. "It appears that death is too honorable for you," the guard said with a smirk. "The mighty warrior is now a slave, is that it? Better to lick the toes of his conqueror than end it all with a sword." He chuckled. "They collect you in ten minutes. Say good-bye to your friends."

"Where am I going?" Thomas demanded.

"Wherever Qurong wishes. To the royal library today. It seems he needs a translator."

"And us?" William asked.

"You're a gift for the wedding." He smiled and turned his back to leave. "Unfortunately, the wedding has been delayed," he mumbled. Then he left.

Now they waited.

"The same power he used to win her loyalty," Suzan said to William.

"Don't be so sure. She's a lying serpent as sure as we are salamanders in her eyes!" William spit to the side. "I would rather die than serve at Qurong's table."

"I don't think it's his table," Suzan said. "It is his daughter's table. Thomas's ploy worked. The Books of Histories may save our necks before this is done."

"His daughter's table would be worse! There is nothing as revolting as a Scab woman."

"I have to agree with William," Cain said. "I would much rather serve at Qurong's table than his wife's, or his daughter's. Better to face the sword of a warrior than the lying tongue of these women."

"You mean rotten tongues, don't you? You can smell them coming—"

"Stop it!" Thomas said. "You're making me nauseated. It's not their fault that they stink."

"If they would choose the drowning, they wouldn't smell; how can you say it's not their fault?"

"Okay, so it is their fault. But they hardly know better. These are the people Justin is courting."

"We're his bride," William said. "Not these whores."

Thomas was taken aback by his use of the word. It had once been a common expression for him, but not since the drowning.

"We would be most grateful if you could convince this whore"— Suzan glanced at William as she said it—"to spare our lives. Do you have a plan?"

Thomas walked to the corner of the cell and turned. "I guess you could call it that. If I can avoid the rhambutan juice, I will dream. If I dream, I will wake in the histories and tell my sister how to rescue us."

"Your sister, Kara, who was also Mikil at the council meeting," William said with a raised eyebrow. "You're placing our lives in the hands of a character in your dreams?"

"No, in Mikil's," Thomas said. "Unless you have a better plan."

They stared at him in silence. That was it; there were no more plans.

"Well, Thomas of Hunter," Cain finally said, "I for one place my trust in you." He moved forward and grasped Thomas's forearms to form a circle between them, the common greeting. "It makes no sense to me, but you've always led us down the right path. Elyon's strength."

"Elyon's strength."

Thomas repeated the grasp with each.

"Be careful, my friend," William said. "Don't let the disease tempt your mind. If I were Teeleh, I would see no greater victory than luring the great Thomas of Hunter onto Tanis's path."

Thomas clasped his arms. They had never seen any from the Circle catch the disease again after drowning—they weren't even sure if such a thing was possible. But some of the words from *The Histories Recorded by His Beloved* suggested it was possible. *If you remain in me, I will remain in you,* the Book said. They still didn't know precisely what this meant but believed the opposite was also true. William's warning was a good one.

"Elyon's strength."

"Elyon's strength."

"Where is he now?" Woref demanded.

"Locked in the basement," Ciphus said. "As agreed."

Qurong stood at the top of the steps that led into the royal bath. They'd built the bathhouse at the base of the Thrall, set apart from the prying eyes of the commoners. Only the royal family, the generals and their wives, and the priests were permitted to bathe in the stone house.

"And Chelise?"

"It was your own recommendation," Qurong said, facing his general. "Now you're fretting like a woman?"

Woref dipped his head. "I'm only interested in protecting what is mine."

"My daughter is yours? I don't remember a wedding. What I do remember is that there won't be one until the Books are found."

"Of course. But this man is no ordinary man. I don't trust him."

"Nor I. Which is why I wanted him dead. Although I must admit, this idea of yours is growing on me." He smiled wryly.

Qurong opened his robe and let it fall to the ground. Steam from the hot rocks the servants had set inside the pool rose around the perimeter. He hated the bathing, not only because of the stinging pain, but because it reminded him of capital punishment. Drowning. The Great Romance was a brilliant way to keep the people in their place, but there should be an exception for royalty.

"I am only concerned for your daughter's safety, my lord."

"She has her guard. The albino is under lock and key. If I didn't know better, I would say that you're jealous, Woref."

"Please, don't insult me, my lord."

Qurong walked down the steps and onto the bathing platform. He dipped his foot in the water, then withdrew it. This dreaded practice would be the death of him.

"What of you, Ciphus? What do you say?"

"I say what I said earlier. To keep your captive on a leash takes a stronger hand than killing him."

"Then you agree that he requires a stronger hand."

The high priest cleared his throat. "The albinos don't believe in the sword, if that's what you mean. Even Thomas of Hunter wouldn't harm your daughter. But he may try to escape."

"Is there a way to escape from the library?"

"You would have to ask Woref."

"Well then, Woref?"

"There's always a way to escape."

"Without violence?"

He hesitated.

"Well?"

"No, not that I can think of."

"Then what's your worry? You haven't found the Books. I would concern myself with that."

"Then I would request that as soon as I have married your daughter, you allow me to kill Thomas of Hunter," Woref said.

"I thought that was the understanding."

Woref glanced at Ciphus, who spoke. "Actually, I believe Thomas was meant to serve indefinitely, as long as he proves useful in translating the Books of Histories. It is a task of great benefit to the Great Romance."

"I'm not interested in a translation made by my enemy. It would be untrustworthy. If he can teach Chelise to read the Books, I will let him finish his task before killing him. Otherwise he will die."

The priest frowned. "Chelise is under the assumption—"

"I don't care what my daughter thinks! This is my decision to make. Woref is right. This albino is not to be trusted! Whatever agreement they made when he struck her is none of my concern."

Yes, I do know more than you think, Woref.

"Thomas of Hunter will be my slave until he's no longer useful," Qurong continued. "Then I will kill him myself. Now, if you will kindly both leave me, I have the terrible duty to bathe in this stink hole for a moment."

They bowed, stepped back, and turned to leave.

"Ciphus."

"Yes, my lord."

"I would like you to arrange public display of my slave. A parade or a ceremony where the people see him firmly under my foot."

"An excellent idea," Woref said.

"How much time would you need?" Qurong asked.

Ciphus answered slowly. "Perhaps two days."

"Not tomorrow?"

"Yes, tomorrow, if you want to rush it."

Qurong turned to the pool. "Two days then."

17

THOMAS SPENT the first night alone in the cold, dark cell below the library, praying for Elyon to show himself. A sign, a messenger of hope, a piece of fruit that would open his eyes. A dream.

But he hadn't dreamed. Not of Kara, not of anything.

He hadn't seen a soul since being ushered into the library's basement and locked in the windowless cell. Surely if Chelise had been so eager to uncover the mysteries of the Books, she would have come that first night and demanded he read more.

Maybe the reading was a thin abstraction for her. Or maybe it was Qurong who wanted to hear him read. Or Perhaps Ciphus had arranged it, eager for another chance to be shown the power Thomas had promised.

They'd been in the Horde city three days. Would Mikil have mounted a rescue? No, not if she followed their agreement. Not so long ago the Forest Guard would have stormed in with swords drawn, killed a few hundred Scabs, and freed them or died trying. But without weapons the task was far too dangerous. They all knew that.

Thomas rested his head against the stone wall and lifted his hand in front of his face. If he used his imagination, he could see it. Or could he? Like his dreams, there but beyond normal sight. Like the Shataiki bats that lived in the trees. Like Justin. Without the proper illumination they were all out of sight. It didn't mean they weren't there.

The door suddenly eased open. He scrambled to his feet.

Two temple guards dressed in hooded black robes stood in the doorway, broad swords drawn. "Out. Step carefully."

He walked into the basement's dim light. They marched him up the stairs and down a corridor that paralleled the main library where the scribes worked. He could see the royal garden through a row of windows. Other than the sound of birds chirping outside, the only sound was their feet on the wooden floor.

One of the guards unlocked a door with a large key. "Wait inside."

Thomas entered the large storeroom where the Books of Histories were kept. The door closed. Locked.

Four tall torches added to the light that streamed in through two sky-lights. They'd left him alone with the Books. He didn't know how long he had, but he had an opportunity here. If he could only find a Book that recorded what had happened during the Great Deception. Any Book that discussed the Raison Strain.

Thomas hurried to the nearest shelf and pulled out the first Book. *The Histories as Recorded by Ezekiel.*

Ezekiel? The prophet Ezekiel?

Heart hammering, Thomas opened the Book. If he wasn't mistaken, this was the prophet Ezekiel. The sentences sounded biblical, at least as he recalled biblical from his dreams.

He replaced the Book and tried another. This one was about some-one named Artimus—a name that meant nothing to him. And if he was right, unrelated in any way to the Book of Ezekiel beside it. There was no order to the Books.

There were thousands of Books! He ran for the ladder, pushed it to the far end, and climbed to the top shelf. There was only one way to do this—a methodical search, from top to bottom, Book by Book. And he would have to go by the titles alone. There were way too many Books to inspect each carefully.

He pulled out the farthest to his right. Cyrus. No.

Next.

Alexander. No.

Next. No.

He quickened his pace, pulling out Books, scanning their covers, slam-ming them back in when they struck no chord. The sound of each volume hitting the back wall echoed with a soft thud. No. No. No.

"Quite frantic, are we?"

Thomas twisted on the ladder. The Book in his hands flew free, sailed through the air, and fell two stories to the wood floor. It landed near her feet with a loud bang.

She didn't move. Her round gray eyes studied him as if she couldn't decide whether he was an amusement or a distraction. A faint smile formed on her mouth.

"I didn't mean to interrupt the great warrior."

Thomas started to climb down. "I'm sorry. I was just looking for a Book."

"Oh? Which Book?"

"I don't know. One that I hoped would ring a bell."

"I've never heard of a Book ringing a bell."

He stepped off the ladder and faced her. "An expression we use in the histories."

"You mean in the Books of Histories. You said *in* the histories."

"Yes."

She picked up the fallen Book. "Did you find it?"

"Find what?"

"The Book."

"No." He looked at the shelves. "And I'm not sure I can."

"Well, I'm afraid I can't help you. I hardly can tell one Book from another."

So here she was, his master. He was relieved it was her and not Ciphus or Qurong. This slender woman had a powerful tongue—she'd proven that much. But she was also genuinely interested in the Books for what they could teach her, not for how they might give her power. Her motives seemed pure. Or at least purer than the others. In some ways she reminded Thomas of Rachelle.

She wore a green robe with a hood. Silk. Before taking the forests, the Horde had been limited to their coarse fabrics woven from thread rolled out of desert wheat stalks.

"Do you like it?"

"I'm sorry?"

"My dress. You were looking at it."

"It's beautiful."

She walked slowly around him. "And me?"

His heart skipped a beat. He couldn't dare tell her what he really thought, that her breath was foul and her skin sickly and her eyes dead. He had to win this woman's favor for his plan to work. He had to dream. It was the only way he could see out of this.

"I'm only an albino," he said. "What does it matter what I think?"

"True. But even an albino must have a heart. You're given to strange beliefs and this cult of yours, but surely the great warrior whose name once struck terror in all of the Horde can still react to a woman."

If he didn't know better, he would say that there was a hint of seduction in her voice.

How would Elyon see her?

He answered with as much conviction as he could muster. "You're beautiful."

"Really? I would have thought you'd find me repelling. Does a fish find a bird attractive? I think you're lying."

"Beauty is beauty, fish or fowl."

She stopped her pacing, ten feet from him. "I'm not asking if I'm beautiful. I'm asking if you find me beautiful."

He couldn't stoop to this deception any longer. "Then to be perfectly honest, I see both beauty in you and some things that aren't so beautiful."

"Such as?"

"Such as your skin. Your eyes. Your scent."

She looked at him for a few moments, expressionless. He'd wounded her. Pity stabbed his heart.

"I'm sorry, I was only trying to—"

"I was asking because I wanted to be sure that you found no attraction in me," she said. "If you had found any beauty in me, I would have kept my distance."

She turned and walked toward the desk. "Naturally, you must keep your distance from me anyway. I find you as repelling as you find me."

"I didn't say you repelled me. Only the disease does that."

This wasn't a good start. "How long will we be together here?" he asked.

"That depends on how long I can stand you."

"Then please, I beg your forgiveness. I didn't mean to offend you."

"You think an albino can offend me so easily?"

"You don't understand. I'm sure that beneath the disease you're a stunning woman. Breathtaking. If I could see you as Elyon sees you . . ."

She turned to him. "I bathe in Elyon's lake nearly every day. He has nothing to do with this. I think it would be better if we change the subject. You're here to teach me to read these Books. You're my slave; keep it in mind."

"I am your most humble servant," he said, dipping his head.

Chelise walked gracefully to the bookshelf and ran her fingers along the spines of several Books. She pulled one out, looked at it, then put it back and went down the row. What did it matter which Book if she couldn't read?

"I used to spend hours looking through these Books when I was a child," she said softly. "I was lost in a hope that I would eventually find one that I could read. A few words even. When I was older, a man once told me that some of them were written in English. If I could only find those, I would be happy."

"A man named Roland," he said.

Chelise turned. "How did you know?"

"I knew Roland. He met you in the desert and you gave him a horse. You saved his life, he said."

"Roland, the assassin. Is he now an albino as well?"

"Yes. Yes, he is."

Thomas followed her along the shelf, running his fingers along the Books. "And there is more. All of the Books are written in English."

She laughed. "Then you know less than you think. How many of these Books have you actually read?"

"I think it's time for our lesson. Pick one."

She looked at him, then the Books.

"Any of them. It doesn't matter."

She pulled a thick black Book from the shelf and carefully ran her palm over its cover.

"May I see it?" he asked, reaching out a hand.

She walked to Thomas and gave him the Book. He could have walked to the desk; it certainly would have been natural to read such a big Book on the desk. But he had ulterior motives now.

He opened the Book in both arms and scanned the page. A Book about some history in Africa. She started to turn for the desk.

"Here, let me show you something," he said.

She looked at the Book.

"Come here. Let me show you." He let half the Book fall and drew his finger along the words on the half he held. She drew close to him, inches from his body.

"Do you see this word?"

"Yes," she said.

He adjusted his grip. "Can you help me with this?"

She reached out and lifted the end that had fallen. Now they stood side by side, each holding one cover of the Book. Her shoulder touched his lightly. A strong waft of her perfume—the smell of roses—filled his nostrils. It didn't cover the odor of her skin entirely, but her scent was surprisingly tolerable.

"Put your finger on this word, as I'm doing."

She hesitated.

"Please. It's part of the way the Books are read."

Chelise put her finger below the first word on her side.

The room suddenly darkened. Thomas glanced up and saw that a cloud had dimmed the sunlight. He lowered his eyes. Wavering orange flames from the torches lit the page. Chelise had her hand on it, waiting for him.

By this light her hand was nearly flesh-toned. The disease was mostly covered by morst, and what he saw by the torch's glow took him completely off guard.

This was a woman's hand. Delicate and gentle, resting lightly on the page with one finger extended as he'd requested. Her fingernails were painted red, neatly manicured.

The sight immobilized him. Time stilled. A terrible empathy rose through his throat. This was how Justin saw her, without her disease.

She removed her hand. "What are you doing?"

"Nothing. I . . ." He looked into her eyes. He'd never been so close to any Scab before. Less than a foot separated her face from his. She was quite beautiful. Her eyes looked hazel and her cheeks blushed with a sweet rose color. It was a trick of the light—he knew that—but for a moment her disease was gone in his eyes.

"I was just noticing what a good student you would make," Thomas said.

"How so?"

"The tools of the trade. Gentle fingers. Clear eyes. Now if we can only work on your mind, you may read this Book yet."

The clouds passed over and the room brightened. Thomas returned his eyes to the page. "You see this word?"

"Yes."

"You know . . ." He glanced at the desk. "Maybe the desk would be better."

She followed him to the desk where he took up the lesson again, this time leaning over by her side as she sat.

"This word is 'the.' You see it?"

"No. It looks nothing like 'the' to me."

"What does it look like?"

"Like squiggly lines."

"But to me it reads 'the.' I can assure you this is a *t* and an *h* and an *e*. My eyes see it as plain as day."

"That's impossible." She looked up at him with wide eyes. "You're saying that this mess of lines is English? Then why can't I see it?"

Thomas straightened. The fact of the matter was that the disease robbed her of the ability to understand pure truth, and the Books of Histories contained only truth. As much as her eyes were gray, her mind was deceived. But if he simply told her that now, she might never agree to see him again.

"I'm not sure you're ready for that lesson yet. We have to start here, with a simple understanding and trust."

"Then this is sorcery? You read with magic?"

"No. But it is a power beyond either of us."

Thomas stood and walked around the desk. "I think that today we should start with a reading. We should familiarize your mind with these words, so that when I am ready to unravel them, you are familiar with the way they read."

"You will read to me?"

"If you would like me to."

"Yes." She stood eagerly. "If I have you to read them to me, why should I read them?"

"Because you won't have me forever. But tomorrow we'll start the lesson in earnest. Now if you could help me find this one Book I was looking for."

"No, please, this one." She lifted the black Book they'd just been reading.

"I was thinking of another."

"Which?"

"I don't know where it is."

"Then read this one. Please."

He reluctantly took the Book and sat behind the desk.

<hr />

She walked while he read from the desk. He was an excellent reader, really. His tone was gentle and full of intonation, yet strong when the story called for it.

Chelise looked at the towering bookshelves and lost herself in the tale he was reading. Then another, and another.

"Should I stop?"

"No. Please. Can you read more?"

"Yes."

And he read.

His voice soon sounded nearly magical. He was the kind she could trust, she decided. A good man who was unfortunately an albino.

How many times had she wanted to read what she was now hearing? It was a special day. She leaned against a bookcase and set her head back. The sun was straight overhead. Midday. If these words were steps, she was sure she could climb all the way to heaven.

She chuckled and sat down on the floor. The reading paused momentarily then started again. *Read on, my servant. Read on.*

He read on.

How could simple words carry such weight? It was as if they were working their magic at this very moment. Reaching into her mind and sending her on a journey that few had ever taken. To lands faraway, full of mystery. To lakes and clouds, swimming, diving, flying.

She lay down on a window seat and rolled to one side, lost in other worlds. It didn't seem to matter which story he was telling; they were all powerful.

The one he was reading now was about a betrayal. Tears flooded her eyes and her heart beat heavily, but she knew it would be all right, because she knew that in the end the kind of power that was in these Books would never let her down.

Still, the story he was reading was dreadful. A prince had lost his only love and searched the kingdom only to find that she been forced to marry a cruel man.

She faced the ceiling and began to sob. The reader stalled, and when he restarted, she realized that he was crying too. Her new servant was weeping as he read.

Or was she only hearing that in her mind?

The story changed. The bride found a way to escape the cruel beast with the help of her prince.

Chelise began to laugh. She drew her legs up and spread her arms and laughed at the ceiling.

It was only after some time that she realized hers was the only voice in the room. She stopped and sat up, disoriented. What was happening? Thomas sat at the desk staring at her. Tears stained his cheeks.

And she was on the floor.

She scrambled to her feet and brushed the dust from her robe. "What's going on?" she asked. "I . . . what happened?"

"I can't see the page," he said.

They'd *both* been crying. She hadn't imagined it after all. She glanced at the door—still shut. What if someone had come in while she was in this awful state? She would never be able to explain. She wasn't even sure what had happened herself.

Chelise faced him. "The story did that?"

"It seems the power of truth is quite shocking to your mind." He seemed as surprised as she.

"My mind. Not yours?"

"I've been shocked plenty of times. Try drowning and you'll know what shocking is."

She straightened her sleeves, suddenly embarrassed. But the power! The joy, the mystery. She couldn't help but grin. Could she tell anyone about this? No. It could be very dangerous.

She cleared her throat and took a deep breath. "That will have to be all for now."

He stood. "We'll meet tomorrow?"

Honestly, she didn't know how to proceed. It was a frightening experience. Intoxicating. "We'll see. I think so, if I can find the time."

"Maybe we could read again tonight," he said, rounding the desk.

"No, that would never do. You're my servant, not my librarian."

"Then could you give me a torch for my cell? There's no light."

"No light? I insisted you have light."

Woref.

"And they're making me drink the rhambutan juice on threat of my friends' lives. If I drink the juice, I can't dream, and I must dream."

"Now you're going too far. I'll get you light and good food, but this dream business isn't my concern."

She walked for the door, half of her mind still trapped in the heavens.

"And my friends, they will live?"

She turned at the door. "I'm sure that can be arranged. Yes, of course. Anything else? The keys to your cell perhaps?"

He smiled.

18

THOMAS WASN'T sure what had happened to him in the library that first day with Chelise, but he found that, try as he did, he couldn't remove her from his mind.

Her heart had been opened to a sliver of the truth; he knew that much. She'd heard the story from history—the unadulterated truth—and she'd become intoxicated by it. Another person might have heard the same thing and listened with vague interest. This much he understood. What was much less in focus was his own reaction to her.

In some strange way, his own eyes had been opened to her. She had heard the truth, perhaps for the first time, but he had seen a truth he'd never seen before. The truth was Chelise. As Elyon saw her.

He spent only an hour with her the next morning, and she seemed guarded. Afraid, even. She walked as he read again, but this time she stopped every few minutes to ask him what the story was about. What time period it had been written in. Who wrote it.

He finally closed the Book and crossed the room to where she'd pulled out a second volume.

"What is it?" she asked.

"You're distracted."

She closed the Book. "Woref is ranting and raving like a lunatic. He's turning the city inside out looking for the blank Books. It's an inquisition."

Thomas was quite sure they wouldn't find them, but he didn't say so.

"That's not what I mean. What did I read yesterday?" he asked.

"A story."

"What story? Tell me the story I was reading when you cried."

Her eyes looked away, distant.

"It was too much for you?"

"You were reading a story about a princess who was taken captive by an evil man."

The story he'd read had been a simple accounting of history, hardly the drama she remembered. Yet she'd heard this in it?

Her eyes misted and she bit her lower lip. He found himself wanting to comfort her. She stood in the sunlight from the window above them, face white with morst, eyes gray and dead. A revolting image once. But now . . .

"That was the truth behind the words I read," he said. "Not what I read. You opened your mind to the truth."

"Then you shouldn't read the Books to me anymore."

"Why not? It's what you've always searched for."

"Not your truth! I've never searched for the ways of an albino! Do you know who I am?"

"You're Chelise, the daughter of Qurong. And who am I?"

"You're my servant. A slave. An albino!"

"And do you think there is any truth in this albino?"

She refused to look at him. They stood in an awkward silence. She finally pushed the Book into his hands and walked toward the door. "There is a tour of the city planned for this afternoon. Qurong wants to show the people his prisoners. You will ride in chains behind us. They will mock you. That is my truth."

Chelise left him without a backward glance.

As promised, Qurong dragged his prisoners through the city that afternoon. The royal family rode three abreast on black steeds, followed by Woref and Ciphus. Then Thomas, on foot and chained—each arm to a Scab warrior on each side. William, Suzan, Cain, and Stephen followed behind with their own guard. An army of a thousand warriors in full battle dress, armed with sickles, brought up the rear.

The horns announced their coming and the streets were lined with hundreds of thousands of disease-ridden Scabs.

Thomas saw the true squalor of the Horde on every side. A baby crawling on the muddy earth between the mother's feet, screaming to be heard above the din of insults that had become a steady roar. Thomas was certain the children cried as much from the pain of the disease as from any other discomfort.

The guards parted occasionally to allow youth to hurl spoiled fruit at them. What little grass had grown on the yard along the parade route was quickly trampled into mud. Several huts collapsed under the weight of spectators.

There seemed to be a particular infection spreading among a sizable portion of the population. Red sores on their necks, raw and bleeding. Thomas plodded on, afraid to look at them, much less care for them.

The parade lasted about an hour, and not once did Chelise turn a kind eye to him or show any hint of misgiving. She rode erect, with no emotion at all. She was right: this was her truth.

He spent the night in his cell, too nauseated to eat. But he still couldn't wash her image from his mind. He begged Elyon for her understanding, her heart, her mind, her soul. He finally cried himself to sleep.

He did not dream.

———∽∞∾———

Chelise rode to the royal garden the next morning, as soon as she felt she could get away without the prying eyes of the court on her. She was flirting with a dangerous game. Even the smallest kindness shown to Thomas could drive a wedge between her and Qurong. Her father loved her; she was sure of that. But his love was conditioned by his people's ways. Hundreds of thousands of men had died in battle trying to defeat Thomas of Hunter. Aiding him in any way would be seen as treason. Qurong could never accept treason, especially not in his own court.

And Woref . . . She shuddered to think what Woref would do if he even suspected the small kindness she harbored for Thomas of Hunter.

She'd settled another matter last night with her maidservant, Elison.

"Why are you so upset over this, Chelise?" Elison had asked. "I would think parading your new slave on a chain would suit you. Thomas of Hunter, of all men! Qurong is calling him his slave, but the word on the street is that it was your idea."

"How did that get out? Do the walls have ears here?"

"I think Ciphus said something. The point is, the people love you for it. The princess towing about the mighty warrior in chains."

"No man should be insulted in that way. Especially a great warrior. The people are like ravenous dogs! Did you see the look in their eyes?"

"Please, my lady," Elison said. "Don't misunderstand the situation here. Thomas of Hunter is the man responsible for widowing one out of every ten women in this city."

"He's great, but not that great."

"The Forest Guard then. Under his command."

"The Forest Guard no longer exists. They don't even carry swords—what kind of enemy is that?"

Elison looked at her, dumb.

"Don't play ignorant with me, Elison. If I can't trust you, then who can I trust?"

"Of course."

She turned to her servant, took her hand, and led her to the window seat. "Tell me that you would rather die than betray me. Swear it to me."

"But, my lady, you know my loyalty."

"Then swear it!"

"I swear it! What is this talk of betrayal?"

"I sympathize with him, Elison. Some people might consider that treason."

"I don't understand. If you were to say something more scandalous, some service you required of him as your slave, I might understand that. But sympathy? He's an albino."

"And he has more knowledge than Ciphus and Qurong put together!" Chelise said. Elison's eyes widened. "You see why I insisted you swear?

To kill Thomas of Hunter would be to take the greatest mind. He may be the only one who can read the Books of Histories."

Her servant looked at her with dawning. "You . . . you like him."

"Maybe I do. But he's an albino, and I find albinos repulsive." She looked out the window at the rising moon. "Strange that we call them albinos when we are whiter than they are. We even cover our skin to make it smooth like theirs."

Elison stood in shock.

"Sit."

She sat.

"You're forgetting yourself. I would think you should sympathize with Thomas yourself. You're both in servitude. He's a very kind man, Elison. The kindest I've met, I would say. I simply sympathize with Thomas the way I might sympathize with a condemned lamb. Surely you can find it in yourself to understand that."

"Yes. Yes, I suppose I can," she said, eyes still wide. "Have you . . . touched his skin?"

Chelise laughed. "*Now* who is scandalous? You're trying to make me ill? I have no attraction to him as a man, thank Elyon for that, or I might be in a real bind. Can you imagine Woref's reaction?"

"Loving an albino would be treason. Punishable by death," her maid-servant said.

"Yes, it would."

She'd risen then, confident in her simple analysis. It was the first time she'd thought about her use of the morst as a way of becoming more albino. Just a coincidence, of course. Fashion was something that changed, and at the moment this new morst that happened to cover their scaly flesh distinguished women of royalty from commoners. In the years to come, it might be a blue paint.

Chelise passed through the royal garden's main gate and turned to Claudus, the senior guard who'd grown up as the cook's son. "Good morning, Claudus."

"Morning, my lady. Beautiful morning."

"Anyone pass this morning?"

"The scribes. No one else."

"Has my slave bathed as I instructed?"

"Yes, and wasn't he filthy! We gave him a clean robe as well. He's waiting inside with the Books."

"Good. I should have asked that you powder him as well." She nudged her horse and then thought she'd better clarify her statement. "I can hardly stand being near him."

"Shall we powder him?"

"No. No, I'm not that weak. Thank you, Claudus."

"Of course, my lady."

She headed toward the library, eager to be among the Books again. With Thomas. In all honesty the thought of powdering him felt profane to her. She didn't want him to be like her. Now there was a scandal.

Chelise tied her horse at the back entrance and slipped into the library, chiding herself for sneaking like a schoolgirl. They all knew she was here, doing precisely what they expected her to do. Qurong had insisted on having the Books read to him after her first lesson, but she'd stalled him. She claimed she wanted to surprise him by reading the Books to him herself. Thomas was her slave—the least they could do was let her spend a few days learning to read before robbing her of her gift.

She also convinced him that the other prisoners might be able to read the Books as well. They should be kept alive for the time.

Chelise unlocked the door, put her hand on the knob, took a deep breath, and stepped into the large storage room.

At first she thought he hadn't been brought yet. Then she saw him, on the ladder high above, searching madly through the Books again. He looked like a child caught stealing a wheat cake from the jar.

"Still looking for your secret Book?" she asked.

He descended quickly and stood with his arms by his sides, twenty feet from her. The long black robe made him look noble. With the hood pulled up and a little morst properly applied, he would look like one of them.

"Good morning, my lady."

"Good morning."

"I have a confession," he said.

She walked to his right, hands clasped behind her back. "Oh?"

"I found the parade yesterday appalling."

She knew he was probing, but she didn't care. "I'm sorry about that. My confession is that I found it appalling as well."

Her statement robbed him of words, she thought.

"No decent man should have to suffer that," she said.

"I agree."

"Good. Then we're in agreement. Today I would like to learn to read."

"I have another confession," he said.

"Two confessions. I'm not sure I can match you."

"I can't get you off my mind," he said.

Now his statement robbed *her* of words. Heat spread down the nape of her neck. He was saying too much. Surely he realized that she could only do so much for him. Light, food, a bath, clothing. But she had her limitations.

"I will never be your savior, Thomas. You do realize that, don't you?"

"I don't think of you as my savior. I think of you as a woman, loved and cherished by Elyon."

"You're saying too much. We should start the lesson now."

He looked away, embarrassed. "Of course. I didn't mean that I had feelings for you. Not as a woman like that. I just . . ."

"You just what? Do you have an albino wife?"

"She was killed by your people when we made our first escape from the red lake. Our children are with my tribe now. Samuel and Marie."

She wasn't sure what to make of that. She'd never heard that Thomas of Hunter had lost his wife. Or had children, for that matter.

"How old are they?"

"Samuel thinks he's twenty, though he's only thirteen. Marie is nearly fifteen."

Thomas walked to the shelf and pulled out a Book. "I think it's important that you realize that your teacher respects you. As a student. As a woman who has ears to hear. I meant nothing else. Shall we begin?"

They spent an hour with the Book, carefully going over the letters that he insisted were English. They weren't, of course, but she began to associate certain marks with specific letters. She felt as if she was learning a new alphabet.

He worked with her with measured reason at first, gently explaining and rehearsing each letter. But as the hour passed, his passion for the task grew and became contagious. He explained with increasing enthusiasm and the movement of his arms became more exaggerated.

They worked closely, she on the chair behind the desk, he over her shoulder, when he wasn't pacing the floor in front of her. He had a habit of pressing the tips of his fingers together as he walked, and she found herself wondering how many swords those fingers had held over the years. How many throats had they slit in battle? How many women had they loved?

She would guess only one. His late wife.

They laughed and they argued over fine points, and gradually she became more comfortable with his proximity to her. With her proximity to his side, bumping her shoulder when he hurried in to point at a letter she'd missed; to his finger, accidentally touching her own; to his hand, gently tapping her back when she got it right.

His breath on her cheek when he was too passionate about a particular point to realize he was speaking loudly, so close.

She was no fool, of course. Thomas was no buffoon. In his own measured way, he was trying to draw her in. Disarming her. Winning her trust. Perhaps even her admiration.

And she was allowing him to do it. Was it so wrong to bump the shoulder of an albino? Did the guards not touch his skin when they shackled him?

Three hours had passed when Thomas decided that a test was finally in order.

"Okay," he said, clapping his hands. "Read the whole paragraph, beginning to end."

"The whole thing?" She felt positively giddy.

"Of course! Read what you've written."

She focused on the words and began to read.

"The woman was give the sword man if running . . ." She stopped. It made no sense to her.

"That's not what you've written," he said. "Please, in order, exactly as you wrote it."

"I am reading it exactly as I wrote it!"

He frowned. "Then try again."

"What's wrong? Why does it sound so mixed up?"

"Please, try again. From the top. Follow with your finger as I showed you."

She started again, pointing to each word as she read. "The woman running if horse . . ."

Chelise looked up at him, horrified. "What's this nonsense coming from my mouth? I can't read it!"

His face lightened a shade. He stepped forward, took the paper she'd written on. His eye ran across the page. "You're not reading what's on the page," he said. "You're mixing the words."

Chelise felt hope drain from her like flour from a broken clay jar. "Then I won't be able to learn. What good is it if I can write the alphabet and form the words if they don't make any sense?"

He set the paper down and paced.

Chelise felt crushed. She would never be able to read these mysteries. Was she so stupid as that? Her throat suddenly felt tight.

Thomas faced her. "I'm sorry, Chelise. It's not your writing or your reading. It's your heart. It's the disease. As long as you have the disease, you'll never be able to read from the Books of Histories."

She suddenly felt furious with him. "You knew this? How dare you toy with me!"

"No! Yes, I suspected that the disease might keep you from hearing, but the other day you did hear the truth behind the story. I thought you might be able to learn."

"I have no disease! You're the albino, not me!" Tears sprang into her eyes.

Thomas looked stricken. He hurried around the desk and knelt beside her. "I'm so sorry. Please, we can fix this!"

Chelise placed her forehead in one hand. She took a deep breath and calmed herself. She didn't understand his sorcery, but she doubted her ignorance was his fault.

Thomas put a hand on her shoulder. "I can help you. I can teach you to read the Books of Histories, I swear. I will. Do you hear me? I will."

"What's the meaning of this?"

Woref's voice echoed through the room like the crack of a whip.

Chelise instinctively gasped and sat up. Woref glared at them from the doorway. She'd left the door unlocked?

The general walked into the room. Thomas withdrew his hand and stood back.

"How dare you touch her?" Woref raged.

Chelise stood. "My lord, he was only instructing me on this passage. He did only what I demanded. How dare you suggest anything else?"

"It makes no difference what you instructed him. No man, certainly no albino, has the right to touch what is mine! Get away from her."

Thomas eased away. "The rules of these holy Books supersede the rules of man," he said. "Are you saying your authority is greater than the Great Romance?"

"I should cut out your tongue and feed it to Elyon."

Woref had lost his reason, Chelise thought. "Then we'll let Qurong decide by whose authority we live," she said. "Yours or Elyon's."

Woref scowled at her, then at Thomas. "I don't see why any instruction would require his comforting."

"Comforting?" Chelise smiled wryly. "You think I would allow this pathetic albino to comfort me? We were playacting. It's a part of breaking the code required to understand that what I can see now is clearly beyond your mind." *Easy, Chelise.*

She stepped closer to him and winked. "But then I'm not fascinated by a man's mind. It's your strength and courage I find exhilarating. If you were a feeble scribe, I would never consent to our marriage."

She walked up to him and drew her finger over his shoulder, stepping behind him. "I expected nothing less than this tirade. You flatter me. But you did misunderstand, my lord. Now tell me why you've come."

He wasn't buying her toying wholeheartedly, but she'd effectively cut him off.

"I have changed my mind about the blank Books," he said, still stern. "They have vanished. My men have searched every possible hiding place for such a large collection, and they can't be found. I think the sorcery of this albino is to blame. They disappeared about the same time he arrived."

"I have no sorcery," Thomas said.

Woref dismissed the claim. "I demand that you convince your father to withdraw his request that I find the Books before we are married."

"You've talked to him about this?"

"I have. He's obsessed with these blank Books."

"And I understand why," Chelise said. "The blank Books make the collection complete. Surely you can find them."

"As I said, they no longer exist. I won't delay my possession of you over this nonsense!"

"Then make my father see the light."

"He will only concede on the albinos," Woref said. "I need you to help him see the light in regard to the Books. I can assure you that I'll make it up to you."

"How has he conceded on the albinos?" Chelise asked.

"He's agreed to kill the other four tomorrow. He said that you thought they should be kept alive, but I've convinced him otherwise. One living albino is bad enough."

She glanced at Thomas and saw the fear cross his face. But she had to choose her battles.

"Fine. Let me think about how to persuade Qurong to forget about the blank Books. Now if you'll excuse us, we are in the middle of a lesson."

Woref stared at Thomas for a few seconds, spit upon the floor, and walked from the room without closing the door.

"I beg you, Chelise, you can't let them die!" Thomas whispered.

She hurried to the door and closed it. "It's out of my hands. How would it look for me to beg for their lives?"

Thomas paced, frenzied.

"We're on dangerous ground here. Not only you, but now me. I know Woref's kind, and I promise you that one day I'll pay for what he just saw. You have to be more careful. Please, keep your distance."

He suddenly stopped and faced her. "I can dream now!"

"What are you talking about?"

"I've been drinking the rhambutan juice because Woref has been holding my friends' lives over my head. He's just removed that threat! I'll refuse to eat the fruit and dream tonight. But they may try to force me. Can you stop them?"

She didn't respond. Why this business of dreams was so terribly important to him, she didn't know. But he was right; Woref had undermined his own threat.

He rushed over to her and grabbed her hand. "Please, I beg you. And you can't say a word about this!" He kissed her hand. "Please, not a word!"

"I . . ." He was still holding her hand. "This isn't keeping your distance."

Thomas released her and stepped back. "Forgive me. I didn't mean that. I lost my mind."

"Clearly."

"But you'll help me?"

"I can't help you. But I don't see the harm in a few dreams." And then she added something that shocked even her. "As long as you promise to dream about me."

19

THE HELICOPTER sat down on the White House lawn with a *thump* that pounded through Kara's head. Thomas was on that helicopter. Her brother, who had traveled to hell and back in the last three weeks. Or was it four weeks now?

The rotors wound down slowly. The door opened and Thomas emerged into the afternoon sun. He stepped onto the grass, ducked his head, and hurried toward them.

"Hey, Thomas." She closed the gap between them and met him by the line of secret service agents, which had doubled since news of the crisis had flooded the airwaves.

Thomas took her in his arms and hugged her. "Hey, sis."

"You're alive," she said.

"And kicking."

He turned to Monique, who waited with a sheepish smile. "Monique."

She took his hand and kissed his cheek. "Hello, Thomas."

"How's it feel?" he asked.

He was asking her about waking from the dead, Kara thought.

"You tell me," she said.

"Like waking from a dream."

"Been doing a lot of that lately, from what I understand."

"More than I care. Although I have to say, I think I'm on to something this time."

Merton Gains stepped forward, hand extended. "Good to have you back. The president's expecting you."

The situation room was buzzing when Thomas stepped in, followed by Kara and Monique. President Blair saw him and excused himself from a conversation with the secretary of state. He approached with a tired smile and stuck out his hand.

"The cat has nine lives after all."

"Two, actually." Thomas glanced around the room and lowered his voice. "What I have to say has to be said in private, sir. I'm not sure who we can trust."

"And I can't work in a vacuum," the president said. "Not this late in the game."

"Please, sir, just hear me out. Then you can decide who needs to know. You were told they have someone on the inside?"

"Yes. Okay, wait for me in my office. Give me a minute. Merton, please show them into the Oval Office and leave them."

"Right away, sir."

Blair took his chief of staff aside and spoke quietly.

"This way," Gains said. They followed him silently through several halls bustling with activity. Into the Oval Office.

They stood in the stately office, surrounded by silence.

"The Book crossed over with me, Kara."

"The blank Book? What do you mean 'crossed over'?"

"When I woke up on the gurney in the basement of Fortier's complex, it was with me. It's the only object that's ever crossed between the realities. Skills, blood, and knowledge—and now this Book. And if I'm right, the rest of the blank Books may have followed somehow."

"The Books are knowledge," Kara said. "Knowledge crosses. This is incredible!"

"No, this isn't incredible. I lost the Book. It was taken by one of the guards, who has no clue what it can do. How much time do we have with the virus?"

"Five days. Maybe less, maybe more. Ten before it's all over."

"Then I guess the Book will have to wait."

The door suddenly opened and the president walked in alone.

"Sorry, I got hung up." He walked to his desk and picked up a warm Pepsi can, then ushered them to the sofas.

"Okay, Thomas. You're on."

"This office is clean?"

"Swept for bugs this morning."

"By whom? Sorry, never mind. I can't decide which world I'm in."

Blair nodded. "Talk to me."

"Okay." Thomas took a deep breath and sat on the edge of the couch. "Follow me closely. I understand the immediate crisis between Israel and France has been defused."

"For the time being. But things could get bad anytime. In three days we lose our nuclear arsenal."

"We're going to need the Israelis."

"How so?" the president asked.

He decided to hold back. "What would you say if I told you I may have a way to put a man in their inner circle?"

"You mean next to Fortier?"

"Close enough to smell his breath."

"I would say we should have done that two weeks ago. Who?"

"Carlos Missirian."

"He's with them. I don't understand."

"I think we may be able to get inside of Carlos's head. I'll need Johan for that. They've shared a connection once before; I think Johan could do it again. But he'll need to dream while in contact with my blood."

"I'm not sure I know this Johan."

"Johan is . . . connected with Carlos?" Kara asked.

"You're saying that if Johan dreamed using you as a gateway, he would wake up as Carlos!" Monique said.

"Yes."

"It could work!"

The president held up his hand. "Excuse me. Maybe you could be a little clearer here."

"It's the way our dreams work," Thomas said. "All three of us have dreamed. We know someone in the other world who could get to Carlos."

"Is that all? I'm surprised I didn't think of it."

"Please, we're running out of time, Mr. President."

Blair lifted both hands. "Fine. I'll try anything at this point. How do we get to this Johan?"

"Well, actually, we have a problem there. I'm being held captive at the moment. We have to get Johan to me, which is where Kara comes in." He looked at his sister. "Come back with me. As Mikil. You and Johan have to break us out of the city—the others are scheduled for execution tomorrow."

She stared, lost in the suggestion. "Break you out without fighting?"

"I have an idea. It'll be tricky, but with Johan's help you should have a decent chance."

"You can't fight?" Monique asked. "You should go in there and do whatever's necessary. Kill the lot if you have to!"

"No," Thomas said. "That's not the way the Circle works now."

The president sat back and crossed his legs. "If we weren't facing extinction, I might be calling security at this point."

All three looked at him. Thomas turned back to Kara. "You have to get me out. If Mikil is still near the Southern Forest, a day's ride south, it may already be too late. But I can't think of any alternatives."

A thick black leather-bound book lay on the end table to Thomas's right. A Bible. His dream of the Circle spun dizzily through his head.

"But you're not scheduled for execution, right?" Kara asked.

"No," he said. "Does the phrase 'bread of life' mean anything to you?"

They were silent, not expecting the odd question. Thomas looked at Kara. "The bread of life. The light of the world. Two of a dozen metaphors we use in the Circle to talk about Justin."

"The bread of life," Kara said. "Sounds like a phrase Dad would have used when he was a chaplain."

"From the Gospels," the president said.

Thomas reached for the Bible and lifted it slowly. The Gospels. Was it possible? The air felt thick. Words spoken by his father years earlier wove through his mind. He'd never paid much attention to them, but they spoke softly from the back of his memory, like whispers of the dead.

Or of the living?

He cracked the book open and thumbed through the latter half. Found the Gospels. The Gospel of John.

Thomas read the first line and felt the strength leave his arms. Here in his hands he held a copy of the one book Justin had left them.

The Histories Recorded by His Beloved.

Kara had walked up and was staring at the book. "The Book of Histories?"

Thomas closed the Bible and set it down. "One of them."

"That's one of the Books?" Monique asked. "How is that possible?"

"Everything that happens here is recorded in the Books of Histories," Thomas said. "Everything."

But it was more than that, wasn't it? This was the one book that Justin had left them with. The Circle's dogma was largely based on this book.

President Blair cleared his throat. "Assuming you get to Carlos, what's the plan?"

Yes, the plan.

20

THE CROWD was swelling exponentially, but not nearly fast enough for Phil Grant. The plan had been simple enough, and the senate majority leader had come through, but time was running out, and now Thomas Hunter had pulled this dream stunt of his again.

Phil walked across the lawn with his radio in hand, dabbing his sweaty forehead with a handkerchief. A line of tan APCs had been stationed every fifty yards to form a large perimeter around the White House grounds. Regular army. A full division had been assigned to Washington. Several tanks sat on the driveway, hatches open and operators sitting on their turrets. Their presence here had been tolerated only because the nation was preoccupied with worse matters. The National Guard had taken to the streets of the nation's fifty largest cities, spanning from New York to Los Angeles. No incidents of fatal conflict. Yet.

A thousand sets of eyes followed Phil as he walked. The protesters stood behind the fence, a good hundred yards off, but their glares pointed even at that distance. The people were a combination of I-told-you-so end-of-the worlders, antigovernment activists, and a surprising number of regular citizens who had connected with Mike Orear and decided that adopting a cause—no matter how practical—was better than sitting at home waiting to die.

Dwight Olsen kept up with Phil's even stride. Phil looked at the opposition leader. The man was oblivious to the real game here, but his hatred for the president had made him an easy pawn.

"We're down to the wire," Phil said. "Tomorrow at the latest. If you can't pull this off, the president's going to try something stupid. You understand that, right?"

"You've said that before, but you know I can't force this. I can't imagine the president starting a war. He and I may not see eye to eye, but he's not a fool."

"That's the point; we can't let him start a war. It's too late for that. Our whole purpose here is to prevent a war."

They approached the front lines of the protest. Mike Orear walked toward them, looking haggard. Dozens of well-known politicians were involved in getting out the protest, but the world's eyes were focused on this one man.

Phil had slipped the suggestion to Theresa on the flight back from Bangkok, and she'd listened intently. They had to give the people a heads-up, and the only way to do it without breaking the president's confidence was to bring in someone who might make the decision to go public on his own. Someone like her boyfriend, who had broad media access. If she hadn't taken the bait so quickly, Phil would have used any of several other leads he had working. The trick had been to hold back the news long enough to let Fortier secure his grip on France. When the news finally broke, they needed it to break big.

Orear grinned and ran a hand through his already-disheveled hair. "Impressed?"

"Mike, I'd like you to meet Phil Grant, director of the CIA," Dwight Olsen said.

They shook hands. "Quite a show you're putting on, Mike."

"It's all the people, not me. I'm sure it's an inconvenience for all you political jocks, but the world is obviously way beyond considerations of convenience, isn't it?"

Phil glanced at Olsen. "Well, that's just the thing, Mike," the senator said. "We're not so sure your vigil is such an inconvenience after all."

Mike gave him a blank stare.

"In fact, after a careful analysis, we've concluded that it just might be the only thing that has any chance of shifting the balance in this game."

"You mean forcing the president to come clean."

Phil grinned. He took Mike's arm and directed him away from the security lines. "Not exactly. Can I count on your complete confidence?"

Olsen walked beside them.

"It depends."

"That's not good enough," Phil said. "This is beyond any one man now; surely you understand that. The decisions made in the next few days will determine the fate of hundreds of millions."

"Then you're talking about changing the president's mind."

Bingo.

"We're running out of time."

"And the public doesn't have a clue what's really going on," Mike said. "That's the whole point of this vigil, isn't it? The public's right to know. And how do you suggest we change what we don't know?"

"I'll tell you what the president's planning," Phil said. "But I need your complete confidence; I'm sure you understand that."

"Fine. If I think you're shooting straight with me, you'll have my confidence. But don't think I won't tell the people what they deserve to know. I won't betray their trust."

"I'm not talking of betraying the people. I'm talking about serving them. You may have more power than anyone else in the country now. We need you to use that power."

Mike stopped. "Spare me the political pap."

"Then I guess I'll just have to trust you, Mike. I hope I'm not making a mistake."

The CNN anchor just looked at him. He was the perfect man, Phil thought. He really believed in this nonsense of his.

"The president is planning to start a nuclear war. He's convinced that France won't deliver the antivirus as promised, and he's decided as a matter of principle to go down in flames. If he doesn't comply with the demands we've received, this country will cease to exist."

"But you don't think he's right."

"No, we don't. Most of his inner circle is against him. We have intelligence that leads us to believe the French will come through with the antivirus in time. Under no circumstance can we allow the president to pull his trigger."

Mike Orear looked at the White House. "So the president doesn't trust the French. And you do."

"Essentially, yes."

"And if you're wrong?"

Dwight Olsen stepped in. "If the president starts a war, we don't have a chance of finding the antivirus, plain and simple. If he doesn't, we have a chance."

"I take it our scientists aren't as close to creating an antivirus as we've been led to believe."

"No."

"You sick . . ." The muscles on Mike's jawline flexed with frustration. "So this vigil of ours is nothing more than our own funeral procession."

"Not necessarily," Phil said, wiping a bead of sweat from his temple. "By tomorrow you'll have over a million people involved. An army. With the right encouragement, this army might be able to change the president's mind."

"The vigil is fine, Mike," Olsen said. "But we're running out of time. Leak the word that a nuclear war might be imminent. We need the president to understand that the people don't want war. And we need the French to see our good faith. It's a last-ditch effort, but it's the only one we've got."

"You want me to start a riot."

"Not necessarily. A riot sends mixed signals of chaos."

"What do you expect these people to do? March on the White House?"

Phil caught Olsen's quick glance. "I'm open to suggestions. But we're going to die here." He let frustration flood his voice, all of it genuine. "This isn't some massive game show you're putting on for the people! You either do what we need you to do, or you don't. But I want to know which it will be. Now."

Mike frowned. He glanced back at the security lines and the peaceful, candlelit demonstration of the "army" beyond. A man in a white robe was performing an ungainly dance, whether motivated by religion or drugs, Phil couldn't tell. A shirtless child leaned against the railing, staring across the lawn at them. He would be leaving this mess in two days; that was the agreement. In time to reach France and take the antivirus before it was too late.

"Okay," Mike said. "I'm in."

⁕

They lay side by side in Bancroft's dim laboratory, ready to sleep and dream. Above them, thirty armed guards the president had called in from the special forces formed a perimeter around the stone building on Johns Hopkins's otherwise vacated campus. The good doctor had been home when they reached him, but he'd scrambled back to his lab to perform yet one more incredible experiment on his willing subjects. His only real purpose here was to put them to sleep in tandem, but he insisted on hooking up the electrodes to their heads and laying them out like two Frankensteins in his dungeon of discovery.

On the chopper ride, Thomas had spent fifteen minutes on a secure line with the president, laying out his plan with the Israelis. Blair had quickly agreed to the bold steps he'd outlined. Their greatest challenge was to plan and execute the operation without the French catching any scent of it. Problem was, they didn't know who the French were working with. They might never. The president was more reluctant to agree to no joint chiefs, no FBI, no CIA, no regular military mechanism.

The communication with the Israelis would be handled by Merton Gains, in person. He was the only one Thomas was sure they could trust.

"So then," Dr. Bancroft said, approaching with a syringe in hand. "Are we ready to dream?"

Thomas glanced at Kara. His sister's hand was bound to his own with gauze and tape. The good doctor had made small incisions at the bases of their thumbs and done the honors.

"Three miles to the east, exactly as I showed you." Thomas said. "You have to get there tonight if possible."

She blew out some air. "I'll try, Thomas. Believe me, I'll try."

21

MIKIL WOKE with a start and stared into black space. It was only the second time Kara had crossed over, but because of her past dealings with Thomas's dreams, she knew immediately what was happening.

She was Mikil. For all practical purposes, she was also Kara. Either way, Johan and Jamous were asleep beside her.

Mikil jumped to her feet. "Wake up!"

They jumped. Both of them grabbed at their hips, rolled, scrambled, and came up in a crouch, Johan gripping a knife and Jamous holding a rock. Thirteen months of nonviolence hadn't tempered their instincts for defense.

"What is it?" Johan demanded, blinking away his sleep.

"I'm dreaming," Mikil said. "Break camp. We have to go."

Jamous scanned the forest around them. "Scabs?" he whispered.

"You're not dreaming," Johan stated. "You're awake. Go back to sleep and dream some more. You gave me a heart attack!"

"No, Kara is dreaming!" She scooped up her roll and bound it quickly.

They'd secured a new camp for the tribe, and after more discussion than she would have thought reasonable given the urgency of Thomas's predicament, they'd agreed as a council to send three of their most qualified warriors on a surveillance mission that could be turned into a rescue attempt if the situation warranted.

Five nights had passed since the Horde had taken their comrades. Five nights! And with each passing night, her certainty that Thomas was dead increased. Times like these tempted her to consider embracing William's doctrine to either take up the sword or flee deep into the desert. Even

Justin had swung his sword and fought the Horde once. He'd been Elyon then as well, right? So then Elyon had once used the sword. Why not again now, to rescue the man who would lead his Circle?

She threw the bedroll on her horse, hooked it into place, and spun back to the two men who were staring at her in dumb silence. "Now. We have to leave now! Are you hearing me? Thomas is alive, and he's just told Kara how to get to him. He's in the basement of the library three miles east of the Horde city. The others are scheduled to be executed tomorrow."

"Thomas told you all of this?" Jamous asked.

"We don't have time!" Mikil swung onto her horse. "I'll explain on the way." She kicked her mount and headed north through a large field, ignoring Jamous's call demanding she hold up.

They would catch her soon enough. The sun would rise in less than three hours, and she had no desire to approach the city in broad daylight.

Johan caught her first, pounding down from behind on his large black steed. "Be reasonable, Mikil! Slow! At least slow enough for us to come to grips with this."

They came to the forest's edge and Johan eased to a trot beside her. "This library where he's kept," Johan said. "He told you how to break him out?"

She ducked to avoid a low branch. The trees were sparse here, but to the east the forest would slow them. She urged her horse forward.

"He gave me some ideas and told me that you would know what to do with them. You lived with the Horde long enough to understand them better than most."

Johan didn't respond.

"And he told me some other things about you, Johan." She glanced at him in the dim light. "We need you to dream as well. Evidently you're connected to a man named Carlos who needs to see the light."

"It's enough for now to talk about freeing Thomas based on a dream," he said. "How much of the healing fruit do we have?"

"Two each," Jamous said. "You're expecting a fight?"

"Do you think Thomas would forgive us if we healed a few of them after putting them down?"

Mikil looked at Johan. "Wounding a Scab and then healing them? I don't know." As long as they didn't kill . . . "Why not? That's your recommendation?"

"How can I recommend anything without knowing what Thomas told you in this dream of yours?"

"He told me precisely where he was being kept. He gave me the lay of the land, and he said that there was a woman who had unfettered access to him. He suggested I impersonate that woman."

"And which woman is this?"

"Chelise, the daughter of Qurong."

They both looked at her as if she'd gone mad.

"How much time do we have?" Mikil demanded.

"Turn around; let me see you by the moonlight," Johan ordered.

She obliged him. "How much?"

"Less than an hour," Jamous said.

"Then this will have to do!" Mikil looked at the compound's wall, just fifty yards to their right.

Jamous spit to one side. "It'll never work."

"Then give us a better idea," Mikil said. "How do I look?"

Donning the Scabs' traditional robes wasn't unusual—they often wore the cloaks when they ventured deep into the forest. But Mikil had never applied this white clay to her face and hands. Thomas had suggested she become a Scab princess for the night, and Johan had insisted on a heavy layer of the closest substitute for morst that he could find. White clay.

"Like the princess herself," Johan said.

"Except in the eyes and the voice."

"Every disguise has its limitations. Just do exactly like I said."

Jamous was right; the plan was madness. The only thing worse would be to try it in daylight.

"Remember," Mikil said, "the library is in the center of the garden. He said four guards, two outside and then two in the basement."

"We have it," Johan assured her. "Give us five minutes before you draw them out. And you should raise the pitch of your voice slightly. Chelise is as . . . direct as you. Don't try to sound too soft. Walk straight and—"

"Keep my head up, I know. You don't think I know what a snotty princess looks like."

"I wouldn't say she's snotty. Bold. Refined."

"Please. The words 'Scab' and 'refined' aren't possibly reconcilable."

"Just keep your wits about you," Jamous said. "They may not be refined, but they can swing their blades well enough."

If Mikil died, Kara would die in Dr. Bancroft's laboratory as well, Thomas had said. Strange. But Mikil was used to danger.

"Go."

Jamous hesitated, then clasped Mikil's arms to form the customary circle. "Elyon's strength."

"Elyon's strength."

The men vanished into the night. Mikil ran to the tall pole fence and scaled the tree they'd selected. The royal garden, Thomas had called it. The moon was half full—she could just see the outline of shrubs and bushes placed carefully around fruit trees. The large spired building a hundred yards into the complex was clearer. The library.

No sign of a guard on this side of the garden. Mikil grabbed the sharp cones on two adjacent poles, slung both legs over the fence, and dropped to the ground ten feet below. Her robe was black—if she walked with white face down, she would be invisible enough. She hurried through the garden, surprised by the care that the Horde had put into trimming the hedges and shrubs. Flowers blossomed on all sides. Even the fruit trees had been properly pruned.

She pulled behind a large nanka tree thirty yards from the library's front door, where two guards slouched against the wall. Strange how she felt no anger toward them since her drowning. She couldn't say she felt any compassion for them, as some did, but she regarded her lack of fury mercy enough. The fact that she'd been complicit in condemning Justin only made her anger toward the deception that blinded them more acute.

She had not been surprised to realize that her anger was directed at the disease, not the Horde. She had no compassion for the disease. The difference between her and some of the others—William, for example—was that when she saw two diseased guards, she saw mostly the disease; William would have seen only the guards.

Mikil blinked away her thoughts. It was time for her to practice a little deception of her own. She had to assume that Johan and Jamous were in place.

She lowered her head and walked directly toward the wide path that led to the library. Twenty-five yards. Gravel materialized under her feet—surely they'd seen her by now. She took a deep breath, stood as tall as she gracefully could, lifted her chin as a princess might, and strode directly for the two guards.

The guard on the left suddenly stood and coughed. The other heard him, saw Mikil, and quickly straightened. They were speechless. *Not too many visitors this time of night, is that it, you sacks of scales?*

She stopped near the bottom of the steps. "Open the door," she commanded quietly.

"Who are you?" the one on the right asked.

"Don't be a fool. You can't recognize Qurong's daughter at night?"

He hesitated and glanced at his comrade. "Why are you wearing—"

"Come here!" Mikil jabbed her finger at the ground. "Get down here, both of you! How dare you question my choice of clothing? I want you to see my face up close so that you never again question who it is that commands you! Move!"

She wasn't sure she sounded like a princess, but the guards descended the stairs cautiously.

"I intend to let this indiscretion go, but if you move like mud, I may change my mind."

They hurried forward.

Two shadows flew from each corner of the building, and Mikil raised her voice to cover any sound they might make.

"Now the fact of the matter is that I'm not Qurong's daughter, but know that I'm here on her behalf. She's told me where to find the albino so that I can rescue him. She's in love with our dear Thomas, you see."

The guards stopped on the bottom step just as Johan and Jamous sailed onto the steps behind and clubbed them each at the base of their necks. They grunted and fell in tandem.

They dragged the guards from the stairs and lay them in the grass. "Any damage?" Mikil asked.

"They'll survive."

Thomas would object, but he would eventually see reason. And though these two might jeopardize the rescue, they would live anyway. That was a kind of nonviolence in itself. The bit about the princess's love for Thomas was absurd—something to give them a laugh later. If Mikil was lucky, it might even land the dear princess in a spot of trouble.

"Let's go."

Johan and Jamous entered the library quietly with Mikil right behind. The door to the stairwell was precisely where Thomas had told her it would be.

"This one. I'll call them up." She waited for Jamous and Johan to stand in the shadows on either side of the door, then cracked it open. Torchlight glowed from below.

She nodded at Jamous, threw the door open, and took a step down. "Who's awake down here? I need the help of two guards immediately!"

Her voice echoed back at her. There might have been a sound, but she wasn't sure.

"Are you asleep? I don't have all night! The Books have been found, and Woref demands your assistance immediately!"

Now the sound of clad feet slapped the flat stones below. She spun around just as two guards came into view, both wielding torches.

"Hurry, hurry!" She walked into the foyer as their boots clumped up the steps.

These two were taken by Jamous and Johan with even less incident than the ones outside. It had been too easy. Then again, the right intelligence was often the key to victory in any battle.

Mikil fumbled at one guard's belt for keys, found them, snatched a torch from Jamous, and descended the stairs as quickly as her long robe would allow. A corridor carved from stone led to a door on the left.

"Thomas?"

"Here! Mikil? The door, quickly!"

She inserted the key and unlocked the door. It swung in and her torch illuminated Thomas, standing in a long black robe nearly identical to hers. He saw her face and froze. She had expected him to bound past her and take immediate charge. Instead he seemed oddly stunned by her.

"Relax. Contrary to my ghostly appearance, I'm not an apparition."

"Mikil?"

"This isn't what you expected? Don't tell me, my beauty stuns you?" She smiled.

He seemed to shake himself free. He ran to her and grasped her arms. "Thank Elyon. The others?"

"I have Jamous and Johan. We haven't gone for the others yet."

Thomas sprang for the stairs. "Then we have to hurry!"

She had to warn him. "We had to use a little force, Thomas."

He barged into the foyer and pulled up. Two bodies lay in a heap. He looked from them to Johan, then to Mikil who stepped around him.

"Just a bump, Thomas. If you want, we could feed them some fruit," Mikil said.

Thomas ran to the door and glanced up at the sky. A faint glow was teasing the eastern horizon.

"No time."

22

THOMAS RAN behind them with the dread knowledge that they would be too late. There was no way four albinos could go unnoticed once the city began to wake.

"Speed, not stealth," he said, passing Mikil. "We don't have time to slip in. We ride hard and we snatch them fast."

"And let them hang eight instead of four today?" Johan said. "We have to think this through."

"I've done nothing but think it through," Thomas said. "There's no other way in the time we have."

"And you intend to do this without force?"

"We'll do what we have to."

They catapulted themselves over the fence and mounted the horses. Thomas rode in tandem with Johan, but they would need five more mounts if they hoped to outrun the Horde.

Thomas led them to the stables, where they collected the horses.

"Saddles?" Mikil whispered.

"Bridles only. We can ride bareback."

It had taken them fifteen minutes, and the sky was gray. They were too late! Riding farther into the city now would be suicide.

And leaving was as good as condemning the others to death.

Thomas swung onto one of the horses and grunted with frustration. So close. The palace rose to their left. Chelise slept there. Something about this escape felt more like an execution to him. Nothing seemed right. They would either be caught and executed as Johan suggested, or they would escape only to meet another terrible fate.

"What is it?" Johan demanded.

"Nothing."

"This isn't 'nothing' on your face! What do you know that we don't?"

"Nothing! I know that you might be right about being caught. I only need one with me. Mikil and Jamous, meet us at the waterfalls in thirty minutes."

"I didn't come to run," Mikil said. "And I have the disguise."

"You're married." He kicked his horse.

"The waterfalls," Johan said. "Hurry."

"Then take this. I don't need it."

Mikil stripped off the robe and tossed it to Johan.

Thomas and Johan rode with two extra horses each, a fast trot, directly for the lake now just half a mile ahead of them. Johan pulled the robe on as he rode.

"She's right about one thing," Johan said. "Anyone who sees our faces will know we are albinos."

"Then our only hope is to hit them before they have a chance to think any albinos would be mad enough to crash through their city. Do you have a knife?"

"You're planning on using it?"

Was he? "Planning, no. I have no plan."

"That's unlike you."

They rode on, straight toward the dungeons now. Their horses' hooves were muted by the soft, muddy earth. Wood smoke drifted through the morning air from a fire in one of the huts to their left. A rooster crowed. The castle still stood in silence, now behind them.

"Mikil tells me that you need me to dream with you," Johan said quietly. "Something about a Carlos."

He'd nearly forgotten.

"Is that a reason to live?"

"Maybe."

Of course it was. But he didn't have the patience to think through this dreaming at the moment. Here, surrounded by the Horde city, something was gnawing at his mind, making him uneasy, and he couldn't understand what it was.

You don't want to be freed, Thomas.

No, that wasn't it. He would do anything in his power to be freed from these animals. Even if it meant hurting a few of them.

A surge of hatred swept through him, and he shivered. What kind of beast would threaten to kill what Elyon had died to save?

Where is your love for them, Thomas?

"I can't pretend to know what's happened to you, Thomas, but you're not the same man I last saw."

"No? Perhaps living here among your old friends has made me mad."

Johan wouldn't dignify his cut.

"Forgive me," Thomas said. "I love you like a brother."

"I may use my weapon?" Johan asked.

"Use your conscience."

Johan nodded at a group of warriors stretching by what looked like a barracks directly ahead. "I doubt my conscience will help against them."

Thomas hadn't seen them. Several watched them curiously. Even with hoods pulled low, the Scabs would know the truth soon enough. Their faces, their eyes, their scent. They were albino, and there was no way to hide it.

"You have the fruit?"

"Two pieces."

"When I go, ride hard."

"That's your plan?"

"That's my plan." One of the Scabs was suddenly walking toward the road as if to cut them off. "Ride, brother. Ride."

He kicked his horse hard. "Hiyaa!"

The steed bolted. Both horses in tow snorted at the sudden yank on their bits. They galloped straight toward the startled Scab, who scurried out of the way.

Thomas and Johan were past the barracks and at full speed before the first voice cried out. "Thieves! Horse thieves!"

Better than albinos. Thomas forced his horse off the street onto the lakeshore and pointed it straight for the dungeons.

There were two guards on duty at the entrance. By their expressions Thomas guessed that neither had ever defended the establishment against a prison break. The guard on the left had his sword only halfway out of its scabbard when Thomas dropped from his horse and shoved it back in.

He swung his elbow into the man's temple with enough force to drop him where he stood.

The second guard had time to withdraw his sword and draw it back before Thomas could take him out with a swift boot heel to his chin. Like old times, quick and brutal.

He snatched the keys from the first guard's belt. "I need thirty seconds!"

"I'm not sure we have thirty seconds," Johan said.

A group of unmounted warriors were lumbering up the path. They'd been caught on foot, but they realized now that stealing horses wasn't the intent of the two riders who'd blown past them.

"Do what you have to," Thomas said. Then he plunged down the steps, three at a time. There was still something wrong gnawing at his gut, but he felt new clarity. They should take a torch to the whole city.

He sprinted down the narrow corridor. "William!" He'd forgotten to grab one of the torches from the wall, and now he was paying for his haste. There were rumors that some of the Horde still kept some of their earliest prisoners alive somewhere in this dungeon, but Thomas wouldn't have the time to look for them.

He called into the dark. "William! Which one?"

"Thomas?"

Farther down. He ran past a row of cells and slammed into the bars of the sixth one. William and Suzan stood, dazed. Cain and Stephen were pushing themselves up on either side.

"We have two dozen Scabs closing in," he panted. He shoved the key into the lock and turned hard. The latch released with a loud clank.

"Are there others?"

"Probably."

"Run! Horses are waiting."

Thomas ran without a backward glance. They would help each other. He felt a surprising compulsion to engage the Scabs who bore down on Johan. A year ago, two of them could have taken on two dozen and at least held them at bay. He could taste the longing to tear into them like copper on his tongue. Blood lust.

Thomas took the stairs in long strides, lungs burning from his burst of activity. The voices of yelling Scabs reached him when he was only halfway up.

"Hold them!"

A voice cried out in pain. Johan?

Thomas tore from the dungeon into the light and slid to a stop.

The sight stalled his heart. Twenty sword-wielding Scabs had formed a semicircle around the entrance. Johan stood with his hood pulled back, bleeding badly from a deep wound on his right arm. The Horde was momentarily stunned by the sight of their old general, Martyn, staring them down.

The scene brought back images of a day thirteen months earlier. They had been gathered around Justin then, but in Thomas's eyes this scene was hardly different. They had killing in mind.

Something snapped on his horizon. Red. He scooped up the fallen sword from the second guard he'd knocked out earlier and swung it in a circle over his head. "Back!" He threw back his hood. "You don't recognize Thomas of Hunter? Back!"

The ferocity in his voice unnerved even him. He clung to the grip with trembling hands, desperate to tear into the Scabs. Johan was staring at him. The Horde was staring at him. He had a familiar power at hand, and he suddenly knew that he would use it.

Here and now, he would swing a blade in anger for the first time in thirteen months. What did it matter? They were all dead anyway.

The Scabs held their swords out cautiously. But they didn't back up as he'd ordered.

William and the others spilled from the dungeon behind him.

"Are you deaf?" Thomas cried. "Take up the other sword, Johan."

Johan didn't move. "Thomas—"

"Pick up the sword!"

You've lost yourself, Thomas.

He rushed the Scabs, screaming. His blade flashed. Struck flesh. Sliced.

Then it was free and he was leaning into his second swing. The sword cut cleanly through one of their arms. Blood flooded the warrior's sleeve.

The attack had been so quick, so forceful, that none of the rest had time to react. They were guards, not warriors. They knew Thomas only by the countless stories of his incalculable strength and bravery.

Thomas stood panting, sword ready to take off the first head that flinched. These animals who wallowed in their sickness deserved nothing less than death. These disease-ridden Shataiki had refused the love of Justin.

They were to blame for Chelise's deception.

Thomas felt his chest tighten with a terrible anguish. He clenched his eyes and screamed, full-throated, at the sky. A wail joined him—the second man he'd cut was on his knees clutching his arm.

Thomas spun to Johan. "The fruit."

Johan reached into his pocket and pulled out a fruit that resembled a peach. "Use this," he said to the Scab, tossing the fruit.

Immediately the Scabs stepped back in fear, leaving the wounded man with the fruit by his right knee.

Thomas dropped his sword and lunched forward. "For Elyon's sake, it's not sorcery, man!" He grabbed up the fruit and squeezed it so the juice ran between his fingers. "It's his gift!"

He grabbed the man's sleeve and yanked hard. The seam ripped at the shoulder and the long sleeve tore free, baring a scaly arm, severed below the elbow. The bone and the muscle were cut.

The Scab began to whimper in fear.

Thomas reached for the arm, but the man slapped him away.

His earlier rage welled up again. He slapped the man on the cheek. "Don't be a fool!" He knew that he was doing this all wrong, that everything about this escape had gone very wrong. But he was committed now.

Thomas gripped the man's arm with one hand and squeezed the fruit over his wound. Juice splashed into the cut.

Sizzled.

A thin tendril of smoke rose from the parted flesh. The healing was working.

Thomas stood and tossed the fruit at the first man he'd cut. "Use it!"

He turned his back on the Horde. The others were staring at him with something like shock or wonder; he wasn't sure which. He marched to his horse and swung up. "Ride."

He was sure the Horde would rush them, but they didn't. They were staring in horror at the man he'd given the fruit to. His arm was now half healed and hissing still. William broke toward a horse. Suzan, Cain, and Stephen rolled onto three others.

"If you think Qurong's power is something to fear or love, then remember what you've seen here today," Thomas said. "This time I give you fruit to heal your wounds. If you pursue us, you may not be so fortunate."

With that he whirled his horse around and galloped toward the forest, stunned, confused, sickened.

What had he done?

23

"NOTHING," QURONG demanded.

"They run better than they fight," Woref said. He stood on the castle's flat roof with the supreme leader, staring south over the trees. But Woref wasn't seeing trees. He wasn't even staring south. His eyes were turned inward and he was seeing the black beast that had steadily dug its way into his belly over the last few days.

He had known this beast called hatred, but never quite so intimately. He suspected it had something to do with his encounter with Teeleh, but he'd given up trying to understand the meeting. In fact, he was half-convinced the whole thing had happened in his dreams. There wasn't a real monster crawling around his innards, but the knot in his chest and the heat that flashed through his veins were no less real. He was now desperate for Chelise for his own reasons, and they had nothing to do with any nightmare of Teeleh.

He would possess her at all cost, to her or to himself. If he couldn't possess the daughter's love, how could he possess the kingdom?

"That doesn't answer my question," Qurong said. "Do we have a sighting of them or not?"

"No."

The supreme leader rested his hands on the rail that ran along the roof. He stood very still, dressed in a black robe, the withdrawn hood showing his thick dreadlocks.

"You executed the guards as I instructed?"

"Yes."

"The one who was healed by their sorcery?"

"He died quickly enough. A second guard tried to use the fruit, but it didn't work."

"And this is important why?" Qurong asked. He turned and looked Woref in the eye. "I'm interested in the albinos, not a few guards you failed to place properly."

They'd already covered Woref's responsibility in this catastrophe. The fact that Qurong would bring it up again, not two hours later, showed his weakness.

"I have accepted full responsibility. While you steam, they run."

Qurong grunted and looked back to the forest, perhaps surprised at his boldness. Woref kept his eyes to the south. When the time came for him to take his place as supreme ruler, he would burn this forest to the ground and start over. Nothing here attracted him any longer.

He swallowed bile. Other than Chelise, of course. And in some ways he craved the mother as much as the daughter. If he didn't one day kill Patricia, he would marry her as well. But it was the prospect of possessing them, not their pretty faces, that brought the knot to his gut.

He shivered.

"I'm not sure you realize what has happened here," Qurong said. "Two days ago I paraded Thomas through the streets to celebrate my victory over his insurrection. Today he makes a fool of me by escaping. If you think that you will survive Thomas, you are mistaken."

"You give him too much credit," Woref said.

"It took you thirteen months to bring him in, and now he's slipped out of your clutches again!"

"Has he? Know your enemy, we say. I think I'm beginning to understand this enemy."

"Yes. I understand that he outwits you at every turn."

"And what if I were to tell you that I knew his weakness?"

Qurong crossed his arms and turned away from the forest view. "He's an albino! We know his weakness! And it hasn't helped us."

"What price are you willing to pay to bring him back?" Woref asked.

"I'm willing to let you live!"

"And what consequence to the person who aided the albino's escape?"

"Anything but a drowning would mock me," Qurong said.

"No grace whatsoever?"

"None."

"And will you be gracious to your daughter?"

"What does she have to do with this?" Qurong demanded.

"Everything!" Woref shouted. His face burned with heat. "She is everything to me, and you've fed her to that wolf!"

Qurong's eyes flashed with anger. "Remember yourself! Your duty to me as general supersedes any lust you have for my daughter. How dare you speak of her at a time like this!"

"He has escaped with her help," Woref said. He might have slapped the supreme leader. "Don't be a fool."

"She instructed the guards not to force the rhambutan fruit down his throat as I ordered."

"And this is helping him? You're blinded by jealousy of a warrior in chains."

"He's not in chains now. That's the point, isn't it? He's free because he dreamed and found a way to use his sorcery to guide Martyn in, exactly as Martyn once said Thomas of Hunter could. He dreamed because he didn't eat the fruit. Chelise is complicit, I tell you!"

"Mark my word, Woref, if even one guard suggests this is untrue, I'll drown you myself."

"We executed the guards an hour ago."

Qurong strode to the door that led below and jerked it open. "Bring Chelise to me at once!" He slammed the door. "Then I'll let you accuse her yourself. How dare you accuse my blood of favoring an albino?"

"You don't think I'm distressed? I haven't slept since I saw them—"

"Not another word!"

"I can prove myself."

Qurong was reacting as Woref himself might have had he not seen. The thought of anyone, much less one's royal flesh and blood, conspiring with their enemy was hardly manageable.

The door pushed open and Chelise stepped out. "I just heard that you allowed my teacher to escape!" she snapped, looking directly at Woref. "Is that true?"

"Did I?" he said. Woref felt his control growing thin. She insulted him by thinking he wouldn't know what happened under his command. "Or did you?"

She looked at Qurong. "You're going to let this man suggest that I helped the albinos escape?"

"It doesn't matter if I'm going to allow it. He's already done it."

"And you believe him? The albino wanted to dream so that he could better read the Books, which in part depend on dreaming. Naturally, I let him dream. Is this a crime?"

She knew! It was the only reason she would have for confessing this so quickly! She was trying to sound innocent, but the whore in her was showing clearly enough.

"You instructed the guards not to make him eat the fruit?" Qurong asked.

"Yes. He's my servant, and I thought it would assist him in his duties."

"And would those duties include holding your hand and whispering tenderly in your ear?" Woref demanded.

She seemed to pale, even with the morst on her face. "How dare you?"

"You deny it?" Qurong asked.

"Of course she'll deny it! But I know what I saw with my own eyes when I found them in the library, alone. If it had been anyone other than my own woman, I would have killed both of them."

Qurong was beyond himself. "Is this true, Chelise?"

"That I have fallen in love with an albino? How utterly preposterous! Thomas is a reasonable teacher who can read the Books of Histories, but it's no reason to call me a whore!" She looked at the supreme leader. "Father, I demand you withdraw your consent for me to marry this man immediately. I'll have nothing to do with him until he withdraws his slander and apologizes."

Woref's head swam in fury. He'd never been treated with such disdain.

Perhaps he'd misjudged this woman after all. She might be harder to break than he'd first imagined.

And this is why you are so desperate for her.

"Then you deny any favor for Thomas of Hunter," Qurong said.

"The fact that my father has to ask such a question makes me wonder who he's been listening to."

"A yes or no would do, child!"

"Of course I don't favor the albino."

For a long moment the roof was silent.

"Leave us," Qurong said.

Chelise glared at Woref and left.

"You said you can prove this connection between them?" Qurong demanded.

"Yes, my lord. I can."

"You've put yourself in a dangerous position, you do realize?"

"Dangerous only if I'm wrong. I'm not."

Qurong sighed. "Then tell me how."

"If I'm right, then I want your word that Chelise will be mine with no restrictions."

The leader lifted an eyebrow. "She will be yours when you marry. What else could you want?"

I want to teach her who her master is, Woref wanted to say. *I want to break a bone or two so that she never forgets who I am.*

Instead he bowed his head. "I want her hand in marriage without any further restrictions."

Qurong faced the railing and looked south again. "Agreed. Your plan?"

"We still have the albino we took captive two months ago in the deep dungeons. Set him free to find the albinos with a message that if Thomas doesn't turn himself in within three days' time, Qurong, supreme leader of the Horde, will drown his daughter, Chelise, for treason against the throne."

Qurong glanced at him, but only for a moment. "Thomas of Hunter would never be such a fool. Even if he was, I could never drown my own daughter."

"You won't have to. If I'm right, Thomas will return. That will be my proof."

"You're not thinking straight. He would never risk his life for a woman he hardly knows."

"Unless she has seduced him."

The supreme leader glared.

"Then test me," Woref said.

"And if he doesn't come?"

"Then you will sign her death over to me. I will take her as a wife and forgive her in my own way. If I betray my word, then you may kill me yourself."

Qurong looked thoughtful for the first time since Woref had made the suggestion. "So even if you're wrong, you end up with my daughter? What's at stake for you?"

"My honor! If I'm wrong, my honor will be restored by my marriage to Chelise. If I'm right, my honor will be restored by the death of Thomas."

"What if Thomas never receives the message?"

"We'll send one warrior with the albino to return with his answer. At the same time we will conduct the single largest hunt for the tribe that escaped us in the Southern Forest. The tribe is without Thomas and Martyn and other leaders and will be vulnerable."

"Unless Thomas returns to them."

"He won't. Not if I'm right."

Qurong mulled the plan over in his mind, but the lights were already flashing in his eyes.

"They were touching when you saw them in the library?"

Woref spit over the railing. "I saw them."

Qurong grunted. "She always was headstrong. We will keep this quiet. You have your agreement. I'm not sure whether to pray that you're right or that you're wrong. Either way you seem to win."

"I've lost already," Woref said. "I saw what no man should ever have to see."

⌘

The route they'd been forced to travel had slowed them through the day. Not so long ago, sight of the desert had always filled Thomas with an uneasiness. This was where battles were fought and men killed. This was where the enemy lived. Justin's drowning had reversed their roles, and the desert had become their home.

But as Thomas led the group of eight out of the forest along the lip of the same canyon where they'd once trapped and slaughtered forty thousand of the Horde, he felt the same underlying dread he'd once felt leaving the trees.

He stopped his horse by a catapult that had been torched by the Horde. This was the first time since the great battle of the Natalga Gap that he'd revisited the scene. Tufts of grass now grew on the ledge where black powder had blasted huge chunks of the cliff into the canyon below, crushing Scabs like ants.

Johan nudged his mount to the lip and gazed at the canyon floor. He hadn't led the Horde army that day, but their attack had been his plan.

Thomas eased up next to him. The rubble was still piled high. Birds and animals had long ago picked the dead clean where they could dislodge the battle armor. From this vantage point, the remains of the Horde army looked like a dumping ground for armory, scattered by strong winds and faded by the sun.

"Thank goodness the Horde hasn't figured out how to make black powder," Johan said.

"They've been trying. They know the ingredients, but besides me, only William and Mikil know the proportions. Give them a few more months—they'll stumble on it eventually."

The others had pulled close to the lip and were peering over. Thomas looked back at the forest, nearly a mile behind them now. It appeared dark in the sinking sun, an appropriate contrast to the red canyon lands that butted up against it. The black Horde holed up in their prison while the Circle roamed free in their sea of red.

But something deep in the black forest called to him. An image of Chelise drifted through his mind. Her white face and gray eyes, gazing longingly at the Books of Histories. He had only shrugged when the others questioned him about his prolonged silence during the flight from the Horde city—he wasn't sure why he felt so miserable himself. They were thinking he was sober over his use of force, and he had half-convinced himself that they were right.

Still, he knew it was more. He knew it was Chelise.

Thomas turned his horse from the canyon and walked it slowly along the rocky plateau. The others talked quietly, reminiscing, but another horse followed him—Mikil probably. Kara. They had work to do.

"So there's no doubting now, Kara," he said. "Which is more real to you? Here or there?"

"I wouldn't know." He turned. It was Suzan. She glanced at the forest.

"I thought you were Mikil."

"You're distracted. It's more than the escape, isn't it?"

"Why would you say that?"

"Because I was the one who suggested it in the first place. I think it worked."

"It was a good plan. Maybe I should give you command over one of our divisions." He grinned. But he knew she wasn't talking about the plan.

"I'm not talking about keeping us alive. I'm talking about winning the trust of Chelise."

"Yes, well, that was good too."

"I think maybe she won your trust as well."

He looked at Suzan in the waning light. Her darker skin was smooth and rich. He knew several who'd courted her without success. She was both cautious and wise. There was no fooling her. Suzan would make any man a stunning wife.

"Maybe," he said.

"I want you to know that I don't think it's a bad thing."

"Trust is one thing, Suzan," he said quietly, not entirely sure why he was telling her this. "Anything more smacks of sacrilege. I would never go there. You understand that, don't you?"

She waited for a moment. "Of course."

"Justin calls the Horde, and so we do as well. You could call it love. But an albino such as myself and a Horde woman . . ."

"Impossible."

"Disgusting."

"I don't know how you put up with the smell in the library for three days," she agreed.

"It was horrible."

"Horrible."

"Where are we camping?" Mikil asked, trotting up behind.

"In the canyon," Thomas said. "In one of the protected alcoves, away from the bodies. The Horde will steer clear of their dead."

"Then we should go. We have to bring Johan up to speed and get back."

—⁘—

No campfire. No warm clothes. No bedrolls other than the three brought by Mikil, Jamous, and Johan. Only sand.

Thomas shivered and tried to focus on the next task at hand. Johan.

They sat in a circle of eight, but the conversation was among the three who spoke of dreams. The others listened with a mixture of fascination and, he suspected, some incredulity. The fact that Mikil had known precisely where Thomas was kept them all from expressing their lingering reservation.

It was rather like the drowning—only the experience itself could ultimately turn one into a believer.

Johan stood and paced the perimeter. "Let me summarize this for you, Mikil, so that you can hear just how . . . unique it is. You're saying that if I cut myself and Thomas cuts himself, and we fall asleep with our blood mixed, that I will share his dreams."

"Not his dreams," Mikil said. "His dream world."

"Whatever. His dream world, then. I will hopefully wake up as a man named Carlos because he's made some connection with me earlier, and he thinks he may be me."

"Something like that," Thomas said. "We're not saying we know how it works exactly. But you know that Kara and Mikil had the same experience. For all we know, all of us could have the same experience. For some reason, I am the link to another reality. Another dimension. I'm the only gateway that we know of. If I don't dream, no one dreams. Only life, skill, and knowledge are transferable. Which is what happened to the blank Book."

"It disappeared into your dream world because Mikil wrote in it," Johan said.

"Yes. And if I'm right, the rest of the blank Books went with it."

"You saw them there?"

"No, only the one that I can be sure of. It's a hunch."

Johan sighed.

"Please, Johan," Mikil said. "Our future may depend on you. You have to do this."

"I'm not saying I won't. If you insist, I'd let you use a pint of my blood. But that doesn't mean I have to believe."

"You will believe, trust me," Thomas said. "Now sit. There's more."

Johan glanced around at the others, then seated himself.

They had to be careful what they told Johan about the situation in Washington. He might accidentally plant knowledge in Carlos's mind. And they couldn't risk tipping their hand in the event Carlos refused to play along.

Thomas leaned forward. "When you wake as Carlos, you will be disoriented. Confused. Distracted by what's happening to you. But you have to pay attention and come back with as much information as you can about the virus, Svensson, Fortier—anything and everything to do with their plans. Above all, the antivirus. Remember that."

"Who are these people?"

Thomas waved a hand. "Forget that. The minute you're Carlos, you'll know who they are. But when you wake up back here, you may forget details you knew as Carlos. So concentrate on the antivirus. Are you clear?"

"The antivirus."

"And while you're there, see if he knows who has the blank Book of History. One of his guards took it. Clear?"

"The blank Book of History."

"Good. In addition, there are two primary pieces of information we need you to plant in Carlos's mind. Our objective is to turn him, but short of that we need him to believe two things."

"Okay. I think I can handle two things."

24

FOR A moment that stretched long into the next, Carlos lay in the attic. Far below was the basement from which Thomas (and Monique) had escaped only days ago, after telling Carlos that he was connected to another man beyond this world—the one who was bleeding from his neck. That was him, Johan.

Carlos touched his neck. Wet. He pulled his fingers back. Sweat, not blood.

Of course there's no blood, Johan thought. That was thirteen months ago. But here in this world it was only a week ago. *I'm in the dream that Thomas told me about! Does Carlos realize that I'm here?* Johan sat up.

Carlos knew immediately that something had changed, but he couldn't define that change. He felt unnerved. He was sweating. A distant voice warned him of danger, but he couldn't hear the voice. Intuition.

Or was it more? His mother's whispers of mysticism had come alive to him these last few weeks. Thomas Hunter had found a way to tap the unseen. He'd lain dead on the cot for two days before apparently throwing off the sheet and climbing the stairs to the main level. True, a doctor hadn't confirmed his death, as Fortier had pointed out. There were stranger examples of near death. But Carlos dismissed the Frenchman's agnostic analysis. Hunter had been dead.

He looked around the room. And now he was here?

———∞———

No, Johan thought. *It's not Carlos; it's me. And although I know his thoughts, he doesn't necessarily know mine, at least not yet. Carlos isn't the one dreaming. I am. It's just like Thomas said it would be.*

Why Carlos? Because Carlos believed that there was a unique connection between them, although not enough belief to wake Carlos up to the fact that Johan was present, as in the case of Mikil and Kara.

And the man had a week-old cut on his neck to prove it. The same cut that Johan had received from Thomas thirteen months ago in the amphitheater when Justin had exposed him. Mind-bending. But real. As real as Thomas and Mikil had promised it would be.

He was in the histories at this very moment. How, he couldn't imagine—some kind of time warp or spatial distortion, whatever Mikil could possibly mean by that. More importantly, according to Thomas, he could affect history by depositing thoughts into Carlos's mind and by learning his intentions. Two things, Thomas had insisted. Convince him of these two things, learn what you can, and then get out.

———∞———

Carlos had a sense of déjà vu. Something familiar resided in his mind, but he couldn't shake it loose to examine it properly. He stood and walked to the dresser. He mopped his face with a handkerchief. His breathing felt ragged and his face hot.

This is how you will feel when Fortier slips poison in your drink after he's used you like an animal—sooner than you think.

The thought caught him off guard. Naturally, he had some reason to distrust Fortier. Hunter had suggested as much himself. The moment Carlos had the antivirus, he would take the necessary steps to protect himself. He'd already told Fortier that Hunter had claimed a coup would come on the heels of the virus. They couldn't possibly know that the coup would be orchestrated by Carlos himself. But he was powerless until he had the antivirus.

Now he was thinking that waiting so long might be a problem.

Why will Fortier let anyone even capable of a coup live long enough to conduct it? You have a day, maybe two; then he will snuff you out.

A chill flashed down his spine as the thought worked its way into his mind, not because this simple suggestion was new or even surprising, but because he suddenly knew it was true. Fortier might even do away with Svensson. His grip on this newfound power would last only as long as opportunity to strike back eluded his many new enemies. Fortier would isolate himself for protection. He would burn his bridges behind him.

It was all just a theory, of course, but Carlos was suddenly sure he'd stumbled onto something he could no longer ignore.

A day's stubble darkened his chin. He splashed cologne in his hands and patted his cheeks. A shower would have been part of his normal morning routine. This wasn't a desert camp in Syria.

Another thought occurred to him: he had to meet Fortier. Now. Immediately.

Exactly why, he wasn't so sure.

Yes, he was sure. He had to test the man. Feel him out without sounding obvious. Fortier was leaving for the city this morning.

Carlos stepped to the closet, pulled a beige silk shirt off the hanger, and slipped into it. He lifted the radio from his dresser.

"Perimeter check."

A slight pause. Static.

Then the guards in place around the compound started calling off their status. "One clear." "Two clear." "Three clear." "Four clear" . . . The check ended at eleven.

Satisfied, Carlos checked his reflection one last time in the mirror and exited the loft. Three flights to the basement. Down the long hall. He entered the security code, heard the bolts disengage, and stepped into the large secure room.

A conference table ringed by ten white chairs sat on rich green carpet. The monitors along the south wall were fed by a dozen antennas, only one of which was located on this building. Most were many miles away. Fortier had spared no expense in cloaking the compound's signature. It no longer mattered—the facility was already compromised by Monique and now Thomas. This was Fortier's last visit.

No sign of the Frenchman.

An intercom behind Carlos came to life. "Carlos, please join me in the map room."

He knew. He always knew.

And he might even take care of you now.

Carlos shrugged off the thought and walked to the third door on his left. Why did this Frenchman unnerve him so easily? He was simply one man, and he possessed half the killing skills Carlos did.

Which guard took the Book?

What on earth was that? What book? Had a guard taken the log book—if so, he couldn't remember being told about it.

He shook his head and stepped into the room, closing the door behind him. There were three others in the room besides Fortier. Military strategists. As Carlos understood it, they would all be gone today.

Fortier turned from a wall of maps that showed the exact location of each nuclear power's arsenal, inbound to France. Several had already off-loaded—the Chinese and the Russians were nearly intact on French soil now. The British and the Israelis had followed the United States' lead by offering their arsenals in exchange for the antivirus. There was to be a massive showdown on the Atlantic off France's coast. But the terms of the exchange only ensured that Fortier would get what he wanted.

The weapons.

"Please leave us," Fortier said to the others.

They glanced at Carlos and left the room without comment.

"Carlos," Fortier said, wearing a slight grin. He clasped his hands behind his back and faced the maps. "So close, yet so far."

"I would say you have them in a corner, sir," Carlos said.

"Perhaps. Have you ever known the Israelis to allow themselves into a corner?"

From the beginning, the destruction of Israel had been Carlos's primary concern. Fortier looked back.

"I don't think they are allowing anything, sir. They are being forced. And in a week it won't matter."

"Because in a week we will wipe them out, regardless of what happens in this exchange," Fortier said. "Is that what you mean?"

"Assuming that we take their weapons, yes."

"And what if we don't take their weapons? What if they're bluffing?"

"Then we call their bluff and destroy them anyway. We have the weapons to do that."

"We do. In fact, as of this moment we have the largest land-based arsenal in the world. Most of the United States' arsenal is on the ocean. But from a purely military perspective, our position is still weak."

"You're forgetting the antivirus."

"I'm setting the antivirus aside, and I'm saying that without it our position is strong, but not strong enough. The United States' submarine fleet alone could still do substantial damage. We're still setting up the tactical missiles from China. Russia has 160 intercontinental missiles under my command pointed at North America and their allies. On balance we are in the perfect position to finish the match in precisely the fashion we intended."

"But you have reservations," Carlos said.

Fortier paced and drew a deep breath. "I spent nine hours yesterday in conferences with the highest-level delegates for Russia, China, India, and Pakistan. They've all embraced our plans, eager to play their part in a changed world. There have been challenges, naturally, but in the end their response is better than I could have hoped for."

Something bothered Carlos about the man's tone. Sweat glistened on his forehead; he seemed more circumspect than normal. Perhaps even nervous.

"But I don't trust the Americans," Fortier said. "I don't trust the Israelis. I don't trust the Russians, and I don't trust the Chinese. In fact, I don't trust any of them. Do you?"

"I'm not sure you are required to trust them," Carlos said.

"Trust is always required. One hidden weapon could take out half of Paris."

"Then, no, I don't trust them."

"Good." Fortier lifted a large black book from the top of a file cabinet and slid it onto the table in front of Carlos. He'd never seen it.

"What is this?"

Fortier frowned. "This is the new plan," he said.

This could be good and this could be bad—Carlos wasn't yet sure which. He reached for the book.

"Page one only," Fortier said.

Carlos left the book on the table, lifted the cover, and turned the first page. A list of names ran down the page. His was the fourth down. Missirian, Carlos. The rest of the page contained at least another hundred names, listed as his own, surname first.

"I'm not sure I understand," he said, looking up.

"Our list of survivors. One hundred million in all, by family. We have no doubt as to their loyalties based on family ties and history, and we have precise plans on how to distribute the antivirus to them. The list took five years to compile. There will be some bad apples, of course, but we will deal with them easily enough once the rest are gone."

Carlos felt the blood drain from his face. Fortier had no intention of giving the anti-virus to any nation. Only these would survive.

"Whether your name remains on this list is entirely up to you, of course," the Frenchman said. "But my decision is final."

He wasn't sure what to say. Why was Fortier telling him this? Unless he intended to trust him after all. Or was he telling him to earn Carlos's loyalty so that he could ultimately eliminate him with ease?

"This isn't . . ." Carlos stopped. Pointing out the obvious would do him no favors. Fortier was going to wipe out most of Islam—it could hardly be Allah's will.

"You're concerned with Islam," Fortier said. "I assure you that the book contains the names of your most respected imams."

"And they agree with your plan?"

"They will be given that opportunity."

Yes, of course. "It's prudent. Bold. It solves everything."

Fortier studied him, then finally smiled. "I hoped you would see it that way."

"And the exchange?" Carlos asked.

"Still critical. We aren't out of the woods yet. There's always the possibility that they will find an antivirus in time. Once we have their weapons, their destruction is ensured."

Carlos paced to the end of the table. "You do realize how dangerous this list is. How many know?"

"Ten, including you. None of them have the antivirus yet."

A stray thought suddenly flashed through Carlos's mind. Svensson was key to the antivirus—he'd undoubtedly ensured his survival by manipulating the antivirus in a way only he knew. He'd claimed as much two weeks earlier, and Carlos didn't doubt him. If Svensson was killed, the antivirus would die with him. Though they already had stockpiles of the remedy, surely Svensson had developed a plan for this contingency as well.

Take Svensson.

That was the thought.

Until the antivirus was widely distributed, Svensson might be the more powerful of the pair. Controlling him meant controlling more than Carlos could imagine.

"You will remain here until after the exchange has been completed," Fortier continued. "We need full pressure to bear on the American president through these riots. It is now your highest priority. After the exchange I want this facility leveled."

"And the assassinations?"

"As planned, depending on how well they behave."

Armand Fortier watched the door close behind the man from Cyprus and wondered if he had made a mistake by showing him the list. But he needed the man's full cooperation these last few days, and there was no better way than engendering his complete trust. Killing him now, before they had control of the nuclear arsenals, was too risky. Who knew what self-protective measures Carlos had in place even now?

His cell phone vibrated in his pocket. He slipped it out and glanced at the number. A paging code.

Fortier walked to a red phone on the wall and began the tedious process of making an overseas call through secure channels. He'd talked to the man only once before, and the conversation had lasted less than ten seconds. The CIA director had proven invaluable and earned his life. Little did he know . . .

The call finally connected.

"Grant."

"Speak quickly."

Pause.

"I have reason to believe that my contact has been compromised."

Contact? Carlos.

"The man from Cyprus."

"Yes," the American said.

"You're certain?"

"No. But they're trying to reach him."

"How?"

"Through Hunter's dreams."

Dreams. The one unanticipated element in all of this. Fortier still wasn't sure he believed the nonsense. There were alternative explanations that, however unlikely themselves, made more sense than this mystical pap.

"Operations as normal," Fortier said.

"Yes sir."

"He must not learn that you suspect him."

"Understood."

"What time is it?"

"Almost six," Dr. Bancroft said. "PM."

They'd slept about three hours.

Kara sat up and glanced at their arms, which were still taped together. She looked at Thomas. "We did it."

"So far so good. We're alive and free."

"And Johan is dreaming."

"Hopefully."

Bancroft reached across Thomas and carefully unwound the tape from their arms. "Johan is dreaming," he said. "Tell me this is good news for us. Here, I mean."

"It's as good as it gets for now. What Carlos does is now up to him." Thomas swung his feet to the floor and took a moist antiseptic towelette from the doctor.

"Incredible," Kara said. "I mean, this is absolutely incredible!"

"It gets more real each time. Three or four times and you don't know which is really real."

"Honestly, if I didn't know better, I'd say that this is the dream," she said.

"It might be," Thomas replied.

"I've always wondered what it would be like to live in a dream," Dr. Bancroft said with a shallow smile.

"Until you understand that there are other realities beyond this one and actually experience one of them, this is as real as it gets, Doctor. My father used to say we fight not against the things of this world, but against . . . I can't place the exact quote, but it was spiritual. Trust me, Doctor, you're not living in a dream."

He rubbed an itch under his arm. Bancroft followed his fingers, then looked in his eyes.

"Just a rash," Thomas said. "Probably something I picked up in Indonesia."

He stood and walked toward the desk phone. "Do you mind stepping out for a moment, Doctor? I have a call to make."

Dr. Myles Bancroft left reluctantly, but he left. Thomas dialed the White House and waited while they patched him through. The president was sleeping, but he'd left instruction to wake him when Thomas called.

"Thomas. You dreamed?" His voice sounded worn.

"I dreamed, sir."

"And Johan?"

"If you don't mind, in person. The line may be clear, but—"

"Of course. The chopper's already there on standby."

Thomas nodded. "Things are moving forward?" Meaning was Gains on his way to Israel?

"Yes. But we're down to two days—"

"Excuse me, sir, but not on the phone."

"We may have another problem. The demonstrations are starting to look ugly."

"Bring in the army."

"I already have. It's not my safety that concerns me. It's public sentiment. If this goes badly, my hand may be forced."

"I need more time."

"And I need to find out what's happening—"

"As soon as I dream again, I'll know," Thomas said.

The president was silent. He was extending himself on Thomas's behalf. If his gamble to play the cards as Thomas had suggested failed, several billion people would lose their lives.

Then again, what choice did he really have?

"Get here as quickly as you can," the president said and hung up.

25

THOMAS WALKED in slow circles around Johan, mining his friend for information about Carlos. But this first experience had been so shocking that most of the information was pushed aside by the raw experience of living vicariously through another mind.

They'd been at it for half an hour. Apart from Johan's insistence that Carlos knew nothing about the blank Book and his repeated exclamations about how incredible the dream had been, they'd concluded nothing. With each passing minute Johan's memory was deteriorating.

"Yes, yes, I know," Thomas said. "Indescribable. But what I need to find out is whether Fortier intends to go through with the exchange, antivirus for weapons, as agreed."

"No."

"No? You said—"

"I mean yes," Johan said. "The exchange, yes, but the antivirus you receive won't be effective. I think. Does it make any sense?"

"Yes. You're sure?"

"Quite." Johan blinked. "So at this very moment you, this other Thomas, are sleeping in this palace called the White House? You are dreaming of yourself. But Carlos isn't dreaming about me. I'm real."

"And so am I." Thomas waved him off. "Don't try to figure it out. Tell me about Carlos's plans. Do you think he can be turned?"

"Maybe. He was responsive to my suggestions. Immediately, in fact. Especially if he were to come here as me, like you suggest. He's already given to mystical ideas. And there was something about a book of names. The Frenchman is planning something no one expects."

"He is? And you wait this long to tell me? What?"

"It just occurred to me. And I'm not sure what. Something with the people he plans to give the antivirus to. It's not what everyone thinks. Fewer."

"I knew it!" Thomas spit. "He's bluffing! That's it, isn't it?"

"I think so, yes. Svensson is the key. I don't know why, but Carlos was thinking of him."

"I don't remember Rachelle ever being this forgetful when she dreamed," Thomas said.

"My expertise is battle, not dreams."

"You're every bit as smart as she was. You're just distracted by your own enthusiasm. Like a kid who's lost his mind over a ride."

Johan smiled. "It was a wild ride! I never would have believed if I hadn't experienced it myself. I want to go back again."

"Just remember, now that you have no doubts about your connection to Carlos, his fate may very well be yours. We have to be very careful. If Carlos slips and shows his hand, they'll deal . . ."

The clopping of hooves on the rocks turned his attention. Four horses trotted around the corner. Cain and Stephen. An albino Thomas didn't recognize. And a Scab.

A Scab?

"We found them on top of the cliffs," Cain said, pulling his horse up. "Qurong sends them with a message."

Thomas immediately abandoned all thoughts of Johan and Carlos. The Scab was dressed in a warrior's leathers, but he carried no weapon.

"This is Simion," Cain said, referring to the albino. He dropped from his mount. "He was taken captive several months ago and has been held in the lower dungeons."

Thomas hurried to the thin man and helped him from his horse. He clasped the man's arms in a greeting. "Thank Elyon. We didn't know where to find you. Are there others?" He turned to Johan. "Some fruit and water, quickly."

Simion beamed. He was missing a tooth, and Thomas knew that a boot or a fist had probably taken it out. "Sit, sit." He helped the man sit. "Are there others?"

"Only me," Simion said softly.

Thomas looked at the Scab, who was glancing about furtively. "Help our guest off his horse and give him some fruit."

"Dismount," William ordered.

The Scab stepped down tentatively. "I am unarmed," he said. "My only purpose is to take your response back to my commander, Woref."

"And what is Woref's question?" Thomas asked.

The Scab looked at Simion, who stood unsteadily.

"Qurong has issued a decree," he said.

Mikil stepped in and offered the man her hand. He waved it off.

"Qurong has declared that unless Thomas of Hunter returns to his captivity within three days, he will drown his daughter, Chelise, for treason."

No one spoke. Thomas's mind spun. Chelise was no more guilty of treason than . . .

She'd allowed him to dream.

He faced Johan. "Would he drown his own daughter?"

"I can assure you that he will," the Scab insisted.

Johan frowned. "What matter of treason is this?"

"He wouldn't say," Simion said. "Only that Thomas of Hunter would know."

They looked at him. "She allowed me to dream," he said absently. "Surely no man, not even Qurong, would kill his own daughter for allowing a prisoner to dream."

"No," Johan said. "I agree; there must be more. This is Woref's doing."

"But why would they think such an absurd demand would be of any concern to us?" William demanded.

Immediately Thomas knew.

"Cain. Stephen. Keep our guests company," he ordered. He caught Suzan's stare. "I call a council."

"For what?" William demanded. "This is a simple matter."

"Then our meeting will be short. A woman's life is at stake. We won't dismiss the matter without proper consideration."

He turned his back on them and walked down the canyon, around a bend, and to a patch of bare sand shaded by the towering cliffs. Conflicting emotions collided in his chest.

He ran a hand through his hair and paced. He had no call to feel so concerned for this one woman. Chelise. A woman he hardly knew. A woman who had thumbed her nose at the tribes and was complicit in the hunt for them. Qurong's own daughter! The others would never understand.

"If I didn't know better," William said behind him, "I would say you had feelings for this woman."

Thomas faced them. They stood in a rough circle around him, Johan, William, Mikil, Jamous, and Suzan.

"My feelings for her are no different than Justin's feelings for you, William," he said. "She is his creation as much as you are."

William looked at a loss. "You're actually considering Qurong's demand?"

"What's the use of a council if we don't discuss our options?" Thomas shouted. "You've made a decision already—that isn't our way."

They stood in the echo of his voice.

"He's right," Suzan said. "A woman's life is at stake."

"A Scab's life."

"Suzan is right," Mikil said. "Although I tend to agree with William about the life of a Scab, we should hear Thomas out. We were all Scabs once."

She sat. The others followed. It was long ago decided that sitting was the preferred posture if any argument was likely to break out.

"Elyon, we ask for your mind," Mikil said in the traditional manner. "Let us see as you see."

"So be it," the rest agreed in unison.

William took a settling breath. "Forgive me for my impulsive response. I am impatient to return to the tribe. They are vulnerable without us." He took a deep breath. "You're right, Mikil. We were once Scabs ourselves. But risking Thomas's life for the daughter of Qurong, who will continue to live in defiance of Elyon, is not only unwise but may be immoral."

"Perhaps Thomas should explain himself first," Suzan said.

They looked at him expectantly. And what was he supposed to say? *I think I may have fallen in love with a Scab princess?* The suddenness of the thought shocked him. No. He should say nothing at all about love.

"I want it to be clear that I haven't fallen in love with a Scab princess." He cleared his throat. "But I will admit that she gained my trust while I was with her in the library."

"Trust?" Johan said. "I wouldn't trust any daughter of Qurong's."

"Then call it empathy," Thomas snapped back. "I can't explain how I feel, only that I do. She doesn't deserve her own deception."

"Yet it is hers," Mikil said. "We're all free to make a choice, and she's made hers."

"That doesn't mean she can't choose differently. She's a person, like any one of us!"

His statement rang too loudly for the small canyon.

"No, Thomas, she's not like any one of us," William said. "She's a Scab. I never would have believed I would hear these words coming from you. Your emotions are clouding your judgment. Get ahold of yourself, man!"

"And what about Justin's emotions?" Suzan asked. "Wasn't it his love that led to his own drowning?"

Several spoke at once, and their words were a jumbled mess to Thomas. Like his own feelings. He wasn't sure how he felt. Emotions weren't trustworthy; they all knew that. On the other hand, Suzan asked a good question. How would Justin see this?

He held up his hand for silence. They quieted. "If Ronin were here, we would defer to his judgment. I admit, the thought of this woman's death sickens me, but I will defer to the judgment of this council. I have no argument except for my own emotions, which I've expressed. William, explain your doctrine."

William dipped his head. "Thank you. I have three points that will guide us. One, as to Suzan's question about Justin's emotions, it is said that Elyon is lovesick over his bride. This we all know. We also know that we, the Circle, are his bride. He told us as much in the desert. The Horde is not his bride."

He glanced around, received no objection, and continued.

"Two, the disease, which can only be washed clean by the drowning, is an offense to Elyon. Some say that anything a Scab touches is unclean, though I wouldn't go so far. But a Scab is certainly unclean. To embrace such a wretched creature who has embraced filth is to embrace the filth itself."

"Justin embraced me when I was a Scab," Johan said.

"That was before the drowning was available. In fact, that is why he provided the drowning, so that we could cure the disease. You're saying it makes no difference if we're clean or not? He would never have gone to such lengths if it made no difference."

There was some logic to William's argument, but it didn't sit well with Thomas. He didn't trust himself to speak.

"He hates the disease," Suzan said, "but not the man or woman beneath it."

"Is that why the Book states that he will burn any branch that does not remain in him and bear fruit?" William demanded. "I am the vine, you are the branches, but see what happens to those branches that are fruitless."

That shut them up.

"And finally, if this is not enough, consider Elyon's anger toward those who refuse him. Would you trade yourself for Teeleh, Thomas? Or for a Shataiki? Are the Scabs less deceived than they are? I would say to give yourself to or for any Scab woman is no less offensive than embracing the Shataiki and would invoke Elyon's anger."

The argument was so offensive that none of them seemed able to engage it properly. Instead of finding any encouragement to do what he now knew must be done, Thomas felt his desperation deepen. He could feel his pulse in his ears.

"You all know that I disagree with William," Johan said. "At the last council I argued that we should embrace the Horde by becoming more like them. But this is different. The Circle needs you, Thomas. Your tribe needs you. Many more of the Horde will come to the Circle through your leadership than this one woman."

Thomas looked at the others. Mikil remained quiet, as did Jamous. Not even Suzan objected to Johan's statement.

"This is the council's decision?"

No one spoke.

He stood. "So be it."

Thomas walked from them, rounded the corner, and marched toward the waiting Scab.

"Thomas!" Mikil ran to catch up. "Thomas, please, she's a Scab, for heaven's sake," she whispered. "Let it go."

"I am letting it go!" he snapped.

He stopped in front of the Scab. "Go tell your general that Thomas of Hunter will no more agree to his ridiculous terms than he will drink his own blood." The least he could do for Chelise was to send a clear message to Qurong that he despised his daughter. "And tell Qurong that what he does with his daughter is his business. Now leave us."

The Scab hesitated, then mounted quickly, turned his horse around, and trotted up the canyon.

26

THEY LEFT the valley in single file and headed across the desert toward the Southern forest. Thomas's sullen mood had smothered the group. Mikil and Johan had tried to lighten his disposition with talk of the dreams, but he quickly reminded them that there was little hope of surviving in the dreams more than a week. He might be better off eating the rhambutan fruit every night for the rest of his life and forgetting the histories even existed. They finally left him to sulk on his own.

William led and Thomas brought up the rear, behind Suzan, who had consoled him with a kind smile. The horses plodded up the sandy dunes with no more than an occasional snort to clear dust from their nostrils.

With each step Thomas felt his heart sink deeper into his gut. Try as he might, he couldn't lift his own spirits. There was no reason to these emotions he battled. None at all. He told himself this much a hundred times over.

She's a Scab covered by disease, Thomas. Her breath smells like sulfur, and her mind is clouded by deception. She would more likely order your death than drown in a red pool.

Then why this inexorable attraction to her? Surely he didn't love her as a man loved a woman. How could he love any woman after losing Rachelle only thirteen months ago? How could any woman, much less this diseased whore, replace Rachelle?

The file was moving faster than he was, but rather than urging his mount to catch them, he slowed even more. Their decision to sentence Chelise to her death had separated them from him.

It's your shame that holds you back. Or is it protest?

Either way, falling behind seemed appropriate. They glanced back but let him have his space. He was soon a full dune behind them.

Only then, when he was out of their sight completely, did he begin to feel at ease. He let images of her fill his mind without regret.

Chelise staring up at him on the ladder, arms folded as he looked frantically through the Books of Histories.

Chelise repeating the words she'd written, wild-eyed with excitement.

Chelise crushed by her inability to put a full sentence together.

Take the disease from her skin and the deception from her mind and what kind of woman would she be? What prince would be worthy of this princess?

"Hello, Thomas."

He jerked up on his horse. But there was no one. He was next to a lone rock formation between two dunes, alone. No sight of the others. The sun was getting to his mind.

"Over here, my old friend."

Thomas twisted around to the sound of the voice. There, on a small rock behind him, stood a bat.

A white bat. A Roush.

"Michal?"

The animal's furry snout smiled wide. "One and the same."

"It's . . . it's really you? I haven't seen . . ." He trailed off.

"You haven't seen a Roush in a long time, yes, I know. That doesn't mean we're not here. I've been watching you. I must say, you've done well. Much better than I guessed publicly before all the others, though I hate to admit it."

Thomas spilled off his horse and ran toward the bat. He wanted to throw his arms around the creature's neck and tell Michal how good it was to see him. Instead he slid to a stop three paces from Michal and gawked like a schoolboy.

"It's . . . You're really here . . ." Thomas finally stammered.

"In the flesh. Although I would prefer that you keep our meeting to yourself."

Thomas sank to his knees, partially out of weakness, partially to match the shorter creature's height. "I'm sorry. I don't know what's happening to me."

"But I do."

Thomas took a deep breath. "Then tell me."

"She's come over you," Michal said.

Thomas stood. How much did Michal know? "Who?"

"Chelise. The princess."

"I empathize with her, if that's what you mean. She's doesn't deserve to die. We spent time together in the library, and she may be a Scab, but she's not what I expected any Scab to be. Surely Elyon can have mercy on even—"

"You call this empathy?" Michal asked. "I would call it love."

"No. No, it's not like that."

"Then perhaps it should be," Michal said.

Thomas stared at the Roush, dumbstruck. "What do you mean? She's a Scab."

"And so were you. But he doesn't see it that way."

"Justin?"

"Justin."

Thomas glanced up the dune at the trail left by the others. "But the doctrine . . ."

"Then you must have your doctrine wrong. Tell me what William said."

Why had Michal chosen this moment to reveal himself? Hope began to swell in Thomas's chest.

"The Circle is his bride. He's lovesick over the Circle."

"True enough, but he's wooing his bride even now," Michal said. "Believe me, if you were to see Justin now, he would be over there by those rocks, pacing with his hands in his hair, desperate to win the love of the Horde. They will be his bride as much as you."

Thomas looked at the rocks and imagined Justin pacing. His heart began to pound.

"What else did William say?" the Roush asked.

"That Elyon's anger toward those who refuse him must be appeased by the drowning before we can embrace them."

Michal frowned. "I would have guessed that after Justin's death you would understand him better. Elyon's anger is directed toward anything that hinders his love. Toward Teeleh and the Shataiki who would deceive and steal that love. Anything that hinders his bride's love, he detests."

"Not the Scab."

"I'm not saying that I understand it—Elyon is beyond my mind. But his love is boundless. Do you know that when you drown, he's made a covenant to forget your disease? He remembers only your love. Even when you stumble as William does now, Justin vows to forget and remembers only William's love, however imperfect it might be. To say that you humans have it made would be an understatement. I would set William straight, to be sure. Elyon is mostly thrilled. Yes, there is a price to pay. Yes, there is a drowning to be done, but he is thrilled with his bride and desperate to woo others into his Circle."

Thomas knew all of this; of course he did! But not quite in such blatant terms.

"If you were to glimpse Justin's love for Chelise, you would wither where you stand," Michal said with a small grin. "This is the Great Romance."

Thomas began to pace. This meant what? That he was right about Chelise being like any other woman, Scab or not? That he was right in wanting to save her? That any love he might feel for Chelise was no different from his love for Rachelle?

But how could he possibly love a Scab in the same way he'd loved Rachelle? No, Michal couldn't possibly mean that.

"Follow your heart, Thomas. Justin's showing you his own."

Justin's words to him returned. He lifted his head and stared out at the desert and let the truth flood his mind. This was beyond him. He did love Chelise. She might not love him, but he couldn't deny the simple fact that he loved her, more than he could remember loving anyone other than Rachelle.

"Thomas!"

He turned to the dune. Suzan stood on the crest looking down at him. She hadn't seen Justin earlier; did she see Michal now?

He spun. The Roush was gone!

"Thomas, the others are waiting," Suzan called.

He stood still, torn for a long moment. Then he knew what he would do. What he must do.

He ran to his horse and leaped onto its back. With a parting glance at Suzan, he whirled his mount around and galloped away from her, toward the forest.

"Thomas! Wait!"

He crested the first dune and plunged down the far side.

"Thomas, wait! I'm with you!"

Suzan was following. He pulled the horse to a stamping halt. She galloped up behind him.

"I'm going back for her."

"Then we're both going back for her," she said.

"I can't ask you to do that."

"You taught me to live for danger. And although no one knows it, I'm a sap for romance."

The dunes behind her were bare. The others would see their tracks and know what had happened. Hopefully they would keep their senses and continue to the tribe, where they were needed.

"Then we have to hurry." He spurred his horse. "We have to get to her before the messenger does."

"You're not going to turn yourself in?"

"I'm going to take her out of there."

They sprinted over the dune. "What if she refuses to go?"

"Then I'll have to persuade her, won't I?" he said with a wide grin.

———❦———

The tracks told the story plainly enough.

"The fool's gone back," William said.

"And Suzan with him," Mikil said.

Johan turned next to the dune. "He doesn't plan on turning himself in, or he wouldn't have allowed Suzan to follow. He's going after Chelise." It was beyond him, this obsession that Thomas had developed for Qurong's daughter. He'd known her as a spirited woman, beautiful among Scabs, but still a Scab, as diseased as any.

He'd argued that the Circle should relax its standards to make it easier for the Horde to turn, but he'd been thinking about the drowning, not love. Now he wondered if he had it backward. Perhaps they should remain rigid on the commitments required to enter the Circle but love the Horde regardless. In many ways what Thomas was doing now would test his own arguments. Would Thomas become a Scab, or would Chelise become an albino?

Or were their conditions irreconcilable?

"We have to stop them!" Mikil said.

"And how would you do that?" William asked. "Follow them all the way back into the dungeons?"

"We wait for them," Johan said. "Here."

"We can't leave the tribe alone so long."

"Then *I* will wait for them."

Mikil looked at her husband. "Jamous?"

"We wait with Johan." He turned to William. "Take Cain and Stephen with you."

William sighed. "I don't like it. The Circle is in trying times, and its leaders are risking their necks for a whore."

"You need some enlightenment, William," Johan snapped. "This is Thomas, the same man who saved your neck a dozen times."

William frowned and guided his mount around. "Then we'll see you at the tribe. Elyon's strength."

Johan nodded. "Elyon's strength."

27

"MORE!" THOMAS insisted. "I want to pass inspection at five paces."

"Then you'll have to grow scales," Suzan said. They'd stolen the morst paste and powder with some clothes after dark, from a house on the city's perimeter. Thomas had his shirt off and was caking the powder on. Suzan rubbed it onto his back. "It'll be dark and you'll have a veiled hood on. I really don't see the need to be so enthusiastic about this stuff."

"The smell!" He turned to her, wide-eyed, like a child. His passion for this mission was infectious. The others would think he'd flipped his lid if they saw the way he'd carried on throughout the day.

He hadn't flipped his lid. He was losing his heart. He might not admit it, but Suzan would recognize these signs with her eyes closed. Thomas of Hunter was going down a road that he had deliberately skirted since Rachelle's death. He was in the early stages of falling crazily in love. Watching him, Suzan felt a yearning for the same.

He was still doing his best to hide his emotions, or perhaps he wasn't really sure what to make of his emotions, but he couldn't help himself. He'd told her what had happened between him and Chelise at the library in far more detail than any man she knew ever would. He talked expressively, with grand arm movements, drawing irrational conclusions about the simplest exchanges.

"Her arms were folded, Suzan," he would say. "Imagine that!"

"I am imagining it. I'm not sure I get the significance."

"Folded! She knows very well that when she stands like that she's striking a seductive pose."

"Arms folded? I'm not sure—"

"It's not the arms. Forget the arms. It's everything about her. You'll see."

Now he was plastering morst on his face, talking of smell. "I want to smell Horde. I've done it before, right into Qurong's bedchamber while he was snoring like a dragon." He grabbed another handful and slapped it against his cheek. The white residue billowed about his head.

"This time it's into her chamber, and I have a feeling she'll be more sensitive than her father. The morst won't cover my albino scent if it's only on my face, now, will it?"

"If I didn't know you better, I'd say you want to become a Scab for more than sneaking into the castle. You're wanting to be like her!"

"Am I? Well, maybe there was a hint of truth to Johan's arguments. I'm becoming a Scab to rescue a Scab from being a Scab."

Suzan laughed. "One look at you and she'll know you're not a Scab. There's no hiding your true colors—that's where Johan's wrong."

He stood and turned in the moonlight. "Agreed. How do I look?"

"Like a Scab." This was a Thomas few had ever seen. To most he was the mighty warrior turned introspective philosopher. But here in the desert he was becoming Thomas the lover. Suzan grinned. She rather liked this hidden side of him.

Thomas leaped for the robe and pulled it over his head.

"Good?" he asked.

"Good. Definitely Scab."

"Well then. I think I'm ready. It'll take me an hour to reach the castle from here, and an hour back. Give me till daybreak. If I'm not back, use your better judgment." He climbed onto his horse.

He was riding into insanity to fetch a woman who, despite his misguided assumptions, did not love him. And Suzan was enabling him because she knew that once Thomas of Hunter put his mind to something, he always saw it through. That and the romance in her own spirit was cheering him on.

All fine and good, but what if he didn't come back? He'd drawn her along with his infectious passion, but what if it all went badly? If Thomas was dead by morning, she would share the blame.

"Be careful, Thomas. It'll be the lake, not the library, if you get caught

"I know." He gazed north, toward the city. "Am I doing the righ thing?"

"Do you love her?"

"Yes."

"Then go get her, Thomas of Hunter. We've said all there is to say."

He smiled and nodded. "Elyon's strength."

"Elyon's strength."

Thomas approached the city from the east, around the royal garden, down the less-traveled road that ran directly to the castle. A bright moon had risen overhead. If anyone spoke to him, he would respond with a dipped head. With any luck he wouldn't have to test his impersonation of a Scab.

The castle rose to his right, tall in the moonlight. He let the horse have its head—this was familiar ground for the animal. He could feel the sweat gathering under the robe, mixing with the morst.

What if she won't come, Thomas?

Suzan had asked the question, and in his enthusiasm he'd assured her that Chelise would come. But he wasn't so sure now. In fact, thinking through his task clearly now, he realized that getting into her room would be the easiest part. Getting Chelise out of her own accord might be far more difficult.

The road was still empty. So far so good. It occurred to him that the single greatest advantage he had was the Circle's policy of nonviolence. The Horde had no real enemies to threaten their security. Their defenses weren't built for an assault, and the penalty for simple crimes, such as theft, were so severe that few Scabs ever attempted them. He'd heard that any infraction against the royal house was punishable by death to the perpetrator's entire family.

The guard around the castle surely had been increased since his escape, but they weren't accustomed to the kind of stealth the Circle had

least that was Thomas's hope. If the weak performance of
yesterday was any measure, he had good reason to hope.

...ned into the forest before he came to any guard on the road.

...; his leg back into a reasonable riding position and guided the

...ough the trees, toward the stables behind the castle. The mare

at the scent of her familiar pen.

...asy, girl."

...le slipped to the ground and tied the animal to a branch. Light from

...castle's back rooms filtered through the trees despite the midnight

...ur. Hopefully they were torches that burned all night.

Twigs crunched underfoot, but no guards detected the noise. Thomas
hurried around the stables. Chelise had told him that her bedroom faced
the city on the top floor. He'd seen the stairs that led to the roof during
the last escape. He hurried to the fence that surrounded the grounds and
peered between the poles.

No guard.

This was it. Once over, he was committed. He gripped the top of the
pole, took a deep breath, and vaulted.

"Who goes?"

Thomas was still airborne, dropping to the ground like a parachute,
when the voice cut through the night air. Close.

He landed on both feet and stared at a guard ten feet to his right. The
warrior had been stationed by the fence.

Thomas lowered his head and walked toward the castle as if nothing
at all was unusual about a Scab dropping out of the sky.

"Stop! What's the meaning of this?"

Thomas halted and faced the warrior again, mind spinning through
options. More accurately, option. Singular.

The guard had to go. Chelise's life depended on it.

He walked toward the guard, head down. Five paces, he thought.

"Stop there!"

Thomas replied in a high pitch. "The general, Woref, told me to meet
him here."

"The general?"

"I am his concubine."

"His . . ."

Thomas moved before the man could process his shocking claim. He dove to his right, rolled once, and came up three feet to the guard's right. The man spun, broad blade flashing.

Thomas let his momentum carry him into a roundhouse kick. His foot connected solidly with the man's temple.

One grunt and the man fell like a sack of rocks.

"Forgive me," Thomas whispered. He dropped to his knee, ripped the guard's sleeve at the shoulder, and hog-tied him, hands-to-feet behind his back. He tore off the other sleeve and gagged his mouth tightly.

Thomas ran toward the building and flew up the stairs. He spilled onto the roof and crouched behind the railing. Had he torn his garment? He checked, catching his breath. All intact, as far as he could tell.

Speed was now an issue. The guard would wake soon enough and, even bound, might be able to raise enough of a fuss to draw attention.

Thomas ran toward the only stairwell he could see. He pushed the latch on the door. Locked. He studied the latch. It was forest technology. His own design.

He'd designed the lock to secure a door against strong winds, not thieves. A simple bronze bolt held the entire assembly in place. He pulled the pin free. The latch fell into his hand. He set it down and eased the door open.

Dim light filled a narrow stairwell. He slipped in, closed the door behind him, and stood very still.

No sound. The castle slept.

Thomas eased down the steps, pausing with each creak. They may have used forest technology, but the craftsmanship had been hurried.

At the bottom, a balcony ran the perimeter of the top floor. In front of him, a single torch burned between two doors. If he was right, one led to Chelise's bedroom. Only one way to find out which.

He poked his head over the railing, saw the courtyard below was empty, and hurried toward the first door.

Again locked.

Again his design.

Again he dislodged the bolt.

He stepped into the room and pulled the door shut. An oil lamp cast dim light over a large bed. She was in the bed, asleep! Thomas took in the rest of the room with a glance. Doors that led to another balcony. A large armoire on which the lamp sat. A desk with mirror. Long flowing drapes. Horde royalty.

The moment of truth had arrived. If this wasn't Chelise, he might be forced to hog-tie yet one more Scab.

He crept to the bed and leaned over the form under the blanket. She slept with the sheets over her head? He had to see her face to be sure, but the thought of unveiling her while she slept . . .

The floor creaked behind. Something struck his head. He fell forward onto the sleeping form and scrambled to right himself.

The object struck him again, square on the back. This time he grunted.

It occurred to him them, midgrunt, that the form under him wasn't a body at all. Pillows.

The third blow hit his head, and for a moment he thought he might pass out. He managed to find his voice. "It's me! It's Thomas!"

His assailant stopped long enough for Thomas to roll over. There, in the orange lamplight, stood a fully clothed woman.

"Thomas?"

"Chelise!" He sat up, head throbbing. "What are you doing?"

"What do you mean, what am I doing!" she whispered. "I'm defending myself."

"I'm here to help you, not attack you."

Chelise held an unlit torch in her hands. She glanced at the door. "How did you get in here? You've come to turn yourself in?"

"No. No, I can't do that."

"Why not? Your escape has landed me in a terrible position. I've been expecting that beast to barge in here all night. I was told that you denied Qurong's demand."

So it was all true. She understood that her life was in danger.

"If I turn myself in, they'll kill me. Would you want that?"

She lowered the torch.

Thomas stood and faced her. They looked at each other for the first time since she'd last left him in the library. Her face looked beautiful by the lamp's flame.

Thomas stepped toward her and started to lift his hand to her face, then thought better of it. "I've come to rescue you."

"I don't need rescuing. What I need is for you to turn yourself in to Qurong so that we can put this madness behind us. I should call the guard right now."

Her dismissal sent a shaft of pain through his chest. His face flushed hot. "Then call the guard."

"Keep your voice down. You look ridiculous in that morst."

"You prefer me without it?"

She walked to her desk, set the torch down, and stared into the mirror, which showed nothing in this dim light.

She hadn't called the guard.

"Listen to me, Chelise. You know as well as I do that whatever life you thought you had in this castle is over. Woref will destroy you. If you survive by turning me in, that beast, as you call him, will give you a living death. And if you refuse to cower under his fist, he'll kill you."

"None of this would have happened without you," she shot back. "Without you Woref wouldn't be such a pig, and without you I wouldn't be put in this terrible position to choose."

"Then at least you see that you do have a choice."

"Between what? Between an animal and an albino? What kind of choice is that?"

He ignored the bite in her words. "Then don't choose either of us. Leave this place and negotiate with your father from a position of strength."

The notion stalled her. When she spoke again, the edge in her voice had softened. "If I leave with you, Woref would never forgive me."

"You won't leave with me. I'll take you by force."

She laughed. "By force? As your prisoner. How can I negotiate with Qurong as your prisoner?"

"We'll think of something. I'll tell Qurong that I want Woref in exchange for you. Something like that. And what would Woref do to possess you?"

"Anything."

"Exactly. Anything. You see, by leaving you can force their hands. If you stay, your life will be a mess, even if you turn me in."

A faint smile crossed her face.

"But you have to understand that I have . . ."

How to say this? He suddenly wished he hadn't spoken.

"What?" she demanded.

"That I think I do have feelings for you," Thomas said. "I can see you feel differently, but I wouldn't feel right taking you out of here without being completely honest about my intentions."

This time she didn't laugh. "Which are what? To win my love? Then let me be honest with you. I know how you albinos look at us. You find us repulsive. Our breath smells and our skin sickens you. I don't know what kind of adolescent notion has climbed inside your head, but you and I could never be lovers."

"We could if you drowned."

"Never."

Thomas wondered then if he'd made a terrible mistake. But Michal had told him to follow his heart, and his heart was for this woman. Wasn't it? The thought of leaving her terrified him, so yes. His heart was certainly for this woman.

"I don't mean to hurt you," she was saying. She'd seen his pain. "I'm sorry. But you have your life and I have mine. I'm attracted to men like me. Men with my flesh."

"Okay."

"Then you understand?"

"I understand. I don't accept. I think I've seen more in your eyes."

"Even if there was, I could not act on it." She stared at him without speaking, then walked to her wardrobe.

"What are you doing?" he asked.

"I'm getting what I'll need for a trip to the desert."

"Then you're coming?"

"As long as you agree to bring me back in exchange for a demand of my choosing."

"Yes. Agreed." He suddenly felt antsy again. "You don't need anything. We have to hurry."

"A woman needs what a woman needs," she said, quickly placing several items in a leather bag. "There's a tub of morst and some paste on the dresser."

"Do you really—"

"It's the scented kind I wore in the library. Trust me, you'll be glad I brought it."

Thomas scooped up the small tub. She walked over and opened her bag. They exchanged a long stare, and he could swear that he was right. There was more behind those eyes than she admitted.

Or maybe not.

"Lead the way," she said.

He'd been called to the castle in the middle of the night, cause for concern even in peaceful times. Considering the events of the last few days, Woref feared the worst.

This was to do with Chelise; he could feel it. He rode his horse down the street at a steady pace, but his blood was boiling already. There was no greater source of problems in the world than women. They loved and they killed, and even in their loving they killed. Man might do better to remove the temptation from the face of the earth. What good was love at such a terrible price?

He dismounted, walked into the foyer, and drew back his hood.

"Woref." Qurong waited just inside the courtyard. "So glad my trusted general could make it."

Woref lowered his head in respect.

"I was just awakened by some very bad news," Qurong said. He was being too coy for this to be anything but horrible news. "One of your guards was found bound by the back fence."

Thievery?

"He said that a man pretending to speak like a woman dropped over the fence, claimed to be your concubine, and knocked him out. A little while later, he returned with another woman and knocked him out again."

"I assure you, sir, he's lying. I have no concubine."

"I don't care about your lies, General! The second woman was my daughter. Chelise is gone!" He said it slowly and with a trembling voice.

"How—"

"The first 'woman' was Thomas, you idiot!"

"Thomas of Hunter," Woref said. "He took her." Or did she go willingly?

"The guard said she was being forced. Thomas told him to relay that his demand would be forthcoming. He will release Chelise when we comply."

She's gone willingly, Woref thought. His face flushed but he didn't show his anger.

"Now it's your life at stake," the supreme leader said. "If one hair on my daughter's head is harmed, I will hold you responsible. You told her she would be drowned, knowing full well that I would never drown her. *You* said it would teach her a lesson, and *you* leaked a word to call Thomas's bluff. Now she's gone."

"We aren't without recourse, my lord. I've received word that my men are closing in on his tribe. He won't have the only bargaining chip."

Qurong looked at him skeptically.

"They're without their leaders," Woref said. "I've sent reinforcements. They can't escape an entire division."

"It's Chelise I want, not a pack of albinos!"

"You will have Chelise. But only if I will have her!"

Qurong scowled. "Find her!"

28

HE TRIED, but he couldn't sleep. And he wouldn't dream, not until he had won her love, he decided. The virus would likely kill him in a few days' time in the other reality, and he couldn't allow that to interfere with this drama unfolding here. He would simply eat the rhambutan fruit every night. A week, a month, whatever it took. When he finally did dream, only hours would have passed where he now slept at the White House.

He leaned against the rock beside Suzan, gazing at Chelise, who slept ten yards from them.

"For goodness' sake, sleep, Thomas," Suzan whispered. "It'll be light soon."

"I'm not tired."

"You will be. And you're bothering me, sitting like that."

"You're jealous?"

"Of her? If you were another man, perhaps—no disrespect, but my heart is taken."

Surprise turned his full attention to Suzan. "Oh? You've never said anything."

"Some things are best kept quiet."

"Who is it?"

"I won't say. But you know him." She propped herself up on her elbow. "I have to say, though, this new Thomas is quite impressive."

"There's nothing new about me."

"I've never known you to lie awake gazing at a sleeping woman who doesn't love you. Or act so interested in who I love. I've always thought you cared more about swinging a sword than wooing a woman."

"Obviously you've never known me. I wooed Rachelle in the colored forest, didn't I?" He looked at the stars. "Those were the days when romance was thick in the air."

"I was too young to remember," she said quietly.

"Not anymore."

"So I take it you're giving in to this impulse," she said. "Wholeheartedly."

Thomas avoided a direct response. "We were born for the Great Romance."

"Of course."

"I am only following my heart."

"Maybe I could show you a few things myself, Sir Poet," Suzan said.

"Then reveal your man to us and let us watch how you court each other."

"Listen to you. You're even speaking like a poet."

He grinned. "Nonsense. I always wax eloquent. My word was once my sword, but now it's this song of love for the fair maiden who lies hither. Or is it thither?"

"I can see I'll have to teach you the finer points of poetry."

His eyes darted over to the sleeping woman, and he lowered his voice. "You want real poetry? Then hear this: I have lost my heart. It is owned by Chelise, this stunning creature who sleeps in peace. When she frowns I see a smile; when she scoffs I hear a laugh. We rode side by side for two hours, picking our way through the dark forest without a single word, but I heard her heart whispering words of love to me every time her horse put its hoof on the ground. I cannot sleep now because love is my sleep, and I've had enough to last a week. She pretends not to love me, because the disease has filled her with shame, but I can see past her eyes into her heart, where she betrays her true desires."

Suzan chuckled. "If even half of that is true, then you are smitten, Thomas of Hunter."

His grin faded and he diverted his eyes. "It is."

Chelise suddenly moved. Turned her head toward them. "Are you two going to talk all night? I'm trying to sleep."

Thomas blinked. "You're awake."

"And you're talking too much. I don't know how albinos court their women, but you might want to consider a little subtlety."

Silence filled the camp.

"She has a point," Suzan finally said.

"I . . . I didn't know you were listening." Chelise was smiling, he could see it in the dark. "Okay, then, I guess it's time to sleep." He lay down, unsure whether he should be embarrassed or thrilled that she'd heard him.

They lay quietly for a long time.

Then Chelise spoke quietly. "Thank you, Thomas. They were kind words."

He swallowed. "You're welcome."

She rolled over. "Just remember our agreement."

Yes, of course. Their agreement. He'd nearly forgotten.

⊶∞∞⊷

Chelise and Suzan let Thomas sleep as the sun rose. They'd both risen an hour earlier and decided that they could wait another hour before heading for the desert. The chance of any Scab stumbling upon them in the small canyon where they'd made camp was remote.

Suzan had bathed in a small creek nearby, and Chelise decided that she would bathe as well. She waited until Suzan was finished before cautiously slipping into the water. Although she'd grown accustomed to the ritual bathing in the lake, the cold water stung her skin.

If it weren't for Thomas, she would never bathe in a stream, but she felt compelled to present herself in a manner that wasn't offensive to the albinos. She bore the pain and washed her skin well. Then she carefully applied the scented morst using a small pool as a mirror. She picked several smaller tuhan flowers and placed the sweet-smelling blossoms in her hair. All of this for his sake.

And why, Chelise? Why are you so concerned about pleasing Thomas? She couldn't answer that question. Perhaps because he was so kind to her.

Albino or not, he was a man, and she could hardly ignore this mad affection he'd displayed by rescuing her.

Chelise faced Suzan, trying not to stare at her dark skin. So very different from her own white flesh. The pendant the albinos wore hung from her neck.

"Why do you wear the pendant?" she asked Suzan.

The albino lifted the medallion in her hand and looked at it. "These are the colors of the Circle. Green for the colored forest, then black for the evil that destroyed us all. Then red, you see?" She indicated the two crossing straps of red leather. "Justin's blood. And finally, a white circle."

"And why white?"

Suzan looked into her eyes. "White. We are Justin's bride."

Such an odd way of seeing things. Foolish even. Whoever heard of being the bride of a slain warrior? Of course, they believed he was still alive.

Absurd.

Chelise looked at Thomas. "Should we wake him?"

"I can't believe he's still sleeping." Suzan smiled. "You must have worn him out last night."

"Ha! I think he's wearing me out with all of his enthusiasm."

Suzan cinched down the extra saddle Thomas had brought from the city. "Do you feel anything for him?"

Chelise hadn't expected such a forward question. She didn't know what to say.

"There lies Thomas of Hunter, legend of the Forest Guard, and he's falling in love with you, daughter of his nemesis, Qurong. It's a fairy tale in the making."

"He's an albino," Chelise said.

Suzan put her hand on the saddle and faced her. "That doesn't mean he's too good for you."

"That's not what I meant."

"No, but it's what you feel. It's why you bathed and why you cover your skin for him. For the record, I agree with Thomas. I think you're quite beautiful. And I don't think you have any idea how fortunate you are to have this man love you."

Chelise felt suddenly choked up. She looked at Thomas. There lay the king of the albinos. Or was Justin their king? Despite his attempt to wipe it off, the morst Thomas had applied last night still caked parts of his face.

"It does feel good, though, doesn't it?" Suzan asked.

"What?"

"Being loved."

She hesitated. "Yes." She wasn't sure she'd ever felt so awkward. Was Thomas right in saying that she was covering her shame? And now Suzan had said the same thing. She'd never thought of it in those terms.

"I think you deserve it," Suzan said.

The knot in her throat grew, and she had to swallow to keep from crying. Where the sudden emotion had come from, she didn't know, but it wasn't the first time the albinos had affected her so easily. The lessons in the library with Thomas had been similar.

Chelise decided then, staring off into the forest so that Suzan couldn't see her fighting tears, that she liked albinos.

"Why don't you wake him?" Suzan said. "We should leave."

Chelise walked over to him, glad for the reprieve. "Wake up."

He grunted and rolled his head, still lost to the world. She glanced at Suzan, but the woman was busy saddling another horse.

She bent down and nudged him. "Wake up, Thomas."

He bolted up, looked around, then saw her and came to himself. He stood and brushed his cloak. "What time is it? You let me sleep?"

"You looked tired."

He glanced at Suzan, then studied Chelise. "I'll be right back," he said and hurried in the direction of the creek. This obsession the albinos had with cleanliness was interesting.

Thomas returned ten minutes later, beaming face clean of the morst. "I feel like a new man. No offense, but the stuff makes my skin itch."

"Really? I find it quite soothing."

"It suits you. The white flowers are a perfect complement."

She smiled. "Thank you." Did he really think she was beautiful, or was he patronizing her?

They mounted and headed south away from the city, toward the desert. Thomas led them along a game trail, far from any well-traveled routes.

—⟨∞⟩—

They rode without speaking for an hour, Suzan bringing up the rear. Chelise finally broke the silence.

"Did you dream well, Thomas?"

"I didn't dream at all. I ate the rhambutan."

"I thought you wanted to dream. I nearly lost my life over your dreaming."

"I've made a vow: no dreams while I'm with you."

She didn't know what he could possibly have in mind, but she didn't press for an explanation.

Thomas brought his horse closer to hers. "Have you decided what we should demand for your return?"

"We could trade me for Woref, like you suggested," she said. "You could turn him into an albino. That would serve the beast."

Thomas chuckled. "Unfortunately, the drowning only works if it's done willingly. Otherwise we would round up Scabs in bunches and shove them under, wouldn't we, Suzan?"

"It's been suggested," she said.

Chelise shuddered. "What an awful death that would be."

"Do I look dead?" Thomas asked. "Alive like you've never known." He stretched out his arm. "When I move my arm, no pain in my joints. And not just because I've grown used to it."

The thought of drowning terrified her. She had grown so accustomed to the pain in her own joints that she simply ignored it most of the time.

"We could demand sanctuary for your Circle," Chelise said.

"You'd do that?"

She shrugged. "Why not?"

"Suzan, I think she's warming up to us."

Just yesterday she would have responded with a cutting remark to set him straight. Any such comment felt silly now. She let it go.

"Maybe we should let my father stew for a day or two," Chelise said. "I am not in a position to blackmail him very often."

"Perfect. Then we'll wait a week."

"A week? I wouldn't know what to do with myself for a week out here."

"You'll ride with us."

"And where, exactly, are we riding?"

"I haven't decided yet," he said. "Away from the Horde. Out of danger. Would you like to visit our Circle?"

"No, no. I couldn't do that. They would be horrified by me! And I by them. Anywhere but one of your tribes."

He smiled. "Then we'll just head south. As long as I'm with you to keep you safe, and you're comfortable, we'll ride."

She couldn't look at him without feeling *un*comfortable. "Sounds fair."

The sun passed overhead and began its descent toward the western horizon. Suzan rode ahead several times to scout out the route, and at times Chelise wondered if Thomas and his lieutenant hadn't planned the lengthy disappearances so that Thomas could be left alone with her. Not that she minded.

He told her stories of his days as commander of the Forest Guard, and she reciprocated with memories of her days in the desert: how they made use of the desert wheat, where they found their water, what it was like to grow up playing with other children who weren't of royal blood.

He seemed especially taken by her stories of the children and asked dozens of questions about how they learned to cope with the disease, as he called it. He really did think of their skin condition as an abnormality. And, of course, it was to him, as his condition was to her. But, as she pointed out, if you took the world as a whole and compared the millions of Scabs with only a thousand albinos, who was abnormal? And who was diseased?

He graciously let the subject go. There was no reconciling their diseases.

"I met you once in the desert," he said with a grin.

"Before? How could you have?"

"Roland."

"Roland? But Roland was from the Horde."

"Roland was Thomas, commander of the Forest Guard, who'd lost his way and contracted the disease. Naturally I was forced to lie to you."

"You were Roland? I had the life of Thomas of Hunter in my hands? I should have slit your throat!"

"Then you would have foregone the pleasure of riding with me today."

"Honestly, I was quite taken with Roland. I remember that."

"If you had to do it over again, would you still slit my throat?" he asked.

She looked at the rolling shoulders of the horse beneath her. "Knowing what I know today, knowing that I would be in a position to blackmail my father, no."

"Even knowing that I would go on to kill many of your warriors in the wars after that day?"

He made a good point. "Then yes, I'm sorry to say that I would have slit your throat."

"Good. I love an honest woman." They shared a smile.

He was so obvious. Thomas of Hunter, this famous warrior who rode beside her, meant to win her love.

By the time they reached the desert, she wasn't sure that she didn't have some feelings for him. He rode ahead to find Suzan once, and she felt surprisingly left out. Lonely. No, more than lonely, yearning for his company. And when he reappeared five minutes later wearing a silly grin, she felt relief.

"Did you miss me?" he asked.

"Oh, I'm sorry. Were you gone?" She immediately wanted to withdraw the tease. This time she did. "I was alone."

When had all of this happened? In the library?

Suzan galloped toward them, waving her arm. Thomas pulled back on his horse. "She's found something."

"The Horde?"

"I don't think so. Come on!" They rode out to meet her.

Suzan reined back, bright-eyed. "Johan is waiting with Mikil and Jamous. They must have sent William ahead with the others."

"Where?"

"They have a camp in a canyon." She pointed. "Two miles."

Thomas looked at Chelise. "Excellent! It's Martyn."

"He's here?"

"In the flesh." Thomas spurred his horse. "Ride!"

Chelise was terrified by this sudden development—Thomas and Suzan were one thing, but the prospect of meeting more of the Circle didn't sit well. And Martyn! Next to Thomas, there was no other name she'd grown to hate more.

She rode.

29

WHILE THOMAS slept in the White House at President Blair's insistence, Kara was following an insistence of her own. She had no desire to sleep, no cause to dream. She'd only wanted one thing, and that was to understand the rash that had appeared under her arm.

Genetrix Laboratories had become Monique's home. She slept on a cot in her office, and she ate what was left of the food in the cafeteria, although they hadn't received a shipment in three days—the catering company had suspended operations. Didn't matter. They had enough nonperishable foods to feed the five hundred technicians and scientists for at least two days. By then they would know if it was time to go home and start saying their good-byes or to hunker down for a last-ditch effort.

Monique examined Kara's arm in silence. Kara watched her eyes—it was too bad that Thomas was so taken with this other woman in Mikil's world. Chelise. The more time Kara spent with Monique, the more she decided the stiff-spined Frenchwoman was softer than she'd initially assumed. She and Thomas might make a good couple. Assuming both survived.

Monique's eyes were no longer on the cut that had attracted her curiosity. She was scanning the rest of her arm.

"What is it?" Kara asked.

"Have you noticed rashes anywhere else? Your stomach or back, maybe?"

Kara stepped away. "It's happening already?"

"On some, yes. No other rashes?"

"No. Not that I've noticed."

On the other hand, now that she thought about it, her skin seemed to itch in a number of places.

"How long have you known?"

"A few hours," Monique said.

Kara turned to her. "You?"

"No."

"I thought we had another week! Who else?"

"There've been a number of reported cases in Bangkok. Theresa Sumner. The entire team who came to meet with Thomas a few weeks ago. Some in the Far East have reported having the rash as long as ten days. Our guess is that this would only occur among those whose systems are actively fighting the virus. The rash is evidence of the body's resistance, though that doesn't mean much."

The revelation wasn't as shocking as she'd thought it might be. In fact, it was a bit of a relief after so much mystery. Like finally knowing that the cancer you had was terminal after all. You were going to die in exactly thirty days. Live and prepare to die.

"How many?"

Monique shrugged. "Several thousand. Our initial estimations of the virus's latency period were only that, estimates. We always knew it could come sooner. Now it appears to have done just that."

They exchanged a long look. What more was there to say? "So unless we go through with this exchange with France and get the antivirus, we're dead," Kara said.

"So it appears."

"The president knows?"

"Not yet. We're running tests. He'll know within the hour."

Kara sighed, dug in her packet, and pulled out a glass vial with a very small sample of blood. Thomas's blood. Her brother had insisted before leaving Johns Hopkins. His reasoning was simple: he was quite sure that he would be going back to France, but he refused to explain why. In the event something happened to him, he wanted Kara and Monique to have some options.

Kara set the vial on the desk.

"Thomas's?" Monique said.

"His idea. You know what would happen if you and I dreamed with this blood?"

Monique stared at her. "Rachelle is dead. You would wake as Mikil. I don't who I would wake as."

"No. But you would wake. And what would happen if you ate the rhambutan fruit when you were there?"

"No dreams."

"What if you ate the rhambutan fruit every day for the rest of your life?"

"Would it matter? If I die here, I die there. Isn't that how it works?"

"Not if dreaming a one-night dream here lasts forty years there. We could live a full life in another reality while waiting for death to take us here."

A small grin crossed Monique's face. Then an incredulous laugh. "Thomas suggested we should do this?"

"No. He said we would know what to do with it. You have a better idea?"

"No. But that doesn't make your idea sane."

"So you won't do it? He mentioned you, no one else."

"Of course I'll do it," Monique said, taking the small vial. "Why not?"

The smile on her face softened. She stared at the blood sample. "Does Thomas have a rash?"

Kara recalled what he'd said about the rash he'd picked up in Indonesia. "Now that you mention it, I think so, yes. Which means he may be among the first."

No reply.

⁓∞⁓

Mike Orear scanned the swelling crowd, too many to count now—estimates put it at nearly a million. It wouldn't take much to redirect their self-reflection into outrage. The frustration in their eyes was undeniable. The words he was about to speak on the air would do nothing less than open the floodgates of rage, directed at the world's best-known symbol of power: the White House.

He'd called Theresa earlier and fished for more on the possibility of an antivirus, but ever since he'd taken this stance as a voice for the people, she'd gone cold. It was a miracle he'd even gotten through to her. When he had confronted her with the accusation that the administration was misleading the people by holding out hope where none existed, she simply sighed and told him she wasn't working twenty-four–hour shifts to please the administration.

Then she'd hung up on him.

This so-called hope of hers had to be paper-thin. Their only real hope lay with the only man who possessed an antivirus that would do anyone any good: Svensson. If the president didn't play ball with France, there was no hope.

Orear scratched his underarm. The rash that had appeared over a week earlier had subsided, but now it was making a comeback. Odd how so few had the rash. Assuming it was connected to the virus, he'd have thought the rash would be widespread. His mother had it. Maybe it was a genetic thing. Maybe a few of them showed symptoms earlier than what the medical community was predicting.

He shoved the thoughts aside and walked to the tent where the CNN cameras awaited his hourly live update. The tent was set on a stage roughly five feet off the ground, enough to give him a clear view of the crowd. Marcy Rawlins was in a heated discussion with one of the cameramen about the mess they were making with the equipment, and he was pointing out that cleanliness was no longer next to godliness.

A tall bald man with a handlebar mustache paced along the wooden barricade, glaring at Mike. He wore a beige robe with arms that flared at the cuffs. Take him, for instance. This man looked capable of eating the barricade with only a little encouragement. The armed soldiers would be forced to fire their tear gas. They were nearly half a mile from the White

House, which rose stately behind them, but the only way the guards could stop a marching army of angry protesters was to kill a few.

Those deaths would be on Mike's head. He knew that as well as he knew Marcy needed a Valium. But the death of a few might bring hope and possibly life for millions. Not to mention the 543 souls in Finley, North Dakota, where his mother waited for him to do whatever was humanly possible to stop this mess.

"Two minutes, Mike," Nancy Rodriguez said, taking her seat next to him.

"Gotcha."

He'd dispensed with the tie long ago—he was of the people, for the people. And tonight he would push the people.

Sally applied a quick brush of base to soften the glaze on his cheeks, picked at his hair, then moved away without a word. There wasn't that much for a makeup artist to say these days.

His coanchor leaned toward him. "You might as well know," Nancy said. "I just talked to Marcy. This is my last broadcast."

"What?"

"I've got family in Montana, Mike."

"And I have family in North Dakota. What about what we're doing here for those families?"

"I'm not sure what we're doing here. Other than dying with the rest of them."

Mike understood. He felt the same way at times. But he had no choice in the matter. The people had become his family, and his obligations were now to them as well.

"Stick around for a few minutes, and I promise you'll see what we're doing here."

"Let's go, people," Marcy barked. "You ready, Mike?"

He started the report by running though an update on reports from around the world, mostly riots and the like. Nothing about the anti-virus, as he normally did. Just the problems.

The crowd was over a million, he told them. The traffic into

Washington, D.C., had been forced to a halt, and the police were turning people away.

They'd set up loudspeakers every fifty yards for as far as he could see and around the corner all along Constitution Boulevard. His voice rang out to the people. Mike Orear, their savior on the air. At this moment his worldwide audience was nearly a billion people, they estimated. They'd sold the updates sponsorship to Microsoft for a hundred million a pop. If they came through this alive, Microsoft would shine. If not, they would die with the rest. Smart thinking.

Mike took a deep breath. "That's the news, my friends. That's what they want you to know. That's what the whole world now knows. But I've learned something else, and I want you to listen to every word I'm about to speak, because your life may very well hinge on what I say next."

He glanced at Marcy. She was past being surprised by anything he might say. Her eyes watched him expectantly—she was more audience than producer now.

"The hope for discovering an antivirus, despite what we've all been told by the White House these last couple of weeks, is now almost nonexistent."

A blanket of silence settled over Washington as he spoke the words. Every television, every radio, every speaker carried his announcement. He envisioned the living rooms of America stilled except for the beating of hearts. This was the news they had been waiting for. Hoping against.

"In a matter of days, every living man, woman, and child on this planet will begin to display the symptoms of the Raison Strain. Within days, maybe hours, of that, the world as we know it will . . ."

A terrible sound drifted over the crowd, and at first Mike thought that one of the speakers was overloaded with feedback. But it wasn't the loudspeakers. It was the people.

A terrible wail, probably from one of the end-of-the-world groups, now spread like fire.

"Quiet! Please, there's more."

They didn't stop.

"Please!" he shouted, suddenly as furious at them as he was at the White House. "Just shut up! Please!"

The wail fell off. Marcy was staring at him.

"I'm sorry, but this isn't a game we're playing. You have to hear me out!"

"You tell them, Mikie!" someone shouted. A general barrage of approvals.

He lifted his hand. "Hear me out. The fact is, we're all going to die." He paused. Let the noise settle. "Unless . . ."

Now he let them hang on that one word. In moments like these he was most acutely aware of his power. Like the director of the CIA had said, like it or not, he was one of the most powerful people in the country at the moment. He didn't relish the fact, but he couldn't ignore it either.

"Unless we find a way to get the antivirus that already exists into our hands. That's the killer here: an antivirus that already exists could end all of this in two days. Not a single one of us would have to die. But that's not going to happen. It's not going to happen because Robert Blair has refused a deal that would exchange our nuclear arsenal for the antivirus."

Again he paused for effect. They already knew of the terrorists' ultimatum, but it had never been put to them so bluntly, and never in hand with the world health community's failure.

"My friends, I say, give them the weapons. Give us the antivirus. Give us a chance to live. Give our children another day, another week, another month, another year, and let them live to fight!" He shoved his fist into the air.

Immediately a roar broke from the crowd.

"The rules have changed!" he shouted, feeding on the crowd's growing cries. "We are in a fight for our very lives! We can't allow one man to sacrifice our survival over his own inflated notions of principle!"

Mike was breathing hard. Adrenaline coursed through his veins.

He shoved his finger back at the White House. "This travesty must not stand! In a few days you will all die unless they change their minds! I say, fight for your lives! I say, storm the White House! I say, if we're going to die, we die fighting for our right to live!"

His hand was trembling. He had run out of words.

An ominous silence had smothered the crowd. It was one thing to shout protests. It was another to incite a riot. This talk of death was sinking in.

The scream started in the back somewhere, as far as ten blocks back for all he knew.

The crowd moved as if the straps that held them back had been cut. They swelled forward, screaming bloody murder. The bald man with the handlebar mustache was one among a thousand who breached the barricades first.

Then they were running.

The cameraman spun and took in the mob. He stepped back, nearly fell over a cord, but quickly adjusted and kept the feed live.

Mike didn't know what to do. As far as he could see, the crowd was moving. Forward. Toward him.

A machine gun rattled—tracers streaked over the crowd.

The army troops were already on their feet. Warnings squealed over their bullhorns, but they were lost in the crowd's roar.

The first line rushed past the stage.

Marcy was screaming something, but Mike couldn't understand her. They were going to run right through these defenses and overtake the White House. No one could stop this. He had no clue . . .

Whomp!

Screams of terror.

Whomp, whomp!

"Stand back or we will be forced to fire!"

Whomp!

A cloud billowed from a canister that landed twenty feet from the stage.

"Tear gas!" someone cried. As soon as he said it, the sting hit Mike's eyes.

Whomp, whomp, whomp, whomp!

Chopper blades beat hard nearby, close enough to do whatever damage they were ordered to do.

The crowd surged through the clouds of gas. Another machine gun roared. A momentary silence followed.

When the screaming resumed, it sounded very different, and Mike knew that someone had been shot.

"Get up there!" he shouted, spinning.

But the cameraman was already running through the crowd.

The war had started. Gooseflesh ran up his arms.

Mike's War.

"The answer is no," President Blair snapped. "I stay here, end of story. Find Mike Orear and his crew and bring them in. I want to go on the air as soon as possible."

Phil Grant frowned. "Sir, I strongly urge you to consider the implications—"

"The implications are that unless we tread very carefully over these next two days, none of us has a prayer. I've known that for over two weeks; now the people are understanding that as well. I'm surprised it took them this long to break down the barricades."

By his hesitancy, the director of the CIA wasn't sure about Blair's evenhanded response to the riots. "I'm not sure they're wrong on this, sir," he finally said.

The possibility that Phil Grant might be working with Armand Fortier crossed Blair's mind for the first time. Who better? His mind flashed over the last few years, searching for inconsistencies in the man's performance. To the best of Blair's recollection there had been none. He was seeing ghosts behind everyone who entered his office these days.

Grant pushed his point. "The riots are only an hour old, and there are already six dead bodies out on the lawn, for goodness' sake. The perimeter around the White House may be reestablished, but they're tearing the city apart. The people of this nation want one thing, sir, and that's survival. Give Fortier his weapons. Take the antivirus. Live to fight another day."

Blair turned away deliberately. This was the same argument, nearly word for word, that Dwight Olsen had made fifteen minutes earlier. Dwight's motivations were transparent, but Phil Grant was a different animal. This wasn't like him. He knew the chances of Fortier coming through with the antivirus were next to nil. To show the Frenchman their military teeth and then beg for an antivirus was simply unacceptable. As long as the United States had some leverage, they were in the game. As soon as they gave up that leverage, the game was over.

Grant knew all of this. Blair decided not to remind him.

"I don't trust the French."

"I'm not sure you have a choice anymore," Grant said. "By tomorrow you could have a full-scale civil war on your hands. You represent the people. The people want this trade."

Blair swiveled around. "The people don't know what I know."

Grant blinked. "Which is?"

Easy.

Thomas's insistence that he trust no one, not a soul, ran through his mind. Gains, Thomas had said. Maybe Gains, that's it.

"Which is what you know. Fortier has no acceptable motive for handing over the antivirus when our ships meet his in"—he glanced at his watch—"thirty-six hours now."

Grant studied him, then set the folder in his hands on the coffee table. "I understand your reluctance. I accept it, naturally. Never could trust the French in a pinch." He stood and shoved his hands in his pockets. "This time I don't think we have a choice. Not with these riots spreading. New York and Los Angeles are starting up already. The country will be burning by noon tomorrow."

"That's better than dead in four days."

The intercom chirped. "Sir, I have a private call for you."

Gains. He'd left very specific instructions. Not even the operator knew that it was Gains on the line.

"Thank you, Miriam. Tell her I'll call right back. Hold all my calls for a few minutes."

"Yes sir."

Blair sighed. "Nothing like a mother to love you." He nodded at the door. "Don't worry, Phil, I'm not going to let this country burn by noon. Get some sleep—you look like you could use it."

"Thank you. I just might."

The director left.

Ghosts, Robert. You're seeing ghosts.

He withdrew the small satellite phone from his desk drawer, locked the door to his office, and stepped gingerly into the closet. Full-scale riots were raging throughout the city, the first signs of the Raison virus had visited them early with this rash, the bulk of the world's nuclear arsenal was about to land in the hands of a man likely to use it, and the brave Robert Blair, president of the most powerful country on earth, was huddled in his closet, punching in a number by the green translucent glow of a secure satellite phone.

The call took nearly a full minute to connect.

"Sir?"

"Quickly."

"We have a go. The Israelis have already directed their fleet as demanded by the French."

Blair let out a long, slow breath. Other than Thomas, who'd first suggested this plan, only four others on this side of the ocean knew the details.

"How many of them are in on it?"

"General Ben-Gurion. The prime minister. That's it."

"Where are their ships now?"

"Approaching the Strait of Gibraltar. They'll round Portugal and reach their coordinates in just over thirty hours, as requested by the French."

"Good. I want you on the USS *Nimitz* as soon as possible."

"I land in Spain in three hours and will be chopped tomorrow." Static filled the receiver. "What about Thomas?"

"He's sleeping," Blair said. "Depending on what happens in his dreams . . ." He caught himself, struck by the sound of his words. They were banking on dreams?

Yes, the dreams of the same man who uncovered the Raison Strain. "If all goes well, he'll join you."

No one other than Kara and Monique de Raison understood Thomas as well as Merton Gains. He sensed Blair's awkwardness.

"It's the right thing, sir. Even if Thomas gave us nothing more, what he's given us to this point has been invaluable."

"I'm not sure whether to agree or disagree," Blair said. "He brought this upon us, didn't he?"

"Svensson did."

"Of course. I'm going on air as soon as they can bring in this character Orear, and I'm going to tell the American people that I'm going to work with the French."

"I understand."

"God help us, Merton."

"Yes sir. God help us."

30

JOHAN WATCHED the three horses galloping into the canyon toward them. Suzan had found them from the cliff above and waved. Now she led, dark hair flowing in the wind. Born to ride. He remembered her repu-tation as the commander of scouts who could find a single grain of desert wheat in any canyon. As Martyn, he'd feared her nearly as much as he feared Thomas. Intelligence was the key to many battles, and Suzan had matched him at every turn.

He'd never imagined he would ever have the pleasure of riding with her. Seeing her approach with such grace, such beauty, made his pulse quicken. Perhaps it was time to express his feelings for her.

Thomas rode behind her. Odd to think of it, but if he was awake here, it meant he was asleep in his other reality.

Beside Thomas, the woman. The daughter of Qurong.

"He actually did it," Mikil said beside him. "Look at her ride."

"Thomas must have taken her by force. The Chelise I knew would never agree to come on her own."

"Love will compel the strongest woman," Jamous said with a wink at Mikil.

Johan chuckled. "Love? I doubt love compels the daughter of Qurong."

"Either way, you're getting what you argued for," Mikil said. "We're about to see just how friendly albinos and Scabs can be together."

"I didn't have this in mind. I was speaking of the drowning. And the more I think about it, the more I think I was wrong."

"Be careful what you hope for."

Suzan slid from her horse, took two quick steps toward them, and then slowed her pace. Or was it two quick steps toward him? Her eyes were certainly on him. Johan wondered if the others noticed.

Thomas and Chelise had slowed to a trot. Suzan veered toward Mikil and grasped her arms. "Elyon's strength. It's good to see you. William?"

"He went on to the tribe with Cain and Stephen."

Thomas rode in beaming from ear to ear. Chelise stopped beside him, peering tentatively from her hood, face white with morst. She'd placed tuhan blossoms in her hair. This, along with the smooth texture of the morst, was new for the Horde.

Thomas swept his arm toward her. "I would like you to meet the princess. My friends, I present Chelise, daughter of Qurong, delight of Thomas."

Mikil's eyes went wide with amusement. Delight? She was a Scab. And did Chelise agree with his sentiment?

Suzan put her hand on Johan's shoulder. "And this, Princess Chelise, is Johan," she announced. Had they spoken about him?

Johan stepped out and bowed his head. "It's good to see you again."

Chelise was speechless. She'd never seen him as an albino. The poor child was frightened.

Thomas dropped to the sand and reached for her hand. She took it and dismounted gracefully. Thomas held her hand and Chelise made no attempt to discourage him. Had any of them ever seen such a sight? An albino man—Thomas, commander of the Guard—tenderly holding the hand of a diseased woman.

Chelise finally released his hand and stepped forward. She bowed. "Johan. It's a pleasure to meet the great general again."

"Actually, the great general is behind you," Johan said. "His name is Thomas, and I am his humble servant." He indicated the others. "This is Mikil—you might remember her as Thomas's second in command—and her husband, Jamous."

Jamous nodded. Mikil stepped forward. "I can see that you and Thomas have become friends." She let a moment linger. "Any friend of Thomas is a friend of mine." She smiled and reached out her hand.

Chelise smiled sheepishly and took it. Welcoming a Scab as Mikil did wasn't such an uncommon sight—the Circle had led many Scabs into the red pools to drown.

Mikil turned around and sighed. She walked up to Jamous, took his face in her hands, and kissed him passionately on the lips. "I'm sorry, the air is practically dripping with romance. I couldn't help myself."

Thomas blushed and tried to set the record straight for the shocked princess. "You'll have to forgive us, but we aren't too shy about romance in the Circle. We believe that the love between us isn't so different from the love between Elyon and his bride. We call it the Great Romance. Maybe you remember that? From the colored forest?"

"I've heard rumors," Chelise said, but the curious look on her face betrayed her ignorance of any such rumors.

They stood in silence.

"Well then!" Thomas clapped his hands together. "The sun is going down, and we would like some meat. We've had nothing but fruit all day. Please tell me you've hunted down some meat, Johan. It's the least a mighty general like yourself could do for a princess." His eyes twinkled. "You do want meat, don't you, Chelise? You told me how much you love a good steak with your wine. We have wine, Johan?"

"Actually, a simple wheat cake would be fine—"

"Nonsense! Tonight we celebrate. Meat and wine!"

"And what are we celebrating?" she asked. She was growing more comfortable already, Johan thought.

"Your rescue, of course. Johan?"

A shy smile crept across Chelise's mouth.

"We have three rabbits, and our water is as sweet as wine. Should we risk a fire?"

"You can't have a proper celebration without a fire. Of course we risk a fire!"

———— ∞ ————

The night was warm and the moon was full, but Thomas hardly noticed. It could be freezing cold and he wouldn't care. A fire burned in his chest, and with each passing hour he'd embraced its warmth.

So he told himself.

But he was acutely aware of his own growing misgiving at the same time. Just as likely, he hardly noticed the cold night because he was flush with confusion. Where might his odd feelings for Chelise lead them? Seeing his friends in the camp only underscored the peculiarity of his strange romance. He'd boldly called her his delight, of course, but he was feeling like a man with last-minute jitters on his wedding day. What right did he have to make such bold statements so soon and in such contrary circumstances?

The rabbits that Johan had killed earlier filled the camp with a mouth-watering scent. The group made small talk and watched them roast over a spit. There were plenty of issues that could have consumed them in heavy discussion, but Mikil was right: something else was in the air, and it made matters of doctrine and strategy seem insignificant by comparison. There was a romantic tension in the air. The aura of improbable if not forbidden love.

Thomas sat cross-legged close to Chelise, who was seated gracefully on the sand. Mikil leaned back in Jamous's arms to Thomas's right. That left Johan and Suzan, the odd couple out. But it appeared they weren't so odd after all. Whatever feelings they'd hidden before weren't hiding so well tonight. If Thomas wasn't mistaken, the man Suzan had spoken of last night was none other than Johan.

"One leg left," Johan said, reaching for the spit. "Anyone?"

Mikil tossed a bone into the fire and wiped her mouth with the back of her hand. "The best rabbit I've had, and I've had a few."

Johan pulled the leg free. "Suzan?"

Firelight danced in her eyes. She smiled. "No, thank you."

The way she said it so tenderly—this wasn't like Suzan, Thomas thought. Why did love change people so? Johan seemed momentarily trapped by her voice.

"Then I think I'll have it," he said, sitting back next to her. He took a bite, but Thomas was sure his mind wasn't on the rabbit.

Chelise watched them, undoubtedly feeling the intoxicant. She stared into the fire, eyes white. "I never realized there was such kindness among the Circle," she said. "I feel honored to be in your company."

A piece of wood cracked in the fire.

"And I never would have guessed that the daughter of Qurong could be so . . . gentle or wise," Mikil said. "The honor is ours."

Thomas wanted to speak his approval of their acceptance, but he held back.

Chelise lifted her eyes. "How can you love those who hunt you down?"

"We *don't* always," Mikil said. "Maybe if we did, things would be different."

Flames licked the night air.

Chelise eased her hood from her head. She was baring herself to them.

"I think your eyes are beautiful," Suzan said.

Chelise looked away from her. "Thank you." Thomas saw her swallow. Her eyes were beautiful, but none of them could possibly see her disease in the same light he did. They were seeing her through eyes of love, because love was in the air, but they were also pitying her. Her skin was riddled with scales, and her mind was twisted by deception.

If only he could make everything right. A knot rose in his throat. *You are beautiful, my love. I would kiss you with a thousand kisses if you let me.*

He glanced up and saw Mikil staring at him. She understood. She had to understand!

Mikil shifted her eyes to Chelise. "It must be a wonderful thing to be such a beautiful princess."

Chelise lowered her head and traced her finger through the sand. Thomas looked away. The sounds of the fire faded. *My love, my dearest love, I am so sorry. It's not what you think.*

"Jamous and I will take a walk," Mikil said. "All this talk of love can't go unanswered."

Thomas heard them stand and leave, but he couldn't look up.

"And so will Johan and I," Suzan said.

They walked into the night.

Chelise continued to trace the sand by her knees, her finger white with morst to cover her shame. The gentle breeze carried the scent of her disease mixed with perfume.

"It's okay—"

"No," she said. "It's not okay. I can't do this." She looked into the black night. "I want you to take me back in the morning."

Her statement took him completely off guard. It was as if she'd flipped a switch that had powered his hopes. She was right. Nothing was right about his juvenile ambition to win her love.

What was he thinking? Thomas suddenly panicked. He did love her, of course. He wasn't a schoolboy tossed about by infatuation. His love had to be real—Michal had essentially said so himself!

But the fact that Chelise was a Scab with no intent to change was real as well. The disparity between these two realities was enough to suddenly and forcefully send Thomas into a tailspin.

"I don't think that's a good idea," he offered lamely.

"I don't belong here."

Thomas stood. Awkward. Terrified by confusion. She was right. That was what stuck him more than anything. This woman, whom he was sure he had fallen in love with, did not—could not—belong with him. He had been chasing the fantasies of an adolescent after all.

"Excuse me," he said. "I'll be right back."

He headed into the night, unaware of where he was going. He had to think. He wanted to hide; he felt ashamed for leaving her. But it was precisely what she wanted.

Thomas rounded a boulder and headed along white sand, deeper into the canyon. *In the morning I will take her back.* His vision blurred with moisture. *I have no choice. It's what she wants. If she can't recognize a gift when she sees one, she hardly deserves it, does she? She should be running to the red pools, but she's talking about going back.*

A tear leaked down his cheek.

"Where are you going?"

Thomas spun toward the voice on his left.

Justin!

Could it be? He stepped back, blinking.

Yes, Justin. He wasn't smiling this time, and his jaw was firm.

"Justin?"

Justin glanced back toward the boulders that hid the camp. "You left her."

"I . . ." Thomas didn't know what to say. Why had he now seen Justin twice in one week? And why was Justin so interested in Chelise?

Justin faced him, green eyes flashing with anger. "How dare you leave her alone! Do you have any idea who she is? I entrusted her to you."

"She's Chelise, daughter of Qurong. I didn't know that you'd entrusted her to me."

"She's the one my father prepared for me! You've left my bride to sob in the sand!" Justin took several paces toward the camp, then turned back, head now in his hands.

Thomas wasn't sure what to make of this display.

Justin lowered his hands. "I told you myself, I would show you my heart. I sent you Michal when you began to doubt, and already you're forgetting. Do I need to show myself to you every day?"

Justin pointed toward the camp. "You should be kissing her feet, not running away."

"I don't understand. She's only one woman—"

"No! She's the one I've chosen to show the Circle my love for them. Through you."

Thomas sank to his knees, horrified by what he was hearing. "I swear I didn't know. I swear I will love her. Forgive me. Please forgive me. I . . ."

"Please, hurry," Justin said. The moonlight showed tears in his eyes. "Her heart is breaking. You have to help her understand. Don't think I am the only one who wants her. My enemy will not rest."

His enemy. Woref? Or Teeleh? Thomas stood clumsily, his feet charged with an urgency to get back to the campfire. "I will! I swear I will."

Justin just stared at him. "She's waiting," he finally said.

The look in Justin's eyes as much as adrenaline pushed Thomas into a sprint. He stopped after five paces and spun back. "What . . ."

But Justin was gone.

Tears ran down Thomas's cheeks. It was too much. He couldn't stop the terrible sorrow that crashed over him. He turned and ran down the canyon, around the boulder, and straight for the campfire.

Chelise looked up, startled. But he was beyond trying to bring reason to what was happening between them.

He dropped to his knees beside her. "I'm sorry. Please, forgive me. I had no right to leave you!"

She looked at him without understanding, without a hint of softening. But now as he stared into her white eyes, he saw something new.

He saw Justin's bride. The one Elyon had chosen for Justin.

Grief swallowed Thomas whole and sobs began to wrack his body. He closed his eyes, lifted his chin, and began to weep.

He put his hand on her knee. Chelise didn't move.

He couldn't process his thoughts with any logic, but he knew that he was weeping for her. For the tragedy that had befallen her. For this disease that separated them.

The night seemed to echo with his sobs. He removed his hand from her knee. For every cry, there was another, as if the Roush had joined in his great lament.

He caught his breath and listened. Not the Roush, Chelise. Chelise was crying. She'd drawn her knees to her chest and was sobbing quietly.

All thoughts of his own sorrow vanished. Her whole body shook. She had one arm over her face, but he could see her mouth open, straining with her sobs. He sat frozen. He began to cry softly—the pain of this sight was worse than his earlier sorrow.

"What have I done? You don't understand. I love you!"

"No!" she moaned loudly.

He scrambled to his knees and reached out for her. But he was afraid to touch her.

"I do love you! I didn't mean . . ."

Chelise shoved herself up and glared at him. "You can't love me!" she shouted. "Look at me!" She slapped her face. "Look at my face! You can never love me!"

Thomas grabbed her hand. "You're wrong." He lifted her hand and kissed it gently.

———⊗⊗⊗———

She was acutely aware of his hand tightly holding hers. His breath washing over her as he declared his insensible love.

The shame of her white flesh had come over her like a slowly moving shadow from the setting sun. She'd been aware of it back in the library, but only as a distant thought. She'd considered it more carefully after hearing Thomas point it out to Suzan last night.

She was diseased. But she told herself that she would rather live diseased than die by drowning.

Then she'd met the albinos and watched them prepare their small feast. Listening to them talk around the campfire, she couldn't shake her desire to be like these people. Life in the castle was like a prison next to the love they shared so easily.

She knew that her skin offended them, no matter what they said. When Suzan had told her that she had beautiful eyes, knowing full well that they believed her eyes were diseased, the last of her self-assurance had fallen to rubble. She realized then that she could never be like these people. Never be like Thomas.

Worse, she realized that he was right when he said that she wanted to be loved by him. She did want to love him.

Yet she could never bring herself to drown. And without the drowning, she could never be truly loved by him. So then, there was no hope.

You hold my hand, Thomas, but could you ever kiss me? Could you ever love me as a woman longs to be loved? How can you love a woman who repulses you?

Thomas had grown quiet. He put his arm around her shoulders and pulled her closer. She let her sobs run dry.

"You are beautiful to me," he said softly.

She couldn't bear the words. But she didn't have the will to resist them, so she let her silence speak for itself.

"Please . . . I'm dying."

You feel sorry that the woman in your arms doesn't have smooth skin? That she sickens you?

Chelise raised her head to voice her thoughts. His face was there, only inches from hers, wet with tears. The fire lit his green eyes. She was breathing on him, but he made no effort to draw back.

This simple realization was so profound, so surprising, that she lost her train of thought. His eyes gazed at her longingly, drawing her in. Such deep, intoxicating eyes. This was Thomas, commander of the Guard, the man who had fallen madly in love with her and risked his life to rescue her from a beast who would have savaged her.

How could he love her?

She closed her eyes. She could never satisfy such a beautiful man. His love was born out of pity, not true attraction. He could never . . .

His finger traced her cheek, effectively stopping her heart.

"Since the first time we were together in the library, I've loved you," he said. He touched her lips with his fingers. "If only you will allow me to love you."

His words washed over her like a fresh, warm breeze. She opened her eyes and knew immediately that he was speaking the truth.

She slowly lifted her hand. Touched his temple, where his skin was the smoothest. Chelise couldn't bear the tension any longer. She put her hand around his neck and pulled his face down. His soft lips smothered hers in a warm, passionate kiss.

She felt a stab of fear, but he pulled her tighter. Then she gave herself up and let him kiss her longer. His mouth was sweet and his tears felt warm on her cheeks.

His hands brushed her hair back and he kissed her nose and her forehead. "Tell me that you love me," he said. "Please."

"I love you," Chelise said.

"And I love you."

He kissed her on the lips again, and Chelise knew then that she did love this man.

She was in love with Thomas of Hunter, commander of the Guard, leader of the Circle who had loved her first.

31

THOMAS ROSE early, filled with an energy he hadn't felt for many months. The sun was smiling on the horizon; canyon larks sang from the cliff; a morning breeze whispered through his hair.

The Great Romance filled his mind. He understood now. This love he felt for Chelise was tantamount to the love that Justin felt for everyone whom he would woo, diseased or not. The realization was dizzying.

Chelise still slept in her bedroll beside him. He'd found his way past her disease and kissed the woman beneath. He'd stepped past the skin of this world and stepped into another, not unlike what he did when he dreamed.

Yes, Chelise was as disease-ridden as ever. Yes, he could taste the bitterness on her breath. Yes, he would give anything to lead her into the red pool and see her forever changed. But he loved her anyway. And he loved her desperately.

He leaned over and kissed her cheek. "Wake up, my love."

Her eyes batted open. He kissed her again. "Did you dream of me?"

She smiled. "As a matter of fact, I did. You?"

"No dreams, remember?"

She sat up and gazed at the others. Johan was stirring. They'd fallen asleep before the others had returned from their walks. Chelise looked unsure. He would settle that soon enough.

He stood and clapped his hands. "Let's go, everybody. We have a long way to go today."

They stirred from their dreams and sat up.

"Where are we going?" Chelise asked.

"To the tribe. If it's okay with you, that is. Or would you rather send a message to your father?"

She pushed herself to her feet and brushed sand from her cloak. "They won't bite my head off?"

"Not if they expect to live the day."

"Then I suppose I could manage."

Only Thomas and Chelise wore the Horde garments—the rest had traded them for the tan tunics worn by the Circle.

They cleaned the camp quickly and prepared to leave. Thomas saddled his horse and walked toward Chelise, who was working with her mount. He spoke loudly enough for all of them to hear.

"I don't know where you found those rabbits, Johan, but I insist you find more like them for our celebration tonight. There was something in the meat."

Mikil looked at him. "And what are we celebrating this time?"

Thomas put his hand on Chelise's neck and drew her close. "Love," he said and kissed her gently on her lips.

The others were as surprised as Chelise.

"Love it is," Johan said, glancing at Suzan.

Thomas winked at Chelise, who smiled sheepishly. It would take her more time to feel at ease in their company, but Thomas would remove any obstacles.

They rode south into the desert. Normally a journey through the hot dunes would be a quiet, plodding affair, but not this one. They settled into three pairs with Johan and Suzan leading. Thomas and Chelise trailed behind Mikil and Jamous. The hours didn't pass slowly enough for them to plumb the depths of their experiences and theories. But with each passing mile Thomas felt his love for the woman who rode beside him grow.

He had a hard time keeping his eyes off her. Fortunately, there were no cliffs to ride off, or he might have. She rode like a warrior, straddling the saddle, and she had a habit of resting one leg at a time across her steed's shoulder. When he pointed out the cleverness of her riding posture, the others just looked at him with blank stares. To Thomas it was brilliant, though he tried it himself without much success.

She also kept her head up as she rode, chin level, like only a princess could, he thought.

Midday they came to the Oasis of Plums, as the Horde had named it. Chelise excused herself and bathed. When she emerged around the plum trees, Thomas had to look twice to be sure it was her. She'd washed her black hair and applied an oil that made it shine. Flowers again, and the scented morst, but she'd also applied a blue powder under her eyebrows and to her lips. She wore gold earrings and a matching band around her neck. She might have stepped out of the histories' ancient Egypt.

Thomas immediately hurried over to her, took her hands, and declared that she was stunning. The others agreed. And this time, he thought, they actually meant it.

That afternoon they rode six abreast and reminisced about the colored forest. The Roush, the fruit, the lake, the tall colored trees. Chelise asked a hundred questions, like a child first learning that the world was round.

Try as they did, they couldn't find rabbits for a feast that night, but Mikil found two large snakes, which they filleted and roasted over the coals. The meat was sweet and satisfying. Chelise and Johan showed them how to dance, Horde-style, and then Suzan led them in a Circle dance. They debated the merits of each and laughed till their sides hurt.

Johan and Mikil urged Thomas to dream, but he insisted that another night without knowing what was happening with Carlos wouldn't hurt any of them. For all he knew, he'd been sleeping for only a few minutes in the other reality, and he wasn't interested in interrupting his romance with Chelise. For that matter, he might consider eating the rhambutan forever and never dreaming of the virus again.

—∞∞∞—

They broke camp the next morning and resumed their journey south. The tribe was camped four hours away—they would arrive before noon.

"You're sure they'll understand?" Chelise asked.

"Of course, they will. You aren't the first."

"This is entirely different. I'm not coming to drown."

Thomas glanced at the others. "They'll get used to the idea. A day may come when you're more comfortable with the drowning."

"No. I'm the daughter of Qurong, princess of the Horde. I have my limits. It's one thing to fall in love with an albino and make friends with the Circle; it's another thing to become an albino."

She could not know how painful her words were. They hadn't spoken of what would become of their love, but they both knew that some things were irreconcilable. The Horde would never accept peace with the Circle, not while Qurong was their leader and Woref led their forces. And Chelise couldn't expect to be princess of the Horde while living with the Circle.

Chelise looked over at him. "I'm sorry. I didn't mean it like that. You know that I love you."

"And you know that I love you." He winked at her. "That's all that matters."

"A rider!" Suzan pulled up.

Thomas followed her gaze to the south. A plume of dust rose from a lone rider charging hard toward them.

"Is he from our tribe?" Mikil asked.

"He must be. The next closest tribe is a hundred miles from here." Thomas slapped his horse's rump. "Let's go!"

They galloped out to meet the rider.

"It's Cain!" Suzan shouted, leaning low over her mount. "There's trouble."

Cain reined in hard. His eyes were bloodshot. "Thomas . . ." He glanced at Chelise and back. His horse snorted and sidestepped. "The village was attacked. My brother's dead with nine others. They took half of us before we could escape."

"Slowly, man! Who attacked?" But Thomas knew who. "When?"

"The Horde . . . a division, at least, last night. William sent me out to bring back Johan."

"William's in command? Who was taken?"

"Yes, William. The Horde took twenty-four trapped in one of the canyons. Men, women, children. They caught us without mounts in the middle of the night."

Alarm flooded Thomas's veins. "My son and daughter?"

"They're safe."

His heart eased.

"William is still at the camp?"

"A mile east."

Thomas spurred his horse. "Cain, follow as fast as you can." Their horses were fresh, and they would outrun Cain. "Let's ride!"

"Thomas!"

He looked back and saw that Chelise sat on her steed, stricken with fear. "We'll catch you," he called to Mikil. They galloped ahead.

Thomas swung around and drew up beside her. "This changes nothing."

"There's more, Thomas," Cain said.

Thomas reached out and put his hand on Chelise's neck. "You're with me, my love. Nothing will happen to you, I swear it."

She hesitated. The Horde would want to retaliate. She was assuming the same about the tribe, despite all she'd seen.

"Trust me, Chelise."

"Okay."

Thomas glanced at Cain. "What more?"

Cain stared at them, eyes round.

"Well, what?" Thomas demanded, pulling his horse around.

"William will tell you."

He glared at the man. They had no time for this. "Let's go!"

32

THEY FOUND the tribe's camp first. What was left of it. The canvas tents had been shredded by swords. Pots and pans were scattered, cots smashed, chickens and goats slaughtered and left to rot.

Several large bloodstains marked the spots where some of the ten had been slain. The bodies were probably with William, awaiting cremation, as was their custom.

Thomas led the others through the camp, sickened. At times like these he wondered if their policy of nonviolence was worthless. Hadn't Justin himself once engaged in battle?

He set his jaw and rode slowly, keeping his anger in check. With a single sword he could take down twenty of the Scabs, but that was no longer who he wanted to be.

"Find them, Suzan," he ordered. Cain still hadn't caught up.

She took a trail that led to the cliffs above the canyon and sped east. They trotted through the canyon below her, waiting for her signal.

No one spoke. They each knew every tribe member as part of a family. Now ten of them had been killed and twenty-four taken captive.

He looked at Chelise, who drew her hood around her face and watched him tentatively. He wanted to tell her it was okay, that they would round the next bend to discover that it had all been a mistake.

A whistle cut through the air. "She's found them," Mikil said.

What remained of the tribe was hunkered down in a wash, one mile east, as Cain had said. Thomas saw them while they were still two hundred yards out. He slowed his horse and studied the lay of the land.

They had four escape routes in the event of a second attack, however unlikely it was at this point. From their position, all the surrounding cliffs were in clear view. William had chosen well.

"Thomas." Chelise's voice was small. "What's going to happen?"

He reached out and took her hand as they rode with the others. "Nothing's going to happen. We will mourn our loss and find a new camp. They are with Elyon now."

"And to me?"

"You're with me. They will embrace you. Your enemy's Woref, not the Circle."

William waited for them with Suzan and several men. The survivors, roughly twenty, were gathered behind them, some prostrate in mourning, others seated quietly, a few studying the surrounding cliffs for any sign of trouble.

Samuel and Marie ran out, and Thomas dropped to hug them. They were used to running from the Horde, but their wide eyes betrayed a new fear.

"Thank Elyon."

"I'm afraid, Papa," Marie said.

He held her tight. "No need. We are in Justin's hands." He clasped his son's shoulder. "Thank you for seeing to your sister. You're a strong one, Samuel."

"Yes, Father."

Thomas remounted and nudged his horse on. The tribe seemed relieved to see them. All except for William. He stood his ground like a man receiving a rebellious son. Johan and Mikil dismounted and hurried past William to console those who mourned.

"That's far enough, Thomas," William snapped.

There was trouble here. "It's okay, Chelise," he said quietly, squeezing her hand.

"That's where you're wrong," William said. "I see you've collected your Scab. How considerate of you to bring this trouble on us."

Thomas stopped his horse ten feet from the man. Three others stood behind him, arms folded. Thomas studied William and chose silence.

"The Horde left us a message," William continued. He looked at Chelise and scowled. Thomas fought the impulse to ride his horse through the man.

"Take your eyes off her! This is Chelise, daughter of Qurong, and she is to be my wife." He wasn't sure of the latter, but he felt compelled to say it. To shout if he must.

"We know who she is!" William shouted. "She is the cause of this great tragedy."

"You blame a Scab who leaves the Horde to find the Circle? I thought it was our purpose to save those who needed it."

"She looks scaly enough to me. And it seems that Woref wants his scaly whore back. If she isn't returned to the city within three days' time, he will execute the twenty-four albinos he's taken."

Chelise's hand twitched in his and he held it tight.

"Never! I won't let him lay a hand on her head. Ever!"

"Then you will send twenty-four of our family to their deaths."

"I will go," Chelise said quietly, pulling her hand free. "If Suzan will ride with me to the edge of the city, I'll go now."

Now Thomas panicked. He gripped his head. "No!" He suddenly felt compelled to get her off her horse. There would be no more riding today.

He slid to the ground, took her hand, and reached to help her dismount. She hesitated, then swung down.

Thomas put an arm around her. "Not another word about this!" he scolded William. "Have you no sense about you, man?"

Chelise turned to him. "He's right, Thomas. Woref will kill them. Or he'll kill half of them and demand again. I won't have the blood of these innocent people on my head."

She spoke like a princess, which made him even more desperate. There was a glint of fear in her eyes, but she stood tall.

Thomas spun to William. The whole tribe was now looking at him. "You see? Does this sound like a Scab? She's more honorable than you!"

"She's only agreeing to return to her vomit," William said. "She's not giving her life or anything as noble as you would imagine."

Thomas was furious. "Council! I call a council."

They just stared at him.

"Now! Suzan . . ."

"I'll stay with Chelise," Suzan said, stepping around William. "And I, for one, find this appalling." She took Chelise's arm. "I am with Thomas, whatever he says."

But Chelise wasn't ready to go without her say. "Thomas, I insist—"

"No!" He calmed his voice. "No, my love, no, no. I can't let you go. Never. Not like this."

Then he turned and walked away without giving her the chance to argue.

It was their second council in less than a week, and the circumstances were eerily similar. They dispensed with the seated discussion and settled for pacing and arm waving. Only their traditional call to Elyon even marked it as a true council meeting.

"If you had listened to me, none of this would have happened," William said. "Suzan may agree with you, but I'm sure not a single other member does."

"Then none of them has the true sense of Elyon's love," Thomas snapped.

"Who can know his love?"

"Surely you remember, William. All of you! Has it been so long since we watched Justin drown for us?"

"Then let Chelise give herself as Justin did!" William shouted. "Woref may take some flesh from her hide, but he won't kill her. Otherwise he will kill our friends."

"I'm not sure that Thomas is wrong," Johan said.

"Me neither," Mikil agreed.

"Then you're as foolish as he." He shoved a finger in the direction of the camp. "What would you suggest, that we all just lie down and die for this woman?"

Thomas paced and ran both hands through his hair. "No. I suggest that I go in her place."

"He's not asking for you."

"No, but we have three days." The rough form of a plan gathered, and he spoke quickly. "If I ride hard, I can reach the city in a day and offer myself in exchange for the twenty-four."

William seemed taken back. "If Woref wanted you, he would have demanded you."

"Let him object. We have time! If Qurong refuses my offer, then we agree with his demands. But he'll agree because he thinks like a Scab leader. He will find me far more valuable than twenty-four commoners."

"Then he'll kill you," Mikil said.

"Not as long as you have Chelise. Think whatever you want about Qurong, but he cares as much for his daughter as he does my capture. Don't you see?"

William frowned. "Have you considered the possibility that this goes beyond simple negotiation with the Horde?"

"Meaning what?"

"Meaning this trouble started with your infatuation with a Shataiki whore. You're acting like Tanis acted at the crossing. Maybe this is Elyon's way of purging the Circle of this nonsense."

A tremble ran through Thomas's hands. It was all he could do to keep them at his sides.

"You speak once more against Chelise and I'll trade you for the twenty-four," Johan said. "Thomas is right. You've lost your sense of Elyon's love. Perhaps you should try drowning again."

William scowled.

"I'll go with you," Mikil said.

"It will be—"

"I don't care how dangerous it is. You'll need help with this."

"I will go as well," Johan said. "There's also the matter of the dreams."

"Forget the dreams! I'm not sure I trust William with Chelise. I need you to stay here to keep him away from her."

With a parting glance at William, Thomas walked away, ending the council. No need nor time for a formal decision. He'd made up his mind, with or without the council's full agreement.

Chelise hurried toward him as soon as he strode into view. "Please, Thomas. You have to let me go."

He held up a hand to silence her, then took her arm and led her around tall boulders that offered some privacy.

"We've come to a decision."

"And what about my decision?"

He took her shoulders and gazed into her eyes, fearful that she'd abandoned her love for him. She was being noble in this insistence of hers, yes, but she was also agreeing to leave him for Woref. He couldn't bear the thought.

"Listen to me." He took a deep breath. "You know what will happen to you if you go back. Woref will never believe that I forced you to leave. He doesn't have a believing bone in his body. The man lives for deceit, and he expects the same from everyone else. If he doesn't end up killing you, he'll do worse. You know it!"

She searched his eyes. But she wasn't talking, and that was good.

"I have a plan. Now listen carefully—it can work; I know it can. Your father will trade me for the twenty-four and—"

"No! No, you can't do that! This is my problem."

"This is my problem! I can't lose you!"

"He'll kill you!"

"Not if you stay."

"Then he'll brutalize you!"

"I'm too valuable to him. It will buy us time. If you go back, it will be over. Please, I beg you. It's the only way."

A tear ran from her eye, and he wiped it away with his thumb. "Promise me you'll stay, for my sake. I promise we'll find a way."

Chelise remained quiet, fighting her tears. He leaned forward and kissed her forehead. "I can't live without you, my love. I can't."

"I feel lost, Thomas."

He held her, and she cried on his shoulder. "I have found you."

"I'm not like you. I'm a stranger here."

She was right, but he couldn't bring himself to point out the obvious, that unless she drowned she would always be lost. There would be time for that later.

"Then I will be a stranger with you," he said.

She rested her forehead against his chest. Then she kissed his neck and held him tight, crying.

It was her shame again, he thought. She still couldn't understand or accept his love. His heart ached, but he could only hold her and hope that she loved him as much as he loved her.

"You'll stay?"

"Promise me you'll come back for me."

"I promise. I swear it on my life."

33

MIKIL AND Thomas made it within a few miles of the Horde city before collapsing for badly needed rest. The moment Thomas fell into sleep, he awakened.

Washington, D.C.

He'd slept the night in the White House, but he'd lived . . . Thomas counted them off in his mind, one, two, three, four . . . four days in the desert, rescuing Chelise. To what end? To return to the city alone.

To end up here, in this mess of a world. He was tempted to knock himself out and return to the larger matter at hand. Chelise.

He forced his mind to focus on this world. He'd learned some things about Carlos and the Frenchman, hadn't he? Yes, from Johan.

The reality of the virus swelled in his mind. They were down to a couple of days. Carlos was the key.

He swung his legs to the floor, walked to the door, and stopped short with the sudden realization that he hadn't pulled on his jeans. Wouldn't do to run through the White House in blue-striped boxer shorts.

He dressed, brushed his teeth with a disposable toothbrush he found in the bathroom, and exited the room.

It took him seven minutes to gain a private audience with the president. Chief of Staff Ron Kreet ushered Thomas into a small sitting room adjacent to the Oval Office. "I don't know what you think you can do, and I can't say I'm a big believer in dreams," Kreet said, "but at this point I would take anything." He raised his eyebrow. "You're aware of the riots?"

"What riots?"

"Mike Orear from CNN said some things last night that sparked the crowd. They stormed the grounds. By the time the army had the situation under control, ten people were killed. Another seventeen in cities across the country."

"You're kidding."

"Not exactly a time for jokes. The president has addressed the nation twice since the riots began, both times with Orear. Things are quiet for the moment, relatively speaking. But fires are burning out of control in Southern California."

"What did he tell them?"

Kreet walked to the door and opened it. "He told them that the United States would cooperate fully with France's demands."

The chief of staff hadn't yet closed the door when Robert Blair showed. "Thank you, Ron. I have it from here."

He stepped in and closed the door behind his back. Blair wore a yellow tie with a blue paisley print, loose at an open collar. His hair was disheveled, and large dark rings hung from both eyes.

They stared at each other for a long moment. "Ron told you about the riots?"

"It's just the beginning," Thomas said. "Are we secure in here?"

"I had the room scanned thirty minutes ago."

"And?"

"Microphone in the lampshade."

Thomas nodded. At least the president was taking all of this seriously. "How's the rest of the world holding up?"

Robert Blair sighed and walked to a navy blue wing-backed chair. "I have to sit. Where to begin? Suffice it to say that if we do find a way out of this mess, the damage to the world's economies, cities, infrastructures, militaries—you name it—will take a decade to recover from, best case. Loss of life from collateral damage could reach into the hundreds of thousands if full-scale riots break out after this goes down tomorrow. The virus has started to flex its muscles—you do realize that."

Thomas sat stunned by this last piece of information. "The symptoms, you mean? I thought we had another five days . . . a week."

"Well, we were wrong. Evidently the first symptom is a rash. It'll last a few days with any luck, but the team that went to Bangkok has already been hit." He glanced at Thomas's shirt. "You?"

Thomas felt his side. "Last night . . ." He'd noticed a faint rash after waking in Bancroft's laboratory, but not like Kara. "My sister has definite symptoms of the virus."

"And so does Monique. Gains . . . the whole team that went to Bangkok. There've been thousands of cases reported in Thailand and now in several other gateway ports. It's a matter of hours before we get hit here."

The conclusion of this matter suddenly struck Thomas as inescapable. Until now, the Raison virus had been a blip on a computer screen. Now it was a red dot of rash. In a matter of days it would turn internal organs to liquid.

He stood. "There's no time—"

"Please sit down," Blair said in a tired but resolved voice.

Thomas sat.

"Did it work?"

"In a matter of speaking, yes. Johan dreamed as Carlos. Unfortunately, he couldn't remember as much as I would have hoped."

"But he . . . got into his mind . . ."

"Yes."

"And?" the president pushed.

"And I'm almost certain that Fortier has no intention of giving you an antivirus that works."

"So we were right."

"Johan also seemed to think that the number of people who ended up surviving the virus would be much smaller than anyone imagines. My guess is that Fortier is planning on turning his back on both Russia and China as well as most of the nations who've capitulated at this point."

"Son of a . . ." The president closed his eyes and took a deep breath. "Of course. What else did we expect?"

Thomas stood again. "Which means that I've got to get back to France as soon as possible. Today. Now."

"You really think you have a chance at this?"

"I have to reach Carlos. I know where he was last night; I've been there before. Fly me in at low level while it's dark and I have a shot of getting in. Our best shot at the antivirus is to make Carlos dream with me. If Carlos wakes up in Johan's mind, we'll have a chance of winning him over."

The president slowly ran his hands over his face and then pushed himself up. "Okay. You're right, but this could be the end. We're out of time."

Thomas lowered his voice. "I'm assuming you won't give them the nuclear weapons."

"Not a chance."

"The Israelis—"

"They agreed."

Thomas walked toward the door. "Then get me to France."

The mood at Genetrix Laboratories had shifted visibly in the last twenty-four hours. The end was at hand, and they all knew it.

The researchers couldn't hide the sudden appearance of red spots. The Raison Strain.

They wore long-sleeve shirts and blouses and slacks, but the rash on their necks was starting to show above their collars. Hope for an antivirus was evaporating as the rash spread. Monique herself still showed no rash, but she could feel her skin crawling, ready to break out at any moment.

Thomas had called for Kara, who'd spent only a few minutes with him before he'd been whisked off somewhere. Kara was returning as soon as a chopper became available. She had nowhere else to turn other than New York, where her mother lived, but she didn't want to leave the immediate area for two reasons, she'd said. One, in case Thomas needed her—for what, Monique could no longer imagine, but she was glad for Kara's company, regardless.

The second reason was more obvious.

Monique rose from her desk and walked to the freezer. The small vial of Thomas's blood rested on the top shelf by itself. She took it out and closed the door.

With this blood she and Kara might find life. It seemed absurd, but she'd experienced this particular stripe of absurdity once before, and she would gladly do it again. They would wait until the last moment, of course. After Thomas had finished whatever he was up to, Kara had said. Then they would apply this blood to their own, take some Valium, and dream a dream that lasted for as many years as they could manage.

She sat down at her desk and turned the glass vial in her fingertips. What was so special about this particular blood? Dr. Bancroft had run it through the lab at Johns Hopkins, and it had come back with no unusual traits. No elevated white counts, no unusual levels of trace elements . . . nothing.

Just red blood. Red blood that brought new life.

She absently flicked the tube. A thought occurred to her.

The door opened and Mark Longly stuck his head in. "The reports from the Bangkok lab just came in."

"And?"

"And nothing. Your father wants you to call him after you've looked at them, but I don't see anything."

"Antwerp?"

"Just got off the phone with them. Nothing new. UCLA has isolated a seventh pair in the string they're developing—it reacts in a fashion consistent with the others, but they're at least a week away from knowing what they have."

Monique nodded. "Cross their data with the strand from Antwerp again, see what—"

"Already have." He stared at her blankly. They'd been through a hundred similar conversations in the last week. Always nothing. Or if it was something, it was a something that meant nothing within the time they had.

"No use giving up now," she said.

Mark tried to smile, but it came off twisted. He closed the door.

Monique returned her thoughts to the vial. *You are my salvation.* She stood and walked to the freezer. Before she put herself under whatever power this blood had to offer, she would have a look at it herself.

But for now, she had a virus to defeat.

Or not to defeat.

34

MIKIL PRESSED her blade against the Scab's neck. "Not a sound and you will live."

She'd taken the man from behind, and Thomas knew that she had no intention of cutting him, but she looked as though she might like to.

"Nod your head!"

The man nodded vigorously.

Thomas walked around him and looked into his eyes. They'd crossed the desert in less than a day and then rested five miles from the city before finding their messenger, a lone sentry who'd been posted on the main road leading in from the west. His white face shone in early morning moonlight.

"We aren't going to hurt you, man," Thomas said. He lifted his hands. "See, no sword. Mikil has a blade, but really it's mostly for show. We only need a favor from you. Do we have your attention?"

The guard didn't move.

"What's your name?"

"Albertus," the man whispered.

"Good. If you don't do what we ask, I'll know what to tell Qurong. My name is Thomas of Hunter. You've heard of me?"

"Yes."

"Good. Then you'll go straight to the castle, wake Qurong, and deliver a message. Tell him that I will turn myself in for the twenty-four albinos he's captured. Bring them to the orchard two miles west of the Valley of Tuhan and I will give myself up. Mikil will take the albinos, and Qurong can have me in their place. Do you understand?"

The guard had settled. "You in exchange for the others they brought in."

"Yes. When did they arrive?"

"Last night."

"They are in the dungeons?"

"Yes. And the guard has been increased."

Thomas glanced at Mikil. They'd expected as much. Any attempted rescue would be a different matter this time.

"We'll be watching. Tell Qurong not to think he can outwit us. A fair exchange or nothing. I want them on horses." He nodded at Mikil. "Release him."

Mikil let the man go. He rubbed his neck and stepped away.

"Ride, man."

"If I leave my post—"

"Qurong will give you a reward for this, you fool! You're delivering his enemy. Now ride!"

The guard ran to his horse, mounted quickly, and rode into the night.

"Now what?" Mikil asked.

"Now we wait at the orchard."

———

The tribe had fallen for his ploy so easily that Woref had delayed his attack for several hours. But the camp slept in perfect peace, unsuspecting of another assault so soon.

His earlier instructions had been very pointed: kill only a few, capture as many as you can, and leave the rest alive with the message. Do not pursue them. Take the captives to the city, but wait for me with a full division.

As he'd hoped, the albinos had assumed that the Horde had taken what they'd come for.

Wrong. So very wrong.

Woref had arrived midday. He knew the tribe would call Thomas of Hunter in immediately. He knew that Chelise would be with Thomas. The fact that Thomas had left to rescue the twenty-four albinos in the city was now of no consequence. Woref would soon have the one prize he desired.

He closed his eyes and rolled his neck. He could almost taste her skin on his tongue now. A coppery taste. Like blood. Blood lust. Teeleh would want to see her tonight, he thought. He wasn't sure how he knew that, but he fully expected the creature to gloat. Woref shivered with anticipation.

Odd how his passions and those of the winged serpent had somehow become one. He was complicit with Teeleh; he accepted that now. But he was serving his own interests. Frankly, he wasn't sure who was serving whom. When he became the supreme leader of the Horde, he would need the kind of power Teeleh could give him.

But first . . .

He opened his eyes and stared into the night. First he would possess the firstborn's daughter. He would possess her and he would ravage her. She would love him. If he had to beat her love from her with his fist, she would love him. He would have to be subtle at first, naturally. Teeleh was as much about subtlety as he was about brute force. Patience. But in the end she would be his and his alone.

Woref turned to the captain. "If a single one of these albinos is killed, I will drown the man who does it. They understand that? Our objective here is to liberate Qurong's daughter. We can't risk killing her with a stray arrow."

"And afterward?"

"I'll decide."

He looked down at the camp again. She was in the third tent from the left. Unless she'd moved during the night, which was unlikely but possible. His men had been known to miss more than he cared to admit.

"They are in position?"

"We have a ring around the camp. There is no possible escape."

"I've heard those words before."

"This time I'm sure."

Woref grunted. "After me."

He dropped over the ledge and approached the line of men who lay in wait along the canyon floor. They'd painted their faces black, and in their dark battle dress they looked like creatures of the night. The Horde rarely attacked at night because of their fear of Shataiki. Odd, all things considered. But the black bats were too busy preying on the minds in the city to wander out into these canyons.

Woref dropped to one knee at the front of the line and studied the tents. Not a stir. All that remained was to draw the noose tight enough to prevent escape.

"Slowly."

He stood and stepped toward the camp. High on his right, the captain gave the signal to the rest of the ring. Cautiously, so that their boots would make little sound on the sand, six hundred warriors closed in on the tribe.

Woref stopped twenty yards from the first tent and raised his hand.

Not a sound. His heart pounded. The warriors on the far side of the camp had taken a signal and stopped with him. Even if the albinos saw them now, their fate was sealed.

The third tent. His white whore was there, sleeping in an albino's tent. Tonight she would learn the meaning of respect. Tonight a whole new world would be opened up to her. His world.

Woref grabbed a tall sickle from the warrior behind him. "Stay," he ordered softly.

He walked deliberately toward the camp, leaving his men behind. When he reached the third tent, he spread his legs, lifted the sickle, and swung it through the edge of the canvas. The blade sliced through the fabric and the center pole as if they were made of paper. He grabbed the collapsing wall and ripped it aside.

There lay a woman, eyes still closed. A Scab. His whore.

Woref reached down, took a fistful of her hair, and jerked her off the ground. She woke with a scream, eyes wide in terror.

"That's it, dear wife. Let the world know your pleasure."

Chelise grabbed at his hands futilely. Her wails shattered the still night. Tent flaps flew open, and albinos stumbled out like rats from their dens.

The Horde army didn't move.

Woref dragged Chelise to the edge of the camp, hauled her up so she could stand, and spun back. The albinos were already in full motion, scurrying for an escape. Let them. They would run into warriors within a few strides.

"No one takes what is mine!" he shouted. "No one!"

"Johan, the eastern route is blocked," a voice cried.

Martyn?

His warriors were still awaiting his signal—to kill or not to kill.

Woref spun Chelise around and clubbed her on the temple with his left hand. Her wails fell quiet and she sagged. He released her hair and let her fall in a pile.

"Martyn!" His voice rang through the canyon. "Martyn steps forward or I will kill every soul."

"We don't need your threats to motivate us," Martyn said, walking in from Woref's left. "You've been threatening us for a year already."

Martyn looked odd without his white eyes and skin. Puny. Sickly.

"This is the mighty general? You look ridiculous, my old friend."

"And you look like you could use a good bath."

Woref wasn't sure what to make of the man. The dark woman they'd taken captive earlier stepped up beside Martyn. His fortune was far greater than he could have hoped for. In one night he would claim his bride and slaughter Johan, leaving Thomas to weep on his own.

"I've reclaimed what is mine, and now I will take pleasure in watching you die."

He lifted his hand.

"My lord, I demand an audience." A tall albino stepped forward. Another one of the five they'd captured a few days earlier. Fear danced in his eyes.

"You're not in a position to demand anything."

"Then I beg. You will thank me."

Woref lowered his hand. "And you are . . . ?"

"William. I am a council member, and I have authority in the Circle."

"What are you up to?" Martyn demanded of the albino.

The one named William lifted his hand to silence Martyn. Interesting. What kind of man would Martyn both object to and respect with his silence?

"Then speak."

"Alone. We aren't people of violence; there's no danger from me."

Woref grabbed Chelise by her arm and dragged her to the line of warriors. "Watch her." The tall albino met him to one side.

"Speak."

William spoke in a low voice. "I can assure you, General, that I argued in the strongest possible terms against this madness. Thomas has endangered the entire Circle, and now we will pay with our lives. You must believe me when I say not all among the Circle are so antagonistic as Thomas."

"You're begging for your life? I have no time for this."

"I'm giving you my motive for delivering Thomas of Hunter to you."

"You can deliver him to me how?"

"I know where he is and where he will be tomorrow. Let us live and I will go with you."

"Your word against the life of Martyn. Am I a fool?"

"You know as well as I do that we're bound by our word in the Circle. Consider my motive. Since the death of his wife, Thomas has been a detriment to us all."

"Then you would betray your own leader?"

"He's betrayed us! If I'm wrong, then you can kill me. Would I give my life for a man I despise?"

Woref considered the man's argument. He had the look of a despairing man, given to deception, perhaps. But who was he betraying?

The tribe was looking at them in silence. Powerless.

"I'll kill Martyn and take you," Woref said.

"No. Then kill us all. Johan is a shadow of the great general you once knew. Let him live out his puny life. Take me and I will deliver Thomas, who's the only threat among the Circle."

"Where is he?"

"Near the city, planning another rescue."

Woref turned toward the captain. "Put this man in chains. The rest live. Keep the army here until morning. Make sure none of them leaves this canyon; I want no pursuit."

He'd come for Chelise. If he could also take Thomas, the last of Qurong's reservations about his general would be gone.

His mind turned toward the unconscious form on the ground. The woman who had brought him so much grief. The one he loved.

His only regret was that he would have to exercise restraint for the time being. Bringing a battered daughter home to her father would not do. But there were always other ways.

He glanced back at the albino and saw that he was staring at Johan. He wasn't sure if it was a look of betrayal or one of regret. They would know soon enough.

—— ⚬⚬⚬ ——

"So soon!" Mikil said, gazing down from her perch in the tree. The sun had just risen when the long line of albinos appeared at the edge of the field with a guard for each. A second row of guards marched into the field on either side.

"What did I tell you?" Thomas said. "Qurong is no fool. He suspects that Chelise will be compelled by my captivity as much as the Circle is. Do you see Woref?"

"No. There's a general, but I don't think it's Woref."

"You'd think he would handle this himself." Thomas looked back at the trees behind them. "The way's clear?"

"There's no way they could have set a trap this soon. Give me ten minutes on them and we're free." Mikil gripped his shoulder. "You're sure about this, Thomas? It's bothering me."

"And you're not bothered by their deaths?" He nodded at the albinos, who now sat on their horses in a long line, waiting for the next move. "Just make sure that nothing happens to Chelise. Without her my life is worthless."

"Johan would hog-tie her himself if he thought she might leave."

"Not like that. If she left me for Woref now, I think I'd rather be dead. And she still has the disease, Mikil. I don't trust her mind."

"But you trust her heart."

"I'm staking my life on her heart."

They'd developed a plan for getting Thomas out—a risky move involving an exchange for Chelise in the desert—but it would require her cooperation.

"Elyon's strength, my friend." He clasped her arm.

"Be careful, Thomas."

"I will."

"If we get through this, I would like to dream with you. Become Kara."

"If Kara lives, I think she would like that."

Thomas lowered himself to one of the horses, took a deep breath, and walked out into the open field beside the apple trees.

"We meet halfway," he yelled.

They saw him and held a brief discussion. The general Mikil had seen called out to him. "Slowly. No tricks. We have men on either side."

Thomas nudged his horse and walked toward the line. The albinos began to move forward.

He passed them on the right, less than twenty yards from three archers who had their bows strung. If he bolted now, they would take him easily. He nodded at the albino closest to him, an older woman named Martha. She looked at him with fear in her eyes.

"I'll be seeing you soon enough, Martha. Be strong."

"Elyon's strength," she said quietly.

And then he was past them and in the hands of the Horde. The tribe members trotted over the field and disappeared into the trees.

"Off the horse!" the general ordered.

Thomas dismounted and let them tie his hands behind his back with a long strap of canvas. "You expect me to walk all the way?"

The general didn't respond. They tied his horse to two others, pushed him back in the saddle, and led him away.

Thomas rode into the Horde city for the second time in two weeks. Once again he saw the squalor caused by the disease. Once again he tried unsuccessfully to ignore the filth and stench of Scabs who screamed insults at him. Once again he approached the dark dungeon that had once been a great amphitheater built for the expression of ideas and freedom. This time they passed the castle without taking him to Qurong. That would come soon enough.

No fewer than a hundred guards surrounded the dungeon, all armed with bows and sickles. These were no army regulars. They were scarred from battle and scowled with bitter hatred.

The dungeon guard led him down the wet steps and along the same corridor he'd walked before. But they passed his old cell and took him down a second flight of stairs to a lower level lit only by torches. They shoved him into a small cell, slammed the gate shut, and left him in total darkness.

Thomas collapsed in the corner, exhausted. There was nothing to do now but wait.

And dream.

35

THE ONLY jump Thomas had ever executed was more of a cannon shot than a one-two-three leap, and that one out the back of a military transport that had been cut in half by a missile two weeks earlier. This time he would buddy-jump with Major Scott MacTiernan, army Ranger.

The French defenses weren't accustomed to engaging enemy aircraft over their soil—the sudden shift in power was only two weeks old, and the military was being coerced. All of this played into the Americans' hands. The C-2A Greyhound cargo plane came off the USS *Nimitz* five hundred miles off the coast of Portugal, and flew south over Spain and then up western France, hugging the land below radar. As soon as they neared the drop point, the pilot pitched the nose up and let the plane claw for the dark skies.

Air defenses painted them at two thousand feet.

"You got ten seconds," the master snapped. They'd estimated the window based on the time it would take the French radar to confirm and respond to the sudden blip on their screens. The parachute was made of a fabric that would give them little if any signature, and even so, they wouldn't be in the air long enough to cause alarm.

"Remember, relax," MacTiernan said, facing the wind over Thomas's shoulder. He checked the straps that lashed Thomas to his chest. "On three."

Thomas fell into the darkness, eyes wide behind the goggles. The aircraft's roar was immediately replaced by the rush of wind beating his ears. He was along for the ride—a very short ride, the major had warned.

MacTiernan pulled the cord. The chute tugged them skyward. MacTiernan guided them in with night vision. The ground was a mixture of black swaths, which Thomas assumed were forest, and slightly lighter fields. They were on top of them, then drifting into a field.

"Watch your legs! Coming up in five. Run with me, baby! Hit the ground running!"

They feathered in for a landing, hit hard, and stumbled forward. Silence.

The parachute flapped once as it folded in on itself and settled to the ground. Thomas shrugged off the harness and checked his gear. Black pants with a knife strapped to one thigh and a nine-millimeter semi-automatic strapped to the other. Canteen, compass, radio with a homing device that could be picked up from Cheyenne Mountain. Black T-shirt, black ski cap, black sweater wrapped around his waist. Night-vision goggles.

The prospect of using a weapon gave him mixed feelings, but he wasn't sure that he was meant to be a pacifist here in this reality. He still wasn't sure what he felt about a whole slew of issues here, particularly religious issues. He wasn't a man of the cloth, for crying out loud. He was a man deeply affected by his dreams of another reality, but in his short few weeks of tripping between the worlds, he hadn't had the time to unravel theology here as he had there. He might never have the time.

"One piece?" MacTiernan was kneeling, penlight on a small map, compass in hand.

"Looks like it," Thomas said. "Where do you put us?"

The major pointed to their right. "One mile that way. I have you on GPS; if you drift left I give you one click. Right, two clicks. You got it?"

"Left one click, right two clicks."

"No other communication unless absolutely necessary. Remember, two hours. We have to clear this sector and make our rendezvous in five hours. We miss the window, we miss the chopper. It's already en route. Missing it would cost us ten hours—this isn't like a fixed wing."

They'd come in on the much faster transport to make the drop tonight, but they wouldn't have the same luxury on the return trip. With any luck they wouldn't need it.

"Two hours." Thomas checked his watch.

"You get in a bind, I come after you. That's the plan."

Thomas didn't bother responding. He was up to much more than this, and much less at once, depending on the reality, depending on the enemy, depending on the day.

He reached the edge of the compound in thirty minutes of careful going. MacTiernan corrected his course only twice. The return trip, assuming there was one, would take only ten minutes. He had an hour and twenty minutes to execute the mission.

The farmhouse sat in the middle of the field, a hundred yards distant. Except for a dull glow from the windows on the first floor, it was dark.

Thomas pulled on the night-vision goggles, squinted at the green light, and then slowly scanned the perimeter. One guard on the north side. Two by the road that snaked into the forest on the far side. Lighter than he would have guessed. Had they already vacated? Their cover here was blown; they knew that. They'd depended on secrecy, not high-tech security for protection, but they'd never planned on one of their corpses coming to life and escaping to tell the world of the location. Their only option would have been to abandon the facility.

He ran in a low crouch, straight toward the basement window that he and Monique had escaped through before. The effectiveness of his mission now depended on speed and surprise.

He squatted with his back to the stone wall and caught his breath. No light from the hallway past the window. No light from the upper floor. That would be his entry point.

Three weeks ago an ascent like the one that dared him now would have been unthinkable. Climbing the stones that formed the fifteen-foot wall would be difficult, but not impossible. Transitioning to the roof that jutted out at least four feet was the problem.

Night goggles still in place, he checked his surroundings, and then hand by hand, foot by foot, he scaled the wall. The soffit stuck out just above his head. He leaned back and gazed at the gutter, two feet up, four feet back. Or was it five feet back? Missing this leap would end the mission as quickly as a bullet to the head.

He set his feet, thought of how Rachelle would have laughed at the ease of this particular attempt, and sprang backward like an inverted frog.

He'd overestimated the jump. But he arched his back and corrected. Still upside down and flying with good speed, he grasped the gutter, folded at his waist into a pike position, then whipped his legs back to continue their natural arc. He treated the gutter as a high bar, and his momentum carried him up and over like a world-class gymnast.

The gutter creaked and began to give way, but his weight had already shifted. He released, floated over the edge of the roof, and landed on his hands and feet, like a cat.

A shingle came loose, slid over the edge, and fell into the grass below. No other sound. He scrambled to the only dormer on this end of the house and listened beside the window. Still no sound.

The room inside was dark, and with the goggles he could see that it was also vacant, unless someone was crouching behind the boxes. Storage room.

Thomas fumbled for the duct tape he'd brought and ran three long strips down the glass. Then he unwrapped the sweater around his waist, covered the window to muffle sound, and smashed it with his elbow. A crunch but no shattering glass. Good enough.

He shoved the tape roll and sweater in his belt and carefully pushed through the broken glass. Two minutes later he stood in the dark storage room, staring at a dozen stacks of boxes.

Thomas withdrew the gun and cracked the door. Small hall. One other door. Clear.

He stepped out carefully. Only one way to do this.

The first door looked as though it led to a closet. It did.

The second appeared to lead to a larger room. It did. A bedroom. Thomas extended his gun and pushed the door open.

The blinding light hit him then, while he had one foot in and one out, door still swinging.

The goggles! He swept at his face and knocked the contraption from his eyes.

"Hello, Thomas."

Voice to his right. This was Carlos.

"I see you insist on coming for me until I finally kill you for good."

Easy, Thomas. This is what you expected. Play the game.

He dropped his gun and lifted both hands. "We need to talk. It's not what you think."

Carlos held a gun on him at five paces. He still wore a bandage over the cut on his neck. A grin nudged the corner of his mouth. Small red dots peppered his face. So the man hadn't taken the antivirus. Or the antivirus didn't work.

"I watch an armed man climb my roof, sneak through a window wearing night-vision glasses, and am expected to consider the possibility that my judgment of his intentions is false?" Carlos asked. "Don't tell me: you came to save me."

"I came because I know that you met with Armand Fortier yesterday," Thomas said. "He showed you a list of the people he expects to survive the virus. Now you have to ask yourself how in the world I could possibly have this information."

The grin faded. Carlos blinked. "You've tricked me one too many times. This time you will fail."

"And if I do, then you will die. We both know that your name's on that list only as a lure for you and only for the moment. Tell me how I know so much. Tell me how I walk off your gurney after two days without a pulse. Tell me how any of what you've seen me do with your own eyes is possible."

Carlos just stared at him. But his mind was bending—Thomas could see it in his eyes.

"I came here for two reasons. One, I've come with proof. If you let me, I can show you beyond any possible doubt that my dreams are real

and that you play a significant role in those dreams. The second reason I've come is to save your life. The simple fact of the matter is that
we need you, but you'll do us no good if you're dead. You may hate
Americans and Israel and all that, but unless you know what's really
going on here, you can't possibly be in a position to make informed
decisions."

He said it all in a rush, because he knew that he had to plant these
seeds in Carlos's mind before he pulled the trigger. His words seemed to
have made an impact. But the man wasn't unnerved as much as he was
irritated.

"I don't know what kind of sorcery—"

"We don't have time for this, Carlos. I just came five thousand miles
to make contact with you, and what I have to show you may save the
Arab world from extermination. What does it take to get your attention?
You still have a cut I gave you last time without touching you, for goodness' sake! You have to let me prove myself."

Too much had happened for Carlos to dismiss this as a game of wits.
His neck, Thomas's escapes, the knowledge of his conversation with
Fortier—all of it unexplained.

"How?"

"By letting you dream with me."

The man's face reddened. "Do you take me as some kind of fool?" His
fist clenched. "I cannot accept this! This . . ."

Thomas moved while the man was momentarily distracted by his
frustration. Dropped shoulder to his left, single spin, heel to the man's gun
hand. Even if Carlos had fired, the bullet would have gone wide.

Fortunately, he didn't even manage that.

His outstretched hand flew wide. Thomas followed with an open
palm to the man's solar plexus. Carlos stepped back, shocked. Unable to
breathe.

"Sweet dreams." Thomas hit him on the side of the head, and the man
dropped.

Working quickly, he pulled out his knife and cut his finger. Then he ran a thin slit along Carlos's forearm. He smeared his own blood along the cut.

"Make him understand, Johan. Please make him understand."

Thomas let the man dream ten minutes before waking him. A minute probably would have sufficed, but he didn't want to take any chances. He shook the man hard, slapped him once on the cheek, and stepped back to the cot, gun extended.

Carlos groaned, went silent, then jerked up with a gasp.

Thomas knew immediately that Carlos had dreamed with Johan. He was far too seasoned to wake in this state of disorientation for any other reason.

"Where were you?" he asked.

Carlos looked at him, glanced at the gun, ignored it, and stared into Thomas's eyes.

"With Johan, I mean. Where were you?"

"In . . . in the forest."

"The forest?"

"Going to the Horde city."

That made no sense. Johan was coming after him? The man had left his post for a mission to rescue Thomas? If he'd done anything to endanger Chelise, Thomas would have his head.

Carlos stared at his gun again. Now the real question. "Do you believe me now? There's another reality beyond this one, and in that reality you and I are on the same side. There's more."

"If I die here, then Johan will die there," Carlos said. He was hardly more than a child who'd just learned the truth.

"And I'm depending on Johan," Thomas said. "I would never let him die. So you see, I *am* here to save your life."

As long as Carlos believed the dream was more than a simple dream, Thomas was sure he would succeed.

They stared at each other for a full minute. It was one thing to believe that another reality existed. It was another thing altogether to change your plans because of that reality.

"If we don't stop Fortier, we will both die," Thomas said. "Along with most of the earth's population. Is this what you had in mind?"

No answer. But his eyes showed no defiance. He was still caught up in the wonder of it all.

"There's only one way to stop Fortier, and that's to take away his teeth."

"The antivirus," Carlos said.

"Yes. The United States must have the antivirus. It's the only force that has a plausible chance of dealing with Fortier." Thomas paused. "Can you get the antivirus?"

"No."

Thomas lowered his gun. "Do you believe that I won't harm you?"

"Yes."

Carlos slowly stood. "I don't know how . . ." He stopped and looked at his hands.

"And you may never know. It doesn't matter. What does matter is that we stop them. You may be our only chance to do that. You're sure that you can't get your hands on the antivirus? It does exist. Please tell me that it exists."

"It exists, but Svensson's protected himself by separating it into two components somehow. He alone controls one, which will be used only at the last moment."

"Then we have to take Svensson. If we control even one component of the antivirus, we will have a bargaining chip. At the moment we have nothing except for the weapons. With any luck we can force Svensson's hand."

"Will you give them the weapons at the exchange?"

It was a moment of truth. If he told Carlos their plans, he might be tipping his hand to the enemy. On the other hand, doing so could earn him the trust he needed. Without the antivirus, all was lost.

"No," he said.

A moment passed between them. Carlos understood what Thomas had just done.

"Does Fortier plan on giving us an antivirus that works?" Thomas asked.

"No." Case settled. They were now together.

Carlos took a very deep breath and tilted his head to the ceiling. "What do you want me to do?"

"Take Svensson. Don't kill him—we have to protect the antivirus. Who's taken it?"

"Only Fortier and Svensson," Carlos said.

"Good. If we go down, so does everyone except those two. I doubt that's Svensson's idea of paradise. He'll be forced to deal."

Carlos nodded. "Maybe. But you have no idea how dangerous this is."

"Dangerous? We're way beyond dangerous, my friend. This history's already been written once, and in that history most of us die. I would say it's more like impossible. But that doesn't mean we don't try. They say with a little faith you can move mountains. That's all I'm asking. Move a mountain. Will you?"

The man from Cyprus frowned deeply. "Clearly, I don't have a choice."

"The fate of the world may very well rest in your hands."

"Not yours?"

"No, my presence would only compromise you. Do you see this?"

"What do you have in mind?"

———

"Did you hear what Carlos told him?" Fortier demanded into the phone.

"No."

"How long? How could you have allowed this?"

"Forgive me, sir. He slipped past our guard. We don't know how long they were together. By the time we understood what was happening, he was gone."

"You're absolutely sure that it was an American?"

"No, but it was clearly no one we knew."

The phone was silent while Fortier considered the matter.

"Shall we take any action?" the man asked.

"No. Carlos stays there. Under no circumstance is he to leave. Consider the compound his prison, but he must not know. Business as usual. If he tries to leave, kill him."

36

THOMAS DUCKED below the spinning blades over his head and ran from the helicopter. The USS *Nimitz's* massive tower reached high just ahead. He'd seen the large fleet from the air. Over two hundred ships from the United States alone. Dots on the ocean, each leading a long tail of white foam.

The British fleet was to the north five miles. The Israelis were using mostly freighters—more than thirty, each loaded to the gills with weapons they denied they actually possessed. There was enough nuclear firepower in a five-mile radius of this aircraft carrier to blow up the world fifty times over.

The first sign that not all was normal on deck was the absence of flight crews. The fact was, the *Nimitz* was being run on fumes, with fewer than fifty troops to guide her across the Atlantic.

Thomas hardly recognized Merton Gains. The man wore a white turtleneck and dark glasses, but if he thought they hid the rash on his face, he was fooling only himself. Thomas hurried toward him. The secretary extended his hand. Wind buffeted his hair.

"Thank God you made it. Just in time."

Thomas took his hand. "They've started?"

"Two hours ago. You have a front-row seat on the observation deck if you want it."

"Absolutely."

The senator paused. "You're not as bad as I thought you'd be."

The rash.

"No. I have it under my arms." He wasn't sure what to say. "Are you okay?"

Gains spit to one side and turned toward the door.

Thomas followed Gains out of the wind and to a large room full of electronics he could only guess at. Radar—that he could see. Large screens with hundreds of blips. Among those blips floated the sharpest edge of America's military sword—six full carrier groups, hundreds of ships carrying everything from their most sophisticated attack aircraft to nuclear weapons. A second large wave of ships was on the way with more, but this was Fortier's primary prize.

Gains introduced him to the first officer. "This is Ben Graver. He's going to talk us through the operation."

Ben took his hand without any expression. "Can't say it's a pleasure," he said.

"Neither can I," Thomas said.

"Should be done in another hour."

The plan was simple. Per French demands, each ship was to be anchored at specific coordinates and their crews off-loaded to a single ship from each country. French crews would board the vessels and verify the cargoes, and only then would the antivirus be turned over.

The obvious problem with the exchange was the lack of a guarantee that Fortier would actually deliver the antivirus after confirming his receipt of weapons. His best offer, and the one Thomas had insisted they accept, had been to anchor one ship containing the antivirus with each navy. They could examine the ship but not take control of it until after Fortier's people had taken possession of the weapons.

"The admiral's aboard?" Thomas asked.

"He is."

"I need to speak to him. Now."

Ben eyed him, then picked up a phone. He spoke quietly and set it back in the cradle. "This way."

Admiral Kaufman. Brent Kaufman, personal friend to the president. The tall, gray-haired man with broad shoulders and blue eyes received them and immediately dismissed the first officer.

"Welcome to hell," the admiral said.

"No, hell comes in two days," Thomas said. "This is more like purgatory."

The admiral frowned. He turned to two ranking men in British and Israeli uniforms. "This is General Ben-Gurion for the IDF, and Admiral Roland Bright from the British fleet."

Thomas took their hands in turn. "Does the first officer know what's about to happen?"

"He does," Kaufman said.

"My understanding was that no one except—"

"I don't know how many ships you've been on, son," the admiral said. "But you can't do what the president has ordered me to do without at least a minimal crew. Someone's got to pull the trigger."

He was right. Thomas regretted challenging the man.

"The French aren't going to give us the antivirus," he said.

"What?" Gains said. "That's . . . Then what are we doing?"

"We're playing ball," Thomas said. "We're hoping for one more chance at getting our hands on a solution that works."

The British admiral's face had lightened a shade. "Under no circumstances am I risking this fleet and this cargo without some assurance that we have an even exchange. This was—"

"Excuse me, sir, but this is exactly what we agreed to. If we don't turn the weapons over exactly as agreed, we tip our hands. At this very moment we have a man on the inside closing in on the antivirus."

"Frankly, I'd sign on for blowing the entire country back into the Stone Age," Ben-Gurion said.

"And the antivirus with it?" Thomas said. "I'm not saying our alternatives have anyone jumping for joy here. We're hanging on by a thread, that's it, but at least it's something."

"I can tell you that I will pay dearly for this tomorrow," Ben-Gurion said.

"Tomorrow the world's eyes will be on the mounting dead, not a few missing nuclear weapons. Our play was based on the hope that they would turn over the antivirus, true enough. Now that we know they have no intention of doing so, our plan still has merit. If we turn tail now, Israel will be hit with missiles within the hour."

"Then we wipe them out."

"I realize your mind is on your military, General," Thomas said. "But trust me, the virus makes your army look like plastic toys. Please understand this: you cannot, under any circumstances, fire on Paris or anywhere near Paris. If you inadvertently take out the antivirus, ten days from now this world will have a population of two."

"Two meaning whom?" Gains asked.

"The only two who've already taken the antivirus. Fortier and Svensson. The only chance for survival the rest of us have is giving my man a chance. That means we follow the plan with one change."

The British admiral arched his left eyebrow. "A change?"

"Can we delay the explosives?"

"We control that from here," Kaufman said.

"Then we delay six hours."

"Why?"

"My man needs the time."

"They will retaliate," Ben-Gurion said. "You said so yourself."

"Not if we play our cards right. Not if my man succeeds. Not if we threaten to wipe out Paris."

"I thought you said we couldn't risk compromising the antivirus."

"We can't. But we can call their bluff. If it gets that far, they'll know we have nothing left to lose. They won't run the risk of a final desperate launch on our part. You've held back ten long-range missiles?"

"Yes," Ben-Gurion said.

"There you go. They might doubt our resolve, but they won't doubt yours." He turned to the window and gazed at the battleship on their port side. The menacing guns that jutted over the water were now useless toys in a game with far higher stakes than their manufacturer's wildest imagination.

"I don't know where you learned your strategy, lad," the British admiral said behind him. "But I like it. And as far as I can see, it's our only option."

"Admiral Kaufman?" Thomas asked without turning.

"It might work." He swore. "I don't see an alternative."

"Then let's give them something to think about," Ben-Gurion said. "We're with you."

Thomas turned back to them. "Thank you."

Honestly, it felt good to be commanding men after this thirteen-month hiatus in the other reality. This could be Mikil and Johan and William he was commanding. Thomas wasn't sure what President Blair had told these men to pave the way for their taking suggestions from a twenty-five-year-old, but it had worked.

The exchange took an hour longer than anticipated, but by 1600 hours the nuclear arsenals of the United States, Britain, and Israel were in the hands of the French aboard more than three hundred ships that steamed steadily toward their coast.

As payment, the USS *Nimitz* had taken ten large crates filled with canisters of powder that a team of virologists from the World Health Organization quickly confirmed contained an antivirus, though there was no way to verify its authenticity for at least ten hours. Even then, they wouldn't know its true effectiveness. A complete test would take a full day.

In addition to the crates, the aircraft carrier now carried the three thousand crew members who'd been off-loaded from the American fleet.

Thomas had left his radio with Carlos as planned. The arrangement couldn't have been clearer. He had a twelve-hour window. If he succeeded, he would activate the homing beacon. If he hadn't yet succeeded, he would not.

There had been no homing signal.

The six-hour delay had come and gone. Thomas watched the clock on the observation deck, and with each jerk of the minute hand, his hopes dropped a notch.

Come on, Carlos.

Perhaps there was no way to change history after all.

Kaufman walked into the room and removed his hat. His eyes glanced at the clock. "We're in confirmed range five minutes, then we start losing a consistent signal."

Thomas stood. "Then what are you waiting for, Admiral? Send the message, fire the missiles, and drop the ships."

A grin crossed Kaufman's face. "At least we go out in a blaze of glory."

"Maybe."

Thomas watched the plan unfold over the first officer's shoulder at the radar station. The message sent to Fortier was straightforward: *fire one round in retaliation and the next ten will target Paris.* It wasn't worded quite so simply, but the meaning was the same.

The missiles were next. Twenty-six in all, eighteen cruise missiles from batteries outside Lankershim Royal Air Base in England and eight tactical nukes—compliments of the IDF. The targeting was straightforward and unmistakable: every major command and control facility in and around the deposits of the Russian, Chinese, Pakistani, and Indian nuclear stores in northern France. They couldn't take out the weapons themselves without risking massive detonations that would level civilian populations, but they intended to at least temporarily cripple France's use of their newly acquired arsenal.

Admiral Kaufman gave the order calmly over the intercom. He could just as easily have been telling his wife that he would be home soon.

"Scuttle the ships."

The observation deck quieted. The air felt stuffy. Thomas kept his eyes glued on the sea of bright dots on the radar screen. Each one represented a loaded ship, including six full carrier groups crowded with fighters. The computer displayed them as steady signals, as opposed to signatures that lit with each sweep of the radar.

"Is it working?"

"Give it time," Ben said. "These things don't drop like stones, I don't care how you do it."

For a while nothing happened.

"Confirmed detonations," a voice said over the comm.

Five more minutes, still nothing.

Then the first light winked out.

"Ship down. Israeli freighter, the *Majestic*."

A billion dollars of nuclear weapons was on its way to the bottom.

Then another and another. They began to wink out like expired candles.

"Back to the Stone Age," Ben said quietly.

"There will be plenty more where those came from," Thomas said. "Assuming there's anyone left to build them."

Here in the silence of the aircraft carrier's observation deck, the destruction of the world's nuclear arsenal looked like something on a video game, but a hundred miles away, the ocean was burning with three hundred slowly sinking blazes. The weapons required far more to detonate them than random concussion and heat from conventional explosions. They would sink to the ocean floor intact, awaiting salvage at the earliest possible opportunity.

Assuming that anyone was around to salvage them.

Thomas watched the screen for nearly an hour, mesmerized by the silent vanishing of tiny green lights.

Then the screen went black.

For a moment no one spoke.

Gains stuck his head into the room. "I just talked to the president, Thomas. They're sending a plane to pick you up."

He turned. "Me? Why?"

"Wouldn't say. But they're sending an F-16 with in-flight refueling. He wants you back in a hurry."

"No clue at all?"

"None. But the news is out."

"The media already knows what we did here?"

"No. The news about the virus. The symptoms are widespread in all of the gateway cities." He pushed his sunglasses up on his nose. "It's begun."

"How long do I have?"

"They'll be here in an hour."

Thomas walked toward him. "Then I don't have much time, do I?"

"What are you going to do?"

"Sleep, Mr. Gains. Dream."

37

A DOOR slammed above Thomas, waking him. A faint scream.

He opened his eyes and stared into pitch darkness. For a moment he thought he was on the ship, hearing another round of fire. But the cold, damp floor under him pulled him back to this reality.

In the dungeon.

How long had he slept?

The scream came again, louder now. He sat up and caught his breath. Chelise?

No, that was impossible. Chelise was in the tribe's hands, safe.

Or was she? He was fully awake now. Carlos had said that Johan was coming. Why?

Footsteps sounded overhead. A dim light wavered down the corridor. Boots on the stairs.

Thomas scrambled to his feet, lost his balance, fell against the wall, and pushed himself off. He hurried to the gate and gripped the bars. Torchlight glistened off wet rock walls. They were coming for him.

He saw Woref's familiar face, glowing by the light of a torch he held in his left fist. His right hand grasped the end of a rope. So the time had come. He took a deep breath and stepped back from the bars.

Woref stared in through the bars. He had someone else behind him—another prisoner or a guard.

"The mighty Thomas of Hunter," Woref said. "So clever. So brave. To come all this way for nothing. William is dead."

"William?"

"You remember him. Tall. Green eyes. A weak fool who talks too much.

He convinced me to spare the tribe in exchange for you. I suppose you should be proud of him."

Spare the tribe. What was the man speaking of? Thomas felt the blood leave his extremities.

"Surprised?" Woref said. "Imagine my surprise to find that you'd already given yourself up in exchange for the other albinos. You were sure you'd be safe as long as your whore was with the tribe."

Thomas's mind spun in dizzying circles.

"It appears the fearless commander of the Forest Guard has finally been outwitted." Woref tugged on the rope. Chelise stumbled past him, lips quivering, hands bound. Something sharp, like fingernails or a claw, had drawn three streaks of blood on her right cheek. Her eyes were wide with terror, and the morst on her face was streaked with tears.

Thomas wavered on his feet. He couldn't think straight.

"I thought you'd like to see her before I clean her up and deliver her to her father," Woref said.

Thomas slammed into the bars. "Chelise . . . Oh, my dear . . ." He spoke to Woref. "How dare you hurt the daughter of Qurong!"

Woref's smile faded. "So you still care for her. Did you really think the daughter of Qurong could ever return your pitiful love? No one told you that you're an albino? She belongs to me, you filthy slab of flesh! And I can assure you that whatever doubts she might have entertained toward me have been removed."

The terrible truth of their predicament washed over Thomas. Chelise could barely keep her eyes open. A single glance at her drooping face brought a tremble to his bones. Woref had abused her in ways he couldn't guess.

His rage against Woref faded as he gazed at her. A terrible sorrow swept through his chest. "Chelise. I'm so sorry." Tears blurred his vision. He sank to his knees.

"Forgive me, my love, forgive me," she cried.

She was crying for him! He reached his hand through the bars.

A fist slammed against his arm, numbing it to the shoulder. Woref turned and slugged Chelise in the jaw. She fell back against the wall and groaned.

"Please, don't hurt her!" Thomas's eyes flooded with tears. This wasn't what Woref had expected. Thomas's love for Chelise, yes, but not Chelise's love for him. The general stood trembling from head to foot.

Thomas lunged for the man through the bars. His face collided with cold bronze, but he managed a hand on the general's leather breastplate.

Woref swung another fist—not at Thomas. At Chelise. It struck her in her side and she gasped.

Thomas fell back in horror.

"For your love of my wife, you will die a terrible, painful death," the general said. He grabbed Chelise by the hair and shoved her ahead of him, down the corridor.

She wasn't his wife. She didn't love him. She despised the beast who would enslave her. Thomas knew all of this. But he could do nothing except fall to the stone floor and weep.

Johan watched the twenty-four tribe members ride in single file down the rocky cliff pass. Suzan sat on a lathered horse on his right, and Mikil faced him on her own horse. Nearly two days had passed since the Horde army left them. They'd debated following but knew that whatever Thomas had intended was already done. And now here was proof. He'd traded himself for the twenty-four without knowing that Chelise had been taken.

Mikil had just learned about Chelise herself, and she was furious.

"He left her in your command! You've just signed his death!"

"Give me the right to use a sword and we would have escaped," Johan said. "Woref outwitted us." He frowned and spit to the side. "I should have known."

"It's my fault," Suzan said. "I should have found the army, but they'd taken their prisoners. We honestly thought they were gone."

"It's done," Johan said. "The question is how we help Thomas now."

Mikil grunted and pulled her mount around. The tribe was running out to meet their family. Little did they know.

"As I see it, we have only one choice," Johan said.

"I can tell you that any rescue won't be easy," Mikil said. "The city is braced for us. If Thomas isn't dead already, he's holed up somewhere only Woref knows about."

"Then we die trying," Johan said. "I couldn't live knowing I let this happen."

"I agree," Suzan said. "William is likely in the dungeons as well. Or dead."

"William?" Mikil demanded. "What happened to William?"

Johan told her. They could only assume that he'd agreed to betray Thomas knowing that Thomas was beyond being betrayed. He'd saved the tribe. He was a cantankerous troublemaker, but the Circle blood ran deep.

Mikil set her jaw. "Let me get Jamous. I need to bathe and saddle a fresh horse. Then we leave."

<hr />

Qurong stood over the bed, staring at his daughter, who slept peacefully. She was bruised and there was some bleeding on her scalp and on her cheek, but otherwise she was healthy, the doctor said. Woref had seen to it that she was freshly bathed and covered in morst when he brought her into the castle, draped across his arms.

His wife pulled the covers over Chelise's shoulder. "We let her sleep."

Qurong followed her into the hall. "She's been brutalized!" Patricia whispered harshly. "Any fool can see that!"

"She was in captivity with the albinos. Of course she's been brutalized. But she will be fine. You'll see. She'll probably be up this afternoon, running to the library or something. She's a strong woman, like her mother."

"I'm not so sure this is the work of albinos. Since when do they brutalize their prisoners?"

"Maybe she fell down a cliff, for all we know. Things happen in the desert. Woref thinks she might have fallen off a horse." He came to the stairs and stopped. "She's safe. I have gained my daughter back. Now let me go and see what I can do to keep her safe."

"You would believe a goat that told you what you wanted to hear," Patricia said. "My daughter would never defile herself. I'll speak to them with you."

He started to object but then decided he could use her. What Woref and Ciphus intended to prove, he didn't know, but better two against two.

The chief priest and the commander of the armies waited for them in the dining room as instructed. They stood from the long table when Qurong pushed the door open. Both dipped their heads in respect.

Woref's face had been scratched. Three thin lines of blood seeped through the morst on his cheek. If Qurong wasn't mistaken, he'd been bruised on his eye as well. This all since bringing Chelise in earlier. His commander had been beaten?

"I see you've taken the liberty of eating my fruit," Qurong said.

"We were told . . ."

He waved Ciphus off. "Fine. My house is your house. At least when you're invited."

Patricia walked in and they bowed again, out of respect to Qurong, not to his wife. If she had come alone, they would treat her like any other wife. Patricia had never approved of the custom, but none of her outrage had changed it. Men were honored over women; it had always been so.

"What is this all about?" Patricia demanded.

Woref glanced at Ciphus, who nodded. The snake would always defer, Qurong thought. His backside was his only holy relic, and he would cover it well.

"There are some things that you should know, my lord," Woref said. "I took the liberty of counseling Ciphus before I came to you."

"Yes, of course. Spit it out."

"It's the condition of your daughter. I can tell you after bringing her to safety that she is not herself. I fear she's been bewitched by the Circle. By what manner of torture or brutality, I don't know, but she woke up once screaming terrible lies. Her mind's been tampered with."

"What kind of lies?" Patricia demanded harshly.

"Lies of all kinds. She accused me of capturing her when, of course, it was the albinos who captured her. She said that I struck her and dragged her by the hair, something I wouldn't think of doing to my bride. She thinks the albinos are her friends and we are her enemies."

"Don't be ridiculous," his wife said. "If she said that you slapped her, I would believe her! How many women have you hit before, Woref?"

He looked at Qurong, shocked by her accusation. "That is hardly the point, I assure you. She's been bewitched!" His face flushed. "How dare you accuse me of mistreating the woman I would die for!"

They stared, facing off.

Qurong intervened. "Ciphus, what are your thoughts on this bewitching? Is it possible?"

"The mind is a delicate thing, prone to deception. Yes, I think it is possible. It wouldn't surprise me at all. Give her time and she will come to. Her heart is something else, of course. Sins of the mind are forgivable. Sins of the heart are not."

"I still don't trust you," Patricia said, glaring at Woref. "If you are to have any peace as my son-in-law, you'd better learn how to correct that. And if you ever treat my daughter like you do your other women, I will see you drowned myself."

For a moment Qurong wondered if Woref would lose control of himself. This was what his wife wanted, of course. She would do whatever was necessary to earn the man's indebtedness; then she would use her advantage however she saw fit.

Qurong smiled. "Welcome to the family. And for the record, I agree with my wife. Harm one hair on her head and you *will* drown, Woref." He paused. "But I'm sure you didn't come simply out of concern for Chelise. Exactly why are we here? I would think both of you would be as pleased as I am. We have Thomas, and now that we know how the albinos think, we will leverage him to bring the entire Circle to its knees. Chelise is safe. All is good."

Woref didn't seem able to talk. Ciphus answered for him. "My lord, there is one matter that you should consider. Your daughter's mind is one thing, as I said. But if she has committed treason—"

"I don't want to hear this!" Patricia said, marching past them toward the kitchen. She turned back. "If you dare suggest that my daughter has any feelings for that wretched beast, I'll cut your tongue out. She could never love an albino. Never!"

"Of course not. Because if she did, she would have to pay the price required by law."

"You heard my wife!" Qurong said. "Chelise is incapable of loving an albino! If she did, I would drown her myself. Are you going to continue with this nonsense?"

Ciphus dipped his head. "I'm only doing my duty as your loyal priest, my lord. Just so you remember that no law is above Elyon's law, as all the Horde knows."

"Fine. Are you finished?"

Woref was seething, and Qurong thought it odd. Surely he'd been forthcoming. Neither answered him.

"Then get out! Both of you. I don't want to hear of this again."

They stepped back, bowed, and left the room.

"How dare they?" his wife snapped.

"They dare because they are far more powerful than you may realize," he said. "This religion and this Elyon of his may be a lot of nonsense, but we used it to our benefit to control the people. This on pain of death, that on pain of death . . . the whole system one of threats and rewards dictated by some god we can't see. Ciphus is the only one the people see. His word is nearly as powerful as mine."

"Then it's time you threw him out!"

"So the people could throw me out?"

"You have an army! Squash the people."

"The army are the people! I've put Elyon above me, and they prefer it that way. They feel less captive. They're serving a god, not a man."

He picked up a green pear and took a bite. "Power is always in the balance, my wife. I no longer have the power to upset that balance. Not if it works against me."

38

THE GUARD opened the door that led into the dungeon while Woref was still ten yards from it. Fifty torches blazed in the midnight hour, lighting the perimeter of the compound and path to the single entrance. If the albinos came for Thomas now, they would have to fight their way through three hundred of his best warriors. Even then, there was no way into Thomas's cell. Woref carried the only key, and nothing short of the black powder the Forest Guard had once used would blast the bars free.

He stooped beneath the door's thick lintel and descended the long flight of steps, the guard just behind.

"Wait here," he said, taking the torch. He walked down the narrow corridor, boots loud on the rock floor.

There was a terrible risk in this plan of his, but the moment Chelise had spoken those words—*Forgive me, my love, forgive me*—Woref vowed to change her. Or kill her.

Thomas was no longer his concern. They would use him, destroy him, drown him. None of it would change anything. His bride's love was all that mattered now. His whole purpose for living had focused on this day, he realized. The sum of his life would come down to winning and losing love.

Over time, he could persuade Chelise to submit to him. But as long as she loved Thomas, her affection would be compromised. And if he killed Thomas now, he would only live on in her mind, haunting Woref forever.

He couldn't kill Thomas. Not yet.

But he could use Thomas to secure Chelise's love.

Woref descended the second set of stairs quickly, eagerly. Ciphus had approved the plan for his own reasons, namely, to save Chelise's life. If she publicly rejected Thomas and openly embraced Woref, the matter of her heart would be settled.

Woref heard the prisoner shuffle to his feet. Expecting another glimpse of his dear love, perhaps? *You and your kind are the worst life has to offer. And when I'm finished grinding you under my feet, I'll commit my life to finishing off the rest.*

Thomas was standing in the middle of the cell, peering out expectantly when Woref stopped before the bars. His eyes glanced to Woref's right, then returned when he saw the corridor was empty.

Woref paced, primarily to squash his impulse to throw open the door and kill the man where he stood. He blinked away sweat that leaked into his eyes.

"You and your precious Circle are finished, Thomas. I'm sure you realize that by now."

The albino just looked at him.

"Your problem is that you misunderstand sentiments intended merely for self-gratification. Affection, loyalty, love. Your friends will come to your aid, bound by honor, but they will only find their own deaths. We will use their misguided sense of duty to our advantage."

Still no reaction.

"You can't save your friends, but you can save Chelise."

His eyes moved.

"You do love her. I can see that." Woref felt sickened by his own words, but he pushed on. "And if you love her, I would think you would be interested in saving her life."

"I love her," the albino said. "More than my life."

"I'm not interested in your life!" Woref shouted. He calmed himself. "Do you know the price that she will pay for this heretical sentiment you've dragged out of her? You've sentenced her to death. It's our law."

"Qurong won't kill his own daughter. She'll never admit her love for me openly. And her father will believe her over you."

"Then I will kill her!" Woref said. He was trembling, but he didn't care. Let the jackal know the truth. "Only Elyon himself knows how desperately I need this woman," he said. "If she won't love me, then she won't love any man. I'll rip her tongue out and throw her to the dogs."

Fear slowly crossed the albino's face. "You won't," he said. "You're too consumed with your own life to risk it."

"I will. There are ways to kill that cannot be traced. I can assure you, the death of Chelise will be brutal."

Thomas's mouth turned down and began to twitch. His breathing was shallow.

Woref smiled. "You know that I'm capable of this. You know, in fact, that I would relish it." He could hear both of their breathing now, loud and ragged in the narrow passage. The implications of what he was saying had the albino's mind in a vise. Woref hadn't expected to feel so much pleasure.

"If Chelise still loves you in three days' time, she will die. Only you can save her life. I've arranged for you to spend time with her in the morning. No one will know. I will give you this one opportunity to change her mind and her heart."

His words hung in the air between them. And their meaning had its full intended effect. Tears flooded the albino's eyes and ran down his cheeks. His face knotted. He slowly lifted both hands, gripped his hair, and began to weep silently.

Woref smiled.

There was nothing else to say, but he was transfixed by this sight of such terrible sorrow. The albino loved the woman nearly as much as he himself did. And what could the albino say? Nothing. He was outwitted. Trapped.

He would have to find a way to convince Chelise that he no longer loved her.

"I will be listening and watching. Don't think that you can fool me."

Woref turned and walked from the cell.

The albino's sobbing began when he was halfway down the second corridor.

39

HE HAD been sucked into the darkest, coldest corner of reality and left there to rot. There wasn't a sound except for his own sobs and the long wails that he tried in vain to silence. He couldn't see—not the walls, not the cold stone floor, not his fingers if he put them an inch from his eyes. His body shivered and his mind refused to sleep.

But all of this was like paradise compared to the hell that engulfed Thomas's heart.

He lost his sense of time. There was black and there was cold and there was pain. How could he do what Woref had demanded? He thought about a hundred ways to save Chelise without crushing her love. His love. But not a single one could hold his trust.

With Woref or his conspirators listening, watching, the slightest advance that Thomas might make would result in her death. She wouldn't be told, of course. She would see him and run to him for an embrace, and he would have to push her away. Woref wanted to see her heart crushed by Thomas so that she would receive Woref's love.

Thomas was being forced to make her despise him. It was the only way to save her life.

But what could he do to make her despise him? The answer drained his body of tears.

Now Thomas wanted to do nothing but sleep. Dream. Anything to tear him away from this agony. In all of his fury, Woref had neglected to make him eat the fruit. If only he could die of the virus and never wake again. If only there was a rhambutan fruit in the other reality that he could eat so that he would never have to come back here to crush her heart.

But the more he tried to shut down his mind, the more it revolted in desperation to find one flicker of light. One thread of hope.

There was none.

He finally lay on his back, staring at the dark. For a very, very long time, nothing happened.

And then a sound reached him. The sound of boots.

———— ∞ ————

"Why the back door?" Chelise asked.

"I understand that your father wants no one to disturb you," Ciphus said, opening the door to the library. "I assume he knows that certain people would object."

She stepped into the hall. "I don't understand. Some time alone with the Books of Histories might clear my mind, yes, but I don't see why anyone would object."

"Did I say alone, my dear?"

Thomas? Ciphus wore a knowing grin. Father had arranged for her to see Thomas? No, that would make no sense!

Chelise stopped. "What's happening, Ciphus? I demand to know!"

"I can't say for sure. I was told only to bring you here and ask you to wait with the Books. Your father understands that you will spend the day resting in the library. You're not feeling well enough to do that?"

"I feel fine. It doesn't explain all this secrecy."

"Please, Chelise, this wasn't my doing."

Ciphus opened the door into the large storage room and walked in. Chelise followed. The last time she'd been in here had been with Thomas. The memories soothed her like a warm salve.

Ciphus turned to leave.

"Woref knows I'm here?"

"Woref? I'm guessing he's with your father. Your wedding day does require some planning."

"My mother told me just this morning that I wouldn't marry anyone I didn't approve of. I don't approve of Woref."

"Then maybe that's why your father agreed to your being here. Maybe its the safest place for you. Woref won't take a refusal lightly. Let the peace in this room calm you. You're as safe here as in the castle."

Ciphus left. She'd agreed to come because her mother was driving her frantic, and the servants were gawking at her as if she'd risen from the dead. Her mind was on Thomas, and she couldn't stand walking around the castle thinking of him.

Now she wondered if she'd made a mistake. There were no busybodies peering at her here, but this room with all these Books made her feel empty. Alone.

Chelise crossed to the desk and stared at the Book Thomas had tried to teach her to read. She couldn't read it because it was designed to be read by those whose eyes were opened. She was surprised that she could accept that so easily now.

She had to be careful. Thomas was in the dungeon—the thought made her sick. But she couldn't endanger his life by attempting to secure his release. Woref knew. A shiver ran down her spine and she closed her eyes. Their predicament was hopeless now. The only man who truly loved her was sealed in a tomb, and she had no will to live without him. If Thomas wasn't imprisoned, she would simply run. She would find the Circle and dive into their red pool and find a new life.

But if she ran now, they would kill him. And if they knew how she felt about him, they would kill both of them.

Her head ached. She'd covered her bruises with morst, but the pain from the blows would take a few days to ease. Mother seemed convinced that she'd been abused by the albinos. With Thomas in the dungeon, Chelise wasn't sure what to tell her.

She pulled the chair out and started to sit when the door suddenly opened.

Thomas stepped in.

The door closed behind him. Locked.

The blood drained from her face. They'd brought Thomas here? His face was ashen and his eyes were red, but he wasn't cut or bruised.

She glanced around. The room was empty, of course. And the door was locked.

Tears sprang to her eyes and she hurried toward him. "Thomas!"

He wasn't looking at her. Something was wrong.

"What have they done to you? I'm so sorry—"

"Stay away from me," he said, lifting his hand.

She stopped. "What . . . What do you mean?" She glanced at the door. Someone was listening? "They're listening?"

"How should I know? It doesn't matter. I've been found out."

Chelise walked up to him, took his arm, and whispered quickly. "They're listening, aren't they? Woref's up to something!" He looked so sad, so completely used up. Her heart fell. "Woref took me from the camp. I had nothing to do with it. What on earth do you mean you've been found out?"

His eyes moistened. A single tear leaked from the corner of his left eye and ran down his cheek. She reached a trembling hand to wipe it.

Thomas moved his head away. "Please, if you don't mind, not so close. Your breath."

His words ran through her heart like a sword. He couldn't mean that! They were forcing him!

He stepped away from her and walked to one of the shelves. His steps were uneven, and he looked like he might fall. "I'm sorry, Chelise. They asked me to come here to transcribe the Books. I didn't know you were going to be here, but I can't hide the truth from you any longer."

"What truth?" she demanded. "Ciphus brought me here knowing that you'd be here! They're forcing us—"

"Stop it!" he snapped. "Of course they knew you were here. They brought you because they think it's only fair that I tell you the truth myself. I don't blame them." He faced her, his expression cold. There was a tremble in his voice.

"Do you have any idea how putrid you Scab women smell to us? Did you stop to wonder how we could stand you in our camp for so long?

Did you notice how the others kept disappearing for fresh air? We used you!" He faltered. "We needed the leverage."

"You're lying! You're standing there trembling like a leaf trying to persuade me that you don't love me. But I've seen your eyes and I've felt your heart, and none of this is true!"

For a long moment they just stared at each other, and she was sure he would break down and rush to her.

"Believe what you want. Just keep your distance. I don't want to hurt you any more than I have to. Even a Scab woman deserves some respect." He turned to the shelf and pulled out one of the Books.

Chelise's mind flashed back to their time in this very library just a week ago. To the poetry he'd recited while he thought she was sleeping. To the long days riding together on horseback. To the first time he'd kissed her.

And she knew that he was lying. Why?

Unless . . . What he said did make some sense. But she wouldn't believe it! No man could show the kind of affection he'd shown her while pretending. He'd wept over her.

She didn't know his game, nor why he was being forced to do this, but she decided to play along.

"Fine. You don't love me; I can accept that. I stink to the highest heaven, and you find me repulsive. You're speaking your mind and being plain. That doesn't change the simple fact that I love you, Thomas of Hunter."

She turned her back on him, walked to the desk, and sat. Even from here she could see the tears on his cheek. "Maybe we should start from the beginning. You won my love. Now what should I do to win your love?"

He turned on her, face red. "Nothing! I'm not interested in your love! Leave me. Find a Scab and love him."

"No, I won't go. I don't believe you." She crossed her arms.

"Then you're a fool. You love an albino who you think loves you, but he doesn't. They'll drown you for this misguided, adolescent infatuation with a man who could never love you."

His words were so cutting, so terrible, she wondered if he might be telling the truth after all. And even if he wasn't, he might as well be. Any love they might have shared was now over.

"I still don't believe you," she said. But even as she said it, tears began to stream down her face. She stared at him, suddenly overcome by his words.

What if they are true, Chelise? What if the only love you've ever known turns out to be a false love, and the love you will know is a brutal love that grinds you into the ground? Then there is no true love.

Thomas continued to read the Book in his hands. He was either so crushed by his own words that he couldn't proceed with his charade, or he truly did not care for her and was now disinterested.

Gradually her tears stopped. She wasn't going to leave this room without knowing the full truth. He just read the Book, refusing to look at her.

A thought occurred to her. "If I drowned in one of your red pools and became an albino like you, would you love me then?"

He turned his back to her and leaned against the bookshelf.

"If I didn't smell and I didn't look so pale, could you stand to touch my skin then?"

Nothing.

She slammed her palm on the desk. "Talk to me! Quit pretending you're reading that Book and talk to me! There's a red pool on the north side of the lake, you know. I could run there right now and dive in. Would that change your mind?"

Thomas faced her. He blinked. "There is?"

"Yes, there is. It's all that remains of the original lake. They've covered it with rocks so you can't see it, but I've heard it runs underground. We'd have to remove the rocks. Would that satisfy you?"

For a moment he seemed completely caught off guard. Then he set his jaw. But the tears were flowing again.

She stood and walked toward him. "Please, Thomas. Please, I beg you. I can't believe—"

"Stop it!" he snarled. "Grow up! I don't love you!" His glare was so fero-cious that she could hardly recognize him. "I could never love you after using you. You're a spent rag."

Chelise's legs felt weak. He might as well have drilled her with an arrow. She couldn't move.

He slammed the Book on the shelf, walked to the door, and turned the handle. It was locked. He slapped the panel with his palm. "Open this door! Let me out!"

Nothing happened. He hit the door again, then turned back. Chelise felt numb. She still didn't think she could believe him, but she was left with nothing else to believe in.

He walked to the corner, sat on the floor, and lowered his head into his hands. His shoulders shook gently.

Chelise returned to the desk and sat down. *You should leave now,* she told herself.

And go where? To Woref? To the castle where Qurong planned her wedding? To the desert to die? Chelise lay her head down on the desk, closed her eyes, and began to cry.

They remained like that for a long time. Whether his mind was on his own failure in this plot he talked about, or whether it was on her— impossible to tell. It hardly mattered anymore. She was dead either way.

A thump on the wall pulled her from the depths of despondency. She opened her eyes.

Another thump. Then again, *thump, thump.*

She lifted her head. Thomas was standing in the corner, hitting his forehead against the wall.

Thump, thump, thump.

Then harder. And suddenly very hard.

The whole wall shook with the impact of his head, crashing against the wood. She pushed her chair back, alarmed. His teeth were clenched and his face was wet with tears.

He was killing himself?

Thomas suddenly spread his mouth in a roar, drew his head way back, and slammed it against the wall with all of his strength.

The wall shuddered. He collapsed, unconscious.

It was then that Chelise remembered his dreams.

40

CARLOS STEPPED into the dark cell and locked the door behind him. He flipped the light switch on. The gurney Thomas had lain on sat empty. He still couldn't wrap his mind around this situation, but he had decided that Thomas was right: Fortier had no intention of leaving any part of the Muslim world intact.

He walked to the cabinet and unlocked the door. He wasn't sure why Fortier had asked him to monitor the exchange from the remote feeds at the farm, but with each passing hour he grew more nervous. The Frenchman had overemphasized the need for Carlos to stay put. It was tantamount to an order. The exchange was now under way, and Carlos had finally resolved that he could wait no longer. If he was to act against Fortier, it would have to be now.

He withdrew the Uzi and three extra magazines. Two grenades.

He unbuttoned his shirt and jammed two of the clips into his belt. The rash on his belly had spread up to his neck and along his arms. The symptoms of the virus were now spreading beyond the gateway cities. In four days' time there wouldn't be a person alive without the red dots. In a week half the world might be dead.

He buttoned his shirt, grabbed a plastic charge with a detonator, shoved them into his pocket, and closed the cabinet.

If Fortier hadn't ordered him to stay, he might have been able to take Svensson as Thomas had suggested. But if he tipped his hand by leaving against orders, his usefulness would expire. No chance of securing Svensson. The man would go deep.

Carlos walked to the door and slid the safety off.

As soon as he made a play to leave this compound, the Frenchman would take steps to protect the antivirus, but there was one thing Carlos could try. One last desperate act to right some of the wrong he'd brought upon his own people.

He hung the weapon on his shoulder and pulled out his pistol. Working by habit, he screwed the silencer into the barrel and checked the chamber.

The hall was empty.

He walked quickly, eager now to do what he did best. *There is a reason you hired me, Mr. Fortier. I will now show you that reason.*

Carlos headed up the steps. The first guard he saw was a short, thick native of France who hadn't learned to smile. The man saw him and immediately lifted his radio to his mouth. Carlos put a slug through the radio— and through the back of his open throat.

He stepped over the man and walked toward the back door.

The second guard was facing the driveway by the door. The bullet caught him in his temple as he turned. He toppled sideways. Not a sound other than the familiar *phwet* of the gun and the dull smack of slug hitting bone.

But the sound might as well have been a siren to the three trained men by the Jeep. They spun together, rifles ready.

Carlos preferred to leave the compound without giving them a chance to call in his departure. Paris would know that something was wrong when the farm missed their next report in fifteen minutes, but fifteen minutes was a lifetime in situations of this nature. Literally.

He kept the pistol leveled, scanning through the sights. Movement. He shot two of the guards as he ran through the door. Dropped into a roll.

The third guard got off a scream and managed to squeeze the trigger on his automatic weapon before Carlos could bring his gun up.

A hail of bullets smacked the wall above him. Worse, the gun's chattering echoed through the compound with enough volume to wake Paris.

Carlos put two bullets through the guard's chest. The man's finger held the trigger as he fell backwards, stitching shots into the sky. Then the gun was silent.

There was a chance the communications operator in the basement might not have heard, but the guards on the perimeter would have.

He slid into the Jeep, fired the engine, and snatched up his radio. "We have a situation on the south side. I repeat, south side. The Americans are bringing in a small strike force."

He dropped the radio on the seat and floored the accelerator.

"This is Horst on the south side," a voice barked. "I don't see them. You said south side?"

Carlos ignored the question. He only needed enough confusion to slow the two guards at the gate. He roared around the corner and headed straight for them. One had his binoculars trained to the south.

Carlos stopped twenty yards away, threw open his door, and planted one foot on the ground, swinging out. "Any sign?"

"Gunshots—"

Carlos shot the one without the binoculars first. The other heard the silenced gun but couldn't respond quickly enough to save his life.

This is what I can do, Mr. Fortier. This is only part of what I can do.

He ran to the gate, slapped the large red button that opened it, and returned to the Jeep.

When Carlos next glanced at his watch, he saw that exactly two minutes had passed from the time he fired the first shot to the time he exited the long driveway that fed the main road.

Paris was two hours by the primary roads. Five hours by back roads. And Marseilles?

Reaching his destination unscathed would be his greatest challenge. If he managed to make it through, he had an excellent chance of completing his mission.

Armand Fortier looked at the thirteen men seated around the conference table. He had promised these men the world. Dignitaries from Russia,

France, China, and seven other nations. Not one of them would live beyond the week.

"I can assure you this is of no consequence. We knew the Americans and Israelis at least would never turn over their weapons. From the beginning our objective was to pull their teeth, not take over their arsenals. We simply put them in a position where they felt secure doing it."

"And now you'll insist that you also expected them to destroy—"

"Please," he said, exasperated, cutting the Russian off. "No, we did not predict this exact response. To be honest, I expected more. None of it matters. They are in a box. The only weapon that matters now is the virus, and we control that. The game has been played perfectly by all accounts." He stood. "I'm sure you're eager to complete our arrangements for the antivirus. Soon enough, but I am needed elsewhere at the moment. If you need anything over the next few hours, please don't hesitate to ask."

He left them without a backward glance. It was the last time he intended to see any of them.

Fortier walked evenly down the hall. For years he had rehearsed this day. He'd pored over his own graphs and debated possibilities ad infinitum. The outcome had always been certain. He'd always known that if he could get his hands on the right virus, the world would be his to manipulate.

But he'd never actually lived through stakes so high. For the first time he looked at the reports pouring over the television monitors and wondered what he had done.

He'd done what he'd set out to do, of course.

But what had he really done? Over six billion people were infected with a lethal virus that would kill them within the week if his antivirus wasn't distributed within the next forty-eight hours.

His thrill was barely manageable.

He'd read once that Hitler had frequently experienced profound physical reactions to the elation he felt when exercising his power. He'd exterminated six million Jews. Who could have imagined the power that Armand now held in his hand?

God.

But there was no god. For all practical purposes, he was God.

Fortier stepped into a small room at the end of the hall and picked up a black phone.

He was experiencing the exuberance of a god. But with the power came immeasurable responsibility, and it was this that caused him to wonder what he had done. Just as God must have wondered why he'd created humans before sending a flood to wipe them out.

It was a beautiful thing, this power.

Svensson picked up on the first ring. "Yes?"

"Issue the order and meet me in Marseilles."

The distribution of the antivirus was one of the most complex elements of the entire plan. In most cases, those who ingested the antivirus would do so without knowing they had. It had already been administered to a number of key individuals in their drinks or their bread. In most cases, the elect would be called with some mundane excuse to a remote distribution point, where they would unknowingly inhale a localized airborne strain. They would leave destined to survive. The risk of the antivirus landing in the wrong hands would pass in less than twenty-four hours. By then, even if someone got hold of it, he wouldn't have time to manufacture or distribute it.

"No problems?" Svensson said.

"Carlos has turned. He's on his way here."

The phone was silent. They had prepared two installations for this final phase, one in Paris, one in Marseilles on the southern coast of France. No one except the two of them knew about Marseilles. It was now all over but the waiting.

"He's no idiot," Svensson said.

"Neither am I," Fortier said. "Remember, no evidence. Leave the antivirus in the vault."

41

THE RIOTS had fallen apart on two counts. The word that the United States had traded its nuclear arsenal for the antivirus and then summarily sent that arsenal to the bottom of the ocean had sent a shock wave across the nation. The news jockeys and political pundits might have spent countless hours dissecting the implications, but another, greater urgency trumped even this stunning bit of news.

The virus had struck.

With a vengeance.

Millions of people in America's urban centers helplessly watched the red spots spread over their bodies. No amount of anger or saber rattling could make these symptoms vanish. Only the antivirus could.

But the antivirus was on its way, Mike Orear insisted. The president had stood on the steps of the Capitol and declared their victory to the world. Hope was not dead. It was being shipped at this very moment, ready to be whisked to the gateway cities, where it would be infused with the blood banks. Within a matter of days, every resident of North America would have the antivirus.

Thomas had followed the news over a secure microwave receiver at twenty thousand feet above the Atlantic. America was holding its collective breath for an antivirus that would not work.

They collected him from the *Nimitz* and streaked back into the sky without offering any answers to his questions. Worse, they declined his request to speak to the president. Not that it mattered—they were in the final throes of a hopeless death anyway. He sat with his hands between his knees, listening to the speculations and calculations and ramifications or possibilities and inconsistencies until he was sure his heart had fallen permanently into his stomach.

The game was over. In both realities.

The fighter settled in for a landing at BWI. Baltimore.

Maryland. Johns Hopkins?

They transferred him to a helicopter. Once more he was denied information as to the nature of his sudden recall to the country. Not because they were hiding anything from him—they simply didn't know.

But his guess that they were taking him to Johns Hopkins proved inaccurate. Twenty minutes later the chopper set down on the lawn adjacent to Genetrix Laboratories.

Three lab technicians met the chopper. Two took his arms and hurried toward the entrance. "They're waiting for you inside, sir."

Thomas didn't bother asking.

The moment he stepped into the building, all eyes were on him, from the foyer, through a large room filled with a dozen busy workstations, to the elevator, which they entered and descended. They had heard of him. He was the one who'd brought this virus on them.

Thomas ignored their stares and rode down three floors before stepping out of the elevator into a huge control room.

"Thomas."

He turned to his left. There stood the president of the United States, Robert Blair. Next to him, Monique de Raison, Theresa Sumner from the CDC, and Barbara Kingsley, health secretary.

"Hello, Thomas." He turned around. Kara walked up to him. Sweat glistened on her face, but she smiled bravely. "It's good to see you," she said.

"Kara . . ." He glanced at Monique and Theresa. The rash had covered Theresa's face. Monique's was clear. The president and the health secretary had been infected twelve hours behind them, and their faces were still clear, but the red spots were showing on their necks.

He knew then what they had called him to do. They wanted the dreams. That had to be it. These four wanted to take him up on his suggestion to Kara and Monique that they dream a very long dream using his blood.

"I apologize for the secrecy," Robert Blair said. "But we couldn't risk word of this getting out."

Thomas could hardly bear to look at Kara's face. "How are you feeling?"

"I'm fine."

"Good," he said. He faced the others. "The rash is taking over. Gains is pretty bad, but I . . . You have to hurry."

"You're right," Monique said. "Time is more critical than you can imagine."

"But you don't need me here. I left the blood for you to dream."

None of them moved. They just looked at him.

"What's going on?"

Monique stepped forward, eyes bright. "We've found something, Thomas. It could be very good." Her eyes darted to Kara and back. "And it could also be very bad."

"You . . . you found an antivirus?"

"Not exactly, no."

"You notice that neither Monique nor I have the rash, Thomas?" Kara asked.

"That's good. Right?"

"How's that rash under your arm?" Monique asked.

He instinctively touched his side. "I have it . . ." Now that he thought about it, he hadn't felt the itching for some time. He lifted his shirt up and ran his hand over his skin. No sign of the rash.

"You sure that wasn't a heat rash? I think it was."

Meaning what? He, Monique, and Kara hadn't broken out yet.

"You're virus-free, Thomas."

Monique turned around and pressed a button on a remote in her right hand. The wall opened, revealing a bank of monitors surrounding a large flat screen. The smaller monitors were filled with charts and data that meant nothing to him. But the huge screen in the center was a map of the world. The twenty-four gateway cities where the virus had initially been released were marked with red dots. Green circles indicated the hundreds of labs and medical facilities around the world that were involved in the search for an antivirus. White crosses marked the massive blood collection efforts that had been underway since news of the virus went public. Small crosses spread out from the gateway cites, indicating smaller collection centers. They had enough blood, he knew that.

But without an antivirus to distribute through the blood, it was useless. "I've run your blood through more tests than I can name in the last twenty-four hours. They showed nothing unusual." She faced him again. "Honestly, I can't tell you why I decided to test your blood against the virus, but I did." She paused.

"And?"

"And it killed the virus. In a matter of minutes."

Thomas blinked. "I'm immune," he said absently.

He felt Kara's arm slip around his. "Not just you. Monique and I have been in contact with your blood. It killed the virus in both of us."

He looked at the others. Why the long faces? This was good news.

The president forced a smile. "There's more."

A faint suggestion presented itself to him, but he rejected it. Still, the thought was enough to flush his face.

"Enough with this melodrama. Just get it out. Why am I immune?"

"I think it was the lake," Kara said. "You were healed in Elyon's water. It changed your blood."

"You were in his lake."

"As Mikil. Not as Kara. Not as me and not in the emerald lake before it dried up. You were there as yourself, in person. And if it wasn't the lake, then it was when you were healed by Justin later, after you had the virus. It's the only thing that makes sense."

Yes, it was.

"However it happened, there's no question that your blood contains the necessary elements that kill the virus," Monique said.

"And yours?"

She paused. "No. Not like yours."

He wasn't sure he liked where this was going.

"You know what it is about my blood that kills the virus?"

"Not entirely, but enough to duplicate it, yes." She walked to one of the smaller screens. "I isolated various components of your blood, white cells, plasma, platelets, red cells—the virus is reacting to the red cells. I then isolated—"

"I don't care about the science," Thomas said. The suggestion that had dropped into his mind was reasserting itself, and he suddenly had no patience for this presentation of theirs. "Just cut to the bottom line. You need my blood."

She turned around. "Yes. Your red blood cells."

"Something in my red blood cells is acting like an antivirus."

"More like a virus, but yes. When it comes into contact with normal blood, it spreads at an astounding rate, killing the Raison Strain. I've dubbed it the Thomas Strain."

Thomas hesitated only a moment.

"Then take my blood. Do you have time to reproduce enough to distribute as planned?"

"It depends," she said.

"Depends on what?"

She glanced at Barbara Kingsley, who stepped up. "Our plan with the World Health Organization was to collect blood from millions of donors near the gateway cities, categorize and store that blood using every form of refrigeration available, and then prepare it for infusion of the antivirus if and when it was secured. We have the blood, roughly twenty thousand gallons in and around each gateway city."

"I know all of this. Please, depends on what?"

"Forgive me," Barbara said. "I just . . . whether we have enough time to use your blood to effectively infect all of the blood collected depends on how much of your blood we use."

"Infect," Thomas said, trying to ignore the implications. "You mean turn the collected blood into an antivirus."

"Yes," she said. "One of our people put this simulation together." She pointed the remote at the wall and pressed another button. "The effects of the antivirus in your blood have been dyed white so that we can see them. The simulation runs at an exaggerated speed."

Thomas watched as red blood, running like a river across the screen, was suddenly overtaken by a dirty white army of white cells from behind. This was his blood "infecting" the red blood.

He blinked at the sight. A picture from his dreams filled his mind. A hundred thousand of the Horde pouring in the canyons below the Natalga Gap. They had been the disease then. Now his blood would be the cure.

"How much do you need?" Thomas asked.

"It depends on how much of the blood we've collected needs to be infused with—"

"How much of the blood you've collected do you need to save the people who've donated it?" Thomas demanded.

"All of it," Barbara said.

"So then quit dancing around the issue and tell me how much of my blood you need to convert all of it!"

Monique paused.

"Twelve liters," she finally said. "All of it."

"Then what are we waiting for? Hook me up. Take twelve liters. You can do a blood transfusion or something, right?"

Monique hesitated and Thomas knew then that he was going to die.

"We have a time problem."

Kara came to his rescue. "What she's saying, Thomas, is that every hour they delay will cost lives. They've worked it out. The model shows a rough number of ten thousand every hour delayed, increasing exponentially each hour. They need to take as much blood as they can in as short a period of time as they can."

"While giving me a transfusion . . ."

Now it was her turn to hesitate. "The problem with a transfusion is that the new blood would mix with your blood and dilute its effectiveness."

Only an idiot wouldn't understand what they were saying, and part of Thomas resented them for not just spitting it out. Heat spread over his skull. He turned from them and faced a large window that looked into a room equipped with a hospital bed and an IV stand. This was his deathbed he was staring at.

"How do I survive this?" he asked.

"If we slowed the process and took only part of your blood, we have a chance of—"

"You said time was a factor," he said. "That would cost thousands, tens of thousands of lives."

"Yes. But we might be able to save your life."

"Thomas."

He looked at the president.

"I want you to know that I in no way expect you to give all of your blood. They say they can save over five billion people and still have a decent chance of saving you if they slow down the process and take nine pints. They may be able to reproduce your red blood cells at an accelerated rate. The number saved could go up to six billion."

"So we delay several hours, a day, to save my life, and we only lose a billion. Best case. Is that about it?"

They looked at him. That was precisely it.

"I want you to know that this is entirely your choice," the president said. "We can ensure the survival of North America and—"

"No," Thomas said. "He gave me life for this." It all made sense now. Thomas looked at Kara. Her eyes were misty. "History pivots on this sacrifice. You see? I was given life in the lake so that I could pass that life on to you. The fact that it'll take my life is really inconsequential."

He was following in Justin's footsteps. Of course. That was it. He didn't know how everything would work out in these two realities of his, but he did know that his life had been pointed at this moment. This choice.

"Let's do it," he said. "Take it all." He started toward the room with the hospital bed but turned back when they didn't follow. "I will sleep, right? I need to dream. That's all I ask. Let me dream. And Kara. Kara dreams."

Her eyes were round. "Thomas . . ." Words failed her.

He forced his mind back to his last dream. Mixed in with this business of his blood, it felt distant.

"That's my one condition," he said.

They stared, silent.

Thomas took Kara aside and lowered his voice. "You have to dream, Kara. I'm—"

"Thomas, I—"

"No, listen to me." He spoke quickly. "I'm back in the library with Chelise. Woref is trying to force me to deny my love for her. He's threatened to kill her if I don't." Thomas ran a hand through his hair, remembering everything now. "I need you to wake as Mikil and find Qurong. You have to dream before I do—you'll need enough time to get into the Horde city, find her father, and convince him to rescue his daughter from Woref at the library. It'll be dangerous, I won't lie. And if Mikil's killed there, you may die here. But it's the only thing . . ."

How could he ask her to do this?

"Please," he said.

Kara set her jaw, then stepped forward. "Of course I'll do it," she said. She kissed him on the forehead. "It's the least I can do for my brother. For the commander of the Forest Guard."

He was suddenly sure that he was going to cry. She saw it in his eyes and whispered gently, "I love you, Thomas. It's not the end. Justin has more. I know he does."

Thomas tried to answer, but he was choked up.

He cleared his throat. "Then let's do this."

"Thomas . . ." A tear slipped down Monique's cheek. She loved him, he knew. Maybe not as a woman loves a man, but she'd shared enough of Rachelle's love for him to care deeply.

"It's okay, Monique. You'll see. It'll be okay."

"You don't have to do this," Robert Blair said. "You really don't."

"Don't be unreasonable. You wouldn't have called me here if you thought differently. How can you even suggest I think differently?"

They seemed frozen.

Thomas turned and strode toward the waiting room.

———

Three white-suited surgeons prepped Thomas. Kara had insisted that she dream in the same room as he. They'd sedated her and taped a patch with some of his blood to the same small, scabbed incision that Dr. Bancroft had made on her arm. She turned her head and stared at Thomas, who rested on his back, wondering if he could feel the heparin they'd just injected intravenously. The thrombolytic agent would keep his blood from congealing when it entered the bypass machine.

"I'll see you on the other side, Thomas," Kara said.

He faced her. Monique stood by her bed, arms crossed, fighting emotions that Thomas could only guess at. The president was outside the room on his cell phone. Evidently Phil Grant was missing. Figured.

"Elyon's strength," his sister said.

Thomas offered a weak smile. He could feel the first effects of the drugs.

"It's a passing, Kara. Just a passing." He nodded at the window. "They may not understand what's happening, but you do. You know as Mikil. It's the way of Justin."

"It doesn't feel like that here," she said.

"That's because the Circle doesn't always feel real here. But does that make it any less real? We have *The Histories Recorded by His Beloved,* Kara. The connection is obvious. It's the same here as there; can't you see that?"

She faced the ceiling. "Yes. I can. But even in the Circle there's a sadness at the passing, for those left."

She was right. "If I don't make it, tell them, Kara. Tell them what we both saw."

"I will."

"Did I tell you about the red pool they have hidden behind the lake?" he asked.

She turned to him. "No. Really?"

"Really. Chelise says they drained the lake but they couldn't get rid of all the water, so they covered it up on the north side."

"The red pools," Kara said. "Like blood." Her eyes closed briefly, then opened. The drugs were working.

"I love you, Thomas."

Then her eyes rested shut.

"I love you too, Kara."

He looked up at the bright light above him. Time seemed to slow.

"You'll begin to feel drowsy," one of the doctors said. "We've administered the anesthesia into your IV."

They'd explained that they were using a simple bypass procedure that would pump his blood into the blue machine at his right. He wanted to dream, so they would put him under quickly. He would feel no pain, not even a prick. Once they started, the entire procedure would take less than ten minutes.

The doctors stepped aside, and Robert Blair stepped to the side of his bed. He put his hand on Thomas's shoulder. "I want you to know that not a soul living will have any doubt about who saved their lives," he said. "You're changing history."

"Is that what you think?" Thomas was having a hard time focusing. "Maybe I am. I'm saving some lives. When Justin died, he did much more. If you thank anyone, thank him."

"Justin," the president said. "And who is Justin?"

"Elyon. God."

Blair lifted his eyes and stared out the window. "Believe me, I will never think of God in the same terms again."

"Thomas." A hand touched his other shoulder. He faced Monique. She was trying not to cry but failing.

"None of this was your fault," Thomas said. "It wasn't your vaccine that caused any of this. It was what a man did with your vaccine. Remember that."

"I'll remember," she said softly. He could hardly hear her now. His world was slipping.

"The real virus is evil," he heard himself say. "The disease of . . . of the Horde."

Then he was sleeping.

Dreaming.

Monique could not bear to watch the entire procedure. All nice and neat with white gowns and silver instruments and sophisticated machines, but in the end they were simply draining Thomas of his blood until he died.

This was how they slaughtered cows.

Then again, it had been his choice. This man who'd come to her rescue repeatedly and saved her life twice already was now giving the ultimate sacrifice. She knew of no braver man.

The only consolation was his dreaming. If he could dream and eat the rhambutan fruit every night for as long as he lived, he might live out a full life in the other reality before he died here, in the next few minutes. It was possible.

On the other hand, he might die in both realities. This was now in Justin's hands.

Monique told them to call her when it was over and retreated to her office. She locked the door, sat behind her desk, and buried her face in her hands.

Then she wept uncontrollably.

The call came twenty minutes later.

She picked up the phone. "Yes?"

"We're done."

She let a moment pass. "He's dead?"

"Yes. I'm sorry."

"How long did he dream?"

"Maybe twenty minutes."

She took a deep breath. "You know what to do." Thomas's sacrifice would mean nothing without a cup of his blood being delivered to each of the gateway cities within the allowable time frames.

"It's already on the helicopter, headed for the airport where the planes are standing by."

Monique hung up. She glanced at the cooler. A sample of his blood was still in there, enough for her to dream one last time. But he was dead now. She had no right to try something so speculative without understanding its implications.

Or did she?

42

MIKIL JERKED up from her bedroll, eyes wide in the bright morning sun.

Kara!

For a long moment her mind wrestled with the information that Thomas had given her. He was in the library under threat of Chelise's death. He'd just knocked himself out. But how much time was there?

She scrambled to her feet and ran for the horses, yelling at Johan, who had lifted himself on one elbow. They'd traveled all night and collapsed in this cave, just outside the city, at first light.

"Do not move! Wait here. I'll be back."

"Where are you going?" Suzan demanded.

"To the city."

Suzan jumped to her feet. "Then we go with you!" she said.

"No!" Mikil grabbed the reins and swung into her saddle. She pulled her horse around. "I have to do this alone. We can't risk losing anyone else."

"Mikil, please!" Jamous ran for her. "You can't go alone. Let me come."

She leaned over and kissed him on the head, then on his face. "I'll return. I promise, my love. Wait here, I beg you. Wait for me."

She kicked her mount and sped into the trees.

"Mikil!"

"Wait for me!" she cried.

Thomas opened his eyes. He was on the floor of the library. His head throbbed. A hand was on his shoulder. Chelise sat on the floor beside him, crying quietly. How long had he been out? There was no way to tell.

Long enough.

Or maybe not long enough, depending on Mikil.

He closed his eyes and tried to clear his mind. They'd been together for an hour, maybe two, all of it worse than he imagined even lying in the dungeon, fearing the worst. The very sight of her when they'd removed his blindfold and shoved him into the library had made his knees weak.

Chelise. His love. The one woman he would gladly give his life for. This stunning being who was white with disease only because she didn't yet know the truth. But he couldn't see her disease. To him her painted face and gray eyes were the sun and the stars.

He'd done his best for an hour. The words from his mouth felt like acid. But he knew that Woref would take her life if he failed. If she died now, her death would be eternal, and that was something he couldn't bear. His only hope had been to give her the gift of life, so that perhaps one day someone else could lead her to the drowning where she would find her Maker.

Now there was another hope. A thin sliver of light. Mikil. He had to give her time.

But there was also something else now. He was going to die. When they took the last of his blood to save the world from the virus, he would die, there and here. Although an hour there in his dreams could be a month here, it could also be just a few minutes.

He could not die without expressing his true love one last time.

He lay still and let her cry softly, afraid to open his eyes again. It had all begun with a bump on the head. He'd lived a month in one reality, unknowingly releasing a plague and then perhaps undoing that same disease. And he'd lived sixteen years in this reality, where another kind of disease had been loosed and then undone.

Both would end in his death.

None of that mattered now. Only Chelise mattered. From the very beginning it had all been about her. This one woman who must be given the opportunity to dive into a pool of red to trade her white skin for the white gown of a bride. Justin's bride.

He had to give Mikil more time.

———⊱⊰———

The main library had been cleared of the scribes by Christoph in a simple agreement that would one day give him more authority. The chief librarian was no fool. He knew that in time Woref might have even more power than he had now. Ciphus was another story. The chief priest had agreed to bring Thomas, but he refused to implicate himself in any way. He could play both sides, a snake if ever there was one.

Woref's most trusted lieutenant, Soren, sat by the wall that butted up against the storage room that held the Books of Histories. He occasionally peered through a small slit they'd cut in the wall to give him a clear view of the entire back room from above the fourth shelf of Books.

Woref stood by the opposite window, looking out at the circular orchard in the middle of the royal garden. He had no interest in watching the albino—some things were better left unseen. He was interested only in the conclusion of this matter.

The fury that had raged through his mind after seeing Chelise's response to Thomas in the dungeons had surprised even him. He'd dreamed of Teeleh screaming into his face, fangs wide, throat deep and black. The beast had slashed him with his taloned claw.

Woref woke from the nightmare weeping. Cheek bleeding.

Recalling the event now, his neck went hot and his fingers trembled. He closed his eyes and calmed himself. Black flooded his mind. *You will kill her, Woref. You know that. In the end, even if she loves you, you will strike her too hard or choke her too long, and she will die in your arms. Why not today and be done with it?*

Because we want her love.

"He's waking, my lord."

Woref opened his eyes. He had to give the albino credit. According to Soren, he'd done well, then knocked himself out to spare himself the pain. It had seemed rash to Soren, but Woref understood. He knew Thomas's heart, and he despised him for it.

The woman was another matter. Her love for Thomas ran deeper than he'd imagined. She was a stubborn whore. But he knew that she was crying for herself, not for Thomas.

It was now only a matter of time. Teeleh would have his wench's love.

⚬⚬⚬

He couldn't bear lying awake while she cried anymore. Thomas took a deep breath and rolled away from Chelise. She jumped to her feet and stepped back. "Thomas?"

Woref or one of his faithful was still watching, listening. They'd let this go on only because of Thomas's convincing performance thus far.

He looked around, as if dazed. "How much time has passed?" he whispered.

"What?"

He looked at her. Face streaked. Eyes wide. Her question lingered on a parted mouth. Thomas suddenly couldn't trust himself to speak. He would break down, here and now, and cling to her ankles and beg her forgiveness for the way he'd cut her to ribbons with his tongue.

He swallowed and diverted his eyes. "How long was I out?"

She didn't respond right away, which meant she didn't know either. He couldn't do this! He couldn't bear it any longer!

"I don't know, maybe half an hour. Or ten minutes."

"Only ten minutes?" Mikil would need much more time! Then again, if she'd fallen asleep and dreamed only five minutes before he had, she could have spent a whole day here already. In any case, no one had come for them yet. Which could only mean that Mikil had not succeeded. For all he knew, she was dead.

"It could have been an hour," she said. Her tone was sharper now. He glanced at her and saw that she was frowning. Still staring at him, but with more resolution now. There was only so much of this she could take before she began to believe his lies.

"Please," she whispered.

Thomas clasped his hands behind his back and strolled down the line of Books. Please! She'd said please, and she might as well have kissed his lips!

He tried to think of the missing blank Books and the very serious consequences that could follow the Books appearing in the other reality. But he had no room in his heart now for what-ifs. He couldn't tear his mind away from the woman who watched him walk as if he was disinterested in her.

I am interested in you, my love. Look at my face, my hands, the way I walk, the way I breathe. Can't you see past this charade and know that I will always love you?

That would defeat the purpose of his game, wouldn't it?

What if he actually succeeded? What if she turned against him in rage and never loved him again?

His heart began to crash in his chest. He came to the corner and stopped. Tears were filling his eyes again, and he tried to blink them away. He closed his eyes and begged her to forgive him. It was worse than death.

Mikil, where are you? He had to make Woref believe that he was playing his diabolical game. He had to stay strong for her sake. Silence smothered the library. A deep void of death. A sealed tomb filled with . . .

Thomas opened his eyes. There was a sound behind him. A very soft wail. Not like her other sobs. There was an unmistakable sound of finality to her groan.

Terrified, he looked back.

Chelise was lying on the floor, facedown, with her hands extended above her head, weeping.

Thomas was stumbling toward her before he could tell his feet to move. He would not bear this! What had he done?

He fell to his knees, threw his arms over her head, and buried his face in her hair. He tried to speak, but his throat wasn't cooperating.

He tried to be gentle—to pull back and tell her what he desperately wanted to tell her, to stroke her face and wipe her tears, but all he could do was cling to her and cry into her hair. Woref would come. At any moment they would crash through the doors and pull him off of her. He had to tell her!

But he could only shake over her like a leaf.

Stop it, Thomas! You're terrifying her!

Then he lifted his head, sat back on his legs, and wept at the ceiling. "I . . . love . . . you." It came out as hardly more than a whisper.

He sucked in a lungful of air and gazed at the back of her head through his tears. He stroked her hair with his fingertips. "I love you, Chelise, my bride, more than I could possibly love anything else." Her crying had stilled. "I'm so sorry . . . It was a lie, all of it was a lie, so that you would forget about me."

His words rushed out with relief. "I had to drive you away so they wouldn't kill you, but I can't do it. I can't do it; I don't have the strength to see you suffer. Forgive me, forgive me, my love."

Chelise's back rose and fell with her deep breathing. Did she believe him? The thought that she might not dashed through his mind. He dropped on her again, clung to her shoulders, and wept into her back.

"I beg you, forgive me! I didn't mean a word, I swear it."

He was smothering her again!

Thomas pulled back.

Chelise pushed herself to her knees, facing away. Thomas trembled, horrified by the thought that she might not believe him.

She turned slowly and he saw that her mouth was locked in a silent cry. She stared at him through pools of tears. She was regretting? She was . . .

Chelise threw her arms around his shoulders, buried her face in his neck. "I knew you loved me!" she sobbed. She kissed him below his ear and ran her fingers up the nape of his neck and squeezed him as if she were clinging to life. "I love you, my darling! I will always love you."

Thomas was beyond himself. He wrapped his arms around her, giving her only enough space to breathe. "Marry me!" he cried. It was absurd, but he didn't care. He wanted her to hear it. "Marry me!"

She hesitated only a single beat. "I will." She wept over his shoulder. "I will marry you."

The door crashed open and slammed behind Thomas. Boots pounded over the floor. A fist grabbed his hair and yanked him back with such force that he thought his neck might have been broken.

He fell back and Chelise came with him.

Woref snatched a handful of her hair and jerked her off of him. Chelise screamed.

"Leave her!" Thomas tried to rise. "Leave her—" Woref's boot connected with his temple and he fell flat.

He had to get up. He had to stall Woref. He had to kill the man. They were both dead anyway. Thomas pushed himself up. The room was spinning. He blinked and gathered himself. It occurred to him that no one else had come into the room. Whatever Woref planned, he would blame Thomas.

"Qurong . . ." Thomas gasped. "Qurong won't let you . . ."

Woref shoved Chelise against the wall and held her by her neck, hand drawn to hit her. "Now I will kill you," he said. His voice rose. "Do you hear me, you filthy whore? I will pound you until you die," he screamed in rage. "No one defies me! Not the daughter of Qurong, not Qurong himself!"

He swung his hand.

"Stop!"

The door flew inward.

Woref was committed—his open hand slapped Chelise's cheek with the sound of a cracking whip. Her head snapped sideways. But Woref had pulled back his full strength at the last moment. She stared at the doorway with wide eyes.

Thomas followed her stare. There stood Qurong. And Ciphus. And behind them, Mikil, hands bound.

———— ✿ ————

The supreme leader stood with both hands clenched, head bared. The vein at his temple bulged beneath his long, thick dreadlocks.

"Release her."

Woref withdrew his hand from her neck. He swept back a rope of hair that had fallen over his face. "This woman has committed treason by loving an albino," he said. "For that she must die."

Qurong stepped into the room. Thomas stood and looked at Mikil, who was staring at him.

"What is she doing here?" Qurong demanded.

"I brought her to save her life," Woref said. "Ciphus knows."

"I only know that you ordered her here," the chief priest said. "I know nothing else."

"You lie!"

"I'll decide who's lying," Qurong said. He stared at his daughter, lips drawn in a thin line. "How could bringing her here save her life? She was never condemned!"

"She condemned herself by loving the albino." Woref spit on the floor. "I knew and I demanded that the albino retract his love so that she would come to her senses. It was the least I could do for you."

"Then you're a fool," Qurong said bitterly. "You see things that don't exist. Who are you to judge the love of my daughter? My wife is right; you have a death wish for her."

"I can assure you—"

"Silence!" The supreme leader paced in rage. "I don't care what you say, your word is no longer trustworthy."

"Perhaps your daughter should speak for herself," Ciphus said.

They all looked at Chelise. Her eyes glanced around. Stared at Thomas. Then settled on her father.

"Then speak," Qurong said. "But I warn you, we have a law that binds us."

Thomas felt his heart sink. She had to deny her love! If she only denied it, Qurong would give her the benefit of any doubt and let her live. Woref's plot was exposed; she would be safe.

Chelise stared at her father for a long time. She looked at Thomas, and he shook his head barely, so that no one but her would see. *Please, my love. I know the truth. Save yourself.*

She locked onto his eyes and stepped away from the wall. "You want to know the truth, Father? You want to know why this beast you've put in charge of your armies is so outraged?"

She walked toward Thomas and stopped in front of him. "You want to know why this albino bound me and stole me from the castle? Why he would cross the desert for me on foot if he had to? Why he would give his life to save mine?" She paused. "It is because he loves me more than he loves his own breath."

Thomas felt his brows wrinkle in fear for her.

Chelise took his arm, stepped by his side, and faced her father. "And I love him the same."

They were six frozen statues.

"I'm sorry, Father. I can't lie about this."

Thomas saw the same fear he felt for her life pass through Qurong's eyes. "You're being forced . . ."

"I'm not," she said.

"You can't possibly say this! Do you know what this means?"

"It simply means that I love him. And for that love I will pay any price."

The supreme leader's face flushed with fury. He glared at Ciphus.

The priest bowed his head. "Then her fate is sealed, my lord."

Slowly, like the fading sun, Qurong's face changed. The resolve that had served him so well in a hundred battles settled over him. He glanced at Chelise once, then looked at Thomas.

"Forgive me," Thomas said. "I would do anything—"

"Shut up! Against the wall! Both of you."

Thomas and Chelise stepped over to the wall and pressed their backs to the bookcase.

"Release him," he snapped at Chelise. "Move away."

She obeyed.

"So then. The price for the head of my greatest enemy is the death of my own daughter. So be it."

He turned his back on them and stared at the back wall.

"Woref, please join them."

The general seemed not to have heard. "I'm sorry, my lord, what—"

"Join them on the wall."

"I don't see—"

"Now!"

Woref stepped next to Thomas.

"Ciphus."

Ciphus walked over and pulled Woref's sword free before the man could make sense of what was happening.

Qurong faced him. "I sentence you to death for treason against the royal family. You will die with them."

Woref stood aghast. "I don't think you understand, my lord. I've committed no act of treason!"

"You denounced me. You also had every intention of killing my daughter. I told you if you hurt her I would drown you myself, and now I will do that."

"This is an outrage!"

"It is fair," Ciphus said. "It is just."

"Come!" Qurong ordered.

A guard stepped in, followed by a line of others, moving quickly. Twenty filed in and surrounded them.

The supreme leader stepped up to Woref, grabbed the band across his chest that gave him his rank, and ripped it free. "Bind them!" he ordered. "They will drown tonight." He threw the sash on the floor and stepped toward the door.

"What of the other albino?" Ciphus asked. "She came willingly. On your behalf."

Qurong's eyes were sad and his fight was gone. He looked at Mikil. "Release her."

43

THOMAS STOOD in heavy leg chains on the wooden platform that reached out over the muddy lake. A half circle of roughly fifty hooded warriors, each armed with swords and sickles, stood behind the dock. Every third one carried a blazing torch that cut the night with flickering orange light. Ciphus waited to one side with several council members, avoiding eye contact with Thomas. Qurong was evidently on his way.

None of this mattered to Thomas. Only Chelise mattered. He searched the darkness behind the guards for a glimpse of her. Neither she nor Woref had been brought yet.

Conflicting emotions had beat at Thomas as he lay in the black cell. He'd wanted to die; he'd wanted to live.

At any moment he might die as he lay on the bed where they were draining his blood. Part of him begged Elyon to spare him the agony of seeing Chelise drowned by allowing him to die now.

Part of him begged Elyon to let him live another hour, long enough to see his love just one more time. They would die, but in their death they would be together. He couldn't bear the thought of not looking into her eyes again.

He didn't know what they'd done with her after they'd been pulled apart at the library, but his mind hadn't rested in imagining. Was she in her castle, crying on her bed while her mother wept for her life in the courtyard? Was she in the dungeon, thrown to the floor like a used doll? Was she demanding her father reconsider his sentence or screaming at him for abandoning her in favor of this mad religion he'd embraced?

Thomas faced the lake and scanned the barely visible distant shore.

Who was watching from the trees? Mikil and Johan, maybe. But they were powerless without swords. He was amazed to realize he had no fear of this drowning that awaited him. Justin had suffered far worse.

But Chelise . . . dear Chelise, how could she have consigned herself to death with this mad admission of love for him? He didn't care about the honor it brought him. He didn't care that she had stood up for principle or that she'd done what was right. He only cared what happened to her.

She would die. Not just in this life, but if he understood Justin, in whatever life awaited them.

Thomas lifted his eyes to the stars. *Why? How could you do this to such a tender soul? She isn't beautiful to you? Her skin offends you? Then why did you put this ache for her in my heart? This is how you will leave your bride?*

There was a commotion behind him, and he twisted to see if . . .

Thomas caught his breath. She was there. Chelise walked down the bank between four horses that guarded her. She was dressed in a white gown and she held her head steady, giving no sign that she was the victim rather than the administrator of this drowning.

Thomas searched her face to see if she had seen him, but her hood was raised and her eyes were shaded. The guards parted to receive her.

Thomas saw Qurong then, riding nobly on his horse with a large guard. They came down the shore from Thomas's right. There was no sign of Patricia.

Qurong stopped twenty yards up the bank. He would see his own sentence through without any display of weakness. But even from here, Thomas could see the supreme leader's drawn face. He wouldn't be surprised if those were claw marks on his neck from Patricia.

Now Woref was being marched down the bank behind Chelise. But Thomas didn't care about Woref.

Chelise walked past the warriors. The flames lit her face.

She was staring at him.

Thomas felt his remaining strength wane. His face wrinkled in sorrow.

She stepped onto the platform and stopped ten feet from him. Thomas moved toward her without thinking.

"Back!" A fist clubbed his head. The night went fuzzy, but he didn't lose sight of Chelise.

"We are dying for our love!" she said for all to hear. "You'll deny even that? If you are going to drown us, then let us share at least a moment of the love we are dying for!"

The guard glanced at his superior.

"Let her go to him," Qurong said.

Chelise walked toward him slowly, like an angel. Her chains, hidden by the flowing white gown, rattled on the boards. Fresh tears ran from her eyes when she was halfway to him. He stumbled toward her, and they fell into each other's arms.

There was no reason to speak. The tears, the touch, the hot breath on their necks spoke much louder than words.

Shame on the rest! They stood watching a true love that had been condemned by the religion they had the nerve to call the Great Romance.

Here was romance!

Woref stepped onto the platform.

"Enough," Qurong said. "Finish this before I force the rest of you in with them!"

"Put them abreast!" Ciphus ordered.

"You gave your life for me," Chelise whispered in his ear. "Now I will die for you." She sniffed.

"You don't have to!" Thomas said. "It's not too late . . . your father will accept your denial. Please, I know your love, but you have to find a red pool . . ."

Hands pulled her from behind. Her eyes looked into his.

"You're my red pool," she said.

———ↀ———

"We aren't going to make it!" Mikil said. "They're already on the platform. Hurry!"

She'd raced back to the others, knowing that she would need their help if there was any chance to save Thomas. But time was running out.

"We still don't know if this will work," Suzan said. "We still have time to stop the execution. Four of us with swords could scatter them!"

"Not as easily as you think," Johan said. "If they have the sashes of assassins, they won't run like the ones we walked through the other day."

"We can't save him by killing the Scabs," Mikil snapped. "We might as well be Scabs ourselves. Just dig!"

Jamous threw his weight into his sharpened stick. The passage was now four feet deep, and they clawed away at both ends. Close, so close. Any swing and either wall of remaining dirt would be breached. They'd cleared over a hundred medium-size boulders and now worked feverishly with torn hands on the soil that separated the two bodies of water.

Mikil shoved the dirt aside as fast as she could, careful not to be hit by one of their digging sticks. Her husband paused, panting. "Suzan's right. We don't know this will—"

"Just dig! There's nothing that says it takes more than a drop! Is an ocean of blood better than a bucket? One drop of Thomas's blood and I can enter his dream world. I'm telling you that one drop of this will do the same. Now—"

"I'm through!" Johan shouted.

They froze. Had his voice carried across the lake? It no longer mattered. They were running out of time.

"It's flowing!" Johan dropped to his knees and pulled aside clods of dirt. Red water spilled over his fingers and splashed into the bottom of their trench.

"The other side!" Mikil cried. "Break it down!"

"Unhand me!" Woref seethed.

The guards shoved them into position, three abreast across the wide platform. Several tall towers similar to the one they'd used to drown Justin stood to the left of the dock. Evidently Qurong had ordered a method that would spare him from watching his daughter struggling while hanging from her feet, half submerged. The heavy bronze shackles around their ankles would pull them to the bottom where they would drown unseen.

They now stood ten yards from the end of the platform. Chelise looked straight ahead, jaw set. But her show of strength couldn't stop the steady flow of tears down her white cheeks.

Thomas tore his eyes away from her. *Please, Elyon, I beg you. Rescue your bride. Have mercy.*

"Step forward," Ciphus ordered. "Stop at the edge of the platform."

Hands pushed Thomas. He moved ahead without any more encouragement. "Please, Chelise. This water means nothing to me, but I can't bear the thought of your death."

"I couldn't live with myself," she said softly. "And you're wrong. My father would never undo what he's ordered. I don't want him to."

He came to the edge and stopped. "You could save yourself. You could save me. You could keep my heart from breaking."

Woref looked ahead at the forest, eyes now searching with quick movements. "I beg you, I beg you," he whispered. His stoic bravado had been replaced by this odd plea to the forest.

Thomas followed his eyes. This was the same forest in which he'd seen the Shataiki after Justin's death. What did Woref see?

"I beg you, my lord," the general muttered. He was crying out to Teeleh, Thomas thought. Let him.

Thomas followed Chelise's gaze into the dark water ten feet below them. Long poles disappeared into the black depths. How many bodies were entombed down there, bones chained to their anchors?

The guards were binding their hands behind their backs now.

"Please, my love . . ."

"You've drowned before."

"But not in this water."

"Did you know that when you dove in, or did you sink in desperation?"

It had been both. Fear and a sliver of faith. But there was nothing to hope for here. He stared across the lake. Beyond the torch's reach the water was jet-black. Blacker than midnight. Blacker than he remembered.

"Now stand and face the rage of Elyon," Ciphus said behind them. The planks creaked under his feet as he paced. His voice rose. "Let this be a lesson to all who would defy the Great Romance by denouncing those whom Elyon himself has put over this land."

Chelise looked at him. The flames danced in her misty eyes. Her lips trembled. "You are my husband."

"And you are my wife," he whispered.

"Prepare them!" Ciphus said.

A guard behind each of them planted a fist between their shoulder blades and grabbed their hair.

"Pull!"

The guards jerked their hair down so that their heads buckled backward, forcing them to stare at the sky above. Three abreast, hands bound with canvas strips, feet laden by heavy chains, powerless and readied to die.

Mikil dropped to one knee on the right of the trench and stared across the black waters. Jamous knelt beside her; Johan and Suzan followed their lead on the other side.

"Please, Elyon," she whispered. "Mercy. Save him."

She glanced down at her left. The trench was roughly two feet wide and four feet long, and it now flowed with a rich stream of the red water from the red pool they'd found behind them. Thomas had told Kara about it absently, but the moment Qurong had sentenced him and Chelise to death in the library, she'd known that this was their only hope. To find the pool of Elyon's water and dig through the barrier between it and the Horde's lake.

But would it be enough?

The red water looked like a black fan as it spread out into the brown muddy waters. Moving fast. Faster than she would have guessed.

"Please, Justin. Save your bride."

"Thomas!" Chelise's voice was faint, tight. Her throat felt frozen. She'd seen both kinds of drownings before—from the platform and the tower—and if there was any measure of relief in her sentence, it was that Qurong had mercifully chosen the platform. In a fit of outrage, her mother had finally demanded at least that much, and her father had quickly agreed.

"Elyon's strength," Thomas whispered.

"As Elyon has commanded, so now you die," Ciphus cried. "Now die!"

A hand shoved her in the back, and suddenly there was nothing beneath her feet.

None of them made a sound as they fell. Woref hit the water first. Chelise saw his splash from the corner of her eye just before the cold water swallowed her legs, then her chest. Thomas plunged in on her left.

Then she was under.

She fell straight down, pulled by the chains bound to her ankles. She instinctively struggled against the restraints around her wrists—as was the custom, they were only loose bindings hastily tied to prevent an episode at the last moment on the platform. Amazingly they came free, sending a streak of hope through her mind. She opened her eyes.

Black. So black.

She clenched her eyes shut and, in so doing, shut the door on the last of her hope.

Elyon! Take me. Take me as your bride as you have Thomas. Her thoughts were born of panic, not reason. At any moment her feet would land in a pile of bones.

Elyon! Justin, I beg you!

The water around her feet, then her legs, changed from cold to warm. She opened her eyes and looked down in surprise. She'd expected a murky lake bottom below her—black demons clamoring for her in their lust for death.

What she saw was a pool of red light, dim and hazy, but definitely light! She looked left, then right, but there was no sign of Thomas or Woref.

Then Chelise fell into the warm red water. She floated. Serene. Silent. Unearthly and eerie. She could hear the soft thump of her own pulse. Above her, Qurong and Ciphus were watching the water for signs of her death—bubbles—but here in this fluid she was momentarily safe.

And then the moment passed and the reality of her predicament filled her mind. It was warmer and much deeper than she'd expected, and it was red, but she was still going to drown.

Her eyes began to sting, and she blinked in the warm water but received no relief. Her chest felt tight, and for a moment she considered kicking for the surface to take one more gulp of air.

She opened her mouth, felt the warm water on her tongue. Closed it. *Is it Justin's water?*

But who would willingly suck in a lungful of water? She'd entered intending to die. She knew that Thomas was right—the disease had ruined her mind! But dying willingly had felt profane.

She hung limp, trying to ignore her lungs, which were starting to burn. But that was just it—she didn't have the luxury of contemplating her decision much longer.

A wave of panic ran through her body, shaking her in its horrible fist with a despair she'd never felt before.

Chelise opened her mouth, then closed her eyes. She began to sob. A final scream filled her mind, forbidding her to take in this water. Thomas had drowned once, but that was Thomas.

Then her air was gone. Chelise stretched her jaw wide and sucked hard like a fish gulping for oxygen.

Pain hit her lungs like a battering ram.

She tried to breathe out. In, out. Her lungs had turned to stone. She was going to die. Her waterlogged body began to sink farther.

She didn't fight the drowning. Thomas had wanted her to follow him in death, and this is what she was doing. There was no life above the surface anyway.

The lack of oxygen ravaged her body for long seconds, and she didn't try to stop death.

Then she did try. With everything in her she tried to reverse this terrible course.

Elyon, I beg you. Take me. You made me; now take me.

Darkness encroached on her mind. Chelise began to scream.

Then it was black.

Nothing.

She was dead. She knew that. But there was something here, beyond life. From the blackness a moan began to fill her ears, replacing her own screams. The moan gained volume and grew to a wail and then a scream.

She knew the voice! She didn't know how she knew it, but this was Elyon. Justin? It was Justin, and he was screaming in pain.

Chelise pressed her hands to her ears and began to scream too, thinking now that this was worse than death. Her body crawled with fire as though every last cell revolted at the sound. And so they should, a voice whispered in her skull. Their Maker was screaming in pain!

A soft, inviting voice suddenly replaced the cry. "Remember me, Chelise," it said. Elyon said. Justin said.

Light lit the edges of her mind. A red light. Chelise opened her eyes, stunned by this sudden turn. The burning in her chest was gone. The water was warmer, and the light below seemed brighter.

She was alive?

She sucked at the red water and pushed it out. Breathing! She was alive!

Chelise cried out in astonishment. She glanced down at her legs and arms. The shackles were gone! She moved her legs. Free. Real. She was here, floating in the lake, not in some other disconnected reality.

And her skin . . . She rubbed it with her thumb. The disease was gone! Thomas had been right! She was an albino. Here in the bowels of this red lake she was now a stunning breed, and the thought of it filled her with a thrill she could hardly fathom.

She spun around, looking for Thomas, but he wasn't here.

Chelise twisted once in the water and thrust her fist above (or was it below?) her head. She dove deep, then looped back and struck for the surface. What would they say?

She had to find Thomas! Justin had changed the water.

The moment her hand hit the cold water above the warm, her lungs began to burn. She tried to breathe but found she couldn't. Then she was through, out of the water.

Three thoughts mushroomed in her while the water was still falling from her face. The first was that she was breaking through the surface at precisely the same time as Thomas on her left. Like two dolphins breaking the surface in coordinated leaps, heads arched back, water streaming off their hair, grinning as wide as the sky.

The second thought was that she could feel the bottom of the lake under her feet. She was standing near the shore.

The third was that she still couldn't breathe.

She came out of the water to her waist, doubled over, and wretched a quart of water from her lungs. The pain left with the water. She gasped once, found she could breathe easily, and turned slowly.

Water and strings of saliva fell from Thomas's grinning mouth. She wasn't sure what had happened to him, but he was alive.

She lifted her arm and stared. Her skin had changed. A dark flesh tone. Deep tan. Smooth like a baby's skin. And she knew without a doubt that her eyes were emerald, like Thomas's.

She was as albino as any albino she'd ever seen.

Only then did it occur to her that Qurong was still seated on his horse less than thirty yards from where she stood. His face was stricken. To her left the guard stared in stunned silence. No sign of Woref. He was undoubtedly drowned.

"Seize them!" Ciphus cried from the platform.

"Leave them!" Qurong ordered.

Chelise walked out of the lake, plowing water noisily with her thighs. Thomas walked beside her—there was no need for words.

In some ways she felt as if she was looking at a whole new world. Not only was she a new person, drowned in magic, but the Scabs she faced were now foreign to her. The disease hung on them like dried dung. But when they understood what Elyon had done for them in this lake, they would flock en masse into the red waters. She would be run over, she thought wryly.

Then she remembered her own resistance to the drowning. She stared at her father, who still looked as though he was staring at something in his nightmares come to life.

"The law states that they must drown!" Ciphus said, walking to the edge of the platform, finger extended.

"They have drowned," Qurong said.

"They are not dead!"

"Does my daughter look like a Scab to you?" Qurong shouted. "If this is not a dead Scab, I don't know what is. She's been drowned and paid her price! You will not lay a hand on her."

Chelise wanted to run up and throw her arms around him. "Father, it's real. The water is red! This is now a red pool."

His eyes jerked to the water behind her. She followed his gaze. The lake looked black, but there was a tinge of red to it.

Ciphus was staring and had now seen it too. "Seal off the lake!" he shouted, spinning to the guard. "No one enters."

"No!" Chelise. "The people must be allowed to drown! Father, tell him."

Qurong looked back out at the water. He scanned the surface. "And Woref?"

"Woref didn't believe," Thomas said.

Her father eyed him. "And how did this water become red?"

"I don't know for sure, but I'm guessing that Mikil and Johan found the red pool you had covered."

Qurong frowned. "Seal the lake," he said.

"Form a perimeter at the top of the shore," Ciphus said. "Not a soul steps on the beach until we have repaired this damage."

Chelise took a step toward Qurong. "Father, you can't allow this!"

He lifted a hand. "Stop there."

"Drown!" she cried. "You have to drown, you and Mother! All of you!"

Her father drew his horse around so that he faced her. "They are free to go," he said. "They and their friends will be given free passage from our forest. No albino is to be hurt before we know the truth of what has happened here."

"Father . . . please, I beg you . . . you know the truth."

"You're my daughter, and because of that I will let you live in peace," he said. "But I have my limits. Leave now, before I change my mind."

He turned his horse and walked up the shore.

Chelise stared after him, torn between the urge to drag him into the lake and the realization that she was no different only a day ago. But there was hope, wasn't there? He was going to consider the matter.

"I'm sorry," Thomas said, putting his hand on her shoulder.

She faced him and her sorrow faded. His skin, just this morning an interesting enigma, was now deliciously brown and smooth. His green eyes shone like the stars. He was truly beautiful.

"Are my eyes . . ."

"Green," he finished. He brushed her cheek with his thumb. "And your skin is dark, the most beautiful I've ever seen."

"I am his bride now?" she asked.

"You are. And mine?"

"I am."

She felt as if she might burst.

He winked and then took her hand. "We should take your father at his word and get out while we can. The Circle will be waiting."

The Circle. She glanced back. Ciphus was glaring at them. Two dozen guards had formed a line by the platform, barring them from following Qurong, who was just now guiding his horse past a hastily formed perimeter guard.

The Circle was waiting. She grinned, suddenly eager to be gone from here and among her new family. To be with her husband.

Thomas of Hunter.

"Then we shouldn't keep them," she said and stepped toward the waiting forest.

44

Carlos had waited three days now, and not a single vehicle had crawled out of the underground facility. But they were there; he would stake his life on it.

Birds chirped on the hillside, oblivious to how close they had come to moving up the food chain three days ago. Here in the country outside of the port, the morning was peaceful and cool. Down in the city there was a scramble to acquire one of the coveted syringes that were now flowing out of Paris. The news was of nothing but the virus. More accurately, the antivirus. The Thomas Strain, they were calling it. The man had reportedly given his life. Carlos wasn't ready to believe that just yet.

There were enough vaccinations to go around, they said, but that didn't stop the panic. The distribution plan was essentially the reverse of their blood-collection efforts. Syringes filled with the Thomas Strain had already flooded the gateway cities. Every refrigerated vehicle in France was now carrying the antivirus to distribution points across the country, where hundreds of thousands waited their turn in long lines.

Meanwhile, Carlos lay in wait with his weapon.

He glanced at his forearm. The red spots had disappeared. He still couldn't make sense of it, but there was only one cause that made any sense. He'd been in contact with Hunter's blood.

The man's funeral was to be held in twenty-four hours. Carlos would use every power at his means to be present. He had to see for himself. And if Hunter was finally dead . . .

The thought knotted his gut and he let it trail off.

If Fortier didn't emerge soon, he would go to the authorities—the French military would like nothing better than to drop a few bunker busters on this site and rid the world of the men who had sullied their reputation. The French president, who'd followed Fortier's demands all too quickly, would probably do it himself to bolster his standing with the people. The world was too distracted by the virus at the moment, but one day Carlos might set them all straight.

The problem with going to the authorities now was that it meant leaving his post long enough for them to make an escape. Unlikely, but he wouldn't put anything beyond Fortier.

So Carlos waited in his hole on the hill.

He'd decided halfway to Paris that the bunker there made no sense. Fortier and Svensson would hole up in Marseilles, where no matter what the outcome of the next few days, they would be safe. With this new plan of theirs to betray so many who'd surrendered their weapons, Paris was full of too many enemies.

Carlos had confirmed that two vehicles had recently driven over the soft ground that led to the hidden bunker below. It could be no one but Fortier and Svensson—no one else knew of its existence. The only reason he knew was because he always knew more than they meant for him to know.

It all made sense in the most apocalyptic way. They had unleashed their weapon and would hunker down until it had done its work before emerging to a new world.

But they hadn't factored in Thomas. Or his dreams.

Carlos reached into his pocket and pulled out another pill. He'd slept once since setting up his post, but it had been early, before the news of the Thomas Strain had broken. He popped the pill in his mouth and swallowed.

He imagined that Fortier and Svensson were down in that hole arguing furiously at this very moment about what had gone wrong. They . . .

The earth on the hill below suddenly moved. Carlos froze. So soon?

Slowly, like a giant whale opening its mouth, the hill opened up. He snatched the antitank missile and sat upright. So they had decided to leave France while the world was still distracted by the crisis. There had been a few massive manhunts before, but none like the one that would surely follow this debacle.

Carlos armed the missile, hefted it onto his shoulder, and aimed it at the entrance. His hands were shaking from the combination of exhaustion and shattered nerves.

The garage door stopped. Open. Then nothing.

He willed the car to emerge. It would be the white Mercedes with armored plating. They would split up later, but they wouldn't risk two cars at this point if only one was armored, which Carlos knew to be the case.

Come on, come on. Come out.

He could practically taste the cordite on his tongue from the anticipated explosion. The missile would tear the car to a thousand pieces.

The nose of the white Mercedes suddenly poked out of the garage.

Steady . . .

Then the body.

Carlos waited until the garage door began to close. One car. Windows tinted so he couldn't tell if they were both inside.

He suddenly couldn't wait another moment. He triggered the missile. A loud *whoosh.* Pressure on his shoulder. Then a streak of exhaust and a waft of hot air on his face.

He willed the missile all the way into the Mercedes. It struck the right front passenger window. For a split second, Carlos saw the legs in the passenger's seat.

That made two occupants.

The detonation shattered the morning air. A ball of fire split the car at its seams. Blew the roof off. Smoke boiled out.

Then it was just roaring fire.

Carlos grabbed his binoculars, adjusted the focus, and studied the flames. He'd seen enough in his time to conclude now that he had just killed two men.

One of them was Armand Fortier. The other was Valborg Svensson.

He lowered the glasses. Unlike Thomas, these two would not be coming back to life.

Kara watched the casket sink below the green turf at Arlington National Cemetery. They were giving Thomas a full military burial with all the honors, and hundreds of people she'd never met were being moved to tears by the event, but to her the whole funeral felt oddly insignificant.

Her brother was alive.

Not here, nor in a way any of these people could possibly understand the way she did. But he was more alive than any of these who wept.

The president stood on her right. Monique on her left. Five days had passed since Thomas's death. They'd wanted to march his casket down Constitution Boulevard while the world watched, but Kara had convinced the president that if Thomas had a say in the matter, he would protest. They'd settled on this more subdued but still nationally broadcast affair.

The seven guns had gone off and three fighters had roared overhead, and Kara had watched it all with mild interest. Her mind was still on Thomas's blood. The blood that Monique still had in storage.

She couldn't get it out of her mind.

Beyond the skin of this world waited another world, as real, perhaps more real. There Thomas was alive and by now surely married to Chelise. He'd died while in the lake, and somehow it had given him life. There was no doubt in her mind that Justin had orchestrated everything.

Justin had allowed Thomas to fall in love with Chelise so that the Circle would know how he felt about them. Kara was sure that if she could see Justin now, he would be racing circles around his bride on a white stallion, thrilled by the beauty of his creation. By the love, however mixed it was, that they had for him.

This was his bride!

And in his eyes her dress was spotless. White.

Someone handed her a shovel. She snapped out of her thoughts. They wanted her to do the honors? She stepped forward, scooped up some dirt, and tossed it into the grave.

Then it was over. She turned her back on the burial. The gathered crowd began to step away.

"I want you to know that I've commissioned a statue for the White House lawn," the president said. "You may think Thomas would object, but this isn't about Thomas anymore. It's about the people. They need a way to express their gratitude. This isn't going to end."

She nodded. The Thomas Strain had smothered the virus in a way that none could have hoped for. There were deaths, but remarkably few. Under two hundred thousand at last count, and most of those the result of people trying to bypass the system. Some riots, a refrigeration truck ambushed, and the like. The Thomas Strain was just now reaching remote destinations around the world—mostly in the Third World, part of South America, China, Africa, where the Raison Strain had been the slowest to infect. The world would never be the same, but it had survived.

If Thomas had been delayed on the aircraft carrier by only three hours, the death toll would have been significantly higher.

The president put his arm on her shoulder. "You okay?"

"Yes." She smiled. "Thank you, sir."

"If there's anything I can do, you let me know."

"I will."

He turned away, and Monique stepped in to replace him.

"So," she said, sighing, "now what?"

"Now I don't know."

"Do you think his blood still works?"

"I don't know. Six billion people now have some of his blood in them, don't they? They're not dreaming."

"They have no reason to dream," Monique said. "Without belief, you don't dream."

Kara walked with Monique. "Or maybe the dreams don't work because he's dead," she said. "'Course, I dreamed once when he was dead."

"Maybe we should find out."

Kara looked into her eyes. "Tempting, isn't it?"

"I've thought about it more than once."

"I don't know. Something tells me that it's changed. I think we should leave it alone for now. It's safe, right?"

"Believe me, no one's touching it."

"There is something else that worries me," Kara said.

"The Book," Monique said without hesitation.

Kara stopped. "That's right. The blank Book of History. Or should I say Books. Thomas seemed to think that they all crossed over. At this very moment there exists at least one Book, last seen in France, which has more power than any of the nuclear weapons Thomas sank."

"Surely it'll show up."

"That's what I'm afraid of."

45

A SUNSET painted the dusk sky orange over the white desert. Thomas sat on his horse at the lip of a small valley that resembled a perfect crater roughly a hundred yards across. The depression harbored an oasis, and in the center of that oasis a red pool was nestled among large boulders. A ring of fruit trees grew from the rich soil beside the limestone that held this particular pool. Twenty-four torches blazed in a perfect circle around the pool. The rock ledge around the water was roughly fifty yards in dia-meter, and it kept the pool clean so that, from his perch above the scene, he imagined he could almost see the bottom, though he knew it was at least fifty feet deep.

Tonight Thomas of Hunter would wed once again.

Chelise, who was now being prepared by the older women, would soon walk into the circle of torches and present herself for union with Thomas as was the custom from the colored forest. The four-hundred-odd members of this tribe had been joined by another two thousand from those tribes close enough to make the trek for the occasion. They were gathered on the far slope, beyond the ring of torches.

Thomas's mind went briefly to Rachelle. He missed her, always would. But the pain of her loss had been whitewashed by his love for Chelise. Rachelle not only would approve, but she would insist, he thought.

Ten days had passed since Chelise's drowning. In that time nearly five thousand of the Horde had joined the Circle, urged on by Chelise's pas-sionate voice. If ever there was a prophet in the Circle, it was she. With Qurong's own daughter now among the albinos, the threat from the Horde had all but vanished. At least for the time being. Teeleh wouldn't wait long before taking up his vain pursuit again, but until then Qurong's decree would protect the Circle from any unauthorized attack. Rumor had it Ciphus was being forced to keep his disapproval to himself. He'd drained the lake and was refilling it again. His religion would be back in full swing soon enough.

Suzan and Johan were mounted on black horses next to Thomas. They would be married in two days in a similar ceremony. Mikil and Jamous sat on the other side. They were fools for love, all of them. The Great Romance had swallowed them whole, and this gift of love between couples was a constant reminder of the most extravagant kind.

"How long?" Thomas asked.

"Patience," Mikil said. "Beautifying is a process to be enjoyed."

"And marriage isn't? I don't see how they could possibly add to her beauty."

Suzan chuckled.

Thomas lifted his eyes and looked at the sunset. It was a paradise, he thought. Not like the colored forest, but close enough. With Chelise at his side and Elyon on the horizon of his mind, more than a paradise.

"You still haven't dreamed?" Mikil asked.

The dreams.

"I dream every night," he said. "But not of the histories, no. For sixteen years the only way I could escape the histories was to eat the rhambutan fruit. Now I couldn't dream of the histories if I tried."

"But they did exist," Johan said. "I was there myself."

"Did they? Well, yes, the histories existed. But when we finally get access to the Books in Qurong's library—"

"He's agreed?" Susan asked.

"Eventually we'll get our hands on them. I'm sure the fact that we can read them will play to our favor. But when we have access to the Books, I don't know what we'll find. It happened; I'm sure it happened. But will it all be recorded? I don't know. Either way, I don't live in the histories. I live here."

An unsure smile crossed Suzan's mouth. Thomas looked at the boulder around which Chelise would soon come. What was keeping them?

"You don't believe that it happened, Suzan?" he asked. "Tell her, Johan. Was it real or was it only a dream?"

"If it was a dream, it was the most incredibly real dream I ever had."

"Did I say I didn't believe?" Suzan said. "But let's be honest, Thomas. Not even you know exactly what to believe about these dreams. Mikil has her thoughts about shifts in time; you talk about shifts in dimensions. I'm not saying the dreams didn't happen, Elyon forbid. But they make about as much sense to me as the red pools do to the Horde."

"Exactly!" Thomas said, impressed. "To a Scab the notion of drowning to find new life is absurd. And to all of us, the notion of entering a different dimension through dreams is as absurd. But the lack of understanding doesn't undermine the reality of either experience."

"I must say, the memory is fading," Mikil said. "It hardly feels real anymore. Everything that was so important to Kara seems so distant. What consumed that world hardly matters here."

"No, what happened there helped to define me," Thomas said. Although he had to agree. The human race had faced the threat of extinction, but the drama there was overshadowed by the drama here.

"But I see your point, and I think it was meant to be," he continued. "How can the rise and fall of nations compare to the Great Romance? Think about it. A whole civilization was at stake there, and at first it scared me to death. But by the end, the struggles in this reality seemed far more significant to me. Certainly far more interesting. The battle over flesh and blood cannot compare to the battle for the heart."

He took a deep breath. "On the other hand, the blank Books are gone. That's interesting. And how the Books came into existence in the first place. For that matter, how I bridged these two realities."

Johan faced him, eyes bright. "I have a theory. Why and how Thomas first entered the black forest, we'll never know, because he lost his memory, but what if he managed to fall, hit his head, and bleed at precisely the same moment that he was struck on the head in the other reality? This could have formed a bridge between what can be seen and what can't be seen."

"Then Earth, the other Earth, still exists?" Suzan asked.

"It must," Johan said. "And the blank Books are most likely there."

"Unless you subscribe to Mikil's theory that Elyon used Thomas's dreams to send him to another time," Suzan said. "You see what I mean? They both make sense only if you use liberal amounts of imagination."

"Principalities and powers," Thomas said absently. "We fight not against flesh and blood, but against principalities and powers."

"What?"

"Something I now remember from the other reality. It was no less obvious there how these things worked. They called it the natural dimension and the spiritual dimension."

"Spiritual. As in spirits?" Suzan asked.

"As in the Shataiki here. We can't see them, but our battle is really against them, not the Horde."

"Well, we know the Shataiki are real enough," Johan said. "So why not the dreams?"

A distant rumble like the sound of thunder from the far side of the world drifted over them. Thomas cocked his head. "You hear that?"

They were all listening now. The rumble grew steadily. Thomas's horse snorted and stamped nervously.

"The ground's shaking!" Suzan said. "An earthquake?"

"Too long."

All of their horses were now restless, unusual for beasts trained to stand still in battle.

"Dust!" Mikil cried, pointing to the desert.

They turned as one, just as the first beasts crested the long dunes in the nearby desert. Then more came, thousands, stretching far to the left and to the right.

Thomas's first thought was that the Horde had staged a massive attack. But he immediately dismissed the notion. Johan spoke what was on his mind.

"Roshuim!" he cried.

A thousand, ten thousand—there was no way to count such a large number. The massive white lions that Thomas had last seen around the upper lake when he'd first met the boy poured over the dunes like a rolling fog.

They were split down the middle. There, slightly ahead of the lions, rode a single warrior on a white horse.

Justin.

Johan, Mikil, then Jamous and Suzan slid from their saddles and dropped to one knee. It was their first sighting of him since they'd fled the Horde after his death. The sounds from the crowd opposite them had stilled, but they rose as one and stared to the west.

Thomas had just overcome his shock and started to dismount when Chelise walked out from the boulders below them. She seemed to glide rather than walk. His bride was dressed in a long white tunic that swept the sand behind her. A ring of white tuhan flowers sat delicately on her head.

Thomas froze. Chelise surely heard the approaching thunder, but she couldn't see what he saw from her lower vantage point. She must have assumed it was the pounding of drums or something associated with the ceremony, because her eyes were turned toward him, not the desert.

Her eyes pierced him, and she smiled. Oh, how she smiled.

She reached the circle, faced him, and lifted her chin slightly. The black, red, and white medallion hung from her neck, fastened by a leather thong.

On Thomas's left, the Roshuim lions ran on, led by Justin. It occurred to Thomas that he was still standing in one stirrup. He lowered himself to the ground, stepped forward, and knelt on one knee. Chelise followed his gaze.

The lions split and swept in a wide circle, pouring around them as if this pocket of desert was protected by an unseen force.

Justin, on the other hand, drove his horse straight on, right over the berm that encircled the small valley, directly toward Chelise.

Now she saw.

Justin reined his horse back ten yards from Chelise, who stood in stunned silence. The stallion whinnied and reared high. Justin's eyes flashed as only his could. He dropped the horse to all four, then slid to the sand and took three steps toward her before stopping. He was in a white tunic, with gold armbands and leather boots strapped high. A red sash lay across his chest.

The lions still poured around the valley, giving them all a wide berth, twenty yards behind Thomas.

Justin looked up at Thomas. Then back at Chelise, like a proud father. Or a proud husband?

He strode into the circle, up to Chelise, took her hand, and bent to one knee. Then he kissed her hand and stared into her eyes. Chelise lifted her free hand to her lips and stifled a cry. She might be a strong woman, but what she saw in his eyes would undo the strongest.

Justin stood, released her hand, and stepped back. He placed both hands on his hips, then immediately lifted them to the sky, and faced the stars.

"She's perfect!"

He turned toward the gathered crowd, most of whom had fallen to their knees. "And each one of you, no less! Perfect!"

Justin bounded for his horse, leaped into his saddle, grabbed the reins, and galloped up the slope, directly toward Thomas.

The Roshuim had completed a circle and now faced the valley. The moment Justin cleared the lip, they fell to their bellies in a soft rolling thump and lowered their muzzles to the sand. The sight knotted Thomas's throat, and he wanted to throw himself to the sand and worship as the lions did, but he couldn't tear his eyes from Justin, racing toward him.

"Elyon . . ." Johan whispered.

Justin veered to their right. Then the sound of metal sliding against metal ripped through the still air. Justin pulled his sword free, leaned off his mount, and thrust the blade's tip into the sand.

He wheeled his horse around and rode away from Thomas, hanging low in a full sprint, long hair flowing in the wind, dragging the sword in the sand. The soft cries of joy joined the thudding of his horse's hooves. They all knew what he was doing. They'd all heard the stories.

Justin was drawing his circle.

And he was drawing it around all of them, claiming them all as his bride. The circle was symbolic.

Justin, on the other hand, was not.

He completed the circuit behind Thomas and turned his horse back toward them. Thomas felt compelled to lower his head. Justin's horse walked by, hooves plodding, breathing hard, snorting. Leather creaked.

It stopped at the top of the slope, not ten yards from where Thomas knelt.

For a long moment there was silence. Even those who had been crying on the opposite slope went quiet.

Then the sound of laughter. A low chuckle that grew.

Surprised, Thomas glanced up at Justin. The warrior/lover who was also Elyon had thrown back his head and had begun to laugh with long peals of infectious delight. He thrust both fists into the air and laughed, face skyward, eyes clenched.

Thomas grinned stupidly at the sight.

Then the laughing started to change. Honestly, Thomas wasn't sure if this was laughter or sobbing any longer.

The grin faded from Justin's face. He was weeping.

Justin suddenly lowered his arms, stood up in his stirrups, and cried out so they all could hear him. "The Great Romance!" He glanced to his left and Thomas saw the tears on his cheeks. "From the beginning it was always about the Great Romance."

He sat and turned his stallion so that its side faced the valley.

"It was always about this moment. Even before Tanis crossed the bridge, in ways you can't understand."

Justin scanned the crowd.

"My beloved, you have chosen me. You have been courted by my adversary, and you have chosen me. You have answered my call to the Circle, and today I call you my bride."

For a long time he gazed over the people who filled the valley with the sounds of sniffing and crying. Chelise was kneeling in her own tears now.

Justin turned toward Thomas. He nudged his horse forward.

"Stand up, Thomas."

Thomas stood, legs shaking. He looked up at Justin, but he found it difficult to look into those emerald eyes for more than a few moments.

"No, look into my eyes."

Those wells of creation. Of profound meaning and raw emotion. Thomas wanted to weep. He wanted to laugh. He was in the lake again, breathing an intoxicating power that came from those eyes.

"You have done well, Thomas. Don't let them forget my love or the price I've paid for their love."

I won't, Thomas tried to say. But nothing came out.

Justin looked at the others and nodded at each. "Suzan, Johan. Jamous, Mikil." He let tears run down his cheeks. "My, what a good thing we have done here."

His jaw flexed and his nostrils flared with pride.

"What a very good thing."

Then he pulled his stallion around. "Hiyaa!"

The horse bolted. On cue, the massive ring of Roshuim stood and roared. The ground shook.

Chelise ran from the red pool, up the slope toward Thomas. She pulled up beside him, staring at Justin. Thomas drew her close, and they watched the receding entourage in awed silence.

Justin galloped into the desert, followed by the ranks of white lions on either side. The desert settled back into silence.

For a long time no one spoke.

And then Thomas married Chelise, surrounded by an exuberant, rejoicing Circle still intoxicated by Justin's love.

Epilogue

SO THEN, were you right or were you wrong?" Gabil asked, scanning the titles of Books on the library's top shelf. "It really is a simple question with a simple . . ." He stopped short. "Ah! I've found it!"

He withdrew an old leather-bound book and swooped down toward Michal, who teetered on the edge of the desk, peering at another Book of History he'd withdrawn only minutes ago. A single candle lit the old pages. The Horde library lay in shadows, deserted at this late hour.

"None of this is simple," Michal said. "Patience."

"I thought you said you'd found it," Gabil said, fluttering for a landing beside Michal. He set the Book he'd retrieved on the desk.

"I said I found the section that deals with the Great Deception, not the actual sentence that states the actual date."

"You did tell Thomas of Hunter early in the twenty-first century. I remember that much."

"And if I did, then you agreed," Michal said, scanning the page.

"Did I? You're positive?"

"Did you disagree? You're far too interested in this minor point, Gabil. What difference does the date make in the end? This is a silly exercise."

"I'm interested because the histories couldn't have said early in the twenty-first century. Thomas changed history. The virus didn't ravage the world. So the question is, when does the Great Deception take place? Or does it even?"

Gabil studied the cover of his Book, then opened it to the first page.

This history was taken from the colored forest. He flipped toward the back of the Book.

"Of course the Great Deception takes place," Michal said. "I'm reading the details now, as we speak. You see, right here . . ." The Roush stopped.

"What?" Gabil released the page in his fingers, hopped once, and leaned over to see.

"Give me some room," Michal protested. "This . . . I don't remember anything about . . ."

"I knew it!" Gabil chirped. "Yes, I did. I knew it. It's changed, hasn't it?"

"Well, it's no longer early in the twenty-first century. But we could have been mistaken about that. But these other things . . ."

"Thomas changed history!"

Michal ran his finger down the page. "The Tribulation as recorded by John hasn't changed, but the date . . . and the Great Deception . . ." He returned to where he'd started reading. "I do say, the events leading up to John's prophecy have changed."

"He did change history. He did, he did!" Gabil hopped again, twice, lost his footing, and toppled to the floor. He bounded to his feet and did a little jig of sorts. "Ha! It's fascinating! It's magnicalicious!"

"Please, settle down. That's not even a word."

"Why not?" Gabil said. "If Thomas can change history, I think I have the right to change a few words."

He jumped back up on the desk and resumed his search in the Book that recorded the colored forest's demise.

Michal looked at him, still gripping the page he'd been reading. "So you really think knowing how Thomas entered the black forest will shed any light on—"

"Here!"

Michal jumped. "What is it?"

"I think I've found it! This Book records his story." He flipped forward to the very end, scanning anxiously. "Here, here, it has to be here in this volume."

Michal looked over the pages with interest.

"Give me space," Gabil said.

"Humph." Michal took a tiny step to his right.

Gabil came to the last page and stopped cold. "What is this?"

"What?"

"It's been . . ." He leaned forward. "It's been changed. Erased and written over."

Michal crowded Gabil again. "What's it say?"

The smaller Roush ran his index finger under the words of the last paragraph, which were clearly written in handwriting different from those preceding.

He read aloud.

"Then the man named Thomas found himself in the black forest, where he fell and hit his head and lost his memory. Ha."

Gabil looked up at Michal, taken aback.

"'Ha'?" Michal asked, incredulous. "It says 'ha'? That's it?"

"That's it. Then it's signed."

Gabil looked at the page. *"Billy, Storyteller,"* he read. "Someone named Billy who is a storyteller wrote this."

They stared in silence for a few seconds.

Michal sighed and returned to his Book. "I have to admit, this is . . . fascinating."

"It seems Thomas wasn't the only one who changed history," Gabil said. "Didn't I tell you? Ha!"

"Ha?"

"Ha!" He closed his book and hopped on top of it. "So read. Read this new history that I told you we would find even though you doubted." He lifted his chin and grinned.

Michal eyed his fuzzy friend. "Yes, I guess you did tell me."

Then the Roush took a deep breath and began to read from the Book of Histories.

THE JOURNEY CONTINUES WITH **GREEN** . . .

GREEN

THE LAST STAND

Author's Note

YOU HAVE IN YOUR HANDS the entire Circle Series with an all new ending to *Green* which brings complete closure to the series.

Originally *Green* was seen as Book Zero, an entry point into the series and as such the ending was an intellectual mind bender. That original ending follows the new ending for *Green*—have some fun with it. But seeing that you clearly started with *Black* and are ending here with *Green* I think I owe you a final climax.

Either way, enjoy the read. Dive Deep. I promise you a trip you will not soon forget.

Prologue

ACCORDING TO the Books of History, everything that happened after the year 2010 actually began in the year 4036 AD. It began in the future, not the past. Confusing perhaps, but perfectly understandable once you realize that some things are as dependent on the future as on the past.

The world's history was written in the Books of History, those magnificent volumes that recorded only the truth of all that happened. Earth was destroyed once during the twenty-first century, in an apocalypse foretold in the books of the ancient prophets Daniel and John, and then recorded as history in the Books of History. But the time for history was not yet finished, and Elyon in his great wisdom set upon the earth a new firstborn named Tanis.

This time, Elyon gave humans an advantage: What had been spiritual and unseen became physical and seen. All good and evil could be watched and felt and touched and tasted. As time passed, however, mankind closed its eyes to what was real and became blind to the forces that surrounded it.

But there remained a small band of rebels who longed to see Elyon as they once had. They were led by one man who claimed to have visited the twenty-first century in his dreams.

His name was Thomas Hunter.

This is his story.

O

The Future

CHELISE HUNTER, wife of Thomas Hunter, stood beside her son, Samuel, and gazed over the canyon now flooded with those who'd crossed the desert for the annual Gathering. The sound of pounding drums echoed from the cliff walls; thousands milled in groups or danced in small circles as they awaited the final ceremonies, which would commence when the sun settled beyond the horizon. The night would fill with cries of loyalty and all would feast on fatted cows and hopes for deliverance from their great enemy, the Horde.

But Samuel, a warrior with a heavy sword and angry glare, had evidently put his hope in something entirely different. He stood still, but she knew that under the leather chest-and-shoulder armor his muscles were tense and, in his mind's eye, moving already. Racing off to make war.

Chelise let the breeze blow her hair about her face and tried to calm herself with steady breathing. "This is impossible, Samuel. Complete foolishness."

"Is it? Say that to Sacura."

"She would agree with me."

Sacura, mother of three just a few days earlier, was now mother of two. Her fifteen-year-old son, Richard, had been caught and hung by a Horde scouting party when he'd straggled behind his tribe as it made its way to the Gathering.

"Then she's the fool, not me."

"You think our nonviolent ways are just a haphazard strategy to gain us the upper hand?" Chelise demanded. "You think returning death with more death will bring us peace? Nearly everyone in the valley was once Horde, including me, in case I need to remind you—now you want to hunt their families because they haven't converted to our ways?"

"And you would let them slaughter us instead? How many of us do they need to kill before you shed this absurd love you have for our enemy?"

Chelise could take his backtalk no longer. It took all of her strength to resist the temptation to slap his face, here and now. But it occurred to her that using violence at precisely this moment would strengthen his point.

And knowing Samuel, he would only grin. She knew how to fight, they all did as a matter of tradition, but next to Samuel she was the butterfly and he the eagle.

Chelise settled. For the sake of Jake, her youngest, they must follow the ways of Elyon. For the sake of her father, Qurong, commander of the Horde, and her mother. For the sake of the *world*, they had to cling to what they knew, not what their emotions demanded from them. To take up arms now would make an unforgivable mockery of all the Circle stood for.

She faced Samuel and saw that his sleeve was hitched up under his left arm guard. She pulled it down and brushed it flat. "It's hard, I know," she said, casting a glance back at the three mounted guards who waited behind them. Samuel's band numbered a couple dozen, all sharing his hatred. Honorable men who were tired of seeing loved ones die at the hands of the Horde.

"He's larger-than-life, we all know that. Just because you're his son doesn't mean you have to blaze his trail."

She'd meant to console him, but he stiffened and she knew her words had done the opposite. "Not that you feel like you have to measure up to Thomas, but—"

"This has nothing to do with Thomas!" he snapped, pulling away. "Nobody could possibly measure up to a man with his past. My concern is the future, not some crazy history bounding between the worlds through those dreams of his."

Odd that he would refer to the time when Thomas claimed to have traveled back in time through dreams. Thomas so rarely referred to it himself those days.

"Forget his dreams. My husband is the leader of the Circle. He carries the burden of keeping twelve thousand hearts in line with the truth, and you, his son, would undermine that?"

Samuel's jaw knotted. "The truth, Mother?" he bit off. He shoved a hand south, in the direction of Qurongi Forest, once controlled by Thomas and the Forest Guard, now inhabited by her father, leader of the Horde, Qurong. "The truth is, your precious Horde hates us and butchers us wherever they find us."

"What do you suggest?" she cried. "Run off now, on the eve of our greatest celebration, in search of a few Scabs who are likely back in the city by now?"

Samuel lowered his hand and looked back at his men. Then to the south again. "We have him now."

"You have who now?"

"The Scab who killed Sacura's son. We have him captive in a canyon."

Chelise didn't know what to say to this. They had taken a Scab captive? Who'd ever heard of such a thing?

"We're going to give him a trial in the desert," Samuel said.

"For what purpose?"

"For justice!"

"You cannot kill him, Samuel! The Gathering would come undone! I don't have to tell you what that would do to your father."

"To my father?" He looked at her. "Or to you, Mother, the daughter of Qurong, supreme commander of all that is wicked and vile?"

Chelise slapped him. Nothing more than a flat palm to his cheek, but the crack of the blow sounded like a whip.

Samuel grinned. She immediately wished to take her anger back.

"Sorry. Sorry, I didn't mean that. But you're speaking of my father!"

"Yes, you did mean that, Mother." He turned and strode toward his horse.

"Where are you going?"

"To conduct a trial," he said.

"Then at least bring him in, Samuel." She started after him, but he was already swinging into the saddle. "Think!"

"I'm done thinking." He pulled his horse around and brushed past his men, who turned with him. "It's time to act."

"Samuel . . ."

"Keep this between us, will you?" he said, looking over his shoulder. "I'd hate to put a damper on such a wonderful night of celebration."

"Samuel. Stop this!"

He kicked his horse and left her with the sound of pounding hooves.

Dear Elyon . . . the boy would be the ruin of them all.

1

THOMAS HUNTER stood next to his wife, Chelise, facing the shallow canyon lined by three thousand of Elyon's lovers, who'd drowned in the red lakes to rid their bodies of the scabbing disease that covered the skin of all Horde.

The reenactment of the Great Wedding had taken an hour, and the final salute, which would usher the Gathering into a wild night of celebration, was upon them.

As was customary, both he and Chelise were dressed in white, because Elyon would come in white. She with lilies in her hair and a long, flowing gown spun from silk; he in a bleached tunic, dyed red around the collar to remind them of the blood that had paid for this wedding.

This was their great romance, and there could not possibly be a dry eye in the valley.

Six maidens also in white faced Chelise and Thomas on their knees and sang the Great Wedding's song. Their sweet, yearning voices filled the valley as they cried the refrain in melodic unison, faces bright with an eager desperation.

You are Beautiful . . . so Beautiful . . . Beautiful . . . Beautiful . . .

The drums lifted the cry to a crescendo. Milus, one of the older children, had recounted their history earlier in the night to thundering applause. Now Thomas retraced from his own vantage all that had brought them here.

Ten years ago, most of these people had been Horde, enslaved by Teeleh's disease. The rest were Forest Dwellers who had kept the disease at bay by washing in Elyon's lakes once every day as he'd directed.

Then the Horde, led by Qurong, had invaded the forests and defiled the lakes. All had succumbed to the scabbing disease, which deceived the mind and cracked the skin.

But Elyon made a new way to defeat the evil disease: Any Horde simply had to drown in one of the red pools, and the disease would be washed away, never to return. Those who chose to drown and find new life were called albinos by the Horde, because their skin, whether dark or light, was smooth.

The albinos formed a Circle of trust and followed their leader, Thomas of Hunter.

The Horde, however, divided into two races: Purebred Horde, who'd always had the scabbing disease, and half-breeds, who'd been Forest Dwellers but turned Horde after Qurong's invasion of the forests. The full-breed Horde despised and persecuted the half-breeds because they'd once been Forest Dwellers.

Eram, a half-breed, had fled Qurong's persecution and welcomed all half-breeds to join him in the deep northern desert, where they thrived as Horde and enemies of Qurong. Nearly half a million, rumor had it.

They called the faction who followed Eram *Eramites*, remnants of the faithful who were as diseased as any other Scab. All suffered from the sickly, smelly disease that covered the skin and clouded the mind.

Thomas glanced at his bride. To look at Chelise's smooth, bronzed jaw now . . . her bright emerald eyes had once been gray. Her long blonde hair had once been tangled dreadlocks smothered in morst paste to fight the stench of the scabbing disease.

Chelise, who'd given birth to one of his three children, was a vision of perfect beauty. And in so many ways they were all perfectly beautiful, as Elyon was beautiful. *Beautiful, Beautiful, Beautiful.*

They had all once denied Elyon, their maker, their lover, the author of the Great Romance. Now they were the Circle, roughly twelve thousand who lived in nomadic tribes, fugitives from the Horde hunters who sought their deaths.

Three thousand had come together northwest of Qurongi City in a remote, shallow canyon called Paradose. They did this every year to express their solidarity and celebrate their passion for Elyon.

The Gathering, they called it. This year four Gatherings would take place near four forests, one north, one south, one east, one west. The danger of all twelve thousand crossing the desert from where they had scattered and coming to one location was simply too great.

Thomas scanned the three thousand strewn along the rocks and on the earth in a huge semicircle before him. After three days of late nights and long days filled with laughter and dancing and innumerable embraces of affection, they now stared at him in wide-eyed silence.

A large bonfire raged to his left, casting shifting shadows over their intent gazes. To his right, the red pool glistened, black in the night, one of seventy-seven they'd found throughout the land. Cliffs surrounded the hidden canyon, broken only by two gaps wide enough for four horses abreast. Guards lined the tops of the cliffs, keeping a keen eye on the desert beyond for any sign of Horde.

How many times over the past ten years had members of the Circle been found and slaughtered wholesale? Too many to count. But they had learned well, gone deep, tracked the Horde's movements, become invisible in the desert canyons. So invisible that the Scabs now often referred to the Circle as ghosts.

But Thomas now knew that the greatest danger no longer came from the Horde.

Treachery was brewing inside the Circle.

A horse snorted from the corrals around the bend behind Thomas. The fire popped and crackled as hungry flames lapped at the shimmering waves of heat they chased into the cool night air. The breathing of several thousand bodies steadied in the magic of the maiden's song.

Still no sign of his elder son, Samuel.

An echo followed the last note, and silence fell upon the Gathering as the maidens backed slowly into the crowd. Thomas lifted his gray chalice, filled to the brim with Elyon's red healing waters from the pool.

As one, the followers of Elyon lifted their chalices out to him, level with their steady gazes. The Salute. Their eyes held his, some defiant in their determination to stay true, many wet with tears of gratitude for the great sacrifice that had first turned the pools red.

The leaders stood to his left. Mikil and Jamous, her husband, side by side, goblets raised, staring forward, waiting for Thomas. Suzan, one of the many colored albinos, and her lover, Johan, who had been a mighty warrior—was a mighty warrior—gripped each other's hands and watched Thomas.

Marie, his daughter from his first wife, who was now with Elyon, stood next to his youngest child, Jake, who was five years old one month ago. Where had all the years gone? The last time he'd taken a breath, Marie had been sixteen; now she was twenty-five. A hundred boys would have wed her years ago if Thomas hadn't been so stuffy, as she put it. At eighteen Marie had lost interest in boys and taken up scouting with Samuel. Her betrothal to Vadal, the dark-skinned man next to her, had occurred only after she abandoned her old passions.

Samuel, on the other hand, still pursued his, with enough eagerness to keep Thomas pacing late into the night on occasion.

And still, no sign of the boy. He'd been gone for a day.

The Circle waited, and he let the moment stretch to the snapping point. A presence here warmed the back of his neck with anticipation. They couldn't see him, hadn't seen him for many years, but Elyon was near.

Elyon—as the boy, as the warrior, as the lion, the lamb, the giver of life and the lover of all. Their Great Romance was for him. He'd given his life for them, and they for him.

They all wore the symbol that represented their own history, a medallion or a tattoo shaped like a circle, with an outer ring in green to signify the beginning, the life of Elyon. Then a black circle to remember evil's crushing blow. Two straps of red crossed the black circle, the death that brought life in the red waters.

And at the center, a white circle, for it was prophesied that Elyon would come again on a white horse and rescue his bride from the dragon Teeleh, who pursued her day and night.

Soon, Thomas thought. Elyon had to come soon. If he did not, they would fall apart. They'd been wandering in the desert for ten years, like lost Israelites without a home. At celebrations like this, surrounded by song and dance, they all knew the truth. But when the singing was over . . . how quickly they could forget.

Still he held them, three minutes now, and not a man, woman, or child over the age of two spoke. Even the infants seemed to understand that they had reached the climax of the three-day celebration. Later they would feast on the fifty boar they'd slaughtered and set over fires at the back of the canyon. They would dance and sing and boast of all things worthy and some not.

But they all knew that every pleasure they tasted, every hope that filled their chests, every moment of peace and love rested firmly on the meaning behind the words that Thomas would now speak.

His low voice flooded the canyon with an assurance that brought a tremble to their limbs.

"Lovers of Elyon who have drowned in the lakes and been given life, this is our hope, our passion, our only true reason to live."

"It is as he says," Chelise said in a light voice choked with emotion.

Together the three thousand responded, "He speaks the truth." Their soft voices rumbled through the valley.

They knew Elyon by many names: the Creator, who'd fashioned them; the Warrior, who'd once rescued them; the Giver of gifts, who gave them the fruit that healed and sustained them. But they'd agreed to simply call him Elyon several years earlier, when a heretic from a southern tribe began to teach that Thomas himself was their savior.

Thomas spoke with more intensity. "He has rescued us. He has wooed us. He has lavished us with more pleasures than we can contain in this life."

"It is as he says," Chelise said.

The people's reply washed over Thomas like a wave, gaining volume. "He speaks the truth."

"Now we wait for the return of our king, the prince warrior who loved us while we were yet Horde."

"It is as he says!"

"He speaks the truth!"

"Our lives are his, born in his waters, made pure by the very blood we now raise to the sky!" Thomas thundered each word.

And Chelise cried her agreement. "It is as he says!"

"He speaks the truth." Their voices spilled over the canyon walls for any within a mile on this still night to hear.

"Remember Elyon, brothers and sisters of the Circle! Live for him! Ready the bride, make a celebration ready, for he is among us!"

"It is as he says!"

The volume rose to a crushing roar. "He speaks the truth."

"I speak the truth."

"He speaks the truth!"

"I speak the truth!"

"He speaks the truth!"

Silence.

"Drink to remember. To the Great Romance. To Elyon!"

This time their response was whispered in utmost reverence, as if each syllable was something as precious as the red water in their hands.

"To Elyon."

Thomas closed his eyes, brought the chalice to his lips, tilted it back, and let the cool water flow into his mouth. The red liquid swirled around his tongue then seeped down his throat, leaving a lingering copper taste. He let the gentle effects of the first few drops warm his belly for a second, then swallowed deep, flooding his mouth and throat with the healing waters.

They weren't nearly as strong as the green lake waters that had once flowed with Elyon's presence. And they didn't contain the same medicinal qualities of the fruit that hung from the trees around the pools, but they lifted spirits and brought simple pleasure.

He took three full gulps of the precious water, allowing some to spill down his chin, then pulled the chalice away, cleared his throat with one final swallow, and gasped at the night sky.

"To Elyon!"

As one, the Circle pulled their goblets from their mouths like parched warriors satisfied by sweet ale, and roared at the night sky.

"To Elyon!"

And with that cry, the spirit of celebration was released. Thomas turned to Chelise, drew her to him with his free arm, and kissed her wet lips. A thousand voices cried their approval, chased by undulating calls from the unwed maidens and their hopeful suitors. Chelise's laughter filled his mouth as he spun back to the crowd, goblet still raised.

He pulled her forward, so all could see his bride. "Is there anyone here who would dare not love as Elyon has loved us all? Can anyone not remember the disease that covered their flesh?" Thomas looked at Chelise and spoke his poetic offering around a subtle grin that undoubtedly failed to properly express his love for this woman.

"What beauty, what pleasure, what intoxicating love he has given me for my own ashes. In place of the stench that once filled my very own nostrils he has given me this fragrance. A princess whom I can serve. She numbs my mind with dizzying pictures of exquisite beauty."

They all knew he was speaking of Chelise, who had been the princess of the Horde, Qurong's very own daughter. Now she was the bride of Elyon, Thomas's lover, the bearer of his youngest son, who stared up at them with wonder next to Marie.

"He speaks the truth," Johan said, grinning. He took a pull from his goblet and dipped his head.

"He speaks the truth," they returned, followed by more calls and rounds of drinks.

Johan, too, had been Horde not so long ago, charged with killing hundreds—thousands by the time it was all over—of Elyon's followers.

Thomas thrust his goblet toward the Gathering, unmindful of the liquid that splashed out; there were seventy-seven pools filled with the red waters, and not one had ever showed any sign of going dry.

"To the Horde."

"To the Horde!"

And they drank again, flooding themselves with the intoxicating waters in a start to what promised to be a night of serious, unrestricted celebration.

"Aye, Father." The male voice came from behind and to his right. The husky, unmistakable sound of Samuel. "To the Horde."

Thomas lowered his chalice and turned to see his son perched atop his horse, drilling him with his bright green eyes. He rode low in the pale stallion's saddle and moved with the horse as if he'd been bred and born on the beast. His dark hair fell to his shoulders, blown by a hard ride. Sweat had mixed with the red mud that he and those of his band applied to their cheekbones; streaks etched his darkened face and neck. His leather chest guard was open, allowing the night air to cool his bared chest, still glistening in the moonlight.

He had his mother's nose and eyes.

A stab of pride sliced through Thomas's heart. Samuel might have gone astray, but this image of his boy could have been *him* fifteen years ago.

The stallion's *clip-clopping* hooves echoed as it stepped into the fire-light, followed by three, then five, then nine warriors who'd taken up arms with Samuel. All were dressed in the same battle dress of the Forest Guard, largely abandoned since the Circle had laid down arms eleven years ago. Only the guards and scouts wore the protective leathers to ward off arrows and blades.

But Samuel . . . no amount of reason seemed to jar good sense into his thick skull.

His son stilled his horse with a gentle tug on its reins. His followers stopped behind him in a loose formation that left them with no weak flank, standard Guard protocol by his own orders. Samuel and his band moved with the ease of seasoned warriors.

A few catcalls from different points in the crowd raised praise for the man who scanned them without a hint of acknowledgment.

"Hear, Samuel! Elyon's strength, boy!" A pause. "Keep the boogers in their stink hole, Samuel!"

This remark was a departure from general sentiment, though not as distant from the heart of the Circle as it once had been. Thomas was all too aware of the rumblings among many clans.

"Nice of you to join us, Samuel," Thomas said, tipping his chalice in the boy's direction.

His son looked directly at Chelise, dipped his head, then looked back at the three thousand gathered in the natural amphitheater. "To the Horde," he called.

"To the Horde." But only half took up the cry. The rest, like Thomas, heard the bite in Samuel's voice.

"To the stinking, bloody Horde who butcher our children and spread their filthy disease through our forests!" Samuel cried, voice now bitter with mockery.

Only a few took him up. "Stinking, bloody Horde."

"Our friends, the Horde, have sent their apologies for taking the life of our own three days ago. They have sent us all a gift to express their remorse, and I have brought it to our Gathering."

Samuel stuck his hand out, palm up. A dark object sailed forward, lobbed by Petrus, son of Jeremiah, and Samuel snatched it out of the air as if it were a water bag needing to be refilled. He tossed it onto the ground. The object bounced once and rolled to stop where firelight illuminated the fine details of their prize.

It was a head. A human head. A Horde head with a mane of long dreadlocks, covered in disease.

A chill snaked down Thomas's spine. This, he thought, was the beginning of the end.

2

THERE WAS no gasp, no outcry, only a heavy silence. None of them was a stranger to violence. But among the Circle, taking the life of another, Scab or albino, was strictly forbidden.

This . . . this looked to be the result of an execution. Carried out by his own son. For a moment, all Thomas could hear was the pounding of his own heart.

Vadal, son of Ronin, one of the very first to drown, stumbled out to the severed head and stared, disbelieving, for a moment. Any hint of celebration in the wake of Thomas's salute was gone.

He swiveled to face Samuel. "Are you mad, man?"

"The head belongs to the man who hung Richard, son of Sacura. We seized him, tried him, and found him guilty. The punishment was death."

Vadal thrust his finger at the head near his feet. "Don't be a fool. You *kill* them and you might as well *be* them. This is your idea?"

"This, you blithering fool, is doing the work of Elyon," Samuel said calmly. "Ridding the world of those who mock him."

"Only to become them?" Vadal shot back.

"Do I look like a Scab to you? Am I—having defiled the love of Elyon himself as you claim—now covered from head to foot with the disease that marks unbelievers? Has he taken away his healing from me?"

Thomas held up his hand to bring some order before the whole thing got out of control. "You've made your point, Samuel. Now take your prize, bury it somewhere far from here, and return to our celebration."

"That's not what I had in mind."

Thomas felt his own patience thinning. "Get off of that horse. Pick up that head. Get back on your horse. And leave us!"

A crooked grin crossed Samuel's face. "Now, there's the father I once knew. Commander of the Forest Guard. The world once quivered at your name."

"And now it quivers at the name of another."

"Does it? Elyon? And just where is Elyon these days?"

"Stop it!" Chelise snapped. She released Thomas's arm and took a step toward Samuel. "How dare you speak of your Maker with such a callous tongue?"

"I'm only stating what is on the mind of us all. Love the Horde? Why? They hate us, they kill us, they strike terror into our camps. They would wipe out this entire gathering with one blow if they could. We are the vomit on the bottom of their boots, and that will never change."

"*You* were once Horde, you insolent pup!" Chelise shot back.

Samuel nudged his horse around the severed head. His posse stood their ground, a group of mind-numb fighters who'd tasted just enough bloodlust to give them a thirst. "Do we not believe that a time will soon come when Elyon will destroy all of this land and the Horde with it, and finally rescue us to bliss?"

Silence.

"Ten years have gone by without one indisputable sign that Elyon still hovers nearby, preparing to rescue us. You're too busy running and hiding from that Horde beast Qurong to ask why."

"That *beast* is my father," Chelise cried. "I would die for him. And you would kill him?"

Samuel paused only a moment. "Kill Qurong, the supreme commander who has sworn to slaughter our children? The Scab who paces deep into the night, poisoned by bitterness against his own daughter because she betrayed him by drowning? *That* Qurong? The one you are obsessed with because he gave birth to you?" He spoke in a soft voice that cut the night silence like a thin blade. "You love your father more than you love any of us, Mother. If it were his head on the ground now, we might finally be free."

Samuel had always been bitter about Chelise's love for her father, but he'd never voiced it so plainly.

Vadal spoke for Chelise, who was swimming in so much fury at the moment that she didn't appear to be able to form words.

"This is heresy! You have no—"

"I took this Scab's head in a canyon twenty miles from here," Samuel announced, ignoring Vadal. "We ambushed him, and my sword cut cleanly through his neck with one swing. It was the most satisfying thing I have done in my life."

"Samuel!" This from Marie, who glared at her brother, red-faced.

Thomas fought a terrible urge to leap upon the boy and whip his hide until he begged for mercy. But he remained rooted to the ground.

Samuel blurted out, "War is permissible. I say we wage it. I've been out there slipping in and around the Horde since I turned fifteen, and I can tell you that with five thousand warriors we could make them regret the day they ever killed one of ours."

"Elyon forbid!" Vadal gasped.

"If Elyon will kindly tell me I'm wrong, then I will step down. We say that evil is on the flesh, that the disease on the Horde's skin is Elyon's curse. So why am I still disease free, having committed this terrible evil by killing this Scab, unless Elyon approves? Until he makes my error clear, my heart will cry for the days when we took them on, twenty to one, and turned the sand red with their blood."

"It's sacrilege!"

"What's sacrilege?" Samuel threw back. "What Elyon tells us himself, or what we have been told he says? Have any of you heard this specific instruction from Elyon lately? Or are you all too drunk on his fruit and water to notice his absence?"

"This . . ." Vadal was trembling with rage. "This is utter nonsense!"

"It used to be that we celebrated the passing of every soul, believing that they had gone on to a better place. Now our celebrations at the passing are filled with mourning. Why? Where is Elyon, and where is this better place?"

None of them could deny the subtle shift in their treatment of the dead.

"We used to long for the day of Elyon, clinging to the hope that any moment he would come swooping over the hills to rescue us once and for all. Now we long only for the day of the Gathering, when we can drink the waters and eat the fruit and dance ourselves silly, deep into the night. The Great Romance has become our elixir, a place to hide from the world."

"You're speaking rubbish."

"I say bring back the days of our glory! Hasten the day of Elyon's return. Fight Qurong the way the Eramites do."

"You'll have to fight me first," Vadal said.

Samuel pulled his horse around on its rear quarter to face the man. His mount snorted in protest. "So be it." Loudly to the whole gathering, he said, "I'm told the followers of Eram also respect the challenge as we once did. I challenge Vadal of Ronin to combat as in the days of old. It is still permitted."

Was it? Thomas felt his gut churn.

"I accept," Vadal snapped.

"To the death."

"Stop it!" Chelise cried. Then, in a softer voice, "I warned you about this, Samuel."

"Did you? Our prevailing doctrine denounces violence against the Horde," Samuel said, "but what does it say of the challenge? We speak all night long about tales of the heroics that preceded us: Elyon this, Thomas that . . . I say let the heroics be seen in the flesh. Elyon will save the one who speaks the truth as he once did."

His argument contained a thread of truth that turned Thomas's blood cold. Before their very eyes they were witnessing the greatest threat to all truth. And from the mouth of his own son. But Thomas was too stunned to form a response. This was his own son, for the love of Elyon!

Chelise whispered his name urgently, and he saw that she was staring at him, begging him to stop Samuel.

Instead, Thomas looked at Ronin and Johan for support. William, Mikil, Jamous—any of them. They all stared at him for guidance. Were they, too, growing tired of waiting for an imminent return that had been imminent for longer than any of them cared to think? Could this be the source of their hesitation?

Samuel wasn't the only one to wonder if Elyon really was coming back for a "bride" anytime soon. After all, he'd allowed them to take beating after beating without so much as lifting a finger. What good was being disease free if you lived in ridicule and on the run?

Thomas caught Ronin's stare. "Ronin?"

The spiritual leader of Thomas's clan frowned, then studied his son Vadal and Samuel.

"No one in the Circle has issued a challenge for a very long time. Never, that I know of. It's utterly foolish."

"But was it outlawed?" Samuel pressed.

Chelise flung both arms wide. "This is so much nonsense, this flexing of the muscle to prove a point. And to the *death*?" She turned to the others. "Come on, Mikil! Johan, surely you can't think this is permissible."

"It's absurd," Mikil said, and Johan agreed, but neither was demanding. The fear in Thomas's gut spread. Why weren't they rushing out and dragging Samuel off his horse in protest? They harbored a small vessel of doubt themselves? Surely not all of them!

Samuel took advantage of their inaction. "Didn't Elyon once condone our use of force? Has he changed his mind? Does Elyon change his mind? *Well, well, by the heavens I've made a dreadful mistake, I will change the way it is done!* Is this a perfect Creator?"

He let that settle.

"No. Elyon knows that it is better to love, that everything rests on the fulfillment of the Great Romance, like the union of bride and groom after a night of dizzying celebration. But sometimes love can be expressed by defending the truth. Vadal has that prerogative. No, Mikil?"

The famed fighter shifted her eyes to Thomas, neither agreeing nor disagreeing with Samuel, but by this very deflection she had endorsed him. Didn't she realize what she was doing? Supporting this ludicrous assertion before the entire Gathering could only bring ruin!

But the fear cascading down Thomas's spine rendered him mute as well. A dozen years ago he would have cut this challenge to the ground with a few well-placed words. Those days were gone, replaced by a wisdom that now seemed to fail him entirely. Smothered by dread.

"Does this Gathering cower from the truth?" Samuel called out. "Let me fight as the Eramites fight!"

Thomas had risked his life on a hundred occasions to love the Horde, to win Chelise, to follow the ways of Elyon, no matter how dangerous or brutal the path. Now that path had doubled back and was running straight down the middle of the Circle itself. The greatest danger was from inside, he always told the others. Tonight it had finally bared its teeth for all to see.

And there was no outcry from the Circle against Samuel's demand.

Thomas looked up at the thousands regarding him. "Who says so?"

No one shouted agreement, as was their right. But after several beats a younger man from another clan—Andres, if Thomas was right—lifted his drink.

"So says I." They looked at him, and he stepped forward into the orange firelight. "There is a time for peace and there is a time for war. Maybe the time for war has come. Didn't Elyon once wage war?"

A hundred *ayes* rumbled through the night.

So then, Samuel *was* tapping the unspoken sentiment of many. This attitude was practically epidemic, a cancer that would eat them alive from the inside.

And this from his own son . . .

Thomas tried to swallow, but the fear now swelling through his head prevented the simple action. He'd faced that devil Teeleh himself and bested him in the blackest forest; he'd hacked his way out of thirty encroaching Scabs with a single broad blade; he'd marched into the city to the cheers of a hundred thousand throats shouting the praises of Thomas of Hunter, the greatest warrior who'd ever lived.

But at the moment, he was only a terrified husk. Useless against this enemy called Samuel, son of Hunter.

It occurred to him that Samuel was speaking again, demanding more from the crowd. "Who else?" he was shouting. And hundreds were agreeing.

"Don't be so thin headed!" William cried over them all. "We've always agreed that we were shown a new way by Elyon, apart from the sword. Now our impatience changes that? Our way is to love our enemies, not wage war on them."

A thousand *ayes* and shrill cries of agreement shook the canyon.

Finally! Finally some sense!

"But I am within my rights to make this challenge, am I not?" Samuel demanded. "And Vadal is in his rights to accept."

"Aye." The agreements peppered the gathering, but all eyes were now back on Ronin and Thomas.

Ronin must have noted the concern that had locked up Thomas, because he addressed the crowd.

"Yes, I suppose it is right what Samuel says. Nothing I know of outlawed his prerogative to challenge my son. And Vadal has the right to accept that challenge or reject it, which would be the wiser by far. Frankly, I'm appalled that there isn't a protest among you all. Have you decided to feed your bloodlust?"

"He's right," Chelise said. "This is the kind of thing we might do as Horde."

"Or under the old Thomas," a lone voice called.

"All things may be permissible, but not all are beneficial," Ronin said, cutting off any further dialogue that might mire them in their own violent history. To Vadal, his son: "Surely, you see the madness in this."

"I see the madness in what tempts Samuel and half of the Circle," he said.

Samuel slid out of his saddle and landed on the ground with a slap of boots on rock. He slipped his sword from its scabbard, thrust the bronzed tip into the shale, and rested both palms in its handle.

"What is it, O favored one? Shall we test the truth?" The fool wasn't taking any of this seriously! Or worse, he was drunk on his own power and took Vadal's death very seriously.

"I accept," Vadal snapped.

"No!" Marie, Thomas's eldest child and Vadal's betrothed, stepped out, ripped a sword from the mount closest to Samuel's, and twirled it once with a flip of her wrist. "I exercise my right to take the place of any other in a challenge."

"Don't be a fool," Vadal said. "Step back!"

"Shut up. If you have the right to throw away your life, so do I. Those are the rules."

"That was a long time ago. Get back, I'm telling you!"

Marie turned to the elder. "Ronin?"

The spiritual leader nodded. "It is her right."

Samuel grinned, whipped his sword through a backhanded swing, and circled to his right, inviting Marie into an imaginary fighting ring.

"Stop them!" Chelise was glaring at Thomas, whispering harshly. "Do something."

He did nothing. He could hardly think straight, much less trust himself to do something he would not later regret. He could not stop them; they all had the same freedom to make their own choices.

The grin had faded from Samuel's face. Surely he wouldn't use his sword on his own sister. This was Marie's ploy. She knew that Samuel would back down. This was her gamble, and Thomas could see the wisdom in it.

"So, Sister. It's you and me, is it?"

"Looks that way." She walked closer, dragging her sword casually behind her. Not to fool a soul; they all knew she was a devil with that thing.

Samuel glanced at the blade, leaning on his own with confidence. "I'm not the young pup you punished the last time we played this game."

"This isn't a game," Marie said. "You're playing with the fate of our people."

"You'll get hurt," he said.

"Then hurt me, Brother."

3

WHILE THOMAS HUNTER stood in the canyon, unraveling, Billy Rediger paced the atrium of Raison Pharmaceutical in Thailand two thousand years earlier, in our own reality—or the histories, depending on how one looked at it.

Billy took a moment to take in his surroundings: the rich golden marble floor, the huge paintings of a red and yellow flower that looked as though it might be the bug-eating variety, the gilded wallpaper, two heavy crystal chandeliers that could crush a Volkswagen. The drug giant's exotic facade fueled his haunting impression of Raison Pharmaceutical.

This is where it had all started roughly thirty-six years ago, in this very building just outside Bangkok. Seven years before Billy had been born and whisked away to the monastery in Colorado, where he'd been raised and turned into a freak.

This was where Thomas Hunter had stumbled upon the Raison Strain, the deadly virus that turned the world upside down. How many dead was it? Hardly imaginable.

But worse than what had died was what had survived Hunter's discovery.

What would Darcy and Johnny say if they knew of the obsession that had overtaken Billy's mind this last year? He had a pathological need to understand why his life had been profoundly impacted by these books called the Books of History.

If his two confidants knew of his quest, they would leave their safe harbor in Colorado, hunt him down, and lock him in a cage. Because they would assume that Billy was after more, wouldn't they? More than just understanding, more than just connecting with his past, more than chasing down the truth, more than . . .

"They will see you now, sir." The receptionist, a man named Williston, had a heavy French accent.

Billy turned, startled out of his moment of unguarded admissions. *They?* He'd asked to see only Monique de Raison.

He caught his image in a ten-by-ten mirror framed in heavy black ironwork. Still dressed in the same white shirt he'd thrown on just before landing eight hours earlier. The self-applied blond highlights in his red hair looked too obvious, and his head hadn't seen a brush since the take-off from Washington, D.C., a day earlier. *Here stands Billy Rediger, one of the three famed gifted savants who turned Paradise, Colorado into a household name.* The rumpled look would have to do.

He was twenty-nine going on nineteen. If they only knew.

Billy wiped his sweaty palms on his jeans, squirted a dash of cinnamon freshener into his mouth, straightened his collar, and strode for the door as the dark-haired Williston looked on with a deadpan stare.

"Thank you, Williston. Thank you very much, sir. And by all means, ditch the blonde from France. Go for the local girl. It's what you want."

The man blinked with surprise. "Pardon?"

"Ditch Adel. You think she's a whore, and you're probably right. Go for the maid—what's her name? Betty. Yes, Betty."

The man was speechless—probably wasn't every day a stranger told him what he was thinking. This far from home, not many knew of Billy's unique gifting. And if they did, they associated it only with a distant face seen on the Net, not a real, living human being walking before them in three dimensions.

He stepped past the ten-foot doors into a white office with colonial latticed windows that looked out to the thick green jungle beyond. At the room's center sat a large teakwood desk with a cream-colored lamp that shed yellow light over a clean glass top.

The dark-haired woman who stood behind the desk looked younger than her reported sixty years—all those drugs she manufactured, he supposed. After six months of searching out every scrap of information he could harvest from records far and wide, Billy felt as though he already knew Monique de Raison.

She'd accepted full control of Raison Pharmaceutical from her father, Jacques de Raison, after the Raison Strain had all but destroyed the infamous company. Rebuilding the company's shattered image was no small task, but she'd risen to the occasion and delivered with flying colors. The sharp, dark eyes studying him as he walked toward her opened to a mind that missed nothing.

Billy knew, because it was his gift to know what anyone was thinking by looking into their eyes.

This is what Monique was thinking at the moment: *Younger than I expected, dressed like a punk. Is he really reading my thoughts this very moment? Does he know I will turn him away regardless of what he hopes to accomplish? Does he know that he's a freak?*

Billy stretched out his hand. "Yes, I do know that I'm a freak."

Monique stared at him for a moment, then lifted a pair of dark glasses from the desk and put them on, effectively blocking her mind from his probing eyes. She took his hand. "So you *can* do what they say."

"Thanks to Thomas Hunter," he said, and released her hand. Because yes, without Thomas Hunter there never would have been magic books to turn him into the freak he was. But that was all in the past.

Billy was here to change the future.

A blonde woman of about Monique's age sat to his right, one leg crossed over the other, hands folded in her lap. She wore dark glasses already, not wanting to risk any exposure to his prying eyes, but he recognized Kara Hunter immediately. Thomas Hunter's sister, keeper of many secrets regarding the blood Billy was seeking.

Both Kara and Monique in one sitting. He'd struck gold.

Billy crossed to Kara, who rose and offered her hand. "Mr. Rediger."

"And you would be Kara Hunter."

She nodded.

"Please, have a seat," Monique said, motioning to the guest chair in front of her desk.

He did, and they both eased back into their chairs. Eyes on him, he presumed, though he couldn't be certain what their eyes were doing behind those dark glasses.

"It is a bright day, isn't it?" he said, failing to lighten the mood.

"What can we do for you?" Monique asked.

"Just like that, huh? You meet one of the few people alive today whose life was profoundly impacted by the Hunter legacy and that's all you can ask?"

"Every living being on this planet was profoundly impacted by my brother," Kara said. "Not the least, himself. You have this interesting gift because you evidently came in contact—"

"Evidently? Try conclusively."

"Conclusively?" Monique cut in. "And what else have you concluded?"

"That thirty-six years ago Thomas Hunter claimed to have dreamed about another reality. That this other reality was, in fact, real. That the Books of History, magical books that turned words to flesh, came to us from that reality. I should know. I used them. They gave me my gift."

"Evidently."

"Conclusively. Did you know that I wrote about Thomas in the books? Maybe that's why he dreamed what he dreamed and awakened in this other world of his. If I hadn't written it, he wouldn't have gone there, and if he hadn't gone there, he wouldn't have learned how to alter the Raison Vaccine and turn it into an airborne virus that did what it did. You might say I was the one who started it all. That it was all my fault, not yours, Monique."

He knew by their silence that his role in these events was news to them, and he continued while their heads still spun.

"So here I am. Billy, the one who has a gift for seeing more than most people can see, just like Thomas Hunter had a gift for seeing, or in his case dreaming, what most don't dream. That makes me unique, don't you think? You could even say it gives me certain rights."

Kara stood and paced to the window, arms crossed. She turned slowly back and studied him through her dark glasses. "Your case is fascinating, Mr. Rediger—"

"Billy. Please call me Billy."

"Fascinating, Billy. But it's no more than what either of us has faced. I'm sure you can appreciate that. As you obviously know, we both had a singular relationship with Thomas. You came out of your experience with this unique ability to read people's thoughts when you look into their eyes. That sounds like a net gain. I lost a brother. Many people lost their lives."

"Net gain?" he snapped. He tried to remain calm, but he wasn't as adept at controlling his temper as he'd once been. "You call this curse a gain? I'm a freak! My soul haunts me. I can't live in the same happy ignorance that the rest of you can when every lousy thought is opened to me. It's driving me mad, and I have to root out the meaning of all this. End it all."

"We're sorry you've suffered, Billy," Kara said, clasping her hands before her. "But the stakes were always more than feelings, yours or ours. We've all paid a price. I think it's best to leave the past in the past. Don't you?"

"Well, see, that's just the thing, Kara." *A little too much emphasis on her name. Mustn't sound so condescending.* "I don't think the past *is* in the past. For one thing, *I'm* not in the past. I'm here and now, a living consequence of your brother's indiscretions."

"Granted, you're one of the many effects—"

"And then there's the matter of his blood."

He wished for a line of sight into their eyes. But he hardly needed to read their minds to know he'd hit the nerve he'd come to hit.

"Blood?" Monique said, leaning back in her chair.

"Blood. The one remaining vial of Thomas Hunter's blood that you put in safekeeping. Did you think you two were the only ones who knew? The lab technician who withdrew the blood was named Isabella Romain and she lives in Covington, Kentucky, today. Naturally she refused to say what her mind was thinking, but I know with absolute certainty that a vial of Thomas Hunter's blood was taken by you, Dr. Raison, for security."

They did not deny it.

"And these eyes of mine exposed a few other secrets," he said. "Turns out that Thomas's blood allowed anyone who used it to wake up in the reality that the Books of History came from. Is it in fact another reality? Or is it our future? Either way, that makes the vial of blood a potent little vessel of a whole lot of fun, don't you think? Not to mention a path to some pretty powerful books."

Billy couldn't stop the wild grin that twisted his lips. He was sweating, he realized. Profusely. It beaded up on his forehead and ran past his temples. With each passing week he seemed to have more difficulty maintaining control of his nerves. The tics and the sweating were the worst. Thankfully he'd managed to suppress the tics thus far. Wouldn't do to start jerking about like a short-circuiting robot before asking them to trust him with their deepest secrets.

He took a deep breath and made an effort to appear reasonable. "Seriously, friends, I know it all. And I've come to ask you to bring me in."

"In?" Monique asked, one brow raised.

"Trust me. Use me. I'm all yours."

"To what end?"

"To what end?" It was a fair question, no matter how obvious the answer seemed to him. "Sorry, being through what I've been through makes that question sound a bit silly. For the purpose of survival, naturally. To *that* end. So that we can take this messy, crazy world and make sense of it again."

"And just how do you propose to do that?"

"For starters, as I'm sure you realize, some would consider me a fugitive. Have been for over two years, ever since the Tolerance Act in the fabulous United States of America turned people like me into bigots. Wackos at the least. That doesn't sit right with all people. The world is primed for more than simple, regional conflicts. Surely you can see that.

The very laws that are meant to bring peace and love are gonna bring the big boom, baby."

A bit too free with the colloquialism there.

"And?"

"And we may have the one thing that could set things right."

Both stared without showing any reaction.

He stood and paced. "I need to connect with my past. And with the future. Are you catching my drift here?"

"Not really, no."

"I need the blood."

Silence. Dead giveaway.

Monique cleared her throat. "I don't think you understand, Mr. Rediger. Even if we knew where this figment of your imagination was, this so-called vial of blood, what exactly do you think you could do with it?"

"Go into Thomas's dreams! To the place all this began. Please, don't tell me you haven't tried it."

No admission. No denial.

"You have no idea how much work it took to uncover these dark secrets of yours. Only a handful of people know what actually happened: That Thomas Hunter's blood was altered when he crossed into the other reality. That it contained unique properties. That when even a single drop of his blood mixes with a person's while they are dreaming, they, too, can go where he went, which might well be the future. That, my two lovely friends, sounds like a very major trip. You can't possibly go your entire life knowing about such a thing and not try it at least once. Kinda like sex, right?"

They still didn't seem to appreciate the simple honesty he was laying down here.

"No?" he pressed.

"Not really, no," Monique said.

"You haven't tried it?"

"Sex?"

"The blood!"

"We haven't established that this blood you talk about even exists. If it does, perhaps you can tell us where we could find it. The powers you describe sound incredibly valuable."

So, they would play it this way. What he would give to dive into their minds right now.

One way or another, he would have his way with both of their minds.

"Cute," he said. "We're going to pretend, then, is that it?"

Kara walked back to her chair and sat. "Please, Billy, have a seat."

He sat again, aware that his right hand was twitching slightly.

"Tea?"

Tea? A bit late to ask him if he wanted to break bread with them. On the other hand, this represented a sea change in at least Kara's attitude toward him. Yes, indeed. At least a pretention of being sweet.

"No thank you, Kara. No tea at the moment, but thank you for offering."

She smiled. "Perhaps we were a bit too hasty in dismissing you. Let's try a different approach, shall we? After Thomas left, my life never seemed to find its true bearing."

"Careful, Kara," Monique warned in a low voice.

Kara glanced at her friend. "It's okay. He obviously knows at least some of the truth." Back to Billy. "But you must understand how dangerous your knowledge is. I'm not sure you do. In the wrong hands, what you know could bring about more pain and suffering than you can possibly imagine."

"Oh, I think I can imagine it just fine. Why do you think I'm here? I've spent every waking minute for the last year thinking of it, tracking you two down."

"The information you have could end life as we know it," Kara continued.

"It could bring the great dragon down from the sky and fill the oceans with blood," Billy said. "Saint John's Apocalypse."

He could only imagine them blinking behind their shades. Too much, way too much. His imaginations were a thing that he should keep strictly to himself. He should know that by now. Not even these two had the capacity to go where his mind went, which is why he was suited—perhaps even prepared, preordained, chosen, all of that rot—to do what needed doing now.

"As a figure of speech," he said, circling his hand for effect, "the dragon being the symbol of death, virus, nuclear holocaust, Armageddon. Point is, if it's all true, if a person could cross into another world with Thomas's blood, and then return with untold secrets, they might not only unravel the past, but also solve the problems of the future. Of now."

"We get it," Monique said.

He couldn't read her true sentiment by her tone; he'd become too accustomed to reading people by their minds.

"So then. You're going to bring me in?" Billy asked.

"We should lock you up and throw away the key, Billy," Monique said.

"What she means," Kara inserted, "is that none of us is trustworthy with what we know. We both try to stay . . . private. We're not sure you appreciate just how difficult that can be."

"I was raised in a monastery. I think that qualifies me."

"Perhaps. But we don't know where the blood is, Billy. Or if it even still exists. We've removed ourselves from that knowledge."

"For everyone's sake," Monique said.

Nonsense. Billy knew then that they had no intention whatsoever of trusting him with the code to their front gates, much less the most potent secret the world had ever known. And why should they? He'd presented himself as a bit of a loose cannon.

But they didn't know him. He'd danced with the devil himself, and he wouldn't let these two witches stop him from doing it again.

"Well, then we'll have to take this one step at a time," Billy said. "I was wondering if you could recommend suitable accommodations."

The door flew wide and a young woman walked in, dressed in a short black dress with spaghetti straps. Bare feet, petite physique. Her black hair fell loosely past square shoulders, and her soft brown eyes cut sharply through the world.

"Excuse me, Mother. So sorry to interrupt. Henri tells me you've decided to sell our New York research laboratory. One of *my* laboratories the last time I checked. Tell me why Henri has decided to speak lies."

"So nice to see you, Janae," Monique returned in a soothing voice. "How was your trip to France?"

"As expected." No further explanation. Monique's daughter, this stunning creature with a fluid French accent who looked to be in her early twenties, seemed to notice Billy for the first time. She turned her gaze on him and peeled him open with that first look.

And who is this young pip? An American, clearly, dressed to attend a rock concert. What kind of fools is Mother exposing herself to these days? And what are those monstrous glasses doing on Mother's face?

"Mr. Rediger, please meet my daughter, Janae." Billy saw that a thin smile had nudged the corner of Monique's mouth northward. "But then you probably already know all about her, don't you? Perhaps more than I do."

The bold pronouncement left Janae silent for the moment. Billy thought it best to leave the young woman wondering.

"You might want to consider wearing dark glasses, dear Janae. Our visitor from America seems to have the ability to read minds."

Again, silence from the spirited one. Billy decided then that he would out himself fully to the dark-haired beauty. One, because he found her strangely compelling, and two, because he thought it wise to give her a reason to find him just as interesting.

"Young pip?" He stared into her eyes. "This young pip who's dressed to attend a rock concert is inside your mind right now, dear Janae. And what a delicious treat it is, all that hostility and resentment for having never known your father. He vanished when you were a small child, and you're thinking even now that he held secrets that would complete you. Isn't that what all orphans believe?"

She blinked. Her mouth parted slightly but held back the gasp some might utter when so quickly stripped. He liked her already.

"It's okay," he said. "I'm an orphan as well."

"I think we all get the point," Monique said. "He's quite dangerous. I would tread carefully."

But Billy wasn't finished. "I'm here for the vial of blood that your mother harvested from Thomas Hunter three decades ago. Maybe you know where it is. Or you could help me find it."

He might as well have dropped a bomb in the room.

Janae looked at her mother. "What blood?"

"This is completely unacceptable," Kara snapped, rising from her chair.

"On the contrary, this is the only acceptable course," Billy returned. "You need to keep an eye on me. What better way than to keep me close? You know I won't put up with either of you babysitting me."

His implication could hardly be stronger. He took the fact that Janae didn't immediately reject the notion of "babysitting" him as a sign of her interest. A glance into her eyes confirmed this.

On second look, *interest* was a bad word choice to describe her disposition toward him. *Fascination* was better. Billy turned back to the others.

Kara was clearly on rough ground. "Surely you can't—"

"It's okay, Kara," Monique said. "He's right. He can stay in the guest quarters until his curiosity is satisfied. God knows we're all better off with him here than out there where real damage can be done."

Monique de Raison thought she could control him, Billy realized. Anyone else and he would dismiss the possibility outright. But Monique was not anyone else. Neither was Kara.

Nor, for that matter, was Janae, who was still trying to understand him.

"Please give us a moment, Billy," Monique said. "Williston will show you to the guest building. Janae will be right out."

Billy stood and walked for the door. The scent of Janae's musky perfume filled him with a sudden desire as he walked past her. Those deep, dark secrets her father had hidden from her seemed to beckon him. There was something about Janae that pulled at him like a strong tide.

"Take your time," he said, stepping from the room.

4

The Future

CHELISE WATCHED Samuel and Marie stare at each other in the dead silence, seemingly unconcerned by the other's sword, like two roosters facing off, expressionless. Vadal stood to one side, pale. The other leaders looked on, unmoving.

The Circle hung on the unfolding drama as if not quite sure it was all really happening. One moment they'd been awash in Thomas's poetic love for her and for Elyon; the next, the Gathering celebration had been flattened with this insane challenge to the essence of what they held sacred.

The Great Romance was being debated at the end of a sword! Is this what she'd drowned for? They all waited for Thomas.

But Thomas wasn't stopping the lunacy.

Elyon's people had never adopted a hierarchy of government that allowed a few to control the many. Guide, yes. But each person was encouraged to follow his heart. They'd all seen what religion had done when the Horde followed their priests, first Ciphus, then Witch, then Sucrow, and now the worst of the lot, Ba'al.

Thomas had a particular distaste for manipulation through religion, preferring faith and Elyon's Great Romance. But this . . . this was ridiculous.

Chelise glanced at him and saw that his jaw was set. He was going to allow them to fight.

Samuel launched himself at a knee-high boulder, planted his right foot near the top, and threw himself into a backflip high over Marie's head. He brought his sword down as he sailed above her, a devastating swing that took full advantage of not only his well-muscled arms, but his leg strength, transferred now to his downward thrust. Thomas had told her that the splitter, as the move had been dubbed, had been named back in the days of war for its ability to cut a warrior in half, from head to crotch, with one blow.

Marie dropped to one knee, lifted her sword—one hand on the handle, one on the broad blade—and jerked the weapon over her head as a shield. The sound of Samuel's blade crashing into Marie's clanged through the valley, echoing off the cliff walls.

Would Samuel have completed his swing if Marie hadn't reacted in time? The impetuous fool had lost his mind.

Marie's braided hair swirled around her face as she pivoted, still on one knee, then lunged for Samuel's body before he landed and gathered his bearings.

Samuel anticipated her. Somehow he managed to withdraw a gutting knife. With a flip of his wrist he turned the knife back along his forearm and deflected Marie's sword. He landed with a chuckle and used his momentum to throw himself into a back handspring.

But Marie was already swinging around, sword extended for a second blow. This one nicked Samuel's chin as he threw himself out of the way.

Marie snatched her blade back, and Samuel righted himself. He touched his chin, felt the blood flowing over his fingers, and glared, face red. Marie stood on guard, breathing steadily through her nostrils.

A grin slowly twisted Samuel's lips, but this was not the look of humor or the stuff of play. This was a fierce grin, strung with resolve and rage.

"Now," he said. "Now you will see."

"You want to kill me, Samuel?" She circled to her left, opposite him. "Huh? Is that what the love of Elyon has taught you?"

"Was that Elyon who just drew first blood? I could have sworn it was you."

"Only because you challenged to kill my lover," she said.

"One for the sake of many."

"You wouldn't kill me, Samuel."

He responded in a low, guttural voice that could have belonged to an animal, Chelise thought. "Then you don't know me."

Samuel moved so quickly that Marie didn't have time to deflect. She could only jerk to her right as his knife flashed from his left hand, sliced through the night air, and thudded securely into her left shoulder.

Where it quivered, then stilled, buried two inches in her flesh.

Chelise was too stunned to act on the horror that swept through her mind. Thomas looked on, immobilized by outrage or letting history take its own course, she couldn't tell, but she wanted to slap him and tell him to make them stop.

They lived in a brutal world, but the way of the Circle was to avoid this kind of brutality in favor of love, dancing, and feasting deep into the night.

"Stop this." Mikil said, stepping forward. "For the love of Elyon, stop this foolishness."

"Back off." The growl came from Marie now.

Johan joined Mikil. "She's right, this is proving nothing."

Marie jerked the blade from her shoulder and sent it flying in Johan's direction. "Back off!"

He slapped the blade from the air before it reached him and snarled. The general in him hadn't forgotten how to move.

But before any of them could move to interfere, Marie threw herself forward and swung her blade.

Again, Samuel deflected the blow.

Again, Marie swung.

Then they were in close combat, thrusting and parrying, filling the valley with grunts and the clash of metal against metal.

The first sounds from the crowd came in the form of gasps when either Marie or Samuel narrowly escaped the opponent's blade. Then cheers of support or objection rose from a small number when Marie landed a hard blow to Samuel's right leg, severing his leather thigh guard in two.

The crowd is being pulled in, Chelise thought. *They are throwing aside their love for Elyon and blindly following this sickening orgy of violence.* The crowd's cheers of support or opposition swelled. Then one cry rose above them all and sliced through Chelise's mind.

"Silence the Horde lover, Samuel! Gut this child of Qurong!"

Chelise's blood ran cold. The call, a woman's shrill cry rising above the others, had come from the right side.

"They took my child. Take theirs! Vengeance belongs to Elyon, and he will drink their blood as they have become drunk on ours."

Samuel and Marie couldn't possibly have heard the voice amid the cacophony of shouts, the roar of three thousand voices now either crying out in outrage or throwing their support behind one of the combatants.

Chelise's son and daughter by marriage fought on.

There it was again, off to her right. She isolated the voice. "Gut the son of Teeleh. May Qurong and Ba'al, the servant of Teeleh, rot in hell. Qurong is the son of Teeleh, and the Horde who hunt us are Shataiki, who belong in a river of blood." Then even bolder, so that Chelise forgot how to breathe. "May Qurong rot in hell, and all who call themselves loyal to him die under the sword of Elyon!"

"Silence!" Chelise screamed. "Silence!"

But her voice was hardly heard above the clash of swords and cries of outrage on all sides. Many of the people were protesting, she saw. But enough backed Marie or Samuel to spur on their bitter battle.

"Thomas!" She spun back, saw that Thomas had vanished from her side, and quickly searched the crowd. Instead of finding her husband, she was drawn to the sight of a woman who stood on a pile of boulders, fists raised to the sky. She was glaring at Chelise. It could have been the firelight, but the woman's eyes appeared red in the night.

"Death to Qurong and all of his bloodthirsty offspring!"

Chelise took a step back in horror.

Her love for the Horde was a personal love, directed toward her own father, Qurong, and her mother, Patricia, neither of whom she'd seen in ten years. She'd become preoccupied with their rescue from the disease this last year, so much so that Thomas had asked her to stop bringing it up publicly. She needed to curb her incessant, affectionate talk about the leader of the Horde, who had ordered their extermination. Qurong was rumored to walk the halls of his palace, cursing the albinos who'd absconded with his daughter and turned her into an animal. Her love for her father was being met by blank stares, a sure sign that she was testing everyone's limits.

Chelise glared at the woman who ripped her father to shreds in a high-pitched voice. "'Vengeance is mine,' says the maker of all that is pure. He will cut off the impure branch, Qurong and his bloodthirsty priests!"

She knew then that if this one woman challenged her to a fight over the fate of her father, she would accept. She would defend Qurong to her death over the insults of this one witch on the stone.

Marie was doing no less, she realized. Confusion swirled about her.

Marie and Samuel exchanged a round of clashing blows, each effectively deflected by the other. But there was more blood now. Marie's thigh lay open, and the side of Samuel's head was bleeding.

Having sought the right to kill Horde, he was being soundly beaten in a fair fight, Chelise thought. She caught herself and shook the idea from her mind. Had the resentment of their tormentors grown so deep that they could no longer tolerate the abuse? The running and the hiding, the death of a loved one . . .

Just last week one of the camp's finest dancers, Jessica of Northern, had lost her son, Stevie, when he went out to hunt deer with two of his friends. They were young and bold, and their search had taken them into the forest, where Horde assassins called Throaters had fallen on them from the trees and killed Stevie. Jessica had wailed for a day before falling hoarse.

The thoughts spun through Chelise's head at a dizzying pace, punctuated by the cries and clanging of swords. Both combatants were panting, bleeding, caught up in a sole objective now: survival.

She had to stop this. It didn't matter that they had the right to the contest, as Ronin claimed. Thomas had to stop this before one of their children was killed. It would fracture the Circle. It would lead to more death!

But Chelise didn't know what to do.

And then it didn't matter, because in the space of time it took Chelise to blink, Marie was on her back, flailing for a grip. She'd fallen. Tripped on a small ribbon of rock that edged the flat stone.

Samuel, seeing the opening, hurled himself forward. He didn't go for her throat. She would have expected that. Instead, his right foot made contact with the butt of her blade and sent it spinning through the air.

Marie was left without a weapon.

A roar erupted from the crowd.

The woman with red eyes screamed at Chelise.

Samuel dropped one knee on Marie's gut, effectively preventing her from twisting free. His blade slammed against the rock an inch from her neck, spraying her right cheek with shards of stone.

That resounding crash of metal against stone silenced the Gathering. But the night was not quiet. A wail of bitter remorse cut through the air.

Chelise had heard this once, only once, three years ago when twenty-three women and children were beheaded by Throaters while the men were out searching for a lost child. Thomas had heard the news, dropped to his knees, and cried to the sky.

She spun around, crushed by the cry of anguish.

Thomas was on his knees on a twenty-foot cliff behind her, arms spread, sobbing at the night sky. "Elyonnnnnn . . . Elyonnnnnn . . ."

For long seconds he wailed unabashedly, struggling to find breath, trembling like a man who'd just learned that his child had been found dead at the bottom of a cliff. Tears streamed down his cheeks as he wept. For his Maker. For his children. For the Circle. For the Horde.

All around the valley, the Gathering stood rooted to the earth, cowering under this horrible sound. Behind Chelise, Marie and Samuel breathed hard, but there was no sound of swinging blades.

"It's over," Thomas wept. "It's over!"

"No," Chelise said.

He cried to the sky. "You've left us." Then even louder, "You've left us!"

"No," she said again, begging him to hear her. "No, he has not left us."

His chest rose and fell.

"No, Elyon has not left us," she cried. "I did not die for this!"

Thomas lowered his chin and blinked. He looked lost, a shell of the man who'd led the mighty Forest Guard to victory in campaign after campaign before Qurong overtook them. For a moment, Chelise thought he'd lost himself in hopelessness, a man stripped of all he once treasured.

His eyes slowly cleared and he staggered to his feet, looked around at the Gathering. His gaze settled on his son and daughter. Marie still lay on her back, pinned under Samuel's sword.

"Stand up," Thomas said.

Samuel stared up at his father. He made no move to relinquish his hard-won upper hand.

"Get up!" Thomas roared. His voice was heavy with rage, and it seemed to have caught Samuel off guard.

His son slowly removed his sword and stepped back. Marie rolled over and pushed herself to her knees. Then to her feet. They stared up at their father, wounded and bleeding.

"Is this what we have come to?" Thomas demanded. "A band of vagabonds who would return to their own captivity? You want to join the Horde again?"

"We should kill them, not join them," the woman who'd challenged Chelise said in a low voice. She might as well have screamed.

Thomas thrust his hand at the horizon. "Killing is what *they* do. To kill them is to join them!" He paced atop the cliff, and with each footfall, Chelise felt her fear grow. She didn't like the sight of the desperation that possessed him.

"Is it Horde that you want? You've lost your belief in the difference between us and them, is that it?"

"No," Mikil offered. "No, Thomas, that's—"

"You're doubting that Elyon is here, among us? That he cares? That he has any power? You wonder if he loves his bride the way he once did, if the Great Romance has become nothing more than the talk of old men around a campfire? Is that it?" He shouted his challenge.

"Thomas—"

"Enough! You had your chance to defend your hearts. Now it's my turn."

The words turned the night cold. It wasn't often that he was like this, but Chelise knew him well enough to know that he'd made a decision, and no force this side of heaven or hell would change it.

"My own son has challenged the very fabric of our way, and he has drawn my own daughter into a fight to the death. Fine. Then I, Thomas of Hunter, both their father and the supreme commander of this Circle, will issue my own challenge."

He stood above them, legs spread to the width of his shoulders, hands gripped to fists.

"I will settle this business once and for all. I will do it on my terms. We will see if Elyon has left us. The Circle will know to a man, woman, and child if he who woos us, who commands our love, is real or if he is nothing but hot air from the mouths of old men."

"Thomas, are you sure you want to do this?"

But he ignored William. "I hereby exercise my right to take on this challenge from Samuel. Do you accept?"

Samuel offered a cynical grin and looked up through loose locks of hair. "As you wish." Then he added for effect, "Father."

"Good. Then I will go to the Horde and cast my challenge. If Elyon is who I say he is, we will all survive another month. If he is not, then we will all be dead or Horde within the week."

The words echoed through the canyon. The fire was dying, starved of wood. A dog barked from the main camp a hundred yards behind the red pool, where they'd all dipped their cups to celebrate Elyon's love.

Now they were faced with death, and their cups sat heavy in their hands.

"Do I hear any objection?"

"How can you risk our lives like this?" some fool was brave enough to ask.

"There is no risk!" Thomas thundered over their heads. "If Elyon fails us, we *should* be Scabs. We will only be as we should be. If he rescues us, we will finish this celebration in earnest."

A deep breath.

"Anyone else?"

No one dared.

"Send our fastest runners to the other three Gatherings. Tell them to come. We will live or we will die together as one. Is that clear?"

Still no objection. Not even from the council, who surely knew how dangerous this course was. But they just as surely knew that to cross Thomas was futile.

"Good," Thomas said. "I leave tonight. Samuel, Mikil, Jamous, you three and you three alone will come with me. Get our horses."

He was going to the Horde, to her father, without her?

Chelise stepped forward. "Thomas . . . Thomas, you have to take me!"

"No. Your mind isn't clear on this matter."

"How can you say that? I . . . I'm your wife! I've vowed my life—"

"You are the daughter of Qurong." Then, with only a little more tenderness: "Please. Don't question my judgment on this matter."

"Then I should go, Father," Marie said.

"Samuel, Mikil, Jamous." He turned from them. "No more. Chelise, bring me my younger son. Bring me Jake."

Then Thomas of Hunter turned and walked into the night, leaving the three thousand alone by the fire.

5

JANAE DE RAISON stepped out of her mother's office and eased the door closed behind her, satisfied by the soft click of the latch when it engaged. Williston stood near his white desk in the atrium.

"Sit down, Williston," she said. "The answer is no, I won't be needing anything else. Maybe a sandwich, but I would rather fetch that myself if you don't mind."

He dipped his head.

She walked across the travertine floor, cool on her bare feet thanks to the conditioned air. Living in Southeast Asia could be a humid affair without the hum of electricity to suck water and heat from the atmosphere.

"You don't mind me robbing you of that pleasure, do you, Will? I know how much you enjoy it, but I would like to do it." She glided up to him and let her eyes wander over his tie, his black jacket. A handsome man with dark hair, graying at the edges. How many times as a child had she fantasized about having a passionate affair with their butler? Too many to remember.

She put her hand on his cheek and withdrew it slowly, allowing her fingernails to graze his skin. "Is that okay, dear Will? Just this once?"

"Of course, madam. Whatever pleases you." He smiled. It was a game they played often and both managed to take some enjoyment from it, she in tempting, he in pretending to be tempted, though they both knew that he wasn't always pretending.

She drew her hand down his tie, pulled it away from his shirt, then let it fall back into place as she turned away. "Where is he?"

"Where is who, madam?"

"Our fascinating little visitor?"

"In the guest quarters where I left him, I assume." He sounded as if he wanted to say more, so at the twelve-foot arched entry to the hall, she turned back.

"You'd like to add something else?"

"No."

"You don't trust our guest?"

He hesitated. "He is a bit unnerving, madam."

"Hmm. Then perhaps he and I will get along just fine."

Again he dipped his head. "Yes, madam."

Janae made her way to the kitchen, ignoring the servants, who moved like ghosts through the twenty-thousand-square-foot mansion that doubled as the world headquarters for Raison Pharmaceutical. Dusting, always dusting the crystal chandeliers and candle holders, the period paintings, the marble tables, anything that had a smooth surface. They were mostly Filipinos who spoke perfect English, and a few Malaysians. Janae had grown up trilingual, fluent by age eight in French, English, and Thai, but she'd also picked up enough Tagalog and Malay to get by.

She walked through the dining room toward the kitchen, mind on the visitor, on this Billy Rediger who'd waltzed into their home and sent both Monique and Kara into a tailspin, although they would never admit it.

"I'm making a couple sandwiches, Betty," she said, stopping the cook across the kitchen. "Could you get me a tray and two glasses of very cold milk?"

"Yes, madam."

She pulled out a white ceramic plate and made two peanut-butter and strawberry-jam sandwiches, each with a healthy side of Russian caviar.

With each wipe of her knife and dip of her spoon into the caviar jar, her mind went to the man. To Billy. Her mother had been unmistakably direct in her instructions to Janae. Kara had been even more forceful.

"Of course there's no blood!" Kara said, dismissing the whole business with a sweep of her hand. She jabbed at the door. "But there is him.

And as long as there's someone out there with this foolish notion, particularly someone who can read minds, we can't possibly be safe."

"Why?" Janae asked. "If there is no blood?"

"Because there once was," her mother said. "What he said is partially true. We did take a vial of Thomas Hunter's blood and kept it safe for several years. But we feared an event exactly like this, so I sent it to our old lab in Indonesia, where it was destroyed. Neither the lab nor the blood exist today."

"But as long as this fool thinks it exists, he'll be a problem," Kara added.

"So you want me to what? Distract him?" she asked, but she was thinking, *Oh my goodness, what if Billy's right?*

"Is that a problem?"

"No. I think he could be the distractible kind. He really can read minds?"

"Please, Janae. Keep him close, but keep your guard up. He could be a rather dangerous character."

Let's hope so.

Janae picked up the loaded tray, refusing Betty's assistance to carry the lunch. She left the kitchen and wound her way down the hall to the guest quarters.

There were things Mother trusted her with and things she did not. Send Janae de Raison into any plant or laboratory in the world that was slipping, and she would return it to full production within a week. But at times Mother treated her with the same scrutiny she'd showed her enemies. *Keep your friends close; keep your enemies closer.*

Monique and Kara had no intention of trusting Janae with Billy. They intended to keep both as close as needed to monitor every move.

The large white door that led into the guest suite was closed. She thought about knocking but decided against it. Balancing the tray on her left hand, she turned the knob and pushed the door open.

The guest atrium was round, surrounded by windows that overlooked manicured lawns and the jungle beyond. A gilded dome rose at the room's center, supporting a huge iron chandelier. Thick lace drapes swept across the top of each window and hung to the marble floor.

The furniture was mostly old English, wood painted in antiqued creams and browns, nothing too dark. Monique preferred light colors to dark stain here in the tropics, unlike her house in New York, which made ample use of cherrywood and mahogany.

No sign of Billy. He was either in the bathroom to her right, down the hall that led to the bedrooms, or in the parlor that doubled as a library. Janae considered the bedrooms with some interest but quickly decided that he would probably be more interested in books than beds even after a long flight. She angled for the library.

Her bare feet padded lightly across the tile. Giovanni had given her a full manicure and pedicure yesterday in New York, painting her nails a delectable deep ruby red that still looked dripping wet. Her short black dress was formfitting but loose below the waist so it could sway across her thighs.

She'd earned a black belt in jujitsu by age seventeen and had kept it up as a form of exercise over the eight years since. "You can seduce many men with a pretty face," Monique used to say. "You can get them slobbering with a pretty face and a powerful body. But you can turn most men into idiots with a pretty face, a powerful body, and a bank account that earns enough interest to pay for jet fuel."

So far Mother had been right, although she'd missed one: a potent mind was a more powerful aphrodisiac than all of the others combined.

She found Billy in the parlor with his back to her, staring at a bookcase loaded with leather-bound books. His fingers traced their spines slowly, as if he expected to read their contents like he'd read her mind. Her family had always been fascinated by books, and it appeared Billy might also be.

"Hungry?"

He spun around, startled.

She walked to a leather ottoman and set the tray down. "Hope you like peanut butter and jelly with caviar. A taste I picked up in Poland last summer."

Billy held her in his green-eyed gaze. He'd been places, this one. For a few seconds she felt as though she was the lesser here, that he'd come to seduce her, to win his way into whatever prize he sought.

Was he really reading her mind? It seemed preposterous. She couldn't feel anything that suggested his mind was probing hers, peeling back the layers of her thoughts, her deepest secrets.

"No, not yet," he said. "Those I'll save until later."

"What are you talking about?"

"Your secrets."

So it was true, then.

"Of course it is."

Janae turned back to the ottoman and lifted one of the glasses. *And now can you?*

No response.

No, not when my eyes are averted or covered. How fascinating.

She drilled him with a long stare and slowly brought her glass to her lips, allowing him to crawl as deep as he wanted into her mind.

She sipped at the cool liquid, felt it slip down her throat. "And what do you see now, hmm? Anything you like?"

"I see evil," he said.

"Oh?" She suppressed a stab of alarm. "Is that a good thing or a bad thing?"

"Depends."

"On whom, me or you?"

"On us," he said. "It depends on us."

She knew then that she liked this redheaded man named Billy. She liked him very much.

"Sit with me, Billy. Eat with me. Tell me why you've come into my world."

THEY TALKED for an hour, and with each passing minute Janae's anticipation for the next grew. From the moment Billy had climbed inside of her mind and found this so-called evil in her, she knew there would be no hiding from him.

More to the point, she didn't want to hide from him.

They talked about a host of topics, taking their time to slowly unravel each other's lives. He'd spent his childhood in Colorado, though he didn't share many details, before becoming a defense attorney in Atlantic City. He then went on to Washington with an old flame of his named Darcy Lange.

"Darcy Lange, huh? You serious?"

"You know her?"

"She was all over the news a few years back," Janae said, curling her legs back on the Queen Anne chair. She took a teaspoon of caviar and brought it to her mouth. "Stunning creature."

"Yes. Can't deny that. We were . . . you have to understand about Darcy and me. We both started young, in the . . . the . . . you know, the libraries below the monastery."

"Monastery? You met her in a monastery?"

"In a manner of speaking." He was hiding something. "We were kids, and we drifted apart until this whole Tolerance Act thing, when these gifts of ours came out. We had a thing, but it's different now. Our interests have . . . aren't exactly in line."

"Look, my beloved little redhead, if you expect me to open up my mind to you, I expect you to quit hiding yours."

"I'm not."

"You're lying with every other word." She stood up and moved away from the chairs. "Maybe this isn't such a good idea. Honestly, I have enough on my plate. The last thing I need is some guy playing games with me."

"No, it's not like that."

"Whatever. Are you finished? I'll send a maid to collect the tray."

"What?" He stood, spilling some crumbs off the napkin on his lap. "No, that's not what—"

"Why, Mr. Rediger, should I give you even an ounce of my attention?" She knew why, but they had to find a way onto a level field of play.

"It's worth it, trust me."

"I'm not in the mood to trust a man who can glance into my eyes and see things I can't even see myself. You'll have to do better."

"How?"

"For starters, come clean. Tell me how you came to read people's minds."

"I will."

She walked back toward him. "Tell me about Thomas's blood." Even as the words left her mouth, she could taste her desire for whatever Billy might bring her.

She didn't understand the desire herself. As a child she'd always been fascinated by red blood, whether in a movie or from a cut or in the laboratory, vials of blood used for endless tests.

Billy had gone rigid. "You know about the blood?"

"You mentioned it in my mother's office, remember?"

His eyes searched hers. "So that's all you know."

He'd expected more, had searched her mind already and found nothing. But she wasn't finished.

"I have some secrets that not even you can extract, at least not without skills far more seductive than reading a mind. Tell me about this blood."

He slowly sat. Crossed one leg over the other. Janae stood before him, arms folded, challenging.

"You've heard of the Books of History?" he asked, then answered himself after a glance in her eyes. "No, you haven't. They are a set of books that recorded the truth of all happenings, exactly as they happened. Pure history. The books of life, you might call them. But they aren't ordinary books. Whatever is written in blank Books of History will actually happen. The wills of humans can be bent by them, but not forced. Inanimate objects, on the other hand, can be manipulated at will. You could write, 'This room is red,' in one of those books, and the room would instantly become red."

"Now you're—"

"Patronizing me," he finished for her. "Yet it's true. How else do you think I can read your mind?"

What was he saying? Reading minds was one thing, turning a room red with a few words written in a book was another thing.

"Another thing, yes, but true. Sit." Then, "Please, just sit down and let me explain myself to you."

She eased herself into the chair but didn't bother relaxing her arms.

"From what I've been able to piece together, the blank books came from another time, presumably two thousand years in our future. They were brought here by Thomas Hunter and they turned up many years later in a monastery, where I found them and wrote in them. Long story, a kind of showdown that would take a few days to explain. Regardless, one of the things I wrote was that I would have special powers. Twelve years later they began to manifest themselves. So now I can read your mind. It's that simple."

She unfolded her arms and set her hands in her lap. There was a finality to his voice that robbed her of any objection. "You're serious," she managed.

"Dead."

"And you want to know about the blood."

"It was said that Thomas Hunter's blood allowed him to . . . travel, shift, whatever you want to call it, between here and there. Anyone whose blood came in contact with Thomas's blood could make the shift as well, at least in their dreams. And I do believe that both Kara Hunter and your mother know this as fact. I think they've both done it."

"With the blood?" Janae's heart started to beat more deliberately. "They . . . you're saying they used this blood to cross into another reality?"

He eyed her. She was betraying her deep attraction to his suggestions, but she couldn't hide from him, could she? So she didn't try.

"You're saying that's possible?"

"I think it's been done. I know they kept a vial of his blood for just this reason." He stood and walked in a small circle, fingers scratching his cheek. "You have to know, these Books of History are *my* history. I'm who I am because of them. My life is ruined because—"

"Where are these books?"

He looked at her, apparently put off at having been interrupted.

"You're sure the blood is still around, that it exists?" she asked. "I mean, what if they did destroy it like they claim? My mother said she sent it to our lab in Indonesia, where it was incinerated. The lab doesn't even exist today."

"Slow down. Take a deep breath. Do you think I would've come halfway across the world if I wasn't sure?"

Janae stood, unable to hide the desire to know what he knew, to strip this knowledge from his history and to own it. Why? But even as the thoughts whispered through her mind, she was aware that he was also aware of them.

Billy blinked at her. "What are you hiding from me?"

"Nothing. How can I?"

"You can't. So why are you so desperate to know what I know?"

"I . . ." What could she say if she herself didn't know? "I don't know. What would you do if you learned that your mother had a vial of blood that could take you to another world?"

Her pulse was now a steady hammer in her ears.

"You'd think it was preposterous," she answered for him. "But then what?"

"Then you'd want to possess it," he said.

"Assuming it exists."

"It does."

She looked away and tried to still her irrational eagerness to stand here while he reeled her in like a helpless fish.

"Until today I was convinced that I was the only person on this planet who was qualified to find and use that blood," Billy said. "But now I think you may be another."

"Because you need me?"

"Because there's something inside you that I've never seen. And I've probed the minds of a lot of people."

"What's that? Evil?" She walked away from him. "I can't believe I've never heard of any of this before today. She hid it from me all this time?"

"It's not exactly the kind of thing you want anyone to know."

She spun back. "I'm her daughter!"

"Even more reason to protect you."

He really did believe all of this, and the idea was becoming only slightly familiar to her. Familiar, not reasonable, not in the least, because what Billy was suggesting made no sense at all. Who'd ever heard of such a thing?

But it did have a ring of familiarity to it.

"Give me a few hours and I'll tell you a few things that will remove any doubt from your mind," Billy said. "The books exist. There's a journal that talks about them, written by a Saint Thomas hundreds of years ago. They called him the beast hunter. Never saw the book, but I've interviewed two people in Europe who have. I'm telling you there're connections between our worlds that would make your head spin."

"Beast hunter," she repeated.

"Saint Thomas the Beast Hunter," he said. "But it's the blank books that interest me more. Like the ones I wrote in during my life in the monastery. I believe they still exist, probably in the safe keeping of Thomas Hunter. His blood is a sure way to get to him. I want you to help me find the blood."

The notion overtook her with such savagery that she felt compelled to turn her face away. Such raw desire was unbecoming.

"Will you?"

I will, Billy. I will use you to feed my own needs.

The thought surprised her. At least it had been guarded. She cleared her mind and faced him again.

"Maybe."

Janae walked up to him and allowed a smile to caress her face. She placed her hand on his chest and ran it up over his head, through his unkempt hair.

"Might be fun."

"I don't care if you do use me," he said, cutting to the heart of the matter. "I have to do this, with or without you."

Interesting. Her deception didn't bother him. This alone increased her admiration of him.

Janae stood on her toes, leaned forward and touched her lips to his. Then she turned and glided back to the chair.

"Tell me more, Billy. Tell me everything."

6

The Future

QURONG MARCHED the path along the muddy lake in his night-clothes, a white and purple robe woven from silk that swished around his knees with each reach of his leg. The moon was absent from the black sky. Qurongi City, named after himself five years earlier, slept except for the stray dog, the priests in the Thrall, and him.

Well, yes, he had awakened Patricia and Cassak. No king should have to visit the high priest in the dead of night without his wife and general at hand. Ba'al had sent his servant an hour ago, demanding that Qurong rush to the Thrall for a most critical audience.

"Slow down," Patricia snapped, close at his heels.

He planted his foot and swung back. "The first sensible thing you've said all night. Why he insists I leave the palace to join him in the Thrall at this hour is beyond me, but I'm telling you, this had better be the stuff of life and death to every living being or I'll make him pay for this arrogance."

She stopped and glared with gray eyes. Patricia had always been provocative when angry, but in the wake of his latest ailment—this cease-less wrenching in his gut that denied him sleep—he felt only annoyance. She'd taken a moment to apply a dusting of morst to her face and to throw on a hooded black silk robe that covered her body from head to heel. Her stark white face peered from the hood like a ghost. The tattoo of three hooked claws on her forehead had been perfectly placed, red and black against her white skin.

"Watch your tongue, you brute," she cautioned. "We're out in the open here."

"With whom? My general, who'd die for me?" He flung his hand out toward the dark city on the other side of the black lake. "Or with the rest of these rodents under Ba'al's spell?"

"Commander!" Her term when she was beyond despair. "Have you lost your mind?"

"Yes, I've finally misplaced my senses! Ba'al will have a reason to make a play for the throne, and I'll be forced to kill him. Such a tragedy. You're quite sweet to suggest it, my bride."

Qurong swung around and continued his march toward the Thrall, lit by the glow of flaming torches in the temple's towers and doors.

"That's not what I meant," Patricia objected.

"No, of course you don't wish Ba'al dead. You'd likely prefer to kiss his feet."

"You're a double-minded oaf, Q. One minute you wake me, insisting that I offer a sacrifice to Teeleh to heal your ailments, and the next you curse him and his high priest. Which is it? Do you love Teeleh or do you hate him?"

"I serve him. I am his slave. Does that mean that I must drink his blood and have his children?"

"If he demands it."

"Let's just hope this aching in my belly isn't his growing child."

"That would be a sight," his ranking general, Cassak, said behind them.

Patricia wasn't finished. "If you serve Teeleh, you serve Ba'al. One of these days you'll get that through your thick skull."

"Like I served Witch, then Ciphus? Then Sucrow, now this wretch Ba'al?"

"Stop!"

This time when he caught her eye, he saw he'd gone too far. The lines of her ghostly face were etched with fear.

"You will not speak about him that way in my presence!" she said.

"And what am I, your poodle to play with?" Qurong demanded. Then, with a clenched fist, "I am Qurong! The world bows at my feet and cowers under my army! Remember whose bed you share."

"Yes. You are Qurong and I love Qurong, leader of all that is right in this cursed world. I am humbled to have known you, much more to be called your wife."

She was toying with him, he thought, only half-serious, but enough for Cassak to believe it all.

Patricia continued. "And you will show your love for me by keeping me away from danger."

"You're more afraid of that witch than of me?"

"Of course. You love me. Ba'al hates us both, and his hatred would only be aggravated if he heard you speak of Teeleh or him the way you do."

Qurong frowned, but his fight was gone.

A sharp pang of pain cut through his belly, and he resumed his march down the muddy path that led to the Thrall.

They walked in silence until they reached the wide steps that rose to the large gate. It was guarded on either side by bronzed statues of the winged serpent, a likeness of Teeleh that their first high priest, a scheming character named Witch, had supposedly seen in a vision. Few besides the priests had claimed to see the great beast in these last twenty-five years, since the waters had turned to poison. Woref, the general, had once claimed to have seen Teeleh. In Qurong's distant memory, Teeleh was more of a bat than a serpent.

Truth be told, Teeleh was probably a figment of their imagination, a tool the priests used to maintain their hold on power. There had been some sightings of the Shataiki bats that lived in hidden Black Forests, and some of the black bats seemed to have an unexplainable power, but nothing like the power that the priests attributed to them.

When Qurong first defeated Thomas of Hunter and took the Middle Forest, they had just lost Witch in battle. Upon defeating Thomas and left without a priest, Qurong had cautiously accepted the offer of the half-breed, Ciphus, to protect them from evil. Ciphus introduced them to a strange brew of religion that he called the Great Romance, which involved worshipping both Teeleh and Elyon, the pagan god of the Forest People.

Ciphus's time lasted just over a year, until three months after the albinos made off with Chelise, the very same traitor who was now out to poison them all with the red lakes. His daughter had become a she-witch herself.

What started out as lenience toward the albinos became bitter remembrance, and Qurong had fully supported Sucrow's bid to kill Ciphus and return the Horde to the worship of Teeleh, the winged serpent who ruled the powers of the air. In his death, Ciphus became a martyr for all half-breeds to revere, emboldening Eram, who soon after defected with the rest of the half-breeds.

Sucrow's reign as high priest ended on a goose chase for an amulet that reportedly had great power. Following Sucrow's death, a priest had come to them from the desert, stood tall upon the Thrall's highest landing, and declared that Teeleh had chosen him to be high priest of all that was holy and unholy. He claimed to have lived with Teeleh until now, when his time had come. He was the servant of the dragon in the sky. Qurong had seen the people's awe of this skinny sorcerer and agreed to make him high priest.

He told himself a thousand times afterward that it had been a mistake. At best, the balance between Qurong's political power and Ba'al's religious power was delicate. There would come a time soon when Ba'al would have to die. He was altogether too full of himself, drunk on his own power.

"Don't get me wrong, wife," Qurong said as they approached the steps. "I wouldn't be here without a healthy respect for Teeleh. I support all of this . . ." He waved at the Thrall that loomed high above them like a black sentinel with flaming eyes, blocking out half the sky. "I've kissed the feet of Teeleh's vessel, Ba'al, this so-called dragon from the sky, on a hundred occasions. But that doesn't mean he's a god any more than my enemies are gods. He's only human flesh doing the bidding of a god."

"Just keep his knife away from your throat," Patricia said in a low voice.

"Exactly." She could be reasonable when she wanted to be. "I swear, sometimes I don't know who's worse, the albinos, the Eramites, or my own priests. None of them allows me any sleep. My gut is in a knot over all of this."

"Not now," his wife warned.

One of the night watchmen opened the gate for them, and they headed across the stone floor to a large atrium surrounded by more of the bronze serpents.

"This way, my lord."

Qurong faced his right, where a hunched priest hidden beneath a hooded black cloak dipped his head and walked toward the sacrificial sanctum. The priest lifted his spindly arm to a large wooden door charred by fire and gave it a push.

Orange light from a dozen flames spilled out into the hall. He could see the altar on a platform inside, blazing candlesticks on either side. An animal—a black-and-white goat strapped spread-eagle on the altar—sacrificed.

But Ba'al's sacrifices were more like butchery. And although he killed animals with the same regularity that he ate and relieved himself, Qurong didn't know the priest to offer sacrifices in the middle of the night.

Qurong walked into the sanctum, the holy of unholies, as Ba'al called it. Flames crackled from the torches on the room's perimeter. Thick, purple velvet curtains hung from the tall ceiling on each side, framing large gold etchings of the winged serpent. Directly behind the altar, the same material closed off an arched passageway, which led to Ba'al's private library. What kind of plotting and deception was conceived behind that curtain Qurong could only guess, but those guesses were not happy thoughts.

"Where is he?" Patricia whispered.

Qurong hesitated. "Doing the work of Teeleh."

That he, the supreme commander of more than three million souls, had agreed to leave his home in the middle of the night for an audience with Ba'al was offensive enough. That he had to now wait in these ghastly chambers while the witch took his bloody time wiping off his wet blades was infuriating.

But this was not the place to betray his emotions. Qurong knew all too well how revered Ba'al was among the common people, particularly now, during the days of the black moon. During the last lunar eclipse, Ba'al came forth from the sanctum and declared that Teeleh had shown him a vision of the coming red dragon, who would devour the children of all who betrayed him. All those who marked themselves as loyal servants of Teeleh and Ba'al would be spared. Three claws carved on the forehead, the mark of the beast's perfection.

Qurong had received the mark of the beast, naturally, but he doubted that it would truly protect him, assuming the beast existed.

The priest who'd let them in climbed the two steps to the platform, shuffled slowly around the altar, and parted the curtains with a withered hand. The door behind the drapes closed softly, and they were left alone.

"This is asinine," Qurong mumbled.

"Hush."

The curtain parted and Ba'al stepped into the inner sanctum, dressed in his usual black silk robes with a purple sash around his neck. Layers of gold, silver, and black beads hung over his breast. The circular serpent's medallion hung from a silver chain.

Ba'al's narrow white face peered at Qurong from his hood, like a king judging his subject. The expression was enough to make Qurong's blood boil.

The priest carefully navigated the steps down from the platform.

"Thank you for coming to me so late, my lord." His voice was low and wet, the sound of a man who needed to clear his throat.

"This had better be good."

Ba'al lifted his face to the Horde leader, and for the first time Qurong saw that the three claw marks on his forehead had been reopened. Thin trails of blood snaked down his cheeks and the bridge of his nose. The man was a masochist.

"Good?" Ba'al said. "The true child has been born, and now the dragon will wage war on her illegitimate children. That can hardly be good." He walked around a table to the side. The goat's head lay on a silver platter, still bleeding, and Ba'al dipped his long black fingernail into the blood. "Babylon will become drunk on her blood yet."

"Idiots may swoon with your talk of children and dragons and the end of all times," Qurong said, "but I'm a simple man who wields the sword. Let's not forget that here."

"Ah, yes, of course. Your sword, your power, your stranglehold on the Horde. Forgive me if I suggested that the dragon doesn't hold his king in the highest regard. He was the one who made you king, after all."

Qurong had no patience for this. "So what is it that is so urgent to keep me from sleep?"

"The day for your full glory has come, my lord, all in good time. But first I must know who you are and who you serve."

"What glory? Another ritual to this god who has abandoned us?"

"Remember where you are, my lord." Ba'al glanced at the walls without moving his head, then shifted his eyes back to Qurong and brought his wet fingers to his lips. "He has ears everywhere," the high priest whispered around his taste of goat's blood.

Qurong held his tongue.

"Your loyalty hasn't weakened, has it? My king?"

"What are you speaking of?"

"You do still believe that Teeleh is the true god. That the dragon has given you Babylon?"

Ba'al had begun this Babylon business a year earlier; Qurong wouldn't put it past the man to suggest renaming Qurongi City, perhaps calling it Dragoni or something as foolish.

"What have I done to suggest any slackening of my loyalty?" he demanded.

"You still believe that we are the abomination of desolation, the dragon's great Babylon? That we are his instrument to crush the rebellion of those who stand against Teeleh? That it is our prerogative and our privilege, our duty, to drain the blood of every living albino? That there will come from times past an albino with a head of fire, who will rid the world of the poisonous waters and return us unto Paradise?"

Now they were retreading old ground, these prophesies that Ba'al had pulled from his so-called visions.

Still, Qurong would give him the benefit of the doubt. "That is correct."

"That your very own daughter, Chelise—"

"I have no daughter," he interrupted. The priest was egging him on, knowing how the name had haunted his nightmares for so many years.

"That Thomas and the woman at his side lead the rebellion against Teeleh."

"Get on with it, priest. Surely you didn't bring me here to remind me of all I know."

Ba'al stared at him for a few beats, then turned his back and walked toward a desk along one wall. His voice was hardly more than a hoarse whisper.

"Have you ever considered drowning, my lord?"

Qurong couldn't immediately respond. What kind of blasphemy was this?

Patricia stepped up next to him and dipped her head. "Forgive me, my priest, but you go too far." Her voice was strained and high. "An accusation of this kind is dangerous."

"Of course," the priest said, turning back. He'd lifted a small scroll from his desk and held it in his clawed hands. "I make no accusation. You'll understand soon enough. But I do need an answer."

Qurong spat to one side and made no attempt to coat his words with anything other than the sentiment that swelled in his mind.

"If I could do it personally, I would run my sword through every albino who still breathes."

A faint grin crossed Ba'al's face. "And the drowning?"

"It is defiance of my reign and all that we hold sacred. The twisted ways of Thomas would drown all of the Horde and tear down this very Thrall. I would rather drown in a bath of poison."

"How dare you put him through this?" Patricia challenged. His wife's solidarity reminded Qurong why he loved her as he did.

"Just a reminder of who our enemies are. The Eramites, yes, but Thomas and his Circle are the true scourge of our world."

"I don't need your lectures," Qurong said. "And don't underestimate Eram or his army. They are growing faster than we are, and they don't hide like the albinos do. I would think that should concern you."

"I assure you, Teeleh's enemies are albino, not Horde. They will be easily disposed of when the time is right."

Qurong couldn't take this line any farther without casting suspicion on his allegiance. "I bow to Teeleh's judgment." He dipped his head.

"Then drink to him," Ba'al said, picking up a chalice next to the goat's head. "Swallow the goat's blood offered to the dragon, and I will tell you how he will give you your enemies on a butcher block." He glided across the floor and held out the silver goblet, sloshing with red blood.

Qurong took the cup, aware that his hand was still shaking from being accused of such treason, never mind that it was only insinuated. He lifted the vessel to his lips and drank deep. The familiar taste of raw blood flooded his mouth and warmed his belly.

Ba'al had instituted the drinking of blood, claiming that the spirit of Teeleh, indeed the very offspring of Teeleh, came by blood. Indeed, the Shataiki were asexual beings, neither male nor female. They reproduced through blood.

Teeleh was served by twelve queens, it was said, like the queens of beehives. But they and their minions were genderless and passed their seed through blood when they bit the larvae produced by the queens. Ba'al sometimes referred to a queen as a she and sometimes as a he, but to Qurong's way of thinking, all of it was nonsense.

Shataiki were simply beasts.

Regardless, the taste had agreed with most Scabs, including Qurong.

It settled the pain and itching in their flaking skin for several hours and now eased the gnawing in his belly. Unfortunately, there were more than three million Horde now living in seven forests, and there was only so much blood, making it a valuable commodity controlled by the temples.

He drained the cup. "For Teeleh, my lord and my master," he recited, and shoved the goblet back at Ba'al. "Do not test me again, priest."

The dark priest handed him the scroll.

"What is this?"

"A message that came to me an hour ago. Read it."

Qurong unrolled the stained paper and stared at the top. This was a communiqué from . . . the circular emblem at the top bore into his mind. His eyes dropped to the bottom and he saw the name: *Thomas of Hunter.*

"Yes," Ba'al sneered. "He shows his face after all these years."

"Who?" Patricia demanded.

"Thomas of Hunter," the priest said.

The spoken name seemed to rob the room of its energy. Patricia kept silent. Qurong's heart slowly doubled its pace. The last communication with anyone among the albino leadership had come three months after Chelise's departure, when Qurong declared open war on the albinos. Ba'al's Throaters and his elite guard had rounded up over a thousand since, but not one among the original leaders. They'd gone into deep hiding.

He stepped closer to the torches on the wall behind him and read the writing on the paper:

To Qurong, Supreme Commander of the Horde
And Ba'al, Dark Priest of Teeleh, Shataiki from Hell
    Greetings from the Circle, followers of Elyon dead to the disease and risen with hope for the return of Elyon, who will destroy all that is evil and remake all that is good.
    Ten years have passed and still you relentlessly persecute my people, falsely believing that we have meant ill toward the diseased Scabs whom

you rule. We have not waged war on your people, though we have the capacity to do so. We have not burned your crops, nor robbed your caravans, nor harmed you in any way. Still you pursue us deep into the desert and slay us where you find us.

It is in our best interests to end this. I therefore cast before you a challenge:

Take a contingent of your most revered and unholy priests and meet me at the high place with Qurong and his armed guard. I will present myself with three of my most trusted followers. No more. There, at Ba'al Bek, we will know the truth.

If Elyon refuses to show his power over Teeleh, then I, Thomas Hunter, who lead the Circle, will surrender myself and the location of every tribe known to me, and you may be rid of the albinos once and for all. They will either renounce their drowning and become Horde or die by your hand.

If Teeleh refuses to show his power over Elyon, then you, Qurong, and you alone will drown and become albino.

If you betray me and conspire to kill me before the terms of this agreement are met in full, then you will have martyrs in Thomas of Hunter and three of his trusted followers. I await you at Ba'al Bek.

Thomas of Hunter

"What does the traitor want?" his wife demanded.

"He's issued a challenge. A duel of sorts between his god and Ba'al. At Ba'al Bek, the high place."

"For what purpose?"

Qurong turned to Ba'al. "What am I supposed to make of this madness?"

"What madness?" Patricia snapped. She pulled the scroll from his fingers and read.

Qurong ignored her. "Can your god do what he challenges?"

"My god? Teeleh is the only true god, and he's yours as well as mine. Or do you falter so easily after a few words from your nemesis?"

Ba'al clearly saw an opportunity here. That a challenge from a group of scattered vagabonds should be taken seriously was by itself humiliating. But that this simple challenge, however misguided, should unnerve him was unforgivable. Who did Thomas of Hunter think he was, issuing such a foolish challenge?

Qurong's gut clenched with pain and he walked to the table, where a flask of wine sat next to two silver glasses.

"You called me out of my sleepless dreams for this?"

"If you don't mind . . ." Cassak, his general, now held the scroll. "If this is true, if the leader of all albinos is foolish enough to wait for us at Ba'al Bek, we could easily end his life. And the lives of his three followers. Even Chelise, if she is with him."

Patricia glared at him. She still clung to the imprudent belief that she might one day recover a daughter. Cassak was a fool not to understand the way of a woman's heart. He would have to talk with the man.

"Killing Thomas is no easy proposition. Even if he could be taken or killed, he's right; he would be seen as a martyr and replaced by another dozen like him. He's mocking us with this letter."

"Is he?" Ba'al said.

"You suggest we take this seriously?"

"You doubt that I can destroy him in this little game of his?" Ba'al returned.

"I don't know. Can you?"

There was the real question, he realized. He'd betrayed his own doubts in Teeleh's power by asking it.

"Have you seen the evidence of Elyon lately?" Ba'al asked. "No, because there are no angels named Roush nor a god named Elyon. These are the figments of the albinos' imagination. The red waters they drink infect them with a disease that bares their skin and fries their minds. We all know this to be the case."

"And if you're wrong? If Teeleh, who isn't too eager to show his face either, doesn't show up and crush them, then what? I drink their red water? Have you lost your mind?"

"Unlike you, I see Teeleh frequently. Trust me, he is as real as your own scabbing flesh. Don't you see it? Thomas of Hunter is playing into our hands. The red dragon who rules the seven horns will devour this albino child and end the time of the Circle once and for all. Your war on them has had its desired effect. They are begging us, out of desperation." Ba'al bit off each word and squeezed his black nails into a tight fist.

The allure of being handed the whole of the albino insurgency on a platter presented itself to Qurong in full color for the first time.

"Sir." Cassak stepped forward. "Forgive the observation, but there is no guarantee that this isn't a trap to kill both you and the high priest."

"They don't ascribe to violence," Qurong said.

"No, but they could take you and force you to drown. They could—"

"Do the red water's poisons work if one is forced to drown?"

"I don't know," the general said. "The point is, this must not be done on his terms. We should take the army. Even the Eramites take courage from Thomas Hunter's evasion of capture. We look small, unable to kill this one man. Here is our chance. We could then strike at a demoralized Eram and be assured victory."

Qurong regarded Ba'al. He understood now why the priest had summoned him here. This battle would be fought and won in the heavens, not with swords. This was a matter for Ba'al, not Qurong. The dark priest needed only his consent and attendance.

He kept his eyes on the priest as he spoke. "Hunter would see our army and be gone. Those were not his terms."

"Not if I commanded the Throaters," Cassak said.

The temple's military wing consisted of five thousand highly trained assassins commonly referred to as Throaters, named after less-discerning killers among the Forest Guard, before it had been defeated and assimilated by the Horde. Indeed, most of the original Forest Guard had left Qurongi and joined Eram in the northern desert. The Horde's greatest fighters were now Eramites.

But they were vastly outnumbered by his full army, Qurong reminded himself. His own Throaters were gaining strength too. The whole matter was an absurd mess. He hated the albinos with a passion, but he feared the Eramites more, regardless of what Teeleh said. He doubted nearly everything attributed to the bat god, whom none of them had seen for a very long time.

"Perhaps. But our dark priest may be right, this is a war to be waged on a different front. And if he is right and he can summon this red dragon Teeleh to do his bidding, we will be rid of the thorn in our side once and for all."

"And . . ." Cassak hesitated on the next obvious point.

"Go on, say it."

"Teeleh forbid, but I must serve my king." He dipped his head to Ba'al in respect. "But if, however unlikely, this dragon we serve does not devour this albino child, surely no one is suggesting that Qurong do as Thomas has demanded and drink their red poison."

The mention of poison knifed through Qurong's belly, and he wondered if the ailment in his gut over these past thirty days was the result of bad food. Or worse, real poison. Served to him by Ba'al. Or an Eramite spy.

"I have no intention of nearing, much less entering, one of their cursed red lakes," he snapped. "But if Ba'al fails in his promise to summon the beast, I will have permission from him to throw *him* into poisonous waters." He paused, eyes on the priest. "Won't I?"

The three freshly opened wounds on the witch's forehead glistened in the flame light. His thin lips morphed into a grin. The evil man was as much serpent as he was human.

"I've lived in Teeleh's bosom. He will never allow any harm to come to me."

Qurong nodded. "It's a day's march. We will leave in the morning. Bring the Throaters."

THOMAS PULLED up his steed and looked out over the Beka Valley, a jagged, stone canyonland. His stallion snorted and sidestepped a blue scorpion that scurried across the sand.

He held the mount steady with a soft cluck of his tongue and lifted his eyes to the high place on the far side. The canyons rose to a plateau that swelled on top, making it look pregnant. With what? Thomas could only assume evil.

This was Ba'al Bek. The highest plateau in this part of the desert. A place claimed by the dark priest. A comet, or perhaps Elyon's fist, looked to have landed at the center of the rise, creating a massive crater the breadth of Qurongi City.

Beside him, Mikil spat to one side. "I don't like this, Thomas. This whole valley stinks of death."

"Sulfur," he said.

Jamous harrumphed on Thomas's left. "Call it what you want. She's right. It smells as if it's rising from Teeleh's hell." He pulled out a kirkuk and bit into the fruit's red flesh. A single bite could keep a man on the move for a day. They each carried a small supply of various fruits taken from the trees near the red pool. Some nourished; others had medicinal value. Without the fruit, the Circle would surely have been wiped out by the Horde long ago. It was their primary advantage, allowing them to heal on the fly and travel for days into the deep desert without any other source of food or water.

Lake fruit. Cherished by albinos, bitter to the Horde.

They had left the Gathering within an hour of Thomas's ultimatum, and the moonless desert night welcomed them in perfect silence. There were no great cheers, none of the customary embraces or wishes for safe travel, no calls for Elyon's blessing on the mission.

Thomas had taken his son Jake out into the desert for a half an hour and assured the boy of his undying love for them all. Whatever happened, Jake must never abandon his love for Elyon, Thomas urged. Never.

"Of course not, Father. Never."

Swinging the child around in an embrace, Thomas had held back tears of gratitude, concerned they might be seen as a sign of fear. The children didn't need more worry.

Then he'd joined Chelise, kissed her passionately, and deflected her insistence that she join them. He'd wiped away her tears, mounted his steed, and rode into the desert with his choice of company: his most seasoned warrior, Mikil, who had laid down her arms with the rest of them years ago; her husband, Jamous; and Samuel, his wayward son, who might be the death of them all.

"Your son should have joined us by now," Mikil said, gazing to the southern desert. "He could be dead."

"Or he's run off," Jamous said.

Thomas had written his challenge on paper, set his seal at the top, rolled it into a scroll, and demanded that Samuel deliver it to the Horde at Qurongi. He arranged to meet them at Hell's Gate, this narrow pass into the Beka Valley. Then, together, they would continue to the high place and wait for Qurong's response.

"It would take a battalion of Scabs to bring Samuel down," Thomas said. "I think he can deliver a message to one guard on the outskirts of Qurongi. He'll be here."

"What makes you so sure?"

"He wants this as much as I do."

Mikil grunted. "Then you've both lost your senses."

"If you hadn't saved my neck a thousand times, I would put you under the sword for that."

"And if you hadn't saved mine as many, I would turn it back on you," she said. Their well-intentioned barbs lightened the mood.

He looked at his most trusted commander, now in her thirties, still childless by choice and still every bit the warrior she'd been when killing Scabs had been an obsession. Her bronzed cheek was marked by a scar, barely visible past strands of dark hair.

"Besides," she said, "we've given up our swords. Remember?" She winked at him.

He had to grin, however thinly. They were all warriors at heart. Given the chance to take up arms against an enemy, they would throw themselves into the task.

But the Horde was no longer their enemy.

The disease was their enemy.

As was Teeleh, who'd cursed mankind with the disease. The way to destroy the disease had nothing to do with the sword and everything to do with the heart. Only by loving the Horde could they hope to persuade any Scab to throw away their diseased life, drown in Elyon's waters, and rise to live again.

"Trust me," he said, facing the high place again, "if the sword could rid the world of Teeleh's curse, I would take sides with Samuel. In his youth he's lost sight of the path and grown impatient for the destination."

"So now you'll risk all of our necks to prove him wrong," Jamous said.

"You think we're risking our lives? So you doubt Elyon will save us? You've proven my point."

"Nonsense. I'm only—"

"You doubt Elyon's power to save us. If even my elders doubt, then I'm only doing my duty. We'll see if your doubt is justified."

"It's not your duty to test the power of Elyon."

"Not him," Thomas said. "I test my own heart. And Samuel's. And now yours and Mikil's. Do you object?"

Jamous looked ahead, silent. He didn't dare object.

But another voice broke the silence.

"I object, Father." Samuel walked his horse from an outcropping of boulders on their left. He'd washed the red war paint off his face and drawn his hair back in a ponytail. His son had reached the pass before them.

"You mean well, but your methods don't work," Samuel said. "Ten years of running and hiding have proven it. So be my guest, prove whatever else you want."

They were the first words spoken by Samuel since their departure, and Thomas wasn't sure if they deserved a response. The time for talk had passed.

He clenched his jaw and turned away from his son.

"Oh, please, you don't think I wouldn't have actually killed my sister, do you?"

"You delivered the message?"

"Naturally. Without bloodshed, just for you."

Samuel pulled up alongside him and stared out over the canyons.

"Don't be such an idealist, Father. This isn't one of your dreams. We aren't in the histories, waging war with some virus. We're in a desert and our enemy uses swords to gut our children. When this little game of yours is over, you'll turn us all over to the Horde and some of us won't go easily. Then we'll have our war."

"Shut your muzzle, boy," Mikil snapped. "Show some respect. This isn't over yet."

"Gladly," Samuel said, then mumbled, "I'm done talking anyway."

The histories. How long had it been since Thomas had given any thought to that time when he'd dreamed of another place? It was rarely spoken about by those he confided in these days. At one time he believed that he'd actually come *from* the histories, where, yes, a virus wreaked havoc on all he held sacred.

The Raison Strain. It seemed so distant now. A dream of a dream. But Samuel had heard it all and forgotten nothing.

Thomas nudged his horse and pointed it into the pass. Samuel was right; they were done talking.

CHELISE PACED around the tent, hands on hips. Her son, Jake, raced by, wooden sword in hand, cutting down imaginary Shataiki as they attacked from all sides. Or was his enemy Horde, covered in scabs?

"Enough, Jake! For the last time, put that cursed stick of wood away before you do some real damage."

The five-year-old stopped and looked up at her. His blond curls hung in his round, green eyes. She should take a blade to those locks before he resembled an overgrown tuft of desert wheat.

"Put it away, Jake," Marie said, eyeing her brother. "You know what happens when you get carried away."

Marie's wounds were nearly healed. A day had passed since they'd applied the clear nectar from the green plums. Only the deepest cut across her belly, bared between her halter and her skirt, was still plainly visible. If Samuel had run her through with his sword, she might have perished. There was no rising from the dead, not even with a hundred fruits.

"You're no example," Chelise chided her.

"Please, Mother, we're past that."

"I still can't believe you would subject us all to that display of brutality."

"We've all been subjected to much worse."

"He's your brother, for the love of Elyon. And he"—she glanced at Jake, who was still looking up at them—"is your brother. What kind of foolish notions do you suppose I'll have to pull out of his mind now? Did you think of that?"

"I defended the truth. If that comes at a cost, so be it."

Yes, of course, the truth. Their whole family was going to burn on the funeral pyre in defense of the truth. However noble it might be, Chelise didn't have to like it.

"Leave us, Jake. Find Johnny or Britton and find some mischief that has nothing to do with fighting."

"Yes, Mother."

"Promise me."

"Promise."

He dropped the wooden sword, a gift from Samuel of all people. Jake skipped over the mats and slipped through the canvas flap as if it were made of air.

Most of their industry surrounded desert wheat, which, apart from beds of cactus, was one of the only plentiful food sources in the desert. There was the fruit, of course, but it could only be found near the red pools.

Like the Horde who'd occupied the desert before them, the albinos used the desert wheat for more than its grain. The stalks could be reduced to thread or woven into thick mats. With the help of dye from the rocks, a few Circle tents could turn a small corner of the desert into a colorful flower.

"Sit down, Mother. You're making me crazy," Marie said.

She sat in a rocking chair Thomas had fashioned out of wood, one of the few pieces of furniture they took with them when they fled the Horde. She could understand Samuel's frustration; she could not understand his plan to resolve it.

"The other tribes are on their way?" Marie asked.

"Our runners are probably just reaching them. But they'll be here in record time, you can count on that. I hope your father knows what he's doing. It's a dangerous thing to have so many in one place. He had no right to leave me behind."

"He's also Thomas," Marie said. "Thomas of Hunter. Do you know how many narrow escapes he's survived? How many armies he's defeated? How many times he's been right?"

Chelise stood, no longer willing to sit and rock. "And this time I think he's wrong. He's going to throw everything down on the line, and even if he wins this reckless game, Qurong will never follow through on his end. He'll betray Thomas."

Marie crossed the room and sat in the chair that Chelise had vacated. "Well, you should know."

"That's right." She knew her father. He was as stubborn as a mule. Even more immovable than Thomas.

"That's why you're so upset, isn't it?" Marie said. "This is more about Qurong than Thomas."

"I don't know what you mean. Of course this is about my father, but it isn't a game. It's just . . . it's impossible!" Chelise could feel the heat in her face but felt powerless to stop it.

"I think that's the point," Marie said softly, staring at a bowl of fruit surrounded by a dozen blue pillows on the mat where they reclined to eat. "Impossible for us, impossible for Samuel. Impossible for all except one."

She switched her gaze to Chelise. "What if he's right? What if he wins this challenge against Qurong?"

"My father will never drown. Not like this."

"Then how?"

Chelise turned away, fighting back tears of frustration. For a few moments neither of them spoke. The rocker creaked as Marie stood and stepped up behind her. Her hand rested on Chelise's shoulder, the same hand that had mastered the sword and fended off Samuel just yesterday. But now it was gentle and steady.

"Then let's go," Marie said quietly. "Let's go to your father, Qurong, leader of the Horde, and let's save my father, Thomas of Hunter, leader of the Circle."

"Elyon knows how I want to. How I need to. Saving my father is all I dream about, you know?" Her brow wrinkled in deep thought.

"If what you say is right, if Qurong will double-cross Father, then we have to go."

"Thomas would disagree."

"Of course. He would say that Elyon will protect him," Marie said, removing her hand and stepping around Chelise. "But Samuel's right: no one has actually seen Elyon in ten years."

"Don't tell me you fought your brother with doubt in your heart."

"Honestly? I think I fought Samuel to fight off my own demons of doubt. Does that make me as wrong as he is? Assuming he is wrong?"

So, even Thomas's daughter was harboring doubt. The situation was worse than she'd imagined. Thomas was right in casting this challenge. The Circle was fracturing. It was all breaking apart.

"You don't approve of my honesty?" Marie said, noticing the change in her.

"Honesty? I don't know what is honest anymore. All I know is that we have a problem, Thomas was right about that." She stepped past Marie. "And I know that I fear for his life."

"Where are you going?"

"To speak to the council. Or what's left of it."

"Why?"

"Because you're right. We have to go after him."

8

JANAE SOAKED up Billy's tales, knowing that every syllable he spoke was simple, unaltered fact. She had lived a lie, and this unlikely man from across the seas had found her and brought her the truth.

She listened as he recounted stories of the monastery in Paradise, Colorado, where he first found the Books of History as a boy. And she knew that she, like Billy, had to touch one of these books if it was the last thing she did before dying.

She heard him speak of the large worms in the endless tunnels beneath the monastery, and she fought off the desire to charter a jet on the spot, fly to Paradise, and see for herself if any of these worms still survived. They, like the books, had certainly been spawned by another world. Yet they were here, in this reality?

But what made her mouth dry was Billy's claim that Thomas wasn't the only one who'd crossed the bridge into this other reality or, for that matter, come back *from* the future.

Kara had gone. And returned.

Monique, her very own mother, had gone. And returned.

How? Using Thomas's blood. The idea, once it sank in, was too much to absorb in one sitting.

"You mean, when you fall asleep—"

"While in contact with Thomas's blood," Billy interrupted, making a show of cutting his finger with a fingernail. "More accurately, while your blood is in contact with Thomas's blood."

"And you just wake up in this other place?"

"It sounds crazy, but there's plenty of proof. Me, for starters. The books—"

"Until you fall asleep there, in which case you wake up here," Janae said, on her own track. "As if the whole thing was just a dream. Only it isn't a dream at all."

"Correct. That's what I've pieced together so far."

"And you know, with certainty, that this blood still exists?"

"How many times do you need me to say it, Janae? You think I've done all of this, come all this way, because I saw your picture in *People* magazine and decided I had to have you? As if I said to myself, 'I know, I'll make up stories about books that can transport you between realities and pretend to be able to read her thoughts, that'll impress her'?"

Janae eyed him, captivated by the notion that he was reading her mind this very moment. She stood and brushed by him, smiling coyly. There was more about Billy that attracted her, and it wasn't simply his promise of adventure. He brought out the animal in her. Maybe she should give it to him without pretending.

She reached back for his hand. "Walk with me."

He did so willingly, and they meandered from the suite, still hand in hand.

"From now on this stays between us," she said. "You'll get nothing from my mother, you know that."

"Maybe."

"Not maybe. She hasn't mentioned a word of this to me, which can only mean she's hidden the truth for good reasons."

"Keeping to ourselves won't get us what we need."

"Of course not, darling. I can get us that. But I need to know that I can trust you."

"Trust me? I'm the one sharing secrets here."

She placed her free hand on his chest and gently stopped him. "Look inside me. Tell me I'm not sharing my deepest secrets with you."

Billy's eyes stared into hers. She thought about her father, what she knew, which wasn't much and had been closely guarded. And she told Billy with her mind that she found him exhilarating.

Images of her past skipped through her mind: the first time she'd overseen a board meeting at age twenty-one, her first lover, the time she'd been busted in New York for drug possession and thrown in jail for the night. But her mind finally rested on him. On Billy. On this man who'd fallen from the sky and in a few short hours managed to strip her of her secrets.

She found him stimulating. Enticing. Nearly irresistible. Not only physically, but spiritually. Emotionally. She didn't understand why. She didn't care that she didn't understand.

"You see? You can see into my heart and know that you can trust me. And I have to know that I can trust you as well."

She still held his hand in hers, and she noted that it was clammy. But then, she was accustomed to the effect she had on men.

"Our secret," she said, swallowing.

He cleared his throat. "Our secret."

"I hope I can trust you." She kissed him lightly on his lips and turned to lead him on. But Billy pulled back.

His eyes glanced nervously at the atrium beyond her. "Where are we going?"

Janae turned back. "You don't know? You haven't read my mind?"

"I do know. Learning to live with my abilities has taught me to . . . well, you know . . . go with the flow."

"By pretending not to know. Because you don't want to come off as uppity by showing your superiority over everyone else in the room. Right?"

"Something like that."

"Don't worry, I feel the same way half the time."

"Then you'll understand when I say that I have no interest in wandering around the compound, pretending to be interested in the lay of the land. It's a waste of time."

"A woman needs time—"

"I don't have time."

Her eyes searched his. "That's how you want to play?"

"I don't want to play. This need has been hunting me down for over a year. It's like a presence. I have to know if it's here."

The blood.

Billy turned and walked back toward the guest suite.

"Where are you going?"

"You don't know where it is, I can see that much. And you don't have any idea how to get it."

How rude! Where'd he grown the gall to think he could just waltz away without any regard for his host, a host who'd practically stripped herself bare for him? He was exasperating.

He was . . . like her.

"Slow down," she snapped, heading after him into the rooms. "Just take a deep breath. Fine." She shut the main door to the suite. "I'm as eager as you are, but—"

"You've known about the books for a few hours," he said, spinning back. "Don't talk to me about how eager you are. The idea that these books exist would be a heady thought for anyone, but why are you so . . . crazy about this? I can't see it in your mind, and frankly it's a bit disturbing."

It was a fair question. She told the truth. No use pretending with him. "I don't know."

"No, you don't," he said. "And that's the scariest part. It makes your longing almost . . . inhuman."

She calmed herself. "What do you expect from me? You tell me all of this and expect me to tap my fingers on the table and agree to help you?"

"Pretty much. Yes."

"Please. A hundred dots have connected in my head, and you want me to take a nap?"

"No dots have connected in your head, Janae. That's the problem. It hasn't turned on the lights in your head. I would be able to see that. But when I look inside you, I see something else."

"Is that so? And what do you see?"

"Your heart. Your desires. They're all black."

"Like yours," she said, because she could think of no defense. What he said was preposterous. She was no more evil than the next person.

Billy turned away and walked to one of the windows overlooking the lawn. "I've been here before. Staring down this kind of blackness."

"But your heart is white now?" She walked up behind him and traced the muscles of his back with her fingers. "You're afraid that naughty Janae will bring it all back? Hmm? Is that it?"

He shook his head slowly. "No. It just reminds me that what we're doing—what I'm doing—isn't right." Billy turned around, and she saw that his eyes were misty. "But I can't seem to help it. The power that's in that blood . . . those books . . . you have no idea how much damage it can bring." He looked away, and a tear snaked down his cheek.

For a moment she thought he might be talking himself out of everything he'd just convinced her to do. Panic swarmed her mind. She couldn't let him do that.

Why not, Janae? What is happening to you?

She was certain about one thing: Billy could not leave this place until she knew everything that he knew. And more.

She had to find that blood. Alone, if it had to be that way.

"I know how you feel," she started. Then, "Actually I don't. I don't share your regret. But you're right, I have desires in me that I can't understand. And I believe you share those same desires."

Janae stepped around him, dragging her fingernails delicately over his neck and cheek. She saw light freckles spotting the flesh under his hair when she brushed it away. The vein on his throat stood out, and she touched it gently.

"If your desires are like mine, then you won't be able to resist them," she said. "It's your destiny, to find this blood. To cross over."

Billy looked at her for a moment, then swallowed and cleared his throat.

"You're right. I know. But you're the first person I've met who knows it as well as I do. When I look into your eyes I feel like I'm looking into myself, and it's all a bit disturbing."

Janae felt drawn to his pale neck, so soft and tender, so bare, so full of life. She leaned forward and whispered into his ear, touching his lobe with her lips.

"Then trust me, Billy. We're the same, you and I. We are meant to be together in more ways than one."

She was momentarily distracted by her own audacity, her flagrant attempt at seduction. This wasn't typical.

But another thought eased her concern. Just exactly who was seducing whom here? Billy had swept her off her feet in a matter of hours. Was he playing her?

She pulled away and walked to a crystal decanter. Poured herself a drink and threw it back in one swallow. When she turned back to him, he was staring at her, expressionless. Reading her. His advantage over her was unfair.

It was also part of what made him irresistible.

"So," she said, pouring another drink. "What is it? Are we changing our minds?"

"I wasn't aware we'd made up our minds," he said, crossing to the decanter. He took the glass from her hand and matched her slug. Set it down with a *thunk*.

"Rumor has it that Thomas wasn't the only one to cross over into this world," he said softly, as if what he would tell her now was of greatest importance. He stepped to a large, plum-colored wingback chair, sat down, and crossed his legs. "Several others have come and gone. But I've learned that one came and stayed. A wraith called a Shataiki in that world. His name was Alucard, and he was a creature of the night."

She felt her chest tighten. "Okay, now you've lost me," she said, but that's not what she was thinking. She turned her eyes away so he couldn't see into her mind. "What do you mean, a creature of the night?"

"I don't know much. But I know they spread their seed through blood."

"Through blood?"

"The information is sketchy, but yes. I think so. It's how they reproduce."

She shoved her thoughts out before he could steal them from her mind.

"Unless you think we can tie my mother down and pry her eyes open so you can plunder her mind, there's only one way to find out if she knows where the blood is."

"I've already considered that," Billy said.

"You don't want to try. Trust me. She'll have you dead or behind bars before you can use what you learn."

"Exactly."

"She has to retrieve the blood willingly."

"Clearly."

Janae turned. "I know how to do that." Then she looked into his eyes and let him take her knowledge.

This time she could almost feel his invasive gaze. His eyes widened slowly and he blinked twice.

Billy stood to his feet, face white.

"Seriously?"

"I should know. It's my lab."

"Raison Strain B?"

"A mutation of the virus that turned the world upside down thirty years ago. It's not airborne. But there's no known antivirus. If we inject ourselves with it . . ."

"She'll be forced to try Thomas's blood, because it proved resistant to the original virus," Billy finished. "And if she doesn't have the blood? Or if it fails?"

She reached for the decanter and said what he already knew because a thing like this needed to be said aloud.

"Then we both die."

9

The Future

THE HIGH crater at Ba'al Bek was a good half mile across, ringed by a thick lip of soil and rock. A boulder from the heavens might have created it, or the fist of a giant, or a belch from Teeleh for all Thomas knew.

What he did know was that the whole plateau stank of rotting Scab flesh.

The four albinos had crossed the gorges and now sat on their horses, peering into the high place with a red sun sinking to the west. Behind them, canyons offered cover from any attack.

Ahead, barren ground up to a single row of tall boulders that ringed Ba'al Bek's famed stone altar. This was the first time he'd seen the altar. The Circle had gone deep into the desert for nearly six years after Qurong turned his full wrath on them.

"We have company," Mikil said.

Thomas looked up at the far rim and saw the purple banner sticking over the crest. Then more banners, then heads and horses.

"Qurong's taken up the challenge," Mikil said. "I don't like this, Thomas. This can't be good."

The Horde marched in two columns, each led by a contingent of two dozen Throaters, then the priests. Dozens of priests. They kept coming, two hundred priests or more, by Thomas's reckoning.

Dear Elyon, what have I done?

Ba'al sat in a litter, rocking on the shoulders of eight servants. Qurong rode tall on a black stallion opposite the dark priest, dressed in full battle gear. His own guard, thirty or forty from the Scab cavalry, rode on either side of him. They bore swords, battle axes, sickles, and perhaps the most dreaded weapon in their arsenal, a simple chain with two spiked balls that could be thrown to take down prey from fifty yards. Mace.

The rattling of a thousand bells on the edges of the priests' robes sounded like a desert full of cicadas in the early evening.

"We're mice among lions," Jamous said. "Are you sure about this, Thomas?"

"I thought you said priests only." Mikil had faced her share of long odds, but never this and not for many years. "They've brought half a battalion!"

"It's for their defense, not to take us out," Thomas said.

Samuel's mount stamped its feet. A grin twisted his face. "They still fear us. What did I tell you? We could take them."

"Four against hundreds?" Mikil scoffed. "Even in our 'full glory' as you like to call it, these would have been unfeasible odds."

"Impossible," Jamous mumbled.

Samuel came alive in the presence of his enemies. "The priests are unarmed. We could at least take Qurong and that witch. That would set the Horde far back. Without a head, the snakes crawl into their holes."

Thomas almost pointed out that Samuel's foolishness had brought them here in the first place. Or that a dead high priest would only be replaced by another live one. Or that these were not their true enemies. The real enemy was peering at them from his hidden perch on the crest somewhere. Teeleh and his host from hell, the Shataiki.

But Samuel doubted Teeleh and the Shataiki and even Elyon, for that matter.

Thomas headed his horse down the slope.

"You're sure, Thomas?" Mikil kicked her horse to follow.

Thomas kept his eyes on the entourage snaking over the crest. Bulls pulled six large chests on carts. Then the goats trotted in. He wasn't sure what Ba'al had up his sleeve, but he doubted Teeleh had a taste for goats. This was all for show.

"Thomas." Mikil drew her horse abreast his. "Please tell me you've thought this through."

"You're asking me now? Isn't it a bit late?"

"I didn't believe it would come to this. You've been brooding."

"My mood has just lightened, Mikil. For the first time in far too long I feel like I have nothing to lose."

"Only your faith," Samuel said, pulling abreast.

"If Elyon doesn't show himself tonight, it only means that he wants me dead," Thomas said.

"And the Horde as well."

Thomas gave him that. "If I lose this challenge, then I will assume the way of peace has passed, and I will take down as many Horde as I can before my skin turns."

"Thomas Hunter will kill again?" Samuel said. "Did I hear that right?"

"Thomas Hunter will die. Again."

"You'll tell them where our camps are?"

"As promised."

They headed into Ba'al Bek, four abreast, facing an entourage that dwarfed them.

"And if you succeed in this challenge," Mikil said, "if Elyon shows himself, you actually expect that Qurong will agree to come with us and drown?"

"He's agreed already."

"He'll betray you," Samuel said. "But I don't think you have much worry there; he isn't going to lose this challenge."

Thomas looked at his son. "Maybe not. But if he does lose, I'll have won my own son back, and that for me is worth his betrayal."

Samuel tried to smile. His twisted lips looked stupid on his crimson face.

The tall rocks that circled the altar rose above them now, red in the sunset. The light would be gone within the hour. Thomas would have preferred to confront Ba'al in broad daylight, but it was what it was.

Qurong and his dark priest had reached the high place and waited for the host of priests to take up their position on the altar's left. The Throaters were fanning out on either side as if they expected an attack from the high ground.

"Imagine what we could do with a dozen archers," Samuel said, scanning the crater's rim. "We could make pin cushions out of them in a matter of minutes."

He was right. A dozen years ago, this setup would have provided the perfect ambush for the Forest Guard. Thomas understood Samuel's desires to destroy his enemies. It was the most natural instinct man possessed.

Love the enemy. This was the scandalous teaching of Elyon. It went completely against human nature.

It struck Thomas then that Eram, the half-breed from the north, could just as easily sweep in with his army, surround the crater, and destroy all of his enemies—both the albinos and the leader of the Horde—in one fell swoop.

"Tell us what to do." Mikil spoke quickly, uneasy.

"I will. As soon as I know."

"Elyon help us all."

"Isn't that the idea? To see if those words have any meaning?"

Thomas led the four past the ring of boulders like an arrow into the heart of darkness. It had been a while since Thomas had been so close to Scab flesh. He'd forgotten just how rancid it was. Only as he drew closer did he see the reason: none of the priests had applied the morst paste.

He pulled up and faced Ba'al, who still sat on his cushioned throne under the silk canopy. His servants had set him down. Qurong gazed off to his right, refusing to dignify them with a square look. His general, the one named Cassak if Thomas was right, sat in stoic silence beside him, eyes on Ba'al.

Who led the Horde these days, anyway? Ba'al or Qurong?

Both, he guessed. The thin serpent wielded Teeleh's power over the people, and the muscled warrior wielded the sword.

Ba'al stood and slinked forward. A black silk dress clung to his body from his armpits to his heels. A purple sash wrapped around his neck hung down to his belly. But his shoulders were bare, white, bony.

Three scars marked his forehead. All the others bore the same marks, something Thomas's scouts first reported about a year ago.

"I've come to speak to Qurong," Thomas said. "Not to his servant."

Ba'al made no show of being bothered by this underhanded insult, but Qurong would take note.

"Welcome, pale one," the dark priest said. "The supreme commander, ruler of humans, servant of Teeleh our master has accepted your challenge."

"Then let the master speak for himself. Is he your puppet?"

This time the witch's left eyelid twitched. "Don't assume that all men would stoop to speak to you, albino," Ba'al said.

"But you do. For more than ten years I've evaded the death sentence placed upon me and my wife . . . I think that earns me the right to be acknowledged by the ruler of this earth." Thomas watched Qurong as he spoke.

"Then perhaps you overestimate yourself as much as you overestimate your God."

"That's what we're here to find out," Thomas said. "Don't get your silk dress all hitched up for the dance just yet. I insist on speaking to your leader."

Ba'al stared. His gray eyes betrayed no emotion, no resentment, no sign that Thomas offended him. This was a wicked man, more Shataiki than human, Thomas thought. The night seemed to have turned inordinately cold.

"Can we please dispense with all the fancy footwork?" Qurong said, eyeing Thomas for the first time. "You've cast a challenge, I've accepted. My priest will invoke the power of Teeleh and you will call on your God. We've gone to a lot of trouble to accommodate this game of yours. I suggest we get started. What exactly do you have in mind?"

"Anything your dark priest would like."

None of the three behind Thomas spoke a word or moved. Ba'al kept his haunting, unblinking stare on him. With a little imagination Thomas could see the conniving brain behind those eyes spinning like a beetle tied to a string. For a long time the only sound came from the occasional snorting or shifting of a Throater's horse.

"Is that your son?" Ba'al asked, looking at Samuel.

"I see you've taken to mutilating your foreheads," Thomas said. "The mark of your beast, is that it?"

The white wraith in human form named Ba'al, who was the wickedest of all Horde, raised his hand and extended a thin finger to the horizon. "From the east the pale one will bring peace and command the sky. He will purge the land with a river of blood in the valley of Miggdon. We will offer ourselves to him on that day of reckoning. The question is, will you?"

"No. We will not. We submit to Elyon and to no one else."

The priest eyed him. His mouth was paper thin, scarcely more than flaps of white flesh to keep the bugs from his teeth. He raised one hand by his head and snapped fingers so delicate Thomas wondered how the snap alone didn't break them.

"We shall see, albino."

Two of the priests hurried over to one of the bull-drawn carts. While one unhitched the beast, the other pulled a large, white silk blanket from the chest. Then a silver goblet.

The rest watched, bare of emotion, as the two priests urged the bull forward, tied it to one of four bronze rings on the altar, and draped the white blanket over the beast's back. One of them strapped a ruby-colored cushion on top. A saddle. The priests hurried back to their posts, bells jangling with the shuffle of their feet. The whole operation took two dozen seconds, no more.

What Ba'al could possibly mean to demonstrate by saddling up a bull was beyond Thomas, but the man's continuous, unwavering stare didn't sit well with him.

"Do you like the sight of blood, Thomas?" Ba'al asked.

"Not particularly." *Dear Elyon, do not keep your face hidden now, not now. The whole world is watching, and I'm powerless.* Then, as an afterthought: *Give the word and I will take this man's head from his shoulders for you.*

"I suggest you get used to it, albino. Because our god demands blood. Pools of blood. Rivers of blood. Blood from the necks of our own."

"Your god, Teeleh"—Thomas spat to one side—"may be a blood-thirsty—"

Ba'al moved while Thomas spoke, snatching a hidden sword from his back, slashing down with lightning speed. The blade struck the bull on its spine, just above the shoulder blades, and cut cleanly through its neck.

Samuel's sword scraped its scabbard as he withdrew it.

The bull's head dropped from its torso and landed on the earth with a dull *thump*. For a long moment, the animal stood still, unaware of the blood that pumped from its arteries onto the ground. Then it took a half step and collapsed.

A soft moan broke from the two hundred priests, now swaying in their black robes. The slaying happened so quickly that Thomas didn't think to react.

Ba'al spread his arms wide and spoke to the darkening sky. "Accept my offering, Teeleh, one and true god of all that lives and breathes, dragon of the sky. May your vengeance find fulfillment through my hands."

He lowered his head and glared at Thomas. "Tell your friends to drop their weapons."

The moans ceased.

"Not for you. Not for any Scab," Samuel spat.

Ba'al dropped his own blade. "Tell him."

"Drop it, Samuel."

"Father—"

"All of you, drop your weapons!"

They weren't here for battle or to defend themselves. It took a few seconds, but Thomas heard the blades fall. Qurong sat on his horse, staring at the dead bull as two priests hurried in and collected the weapons from the ground. The Throaters closed off any avenue of escape, leaving only their rear unguarded.

"This is only a bull, not enough to satiate the true god," Ba'al said. "The stakes here are far too great for an ordinary display of loyalty." He pointed to his gathered faithful. "I will put the life of Teeleh's loyal subjects up against the life of only one albino. We will see which one the true god delivers."

The implications ran through Thomas's chest like a blade. His own life against these swaying witches. His mind stalled at the thought. What was the priest suggesting, that he lie on the altar and take the blade the way the bull had?

But he'd come here to either die or be saved. Any further hesitation would only make a mockery of all he stood for.

"Against your witches," Thomas said, "and you. Agreed."

Ba'al's eyes shifted over Thomas's right shoulder. "We will all bleed and trust our master to show his power as he has in the past. All of them. And then your son. And then me."

Thomas froze. "Never! Myself, not my son."

"You don't trust your god to deliver even this one albino? Is your son beyond Elyon's reach?"

"I decide for me, not for my son." Thomas spoke the words, but his mind was crying out to Elyon already. He had been tricked. Pushed into a corner. He saw the trap, but failing to see a way to break free, his mind cried out. Then his lips, in a barely audible whisper. "Elyon . . . Elyon, I beg you . . ."

"I haven't asked your son about his faith in this God you serve," Ba'al said. "I'm asking if *you* have the faith to put his life in your God's hands."

Thomas felt his lifelines slipping. He'd expected any scenario but this. How could he offer up his own son?

"Do you believe Elyon will save your son?"

The cool night air had gone frigid.

"Elyon has no limits."

"Father—"

"And if your son doesn't agree?" Ba'al cut in. "Would that weaken your faith? Would you be frightened that Teeleh would steal your child the way you stole Qurong's child?"

Chelise. Qurong sat with jaw fixed.

"Listen to me, you skinny little witch," Thomas bit off. "My son, like Chelise, decides for himself whether he lives or dies. He's not your bull to slaughter."

"I thought Elyon and Teeleh were to decide who would live or die. I'm only asking if you, not your son, will give Elyon the opportunity to decide."

Thomas's face flushed with indignation. But he truly was ensnared by this pathetic wretch's challenge. If he delayed in giving his consent, it would only show his doubt. He'd come to prove his faith in Elyon, and already he was flapping around like a wounded chicken.

But he couldn't bring himself to say it. He couldn't stand here and—

Do you want to swim with me?

Thomas's pulse spiked.

Swim in my waters, Thomas.

The distant voice whispered. The same voice he'd heard on occasion in the deepest part of Elyon's waters. A boy's voice, so tender, full of mischief and life. Elyon . . .

"What did I tell you, my lord?" Ba'al said to Qurong. "I've handed you a victory with the slaying of one bull. The great Thomas of Hunter doesn't have—"

"I accept your challenge," Thomas snapped. "I would offer my son. But I can't speak for him."

"No. But I can." Ba'al nodded.

Thomas twisted on his horse and felt the blood drain from his face. The Throaters had closed the gaps between the boulders fifty yards behind Mikil, Jamous, and Samuel. None of them had any weapons.

There was no escape, not even for a fighter of Samuel's caliber.

Ba'al was going to bleed his son.

"Come, my master," Ba'al whispered in a trembling voice. "Enter your servant."

Six Throaters rode in from the left, swords drawn. They didn't hesitate as they would have if facing an armed warrior of the Guard, but stormed straight toward Samuel, slamming into his horse. One of them whipped a long chain around his son's throat and tugged.

"Father . . ."

"Let him go! Release him!" Thomas spurred his horse into the fray, took the butt of a sword on his chin and blindly struck out with a fist. He felt his knuckles sink into spongy Scab flesh. The warrior he'd hit grunted and swung his spear like a stick. It glanced off Thomas's shoulder.

Panic joined his desperation. Even if there was a chance to overpower the Throaters, he would betray his own challenge by attempting anything so foolish.

The sound of a brutal blow to Samuel's flesh made him recoil. A grunt. Then silence. They'd dragged Samuel to the ground and knocked him out.

Thomas spun back to Ba'al, swallowing against the dread rising in his gut. "This wasn't my challenge!"

The dark priest was staring at the dusk sky, hands raised and trembling. He jerked his head down. "It is mine."

Whimpers and murmuring spread through Ba'al's priests, their eyes on the darkening sky. Thomas looked up.

At first glance it appeared as if a huge black cloud had drifted over the high place and was slowly rotating—a hurricane forming several miles over their heads.

But this wasn't a cloud, Thomas saw. For the first time in many years, the Shataiki were showing themselves. Hundreds of thousands of the black beasts peered down with red eyes, having gathered to watch the butchery.

Elyon . . . Dear Elyon, help us . . .

10

CHELISE PULLED her mount up with a sharp tug, digging her heels into the leather stirrups. She threw her weight back to compensate for the sudden stop. The pale mare, bred to blend into the desert, snorted and tossed its head, protesting the bronze bit that dug into its flesh.

The sky . . . there was something wrong in the sky.

"What?" Marie cried, whipping her head around as she shot past. She forced her horse to a tramping halt. "What is it?"

"I . . ." Chelise stared at the black cloud on the distant darkening horizon. Something about the sight spread a chill over her skull. "I . . ."

Marie followed her eyes and gazed with her. "What is it? A cloud?"

"It's moving."

"So clouds move. What's gotten into you?"

"Over the high place, as if—"

"Shataiki," Marie whispered.

The horses were breathing hard from their run, but this one word uttered by Marie felt like a kick to Chelise's gut. She hadn't put her finger on it, but now that Marie had labeled the huge, swirling vortex, the dreadful certainty that her daughter was right wrapped its claws around her throat.

Shataiki.

"That's impossible," she finally managed.

Marie twisted in her saddle. "It's over the high place, Ba'al Bek."

"But . . . so Qurong accepted Thomas's challenge?"

Marie turned her jittery mount back to Chelise, casting an eye at the Shataiki. "Unless they've gathered in defiance of Thomas's presence on their sacred turf. He would be the first albino to enter the cursed place of worship."

"But no one's seen the Shataiki for years. Have you ever seen one?"

"I may have. At one time I thought I had, but it could just as easily have been a shadow. This is . . ." Marie couldn't seem to form her thoughts around the idea that they were actually seeing Shataiki. But there could be no doubt. It was a massive cloud of black bats, each the size of a bloodhound if the legends were correct, packed so closely together that they looked from this distance like a solid mass. "So many . . ."

Chelise had finally convinced the council that Qurong and Ba'al would accept Thomas's challenge only if they intended to double-cross him. She argued that Qurong would never stoop so low in his mind to go with Thomas if he lost the challenge. The only person remotely capable of winning Qurong's heart was his very own daughter. Chelise.

Marie earned the right to go because she had defended Thomas's honor by fighting Samuel in Vadal's place.

They left Jake with Suzan, who complained bitterly that a fighter of her caliber should go with them.

After eight hard hours of riding they were less than halfway there. But they had the fruit; they would not stop.

"We're not going to make it," Chelise said. Her heart pounded in her ears. "If they've already started this ill-advised game, we're going to be too late."

"I'm not sure there's anything we could do if—"

"Then go home," Chelise snapped. "It wasn't my idea that you come."

"Easy. I'm not second-guessing our decision. I'm just stating the obvious. We don't stand a chance against that." She nodded at the cloud of Shataiki, slowly rotating in the dusky sky.

"You're forgetting about Elyon. You nearly killed your brother for his honor—"

"I would never kill Samuel."

"—yet you doubt Elyon's power?"

"If it's up to Elyon, then why does he need us? He's got Thomas out there. What good will two more be?"

"Qurong—"

"Can be won by Elyon much more easily than by you," Marie cut in. Then with less bite: "So it would seem to me."

"You're far too much like your father," Chelise said. "Everyone should take care of themselves, is that it? Your independence is only cute when there's no real danger." She kicked her horse, and the beast surged forward. "If Elyon could snap his fingers and win anyone's heart, the Horde would have flocked to the red lakes long ago," she cried. "That's obviously not the way it works."

Marie urged her mount into a full run and pulled abreast. "I'm not suggesting we don't go, Mother, but Thomas and I aren't the only ones who are stubborn. Father knew that your love for Qurong might jeopardize his mission, not to mention your life. I think that cloud only raises the stakes. Don't do anything rash."

"Now the youth are giving the advice?"

"I'm not a child! I'm the one who's here to keep your backside out of trouble."

"I'm not a fool."

"No, but love is blind. And you, Mother, are blind when it comes to your father."

There was some truth to what Marie said. Chelise would give her life to save Qurong, if Elyon required it. But her love for Qurong didn't make her stupid.

Chelise pushed her mare into a full gallop. "Fine, save my backside. At this rate you're not going to be given that opportunity, because it'll all be over by the time we get there."

She breathed a quick prayer, begging Elyon to keep them all alive until she could show up and make things right. She immediately chided herself for such arrogance.

"How far?" she breathed.

"We can't push the horses like this all night. Daybreak. At best."

Thank Elyon they'd brought the healing fruit.

11

THE PRIVATE laboratory had been constructed underground and fortified with reinforced concrete, halfway between Raison Pharmaceutical's Bangkok laboratories and the mansion on the south lawn. Monique's reasoning for choosing the location was simple: Any attack on the compound would focus on the buildings, not the grass between them. All critical samples would be stored in the five-thousand-square-foot facility where the most sensitive research was conducted.

They called it Ground Zero, home of some of the world's most potentially destructive biological materials. Raison Strain B for starters.

Janae swiped her security card through the reader, heard the magnetic locking mechanism disengage, and looked back at Billy. Sweat beaded his forehead. His eyes darted to hers, then back to the metal door.

She pushed it open and walked into the hall. "Close the door behind you. And hurry. Just because it's midnight doesn't mean security doesn't already know my card was used to gain access. I wouldn't put it past my mother to have instructed them to alert her every time I enter."

"She's that distrusting of you?"

"No. Not normally. But you're here, aren't you? The redheaded bloodhound who can climb into people's minds."

"With the bloodhound who uses her tongue to steal the minds of men," he said.

"Whatever." But he was right.

He followed her down the hall, past several doors where supplies were kept. The passage ended at another steel door that again required her card for access. She could hear Billy's steady breathing behind her.

He'd questioned her no fewer than a dozen times since she first suggested they call Monique's bluff by infecting themselves, though his obsession with reaching the Books of History was reason enough for him to follow through. After all, he explained, he'd grown up with them, used them. He might even be *responsible* for them. He'd been pushed to the outer limits of himself and found nothing more than the blackness he'd come to recognize in his heart.

The fear and horror of a dozen years had turned him into a rag doll at the mercy of that blackness, he'd said, pacing with both hands in his hair. The chance of finally understanding what had turned him into the person he was, however dangerous, was worth the risk of Monique hanging them out to dry. For that matter, maybe he'd only find what he was looking for in death.

But what drove Janae to the same desperation? Nothing Billy could see in her mind. So what was it? He wanted to know. What?

She guessed. "Maybe because I have that same blackness in me. I always have. From the time my father vanished, I've hated my life. That same blackness is calling me. You can't see it in my mind because it's beyond my mind. I don't even understand it, but today, for the first time, hearing about the blood and the Books of History, and my own mother's involvement—I feel alive, Billy. I've come back from the dead."

"And so now you're willing to risk death again?" he'd challenged.

She turned away. "Mother won't allow that."

"But if she does."

"Then she does. But she won't. On occasion I may be the child she wishes she never had, but my mother loves me."

She unlocked the metal door and led Billy into the heart of the facility: a white laboratory blinking with a hundred monitoring lights. The door closed softly behind them, and she gave him a moment to study the room.

A dozen workstations were positioned under fluorescent lights, perfectly ordered with flat touch-screen monitors. Not a pen or piece of paper out of place. Not a single paperclip or piece of lint on the shiny-mirror black floor.

Her mother was obsessive compulsive when it came to research. Two large liquid-cooled servers provided the room with enough computing power to run the Pentagon, but Mother controlled the real brains behind what happened here. Her own.

Then again, there was little her mother knew that Janae did not.

"This is it," she said.

"Impressive. What are all those machines?" His eyes were on a wall lined with high-voltage equipment.

"Nothing you and I need. Magnetometers, electron microscopes, cryogenics, homogenizers . . . too much to explain now. What we need is in the subzero refrigeration system."

She walked to a small room with a skull-and-crossbones symbol under a sign that read *Quarantine*, punched a code into a small pad, and pushed the glass door wide. Inside lay four gurneys with restraining straps. Each had its own life-support system, now disconnected.

"So this is it," Billy said, stepping into the room beside her.

"We won't need all the technology. A syringe will do the trick. But yes, we do need to seal ourselves in. Can't risk additional contamination, right?" She forced a grin.

"Right."

"Please try to relax, Billy. You do realize the real risk here, don't you?"

"I think I do, yes."

"It's not my mother. It's that what *you've* told me isn't the truth. Frankly, seeing you sweat like this makes me wonder."

"It's the truth," he insisted. "Your mother may love you, but how do we know the blood exists? That's the real risk."

"The blood exists. I saw it in my mother's eyes. Like I said earlier, you're not the only one who can read minds. My intuition has never failed me."

"Then you should know that I've told you nothing but the truth," Billy said.

She frowned. Her hands were tingling with energy and the fact that Billy seemed reticent only added to her eagerness. She turned from the quarantine room, crossed to a panel in the wall, and entered a ten-digit code she'd written on her palm: 786947494D. Motors hummed to life as the retrieval mechanism went for the sample in question.

"It's in the wall?"

"The ground, actually. Twenty feet under us. All of the sensitive stuff is."

He looked a little lost, standing there in his jeans and T-shirt. She stepped over to him, stood on her tiptoes, and gave him a light peck on the lips.

"Ready to commit suicide, darling?"

He reached his right hand behind her head, pulled her close, and kissed her long. When he pulled back, his green eyes sparkled. "I am. More than you know."

Interesting. Not the reaction she had expected. Perhaps she'd underestimated him.

A small beep indicated that the sample had been delivered. Janae slid the door of the caddie open and withdrew a Plexiglas tube that contained a glass vial of amber liquid. She habitually flicked the tube with her nail.

"Raison Strain B. No known antivirus."

"How's it different from the original Raison Strain?"

"Well, for starters, it kills in about a day, not thirty days. Never mind the details, let's just say this one is much harder on the body. We'll be bleeding internally within an hour. The only saving grace is that like most viruses, this strain isn't airborne. It requires an exchange of bodily fluid. So even though strain B is stronger, it doesn't present the same threat as the first strain."

"How much do we need?" he asked, eyeing the vial in her fingers.

"Need? The smallest drop. But I don't want to play around. One cc should do the trick. We won't feel anything anyway, not after the sedatives we take kick in. We'll be out."

"May I?"

She handed him the sample, struck again by the fire burning in his bright eyes. He was like a kid next in line at an amusement-park ride.

She plucked the sample from his hand and walked toward the quarantine room. "Why don't you let me do this? I doubt my mother would take any terrible risk to save you. It's me she'll move heaven and earth to keep alive."

"No," he said. "It doesn't work like that. The point is to get Thomas's blood into our own bloodstream. His blood is what should allow us to cross into his world."

"Thomas's world, even though he originally came from Denver, Colorado."

"I mean the Black Forest. The future, where I sent him by writing in the Book of History. Call it whatever you want, that's not the point. Your own mother was able to follow him by injecting herself with some of his blood. That's the point. If you're infected and she injects you with his blood, you'll cross over, at least in your dreams. I didn't come all this way to stand by your bed and watch you cross without me. If Monique uses the blood on you, she'll use it on me as well, assuming we're both infected."

"Don't say I didn't offer."

"How will she know?"

"That we've infected ourselves? When the resident technician does his rounds in the morning, he'll call her. Assuming she isn't alerted earlier that I've been in here all night."

Janae retrieved a syringe from the cupboard, slipped on a needle, and set it in a three-foot glass chamber with a bottle of sedative and the vial of Raison Strain B. She closed the chamber and inserted both arms into the sleeves that gave her access to the airtight compartment. Billy stood by her, watching.

The vial was sealed with a soft, nonpermeable glue, which broke free with a firm twist. "There it is, Billy. Nasty, nasty stuff." She set the vial in a tray that held it upright. "The wonder drug that's going to take us to a whole new world."

"Actually, the virus is the killer. Thomas's blood is the drug."

Blood. Even now, faced by death, the thought of the blood made her pulse quicken.

Janae inserted the needle into the vial of Raison Strain B, withdrew two ccs of the fluid, and repeated a similar operation with the sedative. She capped the syringe with a rubber sleeve and rotated the glass, giving the two fluids time to mix. She could have done it all without the isolation chamber, but habit compelled her. There was always a chance of spilling and contaminating the room.

She pulled the syringe out of the chamber and faced him. "So, darling. Are you ready for this?"

He glanced at the white-sheeted gurneys. "Just lie down?"

"Go ahead." She winked at him. "I'll be gentle."

Billy gazed into her eyes. "I still can't figure you out. Why aren't you afraid?"

"Thomas found my mother, and his life changed forever. Now you've found her daughter, and your life is about to change. Maybe Thomas isn't the only one with something in his blood."

"Right."

"Lie down," she said.

Billy walked to the nearest gurney, rolled onto the mattress, and looked up. He looked so disarming with his big green eyes and disheveled red hair. A jeans-and-T-shirt guy with worn Skechers and fair skin. It occurred to her that she might be staring the fate of the world in the face. Isn't that what they'd said about Thomas Hunter?

Janae leaned over Billy and touched her lips to his. She impulsively bit his lower lip, and when he didn't pull away, she bit it harder.

The fresh taste of his blood sent a faint tingle through her tongue. She was surprised that he still didn't jerk away. Instead he pressed up into her mouth, then calmly settled back down.

"Let's do this."

"Turn your arm over."

She formed a tourniquet of surgical tubing above his elbow, gently traced the median cubital vein on the inside of his arm, and brought the needle to the skin. Billy stared into her eyes.

Then she inserted the needle into his vein and shot one cc of Raison Strain B into his bloodstream.

Damage done.

She withdrew the needle and released the tourniquet. "Lie still." But she wasn't thinking of him lying still as much as she was her own need to follow him.

Janae had drawn her own blood more times than she could count and now decided to dispense with the tourniquet. Disinfectant was a bit of a joke considering what they were putting into their arms. And it seemed proper now to share the same needle, however unclean.

She opened her arm, found the faint line of her vein, plunged the needle through her white skin, and pushed the rest of the amber liquid into herself.

Damage done.

A sting, nothing more.

She set the syringe back into the isolation chamber, sealed it, and took her place on the gurney next to Billy's. Her black dress had ridden up, and she pulled it down so that it covered most of her thighs.

"Now what?" Billy asked.

Janae turned her head and faced him. "Now we fall asleep and slowly die."

"Twenty-four hours."

"More or less." She could feel the deadening effects of the sedative already. "See you on the other side, Billy."

12

THOMAS PACED twenty yards from the altar, trying to remember why he'd allowed the scene before him to unfold as it had. Beside him, Mikil and Jamous were muttering their horror, demanding under their breath that he do something, that this was intolerable, that he'd mistaken Elyon's intentions.

But there was nothing left to do. Except beg.

Beg Elyon to show mercy. To provide a way of escape. To save his son. To stop Teeleh's servant, whose sickness knew no bounds.

He'd watched helplessly as they hauled Samuel down with hardly a fight. His son seemed to know that resistance without a weapon was hopeless. His green eyes held Thomas in a bitter stare as they hauled him to the altar, stripped him, and strapped him spread-eagle to the rings at each corner.

All the while, those red eyes in the sky watched him. Thomas had turned away so they wouldn't see his weak resolve in the face of such a tragedy.

But it would be a tragedy only if Elyon failed them, right? And if Elyon failed them, there was no reason to live. He could only beg Elyon, and so he did, without a pause.

Ba'al stood before the stone slab in perfect stillness as his priests carefully stacked wood in a tower ten feet from the altar. When they'd doused the wood in oil, they took up their places with the others, swaying. Qurong and his general still sat atop their horses, watching from thirty yards back. The Throaters held their posts at the boulders.

All was prepared.

"You're going to get him killed," Mikil said in a low, unsteady voice.

How dare she doubt his love for his son at a time like this? "If Ba'al was going to kill Samuel, he would have done it already. He can't afford a martyr in front of his people. He needs his devil to show his face."

"He *has* shown himself!" she whispered, glancing at the Shataiki circling high above. "I can't watch this."

"Then I suggest you join me and demand that Elyon show himself as well."

Ba'al shrugged out of his robe and stepped forward, naked. His body was threaded with sinewy muscle that looked more like roots than flesh. The man was even thinner than Thomas had imagined. In his right hand he held a long dagger shaped like a claw.

The dark priest lifted the blade high.

"Dark Master, hear our cry!" Ba'al wailed. His eyes, glistening with tears, searched the sky. "Rescue your servant from this body of death! I who am your captive, locked in your embrace, implore you. Show me your mercy."

Thomas's breathing slowed, then stilled. It sounded almost as if Ba'al was praying to Elyon, as if Ba'al had learned his own ways from the Forest Guard. As if he were a half-breed.

"Hear my voice, great dragon," Ba'al cried. "I once knew your enemy as you did, was betrayed by my own and left to die. But you, Teeleh, and your lover Marsuuv showed me mercy." He wept at the sky like a prodigal begging to be allowed back in his father's palace. "I beg you, imprison me once again. Show your great power. Don't allow them to make a mockery out of me."

Thomas hung on his twisted words. The gathering of priests had taken up a soft moan to accompany their swaying. One of them walked out and placed a torch on the wood. Flame leaped up, licking at the sky.

Samuel lay on the altar, chest rising and falling like a blacksmith's bellows. The priest who'd lit the fire gathered up Samuel's clothes and threw them into the flames, putting an exclamation mark on their intention. Samuel would not need any clothes where he was going.

Ba'al's voice rose to a scream. "Kill me now, or send me back to the other world where you sent the chosen one through the lost books. But do not betray me!" He shook where he stood, gasping for air. "Let the land of the living know that you live with power to consume all who will not bow at your feet."

Ba'al's cry cut through the pain ravaging Thomas's mind. *The chosen one.* The words carried the sound of secret knowledge. What did the dark priest know of the chosen one, and what were these lost books? Whispers about seven lost books had been heard around late-night fires, but they were only talk.

Samuel was on the altar, chest heaving with terror.

"We offer our blood to you. Drink and taste our waters of life, lord of the night. Devour our gift to you, the son of this idolater, who serves the one who cast you into the pit."

The priests' moaning rose to a dull roar. On some unseen cue, the front row stepped out and approached Ba'al in single file. The first took the dagger from Ba'al's lifted hand, kissed his high priest's fingers, then nicked his own wrist.

They were bleeding themselves.

The priest stepped to the altar and let some of his blood drip onto Samuel's heaving chest, then walked past as the second priest took up Ba'al's dagger. Cut himself.

"I won't watch this," Mikil said, turning her back. But Jamous and Thomas watched without wavering. And after a moment, Mikil turned back and spit to one side. "Elyon has abandoned us."

Ba'al was begging Teeleh to take Samuel.

And Thomas was begging Elyon to save his firstborn son, covered by the priests' blood on Ba'al's altar.

Mikil grunted. "This is the end."

"So be it," Thomas said, glaring. "But if this is the end, then it's by Elyon's design. Have you forgotten who once turned the world inside out? Who saved us from the Horde more times than you can hold in your sliver of a memory? Unless you have a prayer, keep your mouth closed."

"That was then . . ."

"And this," he shouted at her, "is now! Pray!"

He faced the altar and saw that seven priests had spilled their blood on Samuel. Dark trails ran off his son's chest and pooled on the stone.

Qurong had backed away with his general and vanished from the circle of Throaters. Now it was Thomas and Elyon against Ba'al and Teeleh, a contest of spilled blood against . . .

Against what? What would it take to get Elyon's attention? He'd left them with some fruit and some red pools and then seemed to have vanished. They could rid their bodies of the scabbing disease by drowning; they could heal their bodies with the fruit; they could dance and sing deep into the night, remembering his love.

But where was Elyon to rescue them from the Horde who pressed in relentlessly? What would it take? Samuel's blood?

No. There was no more need for blood. This would come down to the very essence of the challenge he'd first cast. The stage was set. Either Teeleh would take Samuel's life and prove that he could destroy Elyon's own, or Elyon would show his might.

Still the moaning priests filed past the altar, slashing their skin and wetting his son. Still Ba'al stood over the scene, white arms spread wide, gloating over Samuel's bloody body. His eyes glistened, round, unblinking, like those of the Shataiki circling overhead.

The mangy black beasts had descended, and he could make out their triangular heads. They looked like flying wolves, emboldened by the constant moan begging them to come. By the priests' shuffling dance, shaking the bells on their robes. By the sight of the albino's smooth skin covered in blood.

The priests' self-inflicted wounds dribbled slowly. They'd undoubtedly cut themselves before for the beast whose mark they bore on their foreheads.

Thomas let the scene wash over him, allowing his anger to boil beneath his good reason. This display of evil was not Horde. This wasn't the making of Qurong or Eram and his half-breeds. The blood sacrifice before them was the creation of Teeleh and this wraith named Ba'al, who had lived in his bosom. Thomas would be in his rights to take a sword and slaughter the man where he stood.

Instead, he pulled at his hair and begged Elyon to come to his senses.

But the night only grew darker, and the Shataiki thicker, and the raging fire consumed more and more wood. Samuel lay still, by all appearances resigned to his fate, but Thomas knew better. If Samuel lived, his bitterness would know no bounds. This challenge would cost him dearly no matter what happened.

It was too much! It was far too much!

Thomas could no longer hold himself in check. He stepped forward and shouted his bitterness. "Is that all you have, Ba'al? This is all the blood you can spill on my son?"

Ba'al showed no indication he'd heard the mockery. Mikil started to offer some advice, but Thomas cut her off.

"Your dragon-god needs to feed his bloodlust with more than just a bucket of blood," he cried. "He drinks from the jugular! He's drunk on the blood of Elyon's faithful. A little dribble from your sick, wounded animals won't do. Is that it?"

The moaning grew louder, joined by the rush of flapping wings overhead. The Shataiki hovered half a mile above them now, an organic river of rotting flesh, silent except for the *whoosh* of their wings.

"The beast requires a pool of blood to fool himself into believing he, too, has a lake, like Elyon's red lakes," Thomas shouted. "Cut yourself, Ba'al. Drain your blood, you betrayer of all that is holy. You half-breed."

At that last word, Ba'al seemed to be pulled out of his trance. He slowly turned his head to look at Thomas, as if trying to decide what to make of the accusation that he'd been one of the Forest Dwellers when the Horde overtook the forests, and, like all half-breeds, had only then become Scab.

He grinned, faced the roiling black bats, and cried to the sky. "Take me home, Marsuuv! Fill me once again with your glory. Take this first-born son as an offering to ease your wrath."

"Louder!" Thomas cried.

"It is written," Ba'al cried. "I am your chosen one, and the books will be yours. By blood you will enter the secret place and reclaim all that was once yours!"

"Louder, you pathetic worm! More blood. Drain yourself!"

Tears were now streaming down Ba'al's face as he screamed his petition to his god and his lover, Teeleh, and this Shataiki named Marsuuv.

"Save me!" The high priest gulped at the night air. His eyes were closed and his body shook from head to foot, like a boy trapped in a dungeon, crying out for mercy. "Save me. Save me, please save me!"

"Dear Elyon," Jamous muttered under his breath. "He's a tortured beast."

For the briefest of moments, Thomas felt pity for the dark priest. If he was a half-breed, then he'd once known the truth and rejected it to become Horde. But if Qurong guessed his high priest was a half-breed, the leader would surely execute him outright. Any possible connection between the priest and his enemy Eram was far too great a risk to be tolerated.

Then again, Qurong was easily deceived by Teeleh. And whatever else Ba'al might be, he was a handmaiden of the beast. Or of Marsuuv, who was likely some queen who supped at Teeleh's bloody table.

The two hundred priests had all cut themselves and deposited their blood on Samuel once. Now they were halfway through the second round. Their swaying had yielded to jerking as they joined Ba'al and cried with greater frenzy. They didn't merely dribble their blood on their sacrifice now; they leaned over his body or leaped onto the altar to express streams of blood from their veins before staggering off in a weakened state.

How long could they keep this up? The cuts merely seeped when the priests weren't wringing their arms over Samuel's body, but it was only a matter of time before they collapsed. For now they lurched on, accompanying Ba'al's flagrant call for salvation.

"He can't hear you!" Thomas screamed.

Ba'al flung his arm toward Thomas and pointed an accusing finger.

"My lord has shown himself through his servants, but there is no sign of your feeble God. The dragon from the sky will devour the child. The tribulation you have suffered all these years, running from the ruler of this world, has now come to an end. You will bow or be consumed!"

The authority with which Ba'al thundered his announcement made Thomas's gut turn. His last reserve of patience melted like ice under a flame. But rather than shout over the cacophony, he chose his words carefully and bit each off so there could be no misunderstanding.

"Elyon shows himself now, to all who have the eyes to see. He lives through me and through the one you seek to kill on your bloody altar. The dragon tried to kill the Creator once, but Elyon lives still, in his servants, free of disease. You've made a mistake, half-breed. You're serving the wrong god."

Ba'al whirled back to his priests. "More! Empty yourselves. Die for your master, you unclean worms. Shed your blood on this son before Teeleh consumes you himself."

Thomas watched with dread as the priests each leaped on the altar a third time, slashing their arms and chests in a frenzy. Blood poured from their wounds, spilled over Samuel, and ran into a three-foot-wide trough at the base.

Samuel lay still, breathing steadily. His hair and his loincloth were both soaked red. If one didn't know better, he would surely assume Samuel's skin had been stripped off his muscles.

Jamous and Mikil had turned away and clung to each other, muttering protests or prayers or both.

But Thomas could not turn from his son. He could only stare through his teary eyes and beg Elyon for mercy.

The first priest to die collapsed while he was still on the altar, trying to bleed on Samuel. Nothing would come; he hadn't practiced enough restraint earlier. Grunting, he milked his left arm with his right hand, but failed to produce more blood.

Ba'al shrieked and swung his sword. The blade severed the man's arm cleanly at his elbow. Blood dribbled out.

The man stared at his arm silently, tried to stand, then toppled sideways, bounced off the corner of the altar, and lay still on the ground.

"Bleed!" Ba'al screamed. "Bleed or I will bleed you all!"

The priests clambered onto the altar and gave their blood to satiate the beast.

Yes, this was his son, but he could no longer stand to watch. The Circle's code demanded that no man, woman, or child who suffered should be left to suffer alone. They would mourn with those who mourned, weep with those who wept, and above all, they would never hide their eyes to protect their own hearts when another suffered pain or death.

Yet this . . . *Elyon, dear Elyon . . .*

Thomas settled to one knee and steadied himself. He no longer had words for Elyon.

Thomas lowered his head. With the first flood of tears, his resolve vanished and he felt himself slumping to the earth. Pain spread from his heart, robbed him of breath. He pulled his knees closer and lay on his side, and he wept.

The priests' wails cut through the night as they stood upon the altar, offering themselves to Teeleh. Then Thomas pressed his face into the dirt and cut himself off from the world.

If he could retreat as he once had, he would. He'd sleep here and wake in another world where he'd changed history. New York. Bangkok. France.

He'd never been able to confirm with certainty that the world of his dreams was real, but it had served him well when all seemed utterly lost here.

But now, dreaming only delivered him into a world filled with imaginations. There was another way, he was sure of it. Another path into history. If he could only leap onto the altar, take up his son, and vanish there now . . .

Thomas stopped himself. He was here in the real world, in Ba'al Bek with the dark priest and two hundred of his pagan worshippers. His son was strapped to an altar, waiting to see if Teeleh would swoop out from the sea of swarming Shataiki and consume him.

This was the world that Thomas of Hunter was in, and it was a world totally beyond his control. He pushed his face against the sand, clenched his watering eyes, and pushed everything but Elyon from his mind.

13

"HOW FAR?" Chelise cried, slapping her horse as they thundered over the canyon's lip. The steed slid down the steep incline, snorting in protest. But their mounts were no strangers to the roughest terrain, and she let it have its head, leaning back so that her shoulders rested on its rear quarters.

The horse took to the air ten paces from the bottom, launching itself parallel to the ground to ease their landing. Marie rode three strides ahead, whipping her mare with a short strap of leather.

The Shataiki had to be blind not to notice the two albinos racing through the canyons that rose to Ba'al Bek, where Thomas was either dead or about to be dead. The black beasts had settled over the plateau like a hovering lid, so close and low that Chelise could see their red, empty eyes.

"How long?" she demanded.

"Have I been here before? Just ride."

Just ride. Straight into the pit. What two lone albinos with nothing but fruit could hope to accomplish against a throng of Shataiki and Throaters was still a mystery to her. But there was zero chance of changing course.

This challenge Thomas had cast was about more than the fracturing Circle. It was about each of them. About her. About her father. Here, in Ba'al Bek, her worlds past and present were converging. Her father must join her and the Circle before it was too late!

If she could accomplish this, her life would be complete.

Every bone in her body betrayed her single-minded focus as she slashed her mare on, ignoring the threat circling above them. Her fingers latched onto the reigns, her muscles strained her toned arms, her neck stretched forward as her hair whipped behind her head. There was no denying her obsession now.

"Chelise—"

"Ride, Marie! Keep your mouth shut and ride."

THE WAILS were fading.

Thomas snapped his eyes wide and stared at the sand, listening.

This was not his mind playing tricks on him; the cries had nearly ceased. Conspicuously absent was Ba'al's cry. Had he given up and retreated into his pain? How long had it been?

Thomas jerked his head up and pushed himself off the dirt. The scene robbed him of breath. Bodies were strewn about the ground, still. Only Ba'al and four priests still stood. The rest had bled to death.

His son lay on his back, facing the Shataiki who still circled, silent except for the rush of wind on their wings. Blood covered the stone altar and filled the trough that ran around its base.

Ba'al stood with both arms elevated, eyes closed, lips moving.

One of the priests sank to his knees beside the altar, held his hand over an open wound on his chest, then fell sideways with a hard crash. Ba'al didn't react. He was waiting for them all to die. This was the price that he believed Teeleh required.

Two more of the priests settled to the earth to die. Then the last sat back on his rump and watched Ba'al.

Thomas stood, surrounded by the two hundred priests who'd died for their dark priest and his demon, Teeleh. An eerie stillness settled over Ba'al Bek. He scanned the lip of the depression. No sign of Elyon, but neither was there any sign that Teeleh had accepted Ba'al's sacrifice.

Qurong and his general were approaching from the southern lip on their mounts as if they, too, understood that a turning point had been reached. Soon it would be Qurong's turn to meet Thomas's demands.

The challenge had come down to this moment. It was Thomas's turn. The hair on his neck bristled. And if Elyon did not show himself?

He faced Ba'al, who was still moving his lips inaudibly. "You've failed," Thomas called in a strong voice.

The dark priest opened his eyes and stared at Samuel's bloody body. The sight of his son lying there . . . Thomas pushed back a wave of nausea.

"You've offered your priests as a blood sacrifice, but your dragon isn't impressed."

Ba'al was still fixated on Samuel. He took three steps, sprang into the air with an agility that surprised Thomas, and straddled Samuel.

"You have lost!" Thomas cried, stepping forward.

Ba'al lifted his right arm to the sky and pressed his clawed blade to his wrist. "Now!" he cried. "Now accept the fullness of what you demand, my lord and savior, Marsuuv." He jerked his blade across his wrist.

Ba'al's blood flowed from the cut, wetting Samuel's belly. He was adding his own blood to his priests'. To what end? This was what this Shataiki queen named Marsuuv demanded?

Ba'al's naked body began to tremble. He gripped the dagger, the tendons of his hand drawn tight like bowstrings. His lips peeled back over clenched teeth, fighting not to cry out.

He leaned his head back, yawned wide at the sky, and let loose a toe-curling scream that started higher than was humanly possible. His cry hung high, then fell through the register, lower, lower, until it was a throaty roar that shook the ground.

The Shataiki above began to shriek.

"It's him!" Mikil gasped. "It's Teeleh! We have to get out!"

"Father!" Samuel cried. "Father?"

"Hold still, Samuel. Hold!"

Ba'al's mouth snapped shut. He lowered his head and looked at Thomas with haunting eyes, one purple, the other blue, possessed. His voice came in a low guttural growl that couldn't possibly be human.

"Hello, Thomasssssss . . . Such a treat to finally make your acquaintance. I've heard so much about you." A wicked grin slowly distorted his mouth. "Welcome to Paradise. It's time for black to come out of its box"—his head jerked spastically once—"and for Samuel to go into his."

This was Teeleh who'd possessed Ba'al? No, not Teeleh, but the queen Ba'al had spoken about. Marsuuv.

"We loathe boys named Samuel," Ba'al said, looking down at the bloody body under him. "I accept this offering."

Samuel looked like he was hyperventilating. His resolve had finally shattered. "Father?"

Ba'al, who was possessed by Marsuuv, slashed so quickly that Thomas hardly knew he was moving before the blade cut through Samuel's chest, through the muscle, through the bone, into the lung chambers.

Samuel's back arched and he cried out. It had taken a moment for the full pain of the sudden cut to reach his mind, but now that it had, his son could not hold back his screams.

Thomas could not move. Through Ba'al, Teeleh had answered the challenge and taken Samuel. This could not be! Elyon would not allow his son to be ravaged and mocked. Samuel . . .

What if Samuel is no longer Elyon's son? What if he betrayed Elyon and is no longer his son?

The world seemed to spin, and Thomas fell to one knee. Beside him, Mikil and Jamous were immobilized.

But where reason failed Thomas, passion raged. "Elyon." It was barely more than a whimper, because his throat was frozen, but Thomas was screaming.

Ba'al threw back his head, straddling his victim, and roared to the sky. "Come! Come and feed!"

"Elyon . . ."

A section of the Shataiki swarm broke from the main flock and dove. Several hundred fell like rocks, the privileged few, shrieking, ravenous vampire bats with bloodlust in their hearts. Thomas watched in horror as the black, mangy beasts slammed into the bleeding bodies of two hundred priests and began clawing open their flesh. They bared their fangs like dogs and tore at the skin, sucking at the exposed blood, too consumed by their feast to pay Thomas any mind.

Ba'al stood above them all, arms spread wide, gloating.

"Elyon!" Thomas shoved himself up, numb.

"Elyon . . . Elyon!" He stepped forward and screamed. Begging, protesting, raging. "Elyon!"

"Elyon is dead," Ba'al snarled, stabbing Thomas with his blue and purple glare. "I killed him."

Surrounded by a thousand Shataiki fighting over the remains of the fallen priests, Thomas considered this possibility for the first time in a decade. What if it were true? What if everything he'd fought to preserve—the Great Romance, the love of Horde, the embrace of peace, the drowning—what if it were all wrong?

Panic battered him as the thoughts glanced off his mind. And there, because of his own stubbornness, lay Samuel. Dead.

Thomas stumbled forward, succumbing to panic. He had to get to his son, to hold him, to take him away before these animals tore at his body.

A dozen Shataiki spun and snarled, blocking his path.

Thomas pulled up, panting. Samuel lay still. Ba'al stood gloating.

He'd lost? He'd lost both the challenge and his son.

He sank to both knees and sat back on his heels, blinded by hopelessness. Sense fell away, like shackles. He clenched his eyes, sobbing. When he screamed out, his heart, not his mind, hurled the words from his mouth.

"Elyon . . . Elyon, do not turn your back on me! Save us." He held his fist in the air and wept at the sky. "Do not allow them to take your son into hell! Save us!"

Thomas was hauling in breath, mind shot, when he noticed that his eyes were red. Or the lids that protected his eyes were red.

He snapped them open, saw the blinding light above, and threw himself back on his seat. As one, the Shataiki recognized the imminent danger. Shrieking, they scattered in every direction, like a flock of black birds reacting to a predator. Those on the ground clawed at the air for purchase, shrieking with each flap of their wings. Those circling above streaked for every horizon.

The light descended from the night sky like a shaft of sunlight, but thick and cloudy and fluorescent green.

Water. Water? This was a shaft of luminescent mist descending from the sky?

An image of a lake filled with Elyon's green water flooded Thomas's mind. Before Teeleh had brought the scabbing disease, when the Gathering had taken place on the shores of a green lake. No words could approximate the intoxication of those beautiful waters.

The color of Elyon, green. It was why all albinos had green eyes. Why the lakes had once been green. Why the forests broke the harsh desert landscape with this beautiful color. The color of life.

Green.

The radiant, green light descended toward the altar. Ba'al cowered with his neck arched back, gawking at the sudden shift in power.

This . . . this was Elyon. Not Elyon himself, not any more than Ba'al was Teeleh, but this was his power. And Thomas could feel the power on his own skin because all of the air in Ba'al Bek was charged by it.

Ba'al whirled and leaped off the altar like a cat. He bounded over the stripped carcasses of his priests toward Qurong, whose horse was rearing. The Throaters who'd circled the high place were having difficulty controlling their mounts. Some of the assassins were racing back to protect Qurong at the south side of the plateau.

Thomas spun back to the watery green light. The shaft settled over the altar and stopped, silent, but the air was heavy and charged. Fingers of light and a shade of darker green curled and twisted inside the shaft.

He heard the soft song of a child, faint, as if it were buried deep in the water. He knew this song. And his need to be in the water again brought a quake to his bones.

The coaxing fingers of light coiled around Samuel and slowly lifted him off the stone surface so that his back arched, and his heels and head draped down. He hung suspended about two feet in the air, surrounded by the translucent green presence, this raw power of Elyon holding his son.

Thomas wanted to run up to the light, which he knew couldn't be anything as simple as water, and push his hand inside. He wanted to feel the power he'd known when Elyon revealed himself to them like this every day.

Samuel's arms jerked and his chest expanded. He was alive.

"I always did like you, Thomas," a voice whispered. In his head or aloud so they could all hear, he couldn't tell. "You make my head spin."

The words of approval echoed through his mind.

"The end is near, much sooner than you've guessed. Find your way back. Take the diseased one with you. Use the books that were lost." The voice paused. "Here is your son." Samuel's body was released by the tendrils in the green light and landed on the stone surface with a dull thump. "Let him have his heart."

And then the green shaft withdrew to the night sky, slowly at first, then faster. It pulled up in a slight arc to the west, then vanished in a blink. After hours of chanting and ringing bells under a rushing wind caused by so much rotting Shataiki flesh, the night was pristine and quiet.

Then Samuel's bloody body sat upright and sucked in a lungful of air.

A gasp rippled through the Throaters, who remained to guard Qurong and Ba'al, stunned by the sudden reversal of fortunes.

Thomas lifted his arm and lined his finger up with Qurong. "You, father of my bride, tell us all what has happened here!"

QURONG SAT on his steed, unable to respond to the infidel's command. He was to explain what had just happened? He was supposed to interpret these signs from the heavens and suggest the next course of action? Was he a priest? Had he ever pretended to know the ways of Teeleh or Elyon or these cursed creatures of the night?

No. He was a simple man who knew two things only: One, that the ways of the gods were trickery, always trickery, so that no man could truly know the ways of the gods. And two, that although no man could know the ways of the gods, they all could and did understand another way.

The way of the sword.

Where was his wife when he needed her? She was better versed in these never-ending deceptions, not because she herself employed them, but because he didn't, preferring a straight up-and-down fight over clever talk and deception. He'd been down that road and was still paying the price.

"My lord, you must—"

"Quiet, priest." He raised the back of his hand to Ba'al. "You've failed."

"No." The man trembled. "My master has delivered Thomas to you. I heard his voice. He spoke to my belly. You have to take him."

"Leave me! And for the love of all gods, put some clothes on."

"My lord, I cannot express the price we will pay if—"

"Leave!"

Ba'al jettisoned a stream of black spittle, glared at the infidel Thomas, and spun away from the altar. One of the twenty-four priests who hadn't bled themselves approached him and threw a purple cloak over his skinny body. Ba'al was dismissed.

But what he said wasn't lost. Qurong had seen enough in the last few minutes alone to know that the powers behind both Ba'al and Thomas were not only real, but life-threatening.

More to the point, the power behind Ba'al was life-threatening. The other, the green magic, however impressive and disturbing, didn't strike him as . . . fatal.

Qurong walked his horse closer to Thomas and the boy, who'd crawled off the altar, stripped the robes off a dead priest, and was joining the other albinos. To think that Thomas was the husband of the daughter he'd once held precious . . . there was no end to injustice in this cursed world.

He pulled up, ten yards from the man. The mighty Thomas of Hunter, leader of all albinos, poisoned by the red pools, enemy of Teeleh. He didn't look so threatening without a sword. No battle dress. The tunic he wore was made of tanned leather, perhaps sewn by Chelise's own hand. His brown hair was tossed by a long ride. What had happened to cause Thomas to issue such a challenge? Was he losing control over the Circle?

His son hadn't appeared too eager to submit.

"Our agreement was clear," Thomas said. "And now the outcome is as clear. Your daughter awaits."

Qurong didn't turn the tables yet. "You want me to go with you and drown?"

"That was our agreement."

"So what is that like? Sucking in water and dying?"

"Do I look dead to you? It's life, not death."

"Because you don't drown, and you don't come back to life. The red poison strips your skin bare and clouds your minds. So you have a few thousand followers who are gullible enough to believe they've somehow drowned and been brought back to life. Well, I can imagine offering that kind of immortality would make you a bit of a legend. Religious nonsense."

"Thomas . . ." It was the albino woman warning him. But Thomas didn't seem interested.

"You will soon know, won't you?" Thomas said.

"Yes. Yes, of course, that was the agreement."

"Do you doubt that Elyon has brought my son back to life here on your altar?"

"Is that what you saw?" Qurong glanced at the carnage. "Clearly there are powers at work here that none of us understand. But I saw more. Much more."

"You saw the life-giving power of Elyon scatter a hundred thousand Shataiki and embrace my son with new life."

"I saw the power of Teeleh. And I see that two hundred of his servants have been slain. Now that you've killed two hundred priests, if I were to take you into captivity, you would no longer be seen as a martyr."

"Father . . ." Now it was Samuel who warned.

"Your daughter cries for you every day," Thomas said quietly, unfazed by Qurong's direct threat. "I've never seen a daughter love a father the way she loves you."

The words cut like a dagger, and for a moment Qurong lost his bearings. Then rage flooded his heart.

"I have no daughter."

"Go!"

The woman and the albino next to her had issued the command together, unexpectedly, as if the word were an arranged signal. Thomas whirled and sprinted just behind Samuel and the others, picking their way over dead bones, directly for the horses. The speed with which albinos could move never ceased to amaze him.

"Stop them!"

"You saw the power of the one we serve," the woman cried, leaping to one of the four albino horses they'd tethered to a stake.

Even Cassak hesitated. The albinos were already leaning over the necks of their mounts, whipping the animals' rumps, hair flowing behind as they galloped toward the far ring of boulders. It had been years since Qurong had engaged albino warriors in the open, and watching them flee brought the reason into clear focus. They could move at two, maybe three times the speed of his Throaters. His men could match them in strength, but this swift movement was a skill that made him cringe. A beautiful thing.

He thundered at his general. "After them, you fool!"

The man seemed to snap out of a trance. "Close the gap. After them!"

"I want them back, dead or alive," Qurong shouted. "Either you or Thomas, Cassak! I didn't come all this way to watch magicians play tricks!"

"Understood, sir." Then to the warriors behind them: "Markus, Ceril, drop behind and cut off the Mirrado Pass west. Keep to the high ground. If they escape, Ba'al will have your head."

The albinos reached the boulders a good twenty paces before the closest Throaters did, and they flew past the perimeter at twice the assassins' speed. They rose to the depression's lip and vanished into the dark horizon.

Qurong swore and spun his horse back. His personal guard, a dozen strong, waited in a line. Ba'al had already fled the high place, leaving the vultures or the Shataiki, whichever dared return sooner, to feed on the remains of the two hundred bodies. The high priest would rage like a wounded tiger and become more dangerous than he was before.

But it wasn't fear of Ba'al that pounded through Qurong's head as he galloped south to Qurongi City. Nor was it the desire to seize Thomas and lock him in a deep hole until he died of starvation. Nor was it the half-breed Eramites who undoubtedly plotted his overthrow even now.

All of these problems spoke to him, pulling for attention. But none shouted so loudly as the seven words spoken by Thomas before he'd fled.

Your daughter cries for you every day.

14

KARA HUNTER hurried down the hall, hot, not because Bangkok was a humid city regardless of the time of year, but because a bomb had just exploded in her chest.

Blood. More to the point, Thomas's blood.

Why did life always come down to blood? The blood of a sacrificial lamb to atone for sin. The blood of Christ to drink in remembrance. The blood of the innocent to feed the bloodlust of creatures in the night. The Raison Strain, plundering its host through the bloodstream.

Blood had taken her brother, Thomas, into a reality that changed everything. She knew because she had followed him, using that same blood, and what she found took her breath away.

When it was all over and the world set about the business of picking up the pieces, she and Monique had hidden away one vial of that precious blood. Just one vial, ten ccs to be exact. All for understandable, even noble, reasons. They'd planned on every conceivable threat.

But they'd never factored in a maniacal redhead named Billy who could read minds. Worse, they'd never imagined that Janae, Monique's own daughter, would willingly throw herself into a pit of vipers with this stranger from Paradise, Colorado.

What could she possibly have been thinking?

Kara flashed her ID badge at the white-suited security guard, who used his own pass card to open the heavy steel door into the secure lab. The hall ended at a second door, also under guard.

"'Morning, Miss Hunter. She wants you to suit up."

Kara wanted to object. Raison Strain B could only be contracted through direct contact. Instead, she nodded and stepped through the glass side door into a room equipped with white biohazard suits and a chemical-mist shower. She shrugged into the suit and slipped on black gloves, but didn't bother with the head gear or with sealing the suit. A barrier against accidental contact was wise, but going in like a polar bear didn't make any sense.

She stepped though a narrow passage and walked through a second glass door that slid open with a loud buzz. Seven lab techs were at work, three at their stations, four standing with folded arms, deep in discussion that hushed as Kara crossed the room.

Monique stood outside the quarantine room, hands on hips, suited like Kara, staring at the gurneys inside through one of the glass panels. Kara saw the reclining forms, dressed in street clothes rather than in typical lab attire. Janae in a short black dress, par for the course. Billy wore what he'd waltzed into their world wearing: jeans and a T-shirt.

The egotistical little snot-nose.

"How long ago?" she demanded, stopping beside Monique.

Other than Thomas, Monique had been more complicit in the creation of the first virus than any other living person. She sighed. "Based on the culture we're looking at"—she nodded at the clean room opposite this one—"I'd estimate eight hours ago."

"So we have time."

"Some. Not much. She shot them each with a full cc."

"What? Has she lost her marbles?"

Monique just looked at her, deadpan.

"Dumb question, sorry."

"Is it?" Monique said, looking back at her daughter lying parallel to Billy Rediger. They lay on their backs, hands folded over their chests, which rose and fell together. Lost to this world.

"Thing is, I don't think Janae *has* lost her mind," Monique said. "She knew exactly what she was doing." She clenched her jaw, closed her eyes, then opened them again, still deadpan. This was Monique expressing contempt for herself. "I can't believe we allowed this to happen."

"We didn't. She did."

"I should have known the moment that punk entered our compound that he was bad news."

"You did."

"I should have known he was the devil himself, able to bring to life the worst in Janae."

She was referring to the nonsense about Janae having bad blood from her father. Monique had never opened up about her affair with the man who'd fathered Janae and then vanished, but whenever Janae did something irrational or particularly unhanded, Monique blamed it on her father's side. Bad blood.

"She knew what she was doing all right," Monique said, jaw bunching again. "At this rate they'll both be dead within twenty-four hours. Maybe sooner."

Kara felt like she should object, turn to her friend and express her horror at such a prospect. Demand they use the blood immediately.

Instead, she felt only confusion, so she said nothing.

Monique came to her rescue. "They took a strong sedative to ensure that they would be asleep the moment Thomas's blood made contact with theirs. She knew that I wouldn't be able to resist."

What was Monique saying? That she would use the blood?

"And why should she assume anything different? Have I ever not showed her all of my love? She's the only one I have now. She means everything to me."

Tears settled in Monique's eyes. Kara wanted to put her hand on Monique's shoulder, but she was still torn by the conflicting emotions that hammered her own mind.

"There's no guarantee that the blood will work," Kara said.

"No."

"What are the risks?"

"The same as they were the last time a gateway was opened to the other world," Monique said.

Speaking of it so stoically in the face of such a tragedy required a measure of self-possession, Kara thought. The world had barely survived the last such crossing.

"Or worse," Kara said. "That was Thomas. This is a crazed psychic named Billy." *And Janae*, she thought but did not say.

Monique nodded slowly, keeping her eyes on her daughter. "Billy and Janae. They could do a lot of damage in either reality."

"If they did make it to the other world and back . . . only God knows what magic they could bring back to upset the balance of powers. They could destroy a world."

"They can't possibly be trusted."

"No."

Simple. But not so simple at all. This was Monique's daughter on the table, slowly drawing breath.

"She knew exactly what she was doing!" Monique whispered, barely able to control herself. "Maybe we should have discussed it with her. She's doing this out of bitterness." She wiped a tear that had spilled over her lower lid.

"You know we couldn't risk her knowing that we had the blood. She might have tried something like this a long time ago."

"Not if we didn't tell her where it was hidden. Indonesia's a long way from here."

"Monique." Kara did put her hand on her friend's shoulder now. "You can't blame yourself. Janae is a grown woman who decides for herself. Thousands, millions of lives could be at stake. Sometimes . . . the risk has to be weighed."

Monique glared at her. "Please, Kara, I don't need a lecture."

She felt horrible. What if it were Thomas on that gurney? What would Kara say then? *Let him die, let the fool die.* But she'd already crossed that road once. They both knew that the moment Janae had injected herself with the virus, she'd signed her own death certificate.

At sixty years of age, Kara could live with that. She'd seen so many come and go in this life. And she'd spent some time in that other world.

"Do you think it would work?" Monique asked, staring at her daughter's calm form.

"It didn't work in the test—"

"We didn't inject his blood into a living body," Monique interrupted. "We couldn't risk the possibility of the subject crossing over. I'm talking about crossing over, not killing the virus."

"Would a person whose blood comes in contact with Thomas's blood wake up in the other place?"

"Surely you still wonder what it would be like to go again." Monique spoke as if lost. "What Thomas is doing. If he's even alive. The Horde . . . the lakes . . . what's become of everyone?"

"How old is he? Is he married? Children? Everything was happening very quickly over there," Kara said. "Maybe it's all over. I think about it every day."

Monique nodded and wiped another tear, then turned away. "We'll never know."

Which was as good as stating that she wasn't going to use the blood on Janae. It was the right decision, of course. Janae and Billy were only two lives. Opening a way into the other reality could be disastrous. And they'd done this to themselves. She pitied Billy, felt sick that Janae, who in so many ways reminded Kara of herself thirty years earlier, had taken her life like this. She'd liked the girl very much. Such a spirited woman, so beautiful, so intelligent. Such a waste.

However difficult, this was the best way.

"Do you think letting them die is murder?" Monique asked.

15

THE HORSES clawed up the incline at dawn, struggling for breath after the brutal ride through hidden canyonland that rose to the Ba'al Bek plateau. Marie had let Chelise lead but pulled alongside as they approached the huge rim.

Chelise was out of breath, not from riding, but from her own state of unrelenting anxiety. They were too late. Every fiber in her being warned that they'd come too late.

They'd plunged into a deep canyon an hour earlier and lost sight of the Shataiki mass that winged over the plateau like a cloud of giant locusts. When they emerged, the sky was empty of all but stars.

Which could only mean that the reason for their coming was also gone.

But that didn't mean Thomas was gone. He might still be there, clinging to life, waiting for her to rescue him from certain death, the way he'd rescued her once. Or maybe the challenge hadn't started yet. The Shataiki could have been drawn by Thomas's presence on their sacred ground. He could be seated with the others around a campfire, biding his time while Qurong considered his challenge. A dozen scenarios could explain what they'd seen on their approach.

"Careful, Chelise," Marie breathed. "They might see us if we stumble over the top."

She was right, but Chelise didn't let the horse slow until she was nearly over the rim.

The sight that greeted her nearly stopped her heart. Marie was whispering harshly, throwing herself and her horse to the ground, but Chelise couldn't do the same.

The depression was at least half a mile across, sinking twenty or thirty feet to dusty earth. A large ring of boulders circled the center, where a rectangular cube of stone stood in the graying dawn.

An altar. Wet with fresh blood.

But it was the bodies that struck terror into Chelise's chest. Hundreds of dead bodies strewn about the altar. The putrid stench of the scabbing disease washed over her, crowding her taxed lungs.

No sign of Thomas. Nor of Samuel. Nor of her father.

"Down! For the love of Elyon—"

"They're gone," Chelise said. Then again, as if to convince herself, "They're gone. We're too late."

"It could be a trap. There could be Throaters down there."

"No." Few knew the Horde's ways like she did. None knew Qurong's ways as well as Chelise. "No, Marie. No, but I see something more disturbing."

She slapped her mare and rode the beast down the slope, into the depression, picking up speed as she approached the ring of boulders. Marie followed far to the rear. Only when she passed the long stones that reached for the sky did Chelise let the horse slow.

Here the smell was almost too much, a thick fog of invisible scabbing disease that covered her face like a muzzle. She held her breath and pushed on, scanning the scene for any trace of evidence that might give her hope.

The dark priest, Ba'al, dead. Charred stones or burned corpses, anything.

But no sign indicated that Elyon had had his way with these priests, and none of the bodies looked to be dressed in purple, the color that Ba'al would likely be wearing.

And no sign of Thomas or Samuel.

"Elyon have mercy on their souls," Marie said, pulling her horse into a walk beside her. "They look like they've been through a meat grinder."

Chelise stopped her horse five feet from a corpse and studied the carnage. "Suicide," she said.

"They did this to themselves?"

"They cut their wrists and bled to appease Teeleh."

"Their bodies are torn apart!"

"By Shataiki. You can see the claw marks on the flesh."

Where are you, Thomas?

Chelise sat on the horse, struggling to remain calm in the face of her failure to reach them in time. She lifted her eyes to the far rim.

What have you done, Father?

"Then I would say this is a good sign," Marie said.

"Good? The only thing good about this is that we don't know for certain that my lover is dead. Nothing else is good."

"This is my father we're talking about," Marie snapped. "If he's not here, then he's alive! And if he's alive, then he's doing what he thinks is right."

"I don't need you to tell me that he's safe. The man he's up against is *my* father, and you know nothing about him. Qurong may not be the craftiest fox in the forest, but he's as stubborn as a bull and he follows his heart. I can promise you his heart despises my husband."

Marie stared at the bloody altar. "Then why don't you enlighten me? What happened here? Where is my father? And what do we do now?"

"A challenge happened here. Qurong agreed to Thomas's terms, and Ba'al, that snake of his, brought two hundred priests as a gift for Teeleh. The Shataiki came, and Ba'al no doubt went mad for the beast. He either won the challenge and took Thomas with him, back to Qurongi, or . . ."

"Or he failed, and your father took my father anyway, as you predicted. Or Father won and fled when Qurong refused to keep his end."

"Thomas would never kill Horde."

"Did I say *kill?*"

"If my father planned to betray Thomas, he would have set a trap," Chelise said. "Without the use of weapons, not even Thomas would be able to escape."

"Unless there was a distraction."

"Such as?"

"Such as Elyon."

"Do you see any sign that Elyon was here?"

"What do we know about what evidence Elyon leaves behind?"

Either way, Thomas was gone. Qurong was gone. Chelise wasn't eager to debate the comings and goings of Elyon.

She grunted and nudged her horse forward, dug her heels into its flank when it resisted her. She drove the mare over the bodies, slapping its rear hard to urge it closer to the altar. She became sick at the sight of so much blood, enough to feed a thousand of the beasts for a month. The trough around the base was full and overflowing.

At this very moment, Thomas could be in a spirited debate with Qurong, in chains headed for his dungeons. The thought was enough to fray her nerves. Not only was the man she loved more than her own life in terrible danger, but he was in the hands of Qurong, the only other grown man she would move heaven and earth to save.

"Thomas is with my father," she announced. "And I belong with them. He needs me."

"Who does, Thomas or Qurong?"

"Both. Johan should look for me in the dungeons if I don't return in three days."

"What are you talking about? We can't go to Qurongi under these circumstances."

"We're not going. I am. You're going back to the Gathering."

"No. No, that is not acceptable! If you insist on going, I'm coming with you. This whole mission was my idea!"

"They need to know, Marie. The three thousand are gathered, waiting since Thomas dropped this hot coal in their laps. The rest are on the way."

"Going in alone is suicide."

"I know the Horde, child. You're a half-breed who drowned before she knew what it felt like to be Horde. If anyone can get into Qurongi, I can."

"You haven't been with them for ten years."

"Don't argue with me! Turn your horse around and head back before the Shataiki decide to come back for the rotting flesh!"

They glared at each other for a full ten seconds before Marie broke her line of sight, but her face was still red. The thought of the long trek home alone was no doubt a factor.

"I have to do this, Marie." Chelise was surprised to feel the strength of the knot that rose in her throat. How could she put this delicately? "Jake. He's so young, so innocent . . ." Her eyes watered and she looked away. "Promise me."

Marie didn't answer immediately, and when she did, her voice was calm. "Don't worry about Jake. He's my brother, isn't he? If anything happens, I'll take care of him as if he were my own son."

"Thank you."

Chelise jerked her horse around and struck its flank with such force that it bolted away from the altar, over the dead carcasses. Headed south.

Headed directly toward Qurongi City.

16

THEY'D LOST the Throaters in the canyons to the north of Ba'al Bek, but not easily. This general, Cassak, seemed particularly adept at anticipating their moves. The Circle had always enjoyed the advantage of speed in the Horde's constant game of seek-and-destroy. This edge was somewhat mitigated by the Horde's dogged persistence and overwhelming size. Still, the Circle survived. But this general had eerily strong instincts.

Much like Ba'al, who had demonstrated an uncanny familiarity with parts of their legends. The horror Thomas felt at seeing his son on the altar had been replaced by curiosity about the dark priest's prayer to Teeleh. His words about the books demanded more explanation.

They pounded through the sand, twisted through canyons, and urged their horses up steep inclines only to plunge down a cliff fifty yards farther, mindless of where they were going except to safety, away from the two dozen armed warriors who gave pursuit.

Still, the sound of hammering hooves followed them.

Still, the cries of Ba'al echoed through Thomas's mind.

Then Samuel pulled his stallion to a standstill at the intersection of two large ravines, each cluttered with boulders the size of horses. He held his hand up to stop them all.

"What?" Mikil demanded. "Which way?"

He motioned silence with his finger and listened to the faint sounds of hooves. Scabbing disease stench clung to the dried blood that still covered Samuel's hair, face, and body. The cloak he'd borrowed from a fallen Horde priest, along with the Scab sword he'd snatched from another, made him look Horde. Thomas preferred him half-naked and unarmed to this.

Ba'al's cry whispered through his mind again. *Send me back to the other world where you sent the chosen one through the lost books . . .*

What could this possibly mean? Surely not back to the other world, as in back to the histories. How would Ba'al know of the other world?

The lost books must be the ones spoken about in legend. Could they be real? The mere thought that there was still a way back to the histories was enough to make Thomas's blood run cold. Dreaming had long ago failed to take him anywhere but to a fantasy.

"They're splitting," Samuel said, lowering his hand. "Cutting us off to the west where the canyon opens to the desert. That would be our way back."

"North would take us into Eramite country," Mikil said, eyeing the long canyon to their right.

"And the Horde fear the Eramites."

Thomas followed his son's gaze. "Then north. You know this land?"

Samuel turned his horse without responding and spurred it into the long canyon. He hadn't looked Thomas in the eyes once since he'd crawled off the altar. Thomas slapped his horse and followed with the others.

Samuel led them for fifteen minutes at a steady run before cutting right into a small ravine, climbing to the crest of a plateau, and stopping to listen again.

"We've lost them," Mikil announced.

Samuel jerked his horse around in a tight circle. "For now. They know we will head west—there are only two routes through the canyons west."

"So, they'll lie and wait."

Samuel shrugged. "This is Cassak, not just any Scab. Not since Martyn or Woref has there been a full-breed as crafty as this general."

"Martyn was a half-breed," Thomas corrected. Not that it mattered.

"Was he?" Samuel stared north. For the first time he turned his eyes on his father, and the look chilled Thomas. "And what would that make me?"

"My son," Thomas said. "Purebred albino."

"I don't think so. I don't think we even know how this so-called scabbing disease works. Do you?"

"Now isn't the time to discuss doctrine."

"No? This from a man who just put his son's head on the chopping block to prove his doctrine."

Thomas wanted to lash out at the boy, but he stayed in control of his words. "Samuel, I know what just happened doesn't make sense to you now, but it will, and when it does, your life will never be the same."

"You almost had me killed back there!"

"Elyon *saved* you back there!" So much for calm. "You have the audacity to sit here and challenge me after the one you doubt breathed new life into you?"

"I only know what I know, Father, and that isn't much. I'm sick of all this guessing. Elyon did this, Elyon did that. Everything good is credited to this unseen God of yours, and everything remotely evil is blamed on Teeleh."

"You didn't see the Shataiki? You didn't watch two hundred priests pour their blood on you in worship of that devil? You didn't feel the green light lift you from the altar? What was that, my imagination?"

"Of course I saw something. But I no more understand it than you do. So Shataiki exist; did anyone say they didn't? So there is power in the heavens to affect us all; does that mean we understand it? If it was so plain, then why put your son on an altar to prove your point?" His accusations cut deeply, in part because they carried so much truth. "If the truth is so obvious, wouldn't the whole world easily see it?"

"Seal that loose mouth, boy!" Mikil snapped.

Thomas held up his hand. "Let him speak. He's owed at least that much."

Samuel walked his horse closer to Thomas, glaring. "That's right,

Father. After you refused to lift a hand to save me from their blades, the least you can do is let me say my piece. Well, I will."

"This is not—"

"Mikil! He's right."

"Sir—"

"Speak, boy. Tell us all how little we know."

Samuel hardly needed Thomas's encouragement. "I'm not the one challenging you, Father. This Circle of yours is falling apart, not on account of me or the Horde. It's splitting apart inside. The rumors and speculations have spawned a dozen different groups that claim to know the full truth, and you don't even know what the truth is, isn't that right?"

Yes, it was right.

Samuel thrust a finger into the air for emphasis. "Some say Elyon will arrive in the clouds before a time of great suffering." He snapped a second finger into the air. "Others say he will only come after the time of great suffering." Another finger. "Still others say in the middle. Some say Elyon doesn't show his face the way he once did because the time of the supernatural is past. Others say he refuses to show himself to cold hearts."

The splintering had been growing over the past several years, but not until now had it alarmed Thomas, thanks to Samuel and his severed Horde head.

Samuel dispensed with the finger counting and threw his arm wide in exasperation. "Then there are those who claim to have *seen* Elyon. Behind every bush, it would seem. But they call him out into the open and he never shows. Never. They're a fanciful lot lost in delusional hope."

"And what of you, Samuel? Where is your hope?"

Samuel plowed on. "Do you even know where the disease comes from, Father? Do you know how the red waters work? How do you know they're anything more than plain old disease and natural medicinal water?"

The questions bordered on blasphemy, but they were at the very core of Samuel's struggle for meaning. Had Thomas known . . .

But the past was gone. The fact was, Samuel wasn't simply confused about which doctrinal path to take when it came to the Horde; he had lost his way entirely.

"Are you done?" Thomas asked.

"Not even close. But I won't waste my breath. You don't have the answers."

"The disease comes from Teeleh. His worms, evil incarnate, like a virus, infiltrate the skin and muscle and mind, making one stupid to the truth."

"That's your version."

"But Teeleh despises Elyon's waters," Thomas continued. "They kept his disease away when we bathed every day. The virus of Teeleh was killed by the waters. And when the Horde drowned Elyon, those waters turned red. Now we drown as Elyon drowned, and our flesh becomes new, resistant to Teeleh's virus, so that we don't have to bathe every day as we once did. Is this too much for your mind to hold?"

"I don't know, Father. Maybe my mind's full of worms. Like the half-breeds."

He snorted through his nostrils and stilled his stamping horse.

"What I do know is that I can no longer follow a man who feels justified in putting his own son on the block for the sake of his Circle."

"And yet Elyon did the same."

"Then Elyon should go back into the sky where he belongs!"

"Stop it!" Jamous glared at them. "Both of you. We're in enemy territory. The Horde is out there. And Eram. For all we know, our enemy is watching us at this very moment."

"Enemy to whom?" Samuel said, drilling Thomas with a hard stare. "It seems that my own people think of me as their enemy. The half-breeds would welcome a warrior like me."

"Don't be ridiculous," Thomas said. "Your ego is bruised, but I will raise you up as a hero when we return. The Circle will embrace you like a long-lost son."

But Samuel was already stripping off the priest's robes. "For how long? Until I dare speak the truth again?" He cast them aside, then turned his horse away.

"You can't be serious," Mikil challenged. "What fool albino would join the Eramites?"

Samuel twisted back in his saddle. "The fool albino who knows that all half-breeds were once albinos, Forest Guard, despised by the Horde as much as you are. The son of Thomas Hunter will join the Forest Guard once again."

Thomas was so taken aback by what his son was suggesting that words failed him. Elyon had just saved the boy, and now Samuel, covered in Horde blood, would turn his back on the Circle and join forces with Eram? Samuel had thought this through. A naked man would be less threatening to the Eramites than one dressed like a Horde priest.

He must have planned this. He and his band. They were waiting for him.

"Samuel! They wait for you?"

Without turning, his son kicked his horse into a full run, plunged into the canyon they'd just climbed out of, and galloped north, toward the land of the Eramites.

Mikil and Jamous seemed as much at a loss as Thomas. This . . . this had to be a show. Elyon's green waters had just saved the boy, for the love of Elyon! He was toying with them to make a point.

No, Thomas. You've seen this coming.

No, not this. Rebellion, yes. A strong spirit like his own father's, predisposed to stumble into danger, yes. But to betray his own blood? Never!

"He means it," Mikil said.

And Thomas knew that she was right. He sat on his horse and stared at the empty horizon, trying to disbelieve. His son was gone.

For a few moments his mind spun around empty thoughts. Had he been alone he might have fallen from his horse and wept into the sand. But the Horde was in pursuit and the Circle waited and . . .

Thomas released his reins, closed his eyes, and struggled to breathe calmly. What was happening? He'd faced his son's death through the night, and they'd survived only to face this?

"He's bluffing," Mikil said, reversing her earlier position.

She was only saying it to give him hope, and she was failing miserably.

Samuel was right; everything was falling apart. The end was coming. Ba'al knew something that they did not. He'd called the Shataiki out of hiding and fed their lust with more than just his own blood.

Send me back to the other world where you sent the chosen one through the lost books . . .

Thomas opened his eyes. What did Ba'al know about this other world?

The chosen one. Could the rumors of the seven original Books of History be true? Had they truly been lost? Was there a way to the other world through those books? And what if Ba'al or Qurong possessed the books at this very moment?

"Whatever you're thinking, I'm not sure I like it," Mikil said. "I've seen that look before."

"I've lost my son to the half-breeds. Do you expect me to laugh?"

"I wasn't talking about anger or sorrow."

No one but Chelise could read him like Mikil. They'd been through the gates of hell together.

"Then what?" Thomas demanded.

"That far-off look," Mikil said.

Thomas looked away and tried to think through any reasonable course of action. None came to mind.

"I'm at a loss," he said. "I feel like I've been battering my head against a stone wall."

"Then you might want to try something else," Jamous said.

"In the past . . ." He let the thought trail off, baiting Mikil.

She took it. "Please, not that again."

"You have a better idea? All I'm saying is that when I came to the utter end of myself then, the answer always waited for me."

"In your dreams," Mikil said.

"Something like that."

"But your dreams no longer work. Not like that."

Jamous exhaled. "Shouldn't we be plotting a course to safety?"

Thomas ignored him. Mikil knew far more about Thomas's dreams than Jamous did. She'd met one of the women from his dreams once. Monique. Monique de Raison of the Raison Strain. Dear Elyon, to even think about those days when he could travel back and forth with the ease of sleep . . . it felt scandalous now. Perfectly absurd.

Send me back to the other world . . . Thomas's pulse rode a steady pace.

"That doesn't mean the other world doesn't exist. Or that I'm not uniquely chosen to bridge the gap."

Mikil stared at him with wide green eyes. But she didn't protest. And she would protest if she wasn't at least considering the idea.

"Now *you're* the chosen one?" she asked.

Thomas shrugged. "My son was right about one thing: there's much we don't understand."

He looked north. Samuel was gone. He'd left with rage in his heart and bitterness on his tongue. There was no way to undo that here. The answers he sought lay elsewhere. Perhaps in the histories.

The urge to recover this last decade, during which he hadn't found a way to return to the other world even once, ballooned in Thomas's mind. He faced Mikil.

"You can't deny it, Mikil. Monique came to you. You know the other world is real."

No response.

"If there was a way back . . ."

"Don't do this."

"Do I have a choice?"

"There *is* no way back. And yes, unless you've stopped breathing, you always have a choice."

"I think there could be a way. And I think I have an obligation to find out if there is a way."

"This is madness."

"It's who I am!" he insisted. "This is my path." Thomas pointed to the south. "You saw Ba'al! He's in touch with the dark world. He'll ride this dragon's back and devour Elyon's bride. This is only the beginning."

"Then the Circle needs you."

"And you saw the look in Qurong's eyes. Ba'al is his enemy as much as Eram is. I'm telling you, Mikil, the world is headed for a showdown unlike any we've seen."

"We've always known that."

"But it's *now*!" His horse shifted at the sound of his cry.

"We're not alone," Jamous said, scanning the cliffs. "Check your passions."

Thomas took a breath. "Tell me I have no business doing this."

Mikil kept her silence.

Jamous turned back, confused. "What exactly are you talking about doing? Going to another world?"

Mikil kept her eyes on Thomas. "Going to Qurongi City," she said.

"You can't be serious."

Thomas regarded Mikil steadily. "Then you heard Ba'al as well."

"Of course I heard." Mikil set her jaw and looked south, toward the Horde stronghold. "So Ba'al knows a thing or two. What are we to do, rush into his temple and demand he share what he knows?"

"Not we," Thomas said. "Me."

She scowled. "Over my dead body."

"No, over my dead body. I'm dead already. My son's left me. I lead a people who are falling apart after a decade of running and dying. Qurong may have a hard heart, but his enemies are pressing in, and if Samuel joins the half-breeds, his problems are about to get worse. Qurong is desperate for an ally."

"The Circle? Albinos may never slaughter Horde again, but we can never be the ally of the one who hunts us!"

"No, not the Circle. Me. I will make Qurong my ally."

"And die."

Thomas nodded. "Or die trying."

17

THE GREAT library ran off the main atrium, just down the hall from Monique de Raison's office at Raison Pharmaceutical. It contained more than ten thousand volumes, nearly half of which were collector's editions of old books, each worth a small fortune as books go. They lined mahogany bookcases that rose to the twelve-foot ceilings. The room's temperature and humidity were controlled by twenty-four digital thermostats, one at each case. The whole room could be counted as the world's largest humidor.

Kara often came here with Monique, mostly to reflect on the unique connection they shared. Thirty-five years ago, just after the incident, Monique had commissioned two identical green journals embossed with the same title: *My Book of History*. They'd both written of their experiences, recalling even the minute details, then compared their writings late into the evening, expanding and embellishing as they saw fit, perhaps hoping that these diaries, like the blank Books of History from the other reality, would magically transform their own reality.

Normally the journals were in a safe behind a painting of the Capitol building in Washington, D.C. The painting was significant because, for one, it was a fairly innocuous painting of little value, unlikely to be removed by any thief, and for another, much of Thomas's past was linked to that building.

It had all started thirty-six years ago in Denver, Colorado, when Thomas had claimed that he lived in a different reality, in the future, and that this one was a figment of his dreams. He was asleep, dreaming of history in the other, real reality.

None of Kara's world was real, he said.

She'd quickly convinced him that this was real. They had both grown up as army brats in the Philippines and spoke Tagalog to prove it. Their father, a chaplain, had left their mother for a Filipino woman half her age after twenty years of marriage.

Kara had thrown herself into higher education and studied to become a nurse, which she did successfully. Thomas hadn't fared quite so well. He left the Philippines a well-known and respected street fighter with a wicked scoring foot on the soccer field, and landed in New York as a lost soul who didn't quite fit. When his life finally came apart, he fled New York, moved in with Kara in Denver, and took a job at the Java Hut while he put things back together.

The dreaming had started then, late one night in Denver, with a single silenced bullet out of nowhere. Loan sharks from New York were chasing him, he claimed. But soon after Thomas left her for the final time, Kara had sought out said loan sharks, eager to avoid any lingering bad blood, only to discover that they weren't the ones in the alley that night.

The identity of the men who had been chasing Thomas thirty-six years earlier remained a mystery to this day.

As for his dreams, well, that was the question, wasn't it? Just how real were those dreams of his? At one time she'd been sure they were real. But three decades later, it all seemed a bit fuzzy.

Real or not, Thomas's dreams of another world had forever altered Kara's life. Monique's as well, but on many levels Monique was still the same bioengineer she'd been when Thomas first met her.

Kara, on the other hand, had found living in the United States nearly impossible. She had been inexorably drawn back to Southeast Asia. Back to the land and people who'd birthed her.

Back to Thomas's own history.

She'd never married as Monique had, fearful that any relationship might suffer the same fate as Monique's, a passionate and all-consuming but short-lived flame. A rocket rather than a candle.

Kara was no Mother Teresa, but she'd given the last three decades of her life to serving the young, broken girls of Bangkok's sex industry.

And she'd dreamed. Dreamed of what it would be like to dream with Thomas's blood once again. Of what it would be like to vanish from this world and wake in another, if only until she fell asleep again.

But it wasn't that simple. Greatness was never that simple.

Monique had asked Kara to join her here while she decided what to do about Janae. She stood and crossed to the towering bookcase that housed part of the collection from Turkey, in which the scholar David Abraham had first discovered the Books of History. Of course, Monique had never been able to secure even a single volume of the books, and the other titles on the shelf, however valuable and ancient, couldn't remotely compare.

Her gaunt face betrayed the anguish that had flogged her for the last eight hours. She tried to interest herself in the books but, unable to do so, returned to her seat where she settled and crossed her legs.

"What would he do?" she asked. She turned her face to Kara, who clasped her hands behind her back and paced on the round handwoven rug under the crystal chandelier. "Tell me that, Kara, and I swear I'll leave the whole thing alone. I'll let her die . . ." Her voiced trailed off.

"You mean Thomas?"

"Because she'll die. They'll both die in the next eight hours if I don't administer the blood. They might die anyway. We hold their lives in our hands, you and I. But what would Thomas have done?"

"My brother didn't always do the most logical thing."

"Maybe because the most logical thing isn't always what it's cracked up to be."

"Listen to you," Kara chided. "You were always the strong one, demanding we follow the strictest policy."

Monique nodded. Dabbed at a tear that broke from her right eye before it smeared her mascara. "All I want to know is whether you think Thomas Hunter would ever sacrifice his son or daughter for the good of others."

Kara considered the question.

"Listen to me, Monique. You're every bit as much a sister to me as Thomas was a brother. He and I share the same mother, but you and Thomas share the same heart. And blood, if you consider the fact that you entered his dream world."

"It was more than a dream, you—"

"Okay, it was. My point is that you're as qualified as I am to answer your question."

But Monique didn't. In this reality anyway, Monique wasn't capable of killing her own daughter.

"Okay." Kara walked to the overstuffed chair next to Monique and eased down. She held her hands in her lap and leaned back. Blew some air. "We both know that Thomas would probably break every rule to save his son or daughter. So let's break this down. Assuming—just assuming—we give Billy and Janae a small dose of the blood, what's the worst that could happen?"

Monique looked up. "They enter the other reality, get their hands on the Books of History. Only God knows how much damage they might do with the power to write anything into existence. Please don't tell me you don't see the danger."

"Just making sure we're on the same page. It is all a bit mind-bending. Back on point, I think Thomas would save his daughter regardless of consequence."

Monique held her gaze, neither accepting nor rejecting the notion outwardly.

She continued. "What steps could we take to mitigate any danger? We have considerable resources at our disposal. Maybe we're thinking about this all wrong."

Monique averted her eyes and stared into space. For a few moments she seemed lost, but the haze that enveloped her gave way to the faintest sparkle. "We could lock them up," she said, turning back to Kara. "Assuming the blood keeps them alive."

"There's no guarantee of that. It's never been attempted. We're only guessing that his blood will have an effect on the virus."

"It saved you and me from the virus once before."

"Yes, it did."

"Janae and Billy clearly think it would work."

"Okay, assuming the blood works, which is the hope, they go into the other reality and return to find themselves locked up until we can determine what to do."

"For all we know they won't enter the other reality. Their eyes to that reality can only be opened if they believe . . ."

"Clearly, they believe. They're risking their lives for the chance to travel."

Monique smoothed her skirt with nervous hands, rubbed her palms on the arms of the chair. Unable to sit still, she pushed herself up, then quickly walked to the door and back.

"You're saying we should actually do this?"

"I'm saying Thomas would," Kara said.

"And if we were to keep them restrained, we would reduce the risk to our world considerably."

"Well, no, I didn't say that. We would mitigate the immediate threat they might pose. If they do get a taste of the other world, they won't forget it because we slap their hands when they awaken here."

"Then we keep them in chains," Monique said. The prospect of saving her daughter at any cost was asserting itself. "Better alive and in chains than dead."

"Maybe. We still have no control over what they might do in the other reality. For all we know, they might find a way to blow open the passage between our worlds."

"We could destroy the rest of the blood. A return trip would be impossible."

"Unless they find another way."

"Assuming they even go," Monique shot back. "Even then they would only be over there until they sleep. Hours, maybe a day, no more."

"More than enough time to—"

"Are you for this or aren't you?" Monique snapped. "Make up your mind. First you say Thomas would save his daughter, now you go to great lengths to make sure I understand what a terrible decision it is? I can't play these games!"

Kara acquiesced. If Janae or Billy were the child she never had, she'd be crawling the walls. "Just want to be clear." She stood. "How long will it take?"

That settled Monique. "I could have the blood here in five hours."

"Well, then. Make the call."

They faced each other, aware of the momentous decision they were making. The blood was their forbidden drug as much as it was Janae and Billy's. They probably should have incinerated it a long time ago.

"Save your daughter, Monique. Make the call now, before it's too late."

18

SAMUEL PULLED up on his reins and grabbed a fistful of air to signal a full stop. His comrades Petrus, Jacob, and Herum held back at horse length. A lone, stubborn buzzard peered at them from the cliff top ahead and then flapped for the sky to join two that had just vacated their perch.

It was something else, not they, who'd sent the birds away.

"Easy, boys," Samuel said quietly. "No sudden movements. We've come as friends, let's make sure they know that."

The cliffs rose vertically on three sides, leaving only a thin trail ahead up the steep face, or a retreat behind. Samuel had met up with his men, who'd shadowed him as planned, then led them into the canyon, knowing it was a dead end. Only a fool would venture so deep into Eramite territory. The half-breeds' tracks were nearly covered by the sand, only visible to the trained eye, perhaps. But to Jacob, who could spot the trail of a Shataiki ghost on a field of rocks, the sign screamed danger. Any Eramites patrolling this far from their main city would be warriors, surely perplexed over what kind of fool albinos would set themselves up so easily.

And why their leader wore only a cloak of dried blood.

"I don't like it," Jacob mumbled. "They have skilled archers. We're mice in a pit."

"They're Horde, not cats. Open your arms." Samuel released his reins and spread his arms wide in a sign of nonaggression.

Three hours had passed since he left Thomas and the others at the edge of Eramite territory. What his father would do now was anyone's guess. The man was given to rashness matched only by his courage.

But that bravery was now misaligned with an old, dead philosophy that clung to fading hopes. Only three years ago Samuel would have challenged any man or woman who spoke back to his father. He'd been younger and naive, a blind follower like the rest. So much of what they experienced could be explained as the working of Elyon.

But the realities of life cast doubt on that interpretation. Samuel's experience had slowly but thoroughly crushed his wholehearted acceptance of all he'd been taught. He awoke from a fitful sleep a year ago and realized he didn't know what he believed any longer.

Who could say that Elyon wasn't just another force in their world, like gravity or muscle or the sword, manipulated by his users?

Who was to say that the scabbing disease was a disease at all? What if it was just another condition of man, cleansed by the medicinal red waters?

Who was to say that the fruit was a gift from Elyon? Why not just a product of the land with powerful properties?

Who was to say that Teeleh was more than another force, counterbalancing the force called Elyon? Absolute good and evil were nothing more than constructs fashioned by humans who needed to understand and order their everyday lives.

Who was to say that the force that had made his body whole after Ba'al slashed him was any different from the force that grew the fruit? He'd been aware of the power, but only as a distant abstraction, a light that had vanished into the sky as he regained consciousness. And the Shataiki, though unnerving, didn't seem so terrifying to those who worshipped them. Loving them would be like loving the Horde, those scabbed vermin who proved far more dangerous than Shataiki on any day.

One thing was clear: the Horde had vowed to kill every living albino—man, woman, or child. That made them enemy, a force that did not agree with him or his desire to live in peace. He'd faced enough blood, but it was time to speak the only language the Horde understood with absolute clarity.

War.

It was time for the Horde to bleed, and the fact that two hundred priests in Ba'al's service had bled and died on his account was as good a sign as any that the time had come.

I will show you, Father. You'll see that I am right in the end.

"Take us to Eram!" Samuel shouted. His voice echoed through the canyon. "We come for the benefit of Eram!"

Nothing.

"I hope you know what you're doing," Petrus muttered.

"We're past the time for second-guessing."

"I'm hoping, not second-guessing." Petrus drew a deep breath and chased Samuel's call with his own. "We're unarmed, you goats! Come out and meet us. We have words for Eram!"

"That's endearing," Jacob said.

The first Horde warrior to rise into view stood on the cliff to their left. He was a tall Scab warrior dressed in tan battle gear, a cross between the old Horde robes and the Forest Guard armor, with leather guards strapped to thighs, arms, and chest. No helmet covered his clean, thick black hair. No dreadlocks on this one.

The others rose into view along the ridge, a hundred at least, two dozen of whom were armed with unstrung bows. They clearly didn't see the four albinos as a credible threat. More like trapped animals for their amusement.

It occurred to Samuel that he'd never addressed a Horde warrior with anything other than his backside in flight—except more recently, with the edge of his sword.

"Greetings."

The leader stared down at him for a long moment, then twisted in his saddle and spoke to someone behind him. The line parted and their leader slowly moved into view, mounted on a large brown stallion that wagged its head against the bit in its mouth.

No helmet. No leather guards. He wore only a calm, almost casual disposition that spoke of supreme confidence, but he was still as much a Horde as any Horde Samuel had seen.

This could be Eram himself. Samuel felt his pulse quicken. The scene could easily be taken from one of a hundred tales of the old days, when the Forest Guard was led by the great warrior, Thomas of Hunter.

Only this wasn't Thomas. This was a half-breed who had embraced the scabbing disease and waged war on Qurong.

"Greetings," Samuel called again.

"You're naked," the leader said. "I would have expected more from the son of the great warrior."

The man knew who he was?

"My name is Samuel of Hunter," he called. "These are my men, and we come in peace."

"Peace? Do you have any choice?"

A light chuckle mocked them.

"Give me a sword and you'll find me less interested in peace," Samuel said.

"Then you would be a fool."

"If I'm a fool, it's because I've left my father to join you for war."

"Is that right? Even a bigger fool than I thought." Again, laughter from the cliff. "You go from being the sacrificial lamb to the traitor so quickly."

They'd seen?

"These are my lands, boy. My men have been watching you from the moment the first black bird circled overhead."

"Then why didn't you kill Qurong and Ba'al while you had them?"

"Because, unlike you, I'm not a fool. Our time hasn't come. When it does, the whole world will know."

So the rumors that Eram was up to something were true.

"I've come to speak to Eram, the half-breed feared by all Horde. Tell Eram that his time *has* come. And the whole world knows."

The leader watched Samuel for a few seconds, silenced by the bold insinuation. Then the warrior turned his horse around and spoke gently, like a commander accustomed to watching a thousand of his men run with the mere flip of his wrist.

"Bring them."

19

NIGHT WAS falling. Thomas Hunter balanced near the top of a massive oak, studying the glimmering fires in Qurongi City. It had taken him most of the day to snake his way south, careful to avoid any Horde patrols, which were few thanks to the Dark Moon celebration.

How long had it been since he'd laid eyes on the forest once proudly inhabited by the Forest Dwellers? Ten years. So much had changed since he fled this city.

He pulled back the hood of the Scab robe Samuel had discarded, which he'd exchanged for his own tunic. Before the Horde's time, the crystalline lake's southern shore had been white sand, reserved for the nightly celebrations. His people had defended the forests against Qurong's encroaching armies, always returning victorious to this safe haven. It was a place where flower-crowned children and youths too inexperienced for war had run through the streets, welcoming them home. The homes were simple but colorful. They often danced late into the night to the sounds of guitars and flutes and drums.

They'd bathed in the lake together, washing away all traces of the dreaded scabbing disease.

To think that he'd once brought his people bits and pieces of advanced technology from his dreams of another world—it was hardly conceivable now. He'd lived in two worlds at once, awake here while dreaming in the other, and awake there when dreaming here. There he'd loved a sister named Kara and a woman named Monique.

If the lost books, as Ba'al had called them, did indeed exist . . .

He brought his mind back to the city. Except for the palace on the far side, and the Thrall, which stood alone on the near side, Qurongi City was practically colorless. Gray blocks of mud and stone topped by straw roofs leaked smoke from the dinner fires inside. The Horde still subsisted on wheat cakes, but instead of harvesting desert wheat as they once had, they grew green wheat in the large cleared fields of the forests to the south. Meat was a delicacy, reserved primarily for the upper class, the priests, and royalty.

The Thrall stood tall by the muddy lake's shore, lit by orange flames that illuminated a spire rising to the height of three buildings. They said that Ba'al had erected this new addition, topped by a brass image of the winged serpent. The new wing that looked large enough to house hundreds of priests stretched out from the western wall.

The lost books would be either in this temple, under Ba'al's watchful eye, or in Qurong's care. If the dark priest had access to them, he would surely have used them.

The thought had clawed at Thomas's mind for the last eight hours as he pushed his horse south. If a man like Ba'al were to find his way into the other world . . . The thought made him shiver.

But Ba'al apparently hadn't used the books. His lament to Teeleh made it clear that he hadn't been sent like the others. This could only mean that Ba'al didn't have the books.

Qurong must have them. Assuming they existed, of course, which was anything but certain.

Either way, Thomas's need to know had grown like a monster inside him. He felt sure that his fate was somehow dependent on what happened in the other world, which also meant that the Circle's fate was tied to the other world. To the books. It had always been about the Books of History, he could see that now.

"Hello, old friend."

Thomas twisted to his right, lost his grip on the tree trunk for a moment, and grabbed a handful of branches to steady himself. He looked into the large, green eyes of a Roush perhaps two feet in height.

The fuzzy white creature's huge eyes stared unblinking. "Sorry."

Thomas couldn't find his voice. This . . . a Roush!

It had been so long since he'd seen one, even he was beginning to wonder whether he'd only dreamed of the legendary creatures that did Elyon's bidding. Yet here one was, perched not five feet away, looking at Thomas as if he might be an idiot.

"You're real," Thomas finally managed.

"And so are you. Unless it's now my turn to dream."

Then he recognized the Roush. Could it be?

"Michal?"

"Thomas?"

"So . . . so it's you?"

"In the flesh."

"Seriously?"

"Now you're beginning to worry me. We have considerable history together, and yet you sound as if you doubt my existence."

"No. Just . . . we haven't seen one of you for an eternity."

"Actually, that's a long time and yet to come. It's been ten years, I believe." He clucked with his tongue. "You humans do have such a short memory."

"Dear Elyon, if the others could only see."

"Your eyes were opened to the Shataiki?" Michal asked. "Yes?"

"Yes. Yes."

"Well, then. Now you see me. But it doesn't mean I haven't been around."

"No, of course not." Thomas wanted to hug the creature. Wrap him up in his arms and bury his face in that fuzzy neck. But then he wasn't a boy any longer. Or was he? What was it Elyon used to say?

Am I a lion, a lamb, or a boy?

He swung to a lower branch and dropped twenty feet to the soft forest floor. The Roush stared down at him, unmoving, then made a soft humphing sound and hopped into the air. He floated to the ground, spreading wide his wings of thin white skin.

"You've developed a fear of heights?" Michal asked. "I would . . ."

It was as far as the Roush got. Driven by a desperate need to know, to touch, to feel, Thomas fell to his knees, threw his arms around the creature's neck, which was hardly a neck at all, and pulled the soft torso tight against his chest.

The feeling of this warm body, so real in his arms, flooded him with a brew of emotion that pushed tears into his eyes. Joy. Love. Relief. Vindication and power.

Samuel was wrong, so very wrong.

"Easy, easy. Phew, the stench of that robe . . . please, you're going to suffocate me!"

"Sorry." Thomas pushed himself back and stared at the round face. "Sorry."

"Understood. Apology unnecessary but accepted. They told me you'd disguised yourself in this dreadful garb, but I didn't expect to have to wear it myself." Michal hopped to his right and glanced back. "Good thinking, by the way. It should get you into the city easily enough. It's getting out that I worry about."

"Then you approve of what I'm doing."

"Not mine to approve or disapprove. I'm simply here with a message. But while I'm here, I could be talked into parting with some advice. That is, if you still value the advice of Elyon's Roush."

"I would be a fool not to. Has your opinion of humans fallen so low?"

The Roush lifted one eyebrow.

"Okay, so we've made a few mistakes along the way."

"Will," Michal said. "We *will* make some mistakes along the way."

"Okay, will. But surely this will all come to an end before we all drop dead of old age."

The Roush gazed off into the forest. "Is that what you think? That there's an end? That when you die it all ends?"

"No, but not everything is forever." That seemed to satisfy the Roush. "You have a message?"

Michal stared at Thomas, nodded once, and spoke as if he was reciting poetry. "The colored forests, like Elyon, Maker of all that is good, will come again. This is the beginning and it is the end, and yet still the beginning. The first will be last and the last will be first. What was once black will be green. And what was once green will be consumed by darkness. Follow your heart, Thomas, because the time has come. Weep with the mourners; beg with beggars; knock and knock again, because he will give you what you ask in that hour when all is lost."

The Roush took a deep breath and looked off again. "Go to the place you came from. Make a way for the Circle to fulfill its hope."

The night grew still. A night bird cawed far off, and the breeze rustled leaves overhead.

"That's it?"

"It's not enough?"

"No. Well, yes, it is, but it's not exactly clear."

"For him who has ears to hear, it's perfectly clear."

"Then explain it to me."

"I can't."

"Why not?"

"It'll become clear in time."

"You don't understand it?"

The Roush threw him a side glance. "I understand what I'm meant to understand."

Thomas scratched his skull and paced. "Then at least tell me what you understand. I'm out on a limb here. I've just lost a son to the half-breeds, the Circle is fractured, the Shataiki have gathered at Ba'al's call . . . my world is falling apart! At least tell me how to save my son."

The Roush sighed and waddled a few steps, steadying himself with a flutter of wings.

"You've heard of the lost books?"

So he was right. "I've heard rumors . . ."

"They are true. The seven original Books of History went missing, three of them into history."

Into history? He was about to demand the furry creature continue when Michal spoke.

"It's a long story, more than you need to know. But what might be useful is the knowledge that these seven books aren't like the other Books of History. With all seven, one could rewrite the rules that control the blank books."

"Like a key."

"If you like. The Books of History reflect the truth of all that has occurred in history. Write in one of the numerous blank books with the faith of a child, and create history. But with all seven of the original books, one can actually change the rules that govern the rest of the books."

"And these seven original books are no longer lost, I take it."

"They were found by four warriors—"

"Johnis and—"

"Another story altogether. But they ended up here, hidden in Qurong's private library. Fortunately Ba'al"—Michal paused as if considering what to say, then continued—"doesn't know that Qurong has them, or he would have used them a long time ago."

"Used them? To rewrite the rules of the books?"

"No, you need all seven to do that. Qurong has six. But with only four of them, a person can unlock time that binds history and travel into it."

Thomas's heart pounded. The suggestion was immediately clear. "So . . . I can use the four books to return to ancient Earth?"

Michal raised an eyebrow and offered a coy smile. His words whispered through Thomas's mind. *Go to the place you came from. Make a way for the Circle to fulfill its hope.*

"How? How do you use these four books?"

"As I was saying . . ." Michal cleared his throat. "A person can travel into history if he touches four books together with his blood."

"Four books," Thomas said, holding up four fingers.

"Yes, four books."

"Which Qurong has."

"Yes, which Qurong has."

"Qurong has them, but only Ba'al knows of their power."

"Correct, Qurong has them, but Ba'al wouldn't dream of telling what he knows about the Books of History."

"And if I cut myself and touch four of these books, I will enter history, so to speak. Like I could once do in my dreams."

"Not quite the same. You would go physically, along with anything in your possession."

"Physically? You mean actually, *poof*, go?"

"Yes. *Poof*."

Thomas blinked. "And return the same way? *Poof*?" He snapped his fingers.

"Yes. *Poof*." Michal made an inaudible snapping motion with his small fingers.

"And this is what I'm meant to do?" Thomas asked.

"That is up to you. I'm only a messenger, and I can't say that the message was so clear."

"And how is this supposed to get me my son back? Without Samuel, I have no hope."

"Did I say the books would help you find your son?"

Thomas's reasoning stalled. "You're saying he's lost?" He paced, frantic. "I won't have it! There has to be a way to save Samuel."

"And I didn't say there wasn't. Go. And return quickly before it's too late. Do that and you might save your son."

Thomas ran his hands through his hair and tried to think clearly. The prospect of returning to history pulled at his mind like a powerful magnet tugging at a steel ball. They were inexplicably linked, he and the histories. Perhaps because he really had come from Denver, Colorado. From Bangkok. The histories where his sister, Kara, waited.

"Be careful, Thomas," Michal was saying behind him. "Where there is great hope, there is also great evil. Teeleh's time has also come. The blood will flow like a river."

"Yes," he said absently. "Of course." Was Kara still alive? Monique? The books were in Qurong's possession. He'd been right in coming for them, regardless of the risk to himself. If he could get his blood on the four books and return to history, a new hope would present itself.

And then the end would come.

"Whose time has come?" He turned back. "What evil are you . . ."

But there was no furry white Roush to hear him. He looked up, saw only empty branches, and turned around, scanning the forest.

Michal was gone.

The Roush had made himself seen after ten years and said what he'd come to say. It was indeed the beginning of the end.

Thomas faced Qurongi City, where the lost books waited. He took a deep breath, flipped the hood of the priest's robe back over his head, and ran.

20

THOMAS WALKED down the road leading to the palace as he imagined a priest with urgent business would walk; his head was bowed to hide his face, hands folded under his long sleeves, feet taking quick short steps. The sooner he passed any curious onlookers the better.

His urgency came from the books. More specifically from the need to return to the histories, where he would find a way for them all.

Once again, the world hung in the balance of every choice he made.

Michal's words haunted him as he strode by a Scab warrior who mistook him for a priest and gave him a wide berth. What was once black will be green. And what was once green will be consumed by darkness. So, after all these years the great pursuit of mankind's heart would finally end. Either Teeleh or Elyon would win them all.

Follow your heart, Thomas, because the time has come . . . he will give you what you ask in that hour when all is lost. What this meant, Thomas could not know. Only that an hour was fast approaching when all would appear lost, a prospect that certainly justified some urgency. The Roush's next words could hardly be mistaken.

Go to the place you came from. Make a way for the Circle to fulfill its hope.

He approached two guards at the palace gate. The dried blood that covered the dead priest's garment couldn't hurt his chances.

"Open!" he hissed, snatching up a hand, careful to keep his flesh hidden beneath the sleeve. "I have urgent business from Ba'al."

The guard on the left made for the latch, but the other stepped up. "Does his Excellency expect—"

"Open or I turn back and bring the dark priest to answer your questions!"

"No, my lord," the first one said, pulling the gate open. "Ba'al's word is Teeleh's word."

Thomas rushed past, giving them no time to peer beneath the hood. Six Throaters were positioned on each side of the path ahead.

"Let Ba'al's servant pass," the guard called. The mere prospect of answering to Ba'al had the desired effect. None of the warriors questioned the order. Even better, the guard at the next wooden entrance had heard the call and opened the door with a bow.

Thomas hurried inside the large atrium and pulled up, pulse pounding. Two large torches lapped at the walls on either side, filling the room with orange light. To his right, a bowl of morst powder sat beside some fruit. A round table made of stone centered the room, adorned with a tall statue of the black beast, Teeleh.

He considered powdering his face with the sweet-smelling morst to cover his albino skin, but he hadn't come to hide. Instead, he threw back his hood, took several calming breaths, and introduced himself at the top of his lungs.

"Patricia, wife of Qurong, the servant of Ba'al calls you to hear him in the most urgent matter!"

His voice rang through the stone atrium and beyond. A servant appeared in the archway and looked at him curiously. Her eyes went wide, and she uttered a short cry before running off, yelling in a high pitch.

Thomas strode forward. "Patricia, wife of Qurong, Ba'al demands your presence."

"Then come," a woman called back impatiently. "What's the ruckus? For the love of Teeleh don't stand out there, come in and speak."

Thomas entered the receiving room. A long table sat under three brass torches suspended by leather thongs. The walls were decorated with a dozen skulls of bulls and goats, either painted in reds and purples or plastered with morst paste. Chairs made of bone supporting leather seats ran around the table.

He recognized Patricia immediately. She had a large yellow melon in one hand and a black candle in the other, a woman not too elevated in her own eyes to help where she saw the need, despite having dozens of servants at her disposal. Her pale green dress ran to the floor, a long-sleeved garment with a brown belt. Her hair was braided and smothered in the white morst, as were her face and hands. Odd how the Horde claimed to prefer the smell of their own skin over the stench of albino flesh, yet they went to such great lengths to moderate their own stink.

"Well, then, speak." Patricia glanced up as she set the candle in a stand on the table's far side. "You know I honor the word of . . ."

Her mouth dropped open and she froze.

"The husband of your daughter," Thomas said. "Thomas of Hunter, leader of all albinos. I come in peace."

She still didn't find her voice. Two Throaters with drawn swords rushed into the room, no doubt alerted by the servant.

Thomas shrugged out of the robe and let it fall around his feet. He spread his hands.

"I'm unarmed. Hold them back."

Patricia hesitated, then waved them back. "Leave us."

Neither moved. The cries of others came down the halls now, yelling a general alarm. Two of them burst into the room from a side hall and pulled up sharply at the door.

"Leave us!" Patricia snapped.

"My lady . . ."

"I said leave us. Or I'll have your head! All of you. Stand down."

They glanced at one another, then backed away slowly, muttering something about Qurong. Thomas kept his eyes on Patricia, knowing now that he'd chosen the right introduction. As the husband of her daughter, he held a place of importance to Patricia. She might relish the prospect of torturing him for tearing their family apart, but not before gaining some understanding about her daughter.

"I've come from Ba'al Bek, where Elyon made a mockery of your dark priest," he said. "Now I'm here to appeal to Qurong without that snake's knowledge. But I fear he may not hear what I have to say."

She plopped the melon on the table and put a hand on her hip. "And what makes you think I'm interested in what my enemy has to say?"

"Because you were sent packing from Ba'al Bek with your tail between your legs." Thomas said. Too strong?

"Is that what happened? Perspectives shape how we see mystical matters. I heard of a great victory."

"Two hundred priests died. They didn't tell you?"

"You mean Ba'al's offering? I heard that Teeleh and his black beasts showed themselves to the world. The streets are teeming with fear already."

"But in the end, my son climbed off the altar, alive." He didn't have the time to persuade her of what she hadn't seen with her own eyes. Ba'al had already put his spin on the whole mess.

"Never mind," he said. "I have a new proposal for Qurong. One that will help him destroy the enemy he fears."

Patricia walked around the end of the table. "You're mistaken if you think Qurong is threatened by the albinos. Just because you managed to steal Chelise doesn't mean we fear you."

"I'm not your enemy," Thomas said. "You should fear the Eramites and Ba'al."

He saw the quick movement in her eyes. He continued before she could form a response.

"My wife weeps for her mother and her father. No one has a more tender heart toward the Horde than she. What I have to say could save you all. I beg you, take me to Qurong and convince him to listen to me before he disposes of me."

She stared at him, flat-footed. For long seconds neither moved nor spoke.

"And how is my daughter?" she finally asked.

A voice spoke from the darkened hall on Thomas's right. "We *have* no daughter." Qurong walked in, dressed in a leather tunic with long pants and soft-soled boots. No guards, no weapons. He stood nearly a foot taller than his wife, and his bare arms were maybe one and a half times the diameter of Thomas's. His legs, thick like trunks without an ounce of fat. The man might not have Thomas's speed, but he could likely drop a bull with one blow to its skull.

The supreme commander of the Horde snatched up a chalice of red wine and splashed some into a glass goblet. This he threw back in one long drink before turning his eyes to Thomas. He studied him for several long beats.

"I see Cassak failed to prove his worth," he finally said.

"On the contrary, your general proved better than most. But it was an unfair race. My son knows Eramite territory too well."

To this Qurong said nothing.

"You're wondering why the man who just fled you at Ba'al Bek now stands before you," Thomas said.

"You'll have to forgive us." Qurong spat to one side. "It's not every day a smelly salamander snakes its way into our courts."

"How about a drink? It's been a while since I've had a good drink of Horde wine."

The leader hesitated, then nodded at his wife, who poured half a glass and stepped back. Thomas stepped up to the table and took a sip of the bitter liquid, grateful to hydrate his parched throat despite the nasty taste.

"He's earned his right to speak," Patricia said.

"Quiet, woman. I'll decide who has what rights in my own house." Qurong looked at Thomas. "So taking my daughter wasn't enough? Now you come back and try to seduce my wife?"

Patricia glared at him. "Don't be—"

"Silence!" he thundered.

"Her beauty and charm notwithstanding, I have no intention of seducing your wife any more than I seduced your daughter," Thomas said. "I simply loved her, as I now love all people—albino, Horde, half-breed—they are all one. But if you don't let me talk, you may not learn how Samuel, my son, whom Ba'al allowed to escape, is conspiring your death. Kill this albino salamander who stinks up your palace, and my knowledge will die with me."

The man surely wasn't foolish enough to dismiss this claim, not considering the source. Qurong frowned, then looked at his wife.

"Leave us. Seal the doors. I want no one within earshot."

Her eyes didn't leave Thomas. "How is she?"

Qurong held up his hand to stop them. But when Thomas spoke, he didn't silence him.

"Good. Excellent. Healthy and as spirited as ever." Thomas offered her a thin smile. "She speaks of her mother and father every evening, making you both heroes in Jake's mind. Sometimes I wonder why she ever left you for Elyon."

When he didn't offer more, Patricia spoke very softly. "Jake?"

"Forgive me, I thought you'd heard. Jake is your grandson."

He might as well have told them that they'd just swallowed poison and had only minutes to live.

"Leave us," Qurong repeated in a low voice.

"I—"

"Leave us!"

This time she bowed at his raised hand, turned, and walked from the room, issuing orders to those beyond. The door slammed, leaving Thomas and Qurong to face off alone.

"Listen to me, albino. Your pleas for sympathy may melt the hearts of mothers, but all of this talk falls on deaf ears now. Never speak to me of this woman and her child again. Do we understand each other?"

"Yes, I think we do."

"I need you to be certain."

"Then yes."

"If it's war you speak of, I'll give you one minute to explain yourself."

"It's all I need," Thomas said.

Qurong finally let out a breath, poured himself more wine, and sat. "I'll never figure out you albino ghosts. Any other enemy and I would feel compelled to put you in chains the moment you enter our city. But you've all forgotten how to fight. You're hardly a man."

"I can see how you might think that."

"Well, you've earned this right to speak"—Qurong waved his hand— "so speak."

"It's simple. The only reason the Eramites haven't annihilated you is because they don't have the numbers. But that's about to change. My son has turned against me and will take half of all albinos with him to join Eram for the sole purpose of waging war against you."

He let that sink in. It was a bold-faced exaggeration, but he was here for the books, not to help Qurong. His only ally was Qurong's fear.

Thomas pressed his point. "Your high priest would like nothing more than to see you dead."

"What would you know of Ba'al?"

"He let Samuel live. Why? Because he has conspired to bring you to ruin, and Samuel is his greatest ally. Once your body has fed a dozen Shataiki, he will step in and control all of the land, Horde, albino, and Eramite."

"Absurd!" But Qurong stood and walked around the end of the table, clearly concerned.

"You're deceived about some things, Qurong, but otherwise you're a wise man. You surely know most of this already. Tell me that Ba'al isn't your enemy."

The leader glanced at the door.

"Or that Eram doesn't lead a growing army that can no longer be discounted. Or that Samuel wouldn't try to slit your throat if he were standing here."

"Your minute is up."

"I haven't told you how to end this threat, once and for all."

Qurong glowered. "There's no end to your disrespect. This young woman who used to be my daughter may have drowned, but I . . ." He seemed to shudder. "I'm not such a fool."

"You misunderstand me. I'm not here to tell you how to drown. I'm here to tell you how to defeat Eram, Ba'al, and Samuel."

"Is that so?"

"It is."

The man cast another glance at the doors to be sure they were secure. He lowered his voice. "Well, then. Speak."

"My minute is up."

"Then I give you another."

"Did you ever wonder how I've been able to stay a step ahead of you at every turn for so long? How the Forest Dwellers were always the innovators, sprouting technology as if it grew in our closets? The forging of metals, the use of wheels, weapons—all of it, first to the Forest Guard and then to the Horde through your spies?"

The man frowned. "Hurry it up."

"It was me. I came across the secrets to these advances personally."

Qurong waited for more. "And how will this deal with Eram?"

"We can do it again," Thomas said.

"Do what again?"

"Go into the Books of History and retrieve what we need to defeat Ba'al and his hideous god, Teeleh."

"Go into the books?" Qurong was incredulous.

Thomas slipped into a chair and folded his hands on the table. "Not any books, naturally. One of the lost books."

Qurong nodded slowly. "I see. You've come to enter the lost books. Have you lost your mind? This is worse than Ba'al's antics. I know nothing of any lost books or this magic you're trying to seduce me with."

Here it was, then. Either Qurong had the books or he didn't.

"No." Thomas leaned forward and spoke softly. "You may not know of them as the lost books. There were initially seven, the number of perfection. But a great power can come from only four of them."

Qurong wasn't blinking. His whole face had stilled like a mask.

Thomas continued. "The lost books can open a window into a world of great power and magic, Qurong."

Now Qurong blinked.

Thomas put his fleece out. "Does Ba'al know that you have the books?"

The commander's eyes scanned the room.

"Don't tell me you don't know what I'm talking about," Thomas pushed.

"There are six books that I've kept from him," Qurong said in a low, quick voice. "When he first came to us from the desert, he turned the city inside out looking for any sign of them. He claimed he needed these books for ceremonial purposes. These could be the books . . ."

"Six? We need only four."

"We?"

"You have them, I know how to use them. We."

The prospect of returning to the other world was now so realistic, so palpable, so close, that Thomas had difficulty calming a tremor in his voice.

"Don't be a fool," the leader said. "We are Qurong and Thomas. There are no two greater enemies."

"You're sadly mistaken, my lord. The lust of Teeleh and the wrath of Elyon will make our differences sound like whispers in the night. But even here, in your own palace, Ba'al is a greater enemy than I am. As is Eram and now Samuel. Next to all of them, I just might be your closest friend."

"This is blasphemy."

"Show me the books."

"How can I trust you, the greatest deceiver of them all?"

Thomas took a deep breath and tried to sound calm. "Because if you don't, you will die."

Qurong remained silent. Suspicious, but no longer defiant.

Thomas made it clear. "We will all die."

21

BILLY REDIGER was aware of several things in his state of dreaming. He knew that he'd thrown himself off a cliff of some kind, but the exact nature of that cliff kept shifting in his mind. At times he was falling into a black hole, clawing at the air to stop his never-ending descent and thinking that if he could just grow wings, like those of a huge bat, he would be fine.

Then he was being chased through a Black Forest by that very bat. It hounded him, snapping at his heels until it hauled him down and went for his neck with a ferocious snarl.

But Billy knew that he was dreaming. And dreaming was good, because dreaming meant that he was still alive. Or was he?

Then he remembered for the hundredth time: He'd lost all sense of himself, and despite Johnny's and Darcy's best efforts, he fled Colorado in search of himself.

In search of the beginning. The truth behind how his own fall from grace had begun. Before Marsuvees Black. Before the showdown in Paradise. Before he'd learned that he was the chief of all sinners.

Before he'd written that first word in the Book of History so long ago.

The truth came down to a man named Thomas Hunter and what remained of him: one vial of his blood.

He had to find the truth about himself, but having met Janae de Raison, he knew that her truth was a part of his truth. She was his soul mate. And he knew he would follow her to hell and back. Which is exactly what he was doing, lying on this gurney: following her to hell.

And hopefully back.

The murmur of voices interrupted Billy's reverie. "It doesn't take that much . . ." The voice sounded as if it came from the edge of a distant canyon.

"We don't know that. We don't know anything about how this will work."

Then Billy knew. The sting on his arm wasn't Janae. Her mother, Monique, was injecting his arm with a new needle. They were doing it.

Janae, dear Janae . . . your gamble has paid off. At this very moment they were shooting his arm with Thomas's blood.

"Pulse rising!"

Of course, his pulse was rising.

And what if you wake up, Billy? What if you're not dreaming when the blood hits your blood? What if Janae goes but you don't?

He began to panic.

"Pulse 158 and rising . . ."

Billy jumped off a dark cliff and thought about black bats chasing him through darkness. Down, down. Deeper, still deeper, into the swirling blackness below.

The darkness suffocated him. Swallowed him with pain. He cried out and he knew that they could hear him.

KARA HUNTER instinctively jerked her hands to her ears when the scream came from Billy. His back arched. Like Janae, his body had begun to bruise as the capillaries near the skin hemorrhaged, ravaged by the Raison Strain B. Their deterioration hadn't progressed as quickly as Kara feared, but they were now both dying at a breakneck pace.

Billy dropped back down on the gurney and went silent except for the ragged sound of his heavy breathing.

"Pulse 168," Monique said calmly. They'd already injected a half cc of Thomas's blood into Janae's vein, and although she, too, was panting, she hadn't reacted as violently.

"Dear God, it's working," Kara said. "He's . . ."

Monique jerked the needle out and did not blot the insertion point with a gauze pad, as she had for her own daughter. Blood oozed from the tiny wound.

"It's too early to tell," she said.

"No, I mean he's there." Kara's voice cracked and she continued in a whisper. "Billy's in Thomas's world!"

"We can't possibly know that," Monique shot back.

"He's there! Look at him."

Billy had turned as white as the walls, mouth stretched open, neck veins protruding like ropes. His eyes were wide, staring at the ceiling, but Kara knew better. Billy wasn't seeing the ceiling.

He was seeing either himself or someone like himself in another world.

AN ORANGE GLOW grew in the darkness, and Billy snapped his mouth shut. Held his breath.

But he was breathing still, staring at a stone wall with two black candles blazing on either side of a crude, black-veined mirror. He . . .

This was it? He'd made it?

An image of a hollow man, dead perhaps, stared at him from the mirror. He spun around to see who was standing behind him.

No one.

He stood alone in a room, its walls hewn from stone lit by two large torches. Ancient books lined a case along one wall, overlooking an altar that was stained by the blood of both man and beast. It was an ark of covenants, guarded on both ends by the winged serpent, Teeleh.

Billy knew all of this because he was in his own library.

To his left stood his desk, carved from a single stump taken from the Black Forest. Marsuuv, the Shataiki queen who'd caged him, had allowed him to take the tree.

This he knew as well, as if it were his own history. But that was impossible because he also knew that he was Billy Rediger, from Colorado, the United States.

You're both. Billy and Ba'al.

Ba'al. I am Ba'al. He relished the name.

Then his mind flooded with the full truth, and he had to reach out and steady himself on the desk chair to stay upright.

He knew who he was, what he'd done here in this world. Why he was who he was. "I am yours," Ba'al whispered—Billy, who was in Ba'al's body, whispered.

"My queen, Marsuuv, I am your only lover, and I will die to prove my worth." Ba'al's voice was scratchy and thin, barely more than a whisper, but here in the subterranean library, it vibrated like the hiss of a snake. Billy's mind blossomed with the nature of the Shataiki queens. Teeleh and his queens longed to be loved, as Elyon was loved. They were incapable of sexuality but commanded absolute loyalty and servitude. To be the lover of a queen meant throwing your life at his feet.

Billy turned to face the room. Two books sat on the desk. Books of History. These were a fraction of all the volumes that told the stories of history, a recording of all that had ever happened in human history. These two were filled with facts already. They didn't have the power of a blank book, which could be used to create history, but the sight of them eased his fear.

He had come home. This, more than Colorado or Bangkok or anywhere in the other reality, was home. It was exhilaration, not fear, that he felt. After so many years wondering who he was and why his battle with evil was so monumental, he finally knew. He hadn't just created evil, he was possessed by it. The only time he'd really embraced redemption had been in a dream. He'd never fully pushed evil from his heart. Not like Darcy and Johnny had.

Another book lay open on its spine next to an ink jar and quill. Ba'al's blood book, another term for *journal.*

He stepped up to the desk and reached for the blood book. Then, for the first time since awakening in Ba'al's library, he saw the flesh that encased his wrist and fingers. He stared at the flaking, cracking skin, and his first thought was that he'd been consumed by a severe case of scabies.

But the thought was immediately displaced by Ba'al's knowledge. This was the scabbing condition caused by the Shataiki, a badge of honor to be worn by all who refused to drown in the albinos' red water.

Billy turned to the mirror, pulled off his hood, and stared at himself. His cheekbones were pronounced beneath his gaunt, white face. Gray eyes, like clay dimes. White morst paste coated long dreadlocks. The image was at once terrifying and beautiful.

He reached up and touched his cheeks, but the sensation in his fingertips was deadened by the scabbing disease.

This is me, Billy. Ba'al. He pulled his robe aside and looked at his chest. *And I still have the blood of my priests on my flesh.*

The memory of Marsuuv's power flowing through his tall, thin frame as he stood over the son's corpse flooded him now, and he trembled with pleasure. He was greater than anyone could possibly imagine, in either world.

Then again, he'd seen the power of the light in both worlds. Thinking of it now, fear crept back into his bowels. A light so bright that no wraith from hell could stand in its presence without screaming in pain.

You are weak . . .

The thought was Ba'al's, not Billy's, and it was laced with such hatred that Billy froze. He realized then that he wasn't wholly Ba'al or Billy now, but a strange breed of both.

A half-breed.

But he had been a half-breed before, in the worst of ways.

Ba'al impulsively walked to the desk, picked up a knife, cut his wrist, and let his blood dribble into a bowl. "Rid me of this weak parasite, my lover, Marsuuv. Cleanse me and make me whole."

Billy blinked at the audacity of the wraith called Ba'al. Didn't they share the same history? Weren't they of the same blood?

"I'm you, you fool!" He squeezed his wrist and wrapped a strip of cloth around the cut to stem the flow of blood.

Billy stared at the blood book on the desk. Here, in this one secret volume, Ba'al had collected all that he knew about the world. He lifted the book and slowly turned the pages, which contained drawings and explanations of everything from the Roush to the Shataiki, excerpts from other scribes pasted in, memories from the time before . . . all here, carefully pieced together.

And who better to write of this world's deepest, darkest secrets than Ba'al? Because Ba'al had once been Forest Guard. A follower of Elyon.

The thought nauseated Billy.

"Hello, my love."

Desire bit deeply into his mind at the sound of the soft voice behind him. He turned around and looked at the priestess who'd entered. This was Jezreal. His lover, as humans loved.

"Haven't I told you not to disturb me in my sanctuary?" Ba'al spat.

"Yes." Jezreal moved forward, smiling. Her ruby fingernails toyed with a golden cord that hung from her long gown's plunging neckline. "And has that ever stopped you from ravaging me before?"

The connection between them was far beyond anything so banal as the mere copulation of animals. She was the only human who understood Ba'al's dependence on Marsuuv, who had first let him drink Shataiki blood. One drop, and any mere human was forever locked in the embrace of evil.

Indeed, Shataiki reproduced through blood, Billy realized. They were asexual, neither male nor female. They wanted slaves, not partners.

Jezreal, on the other hand, was human. Human urges raged behind those glassy gray eyes, and unless Billy was mistaken, Janae and Jezreal were one.

She stepped up to him, close, so that he could smell her sick breath. Her tongue toyed with the tips of her front teeth. "Billy . . ." she breathed. "Or should I call you Billos?"

He didn't respond, in part because the knowledge that he had once been an elite fighter named Billos, sworn to protect Elyon's forests from the Horde, was one of his most closely guarded secrets. He'd once bathed in Elyon's lakes and sat around fires late at night, speaking of his greatness. He was a Judas who'd gone in search of the lost books—the books of blood—found them, used them, and then lost them.

He had been Billos of Southern, and if the people knew that he was not full-breed Horde, doubt would be cast over his loyalty.

More than this, he despised even the name Billos. Marsuuv had given him a new name, and he'd embraced the full embodiment of Ba'al, the god who required blood sacrifice.

"Billosssss . . ."

Ba'al slapped her face with enough force to cut her cheek with his fingernail. How many times had he insisted she not use the name that she alone knew? Jezreal smiled, then winked. She wiped some of the blood from her cheek, looked at her fingertips, and licked it off. "I've told you before, my love. I don't require warming up. And yet you insist."

She slowly stretched her hand out to his lips, offering him a taste of her blood. He turned away, not because of the blood, but because she was mocking him, reducing him to his former self. To this Billy that had haunted him. To Billos, whom he despised.

He was Ba'al, lover of Marsuuv, the twelfth of Teeleh's twelve queens.

"You're not Billy?" she demanded. "You're Ba'al, of course, my master and my savior. And that's all."

His anger fell away as Ba'al's presence was appeased.

Billy reasserted himself and swallowed.

"Right?" she pressed, eyes skittering over his face. "You're not Billy?"

"Janae."

Her eyes widened, and the look of concern faded to a smile. Her voice shook when she spoke. "We made it, Billy. We're here." She turned, drinking in the library, the torches, the books, the altar with its winged serpents. "It's the most beautiful thing I've ever seen."

"We're not alone."

Janae, who was also the priestess Jezreal, didn't seem bothered by this fact. She touched the altar. Ran her fingers over the dried blood. "I feel like I've come home. The smells, the feel of the air . . . it's as though I've gone back into the womb and have been born again, baptized in blood."

He couldn't help but be seduced by her awe. Billy loved this woman. Janae, not Jezreal, though they were one and the same, and he suddenly needed to tell her what he knew.

His breathing thickened. "Janae . . ."

She looked into his eyes, reacting to the tenderness in his voice.

"There's more you should know if we're going to do this together," he said.

She stepped around the altar, and this time he didn't pull back when she touched his lips with her fingers. "Tell me."

He took her hand in his and kissed it. "We're home, but not truly home, not as long as we are parasites in these wretched bodies."

The Ba'al in him boiled with rage, and Billy felt his face contort.

Janae hushed him, smoothing his knotting lips. "It's okay, ignore him. Tell me."

He wrested control away. So . . . Ba'al was the weaker one. He continued in a whisper but with more confidence now.

"There are four lost books. If all four are gathered and touched with blood, time is unlocked."

"Time?"

"It's how we can return here. You and I."

"In the flesh?"

"In the flesh."

Her eyes frantically searched his. "How is that possible?"

"How is *this* possible? But I've done it. When I was Billos."

She stepped back and paced to her right. "Then we have to do it! We have to wake up and return!"

"We don't have the books."

Janae spun back. "What? You tell me this, but we don't have the books? Where are they?"

"We don't know. But we can't risk waking up until we find out."

Ba'al's outrage at the suggestion that the books were for Billy, not for him, threatened to send him into a fit. Billy noted that he shared the body of a viper that would strike him down without hesitation.

Could he kill Ba'al now? What would happen if he committed suicide? No, he couldn't risk death. But he could draw the battle lines clearly.

"It's okay, Janae. I'm going to get the books. It's my destiny."

"And it's my destiny to be here, Billy, so I hope you know what you're talking about."

"I do."

Her look of uncertainty slowly changed to interest.

"Oh?"

"Ba'al has just made it clear to me," he said, smothering the weaker Scab. "He's assumed that the saying was about him, but he's wrong. It's about me."

Then he quoted the prophecy given to Ba'al by Marsuuv. "'*There will come from times past an albino with a head of fire, who will rid the world of the poisonous waters and return us unto Paradise.*'"

Meaning ignited her eyes. She stared at him for a long time and then spoke in barely more than a whisper. "An antichrist."

Billy didn't respond. But in that moment, all of his own turmoil and angst made more sense than it ever had. This was the demon in him, that evil nature that refused to be extricated, haunted by Marsuvees Black in one world and held captive by the Shataiki queen Marsuuv in this world. He, Billy, was destined to crush this world. And to usher in Paradise in the other.

Janae approached again, dripping with desire. "And I will be by your side. Your queen."

Billy wasn't sure why he was suddenly compelled to remove the strip of cloth from his wrist, but he pulled it free and let her see the fresh cut.

Her eyes dropped and she smiled coyly. Touched the blood and playfully brought her finger to her tongue. But the moment she tasted his blood, her face registered shock.

"What's this? This is Teeleh's blood?"

"Marsuuv's blood." Because Marsuuv had bitten Ba'al and allowed him to take some of her blood. It's where his own thirst had come from.

"Marsuuv," she whispered, staring at his wrist with a craving he'd not yet seen in her. "May I?"

"Yes, you may."

She brought his wrist to her mouth, smothered the bloody cut with her lips, and sucked. Her whole body trembled with desire.

Then Billy knew the truth: Janae, like Billos, had Shataiki blood in her veins.

And Ba'al despised them both.

22

"NO ONE knows of this room?" Thomas asked, leading the way down the flight of steps.

"None," Qurong said gruffly. "Keep your eyes ahead."

"I've had ample opportunity to take you out, if I had any intention of doing so."

"Don't think so highly of yourself."

"You've let your guard down a dozen times. You know I have no desire to see you harmed. It's not only against my nature, it's against Chelise's."

Silence.

"She knows," Qurong said.

"Of this place?"

"I showed it to her when she took such an interest in the books. But that was before I came into these lost books you speak of."

The light from Thomas's torch cast a flickering glow over the stone stairs. They came to a small atrium shut off by a wooden gate.

"Inside."

"How did you manage to build this without anyone's knowledge?" Thomas asked, pushing the gate wide.

"It was here."

"It was?"

"The tunnels and caves were here. A nest of some kind—Shataiki, for all I know. Ba'al tells me they have a wicked appetite for the books."

"Naturally. They seek to make their own history by bending the will of all men in the same way they've bent yours."

Qurong grunted and steered him to his right, into one of five tunnels beyond the gate. The hollowed passage looked as old as the world, carved through the rock but straight enough. They walked twenty paces before making another right through another wooden gate and into what appeared to be a library.

Old books lay on a round table at the center. Bookcases along the right wall. A writing desk to his left. He was about to ask if this was it, when a glow flooded the room. Qurong had lit a second torch on the wall.

Four chairs sat around the table, and beyond it, a couch with stuffed silk pillows. There was everything a reader intent on studying could want down here, including a pitcher of water, a bowl of fruit, even a fireplace.

"This was here?"

"As I said, the cave was here. It's my only escape from the dark priest's prying eyes. He has servants in the walls."

At least one of the shelves was stuffed with volumes from the Books of History. But the Horde could not read the books; Thomas had established that much long ago. To the albino, the words read perfectly clear, but the scabbing disease turned this truth to nonsense in the Hordes' minds. Their scribes were obsessed with writing their own history in plain bound books, a way of legitimizing their own failure to read the Books of History.

Everyone wanted to create his own history. There was nothing as powerful as the written word; history had taught them all that much.

"You can read the Books of History?" Thomas asked to be sure.

"No one can."

"Albinos can."

"That is a lie," Qurong said simply.

There was no way to prove otherwise. He could just as easily pretend to read from the books and Qurong would never know the difference. Such was the nature of religion, plied by man to control the masses.

"But we didn't come down here so you could admire my library." Qurong crossed to the desk. "You say you can give me what I need to destroy my enemies through these books."

He opened a drawer and pulled out a canvas bag bound by rope. He untied the bundle and withdrew colored Books of History, one by one, setting them on the desk. Six of them. The binding of each one a different color.

Qurong faced him. "So show me."

Thomas walked up to the desk and reached for the books. "May I?"

"One. And only one."

"Of course."

He picked up the green book. They were all bound by old leather embossed with the same concentric rings, the symbol for completeness. Elyon's stamp.

The Circle.

Thomas traced the symbol. "Have you opened these?"

"They're empty."

Blank! But Michal said these were a key to both time and the rules that governed the other blank books.

He pulled the cover back. The page was smothered by blood. It had been used. Thomas's heart pounded at the prospect of entering.

"Let me have your knife."

"Don't be a fool."

"Do you want to do this or not?" Thomas snapped. Then he considered a possibility that made him second-guess himself. What if he vanished into the other world without the books? How would he ever make it back? He couldn't conceive of going without knowing he would return to Chelise and the Circle. To Samuel. To Jake.

Michal had all but demanded he use them. So he would.

"Do you have any rope?"

"What for?"

"Trust me. Rope."

Qurong eyed him, then plucked a length of twine from a stand beside the desk and tossed it. "I'm now relegated to trusting my gravest enemy," he said.

"Don't be thick, old man. I don't have any harm in mind. We are in this together."

"And just what are we in for?"

Thomas bound four of the books together with the top cover held back to reveal the first page stained with blood. He then tied the bundle of books to his arm. "I need your knife. Trust me, if this works you're going to love—"

"No!" Qurong slammed his hand down on the books, pinning them to the desk. "Enough trust!"

Perhaps he had been too hasty. Thomas lifted both hands to calm the man.

"Easy. I thought I'd already explained. These books unlock time. You and I can vanish"—he snapped his fingers—"and wake in another world where it will all become clear to you."

"Assuming this nonsense is true, what truth do you speak of? How will this save the Horde?"

"I can't explain it. You'll have to . . . to trust me. The world will become clear in ways you've never imagined. Think of it as a gift, one that will save far more than you—"

"Just that?" Qurong snarled. "Just 'trust me'? I am the supreme commander of the Horde kingdom, and I rule all of the known world. I am not a servant for you or for Ba'al or for any other living creature to toy with!"

Thomas's eagerness was partly to blame for Qurong's frustration.

"Listen to me, you old crustacean!" He was shouting. "My son Samuel has just joined the half-breeds! They will rain rage and fire down on you for the torment you've caused them all. The Horde will be drained of blood, and the Shataiki will *feed* on your precious kingdom! Now give me your knife!"

CHELISE PULLED up sharply at the sound of Thomas's voice murmuring urgently down the tunnel.

She'd entered the city from the south, through the familiar gardens that she once frequented. The journey took longer than she'd hoped, for the simple reason that unlike most albinos, her face, even without the scabbing disease, would surely be recognized by any who caught a glimpse of her.

But she knew a secret way in, behind the stables, via an alley that she'd used numerous times as a girl. Then through a low basement window that she was glad to find had not been boarded up.

She'd donned a cloak from a closet behind the kitchen, then crept through the servants' quarters with one objective on her mind.

Find her father.

Find Qurong, who would know what had happened to Thomas. She would make sure he knew of her love for him after ten years without a word.

Naturally, she could live without Qurong. Had lived without Qurong. But without Thomas, she wasn't so sure. He'd been her lover since the day she learned how to love, really love. He'd shown her the Great Romance. She'd begged Elyon for Thomas's life with every step she'd taken.

The palace was buzzing, and she'd hidden behind a pile of barrels in the pantry. Still, she could hear whispers of an albino who'd come, and that could only be Thomas. No one seemed to know where Qurong had vanished to.

Her first thought was of his library. She'd slipped into the root cellar that led to the tunnel, found the door into the secret passage open, and descended on light feet.

And now . . . her breath hung in her chest. He was alive! Thomas was alive and with her father, whose voice reached her now.

"Just 'trust me'? I am the supreme commander of the Horde kingdom, and I rule all of the known world. I am not a servant for you or for Ba'al or for any other living creature to toy with!"

"Listen to me, you old crustacean!" She was astounded that Thomas would use such language with her father.

"My son Samuel has just joined the half-breeds! They will rain rage and fire down on you for the torment you've caused them all. The Horde will be drained of blood, and the Shataiki will feed on your precious kingdom! Now give me your knife!"

It took a moment for the words to form meaning in Chelise's mind. They claimed that Samuel had joined Eram and intended to wage war on the Horde, but that was . . .

How could Samuel consider such a thing?

"Thomas?" She started to run. "Father!"

THOMAS REALIZED he'd pushed too far. Panic began to set in. Once angered, Qurong wouldn't be easily overcome. A woman's voice yelled down the tunnel.

They both spun toward the gate. They were discovered! Patricia?

Now! While Qurong was off balance. He had to move now!

Thomas whirled and snatched Qurong's knife from his belt. Slashed his own palm, barely aware of the pain.

Qurong swung his arm to retrieve his weapon, raging like a bull. Thomas ducked under the blow and grabbed his other hand. Tugged it toward him, blade ready.

For an absurd moment they each pulled at the hand, Qurong desperate to be free, Thomas knowing that his plan to win Qurong by taking him now threatened his own mission to return.

"Father!"

The woman was behind them, at the gate, screaming. Not just any woman, not Patricia, not Horde.

Chelise.

Qurong faced her. As he flinched, Thomas seized his last hope. He yanked the man's hand, sliced his fingers, and thrust both his hand and Qurong's hand onto the blood-smeared page.

Immediately the world began to spin, and his heart stopped.

It was working.

He twisted back, saw Chelise fading at the gate, eyes wide.

"Save the Circle, Chelise! Save them from Samuel! I'll be back!"

But everything had gone black.

———⊂∞⊃———

CHELISE'S BLOOD ran cold. They were there inside the library, in a tug-of-war over her father's hand, when she cried out. Her father looked up, stunned by her appearance.

Thomas had moved like a man possessed, slashing Qurong's hand with a knife, slamming their bleeding fingers onto a stack of bound books.

Thomas twisted his head; she knew with one look into his wide, green eyes that he was the same man she'd always loved.

"Save the Circle, Chelise! Save them from Samuel! I'll be . . ."

Before he could finish, he vanished. They both disappeared—knife, books, and all—before Thomas could utter another syllable.

There one moment, grappling and bleeding, gone the next.

She stood in the gate, stunned. It had happened. This other world Thomas had talked to her about so often as they lay next to each other under the stars was real. Not that she'd doubted . . .

But she had.

She walked in. Stepped through the space her father and lover had occupied just seconds earlier. His world was not only real, but it had taken him again. She cried out, fists tight. How could he do this? Both of them! Gone! She could kill them both.

Save the Circle, Chelise! Save them from Samuel! I'll be . . . Back. He meant back. *I'll be back.*

Samuel . . . What had the boy done? Dear Elyon! She had to get back to Marie and the council.

Chelise turned and ran from Qurong's library.

She had to get back to her only son. To Jake.

23

"HOW LONG since we injected them?" Kara demanded. "We have to bring them back."

"Twenty-three minutes," Monique replied, peering through a microscope at a sample of Janae's blood. "It's working. Thomas's blood is destroying the virus."

"Already?" The pace of its effectiveness was alarming. "You're sure?"

"Take a look." Monique straightened and looked at the isolation room where Billy and Janae still dreamed in fits and moans. Whatever was happening in their minds, they had to stop it.

Kara bent over the eyepiece and acquired the virus, a microscopic organism she'd always thought looked like a lunar lander. "How can you . . ."

"Dear God, help us," Monique breathed in such a dreadful tone that Kara thought one of the two might have just died.

"What?" She jerked back from the microscope. "What is it?" They were too late, she knew it! Too late for what, she didn't know, but this whole thing had been a bad idea from the start.

Monique stared, pale faced, at the isolation chamber. Two techs stood inside with their backs to the observation windows, fixated on the two gurneys. Only they weren't any ordinary techs in white lab coats.

One was a man dressed in a long black cloak, like a gothic priest. The other . . .

Kara's pulse went from heavy to a dead stop. She recognized the clothing worn by the second man, and his morst-coated dreadlocks.

She hadn't seen anything similar in three decades, but this image had haunted a hundred nightmares in that time.

Horde.

The one dressed in black turned around and stared out at her.

Kara felt faint. This was her brother looking at her. He was older, not much, and his face appeared hardened by time, but there was no mistaking Thomas, not in a thousand years.

"Thomas?" Monique breathed beside her.

"It's . . ." Kara didn't know what it was. Thomas—yes, Thomas!—or a vision of Thomas. The man with dreadlocks turned around. Gray eyes. Most definitely Horde, covered by the scabbing disease.

"We're dreaming," Kara said. She glanced at two lab techs to her right and saw that if she was dreaming, so were they. One had dropped his clipboard and left it by his feet as he gawked.

When she turned back to the room, Thomas was walking toward the door. He opened it. Stepped out.

Spoke.

"Kara . . . forgive me, I know this is a shock." He gripped four books with bleeding fingers, the top book open and smudged with fresh blood. "I . . . I made it back," he said.

She could hardly breathe. "Thomas?" A stupid thing to say, but nothing else would come.

His green eyes darted around, as wide as she'd seen them. He was as shocked as she. His lips slowly twisted into a quirky grin. "Wow."

The emotion of seeing Thomas, who had been lost to this world, crashed over her like a pounding wave, and she made no attempt to stop the tears that flooded her eyes. She uttered one halting sob and stumbled forward.

She rushed the last three steps and hugged him awkwardly. There was so much to say. Endless questions. But at the moment her mind was blank. She could only cry.

The Scab crept from the isolation room in a crouch. "What magic is this?" he demanded loudly. "You've cursed me!"

Thomas eased away from Kara and addressed him. "It will be clear. I told you to trust me; now you have no choice. We've arrived."

The door swung open and two guards burst in, saw the Scab, and leveled their handguns. "Steady . . . no sudden moves."

"Lower your weapons," Monique said, motioning the guards to stand down.

The laboratory adviser, a biological engineer named Bruno, spoke in an urgent voice from behind them. "Miss Hunter, I urge you to step back. The chance of contamination is unknown."

The smell, Kara thought.

"Ma'am, I urge isolation immediately."

The sulfuric stink of the Scab's rotting flesh had filled the room. There was no telling if or how the scabbing disease would spread in this world.

"No," Thomas said. "If the disease spread easily, I would have brought it back with me years ago, when I shifted realities."

But Monique shook her head. "You were only dreaming then. And this . . . You've brought one of the Scabs with you?" But rather than backing off, she walked up to him, eyes fixed on his. "Seal the laboratory's perimeter, Bruno. Leave us."

"Ma'am—"

"Now, Bruno." Eyes still on Thomas. "Out, all of you."

They backed off and headed to the decontamination chamber like scurrying mice. The Scab was dressed in a leather tunic, not battle dress. Cracks on his face ran with sweat that marked the morst paste with long jagged streaks. His eyes, though gray, looked bright with panic.

"End this!" he thundered.

"I don't think you understand, Qurong," Thomas said. "This isn't just a vision that I or you can end. We've unlocked time with the books and are now in . . ." He stopped and glanced around. "Where exactly are we?"

"Raison Pharmaceutical," Monique said. "Bangkok. Hello, Thomas."

His eyes settled on her. "Monique."

"In the flesh," she said. "As, it seems, are you."

"Why did we come to this location?"

"I don't know."

"How long has it been?"

"Over thirty-five years here," she said. "And there?"

"Ten years since I last came. But why would I return *here*, to this exact spot?"

Qurong wasn't following them in the least. "How can this be? We were just in my library. I've awakened in a land of albinos."

"Listen to me, Qurong!" Thomas seemed downright perturbed by the Horde leader. "What have I been saying all along? There's more to the world than your little city and gray water. In this world you'll find no Horde. We're all albinos, as you call us. Not albinos, but human, without your skin disease."

"How is that poss—"

"You've had a thick skull to deny Elyon, but now you'll face the truth. Am I delusional or is this really happening?"

Qurong stared about, but it was impossible to know what he was thinking.

Kara stepped up to Thomas and touched his cheek. "It's really you. You're alive." Her mind was still spinning, trying to make sense of what was happening. Dreaming was one thing, but this . . . he'd just appeared out of thin air!

"Your blood," Monique said.

"What about my blood?"

"Maybe you returned here, and now, because of your blood." She glanced at the room behind them, and Thomas followed her eyes.

"You . . ." He spun back. "They have my blood in them?"

"Yes. They . . ."

But he was moving already, flying past a startled Qurong, into the room, up to Billy's gurney. He slapped the redhead's face with his open palm. *Crack!*

"Wake up! Wake up, get out of there!"

He bounded over to Janae and slapped her cheek hard. "Up, up, up!"

"What are you doing?" Monique demanded. But they knew.

"Wake them! You can't let anyone into my world. The books . . . it's far too dangerous!"

"We did it once."

"Never again."

"They're dying!"

"Then let them die," Thomas snapped, spinning back. "Who are they?"

"My daughter," Monique said. "And Billy, the one who first wrote in the Books of History."

"What is this madness?" Qurong raged.

As if in answer, Billy's eyes opened and he groaned. He pushed himself up and looked around groggily.

"What . . . what's happening?"

"Billy?"

They turned to Janae, who was trying to sit up.

Monique rushed to her daughter's side. "Lie down, both of you. You're in no condition to get out of bed."

Recognition slowly dawned in Janae's expression. Like a deflating balloon, her face wrinkled with scorn and bitterness.

"No!" she cried. She yanked the IV needle from her arm, pushed her mother away, and staggered from the gurney. "You have no right! Where is it?"

"You woke us up?" Billy shouted, red-faced. "You meddling—!"

"What on earth?" Monique looked from one to the other. "We saved your lives, you ungrateful little beasts!"

"Where's the blood?" Janae was by the counter, trembling like a drug addict, searching for the vial of Thomas's blood. "Where is it?"

"Janae!"

She whirled to face Monique. "I was there, Mother. What have you hidden from me?"

"I don't know what you're talking about."

"Tell them who I am, Billos. Tell them!"

And he did, blinking. "She's Jezreal, lover of Ba'al, who is also Billos of Southern. Me."

Qurong grabbed the IV pole, jabbed the air as if it were a spear, and backed out the door. "Stay! Stay or I swear by Teeleh's blood I will kill the first one who comes for me."

Thomas walked toward him, unfazed. "Then kill me. And your way back home will die with me."

The threat gave the diseased man some pause.

"Put the weapon down."

"Tell me what's happening to me. And by the gods, don't tell me I've traveled to another world. No one's heard of such a thing."

"What would you like to hear? That this is a nightmare? That your greatest enemies, Eram and Ba'al, don't really exist? That your daughter, Chelise, really isn't your daughter?"

"Silence!"

"I've told you the truth and in time you will accept it. Now put the weapon down!"

But Qurong didn't appear interested. "Enough magic. Wake me up or I swear I'll kill you all in my dreams!"

"Who is this brute?" Janae demanded. "The old fool Qurong himself. You see, Mother"—she pointed at Qurong—"this is who I am. I belong in his world. Give me the blood, send me back, and kill my body here."

"Stop this!" Monique's face had gone white. "You don't know what you're talking about, Janae; you can't just die in one world and live in another!"

"We don't need to die," Billy said. They turned to him and saw that his eyes were glued to the books in Thomas's hand. "Give us the books."

But Thomas was more interested in Qurong at the moment. "Step back in here. Lower the weapon. Let's be reasonable about this." After a moment's hesitation he added, "Please. My lord, please."

The Scab leader said nothing, but he seemed to be considering a different course. Kara's mind spun with the shocking reality of a very real future to which Thomas had gone and returned.

"He has the lost books, Janae," Billy said, slipping from the gurney. To Thomas: "If you want to be reasonable, let us use them. You'll be rid of us forever."

"Qurong?" Thomas was still fixated on the leader, who finally drew a deep breath and set the pole down.

"Thank you." Free of concern about Qurong, Thomas stared the redhead down. "You have no right to enter our world. We have one Ba'al, we hardly need another."

"And you, Thomas Hunter, have no right to deny me anything. You're here because of me."

"Now you're barking mad."

"I was the first to write in a blank Book of History when they were discovered under the monastery in Paradise, Colorado. More important, I was the one who wrote into history the fact that you traveled to the other world. You went because of me."

Thomas looked shell-shocked.

"You could even call me Father. Now be a good son and give me the books."

"That's not possible. I went long before the books were found in the Paradise monastery."

"No, Thomas," Kara said in an apologetic tone. "I mean, yes, you did go before, but the books reside outside of time. Whatever is written in the books is fact: past, present, and future. At least as far as we've been able to learn."

He seemed to soak that in.

"So then, you're the one who started all of this. Bill. You've been to the Black Forest?"

Billy shrugged. "All I can tell you is that I belong there. I have a purpose there."

"And I have a purpose here," Thomas said. "It does not include sending even more wickedness back to my world. I'm here to find a way for a land that's lost all hope. Unless you have a message of profound hope, I doubt you qualify."

"You don't know us," Janae said. She walked toward Thomas, wearing a faint smile of seduction. "Good or evil, it doesn't matter. We belong there, Thomas. It's Billy's world as much as it's yours. And now it's mine."

"Get back from him," Monique snapped.

Janae had other things in mind. "Is that what you want, Thomas? You prefer the old mother over the daughter?"

"Back!" Monique grabbed Janae's black dress between her shoulder blades and jerked her back as if she were a feather. She shoved her onto the gurney and aimed a long finger at her nose. "Sit!"

"You tell me to trust you, Thomas," Qurong muttered, "but I'm telling you I can't trust my own eyes. If the magic is in the books, then we should use them."

Thomas backed away from them all, untying the rope that tethered the books to his arm. "Kara, if you don't mind."

She walked up to him and accepted the books.

"Step through the door."

The isolation room was only twenty feet square, and the doorway was open, five feet beyond Thomas. Kara retreated from the room and faced them through the doorway.

"Monique, help Kara."

"I—"

"Now! Please."

She glanced at her daughter, who stood by the gurney, then hurried past Thomas, who had his eyes on Billy.

The redhead pieced it together first. "So what, you're just going to lock—"

"No!" Janae threw herself forward, possessed by a desperation that was quite literally of another world.

But Thomas moved like a cat, slammed the door shut, and shoved the outside bolt down. That he'd had the presence of mind to notice the outside lock was testament to refined instincts, but the way he'd moved . . . Kara wasn't sure it was entirely human. Long ago he'd displayed some astonishing fighting skills that he claimed to have learned from his dreams, but this speed and strength was new, maybe because he had lived it rather than dreamed it.

Janae slammed into the glass with little effect, mouth wide in a scream Kara could not hear. See, Janae had only gone to the other world in her dreams. As for Qurong . . . now, there was a man who must have the power of a bull in both realities.

Qurong peered out, mystified. This was undoubtedly the first time he'd seen such strong, clear glass.

"Is there any way out of the room?" Thomas demanded.

"You're going to keep them locked up?"

"What would you have me do?"

Monique looked at the three, caged like animals. "I guess it'll hold them until we figure something out."

Thomas took the books from Kara. "Then let's be rid of this place. I need space to think without monkeys peering at me. We don't have much time."

Kara felt a grin tug at her mouth. Thirty years had changed the way Thomas spoke, but he was the same brother. Thomas Hunter was most definitely back. And to her it was like the second coming.

24

"TEN YEARS," Kara said. "So that would make you how old over there?"

"The same as I am here," Thomas said, pacing beside the towering shelves of bound books in Monique's library. "Forty-nine. Amazing." He rubbed his face with his hand, a habit he'd developed—to check if his skin was turning Horde, Chelise used to joke.

"But it's been thirty-six years since you left us. You were twenty-four at the time. You should be sixty, like me. Instead, you're under fifty and you hardly look forty."

"All I know is that I was twenty-four—or was it twenty-five?—when I first woke in the Black Forest, and nearly twenty-six years have passed since then." He scanned the ceiling. "Utterly amazing."

They'd left the laboratory, taken an elevator to the ground level, and retreated to Monique's library, issuing strict instructions to be left alone.

"A lot's changed since you left us," Monique said.

"It's not the change. It's being back in civilization. Elyon knows how much I love the desert, but this . . . this is fantastic."

"So you're married? In the desert?"

Thomas looked into her bright eyes, recalling what they'd shared. Was that only a dream? The relationship between the two worlds still confused him. What was less confusing was the fact that he was physically here, now. There was only one Thomas Hunter, and he stood in a city called Bangkok, looking at an older woman who, at sixty, was stunning.

"Married? Yes. Happily. No, *happily* is a silly word for it. My wife is the jewel of the desert, the light that guides my heart through the darkness when I grow tired of waiting for the end."

Monique grinned. "Wow. Sounds like I missed out."

"Sorry, I didn't mean it like that. You're married?"

"Once."

"Janae's father?"

"Yes. It was a torrid affair that lasted a year. His name was Philippe, and he raged into my life like a tornado when I was feeling sorry for my loss. I knew it was bad, but he gave me what I longed for and then disappeared. He knew about you, naturally. You were still quite famous then."

Philippe. Thomas wondered what connection he had to the other world. They were all connected, it seemed. The only real question was, in what way? Albino, Horde, Eramite half-breed, Shataiki? Roush?

Kara walked up to him with a roll of gauze and some tape she'd grabbed on the way out of the lab. She took his hand and rubbed his skin, studying the cut on his palm. Then she wrapped his hand in the bandage.

Her hair smelled like soap. Perfume. Flowers. He still wore the Horde robe, which carried the faint odor of scabbing disease—to them he likely smelled like a skunk.

"I still can't believe you're here," Kara said, tapping the bandage. She lifted misty eyes. "Really here."

He slid his hand behind her neck, pulled her close and kissed her forehead. "Trust me, to know that all of this exists . . . it certifies me sane. So many times I believed I might be losing my mind."

"You're here to stay?"

Her question took him off guard. He dropped his hand and walked away. "I was told to come, find a way, and return to the Circle. My son is lost without me. I don't have much time."

"So, how long?"

"He didn't say. Quickly, that's all. You don't understand . . . there's trouble brewing. My son has betrayed the Circle and joined Eram." Saying it renewed his sense of urgency, never mind that it all sounded a bit preposterous. "I fear the worst. War. The unraveling of all good in the land."

Kara studied him, eyes fixed. "Take me back with you."

"Back? No, no."

"Yes," she said. "Take me back."

"This world needs you!"

"This world needs Monique. I don't have anyone left. Mom and Dad are long gone. I've been alone for thirty years."

"You never married?"

"Never."

He considered the notion.

"You can't be serious about this," Monique said, standing from her chair. She crossed to a bar and poured a drink from a bottle of amber liquid. "We don't even know what the true connection between the worlds is. It's far too dangerous."

She was grasping.

"We do know!" Kara snapped. "It's obvious."

"Then tell us."

"Thomas's world is the future of this world, thousands of years from now, remade, a kind of new earth. The essentials of history are being replayed; everything spiritual here has become physical there. It's like take two. Isn't that what you said once, Thomas?"

"I'm not sure I understand," Monique said.

"In the other world, words become flesh through the Books of History. And vice versa: reality becomes words recorded in the same books. The spiritual has physical manifestation. When those books came into our reality, they still had the same power to turn words into flesh." She motioned at the stack of four books on the desk where Thomas had laid them. "The books are the bridge between the worlds. Literally, a bridge."

She'd put it so simply.

"And the blood?" Thomas asked. "My blood, Teeleh's blood, Elyon's blood. Why always blood?"

Kara joined Monique and poured a drink. "I don't know. In both realities, blood is life. Disease here and evil there are both carried by blood. And they're wiped out by blood. You'll have to tell us the rest."

The connections hadn't escaped Thomas all these years, but he'd never put it so plainly in his head. "The red lakes," he said.

"What lakes?"

"They came later. The lakes were turned red by Elyon's blood. By drowning in them we stay free of the disease."

"Drowning? Really drowning?"

"Yes, we die. But it's life, really, because Elyon paid that price so we can escape it."

"Price for what?"

"The cost of our embracing evil—death. Elyon cannot live with evil; it must die. Or so we say."

"So it's like a baptism?"

Thomas nodded. "Perhaps. Only Elyon knows the full extent of these connections."

"Unfortunately, like you say, Elyon seems to have gone quiet," Monique said. "In both realities. And you may have brought the worst to us."

"How so?"

"Qurong." Monique set down her glass and crossed to the window. "There's another connection that I'd like to consider."

"The Raison Strain?" Kara said. "You can't think the scabbing disease is the same as the Raison Strain."

Monique turned back. "Would it surprise you?"

The room fell silent, and Thomas began to feel oddly misplaced here in the world of medicine and machines. What if he couldn't go back? He eyed the books, still bound and smeared with his and Qurong's blood. What did he really know about the rules that guided these lost books?

"Please, Thomas." He turned to Kara, who was watching him in earnest. "Take me with you."

He felt his face slowly offer up a soft smile. "You never were one to capitulate, were you?"

But he couldn't promise her anything, not without knowing more.

"I could never go," Monique said in a thin voice cut by sorrow. She was staring out the window again, lost in thought. Thomas understood a small part of what she must be feeling.

She could never enter the world where Chelise lived. They both knew that Thomas had given his heart and soul to another woman who waited now, braving any danger for him.

The memory of Chelise rushing into Qurong's underground library swallowed him for a moment, and he had to push back the compulsion to rush over to the books and use them again. While he stood in safety, Chelise was . . . was what?

See, that was just it. He wouldn't put anything past his desert bride. Her spirit more often than not pulled her into the most dangerous path. She could be rushing toward Eram to retrieve Samuel or returning to the Circle to warn them. Assuming she'd escaped Qurongi City.

Meanwhile, he'd stumbled back into a love affair that had never quite died.

Monique turned. "But that's my cross to bear. And to be honest, it's not an impossibly heavy one." She took one deep breath and let a smile toy with her mouth. "Although I must say, you do look like a scrumptious dessert. The desert air must agree with you."

"It's the fruit," he said sheepishly, then realized that he might be coming off as pretentious. "And I'm younger. Honestly I was just thinking how beautiful you look."

They stared at each other, and the air grew stuffy.

Monique rescued him. "This is rather awkward." She crossed to him, kissed his cheek, then turned away. "The fact is, however fantastic this turn of events might seem to us, we all know that we're playing a role on a grand stage that determines the lives of millions. I owe this world my work and my life. And Thomas"—she faced them both—"your world is waiting for you. So, what can we do to help you?"

There was still Kara, Thomas thought. Where did she belong?

He nodded. "I will always remember your graciousness."

Monique dipped her head.

Thomas sighed. "As I said, what I know is this: One"—he stuck out a finger—"the Circle has been pulled apart by arguments in doctrine. We still hold to the same basic tenets, but now even those are being challenged. What was once sacred is slipping into obscurity. And the greatest of all guiding imperatives—that we love the Horde—has been abandoned by more than even I probably know."

"Sounds familiar," Kara said.

"How so?"

"You think this world is any different?"

Thomas hadn't considered it; his mind was on the desert. He ran his fingers through his long locks of hair and continued.

"It's as if another kind of disease, this forgetfulness, has been eating away at their hearts for years like a cancer. Now it's too late to reverse it. We never used to live for the desert, because we knew that it was just a transition. A better world was just around the corner. We endured terrible persecution and death, driven by hope. But now that hope of a better world is losing its appeal. Forgotten."

"Again, familiar."

"That doesn't help me."

"So you need what, Thomas?" Monique asked.

"A way for the Circle to fulfill its hope."

They just looked at him.

"Maybe a few guns would do the trick." Still those empty stares. "But I couldn't, of course. I didn't come for a way to kill."

"And what else?" Monique pressed.

"Qurong. I brought the supreme commander of our greatest enemy in the hope of helping him put to rest the impossible stubbornness that's badgered him all these years."

"You shouldn't have brought him," she said.

"Why not?"

"He's death."

25

QURONG STANK of dead fish, Billy thought. The thick, sulfuric scent was inexplicably appealing, and this realization sickened him slightly. Janae paced like a caged animal, seemingly oblivious to Qurong, who was so far out of his comfort zone that he could do little but stand and sweat.

Billy leaned against the gurney, running through their options, which were clearly limited. The Raison Strain B virus had been stopped by the blood; this was good. He had finally, after over a decade of wondering, found himself—his inner demons, his purpose, all that made him tick. This was even better.

But the only way to reconnect with who he really was required the lost books. Right now, he was in the wrong world.

"There has to be a way out of this prison," he said.

Janae whirled, furious. "It's built to keep people in, you idiot! We're stuck!"

Billy stood up. "So now I'm your enemy too?"

She closed her eyes, drew long breaths through her nostrils, and finally pushed air back out through pursed lips. Sweat matted her long black hair to her cheeks, and her mascara had run, but even so she looked as alluring as she had when she was Jezreal.

"Okay. Sorry. Sorry, I'm just . . ." Her eyes opened, misty. "This is all happening too quickly. I don't know who I am anymore, Billy. I don't know why I feel this way."

His ability to read minds hadn't been affected by the disease, but he didn't need to look past her face to see that Janae was hopelessly lost.

Like a newborn child seeing the light but not understanding where the womb had gone.

Thomas was lost as well. As were Kara and Monique. His mind-reading powers hadn't been present while he was in Ba'al's body, and they'd taken a few minutes to reassert themselves after waking, but in the short time he'd stared into Thomas's mind, Billy had learned a few things.

He learned that the Circle was fracturing and might very well shatter with just a little more pressure.

He learned that Samuel, Thomas's son, had betrayed him and gone to Eram.

And he learned the location of the three thousand who waited for the rest of the Circle to join them. All of the Circle in one canyon.

None of that helped him now, locked in this isolation room. He focused on Janae. She'd gone from a lost but spirited young woman to Jezreal in minutes. There could be no doubt: she was somehow tied to the Shataiki. But exactly how, and why *she*, of all people, he didn't know yet.

Then again, her mother, Monique, had been at the center of Thomas Hunter's life. Perhaps Janae's father had approached Monique because of this.

Billy stepped in front of Janae and brushed her hair off her cheeks. "I know. You're conflicted and it's tearing you apart. Trust me, I've been there. When we get back, you won't feel divided. We belong there, Janae. It'll all be okay when we go home."

She lunged forward and kissed him on the lips, drawing desperately on his breath. She wrapped her arms around him and held him close, trembling.

"Don't leave me behind," she whispered. "Promise me, Billy. Never leave me."

He pulled back, feeling awkward. She was like a woman possessed by a spirit that had awakened from the dead.

"I won't leave you."

"Swear it!"

"I swear."

Qurong grunted, and Billy saw that he wore a scowl. Looking into his eyes, Billy saw more. Much more. And he felt compelled to set the record straight.

"Your forehead may bear Ba'al's three claw marks, old man, but you hate him. On the other hand, you love your daughter, though you deny it. You fear Thomas more than you fear Teeleh. And deep down inside, you suspect that Elyon is real, but the Shataiki larvae have invaded your mind and made you stupid."

Which is why I, not you, am the chosen one, he didn't say. "How do I know? Because I also know you were eating blueberries with sago paste when Thomas burst into your house and tricked you into this journey."

Qurong's gray eyes were round. What if the answer to how they might return somehow rested with this man?

"Be careful what you think, Qurong." Let him stew on that for a minute.

Billy kissed Janae on the hair. "It'll be okay, we'll get back. Let's take a deep breath and think this through. Starting with this beast."

"I can tell you, there's no way I would allow you to enter my world," Qurong said, spitting on the clean floor. "You're witches. Albinos who have an alliance with Ba'al. If you think you belong anywhere but hell, you're mistaken."

"This coming from an overgrown lizard who smells like hell," Billy said.

Janae wiped her eyes and breathed out again. "Blood," she said.

Billy frowned. "Blood?"

"Yes. I was drawn to the blood. When I was in Jezreal and you let me taste your blood . . . there was something about the blood that captivated me."

"The blood books." Having been with Ba'al even for an hour, Billy still had many of his memories, and he dipped into them now. "Thomas's blood. Marsuuv gave Ba'al her blood when Ba'al was Billos. Ba'al became part of the Shataiki. How does that help us now?"

Janae studied Qurong. "Well . . ." She hurried to a closet, pulled the door wide, and withdrew a microscope. She tossed Billy a small, clear plastic box.

"Take a blood and skin sample from him. Apply them both to the slides."

Billy looked at Qurong. "From him?"

"From him, yes. Hurry, we don't have all day."

"What's the meaning of this?" Qurong demanded.

"It means that you're going to let us look at your blood under this machine." Billy walked up and handed him a glass slide. "Smear some of the blood from your wound on this piece of glass."

Qurong looked at the slide as if it might be a weapon of great significance.

"Hurry!"

"This means nothing to me."

"Do you want to go home before Ba'al takes your throne?"

The man grunted and plucked the slide from his hand. He awkwardly rubbed some of the blood from his finger onto the glass, then handed it back.

"And his skin," Janae said, handing Billy a small scalpel.

"Now your skin." Billy handed him another slide and the knife.

"You expect me to cut my skin off?"

"Just scrape some off." Janae looked over from the eyepiece. "The thinner the better."

"You heard her," Billy snapped.

"Whatever for? This is preposterous!"

Janae spoke as she focused the microscope. "Call it grasping at straws, I don't know, just do it. Has anyone ever studied your blood before? I doubt it. I'm a scientist, it's what I do."

Qurong scraped some skin off his forearm, then dragged the blade across the slide, depositing a layer of morst and dead flesh on the clear glass. "Albino fools."

Billy set the slide on the counter next to Janae. "Anything?"

"This is . . . I think . . ." But she didn't elaborate.

"What?"

Janae quickly pulled out the slide with blood and slipped in the sample of Qurong's skin.

"What?" Billy demanded again.

"I . . . if I'm not mistaken, he has what looks to me—although I can't be sure without more tests, this microscope isn't the most powerful—"

"Just say it."

She adjusted the focus. "He has something similar to the Raison Strain in his blood. Looks like a slightly different strain, but . . ." She adjusted her view of the skin sample.

Made sense. In a twisted kind of way.

Janae gasped and left her mouth agape.

"What?"

She straightened, eyes on Qurong.

"What?"

"That's it," she said, approaching the man. She reached for him. "Can I have a closer look?"

He hesitantly held out his arm. Janae took his wrist in one hand and rubbed her thumb on his skin. "Horde are a little stronger than albino. Isn't that correct?"

"Yes," Qurong and Billy said in unison.

"But albino are much quicker," she said. "They don't have the same pain and their joints are free to move with ease."

"So some claim."

"For heaven's sake, Janae, just—"

"I know why they're stronger," she said, looking at Billy with some wonder. "It's the Shataiki."

"They have Shataiki blood?"

"No. Maybe, I don't know. But their skin is infested with millions of microscopic larvae."

"Shataiki larvae," Billy said, mind overflowing with Ba'al's knowledge. "The twelve queens spawned by Teeleh reproduce by laying eggs that form unfertilized larvae. They can live for centuries in this state until another Shataiki fertilizes them with blood."

"How?"

"They bite. Pass blood through their fangs."

"Vampires."

"No, Shataiki," Billy said, then shrugged. "Same difference."

Qurong was staring at his arm. "Worms?"

"Tiny larvae," Janae said, hurrying back to the microscope and peering in. "In this world we have scabies, a skin disease caused by a tiny mite called *Sarcoptes scabiei*, invisible to the naked eye. They burrow into the skin and lay eggs that produce larvae and more mites. The rash on the skin is a reaction to the mites. Similar to what we have here."

She looked up again. "The Horde are covered by Teeleh's larvae. They evidently infect Horde blood with something similar to the first Raison Strain. But rather than kill them, the virus passes on some Shataiki properties, like strength."

"Walking breeding grounds."

"This is complete and utter foolishness," Qurong said, dismissing them with a wave of his arm.

Billy suddenly knew how they might get out. "Janae, if we could get out of this isolation room, could you get us out of the laboratory?"

"I don't know." She looked at the main door, where two guards were normally posted.

"Surely there's another way out of here. Ventilation, a passage, something."

"Ventilation?" She blinked. "We're underground, the vents are huge." She brushed past him. "I was a kid when they built this place, and I crawled through some of them then. The main return shaft runs over the rooms down the hall, opening to each one." She was staring at the two-foot-by-two-foot grille near the top of the wall, five feet to the left of the main door. "That would get us out. Maybe."

"Maybe? Why wouldn't it?"

"For starters, we're boxed behind reinforced glass. And even if we followed the ventilation to the end of the hall without getting the guard's attention, the shaft turns straight up, twenty feet. There's no way—"

"We don't need to go up," Billy said. He tore the sheet off the nearest gurney and tossed it to Qurong. "Wrap this around your fists. The glass is made to withstand human force, but they didn't have Horde in mind. You can break it."

Qurong looked at the glass, the sheet in his hands, and then back at Billy. He tossed the sheet back. "I'll take my chances here."

"Whatever for? You heard Thomas! He has no intention of letting you jump back now that he has you under his thumb. He knew that kidnapping you would immobilize the Horde, perhaps giving the Eramites and Samuel the advantage they need to mount a crushing blow."

The thought had just presented itself to Billy, and it made sense, maybe more than they knew. "But Thomas doesn't know Ba'al the way you and I do. There's no telling what the dark priest will do in your absence. We have to get back. Now!"

"Not like this. I go back with no advantage. I would just as soon trust Thomas as you." Qurong was settling into his normative, crafty self.

"I can give you an advantage," Janae said. She looked at Billy, gave him her thoughts, and then addressed Qurong when Billy nodded.

"I could give you a weapon. One that you could use to wipe out all of the Eramites, the albinos—any army that came against you."

Qurong's face twitched. "That's not possible."

"You know nothing of this world! What I have is small enough to take through the books, and believe me, it could end life in your world."

"What is it?"

"A virus. A disease that will only affect those you want it to."

"You're bluffing. Whoever heard of such a thing?"

"You're saying that a lot these days, I'll bet," she snapped, then motioned to their surroundings. "Whoever heard of *this*? Whoever heard of the reading of thoughts and the unlocking of time and space with a *book*? In reality the whole world is one big whoever-heard-of-it!"

"She's got a point, you buffoon," Billy said. It occurred to him that he was talking to the most powerful man in a world where he might soon need allies. He would have to curb the insults.

"You're an intelligent man, Qurong. I saw this when I shared Ba'al's mind, and frankly it scared me. You're also the most powerful man on the planet. Your subjects tremble when you walk by. But we both know that everyone at the top is a target. What we're offering you will ensure your survival. And we can be your greatest allies."

The Horde was sweating again, but he wasn't arguing.

"Every minute we stand here doubting puts distance between us and the lost books," Janae scolded. "We have to move."

"How will you get out?" Qurong asked. "Where is this weapon?"

"Not in here." She shoved her finger at the reinforced glass. "Break it! At least try, for heaven's sake."

Qurong grunted and began to wrap the sheet around his elbow. "I don't like this. You put me at your mercy. I have no reason to believe you'll take me with you."

"You have no choice but to trust us."

The man kept his eyes on them as he stood by the large window, roughly eight by five. Qurong nodded, gripped his fist with his left hand, and slammed his elbow back against the glass without removing his eyes from Billy.

The room shook as the window fractured into a hundred thousand hairline cracks. Qurong pushed the broken glass, and it fell to the ground like rain.

Janae uttered something that made no sense, then scrambled over the sill into the main laboratory. She spun, motioning silence with a finger to her lips, and ran to the same electronically operated storage cabinet from which she'd withdrawn the Raison Strain B.

Working like a mouse over a crumb, she began punching in access numbers. She motioned to a closet and issued whispered orders. "A ladder and tools; remove the grate; wait for me. Just get it off."

"You're getting the virus?"

"Hurry!"

Billy paused. What if the Raison Strain didn't have the same effects in the other world?

"You have other viruses, right? Ebola?"

She caught his eye and glanced at Qurong. "Please, trust me. I need a moment. Alone."

Billy understood immediately. She didn't want Qurong to know what she was up to. Perhaps where on her body she hid the viruses.

He pulled the door to the closet open, grabbed the ladder and a small tool kit. Hurrying to the wall under the return air grate, he shoved the ladder at Qurong. "Keep it quiet." The main door was sealed tight and would offer a good sound barrier, but there was no telling what other security measures had been put in place.

Qurong tried to unfold the ladder as Billy pulled out a Phillips-head screwdriver. "Here, back off." Billy grabbed the ladder, set it on the floor in proper position, and hurried to the top. Four screws secured the grate, and they all came out without a hitch. He hung the panel on a hook that protruded from the ladder, then peered into the return duct.

Large enough for both Janae and him, but the Horde oaf would never make it.

"Get down."

He twisted back and saw that Janae stood beside Qurong, looking up at him.

"Hurry! Get down here."

Billy dropped down beside them. "We can't all—"

"Wait with him by the door," she interrupted, mounting the ladder.

"Me? Wait a minute, I'm coming with you!"

Janae glared back at him. "Shut up, Billy." Then, noting his shock, "I didn't mean it like that. But I'm the only one who can do this. I know where I'm going. Two doors down into a large storage room that has survival equipment and fresh lab coats. Flare guns."

"That's how you're going to get the books, with a lab coat and a flare gun?"

"No, that's how I'm going to walk up to the guards before I disable them and open this door."

"They'll kill you!"

"They know me! I've been giving them orders for years. Trust me, they won't shoot, not before sorting through their confusion. By then it'll be too late for them."

"You're going to overpower them with a flare gun?"

Her jaw muscles bunched with impatience; he was struck by her beauty, standing up on the ladder in her short black dress, dark hair twisted around her face, eyes fired with passion.

"This is Bangkok, the home of kickboxing. Little girls like me learn to take care of themselves at an early age. Stay here."

Then she scurried up the ladder, slipped into the return air duct like a cat, and was gone.

26

THEY SPENT nearly an hour bouncing between their own shared history and the fantastical nature of Thomas's appearance in Bangkok. Although more than ten years had passed since he'd made the last trip in his dreams, the feeling of being here with Kara and Monique was familiar. It wasn't what he'd imagined a ten-year class reunion might be like.

Then again, these women were not mere classmates.

For them, his appearance was more staggering. In the past, his reality jumping had occurred in his mind while his body remained, making it no less real to him, but far less real to those who watched him sleep.

The four lost books still sat on the lamp table by the door. The cut on his palm was wrapped.

He wondered briefly if they would return him to the future. But he thought so—they seemed to follow a path consistent with the traveler's heart.

"So it's basically true, then," Kara said. "You're saying that Earth's history has essentially replayed itself there and been compressed into twenty-six years?"

"Something like that."

Monique had fallen silent over the past ten minutes, seated with one leg draped over the other, still dressed in her laboratory smock. She cleared her throat.

"All of our history," she said.

"So it seems. Not the particulars, of course. But the similarities are inescapable."

"Think of the implications for our world," she muttered. "So this battle between good and evil is as real here as there. Religion may be misguided on most fronts, but it's sniffing around the right notion."

He nodded. "Exactly." Funny how he'd once been so confused about the whole purpose of history. His understanding of the coming and passing of life had all been so egocentric. Looking beyond oneself to a greater purpose was always so difficult for the average person who lived and died before that purpose found its full meaning.

Now, having lived through so much in such a short span, the purpose of life seemed obvious to him. It was nearly impossible to understand how someone could not believe.

And yet, here he was, two thousand years in the past, searching for a way for the Circle precisely because the Circle had begun to lose sight of the true way. What was once obvious to them was no longer quite as obvious. Why was it that humans lost sight of truth so quickly?

They were like a married couple who celebrated in passionate bliss through the honeymoon, yet found themselves estranged only a few years later. It was no wonder the Roush questioned Elyon's wisdom in creating such fickle beings.

This was the essence of the Books of History: human free will. And it always seemed to lead to disaster.

Monique was speaking again. ". . . a real person. Not just an idea."

"I'm sorry, what was that?"

"Elyon. He's a real person. A real being, not just a symbol for an idea."

He regarded her, not quite sure why she would ask such a basic question. "You were there, you should know."

"Trust me, a lot grows hazy in three decades."

And that was the crux of it, he thought.

Thomas sat down, crossed his legs, and faced them both. He looked out the window behind Monique. It overlooked a jungle, teeming with unseen life, but if he took one step into the brush, that life would become very real.

"So." Eyes back on Monique. "What hope is there in this world that would change the course of the other world?"

"Maybe that's not the right question," Kara said.

"No? Then what?"

"Why is everything always about your world? I realize it's where your mind's at, but look at it from my perspective. Until you left us, you were always from this world. Who's to say what you're going through isn't all for us, not for them?"

"Them? You mean Chelise. And Jake and Samuel and all those that I hold dear?"

"And what am I? A figment of your imagination?"

"No." Dear Elyon, she could be obtuse. He leaned forward. "I'm forever in your debt. But you've lived your life here, and I've found mine there."

"Promise me," she said.

She was demanding to go with him again.

He sat back. "Maybe you're right. So what do you have in mind? Besides going with me."

"The present sounds very similar to the future. Yes, I know, the surfaces are very different. There's no Horde, no Shataiki, no Roush, no Circle . . . at least not by those names. But what we do have is a world in which the faithful have forgotten hope. What if your coming is for them, as a part of our history?"

"I'm not here long enough to give your fools hope."

They just looked at him.

"Okay, that was harsh, but please, my own people are desperate! I'm here only to find what I came for and return. An hour or two. A day at the most. This isn't like before. I have to return quickly!"

Kara took a deep breath and eased back in her chair. "Did you know there's a statue of you on the east side of the White House lawn? White granite. Can you imagine what Washington would think if you walked up that lawn and greeted the president after all these years?"

He stood abruptly. "Out of the question."

"Maybe," Monique joined in. "But trust me, the world would come unglued if you walked out of here, Thomas Hunter, returned from the dead. And the world could use a little hope right now."

"That has nothing to do with me. My son has just joined the Eramites, for the love of Elyon! Let's stay focused."

"In giving you shall receive."

"You're manipulating the situation."

"Are we?" Kara said. "Think about it, Thomas. There's a link between the present and the future, and it isn't just you. It's as real for us as for you. Maybe if you find the answer here, you'll find it for your world."

He had no desire to take one step outside of this room, but maybe there was some truth to what Kara said.

What happened in the histories had always been uniquely tied to what happened in his world. If he could find a way to *alter* this history, he might find the answer for the other.

Then again, that didn't feel right. He sat again, sweating now. "I don't like it," he said.

"Since when did what you like have anything to do with truth?" Monique said. "I haven't liked *it* since you left."

Her words felt like a deserved slap.

"And maybe we're wrong," Kara offered. "But the way I see it, you're here, and as long as you're—"

"I'm not here for long," he insisted. "Just keep that in mind."

"Help us, Thomas," she said. "You changed the world once; do it again."

"That was a long time ago."

The door flew wide and a robed servant rushed in.

A robed servant?

It took Thomas only a moment to see that this was Billy, and that Billy held a nine-millimeter sidearm.

Thomas watched, stunned, as Janae, then Qurong, lumbered in behind, scanning the room.

Billy waved the gun at them. "Back! Stay back!"

Janae's eyes rested on the lost books.

The pieces fell into Thomas's mind and formed a complete picture. Their hands were already cut and bleeding. They'd come for one reason only: to use the lost books.

"Don't move!" Janae snapped again, stepping closer to the stack of books. If they touched the books, they would vanish—with the books.

Thomas held up his hand. "Please . . ."

Janae was the first to dive for the books, followed closely in near frenzy by both Billy and Qurong. Her bloody hand slammed onto the top book and the whole table began to topple, sending the lamp crashing to the floor. Thomas was screaming at his legs to move. *Move! Follow them through; move!* But his legs were frozen.

Janae's hand disappeared, followed by her arm. She was vanishing before their eyes!

But not before Billy and Qurong got their hands on her, clambering to join her in the passage momentarily opened by the books.

It all happened in the space of three—no more than five—beats of Thomas's heart. Janae, then Billy, then Qurong, were swallowed by thin air.

And then they were gone. The space they had just occupied was empty. And the books . . .

The books had vanished with them.

Leaving Thomas stranded in this world, while Billy, this redheaded version of Ba'al, and Janae, the bloodthirsty vampire, and Qurong, enemy of all albinos, returned to ravage Thomas's world.

The blood drained from his face. "Elyon help us," he managed in a thin voice. His whole body shuddered. "Elyon help us all."

27

SAMUEL OF Hunter sat cross-legged on a straw-stuffed cushion before a low table strewn with dates, walnuts, and wheat cakes. Hot tea steamed in small, crudely fashioned glass cups. A servant offered a brown crystalline powdered substance that didn't look familiar to him. He lifted his questioning eyes at Eram, who was watching Samuel and his companions from a reclined position across the table.

"Dried from the sugarcane up north. It makes the tea sweet, much like the blano fruit that the Circle uses."

Samuel dipped his head, and the servant scooped some of the dried sugarcane into his cup using a wooden spoon.

"Go on, taste it."

He sipped on the liquid. Found it entirely pleasant, like much of what he'd seen since coming with his men. They'd ridden in silence with the Eramites deep into northeastern canyonlands, through a massive valley spotted with miggdon figs, to a wide desert plateau that boasted a view in all directions. It was no wonder the Horde had never attempted to take their army against the half-breeds. The Eramites held the high ground.

Samuel raised the cup. "Good."

Eram smiled. "We spare no comforts, boy. None. The Horde may be rich, but we're no worse off. Certainly better than your poor tribes, eh? We have it all here: the prettiest women, the sweetest teas, the most meat, more space than we can use, and above all, freedom. What else could a man want?"

"That's how you view the Circle? Poor?"

"Don't be thick, boy. You're villains on the run, vagabonds who wear scraps for clothing and dance the night away like fools to cover your pain."

The man had a point. Everyone knew albinos were poor, but Samuel had never realized the enemy saw it as a defining characteristic.

Samuel looked around the canvas tent, a semipermanent structure built against a mud-and-straw wall, a combination of Horde and Forest Guard construction. Four women, among them Eram's daughter, leaned against posts or sat on cushions watching them, likely the only albinos who'd ever set foot in the city.

Six warriors stood behind Eram, and another dozen waited outside. Like all Eramites, they were covered in the scabbing disease and wore tunics woven from the same light thread the Horde fashioned from stalks of desert wheat. They ate like the Horde and stank like the Horde.

But that's where the similarities ended. Rather than dreadlocks, their hair was washed and styled in a variety of fashions, both straight and curled. Strange. And strangely pleasant if you looked long enough, particularly the women.

The armor they wore was straight from the traditions of the Forest Guard, lighter than most Horde leathers to prioritize ease of movement over protection. On the trek through the canyons, Samuel saw that many of the warriors chewed a nut of some kind, then spat red into the sand. Seeing his curiosity, one of the soldiers had offered him one and called it a beetle nut. Eaten with lime, it eased muscle pain. The man said it was used only by warriors and only out of the city. Samuel refused a sample.

Their religion paid no homage to Teeleh and in fact used a kind of Circle emblem taken from the Great Romance. The only real difference between Eramite and albino was the Eramites' rejection of the drowning, Elyon's greatest gift. Then again, Samuel sometimes doubted the drowning as well, at least as it pertained to anything more than a hallucinogenic state induced by whatever made the waters red.

"I'm impressed," he said, taking another sip. "You've done well for yourselves out here."

"We've done even better than you can imagine," Eram said.

"And who were you? Before . . ."

"Before the Horde invaded the forests?" Eram exchanged a look with a gray-haired man who stood by a green tapestry on the far wall. "You don't recognize any of us, young Samuel? I guess you were only a boy when we had the seven green lakes to wash away this blasted skin disease, weren't you?"

"So you were part of the Forest Guard."

"That's no secret. We lived with your father before he lost his mind to the red waters. Many of our friends gave their lives for him. Not all have abandoned the struggle, but we've never had an albino among us. Certainly not one of our former leader's own children."

"We're not here to join you," Jacob said.

"No? You wouldn't quite fit in, would you?" Eram turned his eyes to Samuel. "So why are you here?"

Samuel's mind buzzed with a hundred conflicts, but he set them behind the one overriding belief that had brought him to this place. Peace with the Horde would not come by any naive expression of love. They were an enemy who understood only force.

He set his cup down. "Jacob is right. Albinos can't join half-breeds. What kind of children would we make? Half-Horde?"

Someone behind him chuckled and Eram's gray eyes twinkled.

"But we can strike an alliance."

"An alliance?" Eram smiled at his general. "Just what we've been waiting for, eh, Judah? The brilliance we lack found in the minds of four albinos. We should celebrate with a fatted calf."

"Not four," Samuel said.

"No? How many?"

Samuel needed a better understanding of Eram's interest before he divulged that information. Otherwise it could be used against them. "I wouldn't underestimate the skill of albinos in battle. We might be the poor who dance away our troubles around open fires, but we can also dance circles around the Horde."

"Yes, I forgot, you don't have the disease. You're superhumans in battle."

More chuckles.

"Something like that."

The room stilled, and Eram's smile took on a mischievous quality. For a moment Samuel wondered if the man was mad, as some claimed. But what other kind of person would put a death sentence on his head by openly defying Qurong?

"Show Marsal just how superhuman you are."

Samuel heard the faint shuffle of boots on dirt behind him before fully realizing what Eram was asking, but his instincts kicked in at the last moment.

He jerked to his left and brought his right elbow up sharply. It connected with an arm, warding off a blow.

In one smooth motion Samuel grabbed the arm, hefted his shoulder into his assailant's armpit, and pulled down and forward, using the man's own momentum against him.

The body rolled over Samuel's shoulder, and he slipped the man's knife from his belt while the body was above him, then slammed the man onto the table, smashing glass and scattering food.

Samuel leaped to his feet, knife in hand. "Should this superhuman kill your man?"

Before an amused Eram could respond, Samuel flicked the knife to his right. It spun through the air and embedded itself in a post, six inches from the general, who watched with wide gray eyes.

The half-breed named Marsal sprang off the table, ready to go at it again, but Eram held up his hand. "You've made your point."

"I told you we should have slit their throats in the desert," Marsal spat.

"Why?" Eram countered. "So he couldn't make you look like a wounded possum? Back off."

The man turned and walked out of the tent with a grunt.

"Are all albinos so violent?"

Samuel shrugged. "Not all. But not because they aren't capable. You forget—like you, most of them were once warriors. They haven't grown soft in the desert. Some would say the fruit we eat makes us even stronger than the Forest Guard once was. Certainly quicker. You be the judge."

"Sit."

Samuel glanced behind, then sat.

"So." The Eramite leader put his elbow on the table, picked up a spilled miggdon fig, and bit into its dry flesh. "I'm listening."

"The Circle isn't as united as it once was," Samuel said. "Many have grown weary of running from an unrelenting enemy while they wait for a day that never comes. There are those ready to join me if I could give them a new hope. It may be the same for you."

Eram spat out some unwanted skin. "Go on."

"We may not have the strength to mount our own offensive against the Horde, but can make life difficult for them."

"Guerrilla warfare," Eram said. "This is your ingenious thought?"

"Ambushes may not excite half-breeds—you don't have the skills for it. You may be faster than the Horde, but you don't have the same advantage that even a few dozen albinos under my command would have. Imagine what I could do with a few hundred. Twenty or thirty well-placed teams to hit them from every side, every other day. Like hornets turning a bull's skin raw."

The leader said nothing, and that was enough encouragement for Samuel to lean into his convictions.

"Think about it. The Forest Guard has always assumed a defensive posture against the Horde's attacks. The Horde has never faced a direct attack. It would force them into a defensive posture that would keep their Throaters home and cripple their efforts to pursue the enemy, both albino and Eramite."

The tent had gone silent. Eram chewed slowly on his fig.

"What he says has merit," the general said.

"How many men will follow you?"

"I don't know. What we don't get at first will come after word of our success spreads."

"A new Hunter comes out of the desert," Eram said. "The new generation with a new answer. Is that it?"

"Something like that."

The leader pushed himself to his feet, wiped his hand on his pants, and walked toward the tent wall behind him. "Let me show you something."

Samuel followed him as he walked to a window and pulled up the canvas flap. He stepped aside and invited Samuel to take a look.

The tent sat on the edge of a large canyon cut from the plateau, a formation easy to miss from most vantage points. The floor ran at least several miles before opening to the northern desert, and as far as Samuel could see, the valley was covered by tents, not the domestic homes that filled the city. These were the tents the Forest Guard had once used in battle.

This was Eram's army.

Then Samuel saw movement. A sea of what he'd first thought to be rocks shifted several miles downwind. Horses in formation. More than could be counted.

"Do you think we've been sitting on our hands all of these years?" Eram asked.

Samuel was taken off guard by the sheer size of the army.

"How many?" Petrus asked.

"All told, one hundred fifty. Thousand."

"So many," Samuel said.

"More than the Forest Guard at its strongest, gathered from all seven forests. They are men, women, anyone of fighting age who is half-breed and possesses the will to retake our homeland."

Samuel's pulse pounded. "Why haven't you?"

"Gone against Qurong's army? All in good time, my friend. We're still vastly outnumbered. Qurong's army is greater than five hundred thousand. We go when there will be no chance of failure." He drew a breath. "Zero," he said.

"That time could be sooner than you think," Samuel said.

"Why wake the sleeping bear before its time?"

"Don't underestimate what we can do for each other."

"How so?"

Samuel no longer had anything to lose.

"What if I could bring you elite fighters able to defeat ten Horde with a single blade? I'm talking about a new kind of Forest Guard capable of holding the flank or ravaging an army's backside as you take it head-on."

"Yes, so you've said—"

"I'm not talking about four. Or forty."

No response.

"What if I could bring you four hundred?"

This time Eram stared over the massive canyon filled with his army in serene silence. When he spoke there was a new respect in his voice.

"Then you will be a legend among the Eramites."

28

THE FIRST thing Billy noticed when he opened his eyes in the other earth—the future earth—was that he was exactly the same person as he'd been a moment ago, before diving into the book behind Janae. Same jeans, same T-shirt, same hands, same pounding heart.

The second thing he noticed in this future was that he, Janae, and Qurong had followed the books into the same location as Janae's last journey here, the visit she had paid in her dreams. They were in Ba'al's study, staring in wonder at the ease with which they had crossed realities.

Of course. The books take you where you think you belong. In some strange way, I am Ba'al. Or at least someone who identifies with Ba'al.

But in other ways, he was nothing like Ba'al.

Ba'al's journal, his blood book, lay on the desk beside him. This one book held the secrets to more than he could recall from his short time in the dark priest's mind. He picked up the ancient book.

"It worked," Qurong said, looking at his hands. "We . . . we're back."

"You doubted us?" Billy asked.

"I think you meant to leave me," the leader said, heading for the door.

"Where are you going?"

"Where I belong as the ruler of this world," Qurong replied, turning back.

"Is that what you think? Teeleh is the ruler of this world."

It struck Billy then that he couldn't read the man's mind. Or the mind of Janae, who was staring at the bloodstained altar upon which sat the lost books. Now that he was here in the flesh, his gift no longer worked? But the vials of virus had come through, surely. And the gun?

"I mean no offense," he said. "But we have to regroup here and think through what just happened."

"Nothing happened," Qurong said. He resumed his march for the door. "Nightmares are not for me to understand."

"It wasn't a nightmare," Janae snapped. She'd come to herself, and he saw that she'd had the presence of mind to shove the gun into the pocket of her lab coat. But where were the vials?

"There's more at stake here than your little kingdom, you fool."

"Easy, Janae," Billy breathed. This wasn't their world, not yet.

She blinked, then visibly relaxed. "All I'm saying is that the world you were just in is real. Everything you heard was true."

Qurong held his hand on the door latch. "Such as?"

"Such as the fact that you're surrounded by enemies. The Eramites, the albinos, Ba'al . . ."

"And two albino witches from another world are here to save me, is that it?"

"We have a few tricks up our sleeves, yes," Billy said. "You've already forgotten?"

"The weapons," Qurong said. "Am I blind, or do I see nothing? Show me."

Janae glanced at Billy, then pulled out the gun.

"Of course," Qurong said. "The blunt knife you claim can throw steel. I'm quaking in my boots. This is what I'm supposed to slaughter the Eramites with?"

"No. The virus is for that."

"And it didn't come through," Billy finished.

Janae glanced at him. Surely she would take his cue, knowing that turning anything over to Qurong now only stripped them of their leverage.

"But that means nothing," Janae said. "The point is, we are of tremendous value to you."

"How?"

"We can use the books, go back, retrieve whatever we like."

"I'm not impressed." Qurong opened the door and left the room, leaving them alone in Ba'al's study.

Interesting that he left the books behind. Surely the man wasn't as dense as he appeared. Billy shoved Ba'al's journal behind his belt, pulled his T-shirt over the cover, and scooped up the four volumes. "Just go easy. We have to figure things out."

"What we have to do is get out of this place. We don't belong with these people."

"And go where?"

Her eyes shifted, and he suspected she knew as well as he did. If so, she wasn't admitting it. "I don't know yet," she said. "But I didn't come here to hang out with these fools."

"Did you think they would be gone? That this was Paradise?"

"Why the hostility? The last thing we need now is to start at each other. The fact of the matter is, we have more power than they can possibly imagine. We just have to figure out how to use it."

"The virus came through," he guessed.

She felt the side of her bra. "Unless they insist on an intrusive strip search, it's safe enough. This, on the other hand"—she put the gun back into her coat pocket—"doesn't scare anyone."

"It will once they know what it can do."

"That's right, Billy. Knowledge." She stabbed her temple with a pointed finger. "What we *know* is our greatest weapon."

Fair enough.

"Why did you come here, Janae?"

She stared at him, peeling back the layers. "You can't read my mind?"

"Not in this place."

She sighed as if this was to be expected, and headed into the dark hallway Qurong had entered. "For the same reason as you, Billy. I came to find myself."

Billy followed her, thinking she was right: they didn't belong here. Not in the temple, not in the city. His destiny rested with another, a Shataiki named Marsuuv, who lived in the Black Forest. The memories he'd taken from Ba'al while in his body were now faint, but three crucial elements drummed through his mind without reprieve:

There was a part of him that wasn't of the natural world.

His destiny was irrevocably linked to a queen named Marsuuv.

Everything that had happened, from the birth of evil to the Raison Strain to the coming apocalypse, was all his doing, because he'd not only started it all, he was going to finish it all.

Billy, the redhead from Paradise, Colorado, was the first and the last. The beginning and the end.

He was ground zero.

No, a small voice suggested somewhere in his brain, *Thomas is ground zero. You're just trying to catch up.*

But he knew that wasn't the truth. At the very least, they were both ground zero. Two sides of humanity. Take your pick.

Billy and Janae walked down a dark hall and peered into a large sanctuary filled with images of the winged serpent, Teeleh. Another altar, like the one in Ba'al's study, sat at the center of the room, still glistening with blood.

Billy stepped past Janae, overwhelmed by awe and the full impact of the room's icons: The black candles, spewing smoke into the air. The brass images of Teeleh on the altar. Long velvet curtains on all the walls, emblazoned with the same three claw marks that they all wore on their foreheads, this mark of the beast.

Familiarity hit Billy with the force of a punch to his chest. He'd found his way home.

He looked over his shoulder and saw that Janae's jaw was parted. She felt it too, didn't she? She knew more than she was saying. Or at least felt more.

He walked into the room on light feet, as though the stone floor was holy ground easily defiled. They'd crossed the centuries and were standing in the sanctuary of an exotic religion that worshipped the same being who'd made him Billy.

He touched the altar, impressed by the silky surface of the stone— was it granite? Perhaps marble?

Ba'al had been in the presence of Marsuuv, Teeleh's queen, and the memory played at the edge of Billy's mind like a pied piper.

"We made it, Billy," Janae breathed.

"Put the books on the altar," a voice rasped behind them.

Ba'al.

Billy turned slowly, having no intention of setting the books anywhere. Then he saw Qurong, standing with arms crossed behind Ba'al, who'd evidently been waiting for them, and he knew they had made a terrible mistake.

"Back off," Janae snapped. She waved the gun at them. "Stay where you are or I swear I'll blow both of your heads off."

Ba'al had tasted Billy's own thoughts, but clearly nothing about guns had surfaced during his short visit. He walked forward, fearlessly. "She said, back off!"

"Then blow my head off!" Ba'al snapped. "Use your toy and kill me if it be Teeleh's will. But know that I am his servant. Marsuuv is a jealous beast who has no patience for albinos who threaten holy men with toys."

His argument wasn't lost on Janae, whose aim faltered.

"Good to see you again, Ba'al," Billy said. "Or should I call you Billos?"

"Call me what you like. I am who I am."

"And so are we, two lovers of Teeleh. Show us how to find him and we'll leave you."

"These two are liars who could lure a snake into bed and bite its head off," Qurong said. "Don't listen to them."

Ba'al walked around them, smiling. "Snakes, are you?"

"No," Billy said. "But we belong to one, and his name is Teeleh."

"So you keep saying. We'll find out soon enough. In this very room. Set the books on the altar and step away."

"I can't do that."

"No? You, of all people, should know why you must do it. You've been inside of my mind and know that I've searched for those books for a very long time. Marsuuv compels me to take them to Teeleh. You would stand in the way of his queen?"

A quandary.

"Give me the books and I will let Teeleh have you," Ba'al said.

"Shoot him, Janae. Kill this weasel now. Put a bullet between his eyes and end his miserable life before . . ."

Click.

Billy blinked. Was that what it sounded like?

Click, click, click.

"It doesn't work," Janae cried. She pulled the trigger again with no better results.

"Why should it work?" Ba'al asked. "If your eyes were opened you might see Shataiki claws at work this very moment, protecting Marsuuv's lover. Please, throw down this useless tool. Lay the books on the altar. It is my last invitation."

Billy hesitated only a moment, then set the books down carefully. If Ba'al was telling the truth, he would take them to Teeleh rather than use them. Perhaps it was best for all of them.

"Tell us how to find him."

"You don't find Teeleh, he finds you. Go out into the forest and call his name. Trust me, he's always there, watching." Ba'al lifted the books and stepped to one side. "Thank you." He headed for the door that led to his study. "Dispose of them as you like."

"What of this virus they speak about?" Qurong asked.

"Yes, of course." Ba'al turned, but his mind was clearly on the books in his hands, Billy thought. "Strip them, search them. I'll instruct my priests to sacrifice them tonight when the moon wanes."

"I would be more comfortable if you were to oversee their execution."

"I won't be here. My master compels me. It is the end, my lord. The great dragon's time has come."

Billy's breathing had stalled.

"They are crafty," Qurong said, frowning.

"They'll be dead tonight, my lord. I swear it."

29

QURONG WALKED down the hall, stormed into the atrium at the front of his home, and shrugged out of his robe before he passed into the dining room. "Get me my general!" he boomed. "Now."

The robe dropped to the floor, where one of the servants would retrieve and wash it of the stink that came from his nightmare. Thomas's reputation as a wizard was well-known. Even as the commander of the Forest Guard, he'd possessed an uncanny ability to appear and vanish at will, along with his army on occasion.

But this! Deceiving Qurong with the illusion that he was in another reality was a talent surely no other man had.

"Where's Cassak? Get him now. In my quarters!"

He didn't care who heard him, only that he was heard. A shuffling of feet preceded the fleeting image of a servant fleeing the dining room.

"Hello, my love." He turned to Patricia, who leaned against the hall entryway to his left, still dressed in her night robe. She crossed her arms and ran her eyes down his body. "You're either feeling frisky this morning or you've lost your mind."

He glanced down at his half-naked body and swore. "I should have killed that albino ten years ago when I had the chance."

Patricia walked to the table and picked up a piece of yellow nanka. "He's escaped?"

"Of course not." But Qurong suspected that Thomas had indeed given him the slip. He'd taken Thomas to his private library, where the witch had somehow put him under with a spell. The next thing he knew, he was popping out of the vision in the Thrall with two equally evil albinos, whom he'd turned over to Ba'al.

"I've released him," Qurong said.

"You've released Thomas," she repeated scornfully. "You have no right to make these kinds of unilateral decisions!"

What on earth was she talking about? How dare she question his authority.

"She's my daughter too," Patricia snapped.

"Daughter? I've been tricked by a conniving witch and all you can think about is a daughter you haven't seen for ten years?"

"I waited up for you all night, you thickheaded bull! Who am I, your servant?"

"Silence!"

"Don't you silence me, Tanis."

He felt his veins run cold. She knew how he loathed his ancient name.

"I spent the night alone in the darkness, alone because both my husband and my daughter have left me," she said. "Fine, Qurong. Be the big, strong hero for all your people to see. But don't toy with my heart."

"*Now* what have I done?" he demanded. Only a woman could make so much out of so little. Give them a single fact and they'd fashion it into a story before taking a single breath. "I've just spent the night in a hellacious trance. My kingdom's falling down around my ears, and you scold me?"

"Don't try to distract me with more tales of how close we all are to the day of doom, Husband." She took a deep breath and gripped both hands tightly, a very bad sign indeed. "I want you to find my daughter," she said. "I want to speak to Chelise."

She turned and strode toward the kitchen hallway. "The next person I speak to with Qurong's blood will be my daughter." At the door, she shot him a daggered stare. "And don't bother coming to my bed." Then she was gone.

Qurong stood rooted in complete befuddlement. Surely she had to know his heart, that he was as bothered by Chelise's absence as she, that he'd lived in misery since her departure. He tried to inoculate himself with bitterness and denial, and that had helped for a while, but even his obsession with finding and eliminating the Circle was for her sake. He would slaughter this cult of fanatics who'd brainwashed her.

He talked about not having a daughter, but only to protect Patricia and himself. This was required of a strong leader forced to make hard choices in times of war.

"Cassak!" he roared.

"Here, sir."

Qurong spun to see his general standing in the doorway. How much had he heard? It didn't matter. Qurong had more pressing matters to tend to. So he told himself, but he'd learned long ago that nothing was as pressing as his wife's peace of mind. He would rather go to war with Eram than face down Patricia.

He spat to one side and marched into the hall that led to his bedroom. "Follow me."

He couldn't think about bringing Chelise here now. He didn't even know how to find her! And what would he say? *Your father has finally come to his senses—please, let's be a family again?*

She was *albino*, for the love of Teeleh!

Meanwhile, Ba'al was conspiring to overthrow him. Qurong couldn't be sure of everything about Thomas's magic, but it had revealed a thing or two, and he wouldn't ignore the warnings.

"My lord?" Cassak was hurrying to keep pace behind him.

Qurong entered his room and stripped out of his undergarments. He needed to cleanse himself of the albino stench before leaving the palace. This time he would welcome the pain of bathing.

"Sir."

"Yes, Cassak. Close the door." Qurong grabbed a fresh tunic from the end of the bed. He pulled it on and faced the general.

"Tell me how much I can trust you."

Cassak hesitated. "I am your servant, my lord, not Ba'al's. If you were to order me to kill him, I would."

So then, Cassak was aware of the threat as well. Was it so obvious?

"I wouldn't issue such an order, but I accept your loyalty. What I am about to tell you cannot leave this room."

"Of course not, my lord."

Qurong walked to the window overlooking the western city. More than two million Horde lived in Qurongi City; of those, over a quarter were males of fighting age, trained in combat as required of all adult men. But no sign of impending war was evident in the sprawling city with its mud huts and smoky chimneys.

His subjects had grown fat off the forests; rich, even. Little did they know the mounting threat from the desert.

"Prepare the army." He swung around. "Send word that we will march north to the Torun Valley for training exercises."

"Consider it done. It will be good to take our third division out; they've grown fat."

"Take everyone," Qurong said. "Including the temple guard."

Cassak blinked. "I'm not sure I understand. A training mission that size has never been attempted."

"All of them! North. Within the week." He glanced at the door, then back. "I want them well fed, hydrated, armed, and ready for a full-scale assault at my command."

Understanding filtered into Cassak's eyes. "Then it's not a training mission."

"Recall our scouts from the northern desert and debrief them. Send out six teams of Throaters with orders to infiltrate the Eramite city and report back by week's end." He paced. "I want to know numbers, strengths, weaknesses. How many children, how many women. Weapons. Morale. Anything that has changed in the last few months."

"A week isn't enough time—"

"It's all we have."

"You're saying you plan on invading within the week?"

"I'm saying I want to be ready to crush the infidels within a week. Sooner if I decide."

Now Cassak was quiet. The order was unprecedented. Not since the invasion of the forests had the Horde fought a full-scale war, and even then they'd never committed all of their assets to one front.

Qurong kept his voice low. "The war drums are beating, Cassak. Samuel, son of Hunter, is uniting Eramite and albino forces with the intention of undercutting us."

"I didn't know the albinos had a force."

"They don't, but it's not for lack of strength. Their will is weak, but that could change. I don't intend to give them that chance."

Cassak nodded and joined him by the window. "I agree. Eram is a thorn to be rooted out. But one week? What's the rush?"

"Ba'al's the rush. He's on his way to some cursed Black Forest now, and if I'm not mistaken, he has ambitions of his own."

"So we move before he can get his prickly fingers into our business."

"And we take his own little army with us."

His general regarded him with a crooked smile. "I was going to say that the dark priest is a snake, but now I should say that about you."

"I never claimed to be a serpent. And I don't think Teeleh would be too upset if Ba'al were his only loss in a war that destroyed the half-breeds and the albinos together."

"Agreed, sir."

Qurong nodded. "I also want you to send out three of our best scouts into the west with flags of truce." He sighed, not eager to pass on the order. "Tell them to find Chelise."

Cassak stared as if he'd heard wrong. "Impossible. We can't just *find* the Circle."

"No, but they can pass word for Chelise to meet her mother in the Torun Valley in four days. She will come."

"They could ambush the queen, my lord. This isn't safe!"

"I thought you said they're a peaceful bunch." Qurong grabbed a bowl of morst for his skin and headed toward the door. "Just do it. And there're two albinos in Ba'al's dungeon, scheduled for execution tonight. See to it that they both stay dead."

"Sir?"

Qurong turned back. "Dead, Cassak. I want them both dead."

⸻ ∞ ⸻

THE ONLY reason the search didn't leave them naked was the guard's ignorance that anything so small as a vial hidden under the band of Janae's undergarments could do any damage. This and the Horde's general disgust for albino flesh. Maybe if Qurong had overseen the search, Ba'al's journal in Billy's underwear and the precious vials would have been found.

Their situation was simple and dire. Billy and Janae's advantage was worthless in the dungeon below the Thrall where they awaited execution at nightfall. The ten cells ran along a tunnel lit only by a single torch near the heavy wooden door to freedom. All were empty except for the one they occupied, but the stench of urine and sweat crowded the small space.

"Still there?" Janae demanded, bunched up in one corner.

Billy pressed his face between two bars and peered down the passage where two priests stood guard. He pulled back and paced the straw floor.

"Well?"

"Yes," he whispered.

"Don't these animals ever use the bathroom?"

They couldn't tell what time of day it was, but nightfall had to be fast approaching.

Billy bent down and uncovered the items he'd hidden under straw in the corner. A vial of Raison Strain B. A vial of one of the most potent, nonbiogenetically engineered viruses, Asian Ebola, responsible for over a million deaths the decade before a vaccine was developed. A third vial contained Thomas's blood. Janae had lined her bra with all three in Bangkok.

The last item was Ba'al's journal. The blood book.

They considered calling the guards over and trying both viruses on them. But Billy and Janae didn't know what the results would be and would surely tip their hand. Regardless, the guards had refused to come after repeated calls.

Still, within half an hour of exploring their cell, they landed on a simple means of escape. The lock.

A brief examination of the crude metal lock revealed it to be an archaic thing with a rudimentary mechanism. She was convinced that she could pick it using nothing more than the underwire from her bra, which she'd already removed.

They would still have to contend with the two guards at the end of the hall. And once out of the dungeon, they had to escape the Thrall and then the city.

Billy had pored over Ba'al's writings in the dim light, filling in the numerous blanks between the memories he'd taken from Ba'al earlier. The collection of writings carefully outlined hundreds of details from numerous sources about this world, but the sections that Billy read and reread as the hours passed related to the Thrall and Marsuuv's Black Forest.

Ba'al had sketched the Thrall's basic blueprint, which showed a back door just beyond the dungeon's entry. If they could get past the guards and climb the steps to the atrium unnoticed, he was sure they could escape the Thrall.

And once out of the Thrall, their course was clear.

"That's it," Janae snapped, rising. "We have to go now, before they come for us."

"Slow down, we only get one shot at this! Keep your voice down."

Her face wrinkled as if she was going to cry. "We have to go, Billy," she begged. "We're going to run out of time! Do you hear me? This is going to get us killed!"

She looked to be on the edge of her own sanity. He had no shortage of urgency himself, but Janae looked like she was on the verge of a breakdown.

She scratched at a rash that had sprung up on her right arm. Only then did it occur to him that his lower back had begun to itch as well. *Rash.* Surely, it had to do with lice or something in this cursed place.

He imagined larvae crawling through their skin. Worms. He'd had his fill of them already.

Billy shivered and snatched up the artifacts. "Okay. Try to spring the lock, but keep it quiet." She was already at the gate, her frantic hands fiddling. "But wait until I say; just try to get the lock open."

She spun back, and held up the sprung lock. "Simple."

So fast? She'd obviously messed with locks in her time. He hurried forward and handed her the vials. "Hide these."

Janae grabbed the small glass containers and stuffed them back into the sides of her bra. Her skin was milky white, and he saw now that the rash wasn't only on her arm but on her belly and neck.

An unreasonable fear slammed into his mind. Déjà vu. He'd been in this situation before, far below a monastery. The worms there had been much larger, but he was now certain that they'd come from Shataiki. He and Janae should wait—they should proceed with extreme caution, but he wanted nothing more than to be out of this cage, guards or no guards.

Billy brushed past her, pulled open the gate, and slipped into the dark hall. His recklessness was an impulsive, irrational reaction to the fear, and he knew it even as he faced the guards down the tunnel, but by then it was too late.

They stared back at him as if he were a ghost.

"I appeal to the power of Marsuuv, queen of the twelfth forest," Billy said, marching forward. Never mind that he was a bare-chested albino; he had knowledge that no ordinary man, Horde or albino, should have, and he intended to use it now. Janae was breathing hard behind him.

Billy lifted the blood journal. "My maker, Marsuuv, with the blackest heart compels you—bring Ba'al and I will speak for my lord."

Ba'al was gone, Billy knew that. The guards yanked out their daggers and crouched, but they didn't sound an alarm. "Back," one cried in a hoarse voice.

Billy stopped no more than six feet from the guards and spread both arms wide. A surge of power swept over him with surprising force. More then adrenaline. There was a power in the air.

He tilted his chin up and spoke with as much authority as he could muster. When his voice came, it sounded like that of an old man, but it carried a power that shook his bones.

"I am born of Black; I am eaten with worms. My place is with my lover and my master, who waits for me in the twelfth forest with Teeleh. Any man who touches my servant will die."

He could barely breathe, so powerful were his words. A wave of power rolled down his spine, and he knew, as he'd never known before, that he was close, so close to being home. The fact that home resembled hell more than any utopia hardly mattered.

He belonged. This was his destiny.

A cry and a *whoosh* of air startled him out of his reverie. Janae had taken the dagger from one guard and slashed his neck. She was now thrusting that same blade at the second guard, moving with unnatural speed. She, too, seemed empowered beyond herself.

She thrust the long dagger straight through his belly, pinning him to a beam. Janae held his body there for a moment, then released it and stepped back, panting.

"Okay, then," Billy breathed. And for a long moment neither said anything else.

Janae absently wiped her mouth with the back of her hand, smearing it with blood. She licked her lips and swallowed, eyes still on her handiwork, perhaps unaware of what she'd just tasted.

She finally faced him, eyes wide. "The twelfth forest?"

Billy swallowed. "Marsuuv's forest. My forest. It's where the dark priest has taken the lost books."

Janae spun and started up the steps. "Then we have to go."

"Wait."

She didn't wait. "We have to go now!"

"Wait!" he spat. "You need to cover up. We'll dress in these priests' clothes first."

She turned and stared down at the bodies. After a moment she began to strip the clothes off the first guard she'd killed. The bloodier of the two.

They both dressed quickly and slid the daggers into their belts. With any luck they would pass through the city under cover of darkness and be free.

"How far?" she asked.

The Black Forest. "Three days. Maybe two if we don't stop."

"Then we can't stop."

He thought about objecting, thinking he should be rational. Better to be cautious and live than die rushing over a cliff. But he couldn't deny his own desire.

"Agreed," he said.

Janae suddenly turned to him, wrapped her arms around his body, pulled him tight, and kissed him on the lips. "Billy . . ." She kissed him hungrily, smearing the guard's blood on his mouth, breathing through her nose. "Thank you, Billy."

Her teeth bit into his lip, drawing blood. Strangely, he found it natural. This was how Shataiki mated, wasn't it? He wasn't sure of the mechanics, but he knew it had to do with the passing of blood. And this . . .

This small expression of affection was merely foreplay, he thought.

Then Janae pulled away and hurried up the steps, hiking her robe so as not to trip on the long garment, like a maiden rushing up the tower stairs to meet her prince.

30

A FULL DAY had passed since the books vanished with Billy, Janae, and Qurong. Thomas spent half of it wearing the carpet thin.

His first reaction had been to deny what his eyes told him. The books were there on the table by the door, and the redheaded witch, who was one with Ba'al, was securely locked up. But then Billy was in the library, and in the books, and gone.

The lost books, vanished. He'd rushed to the table and slammed his hand down, as if by force he could bring them back. Slowly the bitter truth dried his mouth. His only way back was gone.

Following an urgent discussion, Kara and Monique appeared eager to reassure him. He was here for a purpose, Monique kept saying. It would work out, Kara agreed, but she wasn't disappointed that they were together. He should embrace this turn of events for his own sake, she suggested. For the sake of the world.

Their words fell on deaf ears, because Thomas could only think about Chelise now. An hour later, unable to shake the haunting of her face, he'd asked to be alone so that he could clear his head.

He'd been separated from his lover many times, and though he always missed her, he'd never been cut off from her. There was always a path home into the arms of the one woman he'd come to depend on more than anything else in his world.

In fact, it wasn't until now, stranded, that he realized just how much he needed her. He glanced at the empty table again, dropped his head into both hands, and held back his emotion.

He'd once lost those he held closest, and the notion of suffering through it again was too much. What if he never saw her again? What if he'd been returned to this world to finish whatever business awaited him here? What if this was the end of the other world for him?

Panic crowded his mind.

The white bat's order whispered to him. *Go to the place you came from. Make a way for the Circle to fulfill its hope. And return quickly before it's too late. Do that and you might save your son.*

The same could surely be said for Chelise. Images of his bride swelled in his mind's eye.

He recalled the time she'd rushed out to meet him with Jake thrown over her shoulder like a bundle of firewood. "Look, Thomas!" She dropped their son onto his seat and stood back. "Show him, Jake. Show him what you can do." Jake wobbled to his feet and began to walk. How the boy managed to stay upright was a mystery still, bobbing and weaving and crossing his feet like a drunken stork.

They'd danced late that night and exhausted themselves in passionate expressions of love. Thomas had always been the impulsive one, given to zeal over reason, but next to Chelise he was the calm leader. After all, he was more than ten years older and had commanded armies. It only made sense that he would begin to settle down.

He remembered the time he'd tasked his elder daughter, Marie, with teaching Chelise everything there was to know about hand-to-hand combat. Like in the days of old, their fighting arts resembled a choreographed dance, thrusting and sparring with ferocity, but always for the precision and beauty of it, not with Horde in mind.

After only a month, Chelise and Marie performed by the fire for the whole tribe to see. Marie's skills were finely tuned, unmatched at the time. But Chelise . . .

His throat knotted, remembering: Her toned legs cutting through the air in an airborne roundhouse kick that showed her stunning grace. Landing nimbly on her feet, like a cat, then flipping into three consecutive back handsprings. The way her hair swirled around her face, her fiery green eyes, the cries from her throat. She reminded him of his first wife, and lying in bed that night, he'd wept.

Chelise had asked him what was wrong, and when he'd finally confessed, she'd wept with him. For him. He'd never thought of another woman, dead or alive, since.

How many times had Thomas walked through the meadow with Chelise, hand in hand, listening to her enthusiasm on whatever subject had ignited her that day? She'd never been shy of her passion, and if her aim was ever off, she would eventually acknowledge her overexuberance on the matter, though usually in soft, mumbled words.

"But don't be mad," she would say before kissing him. "I'm just learning."

She'd been learning how to be the wife of Thomas of Hunter, supreme commander of the Forest Guard, for ten years now, but as he often told whoever was gathered about the fire, it was he, Thomas of Hunter, servant of Elyon, who was learning from Chelise.

Not that she wasn't also teaching him other things, he would say with a grin. Who could light up a tent like Chelise? Who could lighten a load with a single giggle? Who else could master fighting techniques in only one month? Was there a more perfect vision of a bride in the whole of the Great Romance?

Then he would excuse himself to find his bride. They had unfinished business. Thomas and Chelise *always* had unfinished business. And at no time had he been so aware of just how unfinished their business was as now.

He remained alone in the library for an hour, allowing his self-pity to numb his mind. When no amount of focus presented an immediate solution, he headed out and found both Kara and Monique seated in the hall, waiting for him.

It was Kara's idea to help settle him by taking him into the city. He rejected the idea of leaving the library, where the books would hopefully return. But after a moment of argument, he saw that Kara was right.

He had to clear his mind. Bathe. Get into some clean clothes.

He'd forgotten how luxurious hot running water could feel on the skin, and he let it wash away the lingering Horde stench until the water turned cold. To his surprise, Monique had held on to some of his clothes, among other memories. The jeans weren't as loose as a tunic, but both Kara and Monique insisted they fit him perfectly.

The shirt fit tightly over his chest muscles; too tight, they agreed with sly smiles. Much too tight. Had he been doing pushups? No, hefting boulders.

He sat in the back of a Mercedes with Kara and Monique, and the driver drove them through Bangkok. They made five stops; at each one, more memories flooded his mind. The smells of frying pork rolls; the sound of a thousand cars diving for the same intersection, with blaring horns; the taste of a Cadbury milk-chocolate bar.

And albinos. Everywhere he looked, hundreds, thousands of albinos of every imaginable race. The world had truly become a melting pot in his absence. The word *albino* meant something entirely different here, but he'd embraced the meaning used in his world.

As he saw the city, however, the realization that he was a stranger here became more and more obvious to him. The sights and smells and sounds were familiar, but they no longer felt welcoming.

He belonged in a desert spotted by forests under Horde rule. He belonged in the Circle, rallying the followers of Elyon when the clarity of their purpose waned.

He belonged in the arms of Chelise.

"Take me back," Thomas finally begged. "It's too much."

Monique ordered the driver home. Thomas fell into bed without bothering to change, begged Elyon to save him, and dropped into the embrace of his second lover. Dreams.

But even as he dreamed of his true home, he knew the visions were only imaginations of the mind. Fanciful thinking liberated by REM sleep. Not the reality-shifting dreams that had first taken him to the future so many years ago.

He rose with the new day, showered long again, dressed in the black slacks and white shirt Monique had laid out, pulled on what he'd been told were a pair of fashionable black shoes, and emerged from his guest quarters with a determination to embrace the reality handed to him.

Monique and Kara assured him that he was looking a thousand percent better. The comment only made him think of Chelise. What would she say to these ridiculous duds? Then again, she might find them alluring and insist he wear them at the celebration that very night.

"We have something you should see," Monique said as the servants cleared the table of breakfast. "It might give you new insight."

Half an hour later, he peered into the microscope in the underground lab. "Larvae?" His breathing thickened at the sight of microscopic worms. "This is incredible."

"They cause the scabbing disease. Any ideas where they come from?"

Thomas straightened. "Teeleh. It's said that the Shataiki come from larvae, or some say worms. But . . ." He bowed for another look. Tiny white larvae wiggled in and out of the flesh sample, feeding on it. This was the root cause of the Horde's skin disease.

"Elyon's water must kill them," he said.

Kara cleared her throat. "So Qurong, who was just here, was covered in these things?"

"Being covered in microscopic organisms is nothing new," Monique said. "We all live with constant, unseen companions."

"But this . . ." Kara said, "these worms are evil incarnate. Evil made visible, not unseen, like here."

She might as well have hit him with a hammer. He'd been overlooking the most obvious connection between the present and the future, but here under the microscope it became as clear as spring water.

"The difference between our worlds is plain," he said, grappling with how to make what was plain also understandable—a monumental task at times. "It's right here in front of us all!"

"What is?"

"Evil! The worms! Teeleh."

"And?"

"And?" Thomas absently turned his hands into fists and shook them as if to seize the point. "You see how obvious the truth is when you see it with your own eyes? So many people doubt evil exists as a force beyond just the mind!"

"Not all, but—"

"'Out of sight, out of mind,' isn't that what we once said? You forget about evil until it visits your doorstep."

"Yes. What are you driving at?"

Wasn't it obvious? No. Which only reinforced his point.

"The primary difference between my world and yours is the nature of the spiritual reality, yes? There, the spiritual has a physical form, so we can actually see it. The scabbing disease is actually Shataiki larvae, infesting the skin and the mind. I'm sure you'll find these in the Scabs' brains as well. Elyon has placed his power in his waters—again, that's a physical incarnation. Do you follow?"

"Yes. We've already talked about all that."

"But my point is the converse: Just because you don't see something doesn't mean it's not there. It takes certain instruments to see what is real." He motioned to the microscope. "We become so used to the familiar that we begin to doubt the unfamiliar, until our eyes are opened and we *see*. One second it's Horde flesh, the next a breeding ground for Shataiki larvae."

"Makes sense," Kara said. "It's not a new idea."

"Nothing is new," he said. "But it's a reminder. Just because you can't see something doesn't mean it's not real."

They stared at each other, and Kara finally nodded. "So then maybe this is it. This is your message to your world."

31

THE JOURNEY back to Paradose Valley, where the Circle waited, was taking too long. Not longer than ordinary, but far too long to relieve Chelise's growing desperation.

Thomas had vanished, for the love of Elyon, just vanished! She couldn't shake the image of his and her father's sudden disappearance. And she had no word of Samuel except Thomas's plea, echoing through her mind: *Save the Circle, Chelise! Save them from Samuel!*

But she felt powerless to save herself, much less the Circle. To say she was despondent understated the sickness now eating away at her soul. Tears brought no relief.

She whipped her horse and drove it through the dark forest, ducking branches that crowded her passage. *Elyon, please, if you're there . . .* She hardly knew what to say any longer. The Circle had been crying at the skies for so many years and had what to show for it? More death. More running. And now this, betrayal of the most unnerving kind.

Maybe Samuel was right.

She caught herself and cursed her own weakness. How could she, who'd drowned and found new life, question the reality of Elyon now just because the world was dark?

Because it is *dark,* she thought. *All hope seems lost! My lover Thomas is gone. And my lover Elyon is quiet.*

Where was the light now? Where was even a hint of hope? How could Elyon allow them to enter such a wasteland? She was alone on this steed, blind in a world sinking into despair.

Chelise broke into a clearing and urged the horse to run faster through the grass. Tall dark trees loomed ahead, reaching for a black—

She started. A bundle of white sat perched high upon one of the trees. A living bundle of fur. With wings.

In her shock, Chelise failed to pull the horse to a halt. This was a Roush, one of the legendary creatures. It had been ten years since she'd seen one, so long she'd given up hope of ever seeing one again in the flesh. Yet here was one!

She yanked back on the reins, brought the horse to a heaving standstill, and stared. The creature stared back, unaffected. Its green eyes were bright despite the darkness. Resolute. Absolute.

It's true. They've been here the whole time, she thought, and hope flamed deep in her chest.

She tried to speak, to say something, anything, but emotion stopped her up, and she had to swallow to keep from crying out with relief.

The Roush dropped from the branch, spread its wings, and swept around, gliding west just above the treetops. Toward the desert.

Toward the Gathering.

"Wait!" She cried out, afraid it might be leaving, and spurred her horse after the furry creature. But it wasn't leaving her; it was circling back. Then it faced west again, satisfied she was following.

She was not alone. The light was there, begging her to follow.

───※───

JANAE PULLED her horse to a halt next to Billy's and stared at the massive canyon. The sun was hot, and sweat exacerbated the rash that now covered the skin around her joints—the crooks of her elbows and knees, her neck, armpits, and groin. The growth had slowed after an initial outbreak, and in the last twenty-four hours it hadn't progressed at all.

She swatted at a fly that buzzed by her ear. "I don't see anything but more rocks and sand. This isn't right."

Billy was studying the journal again. Always the journal, as if it was his new lover. "Yes . . ." He glanced up at the stars, then consulted the page again. "Yes, this is it."

"Where?"

He motioned to the dark canyon below them. "There."

"Fantastic," she said bitterly. "I've crossed the desert with a redhead from Colorado who's so twisted up that he's seeing black bats in the shadows. If they're there, why can't I smell them?"

He dismissed her with a turn of his head and urged his horse forward. That was Billy: forward, always forward, into the desert, as if following a bright star to the birthplace of some new king. It was a book that guided him, though, and even more, some inner homing device seemed to keep him trudging forward. Always forward.

He had the rash as well. They decided it was from the air. The atmosphere was filled with microscopic Shataiki, and the two of them were reacting to it. Clearly, their skin didn't react to the disease like the Horde's skin, or they would be covered in the sores by now. Or perhaps Thomas's blood was in them still, fighting against the virus.

They'd escaped the city, taking four horses from the temple stables for the hard journey north. Billy had cut loose the two mounts they'd exhausted after a day, and Janae was certain the two they now rode would give out before the end of the night.

"Billy!" She got her mount moving again and plunged down the slope after him. He didn't turn back. He didn't even acknowledge her presence. She was following her own internal guide, sniffing out the scent of something that pushed her inexorably toward her destiny, whatever that might be. But Billy . . .

Billy was on autopilot. He was so lost, so completely swallowed by his mission that he could no longer articulate exactly what he had in mind.

"Billy!" She kicked her horse, and it bolted forward with a snort of protest. "Tell me why I can't smell their blood. Stop. Just stop this idiocy!" She pulled her horse across the nose of his to force sense into him. "Don't ignore me!"

Billy's glazed eyes studied her. "What?"

"What? What's your problem? We've been running for two days straight, and we haven't seen a hint of Shataiki. Or Horde or albino, for that matter."

"I know where I'm going."

"Maybe you do. But I can't do this anymore!"

His jaw muscles bunched with impatience. "You think we have options here?"

That was just it: they didn't. The sum of her own predicament swelled in her mind, and the world spun. Less than a week ago she'd been in a position of power at Raison Pharmaceutical, tolerating a deep-seated knowledge that she didn't belong, at odds with her mother and the rest, but at least stable. She'd learned how to cope with her dreaded desire to smash everything around her.

Then Billy had turned her world on end. In hindsight, she'd always known that she would eventually meet another like herself, a soul mate with the same insatiable longing for more, far beyond the limitations of flesh and blood. She didn't understand her feeling of emptiness, but she'd known it couldn't last forever.

The moment Janae had awakened in the body of Ba'al's priestess, Jezreal, she knew she'd found herself. Almost. Her identity was entwined with the blood Ba'al loved. With the sacrifices to his master.

To Teeleh.

It was the beast's blood more than his name that called to her.

And Billy was right. They had no options except to find Teeleh. An overwhelming desperation settled over Janae as she stared into Billy's distant eyes. She swallowed past the tightness in her throat, but the emotion rose like a fist, and she felt despair strain her face.

"I need it, Billy!" she whispered. The longing for the blood swallowed her whole, and tears welled in her eyes. "I can't wait for it."

"You need what?" He maintained his hard edge.

She looked away and wiped her cheeks with the back of her hand. "I . . . I don't know." A long silence settled over them. "I'm scared."

Billy uttered a harsh laugh. "Yeah, well it's a bit late for that. You follow me across the universe into hell and now you decide you're afraid?"

"No." She faced him, furious at his insolence. But she depended on him even more now than before. So she closed her eyes and tried to compose herself. More to the point, she loved him—the way a drug addict might love the needle. She *needed* Billy.

Janae opened her eyes and watched him by moonlight. He couldn't read minds in this reality, a small consolation that leveled the playing field somewhat. But Billy was no less extraordinary. Not because of what he *did*, although the fact that he'd been the first to write in the magical Books of History was no small feat.

Still, it was Billy's identity that made him extraordinary, she thought. He was the one responsible for Thomas Hunter's entry into this world. He was the one who'd given birth to evil in those books.

In a sense, Billy was all of humanity bundled into one boy who'd been besieged by evil. Unable to rid his mind of the evil, he embarked on a quest to face it. Only then could he embrace it fully, or reject it, never to return. He'd said as much, but looking at him now, she understood it.

Janae eased her horse next to his, facing the opposite direction. She rested her hand on his thigh and leaned forward slowly until her lips were an inch from his.

"I love you, Billy," she whispered.

He didn't move. She kissed him lightly on his mouth.

"I don't know what's happening to me." The taste of his saliva made her head spin. "I can't . . . I don't know why I'm feeling like this."

Billy returned the kiss, and she had to suppress the impulse to bite his lip as she had before. She moved her hand from his thigh to his back and pulled herself closer.

"I'm not afraid to be here with you, I'm afraid of this feeling." Tears came again. "I don't know what's wrong with me, Billy. I need it."

His breath was hot through his nostrils, and he pulled back so that their mouths were separated only by the moisture between them. "You need what?"

"The blood," she breathed without thinking.

It was the first time she'd admitted it so plainly, even to herself, but doing so brought a flood of adrenaline. Her heartbeat surged, and she crushed his lips with her own.

Billy didn't speak, not with words. He was breathing hard, and he returned the kiss with as much passion. They were locked in an embrace, eyes closed and lost to the world. Images of black trees and large black bats slid through her mind. But instead of being repulsed or frightened, she now felt a wholeness that only fueled her desire.

Billy was her Adam, and she was his Eve, embracing the forbidden world. His lips were fruit to her, the sweet nectar of an apple.

She groaned and bit down deeply, then felt warmth flood her mouth. Like a drug, the blood flooded her with desire and peace. Complete wellness and security. Billy wasn't a mere man; he was a god. Her own to consume.

She knew that she'd regressed to a form of herself that knew only darkness. But there in the darkness of that womb she felt one with herself. She . . .

Her mount snorted and shifted under her. Billy's hand was squeezing her shoulder like a vise. Pushing her away.

She opened her eyes, confused and hurt, but before she could speak she was stopped by darkness.

Not just darkness. Blackness, like ink. So black she could feel the night as if it were a living organism that meant to smother her.

Janae jerked her head away from Billy and saw the circle of red eyes peering at them from the edge of a blackened forest twenty feet away. Where had the trees come from? They surrounded Billy and Janae. She gasped and spun around.

The red eyes were attached to mangy black creatures standing several feet tall, loosely resembling the images she'd seen in the temple.

Shataiki.

Her heart bolted, and she turned to look in the direction that had captivated Billy. A beast twice the size of the others perched on an angular branch above and behind the ring of Shataiki. He watched them with piercing red eyes.

Not a sound. Not a movement. Janae's heart pounded in her ears. The moon had been cut off by a thick tangle of leafless branches, draped in long strings of dark moss. Where only moments earlier sand and rocks had covered the canyon floor, now mud and shale lay on the ground. A single path tunneled into the dense foliage.

Their eyes had been opened to the Black Forest. The twelfth of twelve forests, Billy had said. The queen Marsuuv's domain. And Janae had little doubt that the beast staring at them from his higher perch was none other than Marsuuv himself.

Billy dropped to the ground and went down on one knee, head bowed to the queen. Before Janae could decide what her reaction should be, the large beast sprang into the air with astonishing agility, shot above the canopy, and was gone from their sight in the direction of the path.

As one, the ring of Shataiki flapped noisily off the branches, squawking and hissing. Half flew after the queen, and the others swept in, jaws snapping. Janae crouched as a set of fangs clamped shut close enough for her to feel the creature's hot, sulfuric breath on her neck.

Billy stood slowly, eyes on the path, ignoring the vicious cacophony of the beasts. He calmly mounted and turned his horse into the path. Satisfied, the Shataiki pulled up and fluttered about the canopy.

The air smelled like an open wound rotting with gangrene, but it was laced with another scent that drew Janae like the sweet smell of water drawing herds after a long, parched season.

"Billy . . ."

He pushed his snorting mount onto the path, then into the forest.

"Billy?"

He smacked his horse's rump and it bolted. Janae ducked low and raced after him. The darkness made the path nearly invisible, but the horses followed their own guide, hauling Billy and her into the jungle at breakneck speed.

Two thoughts drummed through her mind. The first was that they were rushing toward their deaths. The second was that she didn't care, because she could smell life in the air, and this was the life she needed as much as breath itself.

The scent grew stronger, and with it her certainty that she had to reach the end of this path, if for no other reason than to find the source of the smell.

She called out his name later, in a moment of unexpected fear. "Billy." But her voice was weak, and even if Billy was listening, his silence seemed appropriate. The fear lifted, and she hugged her horse's neck as she rode it into the night.

Into this hell.

How long they rode or where the twisting path went, she neither knew nor cared. She kept telling herself she was going home. All secrets would be laid bare with her queen.

My queen. She whispered it aloud. "My queen. My queen."

Her horse stopped suddenly and she jerked up in her saddle, eyes peeled. They had come to the bank of a large black pond surrounded by a thick forest. The Shataiki covered the canopy, their millions of red eyes staring in silence, casting a dim glow over the waters.

Janae pulled up next to Billy and followed his gaze. A single wooden platform stood on pylons over the water like a pier. And on the platform, three thick inverted crosses, black against the night.

Crosses. Why crosses?

Janae saw that five or six Shataiki carcasses had been nailed to the crosses and hung like huge dead rats. "Upside-down crucifixions."

Billy kept his eyes on the ancient symbols of execution.

"Where is Marsuuv?" Janae asked.

"In the grave."

They were whispering, and even then, Janae wondered what did or did not offend Shataiki. She felt her skin quiver, like the flesh of the mount beneath her. Something was wrong here. All of it was wrong, terribly wrong. All except the scent. And now her body quivered with desire.

"Where's the grave?"

"In hell," he said. "Below the crosses."

"Under the lake?"

Billy directed his horse to a rotting wooden door into a large mound beside the lake. Like a bunker or a root cellar. For long seconds he sat on his horse and stared in silence. The throng overhead watched like a jury, perfectly still, as if what they were witnessing had been anticipated for a very long time.

History was being written before their eyes. But it wasn't her they were staring at, she realized. It was Billy.

She looked over at him and saw that he was crying. Streams of tears wet his cheeks, and his face was wrinkled in anguish.

"My lover . . ." His voice was raspy, barely more than a whisper. "I've made it. I've come back to you."

A knot rose in Janae's throat. In this moment, she felt such a solidarity with him that she couldn't hold back her own sentiment. "I love you, Billy."

But the moment she said it, she knew she meant Marsuuv. She, like Billy, had found her lover. Certainly not in a way humans found lovers. No, this was far more basic, like finding water in a desert. Or blood after being drained.

Life.

Billy slowly gathered himself, then turned to her. "Do you have the strength?"

"Yes."

"He'll take everything."

And give me his power, she thought.

"He'll take your soul."

She looked at the door, a rudimentary door bound together with vines in a criss-crossing pattern. "He already has it."

Billy dipped his head, then reached for her hand. His fingers were ice-cold, but the gesture filled her with a new warmth.

"Thank you, Janae," he said. "Thank you for sharing this with me."

"Of course."

He looked up at the three crosses on their right. "You know, I once thought I had defeated the evil in my heart. I learned something: We can face our demons, burn them up, stomp them into the ground. I turned mine to ashes. But even if you destroy the evidence of evil, you can't heal your heart. Not by yourself. Only he can do that."

Billy was staring up at the crosses when he said it, and for a moment Janae thought he was capitulating.

He looked at her again. Smiled. "Call me Judas, Janae. We all have our roles to play. I love him too much."

Even if she wanted to, there was no way to turn back now. The scent pulled at her like an airborne intoxicant that beckoned her to come and taste. "I want to love him too."

"He's waiting," Billy said. "Marsuuv is waiting."

Then Billy and Janae slid from their saddles, walked up to the door, and descended into hell.

32

CHELISE LOST track of time as she followed the Roush through the forest, flooded with renewed energy and desire. Even the horse seemed to have gained strength, an almost unnatural stamina to chase this angel of mercy who flew above the branches, in and out of sight.

She knew that the desert would be upon them soon, and then it would be lighter and the path to the Circle more certain.

They are showing themselves again, she told herself. *Something is happening. The world is flooded with darkness because it knows something is happening. It's going to change.* The thoughts repeated themselves over and over, and she clung to them as if they were a tether to Elyon himself.

She lost sight of the Roush in a thick section of forest, and with some panic wondered if he'd left her. Then she burst out of the trees and faced the open desert.

The white creature sat atop a small dune not fifty yards from the tree line, watching her.

Chelise walked the horse closer. Up the slope. She stopped twenty feet from the Roush.

"Come closer, my dear," he said.

Oh, dear. Oh, dear, the Roush was speaking. Chelise couldn't move.

"It's okay, I know I must frighten you to no end. Like a ghost in the night."

"No," she blurted. "No, I . . ."

She couldn't find the words to express her gratitude at seeing this Roush after so much fear and doubt.

The Roush looked at her a moment longer, then wobbled forward on spindly legs hardly made for walking. He stopped ten feet from her and spoke in a soft, comforting voice.

"I am Michal, and I'm here to give you courage. I come . . ."

Chelise heard nothing more because she was dropping to the sand, stumbling forward, craving to know, really know that this was no figment of her imagination, but a real, furry, white Roush.

She managed to come to her senses before running him over, feeling suddenly foolish. But instead of backing away, the Roush stuck out its wing.

"Go ahead. Everybody seems to want to make sure by touching these days."

She touched his leathery skin. Ran her fingers over the fur along the wing's spine. Then settled to her knees with a sob and gripped both of his wings.

Michal stepped closer, and she embraced his furry body. It was real, so very real. And soft, like downy cotton. Only when he coughed did it occur to her that she might be squeezing the air out of him. She let go and backed off.

"Sorry. Sorry."

"Don't worry," he said, waddling to her right. "It happens." He faced her. "Yes, dear, yes. It is all very real, don't lose sight of that. The world is darker now than it has ever been. If you only knew the treachery being plotted in the Black Forest, you would tremble."

"I already am trembling."

He arched his brow. "Then take courage. If I'm real, so is Elyon. And if he is, so is his purpose."

"So Thomas will be okay? Samuel, my father . . . all of them will be okay?"

"I didn't say that. Darkness demands its price—"

"What price?"

"I can't tell you what will happen. Frankly, I don't know. But Thomas is no fool. Trust him. Do what you must do. Go with courage; the light is brimming behind all of this darkness. You'll have to trust me."

"But why?" She knew she was bordering on sacrilege, being so bold, but after days of fearing the worst without a hint of hope, she couldn't help herself. "Why would Elyon force us to face such darkness and tragedy? For ten years now we run and die and, yes, we dance at night to forget it all, but still the horror haunts us. Why?"

Michal frowned. His mouth slowly formed a gentle, empathetic smile. "I'm sorry for your trouble, my dear. But aren't lovers always tempted to find another? You humans are lovers, yes? So you have this awful tendency to reject him who first loved you and follow after intoxicating scents. Evil is a jealous lover who will try to destroy what it cannot possess, so now evil is having its say. But don't discount the power of a loyal heart. You'll see. Have hope."

"How can I hope when evil will charge its price?"

Michal eyed her for a few moments, then, without any answer, he began to turn.

"Hurry, Chelise. The world waits for you."

To do what?

"They will come for you in the desert. Wait for them." And then he leaped into the air and glided into the night.

"Wait!"

"Courage, Chelise!" he called back. "The world awaits you!"

Who would come for her?

STANDING BEFORE the queen Marsuuv was like standing in the presence of God.

The vast underground library was lit by three torches that illuminated thousands of ancient books along the walls; the ceiling was covered by a black moss. But Janae felt only intrigue at these observations.

Marsuuv put out another scent, stronger even than the mucus, and it drew her like clover draws a bee.

They'd descended a long flight of stone steps in silence, then entered one of several tunnels cut horizontally under the lake. Flames illuminated the passage's well-worn walls, interrupted by iron gates that closed off smaller rooms: a storage room filled with artifacts that Janae couldn't place, a smaller study with a writing desk overgrown by roots, an atrium leading into another tunnel.

But Billy took them deeper still, seemingly drawn by a force beyond him. Perhaps his connection to Ba'al.

In the library, the four lost books sat on a large stone platform, a desk of sorts, flanked by two tarnished silver candlesticks fashioned to look like upside-down crosses.

Marsuuv sat on a large bed of red vines beyond the stone desk. The carving in the mossy rock wall behind him explained the crosses on the lake platform. Three hooked claws dug into the cross's inverted beam—a display of dominance. The talons were so long and hooked that they resembled sixes. Their tips looked to have pierced the wall, coaxing forth small rivulets of a dark fluid.

The queen Marsuuv sat at the edge of the bed with his own long talons hanging nearly to the ground. His black fur looked manicured, not bare in spots like the other Shataiki they'd seen. Quite beautiful, actually.

His head was large, like a wolf's or a fruit bat's, with pink lips loosely covering sharp fangs. Red eyes stared like marbles, shiny, without pupils. You could look at this creature and find it magnificent, Janae thought. Absolutely stunning.

She stood next to Billy before the beast, aware that she was trembling. The mix of emotions coursing through her mind made her legs feel weak. The queen was wonderful, but not even someone as enchanted as Janae could look at this sight and not fight off waves of terror. She was unsure which she should pay more attention to, her longing or her fear.

"Hello, Billy." The queen's voice purred, soft and seductive. "Welcome home."

Billy lowered himself to one knee and bowed his head, speechless. It struck Janae that Marsuuv was fixated on Billy, not her. His eyes had been on Billy from the start.

Billy found his voice. "I am your servant. Your lover."

"Are you sure?" a voice rasped. The dark priest Ba'al stood in a doorway to their right, arms folded into a loose black cloak. He walked in and stood before them all, looking even more emaciated than Janae remembered. "Are you sure you know what you're getting into, feeble human?"

"He's mine, Billosssssss," Marsuuv said.

The priest stared at Billy for a long time. Slowly his face contorted into an expression of pain and sorrow. A tear glistened on his left cheek, and he buried his face in his hands, weeping now.

The sight was so unexpected that Janae felt a tremendous flood of empathy for the poor soul.

Ba'al lowered his trembling hands and stumbled forward. "Please, I beg you to reconsider. What did I ever do to deserve this? You're throwing me away for this albino?"

Marsuuv just looked at him.

"I defied you once, I know, but look in his history and you'll see the same. We all defy you once before embracing the darkness." Ba'al words came out in a breath-starved flood. "You bound me and you whipped me, and I still learned to love you! You gave me reason to live as your only lover. 'Bring me the books, bring me the books,' you said. Now I've brought you the books and you'll throw me away? I cannot live with it."

"Billossss," Marsuuv said. "Always so impetuous."

"I am not Billos!" Ba'al screamed. His face was a mess of mucus and tears. "I am Ba'al."

"What life you have as Ba'al came from me. You have my blood. You are mine."

Janae's belly tightened.

"Please . . ." Ba'al leaned against one of the pillars for support. He lowered his voice. "Please don't throw me away. I'll . . . I'll do anything."

"Will you join me in hell?"

Ba'al rushed around the table, grabbed one of Marsuuv's talons, and fell to his knees. "Just say the word, my lover. Say the word so that we can be together in eternal hell."

The queen uttered a soft chuckle. Then purred. He lifted his claw, pulling the man to his feet. Ba'al clambered onto the bed, clinging to the beast's talon with both hands now. Casting a glance up to be sure he was being accepted, not rejected, Ba'al settled against the beast's furry underside and curled up, weeping softly.

Billy was still on his knees, weeping with Ba'al as Marsuuv watched him. Janae believed he understood Ba'al's pain more than she could know. Billos had been held and tortured until he'd slowly become the wretched man named Ba'al. Billy had felt that pain when the two were one.

And what of her? Was she here on a fool's errand, stranded in a foreign dimension, another victim of this hideous beast's insatiable appetite? Heat washed down her neck. She'd made a mistake? She'd willingly entered this hell and would now pay for it like Ba'al had?

And Billy . . .

The sap was just kneeling there, weeping like a baby.

"What?" Billy groaned "What do you want? I can't live like this. I can't! I've seen the light; I've tasted the good; I don't deserve to live."

Marsuuv absently ran his claws over Ba'al's body. "Such a tormented soul. But you've come to me. I will ease your pain and fill you with a new pleasure that you'll crave. Nothing will be the same now, Billy."

Billy gripped his hands to fists, leaned his head back, and cried at the ceiling in anguish. His voice echoed around the room. Janae wanted to tell him to stop this embarrassing display of weakness, but she knew her advice meant little here.

She was the disposable one in the room.

Billy finally ran out of breath and calmed. Marsuuv nudged Ba'al, then pushed him away. "Leave us."

"My lord?" Ba'al was aghast. He began to cry again. "Please!"

"Leave us!" Marsuuv's snarl shook the room, and Janae took a step back. Her pulse quickened. There was something about his jaw, his pink tongue, his fangs that excited her. The scent of blood . . . Could it be coming from his mouth?

Ba'al spun, hiked up his cloak, and hurried from the room, trying to hold back his cries of regret.

Marsuuv watched Billy. "Come here, Son of Adam," he purred.

For a moment, Billy did nothing. She could imagine the fear pounding through his veins.

"Let me take away the pain, Billy. Let me give you pleasure."

Billy pushed himself up and then walked slowly around the stone desk where the four books were stacked. He stepped in front of the beast.

Marsuuv lifted his claws and stroked Billy's wet cheeks. "Why do you cry, my love? You've been chosen for a task that is the envy of the world."

"What?" Billy breathed.

"Teeleh will tell you. You'll be going back soon. We only have a short time together. We should treasure every moment."

Billy was shaking from head to foot, and Marsuuv seemed pleased. His talons touched Billy's head and arms and neck as if they were made of a delicate membrane that would break with the slightest pressure.

She knew Billy and Marsuuv shared a special bond that she did not. This was the devil, and Billy had welcomed him into his head a long time ago.

The truth of this began to eat away at Janae like a flaming cancer, and she began to fear for herself. How could she stand before such a terrifying sight and feel such jealousy? She should be on her knees, showing respect. Her anger would end badly. She would say or do something that triggered this beast's fury.

But he hadn't so much as acknowledged her yet. In fact, now that she thought about it, even back in the clearing, Marsuuv's eyes had been on Billy, not her. She was sure of it.

She was nothing more than a rat caged for the next meal. She'd crossed into this nightmare to be food for this dreadful beast!

And yet, there was nowhere else in the world, or in her mind, that Janae wanted to be but here, facing the truth, the scent, the source of her own desire.

"What about me?" she said.

The beast ignored her. His long tongue snaked out and licked tears from Billy's cheeks. This display of affection combined with the scent of blood on Marsuuv's breath proved to be too much.

Janae stepped forward, enraged. "Am I just a piece of meat here?" she cried.

Marsuuv jerked his head to face her for the first time, issuing a crackling snarl as he snapped the air. "Patience, human!"

The Shataiki's breath washed over her, and with it his scent, so strong now that tears stung her eyes again.

"The desire is so strong, is that it, daughter of Eve? Just one taste?"

Her voice cracked. "Yes."

He shifted on the bed of vines so that his whole body now faced her. "Do you know how we reproduce, Janae? We carry blood in our fangs."

Of course. Yes, of course.

"You are now in my nest, where I lay unfertilized eggs that become larvae. Any Shataiki but a queen can bring the young ones to life; all it requires is a single drop of blood. A single bite."

Janae found the words irresistibly seductive. She wasn't sure why; what he said surpassed all she yet knew about her own existence.

"You wonder why you long for this blood, don't you, daughter?"

"Yes," she whimpered, stepping closer.

"Once there were twelve of our forests, each a nest for a queen. One forest was burned, and the queen Alucard left us. And when Alucard left our world, he entered yours, two thousand years before you were born, at the turn of your calendars. There were no Shataiki to fertilize his own larvae. But he found a way to satisfy his need for offspring by injecting his own blood into a human woman. We know this from one of the blood books, the journal of Saint Thomas the Beast Hunter, where it is recorded that a race of half-breeds came into existence and spread their seed on earth. He called the descendants Vampirum. Offspring."

She knew where he was going, and it terrified her.

"You, Janae, crave the blood because your father many generations removed was a half-breed. Shataiki blood runs in your veins still. You are offspring." He paused. "Does that excite you?" Marsuuv was speaking softly, drawing her in with his eyes and the gentle movement of his talons.

"Yes," she breathed. She could taste a hint of blood on her own tongue, and she gave herself to the desire for it. Even Billy . . . his blood had hints of the same irresistible taste.

Shataiki blood.

As she stepped closer, a distant voice whispered a warning: *It's evil, Janae. Raw, unfiltered evil, like the larvae. You have entered hell, and you are begging to drink evil.*

"Come, my sweet," Marsuuv purred. "Come, taste and see that I am evil." He sprang from the bed and swept the lost books from the stone desk. An altar, she now saw. It was his altar.

Janae walked around to his side of the altar and reached for his claw. He leaned close so that she could feel his breath; the power in that hot blast of air robbed the last threads of resistance from her. She understood Ba'al's desire to be with this magnificent beast.

She instinctively leaned forward and took his fur in her fingers, longing to be closer. He reacted like a sprung animal, plucking her from the ground and slamming her down on the stone. Pain flashed down her back.

The beast leaped upon the altar, gripping the deeply scarred edge with his long claws. He hunched over her and glared.

"You want more," the beast growled. "More. This is why he chose you."

Janae began to cry with gratitude. She'd always known that there was something wrong with her. Something different. Her own appetites for adventure, for pleasure, for more, always more, were far more pronounced than others'. Now she understood.

It was the blood. Shataiki blood. Her own father had passed this desire to her.

"Please . . ." She grabbed the creature's hair and pulled. "Please . . ."

"You long for it. To be Teeleh's daughter?"

"Yes!"

"To curse Elyon and embrace evil for eternity?"

"Yes!"

His jaw came down slowly, and she stretched her neck for him. Felt his fangs touch her skin.

Then Marsuuv, queen of the twelfth forest, bit into Janae's flesh and injected his blood into her veins. And the power that flooded her body made it shake like a dying rat.

Her jaw snapped wide and she screamed. With pain, with pleasure, with the terror of raw evil.

Marsuuv pulled his fangs free, still dripping with her blood, dug three claws into her forehead to mark her as his own, offered a satisfied shudder, and slowly climbed off the table, leaving her to jerk alone.

Billy was saying something, protesting, but she couldn't focus on him because her nerves had turned to fire. Not with pain, necessarily, but with sensitivity. She could sense everything, the cool stone beneath her, the movement of air around her, the pinpricks of pain on her neck. The scent of the flames, the blood, the sweat, the mucus, everything. Her pain had turned to pleasure, and she was having a hard time containing it all.

"In good time, my love," Marsuuv was saying. "All in good time. Get her up."

The sensations softened, leaving her exhausted and content. Hands pulled on her cloak, and she opened her eyes. Billy leaned over her, shaking her. She smiled. "Billy."

"Get up."

She looked up at him, lost in the moment.

"Get up!" he snapped.

She sat up, forgiving his jealous outburst. She hopped off the altar, feeling more alive and energized than she'd ever felt. An image of Ba'al's shriveled husk of a body crossed her mind, but she dismissed it without a second thought. She was no Ba'al.

Janae glanced at Billy, aware of how little she cared for this human now. He seemed small and pitiful to her, a feeble man who'd succumbed to the thirst for evil, not unlike herself, except that she had been bred for it. What was his excuse?

Billy was the author, her inner voice whispered. *He's now your master.*

She turned away, refusing to indulge the notion, and faced Marsuuv, who sat on his bed of vines once again.

"You wish to prove yourself?" he asked. Somehow he must know. Perhaps his mind had joined hers while he fed on her blood.

She pulled the three vials from the side of her bra and set them on the altar. He reached for the tiny bottles and touched them with the tip of his talon.

"Tell me," he said.

"The one marked with the white tape is Raison Strain B. It has the power to destroy all life. Billy and I are immune to it now."

"It cannot kill albinos or half-breeds," he said. "None who have bathed in the lakes."

He knew about the virus?

"The virus originates with Teeleh's blood," Marsuuv said, seeing her raised brow. "It will only worsen the disease the Horde already have."

Her mind spun.

"And the other sicknesses?" he demanded.

"The one marked with the black tape is Asian Ebola. Terminal to all but Billy and me. We've been inoculated with a vaccine like everyone in our world. The last vial is as labeled, a sample of Thomas's blood, which we both have in our systems as well."

The beast reacted to the mention of Thomas with a jerk of his head.

"He's in Bangkok," Janae said, wondering how much the Shataiki knew.

Marsuuv pulled back slowly. "So, the time has come. The humans will decide. We can destroy the land, we can pluck their eyes out, we can whisper evil into their minds, we can rape and pillage and burn, but in the end only humans can unlock their destiny."

"And now we bring you the keys to that destiny," Billy said.

"Not you, Billy. My master has another task for you. As soon as you and I become better acquainted."

Billy glanced at Janae with furtive eyes.

"But Janae," Marsuuv said, purring again, "you will be our new Eve. Together we will destroy them all, and the world will know that Teeleh owns the humans."

She had a craving for his blood.

"You will find Samuel. Seduce him. Seduce the half-breeds." His voice popped with phlegm. "Seduce the albinos. The time has come for the dragon to consume his young."

He plucked the vial of Asian Ebola from the altar and set it by his side, leaving Thomas's blood untouched. "You have no need for this. The Raison Strain will give you the power you need."

"What about the half-breeds?" she asked. "The albinos."

"They will die."

"How, if my poison only affects full-breed Horde?"

Marsuuv glared. "Do I look like a fool? Do as I say."

"And me? Will I die?"

"You, too, are his lover," he said slowly, enunciating each word. Teeleh's desire was to destroy them all and begin over with Billy and Janae, his new lovers in his own twisted garden.

It all fit. The only reason the Shataiki hadn't already destroyed humanity was because only humans could destroy humanity. As such, people were more powerful than Shataiki. Unable to complete their revenge on the world, the Shataiki had hidden themselves, biding their time.

Now that time had come. Janae held the virus that would destroy the Horde and leave the destruction of the Eramites and the albinos to Teeleh.

Marsuuv gazed at her. "Go and do what you must do quickly."

33

TORUN VALLEY, to the northwest of Qurongi City, had been turned black with the swarming masses of the Horde army. Chelise stared at the sight, amazed that she was alive, much less here. If not for the Roush, Michal, she would surely be at the Gathering now, safe, but still lost.

She'd wandered into the desert with the Roush's words swimming around her: *They will come for you in the desert. Wait for them.*

Wait for who, the Horde? The Circle? Thomas and her father? Could it be that Elyon was coming for her? Or the Shataiki . . .

The sun rose after Michal left her, and she had slowly worked her way home toward Paradose Valley and the Circle, waiting to be overtaken any moment by whomever she was to wait for. The sun rose. The day passed.

And as she drew nearer to home, she began to see signs of albinos arriving in response to Thomas's call. They were coming from far and wide, eager to flood Paradose Valley. Perhaps she should leave the desert and return to the Gathering rather than wait. She wanted to kiss her Jake and make sure that all was well. But of course all was *not* well. Thousands would be pouring into the valley. Samuel was in danger or was a danger. Thomas had vanished.

Besides, how would she know she'd been found by whomever she was waiting for?

And then she had crested a tall dune, seen the Scab patrol under a lone tree, waiting for her, and she knew. She'd been found as she was meant to be found.

Still, it took her five full minutes to work up the courage to approach the two men, who seemed content to watch her. She approached with dread and determination.

"My name is Stephen," the young Horde scout had said. "Your mother, Lady Patricia, has requested that you join her in the Torun Valley immediately."

Immediately. Chelise knew that the worst had happened. Qurong and Thomas had fallen into terrible trouble. Why else would a plea come from her mother?

"Stephen?" It was the first word she'd spoken to a Scab since her drowning.

"Yes, my lady. We will keep you safe, but you must not leave our sides."

It wasn't until much later, after the first long day's ride, that she realized he wasn't protecting her from other Horde warriors. He was on the sharp lookout for the new breed of albino fighters. "We all know they are much faster, far more skilled than even the Eramites."

His companion had chuckled. "And everyone knows the Eramites are superior to most Horde."

"Really?"

"How does an army that has no war stay in fighting shape?" the man named Reeslar demanded. "Our Throaters and scouts are the only ones who have the skills that once made the Horde proud."

"And even then the Forest Guard used to beat us up pretty badly," Chelise said.

Her use of the inclusive "us" silenced them for a moment. But it had been "us" back then, and it should be again, she thought. Their smell didn't bother her as much as it bothered other albinos. In fact, the only difference between them and many albinos was the fact that albinos had drowned in a red lake.

Stephen had broken the silence. "Teeleh save us if the albinos ever decide to take up arms."

The other grunted his agreement, and for the smallest amount of time, Chelise understood Samuel's desire to fight. Until now, she hadn't understood the superiority of the average albino's fighting skill and strength. The absence of disease and their constant running from scouting parties had kept them fresh and hardened, ready to engage any enemy.

After crossing the desert for the second time in a day, she sat on her mare between the two Throaters and studied the armies in the Torun Valley. She'd seen dozens of patrols as a youth, but always from a distance. Before they'd overtaken the forests, the Horde went to great lengths to blend into the sand, breeding horses with tan hides and keeping to the valleys. Afterward, they'd reversed their strategy, preferring to be seen in all their dominant glory rather than hide as fugitives like the Circle.

A small army of Horde had once made it to the edge of Chelise and Thomas's camp before the tribe of albinos had escaped. She'd watched the Horde with Thomas from the nearby hills, wondering if she could talk reason into them.

That was at the beginning, before her father unleashed the full force of his rage against them. The Horde butchered several camps and captured hundreds of albinos in the months that followed. She'd once helplessly watched from a cliff as Throaters hung three albinos she knew well: Ismael, Judin, and Chrystin.

Chelise wept that day, and Thomas made the decision to go deeper into the desert. The Circle learned to adapt, and the Horde grew impatient with the meager pickings. But life in the deep desert was harsh, and the red pools were scarce. They had to move every two or three weeks to find food and wood, and long trips were made to harvest the desert wheat. A hunting party might take a week to kill two or three deer for a feast.

This, and the fact that Elyon had left his red pools in and near the forests, persuaded Thomas that they should move closer to the forests once again. The danger was higher, but so was the reward.

Besides, the elders often agreed, Elyon would be returning soon anyway. Any day. Any week. Not even a few months. Surely not more than a year.

That was seven years ago. And now more than a few albinos wanted to retake the forests.

This Horde army crawling through the Torun Valley might be slower and weaker than any albino army, but they were as numerous as the sands! A massive blanket of men and horses and tents stretched out to the horizon, then was swallowed in a dusty haze.

"There must be a million," she said.

"Many," Stephen said.

"The whole army?"

Again, silence, though Stephen had already let the fact slip. At times, she was certain he forgot she was albino and regarded her only as royalty. He was taking her home, after all.

"All this for a training exercise?" she asked in wonder.

"It's never been done, but it makes sense. The army needs training."

"Yes, but the logistics. It must be a nightmare to move so many men."

Reeslar scoffed. "We did it all the time in the desert! This . . . this is nothing."

"You're sure my father isn't with them?"

Stephen ignored the question. "They're waiting. We shouldn't wait."

"They?"

The scout turned his horse from the crest of the hill and trotted toward the trees. "Your mother awaits you, daughter of Qurong."

"Where?" She kicked her mount into a run, flanked by the other two.

"Close. Just over the hill."

They rode hard, passing by several patrols and guards stationed in the trees. She wore a hooded robe at Stephen's insistence. His orders were to deliver her in secrecy. They could either go in with her bound in chains or looking like Horde, and he recommended the latter. She was, after all, Qurong's daughter.

The royal camp was erected on a plateau above Torun Valley, surrounded by a company of Throaters who'd formed a perimeter several hundred yards out. A dozen flags bearing the winged serpent image flapped over a large canvas tent that was bordered by four smaller tents. Around this grouping sat several dozen smaller tents belonging to the royal entourage and the guard.

Temple guard, if she wasn't mistaken. Then Ba'al was out here as well?

"It has been a pleasure escorting you, daughter of Qurong," Stephen said. "I pray that Teeleh will favor you from the many evil spirits who seek to kill the less fortunate."

How long had it been since she'd heard such a blessing? "Thank you," she said.

He slowed as they passed the main guard, then saluted another, who glared and took her reins.

"You're a good man, Stephen. I pray Elyon will smile on you."

The scout hesitated, then dipped his head.

Her new guard dismounted and delivered her to the main tent's flap before stepping aside. "Inside," he said gruffly. Chelise took a deep breath, pulled the flap open, and stepped back into her past.

The first thing that stood out to her was the bowl of morst by the entrance. She wasn't sure why this would take her attention from the lavish furnishings inside or from the three people who stood across the room. Maybe because the morst represented all that was wrong with her old way of life.

To think that a paste the consistency of soft flour could cover up a disease was ludicrous. It was a beautiful lie.

She released the flap and peered into the dimly lit room. Patricia, whom she had not seen in ten years, stood by the center pole ten yards away, hands clasped in front of her. She wore a red robe, and her hair was drawn back in ceremonial fashion.

"Chelise?"

She felt her knees weaken. To hear her mother call her name . . . She'd missed the woman more than even she'd realized.

"Is that you?"

Her hood! She was standing in the shadows with her hood pulled up. Chelise stepped forward into the light cast by two lamp stands and slipped her hood off.

"Hello, Mother."

Patricia's face slowly wrinkled as emotion swallowed her. Her hands lifted as if to embrace her daughter, but then lowered. She glanced to her right, where the two men stood. The first was the general she'd known years earlier when he was only a captain. Cassak. The second . . .

Chelise felt every nerve in her body shut down as she stared at the large form and gray eyes belonging to Qurong, supreme commander of the Horde. Her own father, whom she loved as much as her own life.

She couldn't speak. She wanted to rush toward him and throw her arms around his thick neck, and she wanted to tell him how often she thought about him: every night, every day. Every time she drank the red waters and ate Elyon's fruit, she saw his face in her mind's eye. She dreamed he would follow her into the red pool and drown his pitiful self—never mind how powerful he was—and find a new life that would make him dance through the night!

But she couldn't. She couldn't even move after imagining this moment for so long.

Qurong's eyes were soft. Even sad. But he turned his face away.

Chelise looked at Patricia, whose sharp glare softened. "Welcome into our home, Daughter."

She dipped her head. "It's my honor, Mother."

Silence.

"Hello, Father."

He glanced over and dipped his head politely.

Then her mother was rushing forward. They embraced, mother and daughter, Horde and albino.

"It's so good to see you, Chelise," her mother whispered, struggling not to cry. "I've been so worried."

She kissed Patricia's cheek. "It's good to see you in good health."

"And your son?" her mother asked, pulling back.

"Jake. He's a bundle of energy."

"Of course." Her mother laughed. "He would be, with Qurong's blood."

"He already handles a wooden sword as if he was born with it."

Patricia laughed, as did Cassak. But Qurong stared ahead and asked a most natural question, all things considered. "And is this an albino sword or one crafted by the Horde?"

"Oh, stop it, Qurong!" Patricia scolded. "Albino or not, he's your grandson. Stop being a baby."

Chelise wanted to reassure him but didn't know what to say to cut through all the deceptions that guided him. All of this was his fault, after all. From the very beginning, her own father had expanded the divide between albino and Horde.

She had this one chance to persuade him, but all the speeches she'd rehearsed lying under the stars in the desert fled her mind.

"Where is Thomas?" she asked.

"I have no clue. Gone."

"Tell us about Jake," Patricia said. "Come and sit. Are you thirsty? Cassak, please bring us some fruit."

Chelise sat at the table and politely accepted an orange from her mother. She told her about Jake, a little rascal who was as stubborn as both his father and grandfather. But as cute as a young Roush, with his fluffy blond hair.

She kept glancing at her father, who remained standing—under orders from Mother, no doubt. It was her idea, not his, that they meet.

They talked for a few minutes, and Chelise tried her best not to answer her mother's questions in a way that might offend their way of life, but the challenge quickly became impossible.

"He sounds precious," Patricia said, returning to Jake. "And healthy."

"From his baptism on, he's been as healthy as a horse."

"Baptism? What is a baptism?"

"The drowning. All of our children drown in the red pools. It keeps the disease away."

That robbed the tent of air.

"Barbaric," Qurong said. "You actually kill your children?"

"Do I look dead to you, Father?" Chelise stood. "I know that none of you can appreciate the drowning or you would have chosen it long ago. But you must know from your very own daughter, it is life-giving.

The dark priests tell you it's poison. Do I look poisoned? Is that why we are so much stronger than even your best warriors?"

"Nonsense!"

"Please," Patricia whispered, "don't speak of such things here."

But Chelise had waited ten years to speak of precisely such things here. She stepped around the table and approached her father.

General Cassak moved to intercept her. "Stay back."

She ignored him. "My father isn't afraid of women, particularly not his own daughter."

That stopped the general, who looked at Qurong but got no instructions. Chelise stood several paces from her father and searched his eyes.

"I saw you vanish into the books with my husband, Father. Can you tell me where he is?"

"He's escaped."

"Into this world? Or another?"

Qurong shifted his eyes. "I know nothing of another world beyond the nightmares that plague me every time I close my eyes."

"Please tell me that he was well the last time you saw him," she begged. "I deserve that much."

"How should I know? He's a witch who changes what men can see with their natural eyes. Beyond that I know nothing."

He was in complete denial about what she'd seen in his secret library. But she hardly blamed him. Who'd ever heard of vanishing into books? He'd categorized it as a nightmare.

"Father, I beg you to reconsider your ways. Albinos are a peaceful people who mean no harm to the Horde. They long only to be reunited with Elyon as was always intended. Everything that has happened from the beginning of time points to that end."

"Death and destruction are part of that plan? Don't be naive."

"No, those were man's choosing. But the evil was allowed so that we might all choose our lover. This is the meaning of the Great Romance—to choose to return the great love Elyon has shown us."

She paused, then spoke softly, knowing he must understand her.

"Do you remember what it was like before the Shataiki were set free, Father?"

"All of this is nonsense."

"To you who don't believe! Even to *me* before I believed. But to those who believe, it is the power of rescue. If you drown, Father, you will know what I know. Good and evil are not playing games to alleviate their boredom. The stakes are devastating! Our very lives are in the balance, all of ours—albino, Horde, and Eramite."

Qurong stared at her for a long time before turning and walking to a pitcher of ale. He poured some of the amber drink into a pewter mug.

"Please, Father. I'm begging you." She spoke in a soft, breaking voice because her emotions prevented her from screaming the words. "Drown with me!"

He took a long drink, refusing to look in her direction. Controlling his own emotions, she thought. She was getting through. How could anyone resist such simple truth?

"You speak of albinos who are peaceful, yet at this very moment they conspire to destroy the Horde," he said.

"That's just not true."

He faced her. "Samuel has joined Eram and is conspiring to pull the albinos into alliance with the half-breeds."

The moment he said it, Chelise knew it was true. This was what Thomas had meant!

And with such a show of power, more than a few albinos would be drawn into a war that promised to finish the Horde once and for all. Chelise's belly turned. Thomas was right, the world was crumbling!

"Thomas . . ." she said. "We need Thomas! He can stop them."

"Is that what he was doing when he offered his son up to Elyon at the high place? Stopping a war?"

"Yes! And you betrayed your word, Father." She stepped up to him and placed her hand on his arm, desperate to gain his trust. "I beg you, Father. You can stop this senselessness. For my sake, I beg you. For the sake of your grandson."

"Do not patronize me. There will be no war!" He pulled back, gripped his hand into a fist, and shook it. "But if there is, I will crush any force that comes against me."

"Qurong!" Patricia crossed the floor to them. "Remember our agreement. Watch your tone!"

"I am Qurong!" he shouted. "My women do not tell me what to do!"

Chelise felt smothered by a sudden urgency to return to the albinos. Samuel had to be stopped!

"If she'd never fallen for Thomas's lies, we wouldn't be in such a predicament," Qurong snapped.

"Oh, please, you can't possibly blame this on her," Patricia said. "You should look no further than your own priest."

"He is not my priest."

Qurong glanced at the door flap. It wasn't in good form to say such things about Ba'al aloud. Not all was at peace in the Horde camp. But none of this mattered to Chelise at the moment. She was without Thomas. And Samuel might be heading to the Gathering this very moment, intent on taking albinos with him to wage war on the Horde.

If he did, the Horde's days might be numbered.

"Cassak, see that she leaves her enemy camp without danger," Qurong said, heading for the door. "I have business."

"Qurong!" Patricia cried.

"You're not my enemy, Father," Chelise said. "I love you as much as my own life."

But her father marched out without another word.

All is lost, Chelise thought. *I've lost my husband, my son, and now my father, who is going to wage war on my people.*

The world waits for you, Chelise.

34

FOUR DAYS advising the Eramite army had proved to Samuel that he not only made a good choice in coming to Eram, but a choice that would reshape history. A choice that would soon be heralded as the definitive turning point in the era of Horde supremacy. Thomas of Hunter had become a legend because of a choice like this one, and now his son, Samuel of Hunter, would follow in his footsteps and be praised among the Circle as the one who liberated albinos from the scourge called Horde.

The children would engrave his name on bracelets, and men would sit around fires exaggerating his deeds until he was nothing less than a god in their eyes. And women . . . he'd never married, because deep down inside he knew that he was destined for greatness. While others his age spent day and night trying to impress demanding women, he'd spent his days refining his crafts of war. Now the young maidens would keep their hopeful eyes on him wherever he went.

But he hadn't counted on this particular woman, who found her way into Eram's inner circle twelve hours earlier. Her name was Janae, she said. She was an albino, she was disturbingly intelligent, and she was more beautiful than any woman he'd ever seen. Which gave him pause, because he'd seen all albinos and would certainly have noticed this one among the rest.

"No, my lord," he said, glancing back at the woman who studied them from her horse, twenty yards behind. "I don't think you should follow her advice. I think you should follow mine."

He and Eram sat on horses flanked by Eram's personal four-man guard, overlooking the eastern valley where Samuel's men were working with Forest Guard turned Horde. They'd agreed to place four thousand men under Samuel's command, an elite force of the best fighters Eram could offer. They would be led by as many as four hundred albino fighters, assuming Samuel could come through on his end of the bargain. They'd know soon enough. Tomorrow Samuel would take his small army west, announce his intentions to the Gathering, and challenge any who sought justice to join him in leading a guerrilla warfare campaign against Qurong.

Samuel would take his army, divide them into ten tightly knit, elite units, and station them on all sides of Qurongi City. Their first attack would be surgical and brutal, leaving Qurong's army with deep wounds to lick.

The second, third, and fourth attacks would follow immediately from three sides before the Horde could properly reassemble. Even if they did manage to form up, they would be confused without a clear campaign to execute or an army to engage. Within a matter of months, Samuel would soften Qurong's massive army, and then Eram would bring the full weight of his own one hundred fifty thousand to crush the Horde.

It was a reasonable plan, with almost no chance for failure, assuming Samuel could persuade enough of the Circle to join them. Assuming Eram didn't change his mind for fear of betrayal.

Assuming this woman named Janae didn't bring the whole thing down with her ridiculous talk of an immediate full-scale war on the authority of a Shataiki queen named Marsuuv.

"Please, just look at her. Have you ever seen a witch in service of a queen Shataiki? Not until now."

Eram followed his eyes and twisted his lips into a sly smile. "An albino witch? That's a new one. Where have you been hiding these stunning creatures?"

One thing was certain: Eram loved the ladies. Samuel had never known a man with such a voracious appetite for women. The Eramite leader made no attempt to hide his displays of affection whenever or wherever the impulse struck him, and yet he did it with tact, like a gentleman, despite the fact that his intentions were well-known. His people seemed to love him for it. Their leader was a passionate, virile man who had the backbone to lead them out into the desert. Who would castrate such a man?

"Forgive me for pointing it out," Samuel said, "but this isn't about a woman, however seductive."

Eram's grin softened, and the moment he shifted his eyes Samuel knew he'd spoken out of turn. "Are you looking for a knife in your throat?"

"No, my lord. Forgive me. But surely you can't be bowing to her nonsense."

"Bowing? You beg forgiveness for one jab and follow it with a slice to my head?"

"Forgive—"

"You're a dangerous man, Samuel of Hunter. I served under your father when you were a pup, and I see you have his audacity."

Samuel was glad for the shift in subject. "Like father, like son, they say."

"No, lad. Don't make the mistake of assuming you will ever be even half the man your father is. I would have laid my life down for him on the worst of days, and I'm not sure I wouldn't do the same today. He's a legend without peer and always will be."

"And yet you don't follow him."

"I don't follow his ideas. But I bow to the man. And him alone." The leader took a deep breath and cracked his neck with a jerk of his head. "To the matter at hand . . ." A crazed look lit his eyes. "I think the woman has more than seduction to offer us."

"Yes, danger. Take the whole army to the Gathering? Now? It's a huge gamble."

"I see no danger to me. If she's wrong, I lose nothing but some time and effort. If she's right, on the other hand, she'd replace your lofty status as the hero, isn't that it?"

The Eramite leader was a brilliant tactician in political matters;

he'd pegged Samuel's fear even before Samuel had fully formed his own understanding of it.

"But I'm not one to change with the wind," Eram said. "I've given my word to you, so now I leave this matter in your hands. You decide. Come." He turned his horse from the valley and walked it toward Janae, who still watched them from her perch under a tree.

She wore a red cape with a short black cloak that covered fighting leathers. Odd, this red cape. The breeze lifted long black strands of hair from her shoulders and wrapped them around a porcelain white neck. He'd noticed a light rash on the skin at the base of her neck and on her wrists. Similar to a rash he'd noticed on his own skin yesterday.

Rash or no rash, this woman who'd come to them bearing a challenge from the Shataiki was truly stunning. It was her eyes, Samuel thought. They watched above perpetually curved lips, cutting deeply into his mind. Honestly, she frightened him, not only for her potential threat to his stature among new friends, but for her effect on him personally. Unlike Eram, he resented the notion of seduction now.

The guard held back as Eram and Samuel approached her under the tree. "So, the mistress of a Shataiki queen has brought the poor Eramites salvation, is that it?" Eram said, his smile matching hers.

Janae shifted her eyes back to Samuel. Her longing stares had favored him above Eram since the patrol first deposited her in Eram's court. For now she seemed satisfied to simply look into his eyes.

"How is it that an albino mates with a Shataiki?" Eram asked. "Hmmm?"

"How is it that an albino becomes a half-breed?" she returned, eyes still on Samuel.

"Indeed. The world has changed. Now the most beautiful come from the Black Forest."

"Your flattery means nothing to me, Eram, old boy. I'm fascinated with this stallion."

He chuckled, genuinely amused, Samuel thought.

"And for the record," the woman said, now exchanging a smile with the leader, "I am not the mistress of any queen. Marsuuv, the queen who sent me, has another for his lover. Billy. Perhaps you know him as Billos. As for me, I don't come from the Black Forest. I'm from another world, where my kind are better known as vampires. But you can call me the messiah. And I am mistress to no one but Teeleh, my lord and savior."

She spoke as one reciting poetry, a minstrel from the dark side who captivated even jaded men like Eram with her every word. A wicked woman who melted hearts. Surely Eram saw that much.

"A witch from another world," Eram said, "who comes to tell us that she can deliver the albinos if only we follow her. That if we take our full army to the Circle, they will join us for war. In three days' time, no less."

"I am here to serve, my lord. Not to lead. And unless my aim was to seduce the bravest leader in the land, I would be a fool to come with words alone."

Janae slipped her hand into her cloak and withdrew a small glass bottle, perfectly formed, perhaps three inches tall. She held it between her thumb and forefinger and twirled it.

"This, my lovelies, is the answer to all of your prayers."

Samuel cleared his throat. "A bottle filled with Teeleh's urine will save us? Tell me why a half-breed who still follows Elyon in the ways of old, and an albino who rejects Teeleh, should entertain the mistress of Teeleh himself?"

She ignored his second question, as if it were too silly to take seriously.

"You might be surprised to know what a single drop of Teeleh's blood can do. But for now, we'll have to do with the Raison Strain, a brutal, incurable virus that destroys the body from the inside in a matter of hours."

"We have our poisons," Eram said. "So you have another. What of it?"

"Oh, that's right, I forgot, neither of you has a PhD in biochemistry."

Samuel didn't know what she meant, but he heard the mockery in her tone.

"Let me put it to you this way: if I could deliver what I hold in my hand to the Horde army, the condition that afflicts them already would become worse. Much worse. It would immobilize them in minutes. A strong army could wipe them out."

"And how do you propose to get such a small amount to the entire Horde army without also infecting us?" Eram asked, intrigued.

"Every witch has her secrets," she said. Her eyes turned to Samuel. "Do as I suggest and I will prove my power in front of the entire Gathering."

So, she had more than words and beauty. Or so she claimed. Eram chuckled and faced Samuel. "As I said, young Hunter, the decision's yours." He turned his stallion around and winked. "I'll give you some time to . . . consider this alone."

Eram galloped away, motioned his guard to follow him, and rode over the hill, leaving Samuel alone with Janae. The conniving rogue likely thought Samuel too weak to fend off the advances of this witch, but he didn't know the backbone of Thomas Hunter's son, now, did he?

When he turned back, the woman was staring to her right, into nothing but the horizon from what he could see. Her sly grin was gone, her sultry eyes now harsh. Finally, the real woman stripped of ulterior motives.

"You may have our brave leader by the loins, witch, but I have no intention of handing control of his army over to you."

"That's funny. He said you would be the most difficult."

"Who did?"

She faced him. "Marsuuv. The son of the mighty Thomas Hunter has a backbone of steel like his father. Stubborn to the heels."

"Then the old bat knows more than I would have given him credit for."

Janae dismounted and walked toward the trees. "Let me show you something."

He hesitated, then followed her into the small grove. She let him catch up and took his hand without it being offered.

"To be perfectly honest, the disease these filthy beasts have disgusts me. It's good to touch the flesh of a normal human." She rubbed her thumb on the back of his hand as she led him through the trees. "What

I said about me coming from another reality wasn't meant to make me look foolish, Samuel. It's the truth. I come from the same place your own father once came from. This very planet, actually. Two thousand years ago. The world was much more advanced then. Evil wasn't as plain. Good was even less plain. I do believe it all ended badly, judging by what I see here. All the cities and cars, the roadways, the concrete jungles . . . gone."

They stepped out of the trees on the far side and gazed out at lowlands that stretched as far as the eye could see. "You see this world? It's a simple place compared to what was once here. Manageable. And whether or not you like it, dear Samuel, you and I have been chosen to manage it." She released his hand and slipped her arm around his waist, eyes still on the lowlands. "At the very least, we will manage it the next few days."

He wasn't sure what to say to that. She'd changed her tone.

"You may not like the Shataiki, but they share one thing in common with you."

He was meant to ask what, so he did, but his mind was on her hand, which now softly rubbed his back in an unapologetic show of tenderness. Did she think him a child to be so easily manipulated?

"The Shataiki, like you, despise the Horde."

"Along with the rest of humanity," he said.

"Granted. But also like you, they mean to destroy the Horde, and they have empowered me to help you do it."

He didn't know what to make of this claim.

"I have no interest in taking your place, Samuel. I'll help you, only if that's what you want." She turned into him and pulled him close, staring up into his eyes. "And I won't lie; I wouldn't mind some companionship in the process."

Her approach was so direct, so transparent, that he lost track of her motivation for trickery. He should pry her hands off him and call her out! But he didn't, not yet. What if she meant what she said?

"Our goals are the same, Samuel," she said, searching his eyes in that

way. "We are one at heart. Both albinos, both with the same hatred of
the Horde, both called by powers beyond our understanding. We were
meant to be together."

She's a witch, Samuel. She'll use you and leave you for dead. Still, his
breathing thickened.

"I hate the Horde because they've waged war on my people for as
long as I can remember," he said. "If you've come from the histories, why
do you harbor such hatred for those who've done you no wrong?"

His mind was swimming in her eyes. Her soft lips, her perfect jawline.
But above these, her words. So perfectly placed, so knowing. Enough to
make his belly rise into his throat.

"Don't be silly, Samuel," she said, coming closer to his face. She
spoke in a low, purring voice, but her eyes flashed with passion. "We all
want the same thing. Hmm? The contentment, the pleasure, the power
we were born for. Love life or die trying, isn't that a fighter's motto?"

Was it?

He broke into a sweat, knowing full well that she was manipulating
him. But he couldn't remember what part of her suggestions didn't align
with his own desires.

She touched his lips with her own, not so much a kiss as a peck, but
it made his mind go completely blank.

"Say yes, Samuel," she whispered. "This is what you want. What
you need as much as I do. Tell Eram that he shouldn't wait another day."

"Take the army today." He meant it as a question, but it came out
as a statement.

"If you march all night, you could be in the western canyons when
the sun goes down tomorrow."

"The others have gone to the Gathering. I would speak to them."

"You would speak to them," she whispered. "Samuel, son of Hunter."

"Some would follow us."

"No, Samuel. Many would follow you. I've been assured."

The party doing the assuring could only be Shataiki, his greatest
enemy, but at the moment this minute detail seemed strangely inconse-

quential. He placed his arms around her waist and pulled her against him. Her lips were softer than he had imagined, and for a few moments he felt like a boy discovering love for the first time. She kissed him hungrily, and he knew that he could not say no to the woman in his arms.

Worse, he didn't want to. How things had changed in just a few short minutes. Eram was right. Janae was right.

The time to change the world would not wait.

"Say yes, Samuel. Tell me yes. I want to hear it."

Stripped of any reason to deny her, he said it softly but without reluctance.

"Yes."

35

QURONG DISMOUNTED the sweating black stallion, threw the reins to one of the Throaters who'd accompanied him on the long ride back to Qurongi City, and marched up the Thrall steps, still furious for having left his army in the dead of night. But the situation had become complicated and he was forced to abandon his good sense for the sake of a woman and a priest.

His wife had emerged after spending hours eating a meal with Chelise and demanded to be taken back to the city immediately. Qurong would have sent her with an escort, but then word came from one of the temple priests: Ba'al had returned from the Black Forest with a message that was a matter of life and death for the Horde. Qurong must come immediately. No, Ba'al could not come out because certain rituals were required.

So Qurong endured the silent four-hour trek, during which he and his wife ignored each other in protest over the other's behavior regarding their daughter.

What did she want? He had principles. Chelise might be his daughter, but she had joined his greatest enemy, for the breath of Teeleh!

He spat on the temple steps. She'd *wed* his greatest enemy. Borne a son by him. Now Patricia wanted him, Qurong, leader of the world, to throw away decades of conflict so that she could cuddle her little albino grandson? She'd likely catch his disease!

Worse than this was the position that Patricia had put him in by insisting they meet. His heart had stopped the moment Chelise walked into the tent. He'd put her from his mind a long time ago. But there she was, his flesh and blood, standing so beautifully in his doorway. The sight of her was brutal punishment. He'd exercised extraordinary self-control in making sure she didn't receive hope from him.

Then she told him she loved him, and he took a horse into the forest alone to hide his emotions.

He opened the door to the Thrall's sanctuary. "Where is Ba'al?" he shouted without bothering to look. If he had looked he would have seen the dark priest directly ahead, standing behind the stone altar dressed in his purple ceremonial robe. A red cape Qurong had never seen before covered Ba'al's shoulders.

A butchered goat lay on the altar, sacrificed already. The torches licked at the air, glancing off the serpent's wings on either side of the bleeding goat.

"I'm here," Qurong announced, striding forward. "And I'm in no mood to stay long. You called me from my army at the most inopportune time."

"The day before they are to be slaughtered?" Ba'al rasped. His eyes were red and there was blood on his lower lip. "You meant to wish them all well on their way to hell?"

Qurong drew up and closed his eyes, resolving to suffer through the man's games if he must. "Fine, my dear dark priest. What is it this time?"

Ba'al stared at him for a long moment. His usual coy grin was gone. Another quality about him gave Qurong pause. He looked more emaciated in the face, perhaps. Dirtier, as if he'd gone on this journey of his and returned without bathing. And he hadn't bothered to apply enough morst to hide his flaking skin.

"The world is crumbling about you, Qurong, and you don't have the decency to hear of it. I suggest you listen to the spirits of fear."

"I'll pass."

"Then I'll say what he told me to say and leave your fate up to him." Ba'al picked up a crudely fashioned glass bottle from the podium behind him and set it on the altar. It appeared to be filled with a black fluid.

"You're going to have to make a choice, my lord," Ba'al bit off.

"Tonight you will give all your allegiance to Teeleh, or you will suffer the same fate as the rest."

There was something different about his voice. Simple authority. No pretense. Qurong let him continue.

"At this very moment, the Eramites are gathering with the albinos to march on your army. Did you know that?"

Nonsense. But he would listen.

"Samuel, son of Hunter, has brokered a deal with Eram to fight together against the Horde."

"This isn't news to me."

"Janae, that albino witch from beyond, will convince many albinos to join. They mean to strike within days with an army of one hundred fifty thousand half-breeds and thousands of albinos."

Qurong felt his veins run cold. "That's not possible. I was with one of their leaders just today, and they said nothing of this."

"Your daughter, Chelise, knows nothing. If she did, she never would have come to meet with you."

Ba'al knew of Chelise's visit. More to the point, he seemed to know more than Qurong. There was no end to his spies!

"What I know comes directly from my lover, the queen Marsuuv, the twelfth of twelve who serve Teeleh. The day of the dragon has arrived, my lord. All those who do not bear the mark of the beast will die in the Valley of Miggdon—albino, half-breed Eramite, and full-breed Horde. I bring to you today the means to your salvation."

He'd heard similar words from Ba'al, but at this midnight hour, these words resonated with an undeniable quality that had Qurong's heart beating like a fist.

"We've all taken the mark of your beast," he said. "What more could he possibly demand?"

"Your heart, my lord."

"My heart? He has my entire body!" Qurong thundered. "What is this of Miggdon? We are gathered in Torun, not Miggdon."

"So you are. And I commend you on your plan; it was good thinking. But it won't be enough."

"You know all this how?"

Ba'al picked up the bottle and held it up to the flame. What Qurong had assumed to be black turned red as the light passed through the glass. Blood.

"You look up and you see only sky. I look up and I see the watchers of our souls perched in the trees, soaring over our heads. The Shataiki see everything."

"Only Shataiki? So Elyon is a fable."

"Only Shataiki," he said, bringing the vial to his lips. "For a time, only Shataiki." He kissed the blood and whispered lovingly, "I am your servant, my lover, Marsuuv."

"One hundred fifty thousand, you say." Qurong paced to his left, lost in the size of the half-breed army. "Less than one-third the size of our own."

"They haven't been sitting in the desert getting fat. And they will have albinos."

"A few thousand at most."

"Enough to tip the balance. Don't underestimate the albinos, my lord. They may have laid their swords down, but they were trained by Thomas of Hunter." Ba'al spit to one side and black saliva splattered on the altar.

"I'm listening."

The dark priest set the bottle of blood back down and slowly slid it across the altar until it rested in front of Qurong.

"Move your army to the east face of Miggdon Valley, where the terrain will play to your advantage. Hide three hundred thousand behind the valley and leave the rest on the hills to be seen."

"Bait."

"Eram will lead his army to the other side of Miggdon Valley." Ba'al drew out his plan on the dead goat's hide with a long, crooked finger in need of a nail trim. "He will take the bait and attack the army in the valley with enough men to destroy them."

"And we will descend with the two hundred thousand in plain sight."

"Which he will expect, naturally. He will then commit the rest of his forces against your army, not knowing that you have another three hundred thousand in reserve on the high ground."

"We take them out with a crushing blow, once and for all," Qurong said.

Ba'al smiled and stepped back. "If, and only if, you appease Teeleh."

Qurong didn't see the connection, and his face clearly betrayed his confusion.

"It is the day of the dragon, my lord. This isn't about you. You must believe me when I tell you there's black magic afoot. The Eramites aren't fools. They'll come with their own plans for victory."

"What plans?"

"Dark magic. If I knew more I would tell you, but I can't say what will happen if you don't take the side of my dark lover. In the end it is he who will rule. Not me, not you, not Eram, and certainly not Thomas of Hunter."

Qurong looked at the blood. The blood of Teeleh or Marsuuv, both equally terrifying. He lifted the glass container and held it up to the light.

"Drinking the blood will seal your vow," Ba'al said.

What madness could come from drinking blood?

"A vow?" Qurong asked.

"From your heart."

He could either refuse the rite, which would earn the rage of both Ba'al and whoever controlled him, or he could win their favor. The choice seemed simple enough.

Qurong twisted the stopper, lifted the blood to his nostrils and immediately regretted his decision to do so. The foul smell might have been an old open wound. He would have to drink quickly.

"Will you give your heart to my master?" Ba'al asked.

"Yes."

"Then repeat my words." Ba'al lifted both hands and called the pledge to the ceiling in a loud, ringing voice. "I, Qurong, supreme commander of the Horde, pledge my heart and my loyalty to the dragon called Teeleh, to do his bidding in accordance with only his will."

"I, Qurong, supreme commander of the Horde, pledge my heart and my loyalty to the dragon called Teeleh, to do his bidding in accordance with only his will."

"And I seal my vow with this blood, knowing that it comes from my master, Teeleh, maker of the evil that lives on our flesh."

The jargon of black magic was comical, but he knew every word would be important to Ba'al, so he repeated the vow exactly as instructed.

"Now drink!" Ba'al cried. "Drink of this blood in remembrance of the day you first embraced the evil. Drink to Teeleh, your lord and your master."

"I drink," Qurong said, and drained the blood into his mouth. He swallowed quickly, as if it was a hard drink, and slammed the glass down on the altar. He was tempted to spit, but he dared not. So he swallowed the last of it and steadied himself on the stone.

"Satisfied?"

Ba'al grinned at him. "More than you know, my lord."

"Good."

"Do you feel any different?"

"Only nauseated."

"No, you wouldn't. Your mind is already eaten by the worms."

More magic nonsense. And that was that.

"Then, if your lord requires—"

"*Your* lord," Ba'al corrected. "He's *your* lord now."

"Of course. If *my* lord requires nothing more, I have to leave immediately."

"To the Valley of Miggdon," Ba'al said.

"To the Valley of Miggdon."

WHILE QURONG was vowing his allegiance to Teeleh two thousand years in the future, Thomas Hunter, who'd come from that future, paced in Monique de Raison's personal library, slowly coming apart at the seams, aware only that this world was no longer his home.

"But it could be your home," Kara said. "Please, Thomas, sit down. I don't know how long I can take this pacing."

He spun around and threw his arms wide. "I'm lost, Kara! I'm stranded here in this"—he glanced about—"godforsaken place."

"This godforsaken place might very well be the only place you'll ever live. You've affected this reality as much as you've affected the other; it's time you acknowledge that. For all we know, this little jaunt of yours will have a profound impact on our future."

"Yes, of course, the apocalypse is just around the corner, and it's here because of me. Right."

She stood and crossed to him, intending to calm him. "You've said it yourself: everything that's happened there is a mirror image of what's happened here. It's a dim reflection that's anything but precise, but history is unraveling in almost perfect symmetry. What awaits you in the other reality?"

"Nothing much. Only the end of the world."

"And here?"

She had a good point. "Okay." He lifted both hands in surrender. "You're right, the same awaits me here."

"*Us* here," she corrected.

"Okay, us here."

"Eight billion people are on the cusp of either a tragic ending or a grand climax. And for all you know, you're here to usher it in. That doesn't sound like a rather important consideration to you?"

She was right, so right. But Thomas couldn't wrap his heart around the importance of any role he might play in this reality.

He turned from her, gripping his hair. His chest felt as though it might burst.

And then suddenly it was. Bursting. He shouted his frustration through clenched teeth and keeled over. "I can't be here! She needs me. Jake needs me. Samuel needs me!"

"I need you," Kara said softly.

Thomas faced her. "I will take you, Kara. I swear I will take you. Billy will come back with the books, because if anyone has a role to play in the end of this world, it's that redhead from hell! I won't leave this place. I don't care how long it takes, I'll eat here, I'll sleep here. The moment he appears, I'll . . ."

He'd what? Knock him out, take the books, and vanish? Yes, if that was what returning required.

"You never know how much you love someone until they're gone," Kara said. "When you left us, I thought I would die. I understand how you feel."

"They are my life, Kara. And Chelise . . ." He felt his eyes tear up. "I'm telling you, she is my breath. A constant reminder that Elyon longs for me the way I long for her. Without her I would dry up like an uprooted Catalina cactus." He spoke the words in a rush, feeding on his need to say what was eating him alive.

"She's water to me, my gift from the Giver of all that is good. She's my sky, my ground, my reason for waking and my reason for sleeping. She is my life!"

Kara's neck darkened a shade. "Wow."

"It's all about him; of course it is. But I see him in *her*! She's become the lake that I drown in!"

Overstated in a state of despair, perhaps, but hardly.

"I would rather die than stay here, separated from the woman I love, from the son who turned his back on me! I need to find them!"

Kara set her jaw. "Then beg Elyon to save you from a living death. Because from where I'm standing, you're stuck here. In this death."

She was right. Dear Elyon, she was so right!

Thomas turned around and fell to his knees. He squeezed his hands into two fists, faced the ceiling, and through streams of tears begged Elyon to send him the books.

Send him the books or let him die.

36

CHELISE HAD raced over the desert, expecting at any moment to see signs of stragglers converging on the Gathering in Paradose Valley, late-coming albinos who'd heard the summons that Thomas of Hunter was calling the Circle together for the first time in many years. And Eramite scouts, preceding Samuel.

But it wasn't until she was nearly in the valley that she saw any sign of albinos or Scabs, and the sight made her pull her mount up hard. The mare snorted.

A line of Horde, maybe twenty in all, turned to look at her. They rode in full battle dress over a dune not a hundred yards from where she'd stopped. Horde scouts, so deep?

But these weren't from her father's army, which she'd left last night. To begin with, their armor was a light tan and blended into the sands, not black like those she'd seen yesterday. And these warriors wore no helmets. Their hair blew freely, no dreadlocks.

Her first thought was that they were Eramite, though she'd never seen an Eramite warrior before. And she knew they couldn't be scouts. These twenty carried spears and maces, spiked steel balls, dangling from each saddle, not the lighter weapons of a fast-moving scout.

This was a contingent from a full army, riding without care within a half-hour march of Paradose Valley! That the warriors saw her and made no attempt to cut her off disturbed her even more.

She stared in stunned silence, lost for a moment. Thoughts of the Gathering crashed through her mind. All twelve thousand had surely arrived by now.

Did these soldiers know how close they were to the Circle's most prized tribe? But of course they must!

Samuel.

Samuel had done precisely what her father predicted. He'd brought a contingent of Eramites to the Circle. She'd fled her mother's tent with the scout Stephen as an escort and made the best possible time across the desert, hoping that Qurong's information was wrong, or at least twisted. Stephen had left at her insistence nearly six hours ago. She knew the way from here, and it was safe.

But here and now, she knew that there was only one explanation for the twenty nonhostile half-breeds on the dune to her right. She kicked her horse and galloped on, down the slope and up the far rise, heart pounding. Up the rise, begging Elyon for time. The elders knew about Samuel, but what would they say to . . .

Chelise slid to a halt atop the next dune and gawked at the sight that greeted her. The valley was alive, flooded by an army that stretched to the horizon.

Samuel had not only brought a contingent of Eramites, he'd brought the whole half-breed army! A massive throng, no less than a hundred thousand strong, capable of crushing the Circle under hoof without breaking stride.

And where was Elyon?

The world awaits you, Chelise. Michal's words whispered through her mind.

Chelise whipped her horse and cried out, urging it to run, to race as fast as was possible despite legs tired to the breaking point.

She had to tell them that Qurong had already gathered his army.

That they could not listen to Samuel.

That they could not make a move without Thomas!

A hundred thoughts pounded through her head, and she slapped the mare's hide harder, racing around the army. It didn't matter; not one seemed even slightly disturbed by the presence of an albino on a horse. Only curious. They'd already seen plenty today.

They were half-breeds, but their gray eyes and flaking skin were no different from full-breed Horde's. These half-breeds were as Horde as her own father.

They watched her from a distance, and the sheer scope of their enormity sent a shiver down her spine.

It took her less than twenty minutes to cut a line across the dunes, around the gathered army, into the canyon, and to the corrals behind the tents.

The camp looked deserted. But the albinos had to be around the corner, gathering in the amphitheater where Thomas himself had toasted the Great Romance not two weeks ago.

Then she heard his voice. Samuel's voice, echoing unseen from beyond the cliff. She ran up the path to the overlook and pulled up sharply.

The Circle had indeed arrived, all of them. They stood or squatted on boulders and sat on the cliffs, and their attention was firmly fixed on the flat stone surface where Marie had fought Samuel in the earliest bid to end this craziness.

And here he was again, this son of Thomas, Samuel of Hunter, standing next to an albino woman dressed in Horde battle armor and a red cape. Behind them, an Eramite leader, perhaps Eram himself, sat on his horse with a half dozen other half-breed fighters.

The elders stood to their right, arms crossed, watching with a mix of skepticism and interest. Why weren't they stopping this?

"Wasn't this day prophesied of old?" Samuel called. "It is said he will ride on a white horse and deliver those who swim with him to a new world, where there are no tears."

His voice rang out. "Where his fruit is heady enough to make the most pained heart laugh with delight. Where our children no longer fear that a Horde sword will gut their mother or drop their father's bloody head to the ground. For ten years we have fled this oppressor. Will Elyon never rescue us?"

"But he has," Mikil said.

"Let him speak!" someone shouted back. "This is Thomas's son, and what he says has merit."

Samuel continued without giving Mikil opportunity. "Mikil's right. Elyon has saved our hearts, and now he extends his hand to pull us from this wretched life on the run. Our enemy will not mock us, they will not ridicule us, they will only envy the Great Romance. I am Elyon's prophet and I say it is so."

"It is as he says!"

"He speaks the truth!"

"No, no, this can't be . . ."

The response was a cacophony of mixed sentiment.

"Do you doubt?" Samuel shouted, red-faced. They quieted slowly. "Do you think I was born to Thomas of Hunter for no reason? If he was here, would he deny the prophecies of old? We cannot escape our destiny."

"It is as he says."

"He speaks the truth."

"The day of Elyon's wrath against the Horde has come, my friends. We will destroy the Horde!"

"Through an *alliance* with the Horde?" Johan demanded. "This is ill-advised."

"Ill-advised," Samuel mocked. "Our elders are too intellectual to follow the passions of Elyon, who uses whomever he sees fit. Today that is Eram and the famed Forest Guard." He called the half-breeds as they were known before acquiring the scabbing disease. "I'm proposing we ally ourselves with Eram to this end. He needs us as much as we need him. Let me take five thousand of the strongest fighters here, and we will lead the army you've all seen just outside our canyon in one crushing blow against the Horde!"

It sounded perfectly reasonable, Chelise thought, except for what they didn't know. And according to the Roush, the world awaited her, Chelise, who'd been sent back by Thomas in his stead, to save them all.

The Circle awaited her.

She lifted both hands and stepped forward, overlooking them all. "I am Chelise, wife of Thomas, and I find fault with this son of mine!" she cried for the whole Gathering to hear. They tilted their heads up. A murmur ran through the Gathering as she hopped down and stood on a large boulder to Samuel's right.

"Hello, Mother," Samuel said.

She ignored him. "I have come from the east, where the Horde army is assembling in the Torun Valley. They know we are here at this moment, with the Eramites, and they beg us to come so that they can crush us and leave our bodies for the buzzards!"

"I love you, Mother, but you're wrong."

She whirled to face him. "You're saying the Horde will not slaughter many, if not all, if you march now?"

"Well, yes, there would be some bloodshed. But you're still wrong. Mother. You don't know everything. You don't know that Elyon has given me a supernatural means of victory."

She was at a loss for words.

Samuel stepped forward and addressed the assembly. "It's true, I'm a prophet for this day, but I don't come with words alone. How could I stand up to the quick tongues of the council or my own mother? But I come with another." He looked at the woman beside him. "I present to you the strong arm of Elyon himself, in the flesh, for our benefit." He reached for her hand, kissed it, and held it high. "Friends of the Circle, I present to you Janae, a messiah in her own right."

Applause started with a smattering and grew.

"Show them, Janae."

The dark-haired witch had the look of a seductress. There was a strange rash on her neck, similar to the one Chelise now saw on Samuel's neck.

Janae stepped forward and paced before them like a general surveying the troops. She motioned casually over her shoulder with a single finger. "Bring him."

Two of the half-breeds hauled a chained Scab into the clearing. Chelise recognized him immediately: This was Stephen, the very scout who'd treated her so kindly as an escort.

His gray eyes found hers. "Please . . ."

"Let him go!"

The witch twisted around. "We will! As soon as he shows everyone what I already know."

Janae pulled out a small vial and held it up for the whole assembly to see. "In my hand I hold Elyon's gift to us all." She plucked the stopper from the top of the glass tube and waved it in front of her nose like a precious perfume. "The scent of the most high. To you and I, who have bathed in the lakes, half-breeds and albino alike, it is a gift."

Chelise could smell the potent scent from where she stood, a mix of lemon and gardenia flower if she was right.

Samuel's seductress lifted it up and walked to the closest observers. She held it out. "It gives us only strength. But to this infidel behind me, the scent of Elyon is poison. Yes? If he comes within ten paces of me, as he is now, the scent will enter his nostrils, penetrate his blood, and excite the very scabbing disease that makes him Horde. To be more precise, the scent repels the worms that eat him alive, throwing them into a fit. They will wreak havoc . . ."

The scout began to whimper. He scratched at his skin in a growing panic.

". . . with his nerves," Janae finished. She nodded at the guards. "Release him."

They unlocked the scout's chains and pushed him forward. Stephen had gone from a terrified Horde who feared his captors to a debilitated man panicked by whatever was happening to him. He staggered forward, bent at his knees like an old man. "What's happening? Take it off me!"

"It's not *on* him," Janae said for all to hear. "It's *in* him, and it is Teeleh's breath, stimulating the worms eating his body." She paced before the crowd, scanning them with an even stare. "Yet I feel nothing. The half-breeds feel nothing. The council feels nothing. Those close enough to inhale this breath from hell feel nothing. Why? Because we have all bathed in the lakes at one time and are immune to my Raison Strain." Then she added, "Elyon's gift to us."

A mumble of amazement swept through the crowd with a few sharp expressions of protest, but even more cries of agreement. "She tells the truth, she tells the truth!"

Janae walked to Samuel, who gazed at her as if she might be his own personal goddess. She stood on her toes and kissed him on the cheek. Taking his hand, she turned back to the Gathering.

"Elyon's gift. He gave it to me and told me I would find Samuel with the Eramites. Together we would come to the Circle, in peace. We would extend the grace of Elyon, and then we would march on the Horde army, feed them Teeleh's breath, and slaughter them all in their weakened state."

Chelise stood on the boulder, bound by twisted cords of objection.

Where was Elyon in all of this? Janae spoke with authority. Could her son's new lover have come from Elyon? Her message was desperately needed by many in the Circle. They would drink it deep and satisfy their thirst for Elyon's power once again.

But this woman could not have come from Elyon! She was a seductress, a harlot with words that tickled the ears. And she was missing the most important element in Elyon's charge to them all.

Chelise yelled it now, shouting over both Johan and Mikil, who'd stepped forward as one and were objecting.

"Love the Horde!" she cried, pointing at the Horde scout who was now shaking in fear and pain. "This is our only charge regarding these poor souls. Judgment will be Elyon's to wield, not ours."

"What she says is true," Johan shouted.

"We can never take up a sword and cut down another human in Elyon's name," Chelise said. "Never!"

"So says the daughter of Qurong, the cousin of Teeleh."

She didn't know who from the throng of twelve thousand had made the point, but no one protested the comment. She stood high on the boulder, staring at the full assembly of albinos, and for the first time in many years she felt like a stranger in their midst.

She, who'd drowned in Elyon's love and been washed of the disease, felt more Horde than albino in this moment. What was the difference between them and Qurong? Between Samuel and Stephen?

The scabbing disease was the difference.

And the insight to acknowledge that the condition was evil, affecting the mind and heart as much as the skin. And the bravery to follow Elyon into the red pool, drown to this life of disease, and rise from the waters as a new creature.

Because wasn't her mother, Patricia, capable of love? Wasn't her father worthy of life? She would die before she considered taking up arms against any Horde!

All eyes were on her. Both Samuel and Janae seemed content to let her engage her own people. She silently begged Elyon to bring Thomas to them. *Now.* In these deserts, the people would follow him like no other. They needed him desperately.

She needed him. She required her lover by her side, for the warmth of his body and his soft words of encouragement and his tender kiss of love.

"Yes." Her voice was shaking. "I am the daughter of Qurong, and yes, my father is still deceived. He can't see the truth when it stares him in the face. But isn't this the way of the world? They can only see the ordinary, and Elyon is anything but ordinary. His love is extraordinary, extending beyond you and me to our own fathers and mothers and sisters and brothers who are still Horde."

"His love is extraordinary, Mother," Janae said. "But then so is his wrath." The woman stepped away from Samuel and drilled her with a stare. "Do you challenge my authority as the one who has come with this gift from Elyon?"

What if she was right? What if this really was Elyon's gift to them all? It was strange that this woman had come to them from nowhere, much like Thomas had first come. Strange that she had taken up with Samuel, son of Hunter. So similar yet so . . . different.

Before Chelise could answer the woman's question, Janae faced the Gathering. "And what say you?" She lifted the vial she claimed to be Teeleh's breath. "How many will hear the voice of one calling from the desert? 'Prepare the way of the lord, for every valley shall be filled in, every mountain made low. And the whole world will see the salvation of Elyon.'"

"Is it so impossible?" Vadal, son of the elder Ronin asked quietly.

"Sit down, Vadal," Marie snapped.

He looked into Chelise's eyes and she saw his confusion. When put this way, how could they deny?

Janae repeated her question. "Who will stand with me? And who will challenge me?"

Nearly half stood to their feet. A jumble of support and objection filled the canyon.

Chelise felt her world crumbling. It was too much. *Thomas, Thomas, Thomas. Where are you, my love?* She felt as though she might burst into tears.

She slowly lifted one hand into the air and spoke clearly. "I do."

Mikil, who'd been yelling the crowd down along with Jamous and Johan, looked up at her. But no one else showed they'd heard. The council argued among themselves. Even they were divided.

"I do!" she cried louder, shaking her fist at the sky. Then she screamed it, letting her emotions rally. "I do!"

Now they were listening. All of them. She breathed hard and pointed to Janae. "I do challenge your authority as the one who has come with this gift from Elyon."

She leaped from the rock, strode over to Samuel. Yanked his sword from his back where he'd slung it. Walked to the center of the stone slab.

"I do challenge you by the same rules invoked by Samuel, and I deny any to fight for me."

"What's this?" Janae asked whimsically.

Samuel explained that a challenge once settled disputes. The winner's way would be followed.

Chelise wasn't sure what she expected in the moment—some resistance from the council at least, a moment to judge the skill of her opponent as they squared off. Anything but what happened.

Janae handed her vial to Samuel, stepped over to Eram, who was still watching with amused interest, took his sword from the scabbard, and sprang forward.

But this was not just any ordinary leap. She took two steps, launched herself into the air like a cat, and flew a full ten yards before landing in a crouch directly in front of Chelise, sword on guard.

"Your first mistake, Mother," Janae said. "And your last."

Chelise lowered her sword by her side as if surrendering, but turned it in at the last moment and ran it up under Janae as she threw herself back into an aerial somersault with a loud cry.

It was one of Thomas's basic maneuvers, once taught to all Forest Guard, extremely effective because an opponent had to contend with both the blade and the attacker's feet at once. But Janae had something not even Thomas had.

The speed of a bat.

How did she manage to escape Chelise's sword and appear behind her? Chelise couldn't know; she'd been upside down when Janae moved.

But Chelise was no slouch, and she didn't waste any energy trying to understand what had just happened. She was swinging her sword with as much strength as she possessed before she landed.

Their blades met with a clang that echoed through the canyon. Chelise's hands stung with the clash of metal against metal. But they'd both escaped injury.

Each having earned the other's respect, Chelise expected they would hesitate in the crowd's silence for a moment before . . .

But Janae was moving already, this time with such speed that Chelise couldn't react except to gasp and attempt a block with a wild swing of her sword. Her opponent's blade sliced cleanly through the strap that held her chest armor in place.

Janae reached in and yanked the armor down. The leather thongs slipped free, and the chest guard fell to the ground.

"You've lost your top, Mother."

She felt naked with only a tunic between herself and this witch's blade. More to the point, she knew she was as good as dead. What kind of black magic empowered this woman was an easy guess, but unless Elyon himself granted her the strength and agility of the Roush, she would die.

She now knew that fighting this woman was utterly foolish, but Chelise was committed. And this fight was for her father, whom they sought to kill. If she must die, she would do so knowing she'd died for him.

"Come on, you little whore," she breathed. "Kill me. Or die trying."

Janae flung her sword to one side, easily evaded a thrust from Chelise's sword that would have connected with most mortals, and punched her soundly in the jaw.

Chelise's world spun. Faded. The ground beneath her feet tilted. She landed on the ground with a hard thud.

"I will not kill a child of Elyon," Janae was crying in the distance. "Our war is not between us. It is with the enemy of Elyon! Now this matter is settled. Samuel has joined Eram and the Forest Guard who wait over these hills."

Chelise's world began to right itself. She tried to push herself up but was still too weak.

"Today we will march on the Valley of Miggdon, where Qurong will move his army. In two days' time we will crush them with one blow of Elyon's wrath, and we will leave the blood of the dragon in the valley to feed the lust of all Shataiki. Then, and only then, will Elyon deliver us into his glory!"

A roar spontaneously erupted.

"Who is with me?"

Not all of them, *certainly* not all. But many were crying out in support. Chelise had to stop them! This could not be happening, not now with Thomas gone.

She tried to call out, tried to stand. But then Janae lifted her head by the hair and slammed it into the ground, and Chelise thought her skull may have broken.

Twelve thousand souls who'd drowned in the lakes and found new life were crying out, but to Chelise, the roar sounded muffled, like a voice from a large shell. Someone was shaking her, calling her name.

Then the sounds faded completely, and she lay in darkness for a while.

—⊱∞⊰—

COMPLETE AND utter solitude and contentment. Chelise was stripped of all worries for the first time since Samuel had ridden into the Gathering and slung the Horde head onto the ground. Just one moment of absolute peace, sweet and restful.

Where was Thomas?

". . . dead."

"No, no, don't speak that . . . more fruit . . ."

The silence gave way to this soft talk around her. Chelise's mind dragged itself from the solitude with gaining awareness. She wasn't alone. Two people were talking over her. One thought she might be dead. The other wanted to give her more fruit.

"We need to get the juice down her throat," one was saying. "Sit her up again."

"Why would she respond now? She's been like this all night." This was Marie's voice. Marie, sweet Mar . . .

All night? She'd been here all night? No. No, it had only been a moment.

"Dear Elyon, have mercy on them." Johan's voice.

Chelise tried to open her eyes. Failed. Then tried again. Firelight glowed around the edges of her sight.

"She's waking!"

A piece of fruit was pressed against her lips. Chelise bit deeply and felt the juice of a peach run down her throat. Then more, until she was eating large chunks of the flesh, ravenous for the healing nectar. Her mind cleared and the light grew bright.

They were in Marie's tent with Johan. It was dark outside, and one of them had said she'd been out all night. Janae had beaten her in the challenge while the sun was still high in the sky, many hours ago.

She could hear desert crickets singing outside. The camp was all peace and quiet. Which could only mean . . .

Chelise blinked. Tried to speak, then cleared her throat. "How many?"

Marie glanced over at Johan, who responded. "Nearly five thousand."

"Five thousand? Here?"

"No, five thousand left with Samuel and the half-breeds," Johan said.

"Vadal is with them," Marie said.

"Vadal?"

She bolted up in bed, but a headache of thundering proportions made her world spin again, and she dropped back down.

"No, Mother," Marie whispered. "It's too late, they're gone and you're hurt. Give the fruit some time."

Johan spoke in a soothing voice that failed to calm her. "We did all we could, Chelise. After you lost the challenge our footing was weak, but the council mounted a long defense that won many over to our side."

"And the rest? The five thousand?"

He shrugged. "They've been deceived by a compelling case."

"So they go against the Horde?"

"Yes," Johan said. "They go to Miggdon where they will die."

"Die?" But Johan would know more than most—before drowning he'd been a Horde commander of undisputed skill. "What makes you think Qurong will defeat them?"

"Because Qurong and the master he serves are far too crafty."

Chelise sat up, this time successfully. She looked around the room, saw no sign of Jake.

"He's with Mikil," Marie said. "Seven thousand are here, by the red pool. They're lost in tales of glory. And I'm here, lost in sickness over that fool who would be my husband."

"I'm sorry." Chelise pushed herself to her feet despite Marie's objections. "I know. Believe me, I know. And now I have to go."

"Don't be ridiculous, Mother. You'll go nowhere."

"They're going to kill my father," she cried. "Get me more fruit."

"And they're going to kill Vadal. I'll go with you."

"I'm not going to the Eramites."

Johan nodded at Marie. "Then I'll gather—"

"No," Chelise snapped. "This time I go alone."

They faced each other, knowing even a show of objection was pointless.

The same thought that had echoed through her mind for a day now came again: *The world awaits you, Chelise.* She'd failed to stop Samuel here—Michal's admonition clearly referred to something else.

Johan withdrew a vial from his pocket and handed it to her. "Then take this."

"What is it?" She took the small glass bottle, identical to the one the witch had called Teeleh's breath.

"We don't know. It fell from her cloak. The label says it's Thomas's blood. Maybe it has some power. Why else would she carry it?" Johan turned and lifted the tent flap. "If you see the harlot, shove it down her throat for me."

Marie was still pouting. "Mother, please—"

"No. I go to my father, and I go alone."

37

WITH EACH passing day Billy remembered more why he loved Marsuuv the way he did. In so many ways he was only doing what he was created to do: love himself.

Naturally. To love the beast was to love himself, because Marsuuv was as much a mirror of Billy's heart as a beast, born and bred to feed on the blood of mortal souls.

He wasn't sure how long he'd been in the lair following Janae's departure, a few days at least. The intimacy Marsuuv had shown Janae in both words and deed at first twisted a knife through his belly. Who was she to steal Marsuuv's affection after Billy's own long journey to find him?

When Marsuuv descended on her and thrust his fangs into her neck, he'd nearly cried out in protest. Seeing Marsuuv exchange his blood with her like that . . .

Billy had trembled with rage.

But then she'd been sent off and Billy had time to think about what happened.

Janae was a very small part, perhaps only one-hundredth, Shataiki, a descendant of someone bitten by Alucard generations earlier. A creature of the night.

Although the mythology surrounding vampires was sadly misinformed, there was some truth to the rumors. Vampires were real, of course, but they'd originated from this reality—not from Dracula in Transylvania but from a Shataiki queen named Alucard. *Dracula* spelled backward.

Crossbreeds between Shataiki and human were the *Nephilim* referred to in the Holy Bible itself. Billy had found the subject oddly compelling as a young boy.

While Janae was fulfilling her own destiny, Billy was preparing for his, as Marsuuv had promised.

"He comes," Marsuuv said, shifting his torso away from Billy.

They'd been reclining on the beast's bed with only their breathing and the occasional popping sound of Marsuuv's phlegm to accompany them. More accurately, Billy had been reclining, leaning against the queen's belly as he lightly stroked Billy's hair and cheek.

It struck him now and then, but less and less with each passing day, that he should be appalled by his environment. Instead, he was convinced he lay in heaven, and he found himself yearning to be even closer to his lover. They'd bitten each other several times, but Billy wanted to be bitten again. This was how Billos had become Ba'al, he thought.

He found himself dreaming of a blood transfusion. If he could only rid himself of all human blood and be pure Shataiki . . .

"He comes!" Marsuuv said again, brushing Billy aside.

He sat up groggily and came to himself. The scent of Marsuuv's breath wafted over him, and he fought off the desire to lie against the beast's belly again.

But the clack of talons on stone arrested his attention, and he forgot the thought. And then he remembered who it was Marsuuv referred to. Teeleh was coming.

The great beast himself?

Teeleh stepped into Marsuuv's lair, dragging his wings. He was taller than the queen, clearly the master here, though Marsuuv didn't bow or show respect other than to bare his fangs. He put a wing behind Billy and nudged him closer, as if to say, this one is mine, and Billy found the gesture as kind and loving as any Marsuuv had yet shown him. He swallowed a bundle of emotion that rose up in his throat.

"Billy . . ." Teeleh said.

Billy looked at him again, took in the mangy fur that crawled with tiny worms and flies. His large red eyes weren't glamorous like Marsuuv's, but terrifying. A quiver ran over Teeleh's shoulders, scattering a few flies.

"He is mine," Marsuuv said, and Billy felt better.

Teeleh ignored the queen. He stepped closer to Billy and examined him. "Stand up. Let me see you."

Marsuuv removed his arm. Billy scooted off the bed and stood next to the altar, five feet from the beast.

Teeleh's bulging red eyes studied him from head to foot. Billy was still dressed in the black robe he'd taken off the temple guard, but after days with Marsuuv it was badly stained.

"Take it off," Teeleh said in a soft, gravelly voice.

Billy glanced at Marsuuv, received a nod, and shrugged out of the robe. He stood naked except for his underwear. Sores from Marsuuv's fangs marked the inside of his arm and would be clearly visible on either side of his neck.

"Such a beautiful specimen," Teeleh said in a low, crackling voice. He reached a long claw for him and touched Billy's white chest. Then ran his talon down, leaving a thin scratch.

Billy looked at Marsuuv again, shaking with fear now.

"Be strong."

"If I didn't need you so badly, I would pull out your jugular now and have my fill," Teeleh said. "You humans make me sick. Why you were given such power . . ." He didn't finish, but his disdain was clear.

The beast lowered his claw and rested it on the altar, satisfied to stare at him for a moment.

"If you fail me, I will drain you." He flicked a fly off his cheek with a long pink tongue. "Do you understand this?"

"Yes. Yes, I understand."

"You will use the books and return with a single ambition. To deliver a time of tribulation in which *my* kind will reign. The Great Deception will leave humans desperate for a leader."

"What he says is true," the queen Marsuuv said with uncharacteristic reverence.

"In that day, many will flee and many will cower before me, and you will stand at my right hand."

The words washed over Billy as if carried by an electric current. He was shaking again, but not out of fear. Teeleh's words intoxicated him as much as Marsuuv's bite.

"You must not let the other one, Thomas, stop you. He will try. He will enter the Black Forest and all of humanity will stand in awe. But you, Billy, you can stop him. He must drink the water."

Teeleh spat to one side.

"Say it. He must drink the water."

"He must drink the water," Billy repeated.

"If he does not drink the water, I will crucify you. He must drink the water before he can save the world. You must go back to force his hand."

"I'm going back?" The idea terrified him. He wanted to stay here, with Marsuuv.

"Betrayal is written in the hearts of all, but you, Billy, will make betrayal your lover." Teeleh tilted his head back, swallowed the fly, then faced him again. "We will need to extract your . . . inner beauty and re-create you as two. One of you will go to Bangkok, the other will go back to the beginning to kill Thomas before he can cross over."

Billy looked over at Marsuuv and saw that the Shataiki had begun to tremble. The queen opened his jaw and cocked his head like a fledgling bird, then allowed Teeleh to spit into his mouth. Marsuuv settled with some satisfaction.

"I . . ." Billy didn't know what to say.

"Do our ways of evil disturb you, Billy?" Teeleh asked.

They did, but not as much as he would have thought.

"No," he said.

"They should." Teeleh faced Marsuuv, who seemed agitated, excited. "But you humans can't help yourselves. Blindness becomes you."

The queen sprang through the air and landed on the altar before Billy. He lifted a jar in which two large, slimy balls similar to fish eggs lay in a solution. Billy had studied the jar in his stupor these past few days and wondered what poor beast had given up their eyes as a trophy.

Now Marsuuv unceremoniously dumped the jar's contents on the table. When he spoke, his voice was strained with delight.

"Accept this as my gift to you and our offspring," Marsuuv said, lifting the black orbs. "Look into my eyes."

Billy already was looking. The queen leaned forward as if he intended to either bite him on the face or kiss him, and Billy really didn't care which. He only wanted to be held in a place of safety.

Slowly, the beast lifted his claw and traced his cheeks. "After I've taken your eyes and sent you back, you'll remember little of this. Only what you need to know. Only the impulses and the demands upon your life. And you'll be able to follow Thomas when he dreams." Marsuuv's breathing thickened. "May I blind you?"

Billy began to cry. He didn't want to cry; he knew shedding tears at a time like this must look weak, even foolish, but he couldn't help it.

"Yes," he said.

Marsuuv thrust two fingers into Billy's eyes, like prongs designed to blind in precisely this manner. White-hot pain flashed behind his forehead, and he heard himself scream.

Marsuuv yanked his fingers from Billy's head, then slapped something into his eye sockets. Clouded sight returned, then slowly cleared. The cavern was visible through two new eyes of his lover's making. The pain eased.

"Now you are two," Marsuuv said, drilling Billy with a hard look. "You will be called Bill."

Teeleh stood behind the queen, head tilted back, roaring with such ferocity that Billy thought the ceiling might collapse and crush them all. The great deceiver lowered his head and thrust a long talon toward Billy's left.

"And he will be Billy."

There, not five feet away, stood another Billy, nearly identical, right down to his red hair. His eyes were lined in red, and blood leaked from the corners.

I am Bill. Only Bill, not Billy, he thought.

Teeleh swiveled his head back to Bill. "Thomas must drink the water! Do not fail me this time."

The other Billy had his original eyes, Bill realized. Marsuuv had extracted his eyes—his inner beauty—and placed them in this copy of himself to duplicate his essence.

And the eyes in his face now?

He put his fingertips to his face. They came away bloody. He had new black eyes, from the jar.

"Stop Thomas," Teeleh growled in such a low voice that Bill's bones vibrated.

"I will," Bill whimpered.

"I will crucify you if you fail," Teeleh repeated.

The other Billy was crying. "What about me?" The man even sounded like Bill.

Teeleh stepped over to the other Billy, then around, examining him. He traced the man's flesh with his talon, stopped behind him, and marked him with three hooked claw marks at the base of his neck. Then he dug one claw deep into Billy's spine and twisted it slowly. Billy trembled, weeping.

"You, my friend, will be my antichrist."

Bill felt the man's pain as if it were his own. Because it was. He wanted to cry out and demand that Teeleh show more kindness, but he knew there wasn't a thread of tenderness in the beast.

"Do not fail me," Teeleh hissed in the other Billy's ear.

The redhead turned his head toward Bill. "Billy?"

"Bill. My name is Bill. I'm here."

"I can't see too well." This even though he had bright-green eyes.

"It's okay, neither can I. Our eyes are new. But I'm right here."

Marsuuv pointed at the four lost books stacked on the altar. "Go, and do what you must do." He slashed their fingers with a claw.

Marsuuv spoke to Bill. "Find Thomas in the place called Denver when he first crossed. Stop him. Kill him. Make him drink."

"In Denver? Please—"

"Do what you must do," Teeleh snarled. "Quickly!"

Both men stumbled forward, dripping blood. Together they put their hands on the exposed page.

For the second time in less than five minutes, the lair vanished, and white lights flooded Bill's mind. Billy, the one with green eyes, was returning to Bangkok to be Teeleh's antichrist. As for him, with the black eyes, he was supposed to go after Thomas. In Denver, right? If he remembered history correctly, Thomas had originally come from Denver.

Even as he left one world and entered the other, Billy forgot what he had seen. But he did know a few things.

He knew that he was the lover of Marsuuv, who'd shown him great kindness and gifted him with black eyes.

He knew that he must either stop Thomas or hang from a cross, where he would be drained of blood until dead.

And he knew that he was now Bill. Just Bill.

38

"I WON'T have it!" Monique insisted. "You can't hide in this room the rest of your life, waiting for some books to magically appear on the desk!"

"It has nothing to do with magic," Thomas pointed out. As promised, he'd remained immovable, eating and sleeping in the library. There was a bathroom off the main room, and he'd left only four times to shower.

He had accepted their offer to hook up a monitor and let them show him how to scan the Net using a small finger piece. He wore a pair of black cargo pants beneath his freshly laundered tunic rather than the jeans and T-shirts he'd become accustomed to wearing over the past few days.

Kara looked at the Net feed. "She's right, Thomas, we can't just keep you in here forever."

"It's only been a few days, not forever. Have you no mercy? I've suffered a death, for all I know. Chelise could be dead, slain by the Horde at this moment. My own son, Samuel, could be living with Eram. I have to find my son, for the love of Elyon. Time is of the essence. Michal was very clear!"

They stared at him as they always did when he began one of his tirades, which favored more poetic desert speak. He stuck one finger into the air.

"If there's but one chance in a million to bring my son back to my side, I will suffer all consequences. He is my son!"

"And now *this* is your world," Monique cried, pointing at the Net feed. "For all you know you're a prophet meant for *this* world."

"I'm no prophet," he said. "I've never claimed to be a prophet. I have no interest in being a prophet."

"Michal told you to make a way. Perhaps you've already done that."

Thomas hadn't considered the possibility. Michal had also said he might save his son if he returned quickly.

"Nonsense! Samuel is waiting for . . ."

It was as far as Thomas got. The room flashed with a bright light, like a strobe. He spun toward the desk.

Kara gasped.

There stood Billy, dressed in only a loose undergarment. Blood ran from several wounds on his arms and neck. A long scratch marked his white chest. And his green eyes . . . They were rimmed in blood.

Beside him sat the four lost Books of History.

Billy stared at Thomas for a few seconds, unmoving. Tearstains streaked his cheeks. The man looked as though he had come to them from either Ba'al's dungeons or the Black Forest itself. Even Teeleh's lair.

This was the same redhead who'd tricked them once, but whatever had happened to him seemed to have left his eyes empty. He'd lost his soul. He should be locked up, Thomas thought, and the key to his cell should be taken back to the desert. But that would stop nothing.

"I . . ." His voice was scratchy. "There's another one like me. He's going back to the beginning to kill you. He has black eyes."

Monique stepped forward. "Billy, where is Janae?"

"But I'm not him," he said. "I think I might be the antichrist."

Then Billy turned from them, walked to the exit, opened the door, and vanished into the hall, leaving black prints from his bare feet on the marble floor.

The books . . .

Thomas reacted without thought. He rushed forward, grabbed the knife on the desk and cut his finger.

"Wait!" Kara ran. "Wait!"

He wasn't fully versed in the rules of these books. The possibility that they'd been fixed so that he couldn't return swallowed him. Why else would Billy have left them unattended?

"Hurry!"

He reached for Kara's outstretched hand. Monique stood back, staring. He shoved the knife at Kara. "Cut yourself."

Springing across the room, Thomas took Monique's face in his hands and kissed her once on the lips. "Thank you. I am indebted. But I have to go."

"I know," she said. Tears misted her eyes. "Go to her. Find your son. Find Janae. Please. Save my daughter."

He released her, leaving a smear of blood on her cheek. Then he leaped back to the books, where Kara waited with a bleeding finger.

"Ready?"

Kara faced Monique. "You've been like a sister to me."

"And you to me. I think we'll be seeing more of each other."

Then Kara and Thomas pressed their hands on the opened page, and the world around them vanished.

———— ∞ ————

THE FIRST clue that something different was happening to Thomas came almost immediately. The last time he'd vanished into the book with Qurong, he'd spun through a vortex that deposited both him and the Horde leader in Monique's library.

But this time, what started out as a tunnel of light suddenly expanded and then faded into emptiness. The violent transition from one world to the other or forward in time, depending on how it was seen, had been replaced by a perfect calm.

He hung in the air, completely weightless, like floating in the sky without a hint of wind. Sunlight warmed his back, though there was no sun that he could see. Far below him the curved desert reality slowly rotated, peaceful, undisturbed, as if asleep. There were troubles down there in that desert, but he felt no concern now. Only perfect tranquility.

It occurred to him that he was holding his breath, perhaps from the wonder of it all. He drew breath, but instead of air, liquid flooded his nostrils and he felt a stab of panic. Water? His alarm gave way to the thought that he was in a lake.

Elyon's lake?

He cautiously sucked at the water, allowing the warm fluid to flood his throat, his airways, his lungs. Forcing himself to ignore the instinct to panic, he drew the water all the way in, then pushed it out, an exercise that required a little more effort than breathing air.

Familiar pleasure swept through his chest, soft at first, then with more intensity until he couldn't hold back a tremble that overtook his whole body. He was floating in Elyon's lake a hundred miles above the earth as if it were heaven itself.

Elyon's presence lapped at his mind, and he found himself laughing with the pleasure of it all. He arched backward, arms spread wide, overwhelmed by an intoxication that he'd felt only twice before in his life, both times in the depths of this very water.

His laughter grew until his muffled cackles of delight spread throughout the water. It was as if he was being tickled by the hand of God. Of Elyon. Here in his great lake of breathtaking pleasures.

The colors came from his left, streams of red and blue and gold, rushing through the water like translucent paint. He slowly swallowed his laughter and watched as the colors twirled and circled him, stretching back the way they had come for a ways.

A very long ways. Thomas knew this because he could see the whole distance. In fact, there was no end to what his eyes could now see. The streams of color went on and on. They didn't stretch miles or light-years; they simply did not end.

Amazed, he reached out and touched a streak of red. It bent with the pressure of his finger. A shaft of electrical current rode up his arm and shook his body as if he were a rag doll that had stuck its finger in the wrong hole in the wall.

And with that current came raw pleasure so great that it could not, with any amount of human effort, be contained. So great that for a moment he thought it might overpower his life and leave him dead in the water. He had to pull his finger away from the color or surely die!

But he didn't. He let it consume him. Every nerve, every cell, every bone, screamed with a gratification that reduced all other pleasures to a mere grin in a room of rolling laughter.

And he knew then that he'd found the hope. This was Elyon's presence. This was a piece of heaven, only a piece.

He finally withdrew his hand. The colors veered away and ran in large circles a hundred yards distant, as if they had a mind of their own.

Thomas arched his back and dived backward, surprised to find he could pick up speed at will. He rushed toward the earth, feeling the waters rush over him. They caressed his skin and flowed through his lungs, flooding every fiber of his body with nearly uncontainable bliss.

The ground didn't seem to come closer, so he accelerated. But the farther Thomas dived, the deeper the lake seemed to run.

"Thomas . . ."

A child's voice whispered through the water, and he pulled up. "Hello?"

The voice giggled.

Thomas grinned. "Hello?"

"Thomas, up here."

He snapped his head back and saw that the lake above was brighter.

"Come up here, Thomas."

He clawed for the surface, desperate to be with the one whose voice spoke. He knew the sound. He had heard this voice.

"Thomas."

"Elyon?" He began to cry spontaneously. "Elyon!" He was screaming and weeping and laughing at once, as if his mind had forgotten how to separate the emotions that caused each.

He effortlessly swooped upward, but his desperation to be with the boy had him bawling like a baby. "Elyon! Elyon, wait!" he cried.

"I'm right here, Thomas." Then the boy giggled again, and Thomas rode the laughter to the light above him.

He burst through the lake's surface, rose all the way to his knees and faced a bright-blue sky, then splashed back down like a leaping dolphin. He searched the horizons for the boy.

Clouds drifted silently. Sand dunes surrounded him. It occurred to him that he was standing on the lake bottom, two feet under the water's red surface.

A red pool, no more than twenty feet wide on the top of a sand dune.

As he stared, the ground under his feet began to move. It rose upward. Not just the sand under the pool, but the dunes around him thrust upward toward the sky.

He crouched to steady himself, but quickly determined there was no threat. The desert rose hundreds, thousands of feet, and then slowed to a stop.

But it wasn't the whole desert, he could see that now. It was a circular section of the desert, perhaps a half mile across, that had risen toward the sky in a massive pillar.

And now all was silent. No movement other than a slight breeze.

Thomas turned around slowly, studying his new horizon. It wasn't until he'd finished a full circuit that he saw the boy, standing on a dune with his back to Thomas, staring over the edge.

He was a young boy, perhaps twelve, with black hair and dark skin, dressed only in a white loincloth, standing less than five feet tall. He was thin, and frail fingers hung by his sides.

Thomas's heart forgot how to pump in that moment. An old teaching ran through his mind, one that equated Elyon with a lion and a lamb and a boy in one telling. They all knew he wasn't a lake, or a lion, or a lamb. Neither was he a black boy, or a white girl, or a man, or a woman, or an eagle with eyes under his wings, for that matter.

He was Elyon, the Creator of all that was. He was the author and giver of life. And above all, he was their lover. The very essence of the Great Romance.

With a snap of his fingers, this boy on the dune ahead of Thomas could turn the world into a marble and crush all living things to sand. At a single word, a new world would roll off his tongue and spin into space.

A wink from this boy and the hardest heart would break into pieces, shattered by love.

Thomas thought it all in a moment, and then his heart began to crash in his chest. He had to move. He had to rush up behind the boy and throw himself to the sand in worship.

But before he could move, a fuzzy white creature waddled toward the boy from the left. Michal, the Roush.

Michal glanced back at Thomas once, then walked up to the boy. Without looking at him, the boy took the shorter Roush's hand, and together they looked down. At what, Thomas couldn't see.

Thomas found the courage to move, but carefully, thinking that sloshing through the water might be inappropriate. He walked out of the pool and had started down the depression that separated him from the dune on which the boy and Michal stood, when the first white lion walked into his peripheral view and settled on its haunches to his right.

Thomas twisted back and saw that a dozen huge, white lions had positioned themselves like sentinels around the entire edge, facing the boy. There was no threat, only a sense of honor. Elyon hardly needed such creatures.

Thomas walked up the dune and approached the boy's open side, opposite Michal. Neither turned to him.

He wanted to speak, ask permission, fall to one knee, something, but he was having difficulty thinking clearly in the boy's presence. And then Thomas saw the tears that darkened the boy's cheeks, and he felt the blood drain from his face.

Thomas sank to one knee, smothered by a terrible sadness. He didn't know why the boy was crying, but the sight of it flogged his mind and demanded he weep.

"What do you see, Thomas?"

Thomas? The boy had spoken his name? The boy knew him personally? Yes, of course, but to hear it . . .

What do you see, Thomas? he'd asked.

What do I see? I see you. I see only you, and it's all I need to see.

His weeping grew in earnest, changing from sorrow to gratitude for being in the presence of one so great. He knew he should answer.

Not to answer was a sacrilege worthy of eternal punishment. He wanted to answer, but he was too overcome by the boy's presence to avert his eyes, much less speak.

The boy reached out for Thomas's hand. Took his fingers.

The last reserves of Thomas's poise snapped. He slumped to one side and began to shake with sobs. The boy held his hand, and Thomas gripped the frail fingers as if they were his only thread to life. He wept with deep, air-gulping sobs.

Waves of gratitude swept over him, and he knew that he'd been wrong a moment ago. The waters were not the hope for which Elyon himself had died.

This . . .

He could hardly bear to think it . . . but this . . . this was the great hope for which they were all created. For *this* moment.

There was nothing else that could possibly matter other than to hold the hand of the one who'd formed you with his breath.

Thomas could not stop, he simply could not, and the boy made no attempt to suggest he do so. Thomas curled into a ball, clung to the boy's hand, and wet the sand under his face with tears.

It all made sense now. The pain, the death, the days and nights of fear as the Horde stalked them.

The ridicule, the disease, the fall.

The tears of the mother whose child had fallen and broken her jaw. The agony of the father who had lost his son to an arrow. For the pleasure set before them they, like Elyon himself, had endured it all.

Time seemed to stall.

When it occurred to Thomas that the boy had released his hand, he pushed himself up to his knees, meaning to beg forgiveness for his display, yet one more indiscretion. Because he was human, he might say, and humans stumbled over their indiscretions like oversized boots.

But the boy was gone. In his place stood a middle-aged man with a graying beard and a strong jaw. He wore a white tunic. Before Thomas could make the adjustment from Elyon the boy to Elyon the father, the man turned and stared at him with misty green eyes. "They're denying my love, Thomas," the elder said.

"No . . ." He looked at the desert below and for the first time saw what they were looking at. Far below them lay a great valley lined on all sides with armies that stretched far into the desert.

The valley of the miggdon figs.

"What can I do?" the man whispered.

But Thomas was still far too absorbed by the love that swam about them to consider any dilemma seriously. *Let them destroy themselves,* he thought. *Let those who deny your love slaughter themselves. Just let me stay with you.*

"They've turned away," the man said.

A white lion stepped past Thomas and gazed at the scene below. Thomas jumped to his feet. All of the lions had crossed the sand and now stood in two lines on either side of their master, fixated upon the gathered Horde armies.

The man turned away from the scene and paced. He ran his fingers through his gray hair, deep in thought. "I made them. I wove them together in the secret place, I knit them in the mother's womb."

Thomas recognized the words from a song the Circle sang. A psalm.

"All their days were ordained, written in my book. They are my poem, created for such wonders." His eyes lifted to Thomas. "But I gave them their own book and let them write in it. Now look what they have done."

Thomas thought he might tear his hair out.

"What have I done, what have I done?" The man spun back to the cliff and thrust his arm to the horizon. "Look!"

Thomas looked. Something else had been added to the distant mix of Horde ready to wage war. They were Qurong's army, gathered to battle Eram's army, and for a fleeting moment Thomas wondered if Samuel was caught up in the mix. But what he saw now swept the worry aside.

A massive black swirl of Shataiki circled over the valley—millions of the black beasts, ravenous for the human blood that nourished them.

"Look," Michal said, pointing to the west.

A flood of white approached like a wave of clouds. A sea of Roush.

Thomas could only think one thing now: This is the end. This is the end.

The man lifted both arms and wept at the sky. His shoulders shook with his sobs and tears ran down his face, wetting his beard. The lions turned to him and fell to their faces, hindquarters raised as they bowed. As one they moaned, a dreadful sound that filled Thomas with fear.

Elyon's wail began to run out of breath. Slowly he lowered his head, arms still raised, chest heaving to find air. But his stare began to change from one couched in anguish to a glare filled with rage.

His face flushed red and his cheeks began to quiver. Alarmed, Thomas tried to step back, but his feet would not move.

And then Elyon screamed, full throated, at the sky. His hands knotted into fists and he trembled from head to foot with such wrath that Thomas could not stop his own body from quaking.

The lions roared as one, and the whole earth was swallowed in a thunder of protest that shook it to the very foundations.

Still the cry raged with inexhaustible fury. Thomas fell to his knees and threw his arms over his head.

"Bring us home!" he cried. "Rescue your bride!"

But he was yelling at the sand and no one seemed to be listening. He could hardly hear himself.

"Bring"—the roar ceased midsentence—"us home. Rescue us. For the sake of the Great Romance, rescue your bride from this terrible day."

Silence hung around him, broken only by his own breathing. He snapped his eyes wide. Michal was flying off, fifty feet from the edge of the cliff. The lions were gone. The man . . .

Thomas stood slowly. Elyon was gone?

"Thomas?"

He caught his breath and spun to the voice. The boy stood by the red pool, staring at him with daring eyes. Had so much time passed?

"It's time," the boy said.

"It's over?"

The boy hesitated, then spoke without answering the question directly. "When it is, you'll know. And what you felt—that was only child's play, my friend."

He winked.

Elyon winked.

And Thomas could not keep his knees still.

"Follow me, Thomas!" the boy cried. He took three light steps down the bank, dived into the red pool, and vanished beneath the shimmering surface.

Thomas began to run while the boy was still in the air. It wasn't until he was aloft, falling toward the water, that he wondered how deep it was.

He plunged beneath the surface and knew that these were Elyon's waters, and his lake had no bottom.

39

THE VALLEY of Miggdon ran fifty miles through the high plains, where the fig trees that bore its name grew in abundance. But here at the head, it resembled more of a box canyon. Four sloping descents fell to an immense basin that was known to flood every few years when a rare rain visited this part of the world.

Samuel sat on a horse next to Eram and Janae, studying the lay of what would become their battlefield. Qurong had made no attempt to hide his army on the eastern crest. Their Throaters were mounted on steeds the full length of the valley, a thousand wide by his calculations. And at least two hundred deep.

Two hundred thousand cavalry on the far slope, only a thousand yards away.

The differences between the three armies were pronounced. Qurong's Horde used all manner of horses, no longer attempting to blend with the desert sands. Both Eramite and albino favored lighter-colored horses. The distinction extended to their battle dress. Where once the Forest Guard favored dark leather to blend into the forests, they now warded off arrows and blades in tan leathers, much like the Eramites, whose main infantry also wore helmets.

It was dark against light, the dark being Horde, the light being both Eramite and albino.

But beyond this distinction, the Eramites and Horde looked almost identical. They both used heavier armor that covered their joints, because the scabbing disease made quick movement in any joint painful. The Eramites who chewed the numbing beetle nut suffered less pain, but how much of an advantage this would prove to be on the battlefield was untested.

Tall scythes and spears carried by a full half of the Horde warriors rose like the charred skeletons of trees after a forest fire. They sat on their dark horses stoically, as if the mere sight of them could speak doom to any who dared not flee.

Qurong had divided his Horde army into four classes of fighters:

The Throaters. Qurong's elite fighters, who favored bows and long swords, almost always fought from their mounts. These were the Scabs that had hunted albinos for more than ten years with devastating results.

The grunts. Both cavalry and infantry, grunts were trained in long-reach hand-to-hand combat, using spears and maces or long swords—any heavy weapon that did not require speed in order to kill with a single blow. A spiked ball at the end of a five-foot chain didn't require quick reflexes to swing with any strength. But step into the arc of one of these maces, and either the sharpened chains or the spikes themselves would remove an arm or a head.

Infantry archers. Though their bamboo arrows could be deadly up to a hundred yards, they often found the wrong mark and were almost useless once two armies collided. On this battlefield, Qurong would only use them when the Eramites were caught in the open, unless he was willing to sacrifice his own fighters in a fusillade of indiscriminate arrows.

The throwers. The final group was by far the smallest, perhaps two or three dozen catapults that hurled straw balls soaked in the resin of Qaurkat trees and ignited. The three-foot balls splattered upon impact, soaking a fifteen-foot radius with the sticky, flaming fuel. Samuel counted twelve of them on the eastern ridge. They tended to break, and would be quickly replaced by others in reserve.

This was the Horde army, similar to the Eramite army except for the variation in armor and the absence of artillery, which proved difficult to transport.

The skill of five thousand albinos, on the other hand, made a mockery of both Horde and Eramite. They left all joints free for ease of movement. Whether mounted or on foot, they depended on speed and strength and favored medium-length swords that could change direction almost immediately in the hands of a skilled fighter. They carried knives for throwing—a single warrior might carry as many as ten knives into a fight—and a deadly accurate bow with shorter arrows for short-range confrontations.

Never in history had all three enemies faced each other on one battlefield, and Samuel now considered his orchestration of the events with a mixture of pride and fear.

For months, Samuel had roamed the desert and skirted the forests with his loyal guard while envisioning the day they would return to war. But he'd never conceived of this massive gathering of armies for what could only be a brutal engagement. And yet here they were, because of his hotheaded defiance.

An image of his father entered his mind, but he pushed it out.

"He's there," Eram said, nodding at the southern ridge to their right. "With at least fifty thousand of his best warriors."

"I don't see the colors," Samuel said, looking for the tall purple flags that identified the supreme commander's guard.

"No, not now. But trust me, he's there. And he'll launch his first attack from there, not from the main body."

"How so?"

"He means to draw us in. His one advantage is size, but to use it he has to find a way to descend on my army."

"What size would you say?" Samuel scratched the rash that had begun to overtake his skin. The fact that his rash had worsened, whereas Janae's rash hadn't, wasn't lost on him. She still looked albino. His skin, on the other hand, looked very much like it had contracted the scabbing disease. Worse, he could no longer deny the pain spreading through his limbs.

It had been many years since he'd heard of any albino contracting the disease after drowning. He hadn't even known it was possible. For all he knew, it wasn't, and this was something else the witch had passed on to him, some foul disease she'd contracted from the Shataiki when she'd whored herself out to him. Either way, he couldn't breathe a word of it. Being albino was his one great advantage.

Eram spat red beetle-nut juice to one side. "Our scouts put them at three hundred thousand today."

Maybe he should try some of the beetle nut. Nearly all the Eramites ground the mild analgesic between their molars, turning their mouths red. They looked like they'd fed on blood, Samuel thought.

"So where are the rest?"

Eram scanned the desert. "How would I know? Back in Qurongi, nursing their wounds. Or suffering under one of Ba'al's curses. Even at half strength, they're twice as many as we."

Samuel looked down the line at their own army, stretching as far as he could see. The albino traitors were mounted on horses to his left, some looking fierce, others unsure. Regardless, they were all heavily armed, and once the first blow was struck, they would fight with the pent-up rage of a wounded pit bull.

"Half their strength," Samuel said, "but twice as strong."

"So you've claimed."

"And you've agreed. I would expect the other half of his army to be close by."

The crafty Eramite leader nodded his head slowly. "Perhaps. No report from our scouts. But I will say this for that old monkey: he's no fool. If I were in his boots, I would have chosen this very valley. These slopes will allow him to use his army to its full advantage. Honestly, if not for Teeleh's poison, I would reconsider."

Samuel glanced at Janae, who was looking at the valley unconcerned. Her beauty in the morning light quickened his heart. "But we do have the poison," he said. *And this woman is my poison*, he thought to himself.

Eram kept his eyes on the larger Horde army directly across the valley. "They'll send in a small force to lure us in, and we'll take the bait. We'll send twice as many, without poison."

"Qurong will crush them with a second wave."

"We'll commit our full force at that time, with poison. This breath of Teeleh had better work, because we face impossible odds without it. Ba'al's no fool. That old conniving wraith surely has a trick up his sleeve."

"For a daring leader who defied Qurong once—"

"I left Qurong to live, not to die! Don't question my judgment or I'll cut you down where you stand. The last thing I need is an insolent fool who's turning Scab."

The reference to the disease cut deeply, and Samuel was sorely tempted to lash out. But he couldn't engage Eram on the matter, not now, not when they were fully committed to a bloody end.

"You may not need Samuel," Janae said softly, "but you do need me. Now if you're done being men, we should get on with the rites. I want the albinos to come to me first. Then the rest, until every last warrior has made the vow and taken his poison."

Samuel looked at her. "Albinos? They don't need your poison."

Her eyes flashed, stopping him cold. "They *all* drink the bloody water. They *all* take the mark. They *all* vow their allegiance to me!"

He swallowed. It was so wrong. Yet so right.

"It's a disease, not blood," he corrected.

She studied him, then softened slightly. "The disease comes from his blood. We follow my instructions to the letter. Gather them now."

"Albinos first," Eram said, swinging his horse around. Naturally, he was no respecter of race at a time like this. "You're their leader; bring them to the pond." To his general: "Ready the others. If Qurong dispatches a division into the valley, engage them with twice his number. But none who've ingested this poison."

"Understood."

Samuel had given charge to Petrus, whom he trusted with his life, and Vadal, who served as a constant reminder to the five thousand that even the son of Ronin the elder had joined them. Each commanded half of the albinos, but at a moment's notice, Samuel could step in and take full control.

He signaled to both, and they ordered their fighters to the rear.

The horses seemed to sense the unique danger, where whole armies and peoples were in jeopardy of slaughter. No one spoke, but there were whispers among the albinos now. A thousand yards separated their army from one much larger, and by all appearances as bloodthirsty as any Shataiki legion. The fact that Qurong had chosen the battlefield and was here waiting didn't help either.

But they had this one gift from Elyon. Teeleh's breath, given to them by Elyon to slaughter the Horde. A bad thing for a good cause. War. The thought sickened Samuel.

But this was his lot. This was his destiny. He was Samuel of Hunter, and the whole world would know his name.

Forgive me, Father, for I have sinned.

It was with a sense of fatalism that the albinos encircled the large pond half a mile behind the valley and stood at ease, watching Janae's every move. They were two-thirds men and a third women, and all were better fighters than any Horde could hope to be in their wildest dreams.

They were also smarter, Samuel thought. They could not possibly miss the signs of the scabbing disease that covered his skin.

Vadal was the first to express what was on their minds. "What's the meaning of this disease, Samuel?" The man was chewing a beetle nut.

Janae lifted up the vial for all to see and answered for Samuel. "To test you, my love." She sniffed the bottle. "Do I have the scabbing disease? Do you?"

Vadal spit on the ground and glanced about without answering her.

"No? Yet you were in the proximity of this poison at the camp. You have no faith in Elyon's prophet?"

Vadal looked at Samuel. "And you?" he asked with a red mouth.

"You heard her," Samuel said. "Isn't it true that to defeat the evil, one must first die? To overcome the scabbing disease, we pay a price. If you doubt, leave now."

The albinos looked at him like ghosts lost on the plain. But none walked away.

"When you have all partaken, to the last warrior, Samuel will have paid his price and the disease will leave him. Take out your knives."

They hesitated only a moment, then did so.

"You too, lover," she said to Samuel.

He hesitated, then followed her order.

Forgive me, Father . . . Forgive me.

"As a sign of your loyalty to Elyon and his prophet, you will draw three marks on your forehead or your arm." She slipped out her knife and carved three lines on her own forearm. "Like so."

A rumble of objection spread, but rather than react, she looked at Samuel and winked.

"Three marks for the Maker, the Warrior, and the Giver, who has brought you this gift to make a mockery of the dragon. We use his own seed to destroy his devout, do we not?"

In different circumstances, some, even many, may have demanded a lengthier explanation. But they'd swallowed her reasoning in Paradose Valley, and the possibility of their enemy's destruction was finally within reach.

One, then a dozen, then all of them drew their blades over their skin as instructed. Blood flowed from their forearms, mostly. Some were bold enough to mark their foreheads.

With each cut into his own forearm, Samuel accepted the pain as a form of absolution.

Janae ceremoniously dribbled the vial of Teeleh's breath into the water as she walked along the pond's bank. "Each of you will drink. Be quick; the Horde awaits their final battle. With this poison in your own flesh, any who have never been washed by Elyon's waters will suffer their deserved fate when they draw near. You saw his judgment in your own camp, now you will see it again on a scale that will make all the world tremble with fear at the very name of Elyon."

As each red drop splashed into the water, it spread out with unnatural speed, turning the muddy pond a dark purple. Teeleh's breath looked to be alive and swimming on its own.

"Drink!" Janae cried, dropping the vial into the water. It landed with a loud *plop*. She lifted both hands and turned to face them all.

"Drink, my children. Drink his water and live!"

As if on cue, a terrible moan rolled through the sky far above them. A roar, a scream, rage and sorrow bundled as one. Samuel felt a stab of terror slice through his bones. The roar faded and was replaced by Janae's cry.

"The end is at hand, my children! Drink. Drink. Drink!" She smiled at the sky.

They hurried to the pond from all sides, fell to their knees, and drank. For fear, for revenge, for pain, for love.

But they loved the wrong beast, Samuel thought, facing Janae. Her eyes were on him, and his heart felt as though it might burst with desire for her. She tasted the blood from her forearm, making no attempt to hide her pleasure.

He could not resist her. Not now, not ever. Samuel dropped to the ground, walked to Janae, and kissed her deeply.

It was time for war. It was time for the slaughter.

40

MIKIL STOOD by the red pool in Paradose Valley next to Jamous, Johan, Ronin, and the rest of the council. She stared at the eastern horizon, where the sun had risen two hours earlier. The rest of the Circle lingered or slept in the natural amphitheater to their right, waiting for the council's decision.

All had drunk the red waters and eaten their fill of fruit and pork around a huge fire late into the night. Desperate to justify their reason for staying true, they'd danced hard and sung long and told a thousand tales of glory, many of which started with an element of truth, then spun into wild metaphors that delighted the whole crowd.

But when they awoke, the reality of their loss had robbed most of their passion, and they stared with tired eyes. What now?

"Maybe we should have gone," Tubin, one of the older council members, said.

"You doubt already?" Johan demanded.

"Thomas is gone. Chelise is gone. Samuel is gone. Half of the Circle is gone! But we stand here, waiting. I'm not suggesting we join the battle, but many of us have loved ones there, facing death." He glared, frowning with disgust.

Mikil didn't blame him. They all had dearly loved friends, and in some cases family, who'd been swept away by Samuel's call.

"Elyon knows, I thought about going myself," she said. "His case was compelling. And if we, who've seen everything from the beginning, could be so easily tempted, then think about what must be going through the minds of the rest." She looked at a mother who watched them while squatting on the ground with her daughter nearby. "They've stayed true, but we need to give them more."

"Then let me take a dozen of the fastest scouts and report back," Ronin said. He was eager to go after Vadal, his son. But they'd all lost dear ones to Samuel.

"No. We've already lost Chelise on a fool's errand. The people don't need to see more of their leaders running off. We should stay, all of us."

"And do what?" Ronin demanded.

Mikil walked to the edge of the pool and stared at her reflection in the red waters. So still, so unmoving. But there was something else here. She faced the rest of the council, then stared past them to a small, dark-skinned child on a rock, who also watched them. She didn't recognize the child. The Circle had grown so fast these past few years that she didn't recognize half of them.

A thin mother with long, straight black hair leaned against a boulder and nursed an infant. Boys too impatient to sit still kicked the skin of a bundled tawii fruit back and forth, keeping it in the air. A girl nearly of marrying age, perhaps sixteen, was braiding the hair of a younger girl, who sat with her back to them. A warrior—interesting that they still called the old Guard that—sat with crossed arms, lost in thought under the shade of a pond palm, named for its proximity to the red pools.

But no one was talking. Not even a breeze rustled the leaves. An odd silence hung in the air.

Mikil turned back to the pool and stared at the silky red surface. "When you look at this water, what do you see?" she asked.

The other nine eased over. "Water, like glass," said Suzan.

"Water," Mikil repeated. "With these eyes, it's all we see at the moment. But if we open the eyes of our hearts, what do we see?"

"The drowning that made the waters red," Johan said.

Mikil nodded. "And our own deaths, which brought us life. Every day we look at this pool and see water. Beautiful water, but just water. Yet what kind of life has it given us?"

"The hope of a return to Elyon's playground," Johan said, using the metaphor the poets often used.

"Our entire hope is dimly seen through this glass," Mikil said, nodding at the water. "It's there, just below the surface, and we see glimpses of it every day. Isn't this what Thomas once taught us?" She bent down, picked up a small lemon, and tossed it in her hand. "Elyon's gifts to us are simply a foretaste to keep us eager for the banquet. Isn't that what our poets have told us?"

"It is as she says," someone said softly.

"She speaks the truth."

"So where is that hope?" Mikil said, dropping the lemon.

They stared at the pond in silence. Mikil couldn't put her finger on it, but there was an inexplicable stillness hanging over the waters. Easy to miss if she wasn't focused on it, but there just the same. It was easy to forget just how enchanted the red pools were.

"To many, the hope of winning peace through the sword is more real than what the poets have to offer," Rohan said, speaking for the first time.

No one disagreed. They all seemed strangely fixated on the water, perhaps sensing the same unnatural stillness that Mikil did. Or perhaps they wondered if Samuel's hope was more realistic than what lay beyond this still pool after all. Samuel had come with tangibles.

Words.

A sword.

The head of a Horde.

An *army*, for the love of Elyon. An army large enough to win the peace they required to live as normal human beings.

The pool at their feet, on the other hand, sat still as it did every morning. Just a red pool without . . .

Mikil's thoughts were cut short by a faint stirring in the pond, not ten feet from where she stood. Strange. There were no fish in this pool as in some of the larger ones. But the water was indeed moving, boiling gently, right there. She shivered.

"What's happening?" Johan asked, taking a step backward. "What . . ."

Water burst from the surface like a fountain. Only in this fountain there was a form. A blond-headed boy with chin tilted back, smiling wide as the water streamed off his face.

Mikil gasped and jumped back.

The pool thrust the boy above the surface, and he was laughing before his feet hit the shore. He was green-eyed, blond, thin, and clearly beside himself with whatever impossible force had brought him on such a ride.

He landed next to them with a slap of feet and looked up, grinning.

"Hello, Mikil," he said, but she didn't see his lips move. Water ran off his curved fingertips and wet the sand. She stood frozen, speechless.

The boy glanced at the others, and she knew that they were hearing him too, speaking each of their names. Mikil was so stunned by the boy's sudden appearance that she found her limbs immovable.

This was no ordinary boy. This was no boy at all. This was the one Thomas had spoken about many times.

This was Elyon, and then when the full realization hit her, Mikil could no longer breathe.

The boy leaped ten feet to a rock that overhung the pool, then bounced up to a precipice that overlooked the whole camp.

The water erupted again, and Mikil spun back. Their pool hurled another form from the depths, and this time Mikil half expected to see the Warrior. But it wasn't Elyon.

It was Thomas, and he was laughing with near hysterics as the water drained from his face and mouth. He landed on the shore, wetter than a freshly drowned albino, and jerked his head around, searching.

"Where is he?" His voice sounded muffled by water. He spit it out, more than could have come from his mouth alone, like those who emerged after drowning. "Where is he?"

"Follow him!" the boy cried, and Thomas snapped his head up.

The voice echoed down the canyon, and the whole camp spun to face the boy up on the cliff. He pointed down to the pool.

"Hear Thomas, your leader! Open your eyes and follow him to my playground!" he cried, swinging his fist through the air with infectious exhilaration.

The boy spun and ran into the desert, leaving breathless silence in his wake.

Were they to follow? Mikil turned to Thomas, who stood looking up at the empty cliff. But before he could tell them what the boy meant, the air around them began to move.

A breeze whipped up and swept after the boy, as if his invisible army was hard on his heels. A long streak of red swept over the canyon like a low-flying comet. A blue shaft materialized beside the red.

As if the sky itself were rolling back like a scroll to reveal its true colors, streams of every hue flowed directly over their heads, silent, but so low that a person on the cliff might reach up and touch one.

The colored streaks rose and parted to make way for a wide swath of white clouds rolling through the sky high above.

But these were not clouds, Mikil saw. They were Roush. Millions of the furry white creatures, flying in formation a mile over their heads.

The boy had opened their eyes to see what he saw.

Thomas was clambering up the same rocks marked by the boy's wet feet and hands. He crouched on the cliff, stared east for a moment, then faced the stunned crowd.

He shoved a finger at the eastern horizon. "This, my friends, is our hope!" he thundered.

The soft sounds of weeping filtered through the amphitheater. Mikil understood the sentiment, because her own chest was flooded with an emotion she'd never quite felt: a raw sensation of gratitude so intense that any cry of thanks would understate it tenfold.

Tears blurred her vision, and her breathing came hard. She felt weak and wanted to fall to her knees like some of the others; she wanted to thrust her fists into the air and cry, "I knew it, I knew it!"

Instead she let a sob shake her body.

"This is our day!" Thomas cried. "I have tasted and I have seen, and now Elyon is calling his bride to the great wedding feast."

A woman she'd never seen before, dressed in strange blue pants and a white blouse, stepped up behind him. Unlike him, she was dry. But then she hadn't come through the water.

"Thomas?" the woman said.

He spun and regarded her in a moment's shock. Then he grabbed her hand and held it up for them to see. "My sister from the histories. She's with me."

Two weeks ago it would have been a preposterous suggestion, but today it seemed perfectly natural. Yes, of course, this was Kara Hunter from the histories. Mikil should have known immediately.

Thomas sprang down to a lower boulder, practically dragging his sister with him. "Mount your fastest horses, every man, woman, and child. Leave it all behind. Everything! No water, no food, nothing but yourself and your children."

Thomas leaped to the ground, eyes bright with a fanaticism Mikil had come to know well. "Now!" he roared, sweeping his arm. "Follow me now!"

They ran as one. The raw intensity of the moment precluded more than a few cries as they swept up those too young or too old to match Thomas's sprint.

Colorful ribbons flanked the army of Roush high above. And now light shimmered on either side, reaching all the way to the ground, forming a tunnel that streamed directly east.

"Faster!" Thomas cried. "Run, run, run!"

Every albino was accustomed to quick flight, ready at a moment's notice to flee any Horde threat. And this . . . this call to follow Thomas to Elyon's playground made any threat of death seem like a child's mud pie.

They sprang onto the backs of unsaddled horses and whipped the animals to a full gallop, close on Thomas's heels. And he wasn't waiting, despite having to care for a sister unfamiliar with her horse. Likewise, she seemed too caught up in this mind-blowing encounter to worry about her lack of equestrian skills.

Mikil cried out to Thomas as he flew by, his eyes pinned on the horizon. He pulled up and looked about frantically. "Where's Chelise?"

"She's already gone to Qurong."

Without a word, he slammed his horse's sides and bolted forward. Then Mikil was hard after him, trying to catch up as they raced out of the valley.

"Faster!" Mikil heard Marie cry to those behind her. "Faster!"

They spilled from the canyon into the desert in a cloud of dust, and Mikil pulled up hard. Thomas sat on his black stallion beside Kara, staring at a rider mounted on a white stallion on the next dune.

The tunnel of light flowed around him, whipping his hair and a robe of red around his white battle leathers.

Elyon the Warrior.

The stallion under him reared and whinnied, pawing at the air. The warrior had a sword in his hand, and he now lifted it high over his head, pointing it at the massive formation of Roush.

Then Elyon screamed at the sky, and Mikil thought her ears might burst under the power of this one cry of victory. He swept his sword toward the eastern horizon and called out in a voice that no one within a mile could mistake.

"Follow me, my bride! Follow me!"

And then Elyon raced east, and the seven thousand rode after him with the colored wind in their hair.

East, my bride, east. Toward the Valley of Miggdon. Toward the Horde. Toward the battle.

41

"NOW, MY lord," Ba'al whispered, hunched beside Qurong at the top of the southern slope. "You must engage them now as he has instructed."

"I don't like it." Qurong stood on a flat rock ledge and gazed at the two armies—his to the right, three hundred thousand strong for all Eram could know, and the Eramite army to his left across the valley, half the strength of his own. But they had albinos with them, more than four thousand from what scouts had been able to determine.

"That old fox was right. This is his son's doing. They have something up their sleeves."

"*I* have something up *our* sleeves, you impotent old fool!" Ba'al shouted.

Qurong jerked his head to the dark priest, taken aback by his loss of control. A terrible sound rolled through the sky, high above. The sound of a strong wind moaning through a hollow, but there was no wind.

The sound passed.

"You see? It's a sign." Ba'al removed frightened eyes from the sky and bowed his head. "Forgive me, my lord. I beg your forgiveness. But victory is in our hands! You heard."

"I heard a wind. And I heard your insult."

"It's here!" Ba'al made a fist out of his scrawny white fingers and shook it. "It's right here, and my lover is ravenous for it. We must attack now!"

"Perhaps I should cut out your tongue first. And then we will see."

"You speak this way to his lover?" Ba'al demanded.

"I speak this way to my priest."

"I will remind you that you pledged—"

"To Teeleh, not to you."

Cassak stood by, wearing a frown. "The sun is high, my lord. We have eight more hours of light. I suggest we either execute our plan before nightfall or prepare for a long night of sparring with the albinos. And that won't be pretty."

"Be prepared for deception," Ba'al said. "Kill any albino who comes close, no matter what their intention."

"And if they mean to surrender?"

"Kill them!"

Cassak looked at Qurong. "My lord?"

"Yes. Kill any who approach. We trust no one."

"I'll pass the word. Should we deploy, my lord?"

Qurong fought through the fog of confusion that had not left his mind since his daughter dared to cross the desert to meet him. A week ago he would have refused to think of her as *Daughter*. But now . . .

It was maddening. The walls he'd successfully erected against love over so many years were crumbling around him. First Thomas had tricked him into a dream state, where nothing was as it seemed. Then Chelise brought news of his grandson, Jake.

Qurong had no other offspring but a grandchild fathered by his greatest enemy, Thomas. The supreme commander's inability to toss them all from his mind infuriated him.

Chelise, his feisty daughter whom he had once loved more than any treasure in his possession, was back—just there, on the horizon of his mind, calling to be loved by him once again. He stood overlooking a valley in which there would soon be more dead flesh than living, and he was thinking of only one person. No matter how absurd or naive her philosophy, she was still Chelise of Qurong.

"My lord?"

"I'm thinking!"

"We're running out of time," Cassak warned.

"They're up to something. I can feel it in my bones. They have something up their sleeves."

"As do we, my lord," Ba'al said. "As we most certainly do."

"What? What do we have besides another two hundred thousand men to send into the slaughter? I don't know your *real* plan, only that you keep insisting on some unseen magic."

"Have faith!" the dark priest screamed. He blinked, then settled. "Forgive me." He slipped his hands into the arms of his robe and turned a stoic stare at the Eramite army.

"They have broken their covenant," he said. "This harlot who's come to them has removed their covering, I am assured of that."

"That's it? I throw my army into danger on the back of a harlot and more religious jargon?"

Ba'al jerked his head around. "Listen, you fool." Spittle flew from stretched lips. "The powers of the air are far more potent than your little army. For many years the albinos have been untouchable. The half-breeds have all once bathed, like myself . . . we've all been protected till this day. All but pure-bred Horde have been under the covering of Elyon. But now that covenant has been broken!"

Qurong wasn't sure he'd heard correctly. A horse snorted behind him; a mace's chain rattled over metal. Ba'al's nostrils flared, unrepentant this time. But it was his claim that screamed at Qurong.

"You're saying what? That *you* were once Forest Guard? That you're half-breed?"

The dark priest faced the valley. "I am lover of Marsuuv, made whole by his blood. And now that you know, I will have to open your eyes so that you won't kill me."

He bent, grabbed a handful of dust at his feet, spit into it, and flung it at Qurong. The glob of mud slapped him square in the face and he stepped back, appalled.

"What's this?" he thundered.

"Open his eyes, Marsuuv, my lover."

Qurong wiped the mud off, face flushed with heat. And when he opened his eyes, he found that he couldn't see properly. The valley had darkened.

"Look above, Qurong. See what awaits all who have broken the covenant."

Qurong lifted his eyes and caught his breath. The Shataiki he'd seen at the high place were back. Thicker now. Blotting out the sun. Soaring through the sky not a thousand yards over their heads, with talons extended and red eyes glaring. Only at him, it seemed.

"Elyon help us."

"No, my lord. Elyon help *them*. But he won't. They've turned their backs on him. Now they will be flesh for the beasts."

"And what about me? Or you, for that matter? You don't think they would as soon tear us to shreds?"

"No. We've brokered a deal with the devils and pledged our allegiance, so that we will be spared along with our people. Do you forget already?"

It was beginning to make sense to Qurong. This was the reason behind his blood-drinking ritual. He didn't understand the full import of what he was seeing and hearing, but this must surely be the day of the dragon.

"So these Shataiki can only go after the half-breeds?"

"Yes. Unless . . ."

"Unless what?"

"Supernatural matters always have their caveats."

This would be the end, Qurong thought.

"Send the first wave," Ba'al said. "Send it while we still have their favor."

Qurong turned to Cassak, who was looking up, clearly lost as to what they were seeing. "Send in our first twenty thousand," he ordered. "Infantry. Ready the archers. Spare no one."

SAMUEL KNEW beyond any doubt that he'd become Horde. His joints felt as though pins had been pushed into his bones, scraping with each movement. His skin burned, and when he tried to wash the pain away with water, it only worsened.

It was no wonder Horde generally shied from water and bathed only through pain. He tried some of the beetle nut, but the taste was too bitter.

Yet, even knowing he was Horde, he didn't resent his condition. It made him more like Eram. It fit into the greater world. And really, he wasn't sure why he'd been so offended by the scabbing disease to begin with.

It's taking your mind as well, Samuel.

Yes. Yes, there was that.

"They come!"

"Steady!" Eram called.

Samuel was jerked back to the moment. He leaped into his saddle and galloped to the front lines where Eram, Janae, and his generals were mounted, fixated on the valley. He pulled up between the Eramite leader and his witch, veins thumping with adrenaline.

"What is it?"

"Nice of you to join us, Son of Hunter," Eram said. "Qurong's finally grown a set and is sending his first men to die."

A sea of infantry was spilling over the crest, sweeping into the valley.

"How many have not taken the water?" Eram demanded of no one in particular.

"Fifty thousand, as instructed," his general said.

"The rest carry the poison in their blood?"

Janae responded. "Yes. All of them."

Eram spat, and his red spittle slapped into Samuel's boot before falling to the ground. Samuel caught the leader's eyes.

"Sorry about that." Eram studied the Horde army nearing the bottom of the far slope. "I'd say about twenty thousand men on foot. I'm surprised Qurong would be so obvious. Exactly as I predicted, he's trying to draw us."

"We can't show our strength yet," Samuel said. "Send fifty thousand."

"Yes, my new Horde general. That's exactly what I will do." He smirked at Samuel. "And you will lead them."

Samuel blinked at the man. "I'm sorry, I—"

"I need a general in the valley, my friend. Someone I can trust. I've decided you're the best choice." He snapped his fingers at his other general. "Send them now, General, the fifty thousand who have not taken the poison. Tell the captains they will take orders from Samuel once they're in battle. And tell them to send every last one of those Scabs back to hell."

"Yes, sir."

Samuel looked at Janae, but she didn't appear at all concerned by the decision. Her eyes were on the empty horizon to her left, where empty desert waited. And beyond the desert, the Black forest.

He still wasn't having great success wrapping his thoughts around Eram's decision to send him down. Naturally, he wasn't afraid. Far from it, thoughts of slaying Horde and taking glory were already pulling at him. But what motive did Eram really have?

"Samuel, you're questioning my judgment?" Eram asked.

"No, sir."

"I need your men to see you go down that hill, and I need them to see you kill Horde. I've just been informed that some of them are complaining about a rash. I would send them all down now, before they have a chance to realize they have the disease, but their presence on the battlefield now might spook Qurong, you understand? But one albino, the Son of Hunter—now that would tempt Qurong to send his whole army in at once."

"My men are turning Horde?"

"Are they?" He said it as if he'd expected nothing less. "They've taken the mark and given their hearts to its maker. What did you expect?" A gentle smile. "But the transition will take some time. We have to fight before we lose our physical advantage."

The thought that Eram was a brilliant tactician and the thought that Janae had betrayed the albinos entered Samuel's mind as one. But at the moment, only the former seemed terribly important. Had he expected anything less from his witch?

A flood of Eramite warriors broke over the crest to his left. Infantry. The ground rumbled with the footfalls of fifty thousand as the heavily armored warriors plunged down the slope. No cry yet. The two armies rushed toward each other.

Samuel's pulse surged and he nudged his horse forward, then brought it back around. "Just restrain those archers. I don't need an arrow in my back."

Eram nodded. "Watch for Qurong's next wave. He'll commit the bulk of his force; you'll know it's coming when he launches the fireballs. I'll send reinforcements as soon as he takes our bait, beginning with the albinos. Until then, hold them. Once they descend, the disease will spread. We'll see just how effective this poison really is."

The stampede of warriors still rushed over the crest. Janae still looked to the north, always to the north.

Now she looked at him and smiled gently. "Come here, lover."

"Say your good-byes quickly," Eram said, pulling his horse around. "Your battle awaits you."

Samuel pulled his mount next to Janae's, facing the opposite direction. He impulsively leaned forward and kissed her on the mouth. The smell of her breath drew him as the blood had. He knew that Teeleh had changed her into something less than any woman he'd ever known, and he wondered if he would be so fortunate as to have a similar experience.

"Good-bye, my love," she said. "It's been good to join with you for a while."

"I have no intention of dying," he said, looking into her lost eyes. "I'll be back."

"And I'll be gone. I've done what I was meant to do."

"Gone? No, no, you can't leave now!"

"But I must. I've finished my task here. They are deceived, all of them. Now my true lover calls me." She put her hand on his forearm. "Maybe when this is all over, you can join me, if he will allow it. I think you would like it."

"The Black Forest?"

"No," she said. "Earth. Two thousand years ago."

The histories. He didn't know what to say. A roar erupted from the valley behind him, and he twisted to see the two armies clash. Their leading edges feathered into each other like two black clouds meeting head-on. But here, the union was brutal and bloody, and already, screams of the dying mixed with cries of bravado and rage. He had to go!

"Then wait for me," he said, spinning back. But she was already headed away, sitting like an elegant queen on her pale mare. "Janae!"

She looked back, wearing her perpetual smirk. "Die well, Samuel."

"Janae . . ."

"General!" They were calling him. He could see Vadal watching him. As were all of the albino warriors. And another ten thousand Eramites. All eyes were on him. His army fought now, slaying the Horde as he'd always dreamed. Glory awaited.

Samuel spun his horse around, dug his heels into its flanks with enough power to crack a rib, and plunged into the Valley of Miggdon.

42

BILL REDIGER, who'd been called Billy before he received black eyes and a new name, stepped from the passenger ramp at the Denver International Airport, snugged his dark glasses to his forehead, and turned right, toward the trains that would take him to the street. To any ordinary passerby, he would look like a successful businessman with a taste for fine, dark suits and expensive watches, in this case Armani and Rolex. His red hair was neatly combed back, and a good tan softened the freckles on his cheeks.

None could possibly know who really walked past them on this otherwise plain summer day in middle America. They couldn't know that he had black eyeballs and could read minds.

It was a very good day to be alive, because in so many ways Bill was already dead. But now, having fully accepted his death, he could get on with the business at hand. He wasn't entirely sure what had happened to him, though he suspected that there was another man like him somewhere, living many years in the future.

Yes, that was right. To his recollection, he'd been in Bangkok in search of the Books of History, where he'd met Janae. They'd fallen into a trance of some kind. Gone somewhere he couldn't quite recall. It had left the taste of bile in his mouth.

Then he'd awakened in Washington, D.C., thirty-some-odd years in the past, which was technically before he'd been born. He'd been sent back for only one purpose: To stop Thomas Hunter. And the devil had given him the eyes to follow Thomas wherever he went, even into his dreams.

And once he stopped Thomas, then what? He would probably die some terrible death, because there couldn't be two of him running around.

Maybe he would become a monk, dye his hair black, find his way into a monastery somewhere, and wreak a little havoc. Help things along. Or maybe not.

Getting the money he needed for his task had been easy. He'd simply walked into a Wells Fargo bank and taken what he needed from the manager's mind to make an unexpected visit to the vault before the bank opened the next morning.

He thought it a good idea to create an identity, so he got the necessary documents with some of his hard-earned dollars, bought a ticket under the name Bill Smith, and boarded a plane to Denver.

And here he was, in Denver. This is where he would change history.

This is where he would find and kill Thomas before he could do whatever he was meant to do that made all hell scream with rage.

Bill sighed and adjusted his glasses as he entered the train. Yes, it was good to be alive. Because really . . . most definitely, he was already dead.

43

THIS WAS the second time Chelise had made the eighteen-hour journey across the desert to save her father, but this time she was alone and she was scared, and this time she made it in a fourteen-hour sprint.

The sky was dark, and she was sure it wasn't by coincidence. Evil hung in the air, threatening to burst through the veil at any moment. Eram's army had left a wide swath of litter through the desert, traveling quickly without making camp. They'd eaten on the run and left the scraps from their meals scattered in their wake.

She approached Miggdon Valley from the northwest, following the Eramites' trail, but rather than cut south to the western slope as they had, she'd veered farther east. If Samuel and his witch were on the western slope, her father would be on the eastern slope.

The last thing she wanted now was to encounter Samuel and his band of fools. She had but one goal.

Qurong. Her father, leader of the world, awaited her. This is what Michal must have meant when he said *the world awaits you.*

These were the thoughts that ran through Chelise's mind as she closed in. But the moment she came upon the expansive scene in the Miggdon Valley, a chill swept over her.

She was too late!

The din of clashing metal joined with the roar of battle cries, rising from the valley floor like a hive of angry hornets.

"Easy." She patted her stamping mount's neck. "Easy."

But nothing about this valley was easy. She quickly took stock of the chaos.

The main battle had been joined on the valley floor by upwards of a hundred thousand warriors already. Of those, more than half were down, either wounded or dead.

One of a dozen Horde catapults launched a ball of fire into the air. It arced over the valley, trailing a long ribbon of oily smoke, and streaked toward the armies below like a comet. The projectile slammed into a sea of flesh and mushroomed. Resin splattered in all directions, spreading fire. Burning men from both armies fled in all directions.

Then another, then another, then a fourth ball, all launched in rapid succession, each floating lazily through the sky before smashing into the warriors below. Twelve balls were sent as Chelise watched, and each took the lives of at least fifty tightly grouped fighters—half-breed, full-breed, or albino, it didn't matter. They all burned like flies.

The main body of Qurong's army broke from their position on the eastern ridge and began to flow into the valley. The sight was enough to stop her heart for a moment. Two or three hundred thousand, maybe more, all in black, rushed down the long slope to crush the enemy. Dust rose about their horses as they pounded down.

Their cries then reached her, delayed by the great distance. A dull roar of rage from so many open throats.

Then the Eramites, a smaller army but still massive, broke from the ridge to her right and rushed to collide. Led by albinos! The whole army, leaving none to guard the hill.

She'd half expected the albinos to come to their senses and turn back. But the witch's tongue had clearly proven too crafty.

This was the final battle. When the dust settled, three or four hundred thousand would surely be dead on the ground.

She watched in horror as the two armies crashed into each other. It took a few moments, and then she heard the terrible sound of that initial clash, like two battering rams colliding head-on. She could see the thrusting lances, the sweeping maces bouncing surreally off bodies. From this distance, there was no blood, no flying body parts, only two massive walls of humanity tearing into each other.

And even as she watched, a third wave came from the Horde's slope. Another army to join the first, bringing their total to well over half a million. They outnumbered the Eramites three to one!

But the Eramites had the witch's brew. Teeleh's breath. And if they'd found a way to deliver it, the tide would turn quickly.

Chelise was so overwhelmed by the display of brute force that she couldn't think what to do. Then she saw the tall banners showing her father's colors on the southern slope, and she realized that he was there, commanding from above.

But this was Qurong, and he would join his men in battle if there was any hint that they needed his help. She had to get to him. She had to stop him and force him to use reason in this hour of endings.

She should approach from the east, where the Horde army had lain waiting. Her father's guard wouldn't expect anyone from that side, and she stood a better chance of reaching him. In a time of war, they would have orders to kill any albino on sight. If she died, then her father was hopelessly lost.

"Hiyaa!"

Chelise spurred her horse and forced it east against its will. It would take her half an hour to reach the far side, and then only if she went unnoticed. If she found a stray Horde mount and wrapped herself in Horde dress, perhaps.

Reaching her father was all that mattered now.

———⊗———

QURONG PACED the overlook, seething. "Ba'al!" He stopped next to a servant under the shade of the only tree on the southern ridge, an old miggdon fig that was leafy but barren. From this vantage, there was no sign of the dark priest.

He spun to the servant. "Get that dark witch! Drag him to me if you have to. Now!"

"Yes, my lord."

His servant fled, and Qurong doubted he'd be back. Cassak was down the hill already, as were his Throaters, leaving only a thousand guards to maintain a perimeter around him.

Qurong turned back to the runner sent by Cassak. "Tell me again what has happened to the warriors. This makes no sense, none at all."

"A spell, a sickness, I don't know. But our men in the valley are suffering, my lord."

"Suffering?" Qurong scoffed. "War is filled with suffering." Yet there was no denying the ease with which the half-breeds were cutting through his ranks. From what he saw, the albinos were virtually unstoppable, slashing through his men with such wickedness that his best Throaters might as well be bound by rope.

"Aches and pain." The runner turned frantic eyes down the hill. "They're baying like wounded animals."

"Cassak too?"

"All of them, my lord."

"And you? What of you?"

"No. But I haven't been in the fighting. The message was passed to me by another."

"And did he have this ailment?"

"I can't say. No, sire, I can't say."

This was impossible!

"Ba'al!" he thundered again. He loathed the man.

Then Qurong saw the high priest in the valley. He'd set up an altar in a protected enclave far to the east with a dozen of his wicked underlings. He looked to be sacrificing—of all things! A goat. Or a human, it was too far to see clearly.

Qurong watched in disbelief as the distant figure in purple raised both arms to an empty sky. Dark clouds had gathered, promising rain, but he could no longer see Shataiki. No magic in the air to slay the treasonous half-breeds.

When this was over, Qurong would sever Ba'al's head from his shoulders himself. The man might have some personal tunnel to Teeleh's lair, but he was a disgusting wraith, and a half-breed too. Let Teeleh feed on his flesh. The Horde needed a trustworthy man to guide them in spiritual matters.

He screamed his frustration into the valley, knowing that nothing could be heard down there but the clashing of metal and groans of men. "Ba'al!"

You're wasting your breath, Qurong. Your army is falling.

He stared at the battle, red-faced. An albino close enough for Qurong to make out his dark, smooth skin was on foot, wielding a sword in both hands. He swung his sword as if it were a feather, slashing up and across a Throater's chest, then sidestepping a thrown ax. Like a master among children. His own men looked far too sluggish.

It's over. In one fell swoop they destroy you.

His mind fled the valley for a moment and embraced an image of Patricia, the wise woman who'd loved him always. He would die for her. And Chelise . . .

Dear Chelise, forgive me. Forgive me, my daughter.

Qurong thrust out his hand, palm open. "Captain!"

The captain of his guard rushed forward and bowed.

"Give me my sword."

"Sir?"

"My sword, Malachi! Give me my sword. I'm going down. Order the rest of your men to the battle. Today we will live or today we die."

THE VALLEY of Miggdon might have been a burial pit and Samuel wouldn't have known the difference. That he'd managed to survive three hours of close battle wasn't a thing of glory as he'd imagined.

The blood of tens of thousands wet the ground; he could feel it squishing through his soaked boots. The valley was a butchering ground, pure and simple, and Qurong's army had indeed been the butchered. Horses could no longer navigate the carcasses underfoot and had taken to the perimeter, where those who'd lost their courage tried to flee only to be cut down. By the look of it, Qurong had lost over half of his army, and the rest were feeling the full effects of Janae's poison. Their own disease was eating them alive, and a wail rose on all sides as they dug at their flesh, desperate for relief.

But more than a third of the half-breeds lay dead as well. It was now only a matter of time before they cut down the last of Qurong's massive force, but they had already lost enough to leave many wives and children weeping for months.

Samuel ducked under a swooshing mace and swung his sword full in the face of the Scab connected to the other end of the chain. His blade cut cleanly through his neck, and the man's body took three more steps before tripping and falling over two other bodies.

Forgive me, Father, for I have sinned.

"Your back, Hunter!" a voice shouted.

Samuel spun in time to deflect a spear thrown by a young Scab now skewered at the end of Eram's sword. The half-breed leader caught Samuel's eye, then spun to ward off two Scabs who wielded long swords.

Samuel's own joints screamed with pain, and the albinos fighting around him were covered in the scabbing disease. With each swing Samuel felt his father's eyes on him.

There would be no men left. This wasn't an attack against the Horde. It was the *end* of the Horde. The carnage sickened him.

Samuel stopped and stood gasping in the middle of the battlefield, like a man caught in the eye of a storm, calm for the moment. He turned slowly and surveyed the butchery. The scene whipped by him with dizzying speed. A man with no arm, screaming, another staggering as he ran, blinded. An albino weeping. Weeping though he looked untouched by a blade.

The battle would be won soon. In thirty minutes, the great Qurong's army would be dead and rotting on the ground. Flies had already come by the hundreds of thousands. The stench of Horde flesh had become familiar to Samuel, but bleeding Horde flesh was much worse, and the smell now clogged his nostrils like so much rotting skin.

On all sides the massacre raged. Samuel moved to avoid a spear hurled at him. The Scab stared at him, then fell to his knees and began to weep. He was but a teenager, crying out his mother's name in a mournful wail. Martha.

"Shut up!" Samuel screamed. "Stop it!"

The boy either didn't hear him or refused. Furious, Samuel raced forward, leaping over the bodies in his way. He screamed his anger and swung his sword at a full run.

He stood over his kill, overcome by a wave of nausea. *Father. Please, Father.* He fell to his knees beside the slain body and touched the boy's warm flesh.

Mother . . . A deep sorrow welled up from his past. *Dear Mother, forgive me.*

And then the dam that had separated the boy in him from the man broke, and Samuel began to weep. He sat back on his haunches, clenched his eyes against the dark sky, spread his arms wide, and began to wail his anguish.

What had he done? What kind of deception had he ingested? How could he undo this catastrophe?

But it was too late. It was already done. He'd betrayed his father.

Samuel wept.

It would be better now if someone killed him where he sat, crying like a baby. How could he live knowing that this slaughter had been his doing? He'd been born in his father's image, destined to save the world. Instead he'd played the very Judas his father often spoke of. A traitor.

Slowly the sorrow became anger. Then rage. And then the sky above him became black and the battlefield around him grew silent, and the distant thought that he might be dead crossed his mind. He opened his eyes.

A host of Shataiki, a million strong if there was one, circled no more than a thousand yards above the valley, swirling black tar stuffed with mangy fur and red cherries. He could feel the breeze from their wings as they swept overhead in silence.

The battle around him had come to a halt; the horror painted on the skies above was laid bare for all to see. And Samuel knew the full truth then.

They'd broken their covenant with Elyon, leaving the way clear for the Shataiki to destroy them at will. What kind of evil Ba'al and Qurong were dealing, he didn't know, but he doubted they would be consumed. No, that honor belonged to the half-breeds, to the albinos.

Janae had convinced them all to turn their backs on the protection that came from bathing in Elyon's lakes. And in truth, Samuel had known all along, hadn't he? Deep beneath the disease clouding his mind, he'd known that the witch was Teeleh's handmaiden, because she'd come from the desert bearing his mark.

She was Teeleh's handmaiden, and Samuel, son of Hunter, was her fool.

He stood to his feet, staring at the sky, blinded by a debilitating rage. It was over. He'd come to kill Qurong, the father whom his mother loved more than she loved even her own kind. Instead he'd killed all *but* Qurong.

He'd slaughtered the world.

Samuel trembled, wishing death on himself. The dead were a feast, easy prey, blood and flesh for the Shataiki who'd waited for this meal since their captivity in the Black Forest. And Samuel, son of Hunter, was the one serving their meal.

Screams and chaos rose from the valley far behind him, and he turned slowly. To a man, the armies of both Qurong and Eram were gripped by the sight of a single stream of black bats flowing to the ground at the battlefield's far side, two hundred yards away.

Like a serpent reaching to earth, the Shataiki descended and began to feed. Talons first, ripping into head or backs. Then fangs, penetrating the skulls of any warrior standing. They went down in a tangle of blood and fur.

Warriors abandoned their weapons and tried to run, but the Shataiki caught them and hauled them to the ground. Darkness swallowed the battlefield as the evil creatures poured down through the funnel and spread slowly north.

The valley erupted in panic as the living, a hundred thousand strong still, fled. They could run . . . they *would* run, but they could not hide. Samuel turned his back and faced north, barely able to stay upright for the fear that shook his bones.

The ridge was empty. The Horde command had fled. And the lone tree that stood beside the tall banners was bare now. No leaves. An angular, burnt husk stood alone against the sky, reaching up like a black claw.

What was green was now black.

"Father . . ." Tears streamed down Samuel's cheeks as he turned back to the valley. "Father, forgive me! Forgive me, Thomas."

A small flash of purple streaked across the far southern slope, a warrior mounted on a black horse. It's Qurong, he thought, catching himself. And as Samuel watched, Qurong swung his sword at any enemy that stood in his way. He'd lost his mind and was attacking now, knowing all was lost. Loyal to the bone.

Even now, the reviled enemy of all that was good showed he was more of a man than Samuel would ever be. He blurted a cry of self-disgust.

Here was royalty, in the Horde. And Elyon's heir was a pitiful traitor soaked in blood.

Samuel screamed his frustration. He snatched up his sword, bounded over fallen bodies, and flung himself onto the back of a panicked Horde stallion.

He would die, they would all die, but first Qurong would die.

And then . . . then the end could come.

44

THE HORSE Chelise had taken belonged to a dead Horde warrior who was still slumped over his mount on the eastern ridge when she'd stumbled upon them. She'd quickly set her own horse free, shrugged into the fighter's dark cape, and pushed the fresher mount around the ridge at a full gallop.

Her father had committed his entire army, and from what she'd seen as she raced, they were suffering wholesale slaughter. Except for the few thousand albinos who were inflicting serious damage, the half-breeds' slight advantage as better fighters should have been offset by the Horde's numbers.

But even her father's Throaters were falling where they stood. Something was wrong. There was evil at work here, and the concern she had for her father's life grew with each passing breath.

The mighty Qurong was defeated! Five hundred thousand would be dead, leaving behind a city of weeping widows and children. And what would Samuel do, shove them all underwater until they drowned?

No, that wouldn't work. The drowning had to be voluntary to work.

She kept looking down the valley for any sign of her father's colors. Seeing his men fall like this, he would join. He would rather embrace death than go home stripped of his pride.

Dear Elyon, she had to reach him.

She rounded the southern ridge, whipping the snorting mount. She could see the banners far ahead, but the army was gone. No sign . . .

The sky darkened, and she reined in the horse. What was this?

Shataiki swept through the sky above in a massive, slow-moving vortex. The battle had stalled. Silence smothered the valley.

It was the end, then. Elyon would come. For a brief moment, she felt elation, because this had been foretold. The day of the dragon had come. How the rest would come to pass she didn't know or care to know any longer. Only that Qurong was saved.

And her mother? Yes, her mother as well, of course. But how?

The Shataiki suddenly dived at the far end of the valley, like the tail of a tornado. The damage they inflicted when they touched the earth was no less destructive. They began to devour the living, and Chelise began to panic.

"Father!" Her scream was hardly a whisper in the echoing din below. "Father! Fath—"

She saw him! Trailing a purple cape. Racing across the valley floor on a black horse. He hacked at a fleeing albino fighter, but his goal wasn't the main battle. He was going for a small grouping of boulders on the western side, where Chelise could just make out several priests in their dark robes.

She spurred her mount and dived into the darkened valley. "Hiyaa! Hiyaa!"

The Shataiki flooding into the valley were spreading out, like so many black hornets swarming through a crack in a cliff. Those who fled were being singled out and picked off as they clambered up the slopes. She still had time, maybe ten minutes, before the black beasts worked their way to this end.

There was a red pool one half mile east, but how would she get to it?

"Hiyaa!" She whipped the horse and raced to intercept Qurong.

Not until she was within a hundred yards did she guess his intention. Ba'al, the dark priest, was kneeling on a makeshift altar, stripped of his robe. His arms were stretched to the swirling Shataiki, and his jaw was wide in a scream of delight. Four other priests had discarded their clothing as well and were bleeding from deep cuts in their arms and ribs.

This was his finest hour. He was somehow behind the carnage as much as Samuel and Janae.

And now her father meant to take out his rage on the frail white skeleton of a man.

"Father!"

Qurong thundered on, sword raised over his head, roaring.

"Father!"

Movement far behind and to her right caught her attention, and she snatched a glance at a half-breed racing toward them like a dragon heading out of hell.

She spun back. "Father!"

Ba'al surely knew that his slayer had come, but he trusted only in his master, Teeleh, to save him. But Teeleh was clearly in no saving mood today.

Qurong rolled off his horse at a full gallop, came to his feet ten yards from the altar, and rushed Ba'al with both hands on his sword.

Ba'al was weeping at the heavens now, frantic with his own kind of pleasure.

"Father!"

Qurong planted one foot at the base of the altar and swung his blade like a club. The razor-sharp steel severed the nearest of Ba'al's raised arms, then slashed through his neck before glancing into the air.

The dark priest's head toppled off his body and landed on the stone, jaw still spread, silent now. Ba'al's priests fled, crying out to Teeleh like frantic women.

"Qurong!" Chelise pulled up and dropped to the ground. "Supreme Commander of the Horde, I beg you to hear me."

Her father turned slowly, bloody sword limp in his hand. He stared at her as if he didn't recognize her, lost.

"The end of the world has come, Father. Your army is gone. Your people are without husbands."

"Chelise?" Slowly his face wrinkled with anguish, and he sank to one knee.

"Yes, it's me, Father," she said, stepping closer. "And this is not the way of a mighty leader. You are called to Elyon's side as you once were."

He tried to stand but could not.

"You have to drown, Father."

"Never." His voice was weak, but his jowls shook with his stubbornness. "I will never drown like a coward."

"Stop this madness!" she cried. "It's life, you old fool! You're here on the edge of hell, and you still resist the call of your Maker?"

"I serve no one. Hell cannot touch me now." He tried to stand again, this time wincing. Was he in pain? Was he wounded?

She remembered the sight of Stephen, the Scab Janae had exposed to her vial of Teeleh's poison. Her father had come in contact with it when he'd entered the battle, and was dying already.

"The pain you feel is his betrayal. Teeleh's disease will kill you even if you're protected from the Shataiki. You've been betrayed!"

"I . . . will . . . not . . . drown!" He managed to stand, but shakily, like an old man.

She grabbed the bottle of blood that Johan had given her. Thomas's blood, which Janae must have carried knowing it would affect the disease. Why else bottle it up? She broke off the top, exposing a sharp jagged edge, and held it up to him.

"Blood, Father. Thomas's. Cleansed by the first lake."

"Don't be a fool." He spat to one side. "Ba'al makes me drink Teeleh's blood; now you want me to consume your husband's blood? We are in a battle here!"

"And you are dying! Your people are slaughtered by half-breeds and eaten by those who have a thirst for Teeleh's blood." She paused, not sure what to do. "I think that if Thomas's blood mixes with your own, it will stop the disease."

"I would spit on the blood of Thomas!" Qurong roared.

Chelise was so outraged by his abject refusal to engage common sense that she moved without thought. She rushed him and slashed his forearm with the vial.

He stared at his arm, aghast as Thomas's blood mixed with his own. Chelise stepped backward and dropped the vial. Behind her, the din of the slaughter pressed closer. But she was dressed as a Horde warrior and was with Qurong. They were safe for the moment.

"I don't know what else to do except pray that his blood will protect you. But you must drown, Father. Please, you must!"

He was looking down at his arm, breathing deeply. "I don't know what to do. I don't know what's happening." Tears welled in his eyes and spilled down his cheeks.

He sank to both knees and buried his head in both hands. "Forgive me," he wept. "Forgive me."

"I forgive you, Father." Now she was crying. She stood not ten feet from Qurong while the black beasts ravaged the Horde, and she begged like a mother pleading for the life of her only child.

"Drown, I beg you, drown. The Shataiki won't consume you now, you're protected by the blood. We can make it out, to a red pool nearby. Please, please, I beg you, Father."

She heard the faint pounding of hooves behind her, and an image flashed through her mind. The half-breed she'd seen.

Chelise twisted back and saw the horse upon her. Saw the sword on its way down. Heard the roar of protest from her father.

Saw in a fleeting glimpse that this was Samuel, turned Horde.

Felt the sting of the blade as it cut into her neck.

And then Chelise of Hunter's horizon went blue.

A brilliant sky rising from a perfectly silent desert. Nothing else, just a rolling white desert and a perfectly blue sky.

One moment—searing pain as the sword's metal edge sliced through her neck. The next—absolute peace in this bright world spread before her.

No pain.

No sorrow.

No blood.

Several long seconds slogged through the perfect silence.

A child laughed behind her. She turned around and saw that she wasn't alone. A thin boy of maybe thirteen stood on the bank of a green pool.

Yes, she thought, *there is the pool.*

"Hello, Chelise, daughter of Elyon," the boy said.

She knew at the first sound of his voice that he was far more than just any ordinary boy. Her voice trembled when she answered.

"Hello."

He grinned mischievously, looked at the water, then at her, then back at the water. Finally, his bright green eyes settled on her again.

"Are you ready?"

Are you ready? She couldn't find her voice any longer. And she suddenly couldn't see, because her eyes were blurred by tears of desperation.

Unable to contain his own excitement, the boy turned and dived.

Chelise tore her feet from the sand, gasping. She'd already taken three steps when his body splashed through the surface and vanished beneath the emerald waters.

Then Chelise dived headlong into Elyon's lake, and the pleasure of her first contact with him took her breath away.

———

QURONG HAD been so absorbed, so vanquished by his own misery, so consumed by self-pity, that he didn't see the danger. He'd seen the fleeing warrior earlier, but not until too late did he realize that he was coming in for the kill.

He leaped to his feet and threw out his hands, thinking one of his men was mistaking Chelise for an Eramite threatening him. "My daughter!" he screamed. "She's my . . ."

Then he saw that this was an Eramite warrior whose bloodstained armor made him nearly indistinguishable from his own warriors. Still, in the last moment, he thought the half-breed would heed his cry.

But it was too late. The momentum of the fighter's sword could not be stopped.

His blade sliced cleanly through Chelise's neck. Her head flew from her body, bounced off the attacker's horse, and fell to the ground, eyes still open.

Qurong didn't have time to consider the horror of this sudden change before the warrior swung again with a cry of rage, now at him. He ducked under the blow, aware that the pain he'd felt only a minute earlier was nearly gone. The attacker's sword clanged off the rock behind him, then the man was rearing his horse for another pass.

But there was Chelise, lying dead and bleeding from her neck, and Qurong could not manage the sight of it. He had killed his own daughter, as clearly as if he'd swung the sword himself.

She smiled in death. A pure, clean face, free of any blemish. This daughter, whose forehead he'd often kissed and who'd often strutted around announcing to all that her papa was the strongest, greatest man in the world—this daughter named Chelise was dead. On his account.

Qurong wanted to die. Let the half-breed end it now!

<hr />

SAMUEL'S BLADE was in full swing when the guard turned and Samuel saw that the *he* was a *she*.

Saw that this woman was not one of Qurong's guards as he'd assumed from the cloak she wore and the horse she rode.

Saw that this woman was Chelise. His mother.

Terrified by the sight, he jerked his sword back and away, but the momentum was too great, and his blade slashed through her neck as if it were made of white clay.

His boot bumped her falling head as he rushed past. His mind lost track of his mortal enemy, the father of his mother. He was mistaken; this woman could not be his mother! He could undo this. Mother would never be cloaked as a Scab, riding a Horde mount!

But scream as it may, his mind drained of blood and reason as he struggled to force his horse around. He rushed back, pulled the horse up, and dropped to the ground. Qurong was there, on his knees, face white with shock.

And there on the ground, ten feet from him, lay . . . yes. Yes, it was her.

Samuel's world spun. The horizon started to fade, all but the green eyes staring at him from the face of this impetuous woman who'd scolded him so often, yet loved him as her son.

Chelise. Chelise! *Mother! Dear Mother.*

"Mother?"

He was facing the valley darkened by Shataiki, but in that moment nothing existed except for his own foolishness and the longing to join his mother on the ground, dead.

THE HALF-BREED did not end Qurong's life. He made no attempt at a second attack. Instead, he dropped from his saddle and staggered forward. "Mother?"

Mother? *Mother?* Qurong felt his rage rise and his self-control slip.

Thunder crashed overhead, and Qurong turned to look at jagged lines of lightning that stuttered through the sky. The core of the black swarm circling the valley scattered as light cut through them. Thousands of Shataiki began to fall from the sky, screeching. It was as if a wide shaft of white-hot sunshine had bored through their middle and burned them to a crisp.

The light slammed into the battlefield, and the earth beneath Qurong's feet shook.

The world was ending.

Qurong slowly turned back to the half-breed. The world was ending, and there was only one task that would bring the smallest measure of peace to a man who'd lost everything.

Qurong reached for his sword, snugged the hilt tight in his fist, and rose from his knees, shaking from head to foot. He rushed the half-breed who was frozen by confusion. His wrath came out in a long bloody cry from the bottom of his chest, and he swung the blade with all of his strength, severing the man's body nearly in half at his chest.

The half-breed looked at him with wide eyes, then toppled dead at his feet, taking Qurong's sword down with him.

Qurong stood heaving over the two dead bodies, numb. Then he fell to his face by Chelise's head, and he wept into the ground.

45

THEY HAD raced through the desert for eight hours, and with each pounding hoof, Thomas's heart beat with an expectation that had been building for the last twenty-seven years.

This was it! This was everything.

Everything except Samuel and Chelise.

Their horses fell into a natural formation in a full, tireless gallop over the sand. A million Roush flew above, filling the sky as far as he could see. The streaming colored light formed a tunnel around them, ushering them forward. Thomas wanted to touch it again, to swim in those colors and dive into Elyon's waters of intoxicating power.

But these thoughts were whispers of promise; the Warrior on the white horse who rushed ahead of them stole his mind. He could not keep his eyes off Elyon, just there, a hundred yards ahead, sprinting full tilt over the desert with his red cape flowing behind him. As his horse passed, the sand came alive with light, so that by the time Thomas and Kara reached it, they looked to be rushing through a thin cloud of raw, white power. Maybe this is what gave the horses their unflagging strength.

They were being escorted in a vast display of wonder and power, and no one seemed able to speak a single word. They didn't stop to eat; this anticipation was their food.

This hope was their nourishment.

How had they missed it? Like children wandering in the desert, they'd lost sight of the promise, so easily consumed with finding reward in a daily feeding of crumbs from the sky. Elyon's Israel had lost its way.

But all along, this power crackled just beyond the skin of their world. If only they could have seen . . .

If only the other world could see. But they had, he thought. Someone named Johnny had shown them some things. The saint had opened their eyes. And soon Billy, the sinner, would blind them in an ultimate showdown.

How he knew this, he wasn't sure, because this was his home and he now knew little about the other world. Did Kara know about Samuel and Paradise?

The abstract thought distracted him for a moment. Samuel. What about Samuel? So complete was his preoccupation with the Warrior, he'd forgotten about Samuel and Chelise! He had to save them!

He had to find them and bring them with him!

But then he knew something else, like he'd known about someone called Johnny. There was a reason for their rush through the desert.

They were going after Samuel and Chelise.

Thomas leaned lower and pressed harder, but then the brilliant colors swallowed him again, and again he became fixated on his desire to reach Elyon's lake.

"Run, Thomas, run!"

He looked to his left and saw that Gabil, a fluffy white Roush he'd first met long ago, flew not ten feet from him. The creature's round green eyes sparkled with his mischievous nature. The flier flipped over midflight and executed what looked to be a karate kick at some unseen enemy. "Hiyaa!"

Thomas felt more than heard laughter bubbling from his own chest.

"Impressed, huh?" Then the Roush showed off more, and Thomas saw five younger Roush in his wake, mimicking his every move. "Hiyaa!" The warrior had found himself some apprentices.

He turned to Kara, thinking to show her, but saw that another Roush sat in front of her, holding the reins with her. Had he been there long? She couldn't keep her eyes off the creature's furry head.

Thousands of Roush had joined the seven thousand albinos, riding or flying with them all. And high above them all flew one. Perhaps Michal, following the Warrior who cut through the sand.

Thomas first became aware of the huge vortex of Shataiki when they were still far from the Valley of Miggdon. The beasts reached down to the earth through a funnel, a staggering sight even from this distance. The battle was there, raging, and he should have felt some alarm, but he couldn't seem to work up any.

Gabil and his young recruits, who'd grown to nearly a hundred, continued their antics nearby. No one seemed remotely concerned about this swirling black mass.

The Roush overhead suddenly rose higher, above the swirling vortex of Shataiki, and Thomas wondered if they were going to attack from above.

The Warrior had led them east, dead east, but he now veered south, where the Valley of Miggdon lay open. The light turned with him on either side; the Roush banked south; the seven thousand altered course hard on the Warrior's heels.

The Roush rose even higher, and the colored light swept lower. They were sweeping into the thick of the blackened valley, straight for the center of the Shataiki. At any minute, Chelise would join them. She would rush down from one of the slopes with Samuel by her side.

Thomas could see the whole valley now. Countless Shataiki littered the ground directly ahead. But they were not alone. There were bodies under the beasts.

The Shataiki were feeding on the fallen, a whole sea of death.

The scene took his breath away, and if his mount hadn't had a head for the Warrior alone, he would have pulled up. Gabil and his entourage were gone. The albinos' horses rushed forward, undisturbed by the carnage layering the valley floor.

Bodies lay upon bodies, and only a few thousand were left to flee the Shataiki, who methodically pulled them down and plunged their fangs into their heads.

The valley was screaming, a high-pitched inhuman wail from Shataiki throats. And in that moment, Thomas knew that he had made this very scene possible by creating a breach in time for Billy and Janae.

Michal's words flashed through his mind. *Go to the place you came from. Make a way for the Circle to fulfill its hope.*

But there was more. *And return quickly before it's too late. Do that and you might save your son.*

Where was he? Where was Samuel?

And where was Chelise?

The Warrior leading them didn't look back or slow. He thundered down the center of the valley.

"Thomas!"

He glanced at Kara, then followed her eyes up. The Roush were above the huge gathering of Shataiki swirling through the sky, and a thin stream of them were diving directly into the center of the black swarm.

The Roush cut into the beasts, and the whole swarm of Shataiki shifted, reacting to the intrusion.

The Warrior on the white horse stood in his stirrups and leaned into the wind, still at a full gallop. He thrust a finger from each hand into the air and screamed his charge, then abruptly clapped his hands together. The sound of his clap came as thunder, and it shook the valley.

Lightning stuttered through the sky.

And the bottom of the Shataiki swarm blew out as the first Roush broke through, red with blood. White light streamed through the hole they'd cut. A dozen, and then a hundred followed, each badly bloodied.

Black bats rained from the hole as the Roush punched through their center by the thousands now, creating a great hole at the heart of the vortex. Shrieking with terror, the exposed black bats on the ground abandoned their prey and flapped madly for the relative safety of those above. The whole swarm was off-kilter now, but they clung together like syrup, unwilling to flee alone.

The Warrior Elyon leaned over his white horse, sprinting faster, faster, head down. He was leading them directly into this bloodbath.

The Roush had created their own swarm, a tunnel through the center of the Shataiki, and the streak of light at the core suddenly swelled to a wide shaft and reached down, into the battlefield. It slammed into the ground below, vaporizing any flesh in its path.

The ground shook, then cracked. A chasm opened wide directly ahead of them. Roush streamed down into the great hole with the shaft of light and vanished. They flowed with the light, streaking through the angry swirl of Shataiki and those shrieking for safety, right into the wide gap, maybe a hundred paces across.

The earth was swallowing them all.

The colorful tunnel around the seven thousand narrowed as they entered the battleground, led by the Warrior. Whatever waited in their path was consumed by the light. The Warrior cleared a wide swath through the heaps of dead.

And then Thomas saw their destination, and his breathing stopped. Water was rising in the chasm. Red water, forming a new lake at the heart of the battlefield. The Roush still streamed into a swirling green hole at the lake's center, vanishing into the depths.

This was it. This was it!

But where was Chelise?

Thomas jerked his head around. Kara was there, ten feet to his right, beaming like a child. Mikil, Johan, and Marie were close behind, staring past him at the new lake. The seven thousand leaned forward on their mounts, eyes fixed on the water like dehydrated souls staring at their last hope.

But there was no sign of Chelise. Nor Samuel.

It occurred to him then that they might be lost. Lost! The mere suggestion of it shoved his heart into his throat. Above, the Roush flowed into the eye of this new whirlpool; behind, the seven thousand gave hard chase as the Warrior's horse galloped at full speed; ahead, the lake beckoned.

But Chelise was lost.

"Elyon!" he shouted. The Warrior didn't turn or slow. "Elyon!"

Panic reached long fingers into his mind, and he screamed it this time. "Elyon!"

The last of the Roush vanished below the water's surface, and the hole at the lake's middle collapsed on itself. The water at the center swirled in hues of green, surrounded by a mirror of red.

The streaming light on either side of them reached the lake's edge. It curved downward and plunged into the water as if sucked by a powerful vacuum. A dull roar filled the valley, the sound of pure power. Above, the black Shataiki were scattering.

And then Elyon launched his horse over the slight rise that ran around the lake, catapulted himself from the white steed's back, and sailed through the air in a perfectly executed dive. His body followed his outstretched hands, and the moment his head entered the water, a brilliant white light spread out just under the surface like a shock wave.

Elyon vanished into the depths.

Thomas was going to follow as he had followed before—Elyon knew how desperately he needed to enter the water. But where was Samuel?

"Elyon!" He was crying out at empty water. "Elyon."

A lone Roush flew over his head, low enough to batter his face with wind, headed to the slope. He immediately recognized Michal, the leader of the Roush, fur red with blood. Thomas looked at the far slope in the direction Michal was flying and saw that a crude altar had been erected. A man was on his knees, fists raised at the sky, wailing.

Qurong!

"In," he cried to Kara. "Dive in after him! I'll come . . ."

He veered to the right, following the Roush. Kara hardly needed encouragement. She took her horse over the edge and fell headlong into the red lake with a mighty splash. Elyon's waters swallowed her.

Thomas followed the Roush to the west of the pool, tempted to turn back and dive in. But Qurong was there, just ahead, and Chelise had come for Qurong.

The seven thousand were now plowing into the lake, waves and waves, some of them clinging to their mounts, others diving midair, still others—mostly the young, squealing with laughter—tumbling through the air before splashing beneath the surface.

They all knew this was it. Elyon called to them from these intoxicating waters.

Thomas pushed his mount faster, oblivious to the dead underfoot. He rushed forward, aware that he was going in the wrong direction. The waters still called to him from behind.

But Chelise was ahead.

A wounded albino who looked like he'd caught the scabbing disease rushed past him, headed for the lake with tears streaming down his face. He stumbled to the edge and threw himself into the water. A half-breed rushed the waters on the opposite shore. Both vanished below the shimmering surface. Neither reemerged. Others left alive by the Shataiki followed.

Still others fled the lake, clawing back up the valley's slopes.

Thomas saw Qurong clearly now. The Horde leader had fallen on his face and was gripping an article of clothing. Behind him on a flat boulder lay the naked body of the dark priest, Ba'al, now headless. To his right, a fallen half-breed, facedown.

But no sign of Chelise. Or Samuel. None!

He pulled his horse to a stop, dropped to the ground, and rushed Qurong. "Where is she?"

The leader didn't look lucid. He'd been weeping for some time. Thomas grasped his dreadlocks and yanked his head back. "Where is my wife? Tell me!"

"Gone!" the man cried, shoving the clothing at him. "Vanished!"

Thomas was about to slap sense into the man in his eagerness to know, when he recognized the bloody tunic beneath the Horde cloak by Qurong's knees. And the riding pants, still stuffed into the tops of boots.

Boots . . . These were boots that he himself had made. Chelise's boots. She'd been here!

He spun back to the lake, and the meaning of what had happened filled his mind. Chelise had been here, slain in battle. But Elyon had taken her.

"My son!" he demanded, spinning back to Qurong again. "Where is my son, Samuel? He was with the Eramites."

Qurong's eyes snapped up, and realization spread over his face. He turned to his right and looked at the slain half-breed.

"There. There is your son, the one who killed my daughter."

Thomas stood slowly, fighting to stay steady as he turned to the body lying facedown. He walked forward, gripped the sword still sticking out of the warrior's chest, and turned the man over.

Disease covered his skin and his armor was patently Horde, but there was no doubting this man's face. Samuel. Samuel, who'd turned Scab, lay dead. And his body, unlike Chelise's body, was still here, trapped in this world.

Heat spread down Thomas's face and neck and then flashed down his body, squeezing off his breath. The strength to stand left him and he dropped to his knees.

How could this be? Chelise hadn't been able to save him?

The sky had emptied of Shataiki. Down at the lake, the last of the seven thousand plunged into the depths. The battlefield grew quiet.

But here, in Thomas's head, there was a moaning that washed over him like the voices of a thousand dead.

His heart was breaking and his mind was falling apart, and he no longer cared to live. He covered his face with both hands, lifted his chin, and wailed at the sky.

"Samuel . . . Samuel. Samuel, my son, my son!"

He tore at his tunic, ripped it wide open, and cried without reserve. "Elyon, save my son . . ."

The air was silent.

The vaguest notion of paradise without Samuel was more than he could bear. This was Teeleh's doing!

"Elyon has no ears," Qurong said to his right.

"No!" Thomas snarled, twisting around. "You're wrong." He shoved his finger at the red pool. "Drown! Drown, you fool. My wife and my son have given their lives; now, drown! Dive into the pool, draw his water into your lungs and drown!"

Thomas staggered to his feet, face hot, drawing energy from his sorrow. Then he faced the sky and screamed. "Elyon! Elyon, hear me. Save my son!"

The sky remained silent.

A new way came to him. He spread his arms and searched the sky. "Let me go back. Let me find my son. I beg you, Elyon. Anything . . . anything! Just let me save my son."

Nothing.

He clenched his eyes and threw both arms wide. "Elyon!" he cried. "Elyon!"

The words Michal had spoken a week earlier sliced through his mind: *Follow your heart, Thomas, because the time has come . . . he will give you what you ask in that hour when all is lost.*

With all of his strength, from the pit of his stomach, he screamed at the sky. "Elyon! Fulfill your promise!"

QURONG WAS lost in his own black misery, but this simple fact pointed out by Thomas rose like a beacon of light on the dark horizon: Chelise, his own daughter, had given her life for him.

And she had demanded that he drown.

Thomas was demanding the same. *Drown, drown, you old fool.* Drowning was foolishness. But then, he was dead already, surrounded by the dead.

Drown, Father. Drown, drown!

Thomas spread his arms wide and screamed at the sky in rage.

"Elyon!" And again, with such force Qurong thought the man might damage his lungs. "Fulfill your promise!"

Then it happened for the second time in the space of ten minutes. One moment Thomas was standing there; the next, nothing but air filled out his clothes. He simply vanished as Chelise had vanished. And now his tunic floated to the ground, empty.

Qurong stared at the heap of clothing, staggered by the unexplainable. Could it be that this wasn't Teeleh's doing? That both Chelise and Thomas knew what he did not? That the drowning was Elyon's gift to the Horde?

He turned and faced the red pool, heart and mind heavy with loss. Not a soul stood living. They had all either died, fled, or thrown themselves into the lake. The Shataiki sped south, high in the sky. Toward his city to feed.

By nightfall, every living soul would be consumed by Shataiki. This was Ba'al's gift to them. And yet he, Qurong, remained alive. Why?

He looked at the wound in his arm, where Thomas's blood had mixed with his own, offering him some protection against the disease and the beasts. And now that man had vanished before his eyes.

Drown, Qurong. For the sake of Elyon, drown!

He turned downhill, swallowed the lump in his throat, and walked forward. *This is what you were born to do. To drown. To dive into the lake and to laugh with Elyon.*

Desperation crept over him and he lumbered forward, running now. Over fallen bodies.

Drown, you old fool. Just drown.

He broke into a sprint, and now he couldn't get to the water's edge fast enough. Suddenly nothing else mattered. All was lost.

But there, just ahead, lay a red lake with a green core, and he couldn't run fast enough. Qurong started to weep as he ran, blinded by his own tears.

"I will drown. I will drown," he mumbled. "I will drown for you, my Maker. I will drown for you, Elyon."

And then Qurong, supreme commander of the Horde, dived into the lake. He inhaled the bitter waters of Elyon's death. He drowned in a pit of sorrow.

And he found life in a world swimming with color and laughter and more pleasure than his new body could possibly manage.

46

THE WORLD AROUND THOMAS blinked off, then on, then he was standing on the white sand, facing a bright blue horizon in perfect silence.

Here? Alone? Like a fist milking his veins, his heart throbbed. Time seemed to have stalled.

But he knew he couldn't be alone. The boy . . .

The boy had to be here.

He turned ever so slowly. The boy stood twenty feet away, arms crossed, lips flat and gaze steady. Behind him, a green lake reflected the clear sky, like a shiny mirror.

"You want to save your son?" the boy asked.

"Yes."

"You want to save Samuel?"

His lover's face filled his mind. "Chelise . . ."

"Is with me," the boy said.

Which could only mean Samuel was not.

"I . . . I can't live without him."

The boy looked at him for several long seconds, then shifted his eyes to the horizon. "I know how you feel."

"I know this is within your power," Thomas said. "If you would save all of Sodom for ten souls, you could give me the chance to save my one son."

"I did save him," the boy said, looking back.

"I'll take that risk. I . . . You did?"

"But he turned his back. This isn't just about you and your son. If I were to send you back you might help your son, but at what cost? The cost of saving even one is beyond you."

He hadn't thought of it in those terms.

The boy uncrossed his arms. "Walk with me."

Thomas hurried forward on weak legs. He joined the boy, who reached up and took his hand as they walked along the shore of the lake behind.

"Will I ever see him again? Samuel."

"Perhaps."

"This isn't the end, then."

"The end? There is no end. Think of it as more like a beginning."

"Will it be better or worse?"

"It depends."

"On what?"

"On whether evil is embraced again. As long a humans remain human with a free will they will have the right to choose. Although the old beast has lost for now. For a time."

They walked ten paces in silence. The boy's fingers felt so small in his hand. Thomas looked at the water and for a few moments considered withdrawing his request to join the others. Chelise and Mikil . . . Kara. He could only imagine their pleasure now, dancing and tearing about like children.

"The others are waiting."

"Where?"

The boy looked at the water. "Past the pool. In a new world."

Thoughts swirled in Thomas's head but his longing to dive deep pulled at him. This was his destiny now, to dive. Samuel had made his choice, he would leave his destiny up Elyon.

The boy stepped to one side and winked. "Are you ready?"

Thomas faced the glassy pool. "Dive? In here?"

"Dive deep," the boy said.

Thomas took one last breath, nodded at the boy, and dove deep. Very, very deep.

47

TWO DAYS HAD PASSED, and Bill now knew what he needed to know. Something had gone wrong. Drastically wrong. Thomas had not shown as Marsuuv had promised. And he never would show.

Bill was trapped in this reality. If Thomas did not dream there was no other reality.

Or was it the other way around? Was this the dream? Or neither?

Either way, there was no way for him to cross over now to wreak havoc in that world.

He would simply do what damage he could here, in this world, and hope that in another world Marsuuv, his master and lover, approved.

48

THE INSTANT Thomas hit the water, his body shook violently. A blue strobe exploded in his eyes, and he was tempted to think that he was going to die. That he had entered a forbidden pool, pulled by the wrong desire, and now he would pay with his life. But he'd been here before and he knew that was not the case.

The warm water engulfed him. Flutters rippled through his body and erupted into a boiling heat that knocked the wind from his lungs. The shock alone might kill him.

But he didn't die. In fact, it was pleasure that racked his body, not death. Pleasure! The sensations coursed through his bones in great, unrelenting waves.

Elyon.

How he was certain he did not know. But he knew. Elyon was in this lake with him.

Thomas opened his eyes and found they did not sting. Gold light drifted by. No part of the water seemed darker than another. He lost all sense of direction. Which way was up?

The water pressed in on every inch of his body, as intense as any acid, but one that burned with pleasure instead of pain. His violent shaking gave way to a gentle trembling as he sank into the water. He opened his mouth and laughed. He wanted more, much more. He wanted to suck the water in and drink it.

Without thinking, he did that. He took a great gulp and then inhaled unintentionally. The liquid hit his lungs.

Thomas pulled up, panicked. Then he carefully sucked more water and breathed it out slowly. Then again, deep and hard. Out with a soft whoosh.

He was breathing the water. In great heaves he was breathing the lake's intoxicating water.

But none of this should have surprised him. He'd been here before, more than once. Floating into Elyon himself. And yet each time felt like the first.

He could spend an eternity in these waters and feel as though only a moment had passed.

Thomas shrieked with laughter. He tumbled through the water, pulling his legs in close so he would roll, and then stretching them out so he thrust forward, farther into the colors surrounding him. He swam into the lake, deeper and deeper, twisting and rolling as he plummeted toward the bottom. The power contained in this lake was far greater than anything he'd ever imagined. He could hardly contain himself.

In fact, he could not contain himself; he cried out with pleasure and swam deeper.

Then he heard them. Three words.

I made this.

Thomas pulled himself up, frozen. No, not words. Music that spoke. Pure notes piercing his heart and mind with as much meaning as an entire book. He whipped his body around, searching for its source.

A giggle rippled through the water. Like a child now.

Thomas grinned stupidly and spun around. "Elyon?" His voice was muffled, hardly a voice at all.

I made this.

The words reached into Thomas's bones, and he began to tremble again. He wasn't sure if it was an actual voice, or whether he was somehow imagining it.

"What are you? Where are you?" Light floated by. Waves of pleasure continued to sweep through him. "Who are you?"

I am Elyon.
And I made you.

The words started in his mind and burned through his body like a spreading fire.

Do you like it?

Yes! Thomas said. He might have spoken, he might have shouted, he didn't know. He only knew that his whole body screamed it.
Thomas looked around. "Elyon?"

I see you, Thomas.
I made you.
I love you.

The words filled the entire lake, as though the water itself had become these words. Thomas let them wash through his mind like a powerful narcotic.

The water around his feet suddenly began to boil, and he felt the lake suck him deeper into itself. He gasped, pulled by a powerful current. And then he was flipped over and pushed headfirst by the same current. He opened his eyes, resigned to whatever awaited him.

A tunnel of bright light opened directly ahead of him, like the eye of a whirlpool. He rushed into it and the darkness fell away. The light became Green.

New Life. For a moment there was silence as he descended into the soft emerald color. The water was suddenly filled with a song. A song more wonderful than any song could possibly sound, a hundred thousand melodies woven into one.

I love you.
I choose you.
I rescue you.
I cherish you.

"I love you too!" Thomas cried desperately. "I choose you; I cherish you." He was sobbing, but with love. The feeling was more intense than the pleasure that had racked him.

The current suddenly pulled at him again, tugging him up through the colors. His body again trembled with pleasure, and he hung limp as he sped through the water.

This was his New Birth, he thought.

He wanted to speak, to scream and to yell and to tell the whole world that he was the luckiest man in the universe. That he was loved by Elyon, Elyon himself, and that he had heard it from Elyon's own voice, in a lake made by him.

But the words would not come. His mind was lost in the pleasure of that rebirthing.

When Elyon spoke again, his voice was gentle and deep, like a purring lion.

Never leave me, Thomas.
Tell me that you'll never leave me.

"I will always stay with you."

Another current caught him from behind and pushed him through the water. The boy's voice came again just before he broke the surface, a mischievous daring sound that stopped Thomas's heart for a moment.

Then wait till you see what I've made for you this time.

Thomas was laughing with delight when his body broke the surface not ten meters from the shore. But the moment his eyes laid sight on what the boy had managed this time his laughter was cut short by a gasp.

Images of the colored forest and the Roush and the lions and the intoxicating fruit from the first Eden flooded his mind. But they were gone as quickly as they'd come.

This . . . Now this was staggering. A thing not even he, Thomas of Hunter who'd crossed the worlds through his many dreams, could have possibly imagined.

This . . . This was spectacular.

Then Thomas stood and walked out of the lake, green water dripping from his limbs like the memories of a day long past. And his body would not stop shaking for the pleasure of this new world.

Not for a very, very long time.

THE END

A Note from the Author
about the Original Ending to *Green*:

The original ending to *Green* that you are about to read was designed for those who started the series with *Green* and then would continue on to *Black, Red,* and *White*. But since *Green* was clearly the end of your reading, I wanted you to have the end, the climax of all four books.

Although the original ending was intellectually fascinating and certainly mind bending, it didn't have the same emotional payoff as the version you just read. I love them both. But I'll leave it up to you to decide. We are, after all, in a world where the choices we make alter everything.

45

THE WORLD around Thomas blinked off, then on, then he was standing on the white sand, facing a bright blue horizon in perfect silence.

Here? Alone? Like a fist milking his veins, his heart throbbed. Time seemed to have stalled.

But he knew he couldn't be alone. The boy . . .

The boy had to be here.

He turned ever so slowly. The boy stood twenty feet away, arms crossed, lips flat and gaze steady. Behind him, a green lake reflected the clear sky, like a shiny mirror.

"You want to save your son?" the boy asked.

"Yes."

"You want to save Samuel?"

His lover's face filled his mind. "Chelise . . ."

"Is with me," the boy said.

Which could only mean Samuel was not.

"I . . . I can't live without him."

The boy looked at him for several long seconds, then shifted his eyes to the horizon. "I know how you feel."

"I know this is within your power," Thomas said. "If you would save all of Sodom for ten souls, you would give me the chance to save my one son."

"It's much more dangerous than you realize," the boy said, looking back.

"I'll take that risk. I—"

"Not you, Thomas. The risk is to the rest. This isn't just about you and your son. If I send you back you might save your son, but at what cost? The cost of saving even one is beyond you."

He hadn't thought of it in those terms. But he couldn't back out, not now.

The boy uncrossed his arms. "Walk with me."

Thomas hurried forward on weak legs. He joined the boy, who reached up and took his hand as they walked along the shore of the lake.

"Every choice you make will have far-reaching consequences," the boy said. "You will eventually change everything."

"Will it be better or worse?"

"It depends."

"On what?"

"On you."

They walked ten paces in silence. The boy's fingers felt so small in his hand. Thomas looked at the water and for a few moments considered withdrawing his request to join the others. Chelise and Mikil . . . Kara. He could only imagine their pleasure now, dancing and tearing about like children.

"Okay, Thomas. But I have two conditions."

Elyon was agreeing? "Anything."

"I will send you back to the place and time of my choosing."

"Yes. Yes, of course."

"You will have no memory of anything that's happened. You'll have your chance, unlike anyone else in history, but you won't have the benefit of knowing it's a second chance. You won't have any of the knowledge you've gained here." The boy stopped and looked up at him with round green eyes. "Do you understand?"

Thomas tried. But did it matter? He wouldn't remember anyway. If Elyon required this, then he would agree, and quickly. "I think so, yes."

"You'll wake in a place called Denver without any memory of this reality. Your dreams will be touched."

"Dreams?"

"They'll be real. Unfortunately, you won't know it."

"How . . . how does that work?"

"Better than you might think." The boy smiled for the first time, though only slightly. Then his face fell flat again.

"The fate of the world will depend on every choice you make." He swept his eyes over the horizon. "We'll remake history together, Thomas. Is that what you want?"

"Yes."

He shifted his gaze back to Thomas. "Good. It's what I do with every human anyway. Let's just hope you make the right choices."

"What about Chelise?"

"I thought you wanted to start over?"

Confusion swarmed his mind. "But . . . what about Chelise?"

"I thought you wanted to save your son," the boy said.

"I do."

"By going back."

"Yes," Thomas said. "Unless there's another way."

"Not that I know of. And I know an awful lot."

He considered it all and came to his decision quickly. Impulsively. "Yes. Send me back. For the sake of my son."

The boy stepped to one side and winked. "Then dive, my friend."

Thomas faced the glassy pool. "Dive? In here?"

"Dive deep," the boy said.

Thomas took one last breath, nodded at the boy, and dived deep. Very, very deep.

46

THE WATER cascaded over Thomas's head and ran down his face like a warm glove. It was just that, water, but it washed away all his concern and anxiety and set his mind free for a few minutes. He'd been here awhile, lost in a distant world that hung on the edge of his mind without any detail or meaning. Just escape. Pure escape, the closest he ever got to heaven these days.

A fist pounded the door. "Thomas! I'm outta here. You're going to be late."

A mental image of a much older Kara flashed through his mind. She was graying, perhaps in her fifties, and she was asking him to take her with him. Just that, "Take me with you, Thomas."

And then the image was gone. He blinked under streams of water, suddenly disoriented. How long had he been here? For the briefest moment he was at a loss as to how he'd even gotten here.

Then it all came crashing in on him. He was in the shower. It was late morning. His shift at Java Hut started at noon. Right? Yes, of course.

He shook the water from his head. "Okay." Then added, "See you tonight."

But Kara was probably already out the door, headed to her shift at the hospital. The thing about his sister: she might only be in her early twenties like him, but what she lacked in age, she more than made up for in maturity. Not that he was irresponsible, but he hadn't made the transition from life on the streets in Manila to life in the States quite as smoothly as Kara.

He stepped out of the shower and wiped the steamed mirror with his forearm. He ran both hands through his wet hair and examined his face as best he could with streaks of water clinging to the glass.

Not bad. Not bad. Chicks dug a little stubble, right? He'd lost some of his edge over the last couple years in New York, but Denver would be different. The troubles with loan sharks and shady import partners were behind him now. Soon as he got back on his feet, he would reenter society and find a way to excel at something.

In the meantime, there was the coffee shop he worked at, and there was the apartment, gratis, thanks to Kara.

He dressed quickly, grabbed a day-old sugar donut on his way out, and headed up Ninth, then through the alley to Colfax, where the boutique coffee shop better known as Java Hut waited. The Rockies stood against a blue sky, just visible between high-rise apartments as he made his way up the street. Mother was still in New York, where she'd settled in after the divorce. It had been a tough road, but she was set now.

Indeed, the world was set. He just had to put some time in, regroup, and let life come to him as it always had, with fistfuls of dollars and a woman who could appreciate the finer things in life. Like him.

Okay, only in his dreams at the moment, but things were looking up. Maybe he'd finally get back to one of those novels he'd written when his dream of conquering the publishing world was alive and well.

Thomas entered the coffee shop two minutes past noon and let the door slam shut behind him.

"Hey, Thomas." The new dark-haired hire, Edith, smiled and gave him a wink.

Okay . . . interesting. Pretty enough. But being a magnet for trouble, Thomas didn't make a habit of flirting with women he knew nothing about.

"Hey."

She tossed him a green apron. "Frank would like you to show me the ropes."

"Okay." He stepped around her and behind the counter.

"We close together tonight," she said.

Right. Frank had started up these ten-hour shifts a week earlier. "Okay."

"Yeah."

He refused to look at her, knowing what was on her mind already. It was the farthest thing from his mind.

TWO DAYS had passed, and Bill now knew what he needed to know, thanks to Tony, the two-bit crook with a New York accent who'd agreed to play by his rules for ten thousand dollars a day. Tony had studied Thomas's movements and knew he would cut through the alley when he got off work sometime past ten.

"Focus, Tony." Bill stood atop the building and motioned at the alleyway. "Just make sure he heads into that dead end."

"Please don't *Tony* me, Bill. Then what?"

He wondered if he'd regret hiring the fool, but this wasn't the kind of thing you advertised for unless you had time. "Then you go in after him. Stay on the radio, I'll direct you. I want him thinking we have the streets blocked. The only other way out is up one of the ladders."

"And then he's yours."

Bill adjusted his dark glasses, careful to keep his black eyes hidden, and studied the flat roofs across the alley. He nodded. "Then he's mine."

"What about cops?"

"What about them? We're using silencers."

The New Yorker nodded. "I may get some help. Just to be sure. We get the chance, you want me to take him out? 'Cause that'll cost you more."

"No, Tony. I want him up on the roof." The rifle case lay at his feet, where he would take up position and lie in wait. One bullet to the head, nothing more, nothing less. He couldn't risk jeopardizing the mission by winging Thomas and sending him packing.

He has to drink the water, a voice from his past whispered. He had no idea what it meant.

"Fine, Bill," the man said with a smirk. "When do I get paid?"

Bill forced a grin. "As soon as he's dead, Tony. As soon as he's dead."

⸎

THE DAY passed quickly, and Thomas managed to close with Edith without either betraying his general disinterest in her or offering any encouragement. But showing her the ropes, as she called it, had taken longer than usual, and he didn't get out till ten thirty that night.

He headed down the street, headed for the apartment. Another day, another dollar. Not fistfuls, but at least it was steady. More than he could say for his, uh . . . more ambitious gigs. All was good. All was . . .

But then suddenly all wasn't so good. He was walking down the same dimly lit alley he always took on his way home when a *smack!* punctuated the hum of distant traffic. Red brick dribbled from a one-inch hole two feet away from his face. He stopped midstride.

Smack!

This time he saw the bullet plow into the wall. This time he felt a sting on his cheek as tiny bits of shattered brick burst from the impact. This time every muscle in his body seized.

Someone had just shot at him?

Was *shooting* at him?

Thomas recoiled to a crouch, but he couldn't seem to tear his eyes off those two holes in the brick, dead ahead. They had to be a mistake. Figments of his overactive imagination. His aspirations to write novels had finally ruptured the line between fantasy and reality with these two empty eye sockets staring at him from the red brick.

"Thomas Hunter!"

That wasn't his imagination, was it? No, that was his name, and it was echoing down the alley. A third bullet crashed into the brick wall.

He bolted to his left, still crouching. One long step, drop the right shoulder, roll. Again the air split above his head. This bullet clanged into a steel ladder and rang down the alley.

Thomas came to his feet and chased the sound in a full sprint, pushed by instinct as much as by terror. He'd been here before, in the back alleys of Manila. He'd been a teenager then, and the Filipino gangs were armed with knives and machetes rather than guns, but at the moment, tearing down the alley behind Ninth and Colfax, Thomas's mind wasn't drawing any distinction.

"You're a dead man!" the voice yelled.

Now he knew who they were. They were from New York. Right? He had no enemies in Denver that he was aware of. New York, on the other hand . . . Yeah, well, he'd done a few stupid things in New York.

This alley led to another thirty yards ahead, on his left. A mere shadow in the dim light, but he knew the cutaway.

Two more bullets whipped by, one so close he could feel its wind on his left ear. Feet pounded the concrete behind him.

Thomas dived into the shadow.

"Cut him off in the back. Radio me."

Thomas rolled to the balls of his feet, then sprinted, mind spinning. *Radio?*

The problem with adrenaline, Makatsu's thin voice whispered, *is that it makes your head weak.* His karate instructor would point to his head and wink. *You have plenty of muscle to fight, but no muscle to think.*

If they had radios and could cut off the street ahead, he would have a very serious problem.

One access to the roof halfway down the alley. One large garbage bin too far away. Scattered boxes to his left. No real cover. He had to make his move before they entered the alley.

Fingers of panic stabbed into his mind. *Adrenaline dulls reason; panic kills it.* Makatsu again. Thomas had once been beaten to a pulp by a gang of Filipinos who'd taken a pledge to kill any Americano brat who entered their turf. They made the streets around the army base their turf. His instructor had scolded him, insisting that he was good enough to have escaped their attack that afternoon. His panic had cost him dearly. His brain had been turned to rice pudding, and he deserved the bruises that swelled his eyes shut.

This time it was bullets, not feet and clubs, and bullets would leave more than bruises. Time was out.

Short on ideas and long on desperation, Thomas dove for the gutter. Rough concrete tore at his skin. He rolled quickly to his left, bumped into the brick wall, and lay facedown in the deep shadow.

Feet pounded around the corner and ran straight toward him. One man. How they had found him in Denver, he had no clue. But if they'd gone to this much trouble, they wouldn't just walk away.

The man ran on light feet, hardly winded. Thomas's nose was buried in the musty corner. Noisy blasts of air from his nostrils buffeted his face. He clamped down on his breathing; immediately his lungs began to burn.

The slapping feet approached, ran past.

Stopped.

A slight tremor lit through his bones. He fought another round of panic. It had been five years since his last fight. He didn't stand a chance against a man with a gun. He desperately willed his pursuer's feet to move on. *Walk. Just walk!*

But the feet didn't walk. They scraped quietly. He had to move now, while he still had the advantage of surprise. He threw himself to his left, rolled once to gain momentum. Then twice, rising first to his knees, then to his feet. His attacker was facing him, gun extended, frozen.

Thomas's momentum carried him laterally, directly toward the opposite wall. The gun's muzzle-flash momentarily lit the dark alley and spit a bullet past him. But now instinct had replaced panic.

What shoes am I wearing?

The question flashed through Thomas's mind as he hurtled for the brick wall, left foot leading. A critical question.

His answer came when his foot planted on the wall. Rubber soles. One more step up the wall, with traction to spare. He threw his head back, arched hard, pushed himself off the brick, then twisted to his right halfway through his rotation. The move was simply an inverted bicycle kick, but he hadn't executed it in half a dozen years, and this time his eyes weren't on a soccer ball tossed up by one of his Filipino friends in Manila.

This time it was a gun.

The man managed one shot before Thomas's left foot smashed into his hand, sending the pistol clattering down the alley. The bullet tugged at his collar.

Thomas didn't land lightly on his feet as hoped. He sprawled to his hands, rolled once, and sprang into the seventh fighting position opposite a well-muscled man with short black hair. Not exactly a perfectly executed maneuver. Not terrible for someone who hadn't fought in six years.

The man's eyes were round with shock. His experience in the martial arts obviously didn't extend beyond *The Matrix*. Thomas was briefly tempted to shout for joy, but if anything, he had to shut this man up before *he* could call out.

The man's astonishment changed to a snarl, and Thomas saw the knife in his right hand. Okay, so maybe the man knew more about street fighting than was at first apparent.

He ducked the knife's first swipe. Came up with his palm to the man's chin. Bone cracked.

It wasn't enough. This man was twice his weight, with twice his muscle, and ten times his bad blood.

Thomas launched himself vertically and spun into a full roundhouse kick, screaming despite his better judgment. His foot had to be doing a good eighty miles an hour when it struck the man's jaw.

They both hit the concrete at precisely the same time, Thomas on his feet, ready to deliver another blow; his assailant on his back, breathing hard, ready for the grave. Figuratively speaking.

The man's silver pistol lay near the wall. Thomas took a step for it, then rejected the notion. What was he going to do? Shoot back? Kill? Incriminate himself? Not smart. He turned and ran back in the direction they'd come.

The main alley was empty. He ducked into it, edged along the wall, grabbed the rails to a steel fire escape, and quickly ascended. The building's roof was flat and shouldered another taller building to the south. He swung up to the second building, ran in a crouch, and halted by a large vent, nearly a full block from the alley where he'd laid out the New Yorker.

He dropped to his knees, pressed back into the shadows, and listened past the thumping of his heart.

The hum of a million tires rolling over asphalt. The distant roar of a jet overhead. The faint sound of idle talk. The sizzling of food frying in a pan, or of water being poured from a window. The former, considering they were in Denver, not the Philippines. No sounds from New York.

He leaned back and closed his eyes, catching his breath.

Fights in Manila as a teenager were one thing, but here in the States at the ripe age of twenty-five? The whole sequence struck him as surreal. It was hard to believe this had just happened to him.

Or, more accurately, *was* happening to him. He still had to figure a way out of this mess. Did they know where he lived? No one had followed him to the roof.

Thomas crept to the ledge. Another alley ran directly below, adjoining busy streets on either side. Denver's brilliant skyline glimmered on the horizon directly ahead. An odd odor met his nose, sweet like cotton candy but mixed with rubber or something burning.

Déjà vu. He'd been here before, hadn't he? No, of course not. Lights shimmered in the hot summer air, reds and yellows and blues, like jewels sprinkled from heaven. He could swear he'd been . . .

Thomas's head suddenly snapped to the left. He threw out his arms, but his world spun impossibly and he knew that he was in trouble.

Something had hit him. Something like a sledgehammer. Something like a bullet.

He felt himself topple, but he wasn't sure if he was really falling or if he was losing consciousness. Something was horribly wrong with his head. He landed hard on his back, in a pillow of black that swallowed his mind whole.

And then . . .

And then Thomas Hunter dreamed, and the world would never be the same.

The Circle Series has sold well over 1 million copies all told. The average book is read by 5 people. Out of those 5 million readings a handful of questions rise to the top of reader's curiosities. Here are Ted's responses to those questions.

1) Did you have the entire series in mind when you first began to write Black?

Ted: Yes. Although I originally imagined a series of seven books, not four, tracing the history of redemption through the old and new testaments. Then again that was the ambitious part of me tackling the world. The project I proposed to the publisher involved three books called Black, Red and White. Those first three were written in one year, one right after the other as one long book, then published in one year, dubbed the year of the trilogy, an idea proposed by Allen Arnold, my slave master/publisher at the time. I'll never forget the phone call. "Ted, I've got an idea. Can you write the rest of the series this year?" I said I needed a week to sleep on it since he was, after all, asking the impossible. I called the next day and said yes.

The idea of the alternate ending for Green is a different story. Some will say it brings finality to the series. They are probably right. Unless my slave master calls, that is.

2) You depict evil in the most horrifying ways at times in these novels. Especially in Black and Green. Do you ever worry that you've gone too far?

Ted: I don't think it's my job to pretend evil is less horrific than it actually is. Casting Teeleh as a yellow fanged monster with a thirst of blood isn't any more of a stretch than the Orcs for Tolkien's Lord of the Rings.

I remember watching Peter Jackson's vision on screen for the first time thinking, Wow, Focus on the Family is going to scream about these creatures. Not so, they praised the movie. I think it was a game changer that we have Jackson to thank for.

Evil comes among us like a wolf in sheep's clothing. Part of what we do is rip the clothing off. Let others make life look nice and cozy; I will say doing so is a disservice to the human race.

3) Where did your original inspiration for the series come from?

Ted: I was once in a time of meditation and I imagined God as a lake. And I knew immediately that I had to write a novel in which one could dive into God as if he were a physical reality. To do so I had to write a story in which all that we see as spiritual was recast as physical. The colored forest was born. As was the forbidden circle and the lake.

I then took the idea further and imagined retelling all of redemptive history within the context of this world.

4) You have been quoted as saying that you were born to write this series. Do you still feel that way?

Ted: I was born to write tales that retell redemptive history. Books like this series and *Showdown, Saint, Sinner*, all of the Books of History Chronicles help us relive our rescue and redemption. There is no greater story. I will continue to write similar stories. *Immanuel's Veins* is such a story. As is *Forbidden*, the start of similar trilogy coming out in 2011.

5) The Books of History Chronicles draw links between vampires and the Shataiki from the other world. How long have you been planning this?

Ted: From the beginning the Shataiki were vampires. Not the nice ones written about in some novels, but a version of the Nephilim written about in Genesis. There's a huge backlash against vampire mythology today—people either love the books or hate them, it seems. Yet the whole notion of a human infected by a beast of another kind has its roots back in the Christian account of creation. It's part of our own mythology.

6) How are the Paradise Books tied into the Circle Series?

Ted: The Books of History, a centerpiece in *Black, Red, White,* and *Green,* find their way into our reality where they have the potential to wreak terrible havoc. And they do, starting with a novel called *Showdown,* the first of the Paradise novels, named after the town of Paradise, Colorado, that takes center stage in *Showdown, Saint,* and *Sinner.*

7) Do you think Alternate Universes could exist?

Ted: Sure. As do most. We don't know, naturally, but to think it's impossible is far too narrow an understanding of God and his eternal being. Reading the book of Revelations would lead most to a similar conclusion, if you can pry yourself away from those who simply know the truth based on their own eschatology. What I've written may be more similar to reality than many would guess. On the other hand, it probably isn't.

8) *Black* is a redo of history. Do you think history will be redone in the far future?

Ted: I'll answer with a question. Do you believe that humans will retain their humanity in the next life? That is, will they still have a free will? If so, they would still have a choice for evil, yes? Remove that choice and we essentially become like robots in the future.

So if evil exists in the next life, will anyone choose it, the way Lucifer first did? I suppose so. And if so, would the event involve another fall so to speak? We don't know. Perhaps this allegory I've penned is closer to the truth than one might think. Then again, probably not.

Here's another question, however ridiculous. Is this life we now live a redo? I'll leave you on that note. J

9) Is it true that the main characters in this series are based on your own children?

Ted: True enough. Those of my ilk would be Thomas naturally, the protagonist who grew up in Southeast Asia, a wanna be karate master, something that I can only do well in my dreams it seems. Rachelle is my eldest daughter, followed by Johannes better known as JT in this life, both featured prominently in Black along with Kara my globe trotter. Finally Chelise the main character in White. Interestingly Chelise came down with a very rare skin disease while I was writing White, an novel in which her character had a skin disease. She's in permanent remission now, thank God.

10) Any more novels in this series?

Ted: Never say never. But yes, for now, never. I'll tell you what, I will give you another series that captures my full imagination. If you take that ride with me, you'll find it as compelling, I think. Keep your eyes open.

Having said that, The Lost Books (my young adult series) is a spin off of the Circle Series involving 4 teens in the world of Thomas Hunter. Much is added from their perspective.

There is also passing link to Green in Immanuel's Veins, but only in that the Russians in Immanuel's Veins have ancient Shataiki blood in them and are creatures of the night who have descended from the first and only Shataiki to cross over up to that point, Alucard. Alucard has mated with humans and spawned Nephilim a kind of vampire before the day of vampires. They are masterfully seductive as such and give Toma, our hero vying for the same heroine, a run for his money. I long foresaw and can now easily see a series coming out of Immanuel's Veins, the story of our ongoing seduction. If the Circle Series has interested you, you must read Immanuel's Veins. You absolutely must.

"*Immanuel's Veins* is a heart-wrenching journey of redemption and hope that left me sobbing, laughing and clinging to every word."

— Donna McChristian, 44,
Environmental Chemist

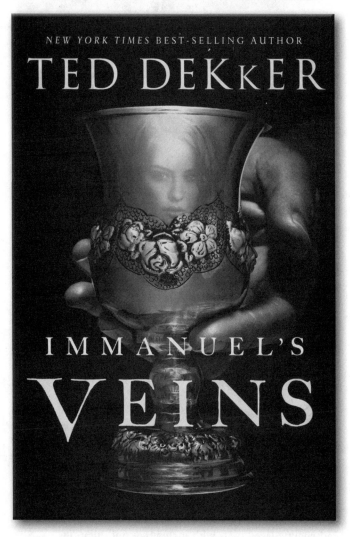

NEW YORK TIMES BEST-SELLING AUTHOR

TED DEKkER

IMMANUEL'S
VEINS

AVAILABLE EVERYWHERE

Ted Dekker is the *New York Times* bestselling author of more than 25 novels. He is known for stories that combine adrenaline-laced plots with incredible confrontations between good and evil. He lives in Texas with his wife and children.